AUDACES FORTUNA JUVAT

SUMMER HILL

SUMMER HILL

by

JOSEPH HONE

SINCLAIR-STEVENSON

First published in Great Britain by
Sinclair-Stevenson Limited
7/8 Kendrick Mews
London SW7 3HG, England

British Library Cataloguing in Publication Data

Hone, Joseph, *1937–*
Summer hill.
I. Title
823.914 [F]

ISBN 1-85619-010-2

Photoset by Rowland Phototypesetting Limited
Bury St Edmunds, Suffolk
Printed and bound in Great Britain by
Clays Limited, St Ives plc.

The Author gratefully acknowledges the help of the Virginia Center for the Creative
Arts in the preparation of this book – and of Macmillan, Publishers, PLC, for
permission to quote from W. B. Yeats. . . .

'Audaces Fortuna Juvat'

For Geraldine
and for
Sally & Stanley

BOOK ONE

1

I T HAD BEEN ominously still and cold all morning under a leaden sky, where the mountains, Brandon and Leinster, remained just visible, grey against darker grey. But, by early afternoon, heralded by the smallest stir of warmer air, these peaks disappeared and the snow storm, broaching the high passes and spreading out along the upper flanks, suddenly rolled downwards, an avalanche engulfing the hunt – hounds, horses, riders all caught in a vicious, windswept drive of blinding flakes.

Frances Cordiner, unable to control her impatience at the slow hunt that morning, had run well ahead and below the field. But now, finding herself quite alone on the bare mountain, she turned in the saddle, hoping to see where the others had got to. Instead, as it seemed just above her, she saw the storm poised, like the crest of a great white tidal wave, about to fall on her.

Defiant then, smiling, she dug her heels in, spurring the mare forward, galloping furiously down the slopes as she tried to outpace the rushing blanket that rolled after her. She took every short cut home, heedless of danger or obstruction, clearing gates, walls, ditches in a dazzle of mad jumps, hooves drumming against the cold earth, a scarlet jacketed blur against the foamy white sea that raced behind her.

But eventually, held back at one point by an impossible hurdle, the storm outran her. Snow stung her eyes, enveloping, blinding her – so that seeing the steeple of the local parish church ahead she wheeled the mare down a farm track, making towards it for shelter.

The small church, near the village of Cloone, lay quite isolated at the edge of the Summer Hill estate, some miles from the great house. Frances knew it well. It was the Cordiner family church. She had been baptised and would hope to marry and perhaps even be buried there, in the family vault behind the building.

Soundlessly, the mare's hooves muffled on the snowy path, she rode up to the porch, dismounted, and, taking the horse with her, sheltered inside. There was room for both of them. But the mare, instead of relaxing, clear of the biting storm at last, became nervous, swinging her rump, tossing her head, whinnying softly.

'Easy, girl – what's the matter?' She tried to calm the animal, peering out into the graveyard. The branch of a great elm, behind the tombstones near the gate, creaked alarmingly in the white storm. 'Silly, it's only a tree.' She stroked the mare's nose again. But she remained uneasy. Then Frances, looking out again, saw the reason and felt a vague tingle of fear pricking her spine.

Across the graveyard, beyond the hollow where the Cordiner vault was, she saw, between the vicious snow flurries, a saddled but riderless horse, quite visible for a moment before the driven flakes swirled back over the vision.

But her fear remained. The beast had been so unlikely, so still and large, a black stallion, come and gone in a moment, invisible now in the bitter white drifts. But it must be real, she thought, steadying herself.

Taking her whip she set out into the storm, dodging between the tombstones, making for the sharp slope that ran down towards the vault. The stallion was no vision. She saw it clearly now, standing on a ditch beyond the line of old elms, reins hanging loose, as if it had broken tether in the storm from somewhere nearby and had come to find its master.

Indeed, it seemed to have found him, Frances thought, with increased alarm, when, turning and looking in the same direction as the horse, she saw the iron barred door leading into the Cordiner vault slightly ajar. The great door was always locked. Someone was inside. An icicle of fear pierced the back of her neck.

Moving diagonally towards the vault door, she noticed the broken lock – then, with infinite care, she peered slowly round the stone jamb. A short brick passage opened into the vault itself and in the bright reflected light from the snow the scene was sufficiently lit. She took it all in, almost at a glance, before recoiling in sheer horror, trembling violently.

The man, with his back to her, some rough tinker type to judge by his torn clothes, had already ransacked two or three of the dozen heavy oak, lead-lined coffins set in tiers about the vault, the lids wrenched off, a debris of old bones and frayed cloth strewn about the place. But, worse than that, at the very moment when Frances peered in, the grave robber had been manhandling the skull of some recently-deceased Cordiner lady – her great-aunt Margot, it might have been, for the flaky brown, parchment-like skin and wisps of long white hair were still attached to the death's head – a woman whom the man had pulled up from her tomb, a broken skeletal doll in her plain shroud, jaws forced open hideously as the man prodded about for gold in her teeth.

Frances, dizzy with horror, eyes closed against the stinging snow, leant back against the wall beside the vault. When she opened them, she saw the second tinker, standing looking at her, not twenty yards away.

He was a much larger man than the first, swarthy, aggressive-looking, with florid, puffy features and strangely protuberant staring eyes under a battered black hat. Taking a knife from his belt, opening his long arms wide and crouching now, so that his hands nearly touched the ground like a baboon's, he approached Frances, moving forward across the snow very slowly, ready to spring to either side as if he was cornering a hen.

Frances, back against the vault, with the sheer ground to either side and the boundary wall immediately to her right, had only one path of escape. She must go left along the earthworks, then up into the main graveyard and back to the church.

She ran for her life – and with a sudden curse he followed, surprisingly agile, a great tattered figure, spring-heeled, pursuing her through the driving snow. She stumbled as she turned, trying to climb the gentler slope further down, slipping on the white-powdered grass. And now, his companion in the vault alerted, the two of them were after her. They nearly caught her before, finding a grip, she clambered out of their way at the last moment, when they slipped themselves in their frantic efforts to catch her.

But now, with the advantage of the high ground, Frances turned and used her riding crop on the two struggling figures beneath her – the whiplash cracking through the snowflakes, mercilessly, repeatedly, as she threw her whole body into the attack, drawing the crop right back, throwing it out from her shoulder, whipping the line straight at their faces, where the cord opened great livid weals on their cheeks, the smaller tinker's eye suddenly pulped and bloodied as the lash bit into it, tearing across his forehead. Time and again, exultantly, she smote them. But the bigger man finally put an end to her attack, catching the lash in his hands, and pulling the crop from her, so that she had to turn and run once more.

Now she was in the graveyard proper, dodging and slipping among the tomb-stones, racing for the porch. But she fell once more, cracking her shin on a metal tomb rail. And this time, as she lay spreadeagled over the hard grave, the largest man, on his feet now and up the slope, seemed certain to capture her.

He lunged forward, arms outstretched again, about to pin her down. But, as he stumbled, she twisted away suddenly, and saw him fall instead on the metal spike at one corner of the tomb, spearing him somewhere high up, between his legs.

He doubled up, bellowing in pain. She had time then to run for the church door, open it and ram the bolt home on the far side before she heard the man throwing himself against the heavy oak, then hammering on the outside. There was no vestry or other entrance to the church, she knew. Only the high windows might offer access – and indeed as she ran back from the door she saw the dark hat and protuberant eyes of the second tinker rising above the sill of the plain east window at the end of the church – a face that raged and glowered at her, as he started to break the glass, continuing his pursuit.

But she soon put herself out of harm's way by climbing up the ladder to the belfry, slamming shut the trap door there, and standing on it firmly before pulling at the bell rope that ran down through a hole in the floor.

The bell tolled violently, a haphazard, ill-rung chime. But riding with the snowstorm, carried by the wind all over the parish, down the river valley, to the village of Cloone, it was soon heard at the great house of Summer Hill.

*

Several days later, though the storm had passed the village, the frozen snow still lay thick on the bridge above the salmon traps, blanketing the river mall and the small tree-lined green behind, preserving a filigree of icicles down the Cordiner memorial in the centre.

The collie dog outside Mrs Ryan's post office sniffed the steaming fresh horse droppings from Hennessy's cob, but feeling the cold soon left his explorations and returned to the post office where he whined against the door. Neither of the two people inside took the least notice of him.

John Hennessy, the grocer from Thomastown, five miles north, dallied over his small delivery – a quarter pound of Lipton's tea, a dozen candles, a small bag of sugar – as he tried to engage the unforthcoming Mrs Ryan in conversation.

'Sure and wasn't that a terrible thing up beyant at the church the other day,' he told the old, yellow-haired woman. She made no comment. 'Did you ever hear the like of it?' he went on knowingly, though in fact he had gleaned little of the events in question, hence his assumed familiarity with them, as a means of putting himself on an equal footing with the old lady and getting her to talk.

Finally she spoke – slowly, with great measure and emphasis. 'Indeed, a terrible thing, Mr Hennessy. A *terrible* thing.' Then, thinking better of it, she stopped.

'And? . . . what happened at all?' Mr Hennessy was forced into a more direct approach.

'Oh, and I wouldn't rightly know now . . .' Silence.

Mr Hennessy took another sugar bag from his basket and put it on the counter. 'A little Christmas box for you, Mrs Ryan.' He patted the heavy brown paper bag, then leant over, offering the old woman a whiskery, cold blue ear.

Mrs Ryan laid a heavy hand on the sugar, as no more than her right in the matter. 'Well, now, mind you I've said nothing, but there were ructions, *ructions*!' she whispered to him. Then she paused.

'What happened? – what happened at all?' Mr Hennessy could barely restrain himself. But Mrs Ryan, even though the appropriate overtures had all been observed, was still loath to ring the curtain up. Finally, she launched into the drama.

'Well now . . . didn't the young Missy take the whole *eye* outa one of thim tinkers, the little fella, all in wan *lash* o' the whip, like an oysther it was, dripping blood, all out on his cheek and he in the county infirmary now, 'till they *string* him up –'

'Sure an' now they'll hardly do that, Mrs – wasn't the oul' one dead already and she in her coffin?'

'Well, now, I don't know about that.' Mrs Ryan was affronted at this imputation that she might have confused the quick with the dead.

'And what about the other lad that went for her and she inside in the church?'

'Ah, sure, an' didn't he run for it, when thim bells got going and the lads from the estate above went for the church. Got clear away.' Mrs Ryan stood back, disappointed. 'Though he took the lash, too, be all accounts, before he went – and he with a great knife on him as well.'

'She's a tough one all right, that young Miss Cordiner.'

'Oh and tough's not the word for it, Mr Hennessy! Clare to God she's – she's the divil itself when she's a mind to it.' Mr Hennessy stood back himself now, licking his cold lips, in awe. 'You wouldn't tangle with *her*, John Hennessy, nor *iny* man, I tell ye!'

'I hadn't the mind to, Mrs –'

'Ah, sure, and wouldn't she take the skin off you as soon as look at ye – just like her oul mother.'

They leant closer, delving deeper into every aspect of the gruesome business.

Outside the cob shifted its weight, back feet clattering on the cobbles, shaking its bridle with a sharp tinkle of bit and chain. The sudden noise might have disturbed the snow on one of the old elms above the village green, for some flakes fell now, floating down through the bare trees, as if through water, confetti against a seaweed of dark branches.

Mr Hennessy finally emerged from the post office, climbing up on the bench of his van to continue his grocery rounds – the last and major delivery to Summer Hill before he returned to Thomastown: a small, red-faced man with wisps of reddish hair peeking out from beneath a worn bowler – his face glowed like a lantern against the white pall. He'd made these deliveries every Friday to Summer Hill for nearly twenty years, and today the usual mug of tea in the warm basement kitchen of the big house, while Mrs Martin checked the order, would be more than welcome.

Pulling a mackintosh rug over his knees, he took the reins, murmured to the cob, and they set off up the steep, twisting hill that led to the demesne gates at the top. It had started to snow again, very lightly – it would come to nothing, Mr Hennessy thought. But, by the time the van reached the top of the rise, the cob slipping on the flint stone past the estate cottages on either side, huge moist flakes fluttered in the air, side-slipping, circling, icing the stone pineapples on the gate pillars, dusting the fretworked gable ends and diamond window panes of the little Gothic lodge.

About to drive through the gates he was startled to see a thin, dark-coated figure ahead of him, shuffling past the lodge, a sack round his head, one empty sleeve pinned to the back of his jacket, tin cans jangling at his belt. For a moment Mr Hennessy feared he might be another dangerous tinker. But when the man turned abruptly, half-raising a stick, his wounded, noseless features staring upwards, shrouded by the sacking, a skull-like vision in the white flurry, Mr Hennessy recognised him: everyone in the locality knew him simply as Snipe – from his fluttery darting speech and equally unexpected movements – a tinker of sorts, but quite harmless, a man of the roads, maimed years before in some harvesting accident and now a regular traveller in these parts, in every weather, who sold tin billy-cans and told fortunes from tealeaves for a few pence. He, too, now and then, was welcomed at the back door of the big house. The cob stopped and Mr Hennessy helped him up on the bench beside him.

The front avenue led due south for over half a mile between white railed fences through the large demesne, past great bare clumps of oak and chestnut, up a slight incline for most of the way so that the house itself was not visible until almost the last moment. To the east, for a quarter of a mile, the pasture fell gradually, before giving way to the steep, forested slope of the valley, the river hidden beneath it as it wound through the limestone walls and buttresses at the bottom of the escarpment.

Ordinarily, in any decent weather, the chain of hills moving against the distant blue mountains on the far side of the valley filled this approach along the high ridge to Summer Hill with wonderful, changing perspectives. But that afternoon in the white drifts nothing was visible beyond the line of tall beech trees – the Beech Walk, a screen which ran diagonally from the brow of the hill down to the first of the thick woods on the lip of the gorge.

The great demesne was foreshortened everywhere, without length or breadth, where none of the spacious eighteenth-century landscaping showed, curtained now by the gentle spirals of snow which muffled every sound, the cob's feet falling on the crunchy flakes, so that the van seemed to be moving through a huge crystal ball, a vast toy, a glass ornament shaken out of its liquid translucent peace, the snowflakes dancing in the orb then, where soon the two travellers would reach the centrepiece of the conceit: the pinnacles and towers of some Gothic fairytale castle.

Summer Hill itself, though, was flat-roofed in the Palladian manner, with a stone balustrade all round, like a fence enclosing a flock of chimneystacks, built in the early eighteenth century from chiselled local limestone – a vast mansion set in the plan of a capital E, designed by David Bindon in his best Irish period for the first Baronet, Sir William Cordiner, on a site set back from an earlier Cordiner castle which had stood there for centuries on the edge of the hill commanding the river and its bridge. Though finely built and proportioned – its flanks, cornices, porch pediment, pillars, sash windows and stacks all precisely balanced, so that it was nowhere heavy, there was little romance in the present building. It was classically elegant.

Summer Hill was very much there on the high plateau, not as ostentation or memorial to colonial plunder, for it was in fact set on land which had been a gift from the Irish themselves: the house dominating this whole middle river valley of the Nore which the Anglo-Norman Cordiners – invited to Ireland with Strongbow by the Irish Chieftain Dermot MacMurrough, hard pressed in wars with his own subjects and rivals – had been given as their reward over 700 years before. And, though the present building had nothing of this blunt medieval age in it, it reflected, in its graceful certainties, the same proprietorial confidence and agreed purposes that had first brought the family to Ireland and had sustained them ever since.

The Cordiners had been Old English originally, Norman Knights in the reign of Henry II – always loyal to the Crown and then, as Barons of Cloone and Kilclondowne, more loyal still to what soon became for them their undivided Irish heritage. More Irish than the Irish themselves, there was nothing of a later plantation family here, no taint of Cromwellian arrogance, loot or murder.

Now, as the snow lay on the house, coating the roof balustrades, edging the long window frames, Summer Hill had the air, not of fairytale romance, but of something very real, a dream writ large, graciously but most realistically cast. Tucked about behind by a semi-circle of dark trees, the house, taking light from the snowy lawns, glowed along its eastern flank, where the flakes glittered on its walls, seeming to fire rather than chill the blueish limestone – a building that triumphed in every weather.

At the back, hidden to the north, a recently built wing in quite a different neo-Gothic style closed the letter E, where first it offered additional bachelor and servants quarters, and then formed one side of a new coach and stable yard. And it was here, turning right off the main drive and going through an archway, that Mr Hennessy and Snipe arrived a few minutes later. The yard was empty. But many windows about the house, already lamp-lit in the gathering winter twilight, confirmed considerable occupation inside.

Lady Cordiner took off her pince-nez, letting them fall on a capacious bosom. She stood up from her desk at the heart of the house, a boudoir of sorts, though furnished rather more as an office, a busy nerve centre that lay beyond the long drawing room.

'But, Mrs Martin, how *could* she have thought to clean the knives in such a manner?' Lady Cordiner spoke angrily of Bridget, a new scullery maid from one of the tenanted farms nearby.

'I really don't know, your Ladyship.'

'Pushing them up and down in the soil!'

'It's a country way, Ma'am. Some of the old men, with pocket knives . . .'

Mary Martin, the housekeeper, understood the enormity of this act in Lady Cordiner's eyes, though in her own mind it was hardly more than a peccadillo. It was one way to remove obstinate stains and the knives had not suffered. But her mistress was not Irish and had never understood such things. She looked at Lady Cordiner, a dumpy formidable silhouette standing against the white beyond the window – a sixtieth birthday celebrated that autumn, but still well preserved, still tightly, fashionably waisted in a long, black, bell-shaped dress whose heavy pleated satin rustled over the carpet as she moved impatiently about the room. Her dark hair, scraped up from behind and piled high in a bun, was only just tinged with white; her skin a soft olive-ivory shade – with plump little hands and small feet that moved dexterously and quickly and lips that were rarely still either, even when she was not speaking; above all the challenging glitter of the eyes which made her face still beautiful, orbs always seeking release from the heavy lids, caged but dangerous, as if, in this small room, here was a hungry animal sensing prey moving about elsewhere in the forest of the house.

Mrs Martin had seen something of the same features and complexion among a few people from her home in County Galway: descendants of Spanish sailors, it was said, wrecked on the coasts there in their Armada hundreds of years before.

And for a moment she pitied the woman, as an exile, far from her real home, and so unable to come to terms with Irish nature. But the sympathy was brief for she knew, in her years as housekeeper here, how well this woman, even if she did not understand local ways, imposed herself on them, reshaped them entirely to her own purposes.

Mary resented this – or rather resented the means, not the ends. For she had to admit that Lady Cordiner ran Summer Hill superbly well. A house, which thirty years before, when she had first come to it as a seamstress, had been quietly deteriorating, was now run vigorously, appropriately, in a way Mrs Beeton herself might have envied.

It was Lady Cordiner's overbearing manner that grated – not an aristocratic thing, Mrs Martin thought. It was more cunning in its form, the attitude of a wardress, so long versed in the wiles of those under her that she knew the likely misdemeanours of the servants in advance, the small tricks which local tradesmen might play, her family's ploys against her – where she would attack first, routing the opposition before it had any chance to order itself.

And yet, although she was high-handed, she was rarely unjust – Mary had to admit that, too. And she never used her power or position distantly. She involved herself intimately with the affairs of the household and before any reprimand or sentence she took great pains to establish the guilt. She was fair in that way, like a hanging judge. And to those servants and tradespeople who did not offend, who accepted her sharp scrutiny and abided by her rules, Lady Cordiner was equally constant – and generous, for she paid better wages and settled her accounts more promptly than any other lady in the county. Thus Summer Hill had become an exception to the rule, or misrule, of the country – and Mrs Martin recognised this and was happy enough in her service, while most of the other retainers, whose backgrounds had been truly poverty-stricken and disordered, were more than grateful: fearful of the ruler, they all appreciated the benefits of the reign.

Lady Cordiner continued with her household business. 'Well, Mrs Martin, the knives are hardly important – beside these household thefts. Nearly three months now. And you tell me the little crystal snow-dome – with the model of the house here inside – that's gone now, from the drawing room mantelpiece?'

'Yes, Ma'am. Yesterday, some time in the afternoon it must have been. As you know, I see to all the small items now, morning and evening.'

'Chinese vases, figurines, silver snuff boxes, candlesticks, Meissen shepherd-esses, Baccarat paperweights . . .' Lady Cordiner pondered this depredation of small antiques about the house.

'Perhaps it must finally be a matter for the constabulary,' she said. 'Though hardly at this moment, with all our house guests and the others about to arrive. We must simply watch and wait, Mrs Martin. But I wonder who it is?' she added, glaring at the housekeeper, venting her annoyance, though she knew it was not her. Mrs Martin was a Presbyterian.

*

That same afternoon Frances Cordiner, quite recovered from her drama with the tomb robbers the week before, and now impatient for further action, knelt by the window, alone in the great hall, looking at the small pane of stained glass which her Aunt Emily had made, inset at the bottom corner of the tall window – her family arms: a spread-eagle perched on a visored helmet with a scroll beneath and the inscription: 'Audaces Fortuna Juvat'.

'Fortune favours the brave,' she murmured aloud, looking out at the frozen snowscape, in the white twilight. The pleasure garden terraces, the sharp lines of the enclosing walls, steps, and box hedges, the exactly charted paths – all these had been smoothed and hidden in the fall, covered in a fluffy white eiderdown now, obliterating the strict patterns which Lady Cordiner, destroying an earlier and wilder Irish garden, had instituted. But the weather, at least, was immune to Lady Cordiner's brutal regimentation, and her daughter was suddenly happy that at least she had an ally here.

Beyond the ascending steps and terraced lawns to her right she saw the huge, white-dusted, Canadian maple, its lower branch just a stump now, no longer reaching out over the frozen croquet lawn. In summer, through many summers, the swing had hung there and she had been happy on it – pushing out, faster and faster, tummy left behind, toes in the leaves, then slowing down in a long glide. But her mother had had the swing removed some years before. 'You are no longer a child, Frances,' she had said. 'And, besides, the branch must be cut back in any case. It's beginning to overshadow the lawn.' That had been only very slightly true.

She had spoken to her father, Sir Desmond – pleaded with him, reminding him of this heritage of exotic shrubs and trees which his great-grandfather, a British Consul in the East, had brought back with him as seeds and cuttings and planted at Summer Hill: how this would be a desecration, a beginning of the end for the maple. And he had spoken to her mother about it. But the branch was cut down nonetheless. Her eldest brother Henry, a botanist and zoologist, might have successfully championed the case, she thought, but he had been away on one of his long expeditions. Or would he have taken a victory there? She loved him but knew how little stomach he had for battle with their mother – hence his long absences from the house.

Frances changed her focus and tried to find her reflection in the window pane. But there was nothing to be seen. She was not there. It made her uneasy – at a loss already, house-bound now for the afternoon. She breathed on the window instead, clouding the glass – then, with her finger, wrote the word 'me' in the condensation. Then she rubbed it out.

She turned impatiently. She must seriously consider the shape of her afternoon. Time for her was a quicksand which would suck your life away unless you fought it, filled it with brave acts, overwhelmed it by force of will. You could stop the clock with one bright deed, she knew. Frances pondered the coming hours, the minutes even, considering their fitness to her purposes as a commander allocates troops in a plan of battle. There were nearly three hours left before her other brother Eustace, his friend Harold Perkins, and the rest of the Christmas house guests arrived off the Dublin train.

She smiled, remembering how little favour any of her purposes had ever found with her mother, closeted just then in her boudoir beyond the drawing room. Frances's schemes, though she was a woman of twenty-two, were still often those of an adolescent, so that they were necessarily secret – her real life, like that of a child's, lived in shadow. Well-born, not tall but beautiful in rather a gypsy manner, with short glossy dark curls, blackberry eyes, full lips, and a very straight nose, versed in every young ladylike manner, beneath these surfaces she harboured quite unexpected appetites: a greedy, inquisitive, uncompromising taste for life. But it was not at that moment any mere animal hunger which she wished to appease. It was a longing for the inanimate, a craving for the spirit of place, a suit which she offered to Summer Hill itself, a house like the Frog Prince now, where she alone, knowing its secret, could work the miraculous transformation.

She wanted to storm the dark and overstuffed place, clearing it of all that her mother had brought here – the massive damask-covered Victorian furniture, heavy grey serge curtains, all the dull red and brown colours that hid the gleaming Italianate stucco of the previously classical interior – now crammed with every kind of fiddly knick-knack and vulgar ornament: wax flowers under domes; small sentimental pictures in fussy gilded frames set like postage stamps all over the walls; gothic-lettered samplers, heavily beaded and embroidered cushions, velvet footstools, Benares brass coffee tables, wrought iron firescreens, starched antimacassars – all in hideous taste.

The house, as she had seen from old aquatints of the hall and reception rooms, had once been spacious, set off in a clean blue and white geometry. It was a musty warehouse now, where most of its fine Chippendale and other Georgian furniture languished in outhouses and attics. Lady Cordiner had laid heavy hands everywhere. Even the white marble statues of Cupid and Psyche in their hall alcoves, considered immodest, had been replaced by togaed busts of Roman worthies. Frances wished Summer Hill a freedom which it no longer had, where she could bring back its true household Gods, rescue these divinities, kiss the sleeping stones into new life.

And it was only during such winter afternoons, when the ground floor was usually empty, that she could offer herself to Summer Hill, when she liked it best. She loved the silence of the great shell then, when she could speak and listen to it, in full possession of it, where she could wander the rooms and corridors, poke into all its nooks and crannies, be possessed by them in turn.

She looked at the long Flemish tapestry at the back of the hall, anchoring her arm about one of the great pillars there, letting her body swirl slowly round it, so that, as she turned, the chivalrous stories in the weave came alive, an animated panorama of fearless hunters and their prey, of medieval courts, of invulnerable Kings and Queens. Summer Hill seemed hers then, where she found faith in these Royal emblems of derring-do, a blessing for her own adventures. She tiptoed away, a wraith moving soundlessly over the floors and carpets, knowing every creak in the wood, where cover lay in each room or corridor, which doors groaned and which were mute.

Upstairs on the top floor, in the first of a suite of rooms which had been the old nurseries, now commandeered for his animal and butterfly collections, Henry Cordiner carefully speared a huge mauve-winged swallowtail with a large pin. Then he fixed it delicately into a glass display case, along with some dozens of other brilliantly winged insects in this particular collection of Nymphalinae. On top of the display, in fine copperplate, was the legend: 'North African Lepidoptera. Morocco, Tunisia, Egypt. March–June 1898'.

He picked up a magnifying glass and carefully examined this last specimen – a thick-set, stooping man in his late twenties, with an attractively broken nose and reels of dark loose curly hair that fell over his brow, partly obstructing his vision. He brushed the strands aside impatiently, trying to smooth them back behind his ears, licking his fingers quickly in the attempt.

'*Nymphalia Jason* – best of the lot,' he said at last to his companion, sitting on a high stool next to a work bench where bell jars, glass retorts and ether bottles were ranged along the surface. 'You remember, in Egypt, that sweltering afternoon in the delta? Near Zagazig. We chased this one all over the cotton field before it escaped into the old man's pigeon loft. What a rumpus – fellow thought we were after his pigeons with our nets . . .'

The younger man on the stool, Dermot Cordiner, a lieutenant in the Hussars and a distant cousin of Henry's, smiled but said nothing – a generous smile flooding his thin pale face beneath the neatly parted frizzy straw hair: a neat young man in everything, a brushed moustache, with the piercing cornflower-blue eyes of most Cordiners, sitting very upright on the tall stool as if he was still on parade and not on leave from his regiment in England.

Henry turned to him, saw the smile and accepted it as an entirely adequate response. The two men either talked a lot or very little. And, that mid-winter afternoon, the warm coals in the grate, together with the permanent rumour of ether in the room, had made them both drowsy and disinclined for conversation.

They seemed an unlikely pair at first – this burly, dishevelled, rather Byronic scion of Summer Hill and his meticulous, frail-looking cousin. What they shared was not obvious but lay near the heart of their relationship, a love of the great outdoors, for adventure there – new worlds to be mastered: lakes, rivers, mountains, deserts and forests to be traversed and charted, rare flora and fauna to be taken and catalogued, where all that they did in this way together was carefully planned and vigorously executed. It was Dermot, with his intuitive grasp of military tactics, who supplied the plans and Henry the scientific vigour. Together they were a happy and formidable combination.

Henry closed the display case, took it up and put it in line with a dozen others on a shelf at the end of the room. An open doorway here led into the old day nursery, a room now given over to much larger glass display cases, filled with stuffed animals and birds.

'Where's Gretel got to?' Henry moved through the doorway, searching the room beyond. On top of one of the glass cases – quite motionless, apparently one of the exotic exhibits – a strange animal lay curled. 'Ah, Gretel – too hot for you in the other room? I'm surprised.'

Henry touched the silky white hairs above a protuberant ear. A round fire-brown eye opened from the middle of a circle of black fur; a smooth, jet-black, puppy dog nose emerged from between prehensile paws – and then a wonderful tail uncurled, fluffy thick, ringed all the way in black and white, longer than the animal itself, before the ring-tailed lemur jumped on her master's shoulder and he took her back to the other room.

But the animal was unhappy there, fretting, chattering in soft clucks and chirrups, nose sniffing, her huge round eyes darting about, searching every corner of the room.

'It's obvious,' Dermot said.

'Yes, I know, Gretel.' Henry spoke consolingly to the animal, picking up half an apple, offering it to her, which she would not accept. 'It won't be long now. Just he's off colour, you see – needs the warmth here and the regular meals. But we'll have him out by morning with any luck, unless the snow stays.'

Henry took Gretel back to the other room, with a basin of cut fruit, setting her on an old patchwork blanket in a club chair at the far end of the room. Closing the door on his return he went to a large, hinge-topped tea chest near the fireplace. Opening it he looked down into the sand inside. A slow, faint hissing noise rose from the olive brown and yellow coils; a very prettily patterned scaly head moved a fraction.

'Feeding time, I think.' Henry moved to a smaller box nearby where he kept a supply of live mice. Dermot remonstrated with him. 'If your mother knew.'

'She *won't* know.'

'But it *is* poisonous.'

'Yes. But it's only a sand snake, Dermot: African Beauty – and isn't he! The fangs are right at the back of the jaws, so he's quite unable to strike with them – has to almost swallow his prey before he can kill it. Absolutely no danger to humans.'

Henry washed his hands in a ewer, then moved over to a large central table where maps were laid out at one end and on the other a Mauser .375 sporting rifle had been dismantled, the mechanism neatly laid out on an oilcloth.

'Shall we take a look at possible routes again?'

Dermot joined him at the head of the table and together they pored over the large army ordnance map, headed 'British East African Protectorates and Territories'. The Arab ports on the Indian Ocean coast were clearly marked – Mombasa, Malindi, the island of Lamu. But the interior, most of the hinterland to the west, was almost entirely blank, apart from two roughly charted red lines, later inked-in additions, running from Abyssinia south-west across a vast space marked 'desert' towards some equally vague shapes marked 'mountains'.

The two men became engrossed in the map, planning their long journey, next year, into the heart of the dark continent.

Emily Cordiner, Sir Desmond's younger sister, maiden aunt in Summer Hill and long resident there, gazed at the snowfall from her studio-cum-bedroom on the west wing of the house. Her windows gave out onto one of the great features of the Summer Hill gardens – long alleys of clipped yew and beech hedging, interspersed with pleached hornbeam arcades, a tall maze of walks, offering surprising vistas, leading to secret bowers and stone grottoes, past antique statuary to little pavilions, a dovecote, an artificial waterfall – each walk terminating at the centre at a great oak tree, beneath which, in summer, pastoral comedies were sometimes presented by the house guests.

Emily loved this permanent conceit just outside her windows, which the snow made all the more baroque, bearding the statues, powdering a folly of broken Corinthian pillars, icing a little Palladian bridge in the distance: the baroque of Vanbrugh perfectly accentuated now in the white glitter, encompassed by this fluffy, pearl-topped regiment of hedges.

Her bedroom decor seemed more rococo. A passionate student and gifted interpreter of the period, she had decorated it herself, adorning the walls with a series of exquisite trompe-l'oeil paintings, turning one end of it, where her big brass four-poster bed seemed a stage now against the wall, into a representation of the little Residenz Theater in Munich, a place which had excited her to a pitch of frenzy when she had first visited it, as a young woman, over twenty-five years before. So here, on either side of the bed, she had faithfully repeated some of those tiers of boxes, exactly mimicking the carved wood and plaster in white and gold, the draped crimson curtains beneath with gold tassels, the cherubs swarming over them supporting coats-of-arms – and above the royal box a vast Imperial crown with glittering gold palm trees rising up each side. These perfect three-dimensional effects, though reduced in scale, gave the room an air of always-impending theatre, where a Mozart overture might break out at any moment.

But now, in the faint white light from the windows, with the help of a tall oil lamp, Emily sat facing away from the stage, intent on another pleasure, bent over her sketch book – skilfully colouring a pen-and-ink drawing there, one of many in the book, the latest in a series of secret books in which, over the years, she had charted her vision of life at Summer Hill, the airs and graces, follies and foibles of its inhabitants. In this instance she had drawn the crowned figure of a Queen, elaborately wigged, processing under an ostrich-feathered canopy up one of the snowy walks outside the window – a rather dumpy, fat-legged but surprisingly confident Queen, since she was dressed only in an indecently short petticoat, followed meekly by her courtiers in their splendidly fussy eighteenth-century costume. The Queen was quite clearly Lady Cordiner, her followers other members of the Summer Hill household, family and retainers. Finishing the watercolour she entitled it 'The Empress's New Clothes' – on a swirly gilt scroll held between the mouths of the two Summer Hill terriers, Monster and Sergeant, trotting in front.

Emily had worked on the painting all day and now that it was complete her body went limp, the earlier animation left her face, the deft hands fiddled uselessly on the table. She was another person, unseeing, vague, released now from the source of her vitality. She said to herself, 'Did I wake at five o'clock this morning? – or was that yesterday evening?' She was worried by the uncertainty of this, day and night confused for her, where she seemed to be slipping out of time, no longer part of its light and dark, lost to the natural rhythms of clock and calendar, adrift without her sketchbook in a world where she had no anchors.

She heard the knock and the key moving on the outside of her door – the door to one side of her bed like a stage entrance – and turning the gilt chair round, facing the bed, she assumed the pose of a spectator in her theatre. Of course – overture and beginners, she thought, seeing the dark tail-coated man enter the room: the conductor, *The Marriage of Figaro*, her favourite.

Pat Kennedy, the young under-butler, came towards her with a tea tray, setting it down gently near her worktable, serving her early as he did most afternoons, giving Molly, her own personal maid, a rest. He smiled broadly, a friend of this thin, bird-like woman in her always-dark wool cardigans – eager-faced and happy with darting blue eyes when she was working, but who now looked up at him vacantly. He knew how, in this state, she would never complain at her incarceration, lost to the real world. But he could not understand why – when he had seen her busy and alive over her sketchbook – why she did not leave her paints and pens and ink, storm the locked door and quit the house. For in that vital mood – and he had seen the results of it, sometimes peering over her shoulder – Emily Cordiner struck him as an oasis of sanity in the great house.

Of course he knew why she was restrained here. Apart from her general vagaries she had recently, when Sir Desmond and Lady Cordiner had gone to Dublin for the Horse Show, run riot with her colours in several reception rooms at Summer Hill, starting to decorate them as she had her own bedroom: barely-clothed nymphs and shepherdesses – unsuitably bucolic murals in the dining room; then a witty trompe-l'oeil, a village band – a collection of quite obviously inebriated old men in bowlers with flutes and fiddles and crates of porter bottles – on the wall behind the Blüthner grand in the drawing room. Lady Cordiner had not been amused.

Sir Desmond Cordiner, in his dark-panelled, rather scruffy study beyond the morning room, considered the shape of the six-bladed propeller set up on a shaft attached to the wall. He turned it sharply, happy with the gust of air that penetrated his short beard, only half-listening to his farm steward speaking on the other side of the desk.

'. . . there's Cooper's wood,' Michael O'Donovan was saying. 'And then the two fields beyond: the ten- and six-acre lots. I believe the price would be right.' O'Donovan leant forward, consulting a map of the Summer Hill estate with its bordering farms. 'The land drops on that west side of the hill – and it's damp, it's poorly at the bottom. But it could be drained. It'll go to auction certainly, but you might consider an earlier offer, Sir.'

Sir Desmond half-turned. 'Yes,' he said. But his mind was elsewhere. The propeller wasn't the problem, he thought. This one, in light ash, together with one like it, would certainly give the required push. It was the engine, as always, that mattered in these heavier-than-air machines. And the petrol engine he was adapting, taken from a new Benz $3\frac{1}{2}$-horsepower motor car delivered that autumn, simply wasn't reliable enough yet. His linen- and wire-strutted machine, he knew – partly set up in one of the coach houses – would certainly glide with a man strapped beneath it, just as an earlier model had done, some dozens of times for up to half a minute on the slopes beneath the house. He was confident about that. He had been in touch with Otto Lilienthal in Germany on that score, using the same concave, bat-like, superimposed wings that the German had done, much more successfully over thousands of glides. But Lilienthal, in a sudden gust of wind, had been killed in his glider two years before.

'The auction is on the 17th of next month, Sir. In Thomastown,' O'Donovan said. 'I'd say it'd go as high as £18 or £20 an acre.'

'Yes.' Sir Desmond nodded absent-mindedly. Of course, what one wanted – and he'd recognised this some time before – was a vertical air rudder like a boat's, where the wind would act like a flow of water against it, though only if the machine was propelled fast enough into it, since of course you couldn't tiller a boat in a calm. And besides such a rudder, which would only take you to port or starboard, there would have to be another means to manoeuvre the machine in its horizontal plane, a rudder that would push it up or down. He had foreseen that, too, and had been working on just such a scheme that afternoon, his plans lying beneath the Summer Hill estate map so that he was mildly impatient now with O'Donovan.

'Make an offer, O'Donovan – do what you think best. Be fair, of course. Be more than fair, indeed,' he added, suddenly thinking of something, looking carefully at the map this time. 'That hill the far side of Cooper's Wood,' he asked. 'It's steep enough, isn't it? And westward.'

'Yes, Sir. But there's good pasture there, if it were drained.'

But Sir Desmond had quite other ideas for it: steep, with an open run from the top, westward into the prevailing winds . . . Perhaps that's what he needed, when the time came to try his new machine. Westward Ho, he thought. And a secret spot, too, away from the roads, with the cover of the wood, for there had been nosy-parkers enough, bystanders and newspaper men coming to the village recently, eavesdropping on his experiments. It would be a disaster, now that he thought himself close to success, if some rival were to pre-empt him. For more than anything else Sir Desmond, though nearly sixty, longed to be the first man in the world to soar aloft in powered flight.

In quite the second best guest bedroom, with its dark, very slightly threadbare velvet curtains, and darker wallpaper, Bunty Cordiner moped and fretted. She would not rest on the plain double bed nor read a society magazine by the low coal fire as her husband, Austin Cordiner, had suggested. Instead she paced the large room, a fidgety, over-dressed, competent little woman, fiddling with her excessive necklace, picking up ornaments from the table, dressing table and mantelpiece – gazing at them with annoyance, talking to her husband the while through the open doorway to their dressing room, where he was at work on some papers, matters concerning his own much smaller house and farm at Wellfield, sixty miles north in Queens county. These Cordiners, Sir Desmond's younger brother and his Ulster wife, had come to spend Christmas with their three children at the family seat.

'And *why* we must spend every Christmas here, I can *not* understand,' Bunty said. Her husband, a taciturn man, much given to serious agricultural thought, remained silent, considering the rotation of next year's crops. 'Your sister-in-law treats me like dirt,' Bunty went on. 'The servants are haughty and the talk is either of these infernal flying machines, or grand opera. Or some quite unsuitable trek among the African heathen. Nothing else, nothing *sensible*. This evening, for example, I hear we are to be regaled by a ballad singer, no less, some saloon bar entertainer.'

Her husband demurred, speaking at last. 'Not *quite*, my dear. This Mr O'Meara is something rather more than that, I understand. Spoken very highly of in Dublin. The *Irish Times* had a very favourable critique of his RDS recital –'

'I should prefer bridge.'

'I think *not* – given Sarah's feelings about card games.'

'See! – how she chivvies you in everything, and you bow under!' Bunty was roused, coming to the dressing room door, holding a little Chelsea shepherdess in her hand.

'My dear, we are guests in her house.'

'*Her* house, indeed! It is your brother's house; and *why* are we always guests? – in the second best guest room to boot.'

'A family gathering at this season . . . is appropriate: besides being a welcome change of scene for both of us, and the children.'

'I should prefer to stay at home.'

This was untrue. Bunty disliked Lady Cordiner intensely, but envied her smooth running of the household, the grandeur of the place, the clever, wide-ranging conversations – envied here all that she did not understand, did not possess, or could not promote in her own home. Summer Hill was thus a continual affront to her lesser status, her inabilities, a permanent frustration, an itch. Yet it offered her a delicious frisson as well, a challenge to her social ambitions. It was a prize only just out of reach, which she dreamt about like a lover. So that to be here, living amidst its wonders, forced her to condemn the house, to sully it, since she could not possess what she wanted.

'Well, if we are not put down here,' she said aggressively, 'why do we spend afternoons lodged in our bedroom? Tell me *that*! We are all of us whip-handed by your sister-in-law,' she spat out. 'Cowering from her like beasts, hidden in our rooms – your brother, sister, nephew, niece – all of you afraid to face her – without a fire in the drawing room 'till teatime, so that we must lurk upstairs as if in some seaside boarding house in Bundoran.'

Her husband, removing his gold-rimmed spectacles, looked up at her at last, wary of her in this mood. 'Bunty, my dear – you are free to wander where you will. You exaggerate, you imagine. Sarah is no ogress . . .' But he let his words die, doubting their truth. Bunty glared at him pointedly, then with equal purpose dropped the little Chelsea figurine; it broke, a mass of splintered colour scattering over the floor. 'Oh, how clumsy of me,' she said, turning away, leaving the bits where they were. 'How clumsy.' Austin turned to his papers. He would like to have sighed, a very audible sigh, but he thought better of it.

Elsewhere in the house, in a distant playroom, Bunty's two sons, Neill and Robert, played snakes-and-ladders under the beady eye of their cantankerous old governess, a Miss Wildeblood from Manchester. Both boys, at twelve and thirteen, would have liked to be outside snow-balling. But that had been forbidden and they were a docile, obedient pair. Bunty's seventeen-year-old daughter Isabelle, though, was not so dutiful. She sat by the playroom window, pouting, pulling her blonde ringlets about, a secret thumb-sucker, her embroidery forgotten on her lap. She gazed out at the snow – not seeing it, seeing something else, thinking of the Honourable Harold Perkins, Coldstream Guards, her cousin Frances's young man, due off the Dublin train with the other guests in a few hours. She had met him earlier that year when he had first visited Summer Hill and had not forgotten one single thing about him.

In his pantry, sitting in an old leather armchair, by the big silver safe beneath the tall green baize shelves with their vast collections of plate and glass, Flood, the ageing butler, stirred in his doze, woken by the sound of horses' hooves on the yard cobbles outside the window. Hennessy's van had arrived. Pat Kennedy, his deputy, was still upstairs with Miss Emily. He would have to check his part of the delivery himself, the consignment of lesser wines, and the spirits, ordered for Christmas.

Mrs Molloy, down in the basement kitchen preparing dinner, heard the van, too, stopped her supervision of the duck-trussing with the three kitchen maids and moved a kettle onto the hotplate of the big range. Mrs Martin was still with her ladyship and Maureen Molloy was pleased that she would have Mr Hennessy to herself, checking the groceries with him. Not that she objected to the housekeeper. No, she was a fair woman who did not interfere. But, like Flood, she was different, quite different. They were both Protestant: there were jokes and gossip with Pat Hennessy which she could never make or share in Mrs Martin's presence.

When she saw Snipe, however, coming into the kitchen as well, she was momentarily put out. Her own girls, and the other scullery and house maids, who would soon hear of his arrival, were always unduly excited by Snipe – as he told their fortunes in the tea-leaves, forecasting unlikely romance, putting all sorts of nonsense into their heads. Well, fair enough, she thought. They had worked like blacks all day: the half-dozen ducks were almost oven-ready, with their braise of chestnuts; the Béchamel Aurora sauce for the sole would not take a moment – the mock turtle soup had long since been prepared and the Kaiser pudding was already gently steaming on a slow plate. The girls deserved their fun.

Flood joined her then, and Snipe sat down among the tittering girls, big earthenware teapot and cups at the ready. Pat Hennessy went to and fro, up and down the steps outside, bringing the order: tea, coffee, cocoa, sugar, candied peel, dried fruit, preserved and canned provisions of all sorts, household requisites: 'Bath brick, beeswax, a dozen blacklead, six plate powder, six polishing paste, a dozen Colman's starch, two dozen carbolic soap, four quarts malt vinegar, one gross candles . . .'

Mrs Molloy ticked off the items, while Flood, more slowly, accounted for his Christmas wines and spirits: 'Two cases Tullamore whiskey, two cases scotch, one case Holland gin, one London gin, two cases sweet sherry, one pale, two Montilla, one Tarragona. One case ginger wine, one orange, two cases Seltzer, two Polly water. Six dozen Smithwick's ale. One nine-gallon stout in cask – can you manage that, Mr Hennessy?' he asked. 'Pat Kennedy will be back in a moment.' But Mr Hennessy could manage it well enough – anxious for his tea and then to be away in case the snow got worse.

Snipe's thin darting voice rose over the end of the kitchen table then, the girls already in his thrall, as he took a first empty teacup, inspecting the oracle of wet leaves inside. 'You,' he said, looking at Nelly, one of the parlourmaids, 'you will meet a stranger, from beyant – from over the sea: yes, I see – a dark stranger . . .' The girls were spellbound, as much by the information as by the scarred and wounded face of the young man who offered it, a face which, reflecting such grim tragedy, must have wisdom in it, they thought, and so more certainly speak the truth in these happy fortunes.

The following morning Lady Cordiner, at her desk, was looking at papers from her family brokers in London, considering financial matters. One of her investments in a Transvaal gold mine had continued to depreciate, but the letter recommended that she hold her stock pending, as her broker put it, 'a settlement with the rebellious Boers'. This was sure to come, the man had added, 'by treaty, not force'. There was nothing to worry about. Lady Cordiner was not so sure. As a Jewess, an outsider herself, she knew the destructive energy and tenacity of the dispossessed from whom, as she saw it, one had everything to fear. She knew this of her own race, of the Irish, too, and so of the distant Boers.

It was a feeling in her blood, not drawn from any first- or second-hand experience – since her own family, the Sephardic Halevys, had been successfully established in England since the Napoleonic wars. Timber, coal, diamonds, gold – the Halevys had not been userers. Like the English gentry, with whom latterly they had sometimes merged, they had taken their money from the land. Unlike them, in the recent steep agricultural decline, the Halevys had seen their stock rise in every quarter. They were rich indeed, though not obtrusively so, living apart from the other greater Jewish clans in England, less orthodox than they, in their Spanish origins, their faith and in their muscular businesses.

Sarah's father, old Basil Halevy, with his mansion outside Leytonstone, not far from his ships and great warehouses on the Thames, had only brief doubts about her marriage over thirty years before to Desmond Cordiner, then a successful mechanical engineer – a brilliant innovator – as well as heir to the baronetcy, house and estates of Summer Hill. Basil Halevy, a Jew of liberal and expansive vision, with two elder sons to secure his own commercial titles, had thought of his daughter's happiness first – and then of other advantages in the match: here was a possible lever, a means of broaching fresh business territory in Ireland.

Besides, he had taken to the young Desmond Cordiner at once, admiring qualities in him which he had not met with in the upper reaches of the English gentry: Desmond's down-to-earth, scientific approach to affairs, yet his gifts of improvisation and lack of stuffy formality, an airy inventiveness. He liked the energy and quick wit of the man, among an Irish landed class that he had previously thought to be merely witty – and lazy. This Cordiner, he had decided years before, might well have been one of his own – one of the Magic People – and he had happily settled £100,000 on his only daughter as a dowry.

The investment, as far as his own business ambitions were concerned, had not prospered: few Irish markets were opened up to him. The Cordiners and their like had no association with, and no need of, the mining industry – coal or precious stones. They burnt their over-abundant wood, and their jewels were more precious family heirlooms. On the other hand Basil Halevy was quite happy to see how his daughter had subsequently made very solid use of her dowry, where the money had brought needed repairs and improvements, including, he thought, a most handsome new yard wing – in the recent neo-Gothic style – to Summer Hill.

On the death twenty years before of Desmond's father, the eighth Baronet, when, as Lady Cordiner, she had become mistress of Summer Hill, she had at once promoted this extra house room as a much-needed addition in familial space, for her own visiting relatives, and for the many other Cordiners – uncles, aunts and cousins of this extended family – who lived elsewhere in Ireland and overseas: a strong Jewish sense of clan, she made clear, which she happily shared with the Irish – it was this which she wished to prosper in her expensive renovations and extensions. In fact what she wanted much more was social advantage, bricks and mortar which would underpin a rampant social ambition.

For what her father or Mrs Martin or few other people had recognised in Lady Cordiner was a vehement desire not only to be accepted by Irish society but more to be seen by them as a great hostess, opening shutters on what for her was a dark outpost of empire, where she would make Summer Hill a glittering beacon of culture and elegance – quite throwing off her mercantile background among the Wapping warehouses – creating a new dynasty of Cordiners, in the hands of her eldest son Henry, who would show the Irish how there was far more to life beyond squabbling with the Land Leaguers and arguing over Home Rule.

Sir Desmond himself had never resisted her ambitions here. He had no interest in them. For him, though he took little active part in the matter, the running of his farms and large estate was everything and the heritage he hoped to pass on to his son was one of well-maintained and endowed lands, not a taste for Schubert duets by candlelight.

His peers in the county shared identical hopes for their male progeny, though few were as likely as him to pass on so fruitful an inheritance. Sir Desmond, unlike his immediate forebears and almost entirely through his wife's money and her restless, dictatorial energy, had become a highly successful landowner. And that, besides his own aeronautical work, was all that mattered to him. His wife's rampant sociability, stamina and zealous interference in all the affairs of Summer Hill left him free to pursue his mechanical obsessions. It mattered little, whenever he had to admit it, that Lady Cordiner had come to bully and dominate him to an extent where, in the running of his own house and estate, he had become hardly more than a figurehead.

Lady Cordiner meanwhile remained entirely committed to her sophisticated hopes, and to this end now, leaving her financial papers, she turned to the guest list for the New Year's ball – climax of the seasonal festivities at Summer Hill. The Waterfords had accepted, but not the Ormondes, and the Devonshires would be away in England. She had not yet reached the top of the social pinnacle. But she would, she thought. Her will, together with her money and social flair, would eventually prevail here, as they had in every other sphere of her life. It was simply a matter of time, of maintaining an unsullied reputation and a strict selectivity in her guests, where she would so increase her social cachet that these other Dukes and Marquesses would readily exchange hospitalities with her – if not Royalty itself.

A moment later she turned suddenly, startled by a noise in the big drawing room next-door – the sound of something falling: some small glass ornament, a figurine, a silver snuff box? She rose from her chair quickly, silently.

The heavily-furnished drawing room, lightened only by a blaze of snowy sun-shine, was deserted. There was no time to discover what might be missing or broken there, for the door at the other end was closing slowly. Someone had just left the room. But the hall, when Lady Cordiner got there, was empty, too. She glanced up at the first-floor balustrades enclosing the stair well: a shadow brushed behind them, disappearing along one of the landings running back into the house. This time the culprit would be caught red-handed, Lady Cordiner thought, picking up her skirts and running as fast as her small legs would allow up the staircase. Once in the corridor, without knocking she stormed into each of the bedrooms, occupied or not, astonishing Bunty and Austin Cordiner and receiving a dazed look from Emily, but without seeing anything suspicious. At the end was her daughter's room. Latterly, she had come to suspect Frances of these thefts. Now, as she flung the door open, impending confirmation of this filled her with a lovely bitter energy.

The pretty bedroom, with its apricot walls and frieze of primroses, was empty – apart from Marquis, Frances's red-tailed African parrot, a gift from Henry, on its perch by the window, cocking its head at her now and eying her impertinently. 'Three bags full, I say!' the bird croaked at her malevolently. She heard the splash of water in the dressing room beyond. Moving to the half-open doorway she saw her daughter, muddy riding clothes on a chair, naked under the portable shower, with its round tank on top supported by three mock bamboo metal poles. Frances's young maid, Eileen, half-way up a step-ladder, was pouring warm water into the tank from several brass cans, where the flow cascaded down through the small holes, straightening and plastering Frances's curls against her head, running off her breasts. Eileen stopped. Frances half-turned, quite unabashed, looking at her mother.

'Yes, Mama – what is it?'

The parrot squeaked from the other room – 'Water biscuits! Water biscuits!' – infuriating Lady Cordiner, so that for answer she turned back into the bedroom and started to ransack the place, stripping the bed, lifting the mattress, peering under it, then pulling drawers out, curtains aside, spilling clothes from a great mahogany wardrobe, tossing and pawing at everything in the room like a bull in a china shop, while the parrot, flapping about on its perch, became equally roused, adding to the furore. 'Nuts! Nuts!' the bird screamed.

Frances came into the room, a towelled figure, curls dripping, her damp face radiant. 'Mama, what *is* it?'

Her mother threw a mauve feather boa on the floor. 'I know it's you,' she shouted. 'You thief!' – and she strode past her into the dressing room.

'Me *what*?' Frances called back to her, picking up the feather boa, putting it on, and doing a little strutting dance, so that Eileen, emerging from the dressing room, could not suppress a giggle.

'It's you!' Lady Cordiner shouted, running amok in the dressing room. 'You who have been taking all these little objects.' Frances and Eileen exchanged looks. Eileen was clearly frightened. But Frances simply smiled at her, putting a finger to her lips. Finding nothing among her daughter's toiletries, Lady Cordiner returned to the bedroom.

'Mama, you are unhinged,' Frances told her, while the parrot shrieked 'Nuts! Nuts!', seeming to add insult to injury, so that Lady Cordiner, goaded beyond endurance, unwisely made for the bird, attempting to sweep it off its perch, perhaps even to strangle it. But the bird pecked her sharply on the wrist, drawing blood, and that was an end of it. Lady Cordiner retreated.

'Be warned, this is *not* the end of it,' she said, confronting her daughter, trying to rescue some dignity in the matter, while staunching her wound.

'No, Mama, indeed not. I think you should lie down. And perhaps I should call Dr Mitchell?'

When Lady Cordiner had gone the two women went back into the dressing room – the petite, rather plump and dimple-cheeked Eileen, normally calm and collected, considerably flustered now. 'Miss, I can't go on with it,' she said. 'She nearly caught me then, downstairs.'

'Nonsense, Eileen.' Frances took her by the shoulders and gazed at her intently, smiling. 'It's my turn next, in any case. And if you like we'll drop it all for Christmas.'

'Yes, Miss.'

'Please don't call me Miss. I told you – I'm Frances.'

'It's dangerous, though – I'd never work again, *any*where, if she caught me.'

'You will *always* work with me, Eileen, wherever I am.' Frances successfully consoled the girl, looking at her so openly and confidently that Eileen's fears subsided. This sort of persuasion was one of Frances's great gifts – an intimate, illicit thing which she could bring to bear against any resistance: a candour of regard which allowed Eileen to feel completely her equal, where at the same time Frances had made it clear to her that what she was offering was something the girl had never dreamt of, a partnership in some vastly exciting adventure. For it was not a simple, flirtatious, one-sided guile, this. Frances always in the end shared in what she willed, made people helpless accomplices in her desires. Like an unsprung trap her mischievous gaze seduced them before they knew it.

As she climbed the step-ladder now, her hair still dripped and glistened – water skating down over the oils of her skin, hesitating on the sudden slopes, finding diversions round her small conical breasts with their retroussé nipples, tickling the dark aureoles there, trickling over her long midriff before swamping the towel at her waist and seeping down her creamy flanks.

Opening a brass water can she picked out the one prize she had for so long coveted in the house and finally gained – a lovely Baccarat snow dome, a paper-weight, with an ivory model of Summer Hill, caught forever in the drifting flakes inside.

She dried the crystal with the hem of her towel, the cloth slipping from her waist – so that, naked now, she held the snow dome up before her like a chalice, the Holy Grail, the secret essence of the house which, in default of possessing the real thing, she would take to now like an adulterous lover.

Then she showed the crystal to Eileen, holding it out, a great victory. Finally she put it away in the empty water tank on top of the shower, among her store of other hidden booty – glass overlay snuff bottles, enamelled colour twist wine glasses, silver snuff boxes, glazed porcelain figurines.

Eileen looked up at her. What's it all for? she wanted to ask – these useless bits and pieces, for a lady who had everything? Eileen did not understand but she marvelled at the cheek of it all. Being with Miss Frances was more exciting than listening to Snipe down in the kitchen: Snipe with his always-hopeful fortunes which for her, at least, had never come true.

But downstairs that previous afternoon, in a last throw of tea-leaves, Snipe had seen an unfavourable pattern. He had not said anything. The girl whose cup it was had looked at him nervously. 'No,' he'd said at last. ''Tis not for you, for there's no spread in it. You see,' he went on, showing her the little compacted hillock inside the cup. 'The leaves – they never moved at all.'

'Glory be! I have no fortune then!' the girl moaned.

'No, 'tis not that.' Snipe looked doubtfully about him, then up at the ceiling. ' 'Tis the fortune out of the house itself, that won't move the leaves, d'ye see? The air in the place.'

Mr Hennessy had called Snipe away then, when he had put his few pennies in his pocket, and the two of them had gone out into the snow, which had eased a little, a soft crunchy carpet over the yard, where Snipe looked back curiously at the great house in the white dusk, the holes in his face where his nose had been twitching sensitively, trying to sniff something in the air, an omen of some sort which he could not interpret at all.

2

'DOWN, SERGEANT! Down, Monster! – down!' Sir Desmond roared at the Jack Russell terriers, leaping through the snow like tiny deer towards the guests, barking furiously, jumping waist high at Eustace, remembering him. As he picked them up, they promptly started a dog fight from beneath each arm.

Two flaming braziers on the porch steps illuminated the scene. The snow had returned with the night, coming thinly out of the darkness, falling into the circles of yellow light as Molloy with the other footmen attended to the luggage wagonette while the household waited to greet the new arrivals from the carriage – Mr O'Meara, the young opera singer, fur-collared, handsome and rather pleased with himself, clasping a small music case; the stoutish, owl-faced Eustace Cordiner and his aristocratic army friend, the Honourable Harold Perkins with the effervescent, well-bearded Mortimer Cordiner, Queen's Counsel and Member of Parliament – Dermot's father – bringing up the rear.

Behind the carriage, from two more hackney traps which had just drawn up, further and obviously unexpected guests were now emerging, small uncertain shapes congregating outside the splashes of light, being marshalled by a tall figure in a very long overcoat. Lady Cordiner gazed anxiously into the night before a stentorian voice made her gasp a fraction.

'God bless all here!' She heard the mock Irish brogue in the darkness, before an elegantly middle-aged man in an astrakhan greatcoat and hat, brandishing a silver-topped cane, strode into the light, followed by a group of strangers, five shawled and shivering young women and a young man.

Eustace turned towards Lady Cordiner. 'A surprise for you, Mama – they were all on the train from Kingsbridge. It's Humphrey, with a troupe of Spanish dancers, can you imagine!'

A boisterous figure approached his mother, arms outstretched, cane in one hand, doffing his astrakhan hat with the other. He enveloped Lady Cordiner in a theatrical bear hug, did the same for Frances, then pumped Sir Desmond's hand, while Bunty Cordiner looked on askance.

'But, Humphrey,' Sir Desmond said, 'we thought you weren't due down here 'till after Christmas. Our *Colleen Bawn* date at the Kilkenny theatre is still on the 29th, isn't it?'

'My dear fellow, with what I've brought now, I simply couldn't wait – knew you'd want to see them first, Rodrigo and his five girls, something quite sensational: flamenco dancers – ever heard of it? Found them out of an engagement in Dublin – absolutely first rate! A rat-a-tat-tat dance to a throbbing guitar – make your blood boil, old man. Saw them at the Olympia last week, brought them down for the date in Kilkenny. But I was sure you'd want to see them sooner. Put a show on here for you – here, on the steps, why not? – tomorrow morning –'

'But, Humphrey, where are they all to stay?' Lady Cordiner interjected.

'Oh, anywhere, Sarah.' And he looked at her, a knowing smile on his weather-stained face, where the snow was melting on heavy eyebrows, running past candid, roving eyes, down whiskery cheeks to a pointed chin. 'These are real Spanish gypsies – stables would probably do, long as they're well fed and watered.' He laughed, a deep belly chuckle, quite at odds with his thin frame, over which the folds of his enormous greatcoat flapped like sails in the chill air. 'In fact, I shall want the best bedrooms for them: your *own* people Sarah, you must remember, from Andalucia – nothing but the best!'

'Really, Humphrey.' Lady Cordiner, taking his point, none the less continued to remonstrate with the gaunt, gay figure, the rich and eccentric Englishman, Humphrey Saunders – amorist, actor, traveller, poet, pamphleteer, practical joker, Irish nationalist and wayward friend for many years: one of the very few people, even though he had loved her once, whom she had never managed to dominate.

'They will have to share quarters in the back wing. But you should have warned us, Humphrey.'

'My dear – surprise! The essence of life, is it not?' He flourished his hands, then warmed them quickly by the brazier, before introducing the troupe, beckoning each to the fire in turn. 'Maria, Concepta, Carmen, Consuela . . .'

The girls, darkly shawled, gave minute rigid curtsies – unsmiling, uncertain but proud, the flickering light showing their cold beauty now, the black eyes motionless, set in the cowled white faces, giving them the air of nuns, untouchable, brides only of a passionate spirit.

Rodrigo, small, with foxy good looks, in his twenties, but with the ease and air of a much older man, took off a wide-brimmed flat hat and bowed slightly, his darkly brilliantined hair, parted straight down the middle, glistening in the light.

'We are . . . honoured,' he said, slowly, with a heavy accent, opening his arms a fraction to include the girls, looking at Humphrey first, then at Lady Cordiner, whose hand he took, brushing his lips above it for an instant. But that was all he said, looking round at the assembled company without a trace of emotion, without pleasure or doubt in the meeting – simply an acceptance of it as something entirely natural and expected.

Frances, forsaking her small talk with Eustace and Harold, stared at the young Spaniard; Henry looked at him – everyone gazed at him in the sudden silence, as if trapped and warmed by his coldness, waiting for a further explanation or greeting.

But he gave none, clearly implying that his very presence there said everything that needed to be said, that he ordered things without words. And indeed it seemed at his unspoken command, when he turned away to see to the girls' baggage, that everyone moved indoors.

'And what do you think of *that*?' Bunty Cordiner spoke to her husband later as they dressed for dinner. 'A band of Spanish gipsies, I ask you! Led by that cheeky ruffian – we shall have our throats cut in our beds, I tell you. And as to those *women* in the house with us, proposing some indecent dance – women of the easiest virtue, I'll be bound – you can hardly think them suitable company, at *any* season – let alone Christmas. It's preposterous! Your sister-in-law is turning the house into a common music hall.'

Her husband rubbed his glasses. He had rather liked what he had seen of the women on the porch steps, but did not care to admit it. 'My dear, you exaggerate. They are merely dancers and musicians of some sort. Sarah is a cultured woman – and of Spanish extraction herself, you must remember, an old and distinguished family there. She will know what she's doing. Besides, it was not her idea – the guests were forced upon her.'

'Yes – by that horror of a man, Saunders: that unprincipled nationalist busybody who so viciously attacked poor Lord Kingston in the *Pall Mall Gazette*, taking sides against his own class, supporting Kingston's blackguardly tenants. I can hardly believe that I must sit at table with him.'

'I believe it was the matter of Kingston's over-zealous evictions in his Rosscommon estates which Mr Saunders complained of there. And he may well have had a point. It does no good to exacerbate the peasantry in that manner – no good at all in the present political climate, where we may see an end to strife in Ireland – with appropriate legislation.'

Bunty knew what he referred to – the distinct likelihood of Home Rule in the new century. 'There can be no "appropriate legislation" which takes control of the country out of the hands of us Unionists,' she proclaimed roundly.

'Yes, dear – a topic you might care to raise with my cousin Mortimer, just back from Westminster. He has a great deal to say on that issue.'

Austin was happy to pass responsibility on to Mortimer in this matter. Mortimer was an astute and vociferous Home Rule MP in the House, as Austin's own wife was an equally vehement, if not so sensible, opponent. He himself preferred not to take sides, though on balance he secretly favoured the Irish Home Rulers at Westminster if only because, loving the land, he despised the absentee landlordism which Unionism encouraged.

'That renegade Mortimer!' Bunty snorted. 'Another fouling his own nest. I can hardly be civil to him. I cannot imagine a more uncongenial house party – gipsies, ballad singers, poetasters, traitorous politicians. Really, Austin, it's too much . . .'

*

'He *was* rather handsome . . .' Frances, in petticoats, looking into the mirror, spoke to Eileen who was combing her hair. 'He plays the guitar.'

'A sort of fiddle?'

'Yes. But you play it with your fingers. Perhaps you'll see it tomorrow – I encouraged Mr Saunders in the idea.'

'And your young man, Miss Frances? – the other one, the fair-haired young man, with that . . . that sly look! Isn't he gorgeous.'

'Yes, Harold. I hadn't thought of him as sly –'

'Oh, I didn't mean sly in a bad way.'

'No, I know what you mean.' But Frances did not quite know. She rose and Eileen helped her into her dress, a long light blue silk skirt with a low bodice trimmed in narrow white lace, a broad, royal blue belt at the middle.

Her eyes sparkled in the lamplight as she flounced her soft curls, adjusted the blue amethyst pendant round her neck, before turning in profile to the mirror, judging the effect. Sly, Frances thought – in a *good* way? Was that possible? She had seen that sometimes supercilious look in Harold's eyes as something commanding and mature rather than sly – a natural attribute of such a man, Lord Norton's eldest son from Oxfordshire, whom her mother hoped she would marry, one of the very few wishes she shared with her. Now the slightest touch of uncertainty crossed her mind in the idea.

Lady Cordiner dressed with more speed than usual, chivvying her maid, as she placed the cloth pads on her scalp, before back-combing, building her hair over them into an elaborate hillock. She was impatient to be downstairs with Mrs Martin, to see the Spanish contingent suitably cared for – by being made invisible. It was too bad of Humphrey, but impossible now to do anything about it. They would have to share rooms in the back wing and eat in Mrs Martin's pantry, no question of having them at table. Tomorrow, after their performance, she would send them on their way, no matter what Humphrey said: the Commercial Hotel in Thomastown or the Club House in Kilkenny could look after them.

Yet there were advantages to be derived from their arrival, she thought. Humphrey, like her, never made cause with the second-rate in culture. The flamenco dancing was likely to be good, another feather in her cap, fresh evidence of her wide and sophisticated tastes. Besides, the whole thing, she knew, would infuriate Bunty Cordiner.

After the ladies had departed, the men took port after dinner, passing the decanter round the evergreen decorations, picking nuts and dried fruit from the delicately latticed baskets that hung from two silver George III épergnes, set in beds of moss and maidenhair fern towards either end of the long table. It had been a tactful dinner with the ladies, Bunty being placed at some remove from both Humphrey and Mortimer Cordiner. But now Mortimer, the port flaming his usual energy and nervous attack, speared the air with his fingers, holding court, altogether the skilled and passionate advocate, whereas the other men rather held their tongues.

'You see it's *land* in Ireland – and the good management of it – which is what really counts. Land is the only gold here. But it's badly used and farmed, without profit, where what little of that there is is simply taken as rent from the hapless tenantry and used to finance a spendthrift, absentee class. For our *own* good, you see, one cannot properly have our vital interests controlled from London. We must have the yea and nay ourselves – must *live* here too – if we are to survive as a class.'

Humphrey Saunders bristled at this word 'class'. 'But it's the rack-rented tenants, along with the rest of the impoverished native Irish who must rather survive, Mortimer – not people like you and Desmond, who do very well, if I may say so.' Humphrey took a large Havana, inspected it pointedly, then returned it to its cedar box.

'*Survive?*' asked Sir Desmond in considerable surprise. 'I was quite unaware it had come to that pass for us – or the tenantry either for that matter, especially with all these new land acts where they'll be able to buy their holdings outright. And there's a point – no government in Dublin would have the money, the financial reserves, to underwrite such land loans as Westminster is planning to do.'

'With Home Rule all sorts of additional funds would be available *within* the country, Desmond – not leaked out straight away to absentee landlords and the Treasury in London. There are a hundred and one inevitable financial and other advantages for *everyone* in Home Rule. But there will be no advantage until we control our own destinies here, free of Whitehall's dictation. We are Irish after all, not English.'

'I grant you that,' Sir Desmond said. 'But it's unlikely that we should remain in control under Home Rule. The butchers, bakers and candlestickmakers would soon be in the saddle then.'

'Well, that would be entirely our fault, Desmond – as it precisely is already, that we have abdicated our responsibilities. And unless we rapidly change our ways it will be our end –'

'Abdicated?'

'Oh, perhaps not you, nor you, Austin. Responsible landowners, no doubt. But the majority of the others have long since done so.' Mortimer looked round the company. This was complete news to them. 'And you do not see it?' Mortimer went on, shaking his head. 'That these latter generations here – the Arrans, Kingstons, Clanricardes, people like King-Harman – where they have not been cruel and selfish, have been quite indifferent, irresponsible over their heritage: fecklessly indifferent – and they will lose it, let it slip from their hands before they know it. Indeed it's these very people, fighting blindly to maintain the Union now, who, through their lazy short sight will make Home Rule inevitable – and, more than that, violent as well as likely as not, a revolution among the butchers and bakers, Desmond, which won't be at all to your taste or mine. Unless we all change our ways our class in Ireland is doomed – finished – a decade or so hence. Mark my words.'

'Agreed entirely,' Humphrey said. 'Only wish it had happened sooner,' he added with smiling malice.

Sir Desmond looked round the great room hung with its rows of solid Cordiner family portraits – rather as Snipe had looked at the house a few days before, doubting something he could not identify, dissolution hidden in the old walls, decay in the rich smell of vintage port and fine cigars, an apocalyptic genie that might rise from the lovely Waterford decanters. But it was not difficult, given reassurance by his ancestors' commanding faces and surrounded by these vigorous, talented men who were his living progeny, relatives and friends, to put all doubts from his mind.

'You exaggerate, Mortimer,' he said easily. 'As you must do, playing to an audience of Fenians and Land Leaguers whose votes you require. But we are not that audience – and so not to be swayed by your cries of "Wolf".'

'My audience *is* the wolf, Desmond, make no mistake. I see it clearly every day, roaming the country, a hungry beast . . .'

There was a moment's awkward silence before Sir Desmond suggested they join the ladies.

But all in Summer Hill, present and future, seemed even more well founded and secure when afterwards they listened to the young tenor, Mr O'Meara, accompanied on the Blüthner by Humphrey, Renaissance man, casually gifted in so many things.

Mr O'Meara's voice, perfectly modulated, floated over the room – a sentimental Thomas Moore ballad which moved his audience for quite another reason, where the sentiment was made believable by the singer's great artistry and control, the over-sweet romance of the words transformed into a pure emotion, almost icy, by the classic voice.

> 'There is not in the wide world a valley so sweet,
>   As that vale in whose bosom the bright waters meet.
> Oh! the last rays of feeling and life must depart,
>   Ere the bloom of that valley shall fade from my heart.'

Lady Cordiner, with a genuine love and appreciation of music, was moved as much as pleased, glancing at Henry, then at Eustace: Eustace, her chubby, owl-faced son – one might have liked a leaner mien there – doing so well with his regiment in Aldershot. His friend Harold, too – they were both fine men. What a future there was there, she felt, before she remembered that the future of Summer Hill, at least, lay in her eldest son Henry's hands. Of course, it was his ridiculously extended travels to all the wrong places, among savages and infidels instead of Society in London or Baden-Baden, that made him unavailable, kept him away from a suitable wife. But he must know of his responsibilities as eldest son, would accept them eventually, even if only in a marriage of convenience. With Frances on the other hand – well, she would soon be off her hands. Harold was suitable in every way – quite apart from the fact that they seemed in love as well. She looked at her daughter then, sitting on a little gilded chair beside and a little ahead of Harold, watching how he gazed tenderly at her now and then, lost to the song, or perhaps inspired by it.

'Tell me the witching tale again,
   For never has my heart or ear,
   Hung on so sweet, so pure a strain,
   So pure to feel, so sweet to hear . . .'

Yes, Frances and Harold would be all right, she thought, Eustace, too – even Henry. There was nothing, indeed, in Summer Hill which, through her own efforts and skills, would not be absolutely fine in the end.

Outside in the hall, Pat Kennedy, making last rounds to see that the shutters and outside doors were secure, stopped a moment by the drawing room door, sunk in race memories, before he pulled himself together and moved towards the back of the house. A camp bed had been put up for him in the butler's pantry, where he slept – as guard for the big safe, which he unlocked now, carefully putting the more valuable silver plate and cutlery away. Flood had retired to bed earlier. The little room was his for the night, warm with the embers of a coal fire in the small grate. He was sorry he had to go out later, a cold tramp through the snow down the drive to the nearest of the estate cottages on the brow of the hill, where he had a meeting. He pulled back the blanket and sheet on the camp bed until the thin mattress was exposed. Then, putting his hand into the side where he had cut the seam, he drew out the RIC Webley revolver, checked it, before hiding it again behind his trouser belt.

Later only Eileen saw him leave the house, a shadowy figure against the snow stealing through the yard, as she watched him from her bedroom window in the servants' quarters. What risks he took, she thought. But then they both did.

The snow had finally moved away in the night, bringing a morning of brilliant blue sky and sun, almost hot, which soaked down on the landscape – an enchantment of pearly folds and meringue twists, a crisp glitter on the garden terraces, nursery slopes pushed up against the windbreak of low hedges, creamy glaciers running down the lawn to the valley where the trees were canopied in powdery foam. It was a day so unexpected in an Irish winter – buoyant, tingling, where land and sky made one vast empty canvas. There seemed no end of things in the air.

'Ah! Where are the pranksters then?' Mortimer said, the company assembled around the breakfast table. He looked at Henry and Dermot, then at Harold and Eustace. It was probably the latter two, he thought, as revenge for his home truths the previous night after dinner. 'The most painfully judged apple pie bed last night indeed! I nearly broke my toes.' He looked firmly at Harold and Eustace who made a poor job of promoting their innocence in the matter.

'Come, Papa – the Christmas spirit!' Dermot, gently ironic, consoled his father – as he did when this could be done quite unobtrusively: an apple pie bed was a poor substitute for a wife, his mother Matilda, who had died two years before, with his younger and much-loved sister Molly, both drowned in a boating accident on the Liffey, above Islandbridge, near Dublin, where they lived. He would have liked to have snubbed Eustace and Harold in some way for their childish jape. He – and Henry, too, he knew – found them both tiresomely juvenile. But it was not the moment.

Humphrey was about to produce his flamenco dancers and, with his unfailing sense of the theatrical, he had arranged the show outdoors on the flagstoned porch, warmed on either side by the two braziers again; and now the household, in fur capes, hats and mufflers, sat with their backs to the hall door and windows – the stage set in front between the great pillars, against a backdrop of intense white and blue, sky and land sparkling like warm enamel, seeming to vibrate in the crystal air.

Rodrigo, without his hat, but with a cape, polka dot shirt and high riding boots, took a stool with his guitar to one side, playing a guarded, tremulous introduction, which gradually rose in sound and pace – until suddenly, on a stamped signal, the five girls, arms high, came in a streaming dancing line through the hall door and out on to the flagstones.

The effect of this sinuous, vigorous arrival, with the increased volume of music and the quick stutter of high heels on the flagstones, quite startled the audience, so that their heads drew back as if from fire – the girls in a weaving semi-circle, closing in around the spectators now, seeming to threaten them in their long bell-shaped skirts, which they picked up, flicking them arrogantly close to their faces as the music gathered tempo. Rodrigo nursed the guitar, bending to and fro over the strings – challenging, stroking, bullying, seducing the instrument as he drew a mounting run of chords from it, only to stop them all suddenly, with the flat of his hand, when the girls a moment later embarked on another, more startling, viciously staccato rhythm with their feet. Dressed in red and black cotton print skirts with tight-laced bodices, they arched their heads back, arms raised, palms facing down, fingers moving intricately, starting to snap them, punctuating the frenzied pace, forming patterns together, then breaking them, advancing on the audience, dark furies against the gleaming snow.

The girls were flagrant and yet indifferent. Their elegant sensuality was quite cold, almost with hatred in it. And when they started to sing, in vicious whiplash voices, the tone, the song, was full of longing and enmity. They revelled in their contradictions. For the audience, as they swirled against the dazzle, they were an insult, a predatory race apart. Most were trapped by their overwhelming physical spell, rabbits facing stoats. But a few others were enchanted, drawn to them, moths to candle flames. And Frances was one of these. She felt their scintillating vigour, passing in the keen air, brushing her face, stirring her blood, bringing a delicious tremble to her whole body. She wanted to emulate them, join the sensuous dance. Their passion – so great but so tantalisingly withheld – provoked her towards some unknown fulfilment of her own. In the rising, maddening rhythms she craved some release, through them, which they achieved in their thrilling finales, but which she did not. She sat there, vastly excited, frustrated. Then she found herself staring at Rodrigo – the fountain head, she realised then, of her excitement. And though, in his surly humour, he had barely glanced at the audience, suddenly he looked up, staring at her in return, with just the ghost of a smile.

Lady Cordiner was alternately rabbit and moth – stirred by it all, then appalled. For her, too, in this music, there was a race memory here which quickened her blood. But a latter world of inhibition and propriety stifled her natural impulses. What would the servants think? She was certain they were there, hidden behind the windows, gazing out. Still, she could hardly make a scene over it. And so, as in all things which she espoused, where she had taken action, she did not retrench, but went forward, undeterred by any qualms – showing all the more appreciation of the dance, the dancers whom, whatever their suitability in polite society, she recognised as being first-rate. Humphrey had not let her down.

'Splendid,' she said as an aside to her husband. 'Really splendid.' Sir Desmond barely agreed. It was not his cup of tea; few of his wife's cultural enthusiasms were. He found this particular business strident and lacking humour. But he was interested in the guitar strings. He would ask the surly Spaniard about them. Drawn from Toledo steel? A stronger, finer wire perhaps for the struts and controls of his flying machine?

Emily, in a high-backed cane chair, with pencil and sketch book, attempted to catch the wild swing of the dancers, thrilled by the swirling movements, the vivid contrast of their dark dresses against the shining backdrop of snow and sky beyond. The air, icy, but shot through with wafts of heat from the braziers, was electrifying. Indeed, when Lady Cordiner rose, after the applause at the end, this combination of heat, cold and excitement proved too much for her. She swayed dangerously on her feet for a moment, before tumbling back into her chair, overcome, in a half-faint. A mild furore ensued, the dancers forgotten, as she was finally helped indoors to a drawing room sofa. Smelling salts and brandy were offered, but refused.

'It's nothing,' she said. 'Don't fuss. The dancing seemed to take me, quite dizzy-making, splendid.' She was pleased thus to make a profit out of her little turn, blaming it on an aesthetic, not a physical, weakness. When the others had left, Humphrey talked to her, drawing a chair up to the end of the sofa.

'Ah, my dear Sarah – I knew it would take you: a true *aficionada*. In Spain last summer, down in the south, I lived with some of these gipsies . . .'

'*Lived* with them?'

'Oh yes – quite wonderful! Wished you could have been down there with me. Too stuck here, you know, Sarah, shut away in this Irish backwater. Such a lot to offer, and not appreciated here.'

He looked at her earnestly – and she returned the look fondly, all the possibilities of another life, which she might have had with him, coming back to her.

'Yes, that would have been nice,' she said, avoiding the issue of her long parochialism, but remembering the woman she had been with him more than thirty years before, a softer, more pliant creature, no doubt. 'But you could hardly expect me to live in some tent!'

'In *caves*, my dear. They live in caves in the rock, not tents. Come back with me to Spain, and see it all again . . .'

'Caves?' She shuddered a fraction. 'Humphrey dear, I think a little brandy *would* do me good.'

The memory of the dance, of Rodrigo and the girls, kept intruding on Frances's thoughts throughout lunch. She longed to get closer to them in some way, talk to them, learn more about it. Humphrey would have given her detailed information, she knew. But she wanted some first-hand explanation of why she had been so intrigued and disturbed that morning on the porch. And it was urgent – the dancers were to be sent off later that afternoon on the train to the Club House in Kilkenny. The men meanwhile were proposing a rough shoot after lunch, which would leave her free – free of Harold, who was likely at any moment to press his suit. She was sure he was going to propose to her at the first suitable opportunity. And there was another urgency – she wanted to be able to say yes, but did not feel any true enthusiasm for the idea now. She must find the right frame of mind before he asked her, a more settled demeanour which she knew she did not possess: there was some itch to be satisfied before she found that.

It was quite simple, of course: she would go to the girls' rooms after lunch – no matter that they did not speak each other's languages. Sign, gesture, smile – these would be sufficient communication to assuage her curiosity.

An hour later, when the men had gone out and the house was quiet, she made her way to the back wing, knocking on one of the bedroom doors where Eileen had told her the girls were quartered. There was silence – until the door suddenly opened and Rodrigo was there.

'Oh, I am sorry – wrong room! I wanted to see the girls before they went. I was so interested – in the dance . . .'

So surprised was she, that she retained the inviting smile she had prepared for the girls, staring at the man, almost mesmerised. He stood there calmly – barefoot, half-dressed, a big carpet bag stuffed with black satin capes and frilly shirts open on the floor behind him.

'Come on in.' The familiar tone was not at all Spanish, clearly English – and common at that. 'Thought you might come round . . .' He held his arm out, gesturing her inside.

'But –?' Frances, in her greater astonishment at this deception, was barely aware of crossing the threshold. The man closed the door behind her, his every movement swift and decisive, as if, indeed, he had been expecting her. He leant against the door then, staring at her in return, a wise smile lighting up his dark features.

'But I thought you were Spanish!'

'Oh, I am. My mother was at least. I've never been to the place. Come from London. Cockney born and bred. Sound of Bow Bells.' He kept his voice at the same even, ironic level, almost sotto voce, and his eyes never left hers – arrogant, inviting, dismissive all in the same hard glance, like an animal trifling with its prey. 'But what was it in the dance that you were so interested in?' he asked intently, without irony, his lips continuing to move after he had spoken, as if he was whispering something to her then, offering some urgent, delicate, thrilling invitation.

The room was hot and oppressive, filled with a smell of brilliantine. Frances's head began to swim as the man approached her. She felt dizzy – trapped by his steely regard, which never left her, a beam of piercing light which she was enthralled by, could not escape from. She stared at the great cleft in his frilly shirt, open almost to his waist. She could not take her eyes off the shapes and colours there, the dark curly hillocks of his chest, the sloping snowy midriff. Eventually she cast her eyes down, only to be confronted by his perfect, alabaster-smooth bare legs and feet.

She backed away, stumbling against the bed, nearly falling before he caught her adroitly in his arms, half-pulling her up to him, holding her there, spellbound. And in those long seconds, winded, almost overcome, she felt she had stopped breathing, as she watched his long delicate fingers rise towards her neck, disappearing over the far side and down her back, deftly undoing the buttons there, as he pulled her to him then, gripping her fiercely with his other arm before kissing her neck, opening the dress now, bearing her down on the bed.

She half-struggled, trying vainly for some leverage against him as he lay on top of her. But for some reason she did not scream. This entirely confirmed the man's initial expectations of her, so that he redoubled his advances, tearing at her collar, pulling the dress right down about her shoulders now, so that her arms were pinned to her sides and her small breasts lay half-exposed beneath her camisole top. With both hands engaged he kissed the nipples through the silk, before taking the material in his teeth and tearing it down, displaying the erect shapes, taking one of them in his lips, while with his other hand, moving it quickly up between her legs, he grasped her sex, his fingers rising into her like a warm knife.

And then she screamed, struggling viciously, clawing, scratching at him. Surprised now, he desisted, rising, letting her free. She stood up, red-faced, gulping air, breathlessly furious.

'You – you filthy brute!' She pulled her dress back up, settling herself. 'I'll have you out of here in two seconds!' She made for the door.

'Will you?' he asked, entirely calm, the dark thin smile still there. 'Don't forget, Miss, it was *you* who came to me. And I'll tell them that. What were you doing in *my* bedroom? – they'll wonder, won't they?' She tried to slap his face, but he held her arm easily. 'I wouldn't tell them if I were you – you little flirt. You really liked it all – before you started yelling!' He laughed as Frances rushed from the room.

She stood outside the door for a moment, chest thumping. She was shocked, horrified by his behaviour – felt dirty, defiled. Of course she would tell, there and then. With her dress torn, there would be obvious proof of his assault. She ran down the corridor, through the great interconnecting oak door, back into the main house.

But then she paused. What *had* she been doing in his room? Harold, inevitably, coming to know about it, would ask just the same question. The whole thing could only result in yet more embarrassment. She went to her room instead, stripping off her clothes and sponging herself all over by the wash basin. Flirting? Had she been doing that? Of course not! – she had simply gone to see the girls, she reminded herself.

'Flirting?' she said out loud. 'No, never!'

But the thrill, renewed now in her mind, and in her body, was undeniable. Standing stock still by the mirror and looking at herself, she started to tremble – at the rashness of her behaviour and its pleasure. She smiled then. She had, at least, an answer now to her curiosity about the dance, the dancers, about Rodrigo, too. Her itch was satisfied. Or was it? Had it only just begun? Frustrated once more, she decided, as a distraction, to visit Aunt Emily.

'Aunt Emily? It's me.' She knocked on the door, before turning the key.

Emily was halfway through a detailed sketch – not of the dancers but of their audience – when Frances came into her bedroom. Emily did not look up, completely absorbed in her work, while Frances stood behind her.

'Why not the dancers, Aunt?'

'Couldn't catch them, you see,' Emily spoke, still bent over the sketchbook. 'And, anyway, I wasn't really interested. Don't know them. Have to *know* the people in my drawings, you see.'

Frances saw how well her aunt knew the people in this instance – her usually uncomplimentary interpretations given a further twist here in that, while featuring their clearly recognisable faces, she had dressed all the household in Spanish costume. So Bunty, with an outraged Presbyterian face, had become the flagrant seductress, a gipsy Carmen in a flounced skirt, and her mother something of an Andalucian crone in a lace mantilla. Harold, she saw, in a stiff gold-braided military tunic, was transformed, lugubrious and long-faced, into a pompous Spanish grandee.

'Aunt! Is Harold really like that?'

'Oh yes.'

Frances, with her aunt, had a fruitful relationship in that Emily spoke to her, at least, as she did to few if any other members of the household. She recognised the cutting honesty and reality in this quite unreal woman. And in return Emily allowed her, alone among the family, access to her bedroom, her drawings, and her startling confidences whenever she wished.

'Should I not marry him then?' she asked. 'Is he pompous as well as sly?'

'Sly? I didn't know it. But quite possibly. Shall I make him sly as well?'

'Oh, aunt – don't joke. You know what I mean. Trouble is, how can one tell what a man is really like until one lives with him –'

'Excuse yourself, girl!' Emily interrupted with a start of her head, the slight brogue in her voice more noticeable now. '*Living* with men – the very idea! – an impossibility in any case. Don't even consider it. They are all far-gone, entirely far-gone.'

'In what?'

'In imbecility. *Tout court.*' Emily began to transform Isabelle, with her blonde ringlets, into a spoilt and pouting Infanta.

'What should I do then?'

'Take to your heels, girl. There's a place in London I used to stay at. Or was it Paris? Respectable accommodation and near some quite decent shops, too. Hotel Crillon, was it? Near our Legation, so it must have been Paris. Go there. The manager was less offensive than they usually are. You'll find it quite to your taste.'

'Yes, aunt. It's an idea –'

'Excuse yourself again, girl – it's the *only* idea. Won't even need spending money either – found them all very accommodating on that score.'

'Yes, aunt.' Frances knew, indeed, how accommodating so many tradespeople and hotel managers had been towards her aunt over the years – knew something of her earlier peregrinations about Ireland and further afield, to places like the Hotel Crillon and the shops in the Faubourg St Honoré, where lavish bills had been run up, which her father's solicitor in Dublin had forever to chase and settle, in person often, since he usually had to escort the spendthrift miscreant home as well, so that in the end doors were locked on her in Summer Hill.

Then, looking over her aunt's shoulder, she saw how, in her own case, Emily had dressed her in virgin white – a frou-frou, many-flounced Spanish bridal dress, her face a study in provocative devilry.

'And who am I supposed to be?'

'Carmen. One of the better operas. She came to a bad end. But they always do in operas, don't they? Have to, wouldn't be much point otherwise.'

Frances returned to her room, slightly chastened by this idea of a bad end. She took out her diary, a secret album *consolatum*, hidden in her dressing table: a locked leather-bound book with a sprig of gilt shamrock embossed on the cover. Opening it, she looked at the last entry: 'I intend *not* to be a good and useful person.' Taking a pencil she crossed out the word 'not' – then, after reflection, wrote it in again. Then she added the sentence, 'I also intend *not* to tell lies about myself,' before closing the book and hiding it once more.

She looked out over the valley, a bright glitter in the afternoon light, where long shadows were creeping down the slopes, the shape of the house darkening the lawn. But Mount Brandon, away to the east, still caught the sun full on, a dazzling, snow-covered peak against the pale blue sky. Did she want all the world out there, beyond the mountains – London, Paris – taking to her heels? Yes, part of her did, and certainly if she married Harold some of all that would be hers – but only intermittently and formally, where the major portion of her life would be spent, eventually, as Lady Norton, mistress of his Oxfordshire home. But, if she lived in the country, she wanted it Irish country, not English. She wanted the country of Summer Hill. What would Harold say to that? He would laugh outright – as it had already amused him that she should want to spend so much time here, with a mother whom she so signally failed to get on with. Harold would offer her the world – he would never understand why she really only wanted this small corner of it.

But why did she? It was love of the place, of course – the house, gardens, river, woods, the secrets she had found and fed on here – a love made the more intense since, perforce, it had been pursued behind her mother's back, against her will. And so her wish to stay here was also partly a matter of revenge; she realised and accepted that. She wanted to pay her mother out for her lack of warmth towards her as a child, her cruelties in such matters as the swing, and many others, small and large – above all for her inability to see and release the true spirit of the house, which she had made into a fortress where everyone was prisoner of her wishes. She had suffered, so had her father and two brothers. But the men had avoided the issue where they had not, literally, like Henry, run away. So it was up to her to stay. Instead of taking to her heels, where she too would share in their defeat, she would remain on the field of battle, waiting her chance somehow to spring a surprise victory.

But how, in what way? Did she unconsciously hope for her mother's early death, she wondered, remembering the curious spasm of excitement she had felt at her mother's faint that morning – a death which, in some measure at least, would make her mistress of the house? Certainly she could see no other way which would allow her victory – such a death seemed the only means, for in a dozen years or so the house would belong to Henry, and he would have his own bride to manage things, not her. Or was Henry a confirmed bachelor, she wondered, so that in time, unmarried, she would keep house for him? But time – that was the bugbear there, time that sucked your life away. She had no wish to wait that long. Besides, what she really wanted of the house was someone loved to run it with. And that, in Harold's terms, would be impossible. Harold would have his own inheritance in England to concern him, to share with her.

So there was the problem, she realised, looking over the waning, clear blue light in the valley: inheritance. The house outside Stow-on-the-Wold in Oxfordshire would never be hers, whereas Summer Hill *was* hers, as a shareholder at least – part of the blood, and the fact that she was a woman should make her no less a partner, she felt, in its future. And that, she knew, was exactly the sort of thing which Harold or any other man would never understand.

*

The men, coming home from their rough shoot, crunched over the snow that rimmed the high woods beyond the house, moving through a silver beech glade where the slanting light dazzled against the timber, finding tints of blue in the bark, where the woods were silent after the sporadic gunfire, several brace of pheasant, some rabbits and a hare accounted for. Harold was happy – he had taken the swiftly running hare. The shooting wasn't as good as at home, he thought, though it wasn't bad. He was pleased with the idea of home then, of England, where really everything, except the fox hunting perhaps, was so much better than things in Ireland. Frances couldn't fail, in the end, to see that. He would ask her to marry him that evening.

'But you don't follow, do you, Harold?'

'Can't say I do, darling.'

'I don't *want* to marry just yet.'

'You are over twenty-one after all.'

Impasse, she thought – just as she had expected. She closed the bound copy of *Punch* on her lap with a louder thump than she had intended. They were alone in the morning room, where it was cold without a fire. 'There are things for me to do here – still,' she said.

'But *what* things, when you might more often be in London – or at home with me. Oh, apart from Christmas and during the summer now and then – I understand your being here then. But why *live* here?'

'It's my inheritance, I'm part of it –'

'But, my dearest, it's Henry's inheritance, not yours. Yours would be my house, when I have it, and our children's inheritance.'

'It's not the same –'

'But you're at hammer and tongs with your mother here all the time. You've told me – and I can see that. So all the more –'

'Well, it's *not* all the more reason. I don't *want* to be at loggerheads with her. I want to settle that somehow, before I marry. I don't want to leave here with that shadow of ill-will.'

'You will surely only increase the ill-will between you both by staying here, for it's that very thing which annoys your mother most – your *being* here all the time.'

'Yes, perhaps. All the same, I have to make the effort. To be on better terms. Perhaps – next year? I simply couldn't marry now, not absolutely *now*. I want to wait, can you see?'

Harold sighed, not seeing. She had been honest with herself, she thought – why couldn't she be the same with him? She was lying to him, of course. She didn't expect to make things up with her mother – rather the opposite: she expected to contend with her for Summer Hill. That was the one thing – hopeless cause or no – that she was set on. The house was her love, and how could she explain that to Harold? What man could reasonably accept bricks and mortar and landscape as his rival in marriage?

A day later, the 24th, when the holly was set up and a tall, green-needled spruce brought into the great hall, Christmas descended on the house. Mr O'Meara had returned to Dublin, the Spanish dancers banished to the Club House in Kilkenny – the artistes had gone. Now, apart from Humphrey and Harold, the family reigned secure from further interruptions – tensions and difficulties put aside, if not forgotten, in the general aura of goodwill.

Though it did not snow again, a sharp frost maintained the earlier fall everywhere, so that on the Sunday Christmas morning, beneath a chilly blue sky, the younger members of the household walked to the little church near the village over the hard earth, their feet sinking into the snow with a crisp cutting noise.

Like stepping through an iced cake, Frances thought, moving a little ahead with Harold in tall buttoned boots, beneath a long sable-trimmed coat and matching Russian hat. They took a back avenue, directly across the lawn, where it twisted down through the forest gorge and met the river before turning sharply along the bank under a heavy canopy of trees towards Cloone. Here the branches above were festooned with icicles and the little rivulets and waterfalls, normally spurting from the steep rocks to their left, were frozen solid, long blueish fingers running down the granite face, with star-encrusted ferns beneath, that had doubled their size in the frost, become solid lacy crystal ornaments.

She loved this walk in every season, this river walk up to the village, or turning right down the bank to the octagonal stone boat house further on – that was a summer walk, where, if one did not take the boats out, the tree-shrouded river avenue went right on for several miles, before cutting up the hill by the southern edge of the estate, back to the house through the long avenue of monkey puzzle trees.

She was so much a tree person, she knew – loved these endless woods and forests that rose up in circles round the house, holding it, a jewel on the hill above, like the lattice work of a crown. In the Cotswolds, beyond Stow, where Harold lived, there was nothing like this. It was all manicured, neat and bare – open sheep pasture, set high up in the winds, with only a few spinneys of breeze-bent beech or elm in the folds. There were no secrets in the landscape there. She needed secrets, needed places to hide. And that was a problem with Harold, too. He was so open and honest, really – and she was simply not used to dealing with such people, where, exposed to their obvious good nature, a similar response was demanded. Her subtleties made that almost impossible for her.

She had been marked by her devious battles with her mother – just as she had by the covert Irish landscape, with its deceptive vistas, hidden views, sudden ruins, screaming rook-filled trees, its wild ragworty fields and moist creeping growths, where so much would always be ungoverned and any imposed order a mere holding operation, a temporary clearing won from a ragged and voracious nature: a restless, cloud-swept landscape, where the colours changed all the time in the wind. It had marked her by her love for it and by her wariness of it, for behind the most placid vision here, she knew, there was always a sense of surprise, disruption, violence. It was a world which had put her too much on her guard, perhaps, so that she thought then that she had been over-severe with Harold the previous evening.

'I'm sorry – if I seemed stubborn yesterday.' She turned to him, neither sly nor pompous in his muffler and greatcoat – just a tall, a nice young man with a good face set against the river light.

'No, no. I wouldn't wish to force you in anything. It must be your own free choice, of course.' His reply seemed entirely felt, reasonable and open. So that she was ashamed of her deceits with him over her mother, and was tempted to tell him so, to explain it all, what her true feelings were.

'Really, in fact, I'm sure it's just a passing phase – these feelings I have for home, for Mama. And a sort of cowardice about the great world perhaps.'

'Perhaps.' He seemed almost uninterested.

'I shall have to embark on it at some point.'

'Indeed.' He looked away, up-river, toward the salmon traps and the approaching bridge.

'You seem – somewhat unconcerned?'

'No, no, my dear.'

But he was, and of course it was probably intentional, understandable at least, Frances thought. He had been hurt by her refusal to marry him at once and was taking mild revenge. And no doubt she deserved it. Yet she did not feel like telling any truths then: he was unreceptive. And, besides, admission here could be weakness; it might mar her relationship with him ever after. At such vital points in life it was always wise to maintain any position of strength.

As they passed the little Gothic lodge, old Mr Kennedy, a widower now, out on the step, took his cap off to the party, wishing them many Good Mornings and Happy Christmases. Behind the small diamond-paned windows, his son Pat Kennedy, with the day off, saw the company pass, then turned to Eileen, watching with him.

'You'd hardly credit it, would you – Miss Frances, with that butter wouldn't melt in her mouth expression, and that eejit Perkins wrapped round her little finger. She's a flyer all right, I'll give her that! Leading him on with the one hand and thieving all that stuff from about the house with the other – and you helping her. Mother of God, if her Ladyship catches either of ye, there'll be ructions!'

'If they catch you, Pat Kennedy, with your Fenian friends and guns and drilling and schemes, there'll be far worse ructions, so you needn't talk.'

He turned from the window. 'No, indeed, you're right there. The both of us,' he added, looking at her very pointedly, 'we'd better keep our mouths well shut.'

*

Christmas soon overwhelmed the household: triumphant carols in the church, presents unwrapped over cherry brandy before lunch, a vast turkey then – before Mrs Molloy, as was the tradition, carried in the two flaming plum puddings and was suitably congratulated on the gargantuan meal. In the afternoon the younger members tried to skate on the ornamental pond at the top of the terraced garden. But the ice cracked when the tubby Eustace launched himself forth on it, pursued by Sergeant, who sank in the freezing water with him, until half the company found themselves dancing about among the ice splinters in the shallow pond. More cherry brandy and hot hip-baths were forthcoming back at the house.

On Boxing Day, at nightfall, the Christmas tree was lit, when the servants, estate workers and their families, well over a hundred of them, accepted their presents from Sir Desmond and Lady Cordiner, the candle flames warming the green needles here and there, filling the hall with an intoxicating smell of burnt wax and pine.

The following evening they played charades in the drawing room, the teams of actors emerging on stage from the hall, where trunks of old theatrical costumes had been taken down from the attics. Sir Desmond particularly excelled here, at this one time of year when, forgetting his flying machines, he gave himself entirely to these seasonal recreations, leting his inventive spirit flow for once in quite another direction, preparing, in these charades, for his own part in Humphrey's production of *The Colleen Bawn* at the Kilkenny Theatre two days hence.

And, when that came, all the Summer Hill household assembled in their boxes in the little velvet and gilt theatre, Frances thought her happiness complete, realising all the more sharply how little she wanted to live in Oxfordshire. She gazed, rapt, at the romantic cavortings on stage, the vivid mix of Boucicault's Irish wit and malice, saw Humphrey excel as the hero, Hardness Cregan, and her father make a splendid fool of himself as the comic rogue, Myles na Coppaleen – the two cheered to the echo by the local populace.

What would Harold, the future Lord Norton, offer by way of similar entertainment, she wondered? Nothing. English county society, she knew, lived at many dull removes from such theatricals, without a spark of this élan, bound up in stuffy isolated formalities. In her life here she had access to any amount of expected or forbidden adventure. England was simply dull, she thought – the people, by comparison with the Irish, quite without character. That was it, that was the worst of it: they were grey, where here, with every sort of person, she basked in always unexpected lights. Was she to spend the rest of her life among dullards?

It was altogether a serious problem. And the only person who might offer sensible advice on it was Henry, her brother, with whom she had shared so many confidences. She would talk to him at the next suitable opportunity.

But when she did, the next day up in his work rooms, after Dermot had gone out for a walk with his father, Henry's answers were not encouraging. He was tinkering with the gruesome cadaver of some oversized bat on his work bench – the slimy furred animal, just released from its alcohol preservative, disembowelled, splayed out with pins on a board, where he was prodding at it with a scalpel and tweezers. The room stank of the chemical, along with some other, even more unpleasant odour, like a freshly suppurating drain.

'Francie, my dear Francie.' He bent over the scalpel, squinting. 'What can I say? – it's so much your life.'

'But you don't really like him, do you?'

'No – I mean, no, it would mean nothing, my liking him or not. Only you can be the judge there. Though, since you ask me about it all, you must have some doubts about him.'

'Not him. Just life in Over Norton House.'

'But that *is* him, or will be.'

'Exactly.'

'You marry the man, though, not the house. If you're really in love – the house, the place, the country doesn't matter. That must be pretty obvious, Francie.' He looked up at her now, the cadaver forgotten.

'But it's not as easy as that – that's in the "blind love" department. And I'm not. That's surely pretty obvious, too, isn't it, Henry?'

'*Touché.*' He left his dissection and moved over to wash his hands. 'But all the same, if it isn't, at least, pretty much in the blind love department, I shouldn't pursue it.' He stopped, arms resting on the basin, thinking of something.

'What?'

'Nothing.'

'Why haven't you anyone, Henry?'

'How do you know I haven't?'

'Some dusky African Princess . . .'

'As likely as not, you think?'

'I've no idea. I suppose it's Mama, makes it difficult for all of us.'

'Not for you. She's keen as mustard on Harry.'

'Yes. And that rather worries me, that we agree over something.'

Henry suddenly drew himself together, dried his hands and moved briskly away from the wash-stand. 'Which is another good reason for moving on from here, Frances.'

'But I don't *want* to move on, you know that. That's really the whole problem – this feeling I have about the place.'

'Yes, I do know. You have the sort of love for Summer Hill that I ought to have, but can't.'

'But why? Mama won't live forever. And it'll be yours –'

'Yes, yes.' He was frustrated now, almost roused. 'But . . . it's not Mama, it's me.'

'Your wanderlust.'

"Yes. Of course – it's that,' he said, his expression softening, surprised and grateful, as if she had been the first person ever to identify his problem. 'That's what I love, travelling with Dermot,' he went on, more easily now, free of some burden.

*

The New Year's ball was a sensation, though not in a way anyone could have anticipated. A small string orchestra had been engaged from Dublin which played at the back of the hall, while the dining room had been made over into a buffet where the long table, elaborately decorated with ferns and evergreens, groaned with devilled lobster, oyster patties, galantines of turkey, fillets of sole in aspic and Neapolitan ice-cream.

Flood ministered over a drinks table at one end, and blue-and-gilt-liveried footmen dispensed a sweet champagne cup in long flutes from silver salvers, with whisky-sodas less obviously available for the men. The drawing room, cleared of most of its bric-à-brac, became a redoubt for the older women, while their husbands commandeered the morning room on the other side of the house as a retreat. The younger company swirled to waltzes or danced vigorous polkas and intricate Scottish reels, under the great candlelit Waterford chandelier in the hall – Frances, rather the belle of the ball, in a ravishing white silk dress with spotted tulle, red velvet bows and streamers. But she was not the sensation.

It was the dog Sergeant who, once more taking aggressive initiative, announced the new revel in a cacophony of furious barking, the sounds first emerging from the landing above the hall, where soon the dog was seen worrying at something behind the balustrade – advancing but as quickly retreating from an invisible enemy on the floor, a rat it seemed, which the dog had cornered, or rather failed to corner, in some vicious game of hide and seek above the company. Eustace, breaking with his partner – he had been dancing with Isabelle Cordiner – remonstrated loudly with the terrier, bellowing above the music.

'Sergeant! Stop that – and come down here at once, you brute!'

For answer, the dog barked more loudly still, while yet making no appearance, leaving that honour to his intended prey, which came in sight just then – first a scaly head, then yellow and brown coils pushing through the landing balustrade, before the reptile suddenly dropped into space, swinging there ominously for a moment as the beast fought to maintain a grip with its tail, unsuccessfully in the event, for it fell sheer away then, onto the floor right in front of the orchestra, lying there stunned, immobile for a moment or two before raising its head with a loud and angry hissing noise.

The men took it mostly in good part, but the shrieks of the women might have been heard in the next townland. Though Lady Cordiner, appearing at the drawing room doorway then with Bunty, remained dumb, unable to credit her eyes. 'It's a menagerie – nothing but a menagerie this house,' Bunty murmured before turning on her heel and fleeing.

Later, when Henry had captured the snake, the ball proceeded – and Isabelle finally achieved her ambition by dancing a waltz with Harold. 'What *can* one think?' she said in a superior tone, currying favour. 'It could only happen in Ireland.' Harold agreed with her in an only slightly less patronising manner.

At midnight arms were linked to 'Auld Lang Syne' and the New Year was toasted in. 'To the year of the snake!' Henry, in high good humour, raised his glass to a doubting Frances.

3

THE VALLEY HAD been wet at first, after heavy spring rains, so that, when the first long days of heat came suddenly, the greenery exploded in wild tropic growths, the daffodils on the lawn below Summer Hill replaced by rampant meadowsweet and cow parsley, while in moist-damp places by the river angelica, pennywort and saxifrage bloomed inordinately. The horse chestnut trees on the lawn and along the estate wall became brilliant green with white candelabra almost overnight; the beech and oak budded early and the grass gleamed, turning glossy sides to the wind.

The house in summer looked over the valley where all this green abundance rising up the slopes seemed to attack it, hoping to overpower it. But such a victory remained a hopeless cause. Gardeners scythed or mowed the grass without remission, woodmen hacked at ungainly branches and overgrown shrubs, gullies were cleared, fences mended, hedges vigorously clipped, weeds viciously attacked and uprooted: armies of men, under Lady Cordiner's obsessive direction, went forth each day to prune, transform or repulse nature.

On the rough pasture, ragged copses and gorse slopes of the small farms across the valley, leading up to the navy-blue mountains, the wind and damp of immemorial Irish weather had long since triumphed, leaving a wild and lovely land. But at Summer Hill, a formal enclave cut from all this indiscipline, the beauty, man-made, was rigorously maintained and manicured.

In front of the house, beyond the gravel surround, the elaborate terrace gardens, with their bedding plants, herbaceous borders and geometric multicoloured box hedges, were most exposed to Lady Cordiner's strictures. She inspected the lobelias, roses, salvias, geraniums and much else each morning with Appleton, the English head gardener, a commanding officer and sergeant major at a drill parade where the smallest irregularity or blemish was pounced upon, noted and subsequently set right or eradicated.

It was sometimes a longish tour for there were four sunken gardens within the main terrace, a good acre of land, perfectly square, divided by a cross of raised red marble chip paths. In the middle of the terrace, replacing a naked statue of the goddess Ceres, a large bronze-ribbed astrolabe had been set up, science ousting myth, the toy of some earlier Cordiner, a man of the Enlightenment, now become a central point for Lady Cordiner's more mundane but no less acute observations.

To the west of these pleasure gardens, a well-shaved lawn led up in a succession of gentle terraces and flights of steps to the tennis and croquet lawns and the walled vegetable garden hidden by the great trees beyond – for this was the area planted out over a hundred years before by Sir Archibald Cordiner, with glades of Japanese cedars, Canadian maples, Spanish chestnuts and American redwoods, trees now reaching some maturity in a spread of perfumed bark and exotic leaf.

Lady Cordiner was not a regular visitor in this higher domain. She disliked the overhanging gloom, the sense of impending jungle, the fact that here was growth in these great trees which she could never control. But, most of all, in the longer grass and thicker shrubs at the top of the rise here, she secretly feared a meeting with one or other of Henry's wild animals or reptiles, for it was against the vegetable garden wall, in a series of wire enclosures, that he had built his small zoo, a menagerie of dik-diks, porcupines, hyraxes, Colobus monkeys, civet cats, mongooses, snakes – and worst of all a Giant Pangolin from West Africa, a dragon-like mammal with a long tail and horny scales big as a man's hand: entirely harmless, slow-moving and confiding, Henry had assured her, with a diet of termites which it searched out in their nests with a long sticky tongue . . . This beast gave her waking nightmares so that she thought no pen strong enough to hold it and always expected the brute to erupt at her feet in these high glades.

But by and large Lady Cordiner managed to dominate these open spaces as much as she did the interiors of Summer Hill, so that for privacy beyond their own bedrooms the household was forced well away from the house and its immediate environs, down the steep sides of the valley or into the wilder woods, to other secret places, or ones inaccessible at least to Lady Cordiner.

Frances stood on the watchtower of wooden scaffolding below the bridge, looking down-river to where the white water, scurrying out from between the bridge piers, gave way to darker pools beneath the trees. She could just see the other men from the estate, up to their waists in the river, standing in to the bank on the same side, hidden by the trees, with the net.

'The flow is smooth enough – and the sight good,' the water-bailiff said to her. 'But will they come at all?'

It was mid-June, an early overcast morning after a night's rain, with a fair depth but with no great current on the river: ideal conditions for the start of the annual two months' salmon netting below Summer Hill, a right which the Cordiner family had enjoyed here since the dissolution of the monasteries, where the fish, when they came upstream in sufficient numbers, could be seen and trapped in the pools, before the others went on up to their spawning grounds: opportunity netting, a patient, skilful business where the water-bailiff or one of his men stood guard on the watchtower for hours each day waiting for a run.

Frances could make out very little in the first of the darker pools thirty yards or so down-river of them. If anything moved there she doubted if she would see it. But Matt Carney, the Summer Hill water-bailiff, gazing on these brown waters for years, knew every calm space and ripple and hidden stone in the reaches below the bridge. And it was he who, some few minutes later, saw signs of the first of the big fish, just the slightest spear-headed disturbance on the surface cutting upstream, so that he raised his hand smoothly to the men lower down on the bank – no noise above the chatter of the river in the silent early morning where the ground mists had only just left the valley.

Behind this first faint chevron on the water other lesser ridges and eddies sprang up, moving slowly upstream. It was a run. They let the fish come right into the last of the pools, Matt with his hand still raised, the men waiting for his signal. Frances could see vague shadows and shapes now, a flash of silver beneath the little curdling movements on the calm surface.

'Yes?' she whispered.

'Yes – a fair run, not big ones, but a dozen or more, I'd say.'

A moment later he dropped his hand and pandemonium ensued. The two men holding the net at either end, up- and downstream, threw it out over the pool, so that most of the fish were trapped in a sudden fury of dancing water, jumping and spinning in the air, trying to leap free, as the weighted cords closed over and round them.

Matt was down the steps of the tower now, Frances following, both of them running along the bank towards the commotion. The other men, hands thrust deep in the pool, were muffling the fish, forcing the net down on them, before circling it together, making a bag out of it, so that they could pull the catch onto the bank.

Frances saw the fish clearly then, arms of reddish silver thrashing about, gills moving furiously, the water a turmoil, as the net closed and the man, up on the bank now with Matt, pulled it ashore. She joined them, heaving the catch in, glorying in the sheer animal energy of it all, clutching, struggling with the fish through the net with her bare hands, touching their fight as they spun and arched, feeling their slippery weight, the chilled scales in her fingers, a fight for life against her own flesh, the thrash of water drenching her, so that she became exultant, carried away by the battle, shouting out, 'It's mine, I have it – I have them!' as if these fish from the bridge of Cloone were hers, not her father's.

The men were not surprised at her force and competence – the way she tussled with the net, threw herself into the fray. For years, in their other work about the estate, she had joined them, watching, helping, as a child – always something of a tomboy. But now, today, as a young woman, they found this passionate involvement strange, that she should so take up with them, keeping no distance, like a man, one of their own. They appreciated her interest, yet were wary, not knowing the reasons behind it.

There were something less than a dozen fish, and most of them smallish peal.

But there was one fully-grown salmon, she saw, thick as a man's thigh, with a great hooked underjaw, that fought to the end – a monster. She turned away as they clubbed it with lead-topped sticks – and then, ashamed, turned back to watch the killing. If you watched, then you watched to the end, she thought: you do not turn away.

They took the fish laid on ferns in a dog cart up to the yard of the house, to Matt Carney's office, where he put them out on a marble slab, weighing them, accounting for each in a big ledger.

'A fair start, Miss Frances. And that one at the end.' He looked at the largest salmon, with its lovely silver and blue sheen, the scales still jewels. 'That's one we've been waiting for – he's been around a time, many a season up and down. Will ye look at him – twenty-six pounds and ten ounces. Ye'll have that for your dinner, I'd say.'

Happy in the business, excited by it, for several weeks afterwards, morning or evening, Frances kept watch on the tower by the river, learning all the signs on the water from Matt or one of the other men, until she became almost as adept as they in spotting a run. As a child she had sometimes watched this netting distantly, the first catch usually, as a family 'event'. But now she took a lonely passion in it, to Matt's surprise and that of some of the villagers looking down from the bridge, who saw her in these early mornings as she stood on the watchtower, a motionless figure, intent on the wavering patterns on the water, in riding breeches and dark hacking jacket, a scarf hiding the ends of her dark curls, so that she might have been a man standing there, a young man, a dark sentinel on the tower emerging from the white mists. 'I am of the trees here,' she wrote in her album *consolatum*. 'And the river too.'

Sometimes Henry came with her, sharing the small wooden platform, where above them, set into the steep slopes of the gorge, they could see the ruins of the old Cordiner castle with its stubby Norman tower, later Gothic arches and mullioned windows – appearing mysteriously as the mists cleared, catching the rising sun in a flash of old limestone, wrapt all round by the sheer green woods: a Lorelei vision commanding the river.

'I look at that old Norman keep,' Henry said. 'And wonder how it's mine.'

'You don't see all the family stretching back? . . .'

'Mailed knights and maidens – and the rough Irishry storming the slopes? Not really.'

'Remember that splendid battle here, when there was no proper bridge, just a ford, and they threw stones at each other across the river – the Cordiners against the Deanes, the rival Knights from Graig. We won.'

'Did we?' He turned to her, surprised, amused.

'Yes. I can see it all – the Cordiners getting their boats back across just in time, then throwing rocks at each other all day, 'till the Deanes retreated, "bootless home" as the account has it.'

'Homeric,' Henry said.

'But you must have heard the story?'

'Yes, yes – must have done. Simply forgotten it.'

'You really are always somewhere else,' she told him. 'Aren't you?'

'No. I've been thinking about this African journey.' He leant on the rail, not seeing anything on the water, pondering quite another landscape. 'And now that Dermot has got himself attached to Milner's staff it may not work out. One of "Milner's young men".'

'What is he? – some sort of military attaché?'

'Yes, exactly. At the War Office in London for the moment. But he'll have to join Milner in South Africa. So he won't have any real leave 'till next year, if then. All a perfect bore.'

'Does he think so?'

Henry looked at her ruefully. 'You're always so sharp, aren't you? I don't know,' he went on seriously. 'It's all a great honour, no doubt.'

'Well, he *is* keen on his career.'

'Of course.'

'And perhaps running round the African wilds with you doesn't help it.'

'Perhaps. But –'

'But that's *your* trouble, Henry – not really having a career.'

'But I do, I do –'

'Just stuffing the old nurseries full of dead beasts and butterflies. And live snakes. You don't work *with* anyone else, quite isolated, like Mama. You ought to do something with *other* people. You're too stuck in yourself.'

'It's not quite like that, Francie,' he said, quietly. 'I *do* do things with other people – with Dermot.'

'Except that you can't now – if he's to pursue his army career in London or the Cape Colony.'

He admitted this with a nod. 'Rather like you, with Harold – both faced with an impasse at the moment. He's coming over next week, isn't he? What will *you* do?'

'What will he do, rather.'

'You can't keep him on tenterhooks forever.'

'No. All a perfect bore, isn't it?' She smiled hugely.

Lady Cordiner considered the summer season – the second annual visitation of uncles, aunts, cousins, friends and fiancées arriving intermittently at Summer Hill throughout the coming months, where they would stay until the Dublin Horse Show, or at least until the grouse shooting opened in Scotland in mid-August.

Meanwhile there was much to be organised. Bunty Cordiner had written a very nearly impertinent letter saying she and Austin, with the children, were expecting to travel to Clifden on the Galway coast for a seaside holiday that year: how the Summer Hill dates offered might clash with this. Lady Cordiner would put paid to that in her reply, by making no allowances to Bunty over her Galway arrangements

– knowing full well how she would come to heel in the end, as she always did. Lady Cordiner was entirely aware of Bunty's social envy – her covert admiration, her longing for all the ordered summer events and niceties of the great house: the tennis and croquet parties, boating trips, fishing excursions, the spirited afternoon tea with the local gentry and more sophisticated foreign visitors on the lawn terraces. Indeed, Lady Cordiner thought, she might well pay Bunty out for her presumption by putting her and Austin in the third best guest room this year.

Frances, on the other hand, she had decided to treat more gently. A wrong move or too much pressure on the girl at this point might destroy the match with Harold – Harold who had explained to her, confidentially last Christmas, how Frances wished to wait before making any formal announcement of their engagement. But they were as good as engaged, Lady Cordiner felt: it was simply a matter of tactfully seeing it through. An announcement, she was sure, would come before the Dublin Horse Show.

But why the waiting in the first place, she wondered? Harold, quite obviously, had so much to offer; and, besides, they were surely in love. Harold had offered no explanation at the time and she herself was none the wiser. What was Frances waiting for? She knew, though without any definite proof, that her daughter had taken the little objets d'art about the house, simply thieved them. What did this signify? What did Frances want of and in Summer Hill that had made her so unaccountably tardy with Harold? Lady Cordiner, quick to identify hidden motive in everyone else, was at a loss here, and it annoyed her considerably that she simply did not know her daughter, a shadow moving quickly about the house and estate, always there but rarely seen, an ominous presence almost, watching, waiting. It was quite unnatural – a girl of her beauty and accomplishments, that she should not be in Dublin or in London for the season, among her own kind. Yes, she was very much banking on Harold taking the girl in hand without more ado. That was what was wanted really: a little male force and decisiveness in the matter and the girl would come to heel. Harold, no doubt, had been too tactful and restrained in his suit.

They arrived, over a week in late June – Eustace with Harold again; Mortimer Cordiner; a distant American cousin of Lady Cordiner, a genial railroad magnate, Wilbur Quince, from Brewster, Pennsylvania, with his pretty wife Mary Ann and her aunt, Mrs Chauncy, a sprightly widow from Lynchburg, Virginia – together with the Austin Cordiners, their two spotty sons and Isabelle, an older, more gracious girl now, just nineteen, her puppy fat gone, less prone to thumb sucking, her adolescent pouts and ringlets transformed and clipped, becoming tools of a flirtatious guile, making her an attractive, if deceptively mature, young woman, for she remained a child.

The dog Sergeant disgraced himself on the arrival of the Austin Cordiners by being sick on the porch steps, just as Bunty emerged from the wagonette, disgorging the gruesome remains of a half-digested rat almost at her feet. Bunty took the greeting generally in bad part.

Sergeant had caught the rat, with Monster, in a spate of furious digging into the bank behind the tennis court that morning, so that the chalk on the base line had been half-obliterated by soil and the end of the court itself partly undermined. The dogs, severely reprimanded, were locked in the stables for the rest of the day and the tennis tournament arranged for that afternoon delayed while repairs were effected.

But when it started Isabelle and Harold, drawing lots as partners, showed themselves dab hands at the game, beating the other mixed doubles, including one with the local curate, the agile and overweening Timothy Birch, who had played for Trinity College and was thus always expected to win, no matter how bad his partner was, in this instance Frances, who hardly played the game at all.

The Reverend Mr Birch took their defeat rather gracelessly and there was a frisson of ill-will in the air before fresh iced lemon-juice was served under the maple tree and the older spectators prepared themselves for an elaborate cream tea, superintended by Flood and Pat Kennedy and carried out by two footmen in their light summer livery.

Lady Cordiner, looking at the willowy Isabelle in her pleated ankle-length skirt and tightly bursting bodice, was surprised at the skill, at the development of the girl in every sense.

'How pretty you look, my dear,' she told her, as she and Harold came off the court before tea. 'The little embroidery there –' She pointed to the trim of daisy chains round the neck and cuffs of the bodice. 'Most becoming. Did you do it yourself?'

'Yes, Aunt – yes, I did!' Her face was peach-coloured, hot and puffed with excitement. Eyes wide, glorying in all her various accomplishments, Isabelle was visibly leaping into life that afternoon. Unladylike, no doubt, yet how attractive such excitement was, Lady Cordiner thought. Yes, Isabelle was undeniably attractive.

It was after tea, as one victory followed another for them, that Harold started to flirt with her – at first tactfully, then quite openly. Frances, on the sidelines, was simply curious to begin with, then astonished: the shouted encouragements, admiring smiles, even the little endearments which he tossed towards Isabelle after a good volley or when she ran like a startled deer for a drop shot – his general ease, his intimacy with her, for it was no less, became so obvious it was shocking. So that Frances blushed when she overheard Cousin Wilbur's tactless remark to Lady Cordiner – 'What a fine pair they make! Shortly to become engaged, I understand?'

Lady Cordiner turned to him, frowning. This mistaken thought of Isabelle as Harold's fiancée quickly alerted her. She had noticed and accepted Harold's fervour towards the girl as mere high spirits. Now, at once, she saw the real purpose behind it. Not male arrogance – Harold was playing quite a different game: raising a little jealousy in Frances by these new attentions, pointing out to her a potential rival, how there were other fish in the sea. How clever of him.

But Frances felt nothing but a growing anger, a fearful indignity, a hatred of this man who could so openly humiliate her. She had never felt like this before – a hot flush of iron resentment rising in her, against Harold, then herself, that she could ever have thought to love someone so ill-mannered and insensitive, so that she snapped at Mr Birch when he offered her a meringue, and later, at the end of the match, was quite unable to control herself – storming away, most pointedly, back to the house, just as Harold and Isabelle left the court after a last victory. Harold's plan, if plan it was, had misfired.

Frances went to her room. On reflection, she was amazed yet proud of her behaviour. It had changed her life, a bright deed certainly, which this time had really stopped the clocks. It was the end of Harold, of course. She would accept no apology – the man was a Lothario, that was it. He was not for her. She could never live with such a person.

In her enthusiasm for her action it did not cross her mind that he might simply have been baiting her in his behaviour – or further, that she had, perhaps, deserved just this, that she had never really loved him. She had been publicly dishonoured. That was all – and that was that.

Insects hummed in the creeper outside her open window. She looked out at the soft, late afternoon sun slanting down the valley, over the lawn with its heavy trees, the cows below in the pasture moving in a long line towards their evening milking, the slabs of light and shade stealing over the blue flanks of Mount Brandon in the distance: the whole, abundant, settled world of Summer Hill.

And she was happy suddenly, wildly happy with a sinking feeling in her stomach, that all this – the land, the house – could remain hers, in secret at least. She would not now have to live in Oxfordshire – blown about, a cold, dull life on those high wolds, among a witless nobility and peasantry. How happy she was – it had really all worked out for the best.

And how unhappy, angry her mother became. Though at first, when she spoke to Frances, she temporised.

'But, my dear, one must expect young men to flirt a little.'

'I do not, *will* not, expect that, Mama.'

'You will find life somewhat difficult then.'

'So be it –'

'Complete fidelity – you will rarely find it, I must be frank with you. Besides, you are not yet actually engaged to Harold. He was simply – how shall I put it? – encouraging you. He didn't mean anything with Isabelle – I'm sure, not for a moment.'

'People *should* mean what they say – and do. I cannot abide such trickery.'

'You have too much pride – lack experience of the world. You are too rigid, my dear. It was nothing – see it as no more than a little tiff on the tennis court. Make it up with Harold. I assure you, he has no real concern for Isabelle, none whatsoever. How could he? She is simply a child.'

'Mama, that makes his behaviour all the more reprehensible – leading the girl on.'

Her mother had no ready answer to this. And it was from then on, annoyed at herself and seeing this splendid match dissolving in front of her eyes, that she became alarmed and thus angry.

'Frances, you cannot throw your life away just because of a little misunderstanding on a tennis court –'

'I'm not throwing it away. I'm regaining it –'

'Don't interrupt. You must pull yourself together – be your age, for once. No more of this childishness. It's all far too serious a matter.'

'Exactly! And I am not to become engaged to a flirt!'

'Harold is a great deal more than that – you know perfectly well – a most distinguished family: Lord Norton himself, peer of the realm, eminent in so many fields, a beautiful house –'

'I was not to have married a *house*, Mama!' Frances rounded on her mother, becoming as roused as she was.

'You were to marry *into* one, a great house. You must not be so literal.'

'I have a great house here – and I prefer it.'

Lady Cordiner looked at her curiously. 'I do not quite understand? You cannot live here for the rest of your life.'

'Aunt Emily does – and will.'

'Your Aunt Emily is – she is touched.' Lady Cordiner was uncertain how to describe her condition.

'With genius, yes.'

'My dear, she is ninepence in the shilling.' Her mother was abrupt and dismissive now, still firmly believing that her daughter could be brought to reason if she spoke firmly, even ruthlessly to her. Frances simply lacked an intelligent grasp of the whole affair – a child who needed some brusque advice on the ways of the world. But this idea that the house, Summer Hill, might lie at the heart of Frances's aberrant behaviour was new to her and worried Lady Cordiner. 'In any case,' she went on, more brusquely still. 'You cannot compare yourself with Aunt Emily – not in genius or vagary. You are a young woman with many qualities' – she went on acidly – 'but not with either of those, I'm pleased to say. And you must go out into the world and express your gifts suitably, which naturally means marriage. I cannot think why you mention the house here as a bar on your life. You dishonour it in no way by marrying Harold. Just the opposite – nothing would make your father and me more pleased.'

'You misunderstand me, Mama.' Frances looked at her, stared at her bitterly. 'I love the house here –'

'But of course, as we all do –'

'No, it's something a great deal more than that.'

'But you would always have it, to visit.'

'More than that.' Frances fell silent. And for the first time, in her daughter's fiercely set expression, Lady Cordiner felt some intimation of her daughter's real desires. She could not identify them, but she saw whatever it was as a threat, to herself as mistress of Summer Hill. And now she was no longer angry, but more afraid, a moment's fear in the pit of the stomach, as when a commander, always victorious in unimportant local skirmishes, is brought news of a whole great army arrayed over the hill.

Harold, despite Lady Cordiner's best endeavours, left the house shortly afterwards – Frances remaining quite adamant. Even her father spoke to her, but to no avail – mumbling about the 'disgrace' of the matter. 'The disgrace is his, not mine,' she told him roundly, before he thankfully retreated to his machinery, the screw propellers, wire struts and rudders of his flying machine in the yard workshops.

The disgrace, too, was her father's, Frances thought. She neither loved nor hated him – he had simply never impinged on her life when she had needed him, another outcast of her mother's, as she had been, where Henry had been so much the favoured person, a cosseted little boy, the pet in old photographs dressed in girl's clothes. Her father had become so distant a figure that she was not even able to pity him now, seeing in his familial cowardice, his lack of warmth towards her, wounds which her mother had imposed, but which he ought to have resisted. That was his disgrace. She at least, she swore, would never suffer such indignity at her mother's hands – and no one would so stunt her warmth either, for she thought that to be her mother's worst crime, the way she proscribed all emotion at Summer Hill which was not her own.

Bunty and Austin Cordiner curtailed their visit, too, amidst a great many self-satisfied cluckings from Bunty, happy that Lady Cordiner should have been so exposed and embarrassed, and that Isabelle had been the cause of it – a much more suitable match for Harold, she thought, in any case, which the events on the tennis court had simply proved. She felt, indeed, that she might well further her daughter's cause in Harold's direction by taking her to England – to Oxford, Stratford and Stow, a little Cotswold tour – in September.

Only Henry showed sympathy for Frances. Indeed, he was obviously happy for her at this turn of events.

'Of course, you were right about Harold: you never did really like him,' Frances told him late one afternoon while up helping feed the animals in his menagerie, the two little dik-diks scuttling about nervously, inspecting the cabbage stalks suspiciously before retreating to their hutch.

'Not so much that, Francie. I was worried about you. You wouldn't have been happy. He was too dull a chap for you.'

'Yes. It was only a dream –'

'So you really knew it too?' He turned to her quickly. 'You were simply playing with him?'

'No. I just know it now.'

'But, Francie, you do flirt yourself, you know. You used to with him, with others as well. I've seen you –'

'Did I – do I?' she asked, only half-innocently.

'Yes, you know you do. You've got great gifts that way. But be careful. Lasting with someone is more important – and more difficult.'

'You speak from experience, do you?' she asked with pointed mischief.

'Yes.'

'Who is she, Henry? Do tell me!'

'She's no one. I just know.' He turned away then, moving towards the brick-floored cage where the Giant Pangolin slept in a box. 'Supply of anthills is getting scarce. Though there are some beyond Cooper's Wood, in Papa's new fields. Come with me and help get some this afternoon?'

Frances followed him, thinking of something else. 'Mama's furious, of course,' she said absent-mindedly, not caring.

'Yes. Obviously. And there's another problem – are\you really going to stick it out with her here, in the present chilly circumstances?'

'What else?'

'Oh, a hundred other things, Francie. Go to Dublin, the Horse Show, stay with Mortimer at Islandbridge, he's home for the summer. Or to London. I'm going on there.'

'To see Dermot?'

'I hope so.'

'I might go away – but only for a bit. And what about your African journey this winter?'

'Doesn't look likely – if Dermot can't come.'

'Can't you go on your own?'

'No. Needs two people.'

'Stanley went on his own, looking for Livingstone.'

'Really, Francie, you don't know the first thing about it. It's much more complicated. I need Dermot.'

The Giant Pangolin, curled in a perfect circle like a huge scaly coil of rope, stirred a fraction in its bed of sandy earth, then continued its slumber. Henry closed the door. 'Must get some more anthills, else I'll have to give him to Bill Lawrence up at the Dublin zoo.' Henry moved on to the porcupine in the next cage. It, too, was half-asleep in the drowsy heat, showing no interest in the chopped carrots which Henry offered.

'Why are they all asleep?' Frances asked.

'The heat or they feed at night. And it's not their natural habitat, of course. We should all be out of here, Francie,' he went on, checking the water, leaving the food. 'It's not natural – clinging to home.'

'Not natural only because Mama makes life such a *prison* here. A caged zoo for us – as much as for them.' Frances gestured back towards the menagerie as they walked away between the glades, the Spanish chestnuts and cedars. When they stopped beneath one of these, Frances scratched some bark out with her nails, crushing it between her fingers, putting it to her nose, breathing the faint perfume deeply. She looked down the sloping emerald lawn to where the house basked in the late sunlight, the old limestone mellow, the gardens in front empty, innocent, with Lady Cordiner somewhere indoors.

'Oh, it really could be such a perfect place,' Frances said impatiently. 'All this – one could fill it with so much *real* life. You could, Henry, with whoever you marry.'

He smiled tartly. 'Don't know that I'm the marrying kind.'

'You see, there's some wonderful spirit hidden there,' Frances went on. 'A frog prince, waiting.' Her eyes gleamed with frustrated emotion.

'All right then, but why do *you* have to release it, with all your own life to lead?'

'Because no one else will! And because it's here – somewhere – my life. That's why. I feel it. I'm tied to the place. Oh, not so much because of what I've had from it as from what I've *not* had from it, what Mama has prevented us from having.'

'But, Francie, it's not really Mama who prevents you from having it: it's the law of primogeniture, the eldest male descendant and all that nonsense. It's Papa and me and Eustace who prevent you from having it, if anyone does.'

'Yes,' she said shortly, turning away from him so that he would not see how unhappy this accident of birth had made her, how much she would so like to have been a man, and the first born at that. 'Well, in any case,' she went on, 'if I can't bring that life to the house, then you must. Which is why you'll have to marry, Henry. What will become of Summer Hill if you don't?'

'Eustace – Eustace can take it over.'

'Henry, that's nonsense. You'll simply let Mama have a final victory over you if you do that.'

'Mama . . .' He paused. 'You always see everything as her fault.'

'I do! She's killing the place, don't you see? And the people – Papa, you, me. There has to be a future, a real life here. And unless we stand and fight her there won't be.'

'A real life?' he asked vaguely. 'What?'

'Oh, don't be so obtuse, Henry! – anything that isn't so neatly and coldly ordered. Chatter, laughter, anything *quite* inconsequential. Nothing so serious, not this spying, this barracks life Mama goes in for, running the whole place like an army. "Do this, do that and you can't do the other thing." – she's always been like that. Can't ever simply relax and *enjoy* it all. You know, how she hardly ever says anything that isn't an instruction, a command or an interruption – and nearly always on some entirely banal matter, like one's dress or hair or being late for tea, just when one's talking about or doing something really interesting. And she kills it. Kills it stone dead,' Frances added, with bitter finality.

'A little hard –'

'But it's true, Henry – you know it is, which is why you disappear aborad so often, won't stand up to her. Oh yes,' she rushed on before he could interrupt her, 'much as I love you, you *do* know that, dearest Henry. You let her ride roughshod over you and I despise her for that.'

'Why not rather despise me?' he asked calmly, a little coldly, not looking at her.

'I told you – I am so very, very attached to you, so the faults don't matter. Attached, more so than ever.' She looked at him gently.

'Why?'

'Confidences – that I can only really ever share with you. And after Harold, well . . .'

'You weren't honest with him?'

'Not entirely. I never told him my real feelings about Mama for example.'

'Never really loved him then?'

'Oh, I did, in a way – and he loved me. But it must have been a game. It wasn't real,' she added quietly. 'Yet if only I could be *sure* I was right in what I did.'

'You were entirely right, Francie,' Henry told her promptly. 'Not because Harold is a flirt but because he is a fool. Oh, a nice enough fool, for dozens of other foolish women. But not for you. That will be your problem – finding some very very *un*foolish young man. Such men tend to come much older, when they come at all.' He reached out and touched her hand, shook it an instant. 'You really are so like me in that way – uncompromising. And you're right. It's painful, but it's the only way in the end.'

'But what are you so uncompromising about, in "that way"? – I didn't know.'

She looked at him intently. But he didn't reply.

'Oh, Henry, you are sly!' She smiled, kissing him impulsively. 'I really, honestly don't know what I'd do without you. All the same, I do wish you'd tell me who she is.'

Frances went to Dublin for the Horse Show, staying with Mortimer Cordiner in his pretty house beyond Islandbridge on the river. Henry came with her, before going on to London to meet Dermot.

By the time he and Frances met again, a month later in mid-September, her brother had changed. He was no longer sly or literal or prompt in his replies to her: he barely spoke to her at all, or to anyone else. And when they did talk he was fidgety and morose, giving little away. The reason for this decline was obvious. Dermot, apparently a considerable success at the War Office, would have no extended leave until the following year, if then. Their long-planned African trip together that winter had been cancelled.

The two men drove up in a hackney sidecar one September afternoon just as the trees were beginning to turn – a thickset man, neatly moustached, in a dark bowler with an unsuitable winter greatcoat, the other smaller, rat-faced, dressed like an undertaker's clerk. They came in by the yard entrance, so that Eileen, up in the servants' wing, saw them arrive and was immediately suspicious. She recognised the hackney driver, old Seamus Newman, who waited on the trains at Thomastown station. The two men weren't country men; they had come some distance. She rushed to find Pat Kennedy, to warn him – there was something wrong, for the men weren't tradesmen or gentry either. But she was too late. Pat, at the back door just then, coming up from the kitchen, was already facing them. She saw the look of fear in his eyes, his whole bearing, as he stood there, trapped.

'Afternoon.' The heavier man spoke, bowler forced down like a helmet over his bushy eyebrows. 'Mr Henry Cordiner – we'd like a word with him, if we may.' The accent was English, Eileen thought. Why hadn't they come by the front door?

Pat Kennedy relaxed. 'Who shall I say, Sir?'

'We're from Dublin. Just a word with him, if you please.'

Pat led them away into the cook's parlour. When he returned to Eileen he confirmed their worst suspicions.

'Police,' he whispered. 'For sure.'

'Not you?'

'No. Nor you either, mercy be. The young master,' he added sarcastically.

'What is it, what is it?' she asked urgently.

'No idea. But something serious – all the way from Dublin Castle, I'll bet.'

'Glory be – what's he been up to?'

Pat shrugged. 'What mischief wouldn't they get up to? – any of these people, with the world in their hands.'

It turned cloudy an hour later when the two men had left. A wind got up and stayed there, coming in gusts and whines before blowing hard from the south-west, the first of the autumn gales getting under way, bending the trees in Cooper's Wood beyond the house, spots of rain starting to fall from a running sky. Summer was ending.

Henry did not appear for tea. But he was often absent then, busy in his workrooms in the old nurseries at the top of the house.

'Who were those men?' Lady Cordiner asked, after Pat Kennedy had brought the tray in, raising a bone china cup, then considering a tiny egg sandwich on the frilled doily.

'What men?' Frances hadn't seen them.

'Kennedy – you saw them in, didn't you? Came by the back door, Mrs Martin said.'

'Yes, Ma'am.'

'Well?'

'I don't know, Ma'am.'

'Something to do with his wretched animals, I shouldn't be surprised,' Sir Desmond grunted. 'Saw Henry walk up there with them. From the Dublin zoo, I shouldn't be surprised. I saw old Newman's sidecar in the yard.'

'Why didn't they come round by the hall door then?' Frances enquired.

'Tradespeople, dear, that's why,' Lady Cordiner said sniffily.

The rain spattered now against the glass, the windows shaking in their frames. Sir Desmond looked glumly out. 'What a wretched change,' he commented. 'Just when we were finishing the harvest so well.'

They forgot about Henry. But, when he did not appear for dinner either, they remembered him again.

They found him later that night, after a frantic search with lanterns, in the howling wind and rain, stretched out in the reptile house attached to his little zoo. At least one of the snakes, a puff adder, had escaped from its glass-sided box, for when Molloy, the coachman, carrying a lantern, with Simpson the head gamekeeper, came through the doorway, they saw the unlocked pen and the brute, in a corner, inflating itself, hissing malevolently, so that they dared not enter, waiting outside in the rain until Simpson's shotgun was fetched and the snake killed.

By this time some of the household – Sir Desmond and Frances with Pat Kennedy – alerted by the commotion, had gathered round the enclosure. But Simpson held them back. 'Wait, Sir Desmond – there may be others escaped.' Sir Desmond pushed him aside, moving in, kneeling by his son, holding the lantern up. Henry had been dead for several hours, his face darkly blotched already, twisted in pain, two clear marks by his swollen chin where the fangs had sunk in, as if he had embraced the reptile. There was an unpleasant smell in the air, so that it was Sir Desmond now who, standing up, prevented Frances from entering.

'No, my dear, no!'

She struggled with him. 'But why?' she shouted. 'Why?'

'The brute escaped – and bit him, simply bit him,' her father shouted at Frances, raising his voice over hers as she fought hysterically in his arms.

The other snakes were summarily executed by Simpson that night. A massacre of innocents? Pat Kennedy wondered. For he had clearly seen the fang marks on Henry Cordiner's cheek. Had he somehow let the snake kill him, as a result of his interview with the two detectives?

The men were identified as such by Sir Desmond the following morning – in a flurry of telegrams, a talk with old Seamus Newman at Thomastown station and a trip to Dublin that same afternoon, where he had a meeting with the Police Commissioner at the Castle. But the details of this he did not reveal to anyone, returning that night a very shaken man.

'It is something I can't discuss with you, my dear,' he told Lady Cordiner, confined to her bedroom, in a state of agonised collapse. 'Believe me, it would be far better not. Suffice to say that Henry got himself into some trouble while he was in London. All charges have now, of course, been dropped.'

Lady Cordiner, the more heartbroken still for hearing some crime linked to her son's death, did not pursue the matter. Frances on the other hand, told the same thing by her father, pursued the reasons behind his sudden, shocking death vigorously. An early opportunity arose with Dermot Cordiner's arrival, among other family members, two days later for the funeral. Knowing him, liking him, she spoke to him at once, outright, going into his bedroom just after he'd got in from the Dublin train with his father.

'Dermot, Dermot, what has *happened?*'

He did not reply. She had cried hysterically at first at her brother's death, astounded, unbelieving. But now, though no calmer in her heart, her emotion had been transformed into a hard-eyed enquiry into the mystery, the injustice of the event. She looked at Dermot in amazement now when he said nothing, thinking that he alone, as Henry's closest friend, must have some explanation for the horror. Dermot moved away from her in his neat dark suit, ruffling his frizzy, straw-coloured hair, then smoothing it nervously. Finally he turned and shrugged.

'But, Dermot – you must know something. You *saw* him in London.'

'Yes. Yes I did.'

'And?'

'And nothing, Frances, nothing.' Dermot coughed, choking a moment, got a handkerchief out, fussed with it. His bright blue eyes flittered about nervously.

'Nothing?'

'He was disappointed, of course, by our African trip not going through.'

'But these two men – two policemen that came to see him, just before the accident?'

'Policemen?' Dermot looked away again. 'I didn't know.'

'About some criminal charge he was involved in, Papa said.'

'I knew nothing of that. Henry mentioned nothing.' Dermot paid full attention to Frances now, bending down, his neat frame leaning over the table, knuckles whitening on the mahogany. 'But I had to be at the War Office a lot. I didn't see as much of Henry in London as I'd have liked –'

'Dermot, something's not right, someone's hiding things – I know it. And the snakes, too. Henry would never have been so careless –'

'He killed himself? Let himself be killed –?'

'Oh, God, I don't know. It's possible. But no one will say, or help. We must find out, we must!'

'Why? He's dead. What difference will it make, Frances? It won't bring him back.'

Frances faced him across the table now, a Gladstone bag open between them. 'It matters, because I want to know why he killed himself – if he did.'

Dermot sighed, picking some stiff collars from the bag, then drew himself up suddenly. 'He loved me, Frances,' he said simply, fingering the collars, moving away to the chest of drawers.

'Of course,' she answered, surprised at so obvious a statement. 'As I loved him. But why should that have anything to do with it?'

'I really wanted my army career,' he said slowly, dully. 'More than the travelling, the exploration. Wanted to make a real career of it – and, when I was offered this position at the War Office, well, I jumped at it – when Henry wanted me to make this East African journey with him.'

'So?'

'Can't you see?' He turned to her.

'Loving you, why should he so mind that?'

'Well, he did, you see.'

'But love is a good thing, he must have wanted your success.'

'With him, though, not with the army or Milner in the Cape Colony. Henry felt I'd betrayed him.'

'Betrayed him?' Frances remembered her angry, agonised feelings when Harold had done the same to her. 'But it wasn't that sort of love – you weren't going to *marry* him!' Frances was astonished.

'It was, Frances,' he told her simply. 'It *was* that kind of love.'

Frances stood back from the table, head swimming. 'Oh, Dermot, how awful, how terrible. I see – I do see now, which is why he wouldn't marry. *You* were the person – when I used to ask him who she was.' She looked at Dermot now in a wholly new way. It was strange, yet it made perfect sense to her. She could entirely understand the feelings between them; she understood, she thought, any kind of love.

Dermot blinked, still standing with his back to the chest of drawers. 'And you, Frances – he told me, if you hadn't been his sister: how you were the only woman he could ever have thought to marry . . . He told me that. And I can see why. He was right.'

The two cousins looked at each other across the room in the dull light, vague ghosts in mourning clothes, before Frances rushed across, embracing him. 'Dear Dermot,' she said. 'How awful – *awful* for you.' He held her briefly.

'How very right he was about you,' he told her again, looking over her shoulder, sadder still now, yet warmed, amazed at this woman's innocent understanding.

'But why the police?' Frances asked suddenly moving back from him, looking at him so bluntly that he could not prevaricate.

'I don't know, but I suspect he may have taken up with some unsavoury – some rough company in London after I left him.'

'I don't understand? Is that a crime?'

'It can be, Frances – between men,' he said reluctantly.

'I'd no idea!' She shook her head in disbelief, curls dancing, eyes wide and staring, so that Dermot saw himself accused then.

'I shouldn't have told you.' He spoke with cold resignation, acknowledging his own guilt and accepting the worst for himself in the whole matter.

'But of course you should, Dermot – if you think it's the truth.' She saw his unhappiness, moved towards him again, touched his hand. 'That's what I wanted, the truth – not lies, from Papa. It's always been lies and evasions here. One must tell the truth.'

'Even if it hurts?'

'But it doesn't. It's the lies that do that.'

'In any case, I feel entirely to blame,' he said, turning away, walking towards the window. She looked at his retreating back intently, as if summing him up in his absence.

Then she said quickly, vividly, 'No, Dermot, loving someone – is not to give your life up entirely for them, to throw away everything of your own. You were right to want to pursue your own career, of *course* you were.'

He turned, surprised. 'I least of all expected to hear that from you, Frances, a woman. You're simply being kind –'

'No, I'm not! That was why I wouldn't marry Harold. I know it myself, because I'd have lost *me* – and all this, here, at Summer Hill, which I love, which is my career, in a way. So I know exactly how you felt – and you were right to do as you did. And Henry was weak – that was the really awful thing. I saw it with Mama over the years. And I told him. I loved him, but I told him and he knew it, yet he went on doing these weak things so that finally he killed himself,' she rushed on. 'And that's what happens when you're weak, it goes from bad to worse and you can't stop it. You have to make a stand against it, from the beginning, and Henry never did. In that way Mama killed him, if anyone did – and that's the truth, too,' she added viciously, working herself up into a state. Dermot looked at her in astonishment. 'You are not to blame for your strength, Dermot,' she went on. 'How can you be? It's what he loved in you,' she added, looking at him now with candour and affection. He returned her gaze in the same way.

'I love you for just the same quality,' he said quietly.

In their shared loss a great bond, a bond of strength, was struck between them then.

The funeral, at which Frances insisted on following the hearse and the plumed horses with the men across the autumn fields to the family vault behind the church at the edge of the estate, was tediously and unnecessarily pompous, Frances thought – the Bishop of Ossory, all the way out from Kilkenny, addressing the packed congregation, offering endless platitudes, both spiritual and temporal.

Lies again, she thought – more concerned than ever now to live her life without them. Dermot had told her the truth about Henry and it had been a breath of fresh air which, though she knew she could not share it with anyone but him, gave her added confidence in all her natural assumptions. She no longer regretted, for an instant, her uncompromising temperament. She missed Henry desperately. But she saw his death, his weakness, as something imposed on him. What a price he had paid to convention – his mother's, his family's, the world's. She would never pay that price, would never contemplate it.

She looked at her father, a broken figure at the end of the pew, then at the porky Eustace, awkwardly mourning. They were living victims of the same impositions. And Summer Hill as well, which Henry would have inherited – the house, she saw then, would not have been freed by him but would simply have come to reflect his weaknesses, to hold his unhappiness and frustration, as it did her mother's now, remaining frigid, unfulfilled. She looked at Eustace, then. The house would come to him. What would he make of it? He was subservient to his mother, in a childlike, disingenuous way – and like his meek father, but lacking

Sir Desmond's inventive gifts. He made the worst of both worlds, Frances thought – without Lady Cordiner's culture or authority or his father's flair. He was conventional – steady, easy-going, biddable and unthinking, largely unaware of others or his surroundings: a model officer and a gentleman. And that was what Summer Hill would come to reflect.

With an equally placid wife, lots of children, army friends and the duller horsy people of the county as visitors, the house would become like a thousand others of its kind in Ireland: staid and unimaginative, a bastion against all real life and feeling. For it was her mother at least, Frances knew, with her intelligence, money, vivacity and arrogance – yes, her Jewishness – who gave Summer Hill its purpose, its glitter and originality now. With Eustace, it would revert into anonymity, a shell echoing with platitudes, with everything conventional.

She held Dermot's hand rather pointedly as they walked back from the church, while she looked east to the clouds running over Mount Brandon, sudden shafts of sun and cloud shadow rolling over the gorse, the valley tinged everywhere with reds and orange, the leaves turning in a soft fire. When the house came in view at the top of the rise she squeezed Dermot's hand and said, just as she had said to Henry a few weeks before, 'Look!' And she gestured towards the graceful limestone rising from the tinted autumn trees, lines of tall shuttered windows mirroring the scudding clouds and sunlight, patterns moving across the glass like changing thought in human eyes: a house so secretly alive, rising so easily above death, offering life. 'Just look at it,' she said again, breathlessly, a pit of emotion opening in her stomach.

'Yes,' he said at once, seeming to know what she felt about Summer Hill. 'And you mustn't see it all as an end, Frances. But a beginning.'

'Oh I do. I *do*,' she answered quickly, as if she was approaching a marriage, not leaving a funeral.

'Open the curtains and shutters, Pat. Where's Flood? – should have been done first thing. And all this black crêpe taken down, too.'

Frances spoke to Pat Kennedy in the darkened hall next morning beneath the covered chandelier. The reception rooms had remained shuttered for the funeral. And afterwards, the evenings drawing in quickly now, it had not been worth opening them again – or so Frances had assumed. But the day was fine and bright, the windows ought to be opened, and Frances in the absence of her mother still upstairs in bed – too unwell to attend either the funeral or the tea – relished the thought of taking temporary charge of the household.

'I'm afraid her Ladyship left strict instructions, Miss Frances, not to open anything or remove –'

'She *what?*' Frances picked up the pile of black-bordered mourning cards and letters of condolence on the hall table, about to put them away.

'Not to touch a thing, Miss Frances.' Pat Kennedy looked at her uneasily.

'That's nonsense. Have Mrs Martin come and see me, please.'

'She's upstairs with her Ladyship at the moment –'

'Never mind. I'll open them myself.'

Pat Kennedy looked at her, amazed, almost fearful, while Frances moved to the hall door, opening it, letting in the brilliant light from the porch, the fresh air of a tingling-sharp autumn day. Attached to the door was a large funeral wreath of glum evergreens. She tried to take it down, but it was firmly nailed to the wood. Returning to the drawing room, she was depressed at the vision. Black sashes hung from all the curtain rails; pictures had been masked with crêpe, every bright thing put away, dustcovers over all the furniture. It was the same in the dining room, the long table entirely obscured by a dull serge undercloth, all the family portraits sashed and shrouded.

In the general emotion of the day before, the crush and heat of people, Frances had barely noticed these exaggerated funerary mementoes: a far too lavish and tasteless indulgence of her mother's, she thought now. It was nonsense. Henry was dead and gone, entombed in the family crypt among his ancestors. He could only be mourned now in thought, not in curling evergreens, tatty black crêpe and black-bordered stationery. She would have it all removed.

Meanwhile, thinking of Henry's effects, and suddenly remembering his pet lemur Gretel, she strode quickly upstairs to his bedroom on the first landing. The door was locked – as was his suite of work rooms in the old nurseries on the top floor. She came downstairs and spoke to Pat Kennedy again in the butler's pantry. Flood was with him now.

'Flood, what is all this about?' She was brusque. 'All this nonsense. My brother's rooms are locked, the whole house like an undertaker's parlour. And Gretel – where has she gone?'

'To the young master's zoo, Miss. And, for the rest, it was her Ladyship's clear instructions, Miss –'

'Yes, yes, I know that. But what?'

Flood looked abashed. 'That – that everything in the house was to stay exactly as it was, Miss, and that nothing was to be touched in Mr Henry's rooms, the doors locked. A period of mourning, her Ladyship said. Some months at least, she said –'

'Some *months*? Is this usual, Flood? You were here when my grandfather died, weren't you?'

'Well, Miss, not entirely . . .' He stopped.

'And? Was the whole house shuttered up – for months?'

'No, Miss, it wasn't. Though her Ladyship wasn't here then –'

'That's all. That's all I wanted to know, Flood. We shall have the house opened again –' She turned. Mrs Martin had just arrived outside the pantry door.

'Miss Frances, her Ladyship would like to see you, with Mr Eustace, in her bedroom.' Mrs Martin, she saw, was still in widow's weeds.

Frances looked at her severely. 'Mary, this is absurd . . .' she started, then thought better of it, looking at the cowed and unhappy faces of the three servants.

Her mother had obviously given them the most strict instructions; it was not their fault. She found Eustace and went upstairs.

The bedroom, completely shuttered, was dark but for one small oil lamp on the bedside table next to a crêpe-bordered photograph of Henry – Henry as a young boy, curly-haired, dressed almost as a girl. Her mother lay propped against an uncomfortable mountain of pillows in the great curtained four-poster – a reduced figure, half in shadow, so that her face was almost invisible. Lady Cordiner, a black lace napkin over her head and black shawl round her shoulders, lay perfectly still on the bed, so that here it seemed was the corpse, the reason for all this mourning. The room, shuttered and airless, smelt of camphor, smelling salts and lamp oil: like a hospital – or a morgue.

'Mama? – are you all right?' There was no reply. 'Mama, we're here. Are you all right?' Eustace stood awkwardly behind her. Finally her mother stirred, leaning forward with a great effort.

'Children,' she began haltingly, a reedy voice emerging from behind the veil. 'We are all quite heartbroken – a tragedy that cannot be overcome, cannot be forgotten, cannot be put right, which we must all suffer . . .' Her voice became stronger as she spoke, more exact and formal, as if she had memorised the words.

'Mama, it's not –'

'Quiet, girl! You will not interrupt,' she snapped. 'A death that has struck at the very heart of our lives, the life of Summer Hill, the whole future – which has been destroyed in a trice, where we cannot make amends other than by our own suffering, where we must share each other's lasting grief . . . I want both of you to realise that, to join me in this deep mourning . . . mourning for a dear soul departed . . .' Her voice, with these Old Testament tones and admonitions, came haltingly again now, seemingly stricken with emotion.

Frances was astonished. Her mother had clearly lost her wits. She looked at Eustace, but he did not react, standing, head bowed, like a penitent at the end of the bed.

'Mama,' she said. 'Of course we mourn dear Henry. But –'

'Quiet, I said, girl. I shall have more to say to you – you,' she added bitterly, 'you who must bear the brunt of responsibility for this tragedy –'

'Me, Mama?'

'Yes, you! – You think I don't see it all quite clearly now? You, who drove Henry away from here, so often in the past, so that he would not stay with me. You, with your thieving designs on the house, as if it were yours and not his, so that he felt unwanted –'

'Mama, I had nothing to do with it. And he was killed by one of his snakes – you know that! I shall hear no more of this nonsense! You are overwhelmed with grief, I perfectly realise. But you shall not accuse me in such a manner. I will hear no more of it. We must get on with our lives now. The house must be put in order – it cannot be kept as a mausoleum, a shuttered, blackened –'

'How dare you! You will do nothing of the sort,' Lady Cordiner shouted, finding her usual strident voice suddenly. 'The house will be kept exactly as it was! Eustace,

I charge you with seeing that *nothing*, but nothing, is altered in the present setting and manner of things. And as for you,' she said simply, turning her livid face to Frances, 'you will go from here! Go from this house, which you have so desecrated.'

'Yes, Mama,' Frances indulged her mother, looking back at her with condescending pity as she left the room.

'She has clearly lost her reason,' Frances said, describing this meeting to her father and Dr Mitchell, the family doctor, who had come out from Thomastown that afternoon. They met in Sir Desmond's study, where her father wandered aimlessly round the gloomy room with its death's head fox masks set above the bookcases, a wraith-like figure himself, clearly less able than ever to cope with these household disasters and disputes.

'Well, I'd not go so far as to say that, Miss Frances,' Dr Mitchell, a bluff middle-aged Protestant from Munster, spoke with a rich Cork accent. 'It's only temporary – the shock has taken your mother that way. Sometimes does, when they imagine all sorts of things –'

'That *I* was responsible for my brother's death?' Frances interrupted vehemently.

'Oh, yes, all sorts of sheer illusions.' He was a big, jolly, horsy type in gaiters and a broad-check suit. He knocked his pipe out now on the grate. 'The maddest sort of things – fire and brimstone, the lot. Seen it often enough before.'

'Come, Dr Mitchell,' Frances continued on the attack. 'My mother has always been malicious – but in an entirely sane and practical way. No hint of such ravings. And they were just that – the ravings of a mad woman. How could she so change overnight?'

Dr Mitchell humphed. 'Oh, indeed she could, just that. Exactly what happens – with some sudden, terrible event like this. But you mustn't take any notice of it. She doesn't mean what she says –'

'Oh, but she does! Tell Dr Mitchell, Papa, what she said to you, when you say she was quite calm, before I saw her this morning.' Her father, over by the small window, winced. 'Go on, Papa.' She glared at his back.

'Well, that you ought to leave the house, dearest. But I'm sure –'

'There – you see!' Frances almost shouted at the doctor. 'And she was quite composed at that point. I have to leave – because I was the cause of Henry's death. She's mad, but she means it all right!' Frances was roused now, bitter at the injustice of it all, barely able to control herself.

The two men, shocked at her outburst, looked at her doubtfully. Finally her father spoke. 'My dear, it would probably be better, just for the time being, if you left for a while . . .'

Frances turned to Dr Mitchell. He was nodding his head – avuncular, wise, understanding. 'The great thing is for her to avoid any upsets. I'm sure you don't want to aggravate your mother, if you can help it –'

'You could go and stay with Cousin Mortimer at Islandbridge, just for a month. Or a few weeks perhaps,' her father temporised. He was more enthusiastic now.

'Indeed,' the doctor said. 'Indeed you could – a grand girl like yourself, find plenty of things to do in Dublin. And that'd be the best of it certainly – from your mother's point of view.'

The two men appeared very reasonable. Yet there was a clear hint in their eyes – of condescension, certainly, as well as mistrust and suspicion – which told Frances that they did not really judge her mother wrong or mad at all in so banishing her. Of course, Frances thought, her father and the old family doctor – they both knew of her long-standing antagonism towards her mother, the temperamental clashes between them over the years. And of course they secretly took Lady Cordiner's side in the matter. Frances, in their view, was an unruly, ungrateful, insensitive daughter – a thorn in her mother's side, much better out of the house indeed, which she ought to have left long before, not hanging round for ever exasperating her mother. She was in the wrong. Her mother, prostrate but still wicked as ever, had won. Frances was absolutely furious, her anger erupting now, uncontrolled.

'Well, if you think that, if you've been taken in by my mother, I really don't know what to say! That preposterous old fraud up there in bed with her evil imaginings. And you don't see it! It was she, if anyone, who brought my brother's death about, with her constant cosseting and nagging; she who drove him away from the house and made him what he was – unable to cope with life, just as she wants to do to me now; get rid of me, too: she, who dominates you, blackmails and bosses you, and both of you submitting to her every whim, every nonsense, like shutting the whole house up with black crêpe for months. And you just stand there, grown men, letting her get away with it, pandering to her! All I can say is – is you ought to be absolutely ashamed of yourselves!'

She glared at them, before turning abruptly and walking imperiously out of the room.

'Tut, tut,' Dr Mitchell said when she had gone, getting out fresh tobacco for his pipe, relaxing. 'The little vixen! But she'll see sense, Sir Desmond, she surely will.' They discussed matters further in a desultory way. However, it was not long before they looked up in alarm, hearing the first of the shutters banging open in the big reception rooms beyond.

Frances threw herself methodically at all the curtains in the drawing room first – dragging them wide, spinning the shutters back, clattering them against the wood, opening the windows, letting the light and air stream in. She tore the black sashes down, took the crêpe from the pictures and flicked off most of the dustcovers before moving into the dining room where she did the same, freeing all the family portraits. Then she tugged the serge mourning cloth from the great table in one vigorous movement, scattering salts and candlesticks before shredding the rest of the grim paper decor. Back in the hall she opened both the great doors wide and simply tore the laurel wreath from its nails. Then, standing on a chair, she tugged away the bag from around the chandelier so that the crystal danced and tinkled. As she worked obsessively, her face reddening, a gusty autumn breeze blowing leaves in from the porch, the house, with its doors and windows open now, became an airy, wind-blown place, small gales coursing through the heavy rooms.

While she gathered together a pile of mourning cards on the hall table, her father and Dr Mitchell appeared, Mrs Martin with Pat Kennedy standing alarmed behind them.

'Here!' she said to her astonished father, throwing the black-bordered cards and envelopes at him so that they streamed through the windy hall like tiny kites. 'Mourn him in paper, if that's all you want.'

She left the two men, moving towards Mrs Martin and Pat. 'Eileen? Have you seen Eileen?' But she did not wait for an answer, striding past them into the back of the house, then taking the stairs down to the basement and kitchen.

'Eileen?' she called. The girl appeared at the kitchen door. 'Eileen, will you pack my things, please? I shall be leaving for Dublin at once.'

'Yes –' Eileen was startled. 'Yes, I will surely.'

'I'll be staying in Dublin for a bit, with my cousin Mortimer. Will you come with me?' She gazed at her forcefully, wide-eyed, happy, offering the girl one more great adventure.

'I –' Eileen was uncertain.

'Not for long – a few weeks. I'll be coming back, don't worry.'

'I will, then, Miss –'

'*Frances*, Eileen.'

'Yes, Miss Frances.'

'Good. Splendid.'

As she turned back along the passageway, Frances saw the long line of sprung room bells on the wall above her. She reached up, hitting each one vigorously as she passed, so that immediately, the metal tongues giving voice one after the other, a great joyous cacophony of sound rose from the basement, filtering up through the house.

Lady Cordiner heard the sounds faintly in her shuttered room, before pulling viciously at her own bell. Aunt Emily heard them, stopping in her grimly baroque drawing of the plumed horses and hearse of Henry's funeral procession crossing the demesne. Eustace heard them in the gun room, morosely oiling his twelve-bore. Nearly everyone in Summer Hill heard the wild bells ring out, felt the breeze flow through the house, the sound and wind of liberation. Mrs Molloy and Flood, parlour, kitchen, scullery and still room maids, laundry maids and footmen – all stopped in their work, or woke from a doze, surprised or alarmed. Some thought there was a fire, others that Lady Cordiner had risen from her bed in vengeance, a few of the more superstitious believed it was the spirit of the young master himself returned to haunt the place. Only Aunt Emily, when Frances came to explain and say goodbye, understood at once what it was all about.

'Well done, girl!' She congratulated her niece. 'Just what I'd have done myself – in better times. So you're off at last. Well, remember that hotel I told you about in Paris, near the shops. The manager is less offensive than they usually are. And entirely accommodating – you won't need any cash.'

Frances kissed her softly. 'Yes, Aunt. But I'll be back – I will. To see you.'

'Of course you will, girl. Now excuse yourself, before you miss the train.' When Frances had gone she looked at her funeral sketch, scowled at it, laughed quickly, then tore it up. 'Yes, indeed, we'll have no more of that nonsense – and quite right too,' she said to herself.

Frances looked back at Summer Hill from the waggonette as Molloy frisked the horse along the avenue. A scatter of rooks rose from the trees around the house, blown about in the sky like tea-leaves, their harsh chatterings thrown to her on the wind – the rooks of Summer Hill, which for Frances had always seemed like household deities, the very spirit of the place, so that for a moment, for the first time, she felt the heartbreak of her departure and thought she was going to cry. But she didn't. She must not. She would not allow herself to be sad. Leaving the house was a defeat, but in a battle not the war. And at last, she further consoled herself, she had nailed her colours firmly to the mast. The endless temporising, the frustrations, evasions and prevarications of her life at Summer Hill were over. Everyone there now knew where she stood. Someone had had to make a stand against the cruel lifelessness of the place, the dictatorship of her mother – she had done that and she was right, she knew. Life was the thing, not death, not mourning.

Frances looked across at the pensive Eileen on the opposite seat, smiled at her, a candid tenderness in her eyes. 'A penny for them, Eileen?'

Eileen, with a glum face, had been thinking of Pat Kennedy, the conversation she had just had with him – the obvious fact that he did not seem very much to mind her leaving Summer Hill. He didn't love her, she decided, or at least he was more concerned with a stronger love, his own secret rebellions, the meetings and drillings in the woods with the other rebels in the area. He had ditched her, that was what it amounted to. So now, in answer, taking courage from her mistress's devil-may-care behaviour, she burst out, 'It was brave of you, Miss Frances. It was a brave thing you did this afternoon – that's what I was thinking.'

'We can't be sad, Eileen. Life's not for that. And it was just as brave of you – to come with me. And fortune favours the brave, so they say.'

Eileen nodded vigorously – and suddenly there were tears in her eyes, tears in the smile as she said, 'Oh, what a lark, Miss Frances – I can't believe it, out of that stuffy old house . . .'

Frances offered her a lace handkerchief and the two women turned then, looking expectantly up the valley, where the wind and the sun fell on the yellowing leaves, rustling them in a lovely dazzle, the cob's hooves echoing in the crisp air, smacking on the hard road now as they drove smartly out of the gates, making for the Dublin train.

*

Frances had telegraphed ahead, so that, when they got to Islandbridge House that evening, Mortimer – and Dermot, who had not yet returned to his work at the War Office in Whitehall – were expecting them. Mortimer stood by the mantelpiece in the small drawing room, Dermot in the bay window, half-open against the twilight so that the sounds of the weir by the bridge some distance away came clearly across the lawn, the engines chuffing in and out of Kingsbridge station further downstream on the other side of the river, the city itself a faint hum to the east. A busy metropolitan life lay just beyond the house and it excited Frances, seemed to justify all her actions at Summer Hill: life – that had been her cause there; and now here she was, almost touching it.

The forthright and caustic Mortimer, when she had told her story, supported her, but with reservations. 'Your mother has never had enough scope for her gifts down there – a frustrated sense of the dramatic among other things, I've often felt, which accounts for her taking to her bed and playing Queen Victoria in a nightcap, trying to turn the place into a mausoleum for poor Henry. But I don't know that you should have so publicly attacked her foibles, dear Frances!'

'I was furious, at the spinelessness of everyone there –'

'Yes, yes – I see that. I've felt the same in my time. But *your* behaviour, look at that a moment, Frances. It simply shows your frustrations as much as anything – keeping yourself stuck down there, head against brick walls, when you should be out and about in the world. You surely see that, don't you?' Mortimer's small blue eyes glittered aggressively with this well-meant advice. He smoothed his extensive beard, eased a thin leg on the fender, picked his sherry glass up.

'Yes, I suppose so,' Frances said at last.

'Simply not good for *you*, Frances, this eternal combat with your Mama, because it's not *producing* anything for you.'

'I suppose not. Except that what I want to produce is for Summer Hill, not for me.'

'Be honest. The fact is you really want to run the house down there yourself, don't you? And that's always *bound* to clash head on with your Mama.' He emphasised the vital words, the voice rising theatrically, as was his habit in the privacy of his own drawing room or in the House of Commons. Trained originally in the law, and a lawyer still, in substantiating his point of view, he followed it up with sharp insight, a seemingly irrefutable argument – and always a brisk energy to drive the nails home.

But Frances was tired, remaining silent now. It was not the moment to explain what she really wanted at Summer Hill, all the myriad feelings she had about the house, her need, her love for it – the house like a lover now whom she had deserted.

Dermot turned in the bow window. 'The obvious answer then, Papa, is for Frances to come with us to London – and help run your little house there, isn't it?' Frances looked from one man to the other. 'You've only got Mrs Moxon coming in in the morning at the moment – the place might do with some running when you go back to Westminster. Why not?'

'Oh, Frances wouldn't want that,' Mortimer said. 'Poky little house . . .'

There was silence, indecision in the air, before Frances filled it with a firm small voice. 'Oh, yes I would,' she said. 'I'd love it, if you'd let me – I really would.'

A train started out from Kingsbridge, a few great bellows from the chimney first, then the fainter, regular rhythm of the wheels and pistons as it got under way.

'Very well, Frances.' Mortimer reached for his sherry. 'It'll be wonderful to have your company in any case. To London, then!'

They all raised their glasses.

4

T HE SUN HAD dropped behind the roofs of Kensington Palace leaving a blowy chill over the deserted park. The leaves scattered in great drifts across the grass, the wind catching them, chasing them round the Albert Memorial, pursuing them over the Serpentine bridge, along Rotten Row towards the empty bandstand where the last concert of the season had finished several weeks before. Now there was only the notice: 'The Park gates will close at five o'clock or sunset, whichever is the earlier.'

Frances shivered, drew her fur collar closer, and turned quickly home. She had lost all track of time in her walk about Hyde Park – an outing which she had made almost every afternoon since her arrival in London with Eileen and the two men a week before. And now, once more, she was astonished by the city, in seeing the notice, that a park – the countryside to her – should ever close. She had not adapted herself to the loss of these freedoms – to roam wherever she wanted, at whatever hour, which she had loved at home. Indeed, more than that – Dermot had warned her not to walk in the park alone at all, at this season and late hour, when almost no one else did: there were rogues and footpads about. Or, at least, she should take Eileen with her. But Frances had wanted to be alone – to think what she might do with her life. But now, all thought abandoned and fearing that she might be locked in for the night, she quickened her step towards the gates.

A great charge of broughams, hansom cabs and omnibuses streamed round Hyde Park Corner, sweeping like chariots into Knightsbridge. She felt safer now among the clatter of hooves, the crowds everywhere hurrying on the pavements. Yet here again, very soon, she found herself losing touch, mesmerised, rooted on the brink of the street crossing, where urchins swept the leaves and dung at intervals between the rush of traffic. A man pushed and jostled her, before leaping past into a gap between the flow of vehicles. One of the ragged boys in the gutter whistled, beckoning her on, gesturing rudely. Now, among so much noise and movement, she was suddenly overwhelmed, at a loss, just as she had found herself in the empty park. London was all hot or cold, frenzy or emptiness, extremes. You took your chances . . .

Lifting her skirts she rushed out into the traffic without really looking – so that a hansom cab, bearing down, swerved at the last moment, the horse viciously reined in, rearing up in front of her, the cabby swearing. She ran for her life blindly, putting her foot in a pile of dung in the other gutter, the waif there laughing at her outrageously. London, this vast throbbing imperial city which she had only been to once three years before, was wonderful yet terrible, she thought – unless you attacked, controlled, dominated it. But how, in her present circumstances, was she ever to do that? As a debutante, it had been very different. With parties and dances arranged for her every day, she had had the support of her mother, a bevy of hired servants and carriages, and a large house in Mayfair which had been taken for the Season. Now she was more or less on her own.

Walking down Knightsbridge, she left the crowds, turning into the quieter Wilton Place. The gas lights had come on in the early twilight and the Italian organ-grinder with his monkey was there again, she saw, near Mortimer's house, on the other side of the street, opposite the church. She was calmer now. She liked the gay music – a polka, then a waltz – echoing in the distance, a touch of coming frost in the air sharpening the piped notes, the footfalls, the coachmen's voices in the ale house on the corner. London was suddenly human again in these quiet little crescents and mewses behind Belgrave Square – where she seemed to have entered a village, a hidden intimate place, the music like an overture promising excitement in the sudden dark in which the street lamps were beacons, directing people home to all sorts of pleasures in the lamplit drawing rooms behind the curtains. London, which they had come to control, was theirs behind all the secret windows. She put a threepenny bit into the bowler that the monkey offered – almost the last of her ready cash – before turning up the short pathway to her cousin's house, getting her latchkey out. She had become accustomed to the key, at least, she thought, with doors everywhere securely locked here: locked against her for the time being, she felt, where she was shut out from all the life that surrounded her.

The smartly painted house – one of a line in a neat Georgian terrace running down to Wilton Crescent – was small but not poky. The front was narrow, certainly. But it was tall enough, rising three storeys over a basement with servants' rooms on the top floor. And the rooms, though narrow, were high-ceilinged and cleverly spacious – lengthy rooms, leading back to a long garden with the coachhouse in the mews behind.

Eileen slept at the top. Frances and the two men occupied bedrooms on the second floor, with a long, light-panelled drawing room-cum-library, divided by sliding doors, beneath – and a similarly gracious dining room with a shiny Chippendale leaf table and silver candelabra on the ground floor. A bijou residence, Frances thought, letting herself in, shouting to Eileen down the stairs in the kitchen before going up to her bedroom.

Neither of the men was home yet. The new session at Westminster had just begun; Mortimer rarely returned before midnight. Dermot was often delayed at the Ministry of Imperial Defence. And that was one of the problems, Frances thought, taking her jacket off in the prettily decorated bedroom: there was little enough house-running to do here, and little to occupy her outside.

She frisked the fire up in the small grate, taking a chair beside it, leaning forward, staring into the brightening coals – not the vast log fires she was used to. And yet it was warm in the house, especially with this new central heating they had. She loosened her high collar, got up and turned the magic electricity on above her dressing table mirror – gazed into the glass carefully and critically, turning her head one way, then the other. She needed some new image for herself in London. A new hair style – new accents, with rouge or silk, in her face and clothes? A new something, she thought. What was it? Clothes, of course, would be one answer. And there were so many of them, lovely new winter fashions in the big stores further down the road in Knightsbridge. But they were expensive and she had little money.

She ran a finger from her forehead down her nose. It was all too straight, the one leading to the other almost without interruption. She longed for a more broken nose, more fashionably retroussé. The forms there now, in brow, high cheek bones and nose, were too stern, regal. It gave people the wrong impression, as her skin probably did, too, with its faint olive tinge, a smoked ivory touch from her Spanish ancestors.

She bit in her too-full lips. They seemed better that way, but her chin rose and flattened in an ugly manner when she did this. Her hair might be the easiest thing to alter, it would add a touch of refinement, make her less a country bumpkin. She ran her fingers through the dark helmet of loose curls. They had lost their country gloss in the grime and autumn fogs of London. She would bath – and wash and experiment with her hair then and there, rearrange it, have it ready for Dermot's opinion when he came back for dinner.

Dermot, she thought, as she lay submerged, luxuriating in the deep hot water, arching one knee, then the other, above the soapsuds, flattening her back right down on the bottom of the bath so that the water rippled comfortingly over her small breasts – Dermot intrigued her: that pale skin, austere face, crinkly straw hair; the delicate bones, slim body; the feeling of something sensitive, almost feminine there, hidden beneath a more obvious masculinity, a careful force. There were contradictions. And they lay in his spirit too. What sort of man was he? What, exactly, had he meant when he talked of 'that kind of love' between men? Only men and women could love each other in that way. He had spoken inaccurately or she had misunderstood him. She might ask him about these things, in time.

She lay still for a while, then raised her flanks and stomach, holding her breath, so that with this buoyancy the water fell away, in rivulets, across the oils of her skin, and she rose from the depths. She looked down her smooth, moistly steaming body where it narrowed dramatically at the waist before splaying out again over her hips. Then she took a fold of skin there, beside the navel, gently pinching it: a ready inch came up in her fingers. Too much, she wondered?

She washed her hair later and had Eileen help her rearrange it – flattening the curls, trimming some of them, pinning them back severely to the sides above her ears, letting the others on the crown of her head stand up as they had been.

'What do you think?'

Eileen stood behind her at the mirror. 'Well . . .' She was undecided.

'Go on!'

'Well, you look a bit scalded, Miss Frances . . .'

'It's the fashion.' She turned and looked up reprovingly at the girl.

'I'm sure it is. Just – you look strange, not like you.'

'Never mind. One must change you know, now we're in London.' Eileen helped her on with her dress then – in red velvet with turned-back white lace, an under-dress in ruched green silk – the only really decent costume she had with her, and even this was out of date, she knew. The *Journal des Modes*, which she had bought the day before at Woolland's in Knightsbridge, was crammed with far more fashionably tantalising things. And more than that, she thought, as Eileen tightened the waist, this dress was too small for her – or was she too fat? The waist really pinched now as Eileen tugged at the back buttons. The twenty-two inch waist, like a wasp's, which she had had the year before, was no longer there. Yes, she had to admit it now – that was what was wrong; here was the real problem which lay against her London ambitions: she was too *fat*, already beginning to take on her mother's plumpness. She had avoided the fact in the bath. But now, with the evidence of the dress, there was no doubt where the trouble lay. She went down to dinner less confident about herself than she had ever been in her life.

Dermot sat opposite, at the far end of the table, the lit candelabra between them. He moved it aside the better to see her.

'Ravishing,' he said, with a touch of irony. 'But then you always were.'

'And the hair?'

'Not quite certain. You . . .' He paused.

'All right, all right – Eileen said it: that I looked scalded.'

'Yes, well . . .' Dermot paused again judiciously, before continuing with sudden enthusiasm. 'But you see, Frances, you really don't need to be other than you are. Absolutely not.'

'But I do! I have to do something – change things over here. And I've discovered I'm getting fat as well.' She was downcast then, fiddling with her cutlery. 'And you know perfectly well – I can't lurk here indefinitely "running" the place. Runs perfectly well without me. You were being kind, that's all, having me here.'

'But of *course* we were being kind – all of us to each other. Distant cousins maybe, but part of the same family after all. You'll find your feet – no great hurry –'

'Oh, but there is!' Frances grasped a knife impulsively. 'I have to *do* something.'

'Well, you can't join the army.' He smiled at her curiously. 'Always so ambitious – thrusting away, when most women would be quite content with needlework and idle chatter.'

'Well, I can't be – even if I wanted to – since Mama will certainly cut me off now, "without a penny".' She resumed her ironic tone. 'And I'm not going to marry,' she went on decisively. 'That's another thing I won't consider. Like you.'

'Like me?'

'Well – like Henry, you're not the marrying sort, are you?' She looked at him with the flicker of a smile.

'Who knows?' he answered brightly, returning a much fuller smile, a touch of flirtatiousness in his eyes. 'Who knows?' he intoned in a deeper mocking voice.

A day or two later, Frances embarked on a regimen of physical training, designed to pare her weight and narrow her waist. Dermot obtained two sets of dumbbells, Indian clubs and a chest expander from the gymnasium at the Household Cavalry barracks – and together, each morning before breakfast, taking over one of the top-floor rooms, they lay on the boards lifting their feet, swirling clubs, and vigorously pursuing various other muscular tortures taken from an army manual. Frances obtained what looked like a circus tight-rope costume for these occasions: thin white woollen stockings that came right up to the tops of her thighs, a tight bodice in the same material, and an indecently small silk skirt that married these other garments together.

Eileen was shocked. Dermot found the whole business diverting. Mortimer, rising late, knew little of it until one morning, curious about the noise over his head, he came upstairs in his dressing gown and discovered them both, in what seemed to him a state of almost complete undress, writhing about on the floor.

'Good God,' was his only wry comment, before he turned back at the door. 'Reputation's bad enough at Westminster as it is,' he added.

'*One*, two, three – *One*, two, three . . .' Dermot sang out the stages of the exercise as they lay on their backs, pushing up from the waist, pausing, then tipping their toes. Now and then, he glanced at this vigorous woman, beautifully flushed, matching him step for step, lying beside him, her whole trunk arching back and forth in a wonderful rhythm. One made love in something of the same way, he thought – with a woman. At least, one might with this woman. The idea, against all his inclinations, excited him vaguely.

Frances hired one of the new safety bicycles, took hair-raising lessons on it at the Royal Cycle School in Euston Road, and, instead of walking morosely about the park in the afternoons, she now rode round its perimeter, much more happily, the wind in her hair, skirts flying. Sometimes she shrieked with joy at the sheer fun of it all so that only the odd horseless carriage, spluttering and back-firing along, attracted more attention from the passers-by. And later, through Dermot's good offices at the Cavalry barracks, she took the loan of a well-tempered chestnut mare called Rosie, and together, on other mornings, before breakfast, they rode in the park.

'What is it about your father,' she asked him one blustery, rain-threatened day as they moved along the Row, 'you both being so opposite – he with his Home

Rule business, you so supporting the Empire – yet you get on so well together?'

Dermot looked up at the lowering clouds. 'Simple enough: we beg to differ. Home Rule in Ireland – he sees that as the right of a nation to do what it wants. And he thinks the same way about individual people. He never objected to my army career – and I like him all the more for it.'

Frances lowered her head against the sudden squall. 'Wish my parents were like that.'

'Frances, you'll have to make it up with your mother – at some point. Why not now? Why not write her a nice letter?'

'If it were that easy – I might. But it would make no difference,' she added, a sudden disgust in her voice. 'You don't know her. She sees me as more than just a wretch: I've despoiled the house, Henry's memory. It's a war – perhaps you should advise me on the tactics.'

'I have. Make it up with her. What other victory can there be?'

Coming to the end of the Row, Frances saw Kensington Palace beyond the Albert Memorial. Suddenly the clouds in the distance parted for a moment and a shaft of watery sun fell on the red brick, spreading a gold halo over the Palace for half a minute. 'The victory of my going back to Summer Hill one day,' she answered firmly. 'And living there.'

'Of your "winning" the house? But I don't see that. How?'

'Nor do I. I don't know "how" at the moment. But that's what I see myself doing in London – finding out. There must be a way,' she added quietly, more to herself than Dermot. He looked at her curiously, wondering at this obsessive longing which could not, he felt, ever be fulfilled, so that it gave Frances, for all her patrician self-confidence and forthright commonsense in other matters, the air of a woman touched, damaged in some essential. But then she had been damaged, he thought – a broken engagement, Henry's death, banishment from the family home by her mother.

All the same, he had seen in the last weeks how, when faced with these setbacks, she had quickly recovered and taken the initiative – with these exercises, the bicycle and horse-riding. And these were surely not prompted by her increased weight which was barely perceptible, mere puppy fat. It was an energy encouraged by a dream of Summer Hill, where she was preparing herself now, just as an army commander might, for a return engagement against the house. He could appreciate all the tactics here; they were straight out of the army manual: retreat in good order, re-form, consolidate a reserve position, renew stores and ammunition, set pickets and observation posts, prepare variations of original attack . . . This was what Frances had come to London for, he saw then: their house in Wilton Place was for her a headquarters in exile where she would plan a victorious return to Summer Hill, on behalf of the true monarchy, when the Pretender would be put to flight. What nonsense it all was, he thought, what sad nonsense – Frances was worth so much more.

'But really,' he said to her as they rode home, the rain dying now. 'All this Summer Hill thing – you're trying to regain a position you've never actually held.

The house is your father's and will go to Eustace now. You're behaving as if you were a man, a son being denied your inheritance. It makes no sense.'

'I suppose not. But I love that house. I just wish I were a man,' she added defiantly.

He smiled at her distantly, hiding the compassion, the tenderness he felt for her in her wrong-headedness. And then he suddenly realised it was just this misguided, do-or-die male quality in her that he found most attractive.

But Frances, despite her physical regeneration through these vigorous activities, found no ease in her mind. She had not heard from her parents, and was not prepared, as Dermot had advised, to write to them herself and make things up. Nor, in this aggrieved mood, would she admit how she missed Summer Hill – missed its populated energy and familiar consolations: its friendships, domestic timetables, seasonal events and rhythms. Summer Hill had been for her a magic city, as London was not, and she would not face this fact. Instead she brooded on things – these contradictory rural and metropolitan hopes – resuming her lonely walks in the park.

She had noticed the rug-swathed invalid half a dozen times before, on brighter mornings or in the afternoon if the sun was still out: a restless young man being pushed along the edge of the Row in a bath-chair, gazing longingly at the Life Guards out exercising in their scarlet tunics and glittering helmets. His visits always seemed to coincide with these equestrian manoeuvres on the Row, so that she thought he might be a cavalry officer himself – and that the heavily bandaged leg propped up at the end of the chair could be the result of some service wound.

Yet the women who took him out on these autumn perambulations – and she had seen two of them – did not appear to be nurses. His family perhaps? There was an older lady, aristocratic-looking, with a fine long handsome face beneath a sensible hat, and someone a little younger, smaller and stouter who yet shared the same rather sallow skin, the same severe features on a reduced scale. Sisters, she thought? Like her mother, there was the same rich dark hair and skin. Were they Jewish, too?

They seemed an exceptional couple, in any case – the older woman especially, with her distant but kindly hauteur, her unfashionable but expensive clothes, her air of cultured regality. They were not nurses, surely – more women of the evening, Frances thought, made for salons, conversaziones, lamp-lit dinner parties; not outdoor women, people of the park, here seen solicitously tending a young man who, Frances saw when she got closer to him one afternoon, did not resemble them at all: an open-faced, fair-haired young man with a wispy beard and a badly scarred cheek, where the women were dark – and mysterious.

Idly curious as to their identity and the arrangements between them, she followed the man and the younger woman that afternoon as they left the park by the Apsley House gate. They crossed Knightsbridge, then turned right into Grosvenor

Crescent, then right again into the mews. Frances saw the wheelchair disappear through an open coachhouse doorway, and walked on down the mews none the wiser. The coachhouse and the small garden beyond presumably backed on to one of the huge and gloomy Crescent houses. Still intrigued, Frances made a long detour through the mews, round by the Grenadier public house, so that eventually she emerged at the bottom end of the Crescent, walking back up the street, glancing at the houses as she passed.

Which house had they gone into? All of them were vast terraced family mansions, with steps leading up to massive doors, sombre grey blinds drawn down over the windows. Only one house, she saw, half-way up on the left, had the blinds raised; indeed some of the windows were ajar here.

And now she heard the music, a piano – something from Mozart – coming from one of the open windows on the first floor: the delicate, precisely-struck notes running forwards and upwards, hesitating, the phrase repeated again and again, before all the themes were gathered together in a thrilling run of sound, echoing forth on the sharp November air.

This, Frances thought, must be the house they had entered: number 23. She stood there on the pavement for a minute, spellbound, listening to the music. And suddenly an extraordinary sense of *déjà vu* or precognition came over her. The music, this Mozart theme, this great grey house with its windows open to the pale November sunlight – somehow she had heard these same notes, stood in front of just this house, at some time before or in a future not yet lived. A sweetness, a lightness, filled the air around her, seeming to emanate from the house – which was offering her something, a gift forgotten from a previous life or, as yet unwrapped, about to be handed to her. This feeling of lost or impending bounty was so strong that she had no hesitation in walking up the tall steps, there and then, and ringing the doorbell.

A rather dwarfish young man in a white coat, flat-headed, owl-eyed with a dank kiss-curl, opened the door, letting her in at once, as if she was expected.

'Excuse me . . .' Frances stood there, at a loss.

'Come this way,' he said immediately and rather uppishly, not the servant type at all, she thought, more like an impatient café waiter. 'Let me take your coat – Sister Ruth has only just begun the recital.'

Beyond her, in the sudden gloom, Frances made out an imposing Florentine staircase, in elaborately cut stone, with rectangular flights leading from the marble floored hall. Tall Chinese vases, filled with dried bullrushes and fluffy pampas grass, rose to greater heights from red marble pedestals. The house was warm and there were strange odours in the air, both brisk and sweet. A touch of carbolic mixed with violets – or orchids, could it be? Warm and heavy. Yet the mood, despite this exotic hothouse atmosphere, the dark and pompous decor, was not oppressive.

'I'm sorry –' She was flustered now.

'Not at all, madam,' the young man interrupted with a confident smile. 'You're not too late at all. Let me show you up.'

She followed him up the dark staircase before turning right along an equally shadowy corridor towards open double doors at the end, where the man suddenly brought her into a dazzle of winter light – sunlight and brilliantly white walls – as if she had come from night to day. She was standing at the back of what must originally have been a large drawing room, or even a ballroom, with a parquet floor and a pillared colonnade down one side facing the tall windows that gave out on to the street: again, a sumptuously decorated room, but here in the Louis XV mode, with stucco walls and ceiling on which gilded sunbursts, cherubs and cornucopias of flowers had been set in bas-relief.

But it was no longer any sort of reception room. At intervals between the pillars lay over a dozen beds, invalid men propped up in them, with a small audience on gilt chairs in the middle of the room, facing the other end, listening to the severely handsome woman whom Frances had seen in the park, playing at a grand piano. Had she arrived in a hospital or at a recital?

Tiptoeing forward, confused yet strangely happy, she took one of the little chairs at the back of the room, which the owlish young man offered her. It was extraordinary, she thought, listening to the sharp cascade of notes, the elegant woman with her back to her, bending to and fro over the piano, nursing the keys, extracting glorious arpeggios: the whole thing had been meant. She was expected here.

The sun slanted through the tall windows, raising delicate motes, falling in yellow shafts against the white walls, picking out the gilt in crowns and cornucopias. There was a swansdown lightness everywhere, a soft glitter, an air of bright repose filled with the scent of orchids which Frances noticed now, hothouse blooms in vases set against the windows. She took her bearings, her arrival barely noticed, sitting behind the fashionably dressed audience, perhaps a dozen other women, admiring their creative hats. But then she lost herself in the music so that after some time her eyes closed in the warmth and she fought to keep awake . . .

'Well – and which young man have you come to visit?'

Frances had woken with a start a few minutes before, and now, the recital over, the tall woman, having moved among the others in the audience, since dispersed to various bedsides, spoke to her kindly, standing with her by one of the tall windows. Frances should have felt awkward, but she did not. The middle-aged though beautifully preserved woman in front of her was so obviously warm, offering her such a genuine smile, so evidently interested, that Frances felt quite at ease, an immediate sympathy flowing between them.

'I do apologise. You won't believe it, but walking along outside I heard the music – you do play so very well – and I simply walked in. I know nobody here. Do please excuse me – my name is Frances. Frances Cordiner. I'm over from Ireland, staying with my cousin in Wilton Place . . .'

As she spoke, the woman's expression changed. At first a rather governessy frown appeared, which alarmed Frances. But then, at once, she smiled more broadly still, the dark eyes crinkling up, almost closing in amusement. 'Forgive my frowning – not at you, I assure you – simply embarrassment at your praise. I hardly play *that* well! More expression, at best, than any technique. But certainly I am honoured that you thought fit to come off the street and tell me so.' Was there a touch of irony in this last statement? Or was this a permanent feature of the woman's hooded, lustrous eyes, a wry and kindly detachment always there? Frances could not decide. The woman, plainly dressed in black silk without any jewellery, offered a long arm, the cream skin running out into delicately elongated ringless fingers: 'I'm Ruth Wechsberg. How do you do?'

They shook hands, the woman's grasp held for a few moments longer than necessary: warm fingers, firm but not as any imposition. 'You really must excuse me,' Frances rushed on. 'I don't know what came over me. You won't believe it either, but something beckoned me – as I stood out there in the street – so that I simply *had* to come into the house, as if I was *meant* to . . .' Frances shook her head vigorously as she spoke, anticipating the other woman's likely disbelief.

But Ruth Wechsberg simply said to her, 'My dear, why shouldn't I believe you? Stranger things have happened. And perhaps something *is* meant. I wonder what, though?' she added as an aside. 'But come, since you're here – let me show you round, let me explain.'

Her voice was easy, low-toned, almost a drawl – again with a colouring of irony in it, knowledge or laughter withheld. The tone, with its very slight German accent, was wry and detached, not in the manner of haughty society chatter, Frances thought, but through knowledge, culture, experience. She touched her dark hair then, where it spread out on either side of a central parting in full gleaming waves. And now Frances saw the polished, strangely-shaped black stone which she wore as a brooch – a charm or amulet, she thought – with a silver inset cut in the shape of a Star of David.

Ruth Wechsberg noticed Frances's interest. 'A fragment from the Wailing Wall in Jerusalem,' she commented, fingering it gently. 'An heirloom.'

'It's so simple and nice,' Frances said enthusiastically. 'My mother is Jewish. Are you . . .?' She hesitated.

'Yes – a small clan, over here since my paternal grandfather left Vienna, many years ago.' They moved away from the window.

'That music you liked,' Ruth Wechsberg went on. 'Well, I try and play a little every week for the patients. Though their relations seem to enjoy it more, I'm bound to say. But, to be frank, we need to make an impression here, make ourselves known. It's a nursing home, you see. Oh, in only a very small way so far: my family home,' she continued as they walked down the room by the end of the beds. 'My father, Nathan Wechsberg – he is a stockbroker and since my mother died and we've grown up – my sister Agnes, you've not met her yet – well, the house has become rather too commodious for our needs! So I persuaded my father to let me open part of it as a nursing home, for officers – there are surprisingly few such facilities for them in London. I completed my nursing examinations at St Thomas's Hospital last year, with Agnes. But I don't know if it will work out. The expense – well, it may be even more than we bargained for!'

They had stopped at the last bed where a middle-aged man, his entire head swathed in bandages, was being talked to by two young women. Ruth turned back. 'Major Williams,' she said softly. 'And his two daughters. A nasty head wound at Omdurman in September. Isn't healing entirely. But he's doing well. And that's Mr Lighthorn.' They paused near a much younger man, with some sort of raised cage holding up the blankets, covering his lower limbs. 'Lost a leg in the same battle. And a little gangrene on the other. But we think we've saved it. We have the doctors in from the Army Hospital at Aldershot – and we employ others from Harley Street.'

They walked up towards the other end of the room.

'Gangrene?' Frances asked.

'Yes – the wound untended. Necrosis. The flesh decomposes, right down to the bone, goes green and putrid. You usually have to amputate.' Ruth was brisk, matter of fact, looking at Frances out of the corner of her eye as she tried to subdue a small grimace. 'Was that what may have been "meant" – what drew you in here, do you think?' she asked her a little sharply. 'A feeling for all that – for service, for nursing?'

'Oh, no. I know nothing about it – nothing at all. As I say, it was the music . . .'

'I simply wondered. Because the music is only the icing here, the officers just wounded men. And some young women are attracted by the idea . . .' She hesitated. 'Of such service – but not by the facts of it, when they see them.'

'Yes, I'm sure.' But Frances was not certain of what she was sure of at all. They came to the end of the room, by the big double doors leading out on to the gloomy landing. She felt the moment had come for her to leave, there was nothing more to be said. But Ruth Wechsberg, interpreting her feelings, had indeed more to say. 'Well, Miss Cordiner, I'm certainly not a *clairvoyant*, but something tells me you came in here because you've found yourself at a loose end in London – on your own, over from Ireland, you say?' She looked at her with an easy, entirely unpatronising regard. 'I've absolutely no wish to pry or presume, but I wonder if that's really what brought you in here – simply a need to talk to someone? If so, I'd be delighted if you took tea with me, after I've seen to the visitors.'

Frances nodded, her face breaking into a smile, a fuller smile than she remembered offering for many months. 'Of course, but I don't want to delay or inconvenience you –'

'You don't,' Ruth Wechsberg replied very promptly. 'I said I would be delighted. And I can assure you of one thing – I always mean what I say.'

When Frances returned, in high good humour, to Wilton Place, she found Eileen, red-eyed and moping, sitting in the basement kitchen over a plate of bread and dripping which she had obviously been consoling herself with.

'Eileen, what's wrong? You don't have to eat that, you know –'

'Well, I *do*, Miss – sure, wasn't it always what we had at home?' Eileen got up and went towards the range, wiping her lips, bosom heaving with emotion.

'Eileen, Eileen dearest – what *is* the matter?' Frances moved to comfort the girl, who was beginning to cry silently now, pretending to occupy herself over the range so that a tear fell on the hot plate, briefly sizzling.

'It's just I miss home. And – and I've heard no word at all from my friend . . .' She sobbed openly then, head bowed, her back turned to Frances who at once went over and put an arm round her.

'Your friend?'

'It's Pat Kennedy, Miss,' she burst out.

'I see. Of course.' Frances understood. She had been aware of this *tendresse*, on Eileen's part at least – Eileen had clearly hinted at it last spring – but, not wishing to pry or embarrass the girl, Frances had never pursued the matter with her. 'And you've written to him?' she asked her now.

'Indeed I have – three times!'

'Oh dear – men can be so insensitive. But it's as much my fault, for taking you away. Eileen –' She turned the girl round, offering her a handkerchief. 'Eileen, you can easily go home, you know, if you want.'

Eileen looked affronted suddenly, annoyed. 'Sure and I don't want to go home – amn't I good and happy here? And I get on grand with Mrs Moxon in the mornings – and there's Mary Lynch from Galway down the street that I walk out with . . .'

'Yes, you told me. You've seemed happy –'

'Indeed I am, sure – in this grand place. And isn't it a wonderful opportunity and experience altogether? – if only I was hearing from him,' she added, the sobs coming back into her voice, 'and knowing he was all right.'

'I'm sure he is.'

'Well, he mightn't be, d'ye see?' Eileen looked at her in a strange way, a frightened look.

'I'll tell you what,' Frances said quickly. 'I'll write home this very night – I should have done before – and I'll ask my father about Pat. Ask him to tell me how he is – and tell him to write to you. Tactfully, of course.'

'Tactfully?' Eileen asked, perking up a bit.

'I mean I won't make a thing of it.'

'That'd be grand, then.' Eileen moved towards the big deal table.

'That's been my problem, too,' Frances called after her, watching the girl starting to pick at the bread and dripping again. 'Not hearing from Summer Hill. And that's my fault too. I see it now, I was too proud to write home.'

Eileen turned. 'Yes, Miss. I suppose you were – though it was the right thing you did, opening the house up that way and putting the air through it. But I wasn't too proud to write,' she added. 'And I should have been.'

'No, you were quite right. And I've been wrong. Pride is such a stupid thing. If you really love something – a person or a place – you lose pride. You have to.'

Frances saw now what had been wrong in her life since she had left Summer Hill: she had refused to admit how much she had missed the place – and Eileen had vividly reminded her of this blindness. She had been proud, arrogant, angry – believing these sentiments entirely appropriate to her condition of exile. Yet they had been mere substitutes for happiness, which she had encouraged vehemently the more to avoid the fact of her great unhappiness. Now, as a result of her teatime conversation with Ruth Wechsberg, she was at ease for the first time since she had left home and so no longer needed to be proud.

'Listen!' she said with the excitement of this realisation, going over to Eileen. 'Forget the bread and dripping. There's that delicious fruit cake we had yesterday. Let's finish it, gorge on it, with strong tea. A little party! – like we used to have in the kitchen at home with Mrs Molloy – and I'll tell you what happened to me this afternoon.'

Eileen was surprised, the dimple sinking in her chin as she smiled for the first time. 'What happened, Miss? Do tell us! You met someone nice – a man?'

'Yes. But a woman, Eileen, not a man. Enough of men – for the moment.' She started to root vigorously about the cupboards and shelves, opening tins, looking for the fruit cake, while Eileen put the kettle on the hob, where it started to sing at once, before she closed the basement shutters against the November night; the two women, happy together, preparing the room for their cosy tea, a homecoming tea, in the mind at least, as they forgot their exile.

Frances wrote to her parents that night before dinner.

'Dear Mama and Papa, I realise now that I was hasty and insensitive in my behaviour to you both at Summer Hill. I do apologise. I have been unhappy since I left but am no longer so, and thus can see my behaviour in a more objective light – and so make apologies for it. But I am happy now, for today I have met a remarkable woman, Miss Ruth Wechsberg . . .'

She paused, looking into the glowing coals of her bedroom fire, remembering once more the conversation that afternoon during tea with Ruth Wechsberg – tea served from the finest bone china in her little drawing room looking back over the mews in Grosvenor Crescent, where she had told her all about herself, her family problems, her reasons for being in London.

It had been an easy confession. Ruth Wechsberg had not in any way encouraged or invited these confidences. She had seemed, in her easy detachment, rather to accept such intimacies as a perfectly normal conversational topic, part of any civilised exchange; she was not in the least surprised or censorious. Other people avoided reality in polite chat about the weather and the crops; Ruth Wechsberg looked on true feeling as the only proper basis for conversation, so that Frances, in talking to her, did not sense for a moment that she was being presumptuous or was divulging any unworthy secrets, freely unburdening herself to her.

'And I have to admit, too,' Frances had said to her later, 'that I noticed you in the Park several weeks ago – you and your sister. And I followed her back this afternoon, before I heard the music.'

'Why? Why was that?'

'Intrigued. And time on my hands, I suppose.'

Ruth had looked at her sharply, summing her up. 'Good observation – and good hands,' she remarked. 'I noticed your fine hands and your eyes at once, when we met.'

Frances remembered how she had held her hand, a fraction longer than necessary, at that meeting. 'And you know,' Ruth had continued, leaning forward, adding more hot water to the silver teapot, 'those are the two most important qualities in the sort of work we do here: careful observation of the patients, and above all feeling for them – with your hands, your mind. The rest can be taught. But not those two gifts. And I think you have them already.'

'Thank you.' Frances had taken these remarks as no more than a social compliment.

'Of course, there is more to nursing – a lot more: the detail, the strict *facts* – timetables, long hours, discipline, all the scientific elements. And this can be irksome – and some of the facts are downright unpleasant. Gangrene for example – or dressing a fresh amputation . . .'

'Yes, I'm sure. The blood and such.'

'The stump shivers, my dear,' she had said, offering her another cup of tea.

'Does it?' Frances had asked, with more curiosity than distaste in her voice, and Ruth had nodded, noting this response favourably.

'But, as I say,' she went on, 'in nursing, it's the need for sensitive enquiry that is paramount: keeping your eyes and ears open, *feeling* things. And I was much struck by your obvious gifts here – when you told me that something had beckoned you into the house, more than simple curiosity.'

'Yes, it was a sense – do you know? – of *déjà vu* as I stood out there on the pavement, that I'd stood in front of this house before at some point.'

'But was it not some other hidden need that gave you that feeling? – a need to justify, to *do* something with your curiosity?'

'Yes, perhaps it was. For I have felt just that: the need to do something with my life.' It had begun to dawn on Frances what lay behind Ruth's comments here.

'Well, then,' Ruth said, a small note of triumph in her voice, 'would you like to learn about nursing here? I believe you might take to it very well. And I believe, too – though as I've said I'm no *clairvoyant*, much more a rationalist – that that is what may have been "meant" by your walking in here today. As simple as that!'

'Could I?' Frances had been genuinely astonished. 'It had never crossed my mind – I assure you.'

'Oh, and I believe you, Frances. One thing I do know, in my own case, is that nursing never crossed my mind either, until quite suddenly I had to deal with my mother, several years ago. I realised then that I should have been doing it from the very beginning, that I had a gift, a love for it – to serve them, the patients. So, you see, I believe you completely. That's the strange thing, isn't it? – how we often don't see what's meant for us. We have to "walk by faith and not by sight" as the Testament has it. The faith came so late for me. But perhaps not for you.'

'I'd love to – I'd love to try it,' Frances had said with shy enthusiasm, a small pit of excitement opening in her stomach.

Now, paraphrasing this conversation, as she had to Eileen, she wrote it down for her mother and father. And, that evening at supper, she elaborated on it once more for Dermot.

'Do you know, I think I have heard of her,' he said. 'A rich woman, Jewish, a nursing home for officers – how very surprising. But do you really think . . . it's *you*, Frances?'

It was. Frances took to the business of nursing almost at once. Though she soon realised that it was the absorbing company and agreeable circumstances that eased her passage here. At the same time she did not bridle at the strict disciplines – arriving sharp at 8.30 each morning, staying until 6.30 or later in the evening, with one hour off for lunch and one day off a week. This surprised her – as it did Ruth – that, having been waited upon all her life, she should so readily accept these long hours of waiting upon others.

Ruth remarked on this one day. 'I imagine, for all that you've told me of your life at home in Ireland, it's perhaps been a matter of replacing one ordered life by another. You must have a need of that.'

'I think I do.'

'It surprised me a little – the one thing that worried me in your work here, for you seem to be, how shall I put it? – impulsive, volatile by nature.'

'Yes, that as well . . .'

'An interesting mix.'

'You mean perhaps – a dangerous one?'

'No – difficult, if you like. A warring nature! But then our bodies rebel. And we are coming more and more to cure that. And I believe that in time we may be able to do the same for problems of the mind. I have long been interested in the psychological aspect of medicine: nervous complaints, neurasthenia, dreams, nightmares. There is a doctor in Vienna at present, a Dr Freud, whose papers on the subject I have been reading with great interest. But enough of that – for the moment we must deal with the obvious ills, and I hope I can help you there.'

So it was Ruth, when they met together in her little drawing room, who outlined the ethics and theory of nursing. 'To care and to cure,' she said. 'There is the whole basis – to nourish, in short. You cannot be a distant figure to these patients. They need you, not as the healthy do, but because they are unwell. And this makes them very different people. You will see men here at their worst – mentally as well as physically in the raw: difficult, demanding, ungrateful – sometimes cruelly so. For they are entirely dependent, helpless, which is what brings out these unhappy traits. And they are dependent on *you*, without wanting to be, which produces this impatience and arrogance – so that you will find yourself retreating from them initially, in your mind at least. But it's precisely your mind, as much as your hands, that they require. So you must cultivate a genuine sociability with them. Be patient, good-humoured – most important that.' Ruth smiled. 'Remember to smile, even in the worst circumstances. A smile can cure as much as anything.'

'I believe I can smile.'

'I'm sure you can – and that can be the greatest tonic. The other gifts, as I've said, you have: observation and touch. But you must develop them, rigorously. *Watch* the patients – there is the real learning. See how they sleep; note any increased restlessness, a difference in breathing patterns. Watch for changes in their colouring, the lips, the ear lobes. Listen to their mildest complaints: why does someone seem to have a headache over one eye in the morning, over the other in the afternoon? Your prompt response to such changes could prove vital – literally. Hence the importance of what may seem irksome or repetitive detail in your work: the adoption of strict cleanliness, method, rule, the exact amount and timing in the administration of medicines. You see, these men must be able to depend on you *entirely* – very much part of their cure, their mental well-being. So you cannot afford . . . to be casual in any way, do you see?'

Frances looked at her pointedly. 'Am I?'

'No,' Ruth replied firmly, yet with an expression that still seemed to doubt something. 'No, not casual. But headstrong, perhaps, as I've said. Reliability is the basis of every other gift in nursing. A patient, you see – he feels his body has betrayed him, become corrupt. So he looks for absolute fidelity, incorruptibility, in you.'

'Which makes it a vocation.'

'Exactly – which is what makes it difficult. It is no mere laying on of hands. One must believe, you see . . .'

'I think I do. I do want to be of some service to somebody.'

Ruth looked at her carefully. 'Yes, I can see that, from all you've told me – your break with your fiancé, your brother's death, your disagreements with your mother, the fracas of your last day at Summer Hill. You've so wanted to serve your house, and have been bitterly disappointed. But I wonder – I hope you'll forgive me: one cannot serve imperiously.'

Frances saw how well Ruth understood her, the contradictions in her nature. 'Yes,' she admitted. 'I do see that.'

'Well, there perhaps is your problem: whether you can resolve such contradictions – whether you will *want* to, which is more to the point, for such disagreements within oneself may seem the very stuff of life. But a divided nature, permanently unreconciled, can become an illness. There is that whole other world of mind, beyond body, which we know almost nothing about. But forgive me again – we must deal with the facts here, not the secrets.'

It was Ruth's younger sister, Agnes, who was responsible for the practicalities of Frances's initial training – Agnes a reduced image of her elder sister in every way: small, seemingly frosty and certainly tongue-tied, who, though she was in charge of most of the actual day-to-day nursing at Grosvenor Crescent, took a back seat in every other way. She was not in the least unkind or dismissive with Frances. But she gave, nonetheless, in her preoccupied reserve, an impression of not really being in touch with her. Agnes lived in her elegant sister's shadow and it was never apparent whether she had chosen or suffered this position.

'The bed,' she told her bluntly as they stood together in an empty room not yet made over as a ward. Then she itemised the coverings, picking them up from a pile. 'Under-mackintosh, sheets, blankets, pillows, cases.' Then, without another word, she made the bed up, and stripped it, before indicating that Frances should copy her. Afterwards they continued the training with a jointed mannequin which Agnes put on the mackintosh sheet, demonstrating a bed bath with it, how to move the patient and administer a bed pan – the whole performance conducted almost soundlessly.

'Here is a typical dressing tray,' Agnes said when they had moved into the nurses' room, next to the long salon, with its medicines and other stores. 'Cotton swabs, gauze, bandages, lint, carbolic, iodine, boiled water, safety pins, scissors, tweezers.' But she said nothing more of their purposes before taking the tray out to the ward where she proceeded to dress Lieutenant Lighthorn's amputated stump. This, since the wound was dry and almost healed, Frances found a relatively easy exercise when she came to repeat it: certainly the stump no longer shivered. Dressing his other leg, though, was something of a shock. The wound, running right down the side of the calf, had been deep and left untended for several days in the burning African bush. It had since been sewn together and there was nothing putrid about it. But the general appearance was still grim: a veined purplish colour, the emaciated flesh hillocky and strangely flaky so that small lumps of it came away like bits of old Stilton cheese.

'How nice to see a fresh face,' Lighthorn said easily while the dressing was going on, looking at Frances in her smart new uniform – starched cap, high collar and white apron with a red cross emblazoned over her chest – Frances, with a very wary face leaning over the man's smashed lower body. 'I'm William – Billy if you like.' He offered her a quizzical half-smile.

'My name is Frances – Frances Cordiner.' She glanced at him quickly.

'Yes, I know. Saw you the other day, listening to the music. Thought you were someone's sister – we all thought so.' He looked round at the others in the long room. 'But then found you weren't – all sorry about that! So it's a pretty nice surprise to find you're going to be here all the time.' His smile broadened. He's flirting with me already, Frances thought.

And so he was. And, soon enough, most of the other men followed his lead, made happier thereby, and Frances thrived on this without taking advantage of it. For she found as the days passed a stronger excitement in the work – a sense, almost, of intoxication: she was needed here, often and obviously, without equivocation. She was a lifeline, literally, in helping these once-vigorous men regain what had been paramount in their lives: their strength and mobility. The fact thrilled her.

And as she learnt, and she learnt quickly, she found another charm in the work. She was able, when alone in the ward and if only to some small extent, to take control, to organise, plan, even dictate. She was in charge. And she saw then how much she had craved this very thing in Summer Hill. Of course it was exactly that inperious feeling which Ruth had warned her against. But she justified the feeling, and its expression then, by reminding herself how the men, in their debility, needed just such control. And they did – soon coming to appreciate her little firmnesses and dictates.

But there was a further and even greater instinctive pleasure which she found in something which she had at first dreaded. She discovered an impersonal joy in handling the men's bodies. Their torn limbs, emaciated torsoes – at first she had touched these with fear and embarrassment. But soon, to her great surprise, she found a solace in it, as the men did. This strange pleasure came, she thought, from seeing for the first time the whole body, beneath the head, behind the clothes, and realising how each part was so wonderfully linked, dependent upon another – how life lay not only in a smile, in the eyes or voice, but in every minute part of the entire envelope and its contents, from toe to scalp. The whole fabric, intimately displayed, amazed and humbled her. Though broken, cut, bruised, cauterised – these bodies seemed all the more precious, vibrant mysteries coursing beneath the flesh. So that when she touched the limbs they no longer seemed mere anonymous appendages to the face but were equally imbued with the miraculous expression of life itself. A toe, she came to feel, contained as much emotion as a heart.

She said as much one evening at dinner with Dermot and Mortimer, who had come back early from the House.

'A toe – smiling? I wouldn't have seen it that way,' Mortimer commented drily.

'Well, it's just that every pore of skin . . . says something.' Frances put her head on one side, looking into the candlelight. 'I can't really explain it.'

'Oh, you have – you've put it very well,' Dermot said. 'A big toe smiling. I like that idea!' He looked at her. 'Listen, you have the day off tomorrow. And I have to go down to Salisbury Plain first thing – watch a new field gun being tested, send a report on it out to Army Command in the Cape. Would you like to come with me? We could take lunch somewhere afterwards, have a look at the countryside.'

'I'd love to.' Frances nodded happily. 'Though I don't know about the gun,' she added as a sudden after-thought.

'No, indeed,' Mortimer broke in. 'I should think not – seeing the results of such infernal weapons each day!'

'My dear Papa,' Dermot responded with a smile, 'your Home Rulers and their Fenian friends are not averse to using them either.'

'Quite different. They do not use field guns –'

'They would if they had them –'

'Besides, as you know, I have no truck with those violent Home Rulers – am concerned only to prosper the right of a nation to choose its own destiny, by peaceful means. The will of the people, dear boy! When will you realise that no gun, in the end, can ever resist that?'

The point was not taken by Dermot. But the two men still managed to exchange smiles before Dermot added, 'A gun, as I see it, is there to defend that very will, Papa, not suppress it. I think we disagree about the Irish destiny there. But never mind, Frances can lurk behind Stonehenge with cotton-wool in her ears – that can be her destiny tomorrow. But you will come, won't you?'

He looked at her, suddenly anxious, and she nodded. She wanted to come, not to see the horrid field gun but to be free and out of town for the day with Dermot.

5

THEY LOOKED OUT at the bare trees and frosty fields, alone in the warm compartment, the land falling away beyond the downs, approaching Salisbury Plain, so that soon the view was one of shallow, rolling hills, without hedges or other boundaries, only a few tracks and coppices to break the monotony of the chilly morning scene. Dermot, immaculate in his Captain's uniform and long brown boots, sat opposite her, his back to the engine, so that Frances saw all that was coming in sight and he could only gaze at its swift disappearance. He let his pipe die and picked up *The Times*. Frances, head against the window, scanned the land ahead attentively, as if expecting something.

'Nothing much to see,' Dermot remarked from behind the paper.

'The spire – Salisbury Cathedral.'

'Hardly near it yet.'

'Did you know? – it's almost 400 feet high and without any proper foundations. No one quite understands how it's stood up all this time.'

'Faith, I should imagine.'

'Are you that sort of person – religious, I mean?'

'No. I think not.'

'Not very?'

'No, I meant not at all. You either are or you aren't. It's fraudulent to sit on the fence. Having it both ways. What about you?' He put the paper down, lit his pipe again, then shook the box of Swan Vestas vigorously, like a rattle.

'You're blunt, aren't you?'

'Like you – saying what you mean, meaning what you say.'

'I don't quite know about religion. I like the *idea* of it . . .'

'Then you're not. It's a faith or nothing. You can't have it as an idea to play around with – that's a philosophy. Now, I like that – systems of thought. Much more in my line.'

'You were so much better educated. Women aren't. I wish I had been – those fearful governesses at home and that awful dame school in Dublin.'

'You shouldn't regret it. You have something else – tremendous intuition. I wish I had that.'

'In battle, you mean? – for killing people, knowing what the other side is going to do.'

'You *are* sharp this morning –'

'Just saying what I mean –'

'Well, your latter point, yes. But I wish I knew more about what ordinary people were thinking, day to day.'

'The whole mysterious business of the mind that Ruth Wechsberg's been telling me about. She talks about that – what she calls illnesses there, dreams, things that happen to you as a child that can affect your whole life. I don't understand her – how people can become quite different, in their behaviour, because of unconscious things, that happened long before. And how you can unearth the real problems of their lives by talking to them, hearing about their dreams and so on. Do you follow it?'

'No. But it sounds fascinating.'

'It is. What makes me so want to annoy and get the better of Mama, for example?' Dermot shrugged. 'Your nature, obviously.'

'Yes, but why wasn't that in Henry's nature, or Eustace's? Same blood. Why only me? And you, Dermot,' she went on enthusiastically, carried along simply by a spirit of pure scientific enquiry. 'Why are you different, from other men?'

He was taken aback. 'I don't know. I've never considered why,' he said at last, lighting his pipe quickly, rattling the box of matches once more. Then he leant forward, craning his neck round, peering out the window. 'Look! That's it – the cathedral spire. Nearly there.'

But Frances, still absorbed by science, was not so taken with this vision of faith when it appeared, much more curious to know – since he must have considered this very question – why Dermot had lied about it.

Dermot meanwhile, getting his army greatcoat and attaché case down from the rack, considered Frances's sharpness and regretted that he had ever spoken to her of this aberration in his personality.

An army staff wagon met them at the station, taking them to the firing range, north of Salisbury on the Devizes road, where they turned off up a track towards the Artillery Ordnance Depot, surrounded by a screen of trees in the lee of the hill.

'You may have to wait at the depot,' Dermot told her, when they arrived at the first of the low brick buildings, a great red flag raised above it. 'I'll ask the Colonel if you can watch.'

It was nearly eleven o'clock, the sun finally piercing through the mists that lay over the higher ground here, dissolving the white cover, pools of blue appearing in the sky. The frosty gravel crunched beneath Dermot's boots as he walked away towards the guardhouse. Soldiers moved briskly to and fro, tending gun carriages, loading ammunition wagons; grooms placated restless horses between the shafts, champing at the bit, the warm breath from their nostrils running in bright plumes into the chilly air. There was a sense of impending sunny adventure in the morning – and Frances, released from the confines and disciplines of Grosvenor Crescent, suddenly wanted to be part of it, not to stay at the Depot. The idea of rash, violent action excited her, a girl playing truant from school among rough boys whose company had been strictly forbidden.

Dermot returned. Permission had been granted. 'But you must keep well back and stay in the wagon all the time,' he said as the two of them, accompanied by their driver, a staff sergeant, left the compound and drove up the hill.

On the far side, looking north over a vast expanse of empty land, a group of officers and men stood in the strengthening sun around two field guns, another red flag above them, a flash of colour set against a sky that was almost clear now, a wash of pale blue running into a milky horizon. A series of large white targets, crossed with black lines, had been placed at varying distances from the guns, disappearing out into the plain. Dermot joined the other officers, leaving Frances in the wagon with the sergeant, an affable local man, getting on in years, who was happy to entertain and instruct this attractive young visitor, producing field glasses, offering them to her.

'Four different targets you see, Miss – the first at a thousand feet, then every 500 feet after. Though it's not the range they're bothered with today. It's a new breech block or some such – so they say. Though I'd be surprised if it were any better than the last guns we tried up here. Can't beat the old ways, I say.'

The guns started to fire then, in tandem, quickly, one after the other, recoiling on their wheels, little gasps of white smoke emerging from the open breech as the men reloaded, stood away, and fired again. There was a splendid rhythm and speed to the business, the gleaming barrels spitting like provoked animals. But Frances was surprised at the lack of noise. The guns, from where she sat above them, seemed like toys, cap guns, harmless. She remarked on this.

'Ah,' the sergeant told her, brushing his extravagant moustaches, 'not at the receiving end, though – I can vouch for that. But there's no charge in these shells today, you see, Miss, when they hit the target.'

'They don't seem to be doing that, though,' Frances put the field glasses down.

'Well, they're only concerned with the speed of firing, Miss, not the aim.'

Frances watched Dermot standing among the other officers – motionless, intent, ramrod-straight, with their braided caps, swagger sticks and red flashes on their tunic collars. It all seemed very unreal, the sun burning out the last of the mists now, warming the tingling air, so that away to the north, swivelling the glasses round, she suddenly made out the great boulders of Stonehenge on the horizon. They're all playing at soldiers, she felt then. Yet she had seen the results of their games at Grosvenor Crescent. It made no sense. Was this what Dermot was going to spend his life doing? Such quick intelligence and sympathy in the man – how could he find reward in these childish games? She turned to the sergeant during a lull in the firing. 'What's it like – being a soldier?'

'Never thought about it, Miss. Never been anything else, leastways.'

The same answer Dermot had given her in the train. They did not really think or feel, these soldiers. That was how they could maim and kill people so easily. But Dermot certainly thought and felt. There was the contradiction and it annoyed her that he should fail to see this. Watching the guns as they started up again, she suddenly wanted to alter his life for him.

'Oh, I loved the colour and excitement of it all,' she said later as they walked around Stonehenge, the sergeant waiting for them in the wagon. 'Liked all that – the little puffs of smoke, gleaming brass, red flags and the frosty blue air – all pretty as a picture. But just as you asked me about nursing – is it really *you*, Dermot? I kept asking myself that as I watched – toy soldiers, that you get over in the nursery.'

They stood beside one of the great monoliths, the slanting sun casting a long shadow of the stone across the grass. 'Oh, I love it all,' Dermot replied simply, turning away, dropping so obvious a topic.

'Yes, but –' Frances continued forcefully.

'Like you love Summer Hill. Same feeling – the army is a whole life for me: mentally, physically, the companionship. That's what you like at home, isn't it? – complete satisfaction all in one thing.'

'Yes, but I don't have to kill people for my satisfaction there.'

He raised his eyebrows. 'I wonder. Your actions against your Mama – that's a sort of mental killing between you both, isn't it?'

'I've left all that, though.'

'Perforce. Be fair, Frances: you've left it because you had to and you haven't forgotten it. You contemplate a return to the fray! And yours, if I may say so, is a hopeless cause.'

She fingered the huge slab beside her. It was cold and damp. She walked out into the sun, lifting her face to it, warming herself, before turning to him. 'Very well then, I've been dissuaded from it –'

'But you haven't! Rather you want to dissuade me, in my army career. That's what's interesting. You have a wonderful need to interfere and try and change people's lives, Frances – with Henry, your mother and now me.' He laughed, not at all cruel in his insights.

'Well, I'm sorry. It's not done with malice.'

'I'm sure it isn't. But it's brick walling, as my father told you. You haven't seen that – that it's really impossible to change the way people are, their natures. You've not seen that immutable plan in the battle.'

'But I don't believe that. People *can* change!'

Dermot shook his head. 'I wish I could save you from the defeats in trying.' He watched her walk away, crunching over the still-frosty grass.

'Oh, but you can, dear Dermot!' Her mood changed completely now – provocative, flirtatious, as she did a little dance back towards him, taking him by the arm, drawing him out into the sun. 'You *can* save me from all sorts of defeats.' She opened her eyes wide, finding his, staring into them, before kissing him briefly on the cheek. 'You can save me with lunch at least. I'm famished. Aren't you?'

He took her arm and they walked away from the great grey circle of stone. He no longer regretted anything he had said to this bright woman, regretting only his nature that forbade him a closer contact with her warmth and vivacity. A longing for her came over him then which, for those moments at least, did not appear hopeless. People could change, she was sure. Perhaps she was right and he ought to believe her, he thought, turning his back on the immutable stone.

They sat in wooden booths over a late lunch in the Bear Hotel at Salisbury, a stone-flagged saloon near a big log fire – a half-timbered chop house in this quarter of the inn, with sporting prints and flintlocks covering the bent and twisted walls. Frances attacked her mutton cutlets, dabbing them with onion sauce. Dermot quaffed a pewter tankard of ale and mopped his brow. Wafts of gravy and burning meat came from the swinging kitchen door behind them. There was a touch of manure in the air as well – local squires and farmers in town for the day, stamping their rough boots, together with a few legal men in frock coats, portly gluttons all, gossiping, arguing the toss everywhere around them.

'We could have eaten in the dining room,' Dermot remarked.

'Nicer here, among the men. I can't bear the cold frou-frou air of provincial hotel dining rooms – anxious maids in pinnies threatening you with *petits pois* and *blancmange*. Can I try your ale?'

He pushed the tankard across. 'I can get you some –'

'See if I like it first.'

She did and he called the pot boy over. 'Lucky Miss Wechsberg's not here to see you,' he told her when the second tankard arrived and she had sucked the froth from it, the foamy beads giving her a brief moustache.

'It's my day off.' She was happily impudent. 'Miss Wechsberg has days off, too. I wonder what she does with them. It's strange she's not married – so elegant and gifted. A little governessy. But men like that, too, don't they?'

Dermot smiled. 'Like you, Frances. A little governessy.' He cut some fat from the mutton. A big tabby cat, wide-eyed and anxious, looked up at them intently from the flagstones. Frances reached across, took the fat from his plate and gave it to the cat.

'Pussy, pussy,' she said. 'I like it here. Yes, governessy . . .' She sat back, considering this appellation. 'It's just that I don't like footlers, can't-make-up-their-mind people – people who won't *respond*.' She stared at him, half-smile, half-glare.

'A little uncharitable?'

'Nonsense! We all have tongues in our head. It's just cowardice, mostly, when people stay mum. *Je Responderay* – "I will reply" – there was a girl at the dame school, one of the Willoughby-Hughes girls; that was their family motto and I've often thought about it, so inappropriate for she was a poor silent creature. Wished it were my motto: "I will answer" – for who and what I am. Well, of course, most people do nothing of the sort – no answer in them at all, no echo, like talking to a log, and so no conversation, no sharing, no truth. Even with highly intelligent people, Dermot – sometimes there's no answer, to the real things.' She provoked him gently.

But he refused to be baited, saying finally and rather formally, 'That's all very well, Frances. But there are some things better hid.' He resumed his meal, looking down intently at his plate.

'I'm sorry.' She leant across and touched his arm. 'You know, I thought nothing wrong of your loving Henry – really not, nothing shaming there, so I don't understand? . . .'

'My reluctance in the matter? But you don't know the world, Frances. They are most reluctant about such things.'

'I don't care about the world! It's the same thing, isn't it? – loving a man or woman – same thing at heart, same feeling.' Warmed by the fire and the ale, she pursued her theme. 'So, if you can love one, that surely doesn't prevent you loving the other.'

'Not for you perhaps. But, well, I've tried the other. And it didn't really work.' He looked at Frances, this candid woman across the plain table, so warm in everything – remembering her face offered to the sun that morning, now flushed and excited by the heat of the room. She lived in warmth and truth, taking certainty from these fires. And he realised then, with Henry's death, how very cold and lost he was in his own life. 'Well, you may be right,' he said. 'Who knows?'

'She probably wasn't your sort, or you didn't appeal to her,' Frances said off-handedly, resuming her meal. 'But I love you, Dermot,' she added, in the casual tones of someone remarking on the weather.

It was a strange courtship. Frances made the running – while he, in response, took a pace forward, then one back. For her the frustration – for him temptation. For he was tempted. But he could not call it love, there was the problem. It was everything else – affection, admiration, a lighter heart whenever she appeared in the room or street. But it was not that head-over-heels involvement, that overwhelming need, which he had felt before, with men. And despite their other great truth sharings he could not tell her this. But she persevered. Though here again she would not admit to him any such effort in the affair, nor the sudden storms in her heart which overcame her in the following weeks as she grew more attached to him. She kept mum on these things, like an angler tempting a trout from a deep pool, experiencing the truth now of what he had told her – how some things were better hid. The process was a strain on her real nature. She wanted Dermot but had to forbid herself any real moves towards this end, withholding herself from him, while he moved in and out of her orbit with wary fascination. In short it was an unsatisfactory business for both of them – a fact which they equally denied to each other, thus feeding a predicament which might have continued indefinitely but for a fortuitous intervention a week later.

Eileen, alone in the house with Frances, opened the door to the stranger one early evening – the stooping, wizened old beggar man, fearfully whiskered in a battered bowler and torn greatcoat tied with string, a rusty campaign medal pinned to his lapel, with a hooked nose and aggressive, staring eyes, a Fagin in the lamplight.

'God bless ye, Miss,' the old horror said with an Irish brogue, a smell of strong spirits on his breath. 'Amn't I travelling the streets since the dawn of day, an oul' sodjer, down on me luck. We'ed ye ever have a few coppers for a cuppa tay – or a pair of boots or iny small thing at all in that line.'

He had put his foot on the threshold. But Eileen held the door against him. 'Well, I don't know now. I'll ask the young lady –'

'Ah ye'd take pity on a pour soul like me. Sure and don't I hear your voice – from the oul' counthry like meself. What part are ye from at all?'

'I'm – I'm from Kilkenny.'

'Sure an' don't I know it well!' He raised his voice now, a nasal enthusiastic whine, pushing further in towards her. 'A grand place altogether – the Marble City, know it well. Sure and if that's the case ye'd have a sup of whisky for me then, and I travellin' the cold streets since the dawn o' day –'

'Well, I don't know about that,' Eileen said firmly, trying to close the door on him. But he had his foot in the jamb now, whining at her still, but in a more aggressive tone.

'Ah, just a sup, Miss – take pity on an oul' man. A drop of the crathur – and may the blessed Virgin and all the saints and angels . . .' He pushed right past her now.

'I'll get the police – I'll call the constable!' Eileen turned back to the stairs then. 'Miss Frances – Miss Frances! Come down quick!'

The beggar, in the hall now, turned into the dining room where he went straight to the sideboard, picked up the sherry decanter and started to swig at it in long draughts, the drink splashing over his chin and neck. Then, just as Frances and Eileen appeared in the doorway and greatly encouraged by the alcohol, he started a little jig, hopping from one foot to the other round the Chippendale table, holding the decanter, starting to sing an Irish ballad in a cracked and raucous voice. '"And on *next* Sun-day morn-ning, I'll meet her, *meet* her, meet her – next Sun-day morn-ning, I'll meet her . . . and I am the *best* of them all!"' he sang out before stumbling and falling heavily on the floor, a bundle of flying rags and boots, the bowler spinning into the grate.

'Get up at once – you brute!' Frances shouted. 'What are you doing here? Eileen – see if you can find a constable.'

The man rose shakily to his feet. 'Arrah now and you wouldn't run in an oul' sodjer,' he whined again drunkenly, touching his campaign medal. 'Look – the Crimea, Miss. And didn't I get a bullet in me back out there from one of those Turkey fellows.' He made a shaky attempt to stand to attention, raising a hand in a wobbly salute, before embarking on 'The Minstrel Boy' in a heavily slurred voice: '"The Minstrel Boy to-o the war-r-r-s is gone . . ."' He piped out a few lines of the song before forgetting it, with a vacant look, spittle running down his chin. Then, pulling himself together again, he started on a stentorian rendering of 'God Save the Queen'.

Frances was enraged. 'You must leave at once. Eileen, fetch a constable!'

'Ah, an angry wumman,' the beggar opined with a crooked smile. 'Nuttin' lovelier.' He leered at her, stumbling towards the sherry decanter on the table. 'Now why don't you and I sit down here and take our eaase over a glass or two. And cripes,' he added, picking up the decanter, appraising the sherry, 'isn't this the finest stuff? A man'd be lacking that and he walking the cold streets since the dawn o' day –'

'Give it me, you wretch! The police –' Frances, trying to retrieve the decanter, started to wrestle with him over the table.

'Oh and thim's fightin' words,' he purred. 'A tough little vixen – nothin' nicer . . .'

The two of them swayed about the room then, each clinging to the decanter. 'Be God, ye can dance too – we'll take a spin surely before we take a sup.' He started to hum a waltz, clasping Frances firmly by the arms, swaying round the floor together. Finally the old reprobate let her go, laughing uproariously.

'My, you do dance superbly,' he said in a completely changed, a most cultured accent. He pulled at his bird's nest whiskers, his hooked nose and tattered grey hair. They all came away in his hands before he wiped his face with a handkerchief and the features of quite a different man clearly emerged.

'Humphrey!' Frances shouted. 'You shocker! – you beast! You had me . . .' She was speechless. It was Humphrey Saunders, her mother's old friend, who had brought the Spanish dancers to Summer Hill – boisterous in quite a different way now, the suave man-of-the-world again, entirely taken with his latest practical joke.

'Ah yes, I had you there – both of you!' He looked at Eileen standing open-mouthed at the doorway. He took off his shabby greatcoat and filthy scarf, found his bowler in the grate and dusted it. 'It's quite extraordinary, isn't it! – what a few old clothes, a different costume, will do. Change the world with a change of clothes, couldn't you? I heard you were over in London, Frances – Mortimer was in touch with me the other day and I thought I'd come round, little surprise, variety the spice of life and what have you. You've rather fallen out with your Mama, I understand?'

'Somewhat, yes.' Frances had regained some of her composure now. Eileen left the room and Humphrey sank into a chair.

'Exhausting business – this acting.' He drew a long breath. 'Sorry to hear about your mother. Never mind – a charming but difficult woman, not unlike you: bound to clash.'

'Am I difficult?'

'Oh yes.' He started to take his frightful old boots off. 'Part of the charm. Like her – when she was young.'

'You knew her well then, didn't you?'

'I was in love with your beautiful Mama – more than thirty years ago, before she met Desmond.'

'Did she marry the wrong man, do you think?' Frances asked pertly.

'No. She would have tried to have her own way with whoever she married. Very forceful character.' He bent down, rubbing his toes. 'These old boots, real shockers. Wore them last for *East Lynne* at the Metropolitan, Edgeware Road – played a very good drunk there, too.'

'You're a wonderful actor, there's no doubt.'

'Ah yes.' He looked up with a judicious smile. 'That's why your Mama didn't finally take to me, I believe. She realised I would always be able to act my way out of her clutches when we married, if I felt like it.'

'Couldn't pin you down.'

'Exactly.'

'But she's quite an actress, too, at heart.'

'Indeed she is – and that was another problem: too much alike in that way, both treading the boards at the same time, you might say, the two of us acting up to each other like one o'clock – to get what we wanted.'

'What did she want?'

Humphrey looked at her in surprise, putting a tongue in his cheek, playing the old roué now. 'My dear, what do you think? What does she want of everyone?'

'Their unswerving obedience.'

'You have it,' he exclaimed. 'You have it!'

'To her every whim?'

'Exactly!' he said joyously.

'So much better – if we could be real to each other, say what we mean.'

'Ah, but would it? Miss out on all the fun then! The cut and thrust, dear Frances – what would life be without it? How very dull, if we were real to each other all the time. And then again, perforce – since most of us have no roles handed out to us – we have to choose, have to create one. Perfectly obvious: all the world a stage and so on. Quite true.'

'And you – what have you chosen?'

He sighed. 'Something different every day, so that I hardly know who I am. The penalty – for so much enjoyment. But I wouldn't have had it otherwise. Acting has got me what I wanted, a means to an end.'

'What end?'

'*Living!* I'm alive, dear girl! A change of scene, a new backcloth, a dash of limelight, a different costume – and I'm *free*. I told you – a dirty beard and an old wig and the world is yours for an hour or two. You saw how it was just now, didn't you?'

Frances nodded. She had indeed seen how it was. And later, over a spirited supper with Humphrey when the other men returned, looking across at Dermot, she pondered the idea of invention and deception in her life. Dermot had praised her candid nature. And she herself, quite apart from the duty she felt towards the truth, believed this might be part of her charm. But perhaps she was wrong – in so far as Dermot was concerned at least. Perhaps the impasse in their relationship was due simply to her being too truthful, too literal, with him. Perhaps, as Humphrey had just done, she should surprise, astonish him in some way.

*

The fog thickened as she walked down Regent Street on her next day off, closing in over the upper stories of the great stores, so that only their bright windows, filled with enticing displays like miniature stage sets, gleamed clearly through the afternoon murk. Laden with boxes and parcels, people staggered, pushed and collided on the pavement, stampeding about in the yellow gloom. Other sounds were hidden – disembodied voices, footsteps, horses' feet and the cries of provoked cabbies, echoing invisibly up and down the street. The fog, and the hide-and-seek it imposed, thrilled Frances – this barely controlled pandemonium, figures appearing and disappearing like excited ghosts through the swirling cotton-wool.

She joined a crowd looking at some of the new clockwork trains in a big toyshop window. A frock-coated assistant wound a green and gold engine up behind the display, before placing it on a circular rail and setting it off in front of a line of tin carriages. She thought of Dermot during the train journey back from Salisbury when she had fallen asleep on his shoulder. But something more than that unconscious intimacy was needed, now.

In a window of Liberty's further down a puppet display was in progress behind a highly-coloured proscenium, the eighteenth-century figures, men and women in various fancy dress, being manipulated on thread through a courtly dance against a Versailles backdrop.

She had been looking, in fact, for some small Christmas gifts – some clothes for herself too, perhaps, though she had little money in hand. Her allowance had indeed been cut off; she had not even had a reply to her letter home. And she was angry when she thought of this now – all her old pride and arrogance returning. Mortimer had advanced her £50 and Ruth Wechsberg had insisted that she take a nominal wage at least during her training. But what did this amount to, in this opulent street? – a mere pinprick of money. Confronted by these extravagant displays and expensive gifts, she wished she was really rich. Money was power – and, surrounded by these wealthy crowds laden with gaily-ribboned boxes, she wanted that now – unbridled power, all her nursing precepts of self-sacrifice forgotten.

She looked back at the courtly puppets again, moving jerkily to and fro in their fancy dress ball. An idea occurred to her then – a plan which found its form a few minutes later when, crossing Piccadilly and going into Leicester Square, she saw the splendid uniform in the brightly-lit window of Nathan's theatrical costumiers: a lovely scarlet Dragoon's tunic, double-breasted, brass-buttoned, swirls of braid on the cuffs, wide shimmering green lapels, dark narrow trousers with red piping beneath.

Frances promptly entered the costumiers and hired the uniform. 'The Rosscommon Dragoons,' the man told her. 'A defunct Irish regiment, I understand' – which delighted Frances all the more, seeing something additionally meant now in her scheme.

The uniform needed taking in here and there and the trousers were too long. But she and Eileen made alterations to it that evening, so that in the end it fitted very well. But it came with a heavy high-peaked officer's cap. She tried this on, sitting down in front of the mirror – took it off, then put it on again.

'You look a scream, either way!' Eileen told her.

'I feel like a lighthouse.'

They giggled. Frances stood up, put her hands in the trouser pockets and strutted round the bedroom. 'Funny having pockets,' she said. 'Should have some money to jangle in them.'

'Funny being a man at all, Miss, isn't it?'

'Yes.'

'What a lark! But what's it all *for*, Miss? Do tell!'

'A surprise. A secret!' she said in considerable excitement.

But the real surprise – the tragedy – was that Dermot, when she went down to the drawing room before dinner dressed as a Rosscommon Dragoon, was not at all amused by her transformation. For several moments, when she entered the room and he first saw her by the doorway, he was obviously taken in by this vision of a slim, dark-haired soldier and his face showed a bright surprise. But, when Frances came forward into the light and he recognised her, his expression clouded; he was annoyed.

'Frances – how could you?'

'You don't like it?'

He had stood up eagerly at first, but now he paced the room nervously, shaking his match box. 'Frances, Frances – I like you as a *woman*, not as a man. What could you have been thinking of?'

'Just a joke,' she said limply. What had she been thinking of? She was not sure now. She had not analysed her scheme completely. It had just been a vague 'plan' – the uniform in the bright window promising her something out of the fog, Humphrey's success in the same manner, the idea of changing one's life, Dermot's life, just an idea, an adventure, a means to an end. But she had never thought it through, to this end.

Dermot cleared his throat. 'A joke? Oh, Frances, you didn't really think, did you? . . .'

'Think what?' she asked rather arrogantly now.

'Think that that would . . . attract me?'

'No, of course not! Just saw it in a window this afternoon – thought it would be a funny thing, like Humphrey in his old beggar's outfit. Spice of life and all that . . .' But she found she could not maintain her conceit or composure now, bursting into tears, rushing from the room. She had fallen in love with a man who could only love other men, who could not be changed. And she suffered the agony then of her exposure, wearing her heart on the sleeve of this stupid uniform – suffering, as she tore the hated clothes off in her bedroom, one more defeat.

*

Frances, having failed at adventure and deception, returned to the literal and prosaic in her life. Dermot's subsequent apologies were profuse and genuine. They were soon friends again. But there was no longer a feeling of impending intimacy between them. That was over. Touching his hand, lips brushing his cheek, head on his shoulder – all the preludes to love were gone. She saw how they could never become lovers.

Dermot, in her most secret thoughts, had offered her a future, a way out: they might have married, lived in Ireland – lived at Summer Hill, even . . . Yes, that fantasy, too, had seemed momentarily possible. Now all this bright invention had betrayed her, and she was hardened by it, sensing, for the first time, how real emotion, towards people, was an idiocy which would get her nowhere in life, something which would always be spurned or wasted. Only objects maintained fidelity, returned it – a place, a landscape, a house.

Her thoughts returned to Summer Hill. There was a world which would not betray her. Christmas was approaching. She would return for the holiday, whether her parents wished it or not. Besides, there was Eileen to think of; she, too, would want to go home for the Christmas season. She had kept in polite touch with Eustace, at Aldershot with his regiment, and now she wrote to him again, telling him of her plans. He replied, agreeing with her in an entirely vague and non-committal way. She spoke to Ruth Wechsberg, who freely offered her the time off, and to Mortimer who equally encouraged her, as did Dermot.

Everyone was on Frances's side. But she felt somehow powerless and unconfident about this homecoming. 'A return to the fray,' Dermot had described her earlier ambitions at Summer Hill. Yet she longed for security and peace there now – not war. Dermot might have offered her this in himself – or at least been a vital support, a means to that end at Summer Hill. But she could not now expect such intimate help from him. Dermot was a friend. Everyone was a friend. None of them really understood the heart of things in her life – her longing for a house, for a hill in summer – so that she gave up thinking she would ever find a true ally in that cause.

6

THE FRONT DOOR bell at Grosvenor Crescent had rung, pulled vigorously several times, breaking the somnolence of the dark December evening. Frances had heard voices in the hall – gruff male laughter, then Ruth's voice and some lively ensuing chatter before heavy footsteps climbed the Florentine staircase, followed by the rich aroma of a cigar, drifting into the nurses' room where Frances was preparing a dressing tray. She had started a week of night duty in the ward that evening, under Agnes's direction. Now she turned to her questioningly.

'Who? . . .'

Agnes looked up knowingly, smoothed her hair, then stroked the side of her nose, as if prettying herself in a mirror. But she said nothing.

'I wonder who it can be?' Frances persisted. 'Visiting just before supper.'

But the footsteps had gone now, disappearing into the back of the house where Ruth had her quarters, her little drawing and dining room: a private guest had arrived, not a visitor to the ward, so that Frances dropped her enquiry and went out to dress Lieutenant Lighthorn's stump. He too had heard the vigorous bell, smelt the rich cigar.

'Thought we were about to see my papa,' he told Frances. 'He puffs at those grand weeds. But Sister Ruth told him very firmly to desist last time he was here.'

'No. A private guest. They went back to Sister Ruth's rooms.'

'A *man* though,' Lighthorn said impishly. She dabbed away some flaky skin with spirit lotion, then ran the clean bandage round the stump. 'Sister Frances –' he went on confidently.

'Not Sister yet.'

'Well, Miss Frances – may I ask you? – do you have a friend, a particular friend?'

'No,' she said firmly.

He sighed. 'Oh, if I only had my legs again, you would have. I wonder who Sister Ruth's particular friend is?'

'He's been here before, you mean?' Frances could not contain her curiosity.

'Oh yes. That same rich cigar, jolly laughter. Every week or so, in the evenings. You've not been here. We've all wondered.'

'Well, I'm sure Sister Ruth does have some male friends, you know,' Frances said off-handedly, finally pinning the bandage, then patting the mummified stump. 'There you are. You'll be quite ready for your supper now.'

'Yes, but *who?*' he asked with mischief, eyes rolling in mock agony. His enforced idleness and lack of mobility among these women had greatly promoted the subaltern's amorous thoughts, a lascivious curiosity, a taste for liaisons – real or imagined. Marooned in bed he lived vicariously – just as Frances did, equally curious now. In their separate despairs, they both longed for answers, access into the secrets of other people's happy lives.

Their curiosity was unexpectedly satisfied – an hour after supper in the ward: an answer introduced by the same rich cigar aroma, followed by a bearded, balding head emerging from a swirl of blue smoke, the beaming figure coming clear, like sun through the fog, as the substantial figure paused resolutely in the doorway, a Holbein grandee, portly and middle-aged, whose evening clothes cut with superb tact did much to disguise both facts.

'Now, Sir, if you'll forgive me, but I really must insist – I must ask you not to smoke in the ward.' Ruth, in a restrained grey silk evening dress, was tactful but no less firm than usual.

'Ah, such a taskmistress! My dear woman.' The neatly badger-bearded man turned and admired her. 'Irish stew, rice pudding – and now no smokes! What a regimen you impose. An evening with you is stricter than a month at Bad Homburg! But as you will – noblesse oblige!' He stubbed the cigar out in an ashtray by the door, then continued the banter. 'As you will indeed – any-thing which may allow me acc-ess to your holy of holies: I am to see it all at last. I have been much in-ter-ested, my dear Ruth, in your ac-tivities – which you have de-nied me!'

He clearly spaced and hit each syllable in longer words, a curious hesitancy which might have disguised a stutter. Yet there was nothing delayed in his general conversational approach. Rolling his r's, he attacked his sentences with a genial and energetic relish, just as he walked down the centre of the ward now – quickly, precisely, despite his considerable bulk – a store of energy and impatience behind the neat steps, someone who knew where he was going, the hooded, blue-grey eyes seeing and appraising everything with equal confidence and enjoyment; a protuberant lower lip moving, tongue flickering, as if testing the air like a food for all its possible surprises.

Frances watched the commanding figure and immediately felt, despite his imperious airs, that here was really a child in a man's clothes. It was her clear impression: a child got up in fancy dress, beard, cigar and tails, who roamed through the rooms of life, as he had come into the ward just then, seeing each room as another and more wonderful nursery.

The visitor stopped finally at Lighthorn's bed. The officer sat up now, both arms rigid by his side, giving him much-needed support in his surprise. 'His Royal Highness,' Ruth presented her dinner guest, 'the Prince of Wales. And this is Miss Frances Cordiner, who is helping us, learning her duties.'

Frances curtsied, a short brief genuflection, the starch in her apron crackling as she bent and straightened. But then to her surprise the Prince offered her his own large square hand. She had done less than glance at him, just an unfocused run over his features, and would not have dared look him straight in the eye unless, as he did then, he had not held on to her fingers, and continued to hold them for what seemed an eternity, so that Frances, fearing her responsibility for some frightful social gaffe, had suddenly stared at the Prince, holding him eye to eye as if pleading for mercy.

'Learning her duties. I say!'

'Yes, she has just started – on night duty.'

'Night duty, of course.' He considered the idea vaguely, preoccupied by some quite different thought, reluctantly letting her hand go at last, his earlier smile gone, but staring back at her now.

'My dear,' Ruth Wechsberg said to her next morning, 'the Prince of Wales has asked that we both take dinner with him – at Marlborough House.'

'Oh – how very kind.'

'Yes. But I fear not.' Ruth turned away, starting to smooth the covers on the one easy chair, set by the fire, in her otherwise spartan little drawing room – the very chair which the Prince himself had occupied the previous evening, Frances thought; a vague odour of cigar smoke still hung in the air. 'I have made it clear to the Prince,' Ruth continued, 'that I prefer not to venture on his territory. His Marlborough House set . . . are not mine.'

Frances wondered, since Ruth had apparently declined the invitation, why she had brought the subject up at all. It was a question, given their open relationship, that she would normally have asked. But that morning there was a slight frisson, a distance between them. However, disguised as advice, the answer was forthcoming. 'I tell you this, Frances, because the Prince is a wilful man, rarely crossed in his social ambitions. He will certainly attempt to make direct contact with you himself.'

'Oh? Will he?' Frances's innocence was well feigned. But Ruth was not taken in. She sighed, opening the window on a dull foggy morning. A damp air crept into the room, a chilly displeasure from the world.

'Yes, my dear, he will.' She sighed once more. It was not like her, repeating a mannerism in this way – she who, in usual times, was so sure of herself. 'He was, apparently, considerably taken by you,' she went on. 'And so I must warn you – since I know him well – that he has a penchant for young unmarried women, a tendency to take them up – and drop them. You would not be the first or the last among his current "virgin band" to suffer in this way. I regard his behaviour as reprehensible, to a degree, and have told him so. I know the risks, in your case –'

'But, Ruth, the risks – I barely spoke to the Prince.'

'It was enough – not what you said but, for him, what you appeared to be. And what you must not be – a mere plaything, to be taken up like his games of baccarat, then dropped for one of whist or bridge. It is his way and I must protect you from it.'

Frances wondered, if this was his way with women, how Ruth, with her sensible disciplines and prohibitions, had ever come to play a part in the Prince's irresponsible life. Again, she longed to ask her before the answer struck her with some force: it had been apparent in all that Ruth had said of the Prince. Her role in his life was one of nanny, a most elegantly attractive one no doubt, but nanny none the less. With Ruth, Frances thought, in that same easy chair by the fire, the Prince could pour his heart out, take succour, or touch faith by making confession for all his misdemeanours in the great world outside this nursery – which was her drawing room. Here, for an evening, the naughty child became the good child, taking his milk and biscuits without tears before bedtime.

Ruth's part in the Prince's life was obvious – as clear as lines written for two protagonists in a drama. And Ruth knew both parts by heart, just as she knew the briefer and less happy roles which lay in store for subsidiary characters, other women who could only achieve mere walk-on roles in the play, to be unceremoniously dumped after the first act. Ruth had cast Frances in just such a part. But Frances was determined on something better.

'Of course,' Frances said, 'I take your point. I understand you perfectly,' she added meekly. But she smiled at her then, the complicit smile of someone who had understood everything that Ruth had *not* said, who had read between the lines of her words and sensed a starring role there. If Ruth was nanny to the Prince, Frances's smile said, and other women mere playthings, then she might offer him something else, neither mutton stew nor caviar, but a dish more to his taste than either.

A chilly pall descended on the room now, the cold of charity. Frances left politely, closing the door behind her, shutting the chill out, leaving the odour of dead cigars, quickening her step along the warm corridor, moving into life once more, mimicking the Prince's energetic progress through the ward, trailing, pursuing, sniffing at the hems of power – certain, though nothing had yet happened to warrant it, that she was moving towards a happy destiny.

She wondered at this confidence, since all her certainties in love were gone. Why did she feel so sure? Perhaps because she felt intuitively that, in this instance, she would not have to put herself at risk or wear her heart upon her sleeve. She felt certain of that from the way the Prince had looked at her – a look that every woman understands.

She had not long to wait for confirmation of her feelings. An anonymous messenger, dressed like a clerk, arrived two days later at Wilton Place: a plain envelope, with a card inside, die-stamped The Marlborough Club, Pall Mall, S.W. 'Dear Miss Cordiner, I much enjoyed our meeting. Would you do me the honour of dining with some friends and myself this Friday coming at nine, 55 Eaton Square? I would send a carriage for you at a quarter to – and can, I hope, look forward to your company. Edward, Wales.'

She saw at once something not only informal but clandestine in the invitation. She was being asked unchaperoned to some anonymous house. An assumption about her morals had already been made by the Prince – a risqué assumption. Yet the Prince, in so clearly and permanently identifying himself in the invitation, had put himself equally at risk. He trusted her. And she was charmed by it all – it was just as she would have had it. The joint risks implied in the note confirmed a fellow feeling – they were conspirators together. And conspiracy demanded secrecy. So she told Mortimer and Dermot that an invitation had come from Miss Wechsberg, for that Friday evening, that they were to dine in town together, with friends. To Eileen she decided to tell the same thing, though she hated any deception with her, when for so long they had been deceivers together. But such was the sympathy between them that Eileen came to suspect something quite out of the usual was at hand.

She had prepared Frances's one good evening costume – the midnight blue silk dress, ruched in narrow green panels, smoothing it down on the hanger before taking a hot iron from the grate to secure the folds. 'Just a dinner party?' she asked. 'But a *special* one?'

'Not really. Just some friends of Miss Wechsberg's.' As she lied she suddenly hated the lie. She felt no need to boast. But she saw the deceit not only as a disloyalty towards Eileen, but the beginning of a whole future of lies, to everyone, a programme which ran entirely against the grain of her nature – she who had made truth one of her hallmarks. She saw, too, how this deception, if she had to maintain it with everyone, would isolate her, would somehow condemn her in advance as a mere plaything of the Prince's. So, for her own peace of mind, there had to be one other who shared the secret – a life raft if the boat sank, a confidante with whom, from the beginning, she would have kept faith if all were lost.

'Just friends of Sister Ruth's?' Eileen asked, ironing the dress now. 'But not all nurses – men as well?'

Frances, in her petticoats, looked into the mirror, wondering about her hair. It had grown out again now, and she would leave it so, unfashionably tossed. 'No, men as well,' she said. 'A man, at least – a friend of Sister Ruth's. The Prince of Wales has asked me to dinner.'

Eileen went on ironing for a moment, then stopped. 'The Prince of who?'

'Wales.'

'You don't mean . . . that old bearded fellow? You're pulling me leg.'

'I *do* mean that old bearded fellow.'

'You're joking – he's old enough to be your father.'

'My grandfather even. But why not?'

'He's married – he's going to be King. You couldn't be . . .'

'What?'

'Going out with him.'

'Well, I *am*. And that's why you mustn't speak a word of it, not to *anybody*, promise?'

Eileen, astonished, picked the iron off the silk before it singed. 'I promise. Oh, Miss Frances – what a lark! Like a fairy tale!'

Frances turned and looked at Eileen with surprise. This was a point which had not crossed her mind at all.

*

She had already decided exactly the advantages she sought from her meeting with the Prince: power – the power she would derive, if she found favour there, from an alliance with this most powerful figure. It was as simple as that. Any other benefits would be entirely subsidiary. But it was not the power of money or gifts, no material thing she sought – least of all was it a fairy tale she wished to be part of. She looked, simply, for the support of such a name in her campaign for a house in another country.

Besides the Prince, there were two other couples and a further man in the light-panelled drawing room in Eaton Square when she was shown in. The Prince advanced energetically, making introductions.

'Miss Jenni Stonor; Sir Seymour Fortescue; Miss Isabelle Marshall-Hall; Major Clarke . . . And, last but not least, Major Augustus Lumley, my mother's Master of Ceremonies – so that I may say you are in entirely appropriate hands, Miss Cordiner!'

Frances barely noticed their features as she was introduced but understood at once that none of the men present was here with his own wife. The two young women were something of her own age, others in the Prince's virgin band no doubt. Miss Stonor was dark and pretty with a hint of plumpness; Miss Marshall-Hall, refined and delicate, was excruciatingly thin, with a wasp waist exaggerated to the point of deformity. Both were superbly dressed and coiffed, leaving Frances feeling frumpish. Yet she did not worry for long, for it was soon clear that her own particular wild dark beauty had made a strong impression all round.

The mood of the party was informal, without being in any way louche – the guests unconstrained in their movements and chatter, no hint of stuffy formality, nor yet of licence. For a moment, though, the Prince engaged elsewhere, Frances had no one to speak to, gazing instead at an equestrian picture above the mantel-piece. But the Prince turned then and, seeing her interest, spoke to her with sudden enthusiasm.

'You like it? I thought you might. You are from Ireland, of course. You will appreciate such things. One of mine. From Marlborough House. Stubbs. "The Jockey on Turf". First-rate man – only painter I can abide. First-rate, don't you think? Look here –' He approached the painting, pointing at the exactly-rendered faces, the minute features of the jockey and groom lost against a large landscape of hills and puffy clouds. 'Actual people – *real* people, you understand, not just in-vented. That is what I so admire – see the scowls on their faces!'

'It is a fine picture,' Frances said simply, for it was. It reminded her of Summer Hill. And suddenly she felt the wound of homesickness, a great emptiness, a misery with London. 'There!' she said before she could stop herself, pointing to the beeches in the picture, eyes alight. 'That beech wood, we have one just like it, on Cooper's hill at home – I used to love it – a secret grove with the wind in the trees!'

'Good! Very good!' he exclaimed. 'I see I have an ally here. I have yet to persuade some of my friends – of the excellence of this man Stubbs. But come, we are not at the Royal Academy – I'm pleased to say. Let me offer you some re-fresh-ment.'

The Prince, wonderfully genial and at ease now as a result of this fortuitous coming together over the picture, led her towards a sideboard where he poured them both glasses of dry champagne. 'You must tell me about yourself,' he said. 'My dear friend Ruth has told me a little. But . . .' He paused, the hooded eyes narrowing in a smile. 'It was very little. She was not actively disposed that we should meet.'

'No.'

'She does not trust me – entirely. But one must be one's own man, do you not think?'

'Indeed. And I am most honoured by your invitation.'

'You did not tell her of it then?'

'No.'

'You would have been quite free to do so. She is a dear friend.'

'And to me – which is why I would not wish to upset her.'

'Exactly.' The Prince nodded his wholehearted agreement and Frances, taking encouragement from this, found more of her voice.

'Nor did I tell my cousins, with whom I am staying.'

'Indeed?' The Prince was surprised at this instance of discretion. 'You have reached your ma-jority, I understand. You may dine with whom you choose.'

'Hardly, Sir.'

'In private, I mean.'

'That, surely, would be the ultimate breach of convention, Sir.'

The Prince suddenly took the point. 'I see, I see. Quite so.'

Could he really have been unaware of these social conventions, Frances wondered. He could not. Was he then simply being forgetful, flustered? There was certainly no irony in his voice. He was preoccupied, Frances decided – a preoccupation, it seemed, with her, for he had barely ceased to gaze at her since her entry.

'I told my maid,' Frances said uppishly. 'That was all.'

The Prince smiled hugely. 'You trust her?'

'More than anyone. We trust each other completely.'

This particular confidence appealed to the Prince. 'Good – how very good! I wish I were such a hero to my valet. But come. We talk too much of meeting, when we are well met already, are we not?'

Frances paused for several seconds, then gave him the slightest nod of her head. He offered her his arm in return. 'Let us to dinner, then. Miss Rosa Lewis from the Cavendish Hotel has prepared something simple.'

Dinner was served in a comfortable, though not opulent dining room, the men's white shirts gleaming in the candlelight, white carnations or gardenias in their buttonholes, Miss Marshall-Hall with orchids in her corsage. Frances sat at the Prince's right hand. The food was not at all simple. It was elaborate and extensive beyond anything Frances had ever experienced. Baked truffles in warm napkins were served first, followed by silver salvers of oysters on ice, which the Prince swallowed at a rush, between mouthfuls of brown bread and butter – like a famished chop house diner, in a manner that astonished Frances who had never seen oysters so dispatched, at such speed or in so cavalier a manner. There was caviare then, with plover's eggs and ortolans in aspic, followed by sole poached in chablis, garnished with prawns. Boned snipe came next, stuffed with a forcemeat of truffles in a madeira sauce; then quail packed with foie gras, followed by the only simple dish of the meal – individual crowns of lamb served with redcurrant jelly, accompanied by cauliflower and celery. Finally came a rum-flavoured chocolate mousse and a raspberry ice cream laced with kirsch. Apart from a Château Lafite with the snipe and the lamb they drank champagne throughout the meal, Duminy *Extra Sec.*

The Prince's appetite and attack remained undiminished to the end of the dinner. Indeed such was his interest in the food that, apart from the short intervals between courses, he barely spoke to Frances. It was clear, in fact, that he wished for no real interruption in his *dégustation*, appearing quite happy to listen to the others round the table, who fed him anecdotes and gossip as he fed himself.

It was clear, too, even when they all adjourned to the drawing room (there was to be no post-prandial division of the sexes, Frances was pleased to realise), that the Prince was no great conversationalist. He preferred the role of benevolent listener and his interjections were mainly in the form of repeated questions – 'Who was it?' and 'Why?' and 'How come?' He lit a vast and pungent Corona y Corona and took his coffee with a chasse-café of cognac, as the other men did, for no other spirits or port were served. Stories were swapped, sporting or military anecdotes, and as if on cue the Prince was tempted to embark on some of his own jokes, well-worn ones apparently, which were received none the less with appropriate silence, then uproarious, if slightly forced, laughter. One story, concerning the Shah of Persia's visit to Buckingham Palace, in which the savage infidel had mistaken the lavatory bowl for a wash basin, went on forever.

He was an indifferent raconteur, Frances thought – ponderous in emphasis, lost in his introductory scene-setting, repetitive, quite without the light touch required in such jovial banter. His friends indulged him carefully. Were he not Prince of Wales, Frances thought, he would have been dismissed as a crashing bore in any company.

She found it all quite unexpectedly pathetic – this Prince wallowing among his toadies – she who, from Irish dinner parties, was used to such real wit and unafraid debate among guests with the sharpest minds. The Prince's mental equipment and agility, by comparison, seemed those of a dullard; his jokes were like lead, his table manners and gargantuan appetite bizarre – a man like a great sleepy bear, who only really seemed to come alive over his food. Being honest, she could only describe the Prince as a vulgarian.

And yet, when he looked at her, raised those sharply-arched eyebrows above the hooded, blue-grey orbs, she saw quite a different man in that kindly gaze – someone almost shy, meek, lost: the gaze of a confused child. This was the hidden quality which attracted her. There was something else in his heart, which explained his frustrated nervous energy – a sadness behind the façade of bonhomie. So that

Frances, sensing and sympathising with this other man she saw in him, thought she might respond to it, search out that real spirit and release it.

He fed himself so, she thought, to satisfy an immaterial hunger. He was a man of questions which had always been misunderstood. She would understand, and respond. 'Je Responderay'. Frog Prince – she would transform the beast – a touch, a kiss – which would return to him his true form.

'So,' he said, when they came to talk, sitting a little aside from the company, 'you wish to become a nurse?'

'I think so, Sir.'

'You are not sure?'

'I may not have the application, the patience.'

'Ruth speaks very highly . . .' He drew on his cigar, looking at her through rings of smoke.

'I am more concerned . . .' She started enthusiastically before letting her hand fall, turning away listlessly. Then, resuming control, she leant forward intently towards him, blinking rapidly. 'I have had problems at home in Ireland,' she said finally. 'Things I should like put right before I consider any other future.'

'Problems? Your mother, Lady Cordiner, is old Basil Halevy's daughter, is she not?' Frances nodded. 'I met him once or twice – and remember more of his reputation certainly: he was a sound and most successful man. So I take it the problem is not one of . . . subsistence?'

'No. No, indeed. Rather of temperament – between my mother and myself. We do not see eye to eye, to say the least. She is a woman of some authority – indeed overwhelmingly so. We – I particularly – find her shadow constricting.'

The Prince, listening attentively, seemed to catch an echo here of something he well understood. 'I see, I see – quite so. I have had some such similar problems in my own circle.' He smiled diffidently.

'But Mama and I have *quite* fallen out. In fact, I have been forbidden the house, our house at Summer Hill.' She laughed at this, as though it had been a minor deprivation, the result of a mere whim of her mother's. But then she changed tack, becoming serious once more. 'And since I love the place dearly – there is the problem.'

Without dwelling on any one incident, nor yet treating the case too lightly, she explained matters further – her break with her fiancé, the death of her elder brother – adding detail to the row with her mother, how she had broken the mourning and rung the bells throughout the house – finally returning to her 'banishment' as she put it, a light reference to it again, the rash dictate of an unhappy woman.

The Prince absorbed her story with increasing interest and sympathy, with few interjections. Yet when she finished Frances was rather disappointed that he simply said, 'I see, I see indeed. Quite so.' He paused for some time, stroking his greying beard, pouting his lower lip, licking it pensively. Then, as if making up his mind about something and sure of her confidence, he spoke with a husky warmth. 'I am dis-tinctly inter-ested. Your history so resembles my own. I, too, was to have married someone much to my mother's taste, but not to mine – lost a father and a brother – and quite like you have suffered the whims and dictates of a dear good mother who, like your own, took to a life of mourning, without respite or con-sid-er ation that others, at least, must go on living.' He nodded his head several times, putting down his cigar, smiling slowly. 'I wish only that I might have had the courage to ring all the bells at Windsor! I have had to be satisfied . . . with less public manifestations of myself!' He glanced round the little drawing room.

'Indeed, Sir.' Frances smiled at him in return. But she said no more.

'I have wished, too,' the Prince continued, warming to his theme, 'always for some rapprochement with my mother – in our differences. Apart from my feelings there, it is so obviously my duty, as it must be yours. I quite see that. In what way, if I may ask, do you intend proceeding to that end?'

'I have written to my parents, some six weeks ago, offering apologies for my behaviour. But they have not replied.'

'Indeed. That is dis-con-certing. I believe though, if I may offer you my own experience in these matters, that you must come face to face with them, with your mother.' He smiled again, with irony now. 'I have found that the actual *appearance* – though it may not be wished – of the penitent prodigal, has much to recommend it! A *mauvais quart d'heure* perhaps. But there is no better way to be forgiven, with a loved one, than that they *see* how one has relented. Letters are a poor substitute.'

'Indeed. One can so dissemble there.'

'But you have not done that?'

'No, I have offered my heartfelt apologies. They have gone entirely unregarded. So that I fear there may now be no reconciliation.'

'My dear,' he said rousing himself now, speaking with brio, 'I have thought just the same myself in the past in my own case – that there could be no real coming together. And I have proved it otherwise. Perhaps, if you will allow me, I may help you in the matter.'

'Sir, it is unnecessary. You are called by so many much more important things –'

'Miss Cordiner,' he smiled a little sadly, reaching out and touching her hand briefly, 'I have been called, for so many years now, on only the *least* important things, I may assure you! What more important than that you should find your home again? You would do me honour.'

'Well, Lumley, what do you say? What do you think of her?' the Prince asked later, speaking to the former Household Cavalry Major, the Queen's Master of Ceremonies, whose task at Court was to decide who was socially acceptable and who was not, and who did the same for the Prince less formally – a man thus much feared in every fashionable circle, who could make or break a person's social ambitions with a turn of his head. More commonly, as a code between the Prince and himself, the words 'Rose' or 'Cabbage' were designated as indicators of acceptability.

Lumley, a small silver-haired man, stiffly military but with clever, darting eyes, stroked his formidable moustaches. 'A rose, I should say, Sir.'

'Good – good.'

'Though I wonder if not . . . too wild a rose.'

'I saw nothing of that – a *most* tactful young woman.' The Prince gave, as an example, her discretion over his invitation.

'But it is there in the eyes, Sir. And you will know how she is Irish –'

'Only half so – old Basil Halevy's granddaughter: she is half-Jewish.'

'Worse still – a most *provocative* mix, if I may say so, Sir. By all accounts there is a headstrongness there. I am reminded of Charles Beresford, all that trouble –'

'She has nothing to do with that intemperate Waterford clan.'

'None the less, there is a distinct air of having her own way.'

'A taking from her mother perhaps, but diluted. She has much grace.'

Lumley pursed his lips judiciously. 'More, she has astonishing beauty . . .' He paused, doubting something now.

'Yes?'

'But she has an equal sharpness of mind. I have rarely encountered so great a mix of beauty and brains.'

'You fear that?'

'I am certainly forewarned by such – if you wish to have your way there.'

The Prince considered this idea. 'I had not intended that, in the manner you suppose,' he said stiffly.

'I am anxious, too,' Lumley went on tactfully, 'that with such intelligence she may be put to schemes. A woman of such mental equipment, not yet married, tends to scheme in some other way. I would fear that.'

'She and her fiancé – Lord Norton's son – they broke their engagement. There is nothing untoward there.'

'I am not surprised. The son is much the pale shadow – no match for her.'

'Besides, she asked for nothing – no hint. It was I who offered her my support.'

Major Lumley became agitated at this news. 'Of what kind, if I may ask, Sir?'

'I offered help – mediation – in effecting a rapprochement between her and Lady Cordiner, her mother. They have fallen out badly.'

'I see. You do not then propose any . . . any informal liaison, which I understood was your thought in inviting her here this evening?'

'No. Not necessarily. Certainly not. I should like to give her my public support.'

'Without her having a chaperone – and I understood Miss Wechsberg has refused that role – how would you intend proceeding in such an open course?'

'She shall have a suitable chaperone, Lumley. We – you – shall see to it. You will arrange that.'

Lumley was much put out. 'But who, Sir? Had you someone in mind? It is not so easy, to simply pick the girl a duenna – out of a hat, so to speak.'

'Not out of a *hat*, Lumley. You will consider the matter most carefully.' The Prince prepared to leave.

'There is one other matter, Sir, in any future you contemplate here. Her cousin,

Mortimer Cordiner, with whom she presently resides, is a most vociferous Home Rule M.P. in the House. It would be as well to bear that in mind. Your support for Miss Cordiner should not be misinterpreted as any support for his policies.'

'Why should it be? Distant cousins merely. And you assured me that, in Ireland, her own immediate family were impeccable, socially and in their politics.'

'Indeed, Sir. It is just that, again, I suspect schemes.'

'*Schemes*, Lumley?' The Prince raised his voice. 'That she has a mind of her own must imply schemes?' he bellowed.

'I have found it so, Sir.'

'Fiddlesticks, Lumley. She is a breath of fresh air in that respect. Her only scheme is to make amends at home. She has suffered much loss. She is in distress. I cannot turn my back on her.'

The Prince turned his back on Lumley instead. As he left, Lumley marvelled once again at the Prince's eager self-deception, his foolhardiness. He could never refuse the role of knight errant in a manoeuvre which, Lumley thought, had a distinctly less honourable end in view. He was besotted with the girl. She would already be well aware of this. Therefore she would have schemes. Lumley had seen it all before – particularly in the case of another Frances, the Prince's Darling Daisy, now the Countess of Warwick – an affair between them that had started in just the same manner, the Prince taking her side as a damsel in distress in the matter of her affair with Lord Charles Beresford. That had been a fracas with a distinctly Irish side to it, resulting in no end of upset, every kind of social awkwardness and upheaval. And Lumley, to his intense embarrassment, had been much involved, in a business that had reflected badly on everyone, himself included. So he looked now with horror on the Prince's demand that he act as go-between – worse, as a sort of maiden aunt – in procuring a chaperone for this girl. He was sure that in so doing he would be aiding and abetting another act of sheer folly on the Prince's part.

Returning home that evening Frances rightly thought that things could not have gone better. She had first of all avoided any indelicate end to the evening – which she was aware, given the circumstances of meeting in this anonymous house in Eaton Square, might have been among the Prince's intentions. Further, she had not openly advanced her plans in any way; the Prince had done all that for her. Only one thing gave her pause for doubt – she liked the man, liked him quite aside from her schemes, quite beyond any idea of flirtation with him. It was a deeper thing. There was a hidden store of real sympathy, affection, a great kindness in the Prince, which worldly appetites and demands had overlaid, she felt. She had glimpsed this from the beginning and he had truly confirmed it now, offering her a sight of this other man, a vision of himself not as Prince but as fallible human, much aware of common hurt, broken familial bonds, all domestic heartbreak, which he had experienced himself, with a grief-maddened, autocratic mother like her own, so that, once he had become aware that they shared these experiences, he had dropped any idea of her as plaything, she thought, and taken to her almost as an equal – two people who understood the pain of family exile.

Eileen had waited up for her. 'Well? Tell us – tell us, do!' She could not restrain the pitch of excitement in her voice.

'Not so loud, Eileen.' Eileen helped her off with her dress.

'Did you, did he – did you *meet* him even?'

'Yes. Yes, he was most kind.'

'*Kind?* Was that all? Wasn't there dancing and things?'

'No – nor midnight chimes, a silver slipper or a pumpkin coach!' Frances turned and smiled at Eileen's disappointment.

'Oh dear . . .'

'It was all much better than that, Eileen. It was *real*.'

'I don't follow? Wasn't there music and . . . and laughing and all *that?*'

'No. We just talked, he and I.'

'But, Miss, you could talk *any* time. But, with a Prince, surely don't you do *other* things?'

'No. The talk was everything.'

'Sure, you'd do better at a crossroads *celidhe* beyant Cloone. It must have been a dull evening. Was there *nothing* else?' she asked desperately.

Frances ruffled her curls, thinking. She was sad now for a moment. 'There was everything else. But we haven't come to it yet.'

Eileen shook her head in bewilderment. 'You're a quare one and no mistake.'

The following morning Frances left earlier than usual for Grosvenor Crescent, in order to avoid facing Dermot or Mortimer with any account of her dinner party. She needed more time to think about her response there.

The Prince had, of course, asked that they meet again – but in a general way, without specifying a place or time, or in what manner she was to appear with him, formally or informally again. She had tactfully alluded to these imprecisions, the general difficulties inherent in both their positions over any future meeting. But the Prince, very much the Sir Galahad, had assured her that matters would be arranged in an entirely appropriate form, that he would be in touch with her. Her impatience lay only in that soon, with Christmas only three weeks away, she would have to leave for Ireland. Mortimer and Dermot were due to sail for Dublin in two weeks' time: she and Eileen would naturally expect to travel with them, if they were going.

But she had told the Prince of these plans, in an offhand way, shuddering briefly at the prospect of a worse than chilly reception at Summer Hill. This unfeigned shudder, these heartfelt words, had rallied the Prince to an increased sympathy and identification with her cause. The joust was in train; his standard, he clearly implied, was at her disposal; she had but to attach her colours to his lance – which she did, on leaving, by shaking his hand and holding it thereafter for considerably longer than convention required, just as he had done with her on their first encounter. He would propose another meeting soon after Christmas no doubt, she thought. Meanwhile she would simply have to wait.

Augustus Lumley reported to the Prince several days later – meeting in his over-furnished, darkly-cluttered study at Marlborough House. The Prince, his long-haired fox terrier Caesar on a tiger skin by the fire, was seated at his small desk, a desk overcome with a confusion of papers and knick-knacks – among which silver-framed photographs of his wife, Princess Alexandra, and his children were the only things clearly to be displayed.

As Lumley entered, the dog Caesar growled, took to his feet and thence, in furious yapping bounds, to Lumley's feet, worrying at his boots and trouser turn-ups, getting his teeth into the cloth, so that Lumley was forced to kick out, swinging the dog round briefly in the air like a conker on a string before the snarling animal released its grip and started instead to bark furiously, head lowered, certain that this rabbit, without further close encounter, could be worried to death.

The Prince, much amused, did nothing to restrain the dog. 'Sir,' Lumley cried. 'Ask the beast to heel!' It was not the first time he, or others in the Prince's retinue, had been so attacked. Though Lumley believed that, in his own case, the Prince was always particularly lax in restraining the brute.

'Caesar!' the Prince eventually bellowed. 'Caesar – come here. You naughty, *naughty* dog.' The dog returned to his master, tail wagging, entirely undismayed, as the Prince himself appeared to be. He was that morning in any case in a particularly genial mood – and the dog's antics had merely sharpened his pleasure. The Prince had been doing what he liked best – surveying and pondering an immense list of intended Christmas presents, to his family, courtiers, staff and friends, both at Marlborough House and at Sandringham, a list which his private secretary had prepared and left with him earlier that day. Now, with Lumley's arrival and Caesar's performance making a very suitable entr'acte to his morning, he dropped these enjoyable considerations and looked at the Master of Ceremonies with a beady eye.

'Well, Lumley, what have you come up with?'

'Sir, in the matter of your Boxing Day shoot at Sandringham, I have to report that Sir Archibald MacIntosh, much the cabbage in any case, is also a most unreliable shot.'

The Prince let him finish, drumming his fingers the while with increasing tempo on the desk. '*Yes*, Lumley.' He spoke with heavy emphasis. 'We shall take due precautions. But I spoke of the *other* matter – of Miss Cordiner.'

Lumley bit his lip. 'Sir, I cannot report any real success there. Lady Filmer, who seemed a possibility, is not the age she was. Nor the Dowager Duchess of Manchester, another possibility. Miss de Vere Trumpington, a distinct possibility, has taken to her bed following a contretemps with her horse – a parting of the ways over a ditch with the Quorn. Then I had thought of the Countess of Berwick –'

'I know you have *thought*, Lumley – it is not beyond you. But who have you come *up* with?'

Lumley, exasperated now, came up with the truth. 'Sir, I must be honest: I have it on the best authority that there is *no* one suitable for such a commission. The matter is altogether too delicate – fraught with difficulty and risk – for anyone in your circle or at court to put themselves in jeopardy over it. Miss Cordiner, for them, is a quite unknown quantity. And it is this factor, as I have said to you myself, that entirely restrains them – as, if I may say so, it should equally restrain your Royal Highness.'

The Prince sighed, stood up, lit a cigar by the fireplace, looked at Landseer's dreamy oval portrait of his mother, with himself and the Princess Royal as children, over the mantelpiece. Then, after a long and ominous pause, he rounded on Lumley – not losing his temper, as Lumley had half-expected, but worse in that he spoke to him slowly, with heavy sarcasm, pitying condescension, spacing his syllables and rolling his r's more than was his custom. 'The Queen's Master of Ceremonies,' he said, 'who can-not ar-r-ange a social matter entirely right and proper and above board; that a young woman most em-inently bred, of grace and in-tell-ectual distinction, the daughter of one of my Irish earls –'

'Her father is a mere baronet, Sir –'

'Don't *in-ter-rupt*, Lumley! – Such a long-established baronetcy outruns most earldoms, as far as I am concerned – a Master of Ceremonies who cannot arrange ac-cess of such a person to Court – Lumley, you are failing at your job. Do you hear? Do you?' The Prince's voice, like an approaching avalanche, had become louder, more threatening as he spoke, so that Lumley knew that he must forestall him somehow if he was not now to be engulfed in a whirlwind of rage.

'Sir,' he put in, an idea striking him, coming to his rescue at the last moment. 'If I might make so bold –'

'Dispense with the preambles, Lumley: pray *make* bold.'

'I take your point, Sir. And mine is this: if it is all to be so much above board with Miss Cordiner, and she is in such palpable need of familial support, I wonder if you might not, with the best advantage, welcome her as a guest in your *own* home at Sandringham for Christmas – where you and Her Royal Highness might, with all due propriety, act *in loco parentis* as it were to the poor girl. In this manner no chaperone would be required: Her Royal Highness would naturally fill that role. And I am sure,' he added unctuously, 'that you could well persuade the Princess of this, given her boundless sympathies – and of course the pitiable circumstances of the young woman.'

Lumley waited anxiously for a response as the Prince walked to and fro between the velveteen sofa and the fireplace. Finally the Prince spoke. 'Capital, Lumley, capital. I shall speak to Alix this very morning. I wonder I didn't think of the idea myself. I am obliged to you. Oh, and I think in that other matter of Sir Archibald MacIntosh – we may dispense with his company altogether on the Boxing Day shoot. I have no wish to suffer the random inattentions of a Glasgow grocer in the line. Besides, I shall have so many more attractive guests to attend to over the season.' He smiled broadly. Lumley reciprocated with a small courtly bow. 'As your Royal Highness *desires*,' he said, moving backwards, before the Prince turned on him once more.

'And, Lumley, a little less of this Royal Highnessing, if you please. You and I have no need to stand on *such* cer-emony, in private at least. We are old friends, are we not? – been through many a little scrap together.' The Prince drew on his cigar, appraised Lumley in a knowing fashion – with a slow smile, perhaps even the hint of a wink.

'Indeed, Sir – quite so, quite so.'

'See him out then, Caesar! See him out!' The Prince nudged the sleeping fox terrier on the tiger skin. Dreaming of other quarry, the dog, waking with a start, followed his master's directions, running full tilt for Lumley's trousers again as the man turned to make a hasty exit.

Lumley heard the Prince's roars of laughter as he passed down the corridor. He was pleased with the way things had gone, but still anxious. His desperate suggestion, given the renowned good nature and impulsive kindness of the Princess, was quite likely to be accepted by her. But if, subsequently, matters degenerated in the relationship between the Prince and Miss Cordiner – and he expected they would – the Prince would be the first to remember that it was he, Lumley, who had first suggested the idea. He, and not Miss Cordiner, would then be accused of scheming.

That afternoon, having spoken to his wife, the Prince returned to his study. At his desk he took the stopper from one of several tubes set in a frame, blew into the orifice vigorously, waiting an instant before shouting down it. 'Fortescue, I have some im-portant e-men-dations to your list of Christmas guests at San-dringham: delete MacIntosh – insert Miss Frances Cordiner. Have an invitation made out straightaway and sent round to her address – 17 Wilton Place. Yes. What? No, she is not to be ac-companied by anyone. She is to be the guest of the Princess and myself: a *family* guest. Good, Fortescue – and I shall be obliged if you will see to it *at once*.'

He returned the stopper, leant back and surveyed the many photographs in front of him, finally picking up the largest of the silver frames, an early court photograph of Alix taken just after their marriage – wide-eyed, girlish, coolly beautiful. 'Yes, indeed,' he murmured to himself. 'You – above all . . .'

He set the photograph down rather sadly before reaching for some notepaper, beginning a short letter which would accompany the formal invitation to Frances. 'Dear Miss Cordiner,' he began. 'It would give the Princess and myself much pleasure . . .' He paused. Would it? Yes, but not of the sort which perhaps he had originally in mind. There was a quite different essence in this girl – not just something to play with, to touch, fondle, make love to, but something more interesting, more exciting even.

Frances brought out a tenderness in him, a compassion that he had only felt before for Alix, his wife. It was uncanny, since the two women were not alike in any way – one classic, regal, considered, statuesque; the other a mix of sharp child and wild gypsy. But the emotions that Frances drew from him were just those that Alix had once inspired. Her loss of home drew his sympathy more than anything. He himself as a child and young man – shunted endlessly between Windsor, Buckingham Palace, Osborne and Balmoral – knew this feeling of homelessness all too well. Frances, by her account and his own intuition, had suffered in much the same way. Thinking thus, with some rage now, of his own suppressed youth, he was determined to give Frances's life back to her before it was too late – offer her, in the first instance, the sanctuary of his own home. He remembered her face, of course, as well – that lovely astonished look when they had first met. All in all the whole thing struck him as a most worthy – and appealing – crusade.

Caesar slept on the tiger skin. The light outside died over Pall Mall. The red coals in the fire, unattended for nearly an hour, turned to ash. The Prince left his desk and stretched himself out on the velveteen sofa. For the first time in years he felt a distinct lack of appetite, of nervous energy – no need to ring for the footman, to see to the fire, to order a lobster tea, or send for Fortescue about the Christmas guest and present lists, or make last-minute rearrangements over his plans for that evening. For the first time in years, thinking of Frances – content with mere *thoughts*, he reminded himself with astonishment – he was no longer bored. He dozed off then, his breath slowing, becoming one with Caesar's, the sleep of the just.

The atmosphere next morning at Wilton Place on the other hand, after the Prince's invitation had arrived in the first post, was electrifying. Frances could no longer dissemble. She met Dermot at breakfast, handing him the Prince's letter and invitation without comment. Dermot glanced at them, read carefully, then threw both aside.

'One of your pranks, Frances. Or someone else's prank. Dear Humphrey Saunders at work again, no doubt.'

'No. It's true. I met the Prince at Ruth's on Monday evening last week. They're great friends. And it was he who asked me to dinner last Friday, not Ruth. I lied – I'm sorry. I wasn't sure of things then.'

Dermot considered the matter. Then he said, 'It's hardly credible.'

'No. But it is.'

Dermot looked at the invitation again, then held the letter up to the light. 'It has the watermarked arms – the ostrich feathers and "Ich Dien". "I serve" – but how will it serve you, Frances?'

'I want to change my life, do I not?'

'Nobody ever really does.'

'This might.'

'For the worse.'

'Why? Don't tell me – I know: his reputation with women is not altogether savoury . . .'

'To put it mildly –'

'But –'

'But how *could* you, Frances? – accept such an invitation on your own, un-chaperoned. It's simply not done –'

'It *is* done. I've done it myself already, and nothing untoward happened. Besides I've been asked by the Princess, his wife, as well – to their *home*, Dermot, not to some lewd house of assignation. So of course I shall accept.'

Dermot looked at her, a touch of envy, sadness in his expression. He was losing her. So that Frances, seeing his feelings, jumped up impulsively, rounded the table and shook him by the shoulders, taking his hand.

'Dermot, it's not a sad thing! I wouldn't do it if it were. It – it will bring me home one day, don't you see? Won't take me away, from you and Mortimer and all the family. It will bring me *back* to you all. In Ireland.'

'So that's the plan, is it?' He looked at her calmly. 'It's really Summer Hill again, behind it all.'

'Yes. The Prince offered to help me make things up at home. That's the whole point. To be friends again with Mama – what you said I should do. Well, don't you see? – Mama would just *love* the Prince . . .'

'Yes, I do see. But what will you have to give in return?'

'Oh, Dermot, it's not like that!'

'I should be very surprised if it weren't – in the end.'

'You'll *be* surprised then – because it won't!'

An hour later Frances had a rather similar conversation with Ruth Wechsberg – though much more chilly in form for most of its duration. But towards the end Ruth seemed to relent, becoming less severe in her strictures. Indeed, she was almost apologetic.

'I'm sorry,' she said, 'I have not been entirely open with you either. I, too, have received a communication from the Prince this morning.' She moved to her little Sheraton bureau, picking up an envelope there. 'A letter in which he explains his and the Princess of Wales's position in your regard. And I must say it corresponds almost exactly with your own account of the matter. He also . . .' She paused, waving the notepaper in her hand, fanning herself with it excitedly. 'He has also offered – has *asked* indeed, that he become patron of the nursing home here, and has enclosed a cheque for one thousand pounds with a promise that he will enlist further financial support from his friends in the same cause.'

Holding the letter and cheque, she turned to Frances. 'I've not told you, nor anyone else either – but without this unexpected donation we should have had to close the nursing home here in the New Year.' She smiled then. 'I believe I may have you to thank for this as much as anyone.' She walked over to Frances then, taking her hand. 'Dear Frances, all I hope is that you . . . will be careful. A life like yours is very precious. The Prince may appreciate this now. But he is a child at heart – of whims and toys.'

The implication was obvious. Frances would, in the end, be a mere caprice of the Prince's. But then, Frances thought, the banker's draft from Coutts for £1,000 which Ruth held in her hand was no doubt a product of the same childish fancy. Whims were not necessarily unproductive.

7

R UTH, AS THANKS for Frances's part in saving the nursing home, made her a gift of £50 for Christmas. 'Besides, you will need some new dresses and costumes at Sandringham – indoors and out. Gloves, scarves and hats. Boots, shoes and slippers! Why not?'

'No, you are too –'

Ruth had looked at her severely, the governess in her eyes again. 'If a thing is worth doing, then it *must* be done properly.' And Frances, overcome by this generosity and by Ruth's stringent stipulation, had been frightened suddenly, realising for the first time all the many implications and pitfalls of this visit. Now she was really broaching an unknown world among Royalty, the cream of the land no doubt. She could not play the flirtatious *ingénue* now, the wild Irish girl or the pretty nurse. She would have to draw on other, more subtle, strengths. There were serious social responsibilities ahead of her, and Ruth must have sensed the fears she had about this.

'It shall be done properly,' she went on in a softer voice, 'because you must have every confidence in yourself. And you must not therefore, for any reason, find yourself at a disadvantage with the Prince and his company. Or, put another way, you must not allow *him* to take advantage of *you*. That, as you know, has been my fear. He should not for a moment be allowed to think of you as being in the "poor relation" department for example – or be given any excuse for indulging an unreal or exaggerated sympathy for you. In character you are more than his equal – and you must dress accordingly!'

With which Frances, much heartened, had gone out to Woolland's and Harrods in Knightsbridge and purchased a new wardrobe: a long white organdie evening dress, with tartan lines over silk, black plastrons on the front, black kilting, piping and cuffs; another dress in red velvet with turned-back white lace, with an under-dress in ruched green silk; a third in maroon voile with a white collar and cuffs and a pleated satin front. For outdoors she already had her Russian hat with the ankle-length, sable-trimmed coat, its rows of Hussar buttons down the front. She supplemented this now with a blue dress in light serge with a mauve waistband, rosettes and a Zouave jacket – and another in brown cloth, a long jacket in brown corduroy velvet with mussel-shell buttons and a velvet hat trimmed with ostrich feathers, together with several pale tea-gowns, assorted silk blouses, gloves, shoes, slippers and a new pair of black lace-up bootees.

When the purchases were delivered she brought them up to her bedroom, with Eileen taking the costumes out from their tissue-papered boxes.

'Oh my,' Eileen said with excitement, holding up the white organdie and tartan ball gown. 'You're going to look a wonder in this, Miss Frances!'

'Am I?'

'Can't fail to!'

Frances saw the longing in the girl's eyes then. There were several other boxes, not yet opened, by the door. Frances went and picked the first of them up. 'And these are for you, Eileen, a Christmas present.'

'Oh, Miss, you needn't –'

'Of course I need. Go on – look at them, if they're all right!'

Eileen opened the first of the boxes, then the second. Inside were four plainer, though none the less smart and attractive, dresses together with various accessories. Eileen held one of the costumes up admiringly.

'I know your size,' Frances told her. 'So they should fit. But if you don't like the style or the colour we can go round and change them first thing tomorrow.'

'No, no – they're lovely. Lovely.'

'Take them with you to Ireland – and I have some small things for your parents.'

Eileen looked undecided, glancing over at Frances's new clothes laid out on the bed.

'What's the matter?'

'Just – I envy you.' Eileen picked up her dresses a little sadly, folding them, putting them back in their fine tissue paper nests.

'You mean?' Frances looked at her in surprise. The girl had a moist glaze in her eyes now. 'Oh, Eileen, you mean – you'd like to come with me?' Frances moved towards her, Eileen nodding her head dumbly, biting her lip. Frances suddenly embraced her – the two women murmuring together.

'Oh, I wish you would, Eileen – I feel so excited, but a little afraid –'

'I would – I really would *love* to come with you.'

'Well, you shall. I told you, wherever I go, you can come.'

Frances's emotion comprised as much guilt as it did joy, for she had bought Eileen's new outfits with the secret thought that, when she saw them, together with Frances's own exciting costumes, she would be tempted to forego her Christmas holiday in Ireland with her family and come with her to Sandringham.

Dermot and Mortimer, prior to taking the Irish Mail that evening from Euston, saw the two women off at King's Cross, in a private compartment on the train for Wolverton in Norfolk. The four of them stood on the platform for a few minutes, among the Christmas bustle, the women's trunks, bags and hat boxes surrounding them, before porters removed most of them to the guard's van. Frances wore her sable-trimmed coat and muff and her Russian hat against the cold. As the engines sighed and roared all round them, spumes of cotton-wool rising to the glass roof high above, Frances fidgeted; Eileen seemed much calmer.

'Well, au revoir,' Mortimer said, clapping his gloved hands, whiskers bristling, smiling kindly. 'The great adventure! What a family we are. I spend my life trying to release my country from the Imperial yoke – and here you are putting your neck right into the heart of it, with Dermot supporting you with his new field guns. What about you, Eileen – what do you feel about it?'

Eileen was flustered suddenly. 'Oh, Sir, I just like being with Miss Frances . . .'

'I really can't win, can I?' Mortimer reflected.

Frances was moved by his isolation from them all. 'Oh, you will, Mortimer,' she told him impulsively. 'You will win in the end – I know you will!' She didn't really know what she was saying at all, offering mere consolatory words to her cousin.

'Oh, yes, I know that, dear Frances – we all have to be free in the end. But will I be there to see it? Perhaps you might speed things up a little, put a good word in for us Home Rulers with the Prince!'

'Yes, of course.' She paused, then added ironically, 'If I ever have the chance.'

'You will, you will.' Dermot nodded his head sagely, as if he foresaw Frances's future in exact detail.

Dermot kissed her goodbye. 'It's extraordinary,' he told her. 'In three months you've lost one house – and gained another. But *what* a house!'

She looked at him sharply then. 'There's only one house for me, Dermot, you know that.'

'Yes,' he sighed. 'I was hoping you might be able to forget that now.'

A few hours later, met at Wolverton in a Royal carriage by a coachman and groom, they were driving through the vast wrought-iron gates of Sandringham, moving through a flat, sparsely-wooded parkland, towards an equally large, rather ugly, red-bricked, bow-windowed Victorian house, set on a slight rise in the distance, surrounded by scrubby trees. A piercing east wind rattled the carriage glass, sweeping across the desolate land from the North Sea. The two women looked straight ahead, dumbly, nervously. Frances thought desperately about what she might do or say on her arrival, what active measures she might take to promote the success of her visit – after all, since she suspected she might be here largely as part of some unrealised intention of the Prince's, she wondered what shape this might take.

At Sandringham it was the Prince's inordinate superstitiousness which, like the Stubbs painting in Eaton Square, formed another of these fortuitous links between them. The Prince, escorting Lady Filmer to her place at the first evening's dinner, noticed how two knives in her elaborate cutlery service were very nearly crossed.

His poise was quite shattered. A footman was summoned and reprimanded. Some fuss was made of it all, to the discomfiture and embarrassment of the other guests.

But later, speaking to the Prince in the big hall-saloon after dinner, Frances sympathised, even tactfully commended his behaviour. 'At home in Ireland,' she said, 'my father has regard for much the same omens.'

'Indeed, I am pleased to hear it. I am thought a great ninny in my superstitious feelings on the matter.'

'Not at all –'

'You feel the same?'

'I am Irish.'

'Thirteen at table and all that?'

'Most especially. Indeed at home in Summer Hill, not so long ago, as a surety of luck an empty place was always laid at dinner for the unexpected guest – some wandering storyteller or minstrel.'

'Excellent – capital! I wonder if I may institute the same procedure here. But I fear I should be worse mocked!'

The next morning, when she met the Prince in the oak-panelled hall after breakfast, he gave her, surreptitiously, a tiny ivory elephant attached by a short chain to a gold ring. 'One of my little mascots,' he told her. 'I was given it in India, in '75. I have rather a collection, over my bedstead. But keep it to yourself – my valet thinks me much the peasant in harbouring such charms.'

Though at first she refused, taken aback by the importance of the gift, she finally accepted it, putting the ring over her finger so that, when she closed her hand, the little elephant was then completely hidden in her palm.

'Exactly the way!' the Prince commended her. 'One mustn't expose one's luck – to every rough wind. And now, my dear, what have you to do today?'

Frances thought the Prince almost rashly attentive. It was not until some time later that she discovered he asked every apparently unoccupied guest the same question, so that the experienced visitor, set on doing nothing, must needs have an immediate plan or excuse to offer – a pressing trip to the library for a book or to the gun room to inspect the Prince's collection of firearms. But on that morning Frances had no plan or ready excuses.

'I shall be busy for the moment – I should like to show you round the estate later,' he said. 'But Alix – she told me herself just now upstairs – she would be much pleased with your company.' Frances was aghast. She had barely spoken more than a few words with the Princess, and that in company. Now she was to face her alone. But there was no mistaking the tones of Royal command in the Prince's voice. A footman brought her upstairs to the Princess's suite of rooms on the first floor, knocking most firmly on the outer door. A maid of the bedchamber opened it, taking Frances across a drawing room, before admitting her to a small boudoir beyond, then leaving her.

At first Frances seemed to have entered an antique shop, art gallery and photographer's display room all in one. Barely a foot of the walls or floor had been left as free space. A vast clutter of ornaments, prints, pictures, photographs, and winter house plants had been set up everywhere, on a dozen occasional tables, glass-fronted display cases, wall-brackets and shelves. A wrong step would send one crashing into a huge aspidistra, set by a portfolio screen filled with Christmas cards; another would certainly result in an earthquake among the hinged silver and tortoiseshell photographs, twenty of them crushed onto a small Benares brass table. A fierce-looking white parrot sat on a perch in the middle of the room.

Frances stood petrified among this jungle of knick-knacks, as the bird inspected her malevolently. A bright morning light streamed in from the one window, blinding her, just as the stacks of furniture and screens obscured her view. Apart from the parrot, the room seemed unoccupied. Finally, almost hidden by a Chinese screen near the small fireplace at the far side of the boudoir, she saw the silk-covered knees, the disembodied hands at some needlepoint, of the seated Princess.

Frances moved towards the window so that she might become visible to her Royal Highness, seeing herself reflected for a moment in the large gilt mirror over the mantelpiece – a terrified spectacle. But the Princess, in an exquisite primrose silk morning dress with high lace collar tightly drawn round her neck, still did not see her, intent on her needlepoint.

'Your Royal Highness . . .' Frances curtsied. But still nothing from the elegantly upright figure. Frances coughed. 'Your Royal *Highness*.'

The Princess looked up, alert now in the eyes at least, offering a most gracious smile. 'Ah, my dear, you've come. So good of you, so nice. Please, please – do take a seat.' She gestured to a spindly gilt chair, which Frances, trembling, drew up beside her. 'That's right – next to me – here!' Her accent retained all the heavier hints of her Danish background. But its tone was wonderfully light, bell-like, full of melody. There was a great repose and refinement about her – the features delicate, beautifully moulded – mouth, high curled crown of hair and small ears all perfect. Though in her mid-fifties, she was still astonishingly thin and well-preserved – looking almost half her age.

'First, are you comfortable, my dear? – the bed not too hard? I have been worried by the mattresses lately. We shall really have to renew some, if not all of them. We've had them since we took the place, over thirty years ago now . . .' She chatted on about the mattresses, the household linens, the general accoutrements of Frances's bedroom, without pause for several minutes, so that all Frances could do was nod her head agreeably. 'You must tell me if you find *anything* uncomfortable or amiss.'

'No. Not at all –'

'I should be most put out to think that you were in any way incommoded.'

'No, I am *most* comfortable –'

'Given the state of some of the beds and mattresses here, I have found the tale of the Princess and the pea often all too appropriate! And the damp, to boot – some of the guttering – we had a fire here some years ago. The repairs afterwards were not what they might have been. On the other hand our new bathing rooms are really rather satisfying . . .'

She wandered on incessantly, through a maze of domestic rigmarole, before embarking on further serpentine résumés, of a familial and dynastic nature. At the end of half an hour the Princess put aside her needlepoint, seeming to indicate that the meeting was over. She stood up and with her slight limp made stately progress towards the window, looking out on the empty flower-beds, the intricate diamonds and circles of low box hedges. The sun had gone in. The Princess shivered a fraction.

'Well, my dear, the main thing is that you stay warm, wrap up well. You must rest and be comfortable here. *Recover* yourself. Nothing strenuous. Consider yourself quite at home here for Christmas. I really do feel for you in your predicaments – and what can I say but that . . . well, that time heals all wounds?'

She offered Frances another of her lovely smiles – so truly sympathetic, tender even, that Frances was genuinely touched as she curtsied before leaving.

Later that morning the Princess spoke of Frances to Lady Melbury, one of her current ladies-in-waiting. 'The poor dear girl,' she commented. 'Most charming. But nothing to say for herself, quite desolate, the pinched face – and looked so *cold*. I was most concerned for her comfort, most touched by her. And quite without guile – I cannot think where that gossip came from. She is a mere child, a babe-in-the-wood. Not the Prince's sort at *all*. Just a kindness on his part – the dear good man.'

Lady Melbury, who had observed Frances with some care since her arrival and noticed, too, several of the Prince's attentive gestures towards her, was less convinced. On the other hand she knew the Prince well enough to doubt that he would bring such a young woman into the bosom of his home if his motives were merely predatory. With all her experience of the Prince's circle, and his liaisons among them, this was one conjunction that she could not fathom. However, she was prepared to give both parties the benefit of her doubts – especially since this charity seemed so to appeal to the Princess, while the Prince himself, she had seen, had been in particularly good humour ever since Frances's arrival.

A babe-in-the-wood? Perhaps that was the key to it, Lady Melbury thought. This girl, with her childish vivacity and wild young looks, reminded the royal couple of their own daughters, similarly untutored and unruly, who had long since left the family nest. It was not only a kindness on their part to have the girl here, she thought – it was their own youthful happy family life revived.

In her bedroom before luncheon, with just time for the letter to reach Summer Hill before Christmas, Frances wrote to her parents, addressing herself to the pale blue notepaper, die-stamped simply 'Sandringham House, Norfolk'.

'I am sad,' she wrote, 'that you have not seen fit to reply to my earlier letter to you both. I cannot think that my previous behaviour, though it may still warrant your disapproval, should also result in your continued silence. However that may be, and though I much wished to spend this Christmas season with you at home – and send you all my best wishes for the season – I have accepted a most kind invitation from their Royal Highnesses the Prince and Princess of Wales, to spend Christmas with them here at Sandringham.

'Mortimer or Dermot, as I have asked them, will I hope already have told you of all this. I am very happy here. The Prince and Princess both have been most kind and attentive. I expect to return to Wilton Place after the holiday and to continue my nursing with Miss Wechsberg at Grosvenor Crescent. My life, it seems, will continue in England for the moment. But I would most sincerely ask you to remember that my *home* is at Summer Hill and that I very much hope that I may see you both there at some point in the New Year. Again, every good Xmas wish, Frances.'

She had thought, perhaps, to have ended with something on the lines of 'Your obedient daughter' – to have offered more fulsome apologies. But, no, the balance was just right; it was not to be too conciliatory a letter, nor yet too provocative. Its purpose was simply to intimate clearly – and the Sandringham heading to the notepaper would do most of that – that in her concerns with her mother she now worked from a position of strength.

It was a large house party at Sandringham, with guests from the most unexpected and varied backgrounds. Frances soon realised: all of them pleasant and civil, all either very rich or equally aristocratic, with a few, such as the Duke of Sutherland, both rich beyond the dreams of avarice and of the most august lineage. One or two others, among them the Bishop of Peterborough and Colonel Higgins – a Catholic, she understood – brought no inherited title or wealth with them but simply an ecclesiastical position or a particular intimacy with the Prince – as did Henry Chaplin, one of the Prince's oldest and closest friends from his Oxford days, who though poor in his own right had made great amends by marrying the old Duke of Sutherland's daughter, Lady Florence Leweson-Gower.

Mr Chaplin, sitting near the Prince at luncheon, had regaled the company at that end of the long table with amusing, highly melodramatic accounts of his expeditions among the warring Blackfoot Indians in the Rocky Mountains thirty years before.

'"Indian country," my guide told me enthusiastically, pointing to one branch of the fork in the track. "*Must* we go that way?" I enquired, finally persuading him that discretion was the better part of valour . . .'

Besides these guests, and the Royal couple's immediate retinue of staff taken from Marlborough House – the Prince's secretary and some half a dozen others – there were several Jews, including Sir Anthony de Rothschild and his daughter; an Italian Countess, originally English, with her daughter, once a Catholic, but now reformed; Lady Filmer, Lady Melbury, the Duchess of Berwick; Lords Cadogan, Carrington and Houghton with their wives, together with a set of younger peers with their ladies.

Nearly all of these guests had been forcibly conducted about the model estate

after lunch on the second day by the Prince, most anxiously proud of his horticul-
tural and landscape gardening achievements in this – as Lady Macclesfield had
rightly observed – rather featureless and desolate spot. After the Princess had fed
the horses lumps of apple and sugar in the stable yard, and then retired, the Prince
led the party off, a most vigorous major-domo, on a long and tiring walk in the
chilly wind. They visited, in turn, the kitchen gardens, the hothouses – for all too
brief a period – the Italian and alpine gardens, the lavender walk, the small zoo,
the joss-house, the kennels where the Princess's dogs were kept and the pet
cemetery where they would be buried. A collection of eminently alive pugs,
beagles, basset hounds, chows, terriers, Eskimo sledge-dogs and French bull-dogs
accompanied them, digging in the cemetery among the bones of their forebears.

On their return to the house, in an even keener wind, chilling them to the
marrow, the Bishop of Peterborough remarked to Frances how he fancied in this
'vigorous marine atmosphere, with its stunted firs and splendid Scandinavian
sunsets' that he was visiting 'Dukes and Princes of the Baltic, Regents of the
midnight sun' – a description which Frances thought quite excessive, though she
admired it for its diplomacy, as the Bishop himself must have done, for a few
minutes later she heard him repeat the encomium in exactly the same words to
the Prince.

The house, when she toured it, was much like the Princess's boudoir, crammed
with furniture in not the best taste. Hunting trophies, together with paintings of
yachts, highland cattle and stags at bay contested the space on every wall with
weapons, ancient and modern – crossed cutlasses, dirks, pikes, ceremonial swords,
muskets and rifles; while at each corner and along every corridor coverts of potted
plants and regiments of cold statuary lay in wait for the unwary: grim Roman
worthies staring out from between the heavy fronds of fern or aspidistra – almost
as unnerving to Frances as the stuffed baboon inside the front door, its paws
outstretched to receive visiting cards.

The huge house, indeed, with its endless poky rooms upstairs, large spaces on
the ground floor, its permanently-stationed or often-moving footmen, pages and
maids, its many guests ambling along the corridors, or darting purposefully through
doorways if the Prince was about – the house had the air of a busy and very grand
railway terminal, where the aristocratic passengers were much intent on their own
pressing journeys, or on avoiding the over-vigilant station-master, so that Frances
did not feel set apart or taken undue notice of.

Indeed, since the Bishop of Peterborough had taken something of a fancy to
her and they were sometimes seen together, she was thought by some to be his
niece or daughter – and by others, more correctly, knowing of the Princess's
interest in her, to be the victim of some family tragedy in Ireland, now an unofficial
ward of the Royal couple. Though in truth, given the air of bustle and festivity in
the house, no one – other than the Prince and his wife – was much concerned
about Frances at all.

Tea was taken promptly at five o'clock every day in the entrance hall – an
elaborate meal ranging from cold lobster and oyster patties to hot scones filled

with clotted cream and raspberry jam – the men in short dark jackets, the ladies in elaborate and flowing tea-gowns, Gottlieb's orchestra in attendance, an unlikely mix of Teutonic and Italian players who fiddled their way through *The Gipsy Baron* and *Die Fledermaus* while the company gorged and chattered under the warm electric lights.

As far as the Prince was concerned, at least, it was a particularly festive tea on the second afternoon in that the first of his several practical jokes proved a resounding success when the Bishop of Peterborough, induced to accept a mince pie by his host, found it filled with Colman's mustard – to his real discomfort and the company's less than genuine amusement. If the Bishop himself was considered fair game for such rough jests what worse might they expect in their own cases?

The atmosphere, though apparently so informal, was trying in such ways. There were severe pitfalls lying in wait for the incautious guest, most particularly in the matter of dress, where the Prince could not bear to see a decoration wrongly worn – or any item, even a button, misplaced. Both the Duchess of Berwick and the Prince's medical friend, Sir Felix Semon, took the whip of a royal reprimand that evening at the formal dinner.

'The Star of the Victorian Order, Sir Felix, is *usually* worn on the *left* breast,' the poor doctor was told with biting sarcasm, while the Duchess, who had appeared splendidly crowned with a diamond crescent instead of the prescribed tiara, was similarly, if more tactfully, rebuked. Frances – the daughter of a mere baronet, in her simple but finely-cut organdie and tartan dress, lovely chiselled features and with only her blue amethyst pendant as jewellery – was beyond reproach. She had had, too, the most careful attentions, in her coiffure and wardrobe, from Eileen, happily ensconced now in the small dressing room next to Frances's bedroom. So that the Prince, at one end of the dinner table, often glanced at Frances, their eyes meeting for a second, before he returned unwillingly to his more immediate concerns.

After dinner, before the party and card games – general post, whist, bridge, carpet bowls and later baccarat – the Prince spoke to Frances in the hall.

'How do you find it all, my dear?'

'Splendid! I am *most* enjoying my visit.'

'I am sorry I have not more time for you myself.' He lit a cigar. 'The general *demands*,' he went on, sighing, gesturing round at the other guests assembling at the card tables set out everywhere now. 'And tomorrow I must spend most of the day with Alix preparing the Christmas presents. Indeed, I am *overcome* with pleasant demands . . .'

'I perfectly understand. I am more than happy –'

'The Bishop – he does not weary you, I trust?'

'Not the least . . .'

The Prince smiled wryly. 'You are being diplomatic. I will admit, confidentially, that he rather wearies me. I fear, for his Christmas sermon, that he will outrun the prescribed ten minutes.'

'Oh, I shall look *forward* to it!' She smiled brightly back at him – and something stirred in the Prince's eyes then, a conflict of appreciation, a mix of tenderness and desire.

On Christmas Eve, after tea, when the Royal couple were to dispense their presents, tension among the company approached one of several climaxes over the holiday season – particularly since, together with other officials of the Court retinue, and according to invariable custom at Sandringham, everyone was forced to line up in the corridor outside the ballroom before being called in one at a time to receive the Royal bounty.

This quite unaccustomed waiting game, this standing about cheek by jowl, for these august, normally well-separated and restless people, led to some indecorous coughing, scuffling and whispering in the corridor – a generally nervy champing at the bit, made none the easier by some facetious remark from one of the younger guests to the effect that he was completely out of brass ink-stands and hoped now for a suitable replacement.

Nor did it help matters when, in the crush and obstructed by the bulk of the Italian countess, Sir Felix Semon inadvertently trod on one of the Princess's pug dogs, causing the beast little pain but great annoyance, so that it promptly bit the ankle of Henry Chaplin, who at once, and with entirely feigned emphasis, took up similar moan.

All in all it was a most trying experience, not eased by the final entrance to the ballroom where, when Frances's turn came, she was confronted by a vast empty space of floor with a long trestle table at one end – the Royal couple, standing at either side of a great line of wrapped gifts, seeming to stare at her ogreishly over the great distance.

Approaching them, she received two beautifully wrapped packages, one of awkward bulk, the other very neat and small. Taking the gifts she blushed, muttered profuse thanks, curtsied and was about to depart when she realised she had committed a great gaffe. There was more to come.

'Wait, my dear!' the Princess said, the Prince concurring, before they both embarked on a lengthy and comprehensive description of the hidden objects.

'You will find this patent sulphur dispenser,' the Princess said, '*most* convenient for your bedside. It but needs to be lit beneath – the little spirit lamp is included – to produce the most *efficacious* fumes, for any chestiness, bronchitis or such –'

'The little lapel watch,' the Prince interrupted his wife, 'is the *best* of timekeepers, I am assured – I should have given it to you, Alix – and further has a most ringing and melodious chime on the hour, if needs be.'

The Prince beamed, blossomed. He was so genuinely and naively pleased. It was clear that nothing gave him so much pleasure as this distribution of largesse – so that Frances, saddened at first that the whole element of surprise in these gifts had been denied her, consoled herself with his joy.

'And you will find it a suitably jewelled timepiece as well –'

'You must beware, however, not to leave the spirit lamp burning –'

'I had the watch from Hunt and Roskill –'

'And, above all, not *all* night, you would be quite fumigated –'

'Made by a Russian émigré there, from Monsieur Fabergé's workshops in St Petersburg . . .'

Frances stood there, sweating, gasping alternately to each of them 'Thank you – thank you, so much, so much.' There was nothing else she could say and it was a stupendous relief in the end to make a final curtsey and leave.

That same Christmas Eve, in the last post delivered from Cloone to Summer Hill, Frances's letter from Sandringham arrived with Lady Cordiner – brought to her boudoir by Flood the butler among a pile of other Christmas mail. She recognised her daughter's hand on the envelope, then the postmark 'Sandringham' – and her heart fluttered dangerously. But perhaps there was some mistake. Other people had country homes in the Sandringham area, friends of this Ruth Wechsberg perhaps . . . But now, opening and reading the letter, she could no longer doubt her daughter's actions, her social success. Frances had reached a pinnacle which she had been denied. The news cut her to the quick.

Lady Cordiner had – or so she thought – not been at all well in the months since Henry's death, spending much of each day in bed or at least in her bedroom. But now, fingering the letter, she felt positively ill – giddy, faint – and worse, there was a sharp pain in her side, as if part of her body had been cut away from her, her actual physical presence diminished. She had thought at first that this Sandringham news was a mere tease, a ploy of Frances's – that in fact her daughter would be spending Christmas with Ruth Wechsberg. Now she would have completely to rearrange her views.

She stood up and walked slowly over to the window. It was already twilight – the trees in the river gorge just a grey pall against the dark sky beyond. Tea would be served in half an hour. Sir Desmond and Eustace would be there, together with Bunty and Austin Cordiner, their two boys and Isabelle – and, distant cousins of hers, the elderly Samuel and Martha Bischoffsheim over from Brighton, staying for the season. Company impended. Was she to speak of all this – how her daughter was spending Christmas with the Prince and Princess of Wales – with the heir to the throne, a man who very soon, and it could not now be long delayed, would be the King Emperor?

Then, thinking of this imminent elevation, she was suddenly struck by an obvious answer to the whole matter. Yes, now that she was calmer, she saw it all: one did not hide one's light under a bushel in such matters. That Frances was at Sandringham for Christmas was an honour: it reflected very well on her daughter. It could no doubt be made to reflect even better on her, Lady Cordiner thought.

At tea, beaming, she announced to the company, 'I am really *so* pleased. We have had news of Frances at last – you know how I've been so worried about her.

But now we hear – she is spending Christmas with their Royal Highnesses the Prince and Princess of Wales!'

Lady Cordiner glanced round the company regally. But there was no response other than a stunned silence.

'Oh, good,' Sir Desmond finally said, at a loss for further words.

'At Sandringham?' Eustace asked in an off-hand way, as if his sister went there quite often for Christmas. His mother nodded.

'Well, good for her,' Austin Cordiner said. 'I didn't know she was a friend of theirs.' He, too, seemed to regard the matter as not unusual.

'Oh, yes,' Lady Cordiner said lightly. 'But I didn't want to speak of it, until I knew the details.'

Bunty, so surprised at this news that she had been unable to comment on it at all, finally laughed – a little uncontrollable titter in the silent room.

'I fail to see the humour in it,' Lady Cordiner addressed her severely.

Bunty regained her composure. 'No. It's just so unexpected – such a *pleasure* for her,' she added, looking at Lady Cordiner pointedly. Bunty had gathered strength from this news – strength in her own battles with Lady Cordiner, knowing now how this malicious woman whom she so disliked had been outdone in her own vast social ambitions by her daughter. '*Such* a pleasure,' Bunty continued. 'Surely a cause for celebration?' she asked finally.

'Yes, indeed!' Sir Desmond broke the silence then. 'We shall have champagne for supper.' He was heartened by his wife's sudden re-emergence as a happy woman – forceful once more, seemingly in charge again after months of gloom in the household. Yet he knew of old how in this mood his wife would soon start to execute 'plans' – how such good humour in her always presaged plans, schemes . . . And this made him uneasy.

'Champagne for dinner? – certainly not,' Lady Cordiner said. 'We are still in mourning, you must remember, for poor dear Henry . . .'

Lady Cordiner had plans indeed. But they did not include any such open celebration of her daughter's social success. Her plan was that she alone of the company, in due course, would celebrate this distinction, by sharing in it, by using it towards her own advancement.

It would need careful planning, of course, she thought later that evening – subtle handling in every way, most obviously with her daughter. How strange it was, Lady Cordiner reflected, that Frances had so played into her hands in this way: this disobedient, ungrateful girl who all unknowing had offered her access now to that social pinnacle. A friend of the Royal couple indeed! How little, in her selfish naïveté, did Frances realise what a prize she had put within her reach.

On Christmas morning in the Sandringham church, the Prince, as was his habit, propped his half-hunter watch up on the pew in front of him – his traditional reminder to the local vicar not to outrun the allotted ten minutes in his sermon.

However, on this occasion, it was the Bishop of Peterborough who was giving the address. And, although the Prince had previously spoken to him jocularly about 'not outstaying his welcome' in the matter, the Bishop had taken this literally as a joke, or had at least come quite to disregard the warning, warbling on now for ten, fifteen, then nearly twenty minutes.

'. . . and I thought to myself,' he intoned lugubriously and unctuously, 'coming here to Sandringham, to this vigorous marine atmosphere, with its stunted firs and splendid Scandinavian sunsets, that I was visiting Dukes and Princes of the Baltic, Regents of the midnight sun; that – as in St Matthew's gospel – "I was a stranger here and you made me welcome". And then I reflected how, finally, it was that King of Kings, the Lord God himself, who had made us all welcome in this lovely place . . . '

A fierce·wind, whipping off the marshes from the Urals, rattled the church windows. The Prince, further annoyed by this suggestion of *lèse-majesté*, could no longer contain himself. He picked up his watch, fiddled with it, put it to his ear, then held it up high, as if to inspect its face, right in front of the Bishop, who paused only for a second before continuing his theme, his view of the testaments as a kind of Almanack de Gotha, in which the Prince, though not paramount, nonetheless occupied a position in direct succession, close to God. 'Yes, indeed, and I thought that even Moses on the mountain top, even Solomon in all his glory . . .'

It was at that moment that Frances's watch, which she wore on her lapel, broke out with its surprisingly loud chimes, starting with an introductory tinkle, then beginning to strike twelve times, the hour of midday. Before going to church she had failed to secure the little catch which silenced the chiming mechanism. And now she fiddled furiously with the timepiece, quite unable to stop it, the melodious notes spreading through the silent church.

The Bishop stopped in his tracks. Others in the congregation stared at her with scorn or embarrassment, seated as she was at one end of the pew behind the Royal couple. But the Prince turned to her and offered her one of his kindest, most heartfelt smiles. The Bishop ceased his long-windedness very shortly afterwards.

Outside, after the service, the Prince took her aside for a moment. 'My dear,' he said, with a twinkly smile, 'you did us all the *greatest* favour. I must have your company more often!'

After Christmas Frances and Eileen returned to Wilton Place, Frances resuming her work at the nursing home. Mortimer and Dermot came back from Ireland, both of them, to various blunt or discreet degree, agog to hear news of her visit to Sandringham. She told them the truth, entirely openly – how much she had enjoyed herself.

Subsequently, in the following months, she and the Prince met again, formally and informally, at Marlborough House and Eaton Square. Yet their need was more to talk than to flirt on these occasions. They talked of horses, of bloodstock in Ireland, of racing at the Curragh, the Prince reminiscing on boisterous times he had spent there as a young army officer forty years before. They spoke of such and such a play, and of real drama seen at the theatre when Frances accompanied the Prince and his party to the Haymarket or Drury Lane, or to a screened box at Evans' Music Hall at Covent Garden. And they spoke alone sometimes at Eaton Square in the evening – of Frances's future, the Prince's concerns, of less indulgent things.

Their relationship grew on such conversations, Frances searching out that secret man behind the façade of forced bonhomie and uneasy practical jokes, so that gradually, with her, the Prince relaxed, became less fraught and nervous, releasing his truer nature. He responded to her, as she had hoped, in many more agile ways, becoming less heavy-handed – in his jokes, his manner, conversation, when he ceased his chaffing, along with most of his huge cigars and gargantuan meals. Under her influence he became a lighter man in every way. Alone with her, or together in company, he no longer merely interjected abrupt questions; he contributed to, shared in the conversation. Frances, with her bright sympathy and intelligence, gave him real speech, where before he had done little more than offer vague comments and platitudes.

'Je Responderay' – that was the secret she had released in him, she thought, as she saw him respond – drawing thoughts, words, from the Prince that he did not know he possessed. He was not a block of wood – there were all sorts of echoes there now, as he sloughed off the carapace of toad in her attentive light and found his true form. The Prince in return offered her support and consolation in her exile.

But their relationship was not only a matter of such shared personal sympathies. The Prince found he could talk to her of public and political matters of the day, among them the ever-present Irish question.

'I should like to travel there more often,' he told her. 'I was most happy, years ago at the Curragh, and with the Irish people generally. But I am entirely discouraged – if not actually forbidden – in my visiting the country, by Mama and the Cabinet. It is thought I might put my foot in it, upset things, negotiations – whereas it is my view that, in any case, the Crown should be presented in Ireland in a more human manner, that bridges might at least be mended, if not crossed in that way.'

'I should very much have thought so.'

'Your cousin, though, Mortimer Cordiner, to judge from the *Times* parliamentary reports, does not see it in the same way?'

'No. But he is quite committed to the opposite view – a complete break between the two countries, without compromise.'

'I fear that will always remain the problem with the Irish – their inability to compromise, as we usually must in the long run.'

'Indeed, for we are both English and Irish in Ireland – and even with Home Rule we would still have to share that rule, in some measure. And I believe we would very likely make a mess of sharing anything. We are – each side – so stuck in our ways.'

Frances, with her sharp thoughts and her beauty, was, for the Prince, an idealised version of any one of his own three daughters – Louise, Victoria and Maud – with whom, though he loved them all dearly, he had never been able to have such conversations. And the only thing that gave the Prince pause in his relationship with Frances was the feeling of disloyalty he had in being able so to take up with her in a way he had never managed with them. In talking with Frances, the Prince achieved a ready equality, a close and easy understanding. And it was this verbal intimacy with the Prince which Frances came to hide from her friends and relations, for this between them she came to hold sacrosanct. Her friends could think what they wished of her association with him, think the worst if they wanted. What they would not know was how easily and calmly she got on with this man. That was the secret – the two of them were involved not only in rounds of pleasure, but rounds of the mind.

Their serious rapport gained momentum with the arrival of Lady Cordiner's letter later in the new year. Frances had met the Prince that evening alone, at his invitation, in Eaton Place, and had shown him the letter.

My dear,

We were so glad to receive your note and to hear that you were happy at last in England. Of course, you have been most fortunate in your social life and it is a great honour indeed that their Royal Highnesses should have so kindly taken you up in this way. I can only hope that you thoroughly appreciate your good fortune and are suitably grateful.

Of course you are forgiven for your earlier behaviour here – and your *home* is, indeed, here at Summer Hill. You must remember that, previously, I never *denied* you this home, merely pointed out to you that you should not, given your virtues (and, indeed, your faults!), think of burying yourself here indefinitely – that you should go out into the world, as you have at last done, and find your happy place there. And I am *most* pleased with that. Your present patronage is a rare gift – I hope you will not misuse it. And I hope we may see something of you and your company at Summer Hill in the not too distant future. Your father joins me in sending every good wish.

Your loving Mama.

'Well,' the Prince said. 'It seems you have effected a rapprochement!'

'It is you who have done that – not I.'

'How so?'

'As my mother suggests – by your patronage, by my staying at Sandringham.'

'Then I am more than pleased!'

They sat at either side of the fire in the small drawing room. Now the Prince stood up, lit a last Abdullah cigarette before dinner, warming the backs of his legs against the bright coals.

'She would not have forgiven me on my own.'

'Perhaps not. But then what are friends for? I think you may regard the problem as solved.' He looked down at Frances, saw a sadness in her face, and realised then how his last words had an unintended ring of finality about them – as if, in having so helped her, their association had no further meaning, so that he said to her now, by way of indicating a future between them, 'And, my dear, I wanted to tell you how there are *other* futures too for you now. You must start to be happy again, in other ways. As your mother rightly says, you must find your happy place in the world.'

'Yes, of course.'

'She is – your mother – perhaps a wiser woman than you realise, or will allow yourself to realise. You have been too close in your wars with her. And she with you. You each fail to see the other's virtues. I have found that myself, so often, in the old days, with my own dear Mama.'

'That is possible – indeed.'

'I am *sure* it is.'

'It's just that I fear she is forgiving me purely because of you – and the Princess – and not for myself.'

'Well, let her do so. It is a beginning. We may cement the relationship in the future – you and I and with Alix herself, indeed. As I said last time we met – I should much like to visit Ireland again, an unofficial visit. And perhaps I might then meet your mother. To tell the truth –' He looked carefully at Frances. 'There is something intriguing about her: the mother of such a daughter!'

'I would not ask that. You have done enough already, Edward.'

'In fact, I have done nothing, as yet. We have hardly begun, you and I.' His eyes twinkled as he raised his glass and she joined him in a toast to this.

But to what exactly, she wondered?

8

THE FROST WAS sharp, but the sun shone from a cloudless pale blue sky. The chill air streamed over her face, biting into her eyes, so that tears blew across her cheeks as the motor bumped down the Brighton road at more than twenty miles an hour. It was the most exciting experience that Frances had ever had.

Covered by a great fur rug, she sat high up on the button-leather seat at the back, the Prince on one side, his equerry, Sir Seymour Fortescue, on the other – with the dog Caesar, nose into the wind like a look-out, on the front seat, next to Henry Stamper, the Prince's motor mechanic in his leather gaiters, knickerbockers and peaked cap. Stamper bent over the wheel now, seeming to coax the motor forward, like a horse, to ever greater speeds.

The claret-coloured De Dion Bouton had just been delivered to the Prince from France. And he was determined, that fine frosty morning in January, to put it through its paces at once, asking Frances and his equerry to accompany him.

The Prince steadied himself – and his excitement – hand grasping the rail above the side-door, as the motor lurched repeatedly, hitting a succession of potholes on the old coach road. They were in the country now, on a long straight stretch, so that they could see the carriages and farm carts way ahead of them. Stamper furiously pumped the rubber ball of the klaxon at these distant obstructions – the sounds, like a flock of startled geese, piercing the cold air, echoing down the straight road, so that other travellers, long before the Prince's motor came near, had made for the ditch, stopping in alarm, the horses rearing, drivers cursing, as the De Dion Bouton sped past in a great swish of air, a clatter of machinery and a fiendish dragon's breath from the exhaust pipe.

'Sir! – it is most illegal,' Sir Seymour shouted across to the Prince. 'You must ask Stamper to slacken pace –'

'Nonsense, Fortescue! We shall drive the motor to its limit. And here is the only stretch of road where we may do so with impunity!' The Prince leant forward now, eyes glazed, staring ahead, just like Stamper, the two of them egging the motor on. 'Are we approaching thirty miles per hour yet, Stamper?' the Prince demanded, shouting over the roar of the engine.

'Not yet, Sir –'

'But we are not permitted to do more than twelve miles per hour, I believe,' Fortescue interjected, highly alarmed now.

'An entirely unnecessary law, Fortescue. In France it is *quite* different. On, Stamper, on!'

'But we are not *in* France, Sir –'

'Soon will be, at this rate –'

The motor hit another pothole, throwing them all to one side, the Prince hitting Frances's shoulder, the dog Caesar toppling over into Stamper's lap, starting to bark loudly as Stamper, watching the little dial in front, finally achieved the desired speed.

'Now, Sir, we have it! Thirty miles per hour. We have it!'

'Well done, Stamper – well done! A fine run, a really fine run!' The Prince was beside himself, in ecstasy as they pulled into the side of the road, stopping by a farm gate. They got out to stretch their legs and to embark on a hamper of game pie and anchovy sandwiches with a flask of brandy, while Stamper opened the bonnet, attending to the steaming engine.

'That really was . . . terribly exciting!' Frances said to the Prince, her face, which had been blue with cold, now turning red as she wiped the tears from her eyes, gasping with pleasure, sipping the brandy, exhilarated, as they both were, by their sensational pace through the tingling cold sunny morning.

'Indeed,' the Prince agreed. 'Nothing finer – the coming age, the age of the motor! What do you think, Fortescue?'

Fortescue, wiping his nose, could not restrain his aggravation. 'I must be honest, Sir – I find it an entirely disagreeable conveyance: shaky, windy and smelly to boot – not to mention the danger to life and limb.'

'My dear fellow, they said just that of the railway – and look what has happened there! We must move with the times, Fortescue. No denying progress.'

'Perhaps not all progress is to be equally welcomed, Sir. Besides, if I may say so, it seems a most undignified method of transportation for – for someone in your position.'

'But I am *one* with the age, Fortescue!' The Prince, in high good humour, lectured his equerry now. 'As I *should* be in my position, with such new developments. Remember, Fortescue, we are approaching a new century.' He looked at Frances. 'Youth at the helm and so on – and I consider I should not be left on the shelf in such matters. I forecast a time, quite soon, when this very road will be *buzzing* with such motor vehicles, up and down, without let or hindrance. I am *impatient* for it all!'

'Indeed, Sir. I cannot say I share your agitation.'

'Ah, Fortescue.' The Prince drained his glass. 'You are not young at heart! Come, my dear.' He took Frances's arm. 'Let us return to our speed-fest. Stamper? How is the engine? Suitably fed and watered?'

'Yes, Sir.'

'Let us climb aboard then. I have an appointment with the Colonial Secretary at Marlborough House – these intemperate Boers again. Caesar?' He called for his dog, still in the field, scouring the hedgerows. 'Caesar! – come here, at once.' They called the dog fruitlessly for several minutes before it finally returned. The Prince shook his finger at it. 'You naughty, *naughty* dog! Denying me the Colonial Secretary,' he said slowly, while Caesar looked up at him very cheerfully, wagging his tail.

A few minutes later they were on their way back to London, the Prince taking Frances's hand under the rug when they lurched into anothe pothole – and keeping it there afterwards, as the wind rushed over their faces and tears glazed their excited eyes once more.

The Prince was increasingly taken with Frances, until suddenly she became indispensable to him. He was in love with her – and told her as much one evening in March as they dined alone in Eaton Place.

'Yes,' he told her, 'from the first moment I saw you, that evening at Grosvenor Crescent – quite changed my life.'

'Surely not, Edward –'

'Yes, yes – it was a *coup de foudre*, my dearest. It was your nose that so took my attention.'

'My nose? But it is my worst feature.'

'My dear, it is sheer elegance: that straight sweep from brow to lip with barely a conjunction. It was your nose,' he teased her gently now, 'which you dislike, that I loved at once. Something quite unique. Indeed, it has been well said that if Cleopatra's nose had been shorter the whole world would have been different!'

Frances on the other hand believed that something less apparent and more designing in her nature had brought about her present position with the Prince. He loved what he saw of her, not what he knew about her or of her designs – while she was more flattered and intrigued than in love with him.

And yet these differences of belief, in what constituted the play between them, made their relationship all the more compelling, led them forward, ever deeper. It gave an exciting, provocative tension to their association – the Prince always taken by what he saw as Frances's mystery, while she was more tempted by what she wanted, and what was so very obvious in him: his forthright power.

It was these cross purposes which led, among other things, to the success of their liaison – in which Frances was bound to withhold the truth, and the Prince, stimulated by this discretion, felt equally obliged to protect or broach it, according to his mood. They were held together by his ignorance of the real situation and her knowledge of it, by his innocence and her deceit, by his obvious and her ulterior motives. In these respects their ploys and ambitions were, indeed, the unadmitted commonplaces of most affairs.

Yet, reflecting an equal commonplace – as a repeated theme barely noticed in this conflicting orchestration – there was, as they both came to recognise, a quieter passage of music through their partnership, the delicate chords of real need and affection. Despite their best efforts at deceiving themselves or each other in the grand manner, they grew together in quite mundane ways. They did so not through any *coup de foudre*, but through often uneventful meetings and habit. And it was this easy regular exposure with the Prince, when they could talk so readily, that allowed Frances one day to realise she loved him. It was speech that brought her love, when she finally spoke the truth.

They had shared a bottle of Duminy *Extra Sec* before dinner one spring evening at Eaton Square. The plane trees in the square had just come into leaf, a late sun was slanting into the drawing room, the window was half-open, bringing a balmy soft air from the city, the sound of carriages, the easy clip-clop of horses' feet coming down Sloane Street. Summer was just an inch away.

'Well, my dear Frances, what of the future?' the Prince had said to her brightly, raising his glass expectantly.

'I am to take the first of my nursing examinations next week.'

'I think perhaps I meant your future – with people. You do not, surely, expect simply to nurse all your life?'

'I had not really thought.' Her eye fell on the Stubbs painting above the mantelpiece. She saw the little beech grove on the hill behind the stallion – so like the grove in Cooper's Wood above Summer Hill. Yes, that was what she was thinking about. That was her future. But she could not start to explain all this again to the Prince.

The Prince walked to the window, gazing out pensively. Now he returned. 'Yes, with people.' He resumed his theme. 'I am curious, for example, given your recent social connections – so many suitable young men – that you have not taken up with any of them. Several, I know – young Wilson for example, Lord Beecher's son – have been more than taken with you!'

'I have not been of similar mind, Edward.' She looked at him openly, spoke without any dissembling. In his company and among his sophisticated friends, she had matured in the past six months – become a woman, far more assured, confident of herself and her relationships. Yet she lied about one thing to the Prince, about what remained most real in her life, what she could not achieve: she wanted her home, and that was why she had wanted him. 'No,' she went on, 'I was not taken by young Wilson, or any of them for that matter. Suitable perhaps, but so gauche!'

'Indeed – and I am grateful for that.' The Prince smiled. 'But still, if I may state the obvious, you are not the spinster type, the maiden aunt. You must expect at some point –'

'A good marriage?'

The Prince nodded. 'It is *most* likely.'

'I am happy as I am. You speak as my mother does, as though marriage were a bounden duty.'

'Not a duty alone – a pleasure, I hope.'

'Yes. But as yet – I have still my mother, my home, to consider.'

'You have made things up there. Surely that is no longer a problem.'

'I have not yet returned there, faced them all – as I remember you said I should.'

'Nothing now prevents you – after your examinations.'

Frances finished her glass in one gulp – stood up impatiently, nervously. It was her turn to walk to the window.

'What is it that still so worries you at home?' The Prince was anxious himself now.

Frances turned decisively. 'Not things there so much, as here, with you: with things . . . I have not told you.' She looked at him with some agitation.

'My dear, you may entirely confide in me.'

'That is my problem – that I have not done so.' She paused, biting her lip. 'I have used you,' she went on quickly, 'used you to effect my reconciliation at home, Edward.' She turned away, in dismay at her admission.

The Prince was relieved. He laughed. 'Is that all? But Frances, it was I who offered to mediate, not you who asked me. How have you used me?'

'I have not been true with you. It was my purpose from the beginning – to enlist your support against my mother. I did not tell you so.'

'But the matter with your mother,' he said. 'That was settled months ago! – in January, when you received her letter, when she forgave you. And you and I have continued to meet since. You have . . . wished to see me?' The Prince, not put out in the least by her admissions, was simply perplexed.

'Yes, I have.'

'Well, then,' he said in an easier tone. 'And we have got on well, have we not?'

'Yes, indeed.'

'So you are not using me in that respect, I can assure you! Your company has been a continual delight,' he added with feeling. 'You have quite taken me out of my old self.'

He approached her, as if to take her hand. But she drew back, annoyed that the Prince should forgive or misunderstand her so readily. Did he not realise her deceit?

'Edward, do you not *see*?' she asked, a bitter frustration rising in her voice, 'that although I have so enjoyed myself with you, none the less my original intention, as regards my mother –'

'Of *course* I see,' the Prince interrupted, rounding on her, angry himself now. 'But you have exaggerated the whole issue, in your usual impetuous manner. I am not such a fool that I do not see how originally, with me, you sought only my support with your mother. But since then we have discovered . . . quite other things to concern us, have we not?' He offered a hesitant smile.

'Yes, but –'

'Well, then,' he was suddenly decisive, 'if that be so, let us drop your Mama for the moment. The matter is done with, except in so far that I am curious that you should bring it up all over again. Why does it so absorb you? She, your home, everything that is behind you – when the *future* beckons, or should do so.' Frances did not, could not, answer. Now the Prince, his anger gone, took her hand. 'Why is it that you so hark back to things when you have the whole world in front of you?'

'I . . .'

'Come, you may tell me. I shall not be surprised or –'

'I have wished my mother dead, Edward!' Frances finally burst out, speaking with great vehemence, a long pent-up emotion. 'Wished her dead, yes, for the way she treated all of us at home – bullying and driving us out of her life, literally in the case of my dear brother Henry. And when he died I vowed to make up for his life, the life he might have had at Summer Hill – by living there *myself*. Do you see?'

'I can't say –'

'I *want* that house, Edward, more than anything else in the world.'

'I don't see how. Your father is very much alive, I understand. And you have told me of your other brother Eustace, who will now inherit it.'

Frances nearly stamped her foot in frustration. '*Exactly!* So now you understand my feelings – that I cannot have the place.'

The Prince was taken aback at this outburst, not knowing how to cope with it. Here was one desire of hers which, given the laws of primogeniture, he could never satisfy. But he rallied quickly.

'Not the house, perhaps – but you can have so much else.'

'What I may have will not be *there*, though.'

'Surely, my dear one, it is simply a matter of your being *between* lives which makes you uneasy – your youth and your future. When you have properly found the latter you will not so crave the other. You will see it all very differently once you have your *own* house – and family, when that is secure.'

'I could have had that already – with Lord Norton's son.'

'But you told me you did not care for him, which was why you broke the match. And there is nothing amiss in that. You will find someone else –'

'I don't *want* to find someone else!' She turned away.

'You will, my dearest – in time, in time.' He took her by the shoulders, gently turning her, then kissing her on the cheek.

'My dear Edward,' she told him slowly and clearly, drawing away from him, but keeping her hands on his shoulders. 'With you, I don't need anyone else – you have so understood.'

'I fear not, in that I cannot see how you may have the house –'

'But that I so *want* it – and you have not mocked me for that.'

The Prince sighed. 'Not mocked you – indeed, I could never do that. But I fear I cannot help you. For women – well, to put it mildly, the laws do not favour them in such matters. Such inheritance descends in the male line – your brother, his children. And if not him, for any reason, then I imagine you have uncles and their male progeny who would expect to inherit. I cannot see how . . .?' He shook his head in bewilderment.

'Yes, indeed, I know – my uncle Austin and his little prim mouse of a wife Bunty and their two milksop boys – there are all of them. Yet they have no *right* to the place!'

'Perhaps not. But your brother Eustace certainly does.'

'He is a tidy little military man, a captain – your own Royal Rifles – presently at Aldershot, entirely bound up in his army career: shortsighted in his ideas generally, literal, mundane to a degree. He has no real love for the place. He has made his career, his life, over here. He looks on home – looks on Ireland – as something second best. When he inherits, at worst, he may close the place down, or sell it up. At best, if he lives there, it will become a dingy mausoleum, a barn, empty of everything – of *life* – just filled with him and his military cronies and their silly wives and children. You've no idea! – how dull and terrible it will all become. At least my mother – well, she gives a sparkle to it, or she did. Yet there could be so much more there, so *much* more! The whole place could breathe, be so wonderfully exciting and happy.'

She paused. Tears had come in her eyes as she spoke. The Prince had listened attentively. He lit a cigarette now, one of his oval Sullivan Egyptians which, in Frances's company, he had taken to instead of his huge Coronas. 'I see,' he said. 'I think I do see. Your view of home is so much mine of Buckingham Palace, Windsor Castle, Osborne, and the rest: all of them mausoleums, for many years now, where nothing has been changed a jot since father's death nearly forty years ago. And I have felt just the same – what a waste it is, how much I should like to change things, breathe a new wind into everything, into *my* inheritance: make it live, just as you say of your own home – make it a happy, not a mournful thing. I am so much of the same mind . . .'

'You, at least, will have that opportunity.'

'I sometimes wonder. I am nearly sixty. My mother, old as she is, retains an iron will and an excellent constitution. She may outlive me.' The Prince was both ironic and sad at this thought, drawing on the cigarette.

'I'm sure not –'

'Oh, just like you,' he interrupted her now, speaking with some of Frances's earlier vehemence, 'I should so like to get my hands on this Royal inheritance! Yes, I long to be king!' he exclaimed, like a boy looking into a shop window full of toys. 'I have been so frustrated, for many years – treated like a child by everyone, forbidden access to state papers, having to *beg* for information from my few personal friends in the Cabinet. You have no idea how this mistrust, this *waiting*, has drained me – made me short-tempered, bitter. I do so understand your feelings there, with your own mother – wanting to change things, longing for the time, for action, fearing it may never come.'

'It *will* come, dear Edward – I am sure . . .'

'We are so alike, with our Mamas, and in our homes – in wanting some action, are we not?' He had walked over to the window again while speaking. Now he returned, pouring himself and Frances the last of the champagne. They drained their glasses in silence, looking at each other.

'Action,' Frances said at last, almost whispering. 'Action, yes . . .' She set her glass down, moved towards him, like a sleepwalker, putting her arms out, embracing him quickly.

And suddenly they had started to make love – there and then, standing up, before supper, in the little panelled drawing room with its window half-open on the spring evening, quite unable to resist or to control themselves, reaching for each other's bodies, touching, caressing, undressing – Frances pulling up her dress and petticoats, discarding her underclothes, suddenly feeling her sex alive when the Prince touched her, falling with her onto the sofa, skirts above her waist now, her stockings down, twisting about in little dizzy spasms as he went on caressing her, between her thighs, high up, higher and higher, so that her legs opened as he fed himself on her, pushing her clothes right up above her hip bones, above the navel so that he could explore it with his tongue, and it was this that offered Frances a forecast of pure ecstasy, making her whole body shake, so that after a few minutes she almost shouted with urgency. 'Edward, yes, please, *please*!'

He moved into her then, gently at first, and slow, then less gently, when it began to hurt, when she thought she would scream with pleasure and pain, when something was stretching and stinging inside her, until suddenly the pressure and pain vanished and he reached up far inside her in one fell swoop, while she lay motionless for a while, before starting to share in his movements, easing herself further down, raising her thighs, so that against his force she could offer her own in return, a gradually rising counterpoint, a seesaw of pleasure – where soon, such was the fluid ease and rhythm of things, that he left her body almost entirely before pushing straight up inside her again, in one long thrust, right into her belly it seemed – rising, rising for minutes on end into a delirious crescendo that suddenly exploded between them as pieces of her body seemed to disintegrate in pleasure.

'Oh, my darling, my darling!' Her head swam. She felt herself sinking through the cushions, falling, observing herself, outside her body, in a long free-floating fall, a dizzy spinning that lasted and lasted, which had no time to it, until finally she was conscious again, in the real world, felt warm and tingling, and immeasurably different – confident, so alive and lighthearted in a way she had never been. 'My darling,' she said once more, in quiet surprise now, shaking her head in wonder, like a traveller returned from a miraculous voyage, glimpsing the infinite, for whom nothing now on earth could ever be the same again.

They lay there for several minutes, youth and age, innocence and experience mingled now, both of them speechless, bewildered by their success. The Prince rose at last. But Frances stayed, letting the soft breeze from the window play over her thighs, arching her head back on the cushions, unwilling to break the spell. She glanced at the Stubbs painting once more, seeing the airy beech grove on the hill. She thought of home again. But now she saw Summer Hill and its lands as something almost within her grasp. With the lovely confidence she felt, the warm sense of relief still coursing through her body, anything was possible. She no longer had to lie to the Prince. They were one together – they understood, they loved, they wanted each other. Her deceit, the tensions she had felt with him, these were

over, replaced now only by another and delicious tension she felt rising in her –
of suddenly wanting him once more, there and then.

Edward?' she asked him smiling quizzically. 'Come to me again . . .'

'My dearest, hardly now –'

'But you *will*?' She sat up quickly. 'We will, won't we?'

He nodded, a little sadly, with a tired smile.

But at supper he had regained his attack, vigorous once more, seeking out all
sorts of other excitements between them.

'My dear,' he told her over the first course, 'I have been thinking: if we are to
see each other happily in the future – we must lay the ghost of your mother. We
must make things up entirely there. Return home after your examinations, speak
to her; ask her if she would do me the honour, with you, of coming with me to
Marienbad this summer.'

'To Marienbad?'

'Yes, a most attractive little spa in Bohemia. I have been there once before. And
given the present delicate situation between this country and Germany – the
intemperate, warlike struttings of my nephew the Kaiser – I have decided not to
patronise Bad Homburg any more for my annual *Kur*. I shall go to Marienbad
instead – I have an excellent relationship with the old Emperor Franz-Josef. And
if you can persuade your Mama to join my party – well then, we may kill two birds:
I may truly effect a lasting reconciliation between you and her, while enjoying your
company openly at the same time. What do you say?'

Frances looked at him uncertainly. 'I . . .'

'It is what you want, is it not? She to be friends with you – and I to be . . .' He
left the definition open, hanging on the air.

'Yes, yes – I do! It's just . . .'

'What then?' He had stopped eating entirely, quite unaware of his food now.

'I had not expected it – the offer. But yes, of course! I will ask her.'

What Frances, in truth, had not expected was how her plans that the Prince
might somehow meet her mother should so readily fall into place, without her
instigating them.

But why did she wish the Prince to meet her mother? What could that achieve,
which his patronage and their friendship had not already achieved at Summer Hill?
And why satisfy her mother's rampant social ambitions in any case? She did not
really want to please her, after all – she recognised that – nor even impress her.
She had no wish to flaunt the closeness of her royal connection, far from it: it was
a private thing, a secret which she wished least of all to share with her mother.

Yet something spurred her towards the idea of their meeting – an intuition, like
that of a gambler in possession of extraordinary cards who nonetheless senses
that he may have to play out the whole hand, down to the last ace, in order to
win.

Frances wrote to her mother the next day, asking if she might come home next
month, saying that she had exciting news for them both – relating to the Prince of
Wales. Lady Cordiner offered her a most heartfelt welcome by return of post.

At the beginning of June, when Frances and Eileen came back to Summer Hill, high summer was already bursting over the valley. An unusually clement spring had brought everything on early, the white candelabra drooping on the chestnuts, the beech and oak almost in full leaf – a day of warm wind that stroked the grass in long swathes of changing green and sent the clouds scudding over Mount Brandon, hiding the sun intermittently before it emerged again, a sudden limelight on the valley, rising quickly up the higher land, a spreading flood of gold against the blue.

Molloy himself, in his best head coachman's uniform and braided top hat, had met them with a groom at Thomastown station. And, instead of the little waggonette and the old cob that had taken them away eight months before, they came home now in the freshly-painted grey landau, with the hood down, pulled by two smart grey mares, the polished horse-brasses and black leather gleaming in the light.

Frances smelt a drift of turf smoke from one of the estate cottage chimneys on the way up the hill from Cloone: a dry, brackish, sweet-and-sour breath on the wind. She could never define it, isolate any single ingredient – a hint of straw, grass, Irish earth and water: all Ireland, which she had so missed, in one smouldering bit of bog – a smell of slow warmth and quiet and security, that tugged at her soul, saying, 'Home, you are coming home.'

They had turned into the long drive at the top of the hill and now they trotted briskly through the tussocky demesne dotted with grazing cattle, up the rise to the brow of the hill until suddenly the long east flank of the house came in sight, a flash of pale limestone through the trees. The tall sash windows sparkled in the noon sun, the rooks cawed clamorously, blown about in gusty swerves and spirals above the flock of chimneys. And at that moment, hearing the harsh melody, Frances could not restrain herself.

'The rooks –' The words caught in her throat. 'I've never heard them so loud.'

'Indeed,' Eileen said. 'Sure they're sweeping them out of them chimneys be the looks of it, that's why.'

They saw the men on the roof then, with chimney brushes and ropes, and heard the dogs barking as they drove round the pleasure gardens to the south front of the house. Monster and Sergeant, the two terriers, rushed forward kicking up the gravel behind them, yapping furiously, as the landau drew up by the porch, the hall door open where Lady Cordiner, composed but somehow less formidable now in Frances's eyes, was on the steps to meet them. Frances jumped out of the carriage and ran towards her.

'Mama!'

'My dearest!' They embraced quickly, spontaneously. And Frances forgot all her old enmities and had the illusion of peace with her mother in this homecoming.

Sir Desmond came on to the porch then, blinking behind his spectacles in the bright light, his short beard teased by the wind, and the dogs, in a tizzy of confusion at this important arrival, leapt up against his knees instead of welcoming Frances and Eileen.

'Down, Sergeant! Down, Monster!' her father roared. It had always been his welcome, Frances remembered: the dogs to be subdued first before the guests could be greeted, as he greeted his daughter vaguely now.

'Papa! – you are here . . .' Frances grasped his hand, feeling the warmth of tears pricking her eyes.

'Where else, my dear?'

'Fiddling with your aeronautical machines, I'd thought.'

Frances wanted to hug him. But she had never done that, and could not now, and already he was moving away from her, taking a back seat.

Pat Kennedy, the under-butler, emerged from the porch with a footman to take the luggage. Eileen stood by the landau, gathering up some hat boxes. She glanced up as he arrived, looking at him calmly, distantly.

'Well, indeed.' His voice was low and sardonic. 'So you're back at last.'

'Indeed, and why wouldn't I be?'

'Too grand now for the likes of us, I'll be bound – and you hobnobbing with Royalty.' He lugged a trunk from the front seat.

'Certainly, and wasn't it a grand thing altogether – the best of times we had, down there in Sandringham.'

'You should be ashamed of yourself – that blackguard with the beard, that Prince of Wales –'

''Tis you who should be ashamed, Pat Kennedy, and you never sending me word at all – all the time I was away.' Eileen stumped off with the hat boxes, leaving him there, deflated, petulant.

'And Aunt Emily?' Frances asked. 'How is she? *Where* is she?'

'Upstairs – of course,' her father said offhandedly. 'On some drawing scheme of hers.'

'Oh, Papa, why doesn't she come down – and greet people?'

Her father shrugged his shoulders. And Frances was suddenly downcast, her happy mood broken, reminded now of all the strictures and impositions in the house – the hatreds, secrets, closed rooms. She rushed upstairs to see Aunt Emily, running to the end of the landing, only to find her bedroom door locked. Pat Kennedy had come up the stairs behind her, helping with the luggage. 'The key – the stupid key, Pat. You have it?' He reached into his pocket, giving it to her. 'It's absolute *nonsense*,' she told him. 'Locking the door on her in this way – we must stop it!'

'Yes, Miss Frances.' He paused. 'Only we had a spot of trouble with Miss Emily, do you see – she ran away a few weeks ago. Her Ladyship insisted afterwards that the door be kept locked again –'

'Ran away?'

'To Waterford, Miss. She got one of the new grooms to drive her to the train. And she was on the boat then, for England, when they got her off it, just before it sailed.'

'I see.'

Pat looked at her superciliously, so that Frances returned his look, encouraged at the same time to take up a point with him there and then which she had thought to speak to him about later, if at all. 'Oh, and Pat, while you're here, I might as well mention it: you never wrote to Eileen, all the time she was away. Now I don't wish to pry – it's entirely your own business – except to say she was most unhappy about it. A little unfeeling of you, surely?' She looked at him coldly.

'Well, yes, Miss – but it is my business.' He was equally cold.

'I only mention it since, as you know, I am so very fond of Eileen.'

'I know, Miss Frances – taking her to Sandry'ham and all.' It was obvious from his tone that he saw this as no favour whatsoever.

'Yes, well, I want her to be happy, that's all.'

'I'm sure she was, Miss.' He was so sardonic that Frances was tempted to reprimand him. But she refrained. 'Well, I just think you might have been more considerate, Pat.' She turned towards her aunt's bedroom door.

'Oh, and Miss,' Pat called out, so that she turned again, hearing him speak in a much quieter voice. 'Another thing, since we're here, I have to tell you. The men this morning – they were sweeping the chimneys, in your bedroom, too.'

He looked at her as if she knew the possible implications of this – and she did. Her heart thumped. 'Yes?'

'They found some stuff hidden in the flue, there's a sort of a ledge there above the grate – little bits and pieces, silver boxes, wine glasses,' he said pointedly. 'And them glass weights with the flowers trapped inside of them that her Ladyship keeps in the drawing room . . .'

'And?'

'The men told me about it – I was up there at the time seeing to Miss Emily. I took charge of the stuff, cleaned the soot off it, and left it all back in your wardrobe.'

'Did you tell my mother?'

'No,' he said wisely. 'I wouldn't want to do that now, would I, Miss? – and get Eileen Donaghy into trouble.' He let his eyes rest on Frances's for several seconds before turning abruptly and walking away, while Frances stayed, covered in shame and embarrassment – caught out, a hostage now to one of the servants, who must know all about her previous thieving escapades with Eileen.

All that other earlier life of hers at Summer Hill – her troubled adolescence as she saw it now, of stealing things – came back to her. She was disgusted, now that she saw herself as a grown woman, to think of the frivolous, dishonest, unhappy girl she had once been. So that, when she unlocked the door and went into her aunt's room, she was almost in tears of rage and frustration.

Aunt Emily, as usual, was completely absorbed in a drawing. She did not look up. But she was aware all the same of Frances's upset.

'So, back again – and unhappy already.'

'I'm so annoyed with myself, Aunt –'

'And so you should be, coming back here, when you were well off where you were.' Her voice was not quite so fierce and scatty as usual; the slight brogue had a kindness in it, an understanding. Yet she remained head down over her work.

'I'm not upset about my coming home. Just annoyed – to find your door locked and all that nonsense again.'

'Ah, that's not what troubles you at all.' Her aunt leant forward, running a fine-pointed watercolour brush along a line. 'And that shouldn't worry you in any case. Fact of the matter is I can get out of here whenever I want – Pat Kennedy and I are the best of friends, we have all sorts of little arrangements.' She leant back from her work at last.

'May I look?'

'Why not? It's for you, in the first place.'

Frances bent over her shoulder. The drawing, full of baroque detail and delicate colour, was a wicked, indeed an indecent pastiche of the Cinderella tale: it showed a gilded pumpkin coach waiting below the steps of a great palace, with Frances disappearing into it, her sequined ball gown all torn and dishevelled, one of her breasts partly visible, with a silver slipper left on the top step, a regal figure emerging in the foreground to pick it up – the Prince of the story, but elderly and rather gross – and in this case very like the Prince of Wales, a coronet askew on his head, in a similar state of undress, hitching up his trousers as he ran.

'Aunt!' Frances exclaimed, her earlier shame quite forgotten. 'It's disgusting. And absolutely nothing like the truth!'

'Excuse yourself, girl. We all know – you're the Prince's mistress.'

'Certainly not!'

'Don't deny it – to me at any rate. And I must say you've done very well for yourself. So why come back here?' Her aunt looked up at her. 'With the world at your feet? That was stupid.'

'It's not at my feet. And I'm only a friend of the Prince's.'

'He has no women *friends* – they're all mistresses, sooner or later. So excuse yourself – you don't have to pull the wool over my eyes. I know what's what these days – here, take a look at this, if you think I haven't my wits about me.'

She opened a drawer beneath her in the table. Inside was one of Lady Cordiner's richest and most attractive paperweights, a posy of dog roses embedded in the crystal. Aunt Emily smirked with pleasure.

'What *have* you been doing, Aunt?'

'Took a fancy to it,' Aunt Emily said shortly. 'And why not? Gives me an interest – when I go downstairs. Oh, I get out and about these days you know. Pat Kennedy and me, I told you – we have nice little arrangements over it.'

Aunt Emily returned to her drawing, chuckling, altogether the happy child now, so that Frances suddenly felt herself to be the older woman. And as such, feeling her maturity, her now well-established balance, she was appalled once more at the prohibitions of Summer Hill, the madness, malice, cruelty and insensitivity that reigned here, introduced and sustained by her mother, which had led to all this eccentric behaviour, her own and Aunt Emily's, not to mention her father's crackpot inventions in the yard with his aerial machines. She would stand it no longer.

'Aunt, it's nonsense – your taking that paperweight.'

Her aunt looked up at her slyly. 'Is it indeed? Speak for yourself, girl – it was *you* who gave me the idea. Oh, don't think I don't know: all the little tricks you and Eileen Donaghy got up to in the old days here. I'm just carrying on the tradition!'

Frances was dumbfounded. 'Who told you?'

'Ah, I have my secrets, too.'

'Pat Kennedy told you.'

Her aunt looked at her blandly. 'Perhaps I guessed. Since it wasn't me in those days, it can only have been you. We're alike after all, aren't we? – in our little tricks with your Mama!'

'The point is, Aunt,' Frances spoke to her very firmly like a governess, 'we don't *have* to go on with them. We can just behave in perfectly ordinary ways here –'

Aunt Emily broke in with a great guffaw. 'Oh, that's a good one, very good –' She spluttered, nearly choking with mirth, before recovering. 'You're out of your mind, girl, if you think that,' she continued now with great acerbity. 'It's only the little tricks that keep you sane here.' She turned back to her drawing. 'I have a few other small items in mind downstairs,' she said in a considered, choosy voice, before taking up her brush and adding a gilt flourish to the pumpkin coach.

Frances was appalled as much as amused. 'Oh, Aunt – I do so wish it wasn't all like this.' After her experience in London she was able to confirm now how far the house had deviated, was void of sensible life, where everything that meant anything to its inhabitants – apart from her mother – was unbalanced, underhand, conducted in secret or out in the yard. Though she had changed, things were just the same at Summer Hill – people made to cringe and steal and hide in the big house, scratching and burrowing about insanely: her mother, as ever, a Gorgon – trapping them all in this bizarre cave.

After lunch Frances spoke to her mother of the Prince's Marienbad suggestion, alone over coffee in the drawing room, her father having disappeared as usual to his study.

'Well,' Lady Cordiner said pleasantly when she heard the news, her usually creased and severe face clearing with a smile. 'And whose idea was it? – tell me, really.' She looked at Frances, her smile changing from the pleasant to the patronising, intent on dominating her daughter once more, as she had in the past – the wise, all-knowing authoritative Mama.

'His – it was the Prince's idea entirely, Mama,' Frances replied with even more authority, determined from the start not to let her mother outface her.

'I am uncertain of your relationship with him, you see,' Lady Cordiner temporised.

'I am simply a friend, a good friend – through Miss Wechsberg, as I told you: a friend to them both, the Princess as well.'

'Why should I be asked, though?'

'Papa, too, if he cares –'

'Oh, I doubt that,' Lady Cordiner said at once.

'Well, then, you and I,' Frances continued pleasantly, playing her mother like a fish. 'It would be a happy change for us both in any case – taking the *Kur* at Marienbad!'

'I should miss the Dublin Horse Show . . .'

'I think not. The Prince will be in Scotland for the opening of the grouse season on the 12th. He would not leave for Marienbad until mid-August.'

'You are well-informed,' Lady Cordiner said somewhat acidly.

'Of course – he has told me.'

Her mother sipped her coffee, silent for a long moment. 'Still,' she said at last, 'I remain unclear as to the *purpose* of the visit.'

'No more than that you should meet. You are my family after all. The Prince, and Princess Alix too – they take a distinct interest in me, my background, naturally.'

'Naturally.' Lady Cordiner echoed the thought suspiciously. She did not trust her daughter an inch. And, though she longed to meet the Prince, she sensed some trap in the whole idea. She had no idea what it might be.

'Well, let us consider it,' Lady Cordiner went on, temporising once more, hoping that in the course of Frances's stay she would identify what made her uneasy in the invitation: Frances would let something drop – or perhaps she would discover it for herself. So that meanwhile, Lady Cordiner decided, she would keep a particularly sharp eye on her daughter.

This was no easy matter, for at once, immediately after coffee, Frances changed into an old riding jacket and set off – first round the house and then, with a mare, about the estate, revisiting all the rooms, the attics, galloping the woods and fields, until late in the afternoon – journeys, taking her well out of her mother's way, which she kept up almost every day of her short visit.

She took to the house and grounds and all her secret haunts there, thirstily, a traveller returned from a desert, making the world of Summer Hill hers again, marking the place – the walls, the lawn, the river walk, the airy beech grove on Cooper's Hill, all the lands running to the mountains – like an animal re-establishing bounds to its territory.

She knelt by the slow, clear stream which joined the big river at the southern boundary of the estate, seeing her reflection there, a woman who had once been a child dabbling in these same shallows, before she bent down, putting her arm through the mirror, drawing sprigs of watercress from the beds and nibbling them.

Later, returning to the house, she ran her hand over the letters carved in the bark of the big maple by the croquet lawn, where she and her brothers had cut their initials years before, growth almost entirely obscuring the incisions now.

In the drowsy afternoons she sometimes went up into the long attic above the old nurseries, gazing at the portraits of her Cordiner ancestors and the fine Irish Georgian furniture which her mother had discarded here from the rooms downstairs. In one dusty corner, behind a pile of cabin trunks labelled 'P & O' and 'Port Said', she found a tea chest filled with playthings she had used as a child – her Caldicott and Kate Greenaway picture books, a small doll's kitchen stove complete with miniature tin kettles, pots and pans. Beneath these she discovered her old nursery music box in a walnut case, a Xylophone, with one of the toothed metal discs still in place. She wound it up, amazed at the sudden sharp memory it brought, a return to the nursery, as the tinkling, bell-like melody emerged – 'The Dashing White Sergeant'.

The toys, like the lovely Irish Sheraton and Chippendale furniture and the portraits of her ancestors, had become irrelevant, lost up here in the attic. But they were not, Frances knew. It was just these qualities of gaiety and play, of a graceful past, which belonged to the rooms downstairs, which she longed to bring back here.

In default of this, at one end of the attic, Frances cleared a space under the skylights and set it up as a happy, hidden room for herself – an oval table and chairs in the middle, with the portraits set round it against the eaves and the music box on an inlaid bureau beside her. And here Frances sat in her ideal home, writing to the Prince, listening to the tinkly music, suspended above the real house like a bird of prey waiting its chance to fall from the sky like a stone.

At night, often going to her room early, she lay on the bedspread, stomach down, looking out on the long summer twilight, southwards, far down the valley, to where the forest at the very end of the estate, rising up on both sides of the river, made a dark V shape against the pink-blue sky: the woods of childhood, she thought, thinking of her years in this same room as a girl, when she had left the nursery, and had stayed awake on just such summer evenings, waiting to see the first star. And so she did now on her return, watching the sky slowly fill with glimmering silver dots, until at last she brought her oil lamp in from the landing, to read for the third or fourth time that day the Prince's latest letter to her.

Marlborough Club
Pall Mall SW

My dear one,

Today we attended the Derby meeting and I write to you now, in quite a hurry – forgive me – just prior to our annual Derby dinner here. I do wish you could have been with us all this afternoon. The racing was admirable, even tho' neither of my fillies took a place. I was given a tip however on a smallish grey in the 4.30 – the unfancied 'La Gioconda' – which (surprisingly for I never fancy greys on short runs) came home in the last furlong, and I collected something of a handsome sum thereby!

It was all most enjoyable – but that you were not there. You are sorely missed, in *every* way. However, from your last letter I see you may expect to return at the beginning of July. I await the day eagerly. May you be here to join our party at Cowes? You are missing the season – unclouded but for the wretched news from South Africa. I fear now that there cannot but be serious trouble with these intemperate Transvaalers before the year is out.

On the other hand it is so wise of you to repair any remaining damage at home and I am so pleased to hear of your success there. I do hope we may all meet together at Marienbad.

My darling one – in my thoughts most often,

E.

Lady Cordiner meanwhile watched and waited, as did Frances. She did not press the Prince's invitation, merely let the idea lie fallow, waiting to bloom. She felt almost certain that her mother – left to her own imaginings and unable to restrain herself – would bring the topic up again, as she did a week later, taking tea in the porch, putting down *The Times* in which, as was her habit, she had been reading the City and financial news. In this instance, though, she had obviously been looking at the sporting page as well.

'I note the Prince of Wales was off racing again yesterday,' she said drily. 'Seems to do nothing but.'

'Yes,' Frances replied nonchalantly, feeding a biscuit to one of the terriers. 'It is his passion.'

'One of them.'

By way of comment Frances merely smiled at her mother. 'Of course if I don't go to Marienbad,' her mother continued lightly, 'you will not be able to travel there yourself – alone. The Princess does not accompany him to these watering places. You would be without a chaperone,' she added with a note of triumph, sensing a victory with her daughter.

But Frances had anticipated just such a move. 'Of course not, Mama – I could not go alone.'

'Which is the only reason you require my presence – it is all most clear – merely that you may enjoy yourself.'

Frances was treading thin ice. What her mother had said was perfectly true. The Princess did not go on these annual visits to the European spas. And without her presence Frances could no longer be seen as *en famille* with the Royal couple. But she staked the game with her mother on the mere possession of these Royal cards which, though she might not play them to the full, she could let drop – apparently unwittingly, innocently, temptingly.

'Mama,' she said, turning to her confidingly, with an air of suppressed brio and disingenuous verity, 'do come! It was the Prince alone who asked – not I who suggested it. And we should *both* so enjoy ourselves. You have no idea – he is *such* good company, so kind, considerate and amusing. His equerry, too, Sir Seymour Fortescue – a little dry, but witty in his own way. He plays a fine hand at bridge. And the Prince's secretary, Francis Knollys – his golf and croquet are really most bizarre!'

'You have done these things with them all?'

'But of course, Mama! I have been at Sandringham several times, and often at Marlborough House,' Frances said wide-eyed.

Lady Cordiner could bear this documentation of her daughter's social success no longer. The bait had been dangled before her eyes long enough. She snapped at it.

'Very well then, if you really –' She stopped herself. 'If the Prince wishes it, how can one refuse?'

'Indeed, one might well see it that way,' Frances replied humorously. 'A Royal command!'

Thus both women took a victory in the matter – Lady Cordiner by allowing that it was her duty to comply, while Frances won through the pure pleasure of besting her mother.

Frances rose early, watching from first light onwards – the strange procession of pilgrims making for the waters, emerging from guest houses, villas, grand hotels and from out of the pine-clad hills that lay all around the little Bohemian spa – congregating in successive groups on the paved promenade that led to the Kreuzbrunnen, the main spring at Marienbad, the holy of holies, under the rotunda at the end of the long colonnade.

They arrived soon after dawn, out of the side-streets, from up and down the hill, strolling players making an entrance on to this gradually brightening, sun-streaked stage, supplicants shuffling along, before reaching out eagerly for their cups at the marble fountain, filling them, returning down the promenade, sipping the water in rapt devotion, celebrating a holy rite.

First, in the half-light, like wood-demons from the forest, came groups of Russian and Polish Jews in black kaftans, their faces gaunt and wasted with expressions of extreme melancholy. Afterwards the monks from the Abbey of Tepl processed in long white robes, gliding ghosts in the pink light, kindly but aloof figures, for the town was theirs after all, its lands and precious waters.

Then came the less important foreign visitors – minor nobility, retired generals, insignificant ambassadors and super-annuated politicians with their overdressed wives. When they had taken their cups and moved into the wings of the colonnade, the stage was free for several minutes, scanned only by an advance guard for the new arrivals – secretaries, valets and ladies-in-waiting – who, like scene-shifters, had come to see the promenade clear for their masters and mistresses, the *crème de la crème* of European society, who shortly made their entry, full of pomp and circumstance: a few kings, from Bulgaria and Portugal; princes and princesses from several other minor dynasties; archdukes, dukes and duchesses from the Habsburg Court, a whole cousinage of the Tsar's from St Petersburg; upper crust English aristocracy, exotic maharajahs and maharanees, mysterious Jewish financiers – all of whom commandeered the stage now, in a secretly expectant mood.

Finally, towards eight o'clock, as it seemed a climax to the overture, a portly, bearded man in a dark blue linen jacket, perfectly creased white trousers and a grey felt hat walked briskly on to the scene, accompanied by his secretary and an equerry – a simply dressed figure, travelling incognito as the Duke of Lancaster, whom yet everyone knew to be the Prince of Wales.

As if on cue the real performance began then, the frock-coated orchestra under the colonnade tuning up on many violins, before breaking into the 'Imperial Polka', when the glittering company filed towards the healing spring, stepping gaily out to the rhythm of the music.

*

It was mid-morning, almost a week after Frances, with Eileen and Lady Cordiner, had arrived at Marienbad. They sat with the Prince on the wide first-floor balcony outside his apartments in the palatial Hotel Weimar, overlooking the little town and the forested hills beyond.

'Ah, Lady Cordiner, you are right!' The Prince raised his coffee cup appraisingly. 'How much better than the waters indeed! No one makes coffee better than the Viennese. My valet Midinger is from that city – I have him make it specially for me. I fear, though, with all this cream on top, we must drink it secretly. My good physician here, Dr Ott, must not know of it!'

'Indeed.' Lady Cordiner nodded in happy agreement. 'I believe, though, that one may overdo the *Kur*, your Royal Highness.'

'True. And some do so, I believe. But I am not numbered among them!' The Prince beamed. He sat very upright on a small gilt chair that seemed impossibly frail under his weight. The weather was warm, even close. He eased his collar a fraction, his hands perspiring.

'Of course, these physicians here,' Lady Cordiner went on amiably, but with a clear hint of teasing authority in her voice, 'I believe they are misguided. They imagine that a single month of self-denial can make up for eleven of self-indulgence. Whereas, it were better the other way about: to live reasonably and rationally for eleven months and "let oneself go" for the twelfth!'

'Wise counsel, Lady Cordiner.' The Prince agreed. 'I am of a mind that these physicians here – they are not adept in the art of living.'

'Oh, they don't know the first thing about it.' Lady Cordiner spoke dismissively. She was happy now, having won the earlier conversational point with the Prince, thoroughly to confirm his subsequent remarks.

Though of course their tastes in the art of living were very different, Frances thought then – yet how well they got on together. They were alike, of course, in their need to dominate, to win – in their sure possession, appreciation and use of power: a characteristic which they could admire in each other without penalty for they shared no social history, had no bones to pick there.

Lady Cordiner, released from the dictatorial poisons which Summer Hill had instilled in her, unbent in the balmy summer air, the fragrance of pine and fir from the hills, the meticulous service at the Hotel Weimar, the aura of social distinction and luxury that lay over everything she touched or looked at – so very different from the rude, rough airs of the Irish and County Kilkenny.

At Marienbad, without responsibilities, free of the bossy round that governed her life at home, her other sophisticated character bloomed. Her wit was no longer frustrated or malicious but used in the cause now of a long-dormant attribute, an informed and cultured mind. An almost youthful, elegant dash – overlaid by years of provincial Irish life – returned to her. She became the person she could once have been, had she not married someone so emotionally bland and socially withdrawn as Sir Desmond. Lacking satisfaction there, her husband's house and lands, and her own money, had come to absorb her love, perverting it.

But now, basking on this longed-for pinnacle of social success, her forgotten better nature was resurgent. Here she found her true station in life, which she was well equipped to maintain – better than most of the Prince's friends indeed, for with her quick Jewish wit and intelligence allied to her sense of occasion and eye for the main chance she outdid them in her social skills.

Lady Cordiner soon emerged as one of the great social successes of the season at Marienbad. The Prince took to her with enthusiasm, while she knew exactly how to handle him, so that the Prince, in turn, assured of her good will, was able to pursue his dalliance with Frances openly – and privately.

Of course, Lady Cordiner's great social acuity was just the factor which soon alerted her to the real nature of the Prince's association with her daughter. And here she was in a quandary. She could not but disapprove of it. On the other hand she saw clearly that her own burgeoning friendship with the Prince depended upon the continuation of her daughter's liaison.

She touched obliquely on the matter one afternoon with Frances, in the drawing room of their suite at the Weimar.

'Of course, my dear, I am quite aware now . . . of the *real* nature of the Prince's interest in you. How it is between you both,' she added distastefully.

'Yes, Mama,' Frances replied coldly, eyes alight. There was no point in denying it any longer. Indeed, now that her mother was aware of the truth, Frances was pleased to confirm it. It was another – and in this case resounding – victory for her, in the several she had recently gained over her mother.

'Of course, a quite passing concern,' Lady Cordiner continued dismissively. 'And it matters not one whit in itself – as long as there is no talk of it, no hint of scandal. You are clear about that, I hope?'

Frances smiled, equally dismissive. 'Oh yes, Mama. We are both aware of *that*.'

And now Frances knew why she had wanted her mother to meet the Prince – why she wished the meeting a success, as it had been. At last, she thought, she could identify the winning card she held. If anything were to go wrong in her affair with the Prince, if any 'hint of scandal' did seem about to emerge, she would have a tremendous lever then against her mother, who would, Frances knew, do anything to maintain her own association with the Prince and his circle. In short, the card she had identified was one of 'scandal', which she could, if the need arose, blackmail her mother with.

They shared an extensive suite at the Weimar, on the second floor, just above the Prince's rooms. And it was an easy matter, when her mother was taking her siesta or late at night when she had retired to her own bedroom, for Frances to walk down the service stairs at the side of the hotel and enter the Prince's rooms by way of his dining room door at the end of the corridor. Further along, at the entrance to the main salon, the Prince's detectives, either Mr Quinn from Scotland Yard, or Paoli, the Corsican, were always stationed. But they had been well briefed: Frances could come and go as she pleased. And that afternoon, after their conversation about the Marienbad physicians, the Prince said to her, 'My dear, your mother is admirable; she is most witty and informed. I cannot think how you ever came to fall out with her.'

'I may tell you, Edward, she is quite different at home.'

She did not wish to pursue the matter. It was enough that both got on so well together. To change the topic she came to him now, touching his collar, settling it, where it had come slightly adrift.

'My fourth collar today,' the Prince remarked. 'It is too hot, too close altogether. Though at home there is a heatwave.' He gestured to the big red dispatch box that had been brought up from the Legation in Vienna, containing various state papers and the last three editions of *The Times*. 'Worse than here, if anything. They have seen nothing like it for years.'

The Prince went over to the dispatch box. He was preoccupied with something, drumming his fingers on the table now as he bent over it. Frances followed him.

'What is it?'

'Nothing . . .'

'Edward, I *am* interested . . . in other things.'

'The fool Chamberlain – and Milner, too,' the Prince burst out suddenly. 'They are pushing us into a war in the Cape Colony – and I can do nothing about it. I have had news today from one of my friends in the Cabinet – they have put us in an impossible position. Already they have purchased hundreds of mules, sent out a dozen staff officers and millions of rounds of small arms ammunition – to provoke the Boers on the Transvaal frontier. The jingo element has entirely taken control at home. And today I learn they have forced General Butler to resign, the Officer Commanding in the Cape, the only voice of reason out there. The Boers have been put into a corner. They can do nothing but fight now. And they will – they are well prepared for it. Yet we are quite unprepared, we have no real troops, no army in the Cape to fight them with. It will lead to disaster – and all quite uncalled for.'

'I thought the Boers . . . were bad?'

'My dear, not *bad*! Uncouth, devious, arrogant, no doubt. But then they have an understandable pride in themselves and their lands they have carved out on the high veldt there. And we have done nothing but undermine that pride, aggravating them quite unnecessarily for years with our sabre-rattling, so that they *must* fight – yet they are not worth the fighting.' The Prince shook his head. 'There is no real *casus belli*. Whereas there is always a cause for peace – I see that as my life's work, indeed.'

'I agree so much.' Frances stood behind him as he returned the papers to the dispatch box. 'You remember my cousin – Captain Dermot Cordiner? He is attached to Milner's staff at the War Office. I imagine, from what you say, he will shortly be leaving for the Cape.'

The Prince nodded. 'Of course. It may be even he, indeed, at the War Office, who had the purchasing of those mules!'

'I have told him – how against his army career I was, for someone of such intelligence, sensitivity.'

The Prince smiled in agreement. 'I am reminded of the staff officer I met, returned from Omdurman with half his head blown away, put out to grass at the

War Office as a result. "Oh, I am quite pleased," he told me, "for I shall not need my brains there." In positions where it matters, they are mostly a shortsighted and incompetent lot – and all entirely without finesse. I fear the very worst.'

Frances moved round the salon fiddling with things, while the Prince lay down on the chaise-longue, taking up *The Times*. 'My brother Eustace, with the King's Rifles,' she said. 'No doubt he would be going too?'

'When it comes, everyone will have to be sent – a vast land. They will need several armies to contain the Boers, let alone defeat them.' He returned to the racing news in the paper.

'And I?' Frances spoke more urgently now. But the Prince did not respond. 'If there is war I shall go, too – as a nurse – I have passed my first exams. They will need nurses.'

The Prince looked up, paying attention now, concerned. 'I could not bear to ... I would miss you,' he said quite openly, looking across the room to where Frances was fingering the handle of his carriage clock on the ornate mantelpiece.

'But, Edward, I must do something with my life.'

She gazed at the clock face, watching the tiny second hand tick by, suddenly feeling her own life ebbing away with it. She had achieved so much in the past year, in work and love. So often the clock had stopped for her – at the nursing home in Grosvenor Crescent – thrilled by the vital needs she found she could supply there; at Sandringham with the Prince, at Eaton Place making love with him.

But now, with his talk of war, she sensed impending change for her as well. Happy in his affection, their need for each other, she knew nonetheless that she could not remain a fixed object in his life. She had achieved her ambition with the Prince, with him and with her mother. Now she would have to go on to something else: fill her life with something fresh, stop the clocks in some new adventure.

'Of course you must do something – I see that,' the Prince admitted despondently. 'Though I wish now –' He laughed half-heartedly. 'I rather wish now that you *had* taken up with young Wilson, who so admired you.'

'Why so?'

'Why, for entirely selfish reasons: you might be married to him soon. And, since he has no concern with the army, that would keep you in London, away from any war – where I could at least *see* you.'

Frances was moved by this admission, coming to him on the chaise-longue, kneeling beside him. 'My dearest dear.' She took his hand, shaking her head, looking at him; he had turned away now, rather ashamed of what he had just said. 'Edward, I cannot take to people I do not love.'

'Of course not, simply a jest –'

'*We* take together in that way – you and I,' she said evenly. 'So I cannot consider others at the same time – I have no need to.'

'Yes, and it surprises me.' The Prince turned to her now, ruffling her dark curls for an instant. 'Most touches me – your single-mindedness.'

'Oh, I know – so unlike you!' Frances lightened the exchange, prodding him delicately in the ribs. 'You and that pretty Frau Pistl for example, who runs the shop in the Colonnade, selling those frightful Styrian hats – your little attentions there, they have not escaped me!'

'My dear, it was nothing –'

'Of course not. But you *are* flirtatious, Edward!'

'I have been – but so much less so of late. And it is obvious why . . .'

'Thank you – and it is the same with me. I had much the same inclinations, before we met. But they don't touch me now.'

'They will, for you *do* have your own life – and I must encourage it. But South Africa . . .' He frowned.

'It may never happen.'

'Be assured –'

'If it does, I will go – and come back. And there is still now.' She pressed his hand. They no longer had to speak.

The carriage clock chimed, the half-hour after three. A close, hot air ran off the hills, through the open windows, stirring the lace curtains. The town, shut down for the afternoon, embalmed the visitors in sleep.

Getting up, undoing the tightly-clasped belt round her waist as she moved across the salon, Frances went through the small anteroom and into the Prince's bedroom, where she undressed completely, lying naked on the white counterpane of the huge bed, leaning back, playing with the Prince's little charms, the silver lizard and other lucky mascots that dangled from the brass bedpost.

The Prince joined her. She rose suddenly while he undressed, stripping the counterpane and the top sheet clear away, and they lay there on the velvet-smooth, cooler sheet beneath, slowly discovering each other again, ever more adventurous explorers through the baking afternoon.

She lay around, beside, on top of him – more skilled now, more loving, in her lovemaking: pushing down on him, rising back, arched above him, rotating in little spasms while he touched her breasts – before she fell on him again, nurturing an ecstasy, letting it become a fever in the warm room, so that eventually, with the heat, exertion, excitement, she could bear the restraint no longer, falling over him finally, pressing down, letting him come far inside her, when for one last moment everything was withheld, unmoving, balancing on a precipice, before her whole body shuddered, seemed to levitate, and she felt herself soaring away in the air in a long arc, melting then, falling, dazed with joy for minutes afterwards.

They slept for half an hour, until a distant rumble of thunder woke them. And half an hour later, just as the glittering company was sitting down to tea on the long terrace of the Bellevue Café opposite, the hog muggy afternoon was suddenly split by a huge clap of thunder, followed by successive fierce cannonades, echoing down from the hills above the Abbey, like a brutal artillery barrage against the town.

In another few minutes the swirling, plum-bruised skies opened in sheets of rain, deluging the women in their frilly lace and silk tea-gowns, and sending the orchestra scurrying with their tubas and French horns. The rain, in glittering great rods, made sudden pools in the empty teacups, set the icing running on the rich cakes, flooded the cutlery, and doused the spirit lamps under the silver teapots.

The customers panicked now – the men clearing the tables, china crashing to the ground, as they pulled the linen table cloths to shroud the women, attempting to herd them out to their carriages, brandishing walking sticks and shouting at the coachmen beneath the terrace. It was a rout. People fell in the aisles or down the steps, the women, clad like nuns in the great cloths, tripping over themselves.

In five minutes what had been a most elegant company, preening themselves, about to enjoy the *café-concert*, had become a bedraggled, vicious horde of animals intent only on survival, pushing and shoving each other without mercy, rampaging for shelter as the thunder crashed and forks of lightning streaked above them, the rain falling in steaming curtains, drumming like an advancing army.

Frances, with just a towel round her waist, watched amazed from behind the lace curtains at this frenzied, cowardly stampede. The Prince came up and stood by her shoulder.

'Just look at them!' she said. 'Wild animals. The Boers are not alone in their uncouth arrogance.'

'A little harsh?' He offered the comment half-heartedly.

'Their manners are only skin deep, Edward, whatever you may say – look at them!'

She smiled, pleased at their discomfiture. They deserved it. There was something over-refined, etiolated, about this society, these people. They had no fibre, no purpose. A rain shower was sufficient to scatter them – this quite insubstantial pageant. Frances suddenly despised them all.

But it hardly mattered. Summer was ending. The season at Marienbad was almost over in any case – the pleasant walks along the winding paths among the hills, the golf, the croquet, the *café-concerts*: all the endless privileged dalliances throughout the warm days – it was all done with and Frances was glad.

Ten minutes later, when she had dressed, she looked out of the window again. The storm had rolled by, all the muggy heat gone, leaving the air deliciously fresh and cool. The debris of upset chairs and tables and crockery made the terrace of the Bellevue seem like a battlefield now, the waiters picking their way over it disconsolately. Frances breathed a great sigh of relief.

9

Dawn came to the vast flat land – first a gleam above the Drakensberg Mountains to the east, then quick flames spreading up into the violet
gloom, saffron and milky gold, before the sun was suddenly there, a half-orb
of fire snuffing out all the western stars, melting the wispy clouds, the hills black
against the horizon now, throwing long shadows as the beams dipped onto the
plain.

The train, which had stopped overnight at Frere station, pushed its way into the
dazzling shafts of light, fountains of white smoke mushrooming up into the keen
morning air. It was the second week of December – unseasonable weather: the
rains had come and gone before their time. And for more than two days – its
passengers alternately chilled and roasted – the train had wound slowly up from
Durban, through Natal, approaching the veldt, making for Chievely Camp where
General Sir Redvers Buller's army was gathering itself, waiting on reinforcements
from the coast, before attempting to relieve the besieged British garrison at
Ladysmith, twenty miles north across the Tugela river.

The Boer commando detachment – some seventy men with their horses – had
camped behind the kopje half a mile away, looking down over the railway, waiting
to ambush the next troop train. Now their leader, the bushy-bearded veldt-cornet,
lying on the brow of the hill, saw the necklace of carriages crawl out of the darkness
and into the sun-streaked valley beneath them.

He tensed, waiting to give the signal to attack. But taking up his field glasses he
saw the red crosses painted on all the carriages: an empty hospital train. He relaxed,
disappointed. The other men in the lea of the kopje dismounted, standing easy
with their Mauser rifles.

'Not for us.' The veldt-cornet spoke to them in Cape Dutch. 'Only for them.
They'll need it.' He turned to the verkenner, the scout attached to their small
group. 'Ride up to the main commando at Blaauwkrans nek – tell the veldt-cornet
there, just a hospital train: no ambush. We'll have to let it through.' He turned to
a companion then. 'It's a pity. We have had such good attacks on those armoured
trains. Last month at Chieveley, what a rout . . .'

His friend agreed. 'We will have no more, I think. After Chieveley, they will bring no more armoured trains up here.'

The two men nodded, smiling, watching the verkenner as he galloped furiously away down the other side of the kopje.

'They have no mobility, these British troops,' the veldt-cornet remarked, looking at the fast-disappearing rider. 'As slow about the place as my old grandmother. Sitting ducks.'

Frances dozed on the bottom bunk next to the window in the carriage of the No. 2 Field Hospital train. She had shivered in the cold, falling in and out of sleep all night while they were stopped at Frere station, lying fully dressed in her crumpled uniform. But now the first bright slants of sun woke her, seeming to offer some warmth. As she looked out of the window, shading her eyes against the great orange rising over the hills to the east, she felt vaguely sick in the stomach. It was the food or the country – or both. There was a vast emptiness and silence in these high table lands which oppressed her, even with the lovely sunrise: an unfathomable, uninhabited plain; yellow-grey, streaked with green here and there, like a scaly beast, broken only by the purple wart of a distant kopje, sprouts of bush and prickly pear: hot, dry, stony, sandy, desolate.

Her older companion, Sister Mary Turner, a big, spiteful, florid-faced woman from Dulwich, with arms like legs of mutton, sat on the bunk opposite, fiddling with a paste brooch at her throat, the small stone at the centre glittering now in the sunlight. Her fiancé had bought it for her at Gamage's on their last day out together before her departure for the Cape.

She and Frances were the only women on the train. The rest of the staff – the twelve Royal Army Medical Corps orderlies and the two Surgeon-Majors, Dodds and Brazier-Creagh – had their quarters in the last carriage next to the Surgery and Dispensary.

'We can't be far now,' Sister Turner said flatly, as if they were on an omnibus between Dulwich and Trafalgar Square. She opened a Fry's chocolate tin beside her and ate most of what was left, masticating, chomping it vigorously with her great jaws. Then she offered the box to Frances. Only one small piece remained.

'No thank you.' Frances picked up the Sherlock Holmes stories she had been reading – the only possible literature she had found during her month at the main base hospital in Capetown.

Sister Turner devoured the last piece of chocolate herself, watching Frances covertly through her spectacles. She did not care for this woman who had travelled out with her on the boat from Southampton nearly two months before – the freshly-converted hospital ship *The Princess of Wales*, originally a pleasure steamer for which the Princess herself had largely paid, and raised a subscription.

Sister Turner did not like Frances because she feared her, both for her class and even more for the influence she must have in first being allowed out to the

Cape without being properly qualified, and then being permitted to take the boat on to Durban and travel up to the front line field hospital at Chieveley.

Sister Turner had heard rumours – on the boat and at the base hospital: Frances Cordiner was in the special charge of Surgeon-Major Brazier-Creagh; she was a friend, perhaps even a mistress, of the Prince of Wales.

It was disgraceful, Sister Turner thought. Miss Cordiner should never have been allowed to leave Capetown, let alone come on to Durban and up to the front. Though she had to admit there might have been some small excuse for this. She herself might not have been going to Chieveley but for the virulent outbreaks of enteric fever which had struck down many of the male orderlies, so that a number of nurses at the base hospital at Wynberg just outside Capetown had been drafted in at the last minute to replace them.

All the same, it was not right – a woman like that, hardly nursing for more than a year and far too refined: she would be of little use in the face of any real trouble, when it came, as Sister Turner hoped it would. She thrived on her work – the more blood and gore the better. She remembered the men back at Wynberg after the battle of Elandslaagte some weeks before – fearful wounds, shot to pieces many of them. She had really thrown her weight into seeing them fit and well again. It was simply bad luck that, even with her care, so many had lapsed in the end – hauled out to the cemetery or shipped back home as senseless mental cases.

War was a funny business. She had seen something of it, serving in a hospital in Cairo after the battle of Omdurman. But one thing she was sure of: to be any good at fighting, or helping afterwards, you had to relish it. And Frances Cordiner certainly did not look the type. Sister Turner peered into the chocolate tin, hoping to find a last remnant.

'It can't be good for you,' Frances said suddenly, looking up from her book. 'All that chocolate, first thing in the morning.' Her own stomach churned again at the very thought of it.

Sister Turner wanted to reprimand her for this cheek. But she hesitated. She had noticed Brazier-Creagh's regard for Miss Cordiner – an interest beyond the merely professional, she thought. The man was a frightful womaniser, of course. She had worked under him before at Omdurman – as quick with women as he was with the knife. But for her own advancement she did not want to openly antagonise either of them just now. Besides, she and Miss Cordiner were not strictly on duty yet. So, saying nothing, she simply glowered at Frances through her gold-rimmed spectacles. She would take revenge later.

They left the train at Chieveley station, moving north-west across the blazing veldt in two mule-drawn ambulance wagons with their stores and medical supplies, making towards the hundreds of khaki tents a mile away, set out in expanding squares and parallel lines over a vast area on slightly-rising ground, looking down on the Tugela river valley two miles away to the north, with a ridge of steep, flat-topped hills towering up immediately beyond the snaking water course. Ladysmith lay behind these formidable barriers.

The heat was intense. So were the swarms of flies beneath the canopy. Frances had stopped sweating long before, her skin dry and abrasive as sandpaper, tasting only the caked saliva now in her mouth as she watched the grey pall of dust rising everywhere above the camp, broken here and there with vicious little sandy whirlpools, whipped up by a baking wind, spinning into the lead-blue dome above.

She heard the dull sound of some big guns then, firing way over to the west beyond the camp – sullen, echoing reports every few minutes.

'What is it? Have they started fighting already?' she asked Brazier-Creagh who was sitting just ahead of her in the front of the wagon.

'No. But they must be about to start, by the sound of it. Those are the big naval guns they took up from the coast – bombarding the Boer entrenchments – there, on those hills.' He pointed to the slopes beyond the river.

'Where? I can't see anything.'

'Just the problem. The Boers are well-hidden. Our guns will do little damage, if any.'

As they drove into the camp, troops were moving to and fro everywhere – collecting mail from home, making for the mess tents, and the water barrels. Some officers and men from a field battery were limbering up ammunition wagons to their twelve-pounders; another group of Kaffirs tried to manhandle an ox team back towards one of the guns, the unhappy beasts doing nothing but swivel round hopelessly in clouds of dust.

Further on a line of tethered cavalry horses, tormented by the flies, foraged restlessly under long khaki sheets. A war-balloon was being made ready, while a civilian technician, kneeling on the ground beside it, adjusted the telegraphic apparatus that it would carry aloft over the battle field. Despite the heat the men were out and about everywhere – a tense but happy expectancy in the air, sharpened every few minutes by the sound of the big guns as they barked imperiously, their great shells whistling over the camp.

A loud, discordant, clanging chime rang out the midday hour as they moved through the centre of the camp towards the field hospital. Frances watched a trooper with an old sword as he struck the empty artillery shell, suspended from a sort of gibbet outside the Army Command Headquarters tent.

'Every convenience, you see,' Brazier-Creagh remarked drily, consulting his own fob-watch. 'Except they're about two minutes slow.'

Brazier-Creagh was a precise little man: heavily side-whiskered, balding, contained, neat – but explosive; either very taciturn or, when he did speak, often alarmingly voluble. He was like a ferret with his quick eyes, his stillness and sudden incisive movements – unpredictable and dangerous, Frances thought, as she gazed at the endless conical tents shimmering in the heat.

'A real army,' she remarked.

'More than enough – for us,' Brazier-Creagh replied. 'But almost certainly too few – for the Boers.' He looked out over the camp, shading his eyes. 'Must be 20,000 men here – fifteen infantry battalions at least, not to mention the artillery companies and the cavalry – the Royal Dragoons and the 13th Hussars.'

'My cousin's with the Hussars – his old regiment, he rejoined them in order to get out here.'

'Oh, is he? I thought that was your brother.'

'No. He's with the King's Rifles.'

'Well, they've been up here some time.'

'I've not seen either of them, since I came out.'

'Quite a little family reunion for you then. If you can find them – in all this.'

Brazier-Creagh looked at her quickly, a smile passing across his face, gone in an instant. He liked this attractive young woman. There was no difficulty about that, of course. And he admired her for her courage. At least, he hoped that was what it was. Certainly he had not understood her vehement insistence, when she had spoke to him in Capetown, that she accompany him and the hospital train up to the front. At first he had refused her request. His tactful but nonetheless firm instruction in London from the Prince of Wales's physician, Dr Makins, had been to see that she was cared for suitably, whenever it was in his power to do so: Miss Cordiner was a very special friend of the Prince of Wales, Dr Makins had intimated.

Brazier-Creagh had told Frances of these instructions in Capetown, when she had become agitated, pointing out to him that, if this was the case, his ridiculous commission would be best implemented by her travelling with him on the hospital train. And he had seen the sense of this. But was she one of those romantic, fluttery women, camp followers, in love with brave officers and the glory of war, never having seen it? He prayed not. He had a horror of such women, though he had seduced them often enough. He had half-asked her about this during their interview in Capetown and now he thought to broach the topic again.

But just then, coming to the dozen bell tents and marquees of the field hospital on the far side of the Camp, they saw the medical orderlies, accompanied by a small honour guard, taking two shrouded bodies out into the veldt on stretchers – a burial party, getting the corpses underground as soon as possible in the fierce heat.

The ambulance wagon stopped, allowing the flies to redouble their attack under the burning canvas. Brazier-Creagh took off his solar topee as the burial party passed in front of them.

'Enteric fever again, I'll be bound. Take more than the Boers will in the end.'

'We brought up plenty of alum on the train,' Frances commented.

'Too late. They should have filtered the water through it from the start on these up-country marches.' The wagon moved forward again. 'So you see . . . Miss Cordiner.' He spoke to himself as much as to Frances.

'Yes.'

'You see.' He turned to her abruptly, a frustrated annoyance flooding his face. 'I've wondered why you want to – you don't admire all this, do you?' He waved his hand round the camp, at the burial party walking through the spinning dust devils out across the veldt towards the makeshift cemetery, where already well over a score of earthen mounds, miniature kopjes in neat lines, rose out of the flat, sizzling emptiness.

'No. I hate it.'

'Why, then? . . .' Frances was silent. 'Have you some love of suffering, some romantic notion about war?' he asked her harshly, his voice rising, his little white-ish eyes drilling into her. 'Why come up here, when you could have stayed in Capetown? No need to come up here, was there?'

'No.' Frances was terrified by the surgeon's sudden anger – terrified, shaking and tortured by the flies now in the confined space. 'But yes, I do know – I want to nurse.' Yet the response was half-hearted.

Brazier-Creagh nodded ironically several times. 'Well, we can't complain about that, can we?'

Frances was suddenly angry herself now. 'Why complain at all?' she answered back sharply. 'I'm here.'

'Because I'm not certain I believe you.' He looked at her closely. 'You don't know what you've let yourself in for.'

'I've seen bad wounds before – amputations, gangrene – men back from Omdurman in London. And tended them.'

Brazier-Creagh cackled drily. 'In *London*,' he said. They drove on. Frances jumped at the sound of the rifle volleys over the graves, after they'd lowered the two men into the shallow soil.

'They do bury them quickly,' she remarked conversationally, trying to lower the tension between them.

'The lucky ones,' Brazier-Creagh replied.

That afternoon Frances walked round the camp, searching for Eustace and Dermot. It was not easy. There was a huge area to cover, the heat was worse for the wind had died, and the men who noticed her did so with mocking or lecherous surprise. One of the medical orderlies had told her that Eustace's regiment, the 3rd King's Royal Rifles, was part of Major-General Lyttelton's brigade, stationed at the centre, and on the northern edge of the camp. But when she arrived at this section she found nothing but a line of empty tents. A slovenly field cook told her that the King's Rifles had been sent out that afternoon, back towards Chieveley station, crossing the railway there on a reconnaissance in force: a Boer commando group had been seen in the hills beyond.

'And the cavalry?' Frances asked.

The cook opened another tin of filthy-looking meat and vegetable stew – 'knock-me-down' stew, with a fearful smell, yellow-streaked like dog's vomit – pouring the mess into a great pan. Frances felt faint, turning away before he replied.

'Ah, Miss, the cavalry – it's over there.' He licked his fingers, pointing eastwards. 'And there.' He gestured towards the west.

'The Hussars?'

'Don't know, Miss.' He looked at her sullenly.

Moving away, she was soon lost again in this city of tents. She walked east, towards where she had seen the horses that morning. In an open space she came on some officers and civilians standing in a semi-circle, watching something intently. Pushing into the edge of the group she saw another civilian in puttees and a solar topee standing half-way up a tall laddered platform, tending a great black box on top with the words 'Biograph Company' stencilled in white letters.

'What – what is it?' she asked one of the civilians standing next to her, a great, swarthy, bear-like man, roguishly bearded, in a slouch leather hat. He looked like a Boer farmer.

'It's a bioscope – one of these new machines – for taking photographs. But running photographs. They move.' He spoke with an American accent.

'They *what*?'

'Yes,' he said coolly, turning and looking at her appraisingly, drawing on a cheroot. 'They aim to show the war back home with it – on a white sheet – as if you were there, or here, I mean. Great new American invention. I'm Clement Springfield, of the *New York Post*. You nursing up here? Didn't know they'd brought any women up to the front line.'

'Yes. Enteric fever took so many of the male orderlies. I'm looking for the Hussars. I wonder if you know where they're camped?'

Springfield looked at her with distinct interest now, sensing a good news item here. 'Yes, I do. They're part of Dundonald's Mounted Brigade, far side of the camp, to the east, right at the edge. Let me show you.'

'Thank you. But I'll find my own way.'

'Oh, go on, be a sport – I know exactly where they are.'

Frances walked away. But the man followed. 'You'll only get lost – I'll show you,' he shouted, before joining her.

Lord Dundonald had attended a battle briefing that afternoon – he and the other four Brigade commanders – with General Buller in his Army Headquarters marquee. Now, back in his own tent, he had called together the senior cavalry officers of his brigade – from the Royal Dragoons, the Hussars and from the three locally-assembled South African mounted regiments. It was time to outline the plan of attack.

He stood at the centre of the big bell tent at a trestle table, a map of the area in front of him, the men grouped round, including Captain Dermot Cordiner – aide-de-camp now to Colonel Baxter, officer commanding the 13th Hussars.

'It's tomorrow then,' Dundonald told the officers. 'The four infantry brigades will move off an hour before first light, Hart and Hildyard's brigades will aim to cross the river here – and here.' He pointed to the two fords, above and below the railway bridge at the village of Colenso. 'Lyttelton and Barton's two brigades will follow on, left and right of the centre – here – ready to give support to either of the advance brigades. We're on the extreme right of the line – here, facing Hlangwane Hill, on this side of the river, just where it takes that big bend north. That hill is our objective, with the 7th Field Battery behind us, softening them up before we attack. We have to take that hill, outflank the Boers on the right, and enfilade their lines from it. If we don't, they can play havoc with our infantry.'

'All looks simple enough,' Colonel Baxter said enthusiastically. 'They've been flattening that hill – and the others – all day with the big naval guns. Can't be anyone left up there.'

'Yes – we saw a lot of Boers this morning, scuttling away from their entrenchments,' another officer remarked.

'I'm sure of it,' Colonel Baxter confirmed. 'They're falling back, all of them. They don't intend holding the line at the Tugela river at all.' Colonel Baxter was very cock-a-hoop.

Lord Dundonald – a canny, mistrustful Northern Irishman – was less confident. 'We should not be sure of that at all, Colonel. Though you certainly share Buller's optimism,' he added drily, eyeing the man carefully. 'The point is, these maps of the area are almost useless and our scouts have barely been over the river, let alone up in any of the hills. We've no idea how many men they may have up there – ten, twenty, could be thirty thousand. And all the time in the world to have got themselves well dug in.'

'But one of our scouts actually stood on the far side of the railway bridge this morning – not a sight or sound of any of them.'

'Colonel, these men are defending, not attacking. Would you give your positions away in such circumstances?'

'But we *saw* many of them running away – they're just a lot of farmers anyway.'

Lord Dundonald sighed. 'Farmers are sly people, Colonel Baxter – especially these ones. A ruse, a trick!' His voice rose in irony. 'There could be many more waiting for us than the few we saw running away.' The officers looked at Dundonald doubtfully, thinking him far too careful an old party, disappointed that he should so prick their optimism. 'As far as I'm concerned,' he continued brusquely, 'we are to assume that Hlangwane Hill is defended in force, and act accordingly. There will be no unnecessary heroics – the infantry will supply that, no doubt.'

Just then there was a commotion outside the tent, the sentry shouting, the sound of another raised voice.

'Good God, it's that frightful Yankee journalist again.' Dundonald looked up. 'Been pestering me for days.'

Colonel Baxter, taking the initiative, turned to Dermot standing behind him. 'Captain Cordiner, go out – see the bloody man off, will you?'

'On the other hand . . .' Lord Dundonald said, almost to himself, suddenly thinking of something.

Dermot pushed his way through the tent flap. The sentry was still remonstrating with Springfield. And Frances was standing behind him, anxious and embarrassed.

'Frances!' Dermot exclaimed. But she put a finger to her lips, gesturing hopelessly. Dermot turned to Springfield instead. 'Lord Dundonald cannot speak to you.'

'He *said* he would. And this young woman wants him –'

'I'm afraid not. You must leave –'

'But he did say he would, I promise you.' Springfield was aggrieved, apparently telling the truth.

At that moment Dundonald himself pushed his way through the tent flap behind them. He was almost genial. 'Yes, indeed, Springfield,' he told the man. 'I may speak to you afterwards. But first I want you to speak to us.'

'I don't follow?'

'Come on, old man.' Dundonald took him by the arm. 'You've been over there recently, haven't you? At Ladysmith – and Colenso as well, I'm sure.'

'Oh, that was some time ago.' Springfield was rattled.

'No – it was *very* recently, I think. I want you to come inside and give my men a briefing – on the Boer strength over there. Come on, old man.' He took him firmly by the arm and led him inside the tent, leaving Frances and Dermot outside.

'Is he a spy?' Frances asked, astonished.

'No. Just he speaks Dutch. And some of the foreign journalists here have been covering both sides.'

'What a funny way . . . to fight a war! He *could* be a spy.'

'Never mind – you're here. I never thought you'd get out to the Cape, after I left, let alone up here. I'd no idea! But I'll have to get back inside. Where are you?'

'Right the far side –'

'At the field hospital? . . . I'll come round this evening, after the mess supper.'

'I have to find Eustace –'

'I'll help you – later.'

'But why on earth *did* you come up here?'

Frances walked with Dermot through the long moonlit alleys between the tents, the camp and the plain behind, flooded with a chill silver air, so that both of them wore their capes.

'Well, I told you – I couldn't find you, or Eustace, anywhere in Capetown. That was one reason – you were both up here!' She turned, smiling at him, his thin face and crinkly hair visible now as they moved out of the shadow of a tent.

'But, Frances, we're attacking at first light tomorrow –'

'Are we? Brazier-Creagh thought that too!'

Dermot saw her eyes glisten in the moonlight. He could not understand her enthusiasm. 'Frances, you won't be safe.'

'Nonsense – it's my job.'

They came suddenly on a group of men, smoking, bending over a small fire at the back of a tent. Seeing Dermot's cavalry mess uniform they hurriedly stamped the fire out.

'Don't be bloody stupid,' Dermot told them.

'Sorry, Sir. Just it's . . . cold.' A young trooper had stood up, saluting.

'Stand easy. Get some rest, for God's sake. You'll need it.'

He walked on with Frances, moving out to the very edge of the camp where the plain ran away seemingly for ever to the west, the moonlight falling on the sandy soil, touching it everywhere like a hoar frost.

'Only thing really worries me,' she said, 'I can't find Eustace. He's been out all afternoon, chasing some Boers beyond Chieveley station.'

'I've seen him – yesterday. He must be back by now. I'll take you round there. But, Frances –' He stopped, taking her by the arm. 'You know, neither Eustace nor I may get out of here alive. And if you're in one of the forward dressing stations . . .'

'I hope I am!'

'But why? – when you could have stayed safely in Capetown?'

'Oh, Dermot.' She glared at him petulantly. 'I'm not going to hide from anything, *ever*.'

Dermot shook his head. 'Strange, when you seemed to have everything going so well for you in London – making things up with your Mama on that trip to Marienbad. And with your friend the Prince of Wales, too. And now you want to risk all that – you, who said you hated everything to do with the army – telling *me* to leave it!'

'Yes, and I still say that. But I couldn't just sit in London when everyone else was coming out here. I have to *move* in my life – forward – don't you see that?'

'Move towards what, though? Bravery? You have that already. You don't have to prove it.'

'Towards you, perhaps? You still don't realise? . . .'

She looked at him quizzically, sadly, her lips trembling a moment in the cold. He ran his finger down her cheek suddenly. 'I only wish I could do something about that.' He turned away quickly and they walked back towards the sleeping camp.

Frances did not see Eustace that night. Stopping at the field hospital on their way across to his station, Sister Turner met her at the flap of one of the fever tents.

'Oh, Miss Cordiner – I wondered where you'd got to. There's a man dying here, enteric fever. I want you to see to him.'

'But, Sister, could you find someone else – *please?* I've been desperately looking for my brother all day. He'll be back by now. We were just going to go and see him –'

'Miss Cordiner,' Sister Turner spoke with harsh cynicism. 'Your brother is alive. There is a man *dying* in there – and no one else available. I'm afraid not.'

'But, Sister –' Frances pleaded strenuously.

'Miss Cordiner, I shouldn't have to repeat myself.' She held the tent flap open, looking coldly at Dermot.

'I'm sorry,' Dermot said. 'I'll go and tell him – how you couldn't come.'

'Will you? And give him my love and tell him I'll see him tomorrow.' She reached up quickly and kissed Dermot. 'And you too,' she added vehemently.

*

An hour before sunrise the infantry moved off in huge shadowy masses, down the long slope towards the river – the dense columns gradually dividing, opening out into skirmishing order as the day began to break, radiantly clear and fine, over the distant ridges of the Drakensberg.

At first light the naval 12-pounders opened fire at Fort Wylie, the nearest of the hills, 4,000 yards away across the river – pouring in a terrific storm of shells and shrapnel.

The impatient, bristling Colonel Long, commanding the 14th and 66th Field Batteries, took up the bombardment with his 15-pounders. To the right, on the extreme edge of the line, Lord Dundonald, mounted on a black charger, held his cavalry regiments back, allowing the 7th Field Battery to pulverise the Boer entrenchments on Hlangwane Hill ahead of him. Dermot had his frisky horse beside Colonel Baxter's, at the head of the Hussars. He tightened the strap of his pith helmet, checked the lanyard attached to his revolver, eased his sword a fraction in its scabbard beside him. There was no more he could do in a material way to prepare himself for his first battle: only his nerves to control now, as he watched the shells burst in a line half way up the hill.

'Bloody range must be wrong,' the Colonel remarked after ten minutes of fierce bombardment, putting down his field glasses. 'Can't see anyone moving up there at all. Or else, just as I thought, there *is* no one there.' He picked up his glasses again. There was absolutely no sign of life from the long, indistinct line of Boer entrenchments, flickering in the heat-mist under the rising sun. He swivelled his glasses round towards the other hills on the left. 'Same thing. Whole place is deserted, not a sound or sight of them anywhere. They've all run – overnight.' Then he spotted something right on top of the ridge, but still well within the range of the guns. 'My God! – I wouldn't have credited it – a group of Boers and some of their women, standing there, just watching us! – like a bloody tennis match.'

At the back, and at the centre of the line, Eustace led his platoon down the slope, behind the other men in Lyttelton's brigade, dispersing gradually to the right, until they moved along beside the railway track, making for the ford just above Colenso railway bridge. To the right, and behind his platoon, Colonel Long's guns were firing rapidly – almost too close for comfort, Eustace thought, more annoyed than ever now that he had been placed at the back of the line here, with his own guns seeming to threaten him and little chance of being anywhere near first in for a crack at the Boers.

Springfield, considering his options, had finally decided to break loose from the other journalists and watch the battle from a point as close to the Tugela river as he could safely reach; that was where the real fighting would be, he was sure.

To this end, he followed General Hart's infantry brigade at the extreme left of the line, placing himself beyond them in open country, as a sort of outrider, hugging cover whenever he could beneath the bank of a small stream running north, which he knew must join the Tugela a mile ahead. He could then move down the big river, hidden in the thick scrub which covered its banks, towards the battle.

He checked his supply of cheroots, his field glasses, water bottle and the Colt

.45 hidden in his waistband, before pulling down his slouch hat against the brightening sun and moving off.

'God,' he thought, 'another blistering day.' He watched Hart's infantry now as they made towards the Tugela, marching down the slope in rigid formation, battle lines precisely drawn, as if on parade on a vast barracks square: all of them sitting ducks. And ducks didn't like the heat either, he remembered.

Brazier-Creagh had given directions to his staff first thing that morning. 'Half an hour after the main advance, we'll be taking No. 3 hospital train down the track – to here.' He pointed to a spot on the map about a mile from the river. 'We then disperse the six field dressing stations we have on board, three to the left of the track, three to the right, moving them as close to the river as we can get them. The No. 1 train will follow us, with the ambulance wagons, setting up the reserve dressing stations behind us.'

He had turned then to the eighty or so turbanned Indian stretcher-bearers who had joined their hospital train, speaking to their headman. 'You people will divide half and half, either side of the railway. The same with the male orderlies.' He turned to these men, considerably increased in force now. Then he spoke to Sister Turner and Frances. 'You both will stay on the train – prepare the operating tables, chloroform drips and so on, for the serious cases we'll hope to get up to you. And keep the train doors open, the bunks ready, for the other wounded.' He looked at Frances then. 'And I don't want either of you to leave the train – that clear?'

Now, an hour later, Frances looked out of the dispensary window as the train nosed slowly down the slope behind the advancing army – the massed lines of grey khaki, spread out below her for over a mile along the valley, a great blanket, the four brigades, each marching to a different rhythm, rising and falling in slow waves across the wide front, rifles angled forward, bayonets glinting. They moved with sure step and wonderful confidence towards the hills where nothing stirred except the sudden greenish blooms of smoke from the big naval lyddite shells as they exploded, mysterious ugly blossoms flowering everywhere all along the hills.

The sun was well up now in a brilliant blue sky, hidden at times by great towers of puffy clouds, illuminating this military panorama with gorgeous colours, ever-changing shafts of light and shade, as the army moved forward in perfect formations, pieces in a vast soldier set. Frances saw the beauty of it all – against her will. She clutched the lucky mascot in her apron pocket, the little ivory elephant the Prince had given her at Sandringham.

She thought of him, and all the endearing – even daring – letters he had written her since she had come out to the Cape. She remembered the anger in them, too, against Chamberlain and Lord Landsdowne and Sir Alfred Milner whose foolhardy machinations had made the war inevitable and taken her away from him. She missed the Prince now, for his indiscreet love, for his peaceful intent. And yet she was excited by this coming adventure in a war he had failed to prevent.

*

An hour after the bombardment had started – and though he had been ordered to keep his field batteries under cover of Barton's brigade – the impetuous Colonel Long, with his artillery in the centre, determined to bring his guns closer in towards the river, where they could operate with better effect, clearly believing that the enemy had retreated everywhere under the heavy British fire. Certainly they had seen no sign of life on the hills, except a few more Boers retreating, and not a single shot had been fired in return.

He gave the order that his twelve field guns, and the six big naval guns under Lieutenant James, should now move forward to a point barely 800 yards from the river and only 1,200 yards from the Boer entrenchments at Fort Wylie on a hill just beyond.

'But, Sir,' an Artillery captain entreated him, 'they may still be there, hidden in force – in that scrub by the river, or up on the hill! Simply a ruse –'

'Nonsense, Captain Jennings.'

'Sir, in that forward position we shall be nearly half a mile ahead of Hildyard's brigade, without any infantry or other cover.'

The Colonel turned on him. 'Forward, Captain. There's no one there – lily-livered lot of bloody farmers. We're not of the same mould, I hope? On, I say! Get the guns limbered up, the teams together. On, on!'

Ten minutes later the two field batteries galloped forward, outstripping their infantry escort almost immediately – Lieutenant James's naval battery following more slowly with their ox teams. Their progress was quite unimpeded as they made right down the slope, getting well ahead of their line, approaching a point about 1,000 yards away from the river.

There was an absolute silence from the hill straight ahead of them now. Nothing moved in the burning sun. Captain Jennings thought the Colonel must be right. The Boers had fled. Yet something made him uneasy. He had noticed the white-painted boulders here and there as they had galloped down the slope. Painted – but why? Then it suddenly struck him: of course, they were range-markers. But the British hadn't painted them – the stones were all on this side of the Tugela, right in the line of the British infantry advance. The Boers must have set out these artillery range points, some time before. He thought no more about it, though. He did not dare think about it.

Just then a single shot rang out from somewhere above Colenso village, and instantly both scrub-lined banks of the river, and the hills beyond, broke into flame with a fearful crackling and roaring, mixed with the rhythmic heavy hammering of the Boer one-pounder Maxim automatic guns.

A piercing deluge of shells from rifle, cannon and machine gun descended on Colonel Long's artillery. The British gunners faced it calmly, as if still on parade – unlimbering the ammunition wagons, picking up the range and opening fire on Fort Wylie without undue haste. But already, within a few minutes of returning the fire, two of their twelve guns, together with most of their crews, had been hit and put out of action.

Behind them, Lieutenant James's naval guns with their ox teams had been lumbering down the hill. The Boers had seen the danger here straight away, directing their fire willy-nilly among the ox-teams and their Kaffir drivers, so that the animals were killed or stampeded in a minute. The sailors managed to drag most of their guns back to a position well in the rear of Colonel Long's artillery, and from here they gave all the aid they could in beating down the fire from Fort Wylie, the hill one continuous cloud of smoke now from the bursting shells.

But the Boer gunners, deep behind their earthworks, seemed immune from the British fire. With their quick-firing Maxims, at this short range, they were able to pour a rain of destruction over Colonel Long's two batteries, completely exposed now in the open space before Colenso. They were in a quite hopeless position: it was a massacre. Within twenty minutes most of their horses and two-thirds of their men, including Captain Jennings and Colonel Long himself, had fallen dead or wounded.

Help was sent for. But none came, the few survivors round the guns held down now by a mercilessly accurate rifle fire. Colonel Long, shot through the arm and liver, was urged to abandon the guns and retreat. 'Abandon, be damned,' he shouted. 'We never abandon guns!'

Yet the fury of the enemy's fire eventually drove them back several hundred yards to the shelter of a dry water course, a *donga*, where they remained, emerging whenever they could, in a lull of firing, to take up their guns again. But it was useless. Each little detachment that ran forward was cut to pieces by the furious Boer fire, so that in the end only one of the twelve guns was left operating, with only two gunners to man it.

The first one bent down to the breech, was hit, and fell over the muzzle. His companion, the last survivor, turned and, disdaining flight, walked slowly back to the *donga* in the rear until he, too, was taken, transfixed with a piece of shrapnel, stumbling forward, struggling along on his knees for a moment, before he fell spreadeagled across an anthill. It was the end of the 14th Field Battery. Colonel Long, delirious now and bleeding profusely, lay propped up on the lip of the *donga*. 'Ah, my gunners! My gunners are splendid. Look at them!' But barely a single gunner of his remained alive.

Springfield, nearing the Tugela with Hart's brigade on the left marching in close order, watched with his field glasses the shell and shrapnel pour into the men. He was not surprised – he had warned Dundonald, at least, of the Boer forces in the hills. But he was amazed at Hart's temerity and foolishness – in allowing his men to go forward in such close order here. The Boers had two huge 45-pounder guns, he knew, on Groblers Kloof and Red Hill just behind Colenso. And now he saw the terrible effect as these shells burst among the closed ranks.

When the smoke cleared each time, not two or three but upwards of a dozen men had simply been cut out of the line, half of them disintegrating, becoming invisible, so that very soon the brigade companies behind had to be deployed, moving forward in steady order, still advancing towards the ford above the railway bridge. But now, breaking ranks, they ran desperately, the men falling singly instead in a hail of Boer Mauser fire.

Eustace's platoon, which had started at the back of Lyttelton's brigade, found they were nearing the front of the line, as the infantry ahead, breaking ranks under the withering fire, fell everywhere. And soon they found themselves right at the head of the line, great gaps in it everywhere now, leaving a wash behind of dead or wounded men, shells still falling all round them. It was literally do or die now, Eustace realised.

'Break!' he shouted to his men. 'And run – run *forward* out of their range, quick as you can – it's our only chance, make for the ford.' Taking his service revolver out, he and the remains of his platoon sprinted ahead, given some cover by a *donga* at first, but finding themselves in the open country as they neared the scrubby bushes hiding the river bank. But now he realised the Boers were hidden there as well, peppering them with a hail of Mauser fire as they ran across the open ground, bullets whining round their ears.

He turned briefly in his crazy run, hearing the strangely mild exclamations from one of his men right behind him.

'Damn it, bloody thing . . .' He watched the trooper, apparently quite unharmed, simply staggering a little as if from a blow of a fist. The man recovered and ran on for several paces. Then suddenly he tipped forward, crumbling at the knees, like an infant stumbling on a garden path, all the life gone out of him.

On the right, Dundonald's cavalry attack on Hlangwane Hill had at first gone forward successfully and almost without incident. But now the three South African regiments of Light Horse, first in the line and breasting the middle slopes of the hill, had suddenly met with an impossible fusillade coming from the sum-mit – maxims, cannon and rifle. The horses, already at an angle on the slope, were hit time and again, so that they reared up and spun back all too easily, throwing their riders, before beasts and men rolled down the hill as so much dead weight.

Dermot, still at the bottom of the slope with the Hussars and the Dragoons, tried to move forward now, up a dry gully, pressing the attack in place of the Light Horse. But with the Boer fire, and the riderless horses retreating in panic down the same gully, it was almost impossible for any of them to move forwards. They were trapped in a great mêlée of rearing, stampeding beasts beneath the hill, the animals charging in circles as the men attempted to force them upwards – meanwhile making a perfect target for the indiscriminate Boer artillery fire. The shells burst among the cavalry then like great dollops of puffy cream, smothering, obliterating the animals and riders at random.

Dermot watched in astonishment as a single horse galloped past him: the rider was firmly fixed in his deep cavalry saddle, the reins tossed loose with the horse's mane, both the officer's hands clenched against its flanks – but his head cut clean off at the shoulders.

Eustace, driven now to such a pitch of heady exhilaration that he was quite unaware of the carnage and bullets all round him, reached the scrub by the river, the first in Buller's army to do so, half of his platoon still behind him. They shot and carved a path through the bush. But the Boers had left this section of the river and the way was clear ahead, down the bank to the mud-coloured water, only a few feet deep, Eustace estimated.

He jumped, followed by his men, all of them plunging boldly in. But the Boers had dammed the river somewhere lower down and in place of three or four feet there was eight or ten now of swirling water. The men, with their heavy equipment, sank like stones. Eustace felt the long gash opening in his thigh, the prongs of submerged barbed wire ripping down his leg as he pushed wildly out for the far bank. Several of his men, unable to swim, remained under water or were swept down-stream, struggling desperately, heads bobbing in and out of the sun-flecked surface, crying out, gasping for life.

Only Eustace, his colour-sergeant, the bugler boy and three other of his men reached the far side, to clamber up the steep bank. But here, on reaching the top, they met with murderous rifle fire from a small Boer force behind an African kraal a few hundred yards directly ahead of them.

Again, inspired by their success, there was no question of retreat. The bugler boy sounded the attack. The Colour-Sergeant came abreast of Eustace, shouting, 'Let's make a name for ourselves and die!' – as the six men left the cover of the river bank, setting out at a rush for the kraal.

Springfield, outstripping Hart's decimated infantry and reaching the Tugela some time ahead of them, had made a comparatively easy passage down the river, under cover of the bush. Now he had reached a point a little above where Eustace and his men had just crossed the stream. Hidden in the bushes, he saw them stumble up the other bank, meet the bullets; he heard the bugle, and then – unbelieving – watched them disappear somewhere ahead into the hail of fire. He jumped into the stream himself then, swimming quickly across, anxious to witness the result of this mad action.

Eustace barely felt the pain of the long gash down his leg as he tore zig-zag across the stony ground. And he felt almost nothing either when the hard, slim Mauser bullet pierced him, just inside his shoulder-blade, half-way in his mad dash for the kraal. The bullet went clean through him, in a straight trajectory, causing little damage. But immediately afterwards, tumbling in the air, the lead struck one of the men behind in the chest, opening a great gaping wound there, killing him in his tracks.

Two more of his platoon fell a few seconds later. Then the bugler boy was hit, in both legs, it seemed, for he crumpled up completely, only his head and torso writhing about on the open ground. Approaching the kraal now, Eustace saw one of the Boers kneeling inside the low entrance, and another behind the hut. He fired his revolver as he ran, but wildly and without effect.

Then he heard the rifle shots behind him – the rapid fire of a Lee-Metford. The Boer at the doorway dropped – and the man behind the hut, just aiming to shoot, fell immediately afterwards. Eustace turned in his sprint. Only one of his men was still running with him, and he was not using his rifle at that point. Then Eustace saw the other man, in civilian clothes and a slouch hat, on the lip of the river bank, using an abandoned rifle with deadly effect.

Arriving at the kraal, firing his revolver at will through the low entrance, Eustace found the Boer inside there dead; two others behind the hut had been killed and two more, who had been with them there, were now running away across the veldt, full tilt, towards Colenso village. Eustace fired after them until his revolver was empty.

He had taken the positon. But it was a hollow victory. He saw now that he was the only one of his platoon to have arrived at the kraal. His colour-sergeant, and the other men following, were all lying dead or wounded out in the veldt behind him. Eustace turned away for a moment, reloading his revolver, considering the position.

He never heard the Boer come up behind him – clutching him with both arms round the neck suddenly, tightening the grip viciously, strangling him. He tried to throw the man off, stooping down, writhing about. But the wounds gave him no strength in one arm and little purchase on the ground with his legs, so that he was hopeless in the grip of his assailant, some big Boer farmer, twice his size and strength.

He felt the man's arms round his windpipe, the breath being driven out of him, choking, gasping, fainting. His head was jerked up into the brilliant sun, blinding him, his last look at the world, he thought.

Suddenly the Boer's arms disappeared, tugged violently away from his neck, so that Eustace found himself free. He turned and saw how the big Boer, with his beard and crossed bandoliers and slouch hat, was in the grip now of an even larger man with a similar beard and hat. It was the civilian who had been firing from the Tugela a few minutes before. The two men struggled, arms clasped around each other's bodies like Chinese wrestlers, grunting, moving in slow circles, scratching the dust with their big boots, the sweat streaming down their grimy faces.

Eustace, still faint and for a moment gathering his strength, watched the contest as the men swayed about above him, both caught in a fierce, vice-like grip. But gradually the civilian got the upper hand, squeezing the man ever tighter in a great bear grip, bending him backwards at the same time, so that finally the Boer fell on the ground, the civilian astride him now, his legs pinning the other man's arms to his sides, as he brought his own hands up to the Boer's face, putting his thumbs in the man's deep-set eyes, pressing sharply, pressing, pressing – so that Eustace had to turn away. When he did glance back half a minute later the Boer's face was just a bloody football, both eyeballs removed, lying out like marbles on his cheeks.

Eustace turned away again. The wounded men in his platoon, out on the open veldt between the kraal and the river – the Colour-Sergeant, the bugler boy and two others still alive, he saw – had all come under heavy shell fire now from a Boer position somewhere in Colenso village, a quarter of a mile north of the kraal. The kraal itself, with its bush and thorn walls, offered no real protection. The only thing was to try to get his wounded men back to the cover of the Tugela river bank a few hundred yards away.

Eustace immediately ran back into the fire, zig-zagging again towards his Colour-Sergeant who was lying about fifty yards from the kraal.

'Get the boy first!' the Colour-Sergeant moaned. He had been shot somewhere in the stomach, and was using both arms to hold his guts in. Eustace bent down, picking the Sergeant up with his one good arm, and together they both set off like men in a two-legged race back to the river. They made it.

Meanwhile the civilian, taking one of the abandoned Mausers at the kraal, had opened fire on the Boer position in Colenso, giving Eustace cover as he left the Tugela again, ran out, picked up the bugler boy bodily and brought him back.

Twice more he managed to do the same thing with the other two wounded men, his strength failing now as he dragged the last one back, so that he stumbled and fell with his load, within twenty yards of the river bank. Then the shell exploded just beside him. His wounded comrade, protected by Eustace's body when they had fallen, was able to crawl on to the safety of the river. But Eustace lay where he was, quite still, hit by the shrapnel, a great jagged piece of metal sticking out from his side, plugging the flow there. He was bleeding profusely now from other smaller pieces of steel that had pierced his temple. He felt no pain at all from these new wounds. He was beyond pain.

The civilian sprinted back across the veldt, picked Eustace up and holding the small plump body in his arms ran on to the cover of the river bank.

Most of the forward dressing stations had come under fire throughout the morning and now four of the surgeons, including Brazier-Creagh, had returned to the No. 2 hospital train and were operating in the relative safety of the surgery there – the most serious cases being brought up the slope to them in ambulance wagons.

The train windows were closed against the dust and flies, so that at midday the heat was intense, the air filled with the sweet reek of chloroform and fresh blood, as the wounded men were brought on to the four operating tables, two in the surgery itself and two other makeshift tables set up in the carriage next door.

Frances was working in the carriage with Brazier-Creagh, holding the chloroform pad over each patient as they came on to the table, making sure the man could still breathe, while the Surgeon-Major, braces hanging down, only a vest on above his trousers, wielded his knife beside her.

Frances had seen operations in London: a slow, meticulous process. She had never thought it possible to work with the speed and precision which Brazier-Creagh showed now on these terrible wounds, as he began the debridement on each patient – removing all the dead or damaged tissue round the wound in great cutting swathes of his scalpel, scything whole chunks of skin and muscle away. It had to be done this way, Frances knew, to prevent subsequent infection or gangrene in the dead muscle. But seeing the brutal process in action for the first time, she was none the less astonished at Brazier-Creagh's apparent butchery.

'Put the bloody drip pad closer, woman!' he suddenly shouted at her. 'He's moving – can't you see? Don't look at me – look at *him*,' he roared at her above the shell fire as he cut away at the man's thigh.

He turned then to a medical orderly behind him, using a syringe, tending an unconscious figure who had just arrived in the carriage, lying out on one of the bunks. 'He's going, that man – I can see from here: shock and blood loss. Stop playing about with three- or four-drop strychnine doses. Give him eight or ten – it's his only chance.'

Frances followed the surgeon's gaze for a moment, looking at the young officer who had just been brought in, most of his uniform stripped away, lying almost naked, covered in grime and dirt, a great piece of shrapnel sticking from his side, blood seeping everywhere from other wounds in his temple, his shoulder and one of his legs.

There was something familiar about the ruined figure, she thought – in the plump, blood-soaked cheeks, the line of nose, the matted curly hair: something familiar indeed. It was Eustace, her brother, next in line for Brazier-Creagh's attentions.

Frances nearly fainted. But she made a supreme effort, pulling herself together, saying nothing. Her hand began to shake, though, the chloroform pad dancing over the patient's face beneath her.

'Hold the pad still, woman!' Brazier-Creagh said. 'I'm almost done here. Have to get that other chap on the table as soon as possible.'

Brazier-Creagh ran his eye over Eustace's wounds when the orderlies had moved him onto the table. He mopped his brow. 'A fresh pad, Miss Cordiner – though I fancy he's too far gone to feel anything anyway. And swabs,' he went on. 'As many as you have – he's lost a lot of blood.' He turned to a male orderly. 'Intravenous infusion of saline here – quick, man! – or he'll haemorrhage to death.'

The orderly brought a large syringe, while Frances set about her business. If anyone could save Eustace this man could, she thought. She swabbed the blood away from her brother's face, laying the pad gently over his nose, while Brazier-Creagh immediately set to work removing some of the shrapnel splinters from around Eustace's ear. But soon afterwards he remarked, 'Too serious – nothing I can do up here. Brain surgery, if he ever gets to a base hospital.'

He transferred his attentions to Eustace's shoulder. 'Smashed shoulder-blade – I think.' He humphed, pausing in his work, seeming undecided for the first time that morning. Then he looked at the jagged piece of shrapnel, three or four inches of it sticking out from Eustace's side just below his rib-cage. 'Can't remove that – bleed to death at once. Patch up the shoulder and leg, maybe.' He considered the long gash in Eustace's leg, then looked back at the mess round his head. 'Hardly worth it – poor blighter would be better off dead.'

Then Frances spoke to him. 'Sir, he's my brother – Eustace, the one I told you about, in the King's Rifles.'

Brazier-Creagh looked up at her calmly, licking his dry lips an instant. 'I'm sorry. But it wouldn't matter if he was the King of England – there's little we can do for him. Real wound is in the head, and we can't begin to deal with that here.'

'But –?' Frances, almost at the end of her tether now, began to plead with the surgeon, looking him straight in the eye.

'Miss Cordiner, with a head wound like that, it's a miracle they even got him up here alive. The shrapnel has pierced the cranium in half a dozen places – not to mention the other wounds. Even if we could operate immediately, in ideal conditions, chances almost certainly are that he'd die. Far too much blood lost, and shock – he'd die if I started any serious operation now. I'll clean the wounds, give him some more strychnine, saline, then put him aside, see what happens.'

He looked at Frances. He had noticed, while he was speaking, how she had left the chloroform pad rather too firmly over the man's nose and mouth. He did not remark on it, starting work again, swabbing the wounds, dressing them. But half-way through he stopped, putting a hand on Eustace's chest.

'Strychnine!' he shouted to the orderly. 'Saline, too.' A few minutes later he raised one of Eustace's eyelids. 'It's no use, I'm afraid. He's gone. I'm very sorry, but it was quite hopeless, from the start.'

Frances looked at him across the bloodied remains of her brother. She was numb, feeling nothing, except that she was swaying, falling . . . Then she fainted. The orderly caught her, just after she had fallen, hitting her head on the side of the bunk.

Poor bloody woman, Brazier-Creagh thought. Her brother would never have lived, of course: might have survived another half-hour or so, at most, if she had not inadvertently suffocated him with the chloroform pad. And the best thing, too – put him out of his misery.

Sister Turner, working with happy vigour at the other operating table in the carriage, saw Frances fall. Silly woman, she thought, pleased to confirm what she had suspected all along: women like that were no use when the going got really rough.

By three o'clock that afternoon, the guns of Colonel Long's two field batteries had been entirely abandoned, while the repeated cavalry assaults on Hlangwane Hill had equally failed. Without almost half their artillery, and lacking this vital hill where they could have turned the Boer flank and enfiladed their positions above Colenso, the battle could never have been won by Buller's army. And now the Boers, seeing their clear advantage, began to win it convincingly for themselves, renewing their heavy fire all along the line, so that the British troops fell further back everywhere.

Yet again, just as in their initial attack, they did so as if on parade – moving in perfect order, slowly, steadily, all the correct intervals between them, officers taking a measured step behind each company. So that again they made an easy target for the Boer Maxims and cannon, and many more were lost on the retreat, killed or wounded – those others left there to endure terrible agony, without water, under the scorching sun.

By five o'clock when the sun dipped at last, and the sky turned pink and violet, the Boer fire slackened and died away: no British troops remained within range to fire at. Only the many hundreds of dead and maimed offered a target now on the slopes leading down to the river, fallen in clusters, like obscene statuary, round the abandoned guns, or isolated in death, lone figures dotted about the veldt, some stretched out quite comfortably, it seemed, as if they had been sunbathing, while others lay in positions of fierce torture, their bodies grilled by a stronger fire.

A sour smell of flame and cordite hung in the air. Soon the battlefield was nearly silent in the waning light, but for the odd sharp cries of the wounded, like bird shrieks, that echoed up the valley as the sun finally disappeared, drawing a curtain over the calamity, sheer catastrophe, this humiliating British defeat.

'Well, do you have any news?' Frances asked urgently, later that night, when Brazier-Creagh came to see her in a curtained-off partition in one of the hospital tents.

'Yes, one of my orderlies spoke to an adjutant in the Hussars. Your cousin is safe. His horse was shot from under him. But he was unscathed, apart from a few cuts and bruises.'

'Thank God! Oh, thank goodness . . .' Frances spoke passionately, leaning up a moment in the bunk. She had barely recovered from her fall, was still in a state of shock, beginning to shiver in the chill night air, so that, while he was examining her, Brazier-Creagh ordered more blankets brought. She was a brave woman certainly – and her brother braver still: news had spread round the camp, how Lieutenant Cordiner, storming the kraal in a hail of fire, had taken the most advanced position of the day, only falling back to save the injured in his platoon, being mortally wounded then himself.

Finishing his examination Brazier-Creagh drew the blankets up, pulling them round Frances's chin. He looked at her for several moments, hiding his surprise, uncertain now as to what he should say. He temporised.

'By all accounts your brother – he distinguished himself, most admirably.' Frances said nothing, looking up into the tent roof. 'And I must apologise to you, for my earlier doubts about your abilities: you, too, especially – given the personal circumstances – behaved with very great courage.'

'I didn't – just fainted. Oh, God, how *awful* . . .' She turned away, lips beginning to chatter. 'And my brother, too, just when we were dealing with him.'

Brazier-Creagh, who had been unsure of his approach, now drew himself together. 'Miss Cordiner, I have to tell you, you fainted because you are pregnant – as much as anything else.'

Frances turned to him. There was little surprise in her dulled eyes as she looked up. 'I thought something must be amiss,' she said simply.

Her cousin, Brazier-Creagh thought: this cavalry officer, of course. That was why she had so wanted to come up here, to be near him – why she was so concerned for his safety. A distant cousin – they were lovers: that was why she had used all her royal influence in London, to join him. It all made sense now and he had been wrong in thinking the girl was one of the Prince of Wales's mistresses. Poor woman. Still, she was alive, as her lover was – and so was the child, he had confirmed – among so many dead and maimed.

'Well, we can all forget Ladysmith for the time being, Miss Cordiner. And it's back to Capetown and home to England for you. I'll have you go out on the train tomorrow morning first thing.'

When he had left, Frances lay awake for a long time in the dark, listening to the cries, the agony of the wounded men in the other part of the tent, some of them obviously living their last hours. It gave her the only hope she could muster just then. She was alive. But how wrong she had been about her brother – about that sallow, plump youth, set in his dull army career. Her brother had turned out to be the bravest of the brave. She cried with guilt and grief. And yet, despite the depths she sank to that night, there was something she could go on towards now with hope: she carried it inside her. A new life had been confirmed, would emerge from the deaths all round her: something had been rescued from all this appalling and unnecessary carnage. The Prince, surely, would see the virtue of that. She clutched his little lucky ivory mascot, pressing it to her stomach.

Next morning Dermot came to the camp hospital, his arm in a sling, as the wounded were being moved into ambulance wagons before taking them down to the waiting train. Frances was gathering her things in the tent, but they had a little time together, since Sister Turner, hearing of Eustace's bravery, had ceased to harry her.

'I heard the news, about Eustace. It's terrible.' Dermot had a cut just beneath the chin, a field dressing round it now, like a helmet strap, so that he spoke with some difficulty.

'Yes – and I never *saw* him before he went out – and I feel so guilty, so awful.'

'You tried, though. And I did manage to see him – and he was perfectly happy and understood. He was very proud – that you'd come up all this way to the front, joining us.'

'But I was so *wrong* about him, Dermot – thinking him just a dull mousy army man, no real spirit. So wrong.'

'Yes. But so was I – all those juvenile practical jokes he used to play, apple pie beds and so on. I was quite wrong about him, too. So you're not alone there. He was very brave. He'll almost certainly be recommended for a Victoria Cross, I hear.'

'What good will that do him? – or us?'

'Your mother and father. It will be some recompense for them, at least.'

'Dermot, there is no reward – it's all just a terrible needless slaughter, without any sense.' She finished packing her case. 'I'll have to go now, help with the men. I'll be going back to Capetown with them.' She looked up at Dermot quickly, 'And then home.'

'Home – to Summer Hill?'

'Yes, I suppose so. You see I'm going to have a child, Dermot, a baby.' She looked at him as calmly as she could.

'Frances,' was all he could mumble through his bandages.

'Yes. But don't worry, it's the only thing I've got to be pleased about.'

'But Frances, whose? . . .'

'His. Who else?' She looked at him, a look that became a glare, then changed again, a mix of tenderness and annoyance. 'Not yours – I'm afraid.' She kissed him quickly on his bandages, before moving away towards the ambulance wagon. But he followed her, taking her by the shoulder.

'If I can do anything, anything at all – you could say the child was mine, if it would help.'

She turned to him. 'Thank you. But the only thing for you to do is not to die out here – dearest Dermot.'

She moved away through the straggling lines of men, the walking wounded on crutches, the many more being taken on stretchers towards the wagons, another gorgeously fine day rising all round the stricken camp, a vast blue sky with puffy white clouds towering away to the west. Dermot watched her go, cursing himself once more for his disability with this woman, with all women, wishing he could have been her lover and the father of the child to come.

Lady Cordiner glanced at the small leather case again, examining the dull brown gunmetal cross and the wide maroon ribbon nestling on a bed of fine white satin. The medal looked so unbright, she thought, so unprepossessing an object to represent such bravery.

Then she read the copperplate citation that had come with this posthumous Victoria Cross for her son: '. . . who on the 15th December 1899 showed conspicuous gallantry at the Battle of Colenso, in being first to cross the Tugela River under heavy fire with some of his company, then taking the most advanced position of the day, and who afterwards, ever mindful of his wounded comrades, returned under equally heavy fire to rescue them: all enterprises carried out successfully and without thought for his own safety, where finally he gave his own life for his men . . . actions far above and beyond the call of duty . . . the greatest courage and self-sacrifice, in the very highest traditions of the army . . .'

Lady Cordiner's eyes clouded over. She could read no more. Instead, she turned angrily to Frances, who was standing by the window of her boudoir at Summer Hill. It was late January, the afternoon of a wet midwinter day, the trees bare and windswept across the valley, the rain falling steadily.

'Well, at least my dear son has gone on – with honour.' Lady Cordiner spoke with bitter sarcasm. 'Whereas you, Frances, can live with nothing but dishonour now. For yourself, of course. But just as much for us, your family. Words fail me.' But they did not. Lady Cordiner rushed on with a torrent of invective. 'That you should have been so reckless, so concerned only for your own sluttish pleasure, so *selfish*, so unthinking – for us, your family, and the dishonour you now bring us.'

Frances looked at her mother calmly. 'Mama, it was not I alone, you know.'

'How dare you! To drag his Royal Highness down into the gutter with you – you little hussy!'

'What nonsense. I did no such thing. Both of us, we loved –'

'Don't besmirch the name of love – with your gross behaviour,' her mother stormed at her.

'Mama, you have quite lost control.'

'Not I, but you – and you shall pay for it! I have only one thing to say: you must leave, as far away as possible – and have your child, out of sight, out of mind – leave as soon as possible. I have considered it already. There is only one possibility – your father's old friends, the Grants, in the West Indian colonies. He is a planter there of some sort, in one of the smaller islands, which could not be more remote, I understand. We shall pay, of course. But you will go there, and stay there. I shall write to them today.'

Frances was astonished. 'The West Indies?' She approached her mother now, fiercely. 'Mama, I may tell you, I refuse to be exiled a second time, to some island. This is my home. I shall stay *here*. Or return to London.'

Lady Cordiner smirked at her suddenly. 'You will not remain here, I can assure you of that. And if you return to London, well, you can no longer work in your condition – and we will not supply a penny to support you there. Unless you imagine the Prince will support you?' She looked at Frances, a clear hint of triumph in her eyes. 'He has offered that?'

'No. I should not ask it.'

'But you have told him . . . of the impending event?'

'Yes.'

'And his reply?'

'He has not replied . . . as yet.'

Lady Cordiner's triumph was complete now. 'Nor will he. He will naturally cease to have anything to do with you. Can you think that he would? – heir to the throne, soon to be King-Emperor – that he would associate himself with your scandal, by admitting or continuing the relationship, or by supporting you in any way.'

'It is his child, as well as mine!'

'Perhaps. But are you so naive as to think he will ever admit it, in *any* way?'

'Not openly, but privately –'

'In no way, *ever*, I can assure you. I warned you in Marienbad – one breath of scandal, let alone *this*, and it is quite finished between you. You are, besides, as good as dead in society, in London or in Ireland. You have only one course left open: you must disappear, abandon the world.' Lady Cordiner, once again invoking all her Old Testament demons, spoke with disgusted finality.

Frances laughed. But it was an uncontrolled reponse. She was losing her grip, forced to admit the plausibility of her mother's argument: it seemed as if the Prince had indeed cast her aside. Though she knew well enough what really angered her mother: the end of her own great social ambitions, so successfully prospered since her meeting with the Prince at Marienbad, if this news got about. However, Frances rallied quickly.

'I may leave for a while, Mama . . . abandon the world, as you put it. But I assure you of one thing, I shall abandon nothing – *nothing* of this house!'

She looked at her mother with stinging contempt, then let her eyes stray to the walls, the ceiling, so that her fierce gaze seemed to penetrate right through the whole house, possessing all the rooms, landings, attics, outhouses – and beyond that the whole landscape of Summer Hill.

BOOK TWO

1

'SEE! THIS WATER is fresh – the other salt!' Frances Fraser explained the phenomenon to her eight-year-old daughter Henrietta and her friend Robert Grant, almost a year older, as the two children sat in the shallow freshwater stream under the palms.

Henrietta suddenly launched herself forward in the current, her bottom sliding deliciously over the sandbank, soon caught by the flow, rushing now towards the sea. Robert followed her. The stream narrowed into a turbulent gully a few yards ahead and once the water took hold of them the children were wonderfully propelled in a cloud of spray out to where the waves roared up to the top of the beach and the two waters met. Henrietta cupped her hands in the sea.

'No! Don't drink it.' But she had and was spluttering now.

'Why is one water salt and the other isn't?' Henrietta demanded. But before her mother could reply the thin, dark-haired, freckle-faced girl had stood up in the sea, shouting petulantly, 'I like the *other* water.' She refused to play with Robert then, running back to the sandy freshwater pool in the stream. Robert stayed where he was among the thrashing waves, preferring them, thinking Henrietta a coward.

'She's just frightened. Hetty is a cowardy cow,' Robert told his mother Mildred, as she dried him later, putting his sun-hat back on, which he hated. Henrietta meanwhile was being fussed over and scolded by her own mother, some distance away by the fire and the picnic table, where Josephine, Robert's creole nanny, was bending down, her great bottom in the air, blowing the sticks alight, with a large black kettle over them. Two of the men from the Fraser estate, Jules the Sailor and Slinky, one of the odd-job boys, were lying out on the deck of the small steam launch, pulled up on the shingle further down the beach.

'No, she's not a coward,' Mildred told her son. 'Hetty just likes fresh water, that's all. People like different things.'

Robert looked over at the picnic table where Mr Fraser had lit one of his small cigars, puffing it, before raising his rum glass again and drinking. Robert was curious. Nobody drank rum in the afternoons, he knew, especially not at a picnic. There was something wrong with Hetty's father. He said so little, sitting there in his white duck suit and dark tie, just drinking, barely ever talking to them. And there was something wrong with Mrs Fraser, too, Hetty's mother. They were both sad, Robert thought – but in different ways. Mr Fraser was grim and silent. With Mrs Fraser – well, whatever it was, it made her angry. She was quite often angry, and very suddenly, over nothing, when she bunched her fingers in and out in a funny way. Robert blotted the hot sun out, burying his face in his mother's neck and arms as she dried his back.

'*Why* are people different, Mama? And why is some water salt and other water isn't?' He mumbled the words quietly into his mother's hot-smelling, frilly white blouse so that Hetty would not hear anything.

'People have to be different. And I don't honestly know about salt and fresh water. It just is. Your father would know.'

'I don't like Hetty – she's annoying. I wish we didn't have to come all the way over this side of the island for holidays. There's no one here and the water's cold.'

'Try and like her, darling. She's really very nice. A little highly strung – and wilful,' she added, looking over to where Hetty was wriggling frantically in her mother's arms. 'She likes you – I'm sure she does. And we can't just not like people because they are different from us.'

'Yes, but *why* is she different from us? I'm much browner – she has freckly spots on her face and her whitey skin.' Robert was frustrated now. He started to struggle, hating his sun-hat and being dried. 'And why hasn't she got a *real* father?' He finally released himself from his mother's arms and looked at her in triumph.

'Robert! What do you mean?' Mildred looked at her son, alarmed. 'Of *course* she has a real father: Bruce – Mr Fraser – over there.'

'That's not what Josephine says. I've heard her talking – round the back of the kitchens at the Hall. She said Mr Fraser wasn't Hetty's *real* father!'

'That's not true, Robert. You mustn't spread lies like that – you're not to talk of it ever again, do you hear? *Ever.*'

'Well, anyway, he doesn't seem like her father – away all the time. He's never here.'

'He's very busy – with his family plantations in Barbados,' Mildred lied.

'Like Papa? Does he work at lime trees and go down to the factory every day?'

'No. They don't grow limes in Barbados. Only here – in Domenica.'

'Is that why Mrs Fraser is so angry? – because Mr Fraser isn't here. And, when he is here, he just sits by himself, drinking all that rum?'

'Robert, you're *not* to talk of it.' Mildred raised her voice a fraction, looking round her cautiously. 'And you must be kind to Hetty.' She lowered her voice, smoothing her son's damp dark hair. 'Because her father isn't often here, she needs *more* kindness – do you see?'

'No. Not really.'

Robert noticed his mother's reproachful look. Or was she just being sad again, he wondered? She sometimes looked that way. But she was never angry. And at least he knew why she was sad, because he was sad himself for the same reason. His father was really an inventor, not a planter. But his inventions usually didn't work, over in their own house, Lime Hill, above Roseau, far away on the other side of the island where everyone lived and the sea was always warm. His father Bertie was always playing with strange grown-up things, just like toys. 'But they're not playthings, you see,' his mother had told him wearily. 'They're real.' But they mostly broke down. Like the funny new machine he'd built in the yard of Lime Hill for squeezing limes, from bits of a washing mangle with chains attached to the pedals of a bicycle – a lovely black brand-new bicycle which had come all the way out on the boat from England, which he hadn't bought to ride, but just to nail down and fix up to the stupid rollers and things in the yard. His father never came on holiday with them over to this side of the island. He had to stay at home – waiting for things from England. Robert could see him now, down on the busy jetty at Roseau, watching the boys load boxes and big crates and things from England, putting them onto the mule cart and dragging them up into the hills.

His father was always looking out to sea, with the long brass telescope, from the terrace at Lime Hill, waiting for the ships, expecting things with a sad face – which often didn't come, and, when they did, he messed them all up so that they didn't work. That was why his mother was sad and spent holidays over on this side of the island – keeping Mrs Fraser company, she said. But he knew the real reason.

His mother turned the brim of his horrid sun-hat down then. He turned it up again. His mother sighed. 'Well, you must just try and be nice to Hetty. People have to *try*, you know, dearest.'

'But she won't play pirates with me, or anything. She just cuddles and cries with Elly. And last night – she hurt me.'

'What?'

'She said there was a big frog, a *crapaud*, in my bed – and Elly didn't scold her, when there wasn't.'

'That's just teasing, not hurting, darling. She teases. We all do sometimes.'

'But she *always* teases me, Mama, so it *does* hurt.'

'Well, you'll just have to try – you are nearly a year older, you know – have to be a rather grown-up boy now and try and understand her.'

'Yes, I suppose so.' Robert so wanted to be older and wiser then. 'It's really because of her father, isn't it? – because he's never here. I know it's that, because last Christmas, when we were over here, she wrote to him, instead of Father Christmas, asking him for things. And I told her she wouldn't get anything, because he never sends her anything, not even on her birthday. And Hetty pushed me then and cried.'

'Robert, you shouldn't – you mustn't say things like that to Hetty.'

'I was only telling her the truth. You said I should always tell the truth.'

'Not when it hurts people.'

They had their picnic tea soon after. Robert did not like it very much. There was a plum cake that was very hard and black on top and all dry and crumbly and not nice inside, because it had come all the way from England. Most things that came from England were nice, he thought. But not this cake. He wished they could bring snow from England – and fog. Fog was thick, like pea soup, his father had told him. But he had never had pea soup either. And never seen snow, of course. Snow was like white rain, his mother had said, even better, like sugar flakes that melted on your tongue, coming out of the sky and covering the whole earth in a great white cold blanket. Could that really be true? It made him tingle with excitement just to think about it.

Later in the afternoon, when Josephine had packed up the picnic things, they all walked down the beach to the steam launch, which Jules and Slinky had pulled up into the shallow waves, turning it about so that the stern and the little ladder there faced inwards, and they all climbed aboard, getting their feet wet. But nobody minded, except Mr Fraser who missed his footing, stumbled about in the shallows and made a fuss about spoiling his smart white suit.

Robert sat next to Big Jules at the tiller in the back, while Slinky stoked the boiler ahead of them. The others sat on either side of the cockpit as they moved out into the surge of Atlantic waves, rounding the headland. This was one thing Robert really liked about coming to Fraser Hall – these lovely bouncy, dippy trips in the steam launch, through these big white-crested waves which they never had on the other, Caribbean, side of the island. Here, with the spray in his eyes, he could really pretend he was a pirate – Captain Morgan with all his treasure – making for the secret cove just below the great white house on the cliff in St David's Bay on the other side of the headland.

Fraser Hall, with its windswept stockade of magnificent Emperor palms, stood on the short cliff, the coral stone façade dazzling white in the sun, patterned with rippling light and shadow, reflecting the endless sea glitter beneath, so that the house seemed alive, appeared to sway and dance, agitated by the prism of colours slanting off the water.

Below it the sea moved in deep swells and crashing breakers, a huge leonine presence, throwing itself on the rocks, exploding in crystal drifts of sunlit spume, retreating in a fizzy turmoil of blue and green, renewing itself further out in menacing rollers of deep purple. But the house mocked the great waves – and the wild land behind it, a startling conceit on this deserted coast, a white vision rearing up from the aquamarine ocean set against a backdrop of jade-green mountains: a large four-square two-storied villa somewhat in the French manner – for the buildings here had maintained that character in an island that had belonged to France less than a hundred years before – with a mansard roof, green louvred storm shutters and metal canopies over the windows – a dozen hooded eyes that gazed dismissively out over the vast Atlantic rollers.

The coral stone had been shipped from Barbados twenty years before, by Bruce Fraser's father when he had first decided to develop this almost uninhabited Atlantic side of Domenica as an agricultural estate: an eccentric, expensive gesture on a volcanic island where nearly all the other plantation houses were set on stilts or ballast brick, built of wood, with shingle or tin roofs.

But then old Alisdair Fraser, though Scottish, never did things by halves. He was cannily extravagant and expansive, which thrust no doubt lay behind the fortune he had inherited and increased from his family's sugar plantations in Barbados. Besides, in the matter of any building in these parts, he rightly feared hurricanes. And so Fraser Hall had been built to survive the worst whirlwind, as it always had, where other houses on the island every five years or so, had lost their roofs and worse, the vicious scything windspouts taking everything away with them: life and limb, wood and tin – everything; lock, stock and barrel.

The sole concession to the elements in the house was the wide verandah with its graceful stone arches, which had been set around two sides at the back, facing inland out of the wind – and the gales when they came with their raging breakers. The verandah, covered in bougainvillaea and hibiscus, with its chairs and chintz sofas, gave out on to a large, sheltered lawn, brilliant green, enclosed by Emperor palms: coarse-grassed, with a mango grove at one end, a lovely casuarina tree with a swing in the middle, and filled with clumps of exotic shrubs and flowers – orchids, anturiums, heliconias – which bloomed fiercely the year round.

Beyond the lawn, to either side, up and down the narrow coastal strip, the land had been cleared years ago for the sugar and citrus plantations. But now, long-neglected, more wild and overgrown each year, the estate was falling into livid decay, a rash of bright weeds rising among the overblown lime and grapefruit trees. The sugar cane had not prospered. The citrus had got withertip, and Alisdair Fraser, cutting his losses, had returned to concentrate on his surer profits in Barbados, leaving the house, its dilapidated estate, and a sizeable income besides, as a marriage gift to his dissolute younger son Bruce – on condition that he never set foot in Barbados again.

Due west of the terrace, less than a mile inland, the great saw-toothed mountains of the island rose everywhere, range after higher range, in ever-deepening perspective, forest-clad, in a variety of astonishing shapes and colours, forming a gaudy green chiaroscuro backdrop to the white house. Green of every shade: jade, moss, yellow, olive, tweed-dark and black green – the steep tropical rain forests running up into cloudy peaks before diving into fathomless dim ravines beyond. Here lay almost uninhabited, impenetrable territory, occupied only by the Caribs, last remnants of the fierce cannibal tribe who had once dominated all these windward islands.

To the left of the high bluff on which the house was set, down a gentler slope, the Belle Fille river ran towards the bay, where, before it reached the sea, water was taken from it along a stone aqueduct towards the old sugar mill with its tall brick chimney, barely used now, except to extract enough cane juice for the boiling coppers to produce a strong rum, once famous throughout the island, but now only produced for domestic consumption.

Beyond the factory, a mile north along the bay, lay the small settlement of Castle Bruce: a few tin shacks, a general store run by a Syrian, and the Catholic church, the parish administered by Father Bertin, a French priest from the Holy Ghost order in Guadeloupe, the next island to the north.

Immediately below the house, down a winding cliff path, lay the sheltered cove with a jetty where the boats were moored – the steam launch *Sisserou*, an unseaworthy sloop *Arethusa*, and two dinghies. Once a fortnight the mail packet, from the capital Roseau, dropped anchor here with supplies, newspapers and letters. The packet was the one link Fraser Hall had with the outside world. Only half a dozen other plantation houses lay on this rugged windward side of the island, and the first two of these were ten miles north and south of Castle Bruce, at Marigot and Rosalie – neighbours in a sense, but never visited now by the inhabitants of the Hall. Roseau, the capital, with its semblance of civilisation, lay two days' journey right round the island by boat. Apart from the few dirt tracks leading out of Roseau, there were no roads on Domenica – and Fraser Hall ruled quite alone on this section of it: isolated, magnificent, secret.

'I don't really care whether you come or go, after your usual behaviour – this afternoon,' Frances told her husband that evening at dinner, as they sat at opposite ends of the long lamp-lit dining table. Mildred had retired early, pleading a sick headache. Frances picked at her dolphin steak. Bruce Fraser had not yet touched the claret decanter, still drinking rum. The high-ceilinged room was hot and humid in this summer season before the August storms. Beyond the open louvred shutters lay the arched verandah and beyond that fireflies danced over the dark lawn, while other insects, despite the muslin netting over the jalousy windows, crowded round the yellow globe of the oil lamp, feinting, buzzing, dying with little spits and pops above the glass chimney. There was an oppressive, sweet-and-sour air in the heavy, dark-furnished room – a mix of paraffin oil, rum and mildew.

'I shall "come", if you put it like that. It is my house, after all,' he said petulantly.

'As you wish. You do me no favour, one way or the other.'

'I did, though – remember that!'

'How could I forget it.' Frances laughed icily.

'We were not so distant then.'

'No. Nor did you spend your time drinking – or months away in the fleshpots of Spanish Town, Jamaica.'

Bruce Fraser sighed, allowing himself a wan smile. Again, he was dressed immaculately – dark dinner jacket, boiled white shirt, black tie, dancing pumps, gold cufflinks that gleamed in the yellow light. This sartorial propriety only served to accentuate his covert drunkenness. He was held up, held firm within the walls of his stiff clothes, so that it was all the more apparent how he trembled and swayed inside them, his brown eyes unsteady beams atop a dark lighthouse. Though only in his early thirties his cheeks were puffy and blotched, enlarging an already-heavy face, still handsome in its way, but with a childish cast to it now, as if the drink had taken him back to a sort of infancy, this rum-formed baby fat spreading about his jowls and chin.

'You were pleased to take my name – and money, once,' he said reasonably.

'Yet since then . . . you deny me – everything. One may drink because of it,' he added shortly, looking down the table, trying to clear his eyes, focus them on her.

'You drank before I met you . . .'

'You have only yourself to blame, then, for marrying me.' He leant forward sharply, the better to insinuate his attack. 'But of course you were not concerned with my morals, my drinking then, not with blame of any sort – merely that you should give your child a father. I see that now, of course. It was your plan from the start – which I failed to see then. Well, she has a father, in name at least – so you may rest content. And I may drink.' He raised his rum glass to her in an ironic salute. Then, puzzled suddenly, he set the glass down. 'Yet it wasn't always so.' He spoke more to himself, than to Frances. 'You saw something in me once.'

Indeed, that was true, Frances thought. Bruce had been witty years before, when they had first met in Roseau, up with the Grants at Lime Hill, only a week after she and Eileen had arrived from England: witty, confident, warm. But she had not seen then how these qualities had largely been the product of his tippling. She bunched her fingers together now, making fists over the elaborate settings of glowing silver cutlery.

'You were a different person then,' she lied to him, for he had not been. She had just failed to recognise his real nature where, under the rum-based bonhomie, he was weak, undecided – and violent, too, because of these defects. Yet he was, and remained, intelligent. She recognised that in his reply.

'I was no different then – drank less perhaps. You want to see me as different now, because you won't admit that it is *you* who have changed, getting all that you wanted – a name, house, money, possessions, a father to your child. You came here an outcast, with nothing but that child in your belly. I offered you everything – I had everything. Now it's the other way around. You've won and I've lost. That's all there is to it.'

He opened the claret decanter then. Frances did not reply. She closed up absolutely – as she always did when her husband confronted her with these drunken truths.

Upstairs, in the children's bedroom at the end of the corridor looking over the outhouses, the kitchens and servants' quarters, Eileen read the poem from the *Irish Fireside and Homestead* magazine, which arrived for her every month from Ireland, Robert and Henrietta in their beds to either side, Eileen on the rocking chair between them.

> '"Come away O human child!
> to the waters and the wild,
> With a faery, hand in hand,
> For the world's more full of weeping
> Than you can understand."

'There,' she said when she'd finished the poem. 'That's grand, isn't it? All the way from Ireland!'

'Are the fairies there real?' Henrietta asked.

'And why wouldn't they be?'

'Like Josephine's and cook's zombies and werewolves – down behind the kitchens?'

'Yes, but the fairies in Ireland are *much* nicer and kinder. Josephine's are real divils!' Eileen shuddered.

'Where is Island?' Robert asked.

'*Ire*land. Though it's an island too. But much bigger than this one. Where I come from – and Mrs Fraser as well. And Hetty in a way, though she's not been there yet.'

'Snow and fog – do they have that there?'

'Yes – sometimes. But not very much.'

'They have it in England, a *lot* of it,' Robert said proudly. 'I'm English. They have real pea-soupers there, in London.'

He turned to look at Henrietta. 'See, you're just from *Ire*land, just a little island.'

'England's only an island as well,' Eileen told him, getting up, tucking him under his single sheet, closing the mosquito canopy over him.

'See!' Henrietta shouted over to him. 'You're only from an island as well – and I don't want to see snow anyway – or pea-soupers, so there! I don't want everything all white and cold. I want it all cosy-warm. Don't I, Elly?' she added, thumb in her mouth, looking up with frail hope, as Eileen came across to her.

'Yes, Mavourneen, of course you do. And you are.'

She settled Hetty down and cuddled her for a minute, her heart going out to this expectant, delicate-featured child with her long strands of wavy dark hair and great blue eyes. A child of such mixtures, so rude one minute, shy the next, you never knew where you were with her – such sudden tantrums and quiet, long silences, eyes gazing nowhere, as if she had gone into another world. Yes, a child touched in a way, Eileen thought, just like the one in the poem. A changeling maybe, that the fairies would take if they were back home. And, God love her, why wouldn't she be like that? – out here in this God-forsaken place with so much to put up with: her mother on edge most of the time, neglecting her, and her father at the rum bottle whenever he appeared. Not her real father, of course. She had always known who that was – the King of England. Hetty was her little princess.

'Now lie down and go to sleep, the two of ye,' she told them. 'And no chitter-chatter, or I'll have Josephine with her divils up the stairs at ye!'

Eileen took the lamp, leaving a night-light burning on a stool by the half-open door leading to the dark landing. Outside the wind had dropped and the croak of frogs everywhere on the lawn rose clearly up into the nursery out of the velvet night.

Robert sighed and bit his lips. Even before Hetty had pretended to put the great *crapaud* in his bed he'd been frightened of the frogs, but couldn't admit it. The huge frogs were everywhere on the island, quite harmless – they ate them even, though he didn't. Mountain chicken they called them. But he had nightmares about them now.

'Hear the froggies, can you?' Hetty whispered over to him.

'No.'

'Yes, you can. They don't hurt, you know. Here, I've got something for you, if you're frightened.'

'I'm *not* frightened.'

'I sometimes am – cook's werewolves and zombies.'

Hetty pushed the mosquito netting aside and tiptoed across to Robert's bed. She held a reel of button thread, taken from Mildred's sewing basket that afternoon. 'Here, you hold one end,' she told Robert. 'And I hold the other. And if we're frightened in the night we can just pull on it.'

She gave Robert one end, returning to her own bed, playing out the cotton-reel behind her.

'That's a stupid idea,' Robert mumbled.

'No, it's not. You'll see!'

In her own bed now, she pulled the thread, gently, reassuringly, several times. After a long moment, grudgingly, Robert pulled it back. They drifted to sleep, the thread still in their hands.

Sometime after dinner, when Frances had gone to her bedroom, Bruce, glass in hand, moved into the hall and started playing the collection of mildewed hurdy-gurdies, barrel organs and pianolas that his father had collected and brought to the house in the years when he had stayed there. Bruce was swaying now as he set them all off in a twanging cacophony of discordant sound: 'Down at the Old Bull and Bush', 'The Blue Danube', 'Pale Hands I Loved'.

Letting the instruments stammer on alone then, moving to the centre of the hall by the mahogany staircase, he danced with himself, swirling around in his stiff evening clothes and pumps – swooping and floundering as he tried to egg on an imaginary partner to ever-greater efforts. The machines gradually wound down; the music stopped. He made for the rum bottle again in the dining room, drank the rest of it, then went upstairs, entering Frances's bedroom where she was well awake.

'Let me – sleep here – with you.'

'No – in no circumstances –' He stumbled, falling through the mosquito netting over the big bed. 'No, you drunken oaf. No, *never!*'

'Ah, please,' he whined. 'It would make it, us – everything so much better.'

He reached forward, lying on his stomach, pawing at her, his sweaty hands sliding over, but failing to grip, her almost equally damp skin. Then, angry suddenly and violent, he tried to force himself on her, clawing up over the sheet, flailing his hands about in the netting. Rising to his knees as he approached her, he stripped the sheet away in one wild movement where she lay before him now in a thin cotton nightdress.

He tried to rape her, pulling at her shoulders, ripping the fine material there, exposing her breasts, tugging the dress down below her midriff. But, before he could do more, Frances leapt from the bed.

She fought him then, nightdress gone, a naked virago, in a tremendous battle up and down the bedroom, as if her life depended on it – as it might have done: a vicious, silent bout which had the air of some condemned sport, the room a gladiator's pit or a cock-fighting pen now, the two of them circling each other, black and white figures, Frances's bare limbs and moist ivory skin shining in the lamplight, confronting this enraged stage-door Johnny in his dark dress suit.

She did not have his strength, but he was drunk and slipshod – while her fury, her terror and horror of the man, released a tremendous energy in her, a long pent-up frustration as she parried his blows, dodged round chairs, lunged at him with a brass candlestick, as he tried to corner her. Finally, seeming to have trapped her, he crouched in front of her, about to spring. She thumped the candlestick down on him. But it glanced off his shoulder – and then he was on to her, only inches between their sweating faces, pinioning her arms to the wall. She bit him deeply on the neck and he yelled out and she escaped into the room again.

Rounding the bed he caught her before she reached the door, dragging her back, clasping her in both arms, lifting her bodily towards the bed. But he stumbled then and they both fell, wrestling over and over on the floor, where, with his weight, it seemed he must finally get the better of her, pinning her arms down now, straddling her.

Looking up at him, she appeared to relax, letting her body go limp. She even smiled a fraction. He moved onto her. Then, at the last moment, she brought her leg up sharply into his groin – a vicious blow with her kneecap – so that he screamed again, doubled up, rolling away from her, writhing in agony.

Frances was on her feet in a flash, opening the door, running down the landing to Eileen's room at the far end, where Eileen, disturbed by the general commotion, was already standing by the doorway. She took Frances inside, locking them in. Frances's skin was bruised, grazed – and coursing with sweat. But there were no tears. She was simply furious.

'What happened –'

'What do you think?'

'No – no.'

'Except that it didn't happen. But I'll kill him all the same. I'll *kill* him.'

'No, be calm –'

'What else, Elly? What else can I do?' she asked venomously.

'Nothing. Wait 'till morning. Stay here with me.'

At the other end of the dark landing the children stood peeking out from the half-open doorway of their bedroom. Henrietta had heard the shouts and seen her mother, a shadowy naked figure running down the landing. She put her thumb in her mouth now, sucking vigorously, wide-eyed. Then she saw her father leave the bedroom, bent over, groaning as he made for the staircase. What had happened? He must have eaten something nasty – that was it. She hoped he had. She hated him. Robert stood beside her. 'I don't like it at all,' he said. 'The frogs – and now this. I don't like it – even with the thread.'

'We could run away.' Henrietta turned to him.

'Where?'

'The mountains. Slinky said he'd show us.'

'No. The Caribs live up there. They eat people.'

'Not now, silly – Mama said.'

'Still –'

'Anyway, Slinky is nearly a Carib. He knows them. We'd be quite safe.'

'We'll see.'

'He must have eaten something very bad,' Hetty said as they went back to their beds.

'Yes. One of those awful frogs, I expect. Serves him right.'

They set the thread up between them again, pulling at it several times before they finally slept once more.

Bruce Fraser left on the packet next day, without speaking to her – and thank God, Frances thought. He would be away for months now, in Jamaica, where he shared a house with some army cronies, or in Fort de France, south in Martinique, where he had a Creole mistress – or back in Europe even, in Paris or Piccadilly. She never knew where. They never corresponded. The old belt-and-braces Scotsman, McTear, who lived by the sugar mill, ran what was left to run of the estate. Bruce came and went as the mood – and his considerable fortune – took him. He would be here again in the winter, no doubt, with his friends from Jamaica, for the shooting – the annual drive on the sheer-sided plateau in the mountains behind the house where Alisdair Fraser had imported some bison and deer from America years before. And the two cougars, which had been heard but not seen since. Meanwhile she had six months' peace and freedom before he returned. Time to think, to plan. But to plan what? How to escape from him? Escape where?

Out on the verandah, she took another crystallised fruit – a Carlsbad plum – from the half-empty box beside her, munched it, biting into its deep sticky juices appraisingly: the last box, but she had ordered another dozen from the Army and Navy Stores in London. So what if she had put on a good deal of weight? – if these sweet sticky fruits and other bonbons had become an irresistible obsession with her in these last years? *Tant pis*. Who would notice her weight out here anyway? It was her one luxury and she needed it more than ever that afternoon.

She lay in the creaking canvas hammock looking out at the great green mountains, another day of humid sunshine, lowering clouds rolling in from the Atlantic, listening to the waves, a faint but ever-present roar on the other side of the house. She had come to love this windward side of the island, where so few people either lived, or fancied living – the several hundred colonial administrators, businessmen and planters with their families who clustered about Roseau. They rarely ventured windward across the island, for it was a quite different world here, a different climate divided by the great mist-topped mountains, looking east towards Europe, sometimes almost European in its weather: a world of cloud-coloured sunrise, moist daybreak, and vivid fresh, rain-damp mornings, sudden downpours alternating with long fierce bouts of sunshine throughout the day. If you looked seaward and forgot the rampant green vegetation – well, one might almost have been in Ireland, on that headland in Kerry, nudging out into the warm gulf stream, which she had visited as a child from Summer Hill, where there were even a few palm trees, tropical plants . . .

Yes, this windy, sea-spumed, rocky coast reminded Frances a little of Ireland, where she wanted to be – whereas the leeward side of Domenica, when she was there, did nothing but suggest a permanent exile for her: a kingdom of torpid afternoons and calm sunsets, ever-clear skies and glittering smooth Caribbean waters, a crystal sea, pellucid lagoons – where coloured fish span and dived languidly. She had come to resent all the lax, unrelentingly tropical beauty there – as if the drowsy, balmy climate over that part of the island might weaken her resolve, disarm her, relax her fierce purpose, which was to return home. So she saw herself, remembering her mother's Spanish phrase *sol y sombra*, as a woman in shadow here, as the sun sank early below the mountains – but temporary shadow, dispelled very early each morning by glorious windswept, spume-drifting day.

These incandescent sunrises – seen from her bedroom window before she went riding along the dew-soaked overgrown tracks across the citrus fields – seemed to offer her sure promise of a change in her life, a place in the sun without shadow, one day, somehow. So, as often before in her life, she saw herself in only temporary eclipse. Meanwhile she thrived on this wild coast, drew strength from its bracing winds, bitter storms and fierce sun – which so exactly reflected the imbalance and vehemence of her own nature now: the anger, the wilful overstatement and exaggeration of the exile.

She moved in the hammock, easing the bruise on her back, looking over at Mildred: Mildred, rather prim and correct, sitting in a high-backed chair nearby, sewing the torn collar on one of Robert's sailor suits. Noticing Frances's gaze, and seeing again the other livid bruise on her cheek, Mildred looked down, embarrassed, concentrating once more on her work. 'He won't need the suit 'till he's back in Roseau next term. But how he does go through his clothes! I suppose you'll be sending Hetty over to the nuns, too,' she added without looking up.

'Yes. No. I don't know.'

'But, Frances, she can't go on running wild over here, just with you and Elly and the priest teaching her – have to have some real lessons. Robert, as well. He'll have to go to school in England soon.' Mildred looked up, touching the mousy curls on the crown of her head, scratching the scalp there, delicately, surreptitiously.

'I want us both to go *home*, not settle here – you know that, Milly,' she told her impatiently. Mildred was kind but poor, Frances thought: fatally put upon by her decent, but impossibly vague husband. She was too yielding, afraid even to think of her best interests there. Though five years older than her, Mildred, with her thin cheeks, watery blue eyes and small mouth, had the air of a simple, uncertain child. She had never criticised Frances for her indiscretions; she had seemed simply unaware of them, as if she really believed babies came from storks or from beneath gooseberry bushes.

Of course Mildred, though she knew of the inappropriate pregnancy, had not witnessed or known any details of Henrietta's birth. No one on the island had. She and Bruce had been married in Jamaica, where he was serving with a West Indian regiment, and they had left at once for an extended honeymoon, lasting nearly six months, in America, where Henrietta had been born in the large apartment they had rented in New York, a house looking over the Hudson on Riverside Drive. And Milly had never since commented on these tactful evasions.

Yes, Frances thought, she had always been kind and considerate in her way, ever since she and Eileen had first arrived on the island. But it was an infuriatingly vague, and therefore an unhelpful, understanding which she had offered, so that the idea of having to live permanently in that indeterminate, discreet atmosphere, where nothing seemed entirely understood or meant, where not even birth seemed important, had appalled Frances.

And so, all the more, she had taken to Bruce – seeing, beyond the man, to the freedom of this big house where she could be her own mistress. Yes, she had rushed into the marriage, for that among the other reasons her husband had mentioned the previous night. It had all been a calculated act of desperation, and she had since paid the price for it with her husband. Yet the house remained at least where, when he was away, she controlled her own destiny. And that had been worth the price. Yet she could not live here forever – not for a moment.

'We must go *home*, at some point, Milly. You do see that.'

'Indeed, the way he treats you . . .' Mildred paused. Then, with a rare tremor of emotion in her bland voice, she said, 'It cannot be *safe* for you here alone with him, Frances. But how may you return? Apart from Bruce, your mother remains adamant, I imagine?'

'I imagine – we never correspond. But these things are sent to try us, Milly. There will be a way. It will happen.'

'But, meanwhile, why not come back with us to Roseau? To Lime Hill – there is more than enough room. Hetty would have Robert and the other girls at school. I cannot think how you *survive* out here alone – just you and the girl.'

'Oh, I have my riding, my walks – the dispensary in the village every morning. And what I can do to keep the house and estate up – with old McTear: a dour fish. But at least we see eye to eye. And there's Father Bertin – my English conversation lessons with him. Not the greatest company – lacks response – but a decent enough young man. And I have Elly – and my letters, books, newspapers from home.'

The letters, Frances thought: yes, they were her real lifeline – the correspondence she maintained with Dermot and with Ruth Wechsberg at Grosvenor Crescent, still running the nursing home. Apart from her mother and Eileen only these two others knew the real paternity of her child – and so, with them, she could be entirely open, about the past, present, future.

So she waited on the jetty eagerly each fortnight for the mail packet – to send out her own letters, taking in those others which meant so much to her. One letter, of course, had never come – from the Prince, now King Edward VII: no whisper of a message, though she had written to him again from New York after Hetty's birth. Silence – as if they had never met, loved, so needed each other: a complete, dead-making silence which had amazed her before the anger had come, a black hatred for him, as for her mother, who had so casually forecast just such a result.

Ruth Wechsberg had explained his behaviour with more tact – but nonetheless as something which Frances ought to have seen as inevitable: of course, the Prince had behaved like a child. But he had become at that point the King-Emperor, as well as a child, and it was simply these combined factors which had prevented him making any acknowledgement of her plight, of his paternity. Surely Frances could appreciate that? Frances had been unable to. As Prince he had managed everything to his – and her – advantage. As King, with all the more power, he had betrayed her. It was as simple as that.

His courtiers – Lumley, Knollys and the others – would have insisted on an absolute break and denial, of course, Frances knew that. But Edward himself, remembering their trust together, should certainly have responded. She had wanted nothing material of him, she had made that clear – nothing but a simple acknowledgement of, and hope for, their child. Failing in this, he had denied his own blood – and that was what she would not forgive him for. Blood transcended everything, she felt – even royal dynasties. She had written as much to Ruth, only to have the reply that unfortunately it was precisely this dynastic element in the matter that had sealed Edward's mouth, and would do so, forever.

But Frances still refused to accept the situation. Instead, she fanned the flames – was pleased to let this betrayal come to obsess her. During these eight years on the island she increasingly brooded on the injustice of her fate, encouraged the running sore, tore the scab off each morning, so that it had become a great wound. She thrived on exaggerating her plight – at the hands of the Prince, her mother, her husband Bruce. She saw herself as a martyr and was happy to feed the urge she now felt for pain – a pain that could only be truly satisfied by revenge.

This seemed to her an entirely natural response. She was not aware that, in pursuing these thoughts so exclusively, her character had changed much for the worse. She was no longer outgoing; her happy, voracious taste for life had almost entirely disappeared. She stopped no clocks now, for she held no bright deeds before her. Time out here, in this rampant green world, enfolded her, immobile, with only one real, if unconscious, aim in mind – to punish others as she had been punished.

Indeed, without her being aware of this either, Frances had taken on all the dark aspects of the island – the malignity, sickness, horror, that lay behind the drowsy beauty – creeping up about her, stifling her, like the vines and lianas over the proud trees. For there was that, too, in Domenica – a haunting sense of menace and evil: in the ever-present mildew, the grotesque phallic-shaped flowers, the huge black copulating toads, the vicious undertow of tides, the Boiling Lake, the Valley of Desolation, the great Devil Mountain. All the vivid, sun-drenched richness here concealed a suppurating decay – and Frances was part of this secret dissolution on the island.

So, in the intervals of nurturing this prized and pure obsession, she sought release only in mundane detail, in hawk-eyed, bullying attentions about the house and estate. She constantly reprimanded the servants, chivvied the cook, complained of the laundry, checked the larders each day against the food consumed – while her exchanges with McTear were not always carried on eye to eye, but in sharp argument. Her conversation lessons with poor Father Bertin were conducted very much *de haut en bas*, and she ran her village dispensary with a hard hand.

Yet to Frances these character changes, when she recognised them at all, were entirely justified. They were part of a higher purpose, foundations to a holy cause; she had purged herself of happiness and pleasure, living in a searing fire now, and thus all the more certain of resurrection. So taken was she by these grim defects, that she never saw how she had assumed what she most scorned: all the worst characteristics of her mother.

She fingered the Carlsbad plums – ate two of them in quick succession, then looked at Mildred: poor Mildred, she thought, accepting her fate, settling for so much less.

'A plum, Milly?' She offered her the last in the box.

'No, my dear, not now.' Mildred looked at her kindly – withholding the reproof she felt. How the poor woman fed herself, she thought, between meals, with these great sticky fruits. Quite shocking really, and what a bad example to the children. But then Frances had always been so wilful and unrealistic – and so unbalanced generally now. It was a charity to be here, to keep her company, to see she came to no harm. She hoped all the more she could persuade her to return to Roseau with her in September, at the end of the holidays.

A mournful horn, a single drawn-out funereal note, sounded then – slowly, faintly repeated on the wind coming from the bay: a conch shell. Some Caribs returning in their canoes from a fishing expedition, advertising their arrival. Mildred felt a shiver of unease creep up over the back of her neck, a cold frisson of fear in the humid afternoon. The Caribs had been tamed long ago, so it was said, and none of them lived now on the leeward side of the island. They had all been moved to a reserve, on the windward side, up in the mountains beyond Castle Bruce, four years ago. But Mildred feared them somehow all the more for that – in that they were hidden now, all together in one group, free to plot any sort of mischief, inaccessible in the vast jungle above them, whence she felt they might emerge one day in force, to rape and pillage or, worse, devour one – for that had been their speciality.

'Those Caribs,' she said to Frances. 'They make me uneasy. You really shouldn't stay here alone.'

'Nonsense, Milly. Unless aggravated, they're quite harmless. Lying in their hammocks smoking that weed, fishing, a little brandy-smuggling, from the French islands: that's all they're up to now – and their snakeskin and basketwork. Quite wonderful. Look at your own sewing basket there, those lovely diamond patterns!'

Mildred looked doubtfully at the snake-skinned basket by her feet, then moved her ankles away sharply. Frances ate the last of the Carlsbad plums.

The children, with Slinky, were at the end of the lawn where he was scything the long grass beyond the mango trees with a cutlass. He paused, suddenly, in his work. Something rustled in the undergrowth of fern and columbine.

'Voyé,' he said, a sly smile spreading over his copper-coloured, slightly Carib-featured face. 'Someone là.' He spoke a rough mix of English and the island patois.

'A *crapaud*?' Hetty asked. Robert retreated a fraction. For answer Slinky put his hand into the greenery and pulled out a large snapping land crab, a vivid orangey-pink colour, holding it judiciously by the back of the shell.

'My!' Hetty beamed, coming up to examine it more closely.

'Vou' mange ça.' Slinky looked appraisingly at the vicious animal.

'It's horrible.' Robert turned away. 'Come on, Hetty – Elly promised to take us to the Emerald Pool this afternoon.'

They left Slinky, running across the lawn towards the outhouses and kitchens to one side of it. Josephine was there, inside the smoky kitchen, talking to Annie, the cook and obeah woman, and Jules the sailor. Cook was at the table, making a paste of bread and water, flattening it out. Beside her, in an open matchbox, Hetty saw the large spider, a furry beast, quite motionless. Annie picked the insect up then, delicately, sitting it on the dough, doubling it over with equal care so as not to kill the spider, making a sandwich of it – and giving the snack to big Jules who ate it down in one mouthful.

Robert looked on horrified. Hetty had seen it all before. Jules was very pleased with himself. 'Dat much good – très bon.' He stretched. 'Ma poor bones – they al' stiffy and crackling from too much sea,' he said, smiling hugely.

'Big Jules – he got the akeanpain,' Josephine said.

'And Slinky caught a great, *great* crab,' Hetty shouted. 'Out in the ditch beyond the mango trees.'

'Good for he,' Josephine said. 'He eat him très bon and fast. Je'spare he don' get that one anaconde là, but.'

Big Jules laughed, white teeth glittering now, as he digested his medicine. He shook, his great dark muscles dancing beneath the old loose blue, brass-buttoned navy waistcoat, which was all he wore above his trousers. 'Slinky,' he said, 'he want no anaconde woun' all roun' lui.'

'There's *no* snakes out there,' Robert said firmly, hoping the wish would stand for the fact. 'Only in the mountains. Where's Elly? She's promised to take us to the Emerald pool.'

'Voyé!' Jules bent down to Robert conspiratorially. 'When you get to Emerpool

– you take that big gommier tree là, you know him by water?' Robert nodded. 'You cut skin off him, petit peu, and you come back and give it here to Josephine. She wan' that one petit peu skin of that tree!' He stood up, laughing uproariously. Josephine scolded him good-naturedly, flapping her arms about over his head. 'Diable homme!' she shouted. 'J'n' veux pas le gommier – pas tou'!' She scolded him some more, chasing him round the kitchen, before the children left.

'What's special about the skin of the gommier tree?' Robert asked Eileen as they walked away beyond the lawn, across a ruined citrus field, towards the forested hills and the Emerald pool half a mile away.

'Who was talking about it?'

'Big Jules – he said I should get some for Josephine.'

'Nothing. Just a charm. One of their medicines.' Eileen hid her embarrassment. The *gommier* bark, in fact, stewed up, was one of their strongest love potions.

'Like the spiders they eat – Jules was having a spider,' Hetty said easily. 'They eat all *sorts* of strange things over here to make them better, you see,' Hetty told Robert wisely.

She picked up a little hard green lime from an old tree as they passed – sticking her nails into it, scoring the skin deeply, putting it to her face immediately, the sharp tart smell fizzing up her nose. She loved this limey essence of the island, loved all this windward part of it with its wild greenery, towering rain forests, mountains, birds, animals; the wonderfully-coloured Sisserou parrot, the tiny humming birds, just like dragonflies, stabbing their rapier beaks into the sweet orchids, the rare *siffleur montagne* with its half-dozen sadly repeated flute-like notes; the possums, land crabs, frogs – even the great cockroaches that crackled across the floor or buzzed over the evening lamps.

She knew every hidden track and grove and stream between the estate and the hills, running wild in this arcadia, touched with dazzling, rain-filtered light – rainbows arching out, one after the other, over each mist-topped hill, a lost world at the end of the wide Sargasso Sea: the ripe fruit dropping everywhere about the estate – coconuts, breadfruit, bananas, mango, papaya, grapefruit, oranges, limes – fallen in the long grass, where she could slake thirst or hunger; the servants round the cook-house in the short twilight at Hallowe'en or Christmas, murmuring of zombies, soucriants and loups-garoux – the mysteries then as she looked out into the shadowy night, velvet-blue, soft, with muted calls and little stirrings.

This was Henrietta's world, which enveloped her, an ever-renewed wonder that took her heart each morning, day long, until she snuggled up with Eileen after sunset. She never wanted to go back to Roseau – or go to England or Ireland for that matter, wherever they were, with all that silly snow and pea-soupers.

They walked now, beyond the estate, up rising ground into the hills, along a moss-slippy forest path towards the Emerald pool. The temperature dropped quickly after they entered the forest – becoming mould-damp beneath the vast, vine-clad trees. Finally, hidden at the bottom of the winding path, lay the pool, crystal-green, with a sheer fall of water from a gash in the cliff fifty feet above it, the rock bowl beneath shrouded by overhanging branches, huge trees, the mammoth-buttressed *châtaignier* tree and the *gommier*, a wonderfully smooth grey, pillar-like hardwood rising a hundred feet. Beneath these primeval giants, in the filtered sunlight, climbing plants pushed and clung everywhere – lianas, vines, growing up from a carpet of silver and gold ferns, gold-dusted on the under-side, leaving a meticulously detailed imprint on your hand when you grasped them.

Henrietta adored this secret bathing place – the 'Shame-lady' tendrils in the moss, withdrawing, seeming to die when you touched them; the tiny mushrooms, which she cupped in her hands, seeing them glow luminously in the dark; the razor grass which guarded the approaches: this no-one-else-in-the-world place, even the air a scented green, she thought.

The children frolicked in the pool, drumming their feet in the water from smooth dark boulders, slipping down into the creamy green foam, splashing in the shallows. Eileen, on the rim of the pool, sat in a brilliant shaft of sunlight, watching them: Hetty, tall for her age, but skinny, with far more of her mother's features than her father's – the raven-dark, gold-tinted hair falling away in straggling ringlets to either side of a high brow, a very straight nose between the perfectly oval blue eyes, the mouth shaped in an equally perfect cupid's bow, a doll's chin jutting out, before receding delicately to the long neck. Yes, like a china doll, Eileen thought, with that pale skin that had never browned or taken on the olive shades from her mother.

Yet in every other way, outside these perfect frail features, she was so far from any cosy repose – the character of a wilful tomboy, forever moving, pushing, dancing about, all a restless twitter, like a bird. All this – and then the sudden silences, striking her down, after some rebuff or rebuke or without reason, when the thumb-sucking started and the deep blank gaze into nowhere. And when you spoke to her then – at best the stammered, strangled response, unable to get a word out properly.

Robert, against this seesaw of busy tirades or silences, kept a ready balance with Hetty most of the time, unmoved by her violent swings of behaviour: a steady boy, slow to anger, Eileen knew – tall for his age, dark, lank hair, mild-eyed, careful, considerate, an ordinary boy. Hetty was lucky to have him as a companion. Most other children would never have put up with her.

She watched them playing tag now in the water – Hetty pushing and feinting about expertly, teasing, even bullying Robert in the game, despite her being a year younger. Robert was stronger. But he did not use the advantage, Eileen saw – allowing her to get the better of him.

'Stop it, Hetty!' Eileen shouted. 'Don't pull his hair like that – that's not tag.' The two of them were locked together, struggling in the middle of the pool.

'Stop it!'

They did – when Robert, using his superior strength at last, simply pushed Hetty over backwards, and she went under, coming up choking, crying.

Eileen waded in, carrying her out of the pool. 'I told you, Hetty, *not* to go on teasing him – serves you right. You must listen to me.'

'Won't!' Hetty screamed between her sobs. 'Won't ever! He's just *rude*,' she screamed.

'It's you who are rude, my girl. Pulling his hair like that – the very idea! Why can't you behave yourself, just for once?' Eileen was angry.

Hetty went all quiet then, apart from an odd choked whimper, sucking her thumb, looking up at Eileen with doleful, tear-filled eyes, an unbearably sad expression, so that Eileen took her in her arms for a moment. 'Now, Hetty, don't – please – go all like that. *Please.*'

'C-c-can't help,' she stammered, before burying herself in Eileen's arms.

High above them, in the deep clotted undergrowth over the waterfall, the young, half-naked Carib gazed down at them through the leaves, puzzled at all this strange behaviour beneath him. His skin was a light shining bronze, minutely beaded with spume-mist from the falls, the hair straight and jet-black, cut in a perfect fringe across his high forehead, a dark curtain over the Mongolian features, wide cheek-bones, slanting almond eyes. He stood there, unblinking, dead still yet intensely alert – the face of an Inca god, a gold disc staring out of the greenery.

He had been lying in wait for the anaconda for several hours. He knew it was there, somewhere about the pool. He had seen it, stalked it down here, all morning. And now these white people had come to disturb it, before time, before twilight when it would come out to feed by the pool. He was annoyed, fingering the cutlass at his side. It was a fine snake, almost as long as his father's fishing dug-out – therefore old and bad-tempered. But he would have it.

Then, in the sloping undergrowth on the far side of the pool, he saw a slow rippling movement, following a line, as if the ferns had been caught in a breeze. A few moments later, the big, questing wedge head came in sight, followed by the great olive-green length of the anaconda with its double line of black spots: the snake was easing down towards the water where the little boy was still playing.

Running and sliding now, half-way down the side of the gorge, the Carib heard the screams. By the time he reached the pool the snake was already in the water, making purposefully for the boy, who had slipped in his attempts to escape it, now on his feet again, but with the anaconda still closing on him.

The Carib dived at it, going straight for the head, grasping it there with both hands, squeezing behind its now-distended jaws, wrenching it away, grappling with it, arching its head up, as the coils, thick as a fat thigh, began to encircle him, its tail thrashing about in fountains of spray.

The reptile tightened its grip, flailing round the Carib's legs like a rope, so that he lost balance, swayed and fell, wrestling with the snake in a fierce battle, turning over and over in a turmoil of foam, snake and man wedded together in one pulsing body – two skins, bronze and green, merging, flashing, fighting for their lives, in the sunlight.

The Carib disappeared underwater altogether, the anaconda in its true element now, crushing, squeezing. And, though the man rose a few moments later, he was half-trussed now, up to his waist, in its glistening, pumping coils, taut string tightening over a parcel.

Robert had escaped unharmed to the other bank – part of a huddled, screaming group there. The Carib meanwhile, his arms still free, had managed to struggle with his great burden to the far side of the pool where he had left his cutlass. Picking it up he started to slash repeatedly at the snake, opening livid gashes in the coils about his thighs and feet. The anaconda relaxed its grip a fraction, blood beginning to colour the water as the young man cut away at his bonds, chunks of skin and flesh flying out like chips from a tree.

But, even so wounded, the snake fought on viciously, continuing to wind its upper coils round his chest. Finally, its body severed almost completely half-way along its length, the snake, losing its anchor, fell away from him. The Carib, covered in blood, some from his own self-inflicted wounds, shouted exultantly. Eileen and the two children fled.

The atmosphere was exhaustingly humid and still on the verandah. The breeze had died entirely in the twilight, and a great blanket of bruised grey cloud had come to hover over the house. 'There's no question,' Mildred told Frances. 'You – we – we cannot stay here. We must leave, all of us, at once – all far too dangerous. Robert is quite devastated, the shock –'

'No, I'm not, Mama.'

Robert, in fact, after his initial terror, had come to reflect on the afternoon's adventure with growing pride: he had escaped the great serpent – why, he had very nearly fought and grappled with it himself. Hetty had been full of praise for him.

'It was *wonderful*,' she told her mother happily. 'The brave Carib, saving our lives –'

'That's just it,' Mildred put in, greatly agitated. 'Think what might have happened!'

'Indeed.' Frances was actually quite relaxed over the matter. 'I only wish we could thank him for his bravery.' She turned to Mildred. 'We shall stay here. You, of course, must do as you think best. Though I wonder if you're not making a little too much of it all? And, remember, it's August, start of the bad weather: hurricane season, storms and gales at least. You and Robert might run far more risk on the boat back to Roseau.'

'Frances!' Mildred summoned up a quite unusual firmness in her attitude now. 'We shall leave on the next packet. And you should come with us.'

Almost as soon as she had finished speaking they heard the first of the thunder, a long gathering rumble out over the bay, which soon moved over the house, in crackling explosions with spits of blue lightning. Afterwards the rain came in solid curtains and during the night a fierce wind, which lasted for days, the sea rising in vast breakers, dashing up over the cliff beneath the house, rattling the storm shutters, the Hall tight shut now all round against the searing gales. The packet from Roseau was inevitably cancelled and everyone stayed indoors for the next two weeks.

Hetty looked at her mother, across the table from her, explaining Consequences. They were playing with Robert and Mildred.

'I do the head,' her mother spoke dictatorially. 'Then fold the paper over – so – then pass on for you to do the neck, a funny neck, then Mildred does the body –'

'Yes, Mama – I *do* see how.'

Her mother frowned at this interruption, bunched her fingers up. Mama was so bossy, Hetty thought. She pushed the lock of dangling hair from her eye, for the umpteenth time.

'You really must wear that hair-clip, Hetty,' her mother said. 'Told you a dozen times – you'll get a squint.'

'Don't want a hair-clip.'

'Eileen will have to sugar your hair again, then – and you won't like that.'

Hetty glowered at her mother. No, Elly wouldn't. Several times, for 'occasions' – the last had been for the funeral of the estate foreman's wife at the Catholic church – Eileen, on her Mama's instructions, had soaked all the wavy frizzle from her hair with a sticky mix of sugar and water, flattening it, letting it dry out in a hard shell: horrible. Why was her mother so beastly – and why did she have such difficult, long, wavy dark hair anyway?

'I'm tired of my hair,' Hetty said, most petulantly. 'Why don't I have easy straight short hair – like you and Papa? Then I'd never have to have beastly clips or sugar in it!'

Her mother did not reply, looked down at her bit of paper, bunching her fingers again.

When Hetty's turn came she drew, as her neck, the long spotted neck of a giraffe – so long that it went right down to the bottom of the paper and they had to start the game all over again.

'You are *difficult*, Hetty,' her mother said aggressively.

'But you said to draw a *funny* neck.' Hetty was genuinely surprised at there being any fault in her contribution. She thought: I don't like these games with the grown-ups – I prefer to play with Robert. After his courage in the pool with the great serpent she had come to like Robert. With all his fuss over that frog business in his bed, she had thought him a cissy. But he wasn't. Yes, he was more fun now. She really liked him – quite a lot.

> '"Oh, soldier, soldier, won't you marry me
> With your musket, fife and drum!"'

Hetty sang out the first part of the game, which Aunt Mildred was teaching them. Then Robert sang his bit.

'"Oh, no! sweet maid, I cannot marry thee
For I've got no hat to put on."'

Then Hetty came in again.

'"So up she went to her Grandmother's chest
And she fetched him a hat of the very, very best,
And the soldier put it on."'

'Now, Hetty,' Mildred said, 'you go out and get a hat for Robert – any hat will do: there's lots in the back hall.'

Hetty left the drawing room. She thought she was going to like this game, for she knew where there were some real army hats, and a lot of other army things, belonging to her father, in the cloakroom beneath the big staircase. She opened the door, smelling a damp mildewy smell, peering into the dark. But soon she found just what she wanted: a tall furry hat with a funny cockade, a red coat with lovely goldy things on the shoulders and a pair of great big black shiny boots. She took the hat out and brought it to Robert.

'Splendid!' Mildred said. 'Where did you get it?'

'In the cloakroom.' She put it on Robert, where it dropped right down over his eyes. But he looked lovely. Hetty cooed with pleasure. 'Go on, Robert – sing the next bits – you need coats and boots and things now.'

'Can't – you have to sing your bit first.'

'"Oh soldier, soldier, won't you marry me
With your musket, fife and drum?"'

'"Oh, no sweet maid, I cannot marry thee
For I've got no coat to put on . . ."'

Hetty left again, bringing back the gold-braided scarlet tunic – and then the tall cavalry boots, until Robert was staggering round the room, the great boots almost up to his waist, arms half-way down the sleeves of the tunic – laughing fit to burst, Aunt Milly as well. Then her mother suddenly came into the room.

'Hetty! – what on earth's going on?' She looked at Robert, gallivanting around like a scarecrow. Her mother was angry.

'We're dressing Robert up – Aunt Mildred's teaching us the game – "Oh, soldier, soldier, won't you marry me?"'

Hetty looked up at her mother, surprised. She was very angry now.

'Who said you could? You're not to dress up in – in those army things. I forbid you – never – they're your father's, he'd be simply horrified.'

Her mother was flustered as well as angry, Mildred saw. 'I'm sorry, Frances,' she broke in. 'My fault – I'd no idea . . .' And nor she had, for she knew that

Bruce could not care less about these old clothes of his, could not care less about anything in Fraser Hall.

Frances relented slightly then. 'No, I'm sorry.' She paused then, at a loss. 'It's just – I'm so much against – army things, especially for children.'

Hetty was upset. The game had to end, just when she was loving it, everyone loving it. Why *was* her mother such a spoilsport?

Mildred spoke to Frances later when they were alone. 'I'd really no idea,' she apologised again. 'Those old army things . . .'

'It's just I don't like them dressing up that way. So much against anything to do with war, the Boer war, you remember – I was there.'

She lied to Mildred convincingly. The pain had come back to her sharply, of course, the moment she had seen Robert dressed up, playing the soldier in the red tunic – so like the Dragoon's tunic she had once worn to capture Dermot's love. Frances hated her past then, all the failures there – and that failure, perhaps, more than any: if only she had been able to marry Dermot, none of this, nothing of it – this exile, this unruly child, this awful betrayal by the Prince – *none* of it would have occurred. How she hated herself, once more, for allowing it all to happen.

'I'm sorry – about the Boer war,' Mildred said. 'I'd quite forgotten. Your brother . . . Of course, I should have realised.'

'Never mind,' Frances said, still rather sharp, hearing the wind batter at the storm shutters. 'It's all a war really, isn't it? These things are sent to try us.'

She repeated the cliché, not in any stoic Christian tone – much more that of an Amazon about to do battle.

'Read us that fairy poem again,' Hetty said to Eileen that night, the two children tucked up in bed, listening to the wind whistle and moan outside.

'That's cissy,' Robert snorted.

'No, it's not –'

'Read us that story about the battle, Elly – the one you read the other night – that Finn man, who was he?'

'Fionn McCool, the great Irish warrior – picked up a clod of earth big as a whole county in the north, and threw it south, where it's a mountain now –'

'That's it!'

'I'll read both to ye – there, how's that?'

Elly got out the Irish *Homestead and Fireside* magazine again and read the tale of Fionn, one of his great exploits from the Gaelic sagas. Then she read the poem.

> 'Where the wandering water gushes
> From the hills above Glen-Car,
> In pools among the rushes
> That scarce could bathe a star,

We seek for slumbering trout
And whispering in their ears
Give them unquiet dreams;
Leaning softly out
From ferns that drop their tears
Over the young streams.
Come away, O human child
To the waters and the wild
With a faery, hand in hand,
For the world's more full of weeping
than you can understand.'

Hetty was not asleep, or near it, when Eileen came to give her a goodnight kiss. She was almost agitated. 'What ails ye, girl?' Eileen leant over her.

'The words,' she said. 'I don't know – not like ordinary words, are they? All slippy and slidy and smooth!' Hetty beamed, alive to something.

'Indeed, sure, isn't that the whole idea of it, girl? That's poetry!'

2

AT CHRISTMAS THE weather was at its best – warm days, a calmer sea, the leaves on the palms around Fraser Hall idly flapping in the brilliant light. The flower beds on the lawn bloomed with amaryllis, and were edged with great sun-struck clumps of silver fern and pink and mauve columbine. And what was left to the fruit from the wrecked citrus fields about the estate fell on the ground now, abandoned, over-ripe, soon rotten.

Flooding showers still came. But they fell from isolated, beleaguered clouds, running helter-skelter across the vast blue sky, pushed on by the fiery warmth of sun and wind, so that they dropped their load quickly, with a sudden drumming hiss, on the hot foliage, before disappearing over the mountains in drifting rainbows.

Henrietta itched and fidgeted in her stiff white blouse, long skirt, black stockings, black buttoned boots and wide-brimmed white hat with elastic under the chin – hating these special clothes, even though it was a special day. She sat on the verandah steps – neatly, quietly reading her book, as instructed by her mother, lying out behind her in the hammock. Hetty turned every few minutes, glancing covertly at her. At last her mother fell asleep.

Hetty stole away then, tip-toeing at first, before running down to the end of the lawn and hiding in the mango grove. She picked a fruit – ripe, deep red and yellow, small, round, very sweet and juicy as she sank her teeth into it. But the smell was even better than the taste, she thought, putting the warm skin, the freshly dripping bite, to her nose: a yellowy smooth sweet smell, like the colour somehow, but with another air to it, a deeper touch of something much stronger, the perfume of roses: yes, some of the garden roses – the ones her mother called Albertine, by the verandah – had the same overpowering, mysterious smell.

Taking the half-eaten fruit, she danced across the lawn, stopping, dipping her nose into various flowers as she went – roses, orchids, heliconias – comparing the flavours, darting from one to the next, savouring each bloom, feeding on it, like a humming bird. But soon, sated and confused by the different odours, she ran on round the house to her look-out point, a flat raised rock on the cliff above the cove, a crow's nest giving out over the bay, where she could wait for the packet steamer.

The breeze tipped and flapped at the brim of her hat, the elastic pinching her chin. Taking it off, she let her hair free, blowing out suddenly behind her, the long dark curls cutting sharply back over her brow, singing in her ears, as she gazed over the deep purple ocean with its dazzling whitecaps.

Free. She always felt a surging ecstasy, here on this rock, the waves moving towards her, rolling in, one after the other in endless succession, mesmerising her, so that after a minute or two, as she gazed steadily at the same point out to sea, she felt as if she was moving, herself, floating away from the island, a strange sinking feeling in her stomach – as though she was swinging above the ocean on the bowsprit of a huge ship.

There was no sign of the packet yet, so she finished the mango and started to count off on her fingers the various exciting, favourite smells in her life. 'Well, there's lime,' she said. 'That's the first. Then mango and cook's ginger cake and those white roses by the verandah . . .' Then the other smells, she thought, quite different, strange – in the tin-roofed church at Castle Bruce where she went every Sunday with Elly.

There was that sort of flower pot on chains that Father Bertin swung about, which smoked and steamed and smelled delicious, a dry nose-tickling burny smell. That was exciting and so was Father Bertin in his green robe and white nightgown thing, his back turned to everyone, raising a silver cup and speaking to God in a funny language – and the little bell that one of the village boys rang every now and then, standing beside Father Bertin, dressed in another shorter white nightgown – and more than anything the statue of a young woman to one side of the table up there, almost a girl, dressed in a very grand gold and blue night-gown, who looked out at everyone with a terribly sad face. All that was very exciting – and strange because she never took any part in it, was cut off from it all.

Father Bertin and the boy were doing something frightfully important up at the table there, and she wished she was part of it all – the funny language, the little bell ringing, the tickly smell and the silences. But she wasn't. She was all kept out of it, and never went near the high table like the others did, sipping wine and eating little biscuity things. It wasn't her church, her mother had told her – that was why she couldn't ever join in on the game. She only went there with Elly because her church didn't exist in Castle Bruce. But she didn't want her church anyway. She longed to be part of Elly's church, to know what was going on up there at the table.

They were praying and offering things to God, of course – she'd been told that. But where was he? Elly had told her he was up in the sky, invisible, very far away. But she thought he must be sitting on the rafters, just above them – as he would have to be somewhere quite close to hear the prayers. And it was strange that people, everyone around her, took so much notice of someone they couldn't see at all. It was certainly some kind of game which these grown-ups played – a game to please God. God liked these games, though it was funny that he didn't seem to play at all in return – just sat on the rafters, invisible.

Some of the estate people and servants at the Hall didn't like God – Cook and Big Jules for example. They had a wicked God and played different games with him, and that was all very bad and secret, Elly had told her – because they were praying to the *devil*, not God at all. And Hetty knew how true this was. She had seen them playing with their strange church things behind the kitchens, beyond the laundry, only a week before, with Cook and Big Jules and some of the others, when they had killed the chicken – broken its legs and wings and then torn its neck off and the blood had spilled out all over the place. Horrible. That was a terrible game to play, but she hadn't told anyone about it, because she shouldn't have been hiding in the bushes in the first place, watching it all.

Well, that was the devil, of course. That was why it was all so horrible, and the church in Castle Bruce so nice, with the burny smell and the little bells and the lovely sad girl dressed all in blue and gold. That was all nice because it was God and it was good. And the other game with the chicken and the blood was bad. It was very simple – she could see that. The only trouble was that Cook and Big Jules were very kind to her and she had lots of fun with them. So why did they do such bad things playing with the devil?

She heard the ship's siren then, several long hoots, from out in the bay. The packet was arriving from Roseau, the last before Christmas: everyone was coming for the holidays – Aunt Mildred, Uncle Bertie, Robert, even her father with his army friends. Christmas was in three days' time – presents, tinsel, carols, crackers, and other good things, plum pudding, mincemeat pies and the big Christmas cake with icy snow on top, all the way from England. Henrietta ran back into the house, joining her mother and Elly and some of the boys, before they all made their way down the winding path to the cove and on to the jetty.

The packet was just dropping anchor beyond the cove, Big Jules and Slinky already out there, idling by with the steam launch, waiting to take the passengers and provisions off. Hetty jumped up and down, skidding on the wooden jetty with excitement.

'Keep still, child,' Elly told her. 'You'll fall in.'

'Can't wait. Look! – look at all those funny boxes and things.'

She had already seen her father, with his two friends, climbing down into the launch, carrying long leather cases over their shoulders. The Grants were already in the launch.

'And look – there's Robert!' Hetty waved at him, but he did not notice her in all the commotion.

'Yes, and you just behave with him this time, my girl. Remember what I said –'

'Oh, I'll behave – with all those presents from Father Christmas, Elly. What do you think he's got?'

'Wait and see.'

'He doesn't come down the chimney here, does he? Because we don't have any chimneys. He must come here by boat – must be on the packet there, somewhere hidden, mustn't he? We won't see him though, will we?'

'Quite right – hidden on the boat.'

'But he can't be *really* hidden, because someone would see him, in his red coat and beard. So he must be invisible – like God.'

'That's right, girl. Invisible. But he comes all the same – you'll see!'

Invisible, Hetty thought – what an annoying word. Why couldn't you *see* things and people that were most important? Why couldn't you *see* a smell? All you had was words to tell you about them, and that wasn't the same thing at all. Words didn't actually give you the smell of the roses or the limes – except perhaps the poetry and the stories Elly read from her Irish book. That was funny – you felt something, you could almost smell things, from those kinds of words.

'Well? – what have you been doing out here?' Robert spoke in a distant, superior voice.

'Oh, the usual things.'

'I've been moved up to the fourth form at school in Roseau. We've been playing cricket this term. And I'm going to England next year – to a much bigger and better school, where I'll *sleep*, a *boarding* school!'

'Oh.'

'Lots of hard work and learning, my father says,' Robert declared with relish.

Hetty sat on her bed, fiddling with the mosquito netting, looking across at Robert arranging his things very neatly on his own bed: school books, exercise books, a wooden pencil box that he had brought with him. Hetty, seeing all this evidence of 'learning' and 'hard work', was a little in awe of him suddenly. Her own lessons, with her mother and Elly and Father Bertin, didn't seem half so grand. She had no pencil box.

'Why don't *you* go to school?' Robert took out a compass and a pair of dividers from the box, inspecting them carefully. 'You ought to. Everyone does.'

'Mama teaches me –'

'That's not *school*.'

'No. But there isn't a real school here – just for the villagers – so I can't.'

'My mother says you ought to be in Roseau with the nuns there.'

'Don't want to go to the nuns.' Hetty stood up. 'I have much better things over here.' She went to her chest of drawers and took out a collection of brilliant blue and green parrot feathers. 'Look! Slinky got them for me, in the mountains – from a real Sisserou parrot. The Caribs wear them in their noses and ears when they have a feast!'

'It's horrid – to kill parrots.' Robert looked at the feathers dismissively.

'And I've got this.' Hetty went back to the chest and pulled a Carib basket from beneath it, bringing it over to Robert, opening it carefully. Inside, on a bedding of stones, was a small iguana, beady-eyed, motionless, very dragon-like. 'A baby one. Lost its mother. I found it in the ditch beyond the lawn.'

Robert inspected it, from a distance. 'I don't like it,' he said finally, turning away.

'You're not frightened any more, are you – of froggies and things?'

'Course not.' He picked up a book he had brought with him. 'Just I'm busy with other things now, cricket – and trains and things.' He opened the book – *The Boy's Book of Railways* with a coloured picture of a steam engine on the front.

'Trains?' Henrietta said, rather bemused. 'Where you sit down in armchairs and get pulled along by a great smoky thing?'

'Of *course*, stupid. They don't have them here on any of these tiny little islands. But they're all *over* England. I'll be going on a train to my boarding school when I go home, Mama said. A *big* school.'

Hetty was annoyed. Robert had gone all grown up. He wouldn't want to play with her any more now – with all his talk about learning and cricket and trains. He wasn't the least interested in her parrot feathers or the little dragon. How could *she* be grown up? You had to go to the nuns in Roseau to be grown up, and then to a grand school in England and travel on trains and have a big pencil box. But she wasn't going to these places and didn't have any pencil boxes or even proper exercise books.

Then she thought, well, I have those picture postcards that Mama's friend Miss Wechsberg and her cousin Dermot sometimes sent her, from all sorts of exciting places in England – photographs of places called Canterbury and Stratford-upon-Avon – and the huge hotel building in somewhere called Brighton.

She took the little collection of postcards from her drawer, showing them to Robert. 'See!' she said, rather huffily, 'I'll be going to all *these* grand places soon, on the train as well, when *I* go to England.' She pointed to the huge building, the hotel on the seafront in Brighton. 'I shall be going to school *there*,' she said stiffly. 'And that's the church I'll be going to, with *hundreds* of nuns inside.' She showed him the picture of Canterbury Cathedral; 'So, you see, I'll be doing much grander things than you very soon.'

Robert glanced at the postcards, bemused himself now. 'Well,' he said, putting them down. 'So what? Everyone goes to big churches and schools – in *England*.'

He believed her! She never thought he would – but he had. She'd told some really whopping lies and he'd believed them all! How terrible of her – but wasn't it funny when you made something up like that and people believed you? Just with words! You could change things exactly the way you wanted them, when they weren't really like that at all. You could be grown up in a moment with words, be anything you liked with them. That was very exciting. It was lying, of course. But what did that matter if it made you feel better – made you feel grown up and happy?

All the same she had qualms then and thought she ought to say something truthful. 'And anyway,' she said, 'when we go back home, Mama and Elly and me, we'll be living in a *much* bigger house than yours at Lime Hill or any of these ones:

our *real* home, in Ireland – Mama's told me and shown me pictures of it – as big as Buckingham Palace!'

Robert laughed at her then, nastily. 'Well *that's* not true,' he said. 'That's a lie! Your home is here – and you haven't got anywhere else.'

'It *is* true – we have!' Hetty raised her voice in desperation. 'Mama's told me, *promise* we have.'

'Rubbish.'

Hetty turned away, shocked and surprised. She started to suck her thumb. She wasn't going to cry, because it *was* true about Summer Hill, the huge house in Ireland. She *had* seen the pictures of it. Her mother had often talked about it, promising her – how one day they would be going back there. Funny, she thought, that people believed your lies but didn't when you told the truth.

Christmas approached with all its traditional local excitements. The strolling Creole carol singers, from Petit Soufriere in the south of the island, came up to the Hall on Christmas Eve, a dozen of them standing on the hot lawn with their banjos, fiddles and a wailing accordion. The women danced, clapping, singing in a wild syncopated rhythm, Africa revived across the ocean now, dressed in bright cotton prints – brilliant blues, red, yellows – with cockaded head scarves, while the men brought a similar frenzy to their instruments. The assembled company at the Hall watched from the verandah, the two children sitting in front of the steps, as the gaudy, loud-mouthed women, in the vivid patois of these Sewinal songs, rent the drowsy afternoon apart.

> Sé pas dòt ki konmpè micho ki di
> Sen Jozef papa Bon Dyé
> Nou ka swété tout moun
> An bon nwèl . . .

The voices swelled in unison, then fell away softly, almost to a whisper; then started up again in a burst – a sudden splatter of words, each hit harder than the last, running away from the music in a crescendo. Henrietta was entranced by it all: being black was warm and happy, she thought – white was cold and sad. She wished she was black.

Afterwards the players were given coffee and rum outside the kitchen quarters, with a hot broth and smoked wild meat, agouti and manicou, to go with it. And later, after dark in the flare-lit space beyond the laundry, there was more dancing and singing with the Hall servants and estate workers, going on far into the night.

At dinner the company heard the wild music, the songs, coming to them clearly on the still air.

'What *do* they sing about? It can hardly be Christian,' Mildred said, a note of unease in her voice, as the noise increased momentarily.

'Oh, yes – it *is* Christian,' Frances told her promptly. 'Those devils – "Diablotin" – they're singing about now: they believe they were all cast out when Christ was born and have been roaming about ever since, looking for somewhere to hide, which is why the locals have to band together now, to stop them getting into their houses. They're defending themselves from the devils with those songs – very Christian!'

Bruce, at the top of the table, looked at her derisively. 'You read far too much into these nigger songs. They have no real truck with Christianity – just to please us – and get their feasting and drinking here afterwards.'

'Not true!' Frances glared at him from the other end of the table. 'You ought to see them at church here – absolutely believing.'

'Just the Catholic mumbo-jumbo – that's what gets them: the Latin and the incense and communion and so on: like a black mass to them. That's why they take to it – and much more because they get baptismal presents for every child. Why, a lot of them move their children from parish to parish here, just to get the presents. But what can you expect from niggers?'

He drank deeply, smiling at his bachelor army friends, Algy Hermon and Roland Stockton. The two men, both a little younger than Bruce, returned the smile nervously. Algy, the taller one, prematurely balding, stroked his moustache carefully, seeming to think of a response. Roland, a nondescript, chubby little man, cleared his throat, as if about to speak. But nothing emerged from either of them.

Frances found both men dull and uncongenial to a degree. But their presence at the Hall occupied her husband, kept him away from her, and that suited her perfectly. Her husband led them by the nose, she could see that: they were in awe of him – his wealth, his possessions, his sophisticated airs. They came here only for the shooting, the annual Boxing Day drive up on the plateau, and thankfully would be gone soon afterwards, along with Bruce.

But meanwhile she was not going to let his last remarks pass. She was not to be so exposed, put down in public without a rebuttal; nor would she accept his dismissive references to the negroes. For all their faults, they were a subject people, just like the Irish: the British had made them so. And ever since her break with the Prince – the so-called 'King-Emperor' now – she had taken violently against his empire and everything to do with it, infused with a nascent republican spirit.

'"Niggers"?' she said tartly, her voice rising. 'They are black because they are African, brought over here as slaves, by you people the British. And you simply dismiss them as niggers!'

'I do, for that is what they are – a heathen horde.' Bruce was getting drunk. 'Though we do our best for them.'

'What nonsense! You have done nothing but disinherit and enslave them, take them from their country, their homes – just as you've done with us, the Irish.'

'Hardly in your case, my dear,' he said sarcastically. 'It was not we – the British – who brought you here. A mere family matter, I believe.'

Frances was furious. A frisson of embarrassment had come over the dinner table. But she persisted – in angrily identifying now, as she had increasingly done during her exile, with both the negroes and the native Irish. 'My case has nothing to do with it. But with the others – they will rule themselves one day!'

'Ah, we have a "Home Ruler" here, I see. Not surprising, I suppose, given your cousin Mortimer Cordiner – up to the same mischief at Westminster! Well, so be it. Except it won't be. A pipe dream,' he added lightly, laughing easily, breaking the tension, so that the company laughed with him.

'The King,' Bruce said to them all then, suddenly raising his glass, getting up, the others joining him, chairs squeaking back on the floor.

Frances could have killed him: not because he knew the King was Hetty's father – he did not; but because he was forcing her now to honour a man whom she loathed beyond all men. Well, she wouldn't. She remained firmly in her seat. The others looked at her expectantly, glasses poised, waiting for her to rise. Instead, when she did rise, she turned on them and walked smartly out of the room.

'The poor woman,' Mildred murmured to her husband afterwards. 'Quite unhinged. As if the dear King were to blame for her problems.'

Bruce and the others had come back late after their Boxing Day shoot and Frances had not seen them that evening. But, the next morning, she sensed that something had gone wrong up on the plateau. The men had taken Slinky with them and a dozen others from the estate as beaters – and Slinky had not appeared for work in the garden that day. Frances went and spoke to Cook, finding her in an agitated state, fidgeting about the kitchen.

'What's happened, Annie – and where's Slinky?'

'Ah, Madame – Sinky, him not bon – he got the akeanpane au'joudi.' Cook rolled her eyes. Frances saw she was very upset about something.

'Not well? And you – what's the matter with you, Annie?'

'Madame, Sinky lui say to you –'

'No, *you* say to me!'

'There is one bad thing up on *morne* last jour.' Cook turned away, head in air, aghast at something.

'What bad thing up on the mountain?'

'The Carib peoples – Sinky lui say deu' shootin' là. Deu' morts.'

'Two *dead?*'

Cook nodded her head. 'Bang-bang an' they lie down and no get up encor.'

Frances left at once, confronting Bruce and his two friends in the dining room where they had just come down for a late breakfast.

'What nonsense,' Bruce told her. '*One* Carib and he certainly isn't dead! Slinky and Cook – exaggerating as usual.' He laughed nervously. The others joined him, picking at their grapefruit.

'One Carib? – well, what happened?'

'Just winged him in the arm – perfectly all right. We were driving a thick covert, full of bushes, by the stream up there. And these two Caribs – well, they were hidden in the bush, and one of them, like a bloody fool, started to move out of the bushes when they heard us, and I winged him. But he's perfectly fine – bandaged him up and gave him some money and he went home pleased as punch.'

Algy and Roland, albeit rather shamefacedly, concurred in this, so that Frances thought to believe them. It was true, after all – the locals, and especially Slinky, did tend to exaggerate things.

She began to think otherwise, though, when she went to look for Slinky down in the labour lines by the old sugar factory, and found he was not there. His room was empty. He had disappeared. She went on and found McTear, standing by the big entrance doors to the factory, the space deserted behind him and the man himself in a considerable state of dour agitation.

'What's happened? Where's Slinky? And all your men?'

'I was just coming up to the Hall to see ye, Mrs Fraser.' He spoke sharply. 'There's no men about,' he went on in his gruff Scots accent. 'They're all afeared – after what Mr Fraser and his party done yisterday up in yon hills –'

'What –'

'Shootin' yon Carib fella. They're all afeared now. And I dinna blame them. There'll be trouble.'

Frances was incredulous. 'But I've just been speaking to Mr Fraser. He told me the Carib was only wounded, just grazed, that he went home –'

'He's no telling the truth then, Mrs Fraser. I talked wi' most of my men this morning, the ones beatin' up there yisterday, and they all say the same thing: the first Carib was shot dead – and the other behind him as well as far as I can tell.'

'I don't believe –'

'Why do ye think all the men have disappeared – only for that? Them Caribs are quiet enough – don't I know it meself these twenty years out here. But if ye cross thim, if ye *kill* thim, they'll take to the rum and the weed – and there'll be ructions.'

'What do you mean?'

McTear humphed. 'More than likely they'll be at us, that's wha' I mean.'

'*Attack* us?'

'That's what I hear – that's why the men ran.'

'But we'll have to get the police at once –'

'Indeed, old Sergeant Alwin and his two dozy men at Castle Bruce: a lot of use –'

'I mean at Roseau.'

'There's no packet for three days, Mrs Fraser – we're on our own out here 'till then.'

'Send the steam launch, then – get Big Jules.'

'I canna do that, Mrs Fraser, 'till the launch is repaired: remember, the boiler is out, since before the holiday.'

'So what can we do?'

'That's what I was just coming up to tell ye: git ready for them, Mrs Fraser, if they do come – that's all a body can do. And in the meantime meself and Big Jules will get on with repairing the launch.'

Frances returned to the Hall. She walked up to the head of the dining table where her husband was still at breakfast, pushing the plate of ham and eggs away from him, sending the lot spinning to the floor. Then, in her fury, she stood back and spat at him.

'You liar, you swine!' she told him, trembling. 'You killed one of those Caribs. I've just seen McTear – he says they may take revenge. You fool – you fools!' She turned and swept out of the room.

Bruce considered the matter. 'I'll go and see the old sergeant at Castle Bruce,' he told Algy. 'I can easily square him.'

The two men looked very ill at ease now. 'We'll have to get to Roseau as soon as possible, Bruce, tell them at police headquarters. It can't be a question of squaring anyone now,' Algy said carefully.

Bruce could no longer bluff his way out of it. 'Of course,' he said amiably. 'Well, we'll do that. But let's not lose our heads, shall we? Remember, it was an *accident*.'

Mildred turned white when Frances told her the news. She was in the drawing room, dallying with a novel, her husband Bertie at one of the open windows, looking out absentmindedly over the bay.

'What?' He turned, only half-hearing the story. 'The Caribs on the warpath, are they? I'd like to see that – hasn't been any of that for years. Caught brandy-smuggling again, have they?' Frances explained the situation once more for him. 'Oh, I *see*: Bruce shot them, did he? How very careless.' He spoke as if Bruce had done no more than poke them inadvertently with an umbrella. Bertie, an awkward, bumpy figure, much older than his nervous wife, rather frail and ageing, with deep-set sea-blue eyes and a careless beard, wore a permanently disengaged expression – always thinking of something else; his mind, like his body, spinning off at tangents. 'So what will they do now?' he asked vaguely, in his rather high-pitched sing-song colonial accent. 'War canoes? – they used to have splendid forty-foot war canoes.' He turned, picked up the field glasses kept by the window, and focused them out over the bay.

'Oh, don't be *stupid*, Bertie,' Mildred yelped at him. 'Not out there! They live up in the reservation, *behind* us, up in the hills. That's where they'll come from.'

'They probably – they won't do anything to us at all,' Frances reassured her. 'Nothing to worry about. It's just that –'

'We shall all of us have to get away at once,' Mildred interrupted her, already in a panic. 'The steam launch, Bertie!' She stood up. 'The children. Where's Robert? We must all get away.'

'That's what I was just about to say,' Frances put in. 'The launch is out of action – being repaired. McTear and Jules are working on it now –'

'No *launch*? Oh, no! . . .' Mildred started to blub quietly then, shaking all over in little convulsions, seeming to shiver in the hot morning.

'My dear.' Bertie came over, consoling her. 'You mustn't take on so. It's nothing.'

'*Nothing?*' Milly was horrified. 'But they are *cannibals*, Bertie! How can you say it's nothing? We shall all be devoured.'

'Dearest.' He put his hand on her shoulder. 'The Caribs have not eaten in years – people, that is. Not in centuries. And this is the *twentieth* century – a Crown colony, magistrates, police . . .' He babbled on. 'And, besides, they eat only – only yams, breadfruit, bananas, a little maize . . .' He tripped on invitingly through a strictly vegetarian menu. 'There is no likelihood of their wanting to eat *us*,' he ended, like a butcher dismissing a very coarse cut.

'None at all, Milly!' Frances smiled quickly. 'There's nothing to worry about. Just that McTear said, well, that we should take precautions.'

'Precautions?' Milly wailed. 'We must do battle with them?'

'Of course not. Just . . .' Frances herself wasn't quite certain of what precautions might be in order. 'Just – we must all keep our heads and be alert – until we can get the launch going. Meanwhile, I'll look after everything.'

And so she did – going straightaway to speak to Bruce, out on the verandah now, smoking with his friends. She confronted them all with cold efficiency, like a sergeant-major. 'The men have nearly all disappeared,' she told them. 'McTear is trying to get the launch going. But until he does, and we can get to Roseau, you three stay out here on the verandah, in case they get drunk up in the hills and decide to do something stupid –'

'They won't,' Bruce told her brusquely. 'You're talking rubbish –'

'Don't *talk* to me! Just do as I say – stay here, outside with your wretched guns, if needs be – have them ready in any case.'

'What nonsense – against a few savages? They wouldn't dare!'

She glared at him. 'I prefer to believe McTear in the matter. Just *do* as I say!' she shouted.

Frances went off to find Elly and the children then. They were upstairs in their bedroom. Robert was playing with a new train set and Hetty reading her Christmas present from the Grants – *The Red Fairy Book*, engrossed in the tale of 'The Princess Mayblossom'. Elly was tidying their clothes in the wardrobe. Frances gave them the news tactfully. Only Elly was disturbed.

'Mother of God, what's Mr Bruce gone and done now –'

Frances, a finger to her lips, stopped her. 'Now, children,' she told them. 'You must not, on *any* account, leave the house. Elly, you'll stay with them, up here, all the time.'

'Will they fight us soon?' Hetty asked brightly. 'Before lunch, I mean. 'Cos I want to play outside with my new kite after lunch.'

Frances was surprised; she had mentioned nothing about any fight or attack. 'Yes, I'm sure you can play with your kite – very soon.'

Robert left his train set and was thinking about something. 'I have my new bow and arrow present,' he said pensively. 'That'll be useful now.'

Frances left them then, going down the hill and along the river to the factory. McTear was there, with the old police sergeant and Father Bertin. McTear was bolting and locking the big doors when she arrived.

'Keep them away from the rum at least,' McTear told her. The sergeant, in his pith helmet and red-piped trousers, bowed shortly to Frances. Father Bertin, the breeze flapping his soutane, said, 'Goo' marnin', Mrs Fraser.' Talking more to McTear than to Frances over the years, he had taken on a Scots intonation in his meagre English.

Frances barely acknowledged his greeting. 'You're locking up, McTear?'

'Aye. It's best. I'll join ye in the Hall, if ye've no objection.'

'And the launch?' Frances asked him, looking over his shoulder, up at the headland to her right above the cove. 'I see you've got steam up again.' They all turned to look at the plume of dark smoke rising above the rocks.

'I'll be damned,' McTear was astonished. 'I was there not fifteen minutes ago an' the boiler was nowhere near ready.'

'Well, it's burning up well now,' Frances said. 'We should be able to get off to Roseau at once.'

'That's no the bloody boiler, Mrs Fraser! That must be the launch itself.' McTear was moving off, up to the headland, before he had finished speaking, the others chasing after him.

The steam launch was in flames, burning fiercely at the jetty, when they got down there, Big Jules standing helplessly nearby. In his hand was a long hardwood arrow, the metal head sheathed with a ball of smouldering cotton. Three or four similar arrows, they could see now, were embedded among the flames along the cockpit and foredeck of the now fiercely-burning launch. Big Jules gestured up to the other side of the cove, to the scrub on the lip of the cliff above them.

'They was là, Madame! Trois, quatre, cinq of them. And I can do no thing 'bout it – 'cept sauvez me!'

McTear took the arrow from him, looking at it closely. Beneath the smouldering cotton a thin strand of red-daubed vine had been twined round the stem. He rubbed his finger over it, the colour staining his skin. 'Fresh,' he remarked easily. 'That's the war paint – the *roucou* dye they use.' Then he sniffed the cotton sheath. 'Brandy – they'll have plenty of that, and drinking it, too.' He held up the arrow, shaking it rather merrily. 'That's the old way with them – tho' it'll ha' little effect on the slates or the coral stone. But that's what they must have in mind: firing the Hall.'

Frances was appalled at this news. She had not thought the Caribs would take any really violent action against them. 'You – you think they intend something serious?'

McTear glanced at the flaming launch, nodding. 'And nay just the Hall, Mrs Fraser. They want us as well – burning yon boat there so we canna get away . . .' He smiled, very matter of fact about the whole business. 'I'll get me shotgun – and join you at the Hall.'

'Mais, c'est vraiment sérieux,' Father Bertin said, rubbing his thin hands together nervously. McTear nodded again.

'Indeed, Father – "an eye for an eye, a tooth for a tooth" – that's the way they see it! They're no Christian up there in yon hills, ye know!' He turned to the sergeant then. 'You go back to the village – see if ye can get any sort of a boat at all – and get someone off to Roseau, soon as you can. Right? Then bring yourself and the two constables and any kinda weapons you've got up to the Hall. Right?' He put his arm on the sergeant's shoulder, enjoying his role as commander, which he had taken over from Frances.

'Yes, Sah!' Sergeant Alwin, half-terrified, half enjoying the excitement, set off running, the other three following him quickly up the winding cliff path.

They barricaded themselves into the Hall, bringing beds, mattresses and heavy furniture out, piling them all up between the pillars of the verandah, making a first line of defence here, where the men could bring their guns to bear, poking through the obstacles, giving a clear line of fire over the wide lawn, and beyond that to the mango grove and the ditch which led out to the scrubby citrus fields.

Bruce and his friends had their Winchester sporting rifles and plenty of ammunition, McTear his 12-bore shotgun, and the sergeant had brought a Webley .45 service revolver which, though not part of his official equipment, he had conveniently unearthed somewhere back at Castle Bruce. He had only six cartridges for it, though. The two young constables with him had ancient cutlasses, jagged and rusty, relics from the Napoleonic wars about the islands, which they carried awkwardly like umbrellas, while Big Jules, with only his brass-buttoned navy-blue waistcoat on over his naked torso, had two cutlasses, along with a red bandanna round his head, which gave him an entirely piratical air.

Bertie had no weapon, nor could he have used one in any case. He stayed indoors with Father Bertin, with the women and children and the remnants of the servants, all of them camped behind further barricades in the hall, for the house, given its very sturdy construction, had no hurricane cellar.

McTear, again, took charge – some fierce old Scottish border spirit happily renewed in him, moving his great bulk around decisively, beard bristling, giving directions right and left, easily usurping any authority Bruce might have offered: organising pails of water against fire, sending one of the constables up with the field glasses on to the roof as look-out, telling Cook to get a strong broth ready and plenty of food in from the kitchens, advising Frances where to set up a first aid post, just inside the dining room door.

'You don't have to tell me, McTear. I did all this before – in the South African war,' she told him testily, and he left her then, returning to the verandah.

'What do you expect, McTear?' Bruce asked him. 'They're not likely to run straight into all these guns are they? – knowing we have them.'

'With enough brandy and that strong *tafia* weed they smoke they could do anything, Mr Fraser – believe you me.'

'In broad daylight? But they'd be massacred, coming straight across the open lawn at us.'

'The *night* – they may well come after dark. That's the danger.'

'But they've no proper guns anyway.'

'They have a few muskets. And those arrows: they can hit a sixpence at fifty yards.'

'We can do better than that.' Bruce patted his rifle. 'Can't we?' Algy and Roland nodded. But they were not so confident. The three men had taken up positions next to each other along the centre of the wide verandah, McTear and the sergeant to one side of them, Big Jules and the second constable on the other, each archway thus well defended.

Bruce turned and drank a noggin of rum. He had a bottle with him, along with his ammunition, on the table. 'Can't be any match for us. Besides, I don't believe they'll attack at all. Just trying to get us into a funk, burning the launch.'

'Don't be too sure,' McTear said. 'It's my hope they'll come in daylight – we can mebbe handle them then. But, after dark, it'd be a different matter.'

'We'll get them anyway, whatever way they come.' Bruce drained his glass. Dutch courage, McTear thought.

He looked up at the mountains then, a darkening green silhouette now as the afternoon light began to dip down behind them. In another hour the sun would have disappeared entirely beneath the peaks and half an hour after that it would be pitch black. If the Caribs had any sense, he thought, they'd attack then, after sunset. He prayed they'd have drunk and smoked enough already to lose all sense – and come for them in daylight.

They waited then, at their fire posts, listlessly fidgeting, through the hot afternoon, gazing out at the vivid, flower-filled lawn with its darting humming birds and butterflies, the placid grove of mangoes beyond. The ring of Emperor palms stirred gently now and then in a faint sea breeze, their great leaves grating together, like sandpaper, in the silence. The sun beat down on them, and after some hours came to slant directly into their eyes, almost blinding the men as they scanned the lawn for any sign of movement.

McTear cursed the strong light, listening intently now for any change in the bird call, since he could no longer see properly into the glare. He had made no allowance for this vast spotlight of sun, which so impaired their vision now, putting them almost as much at a disadvantage as if they had been in the dark.

Still, he thought, another fifteen minutes and the sun would have dropped behind the hills, and there'd be a further half-hour's perfectly reasonable light after that. He put his shotgun down, taking a handkerchief out to wipe the sweat from his brow and eyes. He'd have to see to the lamps soon – they weren't going to come now: they'd attack after dark. He stood up, head and shoulders rising a little above the parapet of sofas and mattresses, turning towards the doorway behind him.

But before he had moved a yard the long arrow struck him fiercely in the right shoulder blade. It was followed by a flock of arrows, interspersed with the heavy thud of musket fire – and then the sharp repeated cracks of the sporting rifles, bolts moving rapidly to and fro, as the men returned the fire, aiming wildly round the edge of the lawn and the ditch a hundred yards ahead of them.

The Caribs, stalking unseen through the overgrown citrus fields, and still invisible, had taken up positions all around them, hidden in the cover of the ditch, the mango grove and behind the great boles of the Emperor palms. Now they raked the verandah at leisure with their muskets and arrows, the defenders barely able to see to aim their guns in the brilliant slanting light.

McTear had stumbled forward through the verandah doors into the dining room, almost falling on Frances by the long table where she had set up her first aid equipment. The arrow, hitting him squarely on the bone, had sheared away to the right then, tearing the flesh in a great gash right down to his armpit. Frances cut his braces and tore at his collarless shirt, removing the arrow. McTear, conscious but in great pain, groaned deeply. 'As long as – as there's no of that *machineeel* poison on it.' Blood spread down his back as he lay face down on the pine floor.

'No – I don't think so. It's quite clean, the arrow.' Frances dabbed and swabbed away at the gash, deftly, quickly, putting a field dressing over it, then a bandage.

McTear sat up, trying to move his arm, while she made a sling for him. 'It's gone,' he said. 'I canna move it.'

Frances, settling the sling, left him then, going into the hall, clambering over the barricades, to where the children and the others were crouching around and beneath the great mahogany staircase. Bertie and Father Bertin were doing their best to comfort Mildred and the servants – all these women, hearing the cannonades, in a great state of fear. Only Elly, with Robert and Henrietta, appeared reasonably calm. They were sitting on the staircase, Elly with her arms about them both, Hetty sucking her thumb, Robert clutching the tin engine from his train set. They were calm enough – Elly was calming them. But they were all very frightened, Frances could see.

'Don't worry,' she said. 'It'll be quite all right. You'll see.'

She comforted them herself then. But suddenly, a hot flush of fear coming over her, Frances realised that it might not be all right at all. McTear, who had been leading and encouraging them all, was wounded, out of action certainly, a gun less on the stockade. And the Caribs, without McTear and worked up into a frenzy with drink and *tafia*, might well manage to storm the house now and that could be the end of everyone. They wouldn't be eaten – oh, no, the Caribs didn't eat people nowadays – they'd simply all be massacred, hacked to pieces by their cutlasses.

Frances turned back then, thinking of this awful fate, a savage anger rising in her – against her husband who had so jeopardised all their lives, against the Caribs perforce, simply because she knew now they meant to murder them, and saw how they might well succeed. It was against all her principles – this warfare she hated: but she would fight them herself. There was no alternative.

Outside the firing had continued, ineffectually, from both sides. But after five minutes the Caribs dispensed with their musket fire and there was a complete silence from the ring of trees. The men waited nervously, Bruce once more taking to the rum bottle.

Then, in the failing light, they saw the little spouts of fire rising here and there all round the semi-circle of trees, followed almost immediately by a whooshing sound as the arrows with their flaming cotton balls sped through the air, a volley in long smoking arcs, striking home into the mattresses and furniture, soon igniting them. But still their assailants remained invisible.

McTear, out on the verandah again, his right arm useless, saw the flames rising from the stockade. 'The pails – get the water pails!' he shouted. Frances, in her bloodstained muslin dress, had just come out on to the verandah. McTear gestured to the line of water buckets. But she did not hear him, or pretended not to. Instead she picked up his shotgun, and cartridge bandolier, took them to the fire port he had been using, and started shooting there herself, then broke the breech smartly, inserting two new cartridges.

'It's nay use, I tell ye!' McTear shouted at her. 'Unless ye git the fire out.' The flames had begun to catch well now, a dense, smoky pall rising from the obstacles, which made it difficult for anyone to see out, let alone aim with any accuracy. And quite apart from that, McTear saw, the flames would soon engulf them, turning inwards, choking them, when this front line could no longer be held.

'Ye'll all ha' to go back!' he shouted again. 'Behind the saloon windows.'

This was their second line of defence, in the dining room, behind the half-dozen jalousy windows. A few minutes later, the stockade burning fiercely now, they retreated into the house, taking up fresh positions, watching the leaping flames all along the verandah. But at least, meanwhile, this fiery barrier would prevent the Caribs making a run at them. They had time to regroup.

'When yon fire dies and the light goes behind them hills,' McTear told them, 'they'll surely come then. Here, gi' me that revolver, Alwin.' He spoke to the sergeant. 'That's all I can use now. You and the boys – you take the cutlasses. Jules, give the boy one of yours. You dinna need two o' them.'

McTear walked along the dining room then, through the acrid drift of smoke, checking the positions at the windows. Bruce, half-drunk and in a high state of excitement, said, 'When we get to *see* the bloody niggers! – they won't stand a chance.' He slapped his rifle.

But they did not get to see them. As soon as the flames began to subside on the stockade, the Caribs, still hidden, let off another volley of burning arrows, aimed at the jalousy windows this time, half of them finding their mark, sailing into the louvred wooden shutters, setting them alight, so that soon the dining room was full of smoke and the men were forced to push out the burning shutters with their rifle butts.

Only then, in the waning firelight, the windows nude, the stockades burnt down and part of the dining room itself now on fire, did the Caribs attack. They rose up all round from the cover of the trees – short, dark, largely naked, war-painted figures, whooping and shouting, red and white circles and lines drawn round their bodies, their hair tied in knots above the crowns of their heads, brandishing muskets, maces, adzes and cutlasses. They started to run across the lawn – not at any great pace, but zig-zagging across the anthurium and orchid beds, so that the men found it difficult to maintain any sure aim.

In their first volley only a few of the twenty or so Caribs fell. The second volley was no more effective. A dozen Caribs were half-way across the lawn now. McTear, with only six cartridges for the revolver, held his fire. He would need those for close quarters. Meanwhile Frances, repeatedly shooting and reloading, blasted away with the shotgun. Two of the leading Caribs stumbled and fell. But half a dozen others, right behind, were almost up to the verandah now, about to jump over the burning debris, flailing around wildly with their assorted weapons.

It was close combat now, as the leading Carib, flourishing a great mace, leaping over the flames, made for the doorway, burst it open with one blow and landed in the room. McTear shot him at almost point-blank range. But there were two more behind – and two others storming the empty windows at the far end, inside now, turning, coming straight for them.

It was time for the cutlasses, Big Jules decided, running forward to meet these two assailants, laying about him – while McTear stood up to the others, in at the doorway now, trying to pick them off. Bruce and the other two with their rifles, had no chance of using them in the cramped, enclosed space. Frances had retreated behind the big table at the far end of the saloon with the shotgun.

A furious mêlée ensued, hand-to-hand fighting about the room, cutlasses, maces and rifle butts flailing. One of the constables was cut down, cleanly, like a stick of sugar cane. The other, pursued by a Carib, tried to flee. Bruce, Algy and Roland – with only their rifle butts now, swinging them round their heads – were being gradually forced back. One of the Caribs cornered Bruce, edging him towards the far wall.

Driven wild by the drink he had consumed throughout the afternoon, he fought the man savagely, but it was clear he would be no match for him. Algy and Roland, still engaged with the Caribs by the doorway, were unable to help. Then the shotgun went off, from the far side of the dining room table – two crashing reports.

The Carib, cutlass raised, about to end matters with Bruce, suddenly jolted away, as if pushed by a huge invisible hand, sprawling several yards from him on the floor, lying there motionless. But Bruce had fallen too, much more slowly, gently, his back sliding down the wall, knees buckling, before he pitched outwards, his skull cracking with a thump on the coral flagstones.

The other two Caribs by the door, seeing their leader dead, fled out into the twilight; the battle was over, the flames in the dining room, running along the wainscoting behind a burning chair, illuminated a Pyrrhic victory. Frances, unblinking, her face strangely lit in the flickering yellow light, dropped the shotgun on the table.

She made no move towards her husband. It was all too clear – everyone could see it: he was dead. In the sudden silence they heard the women wailing in the hall, the children crying. Of course, McTear thought, she had tried to save her husband, not kill him. That was perfectly obvious. That would be his version of events anyway. Otherwise, with Mrs Fraser put away for murder and the estate sold up, he would be out of a job . . .

'It was an accident – the whole thing: all a dreadful accident.'

Frances's aggressive tones to the chief inspector from Roseau quite belied her apologetic, explanatory words. McCracken – a dry and cleverly evasive northern Irishman who knew all about the Frasers, and the chilly relationship between them – had arrived on a Revenue launch that morning from the capital, some days after the battle, with a posse of armed policemen, who had at once set off in hopeless pursuit of the Caribs back into the mountains. Bruce had already been buried, with the young constable, in the little Catholic cemetery at Castle Bruce, while the eight Caribs who had died had been set in ground just outside it and three others, wounded, sent to the dispensary. Now, in the front drawing room, with McTear and Bruce's two friends, McCracken conducted his preliminary enquiry.

'An accident indeed,' McTear vigorously confirmed Frances's words. 'Yon Carib, he had the cutlass right up – above Mr Fraser. He would have had no chance . . .'

'Who would have had no chance, Mr McTear – the Carib or Mr Fraser?' McCracken asked studiously.

'Why, Mr Fraser of course.' McTear pretended to be mystified by McCracken's question.

'Of course,' McCracken said with the faintest hint of a smile. 'All most unfortunate – and you have my deepest sympathy there, Mrs Fraser, in your loss.' He looked across at her blandly, licking dry lips for an instant like a lizard in the heat of the shuttered room. 'And I'm sure the court of enquiry will fairly set aside the circumstances of your husband's death – as quite unpremeditated manslaughter. Except . . .' He paused, consulting some papers. 'I have the evidence from the sergeant here – Sergeant Alwin – that you fired off *both* barrels of the shotgun, Mrs Fraser, when one might have been thought sufficient?' He glanced at her coolly again, removing his half-moon spectacles.

Frances was outraged. 'In the heat of the moment, Inspector – in the literal heat of the moment, for the dining room was ablaze – I had no idea of *how* many barrels I was firing off. I was intent only – on firing!'

'To save him, to save your husband. Of course. I ask, just to remind myself – of how things were.'

'Inspector,' Frances told him, openly aggressive now. 'It was a matter of kill or be killed. You can have no idea of the situation here: there were children and helpless women in the next room, twenty or so Caribs out to murder us, the verandah, the dining room, in flames. We were all of us about to be –'

'Of course, I see that – as you say: a matter of kill or be killed, Mrs Fraser. And, as I said, you have my deepest sympathy in . . . your loss.' He looked at her, the eyes very penetrating, but the face empty, expressing nothing. What did he mean, she wondered? What was he getting at, with all these ambivalent questions and condolences?

'I'm afraid I don't follow you, Inspector,' she said very coldly.

And she did not. It was a genuine incomprehension. As with her long exile, being the instrument of Bruce's death had greatly changed her: it had blinded her to any doubts whatsoever about her action. Faced with a choice of guilt or complete self-justification in the matter, she had taken the latter course, quite blocking out of her mind that she might have intentionally killed him, by firing both barrels. That was impossible, she had assured herself: despite people's worst faults, one didn't *kill* them. The idea was preposterous. She had, as she had explained, fired in the heat of the moment, quite unaware of how many barrels had been despatched. That was perfectly obvious. McTear had already confirmed the point. Bruce's death had been a piece of sheer bad luck, a subsidiary incident, dependent on the much more urgent imperatives of the moment – which had been to save him, to save themselves, the women and children. Bruce had simply been a casualty of war.

'I was merely confirming your points, Mrs Fraser,' McCracken said easily. 'I'm very sorry . . . for your trouble.' He used the Irish form of condolence – knowing Mrs Fraser shared his own nationality. But, in turn, his eyes quite belied the words: they were knowing, lightly ironic.

As McCracken had forecast, the subsequent court of enquiry at Roseau cleared Frances entirely – and her husband – of any criminal actions in the whole business. While the Caribs – insofar as they could be, hidden again in their mountain vastness – were variously punished: several were executed, others sentenced to penal servitude in Jamaica, the Carib kingship abolished, their royal mace removed to Government House at Roseau, and their ten shilling a month grant-in-aid from Westminster discontinued.

Frances meanwhile was confirmed in a new role – as owner of Fraser Hall and estate, and inheritor, since Bruce had made no will, of all his other financial assets: a considerable sum, approaching £30,000. But something much more important had also been confirmed in her now – a taste for victory through physical action, through forcibly, violently asserting herself, which she had not done before.

She related these new ambitions to herself, to women generally, to subjugated races and nations – but also, and more importantly, to Summer Hill. Here was a final, long-dormant cause which attracted her new uncompromising feelings: by indulging these qualities further, she thought, she might regain her home.

So that, far from being appalled by her battle with the Caribs or by her responsibility for her husband's death, these violent events liberated Frances. Since she could not admit her guilt in Bruce's end, she obliterated her crime there by giving herself no pause to think about it, by maintaining, even increasing, her aggressive stance. Attack became her entire defence, both as a frenetic means of suppressing her guilt and as a way of life, of achieving future goals.

In short, she gave herself over entirely to the idea that the end justified the means – an equation which her earlier better nature would have led her to dismiss. She was liberated indeed.

3

S IR DESMOND CORDINER, to his bitter regret, was not the first man to achieve powered flight. In 1903 the Wright brothers pre-empted him there – and by 1905 they had developed a safely manoeuvrable flying machine, which could do figure eights, fly half an hour for up to thirty miles or more. The American government, blind to the importance of the Wrights' achievement, saw no reason to encourage these two bicycle-manufacturers, while officials in Europe, where aviators had never managed more than short hops in straight flight, were in a much stronger position to condemn them as naive maniacs and their machines as mere toys.

Only Sir Desmond, J. W. Dunne, his rival at the Balloon School in Farnborough S. F. Cody, Louis Blériot and a few other intrepid individuals persevered, knowing better. Sir Desmond himself had been one among these 'straight hoppers' for several years, without ever managing more than low flights of a few hundred yards above the meadow across the river from Summer Hill.

However, in the summer of 1908, when the Wright brothers arrived in France with their demonstration flights in a passenger-carrying machine, this general lack of interest vanished overnight. Flying machines became all the rage. Sir Desmond, attending these astonishing demonstrations at Le Mans, had met the Wright brothers, carefully inspected their machine and had taken several glorious, stomach-turning trips with them as a passenger.

Their 'Flyer', like his own machine, was a bi-plane. And indeed, at a casual glance, they seemed to resemble each other in many other ways: the two broad, superimposed, linen-covered wings giving them the shape of an elongated box kite – engines amidship, the controlling planes jutting out fore and aft. But on closer inspection, as Sir Desmond saw, there were vital differences: the Wrights' more powerful aluminium 30-horsepower engine, ingeniously water-cooled, was a light-weight which did not overheat; the crucial elevator which they had mounted forward of the wings, instead of behind – and above all the fact that the 'Flyer' had intentionally been built to an unstable design. The wing-tips, via a series of pulleys and wires, had been made to warp in flight, thus providing essential lateral control, so making the machine very much safer and more manoeuvrable than any European model. It was the lack of this warping factor in Sir Desmond's aeroplane, built to a rigid design, which had never allowed him to do more than swoop and fall alarmingly in a more or less straight line, a few dozen feet above the meadows at Summer Hill.

But now, armed with this new knowledge, Sir Desmond returned home, re-designing his own machine in the following months, so that by late in the year 1908, having introduced warp control, a more powerful 'Antoinette' 50-horsepower engine, and re-positioned his elevator forward, he was impatient – more than impatient – to get his new machine into the air.

The weather over Christmas was entirely against him: cold, windswept, rainy – conditions likely to last well into the new year, everyone thought. However, in February a calm spell arrived, a false spring, a succession of mild fine days with a light southerly breeze, conditions which seemed set fair for a week. And the ground, the short-cropped grass in the long meadow, soon dried out, leaving a firm even surface. Sir Desmond could not resist the temptation.

At first, in the early days of that week, he simply made trial runs – taxiing his new machine, which he had christened *Zephyr*, up and down the meadow, taking off on a dozen occasions, rising fifty feet or so, and travelling easily for several hundred yards, before descending. With his new warp control, forward elevators and increased power, he seemed to have achieved almost perfect stability and manoeuvrability now. It but remained to get properly airborne above the trees at the end of the meadow, so that then, with sufficient height, he could turn *Zephyr*, make a few circuits and land again. If the weather held, he would do so next morning.

Daybreak, when he went down to the meadow before breakfast, confirmed his best hopes. The ground remained hard, the wind in the south, blowing straight up the valley, which would give him all the lift he needed in taking off – and the sky was almost cloudless, a pale blue, rising in a great dome over the bare trees by the river, where the birds, deceived by the weather, took voice in the warm sun.

'I'll take her up,' Sir Desmond said to Lady Cordiner after breakfast. 'Take her up today!'

'But we have our important lunch party today!' she reminded him vehemently. 'Have you forgotten? The Aberdeens and the Wandesfordes. You cannot appear with your overalls – drenched in castor oil, stinking of benzine!'

'Oh, I shall be back long before that. Plenty of time to clean up. Have no fear.'

'But is it wise in any case – your flying so early in the year?' she asked him then, though there was no real concern in her voice since, for her, his passion for these aerial toys had never been wise. The whole thing was an aberration, she had always thought, one more flaw in the Cordiner make-up.

'My dear, if not now – when? I am getting no younger.'

'To the contrary, I believe in the whole matter that you have entered a second childhood.'

She did not smile in saying this, which might have offered Sir Desmond some encouragement, some hope in his enterprise; that was not her way with her husband. It had not been for many years. Nonetheless, he maintained his enthusiastic approach with her.

'You will not come down with me then – to the meadow?'

She shook her head. 'The fumes, the noise of your machine – they give me a headache. In your success, which you so expect, I may surely see you from here, rising above the trees, in all your glory.' She smiled a fraction now, but with sarcasm not favour.

Sir Desmond was still not disheartened. 'You will come out on the porch then? Good. I shall hope to fly right over you, over the house.'

Lady Cordiner was aghast. 'Not over the stables, I trust. You would stampede the horses.'

'No. Straight across the pleasure garden: I shall pass *directly* over the centre, the old astrolabe.'

She looked at him mockingly. 'I very much doubt it – that you could achieve any such exactitude in that foolish string and canvas contraption of yours! Why, it can barely leave the meadow . . . The idea that it could rise directly above us, up here: ludicrous!'

'You will see! You will see, my dear – how wrong you are,' he told her brightly. In fact he was hurt, even angry. But he hid it, as he had for years, putting up once more with his wife's sarcasm and disbelief in his flying abilities. She was arrogant and heartless, he knew. But she was not a fool. Could she be so entirely unaware of the vast potential and importance of these new flying machines, which would soon enable whole numbers of people to travel regularly from city to city, indeed from one country to another – machines which would liberate mankind, make them as birds, which would annihilate all distance and inconvenience in travel?

Yes, she was blind to all this. Well, he would show her – and the Viceroy Lord Aberdeen and the wealthy Wandesfordes, too, as an added bonus – by undeniable example, that very morning, how wrong she was, how his life had not been wasted with 'foolish string and canvas contraptions' but in pursuit of a dream which, albeit late, he would finally achieve himself, participating in the reality of flight which would soon change everyone's lives, the world over. He would take *Zephyr*, with all the precision of a ship's navigator, directly over the great astrolabe in the centre of the pleasure gardens: the old astrolabe – so appropriate a goal – a device once used to measure the height of the stars, which would now meet, soaring above it, a new machine which could actually take men into the heavens.

Sir Desmond, with his leather helmet, goggles and his thick blue dungarees, left the house shortly afterwards – driving down to the meadow with Dick Gregory, his chief mechanic, and the two terriers, Ginger and Billy (direct descendants of the old dogs Sergeant and Monster), yapping excitedly in the back seat of the open Daimler.

Lady Cordiner meanwhile went to her office-boudoir to see the housekeeper, Mrs Martin, giving her instructions for the day – and more importantly for the lunch party that afternoon. Lord Aberdeen, the Viceroy, and his wife, were stopping off en route for the Devonshires at Lismore; while the Wandesfordes, coal barons from Castlecomer, who were joining them, were friends of all concerned. Nothing must go wrong. So that, when she had finished her domestic business, Lady Cordiner advised Mrs Martin of Sir Desmond's plans. 'The Master is making one of his aerial voyages this morning. He believes he will actually fly up here – directly over the house. And, though I very much doubt he will succeed in this, you will warn the servants: the noise may surprise them. I want no breakages or any other unseemly behaviour – and they must keep away from the windows. The guests are expected at midday.'

Mrs Martin duly warned the household staff, with the result that most of them straightaway became excited, broke things and took to the windows, lurking expectantly behind the curtains for the rest of the morning.

They brought the *Zephyr* out from the barn which Sir Desmond had extended as a workshop and hangar at one end of the long meadow – pulling it gently on its two landing skids and central wheel, through the dark doorway, out into the sparkling morning light. It seemed a cumbersome affair – this clumsy kite, elevator and rudder projecting awkwardly fore and aft, the body filled with a confusion of wooden struts, pulleys, criss-crossed wires and chains. It had the air of something fated to stay on earth, a da Vinci doodle rashly translated into physical shape.

And yet, as the sun glinted on the aluminium four-in-line engine, dazzling the primrose-yellow canvas, the breeze trembling the wings, the machine appeared pregnant with a beauty, a power, a purpose, which, though not evident in the design, somehow lurked in it: a glimmer of future life.

They took photographs of the company in front of the machine: Sir Desmond in his flying suit, a terrier in each arm, together with Dick Gregory, the other two mechanics and several of the local villagers from Cloone who had turned up to gawk – though there were not many of these since Sir Desmond's limited swoops and falls along the meadow had become a commonplace in recent years. The terriers, true to the tradition of their bellicose parents, started a fight in Sir Desmond's arms almost at once, so that he rapidly dispensed with them, before attending to the machine, walking round and checking it.

There was a fault in the pitch control wire; it was slack, allowing the forward elevator too much play. And the same problem was found with the back rudder. It took them an hour or more to make suitable adjustments, so that it was not until nearly midday that they were ready to take *Zephyr* up, and Sir Desmond, quite forgetting his august guests and the lunch party, finally climbed into the wicker seat in front, sandwiched between the two wings. He ran over the controls for the last time, the levers to either side of his seat, one for pitch, the other for roll: both were in perfect order now.

Meanwhile Dick Gregory had primed the engine, checked the oil and the small petrol reservoir, before going forward to swing one of the propellers.

'Ready?' he called out.

Sir Desmond confirmed that his engine cut-out was just in the advance position. 'Contact!' he shouted back.

Martin spun the wooden blade and the motor sprang to life, an easy throb, *Zephyr* vibrating steadily now as the two six-foot, scimitar-shaped propellers rotated evenly, already tempting the machine forward. Finally, ensuring that the vital oil flow was satisfactory – the drips of yellow castor already spinning out in misty spirals behind him – Sir Desmond pushed the ignition lever to 'Advance', the engine roared and *Zephyr* moved sharply forward, hesitating for an instant before it turned into the wind and started to rush along the grass, the two terriers barking furiously, pursuing the machine hopelessly down the bright meadow.

As it gathered speed, the wings juddered alarmingly, the tail plane swinging to and fro, the whole machine bumping and slewing about for long agonising seconds: the earth would not release it.

But suddenly the magic came, lifting it off the grass, transforming the machine, as it lost its shadow life, and *Zephyr* was born, free of all its agony, its ponderous weight. Now, without any awkwardness, it climbed gradually into its true element, a primrose bird against the blue, quite sure of itself, easily clearing the trees at the far end of the meadow.

Gaining height then, rising some hundreds of feet above the winding river, Sir Desmond flew down the great wooded valley. After a minute he put *Zephyr* into a first turn, a delicate mix of rudder and warp, going left. The port wings dipped, the controls responding perfectly, as he moved gradually round by 180 degrees.

He flew back up the valley then, towards the barn and the men beneath, waving at them vigorously for a moment, gaining height now for another turn, to starboard this time, which would take him back along the same course. And, again, it was all perfect – a lovely gravity-defying turn, giving him a delicious shiver in the stomach, and then an extraordinary sense of buoyancy as the machine took height again on the straight.

Three or four hundred feet beneath him, he saw the glinting river, the long bridge at Cloone, the salmon traps, the little village square and the church spire brilliantly outlined in the midday light – things which he had known and looked on all his life at Summer Hill but which now appeared in such a totally different configuration and perspective that they seemed objects in a dream, recognisable, yet unrecognisable, familiar, entirely new. Away to his right, almost exactly on a level with him now, lay the house of Summer Hill, rising up out of the bare trees, the sun shimmering on the blue limestone.

As he soared above all this topography of his life, the machine riding the waves of balmy air, the wind streaming through his beard, flapping his collar, tickling his neck, the long-lost exhilaration of childhood returned to him, when everything in the world was quite new, as it was now: a feeling without memory, where all hurt and disappointment were obliterated, where there was only limitless joy.

He had been born again, with *Zephyr*. Here I am, he thought, where I ought to be. Now, at last, he understood the world unfolding beneath him. All partial vision gone, the river valley and the hills struck him as a map of Eden. He saw the master plan: *this* was how it was – no other way but this. Happy at last.

He turned again towards the end of the valley, making several more trips up and down, gaining height all the while, so that finally he was well above Summer Hill. Then he noticed the two large motor cars drawing up in front of the house. The lunch party, of course: he had quite forgotten it. The Aberdeens and the Wandesfordes had arrived. And then, he remembered, he had promised his wife: he would fly directly over the house, and at just the right moment, too, now that the illustrious guests had arrived. Lady Cordiner would cease to scoff – all of them would see just what these flying machines were capable of. He turned *Zephyr*, high over the river, flying above the ruins of his ancestor's castle on the steep side of the valley, heading straight for the garden terrace and the great astrolabe, seeing the dark-dressed, frock-coated figures emerging from the vehicles, half a dozen people already looking upward.

'My word!' said Lord Aberdeen. 'I had no idea we were to be regaled with an aeronautical display!

'I do apologise,' Lady Cordiner told him on the steps of the porch, hiding her outrage. 'I had no idea myself. My husband – Sir Desmond – he should have finished long ago – here to greet you all. I had no idea –'

'Not at all, Lady Cordiner, make no apologies – I am most intrigued!'

The company moved from the porch steps out on to the middle of the gravel surround for a better view of *Zephyr*, a yellow smudge against the blue, growing bigger, the throb of the engine increasing, as it drew near the house.

'What a brave fellow!' Mr Wandesforde remarked, agog with enthusiasm. 'I do so admire him. I had no idea these . . . these machines could actually achieve *real* flight. Quite splendid – I must have one myself. At once, do you hear, Molly?' He turned to his wife. 'We shall have one at once.'

'Dearest, they cannot be safe,' she responded with some agitation as the machine approached them.

'Nonsense – look at Sir Desmond: safe as houses up there!'

At almost every window of Summer Hill now the servants were gathered – chamber, still room, scullery, laundry and dairy maids, cooks and grooms, stewards, butlers, under-butlers and footmen: the whole vast household eyes out on stalks as the primrose machine approached.

'Holy Mother of God!' Bridey, one of the scullery maids exclaimed. 'The Masther's comin' straight for us!'

And, indeed, this was so. Nothing had gone wrong with *Zephyr*. Simply, in Sir Desmond keeping it up too long, extending his trip to fly over the house, it had run out of its small supply of benzine. The engine stopped suddenly, just over the astrolabe. The machine glided on for a few seconds, clearing the parapet of the house, before it dived steeply, crashing into the flat roof of Summer Hill with a terrible rending and splintering.

The company on the gravel, craning their heads round, saw the machine disappear over the parapet, then heard the commotion as several chimney stacks were demolished, high above them.

'My word,' Lord Aberdeen said again, puzzled. 'I had no idea . . . that that was how they landed. Home for luncheon – how droll!'

'You idiot,' his wife advised him in a strong whisper. 'He cannot have intended it – unless he is made of iron.'

Lady Aberdeen was right. Sir Desmond had not intended this and had been made of flesh and bone.

Some few weeks later, Frances, down on the jetty beneath Fraser Hall, waited impatiently for the fortnightly steam packet with the mail and provisions. Instead, before anything else was unloaded, she saw two men disembark and get into the steam launch, followed by a number of crates and boxes, some of them evidently with very fragile contents, since they were lowered to an accompaniment of strident directions and imprecations from the taller of the two strangers, a handsome bear-like man in a leather jerkin, jodphurs and army boots. His bearded companion – a much smaller figure in grubby linen tropicals, his servant or assistant to judge by the sound of things – finally stowed all their luggage in the cockpit, together with the mail, and Big Jules turned the launch towards the jetty. Frances shaded her eyes against the sun, not recognising either of them, curious.

'Hello there!' The big, tousle-haired man in his late thirties, a dead cheroot in his mouth, leapt with great agility on to the jetty before the launch had been moored, coming towards Frances with easy, indeed over-familiar purpose, offering his hand. 'I'm Clem Springfield – sorry I couldn't get word to you in advance – only arrived on the island three days ago.'

Frances looked at him, surprised, withholding her hand, saying nothing.

'Clement Springfield – of the *New York Post*.' He repeated the name, adding his employer, as if he expected Frances to know both. And then, having gazed at each other for long seconds, they both did know something – they were not certain what – of each other.

'Why?. . .' Springfield screwed up his bright brown eyes in a quizzical smile. 'Why, we *have* met, somewhere before – haven't we? Somewhere . . .' He turned away momentarily, clicking his fingers, concentrating. 'Why, yes!' He looked back at her, with a happy smile of recognition. 'You're the nurse I met out in South Africa, at Colenso. The war . . . your brother. Yes, your brother Lieutenant . . . Cordiner. Yes, that's it! I carried him back from the Boer lines – and met you before that, took you to Dundonald's tent! Remember?'

And Frances did remember now, softening, offering her hand. 'Yes, of course – we did meet. And they told me afterwards, how you'd carried my brother back across the river to the dressing station. How extraordinary! But you had a huge beard then and a slouch hat and you looked like a Boer, Mr Springfield!'

'Clem – call me Clem. I knew we'd met before. Couldn't forget – all that dark hair, the face!' He took her hand appraisingly. Then he turned, lighting his cheroot, before introducing her to his companion. 'And this is Oscar Stein, my picture photographer. Oscar, meet – Mrs Bruce Fraser, isn't it?'

'Yes – Mrs *Frances* Fraser,' she replied correcting the American, happy – in her new liberation – to point out her status as a widow. Then she greeted the curly-haired, busy little man who had been supervising the unloading from the launch.

'I'm very sorry to hear about your husband, Mrs Fraser. They told me in Roseau – and of course we read about it in New York. You have all my sympathy there.'

She believed him; he meant it. Perhaps it was his refreshing American accent that lent credence to his words, she thought – the easy, out-going tones, the generally open and confident bearing: so unlike the pompously cagey attitudes of the British on the islands.

'Yes, well, it was all a fearful business. But really I have nothing more to say about it, if that was –'

'Oh, not at all, Mrs Fraser. As I said, we heard all about the Carib attack in New York. We came here to get a feature story on them and a few pictures. Not to interview you,' he added, lying, but with such smiling conviction that Frances believed him once more.

'I see. But I doubt you'll get near any of them now – they've apparently left the reserve and gone to ground, somewhere way up there in the mountains.' She gestured to the great wall of green, towering inland, just visible above the cove.

'Oh, we'll find a way, Mrs Fraser. We have ways. The paper is very keen to get a story on them – cannibal tribe and so on!'

'But that's not true, Mr Springfield – an entirely peaceable tribe, unless goaded.'

He looked at her sympathetically, drawing on his cheroot. 'Yes, I heard about that: how your husband shot – had an accident with one or two of them. Great tragedy. All the same, there's a story my editor wants there, but from the anthropological point of view: mysterious lost tribe from the rain forests, a sort of Conan Doyle "lost world" up there, I understand. Your husband imported a lot of wild animals –'

'My husband's *father* –'

'Yes, of course – buffalo, deer, cougars. You can see the sort of thing I have in mind – obvious attractions. But nothing to do with you, Mrs Fraser.'

'I'd rather you didn't all the same. There have been enough problems already.'

'Mrs Fraser, I really don't want to impose,' he said nicely. 'But we've both come a long way.' He looked at Oscar, sweating in his subfusc suit, manhandling the trunks and boxes on to the jetty. 'We have a job to do, a living to earn – and my editor was particularly keen that I should come out here, do the story. And of course I'd no idea that I'd meet you here. Old friends – in a way.'

He smiled disarmingly, the earlier sympathy still in his eyes. And that was true,

Frances thought – they had met and, much more than that, he had risked his life in trying to save her brother at Colenso. She could hardly, in the circumstances, refuse to help him.

'Very well then, as long as you see my own position in the matter –'

'Nothing to worry about there, Mrs Fraser. The *Post* has a reputation for discretion,' he lied once more. 'You can rely on me.'

He smiled again, almost over-familiar, coming towards her, a great bulk of a man, hand outstretched, as if he expected to take her arm and lead her up the cliff path straightaway. Frances withdrew a fraction, but he touched her arm all the same, resting his hand there a second. 'Don't worry. It's just the Caribs we're interested in – nothing about you, I assure you.'

Their eyes met – cornflower-blue and dark brown, unblinking for a long moment in the bright sun. And something vaguely electric passed between them, a flicker of mutual attraction, which Frances dismissed at once. All men, as she saw it now, were her enemies. They were violent, insensitive, deceitful. They had betrayed her time and again. And here was a man who, in his throbbing, easy confidence, seemed quite capable of the same sins, of following in that tradition. Yet she could not deny that he had considerable charm, seemed honest, and was certainly brave. She would bear with him.

'Well, then, perhaps you'd care to stay with us for a few days? McTear, our estate manager here, may have some ideas.' She had turned away while speaking, but now she faced him again suddenly. 'But where *had* you intended to stay over here?'

'Oh, we have tents and supplies, Mrs Fraser – in those cases. And I'd intended hiring porters.'

'You've certainly brought enough equipment with you.' Frances looked at the baggage piling up on the jetty.

'Well, there are the big plate cameras, you see, that's the main thing – and a dark room tent and chemicals for developing the pictures. All quite elaborate. The *Post* prides itself on its pictures, you see, Mrs Fraser – Oscar here, a great photographer. I just supply the captions,' he added deprecatingly, crinkling up his eyes again in a smile, letting a whiff of smoke curl from his lips. Frances watched the misty blue spirals rise over his face, up into his tousled hair, as if mesmerised. 'But that's no matter,' he continued. 'I haven't thanked you –'

'For what, Mr Springfield?' Frances was lost.

'Why . . . why for your offer of hospitality, of course. Most appreciate it!'

'Oh, that – yes, of course.' Frances came back into the world. 'You're welcome, Mr Springfield.' She smiled at him, a free and open smile such as she had not given a man in years. But then, thinking she had gone too far, she added, 'You – and Mr Stein.' She looked over Springfield's shoulder to where the little man, with Jules and Slinky, had finally established a base camp on the jetty. They left shortly after for the Hall, walking up the cliff path together, the other men stumbling behind them, carrying Springfield's equipment, the provisions and the mail.

Having settled them both in, showing them their bedrooms, Frances brought the mail to her bureau in the drawing room. There was a letter from Ruth Wechsberg – and another from her cousin Dermot Cordiner. She recognised his handwriting at once, assuming it was his reply to her own letter – letters to him, his father Mortimer and to Ruth – telling them all of the Carib attack and Bruce's death.

She opened it and was surprised to see that it had been written from Summer Hill. The contents of the letter – nothing to do with her own, which he could not have received – were more startling still.

'My dearest Frances,

Forgive me – a harbinger of bad tidings. I write to tell you that your father has died. Poor man, he met with a flying accident, just three days ago, while taking his machine over Summer Hill – colliding with the roof there for some reason – killed instantly, the doctor says.

We both, Papa and I, were over in Dublin at the time and came down at once, of course, and I write this the morning after the funeral at Cloone.

Anyway, I know it will be a great shock to you – and Papa and I want to send you every sympathy. I know you were never very close to your Papa. None the less, these things cut deeply. And Mortimer and I (his letter is enclosed) particularly wanted to write to you at once, since your mother, I'm afraid, refuses to send you any word of this – continuing her foolish policy of having nothing whatsoever to do with you. Papa and I spoke to her this morning. She remains adamant in regard to you. And it really is a sad business – that she should continue so to behave in this bitter, unforgiving manner, especially in the present circumstances, which might have been expected to bring you together.

However, there is little to be done about it as far as I can see. And worse, as I must tell you, she sees you as permanently outcast. My Papa took pains to speak to her on this very point, suggesting that it was time for her to forgive and forget – and that she should consider, at least, the idea of your returning to Summer Hill now, with Hetty.

After all, as Papa tactfully reminded her, you are their one surviving child. And with your father's death Mortimer now assumed that you would inherit Summer Hill. At this surmise, however, your mother became most vindictively roused, telling us something we were both quite unaware of – and you will be too, I imagine: that Sir Desmond, in the event of his pre-deceasing her, had made over the house and estate to your mother quite some years ago – after Henry and Eustace died – to use during her lifetime, and with the absolute discretion to dispose of it afterwards as she sees fit.

The place has not therefore, as we expected, either been left to you or entailed to your uncle Austin – which was the other expected eventuality. However, your mother then went on to say that this latter course was the one she intended taking now: Summer Hill would be left to Austin and Bunty, and she had informed them of this while they were down there for the funeral.

Now I know your views on Austin and Bunty. He is a decent innocuous man. But she is something quite else – grasping, small-minded, pretentious, I'm afraid – not at all the sort to take over Summer Hill. And besides, if they did, they would still have their own substantial house and estate in Queen's county, while you would have nothing.

It is all most unjust of your mother – and we feel she cuts you out in this way largely out of spite, for we all know how little regard she has for Austin, much less for Bunty.

– 244 –

However, there it is and you should know the situation. We both think you should return here and see what could be done – perhaps you might talk her out of this course? But perhaps in any case you should come to London first and talk to Papa? I think you should do that.

In haste, ever most affectionately,

Dermot.'

Frances was outraged. She had recognised the possibility that her father, if he died before her mother and did not leave Summer Hill to her, might entail it to Austin and Bunty. But that her mother should inherit it, in the first place, without any strings attached, had not occurred to Frances. The house and estate had been restored with her mother's money, of course. And Lady Cordiner, ever the schemer, had ensured her pound of flesh in return. What a fiend she was – and Dermot was right: she had obviously manipulated Sir Desmond, gaining this control over Summer Hill, just so that she might disinherit her, if the opportunity arose. It had, indeed, been pure spite, guile, enmity. And Frances, in return and tenfold, felt the same acid emotions rising in her once more against her mother. Her father's death, by comparison, upset her much less. It was this impending loss of Summer Hill that cut her to the quick.

Her whole life – at home and in exile – had gravitated about this house, which she so loved, which she thought – somehow, one day – she might possess. And now, finally, irrevocably, it was slipping from her grasp – to be given over to the banal ministrations of her uncle Austin and, worse, to the frightful Bunty.

She rose from her desk, paced the room a minute, then went to the window, opening the louvred shutters, looking out at the dark spume of smoke from the disappearing packet steamer. Yes, she could return to Europe, speak to Dermot and Mortimer – and see her mother. But to what avail? Her mother would not change her mind. She could not force or cajole her – she was certain of that. Was there any other way of saving the situation?

She returned to her desk, opening the letter from Ruth Wechsberg. And there, a few minutes later, in the last paragraph, she thought she recognised something – a ploy, a lever, a desperate move which she might make. Ruth, who had received the news of Bruce's death, had replied with her sympathy, adding later, 'I wish I were with you, to *speak* these words, rather than having to put them in a letter, which I feel is so distant a means of communicating, at least for me, who am not good at them. All one can really say of letters is that, in default of the person, they are lasting evidence of feeling, of my feelings for you in your many hardships . . .'

It was the idea of letters as 'lasting evidence' that struck Frances then: letters, thinking of her father's will, almost as legal documents. And from there it was an easy step: letters . . . the Prince's letters, some dozens of them that he had written to her during their love affair.

These, too, were 'lasting evidence' of that affair – and, more importantly, of the Prince's amorous and political indiscretions in conducting it. There was the lever.

Of course! And here, she thought, if needs be – right here in Fraser Hall at that moment – was the means of activating it: the journalist Clement Springfield.

She picked up the month-old copy of the *New York Post* which he had given her on arrival at the house, reading the huge headline – '200,000 DEAD IN ITALIAN 'QUAKE' – turning pages then to look at the accompanying photographs of the catastrophe, completely devastated buildings in Calabria and Sicily. Well, she had material just as explosive.

She took a key, opening a pigeonhole drawer in the back of the desk, taking out the cache of old letters from the Prince, together with the other once-loved mementoes which he had given her – the little gold-ringed ivory elephant charm, the chiming watch from Hunt and Roskill, some elaborately decorated menus from Sandringham and the Weimar Hotel in Marienbad.

She had not looked at these things in years. Now she skimmed quickly through a few of the letters, noting some of the phrases: 'My dear one, my dearest . . .' 'Of course, Milner and Chamberlain have both behaved outrageously . . .' 'My lovely girl, in *every* way – I so think of you out there at the war, fear for you, wish you were back close to me. Oh, what I should have missed had I never met you! Sad . . .'

Frances, just for an instant, was filled with happiness in re-reading these endearments, feeling again the joy of their relationship, the trust and the love. But in a moment these memories sickened her, made her shudder with embarrassment and anger, giving her almost a physical shock, as if some lecherous old man was pawing her at that very moment with these words. She threw the letters down, where they landed among the opened pages of the *New York Post*. She almost laughed aloud, seeing the lethal combination at once.

Why had she not thought of using these letters in this manner before? Simply, she supposed, that she had so entirely put the Prince from her mind, despising him. And then again the idea of such blackmail would have been abhorrent to her. But it was not now: she saw it as her only chance. It was not the King-Emperor she wished to blackmail, of course. It was her mother.

It would need careful handling, she realised. She would return and confront her mother with the letters – threaten to publish them if she did not change her will in her favour. Meanwhile she would say nothing on the matter to Springfield – merely sound him out, perhaps hint that she had some interesting 'memoirs' to offer. There would be no harm in that. Springfield, after all, would know nothing of her past, least of all of her relationship with the Prince of Wales. There was a knock on the door then. She quickly hid the letters, closing the newspaper pages over them. It was Eileen. 'Those visitors,' she said. 'Cook wants to know if they've to eat with you – or on their own?'

'Oh dear, do they look that common?'

'Cook must have thought so.'

'True, they are just newspaper men. But they can eat with me.' Frances smiled regally: newspaper men indeed, but they might well have their uses.

Upstairs, as soon as Frances had left them, Springfield came into Stein's bedroom in a high state of excitement. Stein, exhausted from his efforts with the baggage and mistrusting the mosquito-canopied bed, lay prostrate on the bare wooden floor.

'Oscar, you bum – get up! I have news for you.'

Oscar groaned. 'I ain't goin' *no* place, Clem – doin' nothin'. I'm *eggs*-hausted.'

'You don't have to go any place – just listen!' Springfield knelt down beside him. 'That Fraser woman, know who she is?'

'No. Yes – you have to interview her, get the news on what she was up to with her husband: "She shot him" – page one – stop the presses – shut up – le' me be.'

'No, you fool. I mean who she *was*! A much bigger story.'

'Who was she, then?' Stein cupped his hands behind his head and looked up at the ceiling blankly. 'The King of Spain's daughter?'

'No – the King of England's mistress, even better. Or used to be. Same woman – I had it all in South Africa, from one of the other nurses there.'

'So what? That's not the story we came out here for.'

'No. This is a bigger story! *Much* bigger.'

Frances waited several days before the opportunity occurred of broaching her topic – days in which the two men unpacked their equipment, tested the camera, talked to McTear and made short and unsuccessful forays into the hills looking for the Caribs.

Then one morning Springfield brought her out to the dark room tent which Stein had set up on the lawn, showing her the equipment there, which Stein was working on just then, developing some plates which he had exposed the previous day. The interior, with its single red lantern, was suffocating, stinking of chemicals, and Frances was pleased to leave the enclosed space, walking back towards the house with Springfield.

'Interesting work, no doubt,' she told him, watching the humming birds hover over the great flowers.

'Mine or his?'

'Both. My elder brother always had a plate camera with him on his travels, just like you. And your writing, of course! I remember my brother reading Stanley's books on Africa with such interest: finding Livingstone and going down the Congo – fascinating. A fascinating profession. I've kept a journal myself over the years,' she added off-handedly.

Springfield showed a quick interest – which he failed to hide. 'Have you, Mrs Fraser? That should be quite something – given your experiences!' He looked at her pointedly as they arrived on the verandah steps – rather too pointedly, Frances thought.

'Oh, just thoughts – about the war in South Africa, for example. Nothing much.' She underplayed her literary endeavours.

'Of course. But there's your recent adventures on the island here – even better! The Carib attack. And your husband . . .'

'That's of no interest,' she told him brusquely.

'And of course you're a friend of the King – the King of England,' Springfield continued easily. 'Knew him when he was Prince of Wales. That must have been quite something.'

Some of McTear's men were repairing the verandah shutters after the fire, hammering about near them, so that at first Frances thought she had misheard him.

'I'm sorry?' She looked at Springfield, half-astonished, then entirely so, realising she had not misheard him. But she hid her surprise. 'I'm afraid I . . . I don't follow you,' she said calmly.

'Well, you must remember the Sister – out there at Colenso, that other nurse you worked with – what was her name? She told me about your being a friend of his. I don't want to pry, of course – but that must have been a very interesting experience, Mrs Fraser. That's all I was thinking, a matter of some public interest . . .'

'Not really, I'm afraid.' Frances, regaining control with an effort, smiled deprecatingly. 'I only knew the Prince very slightly, before the South African war. He was a friend of the woman whose nursing home I worked at in London. I met him there once or twice, that's all.'

'All the same, you've led an extraordinary life – for a woman. Had you thought to publish anything on it? Write your memoirs? My newspaper would certainly be very interested.'

They had moved indoors now, away from the noise on the verandah, walking through into the cool of the hall.

'No, I'd not thought of that, Mr Springfield. Besides, I can't really write.'

'I'd be pleased to help you there, Mrs Fraser. Put your experiences down for you.'

'Most kind,' she told him distantly. 'But really I have nothing to say – for the moment. And now, if you'll excuse me, I have some letters to write.'

Closeted in the drawing room at her desk, Frances tried to compose herself. She remained astonished. How much did Springfield really know about her relationship with the Prince? No more than the little he'd said? – mere gossip, simply, from that spiteful, ignorant, chocolate-gorging Sister Turner, who had picked up some rumour of her royal association from Brazier-Creagh? It could not have been more than that, she decided. And it hardly mattered in any case. Such ancient gossip could not be made to mean anything now, years later. And Springfield could have no other firm evidence to go on, which might make trouble for her.

In fact, he had simply made things easier, if and when she wished to use him; he had agreed in advance to take her 'memoirs' – even help her to write them. She now had another genuine lever with her mother – an offer, in effect, from the *New York Post* to publish this scandal which, when word of it got abroad, would ruin Lady Cordiner's life, set all her social success at nought. Though, of course, it would never come to that. When her mother saw the letters, realised their explosive nature, she would capitulate. So there was really no problem with Springfield. He would never get to see these 'memoirs', let alone publish them.

Springfield, in his greed for a sensational story, made the best of the way their conversation had gone when he spoke to Stein in the dark room tent later, telling him what had passed between them.

'So what?' Stein said. 'So, she was a girl friend of the old guy. But he had *hundreds* of girls – well known – always the Lothario. No story there – forget it.' Stein held up a plate of the Emerald Pool, gazing at it intently against the red lantern.

'I don't know – there's something special here. I can feel it. Those rumours in Roseau, remember? That she did her husband in, on purpose. And that child of hers, with the awful stammer – that it wasn't Mr Fraser's child at all. Remember?'

Stein nodded mechanically. 'Yes, yes, I remember.'

'Well, you know something? I think the King might have been that girl's father. The dates fit – roughly. She must be nine or ten years old – just when Mrs Fraser knew him, before she went out to South Africa. And another thing, Oscar: why would a woman like that – rich aristocrat, so well-connected at home – come out and bury herself in a dump like this? Unless maybe to get away from the scandal of having an illegitimate child back home?'

'Why wouldn't she come out here? A vacation. And then she met Fraser, with this great house, and married him – and stayed here, naturally. That makes sense.'

'Not entirely. She didn't get on with him at all –'

'That happens *plenty*, Clem. Nothing unusual there. I tell you – you're going up a dead end. Let's find these savages, take a few pictures of 'em and get the hell outa here.'

But Springfield was not persuaded. 'Yes, it's that girl, you know,' he said pensively. 'I'd lay money on it. Why, the kid even looks something like the King – those big blue eyes and the high brow –'

'And the beard and the big cigar – Clem, you're outa your mind. Come on, let's do some serious *work*.'

Springfield, with nothing more to go on, might have left it at that – but for Frances's carelessness and the lucky chance he had in benefiting from it that afternoon. In the drawing room, taking coffee with Frances after lunch, he saw the copy of the *Post* which he had given her, lying on top of some other magazines and papers on a small occasional table beside her.

He picked it up casually, remarking on the headline, the frightful earthquake in Italy a month before. 'Terrible business,' he added, as a vague afterthought.

'Indeed.' Frances spoke from over by the window, her back towards him. 'I'm surprised you didn't go straight out there yourself, instead of coming here.'

'Oh, we have several people in Italy already, Mrs Fraser. No need for me.'

He continued to turn the pages over idly, flicking through the paper. And then the letter fell out, landing in his lap: 'Marlborough House, SW. My dearest one, how I have missed you, without any news, and fear for you in that dreadful war. I do so wish you could return, be near me once more. I miss you – in every way – and long to do again all the things we did . . .'

Springfield restrained himself admirably. He pocketed the letter quickly, while Frances was still at the window, continuing to glance through the paper. Frances turned to him then, seeing him reading.

'Ah, rummaging through your old work, are you?' She remarked on the article by Springfield in the paper which she had read that morning herself. 'Your account of floundering about in those hot baths at Saratoga Springs sounded . . . fascinating!' She looked at him almost suggestively, eyes narrowing in a smile.

'Oh, that was nothing, Mrs Fraser. I can do much better than that – I assure you! Let me show you some other things I've done.' He stood up. 'I've got some cuttings upstairs.'

'Oh, don't bother.'

'No bother. I'd like to.'

He left the drawing room, still holding the copy of the *Post*. Upstairs he read through the Prince's letter carefully. There was no doubt about it. They had been much more than mere acquaintances. Mrs Fraser had been his mistress. And the child? Well, he was probably right, it was theirs. But he needed more information – if he could get it, which seemed unlikely. He was in a quandary. Finally, getting out some of his old cuttings, he went downstairs again, deciding he had nothing to lose by simply putting his cards on the table.

'Mrs Fraser,' he told her, holding up the letter. 'Upstairs – this letter fell out of the paper. I think it must be yours.'

He handed it over. She glanced at it – managing with equal skill to restrain herself, showing no concern. 'Oh, how careless of me.' She put it down on the desk. 'I must have left it inside when I was looking at your article this morning. Now what are your plans for this afternoon, Mr Springfield?'

'Mrs Fraser, I'm afraid my journalist's curiosity got the better of me. I read that letter.'

She turned to him coolly. 'How very ill-mannered of you – people's private correspondence. Still, as you say, it's to be expected – from a journalist.'

'Sheer chance it fell out of the paper. I apologise. I really didn't want to pry.'

He spoke meekly, and apparently truthfully. Like Frances, he had the charm to lie with absolute conviction. Frances meanwhile was preparing her own lies, her next move: yes, she would humour him – or better still, now that the cat was out of the bag, she would manipulate, control, trap him in return.

'Well, so you've read it!' She laughed easily, with a sigh of relief, as if pleased that he should have discovered her secret, which now allowed an openness between them. 'But it's of no real importance. It all happened a long time ago, over and done with. Though naturally . . .' She looked at him steadily, with an expression of conniving intimacy. 'It's not for public consumption. I can rely on your discretion there – of course.'

'Of course – absolutely.' There was silence then. They had both produced their lies now. Yet neither really believed the other, and each knew that. The room was hot and still, the louvred shutters spreading bars of bright light over the floor and the heavy furniture.

They looked at each other amiably – an agreement, an understanding reached between them, an apparent trust formed. There was a distinct hint of conspiratorial mischief in Frances's face now, a knowing smile, which Springfield responded to in kind. They were suddenly enjoying each other's lies, excited by their mutual deceits, and the burgeoning conspiracy it suggested.

'On the other hand . . .' Springfield said, returning her gaze. He paused.

'What?' Frances moved towards him, stopping just a few feet away. 'On the other hand *what*, Mr Springfield!' She ran a hand quickly through her dark curls, looking up at him coquettishly.

'Well, it is an extraordinary story,' he went on, shaking his head in genuine astonishment now, sensing something even more unexpected in Frances's expression and approach to him.

'What? – that the Prince was my lover?' she said provocatively. 'Why should that surprise you?' She narrowed her eyes in a canny flirtatious smile, opening her lips a fraction, a wonderful demon rising in her, sure of her power over him, taking a vast pleasure in it. She had not so tempted a man like this in years, and the pleasure was all the greater since, whereas before, with the Prince, she had done this with love, now she offered herself to Springfield out of pure physical hunger, mixed with derision, spite, hatred. It was a new and exceedingly satisfying feeling, for she controlled him now, and so she let him take her, partly in pleasure, partly as a poisonous flower tempts an insect to destruction.

And he took the bait greedily, falling into her, over her, trying to kiss her – one cheek, then the other, searching out her lips as she twisted to and fro, avoiding that contact, letting him crush her instead, feeling his mouth on her neck, tongue exploring her ear, her head arched backwards by the force of his body against hers, feeling him rising against her thighs – and feeling her own mounting excitement, too, so that she made no resistance as he started to fumble at the buttons of her fine muslin blouse, picking at them, unable to undo them.

Frustrated eventually, she stepped away from him, flushed and impatient, looking at him with a vehement mix of desire and an enmity which he did not recognise.

'Lock the door,' she told him breathlessly. He left her, fumbling with the key there as well, so that by the time he returned she had taken the blouse off herself, together with the silk half-bodice beneath, and was standing there, naked to the waist. Then, impatient to be freer still – of the rest of her clothes and his bungling attentions – she was already picking at the hooks and eyes at the side of her starched linen skirt, turning her head round, one arm squeezed tightly round her breast, as she fiddled with the clips.

'Let me,' he said easily. He prised her arm gently away, so that her breasts were open to him now, offering him the dark, tumescent aureoles, which he kissed as he undid the last of the catches, stooping, running his hand down her midriff, pulling her skirt down at the same time.

And then Frances, again pre-empting him – her passion rising, in desperate hurry now – did the rest for him, pulling away from him, stepping out of her slip and cami-knickers, before going over to the long sofa, naked. He followed her, hurriedly undressing as he went.

She lay down on her back, looking up at him as he came towards her, quite startled by his size, in every way – his taut sex, vast, curving in a great arc, as he knelt between her thighs and she grasped and stroked the extraordinary instrument which he offered to her.

And then marvelling, and marvellously excited, she quite forgot how she despised this man and, sitting up quickly, arching her back forward, she bent down into him and took it in her lips, letting it run into her mouth, realising what a small fraction of it she could contain. It had been years since she had last made love. And, just as she had so completely repressed all desire during that time, so now, going to the other extreme, she threw all caution and propriety to the winds.

She mouthed and fingered him wildly, with an excitement that was all the greater since he was nothing but an object for her, whom she cared nothing for, whom she hated. There was only his body and she exulted in that alone and all its possibilities, pushing her mouth right down, feeling him in her throat.

Then, wilfully, she pulled away from him and lay back, put her hands at her hips, pushing herself up there, offering him her own sex. And when she first felt him she thought she might choke or scream, a great surge of expectancy coursing through her. It was a sheer physical joy, quite divorced from any emotion, which she could not have thought possible; smooth, liquid, intense.

He moved forward then, holding himself over her, bracing his arms, to either side of her head, his body suspended high above her, quite motionless as, lower down, he began to glide and explore between her thighs. She could feel his sex, moist-topped, teasing, pushing, retreating, sliding up in front, then behind, intentionally missing the mark, she thought, so that she gasped in frustration, opening herself to him, arms writhing behind her neck, head twisting about in a delicious agony. So that when he did finally come into her, pushing gently, she gasped again, then held her breath, unbelieving, waiting.

But he suddenly stopped, stayed there at the just-opened door, so that she shivered, anticipating the pain. And then she felt what she could not believe, what she thought she could not contain, as he quietly moved forward again, fraction by fraction, and there was no pain – just an endless smooth sliding movement, a widening and a deepening, right down, until he seemed to come to the end of her. And, when he had, she gripped him, contracting her muscles, tightening all round him, so that, when he started to move again, the joy was intense as she enclosed him, the whole deep length of him, she thought. But it was not so. There was more, and more to spare, so that she realised she could never have him all, even when, eventually, frenzied now, they charged right into each other, time and again, and he finally flowed into her and she responded, in spasm after ringing spasm, one exploding firework igniting the next, seemingly without end. Frances had never experienced such a thing, never believed it possible: this cataract, these successive bursts of pleasure, exploding one after the other deep inside her.

4

S RINGFIELD WAS PLEASED with his performance, believing that it had given him a power over Frances more important than the sexual: that he could now, presuming on their intimacy, the more readily persuade her to indulge the full story of her affair with the Prince. Frances was pleased, too, in that, knowing he would make just such a presumption, she could forestall him, yet at the same time learn what he knew and intended in advance.

What she had not expected was that he would so soon, so brashly, take up the running and try and push her on the matter. And it was in this crass hurrying that Springfield, quite unaware of the vital plan Frances had with her mother, made a serious mistake. For of course if anything were made public of her affair with the Prince, before Frances had the opportunity of showing the letters to Lady Cordiner, there would then be no lever in them and her last chance of rescuing Summer Hill for herself would have disappeared.

So it was that Frances, when Springfield started to push her, reacted with violent alarm. And, since she could not delay his ambitions by explaining her real plans for the letters, it was then that she first realised that she might have to consider some other means of ensuring his silence.

Springfield had taken up the subject very soon after their bout on the sofa – that same evening after dinner, when Stein had gone to his room and they were both on the verandah, lying back in the cushioned steamer chairs, taking coffee, looking out on the dark lawn with its polka dots of dancing fireflies.

'Well, Frances! . . .' He stared knowingly across at her in the lamplight, drawing on a cheroot, his previous confidence strengthened now by an air of sexual dominance which infuriated Frances.

Nonetheless, flickering her eyelids, she maintained something of her earlier flirtatious attitude. 'Well – what?' She picked out a Carlsbad plum.

'Well, it was wonderful,' he told her frankly and simply. They had not been alone with each other since their coupling. Frances responded with a minute nod. Springfield sat up then, leaning over enthusiastically. 'Really – wonderful . . .' He admired her, undressing her with his eyes, hoping to confirm how they had both caught sex like an infection, a raging fever, which they must now inevitably continue to suffer: sex – which would guarantee his own professional future, so that he spoke now with exactly that advantage in mind. 'But the future,' he went on in the same caressing, yet slightly overbearing voice. 'I can really help you there.'

'I don't see –'

'Well, with your husband gone, you can't just bury yourself here for the rest of your life, can you? Come back with me to New York!'

'What on earth for?'

'Why, we could do things together, go places. And those letters,' he added as an apparent afterthought. 'Your memoirs – I could fix those up for you. They'd be worth a fortune, you know – start a whole new life in America. Why don't you?'

Frances had reacted to his sly enthusiasm with a first real spasm of alarm – knowing exactly what lay behind it: not her, but her 'memoirs'. 'I don't know that I want to live in America – Clement,' she added nicely.

'Well, not forever maybe. But, Frances – look at the *opportunities*! Your story, you and the Prince – why, it's worth fifty, a hundred thousand dollars, I tell you.'

'*Is* it?' she asked innocently, yet with a suitable hint of greed, hoping to encourage him in further disclosures.

'Why yes, and maybe more. You must have dozens of those letters?'

She did not reply. But she smiled broadly now, as if agreeing with him silently, prodding him to other surmises.

Springfield took the bait – and then a most dangerous plunge. 'And little Henrietta,' he said, confidently playing what he thought to be his ace. 'She's his child, isn't she? Why, that alone makes it all – really so much better. She is, isn't she?'

Springfield looked across at her intently, hoping to discern the answer in her eyes, if not in her voice. Frances was astonished, raging inwardly at this loathsome man – for his greed and his insights. Yet again she said nothing – while again repeating her look of implicit confirmation.

'I knew it!' he said triumphantly. 'So you see – I see it all. We've no need to beat about the bush any more. We can set your story up together – right away and publish it. We have it all in front of us – a future!'

What Springfield could not have seen then was that, in so displaying his dangerous intuitions and his grasping ambition to capitalise on them as soon as possible, he might not have a future at all.

Yet Frances initially had to play for time. 'All right,' she assented. 'It's a possibility – we'll consider it. But meanwhile tell no one: not anybody, not even your friend Stein. Fair?'

'Fair enough. The fewer the better – for the moment!'

They exchanged a final knowing smile, as a seal on their present silent collusion and future co-operation, and Frances had gained a respite in the game.

But her quandary remained – and she saw how deep it was. Even if she offered him no future help, Springfield already knew enough of her affair with the Prince to embroider or invent the rest, in anything he might publish – as he surely would, whether she co-operated with him or not. And once he left the island, if she did not accompany him, she would have no further control over his designs. And, of course, she had no intention of going anywhere with him. If this was the equation – and she saw no other – then there was only one answer to it: he must not leave Domenica. That answer was very simple. But it immediately produced a much more difficult problem: how could he be prevented from leaving the island?

There was a truly delicate point. And Frances considered it in that exact manner, without any malice aforethought, wondering if he might meet with some accident, out boating or in pursuit of the Caribs . . . God knows, she thought, the island, with its violent and unpredictable natural elements, was a dangerous enough place . . . Yet she was forced to admit that even she could not expect to bend the natural order to suit her own immediate purposes here.

In the event Springfield himself offered a possible answer to her problem when he told her next morning of his plan to make a long trek, in pursuit of the Caribs, up into the mountains in the heart of the island.

'You see, they're nowhere in their reserve right now,' he told her. 'From all the evidence, they've scattered – here and there.' He pointed to the map he was showing her. 'Up round this Trois Pitons mountain apparently – and beyond: this Valley of Desolation and the Boiling Lake.'

Frances suddenly paid attention. 'Yes, no doubt they have. You should look for them there, why not? Around that valley – and the Boiling Lake. Fascinating places in any case. We visited them, soon after we were married. Terrify –' She stopped herself. 'Unbelievable!'

Frances, indeed, had stood amazed – and fearful – on the high rock above the sulphurous lake eight years before, and shuddered at its boiling horrors, just a false step away, gurgling and erupting some hundreds of feet beneath her. The journey itself had been dangerous enough – along knife-edged ridges with sheer falls to either side, across crevices on makeshift rope bridges: a journey up through the fetid rain forest and along the treacherously slippy paths over the corrugated volcanic peaks, where one of their porters, taken by a loose stone on the narrow ridgeway, had tumbled to his death, smashed on the rocks far below. Springfield, she thought, might just meet with something of the same fate. It was certainly not a journey she ever wished to repeat herself.

'Right then!' Springfield beamed powerfully. 'We'll start tomorrow.'

'You and Mr Stein.'

He turned to her quickly, something very sly in his smile. 'Why, no – all three of us, of course.'

'But, Clement, I can't come.'

'But you must, Frances. Show us the way – you've been there before. Besides, I'll need you along with me – we can talk over our plans for your "memoirs".'

Springfield, overnight, had considered his relationship with Frances and had decided he did not trust her. He thought he had seen through her amiable consent to his publishing plans. She had been too quick in agreeing with him, had simply been toying with him for some reason – and he thought now he knew why. Quite ignorant of her assets until he had unearthed and valued them for her, she would now, if left alone, simply take the first opportunity of quitting the island and placing her memoirs elsewhere. She was just that sort, he had seen it from the start – calculating, devious, dangerous. He would keep a strict eye on her, keep her with him at all times.

Frances, on the other hand, confronted by this *force majeure*, decided not to contest it. She would make the trip again. Indeed, by accompanying him, she saw how, in some as yet quite undetermined manner, she might turn Springfield's invitation not to his, but to her own, advantage.

They set out at first light across the citrus fields, before rising gently up into the hills, soon entering the cavernous rain forests. It was a full day's journey to the Lake. They rode three scraggy ponies to begin with -- two mules behind carrying tents and provisions and Stein's plate camera, with Big Jules in charge of half a dozen armed porters conscripted from the estate.

But by mid-morning, making a base camp at the foot of the Trois Pitons mountain, they were forced to abandon the mules and ponies, taking to their feet up into much denser rain forest. Here, as they scaled the lower mountain slopes at an angle of forty-five degrees, there was nothing but a narrow, muddy, undergrowth-tangled path to move on, interspersed with log steps, ladder-like, rising almost vertically.

Later the going became even more exhausting since soon, emerging from the tree line, they found themselves on the loose-stoned mountain ridges. On this section, struggling upwards for half an hour, then forced to descend for the same length of time, they moved forward in such an up and down manner for several hours, apparently rising no higher. Finally, however, coming to the top of a ridge, they saw how far in fact they had climbed – for there, miles below them to the west, they could just make out the tiny white speck of Fraser Hall and the sea beyond.

But now there were other problems. They were on the knife-edged ridgeway skirting the summit of Trois Pitons, which led round the mountain to the Valley of Desolation and the Boiling Lake beyond – a twisting track no more than a yard wide in some places, where the crest dropped sheer away on either side, hundreds of feet into deep, tree-filled valleys beneath.

Ahead of them, higher peaks loomed, covered in swirling mists, rain clouds sweeping in over the top of them. And soon the storms had engulfed the party, drenching them, buffeting them, as they crouched on the tiny path, clinging on while the rain swept over them. Then, just as suddenly, the clouds and mist disappeared and a brilliant sun emerged, drying them, allowing them to proceed, as the party took a second wind, rounding the mountain shoulder eventually, getting right into the heart of the island. Now the travel became easier as they descended a great boulder-strewn slope towards the Valley of Desolation below.

And so it was. Here all the lush vegetation of the island disappeared completely, replaced by jagged bleached white stones, flaky or pumice-like, with hot streams oozing slowly through these outcrops; everywhere sulphur geysers sighed and hissed, slowly erupting with a noisome, choking smell of rotten eggs. Nothing moved or lived here, a true slough of despond, a world's end.

Eventually, crossing this nightmare landscape and rising up the other side, they reached the top of a plateau, a smooth square of rock, with damp mists and a choking steam vapour swirling all about them. They could see nothing, wrapped and sweating profusely in these stinking folds of warm cotton-wool.

'So?' Springfield said. 'All that – just for this? There's nothing to see.' He looked at Frances, standing in her filthy, mud-spattered jodhpurs beside him, throwing down her pith helmet, mopping her face.

'So – you wanted to come.'

Stein joined them, with Big Jules and the porters carrying his plate camera. 'Nothing to see – and not a sign of any Caribs either. Crazy.'

Stein wandered away from the group, towards the swirling vapour. 'You no go too much that way, Sah!' Big Jules called out.

Stein turned, puzzled. 'But there's nothing there, is there?'

'You see – if it clear comes.'

A minute later, in a change of wind, it did – all the smoky vapours suddenly dispersing. Everyone stepped back quickly; Frances, suddenly alarmed, kneeling down for safety.

They had, they saw now, been standing near the edge of a vast cauldron of rock, with a lake at the bottom of it, a quarter of a mile in diameter: a lead-grey expanse of thick, porridge-like water – all bubbling, boiling steadily, rising and spattering, fuming with clouds of steam. It was an awesome sight, an Old Testament vision, symbol of Jehovah's wrath, the very mouth of hell where the damned would fall and boil for eternity. Everyone stepped even further back from the sheer edge.

'Sweet Jesus,' Springfield said simply. Stein, unpacking his big camera, prepared to photograph it. Frances, still crouching, sweating in the sticky, oppressive air, listened to the awful gurgles, invisible to her now, beyond the edge of the rock.

'Has anyone ever fallen in?' Springfield asked Big Jules.

'Yes – one homme! He once do that – boiled too hot très tôt!'

'What? – he fell right over, here?'

Big Jules nodded.

'How hot is it, do you think?' Springfield turned to Stein then, fiddling with his camera.

'What d'ya mean – how hot? You can see: it's *boiling*, isn't it? You wanna test it or sometin?' Springfield considered the matter.

Then, without warning, in another change of wind, they were suddenly enveloped in the sickly vapours, which turned off the lake and swirled around them. Frances, still sitting on her haunches, could barely see her hand in front of her face. But she saw her opportunity. Or, rather, she considered it: the problem was, if she were to stand up and make any movement, she ran the risk of falling over the edge herself . . .

'All of you – stay where you are! Don't move an inch!'

She heard Springfield's voice. Before the mists had closed in, he had been standing some half a dozen yards away from her. But now his words came from a closer point. Springfield, at least, disobeying his own instructions, was moving. Indeed, she could hear his footsteps on the rock – treading softly, coming straight towards her. And then, as the vapour cleared for an instant, looking up she saw him looming above her, making for her, reaching out his arms.

She half-rose to her feet, hoping to avoid him, scuttling away sideways like a crab from the edge. Then the fog closed round the eerie face and he was gone and she thought she had escaped him – until she suddenly felt a hand grasping her shirt collar, behind the neck, dragging her to her feet.

'Oh, no – not so fast!' She heard the soft voice out of the mist as he yanked her face round – then saw his great bulk towering above her, a look of ominous malice in his ghostly features. 'You think I don't know why you came all this way with me? – when you were terrified of the place: look at you now! – on your knees with fear. You never wanted to come – except maybe you thought you could ditch me here, push me over the edge or some such. That's why you came. Well, I'm going to keep you *right* with me, Frances!' He tightened his grip behind her neck.

'Where the hell are you, Clem?' It was Stein, calling out urgently from some distance away.

'I'm fine, Oscar. Just stay put,' he shouted back. 'I'm with Mrs Fraser – looking after her. Seeing she comes to no harm.'

Frances struggled a moment, but it was useless. 'You're talking nonsense,' she told him sharply.

'Am I?' He lowered his voice, full of icy sarcasm now. 'You killed your husband – so everyone says. So why not me, if you got the chance? I know too much, don't I? I saw it all afterwards, thinking about it. You agreed to everything far too easily, didn't you? You don't really want your "memoirs" published at all – or not by *me*, leastways. And all that flirting – and romping on the divan – that was some other game you were playing. Took me for a complete fool, didn't you?' He wrung her collar, like a tourniquet, closer round her neck.

'I *do* want them published, I will –' she gasped out, ashamed by her fear, which made her furious.

'Why, you little –' He tightened his grip.

'You can have the letters!'

His face emerged suddenly from the fog, then disappeared again. 'Oh, I can, can I?'

'Yes, yes – you can have them!' She hardly realised what she was saying, sensing only her violent fury, caught by the neck, dangling like a cat, in the grip of this horrifying man.

'So, maybe I don't need you at all then?' He jerked her forwards, towards the edge of the chasm, so that she cried out then.

'Help! Help me – Jules, Mr Stein –'

'You all good an' safe là, Madame?' Big Jules called back.

'She's fine, Jules. Just slipped. But I've got her safely now. Don't any of you move – I've got her quite safely.'

In fact, without his noticing it in the thick fog, he no longer had her safely at all. In gripping her collar so firmly – pulling at it, some of the buttons snapping – the blouse had eased its way out from her waistband and begun to ride up her midriff.

Frances saw her chance. In an instant, bending down and straightening out both arms, she pulled herself violently away from him. And, though he hung on to her viciously, the blouse tore away, sliding over her head, and she was free. A second afterwards she lunged forwards into the choking mists, arms still outstretched, her hands meeting him full on his chest, pushing him violently, so that he overbalanced and fell away from her, disappearing into the swirling grey pall, launched out into space over the edge of the rock, without a sound as he fell into the boiling, gurgling depths far beneath.

Frances knew at once that he had gone over the precipice. It was only ten minutes later, when the mists cleared again, and the others had searched for Springfield everywhere on the high plateau and the rocks behind it, that they, too, realised he had gone this way.

Frances crouched down again then, kneeling, covering herself, half-naked, her body glistening with warm beads of vapour – the smudged, sweaty marks of his hands about her neck. She swayed to and fro gently, crying, gulping back sobs, as if in a state of shock. But they were happy tears – tears of relief and joy. Beyond her, on the lip of the chasm, lay the torn remains of her bouse. Stein reached for it gingerly, brought it back and considered it. The implication appeared obvious to him. But he turned to Frances for confirmation.

'What in hell happened? Did he . . .? Was he trying to . . .?'

Frances nodded. 'Yes, he tried to take me – he had me by the collar, just tore the blouse straight off, then fell back . . .'

'The crazy fool.' Stein turned away, gazing over the precipice where the wind, changing once more, had cleared the air above the lake, the sullen grey waves and eddies visible again, burbling and spitting. There was not the slightest sign of Springfield, swallowed up and drawn down into the seething depths of the cauldron. 'The crazy fool,' Stein said again to himself. 'As if he hadn't had enough women in his life already.'

An accident – everyone agreed to that. It was obvious: Springfield had slipped, lost his footing in the mists. And Stein, with Frances, was happy to say nothing of how, before he went, Springfield had ripped her blouse off, trying to molest her. So Frances conveniently came to believe this was the entire cause of his death: that Springfield had spun out into space simply as a result of hanging onto her blouse, like an anchor, which, when it had come adrift, had catapulted him over the edge. She saw her own part in his death as quite secondary, so that she readily forgot about it. It was unimportant – Springfield was gone. The island, with its unpredictable natural hazards and elements, was indeed a dangerous place.

Leaving Hetty and Eileen with the Grants in their house on the hills above Roseau, she took the packet for Jamaica a week later – and then the Royal Mail Steamship *Orion* from Kingston to Liverpool. And with her she took the Prince's letters.

Ten days later, crossing direct from Liverpool to Dublin, she arrived without warning at Summer Hill, taking old Newman's hackney trap from Thomastown station, trotting up the long drive, the trees in the demesne still bare, the land cold and uninviting.

But the great house when she saw it at the top of the rise – with its long façade of tall windows reflecting the soft spring light – seemed to her full of warm promise. Sheltered by its necklace of old trees, it ran along just below the crest of the hill, formidable and serene as ever – surveying, dominating the valley, all unsuspecting, as Frances approached it, an army of one, about to ambush it. It lay there for her, waiting to be taken, the ultimate prize of her life.

Disturbed by the trap, the rooks threw themselves into the pearl-grey sky – wheeling in great cawing flocks above the chimney stacks: the sound of Summer Hill, so that Frances knew she had come home – to this house that would be hers. She would make sure of that this time. Surviving every setback in the long years of exile, she was more than hardened by adversity now: she was lightheaded, intoxicated with confidence. After all she had suffered, her mother would no longer prove any match for her.

'Yes, Mama – *publish* the Prince's letters, in full, in America. I have already hinted of it to the press there: they will be snapped up. That is my intention, if you deny me the house.'

'Really, you are pathetic – of unsound mind. You should seek medical treatment.'

Lady Cordiner, to begin with, had been sardonically dismissive – dealing, as she thought initially, with a dazed and damaged child who offered no threat. She remained unconcerned, sitting quietly at the desk in her boudoir. 'Your proposals – your threats – can have no source other than in some acute mental derangement.' She turned then, raised her pince-nez, inspecting Frances as though studying some medical curiosity.

'I should say the same of you, Mama – with your monstrous behaviour over the years.' Frances spoke with equal sober irony. 'But we must face facts here: we are neither of us the slightest bit weak in the head. Just the opposite. We both weigh things most carefully, mean exactly what we say – as I mean what I have just told you. Every word of it.'

'Then you are criminally insane – and may expect soon to be confined in an institution for such people.' Lady Cordiner dropped her pince-nez. 'Now, if you will please leave. I, at least, have many real and pressing concerns.' She resumed her correspondence.

Frances noticed the array of black-bordered condolence cards on the mantel-piece: from the Aberdeens, the Ormondes, the Devonshires – with a similar collection of mournful letters lying on top of her desk: society everywhere offering sympathy in Sir Desmond's demise, letters which Lady Cordiner was still acknowl-edging over a month after his death.

Frances, deciding it was time to engage her mother more actively, saw her opportunity here. She picked up the card from the Viceroy, Lord Aberdeen, and his wife, headed by a gilt crown surmounting the simple copperplate legend 'Dublin Castle', and held it out to Lady Cordiner like a writ.

'I have to tell you,' she said much less blandly, a cold command in her voice, 'if you refuse to take any note of the Prince's letters, how all your treasured associations here, at the Castle' – she tapped the card – 'with the King's meddlesome Viceroy, and with all your other aristocratic friends, will cease immediately. If these letters from the King are published you will be *dead* socially. Quite dead. You have only to read them, just one, to see what I mean.'

Lady Cordiner, unable to resist this bait now and feeling a secret alarm for the first time, rose from her desk, drew herself up on her small feet with immense scorn. 'You threaten me!'

'I do, believe me –'

'But it is *you* who are, and will remain, the complete social pariah. Not I. You have quite lost your senses. As if I should want to see those letters! – or be reminded in any way of your squalid *affaire*, which remains utterly repugnant to me.'

But Frances, in so graphically offering this threat of social extinction, and thus getting her mother to her feet, knew she had struck a most raw nerve. She returned to the theme and proceeded to open the wound, picking up the other cards on the mantelpiece. 'The Ormondes, the Waterfords, the Devonshires, Clanricardes, de Vescis . . .' She shuffled through the black-bordered missives, offering each one up as a harbinger of quite another doom for her mother. 'You will never show your face again – at the Castle, Curraghmore, Mount Juliet, Jenkinstown . . . No more Court levées, society luncheons, dinners, *soirées musicales* or tennis parties on the lawn. They will all be forbidden you! Every one . . .'

Frances, her voice cruel with opulent suggestiveness, and reversing the earlier roles – playing nanny to a recalcitrant child now – taunted her mother with this horrifying vision, this exile from Eden. 'Why, given the quite misguided royalist sentiment generally here in this county, most of the local tradesmen will boycott you. You will lose all face – even with your grocer and coal merchant!'

Lady Cordiner, like a rabbit smelling the ferret for the first time, became roused now, genuinely alarmed. She decided to retreat – in strength. Her satin widow's weeds rustling over the floor, she opened the door and moved briskly out into the heavily-draped drawing room which, together with the rest of the house, was still festooned in black crêpe and other grim evidence of her traditionally exaggerated mourning.

Frances, seeing this exit, the predatory animal now sensing blood, took a first point in the contest: she had goaded her prey from its secure lair. She would pursue the attack – from room to room throughout the house if needs be: follow her mother to the kill. She left the boudoir swiftly, snapping at her mother's heels, as it were.

Lady Cordiner, hearing her steps so close behind, turned half-way across the drawing room and rounded on her, renewing her own response, which was to counter attack, choosing this as her best means of defence, pince-nez dancing over her bosom, her face colouring, voice rising, as the whole pace of their exchange increased subtly.

'You will desist from following me!' She almost shouted, thus confirming that battle was joined, that she was no longer dealing with a harmless idiot, and so Frances won another advantage: she had at last forced her mother to admit the reality of her threat. 'I have no wish to see your sluttish correspondence,' Lady Cordiner continued. 'Or you, which is more to the point. How dare you come here! You are not wanted. I have not the slightest intention of collaborating in your evil schemes – nor the least interest in you or your bastard child. And that you should so presume this house as yours and attempt to blackmail me in the matter – well, it is simply laughable, insane! You will leave at once – now, today, this instant. I shall have you forcibly ejected.'

While her mother stormed on, Frances had been slowly and menacingly approaching her, so that now only a few feet separated the two women. Finally they met eye to eye, in silence, as Lady Cordiner's tirade eventually died.

'Do you think I care in the slightest what you think of me? Or Henrietta – or my actions?' Frances said evenly, but weighing each word with ominous intent. 'The issue is quite other: what will you think – and *do* – when these are published?' She brought out one of the Prince's letters which she had been carrying with her, dangling it provocatively beneath her mother's nose.

Lady Cordiner snatched the letter and tore it into shreds. 'There! – that's what I think of your letters. And let that be an end to it. Now you must leave.'

Frances smiled with happy condescension. 'You have simply destroyed a copy of the letter, Mama – not the original. You cannot think me so foolish as to –'

'Wicked, not foolish. Your idiocy is something entirely malign.' Lady Cordiner pushed her aside then, making for the bell pull by the fireplace, tugging it vigorously.

'If you wish to conduct our business in front of the servants, I am *quite* willing,' Frances taunted her once more.

Her mother turned, her great dark eyes ablaze now beneath a cowl of starkly-greying hair. 'We have *no* business to discuss.'

'Oh, but we have! Your future – and mine: this house.'

Frances looked round the shrouded drawing room – and beyond that, her eyes lifting, she seemed to stare through the walls, the ceiling, her gaze roaming and encapsulating the whole vast building and estate beyond.

The two women glared savagely at each other, both openly acknowledging the real nature of their battle now. The issue, which had been avoided or denied between them until then, was at last brutally clear: the prize they fought for was not the Viceroy's or society's good opinion, but the house itself – the ultimate resource, the fountainhead of both their lives. Victory lay in its simple possession – and whoever lost would lose everything. Now, both recognising this, their battle became the more desperate – no longer concerned with mere social, but with literal, survival.

A footman had arrived in the room and Lady Cordiner, unwilling to take up her daughter's challenge in front of him, pushed past her, past the servant, leaving the drawing room, almost running now.

Frances, matching her pace, pursued her into the hall. 'If you refuse to discuss it – so much the worse for you,' she called to her across the echoing, pillared space.

There was silence, before the grandfather clock chimed the hour of noon – twelve imperious, doom-touched notes – as her mother, undecided for a moment, hovered at the foot of the great staircase. Two housemaids, polishing the landing balustrade high above them, observed her down the stairwell. Lady Cordiner, seeing her way blocked there, herself turned sharply, making for the privacy of the dining room. Frances tracked her quickly once more, the pace increasing as the two women scurried across the wide hall.

Her mother, she thought, was mistaken in seeking this as a sanctuary, for the dining room, apart from a passageway leading to the pantries and the kitchens, had only one entrance – and Frances shut this now, closing on Lady Cordiner again as she made for the green baize servants' door at the other end of the room. 'Of course! – we may continue our conversation in front of Mrs Molloy and all the kitchen maids!' she shouted after her.

Lady Cordiner, ever aware of the domestic proprieties, hesitated again and turned. A small, frail figure now, she felt a spasm of fear as she watched her daughter take up a commanding position at the other end of the long table – a fear which, though she remained outwardly calm, prompted her to move and take up refuge by the great Victorian Gothic sideboard with its collection of silver-topped meat dishes and carving implements. She glanced at the bone-handled cutlery here, drawing confidence from the sharp instruments, before turning and facing her daughter.

'I must tell you,' she said, puffing herself up, renewing the attack, taking further strength from the vast piece of furniture which formed a rampart behind her. 'If you continue to follow and badger me in this matter, I shall take steps – forcible steps . . .' Her voice rose in angry tremeloes, her lower lip trembling.

But Frances mocked her. 'I am not afraid of you, Mama – never have been. Which, of course, is what you cannot bear in me. I alone, among all the family, you were unable to hurt or dominate in your long reign of terror here. Though you tried hard enough –'

'What ravings!'

'With that swing on the maple over the croquet court. Remember? Knowing, as a child, how much I loved it, you had it cut down –'

'You were not a child then – merely a spiteful, difficult, ungrateful young woman –'

'And before that, my dappled grey pony you sold –'

'You were too grown for it –'

'And the dances you forbade me at Kilkenny Castle –'

'You were not asked, far too young.'

'I was a young woman then, you have just said.'

'Yes, a thieving young woman, stealing my little objets d'art all over the house: nothing but a common thief!'

Frances paused, disturbed by this reminder, and her mother, sensing the advantage, counter-attacked vigorously. 'Do you think I would give this house over to such a person? Why, you would have the place cleared with the auctioneers within a month!' Lady Cordiner, pressing her attack, advanced a few feet towards Frances. 'You,' she said with deep scorn, 'you are no fit person to run a hovel, let alone a great house and estate like this. You have not the slighest household knowledge, nor business acumen. And, besides, have you not thought? – without me, there would not be a penny to *run* the place! The estate was near bankruptcy when I married your father: all the capital in it now is mine – which, of course, is why he left it to me to dispose of at my discretion. And be assured – that discretion will never favour you! So you see, quite apart from me, your plan to take over Summer Hill is entirely illusory: you would not have a penny to maintain it.'

'I am not concerned with your money. You forget, I have been left rather well off myself: enough, certainly, to continue things appropriately here – if not in the vulgar, ostentatious manner you have always promoted in the house.'

Lady Cordiner, badly pricked by this comment, was furious. 'You – you despicable little hussy. You harlot!'

Frances laughed. Yet she, too, was almost losing control, speaking with stark emotion now. 'Harlot? – there is life to that, at least. You have always been death to this place: a *monster* of cruelty, selfishness – to all of us. The others have gone now, and you had so much to do with their going. But you will not get rid of me so easily.'

'You venomous little . . . bitch!'

Their engagement had reached a crescendo – the two women revelling in their mutual hatred, sustained by an oxygen of pure joy in expressing it, taking an almost delirious pleasure in the wounds they caused, in the other's pain – concentrating all their years of enmity in this final confrontation: feeding their malice, letting it bloom and grow as an evil flower, adorning it with every lethal barb. They were, for long moments then – quite forgetting the real cause of their battle – both wonderfully fulfilled and happy.

It was Frances, taking a grip on herself, who brought things down to earth. She sighed, unwilling to relinquish the heady joy of this character assassination, then said, 'This takes us nowhere. Let us concentrate on the real issues. Blackmail? You may regard it as such – but that is irrelevant. The letters? You refuse to look at them. Very well then, you should simply take my word for it: they are revealing and indiscreet to a degree – there is no doubt of that. The Prince is now the King-Emperor. Their publication would cause a major constitutional and political scandal – perhaps even his abdication. I should not be affected. I have no connection with society here – I should simply return to Domenica, or go to America and start a new life. You, on the other hand, will hardly be able to show your face again in public, let alone in society –'

'You would not do such a thing?' Lady Cordiner cried out, seeming to command Frances, unaware of the alarm in her voice, or how her questioning words contradicted her imperious intent. 'The disgrace –'

'Exactly! But it would fall entirely on you, not me –'

'And the whole family.' Lady Cordiner glanced at the Cordiner ancestral portraits hanging round the dining room walls, Frances following her gaze.

'Indeed. I realise that. But then that is the whole point of my business here: exactly that – the family! And its preservation. My father, my two brothers, are all dead. Hetty and I are now the family, *my* family, not yours – and so my wish to inherit what rightfully belongs to me and ensure the continuation of the line, the house itself. And you deny me that right, my birthright –'

'I deny it to a slattern, to a vile blackmailing hussy.'

'That, too, is quite irrelevant. We talk of blood, not character, here, Mama: *my* blood, and therefore my house and Hetty's, not yours, or Austin's and Bunty's. It's all quite simple. There is nothing improper in my demand. I am merely forced, given your spiteful, wicked intransigence, to consider extreme measures in obtaining satisfaction.' Frances left the table and approached her mother slowly. 'And, believe me, I will take those measures – be in no doubt of that. I have nothing to lose. You have everything: your whole life here – and everwhere else for that matter.'

Lady Cordiner considered things. She still refused to believe that Frances would take the action she had promised. She decided to call her bluff. 'Very well then,' she told her grandly. 'Do what you will with your squalid letters. Publish them! You do not intimidate me. I shall not be blackmailed – I shall take the consequences.' She glared arrogantly at her daughter, who remained silent for a long moment, so that Lady Cordiner, for the first time, sensed the possibility of victory.

But Frances had prepared herself for just such a response from her mother. 'Very well, then – I shall take the mail boat for London this evening. The letters will be in the hands of the *New York Post*'s American correspondent there by this time tomorrow.' She turned abruptly, opened the door, leaving it wide open as she marched with ringing steps across the hall. Lady Cordiner remained, motionless at the end of the long table, fingering her pince-nez – suddenly aware how isolated and vulnerable she was, alone in the great room, surrounded only by the dismissive faces in the Cordiner family portraits, staring down all round her, seeming to laugh or glower at her: as an interloper finally repulsed.

Then, after half a minute, she started to scream.

Her face convulsed. She bit her lips. She yelled. She threw a pettish fit, which rapidly became real as she added to the invention – embroidering it, feeding, stoking it, with every sort of real and imagined persecution: fanning the flames of her outrage and defeat, so that very soon she was possessed by a genuine mania, gripped by an overwhelming, teeth-grinding energy, in which all her malice and repressed unhappiness was translated into vicious physical action.

She threw herself across the heavily-draped dining table, clutching at the dark serge there – tugging, pulling the cloth towards her, so that the two candelabra at the centre crashed to the floor, and she with them, ending up half-covered in the material, writhing about, folding herself in it, then rolling out of it.

She stood up, her pince-nez broken, hair dishevelled and started to sway about the room, resuming her piercing wails and shrieks as she moved towards the sideboard. She picked up one of the long carving knives.

Frances had returned to the room, followed almost immediately by Pat Kennedy, now head butler at Summer Hill, and by one of the footmen. Grouped together at the doorway, they watched amazed as Lady Cordiner flourished the knife.

From the other entrance – the green baize door leading to the kitchens – Mrs Molloy and two kitchen maids had emerged timidly – looking on with fear and astonishment as Lady Cordiner moved towards Frances. She had stopped her screaming now. Instead she had a much more direct and obvious intent – to attack her daughter.

'You!' she shouted. 'This time – too far! A thorn in my side – too long, too long!' She advanced, holding the knife awkwardly, clutching it downwards in her fist, like a dagger.

'Stand back, Miss Frances!' Pat Kennedy warned, taking up one of the heavy dining room chairs and using it as a protective screen, prodding the air with it like a bull fighter with a cape, as Lady Cordiner moved inexorably forward. 'Michael!' he shouted to the footman. 'The table cloth – get hold of it, get behind her Ladyship – quick, man!'

The footman, circling round the other side of the long table, picked up the vast serge cloth, and attempted to manipulate it as a sort of net to trap this wild woman. But the material was far too cumbersome. Instead it enveloped him completely, blinding him as he staggered forward with it, nearly tripping in its folds.

Pat Kennedy meanwhile, advancing slowly with the chair, hoped to pin Lady Cordiner between its legs against the sideboard or the wall.

Frances suddenly smiled. Her victory was nearly complete. The situation was comic. She touched Pat Kennedy's arm, pushing him gently aside. 'Let her be,' she told him. 'Let her face me.'

'But, Miss Frances –'

'No – it is all quite undignified. Put the chair down, Pat. It's all an act – can't you see? She is simply pretending.'

Pat Kennedy set the chair down and Frances moved in front of him, to stand facing her mother. There was complete silence in the big room.

'Mama, you know well – this is no answer.' She spoke firmly to her mother, but softly, a sad nanny to her once more. 'Hand me the knife.'

In these last moments of the contest Frances never let her gaze stray a fraction from her mother's eyes – holding her fixedly, hypnotically, letting her own sense of superior power and impending victory pour into the other woman, willing her to hand over the knife.

But her mother, having gone thus far, was determined on one last flourish. Turning quickly to the wall behind her, and using the knife as a flailing scythe, she proceeded to cut and slash at the Cordiner family portraits, reaching for the first one, the canvas ripping as Sir William Cordiner took the brunt of her attack.

'There!' she cried as she criss-crossed the elegant Georgian painting, shredding the bewigged and dignified old face. 'I think *that* of you and your family! That I should ever have become involved with them. Take them! Take everything to do with your wretched family.'

She slashed again, cutting deep down Sir William's blue and gold-braided tunic, then running a line round his wrist, so that his tattered remains fell from the frame. 'I want *nothing* to do with you or them – or with anything else in this vile, ignorant, godforsaken country. Good riddance to you and your feckless, spendthrift family – whom *I* saved, *my* family, with our money. Without me this place would have gone years ago.'

She paused in her mayhem, turning to Frances. 'Well, you can have the house now. I will leave. But remember one thing: you will have it without a penny of mine. And remember something else – the house remains in *my* possession. I may dispose of it as I want – now or when I am gone. And you will not have it, nor your child, nor any other Cordiner. I spit on you – I spit on your family!'

She turned back then and had moved onto the next portrait with the knife, before Pat Kennedy, with the footman, managed to overpower her – though she struggled to the end, falling over and twisting her leg painfully before she surrendered.

Frances took her victory gracelessly. 'Get a chair. Carry her up to her bedroom and stay there until the doctor arrives.' She spoke to Mrs Martin, the housekeeper – commanding her, already assuming the role of mistress in Summer Hill.

Lady Cordiner, slumped in one of the long chairs from the porch, a liveried footman at either end, was manoeuvred out of the room with ignominious ceremony – Frances observing the little ambulance procession with unconcealed satisfaction.

Later, when old Mitchell, the family doctor, had visited, he came downstairs. Frances interviewed him in the drawing room.

'Your mother,' he began diffidently, in his soft, slight Cork brogue, 'she appears . . . she's very disturbed.'

'I am not surprised. She has behaved most foolishly – dangerously.'

'But, apart from the leg, nothing really wrong with her.'

'She is mad, Dr Mitchell.'

'Ah, now, I wouldn't go that far, no. But I've given her a sedative – Frances.' He tried to get on more familiar terms with this cold and harsh woman. 'But I wonder – if you mightn't go a bit easier with her, making things up in some way? She's taken a lot of bad knocks recently.'

'Doctor!' Frances was impatient now, bunching her fingers together, making fists of them. 'She attacked me, intent to murder me – with a knife!'

'Ah yes, well . . .' He hesitated. 'A formidable and difficult old lady, I'll grant you that. But she . . . she meant no harm.'

'Meant no harm? She might have killed us all, besides destroying half the dining room! She has obviously lost her wits completely – is a danger to herself and others. She must have treatment, be confined somewhere. She cannot be left alone for an instant.' Frances harangued the man now.

'Oh no, dear me, no – I don't think it's anywhere near as serious as that. A few days, a week's rest upstairs here and she'll be right as rain. And perhaps . . .' He took out his pipe, tapping the bowl easily. 'Maybe you could spend a bit of time up in Dublin meanwhile.' He smiled, hoping to initiate a mild conspiracy between them. 'You know what I mean. Take the pressure off her, allow her to recover.'

Frances rounded on him. 'Dr Mitchell, you don't understand. It is my *mother* who will be leaving here – not I.'

'No.' He was startled. 'No, I don't think I follow you there.'

'Yes, indeed. She is leaving Summer Hill – permanently. She confirmed as much, in front of witnesses.'

'Ah, now!' The doctor was almost jocular in his alarm. 'I'm sure she didn't mean a word of it.' He laughed uneasily. 'Not a word of it! Give her a week or two by herself and she'll be right as rain –'

'But *I* mean that she leaves here – and will ensure she does.'

'But, Frances –' Dr Mitchell was thoroughly put about now.

'There is no point in discussing it. Did you imagine that I returned home – all this way from the West Indies – merely to temporise with my mother once more? We have come to an agreement: she has disowned me, this house, all the Cordiners – in front of everybody. Therefore it's all perfectly clear: I, as rightful heir, now assume control of Summer Hill.'

The doctor puzzled over this legalistic statement for a moment. 'Forgive me, but I understood – your father and I were very old friends – that Sir Desmond had left the house and estate to your mother, to use during her lifetime and to dispose of afterwards at her discretion. Has she left you the house formally then?'

'No, not formally.'

'Then – forgive me again – I don't quite see the grounds you have? . . .'

'That will be a matter for the solicitors. But there are obvious grounds already: "unsound mind", Dr Mitchell.'

'Ah, now, Frances, that's going a bit too far altogether. As her physician I couldn't really support you in that theory. Simply a temporary lapse. As I said, she'll be right as rain in a week or so. You'll see!'

'I have no wish to see, Dr Mitchell – nor to seek your advice or support in the matter. Lady Cordiner will leave here at the soonest opportunity. You may depend on it.'

The doctor departed shortly afterwards. And Frances, alone in the great room, the light waning beyond the shrouded windows, considered her position. Of course, the doctor was right: her grounds were insecure. He had, in fact, simply confirmed the flaw in her victory, the real threat in her mother's last words to her. She might possess the house for the moment. But it was a quite impermanent possession. Lady Cordiner, legally, still retained absolute and final control of its destiny.

As well, given the possible stipulations in her father's will, Lady Cordiner might – when she regained her senses and with a good lawyer – have her evicted from Summer Hill, almost at once or at some point in the future when, with the King dead, his letters would no longer form the threat to Lady Cordiner which they did at present.

Thinking of all this, Frances realised how precarious her position was. She had merely won a battle, not the war. She must, she saw, take steps at once to secure the position. Before her mother left Summer Hill, she would have to change her will – would, of course, have to be forced to do so. Frances considered possible means to this end.

She would have to confront her mother again in any case – make out a codicil for her to sign, there and then. Going into Lady Cordiner's boudoir, Frances set to work immediately, preparing just such a document in which, apart from her mother's possessions and capital, all of Summer Hill and its estate were to be left to her, and any previous legacy made of the property be revoked.

That same evening she took the document upstairs. Her mother, sullen-faced, in a night cap and heavily shawled, lay propped up in the great four-poster bed, the curtains drawn, a lamp burning on a table, another by her bedside. Bridey, her maid, was sitting nearby. There was a fuggy air of sal volatile and paraffin in the room.

'Bridey, if you will leave us please. I shall stay here for the moment.'

Her mother barely noticed her, glancing in her direction then turning away. Frances presented her with the codicil. 'Mama, you will please read – and sign – this.' The old lady did nothing, continuing to gaze sideways at the lamp, allowing the paper to fall unregarded on the counterpane. 'It sets out the new arrangements over the house – a codicil to your will.'

Lady Cordiner made no response whatsoever, maintaining her steady gaze at the red lampshade, as if at some nirvana, the rays of light casting an orange glow over her sour features. Frances became impatient. 'It will do you no good – this dog-in-the-manger attitude. I have prepared a perfectly fair document, in which you retain all your possessions and capital here, but where I become the legal owner of the house, now and in the future. I have no intention of allowing you to hold a sword of Damocles over me in the matter. You will sign this – or else, as I promised yesterday, I will publish those letters, without hesitation.'

Lady Cordiner finally turned and looked at Frances. She laughed drily. She cackled. She spluttered and coughed in her glee. But still, as she ignored the paper on her bed, there was no word from her. Frances played another card.

'Of course, if you refuse to sign – and quite apart from the Prince's letters – you will lose all control of the house in any case. Your behaviour this morning, in front of everyone, makes that perfectly obvious: unsound mind – a danger to yourself and everyone else. You will be confined in an institution in Dublin. I shall see to it. I have already spoken to Dr Mitchell.'

Lady Cordiner laughed again – a full, entirely sane laugh, followed by a most satisfied smile. The siege appeared to have failed – and her mother revelled in the victory, relishing it now in continued silence.

Frances stood by the bed, considering the impasse for a moment. Then, deciding upon something, she moved abruptly to the door, locked it, turned and confronted her mother.

'Very well then, if you refuse to sign, we shall neither of us have the house.'

She walked swiftly forward to the mahogany drum table in the centre of the room, lifted the globe from the second lamp there, turned the wick down, extinguished the flame, removed the glass funnel and then unscrewed the cap from the oil reservoir.

Holding the pedestal, she approached her mother, then tipped the lamp over, letting the oil fall on the carpet, making a circle with the paraffin right round the great bed. She spoke calmly as she went.

'You still have a chance to sign – or see this house burnt.'

Now at last, understanding how Frances's intention was that she, as well as the house, should burn, her mother spoke. 'Don't be stupid! What folly are you up to?' She struggled to get out of bed. But her twisted leg prevented her. 'How dare you!' she shouted impotently. 'You will ruin the carpet. Bridey?' she shouted, floundering about. 'Bridey!'

'Bridey has gone down to the kitchen for her supper. No one will hear you.'

Lady Cordiner stretched an arm out then, reaching for the long tasselled bell rope hanging above her bedside table. Frances removed it, pulling the cord right away from her and tucking the end behind a picture on the wall. Then she moved back to the table, picking up a box of matches, rattling them ominously.

'You wouldn't dare!' her mother advised her scornfully.

'I would – I *will*.'

Lady Cordiner, though still in control of herself, was alarmed now. 'Why, you think to murder me! – you imagine you would get away with that?' she scoffed.

'Not at all, Mama. Simply the house will burn down around you. An accident, with the lamp here. You were trying to leave your bed, it fell on the floor. With your leg you were unable to reach the door. I shall have left the room by then. I shall try and save you, of course. We shall all try and save you. But we will be too late.'

Frances struck a match then, allowing it to flare brightly. Then she blew it out. 'Well, what do you say?'

Her mother struggled up in the bed once more, but again could not summon the strength to leave it. 'I forbid you!' she shouted.

'You are quite past forbidding me anything. If you value your life, you have only one course of action open: sign that document – and I shall then have your signature witnessed.'

Calling her daughter's bluff once more, Lady Cordiner still resisted. 'No – never!'

Frances moved forward calmly, bent down, lit a second match and set it to the trail of oil on the carpet. It took several moments to catch and then only slowly. But soon, gathering appetite, the flame licked along the path, running like a fuse, turning the corners of the bed neatly and speeding up the far side, so that within a minute Lady Cordiner and the great four-poster were held in a circle of hungry fire.

Frances calmly watched the flames rise, seeing her mother's agonised features now beyond the smoky pall – the great eyes wide, her face alive with impotent fear. Lady Cordiner screamed. But, with wafts of acrid smoke blowing towards her, the screams soon stopped and she began to cough and choke.

Then, and only then, did she capitulate. 'Yes!' she cried out finally. 'Yes!'

Frances seized the big water jug from its bowl on the wash-stand, doused the flames with it, before stamping them out all round the bed. Then, retrieving the codicil from a fold in the eiderdown, she took it to her mother, together with a pen she had brought upstairs with her.

'You will live to regret this,' her mother told her bitterly, as she signed. 'Every single thing you have done here today. I promise you that.'

Frances, taking the document, leant forward then, peering coldly into her mother's eyes, shaking her head slowly. 'You obstinate old woman,' she told her quietly. 'Will you never learn? It was the way you always *threatened* us in the old days – even by your simple presence – that made us hate you. And *still* you do it!'

Lady Cordiner seemed about to embark on another tirade. 'I shall inform the police – how you extorted this signature from me, attempted to murder me.'

'After your insane performance in the dining room today, they will not believe you. Besides, remember the Prince's letters. If you attempt to make any more trouble, I will have them published. As I've said, the scandal will not affect me. I have no wish to hobnob with society here – just the opposite: I want the British Crown out of Ireland, as soon as possible. That lackey the Viceroy, people like you and all your cronies – all the years of misrule: you in this house and the others up at Dublin Castle. Your time is over in Ireland. So why jeopardise your future in England? – where I imagine you will now return. A house in London or Brighton? A pleasant retirement . . . Why not? You have many friends over there already. But there is no doubt they would all cut you dead if one word of this royal scandal emerged. So my advice to you is that you say nothing of all this' – she glanced round the smoky room – '*ever*. If you hold to that, I shall do likewise: no mention that the King is Henrietta's father, ever, not even to Hetty herself. Your social prospects will remain intact thereby. But if you think to prolong this battle – in *any* way, now or in the future – you will condemn yourself to a lonely and miserable old age.'

Lady Cordiner, still brooding and malevolent, said nothing. But it was clear from her silence, from the look of resignation in her tired, bloodshot eyes, that she was considering her assent to all this, that she thought – soberly now – to cut her losses, be done with the whole affair, and leave Ireland for just such a pleasant retirement.

Frances, in any case, took her silence for agreement, turning then, unhitching the bell pull from the picture and tugging at it vigorously. Then she went over and unlocked the bedroom door before facing her mother once more.

'So! We have an agreement – at last . . .'

Her mother still could not bring herself to say yes. But for Frances the message was now entirely clear: Summer Hill was hers. All the years of thwarted desire and waiting were over. She had come into her inheritance at last. And it was like a marriage for her just then, standing at the threshold by the doorway, a bride at the altar of the house; she would now enter it – all the other rooms, from attics to cellars and the land about – possessing it, being possessed by it; now and always, hers.

'*Mine*,' Frances said simply, opening the bedroom door wide, letting the air into the smoky room, going across and opening the window then, so that a soft evening breeze filled the murky space, a mix of turf smoke and sweet wind running off the moist river valley: renewed life, fresh life, a hint of all the different life to come to this beautiful house which for so long had remained sealed and dumb, asleep, caught in the briar-like toils spun by the old witch who lay defeated in the great bed now. Frances, at last penetrating the evil thorns, had broken the spell, would now – just as she had promised so long ago – kiss Summer Hill back to life.

Two thousand miles away, in the humid air lying just above the warm waters of the Caribbean, another less benevolent wind was taking shape.

At first there seemed little to it. The over-heated air, spiralling lazily upwards, cooled and condensed rapidly, so that, high over the ocean, clouds formed and some rain fell.

But soon more and warmer air, great swathes of it, was sucked into the updraught, reinforcing and enlarging it, creating vicious eddies and a sudden drop in the air pressure. The phenomenon, like an evil genie released from a bottle, took a first hesitant shape – an uncertain brew of wind, heat, motion and energy – until all these forces coalesced, sustaining, provoking each other furiously, rising up and darkening the whole atmosphere, where the cloudy commotion showed its true colours as a hurricane.

The funnel of air became a whirling cauldron, filled with sea birds trapped in the eerie calm at the centre, widening out and spiralling up, fed by violent winds now, forming waterspouts over the tossing ocean: a billowing monster, erupting, climbing, an implacable engine of destruction which finally – establishing itself as an immense black pillar over the ocean, surrounded by a coliseum of clouds – moved towards the first of the Caribbean islands, Domenica, which lay directly in its path.

The sea in the bay beyond Roseau became strangly quiet, the air unnaturally calm. The waves changed their pattern, retreating from the shoreline, and then lapping on the shingle beaches only three or four times a minute now, as if fatally weakened by some great force pulling them in the opposite direction far out to sea.

In the hall of the tin-roofed Carnegie Library on the sea-front the barometer fell astonishingly. But Miss Oliphant, the librarian, chatting softly of the new Galsworthy novel to Mildred Grant by her desk, failed to notice it.

At Fort Young, behind the bandstand in Marine Gardens, the sentry on duty between the two great cannon felt his ears pop, but took no account of it. He yawned and swallowed several times, wiped the sweat from his brow, and remained surprised only by the complete silence in the air, even when he had cleared his ears. He looked over the parapet, noticing how the waves had receded, far below their usual level, half-way down the moist shingle, exposing a collection of old boots and beer bottles. But it was his first tour in the West Indies and he thought little of it.

Further along the seafront though, at the bar of the Club by the Botanical Gardens, just before lunch, one of the older members, gulping the last of his whisky, remarked to Bertie Grant how he tasted blood in his mouth and Bertie commented how his eardrums had begun to sing. At the same moment the two men, both old-timers on the island, realised the cause of their discomfiture – and joined by the other members, all making for the terrace, they saw the first of the great waves, riding ahead of the storm, travelling in a wide semi-circle round the small bay, heading straight towards them. And, beyond the wave, they saw the huge swirling bar of cloud, rapidly obscuring all the light, a heavy black wall closing in upon them like a curtain of doom.

The first wave sank half a dozen small boats and demolished part of the wooden jetty down by the port at the end of Main Street: a small wave. The others, roaring in behind it, were five and ten yards high, vast hills of tidal water. They crashed all along the shore line, destroying the rest of the jetty, capsizing a big sloop moored there, wrecking the terrace and seafront windows of the Carnegie Library, and riding in colossal drifts of spume right up to the top of the ramparts of Fort Young.

Then, the great funnelling cloud closing on the little town, the rain came in vicious squalls, the water falling with the force of hailstones – to be followed at last by the demon king in the storm: an unbelievably venomous wind, that hit Roseau like thunder, a successive slapping of vast hands which altered everything, where the earlier waves and the rain had been mere pinpricks; a circling, thrusting, implacable, devious wind – lifting the roofs, seeking out and laying bare every secret place, toying with everything before destroying it.

Establishing itself with a noise like the manic rattle of hundreds of engines rushing through a tunnel, the wind began to suck the town up, a famished beast leaving the barren ocean, feeding voraciously now for the first time on dry land – gorging, making a single mouthful of whole warehouses, villas, the Anglican church on the hill.

The hurricane, settling to its meal, and having strolled before, now started to gallop through the streets, swallowing everything. Houses were picked up, suspended in mid-air, inspected for a moment, then digested, disintegrating, the bones spat out hundreds of yards away.

The church spire disappeared like an arrow northwards, shooting out over the bay. The great *châtaignier* tree in the Botanical Gardens keeled over, all its roots free above the ground, before it rolled down the emerald lawn, pulverising the shrubs and flower borders, and killing a number of unfortunate people unable to escape its path.

Then, as the eye of the hurricane passed directly over the town, in the airless heart of the storm, the pressure fell to zero and there was a sinister calm in which another sort of destruction bloomed. The better stone houses, with firm walls, windows and foundations, built to resist just such a wind, seemed to explode.

The walls and glazing of the telegraph office in Brunswick Street, unable to cope with the enormous difference in air pressure, simply burst apart like rotten fruit. The chickens in the compound behind the post office in Hanover Street, caught in the same airless funnel, expanded like balloons before detonating – the air sealed in the quills of their feathers released now like machine gun shots.

At its circumference – in the whirling circle of sharp rock, shingle, brick, pieces of wood and mud – people were caught up: beheaded, torn apart, maimed, carried aloft; stripped of their clothing before being thrown out of the murderous carousel, naked, encrusted with sticky dirt – riddled, as if by gun-fire, with stones, nails, splinters.

In the Carnegie Library, Mildred Grant, with Miss Oliphant and a few others caught there, all took shelter between the interior walls of Miss Oliphant's small office, huddling between stacks of new books and fresh copies of the *Sphere* and *Illustrated London News*. But, when the wind got beneath the eaves of the corrugated roof, gripping it boldly from one end and tearing it back like the lid of a sardine tin, they found themselves crammed together like fish, taking the brunt of the weather on their heads.

Mildred never saw the great iron rafter which, released from one side of the roof, fell towards her, spearing her from behind, striking her in the back, beneath the neat bun in her wispy hair. Miss Oliphant screamed, seeing her friend impaled, like a butterfly in a collection case, secured by a pin.

At the Club they tried forcibly to restrain Bertie Grant from leaving the building, where those members who had not escaped immediately were now taking shelter in the cellar stores beneath the bar.

'Don't be a damn fool, man! Milly will be perfectly safe – the library is well made of stone. Stay where you are!'

But, his absentmindedness forgotten and overcome by a sort of guilty panic, Bertie insisted, struggling free and running up the cellar steps.

Behind the bar, bottles shook and broke – while in the dining room next-door plates and cutlery flew off the tables, taken by a fierce wind from the broken windows, as if the whole Club was a ship at sea about to founder.

Bertie ran out into the choking, dust-filled air of the Botanical Gardens. The *châtaignier* tree had rolled down the lawn, coming to a stop near the gates. Beyond them he saw the roof ripped off the library. He quickened his pace. He ran with wonderful speed, taken by the wind pushing him forwards, the long jacket tails of his white tropical suit swirling above his head. But the tree completely barred his exit from the gardens. Beneath it, as he approached, he saw the body of one of the Club staff, the Goanese cook, just the legs sticking out, the rest of the man invisible.

Deciding to conquer the obstacle, and sheltered against the bole of the tree for a moment now, he scrambled up on to its trunk – the wind helping him again, like a comrade. But, once he was on top of the smooth bole, crouching, beginning to stand, quite clear of any shelter and taking the full force of the storm, the wind behind turned traitor and in a sudden burst of energy picked him up like a doll.

Caught by the terrible wind, he sailed straight off the tree trunk, white tails flying, arms outstretched, a dozen feet off the ground, like a bizarre angel – out over the wall, high across the road and into Marine Gardens, where only a bandstand pillar prevented him from disappearing out to sea.

He lay there, half-naked, eyes and nostrils filled with mud, impaled everywhere with sharp debris – spreadeagled on the bandstand platform, where still the wind nudged and pushed him, sliding him across the tiles, moving his broken limbs about as if there was still some life in him.

The hurricane, continuing its feast, contented itself with the rich pickings of the town, avoiding the interior, moving slowly north now along the coast towards the top of the island.

High up, four miles away in the hills above Roseau in the Grants' house at Lime Hill, Hetty with Robert, Eileen and the other servants watched the hurricane move over the town far beneath them – a great tormented cloud, obscuring everything, raging along; at Lime Hill, though the air was dark and turbulent, they had been barely touched by the storm.

'Isn't it *exciting*!' Hetty exclaimed, the wind running in her dark hair, looking over the scene from the long verandah of the house.

Eileen said nothing. The other servants were equally grim-faced.

'I hope Mama and Papa are all right, though,' Robert said, less happily. 'I so wanted her back. I've all my things to get ready, haven't I, Eileen? – for school in England. All my packing!' He turned to Hetty joyously then. 'Packing! – so yah-boo and sucks to you! *I'm* going to *school* in *England*!' he chanted. 'Mama's coming with me the day after tomorrow – and you'll be just left here on your own.'

Hetty glowered at him. 'Oh, no, I won't. *My* Mama is going to take me to Ireland soon. She's over there now seeing to it – isn't she, Elly? We're all going back – to live there in my *real* home. A much bigger place than this. And far better than your old school in England. Isn't that true, Elly? Elly's been there before – she knows all about it. It's wonderful, isn't it, Elly? As big as Buckingham Palace. So sucks to you, you stupid little brat of a colonial boy!'

The two children nearly came to blows before Eileen separated them, taking them both smartly indoors, as the storm raged on, moving away up the coast.

'I'll have no more of it,' she told them sharply. 'This fighting and squabbling. You two are going to behave yourselves and get along together – as long as I'm around and wherever you are. Yes, get along together – that's the ticket!'

She kept them apart, holding their collars, like two fighting cocks, as the children continued to look daggers at each other.

BOOK THREE

1

HIDDEN BEHIND THE curtains and sitting quite still on the window seat, alone in the great hall at Summer Hill, Hetty saw the big rat. Shiny-grey, glistening-eyed, with a long, long tail, it emerged from somewhere behind the tall stairway, frisked its whiskers an instant, seemed to gaze at her, quite unafraid, then came clear out into the open – stopping, sniffing the air, before lolloping over to the big wickerwood basket on the far side by the hall door, where it disappeared.

'Mr Rat!' Hetty said to herself in approving wonder. It wasn't half as big or wild as the rats in Domenica: a friendly Irish rat. Perhaps she might make a friend of it. She badly missed her pet iguana.

Then she heard the green baize door behind the staircase opening softly, and soft footfalls as Pat Kennedy, with the funny curls over his brow – 'kiss curls' Elly called them mockingly – came into the hall, in his dark tailcoat and trousers. Pat was the butler here – whatever that meant. He was the head servant anyway, she knew that. He put his hand in his trouser pocket now, moving quickly across the hall, glancing up the stairway, then to either side, as he neared the basket of logs. Bending down then, he sprinkled a handful of yellow corn all around the bottom of the basket, before returning, just as silently, the way he had come.

Hetty smiled. A nice man! He'd been leaving food out for Mr Rat! And sure enough, a minute later, the same great rat emerged to feed greedily on the corn. Hetty was spellbound, watching it eat – thinking of Pat's kindness: at least there was one nice man in this huge frightening house.

The rat disappeared and Hetty, emerging from behind the curtains, drew up the long hem of her muslin dress, turned and, kneeling on the window seat now, noticed the tiny pane of coloured glass in the bottom corner of the tall window. It was a picture of some great bird with its wings spread out – like one of the frigate birds in Domenica, sitting on top of a strange tin hat, with something written beneath it in funny wiggly letters: 'Audaces Fortuna Juvat'.

She mouthed the words to herself. What could they mean? It wasn't English anyway, not even the strange sort of English most people spoke here in Ireland. But the bird was interesting, with its great beak facing sideways and fierce yellow eye which gleamed brightly in the cloudy autumn sunlight from beyond the window. She thought of the frigate birds – endlessly, lazily sweeping over the bay at Fraser Hall against the huge, always-sunny blue sky. Big Jules had told her they were the spirits of dead sailors drowned at sea, looking for their old homes, their wives, families and friends. And, thinking of this and of Big Jules and Cook and Slinky the garden boy, Hetty was suddenly terribly homesick again.

She sucked her thumb fiercely, digging the other thumbnail into the little, perfectly round lime fruit which she carried about with her everywhere now, ever since she had arrived at Summer Hill a month before; then put the fruit to her nose, loving the prickly sweet and sour smell of her old home, a smell that was dying now, the skin pricked nervously all over with her nails since she had left Domenica and come to this strange, cold place.

Outside, in the racing clouds and sunshine, she saw the quick shadows running over the squares and terraces and diamond-shaped flower beds of the 'Pleasure Garden' as they called it. Though she could see no pleasure in it. She wasn't allowed to play anywhere there, among the rose bushes, the tiny little hedges, the shiny red gravel paths and the stone steps – so many stone steps – going up to a big tree whose leaves were turning a bright yellow. Next to the tree she saw the flat bit of very short grass with white hoops and a coloured pole scattered about it – a game the grown-ups played here, Elly had told her, called 'crocket'.

Beyond this was another piece of grass, the 'tennis court', with a sort of droopy fishing net spread across it. That sounded great fun, though no one had played either of these games since she'd arrived, because there weren't any family grown-ups in the house now, only her mother and the funny, straggly-haired woman, her great-aunt Emily, who wandered about the house and gardens all the time, singing nursery rhymes and laughing to herself.

Elly had told her that her great-aunt Emily was 'touched'. Touched? Who had touched her to make her like this? Elly couldn't tell her. God had touched her, Hetty supposed, and made her silly like this. But how silly of him.

Anyway, great-aunt Emily never played at these outdoor games, she simply drew and painted all the time in a big white drawing book like a child; nor did her mother, far too busy changing and 'planning' things about the house. And Robert, of course, couldn't play at all now, upstairs in bed coughing all day and night, with Elly looking after him for the past week.

She had been on her own most of the time ever since she'd arrived, hiding, running around, exploring. Anyway, these outdoor games were soon going to be put away for the winter, Elly had told her before she'd disappeared into Robert's bedroom: the 'winter', when the ice and the cold and the snow came, though it was only the start of 'autumn' now. There were four of these funny 'seasons' here, when there had only been one in Domenica.

In autumn here the leaves turned yellow and red, when they had been green before. That was what autumn was, Elly had said happily: when the fruit was ripe and the corn gathered in and squirrels and people stored everything away for the winter. They'd be cutting and threshing the corn any day now – a big steam engine was coming to do that, Elly told her, which she hadn't understood ('The same great engine that took us down from Dublin?' 'No.'). And, as for the autumn fruit at Summer Hill, well, she hadn't known what to make of that either: all the trees in the great walled vegetable garden and orchard behind it.

The fruit was extraordinary here, like nothing she'd ever seen in Domenica – small, all funny shapes and colours. It had looked poisonous to her: apples, pears, quinces, plums, damsons, medlars, they were called – and grapes in the vine house.

At first she hadn't even touched any of it, until one hot afternoon an old gardener man, a kind man really, called Martin, with a moustache, had told her in his strange Irish voice that all the fruit here was 'the best of eating'. Then he'd shown her a special tree in a walled-off corner of the vegetable garden with tiny round apples on it, light yellow, with a faint crimson blush: crab apples, Martin called them, eating one himself, before giving her one.

The taste was strange, not entirely nice; sour, pricking her tongue, but then a small strange sweetness. The tree, Martin had told her, was the 'childer's tree'. It had been planted a long time ago, by her grandfather when he was young – 'God rest his soul,' he'd said, before crossing himself in that funny way that Elly did – 'And then it was for your mother here after him, when she was a child, and her two brothers, God rest their souls as well.'

'Why should God have to rest their souls?' she'd asked him then and he'd looked at her in a sad way and said, 'An' sure aren't they all dead and gone from here.' He sighed, polishing another of the little rosy apples. 'An' they all eating in their time from this tree – an' that's why it's called the childer's tree, an' you the only child left in the family now.' She'd been frightened then. 'We-we-were they killed by these apples?' and she'd tried to spit the last mouthful out.

'Ah, sure, not at all, at all. 'twasn't thim apples that took thim. Thim's special little apples – the Apples of Life we call thim here in Ireland, growing wild all over the place, and a great cure for the ague or a cold or iny kind of chestiness.'

'Magic apples?' Hetty had asked him. 'Like the ones in my *Red Fairy Tale* book?'

'Indeed – indeed you're right. That's what they are – ye could well say: magic apples!' And they'd held the happy secret between them then, in the hot, high-walled space in the corner of the garden. 'No, indeed,' Martin had said sadly, ''Twasn't thim apples that took thim – 'twas God took thim, all in his own good time.'

Hetty thought about this now, kneeling on the window seat of the hall: the magic apples and God taking people like this in Ireland in his 'own good time'. Well, it wasn't a good time over here at all that God was managing. At home in Domenica the fruit and the weather had been pretty much the same all the year round. But here God changed the wind and sun, the heat and cold, every few months. He killed people to 'rest their souls' – hadn't they been able to have a good sleep in their own beds when they were tired? – and he 'touched' other people and made them silly, and he fiddled about with the sun all the time. Why couldn't he leave well alone, as he did in Domenica? – apart from the hurricanes.

But of course, she realised, like everyone else she had seen in England and

Ireland since she'd arrived, God was *extremely busy* over in this part of the world, always doing things, mile-a-minute as the trains went, an interfering old busybody. She decided she didn't like God in Ireland. He was a much better person in Domenica.

She heard her mother's voice then, coming from the drawing room behind her – loud words, speaking to Mr O'Donovan, the tall, white-haired, bushy-bearded man in a stiff black suit who was the head man outside the house, who ran everything in the yard and farm. The 'Steward' he was called – he did the same things as nice old Mr McTear did at Fraser Hall, but he wasn't at all as friendly. Mr O'Donovan looked rather like God, Hetty thought – or the one they had over here anyway. He was always frightfully busy. The voices were coming toward her, and she hid behind the long dark window curtains again.

Ever since she'd arrived she'd taken to hiding from her Mama, since whenever they did meet, and with Elly hidden away with Robert who had an 'infectious disease', Mama had found nasty things for her to do, or told her to stay in her room, when what she had wanted to do was roam the house, discovering things. Because, one good thing at least, unlike Fraser Hall, there were so *many* absolutely wonderful places to hide, in this huge dark house: endless rooms and landings everywhere and all filled with cubby-holes, nooks and crannies – and with great dark furniture and long curtains and heavily-draped tables, which she could hide behind or beneath, all cosy and warm, for the cold here was *terrible*, even though it wasn't yet winter, when it got *worse*.

'So that's settled then, O'Donovan,' she heard her mother say as they came into the hall. 'I shall need half a dozen of the yard and farm men in here for the next few weeks – to clear out all this frightful furniture, curtains, pictures and things. Store it, sell it, burn it – anything. And then help me get all the good old furniture down from the attics. I shall clear the house out by degrees, then redecorate the whole place – white and blue limewash for the most part, so we shall need the painters in then, ladders and so on.'

'Yes, Mrs Fraser.' The man spoke rather crossly as the two of them stood in the hall. But her mother's voice sounded even more cross.

'And these gloomy Roman busts everywhere in the hall, O'Donovan – I shall want them all removed – and replaced, in those niches there, with the two original statues, "Cupid" and "Psyche".'

'Statues, Ma'am?'

'Yes, the two here originally: classical Greek, in white marble.'

'I don't know, Mrs Fraser – not in my time.'

'But of *course*, O'Donovan, they were here in the old days, before my mother took over. They must be somewhere about. I think I remember seeing them up in that garden store beyond the vine house: two white marble statues. Two young people, O'Donovan – naked, you know.'

'Two . . . young people. Yes, Mrs Fraser. I'll see if I can find them. I'll . . . I'll ask Appleton to go through the garden outhouses.'

'And don't forget the tennis court – I want to get that in hand straightaway:

don't want it any more – want it planted out in some fashion, young willow saplings, I'd thought. I want to make a willow or rock garden out of it with a waterfall.'

'I don't know if it's quite the season, Ma'am, for planting out saplings –'

'Talk to Appleton about it, get the ground prepared anyway – I want *rid* of that tennis court, that's the main thing.'

'Yes, Ma'am.'

'Oh, and O'Donovan, what about all these rats? There seems a plague of them – Mrs Martin has told me. In the kitchens, cellars – and I've even seen them here in the hall.'

'In the yard as well, Ma'am.'

'How do you account for them? – is someone *feeding* them?'

'Can't account for them, Ma'am – not this early in the year. Unless it's the wet summer maybe. They've come in to feed early about the house. I'll put poison down – and we'll have the terriers at them.'

'Whatever, O'Donovan. Get rid of them. Can't have a lot of *rats* about the place.'

'No, Mrs Fraser. I'll see to it.'

O'Donovan left the hall and Hetty, still crushed in behind the long window drapes, heard the motor car drive up outside on the gravel surround. Peeping through the curtain, she saw the terrifying spluttering machine come to a halt in front of the porch. It was the old doctor. He had come every day, once or twice a day, ever since Robert had started coughing. Hetty stayed where she was as the man walked up the steps and into the hall.

'Ah, Dr Mitchell.'

'And how is the young man today?'

'No better. I'm worried.'

'Poor chap, he's taken a lot of knocks recently, what with his parents going in the hurricane like that – and generally run down. The whooping cough gets a real grip then. You're keeping the little lass well away from him, I hope?'

'Of *course*, Dr Mitchell – I was a nurse myself, you know.'

Her mother's voice sounded very rude. They went upstairs then and Hetty emerged from her hiding place, outraged. What a *frightful* busybody her mother was. Mr Rat was to be poisoned or gobbled up by the nasty, bitey little terriers – the tennis court, where she had hoped to play with Robert, made into a stupid wood of some sort, and, worst of all, all the nice old dark furniture and curtains which she could hide behind taken out of the house and *burnt*! What a *terribly* stupid thing to do. It was 'criminal', that's what it was, like Elly said about some *very* stupid things people did.

Could she rescue some of the furniture, take it, hide it, before it all went? Yes, perhaps she could, and find some secret place to keep it, just for herself. She moved off at once, starting her explorations again, going down the dark, warm-woody-smelling passageway behind the great staircase and into a murky, book-lined room with a huge desk in the middle. It was her grandfather's study, she knew. He'd fallen off the roof of the house in a flying machine, which was something like a motor car with wings, Elly had told her. But that was impossible, motor cars couldn't fly. So mustn't he have been 'taken by God' and been flying up to him in the first place, she'd asked Elly? But no: he'd just had an 'accident'. It didn't make sense.

Then she saw a toy of this flying machine on a table by the window. She gazed at it, most curiously. So it had been real – a motor car with wings! An insect of a sort she had never seen in Domenica, like a tiny bean with red spots dotted all over it, was asleep on the toy. She touched it very delicately and it flew away suddenly, making her jump. Only birds and insects and things could fly. No wonder her grandfather had gone up to God, thinking he could fly. What a stupid thing to do. People really were very stupid over here in Ireland. And she knew why: like God, they were always so *busy*. Well, she wouldn't be. She determined then and there not *ever* to be busy. It killed you.

Going on then into the billiard room further along the passageway she saw the great table with funny net pockets all round – another grown-up's game, for *men* only, Elly had said. What *could* they do here? She set her lime fruit on the green cloth and pushed it around, trying to get it into one of the pockets. But it wouldn't. It squiggled all over the place. Only men played this game, so she supposed that was why she couldn't. And there weren't any men in the house now. Though there had been a lot once – her grandfather and her two uncles. But they had gone up to God as well, resting their souls.

She hated this God more and more. But she feared him just as much. Was he going to take Robert away, too? How *awful* if he did. She could play with Robert, at least. Sometimes, even, she quite liked him. And she really *did* like him now, because . . . because, well, she'd been bad to him often enough in Domenica, and on the boat over, and perhaps this busybody God was going to punish her for that now by taking him away.

'Oh, please God,' she said out loud suddenly, firmly, not pleading, 'please don't take Robert away from us. Please don't make him rest his soul. Let him rest nicely, just here, and get better in his own cosy-warm bed.' She could hear Robert coughing now, faint awful whoopy-whoopy coughs, somewhere above her. 'Please God,' she said, remembering the crab apples. 'I'll give him some of those magic apples. Shall I?' But there was silence. Then she made a great effort and a great promise: 'God, if you don't take him away, I won't *ever* think you are an awful busybody again. I promise, never ever.'

She went back into the hall then, running upstairs and round the first floor balustrade into the upper hall, where two landings on either side ran back into the depths of the gloomy house. Hesitating – and very daring, for she had been strictly forbidden this floor and these landings by her mother, even before Robert had been moved down to one of the grown-up bedrooms – she chose the right hand corridor which she thought must lead to Robert's bedroom, tip-toeing along it in the gloom.

But half-way down, hearing footsteps coming up the servants' stairs at the far end, she ducked behind a heavy chest of drawers. Peering out she saw one of the kitchen maids carrying a tray, turning away from the end of the landing and going back somewhere further into the end of the house. Where was she going – with a tray and food? It could only be for Robert. That's where he was, right at the back of the house somewhere.

Hetty silently followed the maid, the woman in her starched white apron and cap just visible in the shadows before she disappeared up some stone steps, leaving this first floor for some quite different part of the house. Running now behind her, Hetty was just in time to see the maid at the top of the flight of steps unlocking a heavy door there, leaving it open, and going on into another much narrower corridor with funny small diamond-shaped windows on one side looking over the yard.

Half-way down the maid stopped again, unlocking a second door, going inside with the tray, before the door was closed sharply. So this was where they'd hidden Robert, Hetty thought, with his 'infectious disease' – as far away as possible from everyone else in the house. Poor Robert. But at least she knew where he was now. She could come and see him, somehow, and give him one of the magic apples. She moved closer to the door then, listening at the keyhole. She was surprised for at first she heard nothing, no coughing, no sound at all.

But then there was a sudden terrible noise and Hetty drew back from the keyhole in surprised horror: it was an old woman's voice, witch-like, screechy, stopping and starting, wailing; then *laughing*. There were no words in the voice, just this crying out, these angry shrieks. Then she heard the maid say something – 'Now, don't take on so, your Ladyship. I've got some nice tea and biscuits . . .'

But by then Hetty was running back down the corridor – it wasn't Robert at all. Someone else, someone she'd never heard of, was living in this mysterious room at the back of the house. Someone locked up all the time, so they must be *very* bad.

She ran down the stone steps, back into the long corridor of the main house and out into the upper hall again. Robert must be somewhere here – she'd taken the wrong landing. So now she chose the one on the left, tip-toeing down it, passing all the great bedroom doors – until she heard Robert coughing: at last – she'd found out where he was and, seeing a great china bowl, she squeezed in behind it and settled down to wait. Her mother and the doctor must be inside with him. She would see exactly which room he was in when they came out.

She heard a rustling noise behind her, a scratching somewhere on the floor further up the landing. Mr Rat again, she wondered? Or a Mrs Rat? Then a window rattled suddenly somewhere – a vicious rattle-rattle – before a door opened ahead of her and she heard Robert coughing clearly now and voices on the landing, her mother and the doctor, and there was a funny smell in the air now. A burnt, sweetish, nasty smell.

'Yes, keep the fumigations going. And the glycerine. And keep him quiet and the room dark as possible. There's little else . . .'

'The poor mite,' her mother said. 'It's painful to see him. Horrid.'

'Doing all that can be done – if he gets through the night.'

Hetty grimaced, a sick feeling coming into her tummy. The smell was awful, a rotting smell. It was the smell of death. That's what happened to people, how they died – they started to rot away. It was death coming to Robert and not getting through the night and this cruel God lurking somewhere, everywhere here, on the landing, waiting to take people up into the sky to their awful rest. It was terrible – unless she could save Robert with one of those magic apples. But it was all the worse now, with that screechy old woman's voice in one room and death rattling at the door of another and she was suddenly too frightened of everything.

When her mother and the doctor had gone downstairs, Hetty ran helter-skelter, as if pursued by this vengeful God, down the landing and up the back-stairs to the top floor of the house, where her bedroom was, a room which she had been given temporarily, which had once been her uncle's room, Elly had told her – her soldier uncle who had been killed by 'bores' in South Africa. Inside, safe at last, she slammed the door very hard, and stood there panting.

Then, unbelievably, the door of the huge tall cupboard next to her started to swing open slowly and she shrieked – shrieked and shrieked.

There was a *man* inside it – a fat great red-coated man with a gold belt and black trousers. And no *head*. Still screaming she ran from the room.

'Ah, now, don't take on so – it's all right now – what ails ye at all, girl?' Mrs Molloy stroked Hetty's hair, holding her in her arms, comforting her in the big kitchen.

'A-a-a. A gre-gre . . .' She couldn't get the words out. Words hardly ever came properly now, ever since she'd been at Summer Hill. And Hetty cried in fear and frustration, great blubby, thick-throated tears.

'What was it? What was it at all – tell me.' Mrs Molloy took her to a cupboard and gave her a ginger biscuit. 'Tell me now, what ails ye?'

'Me-my-be-*bed*room. A me-me-*man*!'

Mrs Molloy turned to Biddy, one of the kitchen maids. 'Go up to her room, Biddy, and see what she's on about at all.'

'Yes! Ina-ina-re-re-red coat!'

Mrs Molloy sighed, shook her head, then stroked the girl's glossy-dark curls, while Hetty looked up at her pleadingly, thumb in mouth, her great blackberry eyes glistening with tears. 'Now, you come along with me, girl, and help me make this greengage jam.'

She led Hetty over to the big range where a cauldron of sugared fruit was boiling away furiously. 'Now ye sit there.' She drew up a high kitchen stool for her. 'We'll be taking the fruit off in a moment, bottling it. And, when it cools a bit, ye can taste it. It's grand stuff.'

Hetty, up on the high stool now, hands on knees, leant forward and watched the fruit bubbling and spitting. There was a wonderful warm sugary smell. Biddy returned from upstairs then. 'Ah, and sure there was nothing in the room at all. The cupboard door was open, with one of Masther Eustace's oul' army uniforms standing up in it. Nothing at all.'

Mrs Molloy explained this to Hetty. 'So you see, it was just your uncle's old army clothes hanging up there in the press.'

Hetty's face clouded again at this news. 'Bu-bu-but there wa-was no *head*?'

'No, well, you see . . .' Mrs Molloy decided to distract her again. 'Come on now and we'll bottle the jam,' she said. And she took her over to the long kitchen table, where soon Hetty became entirely absorbed, watching Mrs Molloy and Biddy and Sally, the other kitchen maid, putting the jam into tall jars, with a ladle through a funnel.

This was good fun, Hetty thought – especially when Mrs Molloy gave her a big spoon and her own jam-jar and told her to fill it up. The greeny-yellow mix slithered down the glass. The green was lighter and cloudier than the lime-green of the fruit in her pocket, Hetty thought. It was 'greengage' green. That was a nice colour, a nice sound. Mrs Molloy showed her one of the greengages, from a chip basket on the window-sill.

'There, that's the fruit itself now. Lovely and sweet – the best of all the plums. Try one!'

Hetty looked up at this big kind fat woman in the long white apron. Then, trusting her, she took out her own little crinkled, pinched lime fruit.

'C-c-c could you ma-ma-make g-g-*jam* with this?'

Mrs Molloy inspected the fruit with great interest. 'Indeed ye could! It's a little lime. I've not seen one in a while. Ye hardly ever get thim over here. But it's a kind of marmalade ye'd make with it and ye'd need a lot of thim. But it'd be *very* tasty!'

Hetty was pleased with this information. She smiled. 'It's fra-fra-from home,' she said. 'My home – in Dom-Dom-Domenica.' And suddeny she was crying again, couldn't stop herself. She longed for that other home now, her *real* home, that warm, sunny, friendly place, with Slinky and Big Jules and the frigate birds in the great blue sky and the Emerald Pool and the long grassy walks through the old lime groves into the wild forest and the glittering white coral house and green shutters, with Cook, that other cook, and her slices of ginger cake.

Mrs Molloy left the jam-bottling and comforted her again. 'Ah, now, don't cry. *This* is your home now – and, sure, ye'll get to like it, ye will –'

'I won't – I hate it, *hate* it!' In her anger and agony of homesickness then, Hetty's stammer quite disappeared.

But again Mrs Molloy managed to distract her. 'Come on then, alanah, we'll have no more tears. Ye've got your own jam-pot now, so you'll have to write a label for it, won't you?' Hetty looked at her doubtfully. Mrs Molloy picked up a label and a dip pen. 'Ye can write, can't ye?' she asked brightly, and Hetty, affronted at this, nodded vigorously. She *could* write – that was one thing she could do. 'Oh, yes,' she said, her tears drying. 'I can write *much* better than Robert.'

'Well, here ye are then, you copy this.' And Mrs Molloy wrote out in capitals 'GREENGAGE – SEPT 1909. Miss Henrietta's Jam'. And Hetty copied it slowly and carefully and very nicely, before glueing the label and sticking it on her own jar.

'Now, there ye are – your very own jam and ye've made it all yourself!' Mrs Molloy held the warm jar up to the light, and Hetty saw all the mottled yellowy-green colours – and she loved it, quite forgetting her homesickness and the headless man. She'd *made* this jam – well, nearly made it. It was hers and she had a wonderfully warm feeling inside her then, which she wanted to speak about, but couldn't, the words trapped again.

When Hetty had left the kitchen, Biddy turned to Mrs Molloy. 'Well, an' there's a strange one and no mistake – and she not able to get a word out edgeways, suckin' her thumb and those eyes as big as saucers out on stalks lookin' at ye all the time. Wouldn't ye pity her altogether?'

Mrs Molloy didn't agree. 'Well, now, isn't it a great thing not to be chatterin' all the time, like ye be doin', Biddy Walsh. And they do say, when ye can't talk at all like that, it's because ye have too full a heart.'

'I-ma-ma-I-ma-made some g-g-*jam*!' Hetty told her mother proudly in her little study room next to the drawing room that evening, when she had come down to see her before her nursery supper – as she had been instructed to do, every evening at six o'clock.

She sat on the edge of a big high-backed chair now, all neat and tidy, hair combed, curls forced together with two blue ribbons, in a horrid navy-blue, lace-trimmed velvet dress, long white socks and shiny black, sharply-buttoned, very pinching dancing shoes. Molly had done all this, helped her into these frightfully tight and uncomfy hot clothes – Molly, her great-aunt Emily's old maid who was looking after her now while Elly was busy with Robert in his sick room. But it was her mother who had insisted upon it, and now Hetty sat there nervously, smoothing her hands over the sticky velvet, trying not to look at her mother sitting at the desk by the window, reading papers, pen in hand.

Finally Frances looked at her daughter. 'Yes, Henrietta,' she said vaguely. Then she suddenly turned to her. '*Jam*, Henrietta. It's not a difficult word. "J" – there is no "G" in it. Try again.'

'G-g-g-g-*jam* . . .'

Silence. 'I can't understand it,' her mother finally said, looking at her crossly. 'You were never so bad with your words at Fraser Hall. You really must make an effort to speak properly. It's *most* unbecoming, to stutter and stammer like that.'

'Yes, Me-me-Mama.' Hetty froze completely then. She had wanted to ask her mother about Robert – and even more about the strange, screechy-voiced old woman in the back of the house. But she didn't dare now.

'Still . . .' Her mother surveyed her distantly. 'When we're more settled here, you'll have to make a real effort. And no doubt this Miss Goulden will make you speak properly.' She held up a letter. 'She's coming next week, from Limerick. The highest recommendations. She is to be your governess – for you. And Robert.'

'Ge-ge-*goverl*ess!'

'Gover*ness*.' Her mother corrected her sharply, standing up now, bunching her fingers, cracking the joints in her annoyed way. 'She's going to *teach* you – French and sums and things. Teach you all *sorts* of lessons,' she added.

Hetty swallowed nervously. 'Ke-ke-*can* I have a pe-pe-*pen*cil box then?'

'A pencil box?' Her mother was surprised.

'Yes, for my pe-pe-pens and pe-pe-pencils. Like Robert has, for his le-le-lessons.'

Her mother shook her head indignantly. 'You shall have a pencil box when you stop that frightful stammering,' she told her even more sharply.

Robert's cough got worse that night. Hetty heard him whooping away long after her supper in the nursery. And lurking at the head of the servants' stairs later she heard the doctor again and whispered conversations on the landing below, people coming and going. Robert was dying, God was taking him away. Only the crab apples – the apples of life – would save him now.

Hetty had a store of them in her bedroom, and she bit into one then, as if to give her strength for what she had to do. Molly, who slept in the next room on the nursery landing, would be easy enough to avoid. She snored when she slept. But what about the others, when she went downstairs? In fairy stories they did magic things so easily. But this was real.

Molly had tucked her into bed, leaving just the dumpy little wax nightlight burning by the door. Then, hours and hours later, it seemed, she heard her going to bed – and, soon after, she was snoring. It was time.

Holding the nightlight in one hand, and a few of the apples gathered up in the hem of her nightdress in the other, she made her way slowly down the servants' stairs, then turned into the dark first floor landing. She waited at the corner, listening. There was just Robert's coughing every so often, no other sound. It must be the very *middle* of the night. She tip-toed quickly along towards Robert's door, then paused at it undecided for a moment. Both her hands were full – she couldn't open it. Kneeling then, putting down the nightlight, she was just about to rise when she heard a rustling rushing noise like the wind coming down the landing towards her, the nightlight flame suddenly dancing.

She had no time to escape. It was her mother, towering above her, her face twisted with anger in the flickering yellow shadows, as she bent down, taking her by the collar of her nightdress.

'You little wretch!' The apples spilled from the hem of her nightdress, as her mother pulled her all the way down the landing to the upper hall. Then she slapped her face. 'What *do* you think you're doing? – at this hour of the night? Waking poor Robert – with those apples everywhere.' She shook her then, in the faint light. 'How *dare* you try and disturb him. And it's you then, who've been feeding these beastly rats everywhere, leaving apples out for them. You little mischief-making wretch!' She shook her violently again.

Hetty was terrified. 'No, Mama! I wa t-t-t-*trying* to help him ge-get better, with those me-me-*magic* apples –'

'What nonsense! You will go straight to your bed now and I'll have Molly sleep with you in future, with the door locked! Don't you know Robert is *very* ill – and here you are trying to wake him up or poison him with those stupid apples.'

Her mother dragged her upstairs, woke Molly, and made a terrible fuss over the whole thing. And, when Hetty was back in bed, she thought how much she really *hated* her mother. It was *she* who was trying to kill Robert, by not letting him have the magic apples. And she whispered to herself, 'Please God – I *will* get those apples to him. We'll find some way of getting the apples to him, won't we? Promise?'

The next morning Hetty thought she saw a way. Her great-aunt Emily was out with her drawing book, up on the high bank beyond the big yellow-leafed tree – a lovely breezy sunny day. Her aunt had a floppy straw hat on, tied over the top and under her throat with a spotted scarf, and was wearing a funny long green corduroy coat. She was humming, singing something as Hetty stole up to her.

Hetty stood beside her. She wasn't frightened of great-aunt Emily at all – didn't even stammer very much with her. She was really like a child herself. The only thing was she never spoke a lot – and when she did it was in a terrible hurry. Hetty stood there now for a minute watching her draw.

'Great-aunt Emily?' she said at last.

No reply. Aunt Emily had a small paint brush in one hand and a big dabby paint box and several little water jars in front of her attached to the wooden stand. She was doing a coloured picture of the tennis court below her and the house beyond. The only very funny thing was that she'd made the tennis court full of people playing and other people in grand frilly long dresses having tea from silver teapots on the bank. And there *weren't* any people there at all. Of course, she *was* 'touched'. Surely she could see there was no one there at all?

'Great-aunt Emily?' she asked again.

'Yes, yes, child, in a minute – when I've got this dress right.'

'But Aunt Emily,' Hetty couldn't restrain herself. 'There *aren't* any people on the tennis court.'

Aunt Emily turned on her then, peering at her haughtily down her very long thin straight nose, two dark little eyes, like mice eyes, on either side. 'Excuse yourself, girl! The lawn is full of people. Just because *you* can't see them, doesn't mean they're not there. You can be sure of it – if I *put* them there – they *are* there.'

Hetty looked at the lawn and tennis court very carefully then, shading her eyes. It must be some kind of magic. Perhaps the people were there after all. 'I'm s-s-sorry,' she said.

'Oh, they're there all right, girl – don't worry about that. But your mother in her great foolishness is having the whole court grubbed up, so I'm remembering it before she does.'

'Yes, wh-wh-why is she doing that?'

'Ah, some other foolishness on the court here years and years ago, before you were born. With *men*.' Her aunt made a sour face then. 'She was jilted on it, that's why.'

'Jilted?' It sounded like falling off a horse. 'Di-di-did she fall down or som-som-something?'

Her aunt smiled. 'You could say that, yes – she took a bad fall! And all her own fault, for I'd warned her of it, having to do with *men*. Told her that, but she took no notice. And now look where they've got her!' Her aunt cackled then.

'I wanted to play tennis here, with Robert. And that's what I wa-wa-wanted to ask you aba-about.' She looked up at her aunt hopefully.

'Robert, yes. There were ructions, I heard, last night. What were you up to?' Aunt Emily had returned to her drawing.

'I wa-wa-was trying to give him awa-awa-one of these.' She produced one of the apples, holding it up. 'They're magic, you see! Old Martin the gardener said: apples of life, he said. But me-me-Mama stopped me. C-c-could *you* bring it him?'

Aunt Emily turned and looked at the tiny apple intently, but said nothing, so that Hetty thought she was going to scoff at her.

'Quite right, girl – magic apples. Wonder they didn't think of them before. My friend Pat goes up to his room now and then. I'll give it to him – and *he'll* give it to Robert.' She took the apple and put it on the ledge by the paint box.

'Oh, thank you, *thank you!* P-p-Pat the butler, you mean? He *is* a nice man. I saw him –' But she stopped. Pat had been feeding Mr Rat. And that, according to her mother, was very wrong. But why, since Pat was so nice, was he doing something so wrong? It didn't make sense. But then great-aunt Emily's drawing didn't make sense either, and she was *very* nice. So it was all quite clear: good people did these strange things, but they had to do them in secret, like she had tried to do with the apples, because it was her *mother* who was *bad* and tried to stop them all the time.

That was how it was. So she was one of the nice, good people really, trying to help, like Pat and Aunt Emily. And they would all just have to go on doing things in secret, and tell no one about it. That was the answer. It was just like in the fairy stories –'The Two Ugly Sisters' and 'Little Red Riding Hood' – which were always full of bad, wicked people like her mother, and nice good secret people who were unhappy – but happy in the end. Well, she was one of these, just like Cinderella who became a princess – and she would go on doing these secret things, because they were right. It was just like Aunt Emily had said about her drawing. You could put people on the paper even if they weren't there! That was all part of the magic thing about good people.

Hetty felt very much better as she went back to the house. Now she knew she was right about things, she would start at once – rescuing those nice old bits and pieces of furniture and curtains and things.

All that day and the next, whenever she had the opportunity or when the yard men, in to clear the house, were taking their dinner, Hetty chose what she fancied and could carry of the dark furniture and drapes. She took a stool, a small, straight-backed chair, several nice little pictures of donkeys and sheep and things, a funny glass dome with pretend flowers inside and – greatest prize of all – a whole pile of dark curtains left in the upper hall over lunchtime. She hid them all in her nursery bedroom at first. And then, in the days that followed, bit by bit, she took them out to the very secret place she had found, away deep in the woods to the south of the house, high on the ridge above the valley where, some time before, she had discovered a sort of hole in the hill, spread over with rotten branches and laurel and tangly briars. Here, burrowing into this undergrowth, and clearing the old sticks away, she made a space for the furniture on the mossy ground, a house in the woods, hanging the big curtains over it, then hiding that with other sticks and leaves and bits of moss. By the end of the week she had made herself a cosy and warm secret hiding place, dark inside but with two half-burnt candles she had taken, and a gap in the curtains giving out to the light when she wanted. And by the end of that same week – since Pat must have got the magic apple to him – Robert was over the worst and getting better. All her magic things had worked!

She lit one of the candles then in the secret place, like she'd seen them do in the church in Domenica, and put it in front of one of the pictures her mother had so disliked, a picture of a bearded man on a donkey – and she said, 'Thank you, God, for not taking Robert away to rest his soul. I won't *ever* think you're awful again – like I promised.' She paused. Then she added – she couldn't not really, could she? – 'But you do see, don't you? – the magic apple I gave him, that must have made it a lot easier for you.'

Hetty watched the threshing in the high field beyond the yard where the hay barns and corn lofts were. There was a huge black steam engine there, a thundering smoky thing, with a great wheel going round and a long belt driving another machine, into which the men were feeding stooks of corn, and the grain and the straw were separated.

The outer yard was crammed with people – extra men from the village and old women helping and others boiling up endless kettles of tea over a fire to one side. Bits of chaff flew in the wind and stuck in Hetty's eyes and it was very hot and noisy, but exciting.

When they stopped for their dinner at midday, Hetty saw a strange one-armed man, in a tattered black coat tied with string, and all his face eaten away in a terrible way. He sat at the long trestle table and some of the women brought their tea mugs to him – drinking them or swirling them round at first, then emptying them, when the man looked inside them, telling them something afterwards. Hetty was fascinated. She stole up to the trestle table to get a closer look.

'Ah, now,' she heard the awful eaten-away-face man say to one of the women, 'I see a dark stranger for ye here, from somewhere beyant . . .' He looked into the big mug again carefully. 'In America, it is – and ye'll meet him out dancin' . . .'

The woman laughed loudly, the others joining her. Then everyone stopped laughing and there was silence. They had noticed Hetty standing behind them. Their faces turned to her – funny, hot, big red faces, looking at her intently, so that she felt shy, but could not move.

'Ah, sure, an' isn't it the young Missy of the house come to see us!' one of the jollier old women said. 'Come on, alanah, and have yer fortune told – Snipe here will tell ye yer future!' Hetty did not move. But the old woman was beckoning to her in a friendly way. Telling your future? Hetty thought. Another sort of magic. She was tempted.

'Come on, indeed,' the eaten-away-face man said. 'Give her a bit of tay there, and lit her run it round the mug.'

An old woman poured some tea into a mug and handed it to Hetty. 'Turn it round there a bit and throw it out,' she said to her. And Hetty, now within the group, did as she was bid, leaving a lot of thick tea-leaves in the bottom. The man they called Snipe took the mug from her and looked into it deeply, turning it this way and that, eyeing it carefully down his nose – which wasn't there, just two holes, so that Hetty couldn't look at him.

'Be'gob,' the man said at last. 'And isn't this the quarest lay of leaves I iver saw.' He looked up at Hetty then, peering at her closely, then back inside the mug. 'Ah, an' sure it couldn't be,' he said at last. The women began to look worried. What was it? Hetty thought. Didn't she have a future?

'Ah, 'tis a great future altogether,' he said and everyone looked relieved. 'Away in the big world ye'll be – and doin' every sort of thing, all sorts of handy-work. But here's the ting . . .' He looked doubtful again. 'There's a man here behind you – well, he's rich – 'deed he's so rich ye wouldn't be talking about it, owns half the world, and he'll look after you.' The man looked back in the mug again. 'But here's the ting I can't follow – an' this man a king or a prince of some sort.'

The old women were mockingly pleased. 'Will she marry him then, Snipe? Is that it?'

'No,' said Snipe. 'It's not so much the marrying, but sure don't she belong to him now in some kind of a way. In the leaves there – clear as day.'

The women laughed. 'Ah, sure, Snipe, and haven't you got it wrong this time!' they cackled.

'I have *not*. Clear as day,' Snipe said again, aggrieved now. 'An' she a princess herself already.'

At news of this, the jolly women were hushed, turning to Hetty, gazing at her, with Snipe – his face a frightening staring mask. Everyone was all serious now and Hetty didn't understand this magic. A secret princess – a fairy story, like 'Cinderella'? She backed away slowly then. And the crush of people who had gathered round the table from about the yard moved aside to let her pass, staring at her, wondering, not smiling any more, as if they were frightened of her. Hetty moved through the crowd slowly at first – then, frightened herself, as they opened out leaving a wide gap, she started to run.

2

IN THE NEXT year Summer Hill and its inhabitants were variously transformed. Frances, replacing Lady Cordiner – who had suffered a mild stroke and was now confined as an invalid to the Victorian back wing of the house – became every bit as dictatorial, but with quite different aims. The rooms of the house, painted in glittering blues and whites and filled with all the old Irish Georgian furnishings and silver, were restored to their original, elegant, eighteenth-century condition. Much of the heavy Victorian furniture and all the other dowdy knick-knacks of the period, were disposed of; the rest went to fill out Lady Cordiner's quarters, where she lived as a confused and bitter recluse surrounded by these dark remnants of her past existence.

To the embarrassment of Mrs Martin, the Presbyterian housekeeper, and the other servants, the delicate marble nudes of Cupid and Psyche, returned to their niches in the great hall. Outside, the tennis court was grubbed up, made over as a rock and willow garden; soon an artificial waterfall flowed through a limestone grotto – forever and completely erasing the memory of Frances's indignity here, at the hands of Lord Norton's son during the tennis party over a decade before.

As well as Lady Cordiner's quarters, some few other parts of the house and outbuildings remained locked, untouched, forbidden: Sir Desmond Cordiner's workshops in the yard, filled now with the scattered debris of his aerial ambitions, and his son Henry's rooms in the old nurseries along the top floor, where he had worked so intently with Dermot on their collection of tropical butterflies and exotic stuffed animals.

Lady Cordiner had kept these latter rooms as an inviolate memorial to her favourite son. And Frances did the same. She was quite unaware that Robert, after his recovery the previous autumn, had found a way into Henry's shrouded rooms, from the children's schoolroom window nearby, moving out along the sloping lead guttering that ran down to the roof balustrade, forcing the catch on Henry's window through a broken pane.

And it was here – in these stuffy workrooms with their dead bluebottles and spiders left untouched since the day of Henry's death, still with his Lepidoptera notes open on the work bench, a great Amazonian Swallowtail half-pinned into the display case – that Robert, and Hetty on his invitation, retreated to escape the stresses and strains of life which, under Frances's ruthless hand, soon enveloped the entire household.

They sat there one afternoon, in the spring of the following year, when their spiteful governess, Miss Goulden, had taken the train to Kilkenny on her day off – Hetty sitting in Henry's shabby chintz chair by the grate, where the old dead coals and ash still lay, Robert standing at the work bench by the window, peering down a microscope.

'Wha-wha-what would we do, if w-w-we didn't have here?' Hetty sighed, rubbing her eyes, for, though it wasn't warm up here, she was sleepy. It was the bottle that Robert had made her smell – 'Ether' it had said on the label. It was for killing insects, he'd told her.

'If *I* hadn't discovered the place,' Robert said proprietorially. 'You have your *own* secret place in the woods.'

'Yes, but it's been winter and far too wet and cold out there. I can go again soon, though, and you can come – and share it.' That was a whole long lot of words, Hetty thought, without a single stammer. Robert was the only person she could really manage that with. Funny. She wanted to be nice to Robert – he had no parents. But it was difficult. He was difficult.

'I prefer it here anyway,' he said abruptly. 'Much more to do. All these stuffed animals and butterflies and things. And *guns*.' He glanced over at Henry's Winchester sporting rifle, still lying, disassembled in bits and pieces, on another table. 'I'll learn how to put that gun together soon – and there's lots and lots of other things here I haven't even *begun* to discover.'

'They'll kill us if they find out.'

'They *won't* – unless you squeal.'

'*I* w-w-won't squeal!'

'Don't talk so loudly.'

Hetty's clothes began to chafe her again. She stood up, hopping about, scratching her legs. Robert turned to her. 'Don't make a *noise!*'

'These horrid Irish clothes.'

'Yes. They *are* horrid.'

On the insistence of her mother, Hetty wore a pleated Celtic tartan skirt now, held together at the side by a big Tara brooch, with a coarse, white woollen pullover whose oily wool tickled her neck. 'Just like all those stupid Irish words that beardy O'Grady man from Kilkenny teaches us,' she said now. 'I *hate* it – can't d-d-do it, at all. What's the use of it? No one *speaks* Irish here. So *why?* Can you do it, Robert?'

Robert, engrossed in the microscope, did not reply. Hetty, as she usually did when she got to these secret rooms, suddenly pulled off the rough jersey, unpinned and stepped out of the tartan skirt, and stood in her knickers and long vest. Then she tiptoed towards Robert who was trying to focus the microscope.

'Can *you* do the Irish, Robert?'

'No. Just pretend I can.'

'But he *knows* you're pre-pre-pretending.'

'I'm not Irish anyway. I don't have to learn the stupid language. You are, though.'

'No, I'm not!'

'Yes, you are – just like your Mama – and she's learning Irish from O'Grady as well. You're *both* really Irish, so now you have to learn everything about the place – those stupid clothes and the words and everything.'

'But Ireland is supposed to be just like England – Elly said so.'

'Well, it's not really. It's quite different. They all want to be properly Irish here now, or something – and they're fighting and rowing about it, have been for years, and that's why she has all those funny people down here, from Dublin, and that beardy O'Grady from Kilkenny – they all secretly want to fight the English as well.'

'Actually old beardy is quite nice. A bit of a fibber, though. He read me a book of Irish fairy tales – which *he* said were all real: about a huge man called Cuckoo Cullen who could pick up whole *mountains* and throw them about.'

'Yes, but they're all doing something very wrong – and if the police knew about it they wouldn't like it and there'd be *awful* trouble, with guns and things. I *know*.'

'How do you know?'

'I heard Mrs Martin talking about it.'

'Well, I just don't like the horrid clothes – and those Irish words. Even the alphabet is all different.'

Robert was not listening. Then, looking up from the microscope, he said more or less to himself: 'They want to fight, you see, fight the English – with *guns*.' He looked over at the bits and pieces of Henry's rifle. 'If I could put that together again, we could fight back, like in Domenica . . .'

'But that would be *awful*!'

'Yes. But we may have to –'

'But the Irish aren't like the Caribs. They don't eat people – and they're *white*, not black.'

'Doesn't matter – they want to do just like the Caribs – take over the house here and the land. They're annoyed, you see. Mrs Martin said. I heard her talking to old Mr Flood, who lives in the yard. Those two aren't like the other servants here, you know. They're like the English, like us. They go to our church. They're Protestant.'

'But if we're all Protestant, like the English, why is Mama trying to make us all Irish, with these awful clothes and words and things?' Hetty tried to engage Robert's attention, but he had returned to the microscope.

'*Why*, Robert?' she pleaded.

'I don't know,' he said at last. 'Your Mama's mad, I suppose. Like your Grandmama is, locked up in the back of the house – *and* your Aunt Emily. Everyone's mad in Ireland – that's what Mrs Martin said to old Flood.' He left the microscope then. 'We'd better get back. I have my piano lesson with Miss Moffatt.'

He left the work bench and went towards a big covered tea chest standing in a corner beyond the grate. 'Come over here,' he called to Hetty. 'Come and see this.' Hetty beside him now, he lifted the lid. And suddenly he drew out a long necklace of whitened bones, the linked vertebrae of a snake, and rattled them fiercely in Hetty's face. She shrieked.

'You idiot!' he whispered angrily. 'Only a dead snake.'

'You *hated* snakes, at home on the island. Remember the one at the Emerald pool?'

'Yes, well, but I'm not frightened of them any more – *am* I?' he added, even more angrily, rattling the bones again. 'Not frightened of anything here, in this stupid place.'

But he looked sadly at her then, Hetty thought. It was so difficult to be nice to him. And when she was, like saying he could share her secret house in the woods, he was nasty back to her. And all just because his parents were dead. Well, so was *her* father, and she didn't make such a fuss about that. But at least she had Elly.

She spoke to Elly later that afternoon, in the schoolroom, while Robert was having his piano lesson.

'Why is Robert having all these piano lessons? He doesn't really like it anyway – and he's no good at it.'

'Your mother wants him to have every advantage. He's lost everything, you see, parents and all. And she's become "responsible" for him now. She's his guardian.'

'Yes, well, why didn't Mama ask me if I wa-wa-wanted to learn the per-per-piano? She's *my* Mama, isn't she?'

'Yes, but, sure, you didn't really show any interest –'

'She never *asked* me – never asks me anything! She just dotes around Robert all the time. And Robert is nasty to me – even when I'm nice as pe-pe-pie to him.'

'Well, we all have to be kind to him, don't you see –'

'But *my* Papa is dead, too – the Caribs killed him!'

Elly, knowing the truth, became slightly tense. 'I know that, Hetty darlin'.' She reached across the table and ruffled the girl's curls for an instant. 'But at least you have your own mother.'

'I wish I didn't.' Hetty opened the book of Irish fairy tales that Mr O'Grady had given her, looking at the pictures of Cuckoo Cullen ripping up the great mountain with all the strange squiggly alphabet beneath. 'All Mama wants me to do is learn this stupid thing. And wear these awful clothes. I do so wish I could go back to my corduroy dresses and comfy things.'

'She wants you to be *Irish*,' Elly said, trying to hide the doubt in her voice. 'You *are* Irish, when you come down to it, after all. You're going to *live* here. This is your home now, your own house.'

'No, I'm not Irish! And I *hate* it here, hate it. And I want to be *English*.'

What she really wanted was to be loved, Elly thought. And indeed it was a cruel thing, how her own mother – when she wasn't chiding her in that high screechy voice she'd taken to now – neglected her, devoting what little time she had to spare from her devilish Fenian activities to young Robert.

Hetty turned and gazed out from the high schoolroom window, then across the woody valley to the green hills and blue mountains away on the skyline. England was over there, beyond those mountains – she knew that from the map on the schoolroom wall. And she turned to Elly with tears of hurt anger and frustration in her eyes, pointing back out of the window. 'That's where I'm going to live, Elly, in England. There's the great King over there and he owns half the world, as well as Ireland, Miss Goulden said so in lessons. And they live properly in England, don't have to learn Irish or wear stupid itchy clothes. So that's where *I'm* going . . .' She paused in her tirade. 'Besides,' she went on, picking up courage, daring now to tell Elly what she had never told her before. 'I don't really belong here. I'm a secret Pr-Pr-Princess!'

Elly was astonished. 'Who-who said? Who told you that?' she asked, her round dimpled cheeks colouring.

'Snipe – you know him, that funny man with no face, last year at the threshing when he told people's fortunes in mugs of tea. And sometimes he comes here with Mr Hennessy's van.'

'Ah, now, don't you be believing him –'

'But he *said* I was. He knows all about what's going to happen to people in the future.'

'Ah, he'd tell ye any kind of nonsense –'

'But he did, he *did*! And I *don't* have to like Robert, when he's nasty to me and has piano lessons all the time and no one asks me if *I'd* like to learn the piano.'

In the event Hetty did learn the piano, first assaulting the instrument in the playroom alone one day, out of sheer spite, before something gradually took her in the sound of the keys – especially the shiny black ones – and she started to tinker with them more gently, creating a crude music, returning and developing this on subsequent days, when Elly was there, so that eventually Elly, sensing this musical gift, persuaded Frances that Hetty should take lessons too – which she did, from Mr Beckett, the organist at the local parish church in Cloone. And soon, under his sensitive tutelage, developing real gifts, Hetty became much more proficient than Robert.

However, that afternoon with Elly, she ran from the room, just to show how annoyed she was about things in general. Though in fact she really left because she wanted to get to the yard as soon as possible.

The horses were going to be shod, when they came in from work, and she ran downstairs and outside to watch. She wanted to see that nice stable boy, too, who helped the blacksmith. Mickey Joe, he was called. He smoked cigarettes – and he'd promised to let her try a few puffs next time they met.

Elly sat at the schoolroom table after Hetty had left. 'God save us,' she said to herself. 'What'll be the end of it all, I *don't* know.'

The rats had continued their depredations about the house all that winter. Neither the poison O'Donovan had laid, nor the sporadic but vicious attentions of the two terriers, had made much difference to the burgeoning population of these voracious beasts that had come to infest the place.

Frances had seen the remnants of corn along skirting boards and in the hall, confirming that someone in the household must be feeding them – trying to sabotage her work, her whole new life, as she felt it to be, at Summer Hill.

But it was not Henrietta. Frances had established that. In the same manner she had assured herself that Aunt Emily had no hand in the matter. And as for the servants – why should they encourage the beasts? They were terrified of them.

Frances was mystified – and much put out. It seemed a thing of great ill omen that her rule in Summer Hill should so begin and continue with this plague. It was an affront to all her cleansing ambitions, to her transforming the house, turning it on its axis, away from everything English – which she had come to loathe and despise – and towards all things Celtic. And these rats had sullied her dream in this renaissance.

By a process of elimination then she reduced the suspects to one of the men, or boys, in the household. And in turn, watching them, she thought she must discount Robert, and Carty Mike the garden boy who brought in the vegetables, as well as the two new footmen, Brian and Billy Walsh, and the under butler, Willy Phelan, whose father had just died and would thus never risk his job in such a manner.

This really only left the saturnine Pat Kennedy, a man whom she had long mistrusted, and – unique to Summer Hill – to some extent feared. Yet she had not replaced him as head butler. She told herself there were perfectly good reasons for this – he was most competent, meticulous indeed, at his job. But she wished nonetheless, that she could get rid of him, find some excuse – and perhaps this rat business might serve – for Pat Kennedy knew far too much about her, about her thefts with Elly in the house years before, when he had found the stolen baccarat paperweights in the chimney flue of her bedroom, and had mocked her with this knowledge on her return from London. He had, of course, as well, behaved badly towards Elly at that time, coldly withdrawing his attentions.

So she determined to stalk him. And when, in the next few weeks, this bore no fruit, she decided to search his room, in the servants' wing overlooking the yard. An opportunity arose the following Sunday morning, when most of the servants had gone to early mass at Cloone. And it was then that Frances went into the back of the house and opened his bedroom door.

It was the same bedroom, she realised, in which, years before, she had gone to see the Spanish dancing girls – and had met their guitar-playing leader Rodrigo instead, when he had so suddenly and expertly embraced and touched her. And the memory of this, together with the vague odours of Pat Kennedy's habitation here – a smell of brilliantine and sweaty linen – excited her now for an instant, reviving the animal instincts which she had so suppressed towards men in the last ten years.

Quickly, in something of a fever, she searched the place – opening drawers in the small dressing table, pulling the mattress up, looking in his boots, finally going through his wardrobe. And it was here, in the pocket of a dark winter overcoat, that she felt the awkward object, before drawing out the revolver.

Astonished but then fearful, thinking she heard a faint rustle of something outside, she rammed the revolver back inside the coat. But the noise ceased and Frances went hurriedly through the other pockets – of his day-time livery, then his evening tail-coat, and here, in one of the pockets, she was rewarded, drawing out half a dozen grains of corn.

So, Pat Kennedy fed the rats! She had thought as much. But what of the gun? What could be his need, his intention here? She didn't stop to think now, leaving the room and quickly returning along the landing. In the urgency of her flight she quite failed to notice Hetty, crouching behind a pyramid of red fire buckets along one wall – Hetty who had followed her that morning, watching her go into Pat's room, equally intent on her own surveillances about the house. And now Hetty was outraged. Her mother, with Pat at church, was trying to trap him in some way – because nice Pat had been feeding nice Mr Rat. Well, there was only one thing to be done . . .

Pat, sorting the silver later that day in his butler's pantry, leant down towards Hetty, not certain that he had heard her right the first time, the kiss curls neatly poised on his brow, the dark still eyes gazing at her kindly, but intently.

'What is it, little one? I didn't hear . . .'

'My Me-Me-Mama, she w-w-went to your re-re-room this morning – because you w-w-were feeding Mr Rat. She awa-awa-wants to catch you!'

Pat bent down on his haunches so that he was on a level with Hetty. Then he broadened his smile. 'Ah, no, sure an' doesn't she check the servants' rooms like that oftentimes, Miss Hetty, just like her old mother used to. She was just inspecting.' He patted her cheek.

'I see. Be-be-but you *do* feed Mr Rat. I've seen you. And that wa-wa-was kind, and I wa-wa-wanted to help, so you we-wouldn't be trapped.'

'And you have helped, little one, you have. But it's nothing. She wasn't up to any harm, your mother. Nothing to worry about.'

'But – but you we-won't tell her I told you?'

He held her by both shoulders now. 'Never, *never*,' he said. 'It's a secret between us – just us two – entirely.'

Frances confronted Pat Kennedy next morning in her mother's old office-boudoir, which she had since redecorated in her own purer taste: free of all its previous clutter, with a light wallpaper and a handsome Irish Sheraton desk in the window, where she sat now, her back to the light.

'No point in beating about the bush,' she told him quickly and coldly. 'Why have you been feeding the rats? – encouraging them into the house, ever since I arrived back here.' She gazed at him steadily.

'The rats, Ma'am?'

'Yes, the rats, Pat Kennedy. No point in denying it.' There was silence – thirty seconds, a minute. Pat seemed never likely to reply and faced with this unexpected response Frances was at a loss, then suddenly angry. 'If you can offer no good reason – and what one could there be? – I take your silence as an admission of guilt. You must leave the household at once.'

'Very well, Ma'am.' Pat Kennedy spoke at last, with utter calm, and turned to go, at which Frances was even more put out.

'Wait!' she called to him. 'I want to know *why*? Have you some hatred of me, that you wish to despoil the house in this way? You object to the changes I have made here?'

At the door now, Pat turned back to her, still speaking calmly, but with a harder, more ominous tone. 'I object to all your sort in Ireland, Mrs Fraser. You English, you landlords here, who've taken everything from us Irish, for centuries.'

Frances suddenly relaxed, even offered him the hint of a smile. 'So *that's* it! Well, I may tell you, you may rest assured – I thought you would have noticed it already – I am *entirely* of your opinion. I am equally against everything English myself, which is part of the change here. I wish the house, indeed the whole country, back in all its old Irish ways.' Frances's voice was touched with passion now. 'I abhor the English treatment of Ireland and am anxious to do everything I can, in a constitutional way, to end their occupation here. Have you not noticed? – my friend from Kilkenny, Mr Standish O'Grady? He has always been of that mind and written much about it. And, from Dublin, Mr Redmond, leader of our Home Rule party at Westminster – and my cousin, Mortimer Cordiner, an MP in the same party. You have seen them all down here, have you not? You must realise I share, am entirely committed to, their aims. And so to yours.'

Pat Kennedy had returned half-way across the room, more relaxed now, but still with an icy tone in his voice. 'Yes, Ma'am, I have noticed these visitors – and know who they are. But if you hope for change through them – or even through Arthur Griffith's Sinn Feiners – you're wasting your time.'

'Why so?'

'We've tried for years, Mrs Fraser, to get our independence through London, in Westminster. But, with Parnell gone, that was the end of that way. Parnell had the following and the power, at home and in London – he might well have won our freedom, constitutionally. But Mr Redmond never will, nor Mr Griffith. And the British know that. They'll stay on here as long as they want now, any old excuse. They'll only be persuaded to leave Ireland by . . . by other means.'

Frances knew what he meant. Of course she did: she had found his revolver. He was not one with Redmond's constitutional Home Rulers. He supported the shadowy and illegal Irish Republican Brotherhood and their secret army, dedicated to overthrowing the British by violence and revolution. But of this she could not speak to him. She must temporise for the moment.

'Well, you may be right – that is another and wider issue. But, for the moment, you and I, have we an understanding? – that I am not a rackrent landlord here; that I wish, like you, for an end to British rule everywhere in Ireland?'

'Yes, Ma'am. We have that understanding.'

Frances stood up, relieved, believing she had settled her differences with Pat; that now she had an ally, not an enemy, in the man. 'So, if we see eye to eye in the matter, I shall hope for your support in my political and other endeavours at Summer Hill, not your hindrance. Do I have your word on that, too?'

'Yes, Ma'am.'

'Good. We must not be divided in our cause, Pat. That way the British will certainly maintain their stranglehold here – indefinitely.'

'Yes, Ma'am.' He turned to go.

'Oh, and what of the rats? – You're feeding them, Mr Kennedy,' she called lightly to him.

He turned again – for the first time smiling a fraction. 'Ah, that was just out of the softness of my heart, Ma'am.'

He bowed briefly before leaving the room. But there was nothing of the servant in his gesture, Frances thought – more as if, at least her equal, he had just been paying court to her. And this disturbed Frances, just as his revolver had done. For she had to acknowledge then the hidden violence in her own temperament which she had repressed these last months in her happy re-possession of the house . . . had to admit how violence had so well served her own purposes in Domenica and in regaining Summer Hill. Perhaps Pat Kennedy was right in his beliefs there – perhaps, for Ireland to be free, it would have to come to revolvers in the end.

In the drawing room of the square, lime-washed Georgian house at Wellfield, some sixty miles north in Queen's County, Bunty Cordiner once more took up the issue of Summer Hill with her gentle, myopic husband Austin, Sir Desmond's younger brother – flourishing that week's *Irish Tatler* in his face.

'You see! – your niece's ridiculous renovations at Summer Hill have even found their way into the *Tatler*! It is too much, too *much*!' Bosom heaving, Bunty's tiny body shook with anger as she stomped about the room, while her husband – fallen asleep some minutes before by the fire over the latest cattle prices in the *Irish Times* – tried to pacify her.

'My dear, we are not responsible for the decorations there –'

'But we *would* have been,' she rounded viciously on him, 'had you shown an ounce of will in the matter. Lady Cordiner, remember – she left the house and the whole estate to *us*. Told us so, the very day after your brother's funeral –'

'Dearest, we have been through that a hundred times: she *changed* her will – not unknown – indeed a far too common occurrence in this country.'

'Yes, for that little hussy – that *harlot* – Frances!'

'I hardly think . . . She *is* her daughter, my dear.'

'Lady Cordiner loathed and despised her. She would never normally have made a will in her favour, least of all disinherited us, if Frances had not brought pressure to bear. Yes, blackmailed her in some manner. I'm convinced of it.'

'Blackmail – so you have said, often enough. But how so? How so?' Austin, as always, to avoid open warfare, tried to reason with his wife; his logic only served to infuriate her all the more.

'The daughter!' Bunty roared at him. 'Henrietta – there was the lever. I believe she is not legitimate!' she added, playing this trump card for the first time.

Austin showed vague but genuine astonishment. 'But, my dear, she must be – the daughter of that Fraser chap, the no-good sugar planter –'

'I doubt it.'

'And besides, if Henrietta were illegitimate . . . all the more reason for Lady Cordiner's not passing the house on to Frances. You cannot be right. It is an unjust surmise.'

'In any case, I am convinced that Henrietta is the key to the whole matter.'

'I should say something rather less dramatic, Bunty dear: you forget . . . the forceful character of Frances and the advice we know my cousins gave her at the time: Mortimer and Dermot – *they* persuaded her, to make things up with Sarah, to maintain the direct family line. She is her daughter after all.'

'You know perfectly well your sister-in-law never took *any*one's advice. And she *despised* Frances. And now, by all accounts, she is locked up, held prisoner, at Summer Hill – supposedly demented, insane! Can you really think that her personality should have undergone such a complete change without some extraordinary reason, pressure, *blackmail*?'

'Granted, dear. But the reasons are surely much more obvious – the successive tragedies she underwent, the death of her two sons, my nephews; then her husband, hardly in his mid-sixties . . . the long estrangement with Frances. It all unhinged her. And I am not surprised! Imagine your own feelings, dearest, had you suffered the same torments and bereavements in our family?'

Bunty turned away. She was not capable of imagining such feelings. She could think only how she had been dispossessed of the great house – and the role she had long imagined for herself there, as gracious hostess to the county. And her bitterness was sustained by an avaricious fire, a constant sense of indignity and injustice, nibbling away at her soul – that this prize, actually in her hands at one point, had so unaccountably been snatched away from her. And so she had spent the intervening months pondering how she could reverse Lady Cordiner's decision, working on various theories, pursuing them secretly, seeking a way in which she could unmask both Frances and her daughter, prove her theories correct, and thus in some manner regain the glory she had lost. Now she turned to Austin, wishing to offer him a hint of her success in this direction.

'I can only imagine one thing – and I have told you it: we have been quite improperly deprived of our rights. And I shall prove this. I have my ways, in Summer Hill itself!'

'In Summer Hill? But you have not been there –'

'No. But through a quite astonishing piece of good luck I have a friend there now, in the heart of the enemy's camp. I shall prove my point!'

Austin was somewhat shocked. 'My dear, you should do nothing rash –'

'*Rash?* Rash to regain what is rightfully ours? It is no more than common sense,' she added. 'A commodity you are not overburdened with, Austin,' she told him, before leaving the room abruptly. Austin had long been embarrassed by his wife. But there was absolutely nothing he could do about it – he had realised that for almost as long.

The following winter Robert and Henrietta, becoming known about the neighbourhood and with Frances's Home Rule sympathies still largely unrecognised by the other county families, were asked to various children's parties. Greatest of these, traditionally, was the juvenile fancy dress ball held every Christmas at Curraghmore, Lord Waterford's family seat.

Frances, given her feelings about the Anglo-Irish aristocracy, did not accompany the children. In the charge of Miss Goulden, with Elly in attendance, they all took an early train to Waterford and travelled thence, in the dim winter afternoon, in several coaches, sent to meet them and other guests at the station.

Hetty and Robert changed into their costumes in one of the bedrooms made over for this purpose, on a landing directly above the great baronial hall: Robert in Lincoln green, a tasselled costume and peaked hat, with leather boots and a bow and arrow, as Robin Hood; Hetty, barefoot, in a loose-fitting, belted dress of the same material, as Maid Marian. Despite the big coal fire in the bedroom she shivered.

'I hate it – I've hardly any ke-clothes on.'

'Should have thought of that when you tried it on at home.' Elly tossed her hair. 'At least you don't have to have ribbons – just out of the great greenwood you are!'

'I've no real arrows in my quiver,' Robert complained. 'Only pretend. It's all too stupid.'

He twanged his bow several times, loosing off imaginary arrows at the Boothby-Smyth twins, Michael and Johnny. They were going as Tweedledum and Tweedledee, wearing cramped school blazers and corduroy knickerbockers, in yellow-striped waistcoats and similarly patterned caps, both with cushions stuffed into their trousers, fattening them out. How stupid they looked, Robert thought. They were his age and had been sent over to play at Summer Hill several times. He disliked them both, a feeling entirely reciprocated. He loosed off a last arrow in their direction – and Tweedledum stuck his tongue out at him in return.

Beyond these two, hogging the warmth of the fire, Hetty saw Priscilla Armitage, being titivated by her fusspot of a nanny, Miss Biggs. Priscilla was a tallish girl, normally with long blonde ringlets. But now she was dressed as a miniature Marie-Antoinette, her hair replaced by an elaborate powdered wig: a spiteful, haughty girl, Hetty thought her, on the few times that Priscilla had come over to play with her. And Hetty was pleased at her obvious discomfiture.

Later, downstairs in one of the long dark corridors that led into the great hall, and before the main events of the afternoon got underway, the children mixed awkwardly in the lamplit shadows, variously disguised, uncertain who was who. But Robert, when he came downstairs with Hetty, recognised the two Tweedles with Marie-Antoinette readily enough: beside a big oak chest where a bran tub waited, they were all three standing together – sniggering at them.

'You couldn't shoot a thing with that stupid little bow and arrow,' Tweedledum mocked Robert as he passed. And Priscilla Armitage laughed outright at Hetty. 'O-o-o-ps! Just look!' She smirked at her. 'Adam and Eve – with no proper clothes on. Straight out of the trees, from the jungles you came from. No proper clo-o-thes!' she sang out, rustling her voluminous, beribboned satin dress and shaking a tortoiseshell fan just beneath a large beauty spot painted beside her priggish chin.

Robert might have walked on. But Hetty stopped, turned back. 'You look like a huge stupid doll in that dress,' she told Priscilla smartly. 'And that wig is like a tea cosy with flour all over it.'

'It's *not* flour! It's just like the French aristocrats had, Mama told me – and it's her best gardenia face powder – so *there*, you stupid little girl.'

Robert had joined Hetty, adding his own riposte now. 'You get your head chopped off anyway,' he told Priscilla. 'All the rich French people did then. Read it in my history book – and *good* riddance to you.'

Tweedledee advanced on Robert, trying to pull the bow away. 'Suppose you think it's all *very* clever coming like that,' he told him. ''Cos you think you're such a famous hunter and shooter – all those fibs and lies you told us about your shooting cannibals and savages on that island you say you lived –'

'Didn't lie – it's true! They did attack us.'

'Like Robinson Crusoe, I suppose, you little liar! Isn't he, Michael?' Tweedledee turned to his brother. 'Just a little fibber, like that big snake you said attacked you and how the savage cut it all up into little pieces –'

'It *did* –'

'Don't even *talk* to them,' Priscilla interrupted grandly, fluttering her fan even more vigorously. 'They're both little savages themselves. Why, they haven't even got proper fathers and mothers – Mama said so. Have you, Robin Hood? *Have* you? No – just two silly little babes in the wood! That's what you should have come –'

Hetty went for Priscilla before she had finished the sentence, grappling with her, sending her wig askew, just as Miss Goulden, arriving on the scene, intervened.

'What *do* you think you're both doing?' She dragged Hetty and Robert away, back down the corridor, to a cloakroom at the far end.

'They were being horrible to us! – saying we were liars and savages and had no proper parents,' Hetty said to her, flustered, but still angry though not crying. Miss Goulden, in a severe grey woollen dress, was an emaciated woman of dyspeptic temper – her mouth a thin, shuttered line beneath hair-sprouting nostrils and bitter eyes, with coarse yellowish hair tightly wrenched back in a hair-pinned bun. But she suddenly softened her approach now, bending down to Hetty.

'Well, that was *quite* wrong of them, my dear.' Closer now, she peered at Hetty, forming a smile through her gold-rimmed spectacles. 'Why, of *course* you both had proper parents, didn't you? But poor Robert's – they went in that nasty hurricane. And your own dear Papa, those fearful savages –'

'He *wasn't* my own dear Papa,' Hetty interjected. 'I *hated* him – always fighting with Mama and drinking rum all day. He wasn't *my* dear Papa at all.' And now tears at last came welling into Hetty's eyes. And Miss Goulden, made more curious by this last revelation, but mistaking Hetty's meaning, leant even closer to her, became even nicer in an oily way.

'My dear, you must not say such things! He *was* your Papa, Mr Fraser. Why, who else could have been?' Then, unable to restrain herself, she added the sudden earnest enquiry: 'Was there someone else?'

Hetty looked at her blankly: this frightening-faced woman with her hairy nose, bearing down on her, asking these strange questions.

'Tell me, girl, tell me what you mean – had you some *other* dear Papa on the island then? Tell me!' Her voice had hardened and she nearly shook Hetty now.

'No, no!' Hetty was confused. What did Miss Goulden mean – 'some other Papa'? There had only been Mr Fraser, that horrid, sweaty man in a white suit, drinking rum, even on the beach at her birthday party.

Miss Goulden, letting her go, was disappointed. But she had hit on something here, she felt. She would, given time, quarry it further. In due course, she would have something to tell Mrs Austin Cordiner, at Wellfield – Bunty Cordiner, such a sensible woman, for whom she had worked many years ago, over a holiday season with Mrs Cordiner's own children in Clifden, Co. Galway – and whom, quite by chance, she had met again, just prior to taking up her post as governess at Summer Hill; met at the Royal Dublin Society's tearooms in Ballsbridge – an afternoon a year before, when Mrs Austin Cordiner, hearing of her new position had, in a most tactful way, explained her own interests in Summer Hill and asked her help, making various and potentially advantageous proposals . . .

Hetty and Robert hated the party – the more so, since Priscilla won second prize in the girls' fancy dress, and neither of them came anywhere, while their turn at the bran tub unearthed no more than an Irish clay pipe for Hetty and a pack of playing cards, with dull views of Killarney on the back, for Robert. Even the conjuror failed to amuse them: a pallid shadow of the voodoo ceremonies both children had witnessed in Domenica, with his babble of brogue-ish talk, coloured handkerchiefs and white rabbits.

'Just stupid rabbits!' Robert said scathingly to Hetty. 'I'd like to shoot them.'

'Yes, it's all quite stupid – you can see, he has them somewhere up his sleeve.'

Only the magic lantern show, given to round off the proceedings, changed their dire opinion of the party. This, at least, Domenica had not offered them. They had never seen such a thing before – the vivid coloured pictures, of Ali Baba and the Forty Thieves, of Little Red Riding Hood, coming one after the other, shining on a white sheet, sent from the other end of the great hall through a dazzling cone of light from a smoking machine. It was all sheer enchantment, especially for Hetty, sitting next to Robert in the darkness.

'How is it *done*?' she whispered to him, grasping his hand involuntarily in her rapture.

'Oh, it's just bright lamplight, magnified through a glass eye – like they have in microscopes,' he told her prosaically.

'Yes, but the pictures, the story, all the *colours* – how can they get over to the sheet?'

'Just told you.'

Hetty did not really believe him. 'No, it *is* magic,' she told him. And yet she wondered. He might be right. He was so good at history and microscopes and things. She looked across at him now, his nose and his Robin Hood hat outlined against the streak of dazzling light. He looked rather handsome. But then she heard him sniffling faintly. Why was he crying? She leant over. 'What's wrong? You're crying . . .'

'No, I'm not.'

'Don't cry –'

'Shush!' someone said.

At the station in Waterford, as they waited for the train back to Thomastown and while the two women were out of earshot, Hetty said to Robert, 'Well, you *didn't* look stupid as Robin Hood. So you needn't be sad. And you really know a lot more than those other awful Irish boys – about microscopes and those rich French ladies and things.' He'd walked away then, towards the slot machine offering penny bars of Fry's chocolate. 'And anyway,' she went on, following him, 'they don't know *anything* and we did *much* more be-be-braver and exciting things on the island, and we were both good and rude to them – *and* I nearly tipped Priscilla's horrid we-we-wig off, so we won't play with any of them ever again, we-will we?'

'No. We won't.' He turned to her. 'Yes, you were good and rude to her,' he said ruefully, admiring her. 'Wish I'd done the same to those fat Tweedles. But look,' he said, in a low voice, glancing up the platform. 'I've got a penny – stand in front, so the others don't see.' He put the penny in the machine then and they shared the chocolate bar quickly and secretly. And later on the train home, both exhausted by the festivities, they fell asleep, leaning against each other, in the corner of the compartment.

But Hetty's peace with Robert did not last. There was too much submerged hurt in both their lives for that. What was unexplained or unhappy in Hetty's past was more than equalled by the stark tragedy in Robert's. And, since Frances was no mother to Hetty, they were both really orphans – though loth to admit it; both searching for some vital contact, trying to establish roots. And to this process, this search for a confiding heart, a sure and certain cornerstone in their lives, they brought an unconscious ruthlessness, with its by-products of mutual anger and antagonism, which at times flooded from the well of their discontent, poisoning their relationship, so that for every happy truce they made between themselves, as bonded allies against the cruelty of others in this cold new world, they found afterwards some hot *casus belli*.

Their knowledge of each other's unhappiness, their parentless state, both repelled and drew them together. They clung to, yet hated, each other, by turns, in equal measure. Thus, their engagements were the more bitter across the traditional battlegrounds of childhood. And in this see-saw of war and peace they ran the gamut between the roles they took and swapped about: mistress and master alternately, to the other's slave – coming, in the process, to know every weakness, where they could most wound by subtle probes or open frontal assaults.

For Hetty, her strength was in her growing, if sporadic, confidence and hauteur – a mind like her features: sharp, adventurous, daringly cut; an outdoor, wind-blown face in one way, poised, controlled, the bright dark eyes full of determination, a will to power. Conversely, with her pale skin, the cheeks touched with high colour, her small, delicate ears, equally sculpted nose and thin, reedy limbs, she had the air of a frail indoor flower. There was a contradictory mix of the Valkyrie and Botticelli maiden in Hetty's looks and bearing – repeated in her mind, for the confidence she often showed there was only skin-deep, her stammer continuing evidence of her limitations, the vocal tip of an iceberg standing for so much repressed fear and uncertainty beneath.

And here, in this stammer, was a weakness which Robert, when cornered or upset by something in himself, would viciously exploit – and tragically, for with him alone Hetty had come to make her words flow, whereas with everyone else speech was a hair-raising, often tear-filled business, the words spilling forth at first bright, intricate thoughts and phrases, avalanche-fashion; only for the whole creation to be suddenly toppled as she fought for breath, failing to achieve the vital word which was the keystone of her offering.

One day – out of nothing, in what seemed so peaceful a site, in the brick-domed dovecote beyond the upper pleasure garden, the birds fluttering in and out from the circle of sunlight far above them – they found a war which, for a time, drove them far apart. They had brought corn to lay for the birds – and Hetty, for some ten minutes, had been trying to tempt one of them, her special dove Matilda, to perch on her arm, an endeavour which came to bore and tire Robert, so that, impatient, he turned away, before noticing the two terriers who had run up to the iron-barred entrance to the dovecote.

'Don't let them in!' Hetty whispered urgently to him as, just at that moment, the dove came at last to perch on her forearm. But in a fit of pique Robert did just that, the dogs jumping and barking furiously about inside, so that all the birds took fright, with a loud clapping of wings and dancing feathers, as they flew upwards, crowding through the dome hole into the light.

Hetty was outraged. 'You *stupid* little brute! – you did it on purpose! What for? – just when I had Matilda on my arm. You stupid wretched little colonial boy – ignorant horrible *beast*!' She stormed at him.

But Robert was quite unrepentant. 'Tired and bored with all this – feeding the stupid birds. You said we'd go to the river –'

'I won't now! Just as I was getting Matilda used to it all – and she'll *never* come again now, and I'll never pe-pe-play any more with you, you little fe-fe-fool!'

'You're the fool, much more – speaking and spluttering all the time – can't even *speak* properly, so why should I do things with you, when you can't even tell me things straight? You can't speak to *anyone*, you little spluttering girl . . .'

They were close, glaring at each other, Hetty's face red with anger and hurt now. 'I –' she started. 'I ke-ke-ke-*can* sp-sp-*speak*, perfectly well!'

Robert laughed outright then. 'You little liar – look at you, you can't as-pe, as-pe, as-speak *at all*!' He mimicked her cruelly, so that she burst into tears then, running from the dovecote, running, running, to the secret house where Robert had not yet been, in the heart of the woods.

Dermot Cordiner, now a major with the 13th Hussars, took part of his leave away from England that spring, by more or less inviting himself to Summer Hill. Frances, though she had remained in vague contact, had not encouraged him in any such visit. More than ever now she frowned on his army career, his implicit purpose there in maintaining the Empire. Nor had she forgotten her love for, and failure with, him, years before in London. Only he, of course, with Elly, Ruth Wechsberg and her mother, knew the real identity of Henrietta's father. And such knowledge angered Frances now, as did any revived memory of her disastrous *affaire* with the King-Emperor.

On the other hand, Dermot was her cousin, and she owed him a considerable debt through his having warned her, in Domenica, of her mother's intentions over Summer Hill. Without his early letter then she might not have had the house at all, so that she could hardly deny him it now.

In any case, she thought, he is simply coming for a holiday; he could form no permanent threat or irk to her. And no doubt, too, he would be interested to see in what splendid manner she had achieved all her old ambitions with Summer Hill – how she had, as she had so long ago promised him, returned there, laid seige to the place and emerged victorious. Dermot, who had always doubted her in this! Well, he would see for himself now, how much a woman of her word she was. Thinking thus, she actually came to look forward to his visit, as a successful commander might, finally offering an allied but disbelieving general a view of the spoils. In fact, for his own part, Dermot's visit was motivated by quite other considerations which, tactfully, he made her aware of soon after his arrival.

But not tactfully enough. As they walked through the beech hedge maze beyond the upper pleasure gardens, on a rain-cleared, bright spring morning, some days after his arrival, Frances rounded on him.

'Dermot, I know what you hint at: you have had it from your father on his visits here – and it is unjust: that I unduly dominate here, that I have neglected Hetty!'

'I said, rather, that your *political* activities seem to have come to dominate your life, dear Frances – as they have my father's, which I've told him many's the time is to his detriment –'

'But that *is* my life now, as it is your father's, which you will not accept: Irish freedom – just as your life, in the British army, is one of *preventing* such freedoms everywhere!'

'We need not argue that. We have done so, often before – to no avail!' He smiled then. His thin, ascetic features had become even more pronounced with age. His frizzy, straw-coloured hair, parted severely down the middle, had whitened over his temples now, which together with his strangely hooded eyes, whose lids had come more to droop over either side, hiding the edges of his pupils, gave him rather the air of a young sage. Yet his neat waxy moustache, generally severe trim and ramrod bearing proclaimed him an active, military sage, which he was – so successful in his career that, not yet thirty-five, he was the youngest major in his regiment. Then, as one briefly repulsed and regrouping, he took another line in his attack.

'What I meant was that . . . it seems to me, with all your other great gifts, your beauty, you are wasting them in these political bitternesses. Or at least,' he temporised, 'denying so much else that is just as worthwhile in your temperament?' He looked at her searchingly, as they paused, undecided, at a junction in the maze.

'You mean, simply, that I have become a termagant, in my attitude, my views?' She looked at him steadily then, with some venom, entirely confirming his views.

'You have tended –'

'You have forgotten, perhaps, the things that may have driven me to this position?'

'No. You have had more to contend with, in what you hint at, than almost anyone else I know. But I can remember another woman . . .' he added vaguely.

'Yes,' Frances burst out. 'And remember, too, how you turned that woman down!' She walked away quickly, blindly, further into the maze.

Joining her at once, Dermot took her arm. 'I could not – I was not the man you thought me –'

'Doubtless!'

'I cannot so change my basic temper – as you have since done, my dear Frances. That is more a comment than a criticism. You have come to let hatred overwhelm you –'

She turned on him sharply again. 'Indeed! – for it was the one feeling I have been consistently faced with in my own life: that and betrayal. And one cannot remain untouched and unchanged by such experiences. One *changes*, don't you see? – returns like with like.'

'Yes, perhaps – I do see that. But surely, now that you have achieved everything

– 310 –

you wanted here . . .' He looked round at the dense, overhanging hedges of the maze. 'Surely now you may be less insistent, more easy-hearted? What of all the laughter you intended bringing to Summer Hill? And what of Hetty?'

They had reached an impasse in the beech puzzle. Frances turned abruptly, back to the hedge, cornered in several ways now. 'My dear Dermot,' she retaliated by avoiding his questions. 'Despite their provocative nature, I take your comments . . . in the best spirit. I realise, too, your concern for my well-being – you have always shown me that, and I am grateful to you. But you do not see,' she burst out loudly again, 'how life does not suddenly cease to offer its challenges – and I have another and greater one now: the freedom of my country. And there, equally, one must remain hard.' On this decisive note she stopped suddenly, her hair feathering about in the windy spring sunshine.

'I do see that, which is what troubles me.'

'You would do no less in your own career, if offered a good war, would you?'

'There is little chance of that! We seem in the midst of another long peace.'

'Well, here in Ireland we are *not* so peacefully situated! There's the difference.'

Dermot looked around him, considering the impasse, both literal and conversational, to which they had come. 'We seem to be lost,' he said, the kind, hooded eyes narrowing even further in a placatory smile.

'Not so,' Frances answered brightly. 'I know my way here!' And she strode forward, more purposefully than ever, seeking the real exit to the maze. Dermot sadly watched her go. She believed she had won everything, he thought – yet the truth of the matter was that she had been thoroughly defeated.

Hetty, unhappy generally and particularly embittered by her last fracas with Robert, retreated more and more into her secret den in the woods. And Dermot's arrival did nothing to improve her sullen temper; indeed, he exacerbated it – some boring army man, a distant cousin, and worse a friend of her mother's. But, worst of all, such a *great* friend of Robert's now: Robert, who had taken to him immediately, badgering him and playing with him at every opportunity, the day long, talking about guns and things. Hetty – loth to admit it – suffered agonies of jealousy, hatred, frustration then. Why could she not be part of all this exciting male world? – do, and talk about, daring things, fiddle with guns? She felt more than ever outcast, and came deeply to resent Dermot.

Dermot on the other hand made every effort to befriend her, but with no success, until one afternoon, finding himself obscured by the artificial waterfall in the grotto and seeing Hetty stalk secretively down the great monkey puzzle avenue and into the woods to the south of the house, he decided to track her, see where she went and perhaps, in some manner, get on easier terms with her.

But, on this occasion, Hetty's fieldcraft outdid Dermot's. She soon realised he was following her and, a plan forming in her mind, decided to lead him on. Instead of making for her secret house she twisted and turned among the woods, leading

Dermot into the thickest, most briary parts, chuckling at his discomfiture, before she left the trees altogether, cutting across the pasture, straight down the valley, into the steep forested ramparts there, finally coming out on the river bank.

Some way behind her, tattered and torn, Dermot felt as if he were pursuing the white rabbit in *Alice in Wonderland*. He thought he had lost her until, emerging near the river himself, he saw the flash of her primrose dress, some way down the bank, as she made for the octagonal stone boathouse.

Just below the boathouse, he knew, the river narrowed in a gorge and with the spring rains the current here, full of vicious swirling eddies, would be flowing fast. Surely, he hoped – surely she was not taking one of the Summer Hill boats out, alone on the river, at this moment?

Which is exactly what Hetty did. Dermot started to run. But, before he reached the boathouse, Hetty had emerged in one of the light dinghies at the other side. She held an oar in one hand, the other not yet properly set in its rowlock, as she swayed about, standing amidships, so that, before she even got set to row, the boat had nosed into the middle of the current, and she was being swept downstream.

'Hetty!' he roared after her, seeing her trying to head the boat into the stream. She might have seen him as he stood on the jetty. But she did not hear him, the dark flood waters rushing by now, sucking at the banks, the boat a swirling leaf, uncontrolled, disappearing rapidly round the river bend.

Jumping into a second boat, Dermot pursued her. Cutting fast out into midstream and rowing furiously, he soon narrowed the distance between them, and rounding the bend he saw her then, some distance away. She was no longer trying to fight the current, simply gripping on to the sides of the boat, both the oars gone, quite powerless.

Dermot redoubled his energies – for he knew, too, of the further and greater danger here: the big weir by the mill further downstream which would whisk her down its steep, torrential slope onto the sharp, half-submerged stones beneath.

Yet when he rounded a further bend, with the brink of the roaring weir in sight now, Dermot suddenly saw Hetty reach into the bottom of the boat, pick out the two oars, put them expertly into the rowlocks, before pulling the boat away from the V of the weir, aiming for the mill race bank nearby. So that it was Dermot, astonished by this turnabout and not quite looking where he was going, who found himself caught in the vortex of the powerful current and, unable to pull his boat aside, disappeared over the edge into the raging torrent.

In the event, and because of the high water generally, he sluiced safely down the weir, the dinghy riding high in the white water, over the hidden rocks at the bottom. He only lost one oar in the process, before managing to pull the boat in to the bank a little downstream.

Hetty, her boat moored upstream at the entrance to the mill race and standing on the bank there now, was enchanted by her ruse. Dermot, when he eventually joined her, sopping wet, was less pleased. But he had decided, in the cause of gaining her friendship, to make very light of his experience.

'My! – you *did* row then,' he gasped, taking off his squelching boots.

'Of *course* I can re-re-row. Learnt all about that from Big Jules in Domenica, in *much* re-re-rougher water.'

'But you didn't have any oars, when I saw you going down. I was worried.'

'Just drifting,' she said very casually.

He looked at her quizzically. 'Indeed . . . But are you allowed to take the boat out . . . on your own?'

'No. Just because you were fe-fe-following me.'

'So! You planned that I should go to a watery grave – down there!' He looked at the rushing white water below the weir.

'Oh, no!' she answered sweetly.

You little liar, he thought. Yet he had to admire her courage and skills in the whole deceit. Just the same sort of wilful, daring, rather spiteful gifts as her mother: a regal disregard for others. And, thinking of this word, he wondered if she had inherited these arrogant traits more from her Royal father?

It was difficult to think of Hetty in that way, and he had to remind himself, with some astonishment, gazing at this unhappy, frail, stammering little girl, lovely but unloved, that he was looking at the King of England's daughter who, if fate had played a different card, he would never have come within a mile of, let alone finding himself at her mercy, here in the middle of Ireland. A granddaughter of Victoria, that so formal and correct old Queen, Dermot considered – and, beyond that, part of a wandering line that led, nonetheless, back to the great Tudor and Plantagenet monarchs. It was a strange thought.

He took off his wet Norfolk jacket, letting it dry in the sun as he sat in the carpet of kingcups. Hetty crouched nearby, then knelt in the yellow blooms, glad that he was not angry, but still wary of him.

Dermot gazed across at her as he pulled off his socks, still with a look of wonder in his wry, hooded eyes. 'You're a clever girl – no doubt!' He smiled faintly, shaking his head.

'Yes,' she said bluntly.

'You spend so much time on your own,' Dermot went on. 'I was curious – to see what you do here.'

'Oh, just like I did in De-De-Domenica. Exploring, de-doing exciting things,' she boasted.

'Indeed.' He got his pipe out and tried to light it, with no success.

'In Domenica I did *lots* of strange things, really strange, up in the hills, with ke-ke-cannibals and snakes and things. Here it's all very de-de-dull. No snakes at all in Ireland,' she added offhandedly.

'Yes, I expect it is rather dull by comparison.' Then he picked one of the kingcups by his side, fingering it vaguely. 'Except there *are* interesting things here, if you look closely. Know what this is?'

'Oh, that's just a stupid little Irish fe-fe-flower. We had *real* flowers at Fraser Hall in the garden, orchids and great red poker flowers which the humming birds dipped their beaks into. Those fe-flowers are nothing.'

'Yes, but what's this one called?'

'It's a primrose or something stupid.'

'It's a kingcup. Marsh marigold,' he told her easily. '*Caltha palustris* . . .' He murmured the Latin name to himself.

'Nothing exciting about *that*,' she told him scornfully.

'Nice to know the names, though. Part of the buttercup family.' He stood up then. 'But look – over there.' He pointed towards a muddy pool nearby, an overflow from the mill race. 'Now, that *is* an exciting flower,' he turned to Hetty who had followed him. 'Greater Spearwort, greatest and noblest of the Spearwort family. Grows up to three foot high in the summer, with flowers twice as big as the ordinary meadow buttercups.'

He bent down, inspecting the flower, before something else caught his eye. 'And look here,' he went on, groping in the water. 'A *real* rarity!' Quite forgetting Hetty then in his excitement, he dredged up a very dull-looking clump of spiky, fleshy, upright tendrils. 'The water soldier! Extraordinary! *Stratiotes aloides*.'

Hetty, attracted by his excitement, followed his gaze, though seeing nothing the least special in what he so praised. 'My goodness! I've not seen that in a long while.' Dermot fingered the slimy growth delicately. 'A perennial – grows all the year round: extraordinary plant – lives underwater, like now, then rises to blossom in midsummer before sinking to the bottom again. It's a *very* strange, rare wild flower, Hetty, I can tell you! Find it in East Anglia usually, no idea it was over here.'

'You do know a lot about flowers.' Hetty began to admire this excited, friendly man, who played about in ponds finding strange things, sharing them with her.

Dermot stood up. 'Yes, your uncle and I, years ago, we did a lot of travelling, looking for rare flowers – insects and animals and things. I know a little about it all. But he was a great botanist and zoologist.'

'A "zoologist"?'

'An animal man, interested in animals – wild animals especially.'

'Snakes and things?'

'Yes.'

'Uncle Henry was killed by a snake, wasn't he? Elly said.'

Dermot's face clouded. 'Yes, he was.'

'So was Robert nearly. But there are no snakes in Ireland – Elly said Saint Pe-Pe-Patrick kicked them all out. So how was he killed by one here?'

'He collected them . . .'

'That was clever of him.'

'Was it?'

'Yes,' Hetty rushed on. 'I *like* snakes. But Robert doesn't. He's very scared of them. And frogs, when we lived in De-De-Domenica, the croaky kind, croaked all night. He was te-te-*terrified* of them.'

'Was he?'

'Yes, but I wasn't frightened at all. Not frightened of things like *that* . . .'

They wandered off down the bank then, to retrieve their boats, Hetty talking to Dermot nineteen to the dozen, telling him everything now, whatever floated to mind, a friendship budding between them – the little girl in the primrose dress, the man with his pipe and lugubrious Norfolk jacket – as they swished through the yellow kingcups.

Before the end of Dermot's leave that spring they had become firm friends, together walking the land and the woods, where he taught her to recognise all the wild things in this temperate landscape: the flowers, birds and animals which before she had despised as pale shadows of their tropical equivalents. He showed how to wait for otters, hidden by the riverbank, in the lengthening twilight; pointed out the secret pattern in the evening stars – the flight of geese in the early-morning sky, the different sorts of birdsong clamorous at dawn in the rising spring.

For the first time since she had come to Ireland, Dermot made her feel at home in the country. He brought her into life, gave her a feel for masculine pleasures, so that a deep and silent understanding grew between them, which others could not know, and they came to feel they were like one another, in a world quite different from them. There was some magic in their rapport which startled Dermot, displeased Frances and Robert, and which for Hetty was a balm. Here, at last, was a keystone in her life, a father.

Dermot recognised this, too, and so found it all the more ironic, that morning towards the middle of May, when news came of King Edward's death. The household would normally have gone into brief mourning. Not so, of course, in this instance. Frances gave strict orders that no such respects should be paid.

She would have gone shopping extravagantly, as a celebration, in Kilkenny, but for the fact she knew all the shops would be closed there for the day. Instead, she took her horse out alone for most of the morning, riding wildly over the land, and spent the afternoon closeted in her office. Here, unable to resist the temptation, she unearthed the King's letters from the locked deed box – the jewelled Fabergé brooch-watch, the little ivory elephant, the elaborate coloured menus from Sandringham and all the other mementoes.

She was tempted to destroy everything, there and then. Something stopped her – not sentiment, certainly. Perhaps hatred? Surely, she thought, one could hold on to such things as a spur to hatred as much as love, as a way of keeping that feeling evergreen?

Hetty, disturbed that day by the doom and flurry and tense atmosphere about the house, asked Elly what had happened. Elly tried to control herself, but tears grew in her eyes.

'The King is dead,' she said at last.

'Oh, well, he's nothing to do with us, is he? Here, I mean. So why is everyone so funny and upset?'

Elly turned away then, unable to face the girl, letting out a great hubbub of tears.

Later Hetty talked to Dermot, out by the artificial waterfall on the old tennis court.

'Everyone's all awfully cryey and sad today! Did you know? – the King is dead!' she told him brightly.

'Yes,' he replied evenly, looking at her delicate, wide-eyed features, her dark curls set against the blowy sky. 'He was quite an old man. Everyone, everything, dies –'

'Oh, I know that,' she put in. '*I'm* not unhappy. But all the others are – in an *awful* tizzy, Elly crying her eyes out. But you're not, are you – unhappy, I mean?'

'Well, I am . . . a little,' he told her honestly. 'He was my king.'

'But *I* needn't be, need I?'

'No. No, you needn't be.' He turned away, hating the lie then, for the death of anyone's father was the sorest thing, even if they had no knowledge of him, no inkling of his blood in theirs.

'Anyway,' Hetty said, 'he *was* rather a fat, ugly old man with a great beard, wasn't he? I've seen pictures of him! It doesn't really matter, does it?'

'Well, yes, it does. He has family, you know –'

'Are they all fat and beardy like him, too?'

'No.' Dermot turned back, running his finger quickly down her straight nose. 'No, some of them are *very* beautiful. Like you.'

3

WHEN DERMOT LEFT a few days later, Hetty was inconsolable. Elly tried to help. 'That present he gave you – a sort of diary, was it? Well, why not write in it? – all the nice things you did with him!'

'Don't want to write in it – not the same as his being here.'

'Or pictures then. Your Aunt Emily does lovely pictures in that kind of book. Why don't you go and see her?'

'Can't draw.'

Nonetheless later she went to see Aunt Emily, taking Dermot's present with her, with its lovely marble-patterned covers – knocking on the door of her room in the west wing of the house, with its funny paintings all over the walls. Aunt Emily never allowed anyone else of the family into the room, but she did not object to Hetty.

'It's me!' she called out.

Inside Aunt Emily, busy at her work table, was concentrating on a watercolour in a book much like Hetty's. Hetty stood behind her for a moment, looking at the picture: a lot of fierce black crows, in the middle of a field, devouring a young rabbit, the red blood and guts of the poor animal spilled out all over the place, a frightful mess on the green grass. Hetty was horrified.

'That's *awfully* nasty, Aunt Emily!'

'Excuse yourself, girl!' She did not turn round. 'That's how things are: red in tooth and claw. Didn't you know that?' She turned now to look at Hetty, her bright little blue eyes beaming under a fuzz of greying hair.

'Yes, everything dies, I know that – Dermot told me.' She brightened then at the thought of him. 'Look! He gave me this lovely book.' She held it out hesitantly. 'But wha-wha-what shall I do with it?'

Aunt Emily inspected the book carefully. 'A fine little sketch book, Combridge's best – and nicely bound.' She fingered the book acquisitively.

'But I can't draw, like you. And I don't want to mess it all up with writing.'

'Tell you what then,' Aunt Emily said sharply. 'I'll give you half a crown for it – then you can buy something you really want.'

But Hetty took the book back then, holding it firmly into her stomach. 'Oh no, I couldn't – Dermot gave it me.'

Aunt Emily considered the implication of this rebuff. 'Ah dear me, so you've taken to him – that's the problem, is it?' Hetty mumbled something incoherent, fidgeting. 'Tell you what then,' Aunt Emily sped on, 'I'll draw pictures on one page and you write on the opposite one.'

Hetty was mystified. 'Wha-wha-what shall I write?'

'Excuse yourself – the *words* of course. We'll make a story book out of it.'

'But wha-what story – I don't know any stories.'

'You will soon enough, girl – stories are always easy to do, once you get a good idea for the beginning. That's the only difficult part. We'll make one up.'

She took the book back, set it on her work table, opening the first page. 'Now then, what'll it be?' She smiled at Hetty mischievously.

'I . . . I don't know!' Hetty felt a tingle of excitement at this proffered mystery.

'Think of something, girl!' But already, with a soft pencil, Aunt Emily had started to draw rapidly on the right-hand page – the figure of a man with frizzy, neatly-parted hair and a small moustache, droopy eyelids, wearing a Norfolk jacket.

And now Hetty beamed hugely at her in return. 'It's Dermot! But what's he *doing*?' she enquired as Aunt Emily quickly filled in the rest of the body, the limbs, the man in gaiters and big country walking boots.

'Ah, that's for you to decide! That's the story . . .'

Hetty looked at the developing figure: the man was dancing, hopping up and down, but quite alone in a room which, as Aunt Emily filled out the background, turned out to be very grand, with cherubs on the ceiling and a chandelier hanging in the middle, a ballroom.

'He's dancing a jig!' Hetty said, laughing.

'And so he is – an Irish jig.' Aunt Emily was drawing furiously now, setting an Irish jaunting car, with a fat pony in the shafts, incongruously parked at the big double doors to the ballroom, the pony wearing a straw hat, ears poking through, head on one side, gazing at the dancing man quizzically.

'But what's the pony doing there – and the funny trap?'

'No idea – that's for you to decide. And it's a jaunting car, not a trap.'

'Shall I be on it then?' Hetty asked tentatively.

'Why not, if you'd like to be – anything's possible.' And Aunt Emily drew a little girl, like Hetty, setting her up in the driver's seat holding the reins. 'That's it now, d'you see? There's your story – there's these two people, in a magic jaunting car, takes them anywhere they want, all over the world, they only have to wish for it. And that's the adventure. Here they are at the beginning of it, at this grand ball –'

'But there aren't any other people –'

'Not yet there aren't! But you can have anything and everything you want in a story. You only have to say the word!'

'Just like that?'

'Of course! Isn't that the whole point of it, when you make up something? It's not a *dull* business, like real life, you know.'

'We can call it "The Magic Jaunting Car" then, couldn't we?'

'Indeed, a grand title!' Aunt Emily returned to the drawing, adding other figures to the dance, stuffy dowagers in elaborate ball-gowns and outraged, blustery old men in tail-coats. 'So we'll have them here at this great ball to start with –'

'Except all those other smart people wouldn't like them there, would they? The man in his clumpy boots and that old pony and trap!'

'Indeed, you're right – they wouldn't like it at all – those sort of people never like anything interesting. So we'll have this grand old fool of a woman kick them out of the place!' She drew a most haughty party, with a pince-nez, very like old Lady Cordiner, remonstrating with the man in the Norfolk jacket. 'And *that'll* start them out on their adventures, just the two of them – and the pony with the straw bonnet. What'll we call the pony? That's important.'

Hetty smiled, completely drawn into the developing fantasy now. 'We'll call him – we'll call him "Awful". He does look rather naughty and awful, doesn't he?'

'"Awful" it is then.' Aunt Emily continued to draw, filling in the detail, Hetty close beside her, spellbound at these ready inventions of her aunt's – a story about Dermot and herself, which somehow returned him to her, so that he was almost there, in the room, doing things with her again: all their real adventures of the past weeks renewed and continued in these magic ones. Through the story she was living with him again. It was quite extraordinary she felt, that a story – just some pictures and writing, really – could bring a person back like that, make everything good and well again, make you excited and happy, just as you had been with that person. There was magic in stories, of course, like all the ones in her *Red Fairy Book* – she knew that. But she hadn't quite seen that you could make the magic up, yourself – that things you made up like this, in a book, could take away the hurt outside, in real life.

She looked at Aunt Emily in admiration. 'I wish *I* could do it all, like you. You *are* clever.'

'And you *can*, girl!' Aunt Emily turned over the page then. 'So what's their next adventure?'

Hetty considered the matter. 'Well . . . Well, if it's a *magic* jaunting car, it could go out on the sea, couldn't it?'

'Indeed –'

'To some island, with palm trees and strange things . . .'

'And gobbly beasts . . . But they'll have to go down-river to the sea first –'

'Or on the railway, couldn't they? That'd be rather fun!'

'*Exactly!*' Aunt Emily proceeded to put the jaunting car on the tracks, next to the platform of a country station, much like the local one at Thomastown.

'And the ticket man can make a fuss about that!'

'Just as they always do . . .'

*

For the next few weeks Hetty went to her great-aunt's room almost every afternoon, working on the story of 'The Magic Jaunting Car' – creating, following the adventures of the little girl and the man in the Norfolk jacket, as they went down the railway to the sea, then across to the ocean isle where the Gobblies and the Marsh Mallows lived: strange beasts – the first with too many heads, so that they did not know which mouth to feed, where or what to look at, venturing forth only by day; the others, frightening, blobbish watery animals, with only one eye, coming out only at night from stagnant, noisome pools. So that quite soon the book was half-filled, the story going like one o'clock.

And, as the days progressed, in her intense identification with the hero, Hetty came to see this man, befriending the Gobblies, doing battle with the evil Marsh Mallows, as her special protector – and more than that she came quite clearly to believe that this man, in reality, was the father she had never had: this figure here imagined, yet equally real, whom she knew to be living somewhere beyond the blue mountains in England.

Here was someone, as his life was renewed each day in the blank pages, through the character of the little girl, in whom she could confide, discuss and plan things: a knight in shining armour, just like the picture in her King Arthur book, though his chain-mail was a Norfolk jacket. But he was exactly the same sort of person as King Arthur, Lancelot and the others – fighting for the good against the bad. That was just it – that was the great thing about him: he could kill the evil, the hurt and the pain.

And so Hetty could as easily remove him from the story, whenever she wanted, and set him up in her mind as a foil against her own unhappy predicaments at Summer Hill. Here, too, the man came to bear her standard, against the wiles of Miss Goulden, Robert's tantrums, her mother's dismissive coldness.

Dermot was the answer, the missing piece in the puzzle of her life. Why, of course, Hetty confirmed the thought: that was it! *He* was her 'real dear Papa' – the man Miss Goulden had asked such strange questions about at the fancy dress party; not the awful Mr Fraser, but Dermot, her mother's old friend.

And with this thought, finally worked out and established in her mind, Hetty, that summer, became much more confident and happy – as well as insolent and audacious. It was so obvious, after all, she thought: that was why he had been so kind to her, had paid her all those attentions, sent postcards now of the horses changing guard in London – *he* was her real dear Papa!

She kept the thought to herself, though, nursing the happy secret, all that summer, until, with the onset of autumn, the children came to play indoors again – in the schoolroom with Elly and sometimes downstairs with Frances and Aunt Emily: card games of Rummy, Beggar My Neighbour, Old Maid, as well as charades and dumb crambo.

Because of her stammer, and since there were no words in this latter drama of acting out some well-known title – of a fairy story, a song, a famous poem – and no doubt, too, because of the histrionic Cordiner gifts in her blood, Hetty, under the particular tutelage of Aunt Emily, soon showed a ready ability in the mime.

One early evening, at a rare Summer Hill children's party, Hetty – when her turn came in the dumb crambo and on Aunt Emily's suggestion – chose to enact 'The Lady of Shalot' – playing the lovelorn maiden, standing, as if in her high tower, on a stool in the middle of the drawing room. She gazed into an imaginary hand mirror, combing her hair the while, turning the mirror then, so as to reflect the view from a window, of some longed-for vision. The other children, with the grown-ups, grouped round the fireplace, hazarded various guesses.

'Helen of Troy?'

'Penelope?'

'Berenice – and her burning hair?'

Some further mythic beauties were invoked, with no success, until the impatient, frustrated, jealous Robert burst out, 'I know! – she's just playing herself, waiting for Dermot!' He turned to a companion then, sniggering, 'She thinks Cousin Dermot's her papa!'

But nearly everyone heard him – including Hetty, who coloured quickly, quite losing touch with her act. She walked up to Robert. 'No, I wasn't! I was doing "The Lady of Shalot", you stupid, stupid brute!' She was furious now, agonised by this public embarrassment, starting to grapple with Robert, so that they had to be separated.

Later she spoke to Aunt Emily in her room. 'How did Robert *know* about Dermot? I never told him anything, or about our story book. And *you* didn't tell him, did you?'

'Of course not, girl.' Aunt Emily was brusquely matter of fact. 'Never tell men *anything* – never trust them, you see.'

'So how did he –'

'Oh, they suspect everything. They're clever that way – always poking their noses in.'

'I'll never speak to him again!'

'Oh, you will, girl, you will . . .'

And she did, for the following day, prompted by Elly, Robert came and said he was sorry. Hetty had been in the schoolroom, Miss Goulden on her afternoon off. 'I'm *not* speaking to you,' she told him.

Robert went over to the fire. He had hidden some chestnuts in the warm ash beneath the grate. Now he raked them out with a poker, fingering them quickly, before offering one to Hetty. 'They're *quite* nice,' he said uncertainly.

'Go away! I don't want your nasty chestnuts. They're horrid – like you.'

'I didn't mean it,' he said rather sourly, but genuinely apologetic. Hetty had gone to the window then, looking out at the steady rain, a dim, cold autumn afternoon. 'I miss Uncle Dermot too,' Robert went on. 'Those guns and things. He was great fun.'

Hetty turned, looking at him grudgingly. 'Why did you think,' she spoke at last, 'that he was my Papa?'

Robert peeled the crackly skin from a chestnut, ate a bit, but did not go on with it. 'Dunno, really. We never liked your real Papa in Fraser Hall, did we? And fat old Josephine there, she said once he wasn't your real Papa, so I thought . . .'

'Well?'

'I thought perhaps Uncle Dermot might be him, always being so nice to you.'

'But he was just as nice to you as well.'

'But I *know* my Papa is dead.'

Robert gazed into the fire and Hetty relented a fraction. 'Wonder why Josephine said that?' She walked over to him then, thinking hard. They both crouched down by the fire, picking at the chestnuts, gazing meditatively into the embers.

'Oh, she was always gossiping and chattering away, old Josy. Probably wasn't true. Why wouldn't Mr Fraser have been your Papa?'

'He was so *nasty*, that's why.'

'Still, he must have been. That's how people *are* fathers, as soon as they marry the mothers. They have to do that first, then they have babies. Elly said so.'

'No, you don't! Animals don't marry – my pet rabbits and things. They just get on top of each other to have babies. Seen them. And Mickey Joe in the stables told me horses do it in just the same way – the men horses with *lots* of other horses, and they're not married *at all*.'

'That's animals, though. People aren't the same. They have to be married first, in church, before they can do it. So Mr Fraser *must* have been your Papa.'

Hetty was not convinced. Nor, indeed, was Robert. But he wanted to humour Hetty, reassure her. 'Anyway,' she said now, 'I don't want him to be my Papa. I hated him.'

'Well, you have to have *someone* as a Papa, don't you? – else you wouldn't *be* here. But it can't be Uncle Dermot, can it?'

'Why not?'

''Cos he's a relation. And you can't marry relations.'

'Only a cousin.'

'Same thing though: can't be a relation *and* be your Papa.'

Hetty was confused. 'Oh, what does it matter, *anyhow*,' she said angrily, though her anger was no longer directed at Robert, but at this still-unhappy, unresolved mystery. 'Here, I've got some more baccy from Mickey Joe.' She got up then and went to the hole in the wainscoting where she kept her clay pipe hidden – the one from the fancy dress the year before. She got it out. 'Goolley's gone to Kilkenny. Let's smoke a bit.'

Lighting a spill from the fire she started to puff at the coarse-cut plug tobacco that Mickey Joe had cut up and prepared for her, before passing the pipe over to Robert. He took a puff, just to show willing, hiding his distaste, then handed it back. He could not understand why it did not make *her* feel sick as well.

But it was quite a mystery, he felt, about her Papa. Hetty didn't have a father, he was dead, killed by the Caribs, everyone knew that. Yet she thought, and some other people did as well, that there *was* someone else, a real father, still alive. And that made Hetty unhappy, which was why she was so prickly and difficult. Robert wished he could help her about it, find this other man somehow, whoever he was. And he was sorry he'd been so bad to Hetty then. He liked her a lot really, as they knelt there now, cosy by the fire, eating the chestnuts as the rain drizzled outside.

'I tell you what,' he said then, by way of cementing this new truce between them. 'I've found another secret thing, now they've moved the hay all out of the stable yard: up in the loft there, at the end, there's a crack in the floor, just above where old Flood used to live, where Pat Kennedy lives now. I'll show it to you.'

'All right,' she said. ''Cept he hasn't gone to live there yet.'

'No. He's just been putting his furniture and things in, since Flood died. But it's still quite interesting.'

Robert took her out there the following afternoon, climbing a ladder from the stables, up into the old hay loft, then tip-toeing right along to the end in the dark, until they got to the space above the rooms once occupied by the old butler. Kneeling on the rafters, Robert showed her the crack in the plaster and lath beneath them. Hetty gazed down into the room beneath. 'It's empty,' she whispered to him. 'Just a lot of old boxes and blankets and things. And a bed.'

'It must be old Flood's bedroom. Pat's moving in there.'

'Yes. But Pat's nice. We shouldn't look – his going to bed and everything.'

'No. 'Course not. Just wanted to show it to you.'

And they left it at that.

But this illicit view of Pat's room remained an unmentioned temptation to both of them: a forbidden gratification of which they could avail themselves, as revenge against the various indignities and prohibitions they suffered in the household. The crack in the ceiling was like a hidden tin of jam tarts, awaiting their pleasure, offering a sure solace against the trials and tribulations of their life at Summer Hill.

And these remained – in the shape of Miss Goulden or in Frances's spite, her Celtic fantasies, which she continued to impose on her daughter, so that it was not long before Hetty, finding herself alone in the stable yard one afternoon, with Robert at his piano lessons, decided to go up in the loft herself – just to take a quick peep, she thought, into the room below.

She heard voices drifting up to her, before she even looked through the crack. And when she did so she was astonished to see her mother there, in the one easy chair, with Pat Kennedy and another fair-haired man in a check suit with a floppy cap on his knee, both sitting less easily nearby. What was her mother doing here, in Pat's new rooms? – and what were they all on about? Hetty couldn't make head or tail of it.

Frances gazed intently at the small, clever-faced young man with the tam-o-shanter cap. With his fashionably sporty tweed suit, serious pale blue eyes and spectacles, there was something both academic and racy about him: a mix of intellect and fun.

She liked the look of this unusual Irishman, whose background or profession she could not begin to place.

'Honoured as I am, Mr . . .?'

'Mr Murphy,' Peadar O'Hegarty lied promptly.

'Honoured as I am, Mr Murphy – I don't quite understand why you've come all this way with your suggestion. You surely know nothing about me . . .'

O'Hegarty shifted the cap carefully from one knee to the other. 'Believe me, Mrs Fraser,' he said pleasantly in a soft Dublin accent, 'I would not have come all this way if we didn't know a good deal about you already. We have gone into your character and activities carefully enough.' He glanced over at Pat Kennedy. 'Indeed, we have first-hand evidence of it. And, besides, there's a deal of quite public evidence – your work with the Fianna youth movement. And with Miss Gonne's Daughters of Ireland, so particularly dedicated to Irish liberty –'

'But just as much to obtaining equal rights for women,' Frances put in sharply.

'Indeed, indeed –' O'Hegarty started to placate her.

'Which is why I remain surprised that you should propose me for membership of your organisation, the Irish Republican *Brother*hood.'

'One need not take the gender there quite literally, Mrs Fraser. You are a good friend of several other women patriots – Miss Gonne, for example . . .'

'Yes, and she is not, so far as I am aware, a member of your . . . your society,' she answered stiffly.

O'Hegarty smiled weakly. 'If she were, and you were not, you would never know it, Mrs Fraser. Naturally, we are a secret organisation, bound by the strictest oath.'

'Indeed! So it would seem that, in presenting yourself here and taking my involvement for granted, you have rather offered hostages to fortune in the matter.' She glared at him then, a proud, rather mad look in her burning eyes.

'Not so, Mrs Fraser, not so. As I said, we have, some time ago, established the most comprehensive *bona fides* as to your character and beliefs. So that we have felt certain, in advance, that we could rely on your co-operation – you and Mr Kennedy here – in creating a more active branch of our organisation in south Kilkenny. We are anxious now to revive the movement in every way we can – younger blood, new people.'

Frances seemed to understand and agree with all this, nodding as he spoke. Yet once more she temporised. 'In my position here at Summer Hill, not to mention my background and religion, I would seem a most unlikely choice!'

'Indeed – and all the better. Because we're not limited by sect or class in the IRB, Mrs Fraser. Oh, no indeed! Not at all! We look only for dedicated people, be they from cottage or castle, who are prepared to *fight* . . .' he paused, 'when the time comes, in the common name of Irish men . . . and women. And you would not be the first member of the English landlord class here to belong to the movement.'

'I, and my family, have always been *Irish*, Mr Murphy, not English,' she corrected him acidly. But she was nonetheless taken by the man's measured use of words, the air of steely purpose behind the mild accents and manner: attracted by his power, too, for she suspected he must, in coming all this way and making such a direct approach to her, be one of the leaders of the IRB. Yet still she delayed her open acceptance. 'I have had my doubts – about the use of force in winning our freedom.'

'We know you have – and close contacts as well with Mr Redmond and his Home Rule party at Westminster. But it is equally true, is it not, that latterly you have had something of a falling out with them? – indeed, that you have largely relinquished such doubts?' He looked over at Pat Kennedy again.

'Yes, I think it is,' she admitted.

'Besides,' O'Hegarty continued, 'you have just the sort of experience we need – more military than political or parliamentary, if I may say so!' He smiled again, a wan smile, putting his hand in his pocket as he spoke, taking out some pages from an old newspaper, unfolding them, glancing down. 'You were a nurse in the South African war, commended at the battle of Colenso. And later . . .' He turned a page. 'Later you handled firearms – evidently with some skill – when you lived – yes, in the West Indies . . .'

She saw what he had been reading: pages from the *New York Post*, the article describing her early career, her part in the vicious battle against the Caribs in Domenica, and the subsequent unfortunate death of one of their special reporters there at the Boiling Lake.

'It seems you are not unacquainted with violent methods, Mrs Fraser,' O'Hegarty said sweetly.

'Where on earth did you get that?'

'As I said, we make the fullest enquiries – our people in New York . . . Will you accept?'

Frances nodded. 'Yes . . . yes, I will.'

'We can have the oath-taking straight away then.'

All three of them stood. And Frances felt a tingling thrill then, coursing down her spine. She was about to be formally accepted into an organisation which would license her violent nature. No longer an outsider, a pariah between two camps, she was soon to be part of the secret spirit of the times in Ireland, joining the ranks of a hidden army with whom at some point in the future – and the day could not long be delayed – she could righteously take up arms against all that she hated – King, Empire, everything that had betrayed her. In short – though this she could not admit to herself for a moment – she would, in a moment or two, receive a commission in personal vengeance.

Hetty, still gazing through the crack, heard the strange words float up to her. 'In the presence of God, I, Frances Fraser, do solemnly swear that I will do my utmost to establish the National independence of Ireland . . . bear true allegiance to the supreme Council of the Irish Republican Brotherhood . . . implicitly obeying the

Constitution . . . and all my superior officers . . . that I will preserve inviolate all the secrets of the organisation.'

What were they doing now, Hetty wondered? Swearing to keep secrets, in some secret game, Hetty could see that: just like children played. But they were all grown-ups.

Her mother must be mad, as Robert had said. Would she tell him about it? Or Elly? No. There was something dangerous about this game. It was *very* secret. She should never have known about it. Perhaps they'd even kill her if they found out.

She waited, frightened in the dark loft, until they had all left the room below. Here was another mystery, a danger, a further source of unhappiness, Hetty felt – one more horrid secret hanging in the air of Summer Hill. A week later, towards Hallowe'en, another experience added to Hetty's sense of hidden disruption in the great house. She had come to know, long before, that it was her grandmother who lived in the back wing of the house. But she had never seen her. Her mother had told her that she was a 'permanent invalid', a 'recluse'. Elly, Robert and some of the servants had been more blunt: old Lady Cordiner was mad, dotty, touched, dangerous even. She could not be let out of her rooms, must be hidden, forgotten – that was what had to be done with mad people in a family: there was something disgraceful and embarrassing about them.

But Hetty had never quite accepted this view of her grandmother. Indeed, she felt for her in a way – all locked up like an animal in a cage, never seeing the light of day. And besides, with her sharp curiosity, she *wanted* to see her, so that she lurked from time to time, hidden near the stone steps by the great locked door that led into her Grandmama's quarters, hoping for a glimpse of her, a sight of *something*.

What did a mad person look like? Like the face on the hollowed-out turnip masks they were making now with Elly for Hallowe'en? – a candle inside, and a ghostly yellow light coming from the slitty eyes and toothy mouth? Oh, how horrible! Or did a mad person look even *worse*?

She asked Robert, as they looked at a finished turnip in the playroom.

'Oh, a *really* mad person would look much worse,' he advised her distantly.

'Like Grandmama?'

He turned away. 'I should think she would look *terrible* . . .'

'Will you? – shall we? Shall we try and see her. Will you come?'

'We're not allowed. It's all locked,' Robert said, taking up a fresh turnip. Going all goody-goody and grown up, Hetty thought.

'But I think I *know* a way – of seeing her, without being seen,' she told him then.

'How?'

'Just like we saw into Pat's rooms. There must be a loft or an attic above Grandmama's rooms.'

'There isn't. Just the roof.'

'Yes, but there must be some sort of *space* there, which we could get into and cut a hole and look down.'

Robert showed no enthusiasm for the idea. But Hetty, the next day, made various investigations, exploring the aerial geography of that part of the house. And by the following day she had found a way in. It had meant climbing out on to the balustraded roof of the main house, walking back its whole length, then down some steep slates – to a valley of leaded guttering which joined the gable end of the roof on the new back wing.

And in this gable end was a small door. The rest was fairly easy. She took a candle and a sharp-pointed kitchen knife with her, treading very gently over the rafters, until she came to a position half-way down the dark space, beneath which she judged her Grandmama's rooms to be. Like the stable loft there was lath and plaster here, but it was tougher, and it was some time, prodding very carefully, before she could make any opening. And, when she did so and looked down, she was disappointed. It was just an empty, a spare, room.

But the following afternoon she tried further along – and here she was rewarded. After the same careful excavations in the plaster, kneeling on the rafters and putting her eye right down to the florin-sized hole, she saw something quite strange and frightening.

The long space beneath seemed like a dining room. But, though it was bright outside, all the windows were heavily curtained, the room lit by a number of candles, an oil lamp and the dancing flames of some logs in a vast fireplace, so that it was filled with eerie shapes and shadows. The dark-panelled walls were covered with dozens of small grimy pictures, stuck about like postage stamps. A great canopied four-poster bed lay at one end, heavy furniture everywhere, with a long dining table down the middle and narrow high-backed chairs running along either side. The table was laid from end to end with rubbish, Hetty thought, until her eyes became accustomed to the flickering light.

Then she managed to pick out some of the objects: crystal balls, paperweights, dozens of heavy-framed photographs, small stuffed animals, sheathed swords, braided military tunics, bear-skin hats and a hundred other vague things, covered in cobwebs and dust.

Hetty, peering down into this cave, was not to know how old Lady Cordiner, before her intended departure for England and the various subsequent strokes which had finally left her immobile and speechless, had removed herself together with most of her possessions and many of the Victorian knick-knacks in the house – to this long room in the Gothic wing at the back, having her great bed set up there as well; insisting afterwards, when she had to remain there, that all this heavy decor, these family photographs and mementoes of Henry and Eustace, should be left untouched, so that she could survey these emblems of her once-proud sovereignty at Summer Hill from her high bed, gorging on these props of her autocratic rule, now falling apart, decaying with the years, become ideal scaffolding for spiders' webs, and bedding for mice.

Hetty saw all this, but couldn't see her Grandmother. Where was she? She couldn't see her, in fact, for the hole she had made lay almost directly above the canopy of the four-poster where Lady Cordiner now dozed. The room seemed deserted.

But a few minutes later one of the maids – old Molly it was – brought in another oil lamp, set it on a table and prepared to take a seat nearby. 'There you are, your Ladyship – a little more light. How are you feeling at all today?' But Molly turned away as she spoke, as if expecting no reply to her question. And indeed there was none – absolute silence from the bed.

Hetty was frustrated. Her Grandmama was there all right, but she would get no glimpse of her at this rate. She was about to give up her vigil when the bedroom door opened again and her mother, carrying a carpet bag, came into the circle of lamplight.

'It's all right, Molly, I'll see to her, stay with her for a while, read to her.'

Old Molly left. Her mother had a book under her arm. But, as soon as the maid disappeared, she put it aside, unopened. Instead, from the bag, she drew out one of the hollow turnip heads which they had been making in the playroom for the past week and placed it on her mother's bedside table. She lit a candle then, before taking the top off the turnip and placing the light inside, adjusting the terrifying mask so that it faced directly towards the head of the four-poster. Then, turning back, she lowered the wick of the oil lamp. The room was plunged in shadow and the turnip head shone more brightly, emitting a jaundiced light from the slitty eyes and mouth.

'I thought you'd like it,' her mother said then, in a pleasant voice, lifting her head in a conquering fashion. 'It's Hallowe'en, you know, tonight.'

She took a seat nearby, so that Hetty could just see the expression on her face. It was happy, as her voice had been, and yet there was something terribly cruel in it – and Hetty was frightened herself now. What was the point of all this? Grown-ups didn't play with these Hallowe'en turnips. They were for children. And why, above all, was there no sound, no voice, from her Grandmama in the great bed? She must be alive there, mustn't she? – so why didn't she speak? And she must be frightened, too. Was that why her Grandmama didn't speak – *because* she was so frightened?

Hetty found no answer to this, for afterwards she did not speak of the incident. Who could she speak to? Who could possibly know why her mother had been playing with the horrible turnip head, offering it to the old lady in this way, with such a gloating face?

On the other hand Miss Goulden, a week later when she met Bunty Cordiner in the tea room of Wynn's Hotel in Dublin, had plenty to say. Bunty, cup raised to her disappointed lips, looked at her askance over the sugared buns.

'You say the girl *admitted* that her cousin Dermot was her father?'

'No, the boy Robert said so – he lived with them on the island.'

'Fancy . . .' Bunty considered the matter.

'Indeed, he was quite clear about it. And Henrietta was much upset – attacked him! Attacked him physically.'

'Just as I thought – she is not legitimate!'

Yet Bunty knew she was little further ahead in her ambitions. She had seen long before that, in order to regain the house, she would have legally to contest Lady Cordiner's change of will – prove her new will to Frances invalid. The fact of an illegitimate child in the family would not alone suffice to this end. She would have to prove, as she herself had long suspected, that Lady Cordiner had made the new will under duress, or while of unsound mind. And here, more crucially, was where she needed the hard evidence: from one of the servants present at the time of Frances's sudden and unexpected return to Summer Hill – or from the local doctor who attended Lady Cordiner, old Dr Mitchell. He, the family doctor for many years, would be unlikely to collaborate. But one of the servants? There was more ready material here.

In a roundabout way she put these thoughts to Miss Goulden, asking her opinion of likely recruits in this cause.

'Oh, the servants were all there – when Lady Cordiner took her violent turn in the dining room, telling Frances she could have Summer Hill and slashing the family portraits –'

'Yes, but what *induced* her to say she could have the house, so that she took to her bed subsequently and changed her will?'

'Ah, that I don't know. As you know there was a fire, the day following, in Lady Cordiner's bedroom, while she lay there injured – might have been burnt alive by all accounts, before Mrs Fraser rescued her. A bedside lamp spilled . . .'

'Mrs Fraser may have tipped the lamp over herself,' Bunty said acidly. 'Were there no servants present?'

'Yes, I believe her maid Molly was there, some time before, but had left for her supper.'

'Left Lady Cordiner *alone*?'

'As far as I know –'

'And not *told* to leave, by Mrs Fraser?'

'That is possible.'

'I wonder if you might make some discreet enquiries of the maid?'

Miss Goulden became nervous, fearing for her position at Summer Hill. 'I doubt if, in my making such enquiries, one could rely on *her* discretion in the matter.'

'I see . . .' Bunty was disappointed.

'I wonder, rather, if you might find some lever in the company Mrs Fraser now keeps?' Miss Goulden said brightly, hoping to rescue something in her commission.

'The company of those dreadful Home Rulers you mean?'

'No, indeed, *very* much worse than that.' Miss Goulden's lips curled in embarrassed disapproval. 'How shall I put it? She is . . . most unsuitably involved with the butler there, Pat Kennedy. I have heard them conversing, closeted in her boudoir.'

'What were they saying?'

'I didn't hear exactly. But I remarked on the excessive duration of his visits there. And, more to the point,' she leant forward eagerly over the seed cake, 'a week ago I saw her emerge from his rooms in the stable yard!'

Bunty was avid now. 'You are *sure?*'

'I am in no doubt,' she said primly.

'The little hussy, the harlot!' Bunty could not restrain her voice, embarrassing some prim women at a nearby table. Yet, despite her agitation, she could not see how this new disclosure would further her purposes either. Frances's current behaviour, no matter how flagrant, was not proof that Lady Cordiner had been of unsound mind, or that her daughter had blackmailed her.

There, of course, was the key to it – Bunty Cordiner was convinced: blackmail. But how? What had been the instrument here? Bunty had long felt this to have been Henrietta in some way – that Frances had threatened her mother with social disgrace by exposing the girl's illegitimacy. But, even if Dermot Cordiner was the father, such exposure would hardly have been sufficient threat for the old lady to have made over the whole place to her daughter whom she despised.

Where was the key to it all?

'If only I could speak to Lady Cordiner *herself*,' she told Miss Goulden vehemently. 'There I would have an ally, I am sure! – and a ready answer to the whole matter.'

Miss Goulden looked crestfallen. 'I am afraid you would be disappointed. In the months since I spoke to you last, Lady Cordiner's condition has deteriorated. She has had another "turn" – her heart. She cannot, as I understand it, speak at all now . . .'

Bunty Cordiner, appalled at this news, was suddenly speechless herself.

Despite all these manipulations, seen and unseen – and with Hetty's consequent fears, sulks and tantrums – her life at Summer Hill for the next few years was by no means uniformly unhappy. Though she was never at ease in the house itself, there were the great gifts in the landscape which she came to love – in the estate, the forests, the river valley, the hills and blue mountains beyond. Here, from the windows of Summer Hill, Hetty grew up with a view of Arcady – and, in the huge green world outside, where she spent so much more time alone, she became almost a recluse.

Dermot, every year in the spring and usually at Christmas with his father, took part of his leave at Summer Hill: Hetty's friendship with him and their growing correspondence when he was away, flourished – so that, at home or abroad, Dermot became one certainty in her life. And there were others.

With Great-Aunt Emily, though 'The Magic Jaunting Car' book had long since been completed, Hetty developed all sorts of close, sometimes bizarre associations. As she became older herself, Hetty came more and more to see her aunt as a child, but adored her no less for that. For the childishness there, she realised, was part of her aunt's magic, a gift which set her quite apart from everyone else in the household, a shield against the world, behind which another and much more interesting reality existed: a life of the mind in which the world could be quite differently ordered and put to rights. In this way, as Elly remarked, her aunt had a 'mind of her own' – a condition which Hetty soon came to emulate. And, besides, Aunt Emily was not all child. She was full of so much, and most surprising, grown-up comment and information, too.

And so, in these years, it was largely from her aunt, and not through Miss Goulden or her mother, that Hetty took her theories of the world. A distorted vision perhaps, but there was a decisiveness, a wit and passion in her aunt's strange angles on life which appealed to Hetty. Talking to her aunt always excited and surprised her. She felt her brain bulging with contradictory impressions – of the world, of men and women, of what all these were *really* like. Aunt Emily seemed to see *through* everything – that was the exciting thing. Her magic gave her a key to everything, which no other person, except Dermot in quite a different way, possessed. Aunt Emily, in a few moments with her words or drawings, could turn life into a balm or thrilling adventure, when life in fact at that point was full of grey, unhappy things.

With Elly, Hetty found a more conventional solace – and in Robert she had a difficult but invigorating playmate. As he grew – and despite, or more because of, their disagreements and armed truces – she came to respect his steady firmness, the good sense which lay behind his sudden acts of unreason and temper. Robert in these years regained most of the nature he had lost with the sudden death of his parents: a balance, already almost academic in its niceties, a mind where intellect and his voracious reading formed a growing bastion against all that was difficult or hurtful in his life. He was someone, Hetty came to see, who could not be bullied indefinitely or in any way finally put down. And though, with her own essentially autocratic nature, her sporadic vindictiveness and passionate rages, she resented her inability to dominate him, she had to admit that this final layer of steel in Robert made him a worthy opponent.

Only with her mother did Hetty fail to make any connections. Their relationship became increasingly bitter – for Hetty felt deceived by her always, cheated, lied to. And of course, in truth, this was just the case. Frances, so long indulging her disappointments and with the advent now of her militant political activities, was entirely unaware of how this core of bitterness in her soul had quite eroded her intelligence. She remained clever and spirited now only in her ability to hurt people: a tragedy which Hetty could not see, but which she suffered nonetheless.

It irked Hetty, too, that only towards Robert did her mother show any semblance of concern or affection. She had heard, or overheard, her mother praise his steady virtues, his boyish good looks – and indeed often suffered quite open and detrimental comparisons with her mother here. Was she not then good-looking? She could not be – and the thought hurt her deeply.

In fact, at thirteen, Hetty, without her mother being able to admit it, had developed in ways which were quite different from, and far outshone, mere good looks. There were in her all the lineaments of a distinctive beauty, the promise of something quite beyond the conventions.

As her features and bearing began to take a final shape and balance – waist narrowing, lengthening thighs, budding breasts – it was clear that the eventual form here would be original . . . and sensational.

No, she was not good-looking. All the qualities in her face now – the risen cheek-bones, perfectly straight nose, the fierce glinting eyes, the long delicately bowed lips, pointed chin, the unruly cascade of silky dark curls running down either side to the jaw – all were coagulating into a beauty which was both arrogant and divine: the flesh machined so finely, yet overlooked by these bold blue eyes. There was a radiance, a startling, almost harsh elegance blooming here; a sudden flush of insolence or rage which could as soon change and soften into lines of humility and grace.

Chameleon in her looks, which so quickly reflected the see-saw in her heart, tortured by her inarticulacy and by the strength of her emotions, she ran between extremes with such mobility and variety of expression that overall the face was difficult to define, other than by the emotions it presented. At few points was there something static to take hold of and identify her by – only a succession of faces, which could enchant or sadden or terrify the onlooker.

Though as dark-haired as her mother, Hetty would be taller and less plump than her – and without that olive-ivory tinge to her skin, which was a very faint, almost translucent pink. Frances's slightly gypsy looks had been refined here – lengthened, teased out, and re-set in a classic mould. And yet that mould was broken, too, and re-cast again in one more exclusive still – by her eyes, which were her most captivating feature: the mix of Cordiner Wedgwood and pale Hanoverian blue, set in great oval saucers, topped by long scimitar-shaped eyebrows, beneath this framing cowl of black hair: so surprising a colour combination of light and dark, where the expected tinges and mixes had never been arrived at, leaving instead these brilliant contrasts of blue and black and pink.

As she stood on its threshold, life, with its larger battles, had not yet engaged Hetty. But what she presented to it already, in her beauty and sharp will, suggested a lively campaign, one in which she would give no ground, where victory of some sort – as it had been for her mother – would always be of paramount importance.

Unlike her mother, though, these dominant qualities were tempered by artistry, by all sorts of fears and sensitivities, betrayed by her stammer which she never quite threw off. And these fierce qualities, which had their virtues too, she tried to hide, as the shadow side of a coin – not knowing then how, in so vehemently pursuing all her choices, she would eventually have to pay on both sides.

But at thirteen, as old as the century, Hetty's first real battleground was chosen for her. Her mother, having arranged for Robert to board at a Protestant boys' college outside Dublin, but with her horror of anything English for Hetty, sent her to a convent school in France.

4

THE TWO GIRLS, in their uniform of starched white linen skirts and severe cambric blouses, had stopped among the tall trees in the beech alley behind the château leading to the chapel. Hetty was beginning to have second thoughts about their plan.

'Oh, come on!' Léonie whispered hotly. 'It's not as if it was a *real* saint's bone – only a bit of rabbit or something.'

'Still . . .'

'And we're not even Catholic *anyway* – don't have to believe in all that mumbo-jumbo, like the other girls.' Léonie swivelled round, stamping her foot, making a little dance on the mossy grass, the thick carpet of bluebells and wood anemones beneath the trees. 'We're only here for the "ed-u-kay-shun" anyway,' Léonie drawled the word out, exaggerating her slight American accent, laughing quickly.

A breeze stirred the scented spring afternoon. It was the middle of Hetty's second term at the Couvent du Sacré-Coeur; the nuns had inherited the vast, rather ugly, red-and-white-bricked Château de Héricourt, on the edge of a village some miles south of Bayeux, in the middle of the lush Normandy countryside.

Hetty had not been there as long as Léonie, and though, in their growing friendship and various escapades, she had rarely been less daring than her, in this instance she felt a stab of real cowardice: the relic above the altar in its gold-and-red-enamelled box – a finger bone from the hand of Saint Matilda, it was said – was so *very* holy . . .

'There'll be real trouble, if we're caught.' Hetty voiced her doubts again.

'We *won't* be caught.'

Hetty gazed – fear overcome by admiration – at this deep-eyed gamine, a year older than her but several inches smaller, the breeze scattering her fluffy dark brown hair, swishing it across her slightly aquiline nose, where it snagged in her long eyelashes. Nearly fifteen, though Léonie was small, she had the body of an older girl, well-developed, rather chunky, full of sharp angles – in a firm jaw line and a jutting chin beneath a generous mouth filled with perfectly-formed, very white square teeth; a waist that already narrowed dramatically, prominent hip bones, a flat behind, strong legs that kicked the linen skirt about restlessly. And she accentuated these aggressive yet sensuous attributes now, returning Hetty's gaze, hand on hip, chin up, lips ajar, looking at her provocatively from the depths of her grey-green eyes.

Léonie's expression, always direct and searching, often reflected the excitement of some difficult decision being weighed in her mind, usually a straight choice between good and bad, when she seemed to savour the thrill of delaying an answer, the more to enjoy the illicit act itself. And Hetty had been attracted by this air of repressed audacity and knowing ardour ever since she had arrived at the Convent the previous autumn, taking the next cubicle to hers in the junior dormitory.

It was a Saturday afternoon, their free hours, during which the thirty or so other girls were dutifully sewing, reading Racine in the great first floor *salon*, or out walking in the grounds in pairs, for they were never allowed to go alone.

'Look, it's quite simple,' Léonie insisted. 'We just go in and sit down and pray and pretend to be holy and then, if the coast is really clear, we flit up, open the box and take a look.'

'What if the box is locked?'

'Then it's *locked*, you ninny!'

Léonie tugged her towards the chapel. This small building, with its blue-and-gilt baroque interior, was empty, and all went according to plan – except that when Léonie tried to open the good enamel reliquary it was, indeed, locked.

'Shame,' she whispered, tugging once more at the lid. Hetty tried then, and to their astonishment it opened easily. Inside, attached by a gold thread to a velvet cushion, was a tiny sliver of grey bone. They both gazed at it in awe. Then Léonie looked at Hetty. 'How on earth were you able to open it – and I couldn't?'

'Don't know.'

Léonie closed the box, then tried to open it herself once more. The lid would not budge. 'A miracle,' she said shortly.

'Come on,' Hetty whispered urgently. 'Let's leave before someone comes.'

The girls ran out into the late sunshine – breathless and flushed with the success of their endeavour, rushing over the deep carpet of bluebells beyond the chapel.

The convent – which some few parents mistakenly saw simply as a finishing school, so that their girls were not admitted or soon left – had, as its real attraction, a reputation for academic excellence. And it was for this reason that Benjamin Straus, a marine lawyer in his mid-forties and graduate of Columbia Law School in New York, had sent his only daughter Léonie there. He was determined that she should have the best schooling available then for girls in France, no matter that it was not Jewish. He held that faith only very lightly now in any case, as did his wife Effi, a dark-haired girl from Brooklyn, whom he had met sixteen years before, married in a month, and taken back with him to France.

The Strauses had a small town house in Paris – where Hetty had stayed with them for a few days before Christmas – in the *seizième*, one of the last of the eighteenth-century village houses still there in Passy, shadowed and surrounded now by heavy *belle époque* apartment buildings.

American Marine Salvage and Insurance, the company of which Benjamin Straus was overseas director, had their European head office in Paris, with a branch at Le Havre, not far from the château convent. And this had been another reason for sending Léonie there. Benjamin loved his daughter and, as often as the discipline there allowed, came to visit her on his business trips to the port.

Unorthodox both in his faith and temperament, Ben Straus was a brisk and genial man of the world. His views were liberal and advanced – traits which his daughter seemed about to inherit in abundance. They were both originals – in their fiery confidence, happy intellect, sharp intuitions. And Straus's business acumen was perhaps sharper still. Through private investments he had made money – and enjoyed spending it, particularly on young women, and especially on his daughter and her new Irish friend, Hetty. He had a taste for beautiful things – one which he hoped to indulge the following day that spring, at the Hôtel Lion d'Or in Bayeux, where he had arranged lunch for the two girls.

The Mother Superior, Mother Agnes, had granted permission – a little unwillingly. But Mr Straus's air of reliability and charm during earlier visits to the convent, and his equally reassuring letter in this instance, had prevailed over the Mother Superior, with the proviso that he should accompany the girls to and from Bayeux.

All went according to plan. Benjamin, in a creamy grey homburg, white spats and with a silver-topped cane, with his chauffeur in the huge Peugeot cabriolet he had just purchased, picked the girls up at the gates of the château – both dressed in their Sunday best: long white, fluttery, layered muslin skirts, fine cotton embroidered blouses and straw bonnets – and within the hour they were driving into the cobbled courtyard of the Lion d'Or, where shortly afterwards, taking lunch at a large round table, decorated with little vases of wild spring flowers, they studied the simple *carte du jour*.

As an apéritif they sipped glasses from a half-bottle of Roederer brut. The girls, agog, savoured the warm smells from the kitchen and watched the bubbles break and rise, the champagne sparkling in the bright sunlight slanting through the half-open window.

'Papa, we finally got to take a look at that old relic,' Léonie told her father, from whom she had few, if any, secrets. 'It *was* a bit of old rabbit bone, I'm sure. But the strange thing was – *I* couldn't open the gold box, but Hetty could!'

Mr Straus looked at Hetty, then raised his glass to her. 'Well, that figures – it's the Irish in her. All sorts of magic there.'

Hetty blushed. Léonie interjected boisterously: 'But, Papa, *we* have magic, too. You always said so: the Jews!'

'So we have! We're both of us – the Jews and the Irish – the Magic People. But Hetty must have even more of it.' He looked at his daughter again, with a kindly, quizzical surmise. 'After all, Hetty's Irish *and* Jewish, isn't she?'

They ate simply but well – a moist *terrine*, fresh *crevettes* with mayonnaise, the local *truite aux amandes*, fruit and cheese, and a light Vouvray to go with it all, a lunch which, for Hetty, vibrated with every sort of pleasure, happiness: the slightly tart smell of the pale wine, the burnt-sweet taste of crackly almonds, the faint perfume of lilac from a tree in the courtyard just outside the window, garlic and piquant lemon in the air, warmth and satisfaction emanating from the other guests – all this, with the wine, seemed to lift Hetty several inches above her chair, gave her a cloudy sensation of ecstasy, the feeling of being in a dream which was yet entirely real, so that life at that moment was better than in her wildest fancies.

The chatter between the loquacious Strauses was nearly continuous and Hetty was quite content to bask in such happy surroundings. Benjamin spoke of Paris, the gossip among his French friends and the American community there – of the theatre and café life, which Hetty had only briefly sampled in her few days with the family before Christmas. They had all gone to the Cirque d'Hiver and a performance of Racine's *Andromaque* at the Comédie Française, and dined at Fouquet's in the Champs-Elysées. It was a life and a city which Hetty had loved, but which existed for her now only as a memorable taste. Mr Straus drew her into the conversation; they had been talking of the future.

'And what would you like to do there, Henrietta?'

'Oh, I'd like to live in Pa-Pa-Paris!' she said at once.

'Well, so you shall – why not? I wanted just the same thing. And look – there I am!'

'But you have a be-be-business.'

'A good wife, too!'

'I mean, I don't have a business . . .'

'Why, you *can* –'

'Or a husband,' Léonie interjected.

'Indeed,' her father confirmed the point. 'Or a good husband, which is more to the point.'

Hetty looked uncertain.

'I want to be a singer – at the Opera! That's right, isn't it, Papa?' Léonie ran on.

'If you work hard at it, why not?'

'Yes, Léonie sings so well.' Hetty spoke out now, her stammer lost for a moment. 'The "Ave Maria" in the chapel choir. But my voice goes all cracked on the high notes.'

'Well, something else then,' Mr Straus said. 'There's plenty of go in your family, as I understand it. And that's the great thing in life, isn't it, girls? – a bit of get up and go!' He lit a cigar. 'So what do you say? I don't much fancy another look at that old Norman tapestry here. Had enough of conquerors. What if we take the auto to the seaside for the afternoon?'

Which they did, driving north-east to Cabourg, running on the beach there and walking along the promenade among the fashionably-dressed crowds with their tiny parasols and vast picture hats, before taking tea in the palm court of the Grand Hotel. And all this, too, was a wonder to Hetty: the promise of a sort of freedom she had never known in her isolated life in Ireland, a freedom linked to other people's adventures. She sensed she was not alone in her desires – that her wild thoughts of future success, of love and adventure, were not unique to her, but shared, with Léonie, Léonie's father, and surely all the other people on the promenade and in the palm court, with their top hats, sticks and feather boas.

Hetty relished life that day. She was loth to return to the convent, where all such life was prohibited, hedged about with so many petty rules, made to be broken. A few weeks later, Hetty and Léonie agreed on a plan. And, this time, they intended they should be caught – taking their weekly bath, in the two screened tubs, without wearing the required cotton bathing shifts. The two girls sat there, in the hot water, naked, splashing about in the soap suds, making a great noise. So that it was not long before Sister Thérèse, their dormitory monitor, arrived on the scene. A diminutive martinet with a brassy Alsace accent, she was horrified.

'Your shifts! Where are your shifts?' she shouted at them, waving her arms through the wafts of steam. The girls grinned at her.

'I can't wash properly in a shift,' Léonie told her promptly, washing herself with exaggerated movements, raising one arm, then the other, in a suggestive ballet, an olive-skinned odalisque, massaging her rib-cage, her neat breasts.

'It's *dirty*, washing in a shift,' Hetty added, soaping herself with similarly provocative vigour.

Sister Thérèse nearly exploded.

But, the next morning, Mother Superior took a quieter, insidious, much more Jesuitical line.

'You say you cannot *wash* properly in your shifts?' She sat behind an ornate Louis Quinze bureau in her study, an incongruously plain crucifix on the heavy fleur de lys wallpaper behind her.

'Yes – just that.'

Mother Agnes sighed. 'That may or may not be so,' she said icily. 'But honesty should compel you to admit that you *also* bathed in such a manner simply to break the regulations and provoke Sister Thérèse – for the *joy* of so doing. Both of you are sufficiently intelligent to distinguish between these quite separate reasons: it is *good* that you should want to wash properly; not good that you should wilfully disobey our rules here.'

'Are the rules more important then than our washing properly?' Léonie asked innocently.

'The two issues are not comparable in the manner you suggest.' Mother Agnes, a tall, grim-faced woman, stood up, clasping her hands, going over to the window. She turned then, with a look of fierce reason in her eyes. 'You must obey the rules *and* wash properly. That is the sequence – and the whole point of law: that it stands *a priori* – you know what that means? – as a first cause, in front of, before, everything else. Therefore you may wash only within the context of the law here. Is that not perfectly clear?'

Mother Agnes returned to her bureau, and took up a quill pen, prior to setting out their punishment.

'But, Me-Me-Mother Agnes, that's not fair,' Hetty tried to forestall her now, breathlessly, pleading her case with a great, but entirely assumed innocence in her wide eyes. 'We w-w-*were* just wanting to wash properly, not just to be bad.'

'Now you lie, girl, and compound the offence.'

'How do you know I'm le-le-lying?' she stammered.

'I know,' the old woman said deeply. 'And, what's more, *you* know you are. Useless to pretend otherwise.' She shook her head. 'You see, Henrietta, *I* know you, your every temptation, every sin – almost as God knows them – everything ... Remember, when you think to perpetrate these sins again – remember what His Son Jesus Christ said: "Behold, I am with you always – even unto the end of the world." You can never escape that final retribution.'

Mother Agnes passed sentence then, confirming it as she spoke in the big leather-bound punishment book. 'You will walk the grounds, commencing this Saturday, every Saturday in free time, from now until the end of term. And of course there will be no more exeats.' She closed the book with a decisive thump. Then she gazed at the two girls, before adding as her lugubrious peroration: 'And your shifts – you will remember your shifts . . .'

'Well, at least she didn't chuck us out.' Léonie picked a kingcup on the first of their punishment walks that same afternoon, munched the stalk an instant before throwing it in the fast-flowing chalk stream. Kneeling down, Hetty gazed at her reflection in the water.

'No. She wouldn't have expelled us.' Hetty stared down into the green shallows. 'She's too clever for that: prefers to make us feel really guilty.'

'Well, I don't . . . I just think she's an old cow.'

'A clever old cow, thought. We *did* do it to annoy –'

'*And* to wash properly –'

'But we *wanted* to be caught.'

'Of course, to make a point, how stupid it all is. Why should we hide everything? Like the other girls – always hiding things and sniggering and keeping little secret bits of mirror in their cupboards –'

'And writing secret *billets-doux* – to imaginary *beaux*, getting old Michel to post them in the village. *We* don't have to do that.' The girls chuckled. 'The men we write to are *real*!' Hetty said, thinking of Dermot, and they chuckled again.

The two girls lay on their stomachs, gazing at their reflections in the water.

'You can see yourself here at least,' Hetty said. 'So stupid, not being allowed to have any mirrors anywhere in the château.'

'All part of the "context of the law",' Léonie leant out, dipping her arm in the water, wondering if she could tickle the brown trout that wavered in the stream some yards upstream. 'Oh, the *agony* of it all,' she suddenly moaned, her voice full of mock drama. 'Are we really going to spend years and years here, being pestered by Sister Thérèse and Mother Superior? Tell me, Hetty, can we *bear* it?'

'I can – if you can.' Hetty lay on her back now, looking up at the blue arc of sky. Then, she put her hand out, vaguely pawing the air before, like a butterfly net trapping an insect, she let it fall over Léonie's mouth. '*We* can bear it . . .'

'Um-m-m-m.' Léonie's lips fed an instant on Hetty's gentle fingers.

Mother Superior might have known better. Her punishment cemented a friendship which, in the giddy reverses of such adolescent associations, might otherwise have waned or lapsed entirely – a friendship in any case which, had the old woman known more of the human heart, she would surely have thought unsuitable from the beginning. As it was, in commanding these long walks together, she bound the girls to pleasure, not to penance.

Perhaps since on the surface they were so unalike – the tall, stammering, gauche but haughty Irish girl and this compact, sweet-sly European – Mother Superior believed them to be quite incompatible as real friends, and therefore no threat to each other. But of course it was just these wide differences in their character which drew them together – this very factor which, like a lit taper held above a jar of pure oxygen, made their friendship dangerously inflammable.

'I do wish I had someone to write to – properly, I mean – like you do.' Léonie was chattering away the following Saturday, a colder day, with grey rain clouds scudding above the poplars, so that the girls wore mufflers with their green serge topcoats, together with tall lace-up boots as protection against the muddy paths.

'But you *do* have – your uncle Eli in New York who sends you those amazing presents, those real Indian beads and things.'

'Not the same . . . as Dermot, in the *army* and everything. That's exciting. You're so lucky! He's so handsome!' Léonie faced Hetty as they neared one of the trout traps. 'Show me that photograph again – do! The one of him on that great horse in his uniform.'

'It's hidden in my cupboard.'

'No, it's not – you keep it under your vest!'

'No, I don't! Anyway, you can see him properly – this summer, when you come to stay in Ireland. I've written to Mama . . .' Hetty's face clouded then.

'But you haven't heard from her, have you?'

'She hardly ever writes.'

'But Dermot does!'

They had come to the trout trap now, a little tributary, with a metal grille at either end, running out and back from the main stream, where half a dozen fish languished, gills palpitating, heads against the flow of the green-dark water.

'Yes, you'll like Dermot,' Hetty went on. 'He's such tremendous fun.' But she turned to Léonie then, biting her lip, a doubt in her eyes. She did not want Léonie to like him *too* much.

'What's the matter?'

'Nothing. And there's Robert, too,' Hetty ran on, changing the topic, thinking to introduce an alternative male friend for Léonie. 'You'll see him, he's nice. He'll be back from school in Dublin.'

'Robert, your brother . . .?'

'No, not really – remember, I told you: his parents were killed in a hurricane. We were just brought up together.'

'Oh yes – Robert.' But Léonie did not seem very interested in Robert, and it was she who changed the subject. 'Shall we let the fish out?'

'Or fish *for* them – wouldn't that be more fun?'

'What with?'

'A bent pin – I've got one – and our boot-laces. And a worm.'

They found a worm, took off their boots, undid all the laces, and Hetty unfastened a safety pin which had been holding up her skirt, so that it collapsed about her ankles. Then they roared with laughter, dancing about the trout trap, terrifying the fish.

Later, Hetty found a small snail on the path, with a wonderfully coloured shell, striped in brilliant green and yellow bands. She gently picked it up, setting it on her hand; after a minute or two, the snail, which had retreated inside its house, re-emerged. Léonie thought it gruesome.

'It's just a beautiful little snail,' Hetty told her. 'Here, you hold it.'

Léonie grimaced, backing away. 'It's all slimy, though – horrible!'

'No, it's not, it's sweet.'

'Put it on your head, then, if it's so sweet. I dare you!'

Hetty did just that, holding the snail there until it seemed to take root, a brightly-coloured emblem like a third eye in the middle of her forehead.

Léonie watched the performance with disgust. But she was impressed. And now she was ashamed at her cowardice.

'All right,' she said finally, steeling herself. 'Do it to me.'

Hetty walked slowly forward. Léonie, her back against the trunk of a tree, stood quite still with her eyes closed, unresisting, as Hetty transferred the snail, placing it delicately on Léonie's brow. The moment she felt its cold touch – she shivered violently, as if about to suffer a delicious agony.

'There!' Hetty said, when the snail had once more taken up residence. 'See, I told you, it's nothing.' Léonie opened her eyes a fraction, squinting upwards, unable to see the snail, but still fearful. 'You did it!' Hetty ran on, excited, happy. 'You did it!'

Léonie smiled briefly then, keeping her head absolutely still. 'Yes,' she said limply, 'I did it . . .'

Afterwards they walked on, arm in arm, true companions now, as if, in this mutual contact with the snail, they had finally put the seal on their friendship.

Back at Summer Hill, Frances's life had gone from bad to worse. Her militant republican career – all she really lived for now – had suffered various setbacks. Like Hetty, she had been kicking at the traces. But for Frances there was no release in any tender friendship, only an increasing bitterness that she could not now, literally, take up arms against the British.

With the surprising advent of Asquith's Liberal Home Rule Bill in 1912, popular support for Arthur Griffith's Sinn Fein Abstentionist Party in Ireland fell away dramatically. And worse, as far as Frances and the other members of the secret Irish Republican Brotherhood were concerned, there was now almost no public support in Ireland for revolution or violence of any sort.

As a result of Asquith's bill, Redmond's old Irish Home Rule Party was once more everywhere in the ascendant, both in Ireland and at Westminster. In return for supporting the Liberal Party in the House of Commons, Redmond had extracted this bill from Asquith and had thus seemed to guarantee Home Rule for Ireland within a year or two – an entirely peaceful transfer of power from London to Dublin. And so all Frances's dreams of violent glory had been set at nothing; Pat Kennedy's too. After centuries of bloodshed the physical force movement in Ireland was now obsolete. The country would achieve its liberty constitutionally, without Pat Kennedy's revolver or Frances's equally vigorous help – and Frances took this setback badly, as a vampire denied blood, kicking her heels about Summer Hill, working off her ire by bullying everyone more than ever.

So that, by the early summer of 1914, when Hetty and Léonie travelled to Summer Hill, they found Frances in a particularly fierce and unresponsive mood. Often she was away, at clandestine meetings in Dublin or Belfast, with her fellow conspirators in the IRB – O'Hegarty, Eoin MacNeill, Padraic Pearse – among whom she found more congenial company, as they pondered their lost revolution. Thus the two girls, since Miss Goulden had long since departed, had the house much to themselves, until Dermot arrived for his annual visit, coming down on the train with Robert, home from school in Dublin, in the middle of June – a month that started with rain, but soon turned brilliantly fine and hot, the flaming cloudless weather lasting day after day, seemingly set fair for the rest of the summer.

Frances was away for the day when Dermot and Robert arrived, so Dermot immediately took the three young people out salmon fishing, wading into the stream with his rod, while Robert and the girls watched from upstream near the boathouse, where a picnic tea awaited them.

The two girls, leaving Robert on the bank with the big salmon net, returned to the boathouse to prepare the tea, setting plates out and putting the kettle to boil on the small grate at the back of the stone building. They were in shadow now, but it was hot, especially when the dry tinder took fire under the kettle and the flames leapt up. Outside, beyond the jetty, the river glittered fiercely in the sun. Léonie ran a hand over her brow, as the sweat trickled down her cheeks. Then she laughed.

'All this making *tea* you do over here – seem to live on it in Ireland.' She drew away from the fire, flapping her hands.

'Well?' Hetty asked with excited impatience. 'Wha-wha-what do you think of him?'

'Oh, he's nice. Quiet, but very nice. How long has he been at school in Dublin?'

Hetty was astonished, annoyed. 'I meant *Dermot*, you ninny! Not Robert.'

'Oh.' Léonie pulled herself together. 'Well, he's very nice as well. But I *knew* that.'

They went out on to the jetty then, shading their eyes against the glare, gazing downstream at Dermot. But Léonie's eyes soon strayed towards Robert: slim, but much taller now and no longer a boy, handsome in a sharply chiselled, rather farouche way, with a shank of thick dark hair running sideways across his head; an isolated but composed figure as he stood on the bank, quite still, holding the salmon net, a sentinel with a spear in the dazzling sunlight.

'Tea's ready!' Hetty sang out to Dermot, longing to set him down at the little bench in the boathouse, minister to him, generally show him off to Léonie. But, when he did come to tea, he seemed preoccupied, taking little notice of Hetty.

'Will you take Léonie and me – and Robert,' she added as a rather unwilling afterthought, 'out in the trap this evening? We could go over to Brandon, climb the mountain . . .?'

'I'd like to, perhaps tomorrow –'

'Or the otters? Come out and see if we can see them this evening?'

'I'm a little tired, Hetty . . .'

Hetty was crestfallen.

In fact Dermot wanted to speak to Frances – when she got back from Dublin that evening, the next morning, as soon as possible in any case: more anxious to do this than to entertain Hetty and her new friend. The business with Frances was far more urgent, he was sure.

He had heard from his father, who had seen and been in touch with Frances regularly during the past year, heard how very difficult she had become. Violent, insensate – these were some of the words his father had used of her. He feared for her sanity. And then there was an entirely certain matter to take up with her: the deplorable incident with Appleton, the English head gardener, who had done so much for the place under Lady Cordiner's earlier directions. Frances had apparently insisted that he undo all his work in the neat pleasure gardens, changing the formal patterns there, demanding a bosky wildness everywhere – and, when the man had demurred, she had struck him in the face and given him immediate notice. It was obvious – Frances was close to some sort of nervous breakdown. So that Dermot, remembering their old intimacies, saw that he must help her if he could, make one last effort to try to ease her many disappointments, set her to rights.

He took his opportunity the following morning, first indulging in pleasantries with her in the porch after breakfast before following her into her boudoir. She showed surprise at this invasion: surprise and then, as he had expected and prepared himself for, scalding anger at his presumption.

'We have had this quite pointless conversation before, as I remember,' she told him in her harsh voice. 'Let me repeat myself: I do *not* require you to come here, to my house, and tell me how to run it – or my life!'

Dermot had taken up position by the door, in case she thought to bolt, for he had decided now that, if it came to it, nothing could be lost in his taking a very firm line with this dangerously intemperate woman.

He gazed at her then, standing against the bright summer light, a vase of huge white peonies on her Sheraton desk. At nearly forty, apart from a few greying hairs, she had not lost her dark beauty: the almost ruler-straight nose, great blackberry eyes, wide proud mouth, the olive-skinned gypsy looks. The beauty was still there, but appeared now only as a lovely and vague illustration seen through tracing paper, as if each of these original designs had been overlaid with cruel alterations: the lips pouted in permanent disapproval, curling down at either side, the chin puckered like folds on a toby jug, the eyes soured with long antagonisms – and her once sweet voice screeched now as she bunched and cracked her finger joints like angry castanets. The gypsy had become a witch.

The transformation was piteous. And Dermot, remembering the other lovely woman, wished desperately to change the whole mould here, wave a magic wand and return Frances to her better nature.

'Frances, dear Frances,' he began, 'that is *not* what I am doing here, believe me –'

'What else –'

'Please don't *interrupt!*' he told her firmly, showing steel. 'You know perfectly well – things have reached a bad pass down here. We must try and do something about it.' She attempted to interrupt again. 'No, hear me out – first this business with Appleton. You put the matter in my father's hands, his Dublin legal office, and he has asked me to speak to you.' He took a document from his pocket. 'Appleton's solicitors have filed suit with the courts here, for assault and improper dismissal. The case comes up in Waterford next month –'

'Indeed! And we will win it. The man was outrageously impertinent, refused to obey instructions.'

'That may well be so. But in your physical assault he has a more serious case against you and it could well go his way. He has witnesses to the event –'

'It will be up to your father's office to see that it does *not* go his way, else I shall take other legal counsel.'

'My dear Frances, that's not really the point – you know it well. We must speak of other things, come to the root of the matter – of what so worries and upsets you. Already you have seriously jeopardised your life here at Summer Hill. You are, I know, losing staff, in the household and on the estate. And other local people will not work for you – soon the whole place will become unmanageable, the farm bankrupt. If matters continue this way you will destroy your inheritance here – and I only speak to you in this way to prevent that happening. The house here is as dear to me as it is to you. Do you not see all this?'

Frances had stared at him unbelievingly as he spoke, speechless with anger, merely waiting for him to finish before answering him viciously. Yet, when he did stop, she said nothing.

Instead, she walked quickly across the room, raised her arm, and aimed a blow to Dermot's cheek. But Dermot, just as quickly, snatched her arm, held it tightly, bent it back, forcing it down as she resisted fiercely.

'Traitor!' she screamed at him, raising her other arm, until he grasped that, too, holding both as if in a vice, so that they swayed about the room together, locked in a grim dance.

'Traitor! Bully! You interfering great bully!' She continued her tirade.

'No,' he told her urgently, his gentle voice quite at odds with his physical dominance. 'I have *not* betrayed you – others have, but not I. I have always been true to you, told the truth, about myself and about you. If you could only *see* that!'

She continued the struggle, more fiercely still – and still he would not let her go. So that eventually, in this violent proximity, something cracked in Frances – and the end of the contest was just as dramatic as its beginning. Suddenly she quite ceased the struggle and fell into Dermot's arms with an almost equal violence, sobbing on his shoulder.

Embarrassed by this sudden emotional volte-face, Dermot nonetheless took every advantage of it. He consoled her, patting her on the back, while at the same time gently trying to ease his way out of her embrace. 'Now tell me,' he said, 'what is it, tell me, that makes you so unhappy, so many years after . . . all those earlier sorrows?'

She continued weeping on his shoulder. Then suddenly she drew away from him, still holding his shoulders, but shaking them now. 'What do you *think* is the matter – if not all those "earlier sorrows" as you politely put them?'

'Dearest, it was all so long ago –'

'Does that alter it, the pain?'

'But the Prince is dead and gone these many –'

She shook him again. 'You can't be so naive! Not so much him, but *you* – you, Dermot.' She turned away then, taking out a handkerchief, mopping her eyes. 'Don't you see? It all went wrong for me *then*, before him, with *you*. I loved you – oh, more than *any*one, ever.' Crushed by so much emotion, she went over to the window.

'I wish I could make it up to you,' he said, rooted to the spot, gazing at her blankly. 'I wished it then – I wish it now. But . . .' He did not go on, fearing another outburst from her.

'But you can't.' She said the words for him, bitterly.

She had altered in the last few minutes – regaining, as if from the warm impact of his body, something of her old self, the bright, happy woman she had once been. And Dermot feared now, in her last acid words, that, unless he made some positive gesture, she would relapse once more into her bitter life.

So he came across to her then, and gave himself to her, in so far as he could, taking her chastely in his arms and holding her there.

'You have me – at least in every other way,' he told her. 'Cannot you see that – feel it?'

'Indeed . . .' She smiled for an instant, looking over his shoulder. 'There is the whole problem.' And Dermot saw then, felt the emotion intensely, how he alone had it in his power to make this woman happy and change her life, take her away from all this emotional and political frustration. But he feared to implement the power, for he knew, because of his real nature, how he could not truly satisfy her. And she knew it, too, without either of them having to express the fact. Nonetheless Dermot recognised the crucial watershed at which they had both arrived, which he had contrived, which it was his responsibility to resolve in some fashion. And he knew, too, how one false word or move on his part at this point would ruin everything.

So he said, 'If you could bear with me – with my nature – we might marry?'

He so accentuated the doubt in this proposal that at first Frances responded in kind, simply shaking her head in disbelief. 'Do you mean it?' she said at last, her face still frozen in surprise.

'Why, yes.'

'A marriage of convenience . . .' She turned away, sad, dismissive.

'No, a marriage of . . . whatever we made it.' He was almost annoyed suddenly, anxious to contradict her.

Her face relaxed then as she laughed abruptly, turning back to him. 'I could bear with your nature, Dermot. The doubt is – could you bear with mine?'

'Yes,' he said with real enthusiasm now. 'The wonderful nature you had, and have only . . . mislaid.'

'No,' she said wanly. 'I have since changed completely in other ways –'

'Oh, if you mean your Home Rule enthusiasms! But why should I object to that now? Asquith's bill will go through before the end of the year and Ireland will be free. There is no problem there, surely? You will have won your cause without violence and there'll be a happy end to it – for both of us.'

'Well, let us think about your suggestion, shall we?'

There was silence. One of the huge peony petals fell limply to the floor and, outside, a cloud raced across the sun, darkening the room for a moment. Then she moved towards him and kissed him briefly, but with a long-forgotten tenderness.

Frances was truly happy for the first time in years. Her foul humours dissolved. She began to take a relaxed and kindly interest in people and in her surroundings. In short, she mellowed in the warmth of Dermot's affection – all of which, as a quite expected consequence, enraged Hetty. She no longer had Dermot to herself – sharing with him only a small part of the fun and adventure she had expected. In this sudden turn-about she felt betrayed by him – and worse was the fact that he should neglect her for her mother, whom she hated.

So that when, partly on Dermot's suggestion, Frances tried to make things up with her daughter, Hetty violently rejected these peace overtures. They talked together one morning on the porch.

'I have tried to explain,' Frances still spoke formally, but not coldly. 'There have been such difficulties from the beginning – your father's death, all the problems with your Grandmama when we came here: I have not given you the attention I should have.'

Hetty fidgeted by the high-backed wicker chair, anxious to join Léonie and Robert playing croquet on the upper lawn. 'Yes,' she scowled. 'So – now you have explained.'

'Hetty, dear, you are so unapproachable: I am *sorry*.'

'But you have *not* explained!' Hetty rounded on her mother. 'My fe-fe-father, for example. People say – how he is *not* my father –'

'But of course he is!'

'And my Grandmama – why is she locked up?'

'She is . . . unwell.'

'And Dermot!' Hetty burst out, unable to contain herself, shaking with frustrated emotion.

'What of Dermot? He has been a great stay to us both – has he not?'

'Wh-wh-why does he – does he now *haunt* you so?'

'"Haunt" me?' Frances was surprised at the word. But it propelled her into an admission she might not otherwise have made. 'My dear, he does not haunt me. I may tell you now – we hope to marry!' She smiled graciously.

Hetty was thunderstruck. '*Marry* him? But you can't – he's a relation!'

'Only a very distant cousin –'

'But you can't, you can't!' Hetty quite lost control of herself then. 'You *can't* – he's my father!' she shouted, before running away, sobbing, to her bedroom.

Later Frances told Dermot of Hetty's fearful reaction.

'Not unexpected – I so wish she could be told the truth . . .'

'That's out of the question, I'm afraid.' Frances tried to disguise her almost brutal rigidity.

But Hetty's reaction to the news of her mother's impending marriage was openly brutal. That same afternoon, waiting her opportunity, she managed to corner Dermot alone, up by the grotto and the artificial waterfall.

'I *am* sorry, Hetty, that it should so upset you, our marrying –' he told her, before she responded bitterly, 'But you *can't* me-me-marry her – you can't me-marry a desperate Fenian!' She used the word that Elly had often used, covering all violent Irish revolutionaries. 'She's part of a secret group here, against the law! I know it! She and Pat Kennedy – they met a man here, years ago, in Pat's rooms, and they took a secret oath – to fight the British. So how can you me-me-marry someone like that? You in the army and all that? You can't!'

Dermot, thinking she must have invented it all, was not as surprised as Hetty had hoped. 'How do you know this?'

'I *saw* them, from the stable loft above Pat's rooms – all together, when she took the oath. So there!' Hetty was breathless with fury. 'If you me-marry her you will be a traitor yourself.'

She picked a fern, growing out from the rocks in the grotto, and fiddled with it violently.

'But, Hetty,' Dermot said at last, 'Ireland is going to be free in any case now, quite soon. The British are going to give us freedom here, quite legally, so your mother won't have to be involved in any of that sort of thing, any more. Don't you see? – it's all over now – that kind of Irish fighting.'

Hetty was not persuaded by this response, so Dermot took a different line. He turned, leaving the grotto, and gazed down at the house, its blue-ish limestone and great windows glimmering in the sunlight.

'Hetty, look at the house,' he urged her gently. 'Don't you want to have it here, keep it – in years to come – as *your* house and home?'

'No. I hate the house,' she told him sullenly. 'Don't like it here in Ireland at all. I like France and Paris me-me-much better. Anyway, what's that to do with me – marrying Mama?'

'Just that I want the house to *be* here – for her and for you later on. And in marrying your Mama I think I can help that happen.'

Hetty was vindictively brusque again. 'You're me-me-marrying her – just to keep the house? That's not a very good reason. Don't you love her? That's why people me-marry, isn't it?'

Dermot found himself in a predicament. So set on the truth in every other way, he could not tell it here – could not begin to explain that he did not love her mother in the expected way, but felt a great tenderness and sympathy for her, a deep affection – and, yes, guilt for all his earlier inabilities and refusals with her. None of this could he tell Hetty, yet he was loth to lie. So he said, 'I love her, like I love you, Hetty. It's more a family love. Can you see that?'

Hetty could not see it. But she was somewhat placated by his answer, which put her, at least, on an equal footing with her mother in his affections, so that she felt emboldened to say, 'In a *family* way?'

'Yes, just that.'

Hetty's eyes were alight with fear and hope now as she rushed on, 'Are you, are you – my fe-fe-father then? My *real* father?' There was a vast silence, as Dermot fiddled with his pipe and matches. '*Are* you?' she asked despairingly.

'No, Hetty,' he said at last, lighting his pipe. 'No, I'm not. Why should you think that?'

Hetty turned away, close to tears now, crunching up the fern leaf. 'People said – oh, they said it, in Domenica – Robert heard. And that awful Miss Goulden was always asking funny questions . . . And my own Papa, well, *he* was so awful . . .'

'Yes, I see that. But think of it, Hetty – I *will* be your father, your step-father at least, when we marry.' He walked back to her, took his pipe from his mouth, and blew a few expert smoke rings into the still summer air, smiled at her, a loving mischief in his eyes, so that he made her smile at last – and they smiled together then, the smoke rings curling round Hetty's ears. 'That's the *great* thing,' he went on, speaking with boundless enthusiasm now, taking her by the shoulder and turning her away from the cold spray of the waterfall, so that they both faced out into the warm sun, looking over the sloping lawns, the glittering house, the lush valley and the purple hump of Mount Brandon beyond. 'The great thing – that we can all be here together: you and I and your Mama, Robert, your friend Léonie!

All of us – live here, come here and *do* things together, so much to do! Life can be so happy for all of us, promise you – unimaginably happy. Just look at the house, Hetty! It's full of peace and *promise* now – look at it that way. Isn't it?'

Hetty bit her lip, trying to restrain her tears, as he held her arm tightly. 'Yes,' she spluttered. 'I suppose it is . . .'

She gazed at the house herself then. And indeed, in the light of Dermot's forthright explanations, his renewed affection, in his plans of a future for all of them here, Summer Hill, for the first time, called to Hetty, offering her something. It was no longer a site of unhappiness, of quarrels and long bitterness with her Mama, but a building that had floated clear away from all that dissension, reasserting its ancient truth, showing its long-dormant character, stone and mortar imbued with love now, not hatred. The house touched Hetty then, invisible tendrils reaching out in the hot summer air, embracing her delicately, offering itself to her, as a freehold possession – something of hers, not just her mother's. Yes, in the last of the golden afternoon light, the house *did* promise her something.

The following morning the *Irish Times* carried the bold headline: ARCHDUKE FRANCIS FERDINAND AND CONSORT ASSASSINATED AT SARAJEVO. Some days later Dermot's leave was cancelled – he was recalled to his regiment at Aldershot – and by the end of July Germany had declared war against both Russia and France, with England's declaration of hostilities following a few days later. Peace and promise disappeared everywhere, for everyone, then.

5

D ERMOT'S REGIMENT OF Hussars was posted to France almost immediately –
among the first of the British Expeditionary Force to land there on the 16th
of August, when they were moved straight up to the Belgian front, making a
temporary headquarters at the Château de Ghislain on the Mons–Charleroi road.
Here, waiting on events in the push towards Mons, and joining up with a squadron
of the Royal Irish Dragoons, they bivouacked on the flat farmland beyond the
château stables, where many of their horses found ideal quarters.

It was scorchingly hot with an eerie silence, as scouts reported no sign of German
troop movements, either around Mons itself, which they held in force, or on the
road to Charleroi. The whole flat landscape seemed deserted, unmoving, except
for an oven breath which now and then stirred the crimson poppy-heads in the
long, gently undulating cornfields to either side of the road.

The war, for Dermot and his men, was somewhere else, or had not yet begun.
The two cavalry brigades were stalled and still in the lazy swelter, flies caught in
the golden amber of the weather; until the afternoon of the 22nd, when one of the
Dragoon scouts rode back furiously into the stable yard, reporting that a troop of
Uhlan lancers – some three miles away when he had last seen them, the officer in
front casually smoking a cigar – were riding down the road from Mons towards
them.

Dermot mustered his brigade with all speed, arranging with his opposite number,
Major Bridges of the Irish Dragoons, to turn out at once, taking a course through
the fields; they would advance across the corn and hope to surprise the Uhlans on
the road in a sudden pincer movement.

In the event their plan did not materialise as expected. The Uhlans, with their
own scouts and sensing trouble ahead of them at the château, had chosen a similar
plan, leaving the road and dividing their men to either side of it, proceeding
through these same cornfields, thus set on a direct collision course with the British.
So that Dermot, riding ahead with 'C' squadron up a slight rise, was suddenly
confronted by some fifty of the enemy already in battle positions, spread out in
line abreast, like mediaeval cavalry, less than half a mile away across the cornfields,

spiked helmets glinting in the afternoon sun, lances angled forward at the ready.

Rapidly Dermot mustered his own men in battle order. '"C" squadron, draw swords, ready to go! Fourth Troop, in the rear to follow up, ready for action! . . .'

His heart fluttered with excitement. His men outnumbered the Uhlans, he thought, and the westering sun shone straight in the enemy's eyes. And, besides these material advantages, he was so confident himself: the Uhlans, he knew, for all their fierce reputation, had never fought in battle before, while he and quite a few of his men had charged and survived at the bloody engagement of Colenso.

For a long moment, as both sides stopped to consider their positions, there was complete silence over the great flat field, broken only by the sudden 'creek-creek' of a corncrake as it flew up into the shimmering air. Then, almost imperceptibly at first, both lines moved forward, very gently increasing pace. Still there was silence, until a strange swishing sound came, gradually rising in volume from everywhere in the field, as hundreds of horses' feet pushed through the dry corn.

Then, quite suddenly, the quiet summer's day changed. The horses, spurred on, first took to a canter, then rode into full charge at a gallop. The whole earth came alive in a thunderous cacophony of sound – hoof beats, jangling harness metal, vicious shouts from the men, egging each other on or cursing the enemy.

The great war had begun – in a hammering, violent tide of men at arms, sabres drawn, pennanted lances rampant, breastplates gleaming: a vainglorious soldiery, on great black and chestnut chargers galloping across the scarlet-flooded field.

The initial clash was a bloody affair, the Uhlan lances picking off half a dozen of Dermot's squadron in the first affray. But Dermot, ahead of the troop, sword drawn, was lucky. His opposite number in the Uhlan line, a less skilled horseman, lost grip of his reins and allowed his mount to rear up at the last moment. So that Dermot, passing him through the line, was able to swing round quickly and, with one blow, cut the man down from the side, behind his breastplate.

Moving on, he despatched several more in the same manner, before he stood in his stirrups, marshalling his troops, from a position now some fifty yards behind the Uhlan line. And it was this high stance of command, head and shoulders above the other men, which undid him. Some distance away to the rear, something which Dermot had not noticed, another mounted German troop, supporting the Uhlans, had been concealed below a slope in the land. Unslinging their Mausers now, they looked ahead for likely targets. Dermot, standing in his saddle, formed an ideal mark.

He heard nothing of the rifle crack, felt only the searing force and smash of the bullet as it pitched deep into his back – and felt that only for a split second as he fell unconscious from his horse.

The repercussions of this event in Flanders were unhappy. Partly as a result of losing their commanding officer, the Hussars failed to hold their early advantage in the skirmish and eventually were forced into a hurried withdrawal, leaving their several dead and wounded behind. And subsequently, in the immediate British push for Mons and in their disastrous retreat from the same town, Dermot's body was never found.

Officially he was posted only as missing. But Frances, when she received the news from Dermot's father in Dublin and with her own experience of so many similar deaths at Colenso, read between the lines, believing the worst. And so did Hetty when her mother spoke to her of it.

'We cannot be sure, of course – he may be safe somewhere, or have been taken prisoner. We must hope for the best.'

They had been talking on the porch. It was a mockingly beautiful September day. Hetty left her mother without a word, going to her room where she sobbed uncontrollably.

Without breaking down Frances took the news just as hard. Dermot had offered her a future. When, through Asquith's Home Rule Bill, her own political and military ambitions had come to nothing, this man, once so loved by her, had, quite out of the blue, offered his own love, in a very late return. And it had changed her whole outlook and demeanour, and she recognised this. He had turned her from war towards peace and hope. And now he was gone, in another war, and all that human hope had disappeared with him.

And, when in the following months no news was received of his whereabouts, she had to believe he was dead. So once again, in a final most awful way, she felt betrayed – by the shabbiest card fate had yet dealt her: a man she had come to love once more, now dead in the cause of an Empire which she despised. She soon returned to all her old bitter ways, but took to them this time with a greatly increased vehemence.

And, in this plunge into vicious despair, the suddenly-changed political situation in Ireland helped her in every way. As a result of the outbreak of war, Asquith's Irish Home Rule Bill, which had passed its final stage in the House of Commons and had only to receive the Royal Assent in September, was suspended, pending cessation of hostilities. Bad as this was, it might not, in itself, have exacerbated matters in Ireland had not John Redmond, leader of the resurgent Home Rule party at Westminster and toadying for British favour, made several disastrous speeches during these months, committing the 180,000-strong Irish Volunteer Army to the British cause, thus appearing a mere recruiting sergeant for the old enemy: a quixotic gesture made without consulting his party and which found almost no support among his countrymen. In any case, as a result of this Home Rule setback and Redmond's naive misjudgements, the physical force movement in Ireland, long dormant, received a sudden new lease of life.

In September 1914, the Supreme Council of the secret Irish Republican Brotherhood met in Dublin, and decided that a rising against the British should now take place before the end of the war. 'England's difficulty is Ireland's opportunity' was the line taken once again. A Military Council was set up to organise an insurrection as soon as possible. By the end of September Frances, informed of these plans and charged with setting them in motion in south Kilkenny when the time came, was set anew on her violent career. Once more, losing life, Frances had taken to destruction.

For Hetty, the consequences of Dermot's death, though not so openly destructive, warped her soul, blighted her growth. For her, too, there was a terrible sense of betrayal – in losing this father, confidant, friend, and all the future he had promised her. But unlike Frances with her renewed militant outlets – her secret drilling and rifle practice in the deep woods beyond Summer Hill – Hetty had no such ready balm to set on her wounds. Instead, when she returned to the convent that September, there was only Léonie to assuage the bitterness that overwhelmed her.

'You *mustn't* be so down – on and on like this,' Léonie told her firmly one day as they left chapel, where Hetty, head deep in her hands as they prayed, had really been hiding her tears. 'Perhaps he's alive . . .'

'I've prayed for him,' Hetty said softly. Then she repeated herself. 'I've *prayed*!' she almost shouted.

'Of course . . .' Léonie turned away, not wanting Hetty to see how little belief she had in such spiritual levers.

But Hetty sensed her doubts. 'No, it *does* work! Once, years ago, when Robert had terrible whooping cough and was very nearly dying . . . I prayed. And it worked.' Yet she looked at Léonie now, searchingly, as if she might absolutely confirm the efficacy of prayer in this case.

But Léonie could only shake her head. 'They all say the war will be over by Christmas,' she temporised. 'They'll surely find out what's happened – where he is then.'

Some Belgian nuns, sisters in the same order, had arrived the day before and now, refugees at the château convent, walked past them: a sad, grey-faced, unhappy group, hands clasped protectively together below their waists.

Léonie gazed after them. 'How awful! – they say the Germans did really *awful* things to the nuns in Belgium.' Then she realised the tactlessness of her words. 'I'm sorry, Hetty.' She grasped her hand then, massaging it firmly. 'It *will* get better, promise you – I'll make it better for you.' She looked deeply into Hetty's tear-flushed eyes, stroking the soft skin on the inside of her wrist.

That evening in the dormitory, hearing her sporadic, muffled sobs late into the night and risking everything with Sister Thérèse outside in her bed at the end of the central aisle, Léonie climbed up over the wooden partition between their two cubicles, got into Hetty's narrow iron bed and tried to comfort her.

'Léa, what on earth –'

'Shsh!' Léonie whispered, for Hetty had sat up startled, flouncing the bedclothes about, before Léonie pulled them back over them both, putting fingers to Hetty's lips in the darkness.

Hetty's face was damp and slippery with tears. 'You can cry and cry,' Léonie whispered to her then under the sheet. 'And say prayers over and over. But in the end there's just us. We're both here and alive and have each other. That's *real* hope, isn't it?'

'Suppose so . . .' Hetty started to sob again.

'No, Hetty, *don't* – it's *me*.' She moved to her then, clasping her as best she could in the awkward bed. 'I love you, like Dermot does, wherever he is. I really do. And I'm *here*, with you – wherever you are.'

Léonie had leant away as she whispered, but now she returned to Hetty, searching out and finding her face with her fingers again, before caressing her lips, her eyes, cheeks, embracing her long hot body, pressing herself gently against the sweet linen-and-soap smell. '*Please*, you won't cry any more, because you needn't,' Léonie insisted once again. And Hetty, finally sighing, seemed to relax at last, saying nothing, simply reaching her hand up, touching Léonie's fingers as they roved about her face, like a magic wand clearing away her tears and sadness.

'You see?' Léonie said. 'Just with us – it *can* get better . . .'

And, indeed, things did get better – through Hetty's vehement prayers perhaps, and certainly by way of Léonie's tender attentions, that night and later. Shortly after Christmas, which Hetty spent with the Straus family in Paris, word came to Dermot's father in Dublin, via the Red Cross, that Dermot, badly wounded in the affray with the Uhlans, had also been rescued by them – taken back to a German field hospital and thence to a military hospital in Berlin where he had made a good recovery. Now he was a prisoner of war, held at an army barracks among hundreds of other Allied officers near Cologne.

Hetty heard the news from her mother at the start of the spring term, the already-opened letter handed to her by Mother Superior. 'I am happy that some, at least, have been saved in this pernicious war,' Mother Agnes told her with as much grace as she could muster. But Hetty, always furious that her letters should be so opened, stamped out of the room without replying.

Outside, Hetty and Léonie danced a little jig – and immediately afterwards, seeking more privacy, putting coats on, and running out into the snow-filled parkland, they hugged each other violently in the icy wind, before sliding over a frozen patch in the big water meadow, their breath like white smoke on the cold air.

'Oh, Léa, it's wonderful!'

'Yes! . . .'

The girls, arms thrashing the air for balance, mufflers flying, waltzed and slid about the ice, before they fell together in a heap, hugging once more as they lay on the cold surface. But Léonie, drawing away and looking at her friend, felt a touch of ice on her heart then – for this man returned to Hetty, at least in spirit, when, for nearly five months, she had been her only love.

*

The war was not finished by Christmas. With both armies bogged down in the Flanders mud, it had barely begun. While in Ireland, that December and throughout the following year, another war against the British was variously and secretly plotted. Though Patrick Pearse, head of the Military Council of the Irish Republican Brotherhood, asked that summer to give the graveside oration for the old Fenian rebel O'Donovan Rossa, clearly hinted in his peroration at the violence to come: 'The Defenders of this Realm have worked well . . . they think they have pacified Ireland – that they have purchased half of us and intimidated the other half. They think they have foreseen everything, provided against everything. But the fools, the fools, the fools! – they have left us our Fenian dead, and while Ireland holds those graves, Ireland unfree shall never be at peace.'

During the same year Joseph Plunkett, another member of the IRB Military Council, went to Germany on a secret arms mission. In January 1916, James Connolly, leader of the Irish Citizen Army in Dublin, who until then had not in any way supported armed insurrection, now – with the threat of general conscription in Ireland – threw in his lot with Pearse and the IRB. Finally, in March, Pearse received a message from the revolutionary directorate of the Clann na Gael in New York: 'Will send you 20,000 rifles, 10 million rounds of ammunition, to place near Tralee between 22 and 28 April.'

The insurgents – Irish Volunteers and Dublin's Citizen Army now united in one Republican Army, largely under the secret control of the IRB leaders – were ready. The rising was set to begin on Easter Monday in Dublin, the bank holiday, when great numbers would be out of town, at the Fairyhouse races, up in the mountains, or at resorts along the coast.

For Frances the news of Dermot's survival had come too late. Already, in her deeply bitter mood during the autumn and winter of 1914, she had committed herself – body and soul this time – to the cause of renewed violence against the British. Forsaking all her last hopes for personal happiness, she became utterly dedicated, ruthless, ascetic, seeking martyrdom now – driven, with the other leaders of the IRB, to an idea of blood sacrifice on the altar of Ireland's freedom: a holy crusade on behalf of the Gael and all the dead generations gone before in the same cause. And, in this thirst for a cleansing, national blood-letting, personal considerations could be of no account whatsoever. Besides, Dermot, she knew, would never marry her when he discovered her role in all this – as he would, of course, quite soon, when the day of glorious revolution dawned.

So, like a fierce penitent – forsaking every worldly convention and all the comforts of her class – she consecrated herself to this purification by fire, this nobility of death, this halo-bright cause, playing an increasingly important role in the secret revolutionary councils of the IRB and, quite openly, in the Citizen Army, to which she was now attached as a Lieutenant.

She had, of course, from her nursing experience under fire in the South African war, vital skills for the insurgents. These had been immediately recognised, as were her natural organisational ability and blazing dedication – so that late in 1914 her responsibilities in the rising were transferred from Co. Kilkenny to Dublin where she threw herself into a fervour of activity, at the heart of events.

She took charge of the Fianna youth movement, drilling the boy scouts there, with wooden hurley sticks in the Wicklow mountains. She contributed to, and solicited, other funds for the war chest. She arranged – among a few other like-minded Irish Protestants of her class, in possession of suitable yachts – for various successful gun-running expeditions from the Continent; she discussed with Joseph Plunkett, in charge of military strategy, the medical and nursing arrangements for the rising. And she took part in all the sheer drudgery of training as well – fifteen-mile route marches and manoeuvres in every sort of weather.

She relished all the work, even going so far as to design a uniform for herself, a superbly tailored, double-breasted green tunic coat with silver buttons, long skirt and a slouch leather hat, side brim set off by a feather cockade. As final and more compelling additions to this dramatic and glamorous costume, she equipped herself with a Luger automatic and a Mauser rifle. Early in 1916 she was promoted to the rank of Staff Lieutenant within the Military Council, and then, with the rank of Colonel, made deputy to one of the leaders, Commandant Mallin, thus joining the very few people – and as the only woman – privy to all the detailed plans for the rising.

Robert meanwhile continued at his boarding college, St Columba's in the Dublin mountains, while Hetty and Léonie remained at the convent in Normandy – Hetty spending many of her holidays with the Straus family in Paris, so as to avoid the danger of German U-boats in the Channel crossings.

This had been Hetty's intention for Easter 1916. However, at the last moment and without her being able to warn her mother, all these plans were changed. At Verdun that spring the war took a grave turn against the Allies. The French army there, hard pressed within this great fortress for many weeks, seemed likely to collapse at any moment, allowing the Germans a free run through the line to Paris and the rest of France. Many people, who had the opportunity, left the capital. The convent, in the light of these grim facts and worse rumours, closed precipitately, the girls dispersed. It was then that Benjamin Straus, fearing for his daughter if she stayed in Paris, and seeing how both girls could find a safe haven in Ireland at Summer Hill, arranged passage for them with a captain he knew, commanding a neutral American freighter leaving Le Havre for Southampton that Easter weekend.

Neither girl was in the slightest alarmed at the prospect of this adventure. They viewed it with avid excitement – the more so when, allowing for delays in England or Dublin, Mr Straus gave them ten gold sovereigns towards hotels, rail fares, or other unexpected expenses. So it was, after an uneventful journey to Southampton and then to London before taking the Irish Mail to Holyhead, they crossed over to Dublin on Sunday night, on the RMS *Leinster*, arriving in the city early on that Easter Monday.

It was a late Easter that year – the morning fine and bright, already warm, with all the promise of a freak midsummer day. Dublin was pervaded by a holiday calm, as the two girls took a horse cab up from Westland Row station to the Shelbourne Hotel on Stephen's Green.

'We might as well wait here – where we can telegraph Mama and your Papa – and have some breakfast, then get the midday train down to Summer Hill,' Hetty had said to Léonie. And now she bounced up and down on the old leather seat inside the cab, unbuttoning the top of her green convent topcoat.

She was excited, now that their journey – dodging the Channel U-boats – had come to a successful conclusion, though it was not quite over yet. There was still a tempting prospect of metropolitan independence before them – this last morning alone together in Dublin: breakfast at the grandest hotel in town, a quick sprucing up in some spare bedroom there, a stroll on the Green – perhaps a look at the smart shop windows in Grafton Street, even if they could not spend anything there of the sovereigns they had left.

They clip-clopped up through the dark shadows between the buildings to the narrow end of Kildare Street. Then suddenly the whole huge bright space of Stephen's Green opened up before them – tall Georgian buildings all round, bathed in warm sunlight, the cherry blossom and green willow in the big square already bursting or almost in leaf.

The girls were enchanted by this vision. It was a day of wonderful promise, it seemed, so that Hetty suddenly turned and hugged Léonie.

'We're home! – almost home!'

Léonie looked at her friend much more calmly as she drew away from her. 'Yes,' she said simply. And then, gazing at her, some slight sadness in her eyes, she said quietly, 'Oh, I do love it all, you know. You, Hetty – being with you, everything.' And she leant forward then, kissing her quickly in return.

The cab drew up in front of the hotel. Passing between the Nubian maidens holding lamp standards at either side of the monumental porch, they entered the spacious hall, their bags in the grip of two diminutive page-boys in bandbox hats. Inside there was a hint of luxury, but more an air of provincial calm . . . of quiet Irish country house good taste: in the Georgian antiques, mahogany and brass furnishings, in the decent but unshowy hunting pictures and sporting prints, the slightly frayed Aubusson on the floor. Money had been, was being and would be spent here – but no one would ever talk of it.

It was too early for the many guests staying at the hotel for the Fairyhouse races to be up and about. Instead a few tail-coated clerks hovered in the background; a maid in a white pinafore was seen moving for an instant at the top of the broad dark stairway; the slightest hint of fried bacon and freshly-ground coffee lay on the air.

The hall porter, genial and discreet in equal measure, looked at them as if their arrival was entirely expected.

'Just breakfast, if you please,' Hetty graciously informed him. 'And if you'd look after our bags meanwhile – we mean to send some telegrams – and hope to catch the midday train for Thomastown. We shall need a cab for Kingsbridge then.'

'Yes, Ma'am, of course – that'll all be grand. I'll have a cab ready, and confirm the train. I believe the Waterford train leaves at two o'clock today – the bank holiday. I'll let you know. Can I take your coats?'

He gestured towards a dark recess in the hall, from which a little woman began to emerge. But, before she had moved half-way across the hall, some slight disturbance was heard from the landing at the top of the stairs – voices risen, a man's gruff English voice and another, chirpier and alarmed with a broad Dublin accent; the source of both tongues as yet still hidden. The girls looked up the stairway.

A British army officer, in full field uniform, commenced his descent. His step was steady enough, if slow, as he stuck resolutely to a path down the very middle of the stairs, eschewing all help from either banister. But his eyes, his whole expression, were vague and dreamy, the girls saw, as he came fully into sight half-way down. He had the air of a sleep-walker – long practised in the movement, gazing straight ahead, yet finding each step unerringly – all the more surprising, since he was a very big man, naturally cumbersome, of great girth, barrel chest, strong tree-trunk legs. But his young face was quite at odds with this pugnacious, wrestler's body: wasted, pinched and sensitive, the pale blue eyes shrunk back in their sockets, unseeing, as if they had long before retreated from some blinding hurt – a confusion and shocking disorder apparent everywhere over his wan countenance. As he descended, he repeatedly shook one shoulder, twitching it vehemently, as if trying to shake off some pest, some bird of ill-omen, some nightmare hand that had attached itself to him.

The girls looked at this chilly vision spellbound. Everything had come to a stop in the hall, and there was dead silence now – apart from a vague clink of china in the distant dining room – for what seemed minutes on end.

'Oh, dear God, the Major's got out,' Hetty heard the porter mutter, before everything started to happen very quickly – and yet in a manner which seemed quite expected, entirely rehearsed.

The Major – resplendent in his full uniform – seeing the two girls, suddenly came to violent life. He skipped down the rest of the stairway in a trice, shouting, 'Mildred! My dear Milly! I knew you'd come!' – making straight for Hetty, running across the hall to her now, arms outstretched, as if to clasp her in a violent embrace.

But before he had gone a yard or more he was set upon, like a circus strong man suddenly infested by dwarfs: two frail clerks, and the page-boys, now joined by others of their kind – all pounced on the man, gripping him at any and every point about his huge body, some going for his legs, others the midriff, the clerks grappling with his great arms, the page-boys jumping up on him from behind, clambering about his broad shoulders, sending his braided officer's cap flying – all of them, faced with his sudden and demonic energy, attempting to bear him down.

It was a difficult task. The man fought like a tiger, swatting at these gadflies, before spinning round like a carousel, his assailants clinging to his arms like conkers at the end of a string, so that half the clerks and page-boys soon found themselves all in a litter, toppled on the floor. But the boys at least, seeming to enjoy the sport, as if it was an accustomed game, part of their job in the hotel, returned with relish to the fray, the marked Dublin accents of all these minders rising now as they set about their task with renewed vigour.

'Git him be t'other lig, Micky Joe!'

'Take his ear, will ya!'

'Oi hav' him be the oxters –'

'Will ya gi' me *leverage* there for the love o' God, Pat – that's *my* arm ye're holdin' . . .'

And then there were strangled interjections in the very different English accent, despair in the officer's voice now. 'Mildred! – Milly! Have them off me – help me!'

With the terrific noise, the hall had been transformed into a prize fight arena. But gradually – a dying leviathan overwhelmed by these pinpricks – the poor proud man sank to the floor. The hall porter had interceded, together with two equally large men in chef's hats from the kitchen, finally subduing the officer, placating him, soothing, almost stroking him – 'There now, Major, calm yerself, ye're all right now' – as they led him gently off into some nether region of the hotel.

Hetty and Léonie meanwhile had retreated, shocked and fascinated in equal measure, before the manager arrived to make pleasant, but not in the least surprised or subservient, excuses – behaving, Hetty thought, as if this was some kind of regular bank holiday treat at the Shelbourne.

'You'll have to excuse the Major,' he told her, quite jauntily. 'It sometimes takes him that way. A very old friend of the hotel's – him and all his family in Ireland. And a very brave man, a real gentleman, quiet as a mouse here in the old days. But it's got to him, you see, this terrible war: entirely shell-shocked, with the French near Verdun. A terrible thing, you wouldn't recognise him. I know you'll understand – in the circumstances.' And then, in just the same pleasant understated tones, he went on, 'Now, if you'll please come with me, I'll show you both to the dining room – famished after your journey, I expect. Or would you like to take a room first? Wash and brush up. We're absolutely chock-a-block for the Fairyhouse races – but I think I can let you use one on the top floor – just for the morning, in the circumstances.'

Then he, too, gestured to the little cloakroom lady who, peeking out to make sure the coast was clear, essayed another light-footed run across the hall, quite unaffected by the furore, taking the girls' coats, before they moved off to the dining room. The hotel regained immediately its air of untroubled calm.

After breakfast the girls repaired to a small, but decent enough room on the very top floor, high up, with a view right over the Green. In an adjacent landing bathroom, they bathed luxuriously in a vast oak-panelled tub, before changing into their proper holiday clothes – high Easter fashions bought just before their departure from Paris – doing their hair and generally titivating themselves for an hour or more.

Later they emerged in the hall again – but transformed, in long, knee-hugging pale lilac skirts, high-throated lace-edged silk blouses, set off by patchwork and

– 358 –

velvet, gilt-buttoned waistcoats and, as the pièces de résistance, impertinent straw boaters, banded and tailed with flowing red ribbons: two most elegantly beautiful summer girls.

Here, by the telephone switchboard, Hetty made out a telegram to her Mama at Summer Hill . . . and Léonie one to her parents in Paris. The woman took their messages – but after half a dozen attempts she failed to make any connection with the telegraph department at the General Post Office down in the centre of Dublin.

'I'm sorry – a fault on the line. I'll have one of the boys deliver your telegrams there, in person.'

'Oh well,' Hetty said, not surprised, happy, indeed, at this further extension of their freedom. 'The train isn't until two o'clock now anyway. Let's go out – a walk in the Green, shall we . . . then the shops?'

Léonie smiled broadly. 'Yes, let's! Doesn't matter too much about the telegrams – mine will get to Paris later and we'll be seeing your Mama soon enough anyway.'

The band was playing – a medley from *The Yeomen of the Guard* floating over the ornamental lake. The two girls crossed the miniature Bridge of Sighs garlanded in budding willow, and strolled towards the music: the green and gilt bandstand, where, the military bands being away at the war, a small civilian orchestra entertained a mixed audience consisting of a few fashionably-dressed promenaders out from the Georgian squares to the east of the Green, staunch *petits bourgeois* from the genteel suburbs, in town for the day, and a number of shoeless ragamuffins escaping the slums behind the College of Surgeons building on the west side of the Green.

The girls stopped, listening to the woodwind and strings – nicely enough played, but not to the taste of a gruff bowler-hatted Dubliner with a big wart on his chin, standing next to them with his prim little wife in a cheap Easter bonnet.

'The military bands were much better. The Royal Munsters now – they had a great band here, every Easter before the war: Pom-titi, Pom-titi, pom-pom-POM! Big drums and all. These creatures – well, a job lot I'd say, from the Rathgar and Rathmines Musical Society . . .'

The man stamped his blackthorn stick on the ground, frustrated at this lack of properly martial music. 'Oh no,' he growled, 'you can't beat the military at this game. The Munsters now, or the old Irish Dragoons. Pom-titi, pom-titi, pom, pom, pom . . .'

He and his wife moved off towards the Grafton Street entrance to the Green, the big mock Arch of Triumph there commemorating Irishmen lost in the Boer War. The two girls took the same direction. 'Might as well take a look at the shop windows at least,' Hetty said. 'It's nearly half past twelve.'

But, before they reached the shops, they were met by a more diverting sight: a group of uniformed boys in green shirts and short grey trousers, with thin neck scarves and high-peaked scout hats, marching two abreast through the

Empire-glorifying gates. Serious-faced, set on some high purpose and by chance perfectly in step now with a martial tune from *The Yeomen*, they yet had an air of rural, woodland innocence, quite at odds with these sophisticated metropolitan circumstances. The smaller boys had wooden staffs and some had hurley sticks; others bore entrenching equipment, while several of the older, taller boys at the back carried rifles still too big for them.

Once inside the gates, these leprechaun-like figures with their picks and spades and hurley sticks continued their neat march to Sullivan's jaunty rhythms before an order came for them to break ranks, when they took up positions in self-conscious groups by the flowering cherry and forsythia bushes along the railings, at a loss to know what to do next. The ability to stand at ease in the middle of Dublin's most fashionable square, being gawked and laughed at by the slum boys and other caustic bystanders, was not among their accomplishments.

'God save us, Maggie,' the wart-faced man said to his prim wife, 'them's those Fianna scouts – young Sinn Feiners – coming in here for some sort of manoeuvres. Ye'd hardly think they'd lit them in here and they usually at their mischief way up in the mountains . . .'

He stopped then, his attention caught by a further, even more troubling manifestation. Immediately behind the scouts another group – some adult militia, it seemed – had appeared, a hundred or so of them, moving in loose file through the impressive archway: a much more business-like lot in that they all were armed with Mausers or heavy service revolvers, suggesting an army of sorts, a designation which their garb did everything to undermine. They were dressed in a motley assortment of outfits and uniforms: some in dark- or heather-green tunic coats, grey serge breeches, or jodhpurs, with slouch leather hats, the brims twisted up at one side, while others sported old British army khaki jackets or trench coats, the tabs and buttons all torn away, and still more were smartly turned out in their Sunday-best dark-blue suits, or in roughest working clothes – collarless striped shirts, baggy trousers, and clumpy boots. It was a raggle-taggle army. But an army it was, with the men – there were women, too – swagged about with crossed cartridge bandoliers, fixing bayonets now to their long-barrelled Mausers, checking their revolvers. Some kind of violent business was obviously meant, but of what kind or to what end was not, as yet, clear.

'Glory be!' The wart-faced man, mopping his brow in the midday heat, was outraged now. 'Ya wouldn't credit it! – littin' them lot of Volunteers and Citizen Army fellows in here. The park keeper'll have somethin' to say on that and no mistake!'

And he was right. A keeper, a tall and haughty fellow in a braided cap and spectacles with a long, sharp-ferruled stick, approached the soldiers now by the archway and started remonstrating with them, shaking his stick, opening his arms out, trying to shoo them out through the great archway like geese.

'Gwan now! I'll not have yees in here!' Hetty heard him call out. 'This is no parade ground – ye'll be outa here this minute or I'll have the constabulary on ye!'

The keeper was speaking to an equally tall man in a slouch hat, apparently the leader of the contingent, who at that moment was sticking up some sort of poster on the side of the gateway. 'Now ye certainly can't put that kinda thing up here!' the keeper yelled at him. 'Rule 4B – ye can see it here for yerself.' He pointed to the notice of park regulations next to the gateway. 'No bill posting – of *iny* sort, kind or description.'

The irate keeper stepped forward, trying to tear the poster from the archway. Then he suddenly disappeared, falling among the group of volunteers, only to reappear half a minute later, crawling out from between the soldiers' boots, his nose bloodied, spectacles and braided cap gone. But he got to his feet quickly enough and started to blow his whistle repeatedly.

'Clare to God, they'll pay for this,' the warty Dubliner said, as the volunteers left the archway, the poster securely in place. They were replaced by a small crowd of onlookers, including Hetty and Léonie, who gazed up at the dark, heavy-inked and printed message.

Poblacht na hEireann
The Provisional Government
of the
IRISH REPUBLIC
To the People of Ireland

Irishmen and Irish women. In the name of God and of the dead generations from which she received her old traditions of nationhood, Ireland, through us, summons her children to her flag and strikes for her freedom ... In every generation the Irish people have asserted their right to national freedom and sovereignty, six times in the past three hundred years they have asserted it in arms ... We declare the right of the People of Ireland to the ownership of Ireland and to the unfettered control of Irish destinies, to be sovereign and indefensible ... The Republic guarantees religious and civil liberties, equal rights and equal opportunities to all its citizens ...
Signed on behalf of the Provisional Government.
Thomas J. Clarke

Sean MacDiarmada	**Thomas MacDonagh**
P. H. Pearse	**Eamonn Ceannt**
James Connolly	**Joseph Plunkett**

The wart-and-bowler man laughed outright before he had finished reading the text and was soon joined by the other bystanders. 'For the love of God – ye'd hardly credit it! A "Republic" now, are you? – right here in the Green of an Easther's day. A Shangri-la for the takin' – with a few oul rifles and hurleys ... and they should be out fightin' Kaiser Bill instead of all this malarkey over a "Republic".' But he stopped laughing now and instead scowled at the poster. 'Begod, there'll be hell to pay all the same if they don't stop their messin' and git outa here straight away.' A nervous look came over his swollen, complacent features. Sweating badly now, he glanced around him warily.

'C'mon, Maggie – we'd better git outa here and back to Rathmines before the peelers come.'

'What's it all about?' Hetty asked. But the wart-faced man with his nervous wife had gone, vanished, and Hetty's question was answered instead by an excitable pixie of a fellow, elderly and breathless, who had just joined the group. 'Thim boyhoes the Volunteers,' he yelped. 'Hevn't they gone and taken over the General Post Office, with barricades and bombs and a new flag run up over the top of it! Oh, I tell ye, there'll be no pinshuns given outa there for a while. I tell ye that!' Despite this monetary embargo, the old man was in a state of high good humour. 'Oh, there'll be ructions and no misthake! Ye'll hav' to keep yer hats on now!' And he did a little jig beneath the poster.

Two stern-faced young Volunteer sentries had arrived to move the group on before taking up position by the archway.

'Suppose we'd better get out of the way ourselves – if we're to catch that train,' Hetty said easily. Both girls were no more than amused by all these activities: it was some kind of military exhibition or protest – typical of Irish life. They turned back to the Shelbourne.

It was then that Hetty saw her mother.

She was striding towards them, evidently on the warpath, splendidly attired in a tight-fitting dark-green tunic coat, Sam Browne belt, with a huge Luger pistol, breeches, puttees, and a felt hat, side-brim up, with a bright cock's feather, a beautiful Amazon, lovely but terrifying, issuing orders, to two men at her side.

'. . . yes, and get all the civilians out of the Green *now* – they've had quite enough time to read the proclamation – for we'll have to get the sandbags and barbed wire up straight away at all the gates, and the trenching started . . .'

'Mama!' Hetty shouted while Frances was some little distance away. 'Mama! – what on *earth* are you doing here?'

Her mother, equally startled, came to an abrupt halt, but only for a moment. She looked at her daughter coldly.

'*Doing?*' Her mother answered in her most clipped and arrogant Ascendancy accent, as if she were rebuking a careless servant in her drawing room. 'Why, we are having our rebellion.'

She spoke of this as if it were some long-established, fashionable annual event in the Dublin social calendar, the Vice-regal garden party, perhaps, or the Horse Show or the Curragh races.

'Mama, you cannot be serious –'

A rifle shot rang out then, followed by others, a ragged volley, from the direction of the forsythia bushes. The *Yeomen of the Guard* medley came to a sudden halt. Groups of Volunteers ran past, carrying sandbags and rolls of barbed wire. There was a flurry of activity, shouted commands, as the Fianna scouts and the Volunteers set about creating barricades and manning the defences.

The civilians in the Green had by now all left or been ejected. But Léonie with Hetty – still confronting her mother – were about to be trapped inside.

A flight of mallard, alarmed by the rifle fire which had broken out now all along the Grafton Street corner of the Green, rose from the ornamental lake, circling fast in the blue dome of sky, then making for more placid waters. It was a quarter to one. The revolution had started. And Hetty, looking again at her watch, realised that they were now very likely to miss the two o'clock train.

6

'MAMA, YOU'VE TAKEN leave of your senses!' Hetty exclaimed, her stammer temporarily lost in her astonishment. 'You can't seriously think to take on all the British army in Dublin with just these few boy scouts and hurley sticks –'

'Nonsense! My boys are brave members of the Irish Republican Army now. And, besides, there are almost no British troops in the city this morning – all out at the Fairyhouse races – which is precisely *why* we are taking them on today. Already, besides the Green here, we have secured half a dozen other vital strongpoints in the city. Everything is going *quite* according to plan!'

'Mama, you must give it up. Come away now, with us. We are at the Shelbourne –'

'Never!' The cock's feather on top of her hat shook violently.

As she spoke, her mother smiled crazily at Hetty. And Hetty suddenly saw in this warlike, deranged performance the essence of her mother, the *raison d'être* for her life – which was death. It was for this ridiculous moment, Hetty felt, that she had suffered all the long years as a child at Summer Hill – the loneliness and neglect, her mother's coldness and anger; her *stupidity*.

Hetty's long hatred of her mother finally exploded. 'Mama, you're a stupid woman! Was it for this – this nonsense – all your beastliness to me at Summer Hill? And can't you see?' She looked round at the Fianna boys stumbling about with heavy sandbags and entrenching tools. 'This is just a game of toy soldiers. But real people will be killed –'

'Indeed, that is exactly our plan: "The heart of a British Tommy at the end of every rifle" – exactly so!'

'That's criminal nonsense! Perfectly innocent people –'

'Have you not read the Proclamation? It is for Ireland and her destiny!'

'It's for nothing of the sort! It's nothing but sheer evil blindness on your part, and your friends – sacrificing these boys and innocent people, against impossible odds. And I *hate* you for it! Stay here then. You'll be killed – and good riddance!'

Her mother shook her head pityingly now. 'You don't understand. But one day you – and the others – you'll see the rightness of our cause, our sacrifice. One day . . .'

For a long instant Hetty stood there, unbelieving but undecided, listening to the increasing rifle fire. Then she tugged at Léonie's arm. 'Come on!' she yelled at her.

The two girls ran together, ran for their lives as they thought – along the gravel paths back towards the Shelbourne. But the exit they needed there was already barricaded and they took another closer by, which gave out across the road to some tall houses with high front door steps much nearer the Grafton Street corner.

Pausing on the pavement, they were just in time to see the reason for the initial fusillade from the Volunteers. A troop of British Lancers, emerging into the Green from a narrow street to their left, and obviously caught quite unawares, had been met by this sudden rifle fire and suffered several casualties. The cavalry had scattered in retreat, galloping back down the narrow street, leaving their wounded behind.

The Volunteers' fire pursued them, then slackened and ceased, so that the two girls, thinking the moment ripe, sprinted out across the road. But, when they were half-way across, a renewed hail of bullets smashed into the windows of the big houses opposite them, so that they fell on to the tramcar tracks. Their straw hats fell off and rolled away, red ribbons spinning over the cobbles into the gutter. They could hear the vicious whirr of bullets, just inches above their heads, it seemed. Hetty reached out, grasping Léonie's arm protectively as they lay there. 'Down! Keep right *down*!' she shrieked.

'I *am* right down, you ninny. *You* keep down!' They pushed their faces ever more firmly into the cobbles, blind and deaf now as the gunfire increased above their heads. Just then, a double-decker tram turned into the Green from Dawson street, and headed straight for them before the driver at the last moment squealed to a halt. The passengers, hearing the commotion all round, disembarked in panic, clattering down the stairs from the open top and, quite disregarding the prostrate girls, ran pell-mell for the shelter offered by the area walls and steps leading up to the houses on the north side of the Green.

Hetty and Léonie, taking advantage of this diversion, picked themselves up, their faces begrimed and their clothes dishevelled, joining the fleeing passengers, finally taking cover beneath the portico of a smart grocer's shop near the corner of Grafton Street.

Here the heavy glass windows had been smashed, either by gunfire or by some of the slum urchins, who, wasting no time over this heaven-sent opportunity, were already shoving through the broken frames, dancing about on the glass inside and helping themselves to the rich provender on display – Parma hams and pots of gentleman's relish, jars of calf's foot jelly, bottles of vintage port and claret, chip baskets of dried figs and dates, boxes of Turkish delight and a host of other exotic delicacies.

'Begob, an' they mean business – doin' for thim Lancers like that,' a big red-faced man from the tram opined, before turning in a trice, helping himself to a bottle of vintage Cockburn's and leaping away in the opposite direction.

One of the Lancer's horses, tipped over on its back and propped against the kerb, lay with all four feet up in the air, its rider prostrate in a widening pool of blood nearby, his pennanted lance, propped against the horse's belly, like a red danger flag denoting some frightful accident.

Two of the barefoot boys, running back to the slums, laden with their booty but seeing the dead Lancer, set down their loot and proceeded to rifle quickly through his pockets.

Almost immediately a shot rang out from the bottom of the narrow street beyond the dead Lancer. And Hetty, peeping out from behind the stone window casement, saw one of the boys topple over, most of his head blown away, as the rest of his meagre body collapsed in a tattered heap. The retreating Lancers, dismounted now and hidden at the bottom of the narrow street, were staging a counter-attack.

But at that point a group of some twenty Volunteers, running out from the Green, commandeered the tram and, under withering fire from the Lancers, drove it down to the Grafton Street corner. Here, they toppled the vehicle over, and it fell with a splintering crash, successfully blocking any advance the Lancers might make up towards the Green.

Taking up positions then, and protected by the tram, the Volunteers renewed their fire, volley after volley, at the remaining Lancers who, surprised again and incurring more wounded in the hail of bullets, made a final retreat, disappearing back towards the centre of the city.

The Green and all its surrounds were firmly in the hands of the rebels. It was half past one. By now, Hetty realised, they had certainly missed their train.

High up, from their top floor bedroom window back in the sanctuary of the Shelbourne, the girls saw the whole drama in the Green develop: the rebels, small figures now, arrayed like set pieces in a game of chess spread out below them in the warm afternoon sunshine – but a game run riot. The whole park was a swarm of little green-clad figures, moving about with apparently manic abandon.

The rifle fire had ceased and in the relative calm the Fianna scouts, Citizen Army and Volunteers were rapidly consolidating their defences, sandbagging every entrance to the Green, setting barbed wire along the top of the railings. Many more were energetically digging trenches.

Hetty could see no rhyme or reason to their efforts, as they struck out in mad criss-crosses, digging hardly more than sunken gulleys – cutting straight across the glowing tulip beds, leaping budding herbaceous borders, doubling back over the central rose arbours, encircling stone monuments to British generals, before coming to abrupt halts: at the ornamental lake, the miniature Bridge of Sighs and the ornate bandstand, now being adapted as a first aid station.

The rebels were as good as moles. Soon a fair part of the Green, its smooth lawns, paths and neatly-flowered borders, had the air of a vast bombed pleasure garden, with great swathes and bunches of uprooted plants and shrubs lying atop and around the mounting earthworks.

And though from ground level the insurgents were well protected, by the tall railings and the thick line of trees that circled the green, from any height – and the Green was surrounded by tall buildings – they were quite exposed.

Hetty remarked on this. 'It's mad that they don't see how easily they can be shot at from above!'

The very same thought had occurred to a British officer, in command of a contingent of Sherwood Foresters, hurriedly sent into the city later that afternoon. A section of these troops, moving up Kildare Street, entered the Shelbourne from the back and commandeered the hotel. So that, shortly after four o'clock, the girls' bedroom door suddenly burst open and this same officer confronted them, a very young man in a state of bristling, almost uncontrolled agitation.

'Lieutenant Hardstaff,' he said. 'I'm afraid we must take over your bedroom at once – the rebels in the park – your room has the best vantage point . . .'

Without more ado he gestured behind him and half a dozen khaki-clad soldiers struggled in behind him, carrying a heavy machine gun with a tripod and a quantity of ammunition boxes. Stooping down, and dragging their gun, they crept over to the window.

Hetty was outraged by the intrusion. 'How de-de-dare you come in here like this! – with that monstrous great gun!' She abused the officer roundly. 'Be-besides, you can't shoot it out there – it would be a massacre. There are be-be-boys out there, tiny boys –'

'They are rebels, Miss – and must take their chances with the others. They've already killed some of our Lancers – those "boys" out there.'

He crouched down himself now, stalking towards the window, supervising the setting up of the machine gun, before shouting back, 'You'll have to leave – we have serious business here!' Shaking with martial anticipation, as if mounting an attack on heavily-defended German lines, Hardstaff was gripped by a fever of derring-do.

The girls tried the room next door. It was not locked. At the window they saw the Volunteers, unaware of this threat from above, going quite openly about their defensive business.

'Your mother?' Léonie asked anxiously.

'Exactly! She'll be shot – they all will, with that awful gun. But I can hardly tell that officer she's my mother, can I?'

'Not the officer – but we might tell your *mother*, though,' Léonie thought out loud.

'She doesn't deserve it!'

'Perhaps not – but we can't just stand by and see her killed – from our bedroom window. Can we? . . .'

'No. Suppose not. But how do we get out into the Green?'

The girls considered the idea – and the dangers of it. For a moment all was calm outside, but for several motor cycle despatch riders who came and went with messages for the rebels, and a few cars, the drivers of which were not yet aware of the situation. Then, moving easily along the road beneath them, the girls saw a baker's motor van. It turned the corner into Kildare Street and they heard it stop somewhere behind the hotel.

'That van – could we drive it?'

'We've driven father's Peugeot, with Albert, in the Bois – we could try it!'

'Come on then! . . .'

The girls, running quickly downstairs, came into the hall, thronged with guests now, and other people, all sheltering in the hotel, peeping gingerly out from the big bow windows of the dining and drawing rooms to either side of the hall. Pushing past the crowd here Hetty and Léonie moved through various green baize doors into the almost deserted kitchens and sculleries at the back.

At the back entrance to the kitchens the baker's man was making his delivery of bread and cakes, handing the big trays to a kitchen boy. The girls hovered, hidden in the background, behind one of the great kitchen ranges.

'Jeez, Mickey,' the delivery man said, 'an' if I'd known that lot were out in the Green I'd niver have come here at all. What's up for the love o' God?'

'Sure and haven't thim rebels gone and taken over the whole Green and the Tommies upstairs with machine guns! Come on till we take a look? – and all the lads upstairs lookin' outa the windeys inyway.'

The delivery finished, the two of them left the kitchen for the front of the hotel. In a second the girls were out of the back door and sitting up in the seat of the van.

Léonie took the wheel, trying the foot pedals before finding the clutch and ramming the engine into first gear with a fearful grinding noise. She smiled at Hetty. 'Oh my Gawd!' she drawled, crouching down over the half-glass windscreen beneath the open canopy. Then she set the engine roaring, let the clutch in, and the van skidded violently, leaping out of the back area.

She spun the van round into Kildare Street, then turned right into the Green. But, in Léonie's inexpert hands, it swerved suddenly, skidding on the tram tracks as she opened the accelerator lever. She tugged at the wheel desperately, managing to straighten it. Now they were careering towards the Grafton Street corner. Here, sitting on the belly of the dead Lancer's horse, a bottle of looted port in hand, an old shawly woman, well gone with the drink, was singing loudly.

> 'Boys in Khaki, Boys in Blue,
> Here's the best of Jolly Good Luck to You!'

She brandished the bottle at them as they swerved past.

Rounding the corner at speed, the van was almost out of control as it skittered to and fro over the cobbles past the College of Surgeons.

In front of them, a posse of women rebels, running out from the Green, faced the van, revolvers raised. But the van was on them in a second and they jumped for their lives. Léonie struggled to stop, but could not, the big outside brake lever being too far from her reach.

The van, swaying violently now, made a dash straight for the kerb. It hit the stone bollards and linked chains there, careered off into the road again, and finally came to a halt, nearly driving up the front steps of the Russell Hotel at the south-west corner of the Green.

The rebel women had pursued it – and now, lowering their revolvers, were astonished to see the two girls, lying about drunkenly on the front seat, bruised but otherwise uninjured. Some of the women, opening the back door, proceeded to ransack the van of its remaining bread and cakes. Two others helped the girls out.

'My mother!' Hetty gasped. 'I must speak to her.'

The women thought she must be delirious. 'Your *mother?*'

'Of course! Frances Cordiner.' She spoke imperiously now. 'I must speak to her.'

'So! – you have changed your mind. And how considerate to bring us all those baker's provisions. We shall need every bit of food we can get –'

'I have *not* changed my mind! Se-se-simply come to tell you they have set up a great gun in the Shelbourne, and there are probably others. You'll have to leave the park – get all the boys out at least. Any minute now they'll start to fire. Can't you se-see? Have you not seen all the high we-we-windows?'

They had met Frances next to the bandstand, where she had been putting the finishing touches to her field dressing station. From where they stood, behind some tall bushes, all the windows in the Shelbourne were invisible. Her mother, showing no reaction, seemed to think the rest of the Green offered similar cover.

Hetty tugged her arm. 'Come over here – and see – out in the open!' But her mother resisted.

'We have trenches everywhere – do you not see *those?*'

'Mere gulleys.' And Hetty pulled her once more, so that finally she managed to get Frances out into the open where she pointed up to the top floor bedroom window. 'There! The gun is there – don't you se-see? It can easily fire down *into* the trenches. You must get everyone out –'

And just as they stood there, by the edge of the ornamental lake, a first long raking burst of machine gun fire came from the window. Once more the girls fell to the ground. The bullets, kicking up a trail of exploding dirt, passed only a few yards away.

'*Now* do you see?' Hetty yelled at her mother.

'Indeed I see it . . . it is *war*!' Frances shouted – and, leaving the girls at the first aid station, she was off then, at the double, to marshal a counter-attack on the Shelbourne.

A number of nurses and a doctor were tending those Volunteers who had been wounded. Hetty and Léonie at once offered help. The doctor showed surprise at their presence. 'You should have left here long ago,' she told them. 'All the civilians –'

'No,' Hetty interrupted her. 'I'm Henrietta *Fraser*. She's my Mama, I'm afraid. We're here – and we'll help now.'

'But you must *leave*. It's not your fight – you've no right to risk your lives in this way.' The older woman, though not in the least agitated, was firm.

'We're *staying*,' Hetty told her equally firmly. 'There'd be much more risk – going out on to the streets now.'

The doctor, seeing that Hetty was immovable, simply held out her hand. 'I'm Dr ffrench-Mullen. It's brave of you . . . very. I'm sure we'll all be grateful for your help.'

It was indeed a war that had started now – but one which the rebels could never win. Later in the afternoon, a second heavy machine gun, set up to the west, on a roof behind the Russell Hotel, started to traverse the other side of the Green – while the first gun in the Shelbourne continued its sporadic depredations, concentrating largely on the bandstand, to general outrage, since a large Red Cross flag had flown from its top almost from the beginning of hostilities.

Frances, arriving back at the dressing station to confer with Dr ffrench-Mullen, was particularly incensed. 'How dare they shoot at wounded men!'

She bristled with righteous indignation, moving off again at once to see what she could do about it. Running over the little Bridge of Sighs, along a makeshift trench, dodging from one flowering bush to another, she came to the trees and railings immediately facing the Shelbourne.

And it was here, in her fury, that she shot the British officer. During a lull in the firing he had emerged from the Shelbourne porch – a big burly man in full field uniform, his chest covered in ribbons, but unarmed. He had ambled across the road, like a sleepwalker, shoulder twitching, straight towards the barbed wire railings. Frances, in the trees behind with several Volunteers, confronted him as he stepped up close to the railings.

'My dear good woman,' the officer told her vaguely, pleasantly, 'you must stop all this at once – they have a machine gun above you – you will be overrun at any moment. You really –'

Taking out her Luger as he spoke, she shot the man between the eyes, at point blank range, so that, though the bullet crashed straight through, destroying the entire back of his skull, it left only a smallish burnt hole in his forehead. The officer seemed barely hurt at all for a long second, his eyes no more glazed than they had been a few moments ago, before he wobbled a bit, then fell backwards, slowly at first, before plunging with a crash to the pavement.

This was almost the last success of the rebels. By evening, the Green, now reeking of spent cordite, had been enfiladed from all four sides by reinforcements of British troops, their rifles and machine guns playing havoc with the Volunteers in their half-secure trenches. Only the onset of darkness prevented a massacre.

The girls meanwhile, with the arrival of more wounded at the bandstand, found themselves fully occupied – boiling up kettles on open fires, opening tins of food, cutting the bread and cakes from the van they had driven.

They sweated in the heat, their smart brocade waistcoats long since abandoned, lace-collared blouses open right down their throats now, hair awry and ash-filled – so that when Commandant Mallin paid an encouraging visit to the dressing station, passing by their fires, he looked at them twice.

'Well done, girls – that's great work!' And it was then that he looked again, noticing their ruined clothes. 'I don't think I know you? . . .'

'Hetty – and this Léonie,' she told him shortly, wiping her brow.

'Indeed, but –'

'We're just over from France – for the Easter holidays,' she informed him casually, but in tones of such cutting arrogance that the Commander simply shook his head, mystified, before passing on.

They camped that night behind the bandstand, on rugs near the fires, waking next morning to another balmy day. As the guns opened up at them again from all round the Green with increased vigour, their situation very soon became quite impossible.

Soon after nine o'clock Frances arrived at the dressing station. 'We are evacuating the Green,' she told the women brusquely. 'Moving to the College of Surgeons.'

'Not before time,' Hetty told her. The girls, though they had had little sleep, were perky enough, getting the hang of things, quite aware of the seriousness of the situation, but relishing it and their small part in the adventure.

'Stretchers then,' Dr ffrench-Mullen ordered. There were some twenty-five or so wounded men in the bandstand now, but only half that number of stretchers available, so that moving them across the Green had to be done in two sorties. And, though again they carried the Red Cross flag in each of these operations, again they were fired upon.

And it was while following behind one stretcher, just before they came to the heavily-barricaded exit in front of the big granite College of Surgeons opposite, that Léonie was hit – a piece of shrapnel, a stray bullet, a ricochet, it was not clear. There was just a fizz of metal in the air before she fell, clutching her calf – her skirt almost immediately colouring with dark blood.

Hetty, next to her, cried out. Léonie, fallen right over now, face twisted round, though not apparently in pain, was strangely mute, her eyes closed.

'Léa! Léa!' Hetty knelt over her, thinking her dead.

But Léonie, opening her eyes then, looked up at her in a dazed way. 'I'm all right – can't feel a thing.' But the blood was soaking through the skirt now, flooding out, before Hetty and another Volunteer nurse pulled her gently to the cover of a big flowering cherry near the railings.

'Léonie dearest . . .' Hetty bent over her aghast, as some cherry blossoms floated down over her friend's bloodless face.

'I'm all right, you ninny – it's nothing.'

The nurse, cutting her skirt up the seam, revealed the wound, a bad gash in the calf.

'Not broken, I think – just a flesh wound,' the nurse said. 'We'll take her over next time round – you stay with her meanwhile.' And, taking out one of half a dozen leather tourniquets she carried at her waistband, she applied it expertly just below Léonie's knee, before disappearing.

'Oh, Léa, what have I done? – getting you into all this?' Hetty, quite stricken now, leant over her, close, whispering endearments, furiously pulling at tufts of grass round her head, trying to make a pillow out of them.

'Don't be such an ass!' Léonie told her. 'It's only a scratch – I could be dead!'

Then she fainted.

The College of Surgeons, closed for the Easter holiday, had been rapidly broken into and taken over. A large elongated building, with its two-storied granite façade and small windows facing the Green, and an equally stout side-wall running back towards the slum quarters behind, it offered an almost impregnable redoubt, which the rebels might far better have occupied from the beginning. It was a natural fortress with ideal fire lines, commanding both the Green and half its approaches, complete with a surgery, medical equipment and spacious lecture rooms. And now, with many more wounded to tend, and Volunteers from other parts of the city who had joined Commandant Mallin's group, it came into its own, prolonging a fight which would otherwise have ended there and then, with a massacre on the Green.

The wounded, on stretchers, were laid out next to the demonstration operating theatre on the ground floor. And here, in the capable hands of Dr ffrench-Mullen and her nurses, they received attention. The other Volunteers, some from rebel positions that had fallen in other parts of the city, increased to over a hundred men and women now, took up positions by the windows, which were soon filled with desks and sandbags, or on the roof, or mustered in lecture rooms on the first floor.

Léonie – the shrapnel removed, wound cleaned, stitched and bandaged by Dr ffrench-Mullen – lay on a blanket next to the unlit coal grate, in one of the first floor lecture-rooms where she had been carried on a stretcher, the walls adorned with medical illustrations – gory posters, charts, blood-red expositions of the human body: the musculature, lungs, intestines, bowels, ailimentary and colonic canals. At one end of the room, behind a raised desk, a complete, yellowing human skeleton, disturbed by all the sudden movement, swayed eerily from a coat hanger.

Léonie, a rug round her shoulders, as Hetty tried to start the fire next to her, looked over at the swinging bones. 'Most suitable, I'm sure . . .'

'Oh, God – I'll move it.'

Léonie laughed up at her. 'Why?'

Hetty turned back, surprised. 'You are extraordinary – a bullet in your leg – yet you're so *calm*.' She knelt down beside her again. 'Your Papa will never forgive me.'

'*Us*, remember. It was my idea going into the Green – and, besides, he *always* forgives me . . .'

The noise of gunfire, to and from the College, increased as the day wore on. And there was the sound now – repeated heavy thuds – of some far larger naval guns down by the river. As a result of this shelling, fires had broken out in houses nearby and some much bigger conflagration had erupted in the city's centre, in Sackville Street, around the General Post Office – great grey-black plumes of smoke billowing up into the sky.

The Volunteers, ensuring that they had an emergency exit from the College, were smashing holes in the interconnecting walls to their left, leading through to other houses on the Green. The noise, the heat, the acrid cordite fumes, the falling brick and plaster dust in the building – all soon became intolerable. And the food, with so many more men to cater for, had begun to run out.

Hetty's mother, on a tour of inspection, came into the fetid classroom later in the afternoon, and stopped by the two girls. Her smart green tunic and cocked hat were covered in a fine white powder and an oily smear ran down beneath her right shoulder, from the Mauser she had been repeatedly firing. But her face was flushed and radiant. 'You will not regret it,' she told Hetty as her daughter ladled out the last of an oatmeal gruel she had concocted. 'I'm proud of you!'

Hetty, quite disregarding the compliment, barely turned her head. 'The food is running out – this is quite the last of the pe-pe-porridge. When will you see the madness of it all? How many more dead and wounded do you need – before you surrender?'

'We are not here to *surrender*,' she told her sharply. 'We can hold this building – oh, indefinitely!'

Frances knew this was not true. Their ammunition, not just the food, was running out – and quite a few of the Mauser rifles, used so continuously, had jammed. On the other hand, they had, just half an hour before, discovered in a locked basement room a whole cache of small arms belonging to the College's Officer Training Corps – some sixty practically unused Lee Enfield rifles, Webley revolvers and a quantity of ammunition. These they were keeping in reserve. And, just then, noticing the wicker basket of carrier pigeons, which they had taken to send messages to the other Volunteers about the city, an idea struck Frances: an idea for a surprise counter-attack.

For there was no doubt they needed just such an event: British troops, having thoroughly consolidated their positions all round the Green, and moving from house to house, were already beginning to close in on them. For the rest of that day, at least, leaving aside the secret cache of arms, they had just enough ammunition to keep them at bay. But what if they pretended they had run out, of everything, exhausted all their reserves, material and moral, and then let the British come to them? . . .

She put the idea to Commandant Mallin straightaway. 'You see, we hardly need the pigeons for anything else now. We can send half a dozen off – with the same message: that we are almost out of ammunition, must soon give in. One of the pigeons, at least, will surely be brought down – you see how they have shot down several already? Gradually we cease firing – and leave it at that, dead silence. Then, with all these new Lee Enfields, when they come for us . . .'

Mallin agreed. Messages were prepared and the pigeons, at five-minute intervals, were sent off from the roof of the building. And sure enough the fifth one, blasted from the roof of the University Club on the north side of the Green, fell to earth by the Club steps, to be hurriedly taken inside by a British trooper. The trap was set. And thereafter, until darkness fell, they eked out their rifle fire with the remaining Mausers almost down to nothing.

Overnight, handing out the Lee Enfields to thirty or so of their best marksmen, they set the men, two to either side of the barricaded front windows and the rest hidden behind the roof parapet in a long line. So that, by dawn on Wednesday morning, the College, quite stilled and silent, without any firing as the hours passed, must have appeared ripe for a final assault by the British.

Frances had taken up position by the window in the lecture-room where Hetty and Léonie were, her Lee Enfield resting on the fire bay of mattresses and sandbags, the barrel just poking out towards the Green, the bay offering a clear field of fire from there down to the Grafton Street corner.

And she waited now, in a state of happy anticipation, a spring wound tight – waited, just as she had all those years ago, at Fraser Hall in Domenica, behind just such a mattress, looking out on the lovely tropic garden into the sunset, waiting for the Caribs to attack. She felt old now in this world of violence, vastly experienced in sudden death. She would freely mete it out. She would accept it, just as willingly, herself.

Hours passed without a shot fired in the Green. But by midday, observing the British troop movements carefully with field glasses, the rebels saw them moving covertly, from one building to another about the Green, gradually getting closer to the College for a final attack. They knew, too, from their scouts, that several British platoons had already moved into the Green itself and were hidden now straight across the road from them behind the trees.

At 12.30, on some pre-arranged signal, the British rifles and heavy machine guns opened up all round them – an intense fire aimed at the College, so that everyone took cover as the hail battered the granite, the mattresses and sandbags. Not a single shot was fired in return. The fusillade stopped eventually and there was silence everywhere, just the noise of plaster falling about the big lecture-room.

Frances got to her feet and peered out into the bright sunshine. There was nothing to be seen, no movement anywhere, the British troops still under cover. Another fifteen, then twenty, minutes went by. Nothing. Perhaps their plan had misfired.

Then, just after one o'clock, the troops came into the open – first running down the near pavements from the Russell Hotel and Grafton Street corners, hugging the cover of the buildings, then, twenty or thirty of them, breaking from the trees and railings in front of the College and storming straight across the road. Suddenly, momentarily, there were some forty or fifty British soldiers in their field of fire – Frances drawing a bead on a sergeant leading his men across the road from the Green.

All the Volunteers opened fire, rapid fire, the British falling like ninepins beneath the brazen blue sky. It was a massacre.

The British retreated in disorder. And thereafter silence reigned again – and it seemed, indeed, as if the College might be held indefinitely.

Hetty, huddled protectively next to Léonie during all this frantic noise and killing, turned to her now. 'All right?'

'Yes, yes – leg's aching a bit, but all right.'

'Oh, God, I can't bear it – I'll get you something,' Hetty almost yelled, rising to her feet. Others among the more badly wounded in the lecture-room were crying, moaning now, as Hetty, distraught, began to wander about the room.

Léonie called her back. 'It's *all right* – just sit down, rest, it's nothing, leg's all right.'

'Oh, Léa, there must be something!' And she went off then to try to find Dr ffrench-Mullen.

While she was gone Frances, leaving her rifle at the window, and brushing some blood from her brow where she had been grazed by a stone splinter, came over to Léonie. 'How are you? I'm so sorry that you should be involved in this – not your fight – and wounded too. You are a brave woman.'

She spoke gently, but with such feeling and concern that Léonie, knowing only her previous sour or arrogant moods, was quite taken aback. She looked up at Frances quizzically. 'I'm all right. And you?' she asked, for lack of anything better to say.

'Excellent!'

'But you can't win . . .'

'Yes, we can! By winning – or by dying. Either way we can't lose.'

'But if you *do* lose here?'

'Oh, I shall be shot – all the leaders probably. But that will be an ever greater victory.' Frances bent down then, looking into Léonie's eyes. 'If, when, that happens, you will look after Hetty, won't you? You are so much her best friend. I have meant so little to her, I'm afraid . . .'

She pursed her lips, but then smiled. 'It's been my hope for many years – this revolution!' She gestured towards the Green. 'And I don't regret it for an instant. Not for myself, but for Hetty – she has really suffered more for it, this cause of freedom. Perhaps, with an American mother, you will understand that. You were first, after all, to rid yourself of the British . . . and so may better put my case to her than I could.'

She knelt down now, even closer to Léonie, who could smell the cordite on her clothes, see the sheen in the trickle of blood that ran down her forehead. 'Yes, I regret nothing of this fight,' she said with gentle intensity. 'But to her I should like to have made some amends, and cannot. You may feel, perhaps, you can speak on my behalf.'

Then, before Léonie had time to reply, Frances was suddenly on her feet and gone. Léonie was astonished at this transformation – in a woman, previously so bitter, insensitive, vicious. She was not to know how such a transformation lay at the very heart of Frances's and the other leaders' philosophy: a holy purification through fire. This transfiguration had occurred in Frances now – with the ultimate joy and release of a martyr's death still to come.

When Hetty returned with some aspirin, Léonie talked of this change, of Frances's obvious bravery, telling Hetty most of what Frances had said to her.

'Bravery?' Hetty was scornful. 'Or blind stupidity?'

'But, Hetty, if you believe in something so completely, *is* it just stupidity?'

'If it so damages you, kills you and everyone else – yes!'

'It's a kind of love, too, though – isn't it? All this freedom thing. And that's often blind.'

'Does love *destroy* people, though?' asked Hetty, more defiance than certainty in her rhetoric.

'Oh yes, of course it can.' Léonie winced in pain.

The College, despite further counter-attacks by the British, held out for the next three days. The nights were the worst. Then, in almost total darkness and without the distraction of firing, there were only thoughts of pain, death, hunger – for the food, but for some scraps found in houses further along the Green, had quite run out by then.

Hetty lay close to Léonie during these nights, the latter's wound, stiffening and throbbing, growing more painful. And conditions were such in the building now – the airless squalor, the rank smell of death and excretion – that its occupants, beginning to lose all material hope, resorted instead to prayer.

Each evening, with the Angelus, and at intervals throughout the night, a single lantern, low down, casting yellow shadow light over the wounded and dying, prayers were intoned, to and fro across the lecture-room.

'Holy Mother of God, pray for us, intercede for us . . .'

'Now and at the hour of our death . . .'

The prayers rose, taken up by many voices, a silver chant floating over the room, a balm and blessing, as everyone waited for some end on that Saturday night, a great peace everywhere, now that it was quite clear to everyone that there could be no military victory.

But Hetty and Léonie, at odds with this native Irish faith, found an alternative way of prayer, simply by clinging to each other in the frail light. And it was then that another faith came to them – one that Léonie had proposed to Hetty two years before in her convent bed: the faith just of themselves, alive and together, in which a schoolgirl crush, that had become a devil-may-care friendship, now became a hunger, a great mutual need – the single means by which they might be saved, not by prayer but in a chant that they set up silently in each other's arms. The Volunteers had been transfigured, taken on the lineaments of martyrdom, by sacrifice and loss; the girls were changed utterly in this war by gaining a deep love.

The rebels, under a flag of truce, finally surrendered on Sunday morning – some 120 of them, walking out in good order from the side-door of the College into York Street where, having handed over their arms to Captain de Courcy Wheeler and his men, they formed ranks and waited.

Then the dead and wounded were carried forth, on stretchers or in makeshift shrouds, and moved into British army field ambulances, standing by in front of the College. Hetty, next to Léonie on her stretcher, emerged into a pearl-grey morning light, rain in the moist air, a much more typically Irish 'soft' day, the freak balmy summer weather of the week all gone.

One of the British officers by the kerb, noticing their age and the remnants of their fashionable clothes, stopped them. 'Civilians? – are you the two girls from the Shelbourne – caught in the Green that first day?'

Hetty nodded. Then she said, 'I'm Henrietta Fraser. My mother –'

But Dr ffrench-Mullen, right behind Léonie's stretcher, interrupted her, so that the officer did not take in Hetty's last words. 'Yes, these are the two girls caught in the Green. We took them to the College with us. This girl has a flesh wound, in the calf – should be seen to at once.'

The officer glared at the doctor dismissively for a second. 'Over here then, with that stretcher,' he told two of his orderlies. 'The civilian ambulance.'

Hetty and Léonie glanced back at Dr ffrench-Mullen, Léonie with gratitude in her eyes. Hetty had very nearly got them sent off with the others. 'You ninny!' she whispered up as they both moved off to the front of the building. 'One martyr's enough in the family.'

Finally, accompanying the last of the wounded, Frances Cordiner, with Commandant Mallin, left the College. Walking over to Captain de Courcy Wheeler, saluting briefly, she presented him with her Sam Browne belt, pistol and ammunition.

The Captain, a rotund and moustachioed figure, held the equipment awkwardly for a moment, embarrassed by this confrontation, this surrender by a mere woman, yet taller than he.

'Would you prefer,' the Captain said diffidently, 'I can drive you to the Castle?'

'Captain, I am second in command here – naturally, I should prefer to march at the head of our men, with Commandant Mallin.'

'Very well, if you wish.'

He saluted, watching her go to the head of the waiting lines of men – as Hetty and Léonie watched her from beside the civilian ambulance: Frances, her smart green uniform with its silver buttons all tattered and torn, but walking like a queen.

And it was then, as the Volunteers set off down York Street for Kilmainham jail, that the bystanders who had gathered to watch – upright citizens of the city, their prim wives, bookies' runners, old shawly women, pixie-faced little men, together with hordes of urchins – it was at that moment that all of them, with one voice, set up their jeering yells, catcalls, oaths of hatred.

'G'wan wi' ye – ye crowd of bowsies!'

'Ya rottin' lot of good for nuttin' gutties . . .'

'I hope yees are all hunged – shootin's too good for ye! Tryin' to stir up trouble fer us all.'

'Ye damn shower of Sinn Feiners – shure didn't yees go and ruin me Easther holidays!'

'And why wouldn't ya go and fight the *Kaiser* now – ya lot o' lily-livered, yellow bellies!'

A great wild paean of laughter and malevolence rose everywhere in the street as the men tramped off – pursuing them, a mocking, cackling, raucous chorus of spite and derision that Hetty and Léonie could hear rising up over the city long after all the Volunteer prisoners had disappeared.

Hetty was almost in tears then. 'I can't believe it – all that fighting – for *them*. And that's what they think of it.'

As they got into the ambulance, the now-ragged Republican tricolour which had been hanging on top of the College all week was hauled down. It started to rain.

A week later, on the 6th May, Frances was court-martialled and sentenced to death. It was a sentence meted out to all the leaders of the rising, a rebellion now brutally avenged – a set-piece of its kind, theatrical in its intention and effects, going through each appropriate stage of farce, spectacle and tragedy.

7

T HE SOUND OF the piano – repeated fits and starts from Mendelssohn's 'Spring Song' – could barely be heard from behind the closed double doors of the drawing room. But gradually, the notes put together more competently and confidently, the music, in these still confused but dazzling staccato runs, seeped out into the other rooms and corridors: a vague imprint, a mysterious half presence – like the shadow of some fabulous animal stalking the empty house. In its urgent uncertainty, the music was an appropriate harbinger of a spring that had not yet really come to Summer Hill.

'Can't quite get the right rhythm . . .' Hetty slumped her shoulders, frustrated. 'Though God knows I played it often enough, with old Sister Marie at the convent.'

'You'll get it!' Léonie spoke from her wicker wheelchair. 'You really *can* play well, you know.'

She gazed admiringly at Hetty sitting at the Blüthner Grand, peering at her through the edge of a vase of white narcissi with yellow, crimson-edged cups and blue grape hyacinths set on a small table between them.

'Though this piano isn't good for Mendelssohn anyway. It's a *singing* piano – more for you, soft and sweet! That's its tone, really lovely.'

And, breaking into a different composer's music, with themes which she knew much better, Hetty encouraged Léonie to sing Pinkerton's early duologue with Sharpless from *Madame Butterfly*, her voice rising and falling with sonorous exaggeration and a wittily guyed emotion, flooding the room with a spirited rendering of their argument over Pinkerton's irresponsible marriage plans. '*E un facile vangelo!*' Léonie thundered. They had seen the opera in Paris with the Strauses. It was one of their favourites.

At the end they laughed and Hetty clapped vigorously. 'You *must* go on with your singing lessons, Léa! There'll be lots of good singing teachers over here – the Irish are wonderful singers! . . .' Hetty was flushed with excitement.

'Yes . . .' Léonie was uncertain. 'You really think . . . we'll be staying here?'

'Of course! Why not? We talked to Mortimer in Dublin. And he's coming down this afternoon to arrange things generally at Summer Hill – and I'm sure when your Mama and Papa get here tomorrow they'll agree. You can do *all* the things here you do in France – well, most of them – and certainly the singing. You sang that *Butterfly* duet perfectly!'

'Not as good as your piano in the "Spring Song".' Léonie turned and looked out over the rain-sodden view. 'Though it hardly looks like spring.'

'No. Not yet – but it will! I *know* it will.' Hetty reached out her hand. 'Oh, Léa, after all that death and disaster in Dublin – when I thought we were gone, too . . . What does it matter, a bit of rain? Just to be alive.'

Léonie reached from her wheelchair and grasped Hetty's hand. The two girls gazed at each other through the cascade of white narcissi. 'Yes,' Léonie said. 'Yes.' Her deep grey-green eyes flickered – an instant smile, as the light brightened for a moment outside the window, a sudden shaft of watery sun illuminating the room.

Léonie suddenly changed the subject. 'Hetty, it's strange, but behind you there, on the wall . . . there are sort of dark patterns, in a certain light – when the sun came through just now, as if there was a mural or something hidden there. Look!'

Hetty turned and they both gazed at the white wall, with the Fantin-Latour flower painting set half-way up.

'Something, yes, those lines here – and there especially.' Hetty stood on a chair and removed the picture. 'Something dark there, a row of dark things. Old wallpaper maybe? Or a mural. Let's see.'

She picked up a silver paper knife from the bureau and started to scrape away at the paint, where the flower picture had been. After some vigorous work, the crown and then the brim of a bowler hat emerged – and further along, as she continued her scraping, another similar hat came to light, on top of a rubicund Irish face, then the bow of a fiddle and the neck of a bottle of stout: a bucolic, bibulous village band, it seemed, was trying, like the spring, to force its way back into life, through the paint, another herald of joy, long-forgotten, emerging from the walls of the old house.

'Hetty, your mother'll be furious –'

'Mama won't be furious here for years and *years*, thank goodness. Look! I don't believe it!' Hetty stood back, displaying her handiwork. 'Not just *one* bowler hat – but a row of them! Playing fiddles and drinking beer. And on the *drawing* room wall!' Hetty considered the matter a moment. 'Unless – it's something of Aunt Emily's, when they thought she was mad and had her locked up. A mural by her, like the ones she has in her bedroom. Looks marvellous.'

'What a house!' Léonie said. 'All sorts of secrets,' she added lightly.

'Nothing but.' Hetty sighed, taking the point more seriously. 'But come on! – let's do some more *Butterfly* before Mortimer gets here.

'Right, I'll do Pinkerton, and you do Cio-Cio San, and we can sing that duet, remember, like we did at the convent – that squashy, sentimental one.'

And so they happily enacted the great love scene, guying it again, Hetty – her histrionic gifts to the fore – putting a narcissus behind her ear, arching her eyebrows oriental-fashion, playing the coy Japanese maiden as she caressed and hit the keys, peeking in and out from behind the vase of flowers . . . while Léonie, with similar mock dramatics, bellowed out all Pinkerton's swelling passion – until, finally, one of the terriers, goaded beyond endurance, started to bark with furious excitement and the girls collapsed in laughter.

Outside, at the hall entrance to the drawing room, Pat Kennedy, the butler, paused at the closed door a moment, listening to the thrilling voices, the soaring music.

He had musical tastes himself – he ought to have enjoyed his eavesdropping. Instead he was doubtful, anxious over something. Before moving on, he hitched his trousers up, displaying for an instant the Webley revolver – once kept hidden in his mattress, but which now never left the holster beneath his waistband.

'But, Mortimer, for all that you are my much older cousin and dear friend . . . it is after all *my* life, my house here. So I do insist I am consulted, that we agree any plans together. I am no longer a child, you know.'

It was over a month since the Rebellion in Dublin when Hetty spoke almost severely to Mortimer Cordiner, down from Dublin to see what he might do over the running of the household and estate, and more particularly to discuss Hetty's future, now that her mother, reprieved from execution at the last moment because of her gender, had started a life sentence in Dublin's Mountjoy Prison.

'Of course, Hetty. I'm not officially *in loco parentis*. Only here to advise, help.' He twiddled his luxuriant beard as they stood in the great hall, below the restored white marble statues of Cupid and Psyche, pondering this formidably assured girl who, when he had last seen her, had indeed been a child.

'Good. Well, let us talk to the others.'

They moved out onto the wide porch – it was another blowy, uncertain late spring day – where the Strauses, Benjamin and Effi, with Léonie in her wheelchair, still not yet fully mobile from her leg wound, were taking coffee. The Strauses, hearing of their daughter's adventures, and with some difficulty and delay making passage from France to Ireland, had finally arrived at Summer Hill the previous evening. Only Aunt Emily and Robert, nearing the end of his school holidays, spent at Summer Hill with a friend from St Columba's College, were absent from the porch; both boys had been out on the river since early morning fishing for trout, Aunt Emily, with her drawing and easel, lost somewhere in the demesne.

'You see,' Hetty said to the assembled company, taking control just as she had with Mortimer a few moments before. 'Where better for Léa and me to stay . . . than here? With the war in France and the awful troubles in Dublin. Though, as you can see, there are absolutely no troubles down here!'

She gazed over the tulip-covered pleasure gardens, the drifts of narcissi and daffodils down the lawn, to the woods above the river and over the blue mountains: the same serene view of arcady.

'Indeed,' Ben Straus agreed. 'But what of *learning*, girls?' He eyed Hetty brightly as he pulled on a small cigar.

'Well, the convent's closed – thank goodness. And, besides, what more should we learn?'

'All the arts and refinements appropriate to young women . . .' Mortimer thought out loud.

'We can surely find some tutor locally, in Kilkenny, to come and teach us sums and history and things – if that's what you're worried about. And as to the other refinements you mention . . .' Hetty looked across at Léonie in the wheelchair. 'We can surely teach each other all that.' She smiled at her friend. She could hardly believe it – it was wonderful to have Léonie here, in her house, but this time without her mother, entirely under her protection.

'But, Henrietta,' Ben Straus spoke slowly, a little sadly, 'what on earth would you and Léa *do* here all on your own together?'

Again Hetty looked out of the window, at the landscape hanging on the edge of summer. 'Why everything – *everything*,' she told him sweetly.

Effi Straus, petite, dark-haired, sensible, put her hand gently on her husband's arm. 'Ben, dearest, it's just you're such a city man yourself, you can't understand country life. There'll be everything for Léonie to get on with here. And you'll miss her, I know – I will too – but we can come visit. And surely, with this dreadful war going on and on, she'd be safer here?'

'Mr Cordiner – what do you feel? I don't want to impose –'

'No imposition whatsoever, Mr Straus. As I said to Hetty, I'm not formally in charge. But I can't see that Frances would object. I saw her last week at Mountjoy – and will be seeing her again when I get back.'

He looked round the company – silent, embarrassed, at this mention of Frances: a ghost at a feast. And indeed it was so noticeable how her absence from Summer Hill had already lightened the mood of every room, every person, the whole air of the house.

Pat Kennedy came on to the porch then, with one of the maids, supervising the coffee clearing and at the same time making enquiries about the wine for that evening's dinner. He addressed himself to Mortimer, as the eldest Cordiner present.

'Ah,' Mortimer twiddled his beard mischievously. 'You must ask Miss Henrietta, Pat – she's in charge here now!' They all looked at Hetty. 'Well, Hetty? The wines – they should be a part of any sensible young woman's education. What would you suggest?'

Suddenly taken out of her reverie she spoke directly to Pat. 'Oh, let us have sh-sh-champagne! – of course, now that we are all here safe and sound, as a c-c-celebration!'

She stared at Pat forcefully as she spoke. And her gaze disturbed the man, just as the girls' singing had done. What was it, he wondered, that made her stare at him in such a knowing, authoritative manner?

Hetty knew well enough why she took this dominant attitude: she remembered watching her mother taking the secret oath to fight the British in his stable rooms years before. If her mother subsequently had become one of the leaders of the rising, there could be no doubt but that Pat was one of the rebels too, as yet undiscovered. She had a power over him there which he knew nothing of. But she would not use it openly yet, for she feared him as well.

Afterwards Ben Straus spoke to Mortimer alone in Frances's study-boudoir off the big drawing room, where Mortimer was going through farm accounts and other household papers, accumulated in Frances's absence.

'I shall expect to contribute to Léonie's keep –'

'Of course not! How many times has Hetty stayed with you in Paris?' Mortimer put his pen down.

Ben Straus had taken to Mortimer at once. In their original views and freedom from stuffy convention they were much in the same mould, men of the world – so that Benjamin felt able to speak quite freely. 'What of . . . Mrs Fraser?' he asked pointedly. 'It's hard to understand . . .'

'Yes, she was always that,' Mortimer replied promptly. 'And very lucky indeed to have been reprieved, along with de Valera. Your country had most to do with it. Lloyd George is scared of American opinion, particularly the Irish there. And, besides, he hopes to get America into the war.'

'I hope not,' Ben humphed. 'Though I suppose it will surely come . . . But the house here and the big farm – can it run without Mrs Fraser?'

Mortimer smiled, thinking of the Appleton case and the other domestic and farming troubles which, as Frances's legal adviser and only real confidant in Ireland, he had had to deal with over the past years. 'I have to tell you, Mr Straus, that without Mrs Fraser things will run a *lot* more smoothly here.'

'And the girls – what do you really think?'

'I think they'll be fine. I'll be down often enough, keep an eye on things. They'll be fine.'

Later, before he returned to Dublin next morning, Mortimer spoke to Hetty alone, the two of them walking through the formal pleasure gardens and up the terraced lawn – another uncertain, rain-squally afternoon. They had been talking of arrangements in the household – Hetty, remonstrating with him almost over the fate of her Grandmama, still incarcerated in the back wing of the house.

'Yes, I've often spoken to your mother about her. And indeed, years ago, she should have been let out into the light and air. Now it's too late – I've spoken to the new doctor in Thomastown: quite apart from her various heart problems she's almost entirely senile. There's apparently nothing to be done, other than the best attention, which she gets here at home, from old Molly particularly. She can't move –'

'But why did my mother have her put away like that in the first place? It was a me-me-*monstrous* thing . . .'

Mortimer, who knew many of the details which had led to this incarceration, said simply, 'They had disagreements, over the inheritance of Summer Hill – your Grandmama had left it all to your great-uncle, Austin Cordiner –'

'Yes, I've heard something of that – when my uncles died, Henry killed by a snake here and Eustace in that Boer war –'

'Yes, and your mother believed that she had a prior right to the house, as indeed she had.'

'But to lock Grandmama up like that!'

'These family rows – they can be very embittering. Perhaps you can understand? . . .' Mortimer waved his hands in the air, gesturing impotently. 'In any case, it is your mother who must suffer the incarceration now. I fear she will not be released – for a very long while.'

Hetty, far from understanding, was scornful. 'Does she deserve any better? Oh, Léonie has told me: how she spoke to her during the battle at the College of Surgeons – apologising for her wretched behaviour to me over the years. But no, I ke-ke-can't understand it! Why, why she should be se-se-such a cruel woman!'

Mortimer, who through Dermot's strictest confidence knew of Frances's affair with the Prince of Wales, of his abandoning her, and how Hetty was their child, thought he understood Frances's behaviour very well. But he could not speak of this to Hetty, and thus show her mother in any better light. Instead he treated the issues vaguely.

'Your mother has been bitterly disappointed in her life –'

'Yes, but *how?*'

'Over Summer Hill here, with her own mother – and later in the West Indies with your father. Oh, and much else. It has driven her . . . in these cruel directions.' He turned to Hetty then. 'But you must know – she was not always like that. When she lived with Dermot and me in London, years ago – what a warm person she was, how happy, enthusiastic, lovely in so many ways.'

Hetty showed surprise. 'How then the cold and che-charmless person she has always been to me – to everyone – since?'

Again, he could not tell her how, in her own case, it was because Hetty reminded Frances of the Prince, and the disastrous end to their affair, that she so frowned on her daughter.

'Hetty, a person's character can become quite twisted by long disappointment. Do you see? Be sure that it doesn't happen to you.' He gazed into her chilling blue eyes. They had left the pleasure garden now and stood higher up on the lawn, beneath the maple tree which, thirty years before, had held Frances's swing, the stubbed branch still jutting out over the rock and willow garden which had replaced the tennis court.

'Oh, that will not happen to me,' Hetty assured him roundly. 'Disappointments, yes, no doubt – but not that I quite change my character!'

'Good!'

They walked into the rock garden then, suddenly glimpsing Aunt Emily at her easel between the pendant willow branches on the other side, the late sun making delicate yellow patterns through the leaves.

'This, all this, was a tennis court once – I remember so wanting to play on it.'

'Yes, another disappointment of your Mama's . . .'

Hetty chuckled. 'Aunt Emily told me – some man, some rich lord, jilted her here: some "nonsense with men", she said! Aunt Emily hates *men!*' She turned and teased her cousin now. 'Well, I don't hate men – or women,' she thought to add for good measure.

Returning, they stopped by the grotto and artificial waterfall, gazing down at the house bathed in a shaft of evening sunlight, the Virginia creeper just coming into leaf, a vague filigree tracing of green creeping over the façade above the porch. 'And I don't hate Summer Hill either, like I used to. But that's just because Mama's not here. That's awful, isn't it?'

Mortimer bit his lip ruminatively. 'No . . . it's understandable –'

But Hetty rushed on, stricken by the spirit of place, 'It was just here, by the grotto, the day war broke out, that Dermot told me how much the house could offer all of us – me and Robert and Léonie, with him and Mama: married! Just think of it, what "nonsense" that would have been. And yet I believed him – when he said what a future I had here . . .'

Mortimer sighed. 'You, at least, certainly have a future here, Hetty. As to Dermot, well, I have news of him regularly now. I'll send you some of his letters. And he gets the food parcels . . .'

A swirl of emotion overcame Hetty then and she turned to Mortimer vehemently. 'Oh, I do hope the war ends soon. Or he escapes. Why doesn't he *escape?*'

'Perhaps he's tried. But he's in some huge walled castle –'

'I would so like to see him!' Her great eyes glistened.

'So would I. And we will. And the house will have all its promise again.' Mortimer, in fact, was not so sure of any of these things, only managing to hide his doubts in his beard. 'In the meantime, there's me, in Dublin, and Aunt Emily and Elly – and Léonie – here. And the war will be over . . . some day.'

They had started to walk back to the house when Hetty paused half-way down the lawn, beneath the great cedar tree. 'How can there be such peace here – and de-de-death and such horrors everywhere else?'

Mortimer shook his head. 'That's exactly the madness of it all, I'm afraid – which we have to make the real fight against.'

'Because we're not mad, you mean? People like us?'

'Yes, I hope so. Just that.'

Robert and Bertie, his tall bespectacled schoolfriend, were preparing their rods in the porch before going out for a last evening's trout fishing, chattering to Léonie in her wheelchair, when Hetty and Mortimer got back to the house.

'Well, go on! You've never properly told *us*, at least, what it was all *like* in the rebellion!' Robert, already in his fishing waders, his hank of dark hair falling repeatedly over his brow in his excitement, was taxing Léonie. 'We saw *nothing* of it all down here. Do tell us!'

'But, Robert, I *have* told you! It was all . . . just awful! I can't describe it. Here's Hetty – she's much better at describing things.'

Robert turned to Hetty. 'Well? What was the most *awful* thing?'

Hetty looked at him, rather *de haut en bas*. She relished having done, and been part of, men's violent things, which Robert, with his love of guns and sport, so wanted to experience. 'Oh,' she said grandly, 'so *many* awful things. I think the worst was the nights, the rotten awful smell in the lecture-room, blood and dying and thinking you were going to die next morning yourself when the shooting started again . . . Yes, the nights were worst. Without Léa, I don't know . . .' She looked over at Léonie, smiling quickly, sharing again in an instant all that they had shared in those nights. Robert was spellbound, his bespectacled friend less so.

'Oh, and the *poor* carrier pigeons – I couldn't bear it, when they shot them down. And then, when the British started to *shell* the building, on the last few days, and it looked like the whole place was going to go up in flames . . .'

Robert looked at Hetty with envy and obvious admiration. 'Oh, I *do* wish I'd been there!' But it was Léonie who gazed at Robert as he spoke, in silent sympathy at his frustration.

In the years since St Columba's, Robert had seen little of Hetty. But, their childhood antagonisms largely forgotten, absence had made his heart grow fonder. As for Léonie, ever since she had first seen Robert that day standing like a sentinel on the river bank, he had come in and out of her mind as a vaguely disturbing presence, a distant figure – but all the more attractive for that. Yet Léa saw how very much less distant he was with Hetty and realised how much he liked her; and she felt a pang of jealousy then.

They had had a life together – oh, for so many years before she had met Hetty. And, for a moment, she was jealous of that, too. But then, she thought, they had surely never shared what she and Hetty had experienced – together during those last nights in Dublin. So there was nothing really to be jealous of. And she allowed herself once more to look at Robert as merely attractive and unthreatening.

Petrol was rationed, Frances's big Daimler immobilised, so Molloy took the departing company to Thomastown station in the old coach and pair; the girls on the porch waving furious goodbyes, the terriers barking, so that with the general commotion the rooks in the chimney-stacks soared and cawed into the bright blue sky, inky tea-leaves against the sun. A minute later, the girls heard the first white gate clang shut.

Sheila, one of the terriers, jumped up, pawing and stretching herself against Hetty's legs, while Chilly, disturbed by everyone's sudden disappearance, gazed down the drive. After another minute Hetty pushed Léonie into the hall. 'So, all gone,' she said shortly.

'All beginning,' Léonie replied.

Turning the wheelchair towards one of the tall windows, Hetty paused in the shaft of sunlight, bending down close over Léonie's head, both girls silent in the great pillared space.

'That little coloured pane there,' Léonie said eventually, looking at the stained-glass inset at the bottom of the window. 'What is it, I've often wondered –'

'Oh, it's Aunt Emily's – the family arms. And the motto: "Fortune Favours the Brave".'

'Whose fortune?' Léonie asked dully.

'Ours, Léa – ours.'

'That eagle . . . frightens me.' And she shivered, craning round, looking up at Hetty.

'Oh, it's nothing – just like the frigate birds we had everywhere in Domenica: the souls of dead sailors searching for their lost homes . . .'

'That's pretty sad . . .'

'No, it's not! – they find them! They all have homes, just like we have, *here!*'

Hetty turned the chair round as she spoke. And now she wheeled Léonie, slowly at first, as if in some courtly dance, making figures of eight around the pillars. Then, at a gradually increasing pace, speeding past the Flemish hunting tapestry, she ran from the statue of Psyche in its niche at one end of the hall, across to its mate, Cupid, on the other side – pushing Lèonie faster now, the wheels screeching over the marble floor, as she turned the chair in ever-tighter circles, propelling Léonie back and forth in a rising swirl of movement, as if trying to obliterate the immediate past, to set a great distance from that moment of departure minutes before, to reach the threshold of their new life.

They screamed and laughed and sang, the wheelchair a carousel, careering madly about. Then, as it made too sharp a turn, the chair tipped over and Léonie was spilled out, in the middle of the chequered marble floor.

'Léa! . . .'

'I'm all right.' She stood up, quite easily, walked, with only the slightest limp, over to the window, and peered out into the bright sunshine.

'But, Léa . . . your leg?'

'Oh, it's *much* better.' She bent down, eyes once more glued to the little stained-glass pane. 'It's just – I rather liked you pushing me about in that splendid thing, these last weeks . . .'

She turned, righted the chair and, with one vigorous push from her injured foot, sent it careering away into the back of the hall. 'Was that wrong of me?' Hetty, surprised and still breathless, shook her head. 'No? Good. Shall we *walk?*'

Léonie took Hetty's hand and, swinging their arms to and fro, they made a beginning, going out through the doors and into the spring sunlight.

Aunt Emily, from her bedroom studio on the west side of the house, saw the girls move through the pleasure garden, up the terraced lawn, to the maple tree, where they stopped, looking at the rock and willow gardens, Hetty gesticulating at the view.

Taking her sketch book, Aunt Emily rapidly drew the old maple, as she remembered it more than thirty years before, when Frances was a girl – showing the big branch with its swing leaning out over what had then been the tennis court. And on the swing she put Hetty, in her long, tight-fitting lilac skirt and frilly blouse, with Léonie pushing her – thus predicting, by twenty-four hours exactly, the situation the following morning, when the Summer Hill carpenter, on Hetty's instructions, rigged up just such a swing on another branch. Soon Hetty was pushing Léonie on it, higher and higher, so that Léonie gasped for her to stop.

'Fortune favours the brave!'

When Léonie got off the swing Hetty told her, 'I'd like to turn that dreary willow garden back into a tennis court!'

Aunt Emily, in her now-expanded drawing, had already done just that, colouring her sketch in light and dark green washes, picking out the white lines, the sloping black net – just as it all would have been years before, except that now Léonie was on the swing, feet swooping out over the court in an arc, and Hetty, hands in the air, was laughing beneath the mottled green shadows of the maple.

Hetty, with the run of the house and relishing her control, moved to a bedroom next to Léonie's – taking over the yellow room which her mother had occupied as a young woman, looking eastwards over the valley and the mountains, a pretty, rather faded room now, still with the daffodil-and-primrose frieze running along just beneath the ceiling and the antiquated bathing machine in the small dressing room adjoining, with its water tank mounted on mock bamboo pole supports, rarely used since the installation of the first proper bathroom.

'What a crazy machine!'

'All very cosy, though, in the winter.' Hetty touched Léonie's arm. 'We ought to try it –' And a sensuous complicity grew between them for an instant, before a sudden noise in the next room disturbed them. The grate was full of soot and twigs. 'The rooks in the chimneys.' Hetty bent down and peered up the flue. 'Can't have been a fire here for ages.'

Then something caught her eye and, picking about in the mess, she drew out a blackened silver teaspoon. 'Of course – the thieves!' She pushed her arm up the flue and encountered a ledge a foot or so above the grate. She emerged with a grimy, discoloured glass paperweight – but, embedded in the crystal, as she rubbed it, a beautiful crimson rose materialised.

Again she reached up, searching the ledge. There were several other paper-weights there. Finally she brought out a spherical snow-dome, with a delicate ivory model of Summer Hill inside; when she shook it, she set the flakes dancing.

The girls studied the treasures, taking them over to the window, cleaning them more thoroughly. 'The rooks and jackdaws couldn't have taken all these in their beaks – someone must have hidden them here.' Hetty gazed in fascination at the snow-dome, rocking it gently in her hand, letting the flakes wash like a tide over the base of the house.

'Someone may have stolen them then, from about the house, and hidden them there,' Léonie said. 'Secrets, you said,' she went on. 'Nothing but secrets here.'

'Yes.' Hetty was thoughtful. 'Aunt Emily'll probably know – but I'm going to keep these. Especially this!' And she caressed the snow-dome, seeing it somehow as a talisman, an emblem of her new life at Summer Hill with Léonie. This indeed, she thought, was a symbol: the promise of the house incarnate, that promise which Dermot had spoken to her about nearly two years before, when life for all of them would be amazingly, unimaginably lovely, as it would be now, for her and Léonie at least, in *her* house.

Later, in her studio-bedroom, Aunt Emily explained the presence of these little *objets d'art* in the chimney. 'Of course!' she spoke caustically. 'That was your Mama's bedroom, when she was your age – always thieving things about the house, just to annoy!' She glared round at Hetty then in her wide-eyed, mad-happy way.

'But annoy who?'

'Why your grandmother, of course – always hammer and tongs together.' Aunt Emily cackled at the memory.

Hetty was taken aback, not by her mother's thieving propensities, but by her own apparent inheritance of exactly similar inclinations towards these objects. Was she *like* her mother then – whom she so hated? What a thought . . . So that, in a sudden burst of righteousness, she said, 'Well, I shall have them all put back in the drawing room.' Though she made a mental note not to release the snow-dome. 'Typical of Mama,' she went on disapprovingly, espousing an adulthood she did not yet quite possess. 'Stealing things . . .'

'Typical, yes.' But Aunt Emily spoke with enthusiasm. 'She was a spirited young woman! Gaudy – know what I mean?' she added in her haughty, brogue-tinged voice.

'Not really.'

'Your mother had *character*, girl. And that's the only thing that counts: knew what she wanted – and took it! If only she hadn't taken to all those *men* . . .' Aunt Emily curled her lips sourly.

'What men?'

'*All* men.'

'Were there many?'

'Excuse yourself, girl – *one* man's too much. But she had those Horse Show Johnnies in the Dublin season, that wretched oaf Lord Norton's son, that no-good Fraser chap. Far too many.'

'I never knew that!'

'*Lot* of things you don't know – oh, she was a stunner, all right, lovely girl, if only the men hadn't done for her . . .'

'My father, you mean?'

'Well, he was the worst by all accounts.'

'*Was* he my father, though?'

'Why wouldn't he be?' Aunt Emily looked up at her, puzzled. 'Though, now you mention it, I wonder. Your Mama had *character*, took what she wanted, did things her way . . .'

Hetty, startled by these revelations, felt faint, her vision blurring and shaking: a feeling she had known before whenever she was faced with these strange intimations of her real paternity, the idea that she might have quite another father – a sense that had been with her for so long, that she was a changeling, perhaps; coming from, going towards, some as yet unidentifiable greatness. It disturbed her, yet also gave her a wonderful feeling of secret potential, of immense power – a *will* to power, which she must soon express, accepting her true inheritance.

She was surprised, too, by this new view of her mother, in her great-aunt's praise which, added to Léonie's earlier talk of her bravery and to Mortimer's commendations, seemed to confirm the existence of quite a different woman in her youth: a woman whom she could still hate, yes, but also, in her better features, perhaps emulate. With all this talk of bravery, loveliness, character – did she not already reflect these qualities of her mother's? But what if she had only inherited her worst traits? – as in this need for thieving they seemed to share.

'Am I like my Mama then – I mean her good points – when she was young?'

'Oh, she was more the daredevil! A real case – took the eye out of a tinker once, robbing the Cordiner tombs, with her riding crop! And threw a fit when your grandmother blackened the whole house up after my curious nephew Henry let all the snakes out that killed him – pulled the curtains down, rang all the bells in the place fit to burst, and then stamped off with Elly to London! Oh, she was a real panic, your Mama. I had a lot of time for her. Besides . . .' She ran her fingers over her sketch book. 'It was she who gave me the run of the place here, when her mother – the old witch – had me locked up in this bedroom! Oh yes, she had character, your mother, and fearless with it!'

Hetty felt chastened, and lessened, by this comparison. She seemed a pale shadow of this daredevil. Feeling the need to assert herself, she blurted out, 'Well, I shall see that Grandmama is moved into the light and air, when the better weather settles. There are to be changes here.'

Aunt Emily cackled. 'Changes, indeed! Of course there will be – just like your Mama, when she got back from that cannibal island! You're so like her, in that way. Always on to change things, when you can't really, no one can. *Just* like her!'

Hetty was now even more determined, like her mother, to assert herself – in whatever bold and impetuous way she could – on the life of Summer Hill.

And she did change things. In a flurry of activity she and Léonie first travelled the house, from attic to cellar, considering every nook and cranny, establishing themselves, as if in a vast new nest. They moved out some of the Georgian furniture, replacing it with heavy Victorian pieces – things Hetty had loved as a child and which her mother had abandoned. They opened rooms which had been long closed, in particular old Sir Desmond's mechanical workshop in the yard, untouched since his death nearly ten years before. They stood among the debris of jagged wood and torn linen, the remains of the bi-plane which had killed him. Its wooden propellers were smashed, the wicker cockpit seat had been eaten away by rats, the long room was tangled in cobwebs, full of musty decay, yet it was still strangely animate with adventure and hope.

Hetty wiped the thick dust off the linen fuselage, so that the still-brilliant blue lettering emerged: 'ZEPHYR'. Then she pulled one of the control sticks; a wire strained and creaked. 'They fly everywhere nowadays. But he must have been one of the very first.'

'What a *family*, Hetty!'

And Hetty was pleased by the comment – which Léonie felt impelled to repeat when Hetty opened up her Uncle Henry's old museum and work rooms on the top floor – rooms into which she and Robert had stolen through the window, as children. Now, with a key, they marched straight in, finding nothing changed: the same desiccated, slightly medical odour, the partly-filled butterfly display case with its last addition, the huge Amazonian Swallowtail still half-secured there; sporting rifles, assegais, military drums and fencing foils, the same snake skeleton in the tea chest by the ash-filled grate.

Hetty lifted the necklace of vertebrae, terrifying Léonie, rattling it in the mote-filled sunlight. 'I used to be terrified of this, too. Robert was such a tease . . .'

Léonie gazed through the doorway at the display cases filled with exotic stuffed animals: a porcupine rampant, sad-eyed, frozen lemurs, a malevolently toothy crocodile. 'Did they ever do anything *ordinary* here?'

'We'll do all these things – and more!' Hetty assured her. 'Oh, Léa, that's just what a huge old house like this is *for*! For everything!'

She and Léonie hugged each other violently, pressing, swaying together in rising spasms of affection, so that for an instant it seemed their love must catch fire. But at the last moment they drew apart, flushed and breathless, half-annoyed at their restraint.

'No,' Hetty said, gazing at Léonie in frustration. Then, by way of excuse, she went on, 'No, let's not change anything here, leave everything. Unless – we took those.' She picked one of the fencing foils from the wall, flourished it, whipping the air briskly. 'Good way of exercising your leg!'

'A most suitable young lady-like accomplishment indeed! Yes, let's take them.'

'And there's rifles, too – in case the rebels come for us! Dermot showed me how to shoot with them years ago.'

And Hetty, remembering those days, early dawns, starlit evenings, out and about the estate or by the river with Dermot – when life had opened out for her as a child in all sorts of vivid adventure – was tempted by the idea of some equally wild existence, here with Léonie now, so that she took another foil off the wall, passing it to Léonie, then faced her, flourishing her own foil inexpertly, measuring up to her.

'"Action!" – is that what they say?'

'The brave!' Léonie responded. Both button-point foils were in the air now, as they mimed the start of an engagement, swords meeting with a sharp clash, blades shivering. They glared at each other, mimicking the anger of wicked ladies, true swordswomen.

And for that long moment of confrontation, as their foils touched, a very different feeling towards Léonie woke in Hetty – one that was not at all tender or protective as it had been hitherto, but another, quite new, dizzy-making urge: a need to hurt, crush, dominate, subdue this young woman, almost as an object, devoid of feeling. Yes, she wanted to possess Léa then, just as she had the paperweights and the other little objects found in the chimney.

Gazing defiantly into Léa's eyes, she was not to know how her friend, at precisely the same moment, felt an almost identical possessive urge.

Both ashamed of these sensations, they laid the foils down.

'Oh, Léa, I'm sorry . . .' Hetty turned away.

'About what?' Léonie approached her now, concerned – as if determined to rescue, underwrite, confirm something vital which they had both felt in these last minutes – touching her shoulder, turning her head round towards her. 'Probably great fun – these foils – if one knew how to do it.' She gazed at Hetty intently.

'But we don't know how – do we?'

'We can, we *will* though. We can learn, won't we?'

'Yes. Oh, *yes*!' They smiled with relief, that they understood their secret feelings for each other now.

8

'ON GUARD THEN, Henrietta!' Major Ashley started the lesson in his dry, strident voice. 'No! – hold the foil *correctly* first.' He stopped her, acidly patient. 'Thumb *up*. You don't grip the thing like a *carving* knife: *lightly!* Just thumb and forefinger – the other fingers only used to guide the blade. The doigté is all important – remember the great master Lafaugère: "Hold your sword as if you had a little bird in your hand, firmly enough to prevent its escape, yet not so firmly as to crush it."'

The Major – willowy, distinguished, with ferociously bushy eyebrows over a cadaverous face – took his stick and hobbled across the great hall. Hetty, in a linen culotte and padded body vest, took off her fencing mask. Léonie, similarly clad, stood at the other side of the hall, towards the end of a narrow hessian carpet laid out along its length for some thirty feet.

'No, girl, give it here.' The Major, cynically dispassionate now, showed her how to hold the foil. '*Lightly!*' He balanced it perfectly for a second between thumb and forefinger. Then, with fiendish exultation, his bad leg anchored to the ground, he stamped the other foot forward, lunging sharply. 'Thus – and thus!' he roared, repeating the action. Then he resumed his pitying manner. 'You are not *pig*-sticking, my dear. It is an *art*, this. Do you *hear* me, Léonie?' He had swung round in a trice and confronted her.

'Yes, Major!' Léonie, her mask still in place, did not have to hide her broad smile. It was their third lesson with the irascible, sweet-and-sour Major – demon-faced, arms darting, bizarre, but with a kind and witty heart, a man they had both taken to at once and now almost adored.

'Right, then. Masks on. First positions. On guard!' He issued instructions, rat-a-tat-tat, like a ballet master, as they prepared to engage. 'Feet together, at *right* angles, head and body *erect* . . .' He hit the crucial words with a sharp nasal bark. 'Head facing *forward*, Léonie – not to the side, you idiot girl! – left arm hanging, in touch with the body, right arm and foil in a *straight* line, button six inches from floor – then *advance* – move your *pins*, Henrietta! – short step forward with right foot, then left – the body position not being *changed*, Henrietta, you're not *waltzing* here . . . then *lunge!*'

The lesson proceeded, the pace increasing with vigour, and soon the hall was ringing with the clash of steel as the two girls lunged and parried, stamping their feet on the hessian.

At that moment Major Jack Ashley – an old friend of Mortimer Cordiner's, graduate and keen fencer at Trinity College, Dublin before joining the British army thirty years before – should have been teaching the girls about Pythagoras or the Crusades. But, for all of them, such academic pursuits, in the past few weeks had proved tiresome. And so, after Hetty had shown Major Ashley the rescued foils from Henry's room, they had instead embarked on these happy fencing lessons.

The Ashleys, the Major and his wife Winifred, came from Dublin, but were now near-neighbours at Summer Hill – having bought a small Georgian property across the river from Cloone, after he had been seriously wounded in Flanders the previous year. So, invalided out of the Army, and with time on his hands, he rejoiced in these educational – though now more martial – visits, which Mortimer Cordiner had arranged with him, as tutor for the two girls.

The Major came to Summer Hill three times a week, in a governess trap, driven chariot-fashion, with a dangerously frisky cob, tearing up the long drive in a flurry of gravel. The scheme was entirely seemly, for sometimes Mrs Ashley – a charming, if rather faded and put-upon woman – came as well, and tea was served afterwards, with the best Spode and Georgian silver, demanded by Hetty who had developed a taste for all sorts of extravagant gestures. All this was supervised by Pat Kennedy in his finest summer livery.

For, although many of the estate workers and farm hands had long before volunteered for life – and death – in the trenches on the Western front, Pat Kennedy had not done so, concerned as he was with more pressing military matters at home. The leaders of the Easter rising had been executed and the rest, some thousands including Frances, subsequently imprisoned in Britain. But the secret Irish Republican Brotherhood, together with the remnants of its dependent Army, had almost immediately been reactivated. And Pat Kennedy, one of the few senior members of the Brotherhood still at large, now played a considerable part in this reorganisation, meeting secretly with other Republican officers from Kilkenny, or down from Dublin, in one or other of the estate cottages in the village or at outlying farms.

Looking through the green baize door at the back of the hall he had watched the girls fencing and was perturbed by these martial arts so skilfully practised. And, later, as he presided over one of the formal teas, he once again noticed Hetty's knowing glance in his direction. Did she know something then? Had her mother told her about him during that week when they were incarcerated together in the College of Surgeons building? Was he at risk from this sword-slashing amazon?

In the event the threat which Pat Kennedy feared from Hetty came, a few days later, from quite a different source – in the shape of two British detectives from

Dublin Castle, arriving in a small motor insolently and unannounced at the front door, where Pat Kennedy admitted them – seeing them for what they were at once, and almost reaching for his revolver, before they asked to see Miss Henrietta Fraser.

Hetty saw them in the drawing room where, equally impertinent, they lolled on the chintz sofa and smoked cigarettes.

'Yes, of course I was with my me-me-mother most of that week in the College of Surgeons,' she stammered at them furiously.

'We had intended to see you earlier about this –'

'That is your affair. But I have *nothing* to hide, and had nothing to do with the whole business anyway, as you well know. Why, exactly, are you here?'

'We have reason to believe,' the older of the two men said, 'good reason to believe that someone, in the immediate locality, even in the house here itself, is closely connected with the rebels, as yet unapprehended. We have to make our investigations . . .'

Pat Kennedy, his ear to the drawing room door outside, listened intently – and was surprised by Hetty's violent response.

'Why, the idea is pre-pre-preposterous! Who could there be in this house? – with most of the men here away at the war. And, besides, have you not done enough damage already? – with your wicked executions! I did not support the rebels, but you begin to make me wish I had!'

Hetty, in her new mood of regal combativeness, was furious. No, she did not support the Republicans, even now, but she was incensed at these British spies as she saw them, these vulgar nosey-parkers, forcing themselves into *her* house, trying to make further mischief. Of course she knew exactly who they were looking for here: Pat Kennedy. But in her new mood – her new role as châtelaine of Summer Hill – she felt a strong loyalty to everyone in the household. These were her people now.

Quite naturally, and without her really being conscious of the transformation, with the advent of these detectives from London, Hetty became anti-British, champion of the Irish underdog. It was not in any way a political conversion; she neither knew nor cared anything for such matters. It was, more simply, a romantic attitude, which she struck that morning against these two commonplace men – one entirely in line with her new dreams of derring-do, in which she would contest every authority which presumed to set itself against that which she meant herself to impose on Summer Hill.

After more questioning, and some uncalled-for advice as to her own safety in the house, she refused the men permission to interview any of the household or estate staff, telling them abruptly to refer any further enquiries in the matter to her cousin and legal adviser, Mortimer Cordiner, the prominent Dublin lawyer, MP at Westminster, and friend of the Prime Minister.

This news of influence on high somewhat chastened the detectives and they left, though still ungraciously, stubbing their cigarettes out on the porch steps. But Hetty was pleased with her victory over them. It greatly encouraged her in the belief that she now controlled her destiny. Immune from all petty outside inter-ference, she, like her mother before her, now felt in supreme command of the great house on the hill.

While, for Pat Kennedy, the events of the morning and the conversation he had overheard quite altered his view of Hetty. Far from being a threat to him, she appeared to be on the Republican side of things in Ireland. Perhaps, in that long week at the College of Surgeons, her mother had converted her to the cause?

Léonie entirely supported Hetty in her stance against the police spies. She reminded Hetty of what her mother had said to her at the College – how important Irish freedom was. 'How, my being an American, I'd understand all that better than you. Well, perhaps I do – and perhaps you should?'

'Yes, and I think I do now. Something of it, at least. Certainly one can't have vulgar men like those two running our affairs in Ireland.'

And that afternoon, when the Major arrived, Hetty worked off her ire against the two intruders with a most vehement performance – this time, by way of extending her reach, against the Major himself who, standing anchored to the spot, was taken almost to the limits of his skill by her repeated lunges, sparkling ripostes, feints, remises, and devious false attacks.

'Good! Good, good.' The Major, removing his mask, wiped his brow. '*Quite* the champion . . .'

Hetty beamed.

But there were clouds elsewhere, lurking over the summer view. The first seemed hardly a shadow to Hetty, so that Mortimer, when he next came down, had to insist on its gravity. 'The fact is, Hetty, there must be economies here. Your mother has spent most of her Fraser inheritance – and has not run the estate with any profit since she took over. True, with the war, there's a boom in agriculture, but it won't make up the leeway in the farm accounts, or with the bank, where much is mortgaged.'

Hetty was mystified. 'But my Grandmama – I thought she was very wealthy?'

'She may be. But not a penny of hers can be touched – she instituted all sorts of legal restraints on her account, years ago.'

'And the estate rents, the tenanted farms?'

'They don't amount to much. And many can't pay at all now – sons, fathers, dead or still away at the war. O'Donovan, the steward, has spoken to me. There's great poverty, you know, all round here, just beyond the big gates.' He looked at her gravely. 'Of course not, you can't be aware of that – the *real* life of the country here, how very stricken most people are in Ireland, always have been: illness, debt, every sort of aggravation and deprivation over the years. Beyond these walls . . .' He looked round the gracious drawing room. 'Things are very different . . .'

'Oh yes,' Hetty said. 'I know they are *poor*. I've seen our cottages, inside, too –'

'Those are *estate* cottages, Hetty – the people there are well looked after. You must see others, quite different, no comparison . . .'

And Hetty agreed – she would do just that, a proposal much in line with her new interests in local matters. The other cloud, though, she could do little about.

As a result of her mother's rebellious activities in Dublin, and the immense publicity attendant on her act of treason there, Summer Hill had become an almost entirely isolated redoubt. Every Protestant and many Catholics in the immediate neighbourhood and county – from shopkeeper to duke – boycotted Summer Hill and all its inhabitants.

The girls first learnt of this ostracism a few days later. Attending a charity bazaar for the war effort in Thomastown, they had wandered down among the row of stalls set up outside the old church in the high street, glancing at the bric-à-brac and garden produce – all in aid of mittens and woolly socks for the troops at the front – when Hetty realised how the greetings she made to neighbours and vague friends of the family, went quite unregarded. She put this down to mere preoccupation on the part of these county gentry – until she stopped at Mrs Morton's stall, the Mortons of Castleton Hall, the big house of the area, just a mile out of the town, where Mrs Morton, a vigorous, horse-faced Englishwoman, in an ill-cut and unsuitably heavy tweed suit, with a Kitchener brooch prominent in her lapel and a Union Jack over the stall, was selling pots of last year's rather mouldy jam and chutney, together with a variety of home-made sweets and barley sugar twirls.

Hetty fingered a jar of discoloured chutney, thinking not to purchase it. But Mrs Morton, at her most cutting and supercilious, immediately broke in. 'I should be obliged if you would put that down at once. We do *not* sell to rebels here.'

Hetty was so startled she nearly dropped the jar. 'Rebels?'

But Mrs Morton had turned away, searching out her husband, the old Brigadier-General close by, who approached the girls now. 'I'm amazed you have the impudence to show your face here,' he told Hetty – whose face coloured quickly in rage and embarrassment. The General helped himself to the fruits of victory, picking a barley sugar stick from the stall, and the girls left immediately. But Hetty, in her fury, soon recovered, walking head-high back through the row of stalls, where everything had come to a stop now, the prim, self-satisfied, arrogant Protestant community gazing askance at the two girls, who more than held their own in this retreat, looking straight ahead with regal unconcern.

So, apart from the Ashleys' visits, the girls experienced no social life whatsoever that summer – and, even had they been able to, with Mortimer's new economic stringencies there would have been barely the money to support any merrymaking.

The girls were nearly paupers and certainly outcasts. And this state of affairs enraged Hetty, encouraging her all the more in her support of the local people – small tenant farmers, labourers, the real Irish Mortimer had mentioned, whose mean farmsteads and cottages she and Léonie took to visiting and where Hetty, as Frances Fraser's daughter among these Republican sympathisers, was made very welcome.

Here, indeed, she was appalled by what she found. In one cottage, with part of the sodden thatch blown away, on the wilder slopes of Mount Brandon, the girls came upon an emaciated, flushed-faced young woman, not yet thirty, but already widowed and with seven children and an elder brother to support – all of them living in utter squalor, a pig in the parlour, a handkerchief of potato land outside the back door, the children half-naked, filthy, some bow-legged with rickets and open sores, grovelling amidst the pig's feed, a mess of damp peelings and cabbage stalks; the brother, old before his time, a useless figure huddled over a barely-smouldering turf fire in the dark, smoke-filled room, a man with a hacking tubercular cough, blood smears on his stubbled chin.

The girls, horrified by the evidence of these trips, did what they could to help, securing medical attention, bringing a little money or parcels of food; but it was all a mere drop in the ocean of this dreadful rural misery.

'And to think of all these rich people sitting in their big houses, helping British troops, but not lifting a finger for their own people, and treating *us* like pariah dogs – it's too much!' Hetty stormed one afternoon as she and Léonie drove back in the trap from a particularly unhappy visit.

'Yes, but what can we really do?'

'Well,' Hetty said, a hard look coming into her eyes, 'these wretched people shall have *more* money and food parcels. And the others, those rich fools, will supply it. Kill two birds! That's what we'll do!'

'How do you mean?' Léonie gazed at her, already excited by Hetty's apparently sure and certain answer to any problem.

'Look!' Hetty pored over the large-scale ordnance survey map of the county later that evening in the library. 'There's lots of big houses – all within easy riding distance of here. Castleton Hall, Brownsbarn, Dangan Mill, Flood Hall . . . Some I know anyway, been there as a child – but we could scout them out beforehand.'

'Riding distance?' Léonie was perplexed.

'Why yes! At night.'

'But what for?'

'To *rob* them of course, you ninny!'

'Of what?'

'Anything we can find – money, silver, jewellery . . .'

Léonie considered the matter, trying to hide her complete surprise. 'But, Hetty . . .' she said at last.

'Why not? They deserve no better. Besides, it'd be great fun. Are you a coward?'

'No!' Léonie said, only half-truthfully.

'So! – "Fortune Favours the Brave".'

'And . . . and if we're caught?'

'We won't be. We'll go over the places first, carefully, in the daylight.'

'But how? You'll be recognised – and everyone absolutely hates us round here anyway.'

'Disguises! We can disguise ourselves – that theatrical stuff here, all those costumes and things in the wicker baskets up in the attics. It'll be tremendous fun!'

Léonie smiled, rather weakly. But then, unwilling to be left behind in any escapade of Hetty's, she agreed. 'Yes,' she said airily. 'Yes, it might be fun.'

'And here's the first place we'll pay a visit to!' Hetty said, happy revenge ringing in her voice. 'Those frightful Mortons.' And she settled her finger on Castleton

Hall, seat of this very wealthy English family, whose neo-Gothic pile lay on a rise, amidst extensive parkland, overlooking the river some five miles up-stream from Summer Hill.

It was, however, a place which Hetty had never visited, so that the house and grounds would have to be scouted out first. The annual cricket match, the Hall versus the estate, due to take place there the following week, would give them the opportunity to both see the lie of things and test the efficacy of their disguises.

'What shall we go as?'

'Not two girls anyway. Man and wife?'

'Hardly, we'll look too young.'

'Well, I'll have to go as your beau then – I'm the taller,' Hetty said decisively. 'And you'll be my sweet young thing!'

The two girls were agog as they discussed their plan up in the attic, picking through the great wicker hampers of theatrical stuff. 'But this is all pretty useless,' Léonie said, lifting out a pile of eighteenth-century tricorn hats together with some braided, gilt-buttoned French military jackets. 'It's not a fancy dress ball, is it?'

They left the old costumes, taking with them only a kit of theatrical make-up. Downstairs, they ransacked two big wardrobes, which still contained many of Hetty's uncles' old clothes, and laid out their selection on the floor of Hetty's bedroom.

There were evening and morning dress, town and country suits of every kind – in serge, tweed, worsted, and fine tropical linen. But what was most obviously required, Hetty decided, was the check Norfolk jacket and knickerbockers, tweed cap, soft-collared shirt, woollen tie, long grey socks and leather brogues – a country expedition outfit of her uncle Henry's in light cloth, smartly cut, still quite fashionable.

'So?' Léonie asked, fascinated. 'What's the idea? Who are we?'

'We're down from Dublin – take our bicycles, and I can have Henry's old plate camera: doing a summer bicycling tour, taking photographs. Easy!' She started to undress, seeing how the clothes would fit, pushing her legs into the knickerbockers first; they flapped about her calves, until she got the long socks on, and belted the waist. Then she tried the Norfolk jacket. It was almost too small when she buttoned it up, so that her breasts protruded.

'You'll have to flatten yourself there,' Léonie advised her. Hetty took her vest off, standing white-skinned in front of the mirror, while Léonie twisted a narrow linen towel round her chest and pinned it at the back. 'That's better!' Hetty put the jacket back on. 'The trousers need a few tucks in the seams – too baggy – and a bit of shortening. Otherwise, it's marvellous!'

'Yes – even the shoes don't pinch!'

Hetty gazed at herself, full-length, in the big mirror, Léonie behind her, smiling. 'Now the cap!' She set it on her head. 'Your hair – that's the only thing.' Hetty tried to push the fluffy dark locks up inside. 'Have to trim it – and pin it. Give me the scissors.'

Hetty sat down at the dressing table and in ten minutes Léonie had amended her coiffure, brushing the remaining strands sharply up and securing them with a grip. 'There – perfect!' She put the hat back on. 'Now for the make-up – don't quite know about that . . .'

'Here, I'll do it – did it for fancy dress, charades and things here in the old days.' Hetty took the kit and with a Leichner kohl pencil exaggerated her eyebrows . . . then with a powder puff and a box of Crystalessence Talc Shadow she darkened her complexion to a dusty bronze tint. Finally, lighting one of the Abdullah cigarettes she and Léonie sometimes secretly smoked, she stood up and, hands in pockets, strolled about the room meditatively, rocking on the balls of her feet.

'The walk! – it's just right. Just like a man!' Léonie roared with laughter at the transformation. Then, as Hetty stopped by the fireplace, put one arm on the mantelpiece, crossed her legs casually, and looked provocatively at her, Léonie was suddenly serious, stricken in her expression. 'Oh no, Hetty . . .' She rushed over to her. 'You shouldn't – you're too handsome by half!' And she kissed her then – so hard that her own face was smeared when she withdrew, breathless. 'Incredible . . .' she murmured.

And, indeed, Hetty was quite a sight. Masculinity became her. She was a young man now, eighteen or nineteen, a beau most certainly. But there was iron in this dandy: her blue eyes, shadowed by the kohl pencil, glowering down over the ruler-straight nose, the lips supercilious as she compressed them, all this giving her a tigerish air. Her beauty, which at other times could so easily become soft and pliant, had everywhere sharpened and hardened now. She had totally taken on the male role – not only the clothes, but the spirit, too.

It was a fine June day, with a high blue sky and puffy clouds over Mount Brandon. The cricket ground below the red-bricked mansion, overlooking a bend in the river, was circled at various points by leafy chestnut trees, benches of spectators, a striped marquee; cream-clad, tie-belted players made strange patterns in the centre of the greensward, the thunk of leather on wood reverberated in the hot afternoon, followed every now and then by polite applause.

The girls, leaving their bicycles behind the tent, and Hetty with Henry's old tripod plate camera, wandered along the boundary, before taking up a position near the house, setting the camera up, pointing out towards the game.

But then, before they had even begun to establish themselves or their act, a whiskery, red-faced, elderly gentleman approached: Brigadier-General Morton himself. He was eating something again, jaws champing ruminatively, before he noticed them.

'I say!' He admired the camera – by way of more readily admiring, and approaching, Léonie, in bicycling bloomers and a faded poppy-coloured linen jacket. 'That's an old Fox-Talbot, isn't it?' He bent down, inspecting Hetty's camera. 'No shutter – how do you manage to take moving pictures with it?' His eyes strayed from the camera to Léonie's bloomers.

'Oh, I don't worry about that!' Hetty told him, in a throttled voice. 'Just press the button.' And she bent down then, starting to fiddle with the plate camera.

'But, my dear chap – it's a plate camera. It has no button!' he told her, rather irascibly.

'Well, you know, I'm not actually ve-ve-very well up on it all. My grandfather's . . .' Hetty was starting to panic, so that Léonie interjected, flirtatiously.

'What a lovely place you have here!' She ogled the General who at once ceased his interest in the camera. 'Really so beautiful – and the house!' Léonie looked towards the ugly Victorian pile. 'Really lovely! – those stepped gables and corner turrets . . .'

'Indeed!' The old fool beamed. 'Glad you like it.' He held his hand out. 'Morton,' he said. 'General Morton,' he went on, glancing at Hetty, so that she suddenly had to make a response.

'Oh, I am sorry! – this is my friend, Miss Amelia French. And I'm Cole – Horace Cole, from Dublin. We're on a cycling tour.'

'Not at the war then?' the General said, only half-jocularly, to Hetty. But Hetty had prepared herself for just such an eventuality, taking off the spectacles with which she had supplied herself. 'Afraid not . . . wish I was . . . but these glasses, you see . . . can't see a thing without them!'

'Dear me, well never mind – most *pleasant* to see you both.' His gaze returned to Léonie. 'I'd be honoured – show you round the place, take tea with us later in the marquee – and perhaps I might offer you a little barley sugar meanwhile? I'm afraid I have a wicked taste for it myself.'

'No, no, thank you!' Léonie declined, at her most winning now. 'But would you, though – would you ever? – I should so like to see the house itself. I do so admire the Gothic revival!'

'Why, of course, Miss French – no relation of our former Commander in Chief, are you? I should be only too delighted!'

They left the cricket ground and, crossing the pleasure gardens, entered the drawing room by way of the open windows. Two big black labradors were fast asleep, and remained so until the General roared at them, 'Out! – out, I say – not allowed in here, you brutes!' They had not much to fear from the dogs in the house, Hetty thought, as she glanced round the room. There were some dull pictures, all in a hunting or military vein, and a number of tasteless items set in a clutter on tables and mantelpiece: silver cigarette boxes, china horses, miniature brass cannon – nothing of real value.

'Now, look here,' the General said to Léonie, taking her arm purposefully. 'Come to the library first and let me show you the original plans of the house – *most* interesting.'

They trooped out of the drawing room, across the hall, filled with hunting trophies, down a passageway and into a smaller, darker room, containing few books but with a quantity of popular magazines on a mahogany drum table by the window.

'Yes, we have a number of *very* interesting bits and pieces here – house was designed by Deane and Woodward, the Cork architects, y'know – disciples of Pugin, the House of Commons fellow.'

And then, to the delight of the girls, he took a key from the third drawer down in a small bureau and opened up a big, metal-doored, walk-in safe, behind a curtain in one corner of the room. Following him enthusiastically, they peered inside as he sorted through a number of rolled papers, no doubt architects' plans. But there were many boxes inside as well – tin deed boxes, boxes for silver, jewel boxes, perhaps just money boxes. It hardly mattered, Hetty thought: there were undoubtedly valuable things there. She smiled knowingly at Léonie.

'Now, here we are!' The General extracted a selection of scrolls, bringing them over to the table and unrolling them. Hetty, meanwhile, had wandered over to the windows, one of them half-open in the heat.

They gave out to the side of the building – on to a narrow gravel path, backed by a dark yew hedge, which led round from the front of the house to the lawns overlooking the river. She inspected the window fittings. The usual brass sliding catch, open now, was the only security.

'Now, see this,' the General said proudly, scanning the papers, as if preparing for battle. 'The *original* plans – before we had them amended of course – and then what they came up with! Much more appropriate!'

He displayed the two plans, side by side, as Hetty joined them at the table. One plan was no better than the other, she thought, both seeming even uglier than the house itself.

Pleading the late hour, and the long ride they still had to make to Kilkenny, the girls excused themselves from the cricket tea in the marquee and left soon afterwards, much to the chagrin of the General, who blustered about as they prepared to leave – offering them sugary sustenance for the journey, gazing longingly at Léonie's bloomers as the girls disappeared down the back drive.

'Almost too easy,' Hetty said, as they changed into their ordinary clothes in a ruined stone barn near Summer Hill. 'All on a plate – knowing where that big safe is *and* the key – and the two dogs as dozy as anything. All we need now is to practise some more night riding – and wait for a moonlit sky!'

And this they did, taking out Hetty's chestnut mare Cinderella and the black gelding Finnegan, which Léonie had always ridden on her visits to Summer Hill: racing each other out along the monkey puzzle alley in the long twilights, then beneath the great overhanging beech trees, which led away into the woods to the south of the house.

They were reasonably accomplished horsewomen already. But during the next week they steeled themselves in practice, riding everywhere about the estate and district – taking the horses out at dawn, just after sun-up, galloping over the water meadows by the river; in the afternoons roving up the gorse-covered slopes towards Mount Brandon; in the evenings going cross-country north to Castleton Hall, planning their route there, so that soon they felt entirely fitted to the task. There was but one matter, Hetty thought – the matter of further disguise . . .

'After all, we don't want to be recognised on the horses, or if they have a lamp or something, suddenly in the house.'

Léonie smiled, pleased to be able to initiate something in the adventure. 'Remember those French Musketeer costumes – the braided military jackets and tricorn hats, up in the attics? Why not be hung for a sheep as a lamb!'

Hetty was charmed. 'Why, of course! – with *masks*, Léa, and foils in our belts!' They shivered with laughter.

Trying on the eighteenth-century theatrical costumes – the dark pantaloons, braided maroon jackets, frilly, open-necked shirts, soft leather boots, and velvet eye masks with elastic bands which they made – they found the disguises perfect.

'Tomorrow then – if the moon is right!'

'It's due full then – or the day after . . .'

It was late in June, midsummer's eve, in fact, with twilight until nearly eleven o'clock, the girls knew, as they led the horses silently out of the stable yard, taking them well down the back drive northwards, before mounting and riding off to the ruined barn where they had already left their costumes.

Half an hour later, with a luminous pearl-pink sky showing above the western horizon, they changed their clothes, then each smoked an Abdullah cigarette, waiting for darkness to come. Towards midnight, with just the faintest tinge of pink in the sky now, the moon came up over the hills to the east, a watery pale orb, not over-bright, glazed by high-running clouds, ideal – enough to see their way by, but not easily be seen.

They settled their masks, shook hands, mounted their horses. 'Fortune Favours the Brave!' Hetty said. Though at that moment neither of them felt truly brave at all. A night bird called out, startling them, as they moved off towards the Hall.

As they had carefully planned and travelled their route – so as to avoid moving along the Thomastown road – keeping to the fields or beside the river, all went well until, crossing this main road, they were suddenly confronted, not twenty yards away, by the bright beam of an acetylene bicycle lamp, wavering at them through the soft-lit darkness, as someone rode straight towards them.

Hetty was caught in the lamplight for a long instant – and Cinderella, startled by the dazzle, reared momentarily. But the bicyclist, confronted by this masked and costumed horsewoman, was far more startled. His machine went into a spin, mounted the ditch, and ended in the bushes; the rider, leaving it there, running quickly down the road away from this ghostly vision.

The girls continued. By one o'clock they had arrived by the dark line of chestnut trees which bordered the cricket ground below Castleton Hall. Here, they tethered the horses to a fence, skirted the field, and soon mounted the steps into the pleasure gardens.

The house, unlit and silent, was just a vague silhouette in the faint moonlight, an eerie castle now, as high clouds scudded across the silver moon.

Tiptoeing over the lawn and round to the side of the house, they came to the yew hedge and the two library windows, some five feet above the gravel path. Hetty had brought a small electric torch and a thin-bladed kitchen knife. Helped up on to the sill and supported there by Léonie, she pushed the knife up in the minute gap between the two sashes, making contact with the sliding brass catch. Then she moved the blade gently, and the catch sprang back, suddenly, with a sharp noise.

They stayed as they were, petrified – Hetty poised dangerously on the sill, Léonie struggling under her weight – for what seemed like minutes on end, listening to the soft wind in the yew hedge behind them. But nothing else stirred.

Hetty, cheek pressed against the glass, began very gradually to bring pressure on the sash. After a minute it slid up easily. Once inside the room, pushing the curtains aside so that the space was faintly lit, they found the key in the drawer, pulled the other curtain aside and opened the walk-in safe. Hetty undid the first of the big leather jewel boxes and peered inside.

It was filled with neatly-packed sticks of barley sugar.

And so were all the other jewel and deed and cutlery boxes, as Hetty opened them, one after the other, in frustrated disbelief: packed with sweets of every kind, an Aladdin's cave of sugary delights – nougat, marzipan, toffee, fruit bonbons, Swiss chocolates, bullseyes, mint humbugs, Turkish delight, and whole wooden cases, like ammunition boxes, bought in bulk and stacked on the lower shelves, of 'Army and Navy Stores Best Liqueur Chocolate Selection'.

Hetty, her face distraught in the torchlight, could have cried. Léonie could barely restrain her muffled laughter.

9

'WHY DON'T WE just drop it?' Léonie said, annoyed now at Hetty's insistence. 'We weren't caught – put everything back in place in the library – but we *will* be, if we go on with it.'

'Coward!' Hetty spat at her, in her most vindictive mood. 'Where's all your "Fortune favours the brave" now?'

'It's not brave – when you're just stealing things.'

'Wasn't for us! That poor woman, remember? – up in the mountains, coughing blood.'

'Oh, Hetty, be honest. Pretending we're Robin Hood or someone – and we're not. We did it just for fun . . .'

'But it was *such* fun!' Hetty turned suddenly, almost pleading now, making a last effort to take Léonie with her, persuade her to continue with these wild adventures.

But Léonie, older and wiser, and exposing this part of her temperament almost for the first time with Hetty, was not to be dissuaded. 'Yes,' she sighed. 'It was such fun. But the trouble is, Hetty, you're really so *serious* about it all, at heart: not finding anything there, except all those candies – you were furious!'

The girls, one morning a few days later in Hetty's bedroom, with a fresh selection of men's clothes and costumes laid out everywhere, considering another foray, were arguing.

'But of *course* I'm serious,' Hetty fumed. 'All those poor people –'

'Hetty, that's nonsense! It's just theft. And we have money now anyhow, with those dollars Papa has just sent me. We can spend some of that on the cottagers – and there's plenty of food and things here in the house to give them. But if we go on with this burglary thing we'll just be caught and end up in jail, like your mama, and that'll ruin *everything* for us here, don't you see?'

'Perhaps . . .' Hetty was still not at all convinced. Though what really annoyed her was her failure to persuade – to dominate – Léonie in the matter.

'And besides,' Léonie went on, sensing this very factor in Hetty's intransigence and trying to placate her. 'There's plenty of other *ordinary* forbidden things to do – where it won't matter if we're caught.'

Léonie tried to join the mundane and the illicit as a working proposition for them. But Hetty saw the contradiction at once. 'Léa, there can't be real fun, unless the things are *extra*ordinary and one *might* be sent to jail for them! That's the whole point –'

'That's just childish. There's lots of other things . . .' But she wasn't sure now what these might be, fingering one of Uncle Henry's linen tropical suits by her chair abstractedly.

'*What* is there?' Hetty rounded on her. 'What can we do? We can't go out anywhere, see people, no social life at all.'

'New people then – new things!' Léonie, seeing how she must make amends in some way for her apparent loss of nerve by offering some fresh diversion, suddenly stood up and taking the tropical linen jacket she went over and held it against Hetty's chest. 'See! It should fit perfectly – we could go into Kilkenny, another bicycling act! – or something?' But Hetty was not to be moved. 'Oh, Hetty, you're so revengeful – relax! You're not giving yourself time to *see* things.'

'Revengeful? Just I hate all these prissy neighbours –'

'Yes, but who *cares* about them? Just let them be. We don't have to fight them, enough wars on now as it is.'

'Perhaps.' Hetty was sullen, still unconvinced, moving away now, walking up and down the bedroom through the shafts of morning sunlight, a caged tiger.

'You're so *restless*, Hetty.'

Léonie was at a loss. But she somehow sensed the real reason for Hetty's restlessness: it was a frustration, not for theft, but of desire. And she sensed, too, how for every moment's inaction in this sun-filled room, the greater the risk was of her losing Hetty, losing her trust, her love.

So, suddenly deciding on something, she picked up the linen tropical suit, took it over to Hetty's bed, and started to undress, climbing out of her long skirt, taking her blouse off, then getting into the new clothes, the jacket and trousers. Hetty, sulking over the other side of the room, fiddling with the snow-dome, surreptitiously glanced over at her friend. But for Léonie, smaller than Hetty, the clothes fitted very much less well. She stood in front of the mirror then, flapping her hands, the jacket cuffs down by her fingers, like a clown.

'You're a fright,' Hetty told her at last, smiling unwillingly.

'Yes.'

'Here, let me try them on.'

Hetty had been tempted, just as Léonie had intended. Léonie undressed again, as Hetty did the same, putting on the linen suit instead. It fitted her very well.

'See, I told you!' Léonie said, standing behind Hetty as she faced the long mirror. 'Now try the shirt and smart striped tie on,' she said, going back to the bed for these additions, before turning again. 'Do it properly! You'll have to take off your vest . . .'

Hetty, encouraged in this charade, half happy again with a tingling feeling of excitement in her stomach, took off the jacket, crossing her arms over then, about to pull off her vest, where it was stuck down into the trousers.

Léonie was behind her once more with the shirt. 'Here – let me.' She undid the belt then, and the trousers fell to the floor about Hetty's bare ankles. Then Léonie pulled her vest up and off from behind, so that Hetty stood there now, her small pointed breasts bare in the sunlight, just in her knickers, with Léonie, only slightly more covered, holding the man's shirt, looking over her shoulder, both facing the mirror.

Léonie smiled into the glass, unbuttoning the shirt meanwhile. Hetty stretched her arms out and back and Léonie pulled the first sleeve on, then the second and Hetty brought her arms to the front then, while Léonie, encircling her chest, did the buttons up again at the front.

But as she did so, starting at the collar, and moving down, her hands, in their fiddle, touched Hetty's breast for an instant. There was a moment's pause, as if this touch might have been a mere accident.

But it wasn't. And there could be no doubt then, a sudden electric charge coursed through them both, a surge of long dammed physical emotion, as Léonie, decisive now and turning Hetty towards her, quickly undid all her handiwork with the man's shirt, taking it off, and embracing her then as they stood by the mirror, kissing her – cheek, chin, neck, breasts.

'Hetty, Hetty – dearest Hetty . . .'

Hetty, giving rein then to that dominant, possessive instinct she had first felt for Léonie weeks before, and soon frustrated by the immobility enforced on them by standing glued together, became almost violent in her attentions, clawing at Léonie desperately, so that Léonie, pulling apart, took her by the hand, over to the big canopied double bed and they lay on the soft eiderdown then, in the sunlight, resuming their love.

'Oh, I so want to hold you close – and yet look at you and *see* you!' Hetty said, shaking her head in wonder.

'Yes!' Léonie gasped now. 'I too – I do, too – just that. Oh, why so long, so long! – to love you like this? –'

'We didn't know –'

'We did! – we must have done!'

Léonie put her hand to Hetty's waist, searching out the buttons on the knickers there, undoing them, then slipping her fingers between the lace and the hip bone, running a finger down her groin, touching her at last in the centre, where Hetty felt her hand like a warm knife moving gently between her legs – moving imperceptibly, gradually.

'Goodness – oh goodness! . . .' Hetty bit her lip, swaying her hips to and fro in the pleasure of Léonie's touch, her own fingers, in just the same way, searching out and finding just the same places in her lover's body.

But then, frustrated again, Hetty almost shouted, 'Oh these wretched bits and pieces, Léa!' And she grappled with the buttons at Léonie's waist – until, almost tearing the fabric away, they ridded themselves of these final flimsy vestiges between them and returned to each other, holding each other, all over, length to length, top to toe, in repeated rising paroxysms – an unbelievable happiness and excitement soon overcoming them.

All their frustrations were over now. They no longer had to hide their need both freely to love or possess each other. This they could do by turns now, see-saw fashion, returning to a balance in the breathless pauses.

If Léonie had taken the initial steps, they seduced each other then, so willingly and well, in scorching fires of rising excitement, learning as they went along, tutored by their nature, finding their roles by sixth sense; Hetty dominant, Léonie pliant, then *vice versa*, as they embarked that morning – only at the beginning then – of a pleasure they already sensed could end only in something utterly sweet and tempestuous.

So, revelling in the ecstasy, they egged each other on until, goaded beyond endurance, Léonie was first to give in – suddenly arching away from Hetty, becoming rigid, gulping air rapidly, then holding her breath for long seconds, before gasping, stretching, twisting herself violently, eyes tight shut as if in pain – when suddenly, crying out, a feeling of incredible joy burst everywhere through her body, which had no weight now, where she was rising, falling, shuddering in this great flood of fire, suspended in some dark, star-shooting ether.

Falling back, and burying her head in Hetty's breasts, she could say nothing, so drained was she, only convulse in sobs, where Hetty felt Léonie's tears then, as she gradually calmed beside her, moist drops tickling her stomach.

And later, in the same great calm they both shared then, they were equally happy, yet unbelieving somehow, frightened almost, in realising how they had just now so confirmed their love, yet at the same time had altered it, deepened it, out of all recognition.

Here, certainly, Hetty thought, was no ordinary excitement – something miles beyond mere fun. Was it then wicked? No, such love could not be that. Yet she sensed nonetheless it was something they should not be caught at. There was a contradiction here which she didn't quite understand.

Robert, down for the summer holidays with his friend Bertie, looked at the girls over the dining room table at luncheon. 'Mean to say you don't *know* about our great push to the Somme?' he asked Hetty in astonishment. 'Started just this month and we took Delville Wood just last week –'

'Oh, Robert, you are such a bore! We don't read the paper down here – much better things to do.'

Robert, who at St Columba's had a map of the Western front, with variously-coloured flag pins, attached under his desk lid, where he plotted the course of the war, was dismissive. 'Well you *should* take an interest in it then. It'll be all our bad luck – yours too – if we lose!'

'Well, we *don't* take an interest.' She looked at Léonie for confirmation. But it was not forthcoming. 'Anyway,' she went on, 'you can talk to Major Ashley about it all, next time he comes, till you're blue in the face.'

'Yes, you've taken up fencing . . .' Robert was surprised, almost admiring now.

'And we're splendid at it. But that won't win the war for us, will it?'

Léonie finally spoke. 'Perhaps we *should* take a bit more interest in it all, Hetty. At least, I should, with Mama and Papa in Paris, almost in the middle of it.' She looked at Robert sympathetically. 'Tell us what's happening.'

'Well, Pozières is one of the next main objectives – show you on the map after lunch!' He turned to Léonie enthusiastically, as a tiny frisson of division came between the two girls.

'What do you think?' Robert asked Bertie that afternoon; they were out in their waders, upstream from the boathouse, fishing for salmon.

'Of what?' Bertie, quite motionless, had his eye on a deep black pool, where his dry fly lay, on the far side of the river.

'Of the girls.'

'Hadn't really thought.' Bertie adjusted his spectacles. '*Must* be a fish there.' The heat was just beginning to die above the river. Soon the fish would surely start to rise. 'Try a wet fly, do you think?' Bertie enquired.

'No, I meant – just wondered what you made of them both.'

'Not very well educated,' Bertie said laconically. He was a youth of few words.

'They're extraordinary, though, in other ways – all that fencing they do, yesterday with the Major.'

'Oh, some girls do things like that nowadays – all to do with the suffragette movement,' he said dismissively.

'Might take up the foils myself . . .' Robert, pretending indifference in the matter, tested his friend's reaction.

'Oh, I shouldn't – look bad, just pandering to them.'

'Yes, perhaps. They are strange though.'

'But you've known Hetty for years, haven't you? – practically your sister.'

'Yes. But I don't really know her.'

'Told you – they're young suffragettes. Very common now. Lot of nonsense.'

Just then the girls themselves came into sight, emerging on the river bank from the steep fall of trees, making for the boathouse downstream, with towels and bathing costumes.

Léonie stopped and waved. 'We're swimming! Coming too?'

'Do wish she wouldn't shout like that,' Bertie muttered. 'Frighten the fish.'

But Robert, rather eager to see the girls bathe, moved slowly downstream as he fished during the next ten minutes, so that finally he was within fifty yards of them as Léonie swam off the wooden jetty, splashing about in the water in her long black woollen costume, almost down to the knees, sticking to the skin in a wet, exciting way.

Léonie waved again. But Hetty, sitting on the jetty, took no notice – which upset him briefly, a tinge of hurt mixed with desire, as he watched her legs in the water. Yes, he thought, she really looked very fine, black moist curls glistening in the sunlight – and really so sporting: fencing – and swimming like that in the river, where no other girls would ever dare! One only swam in the sea.

But she ignored him, untouchable, unobtainable, that was the problem he could not admit to anyone – hardly even to himself – that he loved her. She dived into the stream then, disappearing, and Robert, rather ashamed of prying, moved back upstream.

The girls, frolicking underwater, could see each other in the clear flow above a patch of silvery stones. Swirling and twining about, bodies glancing, hands touching, they seemed to dance together.

Hetty, watching Léonie – the more expert swimmer – twist and dive so sinuously, noticed how all her usual grace and elasticity was wonderfully released and exaggerated now as she somersaulted in this free-floating element: the sharply-narrowing waist, arching back, long kicking legs, the tight bodice of the costume flattening, sweeping over, her firm breasts.

And then, jealous of Léonie's graceful athleticism – and just for the rebellious excitement of it, wanting to taunt and compete with her – Hetty, most of her body still underwater, started to pull her bathing costume off, tugging at the shoulders, grabbing the material away as she trod water, before finally kicking herself out of the rest of it, laughing at her friend . . . then suddenly diving away, a naked Ondine, into the silvery depths.

Léonie saw her in a new light then, as Hetty swooped and fell, trailing bubbles, in these green shallows – her body almost ethereal, so volatile and fancy free that it could not be described, possessed indeed, in any earth-bound manner. And she was jealous of the stream which so confidently embraced Hetty, but divided them, kept them in worlds apart. She longed for Hetty then.

Yes, how much she *valued* every twist and turn in this sensuous body, the lovely ease Hetty displayed, embracing this watery element even more fluently than Léonie herself had been caressed by her in the last weeks. Quite simply, Léonie felt, she adored her. She opened her lips, mouthing the words, 'Je t'aime!' But only clouds of bubbles rose – as both of them, breathless, shot to the surface before returning to the crystal-green shadow-world beneath.

And it was then that Hetty, playing some game, or genuinely caught in the current, her hair trailing out like river weed behind her, began to drift down-stream, slipping away from Léonie, her body motionless now as the current took her.

Léonie felt a nightmare surge of horror cutting her to the heart: Hetty was leaving her, a water sprite, her time among mortals over, disappearing now, forever, back to some cavernous kingdom in the sea . . .

'Come back!' Léonie clawed after her, trying to reach out and pull her back. Out of breath, she rose to the surface, only to see Hetty rocket into the air a few seconds later, smiling broadly.

'You mustn't do that!' Léonie bellowed at her. 'You frightened me – you really did! Thought you were drowning.'

'Oh, Léa, I never meant to –'

'But you did – and you mustn't!' She swam over to her. 'Hetty!' She took her face in her hands. 'You mustn't *ever* leave me like that!'

Later, with her costume restored, sitting on the jetty, and seeing Léonie glance at the boys upstream, Hetty said acidly, 'You do rather go out of your way with Robert.' She had noticed Léonie's vague attentions to him before and was more than a little jealous.

'Oh, Hetty, it's just because you're so . . . well, cold to him, ignoring him.'

'No, it's not – it's just that *you* like him! I can see it.'

'I do like him. Shouldn't I?' Hetty did not reply, lifting her knees right up, drying her toes, then inspecting them carefully, splaying them out. 'You think I shouldn't?'

'Oh, he's such a tease and a bore,' Hetty said at last.

'Not to me he isn't. And, with you, he only does it because he's fond of you – *I* can see that.'

'But I'm too fond of you, for that – for you to think of him,' she said in a low voice.

Léonie touched her arm then. 'Yes, and so am I – of you. But one can just *like* other people as well . . . surely? And our being so happy makes that all the easier, doesn't it?'

'No, I like you *so* much,' Hetty said softly. 'I de-de-don't like you liking other people.' She stammered now, something she had almost entirely ceased to do with Léonie.

'Yes, but I like . . . I love you, Hetty,' Léonie reassured her.

'What do you *really* like in me – and hate?' Hetty took Léonie by surprise with her vehemence, as if her life depended on the answer.

'I don't know – I like everything.' Léonie avoided the second part of the question.

'But *what* – and why?'

'Well, your courage, I think –'

'But you think that just foolhardiness.'

'Sometimes. But, when you're sensible with it, it's marvellous –'

'You can't be sensible *and* courageous!'

'You can! But . . .'

'But what?'

'Depends what it is. Some things aren't worth doing at all. Yet you push and shove and insist on them.'

'I want to be *different* people all the time,' Hetty was more pensive now. 'That's why I push and shove at things.'

'Why not just be *yourself*?'

'But who is that?'

'It's you, you ninny! And, when you're that, you're wonderful. It's just . . .'

'Go on!'

'When you're all those other people – sometimes it worries me. That I don't know you somehow.'

'And that's what you hate in me . . .'

'No, don't hate it. Just don't quite understand – why you want to be someone else. That restlessness, when you have so much in *yourself.*'

The warmth was fading, with hints of twilight.

'Yes, you're so calm,' Hetty said admiringly. 'But what am I? *Who* am I?' she asked then, looking over the river.

'Who or whose? . . . You are mine and I am yours!' Léonie said lightly, finding that her reply had turned into a little couplet. She smiled at her success, looking at Hetty, who had pulled a splinter from the wooden jetty, throwing it out and watching it twirl away in the stream.

> '"And when I die in the long green grass
> Death will be but a pause.
> For the love that I have is all that I have,
> Is yours and yours and yours."

I like that poem,' Hetty added, much brighter now. 'Almost my favourite.'

They left the jetty then, going inside the boathouse to change. 'Shall we watch them fish?' Hetty asked, in possession of a real identity for the moment, apparently at ease in the idea that, with their own secure love, they could share their affection – with the two boys, with anyone.

'Yes, let's!' And Léonie kissed her then as they dressed, a tinge of passion rising with the gesture. But she had to repress it, she did not want to upset the balance of calm reason which she felt she had brought to Hetty in the previous minutes.

Léonie sensed then, so clearly, how she had the gift, the knack, the spirit – something, whatever it was – to change this girl's life: she could make her happy. And yet this wisdom brought with it another quite opposite and sad intuition: that she might only be able to share this content with one part of Hetty, whereas there were so many other parts to her, which she could not help her in – roles which this wayward, seemingly orphaned girl had not yet lived.

Living with her, loving her, Léonie felt, was so precious because what thrilled her most in Hetty was what most eluded her: her mystery, lack of identity, what she was not, the person she could become, when she might lose her. And these were things she could not tell her, for it was ridiculous – so to cross bridges before one came to them.

Léonie, in this love, had found herself wonderfully released – in body, but just as much in spirit. She felt a lightness in her life now – a glorious spreading fertility, a quickening sense of God-like certainty and confidence: she could do, she could create, anything. And she wanted these feelings, which Hetty alone provoked, to spread and grow, find anchors in the future. Yet she feared loss in that future. She wanted, in short, to guarantee Hetty's life with her forever. That was the problem.

Léonie, in the light of the four candles they held, could see the quick shadows of the bats as they dipped and swerved above them in the moist dark air of the caves. She bowed her head, put her free hand up, alarmed at the idea that these animals might suddenly tangle in her hair.

'Here! – we're up here!' Hetty's voice echoed deeply. Léonie with Bertie, some way behind the others, could only just see the wavering candle flame ahead of them, at the top of a rock slope, where Robert and Hetty had stopped at the beginning end of one of the long cave galleries.

Catching up with them, all four standing together with their flickering candles, they found themselves confronted by a solid wall of shiny limestone, a dead end. But Hetty, with her electric torch, illuminated a column of great boulders above and to their right, with a vague opening at the top, forming an almost sheer ascent into another hidden gallery.

'Oh, let's not bother,' Léonie said, realising this was the worst thing to say as Hetty immediately started to clamber up the narrow aperture above them.

They had made an expedition, with a picnic, in the trap, north of Kilkenny town, to the caves of Dunmore – a great yawning entrance in a field a mile from the main road, which led steeply downwards, through ferns and bushes, into the depths of a flowerless earth, opening out then into a series of limestone galleries, most of which they had already explored, slipping about on the wet boulders, until they had discovered this last obstacle at the end of a chilly cavern.

Hetty having started the climb, the others were forced to follow. 'Come on!' she shouted back at them. 'Bound to be something fantastic! . . .' They all, with varying degrees of effort, managed to climb and pull each other up through the narrowing cone of rock.

At the top they found themselves on a narrow, sandy, pebble-strewn path. It had once been the watercourse of an underground stream, and led forward into the darkness, towards an existing stream, which they could hear rushing in the distance.

They moved up the old water-bed. After twenty yards or so they suddenly felt a breath, it seemed, of damp air, a feeling of space about them. Holding their candles up, they saw they had come into a great nave, a domed, yellowing roof just visible above them.

They stood on a lip of rock. The extraordinary vision lay below and all about them. They were standing on the edge of a saucer-shaped amphitheatre, where stalactites and stalagmites, meeting together over aeons, had formed wonderfully ribbed and coloured pillars, ochre and smoked ivory, frozen cascades which glimmered in the candlelight – pillars as in a cathedral, which ran from floor to roof way above them. The stream they had heard was just visible now, flowing swiftly beyond the pillars, before disappearing into a stygian hole in the furthest rock.

Even Bertie, removing his spectacles, was impressed, as they stood there in the icy air.

'No bats here, no fungus, nothing!' Robert said, awed by the surroundings. 'End of the system – sort of end of the world!'

'No, it's not,' Hetty said. 'Look over there! – there's a passage, a hole, beyond that pillar!' She skidded down the saucer slope to the floor of the cathedral. Then, torch in hand, she moved between two of the pillars, coming to the edge of the narrow, underground stream, close to where it gurgled away into a hole in the rock wall.

'No, Hetty, don't be such a fool!' Léonie urgently called after her, starting to follow, herself slipping down from the rim.

'It's perfectly all right – easy!' Hetty called back.

'No, don't you go – I'll go,' Robert said to Léonie. And he slid down the slope, moving between the pillars, his candle visible before the flame disappeared and Léonie heard a splash.

'Hetty!' she roared. 'Robert – are you all right?'

'Yes, we're fine!' She heard Hetty's voice. 'Just lighting the candle again.' They must have turned some corner now, for no further light could be seen. 'Yes!' They heard Hetty's voice again, but fainter now. 'There's *another* sort of cave here, a drop in the floor, going straight down. Robert! Bring your light here and we can see –'

Suddenly her voice stopped and Léonie heard a cracking, a tumbling noise, of rocks falling, then silence, but for the rushing noise of the stream in the darkness. She started to clamber down the slope. But Bertie held her back. 'No, *don't* hold me!' she yelled at him. 'We must go and see . . .'

They slid down together then, crossing through the pillars, jumping the stream and rounding a corner in the rock face, before they came to a sudden drop in the floor of the narrow cavern beyond. There had indeed been a hole there. But now the declivity was filled with a debris of fallen rock which had almost entirely blocked up the descent. Léonie shouted down. 'Are you all right? – Hetty, Robert!'

But there was no reply.

Hetty's forehead throbbed as she vaguely regained consciousness. Everything was quite dark in her mind. But she was under water, she knew that – naked in the cold black watery depths, swimming about, trying to escape something, with Léonie near her, an equally shadowy figure, twisting and twining beside her. But Léonie was drifting, slipping away from her in the dense flow.

She reached out her hands, tried to follow her, but found herself rooted to the spot. 'Oh, Léonie, Léa! Come back, come back,' she seemed to yell out.

Robert in the pitch darkness next to her – bruised but otherwise uninjured – felt Hetty's cold fingers touch his face. And Hetty, nearer consciousness now, breathed a sigh of relief. 'Oh, Léa! You're there. For an awful moment you were going away, leaving me . . . Please, don't ever go away like that. Oh, Léa, I do so love you –'

'It's me, Robert, not Léonie.' She heard the abrupt male voice.

'Robert?' She could not disguise her disappointment, stretching up, before falling back with a gasp of pain. 'Oh, my side, my hip, I think . . .'

'It's all right – don't move.'

'What happened?'

'We fell – *you* fell. I'm looking for the light.' Robert moved away from her in the darkness, scrabbling about on his hands and knees, looking for the two candles or the torch. Then he realised: of course, he had a box of safety matches in his coat pocket.

He lit one and had a first glimpse of their precarious position. They were perched on a sloping rock floor which, had they fallen a yard or so further, would have sent them tumbling into some bottomless abyss. He lit a second match, turning back then, holding it up to a ragged slope of rock, seeing how a collection of these small boulders, some ten or twelve feet above them, had stuck in the mouth of the drop, almost completely blocking it. But there was no sign of the candles or the torch. And he had only six matches left.

'Well?' Hetty called out.

'Nothing yet. But I've lots of matches. We'll find them.'

But he did not. He lit match after match, until there was only one left. Returning to Hetty he tried to keep the desperation out of his voice. 'No luck,' he said.

'Oh, Robert, they *must* be somewhere. Light another match.'

'I daren't – I've only one left.'

Hetty groaned. Then she twisted in pain. 'Ouch!' Then, even more suddenly, she moved again. 'Robert!' she shouted. 'It's the candle! – I think. But I can't get at it.'

'You idiot!' he told her, running his hands under her in the darkness, fumbling through her skirt, until he felt the candle. His fingers trembled in the deep damp chill, and for agonising seconds, on this last match, the wick would not take the flame and they thought they were doomed. But at the last moment the candle brightened and very carefully he held it aloft.

The vision was incredible. They had plummeted down into a narrow chamber, some twenty feet high. The sloping floor suddenly fell away a few yards from them, to the pellucid waters of a small pool, how deep they could not tell, though the water, set in a whitish limestone basin, was crystal-clear and tinged with a perfect blue.

Then, as he moved the candle about him, they saw the walls of the chamber. They glittered with every sort of colour and icy fire, decorated as they were with hanging calcite formations – small stalactites, frozen rivulets and excrescences. Most were crystalline, translucent, flashing like diamond pendants; some were a deep gleaming ruby, a few pale blue. And it was as if the flame was circling the interior of some vast jewel box.

'Crystal!' Hetty gasped. 'A crystal cave!'

Robert turned to her with the candle. 'Oh dear – you're cut. And cold.' He took off his coat, wrapping it round her shoulders. Then, with his handkerchief, he mopped her brow where there was a gash just above the hair-line.

'It's nothing. It's my hip that hurts.'

'May be broken – don't move. They'll have gone to get help. Just lie back and I'll see if I can find the other candle.'

'Oh, Robert, what an idiotic thing to do – I do feel such an ass!' she called after him, as he moved about the chamber.

'Doesn't matter. We're alive anyway,' he said a little sourly.

'I thought you were Léonie – so lucky it was you!' She tried to placate him for her earlier error.

'Yes, so you did,' he told her coldly.

'I'm sorry. So glad it was you! Léa would have *hated* it down here!'

'No doubt.' He held the candle up above her head. 'No bats anyway.' Then, some yards behind where Hetty lay, something caught his eye and his expression changed.

Hetty looked up at him. 'What is it?'

'Nothing. Just some . . . can't quite make it out.' He leant forward with the candle and Hetty twisted round.

'Oh, God!' she screamed.

Behind her, in the frail light, she saw the skulls, the ribs and other bones – a collection, strewn about, of hideously-broken skeletons.

'Oh, Robert!' She clutched up at him suddenly, violently, so that he felt her hot breath on his cheeks. 'They're *dead*!'

'Course they're dead, idiot. It's perfectly all right.'

She yelped at him then, almost in his arms, pinching him violently in her alarm. 'But that's what's so *frightening*, you ass!'

'Only the bones of some . . . ancient people,' he told her reassuringly, knowledge-ably. 'Celts probably – escaping the Vikings when they raided Ireland in the fifth century. They often hid in caves then.'

'Oh, you do find just the right time for a history lesson,' she told him brusquely, regaining some of her attack.

'Well, you were frightened, so I explained. Nothing strange – just old bones.'

'Not strange to you, with all your history books. But *I* don't know all these things.' She shivered, refusing to turn round as he moved to inspect one of the skulls.

'See, it's been pierced – a hole in the cranium,' he told her prosaically. 'Some heavy implement – probably a massacre nearby and they buried them here.'

'Don't *want* to know. How long will they be?'

'As long as it takes to get some men – ropes and picks and things. An hour perhaps.'

He returned, setting the candle carefully down between them. There were still several inches left to it. 'Should last out.' He looked at her quizzically through the flame. 'But let's try and get your head up and off the cold stone.' He moved away again, finding a small boulder and propping her head up against it.

'But it's my *legs*,' she moaned. 'They're all cold – all freezing and funny. Maybe if you rubbed them?'

'Nothing to put round them, I'm afraid.' But he started to massage them then, warming them, while she tilted her head back, closing her eyes, feeling some of the circulation return.

'Thanks, that's . . . ah! that *is* better. If I'd fallen in here alone, might have been dead by now.'

'Possibly. But then running away on your own like that –'

'I *told* you already – I'm sorry I was such an idiot.' The warmth began to flow in her legs again now as he rubbed them vigorously.

'Still,' he said to her more kindly, 'you do get up to such madcap things, you and Léonie – one shouldn't be surprised.'

She sensed envy more than condemnation in his tone. 'Don't you ever get up to madcap things – at St Columba's?'

'Not much.'

'Always so serious . . .'

'I'd like not to be. But I suppose . . . I am.'

He had reached her knee and she put her hand down and touched his encouragingly. 'That's nice. And that's what's so *nice* about you, you're so reliable –'

'I don't *want* to be reliable, not all the time.' There was a touch of shame, of anger and frustration, in his voice now, as he urged his hand just above her knee, rubbing her thigh, where she let it roam – until eventually, as his hand rose, she took it and drew it to her cheek. The flesh there was ice-cold.

'Oh, Robert,' she gasped between chattering teeth. 'Come up here – no, *here*, this side away from the bad hip – come and warm me, I'm *freezing* – up here now!'

He slid up beside her then on the rock, putting his whole body along her length, pressing gently round her, circling her with an arm, protectively, and trembling himself then, but from excitement as much as cold, as she pulled him to her. 'Closer!' she said – so that their faces touched in the yellow light and he felt and smelt her breath.

'Oh, that's so close and warm, Robert!' Her voice had deepened now, soft, comforting. 'I'd have frozen – I really would! Frozen alive without you.'

'Yes, well, you won't now.'

And in their trembling embraces then – so entirely innocent and proper – they yet both felt a wonderfully new, illicit and transforming thrill. He had the illusion of loving her, and of being loved in return – while she, for the first time and equally surprised and happy in the event, had the illusion of being possessed by a man. They both cherished their illusions, but could not speak of them.

'Well, you were just so lucky – again,' Léonie told her, as she pushed Hetty down the front drive in the wheelchair. Hetty's hip and thigh bone had been badly bruised, and her ankle, in plaster now, chipped and twisted, nearly broken. She could not walk. She was the invalid now.

'If it hadn't been for Robert . . .' Hetty said, savouring a particular memory of him.

'Yes, so you keep saying.' It was Léonie's turn to feel jealousy.

'Well, he *was* very nice. And, without him, I'd . . . well, I might have died!'

'Yes, I know –'

'You should be thankful to him!'

'I am – I am thankful.'

'You accused me of ignoring him – well, I didn't! Not in the caves . . .' she added mischievously. But Léonie, though curious as to what exactly she meant by this last remark, was not to be baited. Hetty wanted some small revenge. And she accepted that. It was part of their relationship, which was so close that they had begun to prey on each other's absences, on each other's thoughts.

It was, perhaps, too close – and Léonie knew she must resist the temptation to delve and pry. And, besides, Hetty's small revenges were so much an expected part of her, and her disturbed background, Léonie thought: Hetty, because of all the old upsets in her life, always making unreasonable demands or initiations – rushing away in the cave like that; Hetty, always thrusting, pushing, shoving, going over the limit in harebrained schemes. Well, she could not do that for a week or two. Hetty would be more or less immobile. Léonie had her to herself. She could soothe all her hurts, spiritual and physical.

'No, I'm sorry – and I *am* thankful to Robert, *very*. And to you, for being back.' She bent down then and kissed her quickly, on her warm hair, warm and sweet-smelling in the August morning sun.

Robert, with Bertie, in Henry's old work rooms at the top of the house, had noticed the two girls from the window going down the drive. And now, with a pair of Henry's ancient field glasses, he focused on the couple, seeing Léonie bend down, muffling her head in Hetty's hair.

'A crystal cave . . .' Bertie said. 'Love to have seen it!' He was studying a treatise on mineralogy, from a collection of natural history books on a shelf nearby. 'What *sort* of rocks, exactly, though? Deep ruby, you say?'

'Yes.' Robert was lost, concentrating on his view of the girls.

'And *translucent* stalactites?'

'Sort of.' Robert turned away from his upsetting vision of Hetty and Léonie. 'I *can't* understand it,' he said to himself, perplexed.

'No, nor can I – when all the other stalactites and stalagmites were just a whitish yellow in the upper galleries.'

'No – I meant . . .' Robert pulled himself together. 'Yes, of course. Well, maybe that book will tell us.'

Half-way down the front drive the postman on his bicycle came towards the girls. He doffed his cap when he neared them and dismounted. Hetty said, 'I'll take the post,' and the man rode away. Hetty shuffled through the letters. There was one for her, a cheap manila envelope, marked 'On His Majesty's Service'. She tore it open. The single sheet of paper, closely written on both sides, was headed 'Aylesbury Prison'. It was from her mother.

August 16th, 1916.

My dearest Henrietta,

At last I have gained the privilege of writing a letter – and you shall be the first, tho' I have always been a pretty rotten correspondent and there is at once too much and too little to say. But what I *really* wanted to say was to renew and emphasise what I tried to tell you, and told Léonie, that last day in the College of Surgeons: I do so ask your forgiveness for my many years' neglect of you.

Something snapped in me, changed me completely that week in Dublin (seeing how *really* brave the others were, the wounded and dying there) and made me realise how little life was worth unless one took account of the *unseen* world, as well as the world of liberty, action and so on. And in this way I realised how I had never properly 'seen' you, seeing only my republican vision all these years, and its end in Dublin that week. Tho' I know it cannot actually *be* the end of that, and others will . . .'

Hetty couldn't read the next two lines which had been crossed out, censored.

. . . so, anyway, I want you to know that you are seen now, for the full and fine person you are, as well as in all your trials and tribulations, many of them brought upon you by me, in my selfishness. You will not easily forgive. But perhaps you will come to understand my *acts* these last years – and more importantly my, yes, *spiritual* transformation, if that's not too pretentious a word, for I have so changed, in the light of all those Dublin events – feel a repose in my life that I never felt before, an end of bitterness, conflict with myself and others, with the memory of them . . . We may not have won yet in Ireland – but *I* have won something – different, but quite as precious – a tranquillity and acceptance, where all I must do now is to prosper it – to this end with Father Lawrence, one of the prison chaplains here, with whom I am taking instruction in the Roman Catholic faith, something I never thought to come to, but which now, so obviously, is the only real answer for me . . .

There was a little more, in a lighter vein: remarks on the hollyhocks in the prison garden and the fact that she had seen a Zeppelin flying over the walled exercise yard the previous day. The letter ended:

Dearest Henrietta, I miss you and everyone – everything – at Summer Hill, of course: so much loved a house. But that apart, and my feelings of sadness over you, I am happy and content. I am patient, now that I know, now that I *believe* everything will happen for the best. Give messages to everyone at home, most particularly remembering me to Elly.
Your loving Mama.

Hetty handed the letter to Léonie, saying curtly, 'She has taken to her dotage – a spiritual dotage!'

Léonie, reading the letter quickly, was equally abrupt, but to quite another end. 'Oh, that's too hard, Hetty. She's not a fool. She surely means it all –'

'More's the pity! It's pathetic – a Roman Catholic! – when she's Jewish. That's their law, you know it very well yourself – they take the faith from the mother's side.'

'Only half-Jewish, though.'

'Yes! – and the other half is *Protestant*!'

'What does all that matter – if she finds comfort in it?'

'It's *betraying* again,' Hetty said roughly, bunching her fingers, just as her mother did when angered, on the arms of the wheelchair.

'Again?'

'As she did before, always has done, with me and my Papa – when I'm sure he wasn't!'

'Oh, so you've said to me often enough.' The rest of the post had spilled from Hetty's lap and Léonie came round, bending down to retrieve it, before confronting Hetty. 'So you always say – about your Papa – but there's no proof. And *why?*'

'No proof! – there would be if there were photographs of him. But there aren't any! She de-de-destroyed all of them, because they would have shown I was *nothing* like him!'

'Oh, Hetty – she probably didn't keep them because he was a bad memory! *You* told me all about that – Mr Fraser, how nasty he was. But you can't really believe your Mama . . . carried on with *other* men?'

'She may have done. Aunt Emily hinted . . .'

'So you've said. But you *know* how she always exaggerates and makes a drama of everything?'

'I feel it,' Hetty insisted. 'He *couldn't* have been my real pe-pe-Papa,' she said, her voice rising and stuttering with emotion. 'I remember him so well on the island. So nasty and *cruel*!' Tears began to glaze her eyes.

'Well, some fathers *are* just that.' Léonie, kneeling in front of the chair now, took Hetty's hands, gently easing their shaking grip from the arm, cradling them in her own. 'Oh, Hetty, it's common, I'm afraid – bad Papas!' she added mock-mournfully, trying to lighten the convulsing sadness that had come over her friend. 'And I'm just so lucky with mine. But just because Mr Fraser was bad – doesn't mean *you* are bad. Don't you see?'

Hetty did not see. Though it was in just this idea of something rotten behind her, of a flawed inheritance, Léonie sensed, that Hetty's real problem lay.

'But why did Mama *marry* such a bad man?'

Léonie had no ready answer here and admitted it. 'I don't know. But it happens, often enough.'

'But *why?* – when she was so beautiful, gifted. Everyone – Aunt Emily, Dermot, Mortimer – they all say so!'

'There's no real explaining, is there? How can we? We weren't there at the time. Your Papa may have *turned* bad, people do. Just as they can turn good, as your Mama has. Oh, Hetty . . .' Léonie leant forward, embracing her. 'You must forgive her.'

Hetty, immobile against Léonie, looked coldly over her shoulder. 'I will forgive her,' she said, softly but icily, 'when she tells me who my real fe-fe-father is.'

And Léonie, feeling this deep rage in Hetty, realised it was something she could never properly calm in her. Only an answer to her question could do that– if the question was real at all. Or was it, Léonie wondered, just part of the dialogue in another long-cherished role, among so many, which Hetty had taken on over the years since she had known her, roles to which all this Cordiner family seemed so partial and performed so adeptly: her grandfather playing Icarus with his disastrous flying machine, her mother swapping between violent revolutionary and saint, Aunt Emily with her endlessly-imagined pictorial fantasies, her fairy tales saturating the house. And now Hetty, trying to vie with them, or just reflecting this dramatic blood, by giving herself the role of Cinderella – offspring of some romantic, mysterious *alliance*, when in fact she was just the product of an unfortunate marriage.

Léonie had no answers herself here, other than that she saw now, with great clarity, how these factors, real or imagined, were the dangerously shifting bedrock of Hetty's life. She would calm, she would try to stabilise, these subterranean eruptions as best she could.

To this end, during Hetty's enforced immobility, Léonie organised card and paper games for her, with Aunt Emily, Robert and Bertie; or brought objects to divert her – Victorian *jeux* with which the house was filled – when Hetty was alone, sitting listlessly in the drawing room or porch: the stereoscopic cabinet with its exotic photographic views of Egypt and India, in which the Pyramids and the Taj Mahal became startlingly real as Hetty turned the handles; and the Zöetrope, the 'Wheel of Life', which Hetty had played with as a child, now brought out again with its dozens of paper scrolls, each with a succession of individual but slightly altered coloured drawings along its length which, when Hetty spun them in the metal cylinder, peering through the slits in the sides, brought the scrolls to extraordinary life, so that a clown riotously juggled balls, a dog chased a cat helter-skelter, and the fabled cow repeatedly jumped over the moon.

Robert, of course, was not slow to explain matters to her. 'It's really very simple,' he told her one afternoon in the drawing room. 'It's the principle of persistence of vision: your eye isn't quick enough to distinguish each individual drawing as they flash by through the slits. So it merges them all together and the drawings *appear* to move. Quite simple.'

'But it isn't,' Hetty told him sourly. 'It's magic!'

'Nonsense, it's just an optical fact.' He twirled the cylinder dismissively. 'Why, they use the same principle everywhere now, in the Kinematograph machine, only there the pictures are all photographed on celluloid – like in the Kinema houses in Dublin. Bertie and I saw one last term, at the Grafton – and they show them sometimes in Kilkenny, too, at the Theatre.'

'Do they? I'd love to see that! Let's go to one, shall we?'

'Yes – it's all pretty rubbishy stuff, though. But, when you're better, perhaps. Why not?'

*

But the summer was drawing to a close and, in those last days of August, before the boys went back to school, they were occupied out on the river, or paying purely domestic attentions to Hetty, still largely immobile, her bruises and sprains taking longer to heal than expected. Plans of going to a Kinematograph display in Kilkenny never materialised.

Instead, the new doctor in Thomastown, the bright young Dr Roche, came out several times a week ministering to Hetty, and seeing old Lady Cordiner, too. Hetty had told him, much earlier in the summer, of her plan that the old woman should be moved outdoors in the better weather. But he had advised against it, indeed he had tactfully insisted. 'Miss Fraser, your grandmother is quite past all that, I'm afraid – you have seen her yourself: so gone in age and with her bad heart – it would likely kill her. She should not be moved, I do assure you.' And Hetty had left it at that.

The Ashleys came, once or twice a week, for tea on the porch in the last of the warm weather. Plans were made for the resumption of their lessons in September with the Major – and Aunt Emily continued to fill her sketch books with endless images, real and imagined, of the household and the glorious summer.

Mortimer came down from Dublin, staying a long weekend, inspecting the accounts, paying bills. The farm still showed no profit. But losses had been stemmed through his economies. And the harvest that year promised well. They would be cutting and threshing the corn earlier than expected and the wartime boom in agricultural prices would make up some leeway in the accounts.

Hetty showed Elly her mother's letter – and Elly, at least, had written to her fulsomely. Hetty merely sent her a short, non-committal note. She had not shown Mortimer the letter, but he had spoken to her of her Mama in any case, tactfully, but generously.

'I shall see more of her in Aylesbury when the House resumes in October,' he had said. 'But already, you know, there is a great ground swell of support for her here in Ireland.'

'Oh, is there? I don't see the newspaper here.'

'Yes, she is much the heroine – she and de Valera, but she especially – quite taken to the hearts of people here. An extraordinary woman!'

'But she is not likely to be set free, of course . . .' Hetty had asked, fearing this but feigning concern.

'No. But she will not be imprisoned forever, indeed not for too long more at all, I feel. The situation here remains very tense. They will probably declare an amnesty for the Republican prisoners at some point soon, repatriate them all.'

'Oh,' Hetty had said dully.

'Hetty, I know your feelings about your Mama. But you cannot expect her to be away from Summer Hill indefinitely, you know.'

'No . . .'

'And you yourself – apart from the caves, it's all gone well with you and Léonie this summer: Major Ashley has told me.'

'Oh, yes indeed!'

'But soon, I feel – there will have to be other things for you. A winter down here on your own –'

'But I *won't* be on my own! There's Léa . . . and everyone. And we're *so* happy here, and the Major teaches us everything – and Léa's parents are entirely content about it all, too!'

'Yes,' Mortimer had temporised. 'I can see that. All the same –'

'Besides, Léa can't go back to Paris with all those German U-boats in the Channel.'

'Oh – so you do read the newspaper!'

'Robert does, all the time – and he told me.'

'Yes, well, we shall see.'

Then Hetty, sensing his concern and seeing how she might turn it to her advantage, suddenly said, 'But if you're worried – couldn't we use your little flat in Dublin, above your offices, for a while this autumn? Get a singing teacher for Léonie, and I could take proper lessons there. We'd be more . . . supervised in Dublin, safer even,' she added in a most convincingly innocent manner.

'Yes.' Mortimer pondered the matter. 'Yes, that's a possibility. There's my housekeeper, Mrs McCabe – comes in every morning. And Mr Watson, my chief clerk, an excellent man, in the apartment opposite –'

'Oh, let's! It'd be se-se-such a good idea!' Only her sudden unexpected stammer might have betrayed Hetty then – how her thoughts of life in Dublin were not entirely educational, and were far from being for reasons of safety. 'And besides,' she finished, 'we're so boycotted down here by everyone: we really *should* meet some new people!'

Mortimer agreed, promising to develop these plans when he returned to Dublin – and the four of them had tea on the porch after he had gone. Afterwards Robert played croquet with Léonie on the upper lawn, while Bertie, not a gamesman, entertained Hetty, over a debris of teacake, with a reading from *Middlemarch*.

'So, you may come up to Dublin?' Robert, playing laxly so that he might keep pace with the less expert Léonie, had played too carelessly – offering her a most inviting cannonade, which she duly performed, sending his ball way into the bushes on the other side of the court.

'Oh, I *am so* sorry!' she teased him. 'Yes, isn't that nice,' she went on when he returned to the game. 'Dublin – lessons for both of us and a singing teacher for me, maybe. And all the theatres!'

'We . . . perhaps we can meet up there. We have three or four Sunday exeats a term.'

'Of course – I'd like that.' She smiled affectionately at him as he lined up another shot. This time he found himself at an advantage, croqueting her, before taking a further shot which would most likely send her far into the bushes. But he desisted, leaning on his mallet, foot on the ball. He wanted to talk to Léonie about Hetty. But he knew no way of beginning. Léonie sensed his frustration and thought she knew its cause. She liked him for it as she said, 'It's really Hetty you want to see, though, isn't it?'

'No, no – you as well.' He was airy, unconcerned now, addressing his ball.

She smiled at his sudden boisterousness. 'It's her, and why not? You're fond of her – I know.'

'Well, I don't know . . .' He was quite offhand.

'Of *course* you are – you were brought up with her.'

'Ha! Very good reason *not* to be fond of people, usually!'

'Well, you are, Robert! And so you should be. I'm . . . very fond of her, too.'

'Yes,' he said, a touch warily, still fiddling with his mallet. 'Well, that's perfectly natural as well.'

'But you're unhappy about it . . .'

'Oh, no – not at all. Why should I be? Girls – often very fond of each other, so many things . . . in common.'

'Well, yes!' Léonie smiled.

'I meant, well – your being at school together in France and all that.'

'Yes. But it's difficult for you, I see that.'

'Why should it be?' He almost laughed then, striking a more confident note. 'You're not a man, after all!'

'No. But I . . . I monopolise her, perhaps, more than I should – as a man might.' She turned away then, somehow flustered, upset by this admission. 'I am sorry – I can't help it.'

'No, no,' Robert responded in a feigned couldn't-care-less voice. 'I quite understand. Very close – and why not? – surviving that awful Easter week together in Dublin and so on. Quite expected.'

'Yes,' she agreed. But the tension was still there in her voice. She turned and approached him, as he stood by the hoop rather crestfallen. In her sudden emotion – about Hetty, about him too – she put her hand briefly on his. 'I *am* sorry, Robert – especially because . . . I like you very much, too.'

He had his foot on the ball, stuck right next to Léonie's then. 'Oh,' he said dully.

There was silence, which Léonie, anxious to lighten the mood, finally interrupted. 'Well, go on then – croquet me! Got me at your mercy!'

And he did just that, with great vigour, sending her ball skimming way into the bushes again. But it made him feel no better, guilty indeed.

'Oh, you brute!' she shrieked at him, laughing.

'I'm sorry,' he told her.

And, seeing his confusion, she came up to him, softening the mood once more. 'Oh, for goodness sake, Robert – we both of us must stop being sorry all the time. What for? It'll all work out all right – promise you, you'll see! Can't but – we're *all* fond of each other. Hetty told me, in the cave, how wonderful you were, saved her life. May not show it mostly, but she really is – she likes you a lot, *really*.'

Léonie had perhaps exaggerated Hetty's affection here. But Robert brightened perceptibly, his rather gaunt features lightening in the hint of a wry smile, his upper lip curling a fraction – his thin face warming now, as if fired by her own candid, affectionate gaze.

It was more than affection that Léonie suddenly felt for him then. She could so willingly have kissed him. She wanted to.

The boys returned to school as hints of autumn crept over the landscape. The Virginia creeper above the porch had turned a dazzling orange-red. And now the leaves of the big maple, lacking sap in the first night chills, joined in this fall of the year – a lighter red, a peachy crimson.

The chestnut trees edging the demesne, in the last windless days of warmth, had been faded, drowsy, fly-blown. But now, within a week, with the first of the September winds, the colours turned and the leaves fell, lemon-yellow in the sharpening autumn light. The mornings were dew-laden, the lawns, in the first sunlight, a glittering carpet, covered in gossamers of spiders' webs. By midday, the heat still there in a bright sun, a few late butterflies emerged, flying among the poppies in the orchards beyond the house. The first fruits had ripened quickly here, early Worcester Pearmains and Victoria plums, and Léonie had wheeled Hetty up to the high land one late afternoon to sample them, parking Hetty beneath a laden apple tree.

Léonie reached up and secured a red-veined Worcester, blowing on it, polishing it on her sleeve so that it shone, before giving it to Hetty.

'So,' she said. 'Alone again!'

Hetty did not reply, leaning right back in her chair, head tilted, gazing up between the branches to the twilit blue sky beyond. 'Yes,' she said at last.

'*Fin de saison*,' Léonie said lightly, after another silence.

'Yes. I suppose we'll go to Dublin, shan't we?' Hetty kept her gaze on the sky.

'Yes, of course, why not?' Léonie, arms on hips, also looked up through the branches, wondering what had caught Hetty's attention there. Then she suddenly saw it – a thin scimitar of silvery moon above the apple tree.

'And yet . . . I don't want to leave here now, Léa, not – oh, this summer, Léa – it's not wanting it to go . . .'

'No. But there'll be others.'

'Mama'll probably be here then – not like this one, alone – not *ever* so much again,' she added, without sadness, almost prosaically.

'But Mortimer was right – suppose we can't spend the rest of our lives down here.'

'Rest of *our* lives?' Hetty was suddenly quizzical now, looking down from the tree, gazing at Léonie, who returned the gaze, an equal worry and query in her expression.

'Yes, our lives.'

'That's what frightens me, Léa . . .'

'What?'

'Not having, not being with you, when you're just *there* in the next room – and I can sleep there, or you with me.'

Léonie came towards her, kneeling in the tall yellowing grass in front of her chair, taking her hands.

'Hetty dearest – there are *other* rooms, you know – everywhere, a room together or rooms next to each other, even in Dublin, I'm sure!'

'But other people, too.'

Léonie drew away a fraction, sighing. 'Yes, of course! Other people, other rooms, other voices – there's always that. But . . .' She was suddenly tongue-tied.

'But what?'

Léonie's lips began to pucker as she tried to dam her rising emotion. 'Well, but – aren't we . . .' Her eyes were suddenly cloudy with tears. 'Aren't we everything "other" – *to* each other?'

'Yes, yes!' Hetty cried out, seeing Léonie's tears, and drawing her into her arms, clutching her tightly, so that her head pressed into her breasts, as they comforted each other, desperately, almost violently, trying to calm each other's doubts.

Léonie continued the reading of *Middlemarch* after supper. And later they played cards by a first log fire in the drawing room, when the lamps were brought in; the big, white-globed Aladdin standard lamp set above the Zöetrope on the occasional table beside Hetty.

She turned the cylinder idly, the lamplight falling directly into the interior of this wheel of life, enhancing the dance set free there as the cylinder span, giving the paper scrolls a golden enchantment. So that, though the images – the juggler, the running dog and cat, the cow – were blunt, even banal now, to Hetty with much repetition, she nonetheless gazed at them, mesmerised. Immobilised over a few weeks in her wheelchair, she longed to jump into the cylinder – yet then felt just as strongly that she did not want this. In this mysterious machine, with its inexplicable movement, its extraordinary offering and mimicking of real life, she was somehow seeing the very cradle of all her joys and fears.

10

M ORTIMER, BEFORE RETURNING to Westminster that October, made arrangements for the two girls to take over his top-floor flat in Crown Alley, a small
courtyard of Georgian business offices off Dame Street, between Dublin Castle
and the river. It was not residential, this legal and financial hub of the city with its
Stock Exchange, City Hall and magnificent façade of the Bank of Ireland at the
other end of Dame Street. But the girls – helped by Mrs McCabe the housekeeper,
who came for a few hours each morning, and under the benign, if largely absent,
eye of Mr Watson, Mortimer's celibate chief clerk, who occupied rooms opposite
theirs – came to relish these unexpected surroundings.

During the day the streets teemed with hectic activity: Stock Exchange messen-
gers, clerks, barristers, top-hatted brokers, journalists from the *Evening Mail*
building nearby – all raucously about their business, chattering on the pavements
or skipping between the clanging trams and the great horse drays rumbling over
the cobbles.

But at night, washed in soft gaslight, the quarter was nearly empty and silent
until, towards eight, the crowds gathered outside the Olympia Theatre not far from
Mortimer's offices; and silent once more until, filled with drink, song and broad
wit, the audience was released just after ten.

But the best times, the girls thought when they came back from the activities
about the city, were those November dusks, the lamplighter moving down the
narrow alleyway into their courtyard, prodding the gas globes into yellow pools of
light above the emptying offices – when soon, they knew, they would have the
whole place all to themselves; soon too, at least for Hetty, when they could dress
up as smart women, or as man and woman, preparing themselves for some
theatrical excitement – emerging from Mortimer's offices an hour or so later, quite
transformed, in all sorts of guises and disguises, intent on testing themselves against
the city.

And for Hetty, certainly, the dextrous lamplighter was a herald of thrilling
change, an unconscious promoter of her hazardous theatricals, the demons that
lurked in her heart. The old man was like a stage-hand, Hetty thought, arranging

a set, turning up the footlights, illuminating the backcloth and props, in front of which the curtain would rise soon on a performance uniquely hers – and Léonie's – when they would step out into the limelight, magic people then, transformed by every artifice which – as wardrobe mistress and actor-manager combined – she had so painstakingly collected and applied in Mortimer's flat beforehand.

So it was, one evening, watching the lamplighter from the front window six weeks after they had arrived in Dublin, that Hetty – fingering through a collection of her uncle Henry's old clothes and others more recently purchased from a variety of second-hand clothes shops in the city – thought to do something properly rash.

'Let's dress up tonight – and go to the Olympia Music Hall!' She looked at Léonie, just arrived back at the flat, where Hetty had been most of the afternoon, pondering the style and form of the evening's adventure.

Léonie, taking her coat off, gave a sigh of disinclination. 'Hetty, I'm tired . . .'

'Oh, *please*, Léa, I've been *so* thinking about it – all afternoon!'

'But all those rough types . . .' Léonie made the limp excuse. 'See them queueing every evening.'

'But that's just what'll be such *fun* – those rough types. Look!' Hetty picked up a smart, chestnut-coloured, check suit and waistcoat of Henry's, then a fawn bowler and red cravat. 'And I've got that pearl tiepin and spats to go with it,' she rushed on. 'And the silver-topped cane. I'll go as a young Dublin rake, out for a night on the halls. And for you . . .' She bent down to the bed again. 'I've something very quaint! Merry young woman's outfit, cheeky servant style – "Bridey from Rathmines": you can be my sweet young thing again!'

She held up the bits and pieces of Léonie's intended costume – a hand-me-down ensemble of slightly threadbare green velveteen topcoat, cheap picture hat with papier-mâché cherries round the crown and scuffed, lace-up black bootees.

'Hardly very merry, is it?' Léonie considered the clothes coldly. 'I'm not going anywhere in that tatty stuff.' Then she was even firmer. 'And, anyway, I'm *tired* of being your "sweet young thing".'

Hetty was quite taken aback by her blunt decisiveness, a quality she had conveniently forgotten in her friend. 'But, Léa, this isn't all of it. There are other things –'

'Besides, if we are playing these charades, why can't *I* go as the man for a change?'

Hetty was uncertain for a moment. 'Well, just I'm t-t-taller than you, that's the only reason.' Then she found her stride. 'But, really, it'd look very stupid if you were the *small* man, out with a *big* woman.'

'Why should it? I've seen *tiny* men out with *much* bigger women, in Dublin. Often.'

'But, Léa, that wouldn't work with us. You'd be far too young-looking a man – to be taking me out.'

Léonie rounded on her vehemently. 'Why can't we *both* go out as young men then?'

Hetty was genuinely astonished. 'Why, Léa, that'd be *awfully* unnatural.'

The two women gazed at each other challengingly. But really there was more doubt in their eyes. Both were confused by these sudden changes and reversals, of sex, age and identity.

'Well, anyway . . .' Léonie flounced away into the front drawing room, taking her coat off, before shouting back, 'I'm not going out in that rubbish – playing the maid or anyone's "sweet young thing". I'm tired of that, so there!'

'But, Léa, wait – wait till you see what else I got for you today!'

Léonie stayed in the outer room. When she had come back that evening to find Hetty fidgeting about the flat, she had clearly sensed a return of that old fierce restlessness in her friend – a frustration over things Hetty so wanted to express: images of a divine discontent in which she, inevitably, would be the empty canvas, the dull clay for these unformed desires, asked to take on some new or old role as lover – pliant menial or *grande cocotte*; saint or slave, the empty page in any case on which Hetty so wished to mark her life, stamping on another all the myriad personas she repressed in herself.

All this Léonie knew or sensed. And generally she had gone along with such fantasies because she loved Hetty and knew how she craved this release. These productions of Hetty's were as life's-blood to her which, if the flow was too long suppressed, would poison the whole body with anger, petulance, frustration – and so, equally, poison their relationship. Yet she would not take direction in every aspect of the production – that was nonsense, bad for her and worse for Hetty: the clay, after all, had a life of its own. Nonetheless Léonie returned then, willing to play audience, at least, in this particular performance.

Hetty had hidden the *pièces de résistance* – and now she produced the first from a hanger in the wardrobe. It was a tea-gown, second-hand, but exquisitely sophisticated, shimmery and well-cut, an airy, flimsy *thé-dansant* dress in smoothest crêpe de chine, with puffed sleeves, black-edged *décolletage*, a loose bodice, billowy and free, caught in at the waist, running down to a tight, sheath-like hobble skirt, cut at an angle up one side, so as to display the leg.

Léonie came forward, inspecting it, astonished, fingering the gossamer silk which crackled faintly in her hand. Pre-war, she thought – nothing of this sort was available or worn in the present austerities – but most definitely *haute couture*. She admired it . . . objectively. The pale green silk seemed all the more smooth and glittering in the lamplight: moonlit waters of the Nile.

'See! – it so goes with your eyes.' Hetty held the gown up proudly against Léonie's chest. 'The grey-green and the bluey-green. Oh, Léa, it's perfect. Do try it on at least.'

'But, Hetty, what can you be thinking! – no maid would ever wear a thing like that.'

'What does it matter – it'll be hidden by the topcoat.'

'Then what's the point of wearing it, if no one sees it, knows it's there?'

Hetty was surprised at this point. 'But *I'll* know it's there. And I've got some brand-new underthings to go with it, from Brown Thomas this afternoon –'

'Hetty, you are an idiot! You can't possibly think – piling all those different sorts of clothes one on top of the other – as if I was a clothes horse. I'd be a complete freak!'

'No you won't, the topcoat will hide it all. And, anyway, it'll be great fun – you'll see. Try it on at least.'

'Yes, a clothes horse . . .' Léonie reflected again on the idea, her head shaking with amusement now. 'And all a jumble of things that don't match, one on top of the other, because you don't know *what* you want me to be!' She paused then, chin jutting, before adding bitterly, 'But why can't I just be *myself*? And why can't *you* be . . . you?'

Hetty looked at her, again with genuine puzzlement. 'But, Léa, *of course* you're yourself. And so am I. This is just . . . dressing up. A game. Can't we amuse ourselves any more?'

She spoke in tones of such patient reason, like a teacher explaining some obvious calculation to a dunderhead, that Léonie, shaking her head again in disbelief, did not pursue the matter. 'All right then, I'll try it on. But I'm not going out anywhere in it, in *any* of it!'

Hetty did not reply, busying herself with the clothes – until finally she said, confidently, quietly, 'You'll see – you'll see.'

Léonie, who had been wearing a tweed suit and flannel blouse, climbed out of her winter clothes, and stood there shivering a moment, just in her woollen underthings, before moving over to the glowing coal grate in the bedroom.

Léonie was uncertain. It seemed in this clothes play as if Hetty was taking some seductive initiative here, just as she herself had done, in something of the same manner, swapping clothes in Hetty's bedroom, some six months before at Summer Hill. Thus she could hardly complain if this were so. Indeed, at another time, she would have welcomed such attentions. Yet, given the present circumstances, there was an obvious flaw in this idea. She cannot wish to seduce me, to undress me, Léonie thought, for she wants just the opposite: to *cover* me with all these clothes.

She was perplexed. But she relaxed . . . stripped off her underclothes, standing naked by the fire, before Hetty, quite clinically, dispassionately, offered her the first of the new silk undergarments, then the others, pausing between each successive covering, observing the rising foundations as a painter might consider the effects of successive layers of colour on a canvas.

Then she gave her the crêpe-de-chine tea-gown, helping her put it on, easing the silk sheath down Léonie's waist and hips, pulling the bodice up, buttoning it at the back. She flounced the billowy silk out, about Léonie's shoulders, neck and breasts, breathing on the thin folds so that they rippled like green waves in the firelight.

'Don't blow so – you're tickling me!' Léonie, despite herself, was being drawn into the performance, feeling the touch of silk brushing her skin, beneath her arms, at her throat.

'See! With a bit of height from the shoes it'll hang perfectly.' Hetty, totally absorbed now in the creation of this model, scurried about Léonie, pinching in the gown, smoothing the hang, straightening the waist, running her hand down the flanks, adjusting, moulding the silk against Léonie's shape.

Léonie played the mannequin without moving, without a sound. But, as Hetty's hands roved about, she found this more difficult. For it was quite clear to her now, as her skin began to prickle with pleasure: Hetty – unconsciously or not, she could not decide – *was* seducing her, not by undressing, but by dressing her. And that, strangely, seemed even more exciting.

Hetty, finally satisfied, drew Léonie over to the long dressing mirror. 'Just one last thing!' She went to the wardrobe, producing a magnificent turban in brocaded satin, an egret feather at the centre, held in place by a large turquoise stone, and placed it on Léonie's head. It fitted perfectly, a metallic silver crown quite covering her dark curls.

'There!' Hetty was beside herself. 'I knew it'd go. Isn't it wonderful?'

Léonie nodded vigorously, biting her lip. She was speechless, with suppressed mirth, sorrow, love – she could not distinguish the feelings. But finally she said the wrong thing. 'You are a real ninny, Hetty – you had that horrid cherry hat before and that tatty overcoat – and now all this magnificence! But none of that . . . would go with any of this!'

Hetty was crestfallen for a moment. Then she was suddenly petulant. 'Oh, what does it matter?' She waltzed over to the bed and, rummaging furiously all round it, she picked up the other old clothes – the Dublin rake's outfit, the cherry hat and the maid's threadbare velveteen coat – throwing them in the air, all over the place. 'What *does* it matter?' she shouted, suddenly bitter now. 'They're all only *ideas*, Léa – so many, many ideas I have about you! Don't you see? And they'd *all* suit – you can wear anything and I'm too tall. You could be anything, Bridey or Madame de Pompadour or Schehérézade. And I can't somehow –'

'That's nonsense! You're a *much* better actress – that's the whole trouble!'

Hetty paused in her rampage, looking at Léonie carefully, rather sadly, and quite deflated now. 'But, Léa – I want all that much more fe-fe-for you.' She stopped again, tripped suddenly by her stammer. Then there was the still, small voice: 'I want everything for *you*, Léa – not for me.'

Hetty turned away then, overcome with emotion, starting to fiddle with her hands, cracking the finger joints. Then she picked up the snow-dome of Summer Hill which she kept by her bedside, and sucked her thumb. Léonie, stricken, saw her wander off into the shadows of the bedroom. She stood up, an odalisque in her oriental headdress and shimmering silk, distraught. She put her head to one side, as if trying to ward off some blow, her eyes screwed up in pain, holding her arms out. 'Oh, Hetty, do come here – *please*. I am so sorry, to be so tactless, misunderstanding everything. *Please* come.'

But Hetty stayed in the corner. So that Léonie swiftly went to her, turned her round and took her in her arms.

'Hetty,' she said, feeling her moist cheeks on hers. 'Oh, Hetty – I want everything for you, too, everything. Love you more than the world – love me . . .'

'That stupid feather,' Hetty said at last. 'It's tickling me . . .'

'I'll take it off, take everything off. *And* I'll go out to the theatre tonight, however you want me – promise I will.'

Léonie removed all her splendid clothes then – and soon she had helped Hetty do the same, before they loved each other again, naked and without artifice.

'The *real* Dublin life!' Hetty exclaimed, excited, a glass of ale in her hand, glancing at Léonie, sipping a cheap sherry, her lips puckered in distaste, as she tried to smile, nervously. 'You look fine. Don't worry!' Hetty added the whispered reassurance.

The two girls stood behind the glass windows of the bar at the back of the stalls at the Olympia Theatre. The lilting music from the small pit orchestra – a Lehar melody sung in an uncertain contralto by a buxom woman – wafted to them as the bar doors swung to and fro. It was a Friday night, one of music hall variety acts, the theatre almost full: suburban men nursing bowler hats with their rapt wives, groups of restless, derisive British Tommies in the back rows, one or two women of easy virtue glancing at the soldiers from behind the glass at the long bar, the intermittent catcalls and whistling of old shawlies, Dublin codgers and urchins just audible from the gods far above.

The misguided contralto finished to ragged jeers and ironic applause. The girls, fascinated, watched the act numbers change, the flash of electric bulbs on either side of the stage, nine to ten, the last act before the interval. A louche Scotsman, in kilt and tam-o'-shanter, knobbly-kneed, with an outsize furry sporran, came on then, amidst a great outburst, and proceeded with a risqué imitation of Harry Lauder, lifting his kilt suggestively as he began to stamp about the stage. Behind the glass the girls could just hear the words of the song: 'Roamin' in the gloamin' wi' a lassie by me side! . . .'

The Scotsman lifted his kilt higher, starting to jig in front of a heather-glen curtain drop, and the house exploded – as his 'lassie' emerged from the wings, an elderly crone, sprigs of heather all askew over a poke bonnet, who lifted her skirts then and, with a simpering smirk, started to scamper about the stage, avoiding the man's lascivious attentions.

The girls forced a smile. It was hot in the bar, the place reeking of stout and tobacco, the great electric globes above the counter fuzzy in the drifting smoke, as the drinkers, attracted now by the excitement on stage, pushed forward round the girls, peering out into the red and gilt auditorium.

Hetty loosened her red cravat, undid the top button of her check waistcoat and, inspecting her vague reflection in the glass, adjusted the tilt of her fawn bowler.

She was dressed as she had first suggested, two hours before in the flat, as a keen young Dublin blade, in a smart chestnut check suit, spats and red cravat, a near gent, out for an evening's slumming in the halls before a bit of slap and tickle later in a jarvey's cab, with Léonie, his little bit of fluff, in the rubbed green velveteen topcoat, cherry hat and lace-up bootees. The tea-gown and turban would await another occasion. They were well enough disguised, Hetty knew. But this was their first occasion in a public bar, cheek by jowl with sharp men and loose women.

Just then two men approached them, pushing in close, viewing the show from the windows: one robust, florid-faced, arrogant in a canary waistcoat, almost bald and narrow-eyed with a few foxy strands of hair over pendulous ears – together with quite a different sort, an elderly, much smaller man, rubicund, a little pixie of a fellow in a loud check suit and bowler.

'I'm afraid not, Mr O'Grady,' the tall man spoke superciliously, in a nasal, suburban English accent, pulling on a wet cigar in a lordly fashion, spewing the smoke out over the bowler beneath him. 'We really have no dates available for you people. The panto's coming up – then right through till the spring we have a hundred and one different acts booked in from England, from the Metropolitan, from Collins' – all booked up, you see!' He bared his discoloured teeth in an ogre-ish smile.

'Ah, Mr Purcell, but a night or two with some of my people – and you'd *really* see something.' The little man spoke with a marked Dublin brogue. He was chirpy, confident, like a bird. Across his pot belly, from one waistcoat pocket to the other, lay the gold chains, heavy and spectacular, of a fob watch. He sipped from a glass of stout, then licked his pronounced cherubic lips. His eyes were unnaturally large as well, great baby's eyes, too big for the pudgy, dewlapped, mischievous face that was quite hairless, smooth and very white, like that of an ivory Buddha.

The Englishman laughed drily. 'But I *have* seen your people, Mr O'Grady – several of your summer seasons out at Bray: know them well – the dwarves, jugglers and the mangy lion too! Fine for the visitors there, the day trippers. But this is the Olympia *Theatre*, you know. Now, if you'll just excuse me a moment . . .'

The cocky theatre manager drifted away, leaving Mr O'Grady humming a tune, sipping his stout next to the girls, as he gazed sarcastically out at the antics in the Harry Lauder imitation on stage.

'Ah, Holy Mother o' God!' He nodded to Hetty. 'Will ye look at it! Thim two edjits out there – lowest of the low, I'd buy oul' Harry himself, but that's a travesty, that kinda o' codology.'

Hetty, who had overheard the entire previous conversation between the two men, immediately agreed. 'Quite dreadful!' she said, her voice several tones lower, upper-class, dismissive. 'Absolute rubbish.' And then, the devil suddenly rising in her, she told him, 'I and my friend here – we do a far better act.' Léonie, horrified, dared not open her mouth.

'Ye do?' The pixie looked up at the tall, imperious figure, the finely-cut features of the dandy – then at Léonie in the ridiculous cherry hat. He seemed doubtful. Yet he was taken by the poise of the young man, the classy confidence, the arrogant control – above all, by the obvious beauty of the couple. 'And what do ye do?' He fed himself some more stout, raising the glass too high, but then leaning over the rim and dipping into it like a duck.

'Oh, we have a singing act – "Bertie and Bridey" – we do imitations, but *proper* ones: popular tunes, operetta. My friend plays the piano, I sing. And sometimes the other way round. And we dance.'

'Ye *both* sing . . . *and* play the pianner?'

'Oh yes – *Madame Butterfly* is our great number.'

'A sort of comedy act?'

'Yes. But we can do it all quite straight, too. My friend's a proper singer – trained.'

'I've not heard of ye. On the boards before?'

'A little – in London.'

'"Bertie and Bridey" . . .' The little man looked at them, first savouring, then seeming to like, the idea. 'Have ye got iny photographs?' Hetty nodded. 'Well, send thim to me – and come out with your act and I'll look at it. Here's me card.'

He finished his stout then, before touching his bowler and waddling away. Hetty looked at the card. 'Mr Alphonso O'Grady' it said in neat copperplate at the top. But beneath, in fancy mock Gothic capitals, was the bold inscription 'FONSY O'GRADY'S THEATRE OF VARIETIES' – before the copperplate was prosaically resumed. 'Bray Promenade, Bray, County Wicklow, Ireland.'

Hetty giggled. 'What a laugh,' she said. '*Perfect!*'

But was it all so perfect, Léonie wondered later that evening, taking off the servant's clothes back in the flat? Had she – for her tactlessness, her love and in the emotion of the moment – given in too readily to Hetty's sensuous vaudeville fantasies? And had she not made amends for her insensitivity – had not they both done so, as real people, in their love-making afterwards? Léonie thought they had. Yet she retained a sneaking suspicion that, when she had dressed to go out as her 'sweet young thing', Hetty had found this an even more exciting gift.

Had Hetty recovered because she had been indubitably loved – or did her later joy that evening stem from quite another sort of pleasure, much more devious, a victory in which she had subtly blackmailed her, Léonie thought, to change her mind and collaborate in this mimic escapade at the theatre?

Did her subsequent bliss in any case justify all these charades? Perhaps, in the short term. But if they became a permanent sport, a constant condition of their lives together, surely they would lose each other? – for who could love a chimera indefinitely, a will o' the wisp, running from one incarnation to another, when the real person was gradually suffocated, submerged, lost.

Or did she really love Hetty for just these volatile qualities, for her personality thus constantly reborn, a wizard's gift in the girl which, far from destroying their love, would, in this necromancy of changing dross to gold, keep it ever fresh?

Yes – that, she thought, was perhaps the truest answer. But it had, as consequence, another less happy facet. Hetty's love would demand constant changes in her as well. They were both to be players in Hetty's games – and she would keep her only if she continued to fulfil the roles offered her – as she had done just that evening with the maid's outfit. She would be sure of Hetty's love only for as long as she played the marionette. That was the truth, too. And Léonie saw it all then with sudden clarity. Well, so be it. She would allow herself to be used. That was the price she would pay, for she could not lose Hetty. She was forced to recognise then that she loved her more than her own independence and dignity.

Hetty pushed the two single divan beds together, as they did every evening, separating them again in the morning before Mrs McCabe arrived. They were aware now that their sort of love was not an accepted thing. But they saw it merely as a social impropriety; that it was in any way immoral did not cross their minds. Soon they were cosy between the sheets, the lamp out, but the room still faintly lit by the dying embers of the fire.

'Well, all that really was *very* funny . . .' Hetty moved her pillow over, laying her head on Léonie's shoulder. 'Wasn't it? – or do you still really feel bad about it all?'

'No . . .'

'But you do. You're not really my "servant", you know – not at all. I'd just as soon go out as that myself – if I were smaller.'

'Yes,' Léonie whispered non-committally.

'But you're still we-worried?' Hetty put her hand out to stroke Léonie's cheek.

'I just wonder about the whole thing. It's always so much more for you than just "fun" . . .'

Hetty turned away then, lying on her back. She sighed. 'Well, is it?' She thought, and then in a much more confident voice she said, 'Yes, I feel I *control* things when I'm being someone else. And I don't when I'm just being me – when I feel nothing, no confidence at all. But the moment I start copying, dressing up, when I start being someone different – I have a we-wonderful feeling of – sheer happiness, because I've walked into someone else's life, someone who knows *exactly* what they're doing and who they are. I suddenly have *power* when I'm someone else. Do you see?'

'A bit.'

'Oh, Léa, it's because I so want to get away from just being me – the weak, stammering, boring, frightened person I am with just myself –'

'But that's not true! You hardly ever stammer with me – and I love the person you *are*, said it often enough –'

'But, Léa, *I* don't like the person I am – because I'm nobody – don't know *who* I am. So I *have* to be other people. I know I do,' she added rather miserably. 'And it won't hurt you, promise. And better still,' she rushed on, vehement now, 'together we can win that way, Léa – run the world, not let it run us, with my Mama and so on. Oh, Léa, I so much want to *win* with you.'

She embraced Léonie then with a fierce tenderness. 'It's not that sort of winning I mean,' Hetty went on, excited, breathless now. 'Not loving you – in that way. It's quite different and just as exciting – it's *doing* so many different things with you, for you. It's the feeling of a future with you in that way that's so exciting. Don't you see?'

'Yes, I do see that.' Léonie responded at last, an urgency in her own voice now.

'Do see it, because – it's that same sense of loving you that I find almost more exciting than the real thing. Mind loving? – yes. You're in my mind all the time, Hetty – *where*ver and *who*ever you are – that's the really wonderful thing. Just sometimes –' She hesitated. 'Sometimes I can't keep up with you changing all the time ahead of me. And I – I think I'll lose you . . .'

Hetty moved to her, touched her. Yet her passion lay only in her words when she spoke – singing, exultant words surging out like a long-dammed waterfall, words as a sudden last ecstasy in an act of love. 'But you won't lose me, Léa, because whoever I am – it's for you. And because I can't be me, whoever that is, *without* you.'

Yes, they needed each other, depended for their very existence on the unequal ties between them. There could be no meaning, no vivacity, no life for them apart. They were indispensable to each other – like puppet and puppet-master.

Léonie recognised all that. But not Hetty, who in Léonie's arms that night thought they had found a greater and more equal depth of understanding and love than they had ever known before.

The top floor pied-à-terre in Crown Alley – a study-drawing room at the front, with the bedroom, small kitchen and bathroom to the rear – had, in Mortimer's infrequent use of it, become a rather grim and spartan affair: the musty, dark-walled front room filled with a large roll-top desk, torn leather armchairs and foxed prints of Georgian Dublin above piles of old legal books and papers, while the bedroom, when the girls had first come there, had been even gloomier, the divans covered with army blankets, decrepit eiderdowns, the curtains frayed and grimy, dampish.

But Mortimer, seeing an opportunity here for change, and telling the girls to make use of his account at Switzers in Grafton Street, suggested they amend the place in a brighter mode. And they had done so, painting the walls a creamy lemon, buying coloured cretonnes and chintzes for the chairs, proper linen for the beds, together with green serge curtains, and organising coal fires. So that within a few weeks of their arrival the whole place had been transformed: a joyful cosy nest under the rooftops of Dublin, from where they looked out at chimney pots and steep slate roofs under pale November twilights – or in the mornings, first thing, when they leant from their bedroom window, seeing the glinting gunmetal water of the river Liffey above the alleyway and the puffing smoke from a Guinness barge on its way down-river to the port. Then, as the day gathered itself, with the clatter of trams and the heavy clip-clop of dray horses, the two girls, in dressing gowns, preparing their own breakfast and sitting over boiled eggs, soda bread, and thick tea, thought themselves in a wonderfully independent seventh heaven.

Léonie took singing lessons from a faded, but still technically adept Italian tenor, a Signor Grossi, who had a meticulously tidy studio, with an upright piano, surrounded by many ferns and aspidistras, off Grafton Street, behind the Gaiety Theatre. Hetty meanwhile spent her mornings at Mrs Wallingford's Academy – a crammer's for those few young women anxious to enter Trinity College – in Harcourt Street beyond Stephen's Green. The girls usually met at lunch in one of the more fashionable cafés in Grafton Street, at Bewley's or Cairo's, visited the National Gallery or the bookshops on the quays in the afternoon, with theatres, concerts or visits to the Olympia Music Hall in the evening.

And – though they had no intention of furthering the matter with Mr Fonsy O'Grady – they went to a photographer, too, whose sign they had seen outside a gaunt Georgian building at the end of Harcourt Street: a Mr Waxman, a satyr-like Englishman, small and somehow suspicious, Hetty thought, who wore a dark beret even while he worked, in what must originally have been a garden conservatory attached to the back of the house, the studio of screens, couches and potted palms roofed in by an expanse of glass. They went, from the very start, as 'Bertie and Bridey', meticulously turned out in the dandy's costume and the maid's outfit – Hetty explaining their need of some new 'artistic' reproductions of their act.

Mr Waxman very willingly provided them with such, in a variety of cleverly-arranged poses around the potted plants, against a Chinese screen for their *Madame Butterfly* act – becoming quite roused as he worked, encouraging saucy smiles and angles, even suggesting they lie together on the couch, directions which Hetty only partly responded to, mistrusting the man more than ever, refusing him their address, saying they would pick up the photographs later.

They were very good – in an unexpected way. Mr Waxman, in his professionalism (and no doubt reflecting his own doubtful tastes), had succeeded, despite Hetty's resistance, in giving the girls a most provocatively teasing and voluptuous air. The sauciness he had wished for was certainly there and made the more compelling by the obvious class of the subjects: Hetty's classically arrogant features touched now by some devil in the flesh; Léonie's usually rather cosy dark looks somehow exaggerated, filled with a slumbrous sensuality.

Mr Waxman was pleased. 'I'd like to see your act – I do quite a lot of theatrical work as it happens. Are you playing at the Queen's or the Olympia?'

'Oh no,' Hetty quickly retorted. 'Just a holiday in Dublin. We work in England.'

A world of other people suited the two girls. Far from losing each other in it, the sophisticated pleasures, company and surroundings of the great city drew them both out from that all-absorbing, too obsessive regard for each other that had begun to threaten their lives alone in Summer Hill.

Here, developing their tastes, their naturally adventurous temperament leading them to entertainment and education of every haphazard kind, they soon found new facets to admire in and surprise each other with. And they came to love these changes in themselves as much as, before, they had taken to what was basic in their character – a need to venture, join hands, in risks against the world.

Now, in Dublin, they could better understand and express their matrix of attraction for each other, name and promote the growing parts, which together seemed to include all things, the whole gamut of emotion: affection, mutual reliance, a complementary wit and intelligence, bedtime company, a deep love of the heart. For the girls at least, not part of the Irish political tensions seething all round them or of the war in Europe, these were days of extravagant hope and happiness.

Léonie's parents, as closely in touch as the sporadic wartime posts allowed, made her a generous allowance; and Mortimer, on Frances's authority, did the same on a lesser scale, from the estate at Summer Hill. Together, their tuition fees paid and the small flat gratis, they had, after giving Mrs McCabe £3 a week for her work, some £12 left over for all their other needs, food, clothes, books, entertainment. Thus, by comparison with most others in the city, a fair sum of free money was available to them. And they made good use of it – buying modern prints from Combridges in Grafton Street and winter hothouse carnations from the old shawly lady at her stall on the Duke Street corner next to the art shop; and their rooms were always full of fruit, autumn pears and apples, which both girls loved to smell and munch.

They entertained Robert and Bertie, too, twice, on their Sunday exeats from St Columba's College in the Dublin mountains: at lunch in the Hibernian Hotel and a second time transporting them in a cab to the Zoological Gardens in Phoenix Park. Holidays, at Christmas and the following Easter, they all spent together at Summer Hill, the mood of their various relationships largely unchanged in that new year of 1917, when Robert, who would be sitting his university examinations, to read modern history in Trinity College in the summer, was more occupied, perforce, with his books than with Hetty.

In early May all four returned to Dublin, and life for the two girls resumed its largely happy tenor, with the added pleasures now of the coming summer in the city, when in the warmth the girls took long afternoon walks to the very far end of Sandymount strand, watching the yachts and sailing dinghies begin to move, from behind the jetty at Kingstown harbour out into the choppy waters of Dublin Bay.

Then without warning – for Mortimer had been away in London and she still rarely looked at a newspaper – the blow fell for Hetty. Returning home alone one afternoon in mid-June she saw the succession of placards outside the *Evening Mail* building in Dame Street: 'AMNESTY DECLARED' – 'REPUBLICAN PRISONERS TO BE RELEASED' – 'MRS FRANCES FRASER COMING HOME!'

11

WHEN THE TWO girls returned to Summer Hill in July, they found Frances changed indeed . . . They had welcomed her off the mail boat at Kingstown on her return from Aylesbury prison – before, it seemed, half the population of Dublin, on the pier and later in the city, had engulfed her with a far more vigorous greeting. Mrs Fraser, among the frantic crowds and cheers, had been the heroine not just of the hour, but for days subsequently in Dublin – when she had visited the ruins of Liberty Hall and other sites of the rebellion, attending endless welcoming committees and receptions. And in all this fervour Hetty – rather thankfully – had lost her. But now, alone in Summer Hill, she had time to take full stock of her mother.

Yes, she had changed – but so completely, like a brilliant conjuring trick, that it was unbelievable. She was much thinner, pale-faced, hair unkempt now, with a relentlessly beatific smile, all her previous vivid attack and anger seemingly quite gone. She was not so much saintly, as Hetty had half-anticipated, but had more the air of a plaster saint: like that passive blue-and-white Madonna remembered from Elly's tin-roofed Catholic church in Domenica. Her mother might have been shell-shocked or sleep-walking; her voice had no edge to it, full of dying falls. And, worse, much of what she said seemed largely nonsensical to Hetty – often mouthing platitudes about the 'holy spirit' and the 'remission of sin' in a way which Hetty found embarrassing.

Hetty was appalled by the transformation. Her mother, in her pliant submissiveness, far from gaining her soul, appeared a broken person. If this was the result of 'coming to God' Hetty wanted nothing of it – God had simply crushed this woman's spirit. Hetty, finding no resistance in her mother, felt disappointed somehow. Here was no worthy opponent, as she had half-wanted her to be, just a broken reed, a woman now firmly embalmed in a spiritual dotage.

But Hetty quite misread these initial, outwardly passive signs in her mother as the final sum of things in her – and grew over-confident thereby, especially with Léonie.

Frances felt she had come to God, certainly, the God of the New Testament, all-knowing, loving, and forgiving – forsaking that other righteous, all-powerful and punishing being in the Old Testament of her Jewish ancestry and upbringing. And it was just this apparent transformation which Hetty observed with such distaste. In fact – though neither Hetty nor her mother recognised this – Frances's new creed was not really a true belief at all. It was an act, one which she had unconsciously taken up, as suitable to her recent incarnations as sacrificial revolutionary, imprisoned political martyr, lost leader and heroine of Holy Catholic Ireland. Hetty was not to know, since she did not admit it of herself, how her mother was just as good an actress as she.

Hetty and Léonie – in their rainy indoor affairs and trysts, and since Robert was away for the first part of the holidays staying with Bertie and his family in Co. Kildare – had taken to using Henry's locked workrooms at the top of the house. Hetty, ever since her childhood when she had illicitly played there with Robert, had always enjoyed the secrecy of these rooms, and even more their aura of drama and romance, the musty ether smells and sense of fabulous adventure they contained. And here, among the African assegais and exotic stuffed animals, she and Léonie sometimes met – to talk, to play, to love, entering the rooms along the flat roof, behind the balustrade, by one of its windows.

Here – just as Henry and Dermot had done – they made a world of their own far above and beyond any interference from the rest of the household. Here, too, on the shabby Chesterfield sofa, when the mood took them, they could love each other, as they no longer could at night downstairs, for Frances had returned to her own bedroom, just beyond theirs on the first floor landing. Here in any case, they thought, Frances, who now showed little interest in the affairs of the house, would never interrupt or disturb them.

But Frances, though apparently only concerned with matters spiritual, had only temporarily lost interest in the house. A month after her return, regaining her strength and temper, she conceived a whole new use for the place, in which the great pile would, she envisaged, play a vital role, become a spearhead of enlightened feminine life in the new Republic – when that came, and the moment could not now be long delayed. Yes, she would start to instruct the young women of Ireland in cooking, household management, arts and crafts. She would clear out and make over the top floors as work- and classrooms, for knitting, needlework, weaving, Gaelic lessons and other essential feminine accomplishments. It was a mission aimed initially at the culturally deprived and generally benighted women of the immediate locality, so that their horizons, thus broadened, would allow them, as fit citizens, to enter the coming Celtic Republic.

It was this optimistic plan which she first set out to implement one muggy, thunder-threatening afternoon in August, taking the keys of her brother Henry's old rooms with her – deciding that, yes, these rooms, too, would have to be cleared out. They could no longer be kept as a mausoleum, a shrine to him. It was not suitable, as much for his unfortunate proclivities – his, as she now viewed it, immoral relationship with Dermot – as for the fact that these rooms, as she knew, so reeked of Henry's imperial enthusiasms, from which corrupt source, no doubt, he and Dermot had contracted their most regrettable tastes. In the new Ireland there would be no room for any such aberrations. Henry's rooms would have to go. So, quite forgetting the all-knowing, loving and forgiving Christ of the New Testament, she stamped up the stairs as briskly as the stifling heat allowed.

Hetty and Léonie were in Henry's rooms that afternoon.

They lay, scantily clad, in the thunderstruck air, drowsily fondling each other, the land beginning to boom all round them, the windows rattling as the weather exploded over Summer Hill in great salvoes and jagged, sky-scorching flashes.

They never heard Frances's footsteps outside on the landing, nor the key turning in the lock, as they clasped each other, half in fear, half in pleasure. The girls had brought a basket of early Worcester Pearmains with them, munching some of them prior to the onset of the storm. The remainder scattered in front of them. And Hetty had been teasing Léonie with the old snake skeleton from the tea-chest so that this sinister necklace of whitened vertebrae lay on the floor as well, just next to the sofa.

It was the first thing Frances noticed as she stepped into the room, then the apple basket, before a vivid flash illuminated the two girls in their *déshabille*. Frances absorbed all these views – fruit, serpent and fallen women – simultaneously with a most vicious thunderclap right above the house, and put the whole together as an apocalyptic vision, a most patently obvious fall from Eden.

Thunderstruck herself now, all her previous visions of Celtic feminine purity in these rooms destroyed, she viewed the two girls with so grotesquely severe an expression that Hetty smiled. Indeed, already deciding that attack was the best means of defence, she nearly laughed.

'Mama! – what *are* you doing here?'

Her mother, for reply, shook convulsively, bunching her fingers uncontrollably. She seemed about to levitate with anger, to grow huge in the darkened, light-flashing room. The looming shapes from the jungle of stuffed animals appeared to snap and glower at her. She felt threatened by an overwhelming aura of nature's malignity. And though at that moment she seemed so much the prophet of doom, taking on all the lineaments of her mother, Lady Cordiner, in her fiercest days, she was suddenly frightened, oppressed by what she chose to see as an ultimate vision of evil everywhere about her.

Hetty meanwhile, believing her mother had undoubtedly regained the form of worthy opponent, did laugh at her then – outright. But Frances span away in the same instant, before her daughter's derision had time to rest on her.

Hetty, on Frances's call, eventually made a tardy appearance in front of her mother, ambling with apparent unconcern into her boudoir later that day. The storm had passed. But Hetty, thinking it would remain in her mother's demeanour, decided she had nothing to lose by taking the initiative again – knowing, too, exactly what line she would choose.

So she said immediately, and with biting reproach, 'Mama, you wrote me several times, from prison, how sorry you were over your insensitive, your difficult behaviour towards me as a child. Yet now you seem intent on renewing it. What can all this be aba-aba-about?'

Her stammer betrayed her confident sally. Her mother, quite composed now, waiting patiently by the mantelpiece, took immediate advantage of the lapse.

'Henrietta, this is no matter of *my* insensitivity, my difficulty – but yours.' She spoke with sad reason. 'You have provoked this, not I. You can have no idea how improper your behaviour with Léonie is. So I must tell you, it is *vicious*.' On these last words, she quite changed, rounding on her daughter, eyes ablaze, lapsing from reason then, storming the heights of all her old insensate fury.

Hetty, pleased by this reaction, regained her poise at once. Now she thought she had her mother where she wanted her – a more than worthy opponent, since it was obvious that she had lost her wits again. Hetty was calm, considered. 'Vicious, Mama? It can't be. I love Léonie.'

'Not love – mere lust.' Her mother moved towards the window, while Hetty stood between her and the door, so that she had the happy feeling of having cornered her mother.

'What nonsense. You cannot feel such for someone loved, who loves you just as much.'

'I shall not debate with with you,' her mother ranted. 'For there cannot be debate over such matters. Your behaviour is wicked, depraved.'

Frances moved to her desk . . . and Hetty advanced a few steps, an animal stalking its prey but not yet quite certain of it. Another show of force was required before a kill – and Hetty had prepared herself for this. 'And you?' she asked with bitter sarcasm. 'You must know of just such love – wicked and depraved – to speak of it, to speak of it so wildly.' Hetty gazed at her mother, letting the words sink in. Frances trembled now, speechless. 'Oh, yes,' Hetty went on. 'For years now you've lied to me – about "Mr Fraser". But he was never my real Papa – I know it. There was someone else. Who was it? And what sort of love was that?' Her mother spun across the room then, slapping her daughter's face. But Hetty remained quite unmoved. 'That's no answer – simply proof of my point: how you have always lied to me.'

Frances, brought up short by this invulnerable girl and the force of her argument, took the only way out she could. She retreated.

'I'm – I'm sorry . . .' She cleared her brow with a hand. 'I lost my temper, for what you say is so preposterous. I will tell you – Robert Fraser *was* your father, but I have never properly spoken to you of him, as I should have done, for the reason that I could not bring myself to think of him myself. It was a rash marriage, taken without proper thought on my part, as a result of my banishment from Summer Hill. He was a brute, in every way as I discovered. Naturally I've not wanted to talk to you of this. But he was your father.'

Her words, Hetty had to admit, sounded convincing enough. Hetty remembered all too well what a cruelly unpleasant man he had been. And Frances, sensing that she had crossed this thin ice with her daughter, took the initiative again. 'And it is just because of my own mistakes – with your father,' she moved towards Hetty now, speaking very earnestly, 'that I must see you do not repeat such folly in the same . . . sphere of the emotions. If you can curb your self-will, Hetty – your most unsuitable unnatural desires – there is a whole world for you, waiting. But not with Léonie. There is no more future there for you than there was for me with your Papa.'

'But Léonie is *not* like my Papa, not for an instant – never cruel, just the opposite. What you say for you is true, no doubt, but not for me. Léa is wonderful.'

Her mother, seeing the force of this argument but unable to admit it, became agitated again. 'Nonetheless, Henrietta, you fail to see the point: for all his faults, your father was a *man*. Léonie is a *woman*.'

'I see no difference. There are no two sorts of love. If one feels such love at all, for anyone, it is the same kind –'

'Henrietta,' her mother interrupted, playing her trump card, 'you shall see . . . how this is no mere cranky opinion of mine. It will be Mortimer's – and that of Léonie's parents, too, I assure you. You will see,' she added ominously. 'There will be changes. None of us can sit by and see you both ruin your lives in this depraved manner.'

Hetty became alarmed now. What was her mother implying? Then it suddenly struck her. 'Oh, no, you can't do that – you can't part us. Not that, never, *ever*!'

But this was exactly what Frances proceeded to do – writing of the event in Henry's rooms, in suitably veiled terms, both to Léonie's parents and to Mortimer, pointing out to him that, in the circumstances, the use of his Dublin pied-à-terre by the two girls must now be discontinued. To Mr and Mrs Straus she wrote more tactfully still. But the message was clear enough: their daughter was involved in a quite unsuitable intimacy with hers and must therefore return to France at once.

Mortimer in his reply, though he privately thought it all a storm in a teacup, was forced to accede to Frances's request. She was, after all, Hetty's mother. The posts to France, with the war, were considerably delayed. There was no immediate reply from the Strauses in Paris. But meanwhile the girls were told of Mortimer's regrets: his flat would not be available to them that autumn, when they had expected to return to Dublin, resuming their studies there. And Frances by now had made it clear to Léonie that she could no longer make her welcome at Summer Hill.

All this alarmed and infuriated the two girls – as much because of their impotency in the matter as for the fact that it seemed inevitable now that they would have to part. Léonie would quite possibly be sent to her Uncle Eli's in New York, while Hetty would remain in what would then be the lonely hell of Summer Hill, cooped up with her frightful mother. For Hetty particularly such a fate was not to be contemplated. She hated her Mama once more, with a barely contained fury; all these monstrous manoeuvrings simply hardened her resolve. But to do what? Neither she nor Léonie had money. Where else could they go?

Frances soon learnt, in the awful silences and air of bitter resentment about the house, how much the girls resisted her dictates – which gave her added proof of their necessity. She gave no thought as to how they might overturn them. How could they? Neither girl had yet reached her majority; they had no resources.

'Yes, they'll probably send me to New York,' Léonie said to Hetty quietly one evening. But Hetty shook her head vigorously. 'We'll never let them do that. We agreed, Léa, we'll not be separated, never, ever.'

Léonie nodded. 'But how not?' she asked wanly.

'I've been thinking: there is one way. Remember that little baby-faced man – Mr Fonsy O'Grady? We met him that night at the Olympia Theatre. "Fonsy O'Grady" and his "Theatre of Varieties"?'

'Yes?'

'Well, I found his card.' She held it out then with a flourish, like a magic charm. 'You remember, we told him we had an act together – "Bertie and Bridey" – and he said to come out and show it to him. Well, we will! That's just what we'll do. And he'll give us a job, I know he will – and we'll go away with them on his tours, and they'll never find us!' Hetty, as she spoke, became more and more breathlessly enchanted with the idea.

'But, Hetty –'

'Of *course* it'll work! "Fortune favours the brave" – remember? I *know* we'll win. You've always been so doubtful about the dressing up thing. But don't you see? – this is the very thing that'll save us now – just that!'

Léonie remained doubtful. But suddenly she was moved by something, almost palpable, hanging in the air between them: a gift of faith it seemed, which Hetty had just offered her, which was hers for the taking if she made the same leap into the dark. So she leapt. Hetty's vast excitement, her surging confidence, convinced her, enveloped her. Yes, it seemed obvious now – with Hetty one could do anything. Yes, they would win. Hetty was right. She gazed into her blue eyes, letting Hetty's certainties flow into her like a balm, her flashing beauty and spirit at that moment a sure guarantee that everything would work out just as she said.

'All right,' Léonie agreed, kissing her softly, briefly. 'Yes! – yes, yes!'

There were careful preparations to be made. They would need money – more than the £20 or so of their earlier allowances which they had saved. They would have to practise their act, invent new ones, plan their actual escape from the house – to which tasks they set themselves throughout the rest of August.

Frances was not suspicious of their sudden musical enthusiasms – indeed she readily agreed when they asked if the grand piano might be moved to the morning room at the back of the house, for here she could keep an eye on them. And the girls spent hours there, with operatic scores and popular music sheets bought in Kilkenny, thumping out renditions and pastiches of the latest songs – 'Tipperary', 'Keep the Home Fires Burning' – together with old music hall favourites, 'Down at the Old Bull and Bush' and 'Knees Up Mother Brown', before refining their duets from *Madame Butterfly* and adding other operas and operettas to their repertoire, flagrantly dramatic passages, which they guyed or sang straight from *The Merry Widow* or *La Traviata*.

'Your tiny hand is frozen . . .' Hetty sang lugubriously, gazing with exaggerated longing at Léonie, before both of them burst out laughing. '*No*, that's just what we mustn't to – that's the whole point – no use unless we do it all *absolutely* with a serious face.'

Hetty loved the whole direction of these rehearsals and showed innate gifts which flowered in the hot August days, as they pursued their variety acts over the piano keys and across the morning room carpet.

For they danced, too, and invented routines against the tinny music from a great horn gramophone – military quicksteps, mimicking strutting soldiers, to the sound of 'The Dashing White Sergeant' and 'Dolly Gray'. And they fenced as well, stamping across the room, creating an act of great brio, foils clashing to the strains of Strauss's 'Thunder and Lightning' polka.

By the end of the month they had got together half a dozen polished and really quite professional numbers – 'Bertie and Bridey', the rakish near gent in loud checks and the maid in the papier-mâché cherry hat who together had such droll and unexpected musical gifts, rendering with tongue-in-cheek vivacity or with genuine emotion a whole range of songs, together with song-and-dance routines, leading to the climax of a dazzling fencing bout, after which, foils dipped, they both practised their final bows and curtseys to an imaginary audience.

Money was a problem in a different key. Hetty eventually decided to steal it – in kind, if not in cash. And so, just as her mother had done twenty years before at Summer Hill, she began to filch small objects about the house – silver teaspoons, gold-topped scent bottles, Baccarat paperweights – soon gathering quite a collection of little objets d'art which they would sell when the need arose. As to their actual escape – well, with all the baggage they would need for their costumes, that presented further problems. They would think about it.

They were forced to think about it sooner than expected. At the beginning of September letters arrived from the Strauses in Paris, for both Léonie and Frances. To the latter, Benjamin Straus, ever the man of the world and not to be intimidated by someone he knew to be slightly dotty, was fairly blunt. He wrote that he regarded the whole business between the girls as no more than an understandable *tendresse*. He had perfect confidence in his daughter's good sense in the matter, he went on. 'But of course,' he continued, 'I would not wish Léonie to overstay her welcome in the present circumstances – and have therefore arranged that she go to your cousin Mortimer's house at Islandbridge. We have exchanged telegrams and he is perfectly willing that she stay with him, pending her return to France – a journey which, given the present U-boat situation in both Channels, she will not make until I am certain that it is absolutely safe to do so.'

To Léonie her parents wrote that she should stay with Mortimer – for the duration of the war, if necessary – and that she could resume her singing lessons in Dublin. And her father added a footnote: he was sorry that, as it seemed, her friendship with Hetty would have to be suspended. But he consoled her by hinting that its termination at Summer Hill was the act of an unbalanced woman and that Léonie could surely resume the association at a later date. Meanwhile, with the present situation in France and on the high seas, she would be safer in Ireland. There was no question of her going to stay with her Uncle Eli in New York. America was already in the war, as much as made no difference, he told her – and any United States shipping across the Atlantic was in jeopardy.

'Well, that's all right for you,' Hetty told Léonie when she had read the letter. 'But I won't be allowed *near* Dublin.' And Léonie had turned to her, saying with soft certainty, 'So what? You'll be near *me*. Because I *won't* be going to Islandbridge. Wherever we're going – we're going together. Remember? We agreed.'

'Yes,' Hetty said simply.

It was Aunt Emily who solved the problem of their escape from Summer Hill. Hetty, as always, often visited her in the studio-bedroom overlooking the hornbeam maze. And she had spoken to her, of course, of her mother's latest wicked machinations, how she and Léonie were to be forcibly separated – just because they were so fond of each other. Aunt Emily had humphed with particular sympathy in her gruff way. Subsequently, with her insights and intuitions, she came to suspect that the girls were planning to escape the house altogether.

So it was that one day, when Hetty arrived in her room, that she found her great-aunt engaged on a most surprising water-colour. She looked over her shoulder at the nearly-completed picture. It showed herself and Léonie – and Aunt Emily with her easel and paintboxes – out in the governess trap, the vehicle filled with other luggage, hat boxes and suitcases and Gladstone bags, piled up between them. The trap, careering along a dusty country road, was clearly making this spanking pace towards Thomastown station on the horizon, where a train waited, the engine puffing smoke impatiently into a blue sky.

Hetty was astonished by her aunt's prescience. 'Aunt Emily! – what can you be thinking of? We're not going anywhere like that!'

'Excuse yourself, girl – I'm not *that* much of a fool. Know all about your troubles. It's obvious! You're off somewhere together. And quite right too. Wouldn't stay here a minute longer, with your Mama up to her wicked schemes again. Quite right to get out. And here's the way: I'll take you both out on a painting expedition, put your baggage and stuff in a ditch beforehand and we'll pick it up on the way to the station. Nothing simpler.'

'But Aunt Emily, why –'

Aunt Emily looked up at her irascibly. 'Excuse yourself again, girl! Haven't I heard it all? – they want you and Léonie out of each other's light. And for why?'

'Why?'

'They want you to have *men* friends, that's the why.'

'I don't know about –'

'Don't interrupt, girl – I know very well that's the reason. And didn't I tell your Mama many times – have *nothing* to do with men, ruination of everything, ruined her. And I've told you the same – and thank God you took the hint. You stick with

Léonie – best move you ever made. And that's why you'll both be coming with me in the trap.'

And so it was. A week later, on a sunny autumn morning, with the leaves just starting to turn and a hint of delicate chill in the changing air, the three of them clattered down the drive, disturbing the rooks from the trees about the house.

Hetty looked back at the long house on the hill, disappearing into its haven of trees, a last glint of sunlight on its tall windows before it was gone and only the ragged cawing of the birds reminded her of all that she had loved and hated at Summer Hill.

Léonie, sensing her emotion, took her hand. 'Don't be sad.'

'Oh, I'm not,' Hetty lied. 'We'll come back.'

'Of course you will!' Aunt Emily frisked the horse along, the ends of the red scarf with which she had tied her floppy straw hat down streaming out behind her in the wind. 'You'll be back, one day, just as your mother was – when she skedaddled off to the colonies years ago.'

Hetty was touched by her great-aunt's happy certainties, so that tears did come to her eyes then, and Léonie offered her a handkerchief as they sped out of the gateway.

In just such a manner, on such a day, Frances had consoled Elly nearly twenty years before, when they, too, had made an equally precipitate exit from Summer Hill. History was almost exactly repeating itself.

Fonsy O'Grady's 'Theatre of Varieties' was just that – a wonderful mix of players and acts: part music hall, part circus, part straight theatre, part knockabout farce, part *café-concert*. The company, as well as its comics, musicians and singers, also included jugglers, clowns, a duo of tightrope artists, a fat lady, a gypsy fortune teller, a ventriloquist, a troupe of acrobatic dwarves and a mangy lion with its keeper – all brought together by Fonsy's whimsical but most comprehensive view of theatre.

Fonsy had been a fine Dublin comedian himself in the old days. But he had never taken dictation easily – had, indeed, taken more readily to the bottle, which combination, together with his generally wayward approach, had led him to form this haphazard collection of players over the years; he spurned all dull uniformity, insisting only that the acts should be quick, daring, vivacious, original – reflecting his own tastes and abilities here.

With such unconventional ideas he had never maintained his place in the big Dublin music halls, the Olympia or the Queen's. But he had been more than content to run things his way, on a smaller and quite different scale, with engagements in out of the way places. His passion – without his knowing it – was for the life of the old strolling players, for *commedia dell' arte*, for improvisation, surprise, a joyous variety in all things. Theatre for him was only this – and the open road; a date in some small market town in the wilds of Ireland pleased him so much more than anything metropolitan. 'Tents under the stars!' he would shout to his troupe when the beds in some local commercial hotel were all filled. Though he himself would invariably find comfort in just such a place, with his much more hard-headed wife Marjorie, who ran the company's finances. Fonsy O'Grady, in his devil-may-care enthusiasms, his cherub grace, charity and unconscious identification with the old Gaelic world of wandering minstrels, always seemed like the last of his kind.

And the two girls were lucky in his eclectic spirit. He took to them and their act at once, seeing how, if both lacked finesse, they were equally without any hint of the tired or blasé. Like him, the girls were originals. Yes, they could join his company of players. Their summer season had just closed in Bray – some of the British artistes, employed only for those months, had returned home. They could do with an extra act or two since, from now on, through the winter and spring, they would be touring the provinces, with dates in small theatres and village halls throughout the country, across its length and breadth, from Wexford to Galway, Cork to Sligo town.

The girls had met Fonsy, not in Bray, but at his permanent headquarters – an encampment in the narrow Dargle valley some miles inland from Bray, where Fonsy, years before, had taken over a small farmhouse, set above the thickly-wooded slopes running down to the tumbling river. And here, on cleared terraces among the beech and elm, he had set up his troupe. Those that did not lodge in Bray lived in the farm outhouses and then, descending the valley, in wooden huts, some bell tents and a few green-roofed horse caravans.

The rehearsal rooms and general centre for the company were in a stone barn, fitted with sprung boards, taken from an old *celidhe* crossroads dance floor, set over the rough earth. And it was here, with a clattery upright piano, that the girls had given their audition.

Without deceit, they had first appeared before Fonsy in their real personae, the 'Bertie and Bridey' costumes still in their baggage – dissembling only in their provenance. They were first cousins, they explained (and in their dark Jewish colourings there was a sufficient likeness here to justify the claim) – Rachel and Sarah Bauer, with homes in the East End of London. They had started careers there, on the boards of the local music hall, the Theatre Royal, off the Mile End Road. Their act had gone well enough. But they had itchy feet, and had decided to try their luck elsewhere. They wanted to tour, fancy free, to see a bit of the world.

Fonsy saw no reason to disbelieve them. But his wife Marjorie was more circumspect. 'I like them, Fonsy – and the act,' she told him. 'But they're too classy somehow. You don't get that sort in the Mile End Road.'

'Ah, ye might well,' he opined. 'Aren't they a class of a Jew to start with? – and the East End there full of them. And then aren't there all sorts of wimmin doin' queer things these days? – what with the war on and them suffragettes and all.' And since they both liked them – Marjorie, maternal at heart, was without any children of her own – they left it at that.

'You can board with us for the moment,' Marjorie told them. 'Though maybe Bella Lynch, now that old Johnny is gone – maybe you might share with her? – in the big caravan below.'

Bella Lynch was the fat woman who did an act with a melodeon. Her husband Johnny had played the fiddle with her, doing Irish jigs. But he had died a month before.

'Yes – perhaps,' the girls had said, taken at once by the romance of this idea. Bella was a huge friendly woman from Galway with a great scatter of red hair and the trusting blue eyes of a child in a face of unmade dough. She lived in a large, untidy caravan half-way down the hill.

And this, before they set off on their first engagement, was what they did. Bella, in her recent bereavement, was happy to have the two girls as company and distraction, and despite her splendid size there was space enough, at one end of the caravan, where, with a curtain pulled across at night, the girls slept in narrow bunks to either side, covered in thick patchwork quilts which Bella with her delicate nimble fingers – so at odds with the rest of her body – occupied her spare time in making.

The girls, almost immediately, had sent letters to Frances, to Mortimer and to the Strauses in Paris. They were happy and well and *together* – and intended to stay that way, until such time, Hetty told her mother, as she saw fit to change her mind about their friendship. Léonie, with her parents, was entirely open and reassuring, at least as to her present welfare. It had been agreed anyway, as she pointed out, that she should remain in the safety of Ireland for the duration of the war. And she was doing just that. But that safety depended as much on her being with Hetty. She left a poste restante address for her parents to get in touch with her in Dublin. To Mortimer Hetty was equally open – he would understand, she knew. And, when he received her letter, he did.

With Frances it was quite a different matter. On the girls' disappearance, in a flurry of all her old dramatic dictates, she had informed the local constabulary and then detectives in Dublin. At first they had taken notice; a few enquiries were made, a watch was put on railway terminals and ports. But, after the arrival of the various letters from the two girls, the police had relaxed. With the present political turmoil in the country they had many, far more pressing concerns.

Meanwhile, throughout the rest of September, the girls sharpened their act. But much more than that, face to face with the real thing now, they began to absorb all the arts of variety theatre. In the big barn – to the varied sounds of melodeon music from Bella, the thump and cries of the dwarf acrobats, the drum-beats accompanying the tightrope act – they soon found friends among the troupe. With a fascination which they tried to hide, they watched these acts, spellbound by all the tricks of the trade, anxious now to mimic them, completely to throw themselves into this vibrant new life.

The two tightrope artistes, a Belfast couple, Jessy and Hal Morton, particularly took to them. And so did the stand-up comics, Billy and Tony Whelan, middle-aged men who did a tramp act. But above all it was the collection of dwarves who really took them in hand – 'The Tumbling Tinies', six small men, two Irish brothers and the rest assortedly from Britain, headed by the eldest brother, Eddy Nolan, hirsute and slightly hunchback, a most deft and vital character who led the troupe in a series of lightning spins, hand-stands, somersaults and whirly cartwheels across the boards, before he ended the act, juggling balls, atop a pyramid of the other five.

With these people, watching everything they did, the girls began to see the essence of things: immaculate physical control, co-ordination, split-second timing, the need for endless exercise, practice, suppleness. They came to love and envy the skills they saw before them. The world quite changed as you watched them, Hetty thought. With the lovely flash and dazzle of their movements, their perfect balance, poise, timing, the tear-pricking beauty of their acts, these people, the moment they took to the boards, entered another dimension – lost to all the dross of reality, entering a pure, exalted ether where they were suddenly in command of life, towering over it, where they had *won* – which was exactly what Hetty longed for herself.

And so she and Léonie, under the excuse of improving their own act, asked to join in, to learn from them. In woollen tights and leotards, the dwarves taught them all the knockabout tumbles and routines – banana slides, pratfalls and the art of giving alternate cracking back-handers to the cheek without hurt. With the Whelan brothers they learnt the three-hat trick, in which shabby bowlers, at increasing speed, were passed between them, from hand to head to hand . . . and their conjuring act which followed, with baggy sleeves, from which an endless succession of carrots emerged, apparently disappearing down their throats with equal dispatch. Hetty, by the end of the month, managed several perilously swaying trips across the tightrope – before she began to master even this act.

Until the year before, the company had toured in a large charabanc, with two lorries and trailers for the props, costumes and the mangy lion. But now, with the advent of petrol rationing, these vehicles lay idle in a big hay barn. The company, without the lion, would have to tour this year by train, Fonsy told them – or, for those who wished and had such, by caravans with their horses. Bella, with the persistent encouragement of the girls (who had no wish to be seen at railway stations), was persuaded to adopt the latter transport. Thus Bobs, a sturdy chestnut farm horse, was fed with daily oats and made ready for the shafts – the journey to their first date in Wicklow town, fifteen miles south, at the end of September.

So began enchanted months for the two girls. They ran away into a life they could never have imagined – of comradeship and breathtaking excitement, stress, tears, happiness, stage fright: all these offered and taken from them in a swirl of vivid days and nights, with hectic moves, set-ups, rehearsals, lugging the great wicker costume skips about, plunging around tiny squalid dressing rooms against broken mirrors, with faint candles or oil light to make up with, before the curtain rose, the dross was put away and the magic began: Bella on the melodeon, strutting out centre stage, her black shawl and lovely red Galway petticoats flowing, starting the show with a helter-skelter medley of Irish songs – 'Phil the Fluter's Ball', 'MacGinty's Goat' and 'The Rose of Mooncoin'.

It was a life the girls came to love, and their own love bloomed in it: the open road, tents under the stars, opening the caravan door in some country byway on to yellow-leafed autumn mornings; dawns in mid-winter when Hetty lit the stove, sending woodsmoke crackling up the stove chimney, flooding the air with burning pine wood and later the smell of sizzling bacon; dazzling frost crystals on the leaded window panes, wafer-thin ice on the wash bowl as Hetty plunged her hands into it, the cold stinging thrill on her cheeks as she cleared the remnants of last night's make-up off, while Léonie gave the horse a haybag and Bella commenced her elaborate dressings behind the serge curtain.

Their act – in Wicklow, Enniscorthy and Wexford, as they made their way south – went down well. Fonsy had got them to shorten it, dividing it in two parts, with their fencing bout in the second half of the show, dressed as two Musketeers in braided jackets, pantaloons and long boots, though still clearly women. And this second act, as they clashed and parried across the stage to the frenzied drumbeats and fiddles in the pit beneath them, roused the locals.

'Good – great!' Fonsy told them one evening as they left the small stage in Wexford. And later, in a smoky, whiskey-laden back room of White's Hotel, he had looked at them admiringly. 'Clare to God, I'd like to get the points of thim swords at the throat of Bob Molloy in Waterford – and he havin' just cancelled our date at the Royal there.'

'Why?'

'Ah and hasn't he gone and put in one of thim Kinema machines instead – the curse of life for all of us it is, bein' put in now all over the country, ruining our dates.'

Fonsy morosely fed himself more stout. All the company was depressed that night. The Waterford date had always been a good one.

But Hetty said to Léonie later, 'That's easy – we can get the date back for them.'

'Easy?'

'Yes, the Kinema thing that shows the pictures – just put it out of action. Then they'll want us as a replacement.'

'Hetty, if the police –'

'The police won't do anything. They'll never know.'

The company in any case went on to Waterford, where rooms had already been booked, and in the hopes of finding another venue. Bella parked the caravan in a field half a mile south out of the town on the Dunmore road. Léonie hoped Hetty might have forgotten her threat. But she had not.

'Smart clothes today,' she told her first thing that morning. 'We're going into town.'

'For what?'

'You'll see – tell you when we get there.'

They dressed in their most fashionable outfits – pompous hats and veils, kid gloves and discreet handbags – in the manner of society ladies. Telling Bella they were going shopping, they took a cab to the Adelphi Hotel on the quays near the Theatre Royal just round the corner. Here, over coffee in the lounge, Hetty explained her plan.

'We'll walk round and see the theatre manager, this Molloy person – tell him we are organising a series of charity concerts in the provinces, for the Society of Protestant Orphans or something, and would like to see round the theatre. We'll do it all very grand and hoity-toity. You keep him occupied and I'll slip away – I'm bound to find the stupid machine somewhere. It'll be at the back probably, in the balcony, and I'll put the kybosh on it.'

'Hetty, it's madness –'

'Léa, Fonsy and the others have all helped us no end. It's the least we can do. Besides, all this Kinema picture show business – it's so cheap and *vulgar*. Locals are much better off without it.'

The manager – a dapper little man, very full of himself – played straight into their hands when, having shown them round the theatre, he suggested they take a look at his sensational new equipment which he had just installed upstairs, in a metal cubicle at the back of the balcony.

'There, now – just look at it!' he told them, puffed up with pride. 'All the way from London – the latest Kalee projecting machine. See –' He pointed out the big drum-spool at the top. 'That's where the film goes first, then right down through this little gate here, past the shutter and lens, then into the bottom spool. Clickety-click! – you'd never imagine it. We've a great Chaplin two-reeler tomorrow night – Keystone Cops, Fatty Arbuckle, Mack Sennett, the lot!'

Hetty noticed the shutter. It was a delicate spinning mechanism, in the shape of a Maltese cross, with four black arms, set between the lens and the mechanical gate. She made eyes at Léonie, gesturing to her to get the manager out of the way for a moment.

'Now, Mr Molloy,' Léonie said with breathless interest, 'I think I understand all that. But what happens out *there*?' She led him to the window of the little cubicle. 'Is that the wall of the stage the light shines on, or just a sheet?'

'Ah, no indeed, Miss – that's a special silver screen, specially treated paint . . .'

The two of them moved away. In the same instant Hetty put her hand into the projector and broke off two of the shutter arms. They snapped in her fingers like matchsticks. She came forward then, joining the others. 'I say,' she spoke in her most gracious Ascendancy voice, 'it really is all *most* interesting, Mr Molloy.'

Mr Molloy's much-heralded Kinematograph performance did not take place that night, nor, indeed, on the four subsequent evenings. Fonsy O'Grady's Theatre of Varieties most conveniently and successfully filled the bill instead.

It was a constant battle and worry for the company on the tour – these new Kinema machines, theatres converted, replaced by hideous picture palaces being set up everywhere in Irish towns, which took away half their audiences when they did play – and, worse, forbade them some dates completely in towns they had performed in for years. Hetty came to despise the whole business of the Kinema which so jeopardised their livelihoods.

'But it is all very *real*,' Léa told her one day.

'But it's *not* real – that's the whole point. Just a childish sort of peepshow. People on stage *are* real, no comparison.'

'They flock to it all the same.'

'Yes, like children,' Hetty retorted petulantly, like a child.

After Christmas they moved on round the Ring of Kerry, towards Limerick and Galway, through isolated towns in the west where there were fewer picture theatres and audiences who still craved their traditional fare. Spring broke in moist, cloudy blue skies over the stony land of Co. Clare: hawthorn blossom flooded sunken hedges along the Shannon estuary and a soft wind blew off the Atlantic in the little seaside resort of Kilkee when they arrived for an Easter date in the ballroom of the Hydro Hotel in late March.

Bella parked the caravan above a sheltered cove behind the hotel, where a huge half-moon of sandy beach ran away southwards. The girls walked it, barefoot, through cloud-dappled sunlight one late afternoon, imprinting their toes on the moist sand, teasing the waves, provoking and retreating from the sea.

'Tour finishes next month in Galway,' Léonie said, scanning the wave-tossed horizon, when they sat down on a rock at the far end of the beach.

'Yes . . . Then Bray and the summer season, I suppose.'

'Summer Hill as well, your Mama – all that. Can't avoid it forever.'

'Perhaps she'll have changed her mind.'

'Doubt it. But we'll have to do something about it.'

'Probably try and lock me up. I wish I was twenty-one. Oh, Léa, it's all such nonsense! Might as well be twenty-one. We can look after ourselves, make a living, so perfectly well.'

'Yes, but the war won't last forever. And I'll have to go back to Paris then, see Mama and Papa.'

'I'll go with you?'

'Yes, of course you can.' But Léonie turned then, a query in her grey-green eyes. 'You will, won't you?'

'Yes, Léa – yes!' Hetty turned then, stroking Léonie's cheek gently, before suddenly cupping her face, staring at her for an age, then kissing her briefly on the forehead. 'Oh, Léa, I do so love you.'

Léonie shivered then, involuntarily – suddenly aware of all the endless ramifications of her feelings for this woman, who was the focus for everything she possessed, in herself and in her life.

In the event the British government most conveniently solved the girls' immediate problem when they imprisoned Frances once more for seditious activities, this time interning her, without trial, at Holloway in London.

In April 1918, shortly after Fonsy's troupe arrived in Galway, the Allied war effort began to totter in France, Ludendorff had made his great push. British and

French lines were stretched to the limit. More cannon fodder was needed – so that Lloyd George, pressured by Sir Henry Wilson, the British Chief of Staff, finally agreed to a Conscription Bill for Ireland.

Nothing could have been better calculated to inflame every sort of opinion in the country. For although tens of thousands of Irishmen had volunteered to fight for Britain, there were – understandably in the light of the recent rising and executions in Dublin – even more able-bodied men who had refused to do so. And for the first time the Irish Catholic Bishops, when the Bill was introduced, took the side of these patriots, many of whom were now supporters, not of Redmond's old Irish Parliamentary Party, but of the IRA or of Sinn Fein, its political wing. The Bishops passed a unanimous resolution against the Bill.

It was a sign the remaining revolutionary leaders had long been waiting for. The Catholic hierarchy, as well as most moderate opinion in Ireland, was now behind them at last. Protest and passive resistance to the Bill would start at once. And, if that failed, force would be used again. The feeling in the country that spring was intense – a lit fuse against a powder keg. As one – with De Valera – of the two remaining leaders of the 1916 Rebellion, Frances felt duty bound to come immediately to Dublin, where she was soon in the thick of things. British machine gunners lined the roof of the Bank of Ireland. Another rising seemed imminent. Frances, quite forsaking her pacifist notions, resumed her role as militant revolutionary once more, involving herself in all the public protests of the moment – while secretly starting to prepare the necessary medical facilities in Dublin in the event of force being used.

Meanwhile the British, aware of these rebellious plans, but unable quite to put their finger on them, or find any cast-iron reason to arrest the leaders, took fright. A trumped-up excuse was needed – and was soon found. The Irish Chief Secretary discovered an entirely imaginary 'German Plot' among the Sinn Fein leaders, and the arrests began. First De Valera and Arthur Griffith were taken; then Frances and a number of others.

This, at least, was news that Hetty read avidly in Galway. So that at the end of the tour, with a month's break before the summer season, she and Léonie returned at once to Summer Hill, on their way through Dublin contacting Mortimer, who joined them a few days later.

'Well, I knew you were both all right,' he told Hetty, as the two of them took tea in the drawing room, after she and Léonie had described their theatrical activities of the past months. 'As did Léonie's parents. We got your various postcards. But *really*, Hetty . . .' Mortimer fingered his great bird's nest beard an instant, looking at her half critically, half in admiration, over his spectacles. 'The whole thing – it really was very rash of you both, you know.'

'But, Mortimer, we had no alternative,' Hetty told him sensibly, but with a happy glint in her eyes. Then she was entirely serious. 'You knew it well – that Mama was quite determined to separate us. And such a hypocrite about it all, too! Having written me those understanding letters from Aylesbury prison, she then quite lost her reason again. And now, worse still, the same madness has taken her back to the rebels – in prison once more!'

Hetty, charmed to be home again, in a home without her mother, was pert and excited – charmed above all by having taken such a victory over her Mama, turned the tables on her mean spirit.

'Yes, well . . .' Mortimer considered things.

'How else can you explain it?' Hetty, switching blame from herself to her mother, spoke with mature concern now, as if they were discussing the problems of a most difficult child. 'So forgiving, reasonable, apologetic – then so vicious all over again?'

'It's difficult for her, Hetty. An unreconciled nature? I believe so. The hurts she suffered herself in the past – she's tried, but been unable to quite erase them. You should be more understanding, now you're older – and certainly so much more experienced! – yourself.'

His eyes twinkled at her over the teacup.

'But *what* great hurt? – just that she was banished to the colonies and the house wasn't left to her?'

'Hurt enough! You see, she loves the house – desperately.'

'But why was she "banished", Mortimer? Such a dramatic word – she used it herself to me. What frightful thing had she done?'

Here Mortimer, who knew exactly what she had done, was forced to dissemble. 'Why, rather like you, Hetty! She and *her* Mama spent most of their time at each other's throats. She refused to marry Lord Norton's son, for example, over some little tiff on the tennis court. And then there was the matter of your Uncle Henry's funeral, when she tore down the crêpe and black drapes in the house before ringing the bells all over the place.'

'How spirited of her! But that was long before her "banishment" surely? For she lived with you in London, didn't she? – worked there as a nurse for several years. And then went out to the Boer war, when Uncle Eustace was killed. She was only "banished" *after* all that. So what had she done to deserve it – at *that* point?'

Mortimer, giving himself time to think, turned away, looking into the grate. 'I can't say – exactly.' He returned to his white lies most reasonably. 'Except, at that point, with both of her brothers now dead, the issue of the inheritance must first have come up, when her mother told her she was not to have the house, that Austin and Bunty were instead.'

'Yes, but Grandmama changed her will after that, didn't she – in *her* favour. I wonder how Mama managed to persuade her?'

Mortimer had often wondered just the same thing. 'I don't know. She persuaded her somehow. A most forceful character – all three of you!'

He twinkled at Hetty again. She went to the window, and gazed at the changing April light for a long moment before turning. 'Just "force of character" you say?'

'Yes. A fine quality, if you can direct it – suitably!'

'And I have not?'

'Not always –'

'But, Mortimer!' Hetty, frustrated now, knelt in front of him by the fire, speaking vehemently. 'Mortimer, there *must* be something else to it all. I've always felt it so: my father – that he wasn't my real father, couldn't have been – and that *that's* at the heart of it all. Isn't it? You'd know if anyone did.' Mortimer was most uneasy then. But with his lawyer's skill, he hid every sign of this discomfort. '*Isn't* it, Mortimer? That's Mama's real hurt – and that was the reason for her banishment, for her not inheriting Summer Hill. Because I'm not – not legitimate. There was some other me-man, before Mr Fraser, and Grandmama knew about it, which is why she disowned her – I'm sure of it. Oh, *do* tell me,' she asked then, no longer vehement, pleading softly.

Mortimer sighed. He wished so much he could tell her – despite the enormity of the truth: that indeed she had another and once most real father, that she was, in fact, half-sister to the present King-Emperor, George V – for he was entirely aware how most of Hetty's difficulties, her tantrums and unhappinesses as a child, her rash and irresponsible behaviour now, must all stem from this central lie in her life. But he could say nothing of this. Instead he temporised. 'Hetty, I really don't know. But I don't believe –' He paused. 'I don't think it's possible. I believe Robert Fraser was your father.'

Hetty had noticed his hesitations. 'But you think I *might* be right?'

'No. I don't think you are.' He stood up then, outraged and frustrated at his lies, anxious to break off this painful inquisition. 'But in any case, Hetty, we must think of the future, not the past. Your Mama is likely to be interned in London for some time. She knows of your return here –'

'And the Strauses in Paris know we're safely back too . . . so you're not thinking of trying to separate us again?'

'No, of course not. Though I can't, obviously, go quite against your Mama's earlier demand by letting you have the Dublin flat back –'

'But Léa can't return to France yet either with all the U-boats about. So! . . . we'll stay here . . . 'till the summer season starts in Bray.'

Mortimer walked over to the window and Hetty joined him. 'Yes, of course you can stay here, Hetty. It's your home after all . . .'

'And I so love it. Without Mama . . .'

Mortimer gave an understanding nod. 'But, Hetty, you must give her that credit at least. Without her earlier efforts with old Lady Cordiner – whatever they were – it wouldn't be your home at all. Austin and Bunty would be living here now.'

'Yes, Austin and Bunty – all that stupid nonsense. Not that I care much for her. She and Austin came here, you know, last time Mama was in prison – to see Grandmama. I wonder why?'

'Oh, Bunty wouldn't have set foot in the place with your Mama here: daggers always drawn, those two!'

'No, I meant – why did she want to see Grandmama?'

'Well, Austin's her brother-in-law. You know – family. And of course Bunty desperately wanted Summer Hill as well in the old days – never forgiven your Mama over that.'

'No, nor me either, it seems. She didn't speak a word to me when she was last here.'

'Indeed ... Because of course, Hetty, unless your mother changes her will, which I drew up for her last year, this house will go to you. Did you know that?'

Hetty turned to him, astonished. 'No! – No, I di-didn't.'

'Who did you think it would all go to then?'

'I di-di-*didn't* think.'

'Well, in that case perhaps you'd better not tell your Mama I told you. But, yes, of course – it must be yours. There's no one else.'

Hetty felt a frisson of stomach-turning surprise, as she laid a hand involuntarily on the tall window shutter. She gazed out over the daffodil lawns, the budding chestnuts, the whole estate around and beyond. She looked at her hand on the shutter, then ran her eye up to the delicately-moulded ceiling with its Italianate bas-reliefs, the gilt stucco of cherubs and harps and cornucopias far above her, the white Georgian room suddenly lit by an intense spring light. All this would be hers? But how could it be? She and her mother had hated each other for so long, and with such intensity, the idea that Frances would ever make over such a great gift to her had never crossed her mind.

Yet now the thought of owning Summer Hill suddenly held a startling, an overwhelming appeal. The cold brick and mortar took on a quite different aura, seemed imbued with human qualities, a confiding warmth and promise, nothing to do with her mother but for her alone. Something had been returned to her in Mortimer's words about the will – something lost, like a person, which she had missed all her life. Yes, the great house proposed itself to her now, as an answer to all her hurts, like a lover who would calm all the searching storms in her heart, fill the emptiness there. Then she saw how unlikely the idea was.

'But, Mortimer, Mama hates me so! One doesn't give things – like this, all this – to people one so dislikes!'

'Come, Hetty, you exaggerate, I think. You forget, sometimes she doesn't hate you at all, when she was in Aylesbury prison for example. With her temperament, her feelings are always something of a seesaw, hot and cold. And then – remember – you *are* her daughter. There's absolutely no doubt about that! And it's blood that counts in the end.'

'Anyway, she's barely forty. Won't happen for years. And she'll probably change her will in any case, after what Léa and I have done. So it's not worth thinking about.'

'Oh, but it *is*, Hetty.' Mortimer took her arm as they walked away from the window, stopping by a vase of narcissi on the grand piano. 'That's what a house like this is all about: keeping it in the same family. You'll marry, surely, have children ...' He paused then, seeing her face sour in an instant. 'You probably will, you know, one day.'

'No ...' Hetty turned away decisively, frowning, starting to fiddle with a narcissus.

Mortimer, quite aware of the strength of her affection for Léonie, knew he might be treading delicate ground here. But nonetheless he gently pursued the matter. 'I'm well aware of your feelings for Léonie, and I've never for a moment come between you over that – you know that. But those feelings – why, they don't prevent you marrying one day, Hetty.'

'Oh, but it would prevent me.' Hetty turned, staring at him with a childish intensity. 'It we-we-would, you see, because, well, I'm really "married" to her.'

Mortimer had not seen – and did not see – that. But he hid his astonishment. For him their relationship had seemed a great friendship, the happy maturing of a girlish crush. The idea of their being "married" shocked him momentarily, not for any moral reason, he thought and hoped, but because, looking at this astonishingly beautiful, dark-curled, vivacious creature, he could not conceive that some man, many men in time, would not pay court to her. And that, one day, finding the right man, she would return the compliment.

Yes, in the year since he had last seen her, Hetty had grown up, her beauty finding mature shapes, dramatic curves, a hard suppleness in her limbs, meticulous poise and control – a result, he supposed, of all her theatrical exercises and activities. The puppy fat had quite gone; her high cheek-bones, more prominent now, sloped into delicate hollows, nostrils flaring over thin lips. Her almond-like, Wedgwood-blue eyes gazed piercingly from beneath a more controlled mass of dark hair. She was a woman. Yet the child in her had not quite disappeared, nor the insecurities of that childhood. There was still the stammer. Always precocious, commanding, unreasonable, moody – now these qualities, though they were still present, had softened, were directed by a much more real and relaxed assurance. She had, at the centre, an inviolate calm, Mortimer felt – such as lovers feel. Yes, that was it, of course! He saw it clearly now. They did love each other. The evidence was perfectly clear, he realised, in all her new radiance.

'Well,' he went on easily, 'there's plenty of time. Meanwhile I should see your grandmother while I'm down here. Will you come with me?'

They went upstairs, down the long landing, up the little Gothic arched stairway, through the great oak door and into the Victorian back wing of the house. Sally, the maid who had taken over from Molly in looking after Lady Cordiner, sat in a wicker chair at the foot of the four-poster bed at one end of the long room. Lady Cordiner, propped up on pillows, lay asleep – still surrounded, in this her last domain, by all the heavy furnishings and mementoes of her own life here: black-bordered photographs of her adored sons Henry and Eustace prominent at one end of the refectory table; the walls covered with banal Victorian prints and pictures; glass-domed wax flowers, Eustace's Victoria Cross displayed in its velvet box, Henry's cavalry sabre on one wall. The room was permanently dark, with thick drapes against the light; it was filled with decay, nothing had been moved or changed in years.

Mortimer and Hetty stood at the end of the bed. 'Her Ladyship has been sleeping *very* well,' Sally whispered to them. 'Like a lamb.'

And indeed the old woman, with her carefully-tended white hair and even paler wrinkled skin, seemed the very picture of unconscious repose. But just then she opened her eyes a fraction, clearly recognising them both, staring at them, before she concentrated her gaze most malevolently at Hetty. Her eyes were bright, red bright in the lamplight, shining out wickedly from the withered mask of her face – just like the Hallowe'en turnip mask, Hetty thought, that her mother had set before Lady Cordiner years ago, when Hetty had gazed down into the bedroom from the hole in the ceiling. Now, seeing the same malice in her grandmother's face, she wondered whether such evil transferred itself between the generations, from one to the other. Appalled at the thought that she, too, might be so infected, Hetty almost ran from the room.

Mortimer joined her in the corridor. 'De-did you notice how she l-l-looked at me?' Hetty stammered.

'Yes,' he had to admit.

'Why should she hate me so?'

'All of us, I think, Hetty –'

'No – just me. Particularly me.'

Mortimer shook his head. 'You must try and forget the past, Hetty.'

'How can I? You said yourself – the past, our family line – that's exactly what a house like this is all about.'

Robert, reading modern history now at Trinity, was down with Bertie for the Easter holidays. He had been annoyed at first, and then dismissive of Hetty's and Léonie's theatrical behaviour. True, Hetty had sent him several postcards. But really, he'd thought, when he heard about it, it had all been a senseless performance – so needlessly antagonising and upsetting to everyone.

But when he saw Hetty again now – so grown, so composed, fulfilled, happy – he was forced to change his mind about her. Hetty had been *living*, while he only lived in history books. And secretly he loved her all the more for this, as he had loved her before in any case. But that had been a hopeless suit – and must be the more hopeless now, he thought, given Hetty's brazen behaviour and obvious attachment to Léonie.

So he was surprised at the attentions Hetty paid him during the holiday, when she acknowledged him as an equal, as an adult himself now, enquiring warmly about his work, his ambitions – so warmly indeed that the hopes he had had of her were suddenly renewed.

'Oh, I don't quite know what I'll do,' he told her one afternoon, when the four of them were out walking the woods together, Léonie and Bertie ahead of them, making down the valley towards the river. 'I've another two years at Trinity. I'd like to be a journalist, but that's difficult.'

'Teaching perhaps?'

'No . . . Well, I may have to, I suppose. But something a little livelier. Like you.'

'But I've no real gifts, no likely profession.'

'Goodness! – that can't be true: all year with that theatrical company. You must be brilliant!'

'At what?' Hetty was genuinely puzzled.

'At acting, of course. I'd love to have seen you.'

'You can – at Bray. We'll be there this summer. But it's not very much.'

'You and Léonie, you're not going to do that as a career?'

'Course not! Just a way of getting out of Mama's clutches – and staying together,' she added lightly.

'Together?' Robert was rather pointed.

'Yes, of course.'

'But – but that's not really a career either, is it?'

'I don't really expect a career. Léonie'll have that – in opera. Wants to study it properly when she goes back to Paris. And I'll go there, too.'

'And help her?'

'Why, yes – I suppose so.' Hetty had never envisaged any precise details of her future life with Léonie; that she would simply live and be with her was sufficient in itself.

'But you'll surely have to do something else, Hetty, won't you?'

'What?'

'Well, there's lots of new things for women these days. And old things, too – like marriage!'

'Oh, I won't marry.' She laughed. 'Just look at all the unhappiness that brings. Look at Me-Mama! And that awful man she married: my "fe-fe-father". Oh, Robert, you most of all – you'll remember!' She turned suddenly, grasping his arm, eyes clouding with emotion, passionate in her remembrance. 'How *terrible* he was in Domenica: on the beach that birthday of mine – and that night, shouting and roaring drunk with Mama. You remember!'

She gazed at him, longing for his confirmation of their joint unhappiness years before. They had stopped in a shaft of dappled sunlight on the pathway; the others were some distance ahead. Robert, remembering the events all too well, and taking Hetty's impassioned approach as a miraculous indication that perhaps she did love him after all, suddenly grasped her, kissing her awkwardly, before Hetty disentangled herself from the embrace, embarrassed, astonished.

But she had the tact not to show her reaction, letting his embrace seem impetuous evidence simply of his deep understanding. She moved, forward, linking her arm in his, but without any intimacy.

'Oh, Robert,' she said easily. 'It's so nice that we're such good friends now. All those rows we used to have!' She swung on down the path, leading him briskly, catching up with the others. 'So nice to have you, because only you – you alone – know all about our past, right back to the beginning, to talk about it, which makes me feel so much better.'

But Robert was less comforted by this bond of shared memories. He wanted a future with Hetty, not a past. And, if Hetty conveniently repressed her knowledge of this, Léonie could not do likewise. She had seen Robert's embrace.

Later, out on the river, Léonie sat in the stern of one of the boats, watching Robert row over the smooth blue-black water. More than ever now, she was reminded of Robert's feelings for Hetty – knowing, too, how Hetty never thought of him in the same way. And she felt for him then, desperately, but did not know quite how to express it.

'So, you're happy at Trinity?' she asked him, putting all her vivacity and enthusiasm into the banal enquiry.

He sighed. 'Yes,' he said brightly, the tone of voice going quite against his sadness.

Léonie felt stricken by his plight – and by her own part in his disappointment. Suddenly, unable to bear her restraint any more, she leant forward and took his hands, clasping them firmly, so that he had to stop rowing, gazing up at him then with a frustrated tenderness.

'Oh, Robert, please don't be so sad. I so hate it, because . . .' She shook her head, unable to finish the sentence, looking away. But then, turning back, she willed her own eyes deep into his. 'Because you're so good and nice and I'm really so fond of you. I do really like you very much,' she added, speaking with almost painful emphasis.

Robert moved awkwardly on the seat. She took her hands away at last. He stared at her then, half-resentfully, yet half-lovingly, with a surprised intensity as if he were seeing her properly only for the first time. But then the curtain fell and he shut himself away once more.

'Yes,' he said, in a dull voice.

'Yes . . . what?' she asked eagerly.

'I like you too.' He frowned again. But there was no half-smile there this time. His face which, for that one moment before, had been filled with light for her, resumed its set, disappointed form. Yet, Léonie knew something vital had passed between them in that moment when, like a sleep walker, he had woken from his obsession with Hetty and seen her properly.

'Robert,' she said, quickly wanting to do or tell him something of vast importance, but then forgetting what it was.

'Yes?'

Suddenly she knew what it was – and could not say it, just as she had been unable to do it: she had wanted to kiss Robert then, just as he had kissed Hetty back in the woods fifteen minutes before. A kiss of sympathy, she thought. Or was it more of love?

She could not tell Hetty anything of these feelings. But Hetty was not slow to speak.

'My goodness!' she laughed when they were in Léonie's bedroom later that evening. 'You and Robert in the boat this afternoon – clutching and clasping! What *were* you trying to do? Teach him to row?'

Léonie saw the touch of worry and jealousy just beneath Hetty's good humour, but nonetheless felt she had to make an honest reply. 'Hetty, it's such a punishment for him. I saw you both, behind us in the woods –'

'It's not *my* fault!' Hetty, suddenly annoyed, flounced over to the wardrobe, opening it, running her fingers through Léonie's clothes there, as if trying to avoid the issue by having them both dress up and escape into some theatrical adventure, one of their 'games'. 'Not my fault – I've been as nice as pie to him these holidays!'

'Yes, you have been nice to him, I've seen that – and I know it's not your fault. And that's why –'

'That's why *you've* been trying to comfort him – as usual,' Hetty spat back. She had a mauve silk evening dress in her hand now, and shook it in Léonie's face, as if trying to will her into it. But Léonie did not respond. She would not play that game, any game, just then. Hetty stamped her foot. 'Besides,' she went on even more angrily, 'you can't love people on demand, you know. There has to be a *special* feeling. And that's what you have for him – else you wouldn't be making the running over it. Well, *you* love him, then, if that's what you want.' She paused. 'And you do l-l-love him, don't you?'

Léonie coloured, but was determined to remain calm . . . and honest. 'Oh, Hetty, only a fraction as much as I love you.'

Hetty shook with anger at this quite unexpected confirmation of her worst fears. 'A "fraction"?' she shouted. Then she laughed – a bitter, incredulous laugh. 'A *fraction*? That's enough – that's the beginning of the end then, isn't it?' she almost screamed.

'What absolute nonsense!' Léonie, herself angered now, but equally determined in this instance not to be bullied by Hetty, still managed to control her voice. 'A loving affection – you can have that for someone. Nothing *like* what we have. You're being very childish.'

Hetty fully expected Léonie to come to her then, as she had so often before, to comfort her and make things up. But Léonie did not move. Instead she said in a chillingly calm voice, 'Nothing like that – like *him* – is ever going to take me away from you, Hetty.'

Hetty continued to sulk. Léonie hoped that for once she might make the effort at reconciliation, by confirming a parallel sentiment. But all she finally said was 'yes' in a small flat voice.

'"Yes" – what does that mean?' Léonie was unable to prevent a touch of anxiety in her voice now.

Hetty, sensing her unease, took immediate advantage, resuming the attack. She turned, eyes ablaze with self-righteousness, so much the injured party. 'Yes – well, I mean it's not something I could ever even *think* of doing with a man, *ever*. That's all.'

At the end of the Easter holidays Robert and Bertie returned to Trinity College, the girls rejoined Fonsy O'Grady's troupe for the summer season at Bray . . . and Frances remained in Holloway. The war rumbled on in France, the Allies regaining some of the ground lost earlier that year in Ludendorff's great push. Situations that had seemed so unstable at Easter, at Summer Hill and on the Western front, seemed to regain a balance once more. But the poise was illusory.

After their row over Robert, matters between the two girls had in fact changed considerably. Hetty for the first time had failed to dominate, to have her way with Léonie. Léonie had stood firm in her admission of love, or loving affection, for Robert. She had failed to recant – and, worse, had failed to make things up with her, Hetty felt. Worst of all, Léonie then, and subsequently, had abandoned their 'game'. At the crucial moment in their argument, when she had offered Léonie the mauve ball gown, when if she had undressed and worn it, or not worn it, they could have loved each other and so reached a reconciliation in the best possible manner – at this vital instant Léa had denied her.

This betrayal, as Hetty saw it, began to fester in her soul, a corruption which, throughout that summer and autumn, brought back, indeed increased, all her old poisonous frustrations, her domineering restlessness, so that for lack of mastering Léonie, she punished her in various little theatrical ways – over 'business' in their act, the sharing of a dressing room mirror, promoting a quite unnecessary aggressiveness in their fencing performance. Hetty felt her soul drying out – all the myriad personas there, which before Léonie had so nurtured and responded to, finding no outlet now.

Léonie, whose great gift was to know what was in the minds of others and to love without making unreasonable demands, saw and understood these changes in Hetty – and did everything she could to reassure her. But Léonie had changed, too.

She thought she would love Hetty all her life. But, after the business with Robert, and Hetty's unjust accusations, Léonie felt she could no longer entirely repress her own personality in this love – and this because she wanted at all costs to preserve and not lose it. For something had moved in her heart then, during their row over Robert, spelling out the clear message at last – confirming, insisting on something she had long felt – that, if she continued to give in to Hetty, pander to her every whim, Hetty would use her up, suck her dry, finally turning her into something despised, a slave, and then drop her. So now, a last chance, it was vital to stand firm and not become that slave. They must both grow into a different love, a love that would have to mature if it was to survive. And she said as much to Hetty, as tactfully as she could, during the following months.

'Don't you *see*, Hetty,' she told her one day, sitting among the gorse bushes on top of Bray Head. 'We dress up every evening for our act. And *that's* why there's no need for all our old games any more. We can have a different love now, an even better sort.' She turned, trying to catch her attention. But Hetty's gaze remained fixed on a ship far out to sea. 'You think, because we don't have our games any more, that I love you less? No! Not true – I love you as much as ever, promise you. Just, if our games go on . . . they'll destroy us. You'll come to despise me for giving in to you all the time. And it's not love – just being someone's mirror for ever and ever. And, besides, you have that mirror every day now in the audiences. You don't *need* me for that any more. Please – just need me as a person – I've so often told you – the one I am, am growing to be.'

Hetty, who had nodded vaguely throughout all this, still gazed out to sea. 'Oh, *Hetty*! – we have to change. You know we do.' She took her hand and stroked it. She would have embraced and kissed, made love with her even, there and then, among the gorse bushes. But Hetty, though she seemed to have agreed with all this, remained cold – stone cold in the warm August afternoon.

Finally all she said was, 'Dermot'll be back soon, from that prisoner of war camp. Everyone says the war will be over in a month or so. And that'll be something at least.' She smiled to herself. 'Wonderful! – I've missed him so much.'

Léonie took this sudden unrelated comment as a small piece of revengeful spite on Hetty's part, as indeed it was. But just as much was it a true sentiment. Hetty really had missed Dermot, writing to him regularly, receiving brief POW cards from him sometimes in return. And now, with this sense of the war's ending, she was excited by the idea of seeing him again.

Father, or father figure: all that still mattered to Hetty in Dermot. But in any case he was her great, her greatest friend, as far as men were concerned. She longed to tell him of all her adventures in the years since she had last seen him, the daring child now become an even more daring woman. Hetty, especially in the light of her present impasse with Léonie, was tempted by Dermot once more. And, though she could not admit it for a second, he loomed on the horizon for her that afternoon as someone, aside from Léonie, whom she might set out, as she had once before, to impress, perhaps to dominate, even to love. Had she been able to admit this to herself, she might have added that Dermot occurred to her now not as a substitute father but as a potential replacement for Léonie. But she refused to bring any such honest self-analysis to bear in the matter.

The war ended in early November. By then the girls were on tour again, moving south along the coast, as on the previous year, towards Wexford and Waterford. Frances remained in jail. But the political situation in Ireland, so increasingly chaotic, was such that it seemed likely she would be released soon – for now she was no mere rebel prisoner, but a member of parliament at Westminster.

She and seventy-two other Sinn Fein candidates, many of them also in prison, were elected as Irish MPs in the British general election that December. The mood in the country, quite forsaking Redmond's old Irish Parliamentary Party, had swung round almost entirely in favour of Arthur Griffith's abstentionist Sinn Feiners, who, though elected, would refuse to take their seats at Westminster, forming instead their own illegal government in Ireland. Mortimer Cordiner was one of only a handful of Redmondite MPs who managed to retain their seats at Westminster. Thus he was in London, at his house in Wilton Street, when Dermot returned to England before Christmas.

12

T HERE WAS ANOTHER young man returning to London from the war, an Irish-American, who had volunteered more than a year earlier, serving with the Royal Canadian Flying Corps on the Western front. But he went on almost at once to Dublin, taking a suite at the Shelbourne Hotel. Now, immaculate in soft Donegal tweeds, sipping coffee in his rooms overlooking Stephen's Green, he sifted through a portfolio of theatrical photographs which Mr Waxman had brought to show him.

'So, Waxman – up to your old tricks again . . .' The tone was quick and ironic, a New York accent – but touched with another and softer melody, a more cultured Irish tone just discernible in the background.

Waxman, still retaining his black beret, smiled. It was almost a leer. 'Tricks?'

'All these girls – *Irish* girls. How do you manage to persuade them into these poses! "Holy Catholic Ireland" . . .'

He adopted an authentic brogue for these last words, using the pleasantry as a cover for his keen interest in some of the more daring situations which Mr Waxman had contrived for the girls on his studio chaise-longue.

'Ah, the temptation of the camera, Mr Williamson – you'll know it yourself. They can't resist it, do anything for it, with a bit of encouragement. They're more than willing. You'd be surprised!'

'No, I wouldn't.' Craig Williamson cut Waxman's familiarity dead as he abruptly discarded the last risqué photograph, going on to something more decorous.

'Of course not, Mr Williamson.' Mr Waxman resumed his obsequious stance behind the armchair.

Craig Williamson, though not tall, still appeared lanky. It was his thin face, delicate proportions and fine bone structure which gave him a willowy appearance. And the well-cut tweeds, green silk handkerchief trailing casually from his breast pocket, the soft cotton shirt and hand-made brogues, all accentuated his natural finesse. He was neat, quick, contained, with a darting precision in his movements – an expression steely and dreamy by turns, dangerously chameleon in mood.

In the same way he seemed both older and younger than his twenty-nine years.

There was a vast maturity sometimes in his faraway gaze, an air of contemplative understanding. Yet just as often he was filled with a dazzling Celtic boyishness, playing the rogue . . . or promoting a biting, sometimes even a cruel, wit, a deceptively sharp intellect and dominant intent which quite gave the lie to his matinée idol good looks.

'There!' Waxman stooped down and pointed to a new photograph. 'Rather nice, isn't she? A Miss Gilchrist – soubrette at the Queen's Theatre here. She would do well in classical costume,' he added with a judicious smirk.

Craig Williamson looked up sharply.

'Miss Gilchrist has the air of a Dublin seamstress, Waxman. This is *Cleopatra* I'm considering women for. Something considerably more regal is required.'

'Oh, I thought you had already cast her.'

'I had. With Miss Swanson. But she's not available. Triangle won't release her. So I'm considering others – on my way through town.'

'Of course, Mr Williamson.' Waxman was unctuous. 'I know your great affection for Ireland –'

'I have very little affection for Ireland.' He cut him dead again, with bitter emphasis. 'Came by only to see my family.'

'Yes, the big house . . . In Limerick, isn't it?'

'No – County Cork.' Craig Williamson turned away, uneasy for the first time about something. 'Anyway, that's no matter.' He returned to his view of Miss Gilchrist. 'Yes, something considerably more regal, Mr Waxman.'

He stood up then, and with something of a belligerent swagger walked over to the big window. But now the image of the matinée idol was somewhat tarnished: he swaggered, but with a slight limp, as he went to inspect a group of Redouté flower prints on the wall. Reaching out, he took one, of a lovely arum lily, gazing at it, then holding it up to the winter sunlight as if it was a chalice. 'Yes, *regal*, Mr Waxman – like this flower.' He turned, confronting the little man, showing him the print, staring at him with his grey-blue eyes – usually slumbrous, relaxed, but fired now with a vivid enthusiasm. 'This lily,' he went on, 'a pure beauty, grace, poise, *innocence*, yes! But at the same time something dark in the heart, mysterious, a hint of evil. *That's* my Cleopatra. And Miss Gilchrist doesn't quite fit the bill, I'm afraid, Waxman.' As he spoke he was unable to disguise his passion for both sides of the coin in this ideal woman: she was someone equally dedicated to the sacred and to the profane.

'Yes, Mr Williamson. But there are . . . other women. Possible Cleopatras.' He gestured to the portfolio.

'So they said in London. But there weren't.' Craig Williamson returned, disconsolate and bored, to the armchair.

'You've been in London, of course.' Waxman resumed his oleaginous air. 'Your war wound – very sorry to hear about it.'

Williamson brightened, vaguely warming towards Waxman for the first time. 'In some god-awful hospital in Eastbourne actually, laid out with weights and pulleys which did no damn good at all.'

– 466 –

'Yes, you've been away at the war some time, haven't you? What? – over a year?' Waxman, attempting subtle revenge now, had a doubting tone in his voice, implying that perhaps Williamson had been away at the war too long, had lost touch with things in Hollywood, that he might not now be quite the powerful figure he had once been there.

'Yes, a year, Mr Waxman. But patriotism counts more with me . . . than it does perhaps for some people.' He glowered at Waxman before returning to the portfolio, about to dispense with it, thumbing quickly through the final few photographs, before one of them caught his eye. It was of Hetty and Léonie, in their 'Bertie and Bridey' costumes, one of the series that Waxman had taken of them over a year before – the girls, in his skilled hands, at their most decoratively seductive. Craig Williamson gazed at the photograph intently, then at the others, his eyes suddenly alive.

'Who are these two?'

'Ah hah!' Mr Waxman was pleased to have struck gold at last. 'An interesting pair. That one,' he pointed at Hetty, 'not a young man at all, you see: a young *woman*, *dressed* as a man!' He looked at Williamson knowingly. 'Yes, a young woman – though she wouldn't admit it. They came to me straight off the street, dressed like that; said they had a music hall act together, in England. Of course I didn't believe them. Her accent was too good – the tall one – and clearly Irish. And both were too classy by half. Just a pair of mischievous Irish girls – *very* mischievous – up to some elaborate party trick.'

'Yes, Waxman. But *who* are they?'

'Ah, there you have me –'

'I'll make it worth your while.' Craig Williamson showed a nakedly dominant intent now.

'They left no address, picked up the photographs themselves. But I kept copies, they were so good – and I followed them when they left the studio. They returned to an office behind the Olympia –'

'I see, so they were playing at the Olympia?'

'No, no – not at all. I checked that. They went back to a lawyers' office in Crown Alley. That's all I know . . .'

Williamson held up the last photograph, in which Hetty, at her most masculine, in cravat, check suit and fawn bowler, with an arm round Léonie, was gazing imperiously into the lens.

'A *woman*, you say?'

'Sure of it. Just look at the shapes there. That's not a man's chest. Nor the waist – or the behind! – I can assure you of that!' Mr Waxman licked his lips.

'It's the *face* I'm interested in, Mr Waxman,' Williamson told him curtly. 'Can't you see it? That's what I meant by regality.'

'Indeed. But with just that hint of, well, something . . . quite "uncalled for" . . .' Mr Waxman gazed at him with narrow, conniving eyes. 'I can take you round there, if you're interested. The lawyers there will probably know about them.'

'I'll go round there myself – if I'm interested.'

Craig Williamson had concluded the meeting, though he still held the photographs. Waxman gestured at them.

'You'll keep those then?'

'Yes. I'll pay for them.' Opening his wallet, he handed over a crisp five pound note. Then, his expression suddenly hardening, he took out another note, holding it up casually. Waxman showed surprise. 'Come now, Waxman – I'm not quite such a fool.' Williamson moved forward, almost threatening him. 'Will you take the extra money, or shall I adopt . . .?' Williamson, though slight, showed all the aggression of a fly-weight boxer.

'I don't understand.'

'But of course you do. If you'd bothered to follow those girls half-way across Dublin in the first place – *and* brought me their photographs – then you must know where I can find them. "Mischievous girls" they may be. But they're obviously stage people as well, have some music hall act here. Where is it, Waxman?' He raised his voice. 'The Gaiety? The Olympia? The Queen's?' He dangled the money in one hand, bunching the knuckles of the other.

Waxman was alarmed. 'No, no, not in any of the Dublin theatres – I checked on that. But I'll tell you,' he said urgently, 'they could be with Fonsy O'Grady's troupe. That's the only other music hall outfit here: "Fonsy O'Grady's Theatre of Varieties" – on Bray Promenade. But they'd be on tour now, Wexford or Waterford. They tour every winter, all over Ireland.'

Williamson nodded, handing him the extra money. 'Thank you, Waxman. "Fonsy O'Grady's Theatre of Varieties" – sounds just their style.' He was happy at last as he showed Waxman to the door.

'I hope you won't be disappointed, Mr Williamson.' Waxman made a last sally. 'They're not really actresses, I'm sure of that. Still, that's not really what you wanted them for, was it?' he added quickly, before scuttling out of the door.

Waxman knew something of Craig Williamson's wayward tastes in young women. He had acted as tacit procurer for this most successful Hollywood picture director, on several of his previous visits to Ireland. His family was Anglo-Irish, he thought – the St John Williamsons, weren't they? – from some big house in the west. He wasn't sure where, for Mr Williamson had only hinted to him of his family background. Why would he do more? – when his private interests, when he came here were . . . well, so necessarily private.

Craig Williamson, taking the photographs round the Dublin theatres that afternoon, learnt that, as far as anyone knew, the girls had indeed never acted at the Olympia, the Queen's or the Gaiety. They must, as Waxman had suggested, work for Fonsy O'Grady's troupe, if they worked for anyone. And then the stage doorman at the Queen's Theatre, who knew several of the artistes in Fonsy's company, confirmed this supposition, after he had seen the photographs. Yes, he told him, he had heard of a comic act, a song-and-dance duo, in Fonsy's company, two women, one dressed as a man. It was supposed to be quite good. Yes, indeed, he said, looking at the photographs, that was likely to be them. But Fonsy was on tour now, the stage doorman went on – probably due to start his annual date at the

Theatre Royal in Waterford, which was usually the first week in December.

This suited Craig Williamson very well. He had to go south the following day in any case, to Cork, to see his father briefly. His boat, from Queenstown to New York, was not due to leave for another week – and with all the returning American troops would almost certainly be further delayed. He had time to spare. After Cork he would come back to Dublin via Waterford. Fonsy's company was usually there for a week, the doorman told him.

Returning to the Shelbourne he looked through the photographs of the two girls once more. Was it worth it all, he wondered? So many would think it sheer madness – this chancy pursuit of a mere image. But then he reminded himself how, in the moving picture business, that was exactly what everyone pursued, producers and audience equally: just a photographic image. In his world that was everything.

It was certainly worth it. He had rarely, if ever, seen so startling or tempting a face as the taller girl's – or one so formidably beautiful, the dead straight nose, the classical arrogant lines. And yet so pure, untutored: a face which, if he could get his hands and his cameras on it, might at one blow regain his fortunes in Hollywood – a face so entirely different, at once more distinguished and seductive than any possessed by the picture stars out there now: the banal shop-girl, spit-and-kiss-curl women like Mabel Normand or Mary Miles Minter, the preposterous vamp Theda Bara, the blonde ringlets and cloying innocence of that false child, the World's Sweetheart, Mary Pickford . . .

And, apart from his professional interest in this woman, he was taken by her in a more personal way. The insolent intelligence in her expression, the cool mischief there, appealed to him. Here, he sensed, was a worthy opponent, a valid quarry in his long hunt. And beyond that there was even something more, in those great liquid eyes – a touch of mystery, of hurt, of anguish even – which drew from him a quite different feeling, one which he hardly dared think about, having suppressed it for so long: a sense of protectiveness, the possibility, even of love.

Yes, something in her expression murmured to his romantic heart, so long overlaid by mere lusts, sad desires, successive failures in the hunt. But in these photographs he thought he heard a voice say to him, 'This one will be happy – this one is for you.'

The chance of finding her in Waterford . . . well, he might be disappointed. Yet she existed somewhere. The photographs proved that. And, since she existed, then he would find her. In that material respect at least, he would win – as he always had. To win: that was the simple motto of his life.

In a dark overcoat, trilby hat and a scarf right up against his mouth as if he was trying to disguise himself, Williamson pushed against the cold December wind, walking into the city from Cork railway station. He passed the Presbyterian church on the corner – knowing it all too well, inside and out, from so many childhood Sundays spent there – before finally turning into the High Street.

He saw his father's grocery shop, with its pretentious rustic wooden lettering: 'W. C. Curtis. High Class Family Grocers & Provisioners'. The shop was half-way down the main street, near the new picture palace where that week Gloria Swanson was starring in de Mille's latest extravaganza *Her Gilded Cage*.

Craig felt a pang of jealous bitterness as he passed the billboards, impatient to be back behind a camera himself, and walked on past the statue of Father Matthew, the great apostle of temperance in County Cork, set in the middle of the wide thoroughfare. Narrow-minded, teetotal Catholics – and a few Presbyterians more prejudiced still; ragged, barefoot children playing by the Mardyke, and dank vegetable shops full of wet cabbages under the misty street lights: the whole city had always been as cold as charity for him. He hated the place.

It was late afternoon and dark, but the windows in the flat above the shop, which had been a chilly home to him for the first fifteen years of his life, were unlit. His mother, Eileen, who years ago would always have been there to welcome him with a pot of Barry's strong tea and a big fry-up, had died almost ten years before.

She had been a Catholic, from Dublin, pregnant with him before her hurried and disastrous marriage to his father, which had resulted in their both disappearing from the capital, moving to Cork and opening the shop there: a misalliance which had resulted in his mother's incarceration upstairs in the flat, feigning invalidism on his father's instructions, so as to avoid meeting the other members of the Presbyterian community in the city. Now there was only his father in the shop. He could see him through the window now, beavering away behind the counter, an area he hardly ever left.

The little bell on top of the door pinged as he entered, moving past shelves filled with the more select brands of jam amd marmalade, jars of sauce, pickles and tins of Colman's mustard. To his right a row of Irish gammon hams hung from the ceiling. He made towards the long pine counter, then hesitated. An insolent county lady in heavy, oatmeal tweeds, was speaking to his father. 'Yes, Mr Curtis – but it must be a *Yorkshire* ham for Christmas. Not these local ones. And I shall need the usual sweetmeats, nuts, dried fruit and so on. Have you any pineapples?'

'I'm afraid not, Ma'am. The war, you know . . .'

Craig Williamson almost turned and left the shop – appalled, as he always had been, by his father's obsequious tone and attitude. But his father noticed him just at that moment – a cold, neat figure in a dark tie and wing collar, impeccably dressed, in a white bibbed apron over his pin-striped jacket, a few dark slivers of hair running across a balding scalp, thin moustache, narrow lips, a man already old in his early sixties.

Craig made a covert gesture, to delay their meeting until the arrogant lady had finished her order. He made the sign seem one of pure courtesy. In fact he did not want to embarrass his father – or himself – by making their relationship apparent.

Eventually, the customer gone, his father spoke. 'Michael – Michael Curtis,' he said to his son, Craig St John Williamson. 'The prodigal's return,' he added drily. There was no welcome in his dull, clipped voice, just a tone of tired criticism and exasperation – as there had always been. And once more Craig was tempted to turn on his heel . . . and quit this sad place, filled with so many old lies and familial horrors, this shop with its flickering gaslight, smelling of bacon rind, sawdust and carbolic soap; its memories for him of such hypocrisy; a stinginess and cruelty upstairs, together with a servile respectability and lavish credit for the county gentry downstairs in the shop.

But he could not leave. For, just as he nurtured a frustrated, twisted romanticism in his heart, so, too, in the same place lurked the shadows of Christian honour and duty, all the ineradicable traits of the lapsed Puritan.

In Waterford the following day he took a room at the Adelphi Hotel on the quays, confirming that Fonsy O'Grady's troupe was indeed playing at the Theatre Royal nearby, and going on there that evening. He paid ninepence for a front seat in the stalls, then a penny for a programme. And there was the act: 'Bertie and Bridey', number six in the first half, the 'The Two Musketeers' – whatever that was – number seven in the second. And the names of the two players in each instance: 'Sarah and Rachel Bauer'. This surprised him. They were Jewish obviously. But had not Waxman clearly mentioned an Irish accent?

Their song-and-dance act, when it came, did not astonish him. Remembering such vaudeville theatre from his days in New York, he found it no more than a routine performance – not amateur, but with too many ragged edges, insufficiently skilled musical backing, and without the proper pacing that would have made it truly professional. One of the girls, the smaller one, could certainly sing – a lovely velvety soprano. And the other – though with no real voice at all, indeed she seemed for an actress to have at moments a strange hesitancy in her voice – played the piano very well. As for their second number, both of them in eighteenth-century French costume as 'The Two Musketeers' – well, it was rousing stuff and the taller girl could certainly use a foil. But it was all more in the way of a fencing exhibition. No, indeed, their performances left something to be desired. But the basic human material there . . . well, that was quite astonishing.

The tall girl, dressed as a man: there was so much more poise, beauty and maturity than the photographs had suggested. Even beneath the bowler and the high cravat he could see the vividly expressive features, all so strongly marked, above all the animal vigour, the spontaneous vivacity of the girl, the thrill she offered in just being alive, which gave her so startling and immediate a presence, a wit or cheek or tender wistfulness, that simply leapt over the footlights, pervading the audience with her spirit.

What she possessed most of all, Craig Williamson recognised at once, was some indefinable quality which, unaware of it herself, she could project, without thought or effort; and, when this happened, made it impossible to take one's eyes off her. No one in the picture business had ever really defined that gift, Williamson knew: a mix of so many natural or identifiable gifts, but essentially something mysterious, untouchable – a radiant spirit, and its most hidden recesses at that, which very few stage people were able to promote, as this girl did now, just by standing there and looking at you.

You could not identify this quality until you saw it. But in his business, when you did see it, you recognised it at once, and your stomach turned over with excitement. Intuition alone told you then, as it told him now: this girl had it – a dazzlingly engaging presence, which drew you like a magnet, something that could never be faked or produced or emulated, a unique, un-put-downable quality given only to the greatest stars in his celluloid heaven.

'No, Mr Williamson. We're not the least interested in working in your "photoplays" or "moving pictures" or whatever nonsense.'

Hetty, at her most dismissive, glowered at Craig Williamson over her untouched coffee cup in the lounge of the Adelphi Hotel where he had brought the two girls after the performance.

Craig sipped delicately, treading the ground with extreme caution. Getting the two girls to the hotel had been difficult enough. Having sent his card up to them, he had hung around in the alley behind the theatre like any stage-door Johnny for nearly half an hour before they finally appeared, surrounded by 'The Tumbling Tinies', a troupe of dwarves in their minute coats and boots against the cold wind.

To begin with, the girls had refused any hospitality or conversation with him, until he had suggested the dwarves accompany them to the hotel; where they were now, happily ensconced over drinks, a row of merry gnomes on high bar stools in a room leading off the lounge. At first he had been quite confident the girls would come back with him. They were actresses – theatre people – after all. And the card he had sent up – 'Craig St John Williamson', from the 'William Fox Picture Corporation, Hollywood, Los Angeles' – had always been a sure bait in the past. But they had refused.

'Is this *you*?' The taller girl had flourished his visiting card dismissively in his face as she left the stage door. And 'yes', he had replied, with something of a wicked smile and an exaggerated brogue – ''Tis me! Who else?' – as if they had met before and she was a bad girl to have forgotten him.

And then, as if startled by some sudden barrier in front of her, the girl had paused in her departure from the theatre, staring at him carefully in his red scarf and trilby, momentarily intrigued. Putting his card between her teeth, donning a Russian fur hat and pushing her curls up beneath it, she stared at him.

Something passed between them then, in that first instant in the lamplight outside the stage door – a moment's acknowledgement, as between duellists, of some future engagement. And that, Craig thought, was the real reason she had finally agreed to come with him: she had been tempted, against his roguish impertinence, by the idea of punishing him for his temerity, and by the prospect of an easy victory there.

So that now in the hotel, while retaining some of this wit, he was much more careful in his approach, favouring the other, smaller, dark-haired girl as much as her companion.

'I wish you'd at least consider a picture test. I can fix it up in London, or Dublin – Miss?' He hesitated, looking at Hetty. 'It's Miss Sarah Bauer, isn't it?'

'No, I'm Rachel.' She gestured at Léonie. 'My cousin – she's the Sarah.'

'I see . . .' Craig nodded wisely. He felt somehow he was being lied to. They both looked Jewish certainly, especially the smaller girl. But the taller one had this distinctly cultured Irish accent, Ascendancy Irish – there was no doubt about it. He could spot it at once, for he himself had longed for just such an accent and background, things he so assiduously pretended to now.

'Nice name . . . "Bauer". Jewish, isn't it?' he went on lightly. 'But of course you're Irish. At least *you* are.' He looked steadily at Hetty. 'Not many Jewish people in Ireland, are there?'

'Oh yes, one or te-te-two!'

Now he was almost certain she was lying: that sudden stammer told him something. The girl was not so confident in this alias. But he let it pass. 'Anyway, as I've told you, I'm on my way back to America from the war . . . and looking for people to cast in a new motion picture I'm hoping to start soon.'

'Oh yes – what's that?' Hetty retaliated at her most haughty.

'*Cleopatra.*'

She laughed. 'Well, you're not suggesting I could pe-play her, are you?'

'No, you couldn't.' He paused. 'Not yet,' he added.

Léonie chuckled. 'Cleopatra,' she murmured. 'What next?'

Craig turned to Léonie. 'Not beyond the bounds of possibility, you know. You can both act. Your friend particularly: wonderful presence. Need more training, more experience, of course. But it's all there for her, I assure you. I don't return to the States for a week or two. So let me fix up a test?'

'But, Mr Williamson,' Léonie interrupted, sensing clearly how he was making a play for Hetty, excluding her, 'we've neither of us the slightest interest in your motion picture business. Indeed,' she leant forward, confidingly dismissive. 'Indeed, more than that, we – all of us in the company – we actively resent your business a great deal. It's been ruining half our dates in Ireland for the past few years, all these new picture palaces – taking the bread from our mouths. And, quite besides that, it's really such *rubbish* you people produce!'

'Yes, indeed!' Hetty took over, though with less conviction than Léonie had shown. 'Far from working with you, I'd like to destroy all your picture palaces!'

'I'm sure you would.' Craig smiled. 'That's just the vigorous quality I like in you. And woman of your word, no doubt, too. Yes, indeed, you'd do *just* that,' he ran on enthusiastically. 'But, Miss Bauer, even you can't stand against this picture palace business for ever. And, with your great gifts in the same field, why, it's obvious: if you can't beat 'em, join 'em!'

Léonie shook her head, answering for Hetty. 'Not possible. This music hall act is only a temporary business, taken up because we couldn't travel with the war on.

But I'm to study opera soon – in Paris. And my cousin will be coming with me. So, you see, it's simply not possible, even if we wanted to get into your motion picture business, which we *don't.*'

Léonie, having delivered this coup de grâce, stood up to leave. But Hetty was less anxious to go.

'Well, thank you for the offer, Mr Williamson. Some other time perhaps . . . I might consider the idea of taking your test or whatever.' She smiled at him briefly. But Léonie was furious.

'Hetty!' she remonstrated with her. 'What can you be thinking of? There's no question . . .' Her voice trailed off. There was silence.

'"Hetty"?' Craig Williamson asked. 'Not Rachel – but Hetty. Short for Henrietta. Not a very Jewish name!'

Hetty was furious now. 'Henrietta is my middle name – and it's none of your business what my friends call me, Mr Williamson.'

She stamped out of the room, Léonie following her. But in her anger she had forgotten her purse on the table, a little blue bead bag. Craig Williamson, opening it very quickly, fingered deftly through the contents, soon finding what he wanted – an envelope with a London postmark, addressed to 'Miss Henrietta Fraser, Summer Hill, Cloone, Co Kilkenny'. He followed the two girls out to the hall and returned the purse.

'You left this behind, Miss Bauer.' He gave her one of his nicest smiles. 'Yes, I do hope you'll reconsider my offer. I'll be in touch with you.' The troupe of dwarves, leaving the bar, surrounded the girls. 'Why,' he went on, looking down at the tiny men. 'You could *all* come to Hollywood – I'll need just such people, for Cleopatra's Egyptian court!'

Hetty, snatching the purse, turned on her heel without another word.

Craig Williamson returned to the Shelbourne Hotel in Dublin. 'Henrietta Fraser, Summer Hill, Cloone, Co Kilkenny'. Who could she be? It should not be difficult to find out. He spoke to the manager of the hotel, someone sure to be well versed in big houses and great families in Ireland.

He answered at once, but without any enthusiasm. 'Henrietta Fraser – of Summer Hill in Kilkenny? She must be related to Frances Fraser, the Republican rebel who caused such havoc here in the hotel and in the Green in the 1916 rising. She's in jail at the moment. In London,' he added thankfully.

'Are you sure?'

'About the woman Frances Fraser anyway. No doubt. She certainly comes from Summer Hill, a big house down there. One of the Cordiner family. But I'm sure you'll find all the information you want here, Mr Williamson,' he said tartly, handing him the hotel's copy of *Burke's Irish Landed Gentry.*

And there indeed it all was, in nearly two pages of the directory – the Cordiners of Cloone and Kilclondowne, with the latest in that line as a final entry: 'Henrietta Francesca Elizabeth Fraser (b. 1900) dau. of Frances Fraser (née Cordiner) and Bruce Fraser, of Fraser Hall, Domenica (d. 1908)', with her address as the family seat at Summer Hill.

Craig was enchanted by all this information. His boat to New York was delayed. He had more time on his hands. He would go down to Summer Hill, make another approach to the girl. She would surely be there over Christmas – with her 'cousin', if such she was. The whole business of these subterfuges – her male disguise, her alias as 'Miss Bauer' – all this only added to her charm for him. And now this additional factor of her aristocratic lineage, with a great house in Ireland, made her more attractive still. There was no question, he would renew his suit. He would not let her go. He would win. This girl, quite apart from her theatrical gifts, her beauty, represented in her background everything he had ever dreamed of for himself in Ireland: 'Henrietta Francesca Elizabeth Fraser – of Summer Hill, Co Kilkenny'. The idea and its ramifications sent a thrill down his spine.

Leaving the hotel that evening, he saw the billboard by the news stand in the porch: MRS FRASER TO BE RELEASED! HOME FOR CHRISTMAS! Buying a copy of the paper he saw the woman's photograph on the front page. Yes, of course, something of the same features – this was the girl's mother! There was no doubt of it.

Henrietta Fraser: daughter of an Irish rebel leader, with some exotic West Indian background to boot, and heir no doubt to a great estate, wonderful comedienne, fencer, outrageous liar, male impersonator and with that clear hint he had had in the Waterford hotel of some unsuitable relationship with her 'cousin' – the mix was almost too rich. The stars in Hollywood, like Theda Bara, had to have such lives invented for them by the publicity departments – and such skills, usually and unsuccessfully, drummed into them. This girl had all this in truth and by nature. Now that the petrol rationing was over, he would motor down to Summer Hill in the next few days.

In normal circumstances – if the two girls had gone to Paris or continued their tour with Fonsy, disappearing into the wilds of Ireland – Hetty would never have had to think of Craig Williamson again. But circumstances changed.

That following day in Waterford Léonie received news from Paris, a telegram from her father: her mother was ill, dangerously so it seemed, with influenza. Léonie, perforce, had to make arrangements at once to return home, booking passage on the boat to England the next morning.

'Of course, you'll come with me,' she had said to Hetty.

But Hetty was unwilling. And later she became adamant. 'Léa – it's rather nonsense: for me to go all that way to Paris, when your Mama only has 'flu. She's bound to recover . . . and you'll be back here anyway in a week or so. And, besides, I *can't* go. I promised to be home next week – for Christmas. Dermot's coming back, remember?' She grasped Léonie's hand reassuringly. 'I just had that wonderful long letter from him. He's expecting me at Summer Hill. I can hardly disappoint him, after four years away. He and Mortimer and Robert – all coming home for

Christmas. It's all fixed. And I could never get back from Paris in time, if I came with you.'

Léonie was distraught. 'But, Hetty, we promised to stay together –'

'Of course we did! And we will. But in this case, just for a week or so, we can't. You know we can't. And you'll be back soon enough, of course you will . . .' Hetty was becoming impatient at what she felt were Léonie's clinging tentacles. 'Don't you *see*, Léa?' she added, a touch impatiently.

Léonie did see, but repressed what she saw – preferring to think that Hetty was tactfully dropping her, that she was trying to push her out of her life, as she always suspected she might, using her mother's illness in Paris now as the excuse, and no doubt intending to take up instead with this awful Craig Williamson and his motion picture plans.

Adding insult to injury, as Léonie felt, Hetty more or less forced her on to the mail boat for Fishguard next morning, propelling her up the gangway, into her cabin, so that Léonie was quite frantic when they got there.

'No, Léa,' Hetty tried to calm her, reason with her once more. 'You have to go. You can't let people down in this way –'

'Me letting *you* down? But it's *you* I want to be with!' Léonie nearly screamed.

'No, I meant letting your parents down, your Mama.'

'But . . . you're just as important as they are. More important . . .' She began to sob – as Hetty embraced her. 'Oh, yes, Léa.' She brushed her ear with her lips. 'And you to me. But this time I *have* to stay. And you really have to go.' Hetty's tone was warm enough. But the words, the balance of the phrasing, could not but give a dismissive impression.

'You're just pushing me out of your life! . . .'

'But I'm not – I'm *not*, Léa dearest. Our life – all that we have together – has to include other people sometimes: your Mama and Papa, Dermot, Robert, Mortimer . . . And we can't be so selfish, just with each other, all the time. Don't you see?'

'No! You just want to be free of me – or go off with that man Williamson. I can feel it!'

'No, Léa, no!' Hetty lied.

'Hetty, come with me – we can have our games in Paris, better than we ever could in Ireland.' Léonie's eyes, filled with tears, took on an extra dimension now – of seductive compliance, a yielding submission.

'No, I *can't*!'

'Why can't you, damn you?' Léonie was desperate now. 'I can love you any way we like, any way you want in Paris. As long as you're there, in front of me, in bed with me. *That's* how I love you.'

'But, Léa, you told me once it was your *thinking* of loving me that meant most to you, not . . . doing it. Well, same here. So it won't matter if we're apart for a bit. We can both *think* of loving each other. You said so yourself! . . .'

'Did I? Well I've changed my mind.' Léonie remembered very well this earlier, happier invention of hers – when Hetty could readily be possessed. Now, losing her, she resorted to every deceit, compromise, exaggeration, approaching her in a clumsy embrace. 'I want you so much – *that* way, Hetty, not thinking of you.'

'Oh, Léa – you're being totally self-centred and indulgent about it all.'

The ship's siren rasped, calling visitors off and drowning out Léonie's next words: 'You don't *want* me to love you then.' And Hetty, thinking Léonie had said something else, something happy by way of goodbye, nodded her head vigorously and kissed her before turning away, leaving Léonie sobbing in the cabin.

So Hetty returned to Summer Hill a week earlier than expected. The thought of meeting Dermot soon obliterated the unhappy departure scene with Léonie. He had written her such a lovely letter. She had kept it in her purse, rereading it every so often, and now she was able to remind herself that, without Léonie, here was someone else, clearly in view, who loved her, to whom she might pay court, who would replace Léonie temporarily. For of course Léonie would get over her pettish, possessive anger. It was so unjustified in any case – for had not Léonie in fact abandoned her, leaving her just because of her mother's silly bout of 'flu? So Hetty conveniently argued her quite justified liberation from her friend, without thought for any possible consequence. It was time she freed herself from her a bit; indeed Mr Williamson had seemed to hint as much . . .

But when she arrived at Summer Hill a real setback awaited her. There was another letter from London, this time from Mortimer: Dermot had succumbed to the same influenza epidemic, was ill in bed, and was likely to remain in London for some time. Neither of them could be expected over for Christmas. Mortimer, unaware of Léonie's departure, hoped that Hetty, with Léonie and Robert, would hold the fort at Summer Hill over the holiday season, and that they might then all meet in the New Year.

Hetty was inconsolable. Robert, alone of the four who had already arrived at Summer Hill, did his best to cheer her up.

'It's really awful – I *do* feel for you,' he told her comfortingly. 'But there's nothing we can do about it really. It's some new form of influenza. I read about it – it's to do with the end of the war: all the troops returning from the filthy trenches, packed up like sardines in ships and trains, then seeing their friends and relations at home – so that it's spreading like wildfire. A real plague apparently. Best thing is just to stay put here –'

'We could travel over to London, you and I, and see them there!'

'Oh, Hetty, I know what you feel. But it wouldn't work. Mortimer'll be busy with Dermot –'

'Exactly! So *I* could look after him.'

'And get the 'flu yourself? Look, it'll all soon blow over. Much better to stay here. And besides, now that your Grandmama is failing, we really ought to stay here. You heard what Dr Roche said this morning – she probably won't last long. And, with your Mama away, *someone* has to take charge here. And that person's really you, isn't it?'

Hetty had to agree. Indeed, given the way Robert had so artfully put it, she was pleased to agree, consoling herself finally with the role she could now play – with every good reason – as châtelaine of Summer Hill.

So that immediately, with Elly and old Mrs Martin the housekeeper, she set about directing domestic details in the household, going ahead with all the usual Christmas arrangements – a quiet Christmas, no doubt, though perhaps she might ask the Ashleys to stay over the season. Yes, that was a plan . . . which would save something from the social wreck. She would make the house as bright and merry as possible, decorate it with lots of holly and ivy, even mistletoe, why not? She could kiss the Major under it. And put lots of lamps about – how she wished they had electricity – glittering lights and fires everywhere in these dank, dark mid-winter days. To this end she went to the lamp room with Mrs Martin and Teresa, the maid responsible, picking out a number of extra Aladdin and other taller standard lamps, asking that they be cleaned, filled with plenty of oil and made ready to set about the house.

'Let's light the whole place up!' she said to Mrs Martin, eyes ablaze, like the effect she intended, speaking with such vehement joy that the old housekeeper, remembering her mother's similarly manic fits, thought her touched now in the same way. 'Yes,' Hetty flew on. 'Let's have lights! And music! Let's all eat, drink and be merry! . . . Don't you think, Mrs Martin?'

Mrs Martin, as a staunch Presbyterian, thought no such thing. But she followed her instructions – so that the house that afternoon, when darkness fell and Austin and Bunty Cordiner arrived quite unannounced, was lit by fires and lamps, sparkling like a catherine wheel, as if for some great reception.

Hetty had only the briefest and coldest of words with Bunty, before she and Austin went on up to the back wing to see Lady Cordiner. They, too, had heard from Dr Roche: the old lady was failing. Austin Cordiner, out of kindness, had come to offer what he could in the way of consolatory gestures towards his sister-in-law. But Bunty, as on her previous visit, had another and entirely devious reason. Taking advantage of Frances's continued absence in Holloway, and the fact that, if she knew she was dying, old Lady Cordiner might somehow speak at last, she would make one final attempt to elicit an answer to the question that had so plagued her since she had been denied Summer Hill nearly ten years before.

Who was Henrietta's real father?

If she had sure answer to this, she could then contest Lady Cordiner's subsequent change in her will – and perhaps, even at this late date, by confronting, even blackmailing, Frances with this truth, secure the house and estate for herself, or at least for her descendants.

Both of them sat in Lady Cordiner's gloomy bedroom, Bunty gazing at the withered old lady, propped up on her many pillows, asleep at first. But soon she opened her eyes. And they were bright again when she recognised them. It was clear that she looked on them both without any of the malice she reserved for Hetty.

'How are you . . . dear Sarah?' Austin spoke gently. 'Are you well?' he added awkwardly.

After what seemed an age, she nodded. Bunty particularly was pleased with this response. The old lady, though unable really to speak a coherent word, could nod and perhaps shake her head, at least. She could thus say 'Yes' and 'No' – like a spirit in a table-tapping session. And that would be quite sufficient for her purpose here, Bunty thought. She would speak to her, alone, when Austin left to visit O'Donovan, the farm steward, as he always did on his rare visits to the house.

A few minutes later Austin rose to his feet. 'I'll go and see O'Donovan, dearest. You'll keep her company a bit longer, won't you?' he whispered.

'Of course, dear.' Bunty was at her most charitable and concerned.

But the moment her husband left the room her expression changed. Taking her chair right over beside the bed, starting her interrogation, she looked fixedly into Lady Cordiner's eyes.

'It's me, you *know* it's me,' she began, in a steely but confiding voice. 'Frances is still in prison in England – and we're quite alone here now. We may talk, or I may – about the house, about everything – the things you'd like me to do for you, and about Frances, who so wickedly took the house away from you. But first you must tell me about Henrietta – her real father. It wasn't Bruce Fraser, was it?'

Lady Cordiner tried to speak. But only a dry warble emerged from her lips. 'Just shake your head.' Bunty could barely restrain her impatience. 'Was it Bruce Fraser?' Lady Cordiner shook her head a fraction. 'Was it young Dermot then – out at the Boer war with her?' Lady Cordiner did not seem to understand. But Bunty had come prepared. She produced a photograph of Dermot and held it up to her. Again, after a long moment, Lady Cordiner shook her head.

'Then it must be him.' Bunty produced another illustration, this time in a torn page from an old *Irish Tatler*, a full-page line drawing of the Prince of Wales, done many years before. 'Was it him?' And at this, seeing the drawing, Lady Cordiner nodded her head, not once, but several times.

Bunty showed a huge relief. 'So, the old King's daughter! I suspected as much . . . not legitimate at all. And so Henrietta has no right to the house!' Bunty, her eyes filled with greedy satisfaction, patted the old lady's hand, still staring at her fixedly. 'Well, now I know – I may do something about it!' And indeed, she thought, what damage she could now do with this information – by blackmailing Frances with it for a start, just as Frances herself had obviously done ten years before with the old lady. 'Of course,' she whispered to Lady Cordiner, leaning forward – confiding, arrogant, condescending, all in one glance. 'It all makes sense now. *That's* how Frances forced you . . . into changing your will . . . wasn't it?'

Lady Cordiner nodded once more, her own eyes strangely alight now, seemingly happy with Bunty's comments. 'Well,' Bunty went on. 'Now we may have the house, just as you wanted, Austin and I – or at least the boys may have it. You'd want that, wouldn't you?'

Lady Cordiner did not nod this time. Instead she seemed to give a smile of assent. She turned her eyes towards the oil lamp on the bedside table, set some distance away, well out of her reach, making a feeble gesture with her arm.

'You'd like the lamp brought nearer?'

Lady Cordiner nodded. Bunty, at her most solicitous now, moved the entire table next to the bed. 'There, you'll see better –'

In the same instant Lady Cordiner, summoning up all her last reserves of energy, reached out with her one good arm and gave the lamp a violent push – breaking the frosted glass shade and chimney, spinning it over on the bedside table, where the oil spurted out across the lacquered surface, immediately taking fire there, flames leaping up in an explosive mix of varnish and paraffin. Bunty, taken by surprise, dithered for a long moment, allowing the fire to get a grip, before finally she picked up one of the crochet-work woollen shawls on the bed and threw it over the flames.

The shawl promptly caught fire, before falling to the floor. Bunty attempted to stamp the flames out, treading and scraping at the burning wool. Within a moment the hem of her dress took fire – and a few moments later the flames, leaping upwards, gorging on the material, had turned her into a blazing human torch.

She screamed then, and started a frenzied, swaying dance about the room, thus encouraging the flames, which soon had a firm grip on her. She thought to extinguish the fire amidst the blankets of the four-poster bed. But that was alight now: Lady Cordiner immobile in the centre, sitting up, perfectly still, a witch in a closing circle of fire, the flames skating over the silk eiderdown, nibbling at her arms, beginning with voracious appetite to feed on her nightdress, the pillows, the shawl around her shoulders.

Bunty, blinded by flame and smoke and in the belief that she was moving towards the door, found herself instead over by the window. She tugged at the velvet drapes, trying to envelop herself in them. But, instead, offering the fire another foothold, the dry curtains flamed in a streak of ascending yellow light, travelling up to the ceiling like the tail of a rocket.

And now Bunty screamed, terrified shrieks, while Lady Cordiner, still conscious, saw her sister-in-law's agony, and smiled, well pleased at her handiwork.

But she saw no more as her eyes closed, the lids seeming to melt in the searing heat rising all about her. The loose folds of skin on her neck and cheeks started to blister and bubble, the little fat left in her face began to crackle – and then, in a sudden tinder flash, her wispy hair caught fire and the old lady disappeared from view in a pall of smoke.

Everything was ablaze now – bed, curtains, floorboards, most of the furniture, the long refectory table with its tasselled velvet cloth, its dusty Victorian mementoes, the silver-framed photographs of Henry and Eustace. Objects sizzled and popped about the room in a series of small explosions. The heat was intense in the sealed space – the air, almost gone now, feeding the conflagration. So that when Pat Kennedy – with Austin and O'Donovan behind him – opened the bedroom door, letting a sudden surge of air inside, they were met by a fireball exploding outwards, which scorched and felled Kennedy and drove the other two men back, before they rallied, managing to return, dragging the butler away with them, and running themselves then, pursued by flames, finding sanctuary in the main house, slamming the heavy interconnecting oak door behind them. In another ten minutes the whole neo-Gothic north wing of Summer Hill was an inferno.

By next morning firemen and the estate workers had finally doused the last of the smouldering timbers. The roof and floors of the north wing had largely collapsed, leaving just the charred walls and gaping windows, the rest a smoking pyre of damp brick and mortar open to the December sky. But, apart from one or two rooms, including Frances's study-boudoir next to the north wing, now a sodden shambles, the men had managed to save the rest of the Georgian house.

The Constabulary were there, picking through the blackened debris. Undertakers had removed the charred bodies of the two women. An ambulance had taken Pat Kennedy, burnt about the face and hands, to the County Infirmary. Austin Cordiner bore up, showing great courage, while the rest of the household stood about aghast. Hetty was with Robert on the front lawn, practically speechless. Then, taking a grip on herself, she said, 'I'll get that telegram off to Mortimer, Mama must be told. Then I'll talk to Austin, see about the rest of his family getting down here.'

The servants, many of whom had had their quarters in the north wing and had lost everything, were still in a state of shock, weeping, being ministered to by Dr Roche and old Mrs Molloy with cups of tea in the kitchen. Teresa, the lamp maid, was particularly distraught – weeping, shaking, in the housekeeper's parlour, where Mrs Martin tried to console her.

'*Of course* it wasn't your fault,' she told her.

'But 'twas I who got out all those extra lamps in the first place, like you said. And I'd just filled her Ladyship's lamp up, right up to the top –'

'You put out all the new lamps in the *main* house, Teresa. And the fire didn't start there. Nothing to do with you at all.' She calmed the girl.

'But how did the fire start then?'

Mrs Martin shook her head. 'An accident – I don't know. But it certainly wasn't you.'

Of course it had crossed Mrs Martin's mind that Hetty's sudden manic enthusiasm about the lamps and fires that same afternoon might have had something to do with the conflagration. She knew very well of the girl's headstrong ways – just like her mother, up to every rash trick when the mood took her. She knew, too, of the enmity between her and Bunty Cordiner – she had witnessed just this during their meeting in the hall only half an hour before the fire had started. And, of course, she had known for a long time how much old Lady Cordiner had disliked her granddaughter and assumed the feeling was mutual. Was it possible? – that Hetty had set the place on fire, getting rid of the two of them in one fell swoop? Anything was possible with the women of this family, she thought.

And this, certainly, was Frances's view subsequently. Hetty had no need to telegram Mortimer. Her mother, released from Holloway the day before, had crossed over to Dublin on the mail boat that night and taken a hired motor down to Kilkenny straightaway next morning. She drove up to the house an hour later.

Frances's reaction to the deaths of the two women and the loss of the north wing was not one of sympathy or resignation but of astonishing anger. From the beginning she suspected that Hetty had been in some way responsible for the blaze. And, when she learnt of all the additional lamps and fires which her daughter had commanded the previous day, her suspicions became a certainty: Hetty, in this covert manner, had tried to set the whole house alight. She was, in any case, still furious with her daughter for her behaviour in running off with Léonie more than a year before. So that now, with arson to be added to her crimes, their confrontation later that morning in the drawing room was electric.

'That *I* tried to burn the house down?' Hetty, astonished, was just as angry.

'But of course . . . as your revenge against me! The one thing you knew was truly dear to me – this house!'

'You are insane. Why should I be-burn down our house?'

'*Our* house? Not yours – *ever!*' Her mother loomed at her viciously and for a moment it seemed they might come to blows. 'And further . . .' Her mother stopped inches away from her. 'I shall have you charged with arson. Oh yes – I shall call the Constabulary.'

'They will take no notice of such ravings – least of all from you, a convicted rebel, just out of jail! Besides – and Robert can vouch for this – I was nowhere near the north we-wing yesterday. Only Bunty and Austin went up there. And it was Bunty who stayed on alone in the room with Grandmama. If anyone started the fire it was *her*! You know perfectly we-we-well how she's always coveted the house, especially since she was done out of it when you got Grandmama to change her will. It was she, if anyone, taking revenge on you, not me.'

They stormed at each other, up and down the long room, just as Frances herself had done, twenty years previously, with her own mother, before her banishment to the West Indies. And now Frances had an identical end in view for Hetty.

'Your behaviour, as I've told you before, is simply *criminal*. But now you have gone too far. If you are not convicted of arson, I can promise you one thing – you will leave this house now, for good and all, never set foot in it again!'

Hetty, deciding to disengage herself from the pointless argument, shook her head and smiled pityingly at her mother. 'Calm yourself. Your threats and theories are all nonsense. We have more important things to do. Austin, for example, we must think of him . . .'

This sensible line of argument only served to infuriate Frances the more. 'How dare you feign concern for a man you have just widowed – you brazen little hussy!'

Frances aimed a blow at Hetty's cheek. But Hetty, far more fit than her mother after the latter's months in prison, caught her arm and held it. Slowly she bent it back, until her mother struggled in pain.

'Madness. Sheer madness,' Hetty remarked casually, letting her go. 'Just like Grandmama – whom *you* made mad. I saw you once, you know, up in that great bedroom, years ago! Oh yes – you had that we-we-wicked Hallowe'en turnip head – and you set it in front of her, with a candle inside, while you just sat there, torturing her. *You* killed Grandmama long ago. You're the criminal, not I. But I'll promise you one thing: you'll not kill me. And another thing . . .' Hetty looked round the room. 'It's *you* who have destroyed this house – just as if you'd burnt it – with your evil temper, your cruelties and ma-ma-mad ambitions for it, your hatreds, your pe-pe-possessiveness.' Hetty turned now, half-way to the door. 'When I have Summer Hill, things will be very different . . .' With these last words, issued without the slightest hesitancy, Hetty turned and left.

But, alone in her bedroom, Hetty showed none of the same confidence and attack. She collapsed, sobbing, on her bed. Finally, with this fire, these deaths, and the return of her mother, it had all become too much for her.

Léonie, as Hetty chose to think, had dropped her. And Dermot, with just the excuse of some silly bout of 'flu, had failed her as well. Admittedly, there were still Robert and Aunt Emily at Summer Hill. But, even if her mother had not just forbidden her the house, she could not have faced staying with this malignant woman a moment longer. She would have to leave – for London, Paris, anywhere. Her world had collapsed. She could fall no further.

At the nadir of her fortunes, she picked up the snow-dome from her bedside table, shook it gently, and watched the flakes rise and wheel over the ivory miniature of Summer Hill. Something touched her heart in this fairy-tale beauty: drifts of snow, memories of childhood. There was an inviolate solace there, embedded in the crystal, beyond all corruption. And a proprietorial feeling for her in it, too – a confirmation of security, power and long tradition, of which she was part. That could not be taken away from her. The house was hers. And, just as she had told her mother, one day she would return and repossess it. Of course she would! Summer Hill was the essence of her life; no one could ever deprive her of that. Here alone – in these bricks and mortar – was something that would never betray her.

And at that moment she regained some of her old confidence – and with it, she realised, came something even better: a burning, surging feeling of anger, then a godlike distancing and independence from all these setbacks. She was immune from them. What should she care for her mother's madness, the frailties of her friends? All that was a waste of time and spirit now. You could not in the end really trust others – could only rely on yourself. And she need not be dependent on anyone now. For it was she, after all, who had the real character, vigour, talent, beauty – she who could make her way perfectly well without them all.

'Let them all go hang!' she said, speaking to the little crystal globe – pure, undefiled emblem of all her hopes. 'Fortune Favours the Brave,' she added, speaking slowly and decisively, her tears drying, a wonderful feeling of command sweeping over her. She would run things her own way from now on. She would win. She stood up, went to the wardrobe and started packing a suitcase, taking the snow-dome with her, placing it carefully, protecting it between the thickest clothes.

Craig Williamson, in the back of the chauffeur-driven Daimler, looked about him as the car wound up the long drive. A pale sun had emerged, running in shafts across the valley, before it reached the great house, spotlighting it among the semicircle of dark trees. He was excited, avaricious for the grandeur of it all. Every prospect pleased him here. This was exactly the sort of great house and estate – a dream of classic ease and order – for which he had always longed; a landscape which, at one fell swoop, would wipe out all the drab, penny-pinching memories, the chilly cruelties and indignities of his own childhood in Cork.

Then, he saw the men, still gathered about the blackened remains of the north wing. Seeing the destruction, he stopped the car near the archway into the yard, and got out to investigate. A constable stood nearby.

'What happened?'

'Ah, a terrible blaze altogether.'

'And casualties?'

'I believe so . . .' The constable was not more forthcoming.

But another man approached him now, tall and elderly, with a prophet's beard. 'I'm O'Donovan, the steward. You'll be from the insurance people –'

'No, in fact –'

But Mr O'Donovan did not hear him. They both turned then, as part of the wall, high up, collapsed, falling inwards with a great crash, so that the man hurried away and Craig, accepted now as someone who had business in the place, was left on his own. He walked up over the lawn towards the south end of the burnt wing, where it joined the Georgian house, stepping over damp rubble. Soon he found himself looking through a gaping hole in the brickwork, giving straight on to the sodden remains of Frances's boudoir.

Charred and broken furniture lay beneath drifts of fallen brick and plaster. Tin deed boxes poked out among the damp paper and splintered glass. Stepping gingerly through the hole, he surveyed the desolate scene inside.

His boot slipped on a morass of damp plaster, hitting one of the deed boxes, half-buried beneath it. The lid, he saw, had buckled in the heat, leaving the box partly open at one end. Then, just next to the lid, something caught his eye, a flash of light in the mess of plaster. He bent down. It was a brooch-watch, barely harmed, an exquisite Victorian timepiece, set in a gold case with a blue glazed enamel face, the pin-clip inset with diamonds. Turning it over, he saw the engraved dedication: 'Frances. From Alix and Edward. Christmas, Sandringham, 1898.' And, beneath that, a miniature coat of arms, three ostrich feathers above the legend 'Ich Dien'. Then it was suddenly clear to him: 'Alix and Edward – Sandringham – Ich Dien'; the watch must have been a gift to Mrs Fraser from Edward VII when he was still Prince of Wales.

He held it in his hand for a long moment, tempted by something – not to steal it, no, but by some other feeling, some sixth sense, which he could not identify.

Then, sensing that someone was looking at him, but unwilling to let the watch fall and disappear again among the smoking debris, he pocketed it adroitly. Looking round, he saw a woman gazing at him. She was dressed in travelling clothes, framed above him in a broken, smoking arch that had once been a doorway into the room. Her face was quite expressionless, without distaste or interest at his presence: a hard, tear-streaked mask. Craig, composing himself, settling his red scarf about his throat, took off his trilby hat.

'I *am* sorry,' he said, looking at the destruction around him, then back at the broken face. There was nothing of the rogue, the actor, no irony in his voice now. The tone was heartfelt. 'Can I help – in any way?'

Hetty considered the offer for what seemed an age. Then, with the same hard tone in her voice, she said, 'Yes – yes, you can. I want to go to Dublin. That's your ke-ke-car, isn't it?' She gestured towards the yard. 'Can you take me to the station?'

'Of course, I'd be pleased to. But I'm going back to Dublin myself. I can give you a lift all the way.'

'We-wait for me then. Don't let them see you. Leave the ke-car where it is. I'll join you in a minute.'

Hetty said goodbye to Robert, then to Aunt Emily. Robert tried to dissuade her.

'It's madness, Hetty! –'

'No! I'd go me-me-mad if I stayed here –'

'But your Mama'll cool down!'

'She won't! She's going to have me charged with arson –'

'Take no notice of her ravings. Where'll you go anyway?'

'London, see Mortimer at least. Then Paris, to Léonie. There's no pe-pe-*point*, don't you see? I can't stay. Mama's told me to get out, tried to hit me. We'd both come to blows. It's impossible. Best to go away for a bit. But I'll be back.'

Aunt Emily, bewildered by the fire, was much more enthusiastic in her old mad way. 'Paris? – I'll come with you. There's a decent enough hotel, near the shops in the St Honoré, just round the corner from our Legation there, a most accommodating manager as I remember –'

'Not now, Aunt. Another time. It's Léonie, you see. Her Mama's very ill.'

'Ah, Léonie, of course. As long as you're not running off with some man . . .'

'Of course not.'

She kissed her aunt – as she resumed the drawing she had started that morning, a most spirited sketch, Hetty saw, of the north wing in flames, violent yellow streaks soaring up against the darkness; an entirely realistic painting, except for the clear shape of a face in the swirling pattern of leaping flame and smoke, the features of Lady Cordiner, an evil genie rising from the ruined wing, spiralling away, with a headdress of sparks, into the night sky.

Hetty left by the back-door. And, as she left, running along the basement corridor and raising her hand, she touched all the room bells, in a line above her head, pushing each one vigorously as she passed, so that the house came alive suddenly, with a joyous, sparkling sound, rising through the floors and stairways, flooding the house with challenging melody.

Hetty, on the journey to Dublin, gradually, in fits and starts, but gathering confidence against the man's attentive and sympathetic demeanour, explained the whole situation to Craig Williamson. So that by the time they arrived at the Shelbourne she had agreed to take a room there herself, at least for that night, and talk further of his propositions.

She was surprised at her change of heart about the man. But then, she argued conveniently, she simply had not known him before. And indeed this was true in quite another way. In her theatrical experience she had not expected, nor so far encountered, anyone so apparently civilised, sophisticated, intelligent. She had loved all the rough-and-tumble of the music hall, the deep camaraderie she shared among her friends there. But this man, part of the same tradition, showed a refinement and sensitivity that was quite new to her.

Above all – the moment she had stepped into the luxury of the Daimler – there was the clear feeling that she had entered a world, not so much of money, which meant little to her, but one of power, which at that moment in her life meant everything.

They dined in the hotel restaurant that night. Wartime austerity was over, there was Veuve Clicquot champagne with the Galway oysters, before the filet mignon.

He wore a smartly-cut dark suit – with a double-breasted jacket of a sort she had never seen before – and she felt frumpy in the few clothes she had taken quickly from Summer Hill. He raised his glass, his hair a dark sheen in the lamplight. 'The future: yours – and mine.'

'But I haven't said I'd take that pe-pe-picture test.' Despite the hesitancy, she returned his look calmly.

'No, you haven't. But hearing your story I think you should. Now's the time – for change.'

'Here?'

'In California.'

She eyed him carefully, putting down her glass, avoiding the issue raised by this implied invitation. 'You think – a test – it's we-worth it?'

'Not really. But you are. That's the real point I made – about California. You should come there with me.'

He studied her then, waiting for a reaction, looking into her blue eyes, an air of incipient fun visible for the first time that day. But she said nothing, joining him in a trial of wills, looking at him coolly in return. By way of response he leant back then, instead of forward, allowing distance to emphasise the authority of his words.

'Test or no, Miss Fraser, you have the qualities that make motion picture stars.' Then, dusting his lips with a napkin, he added casually, 'I can make you a star.'

She laughed. 'As easy as that . . .!'

'No. A lot of hard work – and mostly yours.'

'And you're so ke-ke-confident?'

'Oh yes. I am. Have to be. Done it before.' He spoke in an abrupt staccato, slightly fretful now. 'It's my business, my life, you see. Think I'd risk it over someone I didn't believe in?'

'No. You wouldn't. I can see that.'

'And I can see the same thing in you, too, Miss Fraser,' he retorted sharply. 'You're *just* as ambitious – for something.'

They smiled, the first intimation of some real understanding passing between them. 'Besides . . .' Craig leant forward into the lamplight then. 'Now the war's over, the picture business in America is really going to go places. You think it's just a thing of nickelodeons and hucksters, a pastime for the lower orders. Well, that's true. But it's a lot more: an art – a real art – as well as a huge money-spinner. And remember that as well, Miss Fraser: now that your mother's pushed you out, how did you think you were going to live? On the charity of your friends in London or Paris?' He took the Veuve Clicquot from its cooler, half-filling her glass.

'Live?' She was genuinely curious.

'Yes. Money – this sort of thing.' He tapped the bottle.

'Oh, I don't need that – have no real te-taste for it.'

'Clothes?' He looked at her pointedly. 'You like clothes, don't you? Love the whole dressing up thing – I saw that in Waterford.'

At this Hetty admitted distinct interest. 'You mean they pay people – I mean really *pay* them – to be in your moving pictures?'

'Mary Pickford, when I left Hollywood last year, was getting ten thousand dollars a week from Zukor's Famous Players . . . And, besides, the whole business is about clothes – and dressing up . . .' He lingered invitingly on these ideas for a moment. 'You should see Gloria Swanson's wardrobes in de Mille's pictures.'

'Ten thousand dollars a *week*?' she asked. Craig nodded. 'But that's *thousands* of pounds, isn't it?' He nodded again. 'Fonsy O'Grady paid most of us ten *shillings* a week!'

'Well, he didn't have a big audience, you see. You don't understand – everyone, the world over now, pays to go see moving pictures. That's why they call the actors stars,' he added with some irony. 'Everyone, everywhere, sees them.'

'But wha-what is it – and why do you think I have it – that makes them that?'

'Listen,' he told her. 'What you have is half a dozen characters churning about inside you trying to get out. It's obvious! – that stammer and telling me you were "Miss Bauer" and dressing up as a *man* at the drop of a hat and all that aggressive sword play you go in for: your general kicking against the traces! And that's the cause of half your troubles – with your mother, your friends, that nice girl friend you tell me dropped you and skedaddled off to Paris. They don't know who you *are*, what to expect next, can't rely on you. But that sort of response, that invention, is just what's required in motion pictures – *if* you can discipline it, get rid of the purely wayward elements . . .' He looked at her quite severely now. 'So you have that. And you can *act* as well, as long as you don't have to do too much speaking, with that . . . attractive hesitancy of yours, which you won't in motion pictures, because they're silent. But the real thing you have, well . . .' He gestured vaguely. 'You can't lay hands on it. Some quality, some secret, nobody quite knows what – you can't put it into words. No more than I could tell you why exactly this champagne tastes so good.'

'Oh, I can,' she broke in enthusiastically. 'It's fizzy and dry and de-de-delicious!'

He smiled. 'Well, there you have it, near enough. That's just what you taste of as well. Get that on the screen – and that's what'll make you a star.' He raised his glass again, looking at her steadily over the bubbles. 'So, you'll come with me to California then?'

'I might – I may.' There was nothing of the tease in her voice. She still had genuine doubts.

'Your friend, Léonie . . . That's the real problem, isn't it? She's more than just a friend, isn't she?' He touched her hand quickly. 'I understand,' he went on. 'It's tough, these break-ups.'

'Oh, no – it's nothing.' But Hetty's expression gave the lie to her words. And Craig, seeing the lie, took advantage of it by lying himself. 'Well then, you don't have to worry about that.' He looked at her with a mature knowingness. 'She's the one who left you – you don't have to worry too much about her.'

'No.'

She was grateful for his quick support. But then she felt awful, a great yawning horror opening up inside her, for this betrayal of Léonie – until, as if he had sensed this, she thought, he broke into her thoughts and calmed them once more.

'No, you can't worry about Léonie,' he said softly, the devil's advocate now. 'We all lose friends sometimes that way. We grow away from them, to places they can't follow. It's tough. But what can you do? Deny your own life, all the gifts there? Well, that'd be crazy! Because you have *so much* there. The truth is there's really no future for you in that relationship – you've grown beyond it, towards every other sort of future, which you *can* have, just waiting for you, out there, in Hollywood . . .'

He had brought her to that high hill then, and shown her the view on the other side, the limitless plains where the beasts of pure self-will and unfettered ambition were free to roam – in pursuit of every egotistical fulfilment and worldly achievement, encouraged to feed on every exotic pleasure, pursue every vanity, forget every old friend. He had shown her this amoral vision, and she had taken it in, he was sure of that. He would let her sleep on it.

That night, in her room, Hetty weighed her opportunities with Craig Williamson. Yes, the man reeked of power: that was the most exciting thing about him – not the power of birth or class, which she was entirely accustomed to, but a force quite new to her, without those inherited trappings or constraints, a power that operated from scratch and without scruple, in the real world: a confidence and command which stemmed not from great houses or inherited wealth but from sheer arrogant will, character, talent, quite free from the constraints of ordinary life or from any emotional commitment there.

And, in these hours of deep bitterness and betrayal, Hetty, sniffing at the hems of power, found the aroma infinitely sweet, intoxicating, drawn by it, seeing clearly how, if she could come to feed off the same magic elixir, she need never again find herself at the mercy of her demented mother, or suffer the vagaries and disappointments of her friends. She could revenge herself on all that – and all the other earlier injustices of her life, putting herself finally beyond reach of hurt and pain.

Yes, that was what Craig Williamson offered her – what she had always wanted for herself, she openly admitted now: the power, without any inhibition, to impose herself on life, on others, on an 'audience' – something on which Léonie in the end had quite failed to collaborate with her. But here, against this new mirror, with this man so obviously taken by her, she could give free rein to her *true* personality. It was so obvious! Craig Williamson, given the nature of his motion picture business, expected this from her, and had said as much. He *wanted* everything which Léonie had tried to frustrate or deny in her – all the many conflicting people trapped in her soul.

Indeed, this was the essence of the whole business: Craig Williamson was offering her the person she really was. He had already half done so – prodding her, long dormant from her chrysalis, into the life she was born for. And she had basked in these first intimations of change, making hesitant wing-beats in these glorious new colours, testing herself in the balmy airs. Now she would go the whole way, leap into that bright world and fly, become that completely-changed being, accept her destiny.

Something finally snapped in her. She could not sleep, tense with a euphoric mood of vast energy, ruthless intent. She sprang out of bed and started walking to and fro. Yes, she had done with all this temporising, these compromises – with her mother, with Léonie and Dermot. She had done her best there. But it was useless. At worst these people, like her mother, were utterly malign; at best, though with good intentions, no doubt, they quite failed to see the real purpose of her life – which was to be free to express these gifts she had been born with; a task, she saw then, in which she must now serve herself alone, a discipline which she must ruthlessly pursue, forsaking her past, as part of the cost, part of the debt she owed to her talent. Craig Williamson saw all that. The others did not. It was as simple as that. She made the firm decision then: she would go with him to California.

In his own bedroom Craig Williamson considered the day. It had gone well – all the chances had fallen his way. The girl was as good as his, he thought. Though he was equally aware that his future success with her would need patience, clever handling, many wiles on his part. But she was worth every effort, every scheme. The re-launching of his Hollywood career, his whole future there, could well depend on this woman. He knew well what a jungle it was over there. A year away from the cameras, and others had jumped into your place, they were *happy* to do so and to forget you, and you could well be finished. But with such a woman, a hidden star in your pocket, you had the one thing no one could resist out on the coast: you possessed the raw material which sustained all their lives in that shallow, dream-obsessed suburb – a rare, deep vein of gold which, when mined and minted through the alchemy of the camera, turned to dollars. It was as simple as that. And that was the sure, indeed the only, means towards any resurrection in Hollywood: dollars.

BOOK FOUR

1

'NO! – DON'T GO in!' Craig commanded Hetty, mock-fierce and still panting from their race up the long steps; because of his slight limp, she had beaten him to the great imitation Gothic doorway. 'You just wait here – 'till I organise the surprises – and carry you over the threshold!'

'Oh, let me come in, too – I can't wait!'

'No! . . .'

She gave way in the end, as usual, and he disappeared inside The Wolf's Lair, the phoney Bavarian hunting lodge on the slopes of Mount Lee above Hollywood Lake, leaving Hetty, in her short silk wedding dress, to twiddle her thumbs on the terrace.

She was momentarily exhausted. It was hot. The air still shimmered and glittered after the long day's heat. Even at this height, nearly a thousand feet above the canyon, the terrace was an oven of burnished wood, spotlit now by the slanting afternoon sun, a gold-hazy orb dipping into the Pacific away to the right.

It was hot and silent.

A small lizard scuttled across the bogus armorial above the hall doors. Cortez, the impertinent Amazon macaw, a wondrous blue and yellow, held in a gilt cage under the awning, broke the silence with a guttural murmur. And Hetty, frustrated and impatient to see what the surprises were inside, suddenly started to taunt the bird, prodding the bars, drumming her fingers over the cage, making faces, so that Cortez began to flap and croak, swishing his long tail.

'Bananas! Bananas!'

'And nuts to you!'

Hetty was tempted to continue bullying the bird, but it was too hot. Instead, moving over to the balustrade with its tall scarlet poinsettias and overhanging sweep of jasmine, she leant right out, hoping to catch some air rising from the valley, looking down the almost sheer slope – a treacherous wilderness of scrubby thorn and wild fig – to the groves of old orange and olive trees, the remains of this now-untended Californian mountain estate.

And, suddenly, cool eddies spiralled up to her, the air touched with orange blossom, the desiccated, peppery whiff of sagebrush and wild thyme. And now she basked in the place and loved it, pushing her face out into the evening light, breathing in these wild scents, absorbing the limitless distances, the vast panorama that lay before her – but immune from it, her feelings of power over this reclaimed desert once more confirmed.

The sagebrush reminded her of the real desert, way to the east beyond the city limits – of the ravishing heat and the crystal light out there, after all the dark tragedy of Ireland, the chilling mid-winter cold of New York. A month or so after she had arrived in Hollywood, nearly eighteen months before, Craig had taken her up for a joy ride from the little aerodrome outside Los Angeles – just the two of them, Hetty in the front seat of the small bi-plane, swooping out over the bay, then back round the studio lots, her stomach turning as he banked and switched about, climbing steeply into the blue, levelling out then, breasting the air for a long moment, gliding, stalling, then diving perilously at full throttle – on, on towards the earth.

So that when they landed on a flat patch of quite empty, hard-sanded desert, way to the east of the city, pulling to a stop near clumps of sagebrush and cactus, she was already dizzy with excitement. He had come to her then, raising his goggles, helping her out, holding her in his arms briefly, kissing her chastely. And she had felt the sudden urge to respond, a wild thrill, which she – and he too surely? – had repressed at the last moment.

And yet, in a way, she thought, he had seduced her in that burning empty desert. 'No,' he had said. 'Not yet, Hetty. Not yet . . . Just to see you.' And then, as she had stood there by the plane, he had taken her goggles off, flying helmet, leather jacket and silk scarf, her blouse and skirt.

He had come towards her, so close finally that she had seen the minute rise of flaxen down just below his dark hair line, his eyelids flickering an instant in the brilliant light, his eyes intent on hers, hard, ironic, caring, all in the same glance . . . had seen his hand approach, felt his neat fingers caressing her cheek, lips, neck, touching the first button on her blouse . . . She could have discouraged, stopped him at any point. But the will was never really there, scorched away in that curious gaze of his, both dreamy and wilful – by his hungry, instinctive movements which were yet full of grace, almost mannered. She had been drawn to him, irresistibly, by some strange chemistry she knew nothing of, and had stood there, barely moving, mesmerised, while he undressed her, until she was naked, leaning back against the fuselage, shaking slightly.

He could have made love to her then. In all her new mood – the fire and release she felt in her life now – she would have let him, liked him, to do that. But he did not. Instead all he said was 'You really are – beautiful . . .' – quite simply, before he added, handing her the long white silk scarf she had been wearing, 'Wrap that round your waist, and just stand out there in the light against the desert a moment.' And she had taken the scarf, winding it like a short shirt around her thighs, and walked away, posing in the light against the scrubby hills and dunes that ran away to the horizon, parading briefly, erect against the great burning landscape, stopping, turning back.

'Why? Why did you want that?'

'This Egyptian picture –'

'Yes, but, *which* one? You're always on about it! And it can't be *Cleopatra* – de Mille made that a few years ago.'

'I'll tell you, later – don't want anyone else to get the idea. In Hollywood they really are rogues and vagabonds: thieve a story from you as soon as look at you. But I wanted to see you against that sort of desert backdrop – like Egypt.'

'And?'

'You were perfect!'

'They won't have me half-naked in it, though!'

'Why not? In costume epics, ancient history, they don't mind at all. Just look at de Mille's pictures!'

Later, on the terrace of The Wolf's Lair that evening, she said, 'Why didn't you? – you know – make love with me out there.'

'Ah, you're special, Hetty! – something quite different . . .' had been his only explanation, ironic, still withholding himself from her, mentally now, so that she was tantalised by him in a different way, by secrets, which she wanted to touch in him.

She had no suspicion at that point how Craig had intended just this – to tantalise, to provoke her – by the whole episode that afternoon out in the desert, which he had produced and directed, cold-bloodedly, like a scene from one of his pictures. She had no idea how, in this initial ploy, this feigned restraint, Craig had been baiting a trap for her, allaying her fears and suspicions, encouraging what he sensed was a repressed but rampant sexuality in her, so that in future, goaded beyond endurance by such refusals on his part, she would one day grab the bait, releasing all her sex for him, when he could feed on what would then be a banquet, not a snack.

Hetty had no knowledge of this regimen of sexual denial which Craig had prepared for her and which, indeed, she came to suffer with mounting frustration during the next few months, so that, when at last he sprang the trap, she responded with a fury and abandonment that surprised even him.

He had taken her one night to his 'Astronomer's Lair', a locked room high up in one of the Gothic turrets of the Lodge, a perfectly circular, faintly-lit eyrie which he had organised for himself some years before, feeding his passion for astronomy, for peering into secrets unobserved, a wily necromancer, a flawed Merlin in a smoking jacket. Here, with a large telescope, he followed the stars and planets, confirming their courses or plotting deviations in the heavenly bodies, staring past Mars, Venus and Mercury, out into the milky way, and further on, ever questing, identifying distant nebulae.

As he turned a winch and chain, the metal roof slid back, opening the room to a warm, starry night. Hetty had been astonished at the whole set-up – the mysterious stellar maps and graphs and photographs of sunspots on the walls, the great telescope, eight or nine feet long, tilting upwards, as Craig lay beneath it on a sort of steamer chair, his head glued to the eye-piece, turning brass wheels on the pedestal, as if manipulating a great camera, so that the long steel tube, rising into the vertical and already poking out above the castellated turret walls, began to swing slowly round, scanning the velvet sky.

'What? – what is it?' she asked, for want of anything better to say.

'An Engelmann eight inch refractor,' Craig had told her easily, leaning back into the softly lit room. 'You really want to know? – nine foot focal length, mounting by Repsold's of Hamburg, the glass from Clark's of Cambridge, Massachusetts. Bought it from them in fact, second hand. It's out of date. But it suits me fine. Here, take a look – I've focused on Venus.'

She had taken his place, lying on the cushioned chair, while he adjusted the back, winding her up towards the eye-piece. The view was amazing: a brilliant white crescent, white as the most dazzling snow, with even brighter points and patches, vast snow peaks they seemed, piercing through a covering of milky cloud. Hetty was enchanted. But she could not understand the shape she saw.

'It's not round,' she whispered. 'I thought the planets were all round. This is just like a crescent moon.'

'Venus orbits the sun. So, depending where it is on its orbit, we see it like a crescent, where it is now, almost between us and the sun, or a full sphere when it gets round the other side of the sun.'

'Those huge mountains, they look like . . . as if they were poking up through cloud!'

'They are mountains, maybe. But the atmosphere is much denser on Venus than here on earth. So we don't quite know what's there . . .'

He babbled on. She barely understood him, her whole attention concentrated, spellbound, on the glittering crescent – until suddenly she was aware of him, standing right behind her, his arms on top of the chair. His hands slid down about her breasts, barely touching her, moving lightly, almost imperceptibly. Yet nonetheless she felt his touch like a sharp current, crackling through her thin voile blouse, prickling her skin, coursing on down her whole body.

'We can only see the cold side of Venus,' he said. 'Never the side that faces the sun, the warm part. No idea what it's like. Maybe it's some sort of paradise . . .'

She had begun to tremble then, the image of the planet starting to dance before her eyes, so that she could no longer concentrate on the vision, leaning back in the chair, seeing his face vaguely inverted above hers, letting him fondle her, until he had slipped his hand through and touched her nipple an instant, and she had jumped in the sudden thrill, supplanted by an agony almost, a twisting in her stomach, as he let the back of the chair down, rounding on her.

But she had writhed as he had touched her again, grasping at him, yet pushing him away, tearing at his shirt – so that both of them had suddenly stood up, undressing each other furiously, until they were naked and she saw him standing there in the half-light, alert, his sex risen, a pale figure, his skin a shadowy alabaster, smooth and white, before he had come to her, taking her in his arms and she had felt the whole warm length of his body and they had seemed to dance a minute, locked together, swaying round the great telescope. He had bent down then, knelt, kissing her stomach, her thighs, her sex. She had wondered for so long . . . What was it like? What was a man like? Now she took his sex in her hand, held it, cupping it, supple yet rigid. It seemed impossible . . . But wonderful.

They lay on the wooden floor. She found herself gazing at the endless freckle of stars, straight above her, just myriad pinpoints of light now, until he leant over, his face masking them, caressing her, putting his hands to his lips, then to hers, taking the moisture there, touching her lower down, so that her legs opened to his fingers, as if he had put some oiled key into a lock – and continued to open as he moved his fingers inside, smoothly, gently, then more firmly, so that she shivered and stretched uncontrollably, raising her thighs, twisting this way and that, as he had knelt between her legs, pausing then for what seemed an age, leaving her in an agony of suspended desire, until she could bear it no longer and had reached out, grasping him from behind, pushing him towards her, pushing him into her . . . And that first long instant of pain had almost undone her when he had come inside and stopped, before gently, insistently, flowing on; then the pain went and he thrust deeper, deeper, far, far up, until he was completely inside her, moving in delirious spasms . . .

And then, minutes later, an eruption – explosions, vast sun spots, flames, on and on, flooding her mind, with a dizzy ringing in her ears, the stars dancing in her eyes: a pleasure she had never imagined possible.

So that afterwards, she turned on him again, feeding on this miraculous source, thinking at last she had discovered the whole meaning of life. Craig – for the first time, the first person, she knew – had found and released all of her, heart and soul, the whole being: he had truly completed her.

She did not see that all he had done, like a canny water diviner, was to tap and encourage a quite exceptional flood of vehement sexuality in her, implicit in her nature, a voracious taste for every kind of exotic sensuality: a thirst for so long denied that thereafter it overflowed with Craig, at the slightest excuse, an explosive chemistry, which overcame them both, often in the least suitable places, so that sometimes, driving home from the studios in his Pierce-Arrow, they were forced to drive off the road and satisfy their cravings.

Hetty became obsessive, adamant in this pursuit of a great discovery: that she could make such thrilling love with a man. It became an overriding imperative in her life. Such a sensational new toy for her, it soon formed an ideal means – one among many – of scrubbing out the memory of her past, her betrayal of Léonie and her own unhappiness there, of beginning life anew in Hollywood, like everyone else in this plasterboard paradise – all exiles, as she was, from the old puritan worlds, all starting again with a clean slate, on which every sensual excess and folly could be writ large. This sex, so right-seeming, so licensed by the world she moved in, eradicated all Hetty's earlier experiences and ideals. She believed the explosive chemistry she and Craig shared was an unavoidable force of nature. And so it was – like an avalanche which might easily engulf her. But she did not see it in that way, spellbound in its path, unable to move, almost unhinged by her passion.

Even though at times, more soberly, she had been touched by vague doubts, and then by direct evidence, of Craig's trickery, this knowledge of his flaws had not affected her obsession with him – had added, indeed, to his mysterious charm. Yet now at last, standing on the terrace in her crumpled wedding dress, she was forced to wonder why she had married him. To make love was one thing – but to marry? For she remembered the party six months after they had arrived in Hollywood, with Craig's friends, his special cronies at Fox, the other members of the Irish brigade there: the production chief Winfield Sheehan, the directors Walter Brenon, Raoul Walsh and Mickey Neilan.

Mickey Neilan had been in his cups, as he usually was. All of them were celebrating her first real success with Fox, *Faith and Fury*, a four-reeler in which she played the romantic lead as the swashbuckling daughter of a French aristocrat executed in the Terror, whose place she had taken, usually masked and on horseback, avenging his death with all sorts of mayhem against the lower orders, involving scintillating duels and ambushes up and down among the orchard groves and hillocks of the San Fernando valley.

Mickey, congratulating her, had told her how far she could go. 'You were great! Even with that mask on – you have it all in the eyes, where it counts. And, as for the duelling, in God's name, where did you learn to handle a sword like that? That whole athletic thing you have . . .' He shook his head. 'As good as Fairbanks – if you could get a picture with him!' He looked at her wickedly, all curly-haired grace and mischief, one of the most immediately charming men she had ever met.

'What are you doing next, Mickey?'

'A real potboiler – *Don't Ever Marry* – and you won't, will you?' And he had leant forward then, enticingly. 'Keep yourself for me . . . Craig's an old rogue, you know. Love him dearly, but there's more fantasy in his life than any of his pictures.'

'No, I di-di-didn't know –'

'Oh yes – he never told you?' Mickey paused for another drink. 'That limp for example, that famous "war wound" – got it tumbling downstairs in some bordello behind the lines, not falling out of any airplane!'

'But he was in the Canadian Flying Corps out there –'

'Yes – but just as a photographer!'

'But he *can* fly. He's taken me up here.'

'My God, he can certainly fly. Fly you to the moon – in his imagination . . .'

That had been a first dent in Craig's armour. But she had not spoken to him about it. Mickey was probably a bigger liar. But from then on she had questioned Craig – tactfully but in more detail – about his past. And in brief, at least, he had been quite open about it. His family, the St John Williamsons, had been plantation settlers in Ulster – an ancestor had been a commander in Cromwell's model army – and his father had been a successful doctor, with a fine white house on the southern shores of Lough Neagh. His mother had died young, and his father a few years later, when Craig was sixteen. He had been an only child.

'Do you have photographs – and things?' she had asked.

'No. They were all lost, when I moved out here from New York in . . . 1915.'

'Didn't your American ke-ke-cousin – the one you told me about, who brought you up when you left Ireland and went to the art school in New York – didn't he ke-keep your things?'

'No, no. Cousin Thomas, I told you – he moved up to Canada, Toronto. That's how I wangled my way into the Canadian Flying Corps.'

'What was it like – in Ireland, growing up on the big lake there?'

'Wonderful. Father took me out with him, most days in the holidays, visiting patients, me sitting up front with him in the trap with the cob, skimming along those little country roads into the mountains. Wonderful collection of old people still living up in the hills there then, mostly too poor to pay, giving him bottles of moonshine instead. Or a bit of mutton. Or a Christmas turkey. Marvellous Christmases by the lake. Frozen over one year, skating . . .' He had made it all sound so romantic, entirely real.

Then one day, as she was taking tea in the Hollywood Hotel with the actress Marion Davies who had become her best friend in Hollywood, Marion had unwittingly torpedoed all these romantic notions. They had been talking about the dancer, Betty Hudson, Craig's first wife, divorced three years before, a platinum, golf-playing blonde from Pittsburg.

'Oh, yeah – I knew her well,' Marion had said in her rowdy New York voice. 'She was in the Ziegfeld Follies with me. That's where Craig met her, when he was playing bit parts with Vitagraph out in Brooklyn – got her into one of the two-reelers he was working on then. But Betty wasn't quite up to it. She could dance, but couldn't act to save her life, couldn't let herself go – know what I mean?' she added, a little wicked edge to her usual great good humour.

'What happened? – the marriage, I mean. Craig never talks about it.'

'Oh, nothing much – other than sink with all hands! You know Craig – all that dreaming he goes in for. And she was rather prim and regimented and on the ball – golf balls, not the other kind. Christ! – they were totally unsu-su-suited,' she stammered, for she suffered from the same hesitancies as did Hetty. 'And Betty was something of a snob, too – father was a big wheel in Pittsburg steel, so when she found out Craig's father ran some crummy fe-fe-food store in Ireland somewhere –'

'A food store? But his father was a doctor, he told me, with a big house, on a lake up in the north.'

Marion had looked at her teasingly then, thinking she was pulling her leg. 'Hell, that's just one of Craig's jokes, Hetty. Father ran a food store, some smelly little joint he hated, way in the backwoods of Ireland somewhere. And when Betty – and her father – found this out, well, there was hell to pay. But by then it was too late. She was "Mrs Mickey Curtis"!'

'"Curtis"?'

'Why, yes.' Marion had looked at her curiously then. 'Of course. That's Craig's real name – Mickey Curtis – 'till he came out here to the coast and changed it.

That "Craig St John Williamson" bit is just a cover. Didn't he tell you?' Marion had looked embarrassed.

'No – no, he never did!' Hetty had laughed it off. 'Just another of his jokes!'

No, indeed, he had never told her, then or later, Hetty thought, coming out of her reverie on the terrace.

Craig pretended to worthy ancestors, an eminent father, a romantic background in Ireland. But Hetty's own pretences were just as bad. She believed that Craig had drawn out her real nature, the whole person, that he completed her in every way. And in return, encouraged by the reckless post-war mood of the times, by Craig himself and by others she met of the same rash disposition in Hollywood, she acted out that nature accordingly, in all sorts of imprudent ways, taking on, at Craig's skilful instigation, one more role, that of libertine and happy hedonist.

But Hetty's greatest pretence was that she had behaved appropriately with Léonie – and in this belief Craig encouraged her most of all. 'Why,' he'd said to her one day driving back from the studios, 'there can't really be anything to reproach yourself with there. Léonie, well, she had nothing herself, so she really had to cling on to you, keep herself afloat – and pull you down with her. She couldn't live with the person you really are, the things you had to do . . .'

Craig had become Hetty's Svengali – tempting, promoting her, so much more successfully than Léonie had ever managed, into a far greater variety of exotic roles: liar, mistress, child, daughter, whore and now wife. He saw in Hetty the essence of everywoman – and had drawn these distillations from her in the past eighteen months. And this was the basis of her obsession with him: Craig had become her substitute for real life, offering her false idols, bad faith. He had lifted all the screens in her, released her devils.

Hetty looked down the valley from the terrace. The steep hills around were quite bare of other habitation – until beyond the canyon some new mansions, just white flecks in the violet-tinged afternoon light, glittered on the edge of Lake Hollywood a mile or so away. Beyond that, on the flat valley floor looking south over the dry plain, lay the studio lots, scattered round a wide area on the outskirts of Hollywood, carved out of the scrubby desert in the last few years and practically invisible at this distance.

You could see them if you wanted to, though. Craig had fixed up another big marine telescope on the balustrade – and Hetty, filling in time, played with it now. The view danced violently as she swung it over the horizon. A studio lot appeared as she dipped the lens: shaking plasterboard illusions, shimmer-white fantasies made more fantastic still in the foreshortened optics; a moat and drawbridge, castellated walls and towers with nothing behind them – the Sheriff of Nottingham's castle. Further along, on the old Triangle lot, at the junction of Hollywood and Sunset, the remains of Griffith's Babylon reared up in front of her, the huge sets from *Intolerance* – Belshazzar's Court: an endless waterfall of steps flanked by two immense colonnades, bulbous pillars topped by winged deities and monstrous elephant gods, set beneath even greater walls, triumphant arches, ramparts and towers reaching up into the sky – a Babylon so vast that even at this distance the lens failed to enclose the vision. Yet Craig, whenever he saw these huge remains, had always said, 'My sets, for the Egyptian picture – they'll be even bigger!'

Further across she saw the Paramount lot – Zukor's studio, which she had first visited, with Craig, almost immediately after their arrival in Hollywood: that morning when he had confronted the British director William Desmond Taylor, doing some studio tests for his *Huckleberry Finn* picture. She remembered that first time in a studio so well: the open stages, all in a line, each filled with a different frenzied activity, carpenters hammering, actors acting, little trios playing mood music, a panic of creation, muslin awnings drawn across against the sun, and some other stages with glass overhead, burning hot, with a wonderful smell of pine resin, lime dust, moist plaster, a pear-drop odour of fresh varnish, the acrid whiff of raw film stock.

Craig had simply stood there, at the back of the stage, watching Taylor work, staring at the tall, impeccably-dressed, dignified man who looked just like a London stockbroker. Eventually an assistant had come over asking what he wanted.

'My picture,' Craig had told him simply. And Taylor, finishing the test, had walked across then, wiping his hands neatly in a silk handkerchief. 'Well, Craig – how are you? Didn't know you were back –'

'Yes, from a war you should have been in, Taylor, instead of stealing my picture.'

'Now, Craig, that's not so – I did *Tom Sawyer* first –'

'I know, that's the one I meant, the one you stole from me. And what a bloody stodgy, cackhanded job you made of it. And now you'll do the same with Huck – and that was my picture, too. Soon as I went away, you just stepped in and took it all, you bastard . . .'

'Now look here,' Taylor said reasonably. 'That's nonsense.' He spoke softly, in a cultured English accent. 'I was too old for the war, you chose to go away and play the hero –'

'Don't give me that bullshit! – with that phoney accent of yours, you two-timing bog Irishman, you.'

Taylor had been unmoved. 'Just down on your luck, Craig – that's how it is in Hollywood,' he had told him superciliously. 'Someone had to make the pictures around here –'

'I won't forgive you, Taylor, remember that. You can't play the cultured Britisher with me. I *know* who you are, from the New York days – and don't you forget it,' he had told him forcefully before turning on his heel. Hetty had been mystified. 'He's just a shit – that's why I never tell anyone my ideas around here,' was all the explanation Craig had given. And Craig's fortunes at that moment had seemed very low indeed. No one really wanted him back in pictures. But he had taken Hetty to lunch that same day, bribing the maître d'hôtel for a best corner table at the Hollywood Hotel, and Winfield Sheehan from Fox had been there, doing some deal, and seeing Hetty, so young and fresh, so original in a room filled with tired and familiar faces, had come over, gazing at her.

'Hi, Craig – didn't know you were back!' Then he had gazed at Hetty more closely. 'And who's this?' He fished for an introduction.

'Wait and see, Winfield – just you wait and see! I'm making some tests on her – show them to you when they're ready . . .'

Hetty left the telescope, bored with these reminders of her workaday world. She turned and gazed up at the hall doors, willing them to open, for Craig to return. But nothing moved in the stillness. She sighed, leaning back on the balustrade, tilting her bronzed face upwards, closing her eyes – a slim dark figure in the white silk dress, chin tilted, neck arched, as if offering herself to some delicious agony. She had blossomed in the warmth and pleasure of these southern California airs, the attentions of studio make-up men, hairdressers, costumiers – the dark curls straightened now, bobbed and fringed across her brow. There was still the tomboy athleticism, the mischief. But in the last eighteen months, under Craig's direction, and in her own sexual release, there was a quite new poise and sophistication; the childishness had been refined into something sensuous, inviting, knowing. She was a different person, in body as well as thought. Apparently resolving her earlier conflicts of temperament, she combined her previous innocence with a precocious maturity. Only her stammer reoccurred sometimes, as evidence of her former torments, from which she believed she had completely released herself.

Now, she thought herself fulfilled and happy. What did it matter if she had married a liar? She was *who* she was with Craig. That was what counted. She had come into her inheritance, which was not a great house in Ireland, but her own unique gifts, released now in expressing her real nature. And in that cause what did a few inventions matter? They had not lied about their passion, or their success in pictures together. Both these had been very real.

But Hetty, fed on vanities, so obsessed by, so seduced in every way by Craig, had quite blinded herself to the realities of the situation. Now, locked in his orbit, she had no independent track across the heavens herself. She did not choose to see how Craig, from the beginning, had been manipulating her. So intent was she on furthering her own power schemes, on justifying her obsession with him and on repressing her guilt about Léonie, that she refused to acknowledge his own wiles, to much the same ends, with her – had not realised how she had been a key card in his resurgence as a Hollywood director, or seen how he used her voyeuristically, through the camera and in private, unaware that what attracted him as much as anything in her was her love of women, or of one woman at least, a delicious aberration for him, which he had sensed in her from the beginning.

So Hetty, knowing nothing of the picture business – of all its usual great hurdles to success – and caring less, had seen her sudden achievements in Hollywood as simply a natural progression of her talent, a mere confirmation of her gifts.

When Winfield Sheehan had stood up in the small projection room, after he had seen Craig's tests on her, and said, 'Well, Miss Fraser, the camera certainly likes you!', she had taken this praise as almost inevitable, not something upon which Craig's career might hang – for she had not been in Winfield's office afterwards when he spoke to Craig.

'Okay, I agree – you've got something quite unusual there. But –'

'But she goes only with me, Winfield. Remember that.'

'Well, I'd like to, Craig – but you've been out of the business quite a while . . .'

'Take it or leave it. Both of us or nothing. Paramount will snap her up, or Universal – and she'll be a star. No doubt of it – see it as clear as the nose on your face. But take us both – and you'll have her with Fox, in on the first floor . . .'

'Okay, Craig . . .' Winfield, drumming his fingers on the desk, had unwillingly seen the light. 'Raoul is still held up on location with *This is the Life*. So I'll give you the new Billy Farnum picture to do. Try her in that small part, the sassy, arrogant daughter from Charleston.'

A Family and Its Fortune the picture had been called, the story of an aristocratic southern household, fallen on bad times after the Civil War, trying to re-establish themselves, in which Hetty, as the youngest of three daughters, falling in love with a Yankee officer, runs foul of her parents, particularly her mother. It was a small role. But it was one which she played to perfection.

She had gone from strength to strenth after that – and so had Craig. Their partnership flowered in a succession of swashbuckling costume pictures, some banal contemporary modern melodramas and one or two sentimental love stories – not the sort of picture that Craig really wanted to direct at all. But they had all made money and Craig was on top now again. And Hetty – as Laura Bowen, the stage name he had invented for her, insisting she use it in real life as well – was already a coming star, with interviews in *Photoplay* and an increasing pile of fan mail.

The era of the vamp was fading in Hollywood – as was the taste for Mary Pickford's old-world home-spun childish innocence. Post-war audiences – emancipated, irresponsible, more sophisticated – wanted something different in their dream women: a greater realism, a modern tone of command, a more available sexuality, bounding arrogance, devil-may-care adventure. And Hetty, with her mischievous regality, supplied just this tempting mix.

But more, for Americans, she was a startling face to conjure with – a quite new sort of beauty for them, in which there was nothing cheap or sentimental, the classic features of old European nobility, yet lit by all sorts of contemporary devilment. With its finesse, hers was a unique face in Hollywood pictures, that of a princess who had come right down into the market place, freely available to all, so that a huge audience of clerks and shop girls could feel themselves mixing with royalty on equal terms . . . at least for an hour in a darkened picture palace. For Hetty's availability to ordinary mortals was finally illusory. She was not one of them. She touched their lives with easy grace and command, which they might seek to emulate, but left them at fade-out, elusive in her fiery independence, unobtainable on any permanent basis, leaving her audience only with a tantalising taste of the power she exuded.

Craig, of course, had seen just these latent images and opportunities in her, and had skilfully promoted them – the right scenarios, parts, make-up, costumes, lighting. But just as much, as she learnt the trade, Hetty had come to inspire him – all her histrionic fancies, so often frustrated before, coming to fruition now, when she could dream in public, licensed in every whim, making love to the camera.

There had, indeed, been something inevitable about their professional success. With Craig directing her *sotto voce* on the stages, they sparked off such magic in each other.

But why had she married Craig, she wondered once more, leaning back on the balustrade? Well, she had fallen in love with him – and he with her, or so she thought. She refused for a moment to acknowledge another and deeper reason: that, in marrying Craig, she could prove her love for a man, thus relegating her relationship with Léonie to the status of a girlish crush. She could put the seal now on the tomb of that dead relationship and so forget her betrayal there. And there was a further reason she was not conscious of at all: in her guilt at this betrayal she wanted as much to wound people as to dominate them. Because wounds, she knew intuitively, must be all the more telling in a marriage. Though in both these ambitions she had made no headway whatsoever with Craig.

She opened her eyes, gazing up at the Lodge. Built on several receding levels it was an absurd Alpine conceit in these burning desert airs. No single feature rhymed with any other. It was a complete hodge-podge of conflicting styles and Gothic excrescences – of fairy-tale steeples, castellated turrets, half-timbered battlements, gargoyles, arrow-slit windows, lattice-work wooden balconies, a mix of thin wood, plaster and some brick – a fragile dream in the glimmering light: paper-thin, preposterous.

But Hetty had never been able to dislike it. How could one dislike something so insistently, compellingly bogus? Craig had bought the crazy place early in 1917, before the building had even been completed, after he had been three years on the coast, working on, and finally directing, two-reelers for Jesse Lasky; then he had moved to Fox and had his first big success there, a torrid six-reel extravaganza, supposedly set in ancient Egypt, *Mistress of the Gods*, with Annette Kellerman. The picture had cost an astonishing $40,000. But it had grossed almost ten times that.

Craig had been in the money then. And the man who had originally built the folly, a geologist taking a fortune out of the South Bay oil boom, had let it go cheap. His wife had died just before they were due to move in and the man had jumped at the chance of unloading it. There had been no other bidders. Access was difficult – the geologist had already spent a fortune just grading the site and hacking the road up to it – and it had been miles from anywhere then, from the studios or Hollywood itself, which was exactly why Craig had wanted it. He loathed Hollywood, its vulgar suburban airs, and the brash studio lots growing up all round it. He had wanted just this, something wild and craggy, as far away as possible from all the charlatans, self-styled geniuses, neurotics and hucksters of the plain.

Which was exactly why Hetty had come to like it, too. On this peak, in the limpid air, she could lord it over all the other hazy creations far beneath her, the shallow, dust-dry illusions of the valley. And, though she herself had come to live in a further rackety illusion up here, that was something quite different: the Lodge was an illusion of arrogant European civilisation – no matter that the place itself trembled now on the edge of destruction above the canyon, already beginning to split in the fierce heat, wood buckling, paint peeling, the back of the lodge never completed and still supported by scaffolding and buttresses, just like a set on one of the studio lots.

They both liked it that way. Craig had made no repairs. What was the point of repairing something so insubstantial? You never repaired things out here anyway. The fools on the plain – they just built afresh every time, always desperate for something new. But he and Hetty both cherished the illusion of power and feudal tradition offered by the gimcrack Lodge.

Yes, Hetty thought, despite the fragility, the youth of the building, everything had a memory for her here. She noticed the long, false marble plaster panel, one of three as a surround for the hall doors, through which Craig had put his elbow one night after dinner on the terrace, just to show how skin-deep the place was. Some of the guests had been quite shocked at this wilful destruction of something they took to be precious and genuinely antique. Craig had smiled at them.

'All just phoney! Only a dream palace . . .'

'And you're the dream king, I suppose!' Betty Nansen, the Danish beauty and now a big star, had said drily.

'And you the queen, Betty . . .' Craig had looked at her lovingly. And Hetty had felt a pang of bitter jealousy then, which she thought she had entirely hidden. But Craig, close by, had noticed it and whispered, 'You needn't fret, Laura.'

'I'm not! – don't fool yourself.'

And he had shaken his head in wonder then. 'You don't know yourself, Laura – it's all in your eyes, just as it is in close up. See all your thoughts, clear as day. You can look so jealous or loving, yet your expression doesn't change a fraction. All in your eyes . . . That's why the camera loves you!'

And was this why she had come to love *him*? – because however much she dissembled, disguised herself, he could still see the secrets of her soul? More reason for hating him, surely? – that she could not escape, was held captive in some way by his knowledge of her, his intuitions, which always out-reached what she knew or felt about him.

For the first time in her life she was with somebody whom she could not, in the end, dominate or wound. And there was the challenge. Craig was a tantalising will o' the wisp, forever dancing away from her, just out of reach, imbued with all sorts of knowledge, secrets, magic – gifts which she longed for herself in the person of someone she could not finally possess. And perhaps she had married him to further that end – as if in such legal possession of him, and of half the Lodge, she might finally command his spirit as well.

Craig confirmed this idea of a shared property, at least, when he emerged on the terrace then, all mysterious smiles, carrying a genuine marble plaque. He turned it round. LAURA'S LAIR, it said, in Gothic characters chiselled deep into the stone. He set it down by the hall door.

'Well . . . Laura Bowen!' He was just in his shirt-sleeves now, sweating, his eyebrows raised. She jumped up and they met in a calm embrace – and she kissed him, half-warily, half-tenderly, brushing the pinpoints of perspiration away from his upper lip. 'You like it?' She nodded as he picked her up in his arms. 'Well, now for the other surprises . . .' And he carried her over the threshold.

As he opened the doors and they moved from the light into the shadows of the mock baronial hall, the music started – a great swirling burst of woodwind, strings and timpani, Lehar's 'Gold and Silver' waltz. In the same instant spotlights illuminated a dais at the end of the hall and Hetty saw the orchestra, some fifteen or twenty men in white tie and tails, with little Eddy Nolan, one of the two dwarf brothers from Fonsy's troupe, whom Craig had taken with them from Ireland, set up in front, in a miniature dress suit, playing the conductor.

'What on earth . . .' Hetty was enchanted. 'How did you get them all up here?'

Craig still held her in his arms. 'Ransacked the studios – there'll be no mood music down on the plains this afternoon! Sneaked them all up here after lunch – Winfield fixed it for me. Isn't it great?' She nodded again, before he set her down and they waltzed away together, quite alone in the wide spaces, circling round in their tired wedding outfits. Their clothes were sweaty and bedraggled. But the new ring on Hetty's finger, one of Craig's wedding presents, a great cornelian scarab with a strange Egyptian symbol engraved on the flat side, glittered like a dark and pristine moon. She looked at it. Yes, she was married.

'They can't get me now,' she whispered, brushing Craig's ear as he held her lightly. 'However hard they try . . .'

'I'd never have let them get you anyway.'

'Mama might have done anything in her craziness. You'd "abducted" me, don't forget! Remember that detective she sent up here – when I was supposed to be living down at the Studio Club – and you locked me in the turret while he searched the place? And you told him the room there had never been opened, some sort of ghost inside, and he skedaddled!'

'I could just as easily have paid him off.'

'Of course you could. But you invented him off instead! You sweet monster . . .'

Her mother, when she had eventually learnt of Hetty's Studio Club address, had threatened all sorts of woe, legal and otherwise, in several letters, half-dismissive, half-revengeful: '. . . who cares what you do with your stupid life . . . I shall have the police in America apprehend you . . .'

Before that she had written to Mortimer, Dermot and Robert. They had replied in reasonable but concerned tones. Was she doing the right thing? Was she happy? Though they were astonished at her behaviour, she at least felt some contact and understanding there. The only letter which cut her to the bone, so that she afterwards completely eradicated it from her mind, was the one from Léonie, received while she was still at the Studio Club.

'. . . Mama died in the influenza epidemic. Then you disappeared. I thought I'd die myself then. I just can't imagine why you did this cruel thing, without a word of warning or explanation, destroying everything we had in a moment . . .'

The hurt, recriminatory tone had changed then, replaced by apt reflections on Hetty's character and the likely consequences of her actions, yet offering a final understanding, indeed forgiveness, so that it was this last part of the letter which Hetty most completely forgot.

I know you well enough – *so* well, indeed! – to know that with this man you'll just betray your real nature. Oh, you'll think you're fulfilling yourself with him, in his world of nickelodeons or whatever. But it won't be anything of the kind. Don't you see? – with him you'll lose all that is best and truest in you, your great gift which is not for acting, pretending, but for being *real*.

I know how you can't face that reality in yourself, because of your missing father, all the rows with your Mama and so on. But with this man you'll only be expressing shallow surfaces of yourself – tricks, vanities, living on thin ice which will land you in all sorts of trouble in the end. Yes, that trite phrase – you're running away from yourself! And don't you see, too, that this man is not the father figure you've searched so long for, but just someone out for his own ends, who'll encourage all that's worst in you? I saw that at once in him, that evening in Waterford. Really, you shouldn't go on with it. You mustn't, because one day, if you go on feeding these pretences, you'll come to hate yourself, for betraying your real goal, which shouldn't be for impressing the world, but knowing your true self and expressing that. You gave that wonderful self to me, often enough. And a thing like that doesn't just disappear. You've only hidden it more thoroughly. But you can find it again. Or we can. I'll wait for you . . .

Hetty had read the letter with angry, tear-filled eyes. Then, in a fury of guilty rage, she had torn it up. She had not replied, nor heard from Léonie since. Instead, asleep sometimes, in nightmares, she moaned her name.

Coming closer to Craig in the waltz, resting her chin on his shoulder, her eyes circled the hall in all its bogus splendour. Flowing round in the dance she saw a blur of hideous sporting trophies – grizzly bear, bison, puma – high above the collection of mediaeval armour, ghostly men-at-arms, opposing rows along each wall of dark, malign figures in visored helmets, great carapaces of steel and chain mail, with crossed lances set between them, double-edged swords, Gothic blunderbusses, miniature cannon . . . Craig had collected these emblems of chivalry and violent derring-do from various studio prop departments – they were all quite unreal, made of tin, papier-mâché or wood, just as most of the lodge was.

But their bogus nature was precisely intended – as a play within the play, further conceits within a greater one, turning the lodge into a huge toy box for them both to tinker with, room by room, sustaining their own bizarre dreams, their 'games'; each separate space presented a different theme in its décor: a Wild West saloon, complete with bar and pool table; a gilded Versailles salon fit for Marie Antoinette; a drawing room decked out in classic Georgian mode, a memory of great Irish country houses, with hunting prints and imitation Chippendale; and, last and most resplendent of all, an ancient Egyptian room, reflecting Craig's obsessions with the Pharonic period, with coloured tomb murals, hieroglyphics and cartouches, all round the walls, two vast plaster busts of Isis and Osiris at either end, a delicious dancing fountain in the middle, with the anachronistic addition of silken cushions and hookahs from a later Arab period littering the floor: all the magpie collection scavenged from the studios over the years and settings now for their own personal productions, where they returned each night from the studios, isolating themselves from the vulgar crowd on the plains, creating exotic dramas in the lodge which would never be captured on celluloid.

Hetty remembered one such occasion, six months before, when she and Craig had returned late from a riotous party at the Ship Café, with two young women, bit-part actresses Craig had picked up there. They had all flopped down in the Egyptian room and Craig had masterminded things, filling the hookah bowls with marijuana, so that all of them, in half an hour, were stretched out, dreamy-faced, on the opulent cushions, Craig lolling next to one of the girls, fondling her.

And Hetty, drawing on this narcotic for the first time, had looked over at him, only vaguely surprised, watching the girl wriggle out of her thin dress; the other girl – called Tansy, she remembered, small, pert, red-haired, adventurous – had leant over and casually touched her lips. Hetty, in a state of happy aerial suspension, had still felt a thump of surprise at this invitation. But instead of resisting it, as she had thought for a moment to do, she had been overcome by a sweet faintness, lying back on the cushions – and the other girl, leaning down, had slipped her hand into her dress, and touched her breast delicately, twitching the nipple. And the sense of rising excitement then, so that she had jack-knifed up, reaching for Tansy, before falling back, stunned almost, as the red-haired girl, kneeling above her now, quickly took off her own blouse, then climbed out of her skirt, and straddled Hetty gently, bending forward, opening her dress wide, kissing her breasts, before running a hand, feather-light, slowly down to her sex. The pleasure, spasm upon spasm, had been delirious.

Though she had considered the whole episode more soberly next morning, she did not allow the idea that she had done anything the least unsuitable to cross her mind. How could there be anything wrong in such pleasure? She had done just this with Léonie many times. The whole business, and its later repetition, she saw simply as a happy extension of their many 'games', all part of the endless tricks and fancies played out between them then, the glorious realisation of dreams, in which Léonie in the end had quite failed her. Such escapades were simply other ploys, joyous sexual conceits, in which they could both extend their reach over the common herd. Now, of course, there was a difference. She and Craig were married. Would that change the game? She danced on with Craig through the great hall.

The party to celebrate both her wedding and the release of *Thunder Bay*, her latest pirate swashbuckler directed by Craig, started a few hours later. The bootlegger's van had arrived some time before, filled with crates of scotch and champagne, which Craig had ordered specially for the occasion, run up the coast from Mexico. The first guests arrived soon afterwards – some straight from the studios even on a Saturday night – roaring up the dark, winding track in their Kessels and Dusenbergs, headlights piercing the night, momentarily illuminating Craig and Hetty as they waited on the terrace – Craig in a white alpaca jacket, Hetty in a sheath dress of black silk, delicately appliquéed with tiny white beads and sequins.

'Hi, Wally! – Dotty!' Craig stepped forward, giving Wally Reid and then his wife a quick bear hug. Wally was smashed already. Was it just drink, Hetty wondered – or had he moved on to the snow? Well, there was that here too, if anyone wanted it.

Wally, with his striking, pretty-boy blond good looks, was with Paramount, the brightest male star in Hollywood just then. And Mabel Normand, who tripped – literally tripped, was she back on the snow as well? – up the steps next with Fatty Arbuckle, was with Goldwyn. But most of the other guests were friends of theirs at Fox – Billy Farnum, Betty Nansen, Virginia Pearson and Betty Blythe, fresh from her success in *The Queen of Sheba*.

Walter Brenon with the rest of the Irish brigade came in a rush soon afterwards – Raoul Walsh, Mickey Neilan and Winfield Sheehan: blond, blue-eyed, flamboyant, with his equally boisterous wife, the opera diva Maria Jeritza.

In couples or excited groups they ran up the steps, pushing into the great hall, hazy with tobacco now, filled with raucous laughter and the sharply syncopated clatter of ragtime – grasping drinks from phoney silver goblets, picking at lobster and bronzed suckling pigs from a mock-mediaeval groaning board. Finally, a vast chauffeur-driven Dodge limousine drew up and the actress Marion Davies, in a long, deep-cut black polka dot silk dress, emerged with her friend William Randolph Hearst, the newspaper tycoon.

Hetty rushed down the steps to greet her. 'Marion!' They embraced. 'How's it going? That director Leonard still murdering you with soft lights and pe-passionate romance?'

'Christ! – don't t-t-talk about it! *The Restless Sex* – you can say that again! What a be-bloody picture. Not an ounce of comedy,' she added in her funny, rowdy voice, before they moved away together as Craig welcomed Hearst.

'And the Boss?' Hetty looked back at the tycoon. 'How are things?'

'Always the be-beady eye on me. Never misses a trick.' Then, making sure she was out of earshot, she went on, 'Laura, I could really use a drink.' She looked at her friend, wide eyes flickering, running her fingers nervously through the stiff perm in her auburn hair.

'I've a be-bottle in my room. Come on up and have a jigger while you take your coat off.'

'I ain't got no coat, you nutty –'

'"Powder your nose" then.'

'Powder my ass . . .'

People looked up as Hearst and his mistress moved into the crowded hall. This was a real catch, they thought – almost as good as Fairbanks and Pickford, who certainly would not be coming to this louche shindig. Hearst, with all his gossipy newspapers, among these crates of bootlegged drink, would be at risk, while Marion Davies, whom he had made one of the social queens of Hollywood, had a bad temptation that way. But Hetty had insisted Marion come – so that Hearst, ever the concerned jailer in their strange relationship, had had to tag along too.

Marion sat at Hetty's dressing table, settling her hair with one hand, taking a shot of scotch with the other. Hetty paced behind her. It was her turn to be nervous now. Drink wasn't her problem. She wished in some ways it was. You could cure it then – by having a few.

'So?' Marion asked, fortified now, even warmer and more scatty. 'What's *your* problem?' She smiled at her in the mirror. 'Marriage – already?'

'Not quite . . .' Hetty, cracking her knuckles, was at a loss.

'Well, it can't be your new pirate pe-picture with Craig. Everyone says it's a real wow, held over at Sloans for a second *week*, goddamit!'

'No, not that . . .' Hetty turned, half-smiling, nervous.

'It's the marriage then, when you have him anyway.'

'Maybe . . .'

'Listen, Laura, you're stalling. Either you're nuts about Craig, I mean really ke-crackers, or you want to sink the ship without knowing it. One or the other. You wouldn't be me-marrying him otherwise. I tell ya, honey – no surer way of falling out with a guy than getting hitched. And being crazy about someone, *that* crazy, well, that'll have just the same result: *finito*, 'cos no man's really worth it. So either way – you're doomed! Have a drink.'

Beaming hugely, she offered Hetty the bottle.

'Pe-perhaps –'

'No perhaps about it! Know it myself all too well. Listen, I'm hooked with Randy. But I know *why*. A lot of weaknesses – 'cos maybe I ain't really no actress at all. So I need him to look after me. But if I *me-married* him, why, then he'd treat me like dirt. *I'd* be doomed! So I hold off, for the good of my health.'

'I de-de-don't need Craig to look after me.'

'Okay, so you're hooked in some other way – in bed maybe. And that's fine. But you don't need to me-me-*marry* a guy to have that!' Marion took another shot of whisky, looking at Hetty now as if at some new species of woman. 'Ya see, that's what I don't get. Ya gotta perfectly good de-deal going with Craig already, in *every* way. Yet here you are digging your own grave. It's crazy – killing happiness that way.'

'Why should me-marriage kill our chances, though?'

'*Your* chances, not his – and 'cos you don't *need* marriage with him.' She looked at Hetty, shaking her head in wonder. 'So you're really hooked on Craig some quite different way altogether, aren't you? I don't know what. But what's worse is *you* don't know either. And that's crazy! Ya gotta resist the hook, Laura – 'cos it'll destroy you.'

What nonsense, Hetty thought. Marion was lovely – but she really did drink too much.

The evening went from strength to riotous weakness. Drink flowed, the Frisco lobster and the suckling pigs were hardly touched. People danced and hugged and kissed, sometimes in step to the ragtime music, more often not. Some of the guests moved to other rooms, darker corners, for assignations with snow or sex. But most remained in the great hall, a brittle, raucous crowd, mocking the chivalrous men-at-arms all round them, flouncing their short skirts in Charlestons, kicking the papier-mâché mediaeval cannon, while Wally Reid, far gone, aimed an Arab blunderbuss at his wife. Others kept close to the long table with its bootlegged drinks, like desert travellers at some miraculous oasis, laughing like schoolchildren, telling tales out of class.

A drunken minor executive from Fox sidled up to Craig. 'So what's your next picture, Craig? Rumour has it you've got some big costume epic up your sleeve.'

'Rumour's wrong. Got a nice little family melodrama coming up with Laura –'

'You should put her in something big, now's your chance. *Thunder Bay* – held over for a second week at Sloans, grossed over five thousand bucks there *last week* –'

'I know, I know –'

'But now you've gone and *married* her, Craig! What was the idea there?'

Craig rounded on him then. 'What's the *usual* idea there, you hamhead?'

The man was surprised, swaying about. 'Search me, search me . . .'

Hetty danced with Mickey Neilan, in his cups as usual, but still entirely graceful and charming.

'So, top of the evenin',' he said to her, making jaunty steps, so that they nearly ran over Eddy Nolan, still in his miniature dress suit, dancing with another midget, a little pixie of a woman, part of a troupe working on a Lon Chaney horror picture at Universal. 'Christ, they really get under your feet here,' Mickey went on. 'What's with Craig, that he has to have all these deformed tiny tots about him? – and in his pictures – often wondered.'

Hetty smiled. 'He likes them. And so do I. Eddy Nolan's a sweet.'

'Yeah – but it's really a sort of fetish with Craig. And his friend Von.' He looked over to the drinks table where the Austrian director, Erich von Stroheim, erect in white tie and tails, very Prussian, with close-cropped hair, was lowering a goblet of champagne in one gulp, jerking his neck back, then coming smartly to attention, clicking his heels, laughing. 'Always looking for the perverse side of things.'

'Do they?'

'You didn't see *The Devil's Passkey?*'

'No.'

'Yeah: lust, malice, torture, obsession – that's the Von. And Craig, too, whenever he gets half a chance.'

'And you? You're pure as the driven snow?'

'Well, I *am*! Directing Mary Pickford all these years you *have* to be . . .' He came to her confidingly then. 'Laura, I'd really like to do a picture with you.'

'Me too. But –'

'But Craig's just gone and got you under permanent contract. Why did you have to go and *marry* him, for Chrissakes? I told you, you shouldn't have gone and done it.'

'Second time tonight! Marion said the same thing. What's wrong with you people? A little drink on board – then sour grapes?'

'Oh no, Laura.' He looked at her winningly. 'In Vino Veritas – Vino Veritas . . .'

He was just drunk, too, she thought. Nicely so. But you had to take it all with a pinch of salt, with both of them, because Marion – well, she'd have liked to marry Craig herself. A lot of Hollywood women would have wanted that. And Mickey? – he was crazy about her. Sour grapes all round. But what was a 'fetish', she wondered? She'd ask Craig. He'd be bound to know.

Later, on Von Stroheim's suggestion, a dozen of them made up another party, taking their cars down the canyon, way out east of Los Angeles, to an old barn, with raked benches all round and a cockpit in the middle, made over now as a boxing ring. The foetid, windowless space was already packed tight with fashionable spectators – picture people, gamblers, some of the Mob – coming on here after other parties in town. But it was a very private function in this isolated spot, where normally, most weekends, cockfights were held, run by Mexicans. Tonight, however, it featured a special bill, a series of prize fights – between women.

Hetty was pushed off her feet in the surge towards the ring as the bell went and the main bout started. Two tall, leggy, well-built girls – attractive, though one had a cast in her eye – in singlets and shorts, with mops of long dark hair down to their shoulders, started to lay into each other, vaguely skilled in the art, or at least mimicking it cleverly, leading with left jabs, hooks to the body. Soon they were in a sweaty clinch, breast to breast, pawing at each other. The crowd roared.

'Break! Break!' The referee, a lantern-jawed man in a dress suit, intervened. The girl with the cast tried to knee her opponent in the groin as they separated. There was pandemonium.

'Foul! Foul!' The roars reached a crescendo. The girl with the cast smiled – before suddenly walloping the other with the side of her glove. 'Foul! Dirty play!' the spectators shouted. They loved it. Hetty did not. But she was not going to show it. The girls set to again, gloves flying, body punching now, getting below the belt, before coming into a clinch again; this time the girl with the cast hammered the other on her back, then got a glove beneath her singlet, trying to rip it off. But the other girl pre-empted her, pushing her glove inside her opponent's waistband, ripping it open, so that the shorts slipped down her thighs and she had to box on, holding them up, with only one hand.

'Foul! – stop the fight!' Wally Reid roared. And they did, while running repairs were made, the girl tying up her shorts with a necktie that had been thrown into the ring.

Soon, sweating heavily, breasts moulded against their singlets now, the girls began to tire. The bell went. The second round was more provocative still. The girls groped at each other voluptuously in their clinches and the fight became more of a perverse wrestling match, the referee trying to part them unsuccessfully. They fell to the floor, rolled over one another. And now the girl with the cast took a clear ascendancy, straddling her opponent, while the barn exploded and the crowd bayed for blood. Instead, the second girl, suddenly recovering, reached up and, taking her opponent's singlet by the neck, ripped the fabric down, leaving the girl naked to the waist, sweat streaming down her breasts.

Hetty could take no more. Overcome with the heat she slumped to the floor in a faint. When she recovered she was outside in the front seat of the Pierce-Arrow.

'What on earth?' she murmured angrily to Craig beside her. 'What *possessed* you?'

'It's all an act, Laura!' Craig was not in the least put out by it all. 'Nobody really gets hurt and they're well paid. Nobody forces them.'

'It's disgusting!'

'Oh, come on, Laura – you're being old-fashioned.'

'It's just . . . degrading.'

Craig started the engine. 'Okay, I'm sorry – we'll go home. I've got a special present for you still to come, a surprise.' He turned to her, a shadow in the darkness, touching her lips a moment. 'Sorry – about the boxing match. Just part of this crazy place. One day, we'll get right away from it . . .'

'But you like it, like all that . . . sort of torture, don't you?'

'Hell, no. It's just . . . all part of the scene here. You know that, honey. *You're* part of it, too. Look at those pictures we make together – revenge, lust, violence, high emotion. You'd think they'd work, think the crowds would flock in, if you were just drinking milk shakes in the pictures?'

'Yes, that's only acting, though.'

'That's life, Laura, only most people try and pretend it isn't. But we have to tell the truth in pictures. Least I do. And the Von. And that's what I want to do, with you, in our next pictures. Come on home and I'll tell you about it – your last surprise today!'

He kissed her softly and they drove off.

'What does a "fetish" mean, Craig?' she asked after a few moments.

He laughed. 'A totem pole, or an amulet in ancient Egypt, that's a fetish – something you think has magic in it, that you worship, an inanimate object.'

'And?'

'That's all. A superstition.'

'Are you like that?'

'Oh yes! Got to be. After all, the whole thing's just a charade here, isn't it? You, us, this.' He gestured round the darkened landscape of Hollywood. 'And the only reality in the end – just a flickering image on a screen – is the biggest illusion of all. So of course I'm superstitious. But I don't worship an inanimate object. I'm lucky that way. I have you.' He gripped her knee gently.

Later, Hetty, propped up in bed waiting for Craig, saw him come through the shadows carrying something, a severed head it seemed, and her heart missed a beat. But when he was in the light, and she saw it clearly, she was even more astonished. It was the portrait bust of an Egyptian woman – a slender, unbelievably elegant face, rising from a lotus-stem neck and pointed chin, in a long inverted triangle, up to a flared head-dress: firm swelling lips, perfectly modelled nose, vast, heavy-lidded eyes, sharply crescent eyebrows, the whole delicately washed in soft pinks and apricot, kohl blacks, the head-dress picked out in bands of gold and blue, centred with some great jewel, crossed with a gold band in the shape of a snake's head.

But the woman's expression was the extraordinary thing. Far more than the sum of its parts, it was animate while yet perfectly still. There was life there, a deep, full, sensuous life – but one could not quite touch it. There was profligacy, yet a severe control, great distance, yet intense femininity. She was both goddess and woman. She gazed at Hetty then, as Craig held the bust up to her, with a look of cold, calm, languorous beauty – a perfect balance between the sacred and the profane, a regard that offered everything, yet promised nothing. Hetty felt the eyes drilling into her, through her, something she could not escape – those beautiful eyes, lit with irony, power, wisdom, love – everything she desired in herself.

'It's Queen Nefertiti,' he said quietly, as if the woman was alive with them in the room. 'And it's you,' he added in an even lower voice. He set the bust down, and sat next to her on the bed.

'But who? –'

'Our picture, Laura!' And now Craig was filled with tense enthusiasm. 'The one I've always wanted to do. And we can – soon; Nefertiti, wife of the heretic Pharaoh Akhenaten, eighteenth dynasty, in Egypt –'

'A costume picture –'

'An *epic*, Laura! Bigger than any yet made, bigger than *Intolerance* or anything de Mille ever attempted. Bigger – and better. It's a sensational story, been working on it secretly for years – it's everything that ever mattered to me, everything that ever mattered in ancient Egypt, too. You'll see!' His eyes were bright, almost manic, as he came closer to her.

'It's not just chariot races and battles up and down the Nile out on some tank on the back lot – like de Mille and the others. This is about a whole new *faith*, the first time in history, fifteen hundred years before Christ, that men came to worship *one* god. That's the great thing. Nefertiti married the boy Pharaoh Amenophis the fourth – a dreamer, artist, pacifist – who changed the whole religion of ancient Egypt. Instead of worshipping all the thousands of animal gods they had out there then, he scrapped all that, sacked the priests at Thebes, and worshipped the sun, as the one true god; became the Sun King, Akhenaten, and built an incredible city for the new faith, way up the Nile at Amarna – the City of the Sun, a city of love, not fear, a dream place, with flowers, lakes, pleasure gardens, fountains, great boulevards, vast temples, royal palaces, literally a paradise on earth, 'till the whole place was razed to the ground twenty years later by Akhenaten's rivals of the old faith back in Thebes. But, for those twenty years, Laura – well, it was the most incredible civilisation ever seen, before or since. And Nefertiti, the most beautiful woman. Look at the inscription on the bottom of the bust – one of the poems Akhenaten wrote about her.' Craig read it out:

'"The heiress, great in favour, lady of grace, sweet of love, Mistress of the South and of the North, fair of face, gay with two plumes, beloved of the living Aten, the Chief Wife of the King, whom he loves, Lady of the Two Lands, great of love, Nefertiti, living for ever and ever." And that's her.' Craig glanced over at the bust. 'Had it made up by Leo Kuter, my art director, copy of the real thing in the Berlin Museum.'

Hetty was enchanted. 'It's incredible . . .'

'Yes. And only you can play her. Born for it.'

'Can I?'

'No one else. I have a scenario. But it's all secret – not talked to anyone yet, so you mustn't either. In a few months, I'll move on it.'

'Cost a fortune.'

'Yes.' Craig relished the thought. 'Akhenaten's Royal Palace alone was half a mile long – have to build it. The most beautiful city ever made. And we'll make it even better than the real thing! Fox has all the money. We'll do it in Egypt, the interiors in Rome or this new studio they have in Nice, get right away from this crummy place.'

'They'd never let you –'

'Let *us*, Laura. They'll let us do it. Because they'll see it, just as clearly as I do: you're Nefertiti, image and spirit. What do you think?'

Hetty looked at the bust again, thrilled by the challenge, the honour, and yet by the rightness of it all. 'Oh, yes, Craig, yes! . . .'

Now at last, she thought, she knew why she had married Craig. Everything fell into place – it had all been ordained. Craig had been secretly working all this time towards this point where her destiny could be fulfilled, where she would become that Queen, not as an actress but as of right. She had felt it ever since childhood – the sense of being a changeling, with royal blood perhaps, a princess. And here at last was confirmation of what Snipe, the maimed fortune teller at Summer Hill, had said. She was about to enter her true estate – as Nefertiti, Queen of the Two Lands.

2

AFTER THE WAR in Europe – and the start of the real troubles in Ireland – the great house at Summer Hill began to languish. Much of the pleasure garden and the terraced lawn, once so meticulously kept, planted, pruned and cut, went to seed. The upper lawns and croquet court, unused, began to seep with moss – and, with the demise of the last of the ferocious Summer Hill terriers, became instead a playground contested between rabbits and moles. The demesne, for lack of milch cows, became ragworty and the high orchards flooded in autumn with unpicked fruit. Moist growths of elder and ivy, the voracious tentacles of Irish nature, began to feed on the ruined north wing, which remained a burnt-out shell. The estate workers, masons and carpenters who, in earlier times, would have at once started to clear the rubble and rebuild the wing, had in many cases never returned from the trenches or had emigrated, leaving their land forever.

Most of the domestic staff had been paid off as well, for there was no longer the money, either to effect repairs or to maintain such a vast household. Lady Cordiner's considerable fortune had gone almost in its entirety to a Jewish charity in London, while Frances – as an abstentionist Sinn Fein MP in the recently elected, but illegal, Irish Parliament – continuously embroiled now in seditious Republican speech-making and other covert activities about the country was rarely at home, staying with friends and sympathisers, often moving from house to house overnight, on the run from the British forces.

The farm lapsed and the estate rents, on Frances's abrupt instructions, were discontinued. Though Mortimer, one of the last of the old Redmondite MPs, but without any real constituency now in Ireland, came down from Dublin now and then and did what he could for the place, keeping an eye on the dwindling accounts with Mrs Martin and old O'Donovan, and selling off, with Frances's agreement, a few of the better antiques – one of the Georgian silver épergnes and a Chippendale table – to pay the few remaining servants and estate workers.

Sooner do this, he had told Frances, than allow the British Army another rout. For in the spring of 1919, searching for Frances, they had ransacked Summer Hill, looting pictures and other valuables. So that afterwards Mortimer had much of the better furniture and effects removed, lodging them with the bank or hiding them in stable lofts and outhouses. This he had done entirely on his own initiative, for in June of that year the police, finally catching up with Frances after a most inflammatory speech in Co. Cork, had arrested her. She was tried in camera, and sentenced to six months' imprisonment in Cork jail.

Apart from Aunt Emily, Mrs Martin, Mrs Molloy the cook, a few maids and Pat Kennedy, now returned from hospital after his accident in the fire, the huge house lay empty. Elly had long since left the house – marrying out of it, to Jack Welsh a railway man who lived beyond Cloone. Dust settled on the great reception rooms and then fell on the sheets that had been put out to cover what was left of the furniture. The Cordiner ancestral portraits had been removed from the long dining room. Mice and even some bold rats returned, allowed full play across the hall, up the staircase and along the landings. On the top floor, in Henry's old work rooms, the stuffed crocodile continued its infinitesimal decay.

Only Aunt Emily remained at Summer Hill, a spry, indomitable figure, still at her pen and ink drawings and watercolours, her illustrated Summer Hill journal, retiring more or less permanently upstairs and making a redoubt of her large bedroom overlooking the uncut hornbeam maze, where young Biddy Molloy, Mrs Molloy's granddaughter, ministered to her with endless cups of strong tea and shortcake biscuits. Mortimer, in these chaotic, violent times, when every day brought some new outrage – an RIC barracks blown up or a village sacked and looted by the Black and Tans – had offered Aunt Emily the sanctuary of his house at Islandbridge. But she had adamantly refused to budge.

'*I'm* the family now,' she had told him firmly. 'Excuse yourself, Mortimer. I'll not be moved by a few blackguardly Sinn Feiners *or* the British Army.'

Aunt Emily had refused to move to Islandbridge. But Robert had readily agreed. Since Hetty had left Summer Hill eighteen months before, he had in any case spent more of his time in Dublin – at the pretty, white stuccoed house by the weir, a long tram ride from Trinity College. With Mortimer's kindness, and Dermot's too, when he was back on his leave from England, the house had become a second home to him. Now, with Frances's most recent incarceration, and having just taken his modern history degree at Trinity, Mortimer had invited him to stay there more permanently, while he decided where his future lay. So, in June 1920, down from Dublin with Mortimer to pick up some of his things at Summer Hill, Robert walked through the empty, dust-sheeted rooms now in the bright midsummer light.

His life in the great house seemed to be coming to an end, another starting elsewhere. But where, he wondered? For so long he had seen Summer Hill as his permanent home. But some time before he had realised that, without Hetty, and alone with her mother, he could not be happy there. And, yes, the thought had also been there – one day, perhaps, he and Hetty might have married and lived at Summer Hill together. That was obviously not to be.

In his bedroom cupboard, picking through some old school books and papers, he came across the precious cedar-wood pencil box, brought with him from

Domenica, the box that Hetty had so coveted then, her mother denying her a similar one, because of her stammer. And he hated Frances as he heard Hetty's anguished stammer again in the silent room – the product of Hetty's rages or just as often of her heart's terror, the hurts she had suffered from her cold and punitive mother, the loss of her father. He had lost both his own parents, but he had never had any doubts as to who they were, or of their love for him.

Hetty: childhood friend, enemy, sister, confidante, partner over chestnut embers by the nursery fire – and then, later, the longing to be even closer to her, when Léonie had usurped his place. Orphaned, he had surely lacked the loving certainties more than she. Yet it was Hetty who had broken . . . taken to all her self-destructive escapades, with Léonie and then with this man in America, whom she had since married. An adult now, Robert thought he saw why, unable to cope with all those early horrors and indignities in her life, she had done this. He understood what caused her folly, objectively. And yet he had been outraged, made quite desolate, at her final betrayal of him, and thought of her now with more hate than love.

But that was his quandary. He loved and hated her, swinging wildly between the two extremes beneath the outwardly calm and studious surface of his life; he hated her for her cruel arrogance, her callous insensitivity, but loved her, too, for her true goodness of heart.

And he blamed himself then for having lost her. He wished he could have allayed those fears of hers, fought more successfully on her behalf against the wiles of her mother, discovered who, if such a person existed, her real father was. Had he succeeded in any of these causes, he might have possessed her now. But he had to remind himself, once again, how he lacked that kind of rash, intuitive bravery, which was at the heart of Hetty's personality – how he lived with too much forethought, delay, prevarication, seeing too many sides to each question; how he lived, in short, through the ever-twisting ramifications of ideas and books and not in the full flow of life.

He went into Hetty's old bedroom before leaving, looking up at the frieze of primroses round the wall. The room, in the hot sunlight, smelt dead, musty. But then suddenly – and inexplicably, for the windows were firmly shut – the door into the little dressing room beyond swung open and there was a faint odour of limes, a smell he knew so well from his early childhood. And equally suddenly, so that he turned sharply, Hetty was in the room with him, a child, laughing, teasing, stammering – 'You ne-ne-ninny, Robert! You absolute de-de-dolt!'

He moved into the dressing room and looked vaguely for the source of the bitter-sweet smell. And there, in a soap dish next to the washbasin, he found a tiny lime fruit, desiccated now. He scratched its surface. There was not the faintest odour.

'But if I put it in water,' he said to himself slowly, remembering his science, 'it'll revive . . .' Then he returned it to the table. But finally he took it up again and pocketed it.

Mortimer spoke on the train to Dublin that afternoon. 'So, "Change and decay in all around I see",' he said lugubriously, but with a keen smile. 'But not for you,

Robert.' His tone changed, became brisk and encouraging. 'All a wonderful beginning now. You're bound to get a good degree. When will you know?'

'A fortnight or so, I think.'

'And journalism – you really want that?' Robert nodded. 'Certainly, I liked that last article of yours in the Historical Society's magazine, about the Dreyfus trials. Not many of us have faced the implications of all that – the fierce anti-semitism of the French, always pushed under the carpet over there, so that one day the whole thing will blow up in some much worse form.' Mortimer licked his lips. 'Shall we take a little refreshment? Think they still do it on this train. A glass of ale? – go well with this heat.' He mopped his brow. The dining car attendant brought them two bottles of Smithwick's, and Mortimer continued. 'Well, journalism – and France. Two of your interests. No reason why they shouldn't go together. Go over there this summer, why not? See how the land lies.'

'Yes, I'd thought to. But the money, well . . .'

'Nonsense! You have that annuity from your parents' estate in Domenica – and I'll advance you £100 here and now to cover any immediate expenses.'

'That's terribly kind. But journalism – in France? I thought I'd be lucky to get a job as sub-editor or something with the *Irish Times*.'

'Yes, indeed, and you might. I have several good friends there. But why not be a little bit more daring? Start where you *really* want to start – you have good French, know the history there backwards.' Mortimer leant forward now. 'And get out of Ireland for a bit, in any case – all the horrors here. I'm afraid it'll get worse before it gets better.' He looked out at the lush summer countryside. 'The Sinn Feiners won't stop now: the elected government here after all, as they see themselves – as they are indeed. And with these new British troops, these thugs of Black and Tans in the country, there'll be much worse to come. So it's obvious, isn't it? You've got just as good contacts in Paris: your friend, and mine, Ben Straus. And Léonie. Had you forgotten all that?'

'No.' But Robert seemed quite absent. He did not want to admit how he still mistrusted Léonie, did not like her even. Then he gathered himself. 'No, it's just . . .' He hesitated again, rather crestfallen.

'Forgive me. But, well, you've hinted at it before – you and Hetty. I'm sorry, sorry about that. But there's really nothing any of us can do about it. She'll have to find her own level, mistakes, virtues, whatever it is. We all have to. You and I, with our books and training, we take so much support from theory and precedent, you see. But she's never had any of that, only practice – and perhaps that's a better way to learn, one has to give her that. Though it'll hurt more, no doubt.'

'Yes, yes . . .' Robert looked pensively out of the window. Then he turned suddenly, intent, animated. 'You understand her so well. I don't know that I do sometimes: all that business about her father, which made her so unhappy, believing he wasn't her real father. That's the root of her problem, of course.'

'Well, maybe.' Mortimer, with the introduction of this sensitive theme, had already started to temporise.

'But what *was* the truth? She's always been so certain that Mr Fraser wasn't her real father. You'd surely know, if anyone did.'

'No.' Mortimer wiped some froth from his whiskers. 'No, I've never had any reason to suppose . . . otherwise.'

'You see, if she's right – and one could only discover the truth of the matter – well, it might put her on an even keel again, stop all this nonsense in America. I'm *sure* it would.' Robert leant forward earnestly.

'Oh, I don't know about that. She'd retain the same character, temperament, whoever her father happened to be.'

'So you admit the possibility then, at least, that she might be right?'

Mortimer, knowing indeed how correct Robert was in his assumptions, was loath to continue the lie. But he had to. 'It's my view – and I have to say it – that it's her poor mother who's caused most of the trouble in Hetty's life, not her father.'

'Yes, of course. But *could* she have had a different father?'

'It's possible, though I doubt it. Besides, you'd know more about that than me. You knew Mr Fraser after all. I never set eyes on him.'

'Yes, he was a brute. So – so quite unlike Hetty, in looks, everything.'

'I can't say.' Mortimer leant back. 'All theory. Not practice. And I think you, we, have to think in that latter term now. Paris? France?' He raised his glass of Smithwick's.

Robert nodded and they drank to it.

Three weeks later, in a new rust corduroy suit, with a good degree, his baggage and French Baedeker, Robert was welcomed under the full-leafed chestnut tree at the door of the Strauses' small eighteenth-century house in the rue Desbordes-Valmore, an old village house once, on the edge of the Bois de Boulogne, now crushed between *belle époque* apartment buildings, off the main boulevard in Passy.

'So! Bienvenu! Willkommen! Step right in!'

Ben Straus, though a little more drawn and elderly, still maintained his brisk and genial air: bushy eyebrows, dark hair silvering at the temples, thin moustache, the busy, quick-thinking, generous American – still the man of the world, still intent, in the most amiable and relaxed fashion, on setting everything to rights.

Léonie, in the shadows behind, stepped forward, wearing a billowy, flower-embroidered skirt and white voile blouse. 'Robert! It's so *good* to see you – really!' She kissed him on both cheeks.

Robert saw her clearly now – the dark, fluffy-haired young woman, shorter than he, the big grey-green eyes, direct and searching in their deep, blue-tinged sockets, the aquiline nose: all the repressed audacity and knowing ardour he remembered coming to the surface then in her quick warm embrace – yet quite grown up now in the eighteen months since he had seen her; a richer, darker, calmer Jewish beauty, the face matured, though touched now with vague lines of hurt, a certain indelible sadness.

'You're honoured, Robert,' Ben told him. 'She skipped singing lessons this evening to meet you.'

'But of course he's honoured, Papa! – my best old friend!'

And Robert, seeing the implications of these last words, felt honoured indeed, thinking a little better of Léonie despite her past relationship with Hetty.

They moved into the narrow hallway, where the evening summer light was reflected and distorted in several mirrors. Robert breathed in a perfumed coolness, the smell of roses – and something else seeping up from the back regions: a whiff of garlic, French mustard? The smell of abroad. He turned back an instant. Léonie was standing dead still, outlined like a statue against the light from the open door, that slightly chunky figure that he remembered thinned out now, the waist narrowing more dramatically, hip bones more prominent, the flat behind – above all that dramatic toss of dark, fine-spun hair, set off by the white voile blouse. She was warm and generous, fruit filled somehow. She stood there, looking at him, unblinking, hands clasped together. Then her firm jaw and jutting chin relaxed and she smiled softly – a hesitant smile, imprecise, like the strangely refracted light from the hall mirrors.

'Come on up and I'll show you your room before supper – old Hortense has cooked up something special for us all: Lapin à la moutarde, then some Normandy pancakes!'

Ben took him up a winding staircase, past a first floor, then on to a small top bedroom, with a narrow balcony directly overlooking the chestnut tree in the tiny front garden.

'Room's a little small,' Ben said. 'All a little small, if you live in Paris – and no real view. But at least it's a house, with no concierge! – and they're the only grim thing about the city.'

'No – no, it's perfect. Perfect . . .'

Ben joined him at the window. 'Yes, it is, I suppose. One forgets, living here. Then someone like you, just coming to it fresh – well, one sees it through your eyes for a moment, gets that first-time view of Paris all over again, that you thought you'd lost. And then you know – there's never really any end to it.'

Before supper Ben opened a bottle of champagne and they toasted each other in the small first floor salon. He raised his glass to Robert. 'Start of a great career! I had your letter and your College articles – I think maybe I have a possibility for you: Jake Schwartz, business manager of the *New York Tribune* here, good friend of mine, spoken to him and he'll see you, introduce you to the Paris editor. There could be something, sub-editing maybe, or some freelance reporting.'

Robert was impressed by the speed of his host's operations. 'Thank you –'

'Think nothing of it. That article you did on the Dreyfus case – I liked it. And it quite took Jake's fancy as well. You surely seem to know your stuff. And the style was clear – especially after a diet of Gertrude Stein. What do you think, Léa?'

'Why, yes, he can certainly write! He can come and do a review at the Academy.'

'What?'

'*Madame Butterfly*,' Ben put in. 'You're looking at her! Yes, her first big lead at the opera school. Great, isn't it? Both of you starting out.'

Madame Butterfly, Robert thought. He remembered Hetty and Léonie singing passionate duets from it, or guying the arias, in the old days at Summer Hill. Did Hetty still haunt Léonie, he wondered? – as she haunted him. It was a theme he did not care to raise. Yet a chord had been struck already in the salon.

Robert met Mr Schwartz and the Paris editor of the *Tribune* at their business office in the rue de l'Opéra. There was no proper position, but there might be later in the year. Meanwhile they offered him a job as glorified office boy at fifty francs a week, with a promise that they would look at anything he wrote and pay him extra if they used it. He settled into the routine well. At two o'clock he went to the office, often staying until midnight, busying himself in a hundred ways, learning the trade. The mornings he had free to roam the city, looking for possible stories. Often he went out with Léonie, whose singing classes took place at an academy on the left bank, or sometimes, for Léonie was already part of the chorus there, at the Opéra itself, just along from the *Tribune* office.

It was some time before they talked of Hetty. Neither had wanted to broach the subject. Their lives in the city were filled with so much else that summer. But Hetty remained a ghost at their banquet. She could not be denied indefinitely.

One day, in early autumn, walking down the boulevard des Italiens, they saw the huge garish poster of her above the Pathé Cinema: 'Laura Bowen – Dans – BAIE DE TONNERRE – Réalisé par Craig St John Williamson'.

They stood gazing up at the display, shocked momentarily, unable to look at each other. Léonie finally spoke. 'It's extraordinary, seeing someone you knew so well, so completely changed, a different name, not real. Look at the size of her!' They stared up at the vast poster high above them, Hetty in a pirate outfit, tricorn hat, red bandana handkerchief, flourishing a cutlass.

'Yes, extraordinary. Horrible . . .'

Léonie was shaking slightly. They went to a nearby café, ordered coffee on the terrace. Robert was equally shaken, all his hatred and jealousy returning. 'I suppose, one never thought – well, that she'd be so successful.'

'Or never hoped, do you mean?' Léonie said lightly. 'Well, I think I did.' Half-rueful, half-happy, she was unable quite to hide the embers of pride she felt in Hetty's achievements. 'She always wanted that sort of adoring crowd thing, you know. Such energy for it – bound to succeed, quite apart from her looks.'

'She was just ruthless, that's all.' Robert was curt.

'Oh, Robert, it's no use being bitter.'

'It sometimes helps.' He turned away.

'I'm sorry.'

'She behaved atrociously.'

'Yes, she did. But you see –'

'Oh, I may see why – but that doesn't excuse her. I lost my parents, home, everything,' he went on quite calmly. 'But that doesn't mean I have to behave like a cruel idiot.'

'No, you've been wonderful –'

'Look at her!' Robert gazed down the boulevard to where the vast poster was still visible. 'A big "star", don't they call them?' His sarcasm was biting. 'You must miss her,' he went on, trying to console, but distant, remembering Léonie again as his rival and wondering if she still loved Hetty.

'I do miss her. But really – isn't it the same for you?'

'Oh no,' Robert lied. 'All that was just, well . . . just a juvenile thing on my part.'

Léonie reached across to him, breaking the formality of their exchange with a quick warmth. 'Oh, Robert – it couldn't have been! We can't pretend that, it's not true. It *was* a pretty huge thing – for both of us.'

Robert turned away, embarrassed. 'Well . . .' He shrugged. 'Anyway, we'll hardly see her again, except in one of her stupid "pictures" – and I certainly don't want to see them. Do you?'

'No, no. But that's the awful thing though, isn't it?' She glanced down the street again at the poster. 'She's here all the time – seen her before like that about town. And now she'll be posted up all over the place again. Sort of hovering over us, not being able to forget her.'

'But we must. Or we'd better. After all, look what she did – just walking out on you, on everyone, in a moment . . . pretty awful thing to do.'

Léonie frowned. 'Yes,' she said at last. 'But there's always some *reason* for that sort of behaviour. One has to look for that.'

'"Tout comprendre, c'est tout pardonner"? I don't agree with that in this case.' Robert was more forceful now, trying to suppress any possible excuse for Hetty's behaviour. 'You can't just blame her mother, or the loss of her "father" for everything she did. It was just . . . wilful, wanting to hurt, on her part.'

'Yes, of course she wanted to hurt both of us. And she did – always succeeds in what she sets out on.'

'So why . . . why do you have any more time for her?'

'Because I can't just drop the past and pretend it never happened. Isn't she still part of you? She's a part of me, always will be. The things we did, shared, they can't be "betrayed". They happened. They're still there.'

Robert was jealous again. Léonie, indeed, had shared things with Hetty, had possessed her no doubt, in ways he never had. He hid his jealousy but not the sarcasm in his next words. 'Of course, you knew her so much better than I.'

'No,' Léonie said dully. 'A different way, not better.'

'Because you loved her in a different way, of course. I've often wondered . . .'

'Yes, I suppose you did wonder. Well, women can love each other – just as much as men,' she told him quite directly.

'Yes,' Robert was non-committal.

'It shocks you?'

'Oh no,' he lied again.

'It must at least have annoyed you. Without me, after all, she might well have taken to you.'

'Perhaps.'

'You see, that's exactly what made me so unhappy at Summer Hill – for you.' Léonie was suddenly ardent again. Then she was resigned. 'But now I don't think I stopped anything for you. Hetty wanted things in us which neither of us could give her.'

'What?'

'Oh, the slave thing, for one – and that's not us.'

'Or the American she's married. He's no slave, I bet.'

'Ah, but he's the other side of the coin she wants: the king thing, all that power, when *she* can play the slave!'

Robert sighed. 'It's all really so very tiresome and childish in the end, isn't it?'

'Yes. But sometimes we love people for that, don't we? – for their faults, not their virtues. That's sometimes more difficult.'

'You still love her then, don't you? – for all her faults.'

'Sometimes, yes.' She turned then, gazing at him intently. 'Sometimes . . . she sweeps over me again, taking me back, like the sea, when I'd thought I was free of her.'

Léonie sat there quite still, then looked away, unable to face him. And Robert saw how deep her hurt was.

'Oh, perhaps I wouldn't miss the person she's become,' Léonie went on, gathering herself. 'But the person she was – and the person she *could* have been, even more: that's the heartbreak. That's terrible – to think what's lost there.'

'For her?'

'For both of us. I'm not so saintly that I didn't hope to share in what was best in her. I wanted to encourage all that, for myself as well as her. Didn't you?'

'I . . . suppose so,' he said indifferently, unwilling to admit the truth of this.

'Well, then – we can both see how much we've lost, can't we? There was something wonderful there. Such beauty – in so hurt a spirit.'

Robert pondered these comments. They were very much ones he would have made himself about Hetty – if he possessed more courage and if he did not still feel so hurt by her. It was perfectly true – all that Léa had said: both of them had been deeply scarred by her betrayal. But betrayal it had been: gratuitous, clear-sighted, precisely intended. There was surely no getting away from that. And so he said, again trying to despoil Hetty in Léa's eyes, 'But the glass was flawed. You said so yourself earlier: neither of us could have really helped her in the end, given her what she wanted. That spirit was broken from almost the beginning, the lack of a real father, all those horrors on the island long ago, her mother's cruelties to her as a child at Summer Hill. I know – I was there,' he added, secretly pleased to remind Léonie of his prior intimacy with Hetty.

'Of course, I see why you feel all that. But I think you're wrong – about her spirit. The flaws were part of its beauty. The glass just needed holding together, with love. That's all I wanted to do.'

Léonie looked at Robert again, with a blazing belief in her eyes. And Robert again had to admit the truth of her last words – for this had secretly been his own view – he who had thought, too, that with his love he could have protected that same essential fragility, while sharing in all Hetty's more purposeful, confident ardours.

'The fact is, dear Robert,' she said sadly, 'she's put both of us in the dumps, deep down, because, well – you too, I think – we both more than loved her. We were kind of married to her already – that close, you know? – so that it's not just she who's gone, but a complete civilisation, sort of, all the comforts there – a lost language, signs, smiles, everything between people that's beyond words. Don't you think?'

'Well, that's all very fine – but are we to spend the rest of our lives playing archaeologists over her?'

'I don't know, I really don't. I don't *want* to – but how can one hold back the tide? Because she's not dead, you know,' she went on desperately. 'It's not an altogether vanished civilisation. She's over there, large as life, behind that poster!'

Robert saw the truth of this, too, and was at a loss to know what to do or feel about it as regards Léonie. On the one hand – liking and feeling for her as he did now – he wanted to support her, get her out of those dumps. On the other, he saw how Hetty remained a barrier between them, saw how great Léonie's attachment still was to her. He felt jealous and excluded by this and wanted therefore to demean Hetty in Léonie's eyes, expunge every memory of her – as a means of furthering what he took to be their joint cause, which was to forget this cruel woman. So he said, 'But, Léa, if either of us is to have any real life – we'll *have* to accept the fact that she behaved abominably, doesn't care a damn about either of us. We'll have to hold that tide back – together.'

Her reply was only half-confident: 'Perhaps . . .'

Robert's impatience, his frustrated jealousies, rose to the surface. 'But we'll have to, Léa,' he said almost angrily. '*Have* to forget her. And not let her sweep over us any more.'

'Yes,' she said then, almost too forthrightly.

'Well, come on then, let's forget about her – let's go and have a good lunch. The paper's going to use that report I did on Les Halles, so I'll have enough – to go to the Grand Vefour! Remember? – I promised we would, when they first took something of mine.'

Léonie smiled. 'Yes, so you did – always keep your word, don't you?'

She smiled again. But Robert was annoyed now. 'You don't have to – you just think I'm Old Reliable, don't you? That's my problem. Well, I can be unreliable too, if you want –'

She reached across to him. 'Oh, no, Robert – I mean – I like you, *because* of that. I do! – really do.' She touched his hand, and they got up and walked away from the monstrous hovering vision of their friend.

Was it in the restaurant that Robert first began to fall in love with her? – or afterwards? – as they strolled beneath the arcades of the Palais Royal in the autumn sunlight, round the gardens, and Robert, stopping outside one of the little antique shops, seeing a Japanese fan in the window, went in and bought it for her.

'There,' he told her. 'For Madame Butterfly.'

Enchanted, she opened it at once, fluttering it against her face, not coquettishly, just gently.

Something moved in his heart for her at that moment. But he was wary, taking it no further.

While Robert had to count his francs carefully that autumn, Hetty had begun to spend money with total abandon. *Thunder Bay* had been a complete sell-out. Hetty was now a big star, already beyond that field of gravity which restrained ordinary mortals. Over half-way through her three-year contract with Fox her salary was a thousand dollars a week; Craig's was twice that. Inheriting her grandmother's hungry social ambitions, but promoting these in an entirely eccentric manner, Hetty luxuriated in this new wealth and the power it gave her to express her material whims and her passion, similar to her mother's, to organise and dominate a household.

So she filled the phoney Bavarian *schloss* with exotic European imports – bulbs and shrubs which bloomed in pots with constant care and watering, smoked salmon from Scotland, Bradenham hams, fine wines smuggled in from France – and threw either impeccably formal dinner parties or Bohemian routs, employing a bevy of Chinese cooks, Irish maids, Mexican gardeners; so that the Lodge, at least for the most talented and amusing among the Hollywood community, became a bran tub of bizarre social surprises.

She and Craig, in their free time, rarely ventured down the valley. But, when they did, to attend some première at Graumann's Egyptian Theatre or a party at the Ship Café, people opened a way for them, instinctively, as if touched by fire. If Fairbanks and Pickford, at their dowdy mock-Tudor mansion on the plains, were the formally crowned heads of Hollywood, Hetty and Craig, their raffish but luminous partnership surrounded by an aura of invincible success, were the envied pretenders to the throne. They were envied, feared, even loved but not universally liked – deeply mistrusted, indeed, by some of the most powerful in Hollywood, producers and studio bosses, who resented their European airs and graces, their unconventional life, their culture, talent, their difficult professional demands. But, as long as their success continued, these criticisms were mute. Hetty and Craig were immune from them – as long as their pictures grossed such fortunes. Which they did.

Hetty's only problem was that she, like Craig, longed to be out of the place, this cultural desert, where, with all the money in the world, there was nothing to spend it on. Sometimes, in short breaks between pictures, they drove down to Mexico and once or twice took the long five-day train ride east to New York. But these trips only sharpened Hetty's appetite to leave Hollywood altogether. Unlike Craig, though she worked just as hard, she never came to see pictures as the be all and end all of her life. They were a holding operation of some sort – and the pictures themselves, however successful, were rarely inspiring: costume romances giving way to contemporary melodramas and society extravaganzas. All the time she longed to embark on her great role in the great epic, *Nefertiti*. So did Craig.

'But we can't, not yet,' he had told her. 'We need the leverage of a new contract for you with Fox. *Then* we can move. Meanwhile, just make as many box office hits as we can.'

Hetty bridled at the delay – became petulant, difficult, demanding, both at home and in the studio. Her attitude towards Craig underwent a change. Unable to dominate him, she started – just as she had with Léonie – to nurture antagonisms, suspicions, hurts. She came to feel that perhaps in some way he was holding out on her over *Nefertiti*, hiding something, postponing the matter unnecessarily, thinking of someone else for the role. More often now he was out in the evening at the studios, in the cutting rooms, or with his friend, the art director Leo Kuter, the only other person privy to the Nefertiti picture, who was already working on preparatory set designs for it. Hetty, on these occasions, left to her own devices in the Lodge, took increasingly to the company of little Eddy Nolan, whom Craig had made a sort of major-domo in the household, and who now became a confidant of Hetty's.

'What's he doing – all these evenings out?' she said to him one night, after the Chinese cooks had gone to bed, and they sat in the kitchen drinking mugs of strong tea and eating slices of fruit cake, just as if they were back in Ireland.

'Working,' Eddy said, at his most direct and laconic. 'The curse of the age . . .'

'I wish I believed that.'

'Drive down and see for yourself then.'

'Oh, I'm not going to spy.'

'Set your mind at ease. Why not?'

'I think he's seeing someone else.'

'Ask him then – put it to him straight.'

'Perhaps. Trouble is, he could just lie, couldn't he?'

'Ah, well, there you have me. Always the problem, isn't it?'

Hetty remained frustrated. That indeed was the problem. Craig, as she knew, had lied about his Irish background. And she had never confronted him over this, anxious to maintain her own deceits inviolate – anxious and secretly frightened of him as well, this man upon whom all her deceits and fantasies rested.

Craig, in the event, was indeed absorbed by something else just then – but not by another woman. While he was researching the Nefertiti material, Leo Kuter had brought him an old copy of the *Illustrated London News*, showing photographs of the German archaeological dig at Amarna in upper Egypt in 1909 and an artist's recreation of the whole original city. Flipping through the magazine, he was suddenly confronted by a large portrait of Edward VII. He glanced at it idly, before being struck by something in the King's expression. The eyes? The shape of the forehead? The whole cast of the upper face said something to him. What was it?

Yes, the shape of the eyes, the hooded lids, the nose and eyebrows, the whole conjunction here, this was Hetty's expression too, he thought – that arrogant, slightly drowsy look she sometimes had. And then he remembered the little brooch-watch he had found in the rubble of the north wing two years before at Summer Hill, with the inscription on the back: 'Frances – from Alix and Edward – Sandringham, Xmas 1898.'

It was not difficult to put two and two together. But did they really add up? Was it possible that Hetty was the old King's daughter, the result of a liaison between him and her mother? And, if it was, did Hetty know of this? Almost certainly not. Should he tell her? Hetty, difficult enough, would probably fly off the handle altogether. So his suspicions would have to be kept under wraps. But it was quite a thought – he, son of a dour, penny-pinching Cork grocer, now quite possibly son-in-law to the old King. He smiled. They might, indeed, be true royalty, he reflected, in their great palace on the hill. One day, perhaps, the family connection might prove a vital counter in their affairs. If it was true . . .

But what was their more likely future? he wondered then. He had spoken to Leo before on this topic, and now he reintroduced it.

Leo had noticed him gazing at the portrait of Edward VII. 'Thinking of doing a picture on him – with Laura as one of his mistresses?'

Craig was momentarily shocked at this incestuous suggestion. 'No. No . . .'

'The Von would get a good story out of it: all that stiff court life, the regalia, then the lusty girls and champagne behind the curtains. They say the old King had dozens of them.'

'Yes . . . No, I was thinking of Laura.'

'Is there some problem?'

'She's getting more and more difficult. And, you know something? – she doesn't really care a damn at heart, whether she works in pictures or not. Doesn't really touch her – all that star thing.'

'What does touch her then?'

'Power, I think.'

'More than you?'

'Oh yes – I'm only a means to an end.'

'That big house of hers back in Ireland?'

'No. She used to want that. But she's broken all the connections there.'

'Listen, she probably just wants *Nefertiti* . . . and to get the hell out of here – like we both do.'

'Yes. Sure. But after that? She wants something else. And it's eating away at her. Oh, it gives her that extraordinary edge on camera – whatever's getting at her, that mix of . . . wistfulness and frenzy.'

'You know something?' Leo looked at him searchingly. 'Often noticed it in her, how she doesn't take compliments, cuts you dead if you try to treat her as a woman. She's got a man's mind in a woman's body. That's her problem. She's going against her real nature all the time – *that's* what's eating her.'

And Craig, knowing full well the truth of this – how Hetty of course, had been the 'man' in her earlier *affaire* with Léonie – had to agree with Leo. But he did so silently, for here was another secret of Hetty's he thought best kept hid.

What Craig refused to see, and Hetty even more so, was the most obvious secret of all in the whole business: how her behaviour, her tantrums, her frenzied sexual and social life, that 'edge' which came across so dazzlingly on camera – all these were the product of her guilt, her betrayal of Léonie, Robert, her family, of Summer Hill.

Craig might well have seen this. But he chose not to, for it was just this fascinating 'edge', inspired by guilt – that mysterious tension, the calm and sudden wild imbalance in her performances – that kept them both so successfully in business. And so he fed all these flaws in her, tactfully, like a concerned zoo keeper, encouraged her illness and her guilt, for without her suffering in this way he felt intuitively that she might leave him and give up the whole picture business altogether. If Hetty held Robert and Léonie in some strange thrall, Craig had just the same power over her; he was the vital link in the chain that kept Hetty apart from her real friends, her real life – the one who, as final puppet master, maintained the hurt and pain for the other three.

3

I N IRELAND, THE Anglo-Irish war deteriorated into horror and atrocity. The Irish Parliament, Dail Eireann, continued to meet clandestinely. But the real management of affairs in this resistance passed increasingly to the Irish Republican Army, and particularly into the hands of its Director of Intelligence, Michael Collins. A large and genial man, behind this façade of Cork bonhomie he was quite ruthless, a born leader and guerrilla commander. Having worked as a clerk in the London post office he had, too, a gift for organisation, besides a genius for disguise, concealment, the creation of every sort of surprise. His IRA flying columns, deployed throughout the country, launched almost daily attacks against isolated RIC barracks, coastguard stations and British Army patrols. In Dublin, British detectives, spies and agents provocateurs were regularly assassinated, on the streets in broad daylight, even in their beds.

The British retaliated. But they had little or nothing at which to aim, as their enemy melted into the woods and mountains or city alleyways. As a result the British Army – and most particularly the Black and Tans, a drunken and ill-disciplined group of veterans from the Great War recruited to help the RIC – took to murderous reprisals, gunning down innocent bystanders, roaring along village streets in their Crossley tenders, sacking whole communities and taking over local strongpoints as fortified headquarters.

So that it was not long before a Black and Tan company of some forty men, passing through Kilkenny in the spring of 1921 and moving south along the river towards Waterford, set their eyes on Summer Hill, an ideal site half-way between the two cities, from which they could control the whole middle river valley of the Nore. Besides, as they soon learnt, the house was owned by Mrs Fraser, one of the most sought-after rebels in the country; they could thus do what they liked with it. At first, they stormed Summer Hill under the pretence of looking for Frances. She was not at home of course, so they commandeered the whole place as their regional headquarters, setting up machine guns on the roof and in the porch, posting sentries at the gate lodges, sending patrols regularly through the grounds and dispatching all the servants. Aunt Emily initially refused to move. But in the end she was forced to seek sanctuary in Mortimer's house in Dublin.

Pat Kennedy, however, alone among the servants, had been forcibly retained. The Tans needed and indeed came to trust him, for he remained on the surface a man of impeccable credentials – impeccably dressed, too, as the house butler. Almost at once he was in touch with the Kilkenny IRA brigade, who in turn immediately advised Michael Collins of the situation.

A few days later Frances, who had been hiding out in the Wicklow mountains, spoke to Collins in a back room of Vaughan's Hotel near the quays.

'I'm afraid the Tans have taken over your house,' he told her gently. To his surprise she was not in the least put out. Indeed, she saw the whole thing as a wonderful opportunity.

'Since I know the place backwards and Pat Kennedy is still there,' she told him, 'we can storm it ourselves now, make an example of the blackguards!'

'I don't quite see, Mrs Fraser, it's your family home, there'd be terrible destruction –'

'Oh, that's of no account. Far more important to teach those Tans a lesson.'

Collins considered the matter. 'There's some forty or more men there, heavily-armed, machine guns, right up on a hill over the river, as I understand it. A bad position, bad odds, Mrs Fraser – from that height they'd massacre us.'

'Of course, if we made an open frontal attack. But we needn't. As I told you, Michael, I know the place backwards. There are other ways of doing it.'

He looked at her quizzically, quite prepared to consider any scheme proposed by this extraordinary English woman, as he still really saw her, who for years now had defied her own class and nation, with that imperious accent, on hunger strike in prison, or with guns – a woman, indeed, who had outranked him as one of the leaders in the Easter rising five years before. And so he listened to her attentively. After half an hour's discussion he agreed to implement her proposals. They had, he saw, the supreme merits of simplicity and surprise.

A few weeks later, when high summer had come over the land, Pat Kennedy seemed to fall ill, finally taking to his bed in the back of the main house, starting to cough and moan. He asked that a Dr Brennan from Kilkenny be called. The doctor came, examined him, left medicaments and reported to the Tans that it was a case of galloping consumption – an endemic and highly contagious disease, he warned them. There was little to be done.

The Tans, fearing infection, thereafter kept well away from Pat's quarters, where he was tended by young Biddy Molloy up from the village; every day she brought him various balms and foods, including a regular supply of what looked like red candles secreted beneath her petticoats. Pat's condition rapidly worsened and within a fortnight, taking the last rites from a priest one brilliant morning in July, he was dead.

The priest called a firm of undertakers in Kilkenny. A motor van, with two men and a large coffin, arrived in the yard later that afternoon. The Tans' Commanding Officer had the men frisked for arms and checked both the inside of the van and the coffin itself before allowing it into the house. And then later, from a safe distance on the landing, he watched the two men transfer the body into the open box. But, having seen the coffin lid screwed down, he did not linger.

The Tans ate every evening in the old servants' hall, just above the basement kitchens, a narrow room which led via various pantries out to the back yard, forming a natural exit here from the servants' bedrooms above.

But the Tans – some twenty-five of them, for the others were on sentry duty or on patrol – were nonetheless outraged when the two undertakers appeared in the doorway at one end of their mess room, carrying the heavy coffin.

'Bloody hell! – get that thing out of here,' one of them shouted, before others round the long table took up the same chorus. The two undertakers meanwhile, already in the room, had started to stagger under the weight, twisting and turning, dithering with it, before setting the box down.

'Look at them!' one of the more drunken Tans observed. 'Bloody Irish – can't even carry their dead. Get the fuckin' thing out pronto, you curs!'

'Yes, sir. At once, sir. Paddy!' the first of the undertakers called to his friend. 'Go back and get that wheel trestle.' His companion left the room, while the first man, bending down now over the coffin and fiddling with something at the head of it, said, 'Just a minute now, sir, till we get the oul' wheel trestle.'

'Go on, damn you! – get it out of here *any* way.' Some of the Tans were on their feet now.

'Mick? Where are you at all – with that trestle?' The first man went back to the doorway, standing there a moment, counting the seconds under his breath. 'Six, seven, eight . . .'

Then he stepped out neatly, closing the door, and ran as fast as he could down the corridor before the tremendous explosion rent the room apart behind him.

Seven men were killed outright and many more wounded. The remaining Tans, none too sober in the first place and now fighting mad, set out to retaliate at once – intent on storming the village of Cloone. But this was exactly what the IRA had anticipated. Two of their flying columns lay in wait, hidden in the trees bordering both the main and the river drive, so that when the big Crossley tenders emerged into the twilight, headlights blazing down the hill, the first vehicle, as it crossed the culvert just outside the main gate, was blown sky high; and the second, racing along the river bank, was raked with fire, so that it skidded, bounced off a tree, then sheared away into the deep water.

The only retaliation the half-dozen remaining Tans could make then was against the house itself and the village, where most of the populace, warned by the IRA, had already made off for the hills. Burning and looting what they could in the village, they returned to Summer Hill and prepared to fire it as well. But half-way through these frenzied arrangements they thought better of the idea. The IRA might attack again, they had their wounded to attend to, were far from any real help just then, and to burn the house down would be to lose their fortified position. So they left things as they were – the back of the house, the old servants' hall, sculleries and pantries, now a blackened mass of debris, windows all blown out, open to the night.

Replaced by another company, who moved into the front of the house, the Tans stayed on at Summer Hill until the autumn, when a truce was called and negotiations began between Sinn Fein and the British government. A month later, in early December, the Tans moved out of Summer Hill altogether, just prior to the signing of the Anglo-Irish peace treaty in London. Apart from the six north-eastern counties, 700 years of British domination in Ireland had come to an end.

The burnt-out shell of the Victorian north wing led now to the partly-destroyed end of the Georgian house; the rest of it, the great hall, gilded reception rooms, library and bedrooms – all these had been terribly knocked about during the Tan occupation.

Water, trickling through broken gutters, slates and chimney flues, soon made deeper inroads, soot-blackened rivulets coursing down the white walls, bringing mould and damp which rose from the floorboards, mixed with the smell of urine, the rank odour of decay. The tall shutters banged against sandbags and broken window glass in the winter gales. Triangles of gilded plaster hung and spun like glittering kites from the ceilings, then fell, littering the silent, empty rooms. The marble statues of Cupid and Psyche, one bullet-riddled, the other decapitated, stood like frozen mutilated corpses in their niches above the great hall. The heavily sandbagged library, a stencilled sign outside saying 'Armoury', was stacked with empty ammunition boxes, old cartridge belts, pools of oil on the floor, soaking into a detritus of ravaged books. Only the rats and rooks maintained, indeed increased, their tenure about the house.

And now, its sustaining Cordiner presence gone, its nobility destroyed, all its lovely things, the art and thought of centuries quite dissipated – the great house finally promised nothing, drifting rudderless through the months that led into that bright new year of Irish independence.

Frances, with Mortimer, arrived there one afternoon in February, driving up to the ghostly house in a light snowfall, early twilight sweeping in with the cold grey flakes. Pat Kennedy, returned now in full health, acting as caretaker and living in the gate lodge, opened up the house for them, leaving them to walk alone through the dreary rooms, Mortimer carrying an oil light, a beacon illuminating each fresh instance of destruction.

Frances appeared quite unmoved by the havoc. She picked up a piece of jagged plaster in the hall. Part of a gilded harp was clearly visible in the lamplight.

'Well, free at last!' she told Mortimer proudly, holding out the broken harp as evidence of Ireland's release. He did not reply at once, looking round at the obscene graffiti on the walls, the statues of Psyche and Cupid.

'Free,' he said finally. 'In a world hardly worth living in.'

'Your way, though – it was never going to work,' she told him briskly, a harsh edge in her voice. 'Force with force. That was the only way.'

'Force – that only leads to worse.'

'So be it! Were we never to be free?'

'Oh yes – I've fought for just that most of my life,' he told her vaguely, lacking conviction, turning away then, illuminating the corners of the hall; there was a scrawled message on the drawing room door: 'Fuck all Shin Faners.'

'Fought with words, though, all you old Home Rulers – just words,' she added with passionate intensity. 'Words could never have freed us, Mortimer.' She gazed at him, a chilling, mad certainty in her pinched features, pale and lined with prison suffering, but eyes still bright with venom.

Yet he remembered the beauty of that face twenty years before: gypsy-touched, yet regal, wild and free. There was a freedom she might better have fought for, he thought – beauty and right mind and not one filled, as it was now, with bitter, ranting nonsense. She and her companions might, with words, have fought for life and not for death, all about them in the house and throughout the land. Oh yes, Ireland might be free, he thought – but at the cost of all her democrats. And now he faced that freedom: a ruined house and a woman, a political leader, equally destroyed, whose wits had addled, with a voice that only shrieked in the dark.

What use to try and rebut her last words? Words for her and her kind had for so long, under the guise of patriotism, been just a means of rabble-rousing, a coinage of ignorance and self-delusion. And that would be their inheritance now: the mob, the blind leading the blind. Instead of pursuing these grim themes with Frances, he opened the dining room door, finding it half off its hinges.

'But does it mean nothing to you, Frances – this destruction – of *your* house, the one you fought so long to possess?'

'I *have* possessed it, Mortimer, fully. I need it no longer. A symbol of British tyranny.'

'This house has always been Irish.' He was angry now. 'And there was no tyranny at Summer Hill. That was never a Cordiner way. We and the more illustrious of our sort – Tone, Grattan, Parnell – how can you possibly think of tyranny there? Just the opposite –'

'But all that's long gone now, don't you see? – Lord Edward Fitzgerald and the rest of those well set-up Englishmen, really only fighting for their own survival here. Parnell!' she added dismissively. 'That adulterous landlord. *We've* come to rule now, Mortimer, the true people, the real Irish.'

'Yes, the butcher, the baker, the candlestick maker . . .' He remembered how, nearly twenty-five years before, at a dinner party in this same dining room, he had forecast just this – the onset of mindless violence, under the flag of the old true patriots, which would bring just such petty people to rule, and the demise of his own race in Ireland as well, largely self-inflicted, through their brutality, negligence, stupidity. And though, at least, these had not been Cordiner faults then, they were now: he was looking at a woman who had just casually thrown away her heritage of seven centuries. He found it hard to forgive her for that.

'Who?' Frances was suddenly rigid with annoyance. 'Who are you referring to?'

'You'll see. The gombeen men will come to rule the roost here now. All your "true people" – Connolly, MacDonagh and the others – they all went in the Easter rising. And the truest long before that, O'Connell and Parnell –'

'What nonsense!'

'No –'

'Besides, we have some Protestants in the Dail. And there'll be more in the new Senate. You might serve there yourself, instead of carping.'

'I'm too old to serve any more. Besides, was there ever a dog that praised its fleas?'

'Words again. Always so good with them, Mortimer. But you lack humility, the common spirit. You've been defeated, by your wit, your class – along with all the rest of your kind in Ireland. You have no hope.'

Oh my God, he thought, looking at the bitter and disappointed woman staring up at him: where is that bright face of hope you once had, dear Frances? – that I remember so well from your early days with us in London. And then the whole tragedy of her life, once again, fell into place for him. She had fought England for so long, believing that the whole meaning of her life had been released in this fight, so that she could not for a moment accept that England, in the shape of the Prince of Wales, had killed her true spirit long before. Ever since, she had not so much been fighting for Ireland, but more venting her fury on the British crown. She had nurtured a personal vendetta, groomed and inflated it, so that it came to shine forth as martyrdom, honour, in all sorts of righteous violence. The old Prince had much to answer for. But then so had Frances. What could the Prince have done about her at the time, given the child? And surely Frances should have realised this basic incapacity of his – and come to terms with a fault for which, after all, they both shared the blame. But she had not. Instead, a blind obsession and vindictiveness had overtaken her, and destroyed her real nature. And there, he thought, was the banal heart of the tragedy: hell hath no fury like a woman scorned.

He should have shown more sympathy towards her for this very reason, of course. Yet her chilly insensitivity made it difficult. Above all he could not countenance her wilful dismissal of Summer Hill, of all that the house had meant – to him, to so many earlier generations of the Cordiner family, to the local people generally. So that he spoke more acidly than he would have wished.

'I *do* have hope, Frances – for this house at least, if not the political situation. It can be put in hand again, by degrees. As you know, I had most of the pictures, and the better furniture, removed before the Tans arrived. Pat tells me it's all still safe, stowed about the lofts and farm buildings. Some of the land can be sold and the rest put in good heart again. You can't just rid yourself of the whole place, with a shrug, and let it die.'

'But it's already dead, Mortimer. And, even if it weren't, there can be no future here for such places in the new Ireland, such ostentatious show. Besides, I don't need Summer Hill any more. I shall buy that little house in Dublin now for myself.'

'That new bungalow in Rathgar Road?'

'Indeed! And that's the future of Ireland, dear Mortimer!'

She laughed at him, a shrill laugh, turning away from the empty dining room, only dark shadows on the walls where once the Cordiner family portraits had hung. Opening the front doors and clambering over the sandbags, she went out on to the porch, standing in the fluttery snow, before doing a little jig on the steps. Mortimer followed her with the lamp.

'But, Frances,' he called out to her across the great divide. 'Of course, you can live where you will. But all this . . .' He swung the lamp round the great hall. 'It's a *family* heritage. And you're only a caretaker –'

'I have no family now!' she shouted back, clutching the broken plaster harp, as the snowflakes drifted down over her, whitening her cape and straggly hair, giving her the air of an old crone. Mortimer looked at her: Cathleen Ni Houlihan, he thought – the true spirit of Ireland indeed, mad as the mist and snow.

4

F RANCES WAS WRONG about having no family. Indeed, she was close to becoming a grandmother that winter. However, Hetty's child had miscarried just before Christmas. The pregnancy had not been intended, but the loss of the child had nonetheless hurt her deeply, greatly increasing her general depression and nervous unease. Craig, secretly relieved, consoled her, as did Marion Davies, during the month she took off from work.

But Craig had been asked to do another picture meanwhile and was not often at home, as Hetty moped or stormed about the Lodge, issuing petulant dictates to the servants, lying restlessly on a day bed on the terrace or drinking endless cups of strong tea in the kitchen with little Eddy Nolan, who was now her constant companion. He was worried for her, particularly one evening when she told him she had a mind to give the whole thing up in Hollywood.

'And do what?' he asked anxiously, flexing his short, muscular arms nervously on the table.

'Oh, go back to Ireland, Europe, anywhere. *Anything!* I can't stand it here any longer.'

This was not Eddy's feeling at all. He had come to enjoy everything of his life in Hollywood – the good money he made now and then down at Universal Studios in one of Lon Chaney's horror pictures, and particularly his role as miniature major-domo about the Lodge, as Hetty's and Craig's particular confidant. He was part of the furniture here. The idea of their giving the whole thing up and his possibly having to return to the cold and violence of Ireland quite horrified him.

'Sure you wouldn't want to go and do that, Hetty.' He poured her another cup of tea. 'It's only temporary. I tell you what! – what you need is a bit of the oul' juggling and cods play we used to do with Fonsy O'Grady!' But she did not respond. 'But you *can't* throw it all up now – what with this big Egypt picture coming up.' Eddy, on the strictest confidence from Hetty, had been told a little of this.

'But it's *never* coming up!' she told him. 'That's the whole problem.'

'It will – it will! Just as soon as you start your new contract. Sure an' amn't I going to play the King's jester in it – cap and bells an' all!' And he did a comic little jig for her round the kitchen table so that she laughed at last. 'Ah, and there's no bad news that you can't do away with a dance,' he told her, finally improving her humour.

But a month later there was bad news. Craig heard it first from Leo Kuter. 'I got rumour of it yesterday from Taylor's art director,' he told Craig. 'Taylor's just asked him to work on some sketches for a new Egyptian picture he's going to offer to Paramount.'

'Just chariot race stuff – on the lot here?'

'Not, not just . . . It's *Nefertiti* – with Mary Minter or Mabel Normand in mind. Thinking of going over to Europe to do it.'

Craig was unbelieving. But Leo was certain. And Craig exploded then. 'Christ almighty! The thieving bastard. The bloody little drug-peddling womanising bastard! Mabel or Mary couldn't play Nefertiti in a month of Sundays. How the hell did he get the idea?'

'Not from any of us, I assume –'

'Picked it out of the air, did he? Well, by Christ, he'll put it right back there again. He thieved Huck Finn from me. But I tell you – he won't take this one, never.'

'How not? He's made big money for them with Huck.'

'I'll go see him.'

'He hates your guts. He'll just laugh at you.'

'Some way then . . .' Craig stood up, thinking, agitated.

'What?'

'We'll go on it first.'

'But you'll have to see Fox himself for that sort of money – in New York.'

'Some way, don't worry. Taylor will only make that picture over my dead body . . .'

That afternoon, when he returned home and told Hetty, the gloom deepened. Hetty relayed the news to Eddy Nolan.

'Now you see! The picture I've most wanted to do – snatched out of our hands!' she cried out in despair.

'Ah now, don't take on so.' The agile little man comforted her. 'There's always a way out. You'll see. Never so black as it looks.' He put the kettle on then, got the teapot out, and opened a tin of imported fruit cake, almost tearing it open with his vast strength.

When he turned back though, offering Hetty the cake, he saw that she had gone quite still, body rigid, eyes glazed, staring fixedly in front of her, barely a twitch of life in her pale face.

'Hetty?' There was no response. She started to shake then, a minute trembling – grinding her teeth, the jaw bones locked together.

'Hetty – what's up?' Eddy waved his hand in front of her eyes. But she saw nothing and there was no speech, no noise but the pulverising sound of her teeth – and soon a small trickle of blood fell from her mouth where she must have bitten her tongue. She was having some kind of fit. Eddy ran to call the studio doctor. But when he returned she seemed quite recovered, still dazed, but entirely conscious, wiping the blood from her lip and looking at the red smear on her finger in a mystified way.

'Where am I?' she asked dreamily. 'Oh, Eddy – it's you. Where – where are we? In Ireland, Summer Hill – yes! We're in Summer Hill, aren't we?' For the first time in many months a beatific smile lit up her face, a gentle, loving expression.

'No, no, we're not. We're in Hollywood, Hetty – your own house here.'

She suddenly became agitated, her face clouding over, bunching her fingers furiously. Then she started to thump the table, pummelling on it with her fists, a vicious drumming, a long-pent-up anger released from everywhere in her body, punishing the wood. Some other sort of fit, Eddy thought, when he finally had to restrain Hetty.

The doctor spoke to an impatient Craig that evening. 'Yes, of course I examined her. Nothing physically wrong. Just generally overwrought. Needs rest. And that must have been a black-out she had. *Petit mal*, they call it. A mild form of epilepsy. They don't know what causes it. But she'll need watching. And no driving the car. Just rest.'

'I'll have Eddy with her all the time. And we can get a nurse up.'

'Yes –'

'But what about the other fit Eddy says she threw? – hammering at the table? That wasn't a black-out.'

'Well,' the doctor considered matters, 'that's just some kind of suppressed anger, isn't it?' He looked at Craig carefully. 'Things not been going too well between you both?'

'No – fine. Just the loss of the child some time back.'

'Yes, sure . . .'

'Can she hurt herself like that – I mean, if she takes to it again?'

The doctor nodded. 'Why, certainly she can. And maybe that's what it's all about. She *wants* to hurt herself, for some reason.' He looked at Craig quizzically again.

'God knows why. Unless it's just that she's not working right now.'

'Could be. Or maybe something deeper. She's under some kind of pressure, that's for sure. Find out what it is, get rid of it – and that's the way to a cure.'

Craig knew what the stress was – the possible loss of *Nefertiti* for her. But he was not going to tell the doctor that. And he might have gone on to admit where the real problem lay: the fact that Hetty, at last, was beginning to face the guilt of her behaviour, towards Léonie, her family. As Léonie had forecast in her letter, Hetty had begun to hate herself.

But Craig did not delve into any of these real causes. Instead, over the next few weeks, he consoled Hetty by blaming Hollywood. 'It's time we got out of here,' he told her one Sunday morning, as they sat on the terrace. 'That's the real problem, for both of us. Need to get back to our roots. Your contract'll be up soon. We'll go and see Fox then – and get the hell out of here, make *Nefertiti*.'

'Yes, but what about Taylor?'

'Oh, he won't count.' Craig turned away then so that Hetty had the impression he was avoiding the issue.

'But you said how he'd thieved those other pictures from you –'

'Not this one, though.'

'*How* not –'

'Because we'll move first. And, besides, no one's going to listen to him. Can you imagine? – Mabel Normand playing Nefertiti? Or Mary Minter? The idea's absurd. Zukor wouldn't countenance it for a moment.'

'He might –'

'He *won't.*'

But Hetty was not convinced. 'Who *is* this man Taylor?' she asked then, a sudden hard calmness in her face.

'You know all about him. What do you mean?'

'I mean – why does he exist?'

Craig looked at her carefully, shading his eyes against the harsh, unchanging sunlight, thinking she might be about to have another black-out. But her expression did not alter.

In Paris that September, the flat August light gave way to gusty skies, as the first of the autumn winds, raking across the Ile de France, began to scratch and nose about the city. Stormy sunsets fell from skies of crimson and silver, setting fire to the bridges, touching the arches, one by one, far down-river. The children, back at school, in their black aprons with fresh white collars and clog-soled boots, ran with a great helter-skelter, feet echoing on the cobbles, racing the early twilights, shouting the latest fables. The wind smelt of rain as the city lurched into the dark.

And yet for Robert and Léonie the autumn had no air of ends, much more beginnings, as they easily resisted each item in the slow decay of the year, building castles against the seasons. They took a train out one Sunday morning to the village of Saint-Germain-en-Laye, crossing the great royal hunting forest before walking on and joining the river again on a narrow backwater, taking lunch at a small café-restaurant, the Cheval Blanc, by a bridge below Poissy.

They ate on the open terrace set above the river, on what seemed like a last miraculous day of fine weather, looking through the poplar trees to the river, listening as the leaves rustled and fell, lemon yellow, in the water. It was a day between seasons, bright with a fine sharpness, a little crackle in the air of an Indian summer. And it seemed to them, through the force of their own content, that they themselves had held back the weather, made a truce with winter.

They had pâté, and *goujons* of the local dace-like fish, washed down by Muscadet.

'You do love the food thing, don't you?' Léonie remarked pleasantly to Robert. 'I've noticed it – ever since you've come to Paris.'

'Love French food, yes – because you should have seen what I had to eat at St Columba's for five years up in the Dublin mountains!'

'Yes!' She leant across to him, as he fingered some more of the Brie. 'But it's not a schoolboy greed. You seem to set into it – with a sort of famished tenderness!'

'Another way of loving, you mean?' he said lightly.

'Yes! Something like that.'

'Perhaps . . .' He looked over the water. A few rowing skiffs passed them, skimming lightly downstream, couples out for a last trip on the river. 'Good food – a constancy that doesn't disappoint?'

'Yes. But "another way of loving" . . .' She picked up a pear from the basket, considering it rapturously. 'That was putting it even better. You do say things well, you're really going to be a fine writer. Oh, Robert . . .' She looked at him, her elbows on the sun-dappled tablecloth, head to one side, frowning a moment, but did not continue.

'Yes?'

'You have been . . . so hurt.'

'Not at all.' He was dismissive, taking up a pear himself then, biting into it, leaning forward as the juice dripped on to his plate. 'Goodness me! I'm alive, sitting with you by the river . . .' He looked about him, through the shafts of sunlight, the freckled patterns which no longer moved, for the weather had changed. The earlier breeze had gone, the leaves had ceased to fall, the water was unruffled, like a mirror. The world was silent, suspended in the yellow calm. 'Who can describe the fineness of an autumn day?' he wondered out loud.

'Only Monet . . . We'll just have to sing – and write – for our suppers.'

She picked up her wine and gazed at him through the glass, one of her grey-green eyes magnified in the straw-coloured liquid. A sense of professional companionship, inspired by her last words, bloomed then between them. Their friendship included a shared artistry, an imaginative endeavour. Yet, frustratingly for Léonie, these warm feelings which she felt between them then evoked no words from Robert in confirmation. Léonie longed for just such a response. She was almost certain he felt for her just as she did for him. But he was holding back for some reason. And she thought she knew what it was.

So, leaning forward once more, she said, 'But at least we're lucky – having each other.' Then, changing her tone, she suddenly added, with complete simplicity and directness, 'Let me help you love again. Because I think I know why you sort of . . . hold back with me. Because you feel I can only love – in the way I loved Hetty.' She looked at him uncertainly.

He wiped his lips, not facing her. 'Well, I don't know . . . But, yes, as I've said, I had wondered –'

'Well, I *did* love her – in that way,' Léa broke in, almost enthusiastic now. 'And I thought it was the only way, for me. But it's not – not at all. Or, at least, it doesn't have to be. I've known that now for quite a while. Remember that day out on the river at Summer Hill, with Hetty and Bertie? – when you were in the boat with me? – I think I knew it then.' She smiled, a hint of triumph in her admissions. 'So you see!' she added proudly.

'I thought your feelings then were much more of pity, at my predicament with Hetty,' Robert said, ironic, still distant.

'No. I thought that, too – but only to avoid the feelings I had for you.'

There was silence. A single poplar leaf spun down towards the table, landing in the fruit bowl. 'Oh, *Robert*!' She broke the mood with a happy impatience. 'Don't you see? I *can* love you – it'd be all too easy! That's what I wanted to say.'

He smiled, glancing at her, but still hesitant, not entirely given to the idea. 'Thank you,' he said awkwardly at last, so that she laughed outright.

'What a formal response!'

'Sorry –'

'Oh, it doesn't matter – I'm not making any demands. Just explaining. We'll always explain things – won't we? So that there's no misunderstanding.'

'Yes, we will, Léa.' Robert was suddenly more confident, involved. 'Absolutely – explain things.'

She took his hand in hers, pleased to have broken the ice with him, without falling through it.

'*You*,' she said, in a happy, mock-bullying tone. '*You* – because you're such easy fun to be with and really so kind and warm and good-hearted – and because we shared so much at Summer Hill, when we didn't really know each other – so we can talk now and truly explain things. *You*, because . . .' She lowered her voice in mock seriousness. 'You're so lanky and handsome and I like your inky printer's fingers and even that frightful *pipe* . . .' She ran on, enumerating his virtues, still holding his hand, thrusting it down each time on the table.

Robert, bemused, said, 'I like you – just as much – too.' He fiddled with another pear then, as if he had said too much, before handing it to her. 'Fruit-filled,' he added. 'That's you.'

'Thank you,' she said simply.

A skiff passed them on the backwater, one that they had seen with a young couple going upstream half an hour before – floating back now, both oars shipped out of the water, mysteriously empty. 'Oh my!' Léonie was ironic. 'What *can* they be up to – that couple that passed us? Come on, let's grab it!'

Before he could join her Léonie had rushed from the terrace, followed by the *patron* with a boat hook, running down the river bank. Together they caught the skiff just before it passed under the bridge.

'Come on!' Léonie shouted back at him. 'The *patron* says we can take it back to them!'

'Coming!' Robert, leaning on the terrace balustrade, called back to her. Then to himself he said, 'And you, too, Léa – I'm sure I love you, too, because you're easy and warm and beautiful – and everything else nice I can think of. So why can't I say it?' He left some money for the bill; then ran down the river bank to join her.

Hetty, in the hall of the Lodge a month later, was beside herself with anger at Craig. She had been trying, with some logs she had ordered up specially, to get a fire going in the huge mock-baronial fireplace, only succeeding in nearly setting the whole place ablaze, before Eddy Nolan had doused the impending conflagration. Now she confronted her husband, just back from the studios, over the steaming mess of wood and smoking cinders by the grate.

'A *fire*? My God – in this kind of weather?' he asked her, unbelieving, looking out through the open hall doors to where the evening sun shone, as ever, with a flat glare.

'Why not? It's autumn at home!' she shouted at him. 'Just the time for fi-fi-first fi-fires.'

'Listen, honey, we don't have autumn this far down here on the Pacific. Why, it was over ninety degrees out on the lot today.' He wiped his brow. 'Come on, let's have a cool drink on the terrace –'

But she rounded on him again. 'Just because you never had any proper fires, in that miserable shop in Cork where you were brought up.'

'In Cork?' Craig turned to her surprised.

'Oh yes, don't pretend! Marion told me. You never had any fine house on a lake in the north of Ireland – father was some little *grocer* in Cork!'

Fully expecting these arrows to strike home and for Craig to further dissemble or contradict her, Hetty was disappointed. Craig, in his own estimation, had never lied about his dingy, colourless past. He had, rather, done something entirely natural and commendable with it. He had improved, embroidered upon it – had invented it, as he might any of his scenarios. Fact and fiction had never been sufficiently separated in his mind for him to see anything remotely wrong in this re-ordering of his past, so that now he let Hetty rant and simply left her, walking round the great hall, fingering things lovingly as he went, the phoney suits of chain mail, the papier-mâché arquebuses and cannon.

'Yes!' Hetty stormed on at him. 'You lied about all that – and your limp, too: you got that fe-fe-falling downstairs in some French brothel. You lied about everything – just as you're lying about *Nefertiti*! Taylor's got the picture and you won't tell me – you just let it go!'

Her face was contorted with anger. But Craig was quite calm, saying nothing. 'Why don't you *speak* to me?' she yelled at him. He was down by the hall doors now, a small shadow against the blazing rectangle of sunlight. Then he walked back towards her, slowly, menacingly, in his jodhpurs and riding boots, before finally he faced her, staring at her, as she shivered there with rage in the close air.

'Listen,' he told her, ice in his voice, 'we're not talking about brothels or big houses or grocers in Ireland –'

'*I* am –'

'No, you're *not*,' he interrupted with a viciousness she had never heard in his voice before. 'Because there's only *one* thing we have to talk about – and that's *Nefertiti*. And the one thing you have to remember there is that, without me, you'll *never* make it – *never*. So, if that's what you want, fine. You can walk out that door'

– he pointed towards it – 'right now and go back to all the fires you want in Ireland – and forget the whole thing. I'll get someone else to play the Queen – if all you can do is play the fool.'

'You'll what?'

'You heard – and, believe me, I will. So, go on.'

He gestured towards the door again. But she said nothing, rooted to the spot, feet fidgeting in the moist cinders. Craig walked away.

Hetty began to weep, great hiccoughing sobs welling up inside her, exploding. Why had she been unable to walk out of the door just then? That was the crux of the matter. Whether she loved or hated him – and she did both – she saw that she could no longer create a life away from him, without him; that she was drawn to him unavoidably, linked with him inevitably, for better or worse, to the end. That was the final indignity – to see how she had allowed herself to be trapped by him, held by his strange power, how she had as good as thrown her own independence away. That was the worst thing – to recognise now how she needed somebody so obsessively that she did not know whether she loved or hated him.

She tried to staunch the tears of defeat, but succeeded only in smudging her face with sooty fingers. She cried out in anguish, weeping fiercely, clenching her fingers in the sodden debris by the grate, fouling her light white dress with it, like a keening savage, punishing herself uncontrollably.

She wandered into the imitation Georgian drawing room, glancing at the reproduction Irish hunting prints, before sitting down at the piano. Then, very hesitantly, for the first time in years, she embarked on a passage from *Madame Butterfly* – singing one part in a duet quietly to herself, the moment where Pinkerton comforts his weeping bride. There was no answering voice.

She stopped playing. The music only made it worse. She slammed the piano lid down. It was better to be furious than unhappy, she decided, as she had so often decided before. Action – action of any sort – was better than misery.

In Paris that very day, Robert with Ben Straus and a group of friends had gone to Léonie's Academy for the first night of her performance as Butterfly. He listened now to her pure soprano tone as Léonie, in a peacock-hued kimono, sang out the happy words – answer, indeed, to Hetty's cry six thousand miles away. 'Vogliatemi bene, un bene piccolino, un bene da bambino . . .'

Later, Ben Straus took them on to dine at Maxims. 'You really made me feel for her,' Robert told Léonie, raising his glass. 'Not as some put-upon little geisha girl, but as, well, someone living and loving – and losing – in the here and now: as if it all really *meant* something to you.'

'I did really mean it . . .' She touched his hand, without confirming exactly what she meant. But later, at home, Robert, plucking up courage, asked her, 'When you sang all those passionate duets with Pinkerton tonight – just as you used to do with Hetty at Summer Hill – were you thinking of her?'

'Yes,' she told him with her usual directness. 'That was really the whole point of my wanting to play the thing in the first place: "living, loving and losing" – just as you said. Getting her out of my system.'

'And?'

She nodded vigorously. 'Yes! I've rid myself of all that at last – the slave thing, the servant, the obsession – just as Butterfly does. She's dead and it's dead and I shan't ever play that put-upon little woman again!'

She kissed him briefly then, brushing his lips. He tasted the last trace of her make-up – but it was a taste which seemed to promise a future for them both, an end to the charades and thraldom of their lives, with the woman who for so long had haunted them. And so it was, as Hetty's life in Hollywood became every day more miserable, theirs in Paris started to climb the heights. As Hetty came to hate herself, they – more openly at last – began to love each other.

And yet it was not quite so easy – certainly not for Robert, so inexperienced in love. Now, he had, for the first time, to contend with realities, the delectable but to him unknown actions of the heart, in a love reciprocated.

For Léonie there was a different hurdle. So sensuous in essence, so given to the physical world, its fruits and flowers, winds and weathers, she held ready the same natural inclinations in her sex. But she had never loved a man: she was equally virginal there. And though, as she had hinted by the riverside, she felt ready to embark on the experiment – longed, secretly, at moments, to devour this man – she hesitated, afraid.

Robert equally feared such a confrontation. So they both fought shy of any serious contact or consummation of their affair, fearing they might destroy what they loved in each other, either by witless inexperience or uncontrolled appetite.

In Hollywood as Christmas approached, up at the Lodge, Hetty, despite the fact that she had largely made things up with Craig, became ever more frustrated and unbalanced. She was due to start another picture – her last on the current Fox contract – with Craig the moment he finished the one he was working on. But that would not be for another fortnight. Then they would see William Fox himself, and negotiate a new contract to include *Nefertiti*. Meanwhile the matter of Taylor, and his possibly pre-empting them on the same idea, began to obsess her.

'But he *won't* go ahead with it,' Craig continually told her.

'So you always say. But what have you actually *done* about it? How can you be so sure?'

'Leo Kuter's keeping me in touch. Taylor's art director is working on another picture with him now – some Civil War story. They seem to have shelved their Egyptian idea.'

'But you're fibbing again – I can see it in your face!'

And Craig had indeed been lying. He knew almost nothing of exactly how things stood with Taylor, simply hoping he could complete his next picture with Hetty as soon as possible, then go to see Fox and move first on *Nefertiti*.

'Okay, if you want to believe that – I'm lying. Have you any better ideas?'

Hetty had but she did not speak of them. Instead the idea that she might lose this one great picture came to dominate her – this picture, so far above all others, which would justify the sacrifices she had made, which would assuage the guilt she felt now, the self-hatred, rising up all round her. It was a matter, she knew then, of sink or swim.

In Paris that cold winter Robert heard the latest news of Frances and her visit to Summer Hill in a letter from Mortimer. It was a Saturday. Léonie had persuaded him to go dancing that same evening with her at the Bal Rouge, one of the little *bals musettes* on the rue Soufflot leading down from the Panthéon. And they sat there now, at a table pushed in against the wall, Robert sipping a pastis, Léonie with a cassis-Chambéry, looking out on the small open space, where a few couples – students and scrubbed young workers with their girls – were holding each other loosely, one-handed, waltzing lazily. The accordion music came from a musician on a small platform, set, astonishingly, on top of a stout pole rising from the middle of the floor. The air smelt of cheap brilliantine, anis and burnt French tobacco. Later everything would change, Léonie knew.

'You're a regular here?' Robert asked.

'Once or twice – with friends from the Academy.' She was elated at her success in getting him there. 'You'll see! It's marvellous fun! Get something for the *Tribune* out of it, too.' But Robert maintained his rather glum expression. 'Oh, I know it's tough – about Summer Hill,' she went on quickly. 'But is there anything – *any*thing – you can do about it?'

'My home, in a way. Hate to think of it destroyed.'

'But it's not! Only a bit of it. And, besides, you can't live there – *and* make a living as a journalist. Isn't there all your own future to think about? Or did you really hope to live there one day?'

'Perhaps I did, in a way.'

'In the way . . . you loved Hetty?'

He smiled faintly. 'Maybe.'

'Well, that's not going to happen now –'

'Yes, but what happens to the house? Frances doesn't care a damn for it now, nor Hetty obviously.'

'It's only bricks and mortar.'

'Limestone actually. And marble – Kilkenny and Carrara,' he told her lightly.

'Well then, it'll last for ever and ever, won't it? And you needn't worry.' But he did. And she saw it. 'Oh, Robert, don't you see? Summer Hill was Frances and Hetty and all that – horror. You really *should* forget it, as I've done. And have your own life, your own house.'

'Not so easy. It's the only home I've ever really known. The whole place for me – it's something important, quite apart from Hetty and Frances. Feel I should do something . . .'

'Tell you what then!' Léonie was bright. 'When you're rich and famous, then you can *buy* it!'

'Poor and unknown, more likely! The other will be more your department – a great opera singer!'

'Right then.' Léonie was serious. 'Maybe we can buy Summer Hill *together* then . . . some day.'

Robert frowned. 'Oh, that wouldn't really do. The man has to buy the home . . .'

Léonie, though she heard the teasing in his voice, came back at him strongly. 'What a lot of nonsense! Don't believe in that – in marriage, in any relationship. People pay what they can, either way, if that's what they're up to!'

'You, too – all part of the feminine *zeitgeist* now, aren't you?'

'Yes. But part of common sense even more. All that old male-dominated world which Summer Hill epitomises – formal marriage contracts, strict male line inheritances and so on. All that world is vanishing fast, Robert! Just look around you – those girls, they pay their few sous to dance here just as often as any of the men. And thank God it's like that now. Look at what the old ways did for Frances – that frightful need she had to *possess* everything, Summer Hill, everyone: always to dominate and control.'

'I'd have thought you might have admired that in her – given your own feminine angle on things.'

'Admire the thought, maybe. But not the results. Frances was really looking for some other kind of bondage all the time. Didn't really want to be free – or for any of us to be free either. Just wanted to punish everyone, for something awful in her own life, and wants to punish herself most of all. And that's not the point about "feminism" – just the opposite: it's to release us from all that sort of self-hatred and feelings of being inadequate.'

'Well, maybe you're right – about Frances. And about the world changing for women. Just, I tend to be a bit . . . old-fashioned about all that.'

'So you'd have to buy the house? Wouldn't let your girl friend – or your wife – help, even if she was stinking rich?'

'No. I don't think I would.'

They were silent then. Robert sipped his pastis. Léonie finally broke the mood, as the accordion started once more, a jaunty waltz, 'Valentine'.

'Oh, *do* dance with me, Robert!' Léonie suddenly asked, head on one side, pleading mischievously to be taken up in the happy swirl of music.

She moved with easy grace. Robert was far less confident. Awkward and gangly, he began to perspire as he swirled furiously round with her.

'Not so fast!' he called out. 'I can hardly see –'

'You're not *meant* to see – just feel!'

'I should have worn my glasses –'

'Gracious sake! – you're not reading a book! Just let yourself go a bit.'

He tried to, but his legs remained stiff and unbiddable, like an automaton toy not properly wound up – until, slackening pace, when the accordionist started a slower waltz, Léonie brought him more firmly to her, resting her chin on his shoulder.

Feeling so close together for the first time, Robert, though fearing the opposite, found himself relaxing. This sort of non-dancing was more within his compass, he decided. Yet in truth there was a different reason for his new feeling of confidence and ease. A scent of warm violets drifted up to him from Léonie's face – from the delicate perfume she used. Encouraged by their exertions, and by their closeness, the perfume seemed to be almost as much a part of his body as of hers: an indivisible odour, creating a heady intimacy between them. And it was this that gave him the sudden confidence, this and the subsequent brief thought of how, if they were sleeping together, the same perfume would so wonderfully cover them both, their whole bodies, skin on skin, all night long.

Rain had threatened for some days in Los Angeles and now the city lay under a boil of humid cloud that would not burst. It was suffocatingly close that afternoon in Hollywood – and later the sky was seared by sheet lightning far out in the bay, an electric storm over the Pacific, with rain and distant thunder, which yet refused to come ashore and cleanse the land.

Hetty, alternating between the bathroom shower and ice-packs in her bedroom for most of the day, had by evening reached a pitch of frustration. She had already found what she needed in Craig's bedroom drawer: the ignition key to her car which, because of her black-outs, he had hidden from her; and the other even more important item in a second drawer. Her special clothes were ready, and Craig had told her he would not be back from the studio until late that evening. Apart from Eddy Nolan, always keeping an eye on her, the situation was perfect. She longed to be off, to break out of this humid carapace, identical to the pall of long inaction which was destroying her life. Now was the moment.

Just as darkness fell, she managed to engineer an argument over menus and provisions between the Chinese cook and Eddy – so that the two of them, disappearing to the larder, gave her just those few minutes she needed. Changing quickly into her new clothes, she ran down to the garage on the lower terrace, reversed her Dodge coupé smartly out, wheels spinning on the gravel, and raced off down the hill into the canyon.

Seeing that there was no one in pursuit she drove more slowly then, past Hollywood Lake, on towards the long suburban boulevards, the twinkling lights of Hollywood in the distance. She was quite calm now. There was no hurry. She knew exactly where he lived, exactly what she had to do. She smiled as she drove.

Coming into Beverly Hills, she took a right by the gas station on the main boulevard, then drove up to the end of a small side-street, and parked the Dodge on some waste ground, leaving it partly hidden in the shadow of an overhanging pepper tree. It was quite dark now, just a few minutes after eight, as she doubled back, walking easily down the street. Wearing a man's light grey mackintosh, felt hat and slacks, with rubber-soled shoes, hands thrust in pockets, she readily mimicked some inhabitant of the suburbs out for an evening stroll. But no one saw her in any case. The street was deserted.

Taylor's bungalow was half-way down, set some thirty yards off the street, part of a courtyard of similar little residences – and the cover here was perfect, all the houses shrouded in trees and bushes.

Turning off the sidewalk, casually she moved up the crazy paving between the other bungalows, before she saw the light in the front window of Taylor's house. Tiptoeing up, pushing in through a tangle of bougainvillaea, she tried to see through the window. But the curtains were drawn and all she could hear were the voices – a woman's voice raised in anger.

'. . . leave my daughter alone . . . hear me! . . .'

'Mrs Minter –'

'You and your drug peddling with her . . . and what else I don't know . . . behind my back. But it's going to stop, once and for all, I can tell you –'

'Mother!' Another woman's voice broke in, younger, in a higher register, even more angry. 'It's nothing the hell to do with you. And nothing of that sort's going on . . . you bursting in here . . . we were just going over a scenario . . . this new Egyptian picture . . .'

Hetty froze in anger. It was obviously Mary Miles Minter, with her virago of a mother having some row with the director – about drugs, seduction, the lot. Hetty was not surprised. It was well-known about the picture colony: Taylor, with his insatiable taste for affairs with young women, had been carrying on with Mary. Mrs Minter had come for a showdown with him now. Taylor deserved no less. But Hetty was frustrated.

She would have to wait, but not here, where it was too exposed. She went round to the back of the bungalow, taking up a position just outside the kitchen door, crouching next to some empty crates of bootlegged beer and spirits. The kitchen door was half-open, she saw, as if one or other of the Minter women had come in by that route. But of course! Mrs Minter had come that way, hoping to surprise the couple at their antics. What a lot of surprising business Taylor had on his plate that evening, Hetty thought. Well, she would not be denied her part in it. She settled down to await developments. The two women could not stay there forever . . .

Up at the Lodge, Eddy Nolan – hearing the coupé swinging round on the gravel – had rushed down to the lower terrace, too late to stop her. There were several cars in the garage, but Eddy could not drive. Instead he put an urgent call through to Craig at the studio.

'For Christ's sake, Eddy, how did you let her go? – *where* did she go?'

'No idea – I thought maybe downtown to meet you?'

'Like hell she is! Maybe Marion Davies or Mickey Neilan – I'll call them. Or maybe worse . . .' Craig considered something for a moment. 'Listen, Eddy,' he said then. 'Get down here quick, will you? I may need you. Get one of the cooks to drive you.'

Hetty meanwhile was becoming impatient, frustrated in her lack of action, and made more uneasy still as the oppressive sky finally broke in a storm above the city, with patches of vivid lightning, and the electric cables on some small pylons nearby sizzling with blue flashes. She could hear no detail of the argument now, only the raised voices from the front room. And suddenly she thought how, instead of waiting for the Minters' departure, she might better use their presence there instead. She had no need to talk to Taylor, after all.

She moved silently into the kitchen, then on down a corridor towards the front room. Turning a corner into a second shorter corridor, she saw a curtained Spanish archway some yards ahead, light from the drawing room shining through a gap in the drapes, shadows moving to and fro beyond, voices clearly heard now – dominated by Mrs Minter's strident tones.

'Don't lie to me! – that's what you've been doing for years, getting decks of coke to every young girl you could lay your hands on about the studios, then seducing them. Well, you won't go on doing that with *my* daughter, you creep, you cheapjack . . .'

Hetty took out the Smith and Wesson .38 she had taken from Craig's drawer. It would surely be an easy shot, through the curtains – then back out of the kitchen door. She would never even be seen. She moved forward, hardly breathing, the gun held straight ahead of her, the barrel moving slowly towards the gap in the curtains. Raising the gun and peering through, she saw them all: the two women across the room, Taylor sideways on to her, hardly three yards away, tall and thin, silvering hair, impeccably dressed in his dark English worsted. But, most astonishingly, there was Mrs Minter, at that same moment, taking a revolver from her bag, aiming it at Taylor.

The shot went off with a sharp report which stunned Hetty. Had it come from her revolver, or from Mrs Minter's? Hetty was not sure. Taylor's knees crumpled, then he fell straight downwards, like a tall building being demolished. Hetty, still behind the curtain, saw the look of fear and astonishment on the faces of the two women, standing there for a moment, rooted to the spot, wild-eyed, before they turned and fled, closing the front door behind them.

Hetty went into the drawing room as the thunder boomed over her. Taylor was stretched out on the carpet between his desk and the sofa. He seemed quite unharmed, as if asleep. There was no sign of blood or other injury. She bent over him, a crisis of alarm and guilt threatening her.

Suddenly she felt a sense of fuzzy distances overwhelming her, until she saw nothing, just a warm blackness spreading everywhere round her, the beginnings of some comforting dream forming in her mind, as she fell herself then, to lie stretched out next to Taylor. Soon there was a knock on the door, but she never heard it.

'The lights are on – she must be here.' Craig turned to Eddy on the doorstep.

'That was her car at the end of the street. I'll stay out front – you go round the back.'

Moments later, coming through from the kitchen, they found her on the floor. 'Where am I?' she asked, dazed but calm. 'We were at home, at Summer Hill. I was speaking to Aunt Emily!' She was happy at this thought, as she glanced vaguely around her. 'Where is she?'

'No, Laura, you're here, with us – in Hollywood . . .' Craig told her. And suddenly, at this news, Hetty was on her feet, pushing and shoving at the men, struggling violently, before Eddy, practically leaping on her, like an animal, gripped her fiercely, pinioning her arms. 'Easy, there, easy,' he calmed her, like a tiny jockey astride a racehorse.

Craig picked his gun up from the floor, checked the rooms for any other evidence of Hetty's presence in the bungalow, and they got her out through the kitchen door and back to the car. 'You go with her, Eddy – she'll have to drive, it's the only way. I'll follow.'

As Craig passed Hollywood Lake, he stopped for a moment in the rainy darkness and threw the gun as far as he could out into the water. Back home, he took Hetty to their bedroom. The storm had passed. The air on the mountain was suddenly cool and refreshing for the first time in a week. He embraced her. 'My God, honey – you shouldn't have done it. It was only a picture.'

'Done wha-what?' She looked at him with genuine astonishment.

'What do you mean? Down in Taylor's house – you just shot him.'

'Oh! Was that where we were just now? *Taylor's* house? – but I don't know him. And somebody *shot* him?' She was entirely mystified.

Craig put his hand to her cheek, calming, stroking her. 'Okay, somebody shot him. Fine. But, whatever you do, if anyone asks, we *weren't* downtown tonight. None of us. Okay? We weren't *in* Taylor's house tonight. Remember that, won't you?' He looked at her urgently. And she returned the look, still curious, but agreeing.

'No, of course not. I we-won't say.'

'Now, get those clothes off,' he told her.

'Yes, of course.' She looked down at her disguise, the men's slacks and mackintosh, suddenly quite bemused again. 'What on earth am I wearing these for? Weren't filming today, were we?'

'No – just some charade we were playing . . .'

She started to get undressed, throwing the clothes about her in a vigorous whirlwind. 'Extraordinary! Don't remember a thing aba-about it all. One of our nice "games" again, was it?' She paused, then turned to him, with a smile of great happiness, like the old days. 'Oh, Craig, it's so long since we played those good games, isn't it? What was it, some frantic party downtown?'

'Yes . . . Yes, but you had a blackout, one of your little turns.'

'Oh, dear. At the pe-pe-party?' Craig nodded. 'Yes, it's funny, because I remember something now – Mary Minter was there, wasn't she? – with her mother. Some sort of row going on. Anyway, I feel fine now.'

The air had cleared, all the mugginess gone, stars visible in the sky through the open bedroom window, a faint breeze running in from the ocean. She came to him, embracing, kissing him seductively. 'I can't te-*tell* you,' she said vehemently, 'how nice it is – to be playing our old games again.' She licked his ear mischievously. She felt so different now, all the mysterious burdens of the last months quite lifted. 'But *what* a party!' she went on, standing back from him, curious once more. 'Someone *shot* Taylor, did they?' He nodded grimly – and she reached out, touching his cheek briefly. 'Oh my God, but *who?*'

'I – I don't know exactly . . . wasn't in the room when it happened.'

'Well, at least we can make *Nefertiti* now, can't we?'

'Why, yes. Yes, we can, honey.' And Craig kissed her tenderly.

Later he spoke to Eddy in the kitchen. 'Jesus – she doesn't remember a thing!'

'So much the better. And no one saw us. And, if anyone saw her, well, look at the disguise she had on.'

'And nothing to link her with Taylor, she's never met him. We may get away with it.' Craig poured himself a drink. 'It's funny, though, when I spoke to her, she thought she'd been at some downtown party, in Taylor's place – with Mary Minter and her mother there, having some row.' Eddy grunted and Craig continued, 'Funny, because it figures in a way, doesn't it? Taylor's been carrying on with Mary for months now, behind her mother's back. Just the sort of thing she'd do – turn up at his place unannounced and try and crack him one, or even shoot him.'

'Yes . . .' Then Eddy thought out loud. 'Yes, indeed – those two, or Mabel Normand. She's been having a long fling with Taylor as well – while he was two-timing her. Any one of those dames might have shot him – they'll be the first people the cops'll think of.'

'You really think that, Eddy? Or are we just out of the frying pan, into the fire?'

Robert and Léonie had been dancing 'Le Fox' – and then, even more daringly, 'Le Java', the latest craze, a mad dance, stamping their feet furiously, so that by the end of the evening they were both heady-drunk, sweating with exhaustion and excitement.

It had started to snow outside, so that, leaving the *bal musette*, they walked straight into the delicious, cooling flakes. Lifting their heads, opening their mouths, they drank in the weather, snow melting on their tongues as they walked through the Latin Quarter towards the river.

By the time they reached the narrow mediaeval streets round the church of St Julien-le-Pauvre on a slight rise above the water, all the traffic had disappeared and the snow had become heavier, colder, falling silently. They stopped a moment by the church doorway, while Léonie adjusted her big red scarf, so that it covered her sugar-dusted hair. Then, looking up at the church, she turned and kissed Robert abruptly, a peck on the cheek.

'Abelard's church!' she told him.

'Oh, I didn't know –'

'Like stations of the cross – one has to mark it!' Robert, stamping his feet, bouncing the snow off his boots on the pavement, had no time to comment on this, before she said, 'Doing the Java again?' She smiled, putting her arm in his, pulling him on. 'You were really pretty good by the end!'

'More the pastis –'

'No! But *no* – it was all you, letting yourself go at last!'

'I'm really no dancer . . .'

'Oh, go on, you old fraud! Do anything if you try!'

She left him then, skipping round him, teasing him, flouncing her arms out in the snow, as he continued his steady walk down towards the Quai Saint-Michel. 'Anything! Anything!' she sang out, lunging at him, tipping at his old felt hat, so that soon they were snowballing each other, both scattering down the street, sliding, and throwing snow, in a great helter-skelter, until they reached the river. They stood by the wall then, at the very edge, arm in arm, watching the white drifts falling, curtain upon receding curtain, against the dark backdrop of Notre-Dame just visible across the water.

'Winter! What a winter!' she said, shivering, wrapping the scarf tighter. 'I love it – just love it when it snows like this! Wish there was never any end to winter . . .'

'Yes,' he said. Then, quite absentmindedly, apropos of nothing, he went on, 'All wrapped up in the cosy-warm . . .'

She turned, looking at him as he gazed pensively into the snowfall. 'Oh *yes!*' she said, huddling up to him quickly, so that he smelt the damp snowy wool on her scarf then, mixed with the distant odour of violets. '*Yes!*' she said once more. They took a taxi back to Passy.

Ben Straus had long since retired when, opening the door silently, Léonie came into Robert's small top floor bedroom, a wraith-like figure, standing in her cotton nightdress for a moment, vaguely illuminated by the street light outside the window.

'Robert?' she whispered.

Robert, thoughts of the evening's song and dance still churning about his head, was wide awake. But he pretended drowsiness.

'It's so *cold* in my room! Can I . . . come in . . . and share your bed?'

Her voice was entirely sensible, direct, without urgency or passion. Yet Robert felt a complete panic. 'Yes,' he murmured, as if waking from a deep sleep.

'Sorry to wake you!' She lifted the coverlet briskly, and hopped into the narrow space beside him. 'But it was quite *freezing* in my bed.' And she shivered next to him then, a long spasm right down her body, as truthful confirmation. Robert had been lying on his side facing the wall. Now he turned on his back.

'Yes, chilly, isn't it?' he remarked in a casual tone, as if sharing views on the weather with a neighbour. He shivered himself in his warm woolly pyjamas – though not from cold, as he felt the long length of this woman, so close to him, the folds and run of her whole body, just as he had imagined, length by length, so deliciously, perilously close to him. He raised his hands carefully behind his head, and they lay there, side by side, straight out on their backs, still as corpses in the dark, until Léonie chuckled.

'What?'

'Just, it struck me – lying like this – we might be two elderly people, being chauffeured out in a motor, commenting on the weather.' And then she shivered once more, her shoulder throbbing next to him, as if a bitter wind was raging through her, before she turned to him, putting her arm across him.

'Oh, warm me, Robert, warm me – in the cosy-warm!'

He thought of the phrase again. And now he remembered its origins. It had been one of Hetty's in their nursery days together with Elly in Domenica and Summer Hill. He had spoken it involuntarily, without quite knowing why, an hour before on the Quai. But now the words, drifting through the snow of the years, had come home to roost. Of course – he saw it then: the little nursery phrase of the girl who for so long he had loved and wanted had been the key to his bed that night, which Léonie, all unknowing, had picked up and turned in the lock. What irony – that Hetty should so make their bed for them that night, a last gift from her. So that when he turned into Léonie's arms, clasping her, he saw instead that other tall, audacious girl, so full of laughter and shadow, seeing what he owed her then, in the shape of this forgotten nursery fable, saw how he still both loved and hated her.

He felt the thrilling flow of Léonie's body then, soft breasts and thighs, hard hips and knees – and soon he found himself shivering for another reason.

'Violets,' he said as he touched her. 'I had this idea, while we were dancing . . .' He stopped.

'What? Go on!' She encouraged him breathlessly.

'Well, just that perfume you use, smells of violets – I'd wondered what it'd be like if one was close to you . . .'

'*And?*' She was impatient.

'Well, it's not there now! Just a sort of starchy linen smell –'

'That's just my clean nightdress, you idiot! Here, I'll take it off!' And, before he could do anything about it, she sat up abruptly, pulling the nightdress up over her shoulders in a moment, then lying down with him again at once, hugging him.

'*Now!* – can you smell the violets?'

He sniffed. 'Yes – yes, faintly.'

She laughted outright. 'You are funny.' Then she added, taking up one of her mock operatic voices, 'You and your violets – like an old gardener!'

'Sorry –'

'Oh, *Robert!*' She scolded him kindly. 'Do stop pottering about in the garden!'

'Yes, of course . . .'

And she worried him again, like a terrier, playfully pulling at his hair, pinching his ear, then hugging him to her.

'It's no use – you're tickling me so. You'll simply *have* to take your pyjamas off!' she advised him haughtily, like a duchess in a comedy.

'Oh – sorry.'

She undid his pyjama top then, putting her arms inside, feeling the soft skin there for the first time, before running her hand down to his waist, and pulling the string, so that soon they were both naked.

Robert was astonished at the delicious warmth and pleasure he felt. Their skin together now was like nothing he could ever have imagined: it was a gliding feeling between them, so smoothly tender, and there was a musky sweet smell now with the violets, as he felt his sex rising, surging towards her, so that he tried wildly to withdraw, before she held him.

'No! No – don't go away! That's perfectly *all right*,' she calmed him. 'It's the best thing in the world! Because I love you,' she said as she touched him, leaning over him now, kissing him gently, down his face, his chest, so that for minutes on end then they seemed suspended together, quite weightless – even when she lightly straddled him, opening herself to him, coming on to him delicately, lightly, imperceptibly at first, so flowingly and inevitably that before he quite realised it he was inside her, moving into her, as she pushed gently, drawing back from him, moving to and fro.

'The *best* thing!' she said again, her passion rising, stretching right back, arms fluttering about before she took his hand and put it to her breast; so that, caught in these separate ways, their bodies forming a rough circle, they struggled together in a confusion of pleasure – before Robert suddenly turned over on to her and made love to her, rising to a pitch when he could no longer contain himself, falling then, falling into her, into a great bank of violets.

'I *do* love you,' he said afterwards, in quite a different, more confident voice – the tones of the inexperienced gardener quite gone. While for Léonie the surprise and change was just as great.

'I was *so* scared,' she said, nuzzling him, 'that I – couldn't do it.'

'You didn't show it! –'

'No – no! Easy as falling off a log – because you wanted me! I felt it – the moment you said that about the "cosy-warm" down by the river!'

'Yes – yes,' he said, without elaborating on what he thought to be the key to their success that evening. But Léonie in fact knew the origins of these words, too. Hetty had often used them with her, when they had lived together in Dublin, as a coded invitation to bed. And now, as she had realised by the river, Hetty had used them with Robert as well, long before, as part of some nursery fable in Summer Hill. How strange it was, she thought, that Hetty's words should so bring them together that night – Hetty, still working for her, invisibly, a hand, a voice, a phrase reaching out to her from the past, bringing her the gift of Robert. And for an instant then she saw Hetty's face ahead of her in the darkness, not Robert's – Hetty in all her vivid tormented glamour.

5

I T WAS THE autumn of 1925, and already nearly two months had passed in Egypt. But now at last – with the help of some hundreds of Egyptian builders, carpenters, stonemasons, plasterers and coppersmiths, together with American, Italian and French craftsmen, set-designers and other technicians – the gleaming city of Amarna, the Pharaoh Akhenaten's fabulous 'City of the Sun', was rising up in the desert, beneath a crescent of jagged forbidding hills on the east bank of the Nile, near the town of Beni-Souef eighty miles south of Cairo on the railway.

'Up! Up! *Mein Gott!* . . .' The art director Leo Kuter broke into his Teutonic mode, yelling in tense frustration, his little goatee beard glistening with sweat.

The fifty or so Egyptian labourers in the current work gang – *fellahin* employed from the villages on the other side of the river – tugged on the half-dozen ropes, running down from the scaffold with its wooden pulleys high above them, gradually easing up the vast ornamental plaque, a central altar-piece weighing well over a ton, one among a roughly similar half-dozen, showing Akhenaten, his wife Nefertiti and their three daughters, exultantly happy under the rays of the sun god Aten. The plaque was to be set above the open shrine at the end of the Great Temple, Aten's 'House of the Sun', an immense half-completed construction, three or four hundred feet square, enclosed by high walls, with rows and clumps of columns inside, supporting decorative architraves, or creating little pavilions, sunshades, in this huge mosaic-paved plaza set some way back from the river.

Leo Kuter looked a mess in a pith helmet and sweat-soiled linen suit, and Johnny Seitz the cameraman, flat cap on back to front as usual, was equally bedraggled; both suffered in the intense midday heat, the blaze of light that cast no shadows and seemed to levitate everything in its shimmer. Only Craig, like the sun king Akhenaten himself, appeared to have entered his true element. Perfectly turned out and tailored – in a dazzling white silk shirt, linen trousers, leather-belted, hatless, his smooth dark hair glistening in the light – he drew the sun's rays to him, becoming part of Aten's fire: sweatless, immune, almost inhuman.

The three men stood on top of a thirty-five-foot-high steel scaffold, set on four doubled sets of automobile wheels, sent out from Hollywood and incorporating a camera lift, with which they were experimenting, while at the same time supervising this final construction of the city, which costumed crowds of extras would fill during the first week's shooting. Leo went over again to the huge megaphone, suspended from a bracket on top of the tower.

'Up – and to zee right!' he shouted to one of his half-dozen assistants, on the ground below and on the balcony beneath the dangerously swinging plaque.

'Christ, Leo – don't let them swing it over too far!' Craig warned him. 'It'll hit that balustrade.'

'*Basta*, Luigi, *basta*!' he called to the Italian foreman high above the altar. Then he shouted down to a second foreman, from the Victorine studios in Nice, who was in charge of the sweating *fellahin*. '*Ça va*, Gaston. *En haut encore. Mais doucement!*'

The Egyptians, set out in long radiating lines, moved again on the ropes – pulling, heaving, until gradually the great plaque came into position, some thirty feet above ground, opposite the niche in the temple wall that had been prepared for it.

'*Ça suffit*, Gaston. *Arrêtez! Ne bouge pas encore!*'

The *fellahin* kept the ropes taut, until some of them began to slip on the smooth stone plaza, so that Leo roared at them again like a slave-master. '*Arrêtez*, Gaston! *Ne bougez* pas!' And Gaston took up the command beneath him, berating the turbanned men in kitchen Arabic, '*Yallah! Ma fische!* . . .' before Leo continued, shouting across the great divide at Luigi, '*Va bene*, Luigi! Take it in now – *ma dolce*, dolce!' The plaque was finally fixed in place.

'My God . . .' Leo wiped his pudgy face with a red bandana handkerchief. 'Verse zan building zee pyramids . . .'

'Yes, but look, Leo!' Craig put a hand on his shoulder. His eyes were glazed with emotion, as he pointed up to the plaque – a spectacular white emblem, reflecting the midday sun, one sun mirroring another, the rays at the end, caressing the five almost naked figures. 'Just look – it's sensational! Better than the original – bigger, better, twice the size!'

Craig was beside himself, his dark sunburned features alive with power and pleasure. Taking over directions with the megaphone, he shouted down to a group of camera grips, standing at the four corners of the steel scaffold beneath him. 'Okay, boys, take it back now. *Mais doucement pour commencer* – and we'll see how it moves.' He moved forward then, taking up a spare viewfinder while Seitz settled down behind the Bell and Howell camera.

Slowly at first, the pace gradually rising to a walk, the whole steel tower moved back, away from the vast altar, along the centre of the plaza. And Craig, kneeling down, peering through the squared-off glass, suddenly, for the first time, saw the screen shape which would contain this immense vision in these long, high-angle tracking shots. The glass danced in his hand. But it was there all right – everything! – the receding altarpiece, giving way to the balcony, with its steps and pennant staffs came into view, and after that, the great columns and pavilions to either side, as the scaffold drew right back to the end of the plaza.

'Great! Incredible!' Craig stood up. 'What do you think, Johnny?'

Seitz left his camera. 'There's a wobble here and there –'

'Hell, Johnny – with the crowds and all the action going on everywhere, it won't notice!'

'Maybe. But we've not tried the lift yet –'

'We wil, we *will*! And look!'

He grasped Johnny's shoulders then, pushing him round. Both men turned in a half-circle, so that they gazed out at a wide street beyond the walls of the temple plaza, the 'Sikket es-Sultan', the Royal Way, crossed by an ornate, covered bridge just in front of them, where men were working on a roof colonnade and a large window at the centre; the bridge leading down the far side to Akhenaten's Royal Palace, an equally vast, nearly completed building, again in glittering white plaster, but here set out with far less austere ornament – a pleasure dome of glinting copper roofs and fountains, palm-filled sunken gardens, lotus flowers, ornamental ponds, two filigreed harem quarters, the whole palace surrounded by walls topped with hanging gardens, fronting on the river bank for nearly two hundred yards.

'See?' Craig went on. 'From here, on the reverse track, when they come across for the inauguration at the temple, we can pick Akhenaten and Nefertiti up, with all the courtiers, moving over from the palace, stopping at the "Window of Appearances", scattering the flower petals, then follow them over into the temple plaza here, right the way through the crowds to the altar – all in one take!'

'Yeah . . .' Johnny was doubtful. 'Maybe. Have to be an early morning shot, though, else we're going to get the sun right at us, like now, reflecting off the river.'

'Jesus, Johnny – we can *do* it, though. The bloody scaffold works! And just look at the view we get from it, up here, over the rest of the city!'

The three men turned about, gazing out over the shimmering bright panorama, high up above the walls and palaces, the streets and houses – here, at the epicentre of this miraculous city risen from the desert, shading their eyes against the tremendous light.

'Jesus! . . .' Craig breathed.

Below them, beyond the palace wall, labourers unwrapped long palm trees, setting them up, boxing their roots in the watered sands of the royal gardens. To their left and right along the Royal Way, painters were decorating the villas of the nobles, setting hanging baskets of flowers above the peach- and lemon-coloured doors and lintels. Further down the street swarms of men made other finishing touches to this enormous complex of buildings.

Yet what was astonishing was not the height or size of the plaster and pasteboard city, but its exquisite detail, design, its perfect symmetry – above all its originality. Designed by Craig and Leo in a new style, it was quite unlike any earlier Egyptian architecture. Here were no heavy repetitions from the old and middle kingdoms at Memphis and Thebes – the bulbous Osirian columns, the monstrous Pharaonic statues of men and beasts, the effigies, obelisks and pylons commemorating all the hundreds of nightmare animal gods. The designs here, in line with Akhenaten's condemnation of the superstitious mummery at the old capital of Thebes down-river, and his departure for the brave new world at Amarna, quite lacked all the earlier doom and clutter. Reflecting his apostasy, his new faith in the one loving god of the sun, the shapes and decorations here had a startling naturalism, freshness, simplicity – straight lines replacing heavy curves, delicate laterals instead of overpowering verticals, the whole city couched in terms of domestic intimacy, an architecture quite new in the world, honouring this warm god, the expression of a free people.

Craig gazed over the palace to the river, watching the heavily-laden barges and feluccas endlessly ferrying across the water, carrying a vast assortment of supplies and props from the invisible wharf, the tented warehouses and railway siding, hidden from view behind an island in the centre of the river.

'And look!' he continued talking to the two men. 'Even from this height – can't see a thing of that messy camp over the water. The palm trees on the island hide it all.'

'Yes,' Leo Kuter warned him. 'And you look after all those damn palm trees! Three dollars a piece, all zee vay up-river!'

'And we can't really shoot the royal barges from the plaza here,' Johnny put in. 'Except as a wide-angle establishing shot – too far away for any detail.'

'I *told* you, Craig,' Leo added. 'Zat Royal Vay is too vide – almost double zee vidth of zee real zing, vhich was only fifty feet, othervise you'd have gotten closer to zee river from here.'

Craig took Leo by the shoulders. 'You know something, Leo – bin on my mind some time. I want you to play Bek, the royal architect. That goatee beard, it's ideal. Put you in one of those Egyptian kilts, knobbly knees and all. Come on, I'll take you to costume and make-up straightaway.'

Leo frowned, taking him quite seriously for a moment. Craig in this mood, he knew, was capable of any brazen conceit. 'I don't know, Craig –'

'Come on, you old kraut! Told you before we started – anything we do will be double the size of the real thing!' He clapped him on the back. '*Double!*' he shouted above the noise of hammering and fervid construction going on all round them.

Suddenly a gong sounded, the reverberation from some distant metal echoing through the midday heat. The men turned back to the great altar of the temple. To one side they saw the huge copper gong, decorated in the pattern of the sun's disc, a tiny figure aiming a second stroke at it with his drumstick.

It was the lunch break – and now the whole busy scene dissolved as everyone downed tools and a silence descended over the city, the last sounds of the gong echoing across the plaza, over the palace domes, setting some doves aloft, to soar into the sky over the dazzling river. And Craig trembled himself with excitement, standing atop the scaffold, lord of all creation, breathing in the smell of warm pine resin and plaster, sensing how, in a few days, all this half-completed artifice, this pasteboard act of faith, would suddenly bloom, become real, filled with the only reality he knew – a world filled with actors and cameras.

'"In Xanadu did Kubla Khan, a stately pleasure-dome decree",' he intoned with mock gravity over the magic city shimmering against the arid hills beyond – this myth which he had made flesh. '"Where Alph the sacred river ran, through caverns measureless to man, down to a sunless sea . . . So twice five miles of fertile ground, with walls and towers were girdled round – and gardens bright with sinuous rills, where blossomed many an incense-bearing tree" . . .'

'What poem is that?' Johnny Seitz asked. 'But I needn't ask,' he rushed on. 'You wrote it yourself.' Craig did not contradict him.

During the somnolent lunch break, Craig took his dozen assistant directors out for a briefing and tour of inspection through the unit's workshops, property stores, dressing and dining rooms – just north of the Amarna sets and hidden from them by a slight dip in the land and rows of imported palms.

And here they entered an even larger city, a vast tented encampment running away across the desert from wharves on the river bank – row upon row of large dun-coloured marquees, army bell tents and scores of smaller haphazard tents dotted about the land, bedouin black, accommodation for the hundreds of *fellahin* who, when the shooting started, would become costumed extras, citizens of Amarna.

The assistant directors, apart from Harry Elmer, the American first assistant and Mark Eldon the second unit director, were all French, Italian or Egyptian, young men taken up from Cairo, or brought over with the unit from the Victorine studios in Nice, where this Fox production had its European headquarters and where most of the interiors would be shot later.

One of Craig's assistants, a young Russian, Mikhail Ostrovosky, was the son of a Czarist exile, Prince Ostrovosky, who lived in a decrepit villa outside Nice – a youth, hardly twenty, who had pestered the company for days at the Victorine studios, asking to be taken on. Craig had finally agreed. Mikhail, or Mickey, had one obvious qualification which he had failed to mention in his earlier approaches. He spoke good Arabic, colloquial Egyptian indeed, for his parents had lived for several years after the Russian revolution in Alexandria, where his father, among many other business failures, had once been director of a now-bankrupt tobacco factory.

Craig had come to like Mickey. He was rather gauche, farouche even – tall and clumsy, like a vaudeville comic with his mobile indiarubber features, gangly arms and legs, his tufts of short damp hair. But, behind this physical awkwardness, Craig soon recognised a fine sensitivity and intelligence, an apparently limitless capacity for hard work and a vast enthusiasm and curiosity for every detailed aspect of the business. At this point, having worked with the unit for nearly two months, Craig had tacitly made him his personal assistant, his interpreter and immediate liaison officer with all the many Egyptians he had to deal with.

Now, in the great silence that had descended over the two cities, the group moved from tent to tent, Craig opening the flaps and ushering the assistants inside with a flourish, like a magician displaying the wherewithal for his tricks, delegating to each assistant his coming responsibilities.

'Costume tents – male, female . . . dressing rooms, ditto . . . stars, feature players, extras ... Make-up and hairdressing ... property tents – furniture, jewellery, chariots, horses, barges, armoury ...'

Moving down the double row of tents he itemised their various concerns, broaching the mysteries, displaying these lavish riches: a dozen spindly chariots flaked in gold leaf, pennanted spears, sling shots, gilt bows and bamboo arrows – 'That's for you, Mario – the battle stuff, against the Theban priests when they come up-river to sack Amarna' – whole chests of sparkling costume jewellery, deep necklace collars, Pharaonic clasps, rings and bracelets, imitation gems and stones, cornelian, lapis lazuli, green and blue malachite, silver and gold. Craig dipped both hands in the studded jewel boxes, letting the glitter run between his fingers. 'Riches beyond the dreams of avarice! ...' he intoned, and the assistants smiled.

Beyond, in further tents, lay other dazzling or bizarre collections: a stock of ancient Egyptian musical instruments, lyres, and reed flutes – 'For the blind harpists and choirs!' – and a tent next to it, set out as a contemporary band room with music stands and modern instruments – 'Mood music, from half the Cairo Opera orchestra ...'

Finally, in a boatyard by the river, they saw the two royal barges. It was a stunning climax to their tour. The builders were at lunch and the boats stood empty, buttressed on their slipways, now transformed into delicately sloped vessels, running up to a peak fore and aft, with small gilded pavilions at the back, surmounted by flying sun pennants and ostrich feathers, the gunwales encrusted with decorative hieroglyphics and cartouches, sun discs, lotus flowers, lilies, enclosed in sweeping lines of gold, all set against a Nile-green background.

The assistants gazed on these recreated miracles, glittering in the light, gilded oars rampant, waiting to slip into the river. Craig climbed a step-ladder and stood by the prow, looking down on the men.

'So – here's our first sequence, I think, unless we do the temple inauguration first – Akhenaten and Nefertiti, with all their court, coming up-river from Thebes – from the two camera launches. And that's for you, Mickey – I want you dressed up on the first barge, with Laura and Clive, just beneath the pavilion there at the back, with the drummer marking time for the oarsmen – we'll work out the signals ...'

Mickey nodded, happy at this honour, looking up at the director, while Craig gazed out on the river – dallying a moment at the end of the tour, delighted by all these paste and plaster props, these papier-mâché toys and baubles, a Merlin once more, turning dross to gold, a lavish spendthrift of the desert.

As they left the boatyard, a man in a heavy suit and homburg, who had been sweating along after the group throughout the trip, now finally closed on Craig, as he walked back alone to his own tent.

'Yes, yes – it's Mr Max Jacobson, our never-to-be-forgotten chief accountant!' Craig told him a little impatiently.

'Yes, Mr Williamson ...' The man took off his hat as they entered Craig's private tent. 'I had a cable yesterday, from head office in New York – came down from Cairo on the overnight train, thought you should see it at once.' Opening an attaché case, he handed Craig the message. It was from the Fox financial controller. 'ADVISE YOU THAT PRE-PRODUCTION BUDGET NOW OVERRUN BY ONE HUNDRED TWENTY NINE THOUSAND DOLLARS STOP BANK OF AMERICA CAIRO OFFICE CREDIT SUSPENDED PENDING YOUR GUARANTEE NO MORE UNAUTHORISED PRE-PRODUCTION COSTS INCURRED.'

Craig smiled. Then he tore the cablegram up. 'Well, that's all right, isn't it? Pre-production is nearly over. First day of principal photography in a few days' time. No mention of suspending that budget, is there?'

Mr Jacobson shook his head. 'No. No – but that deposit can't be touched, of course, until you start –'

'And what do we have there – two million dollars?' Jacobson nodded. 'Well, since we're all still technically on pre-production – all you'll need is your train fare back to Cairo . . .' Craig put his hand in a pocket, jangling some piastres. 'Here you are.' He made to hand over some of the coins, then paused, looking at them. 'Trouble is, Jacobson, I don't know about you, but I can never get to trust this Egyptian money – every damn coin's got a hole in it . . .'

Mr Jacobson was unamused as Craig ushered him out. 'Cheer up, Jacobson!' he told him brightly. 'Just wait till we get our hands on the production budget proper – then we'll *really* start to spend money!' Jacobson was horrified, and Craig took pity on him. 'Listen, Max,' he went on. 'You look all done in. Use my steam launch back over the river – take a shower, get them to give you a proper meal, in my *wagon-lit* carriage on the siding. You know the one – the one with King Fuad's arms over the window.'

Craig's tent was sparsely luxurious, set out in the bedouin fashion. Apart from some office chairs and a large trestle table covered in set and costume designs, photographs and scripts, the furnishings were largely hanging silks and exotic cushions, red and cool lemon, with intricate Persian rugs layered over the desert floor and an ornate silver hookah in one corner. Beyond a crimson partition was a low broad bed and a brass-bound army travelling chest. There was an outer hallway, too, and now, as he took off his silk shirt, and his servant Abdullah, a tall Nubian with a red cummerbund, laid his lunch for him, there was a knock on the tent pole outside.

'What is it?' he said impatiently.

'Craig, can I talk with you a moment?'

Christ, he thought – it was Howard Southham, the dull but popular scenario writer, a man he had employed on and off, for over a year, preparing a final blood and thunder chariot racing photoplay to show to Fox and the rest of the big wheels in the company. He would have to humour him.

'Come right on in, Howard!'

'Hi, Craig.' The tall, white-haired man, prematurely middle-aged, looked worse than Jacobson – shaking, bleary-eyed, sweat coursing through a day's stubble on his chin. With Jacobson it had been the heat. But with Howard, Craig suspected, it was drink.

'Some lunch, Howard?'

'No. No thanks. I just came down on the train with Max Jacobson –'

'Great! How are things in Cairo? Brought all the final typed scenarios with you?'

'Yes. As final as we can get them.' He put one of them down on the table. 'The rest are outside.' He lit a cigarette with a trembling hand. 'Trouble is, Craig . . .' He paused, bending his neck to and fro as if to ease a headache. 'Say, Craig,' he went on, 'you don't happen to have a drink hereabouts, do you?'

Craig laughed good-humouredly. 'Wish I did, Howard. But as you can see.' He glanced around him. 'All strictly teetotal here, in the Arab manner! Not a drop this side of the river. I've given strict instructions all round. Got some sherbet, though. Or some iced lemon! Abdullah!' He called his servant. 'Get Mr Southham a glass of that bitter lemon, will you?'

Southham grimaced at the very thought before continuing. 'Trouble is, Craig, as I said before, in this final script, well, the material – apart from the big action scenes – it still doesn't seem quite to fit together, one scene with another. Gaps. Yes, well – just gaps – doesn't altogether make sense.'

Craig, picking at his simple lunch of unleavened bread, beans, sliced onions, tomatoes and anchovies, lifted an onion sliver to his mouth, delicately, pensively. Then he sprang to life. 'Hell, Howard, that's no worry. Lot of it'll have to be changed anyway – and it'll all fit on the day.' He picked up the new scenario on the table, flicking through the pages. There weren't many, barely eighty, for a picture that was planned to run out at eighteen reels, or nearly two and a half hours. 'No, you don't worry. You've done a great job, Howard. I hear you're moving on to Brenon's new picture back home – when do you leave?'

'Monday, from Port Said – Jesus, Craig, I wish to hell I could stay, but . . .'

God forbid, Craig thought. 'Me too, Howard. Never mind. You've done a great job. Great!' He stood up now, taking his hand. 'No, you couldn't have been more constructive or imaginative,' he lied convincingly. 'And I'll tell you what, Howard – don't bruit it around – but if you go over to my *wagon-lit* carriage, you know the one with the Khedival arms, in the siding, ask Mabrouk there, my waiter, tell him I said so: he's got a bottle of brandy – one I keep for emergencies. He'll give you a drink.'

Howard's face suddenly cleared with pleasure. 'Why, Craig –'

'No, no – you go ahead!' And Southham left, offering heart-felt thanks for this impending alcoholic cure in the barbarous desert.

'Jesus!' Craig muttered when he had gone. 'These goddamned rummy writers – nary a one of them ever sober.'

Then he picked up another scenario, hidden on the table, typed, but with very many more additional pages bound in, written in his own neat hand, a scenario nearly 150 pages long, running out at over thirty reels, with dozens of new scenes, which neither Southham nor William Fox, nor Winfield Sheehan nor anyone else, had ever seen. No, not even Laura.

He opened the scenario haphazardly then, reading the handwritten start of one of these new sequences: 'ESTABLISHING MID SHOT: INNER SANCTUM,

THE ROYAL BEDCHAMBER: The Queen, half-asleep, without her wig, naked under the diaphanous covers, delicate toes emerging at the end of the bed, wakes to see Akhenaten moving towards her. She smiles dreamily as he bends down, his elongated deformed head and bulbous lips touching the end of the bed in a sort of famished obeisance, before, taking her toes in his hands, and gently massaging them, he starts to kiss them.'

Smiling briefly, Craig closed the scenario and returned to his austere meal.

Way down-river, a day out of Cairo, the teak-decked Nile paddle steamer *Omar Khayam* churned through the water, a contemporary royal barge, one of several belonging to King Fuad, which, along with the Khedival *wagons-lits*, he had lent to Craig and Hetty, as additional accommodation on the picture.

Hetty, in cool khaki bush shorts and shirt, lay out under the foredeck awning on a luxurious steamer chair, drowsily watching the passing scene on the river bank and the water – great lateen-sailed feluccas gliding by, pyramids and ancient temples, *fellahin* in the cotton fields, oxen forever turning *sakias*, irrigating the billiard-table green, the fields of berseem clover.

In her lap lay one of the new scenarios. Eddy Nolan had just brought her out a pot of tea and some of her special fruit cake. But she left it all untouched. Clive Brook, the British actor cast as Akhenaten, was in his cabin resting. She was alone on the great river, moving towards her destiny.

Of her own past now, in this sensuous dream time, she had no memory. Merging with the fabulous landscape, there was only an eternal present for her shaped in these ageless, ancient river monuments, sliding by her in the vivid turquoise light. She was no longer Henrietta Cordiner nor even the famous Laura Bowen. Already lost to those earlier personas, she had entered a pantheon of Gods, impervious to all mortal commonplaces, as Nefertiti – 'Lady of Grace, Sweet of Love, Mistress of the North and South, Queen of the Two Lands, Nefertiti, living for ever and ever . . .' She dozed off in the glaze of heat, already cradled in immemorial dreams. But the dream then was of more recent events.

Dermot – Dermot Cordiner – suddenly came into her suite at the Semiramis Hotel by the river where she had been staying in Cairo, dressed in his major's uniform; Dermot, somehow stationed in Egypt then – Dermot, not seen in years . . . They shook hands, formally, and he did not really smile, putting his cap down on the sofa.

'So, at last . . .' he said awkwardly. 'So many years.' He smoothed his crinkly straw hair, greying a little now. 'Who would have supposed it! Nefertiti! Thought I'd call round – regiment's quartered just next door at the Kasr el Nil barracks. All right, I hope?'

And Hetty wanted to speak in the dream, but found she could not, so that Dermot ran on, in his staccato. 'You used to write, of course. But it's been so long now, since we heard anything. Seen some of your pictures, now and then – even here in Cairo!' But still she could not speak in return, trying desperately to voice her apologies, her guilt. It was torture. 'Hetty?' He came nearer then, wondering at her silence. 'Hetty – why didn't you write? You still have a family, after all. Me and Aunt Emily and Mortimer. And Léonie and Robert, of course – they're married now you know! . . .'

On the foredeck of the steamer, Hetty woke with a start. *Married?* Léa and Robert married? 'Oh, my God,' she said, blinking in the strong light. 'What a nightmare!' But then, gathering herself, she had a worse shock still. The dream had simply been a slight variation of the reality. Dermot had indeed called on her at the Semiramis, and almost everything in her nightmare then – the words, the actions – all had happened in fact a few days before.

She picked up the cooling pot of tea, fiddled with the fruit cake, lit a cigarette, trying again to obliterate everything in her earlier life, the memory of this meeting two days before in Cairo, dispel all her demons once more. Someone moved in the grand saloon behind her. The exotic songbirds in the royal aviary trilled and called. She steadied herself as she drew on the cigarette.

It was all right, she thought then, running her hand along the richly-inlaid marquetry of the steamer chair, looking about at the other wonderfully-crafted riches and luxuries which surrounded her. Here she was, in the only reality she need consider, regally indifferent, quite insulated from all such nightmares, a woman with no past dooms or connections. Now she remembered her actual words at the meeting in the Semiramis Hotel, her gracious but distant response to Dermot. 'How nice that you should have called . . . But I no longer have any connections in Ireland . . . Robert and Léonie married? How suitable!'

At the memory of these last words, she bunched her fingers and cracked her hands violently on the arm of her chair, stood up and walked about the deck, angry and frustrated. Her stamping footsteps disturbed the afternoon calm, reverberating about the steamer.

Below deck, in a provision hold to the rear of the boat, the snakes stirred, locked in several glass-sided boxes, their keeper nearby, from the royal zoo in Cairo. The reptiles, hired for certain scenes in the picture, had been put on board at the last moment, without Hetty's knowledge. They, too, like Hetty – these puff adders and pit vipers – sought some destiny in the paradise of Amarna far up-river.

Robert and Léonie had married earlier that year in Paris at the American church on the Quai d'Orsay, with some thirty guests entertained for lunch afterwards at the Plaza-Athénée Hotel across the river. Robert now had a more secure position as a reporter on the *Herald Tribune* in their main printing office next to Les Halles, while Léonie had joined the Paris Opéra, promoted from the chorus and taking on some small feature roles, keen to succeed there, but more anxious still to make a good marriage with Robert.

For, although she had no qualms or hesitations in her loving there, she feared something in her soul: not so much Hetty, or the memory of Hetty, for there was still that from time to time – but more a resurgence of that kind of love. For sometimes, quite out of the blue, she found herself attracted by other women, by girls in the Opéra chorus or by others – sometimes just seen passing in the street or glimpsed at a café table. She had only to look at such women, and they at her – even briefly, noting a particular fall of hair, a slant of eye, some wayward design in the lips or nose – for a sudden distant echo of that sort of passion to spring from her heart, unstoppable. She knew how easily she could fall for such women, though it would not take away one iota of her love for Robert, might, indeed, increase it; but she dared not talk to him about, or succumb to, it.

Robert for his part had no inkling of all this. Léonie had got Hetty out of her system; that he knew. And so, he assumed, all that kind of love had died in her as well. It never crossed his mind that Léonie's fervour and devotion towards him, though entirely genuine, was increased by this need to blot out another part of her nature. So Léonie devoured him now, within all the appropriate bonds of marriage, in part to dam up other less appropriate hungers.

They rented a small two-roomed apartment on the left bank, six floors up, on the narrow rue Saint-André-des-Arts, next to the old hotel there, looking out on the rooftops, a crazy chiaroscuro of drunken chimneys, gutters, louvred shutters, balconies and geranium pots. Money was short and they were both hard at work. But Ben Straus insisted they take a proper honeymoon, when they were free to do so, later that year.

'Now, what would you most like to see, to do, in all the world? Go on! Anything! – part of my wedding present to you. May never have the chance again!'

'Oh, I don't know . . .' Léonie smiled. Then it suddenly struck her – they were soon to start rehearsals for *Aida* at the Opéra. 'Egypt!' she said. 'All those temples and pyramids and things – up the Nile in a steamer!'

Her father readily agreed. 'And so you shall – nothing easier!'

Frances, siding with de Valera and the other republicans in their refusal to accept Michael Collins' partition treaty with the British, had survived the ensuing vicious civil war in Ireland largely by dint of spending much of the time in and out of jail, successively sentenced by the emerging Free State government, first under Collins and subsequently, after his assassination, headed by the new President, William Cosgrave.

Finally released, her friends and supporters defeated, at the end of a murderous internecine struggle, Frances had no part to play at all in the new government. She and the other republicans, beaten at arms and discredited politically, returned to a shadow life in the country, under what rapidly became a staid and cautious régime that had no use whatsoever for any of their old republican fire.

De Valera bided his time, repairing old allegiances, mustering new support, generally scheming for eventual power in the land. But Frances, far less politically adept and without de Valera's executive skills and devious acumen, twiddled her thumbs in the ugly little pebble-dash bungalow off Rathgar Road in the Dublin suburbs. She took up good works on behalf of republican ex-prisoners and their families, and the Dublin poor. The bungalow became a clearing and meeting house for these charitable activities, filled with vagabond old suits, shirts, hats and boots. The rooms smelt of damp and stray cats, which she took on in abundance to share her essentially lonely existence.

Emaciated, suffering from intermittent bronchitis, arthritis and other ills consequent on her long and various imprisonments, all her earlier fires, in mind and body, had burned low. She was sustained nonetheless by her Catholic faith, by a continuing dream of a united Ireland, by the respectful attentions of old and new republican friends and by the ever-increasing admiration of the Dublin indigent – to whom, in a small Ford motor, she delivered sacks of coal at their impoverished tenements, and for whom she rapidly took on all the lineaments of a martyr and saint.

This was precisely the role she had always subconsciously sought, ever since the Prince of Wales had betrayed her, and she played it now with a pale, ethereal vigour, in a submissive yet somehow self-righteous manner, an act which sustained her in a premature old age, for she was still barely fifty. The faith became for her a professional stage on which she elaborated her already-fervent amateur devotions, sometimes now to the point of mania – especially favouring the Virgin, with whom she more and more identified in a flagrant excess of Mariolatry.

In these obsessive activities, spiritual and temporal, she, like Hetty, quite lost sight of her own personal and familial past. Blindly dedicated to God's work – just as her daughter was to the pursuit of false gods – the memory of Hetty rarely clouded Frances's mind. Nor, in any immediate way, did she concern herself with Summer Hill, never visiting the place – though Mortimer, still believing in some possible future there, had prevailed upon her not to sell it, at least, for some nunnery or convent, as had been her intention. Some of the estate she was forced to sell to the new Land Commission, but the house lingered on, under Mortimer's stewardship and Pat Kennedy's more immediate care, with only Aunt Emily and a few maids still living there.

Sun and winter, and long Irish damp, took their toll, together with gathering ivy, lichen, elder. So that when curious village children in summer, pushing through the rampant briars and ragwort of the demesne, saw the house on the hill, it appeared as a green-girt ruin, an enchanted castle, which they dared not approach further; for inside lay no sleeping princess, they knew, only an ugly old witch.

Aunt Emily, in truth, was no such thing, still bright and spry in her mid-sixties, with a remnant of fine looks, she and Pat Kennedy got along famously alone together: she at her illuminated diaries, drawings and watercolours, maintaining every continuity there; Pat ministering to her few needs, taking her out in the governess cart through the lush valley to some choice spot, where she would set up her easel, or sometimes to Stallard's new cinema palace in Kilkenny to watch one of Hetty's pictures when they came to town. Aunt Emily had not forgotten Hetty – had forgotten nothing, by still commemorating everything.

Pat, who after the Black and Tan depredations in the house, had retired to the gate lodge on the river drive, now returned to Summer Hill, taking perforce, and for the first time, a room in the main Georgian building. He did so somewhat hesitantly, feeling uneasy in the grand guest room, not far from the great staircase.

He need not have worried about this occupation. A letter arrived for him that autumn from Frances in Dublin. 'I believe,' she wrote, 'that you, as an old Republican and companion-in-arms with me, should now take over Summer Hill on a formal basis – a house which I no longer can, nor care to, administer, but which you do so most competently at the moment. Therefore I intend making over the house and what is left of the land to you, as a legal bequest, as of the first of next month. Of course, you have no family at the moment. But perhaps, with this gift, where you could farm what is left of the estate, you may now consider a marriage? I should so like to think of you and your descendants, people of the real Ireland and not the British usurper, making use of the place . . .'

Frances, with a local solicitor in Rathmines, had quite by-passed Mortimer in the drawing-up and signature of this new deed, one which now revoked her earlier testament, still retained in Mortimer's office, in which she had left Summer Hill to Hetty. Nor did she inform Mortimer of her decision. That task was left to Pat Kennedy himself, on Mortimer's next visit to Summer Hill, when Pat showed him Frances's letter. Mortimer, on reading it, was just as astonished as Pat had been. More, since he wished to avoid any immediate bluntness, he was forced into an unaccustomed speechlessness – since it was obvious that Pat, with no apparent farming abilities, could never in any case keep on such a vast place, and would obviously sell the house, at least, at the first opportunity. When this thought, in the butler's subsequent words, was quite openly rebutted, Mortimer was even more astonished.

'Well, Pat,' he had said to him, 'she has rather put a millstone round your neck . . .'

"Oh, I don't know, sir,' Pat had replied, gazing greedily out over the valley from the butler's pantry window. 'There's more than enough land left about the place to make a fair living out of it . . .'

Mortimer, for once, had misread the man – discounting, in this old house servant, the much older Gaelic land hunger. Still, in this instance, he could not be so stupid. 'But the house, Pat, it's far too big to maintain on just the income from what's left of the land.'

Pat had considered this point, but only for a moment. 'Ah, well,' he said nonchalantly, 'sure there'd be no income from the house anyway. That could go.'

Mortimer saw then the depths of Frances's insane enmity – against her family, her class, her past, against the disaster she and the old Prince had contrived in the shape of Hetty. She would take revenge on all these things through the instrument of her servant who, she must know, would more certainly and completely destroy the place than even the most insensitive religious institution. In Pat's hands, unmarried and likely to remain so, the great house would be guaranteed to end with him, sold to some timber merchant, with the roof off within a year. It was sheer wilful malignity.

When Craig had finally gathered together all the major figures in his cast at the remote bend in the river – far from Cairo and further still from the various Fox headquarters in Nice, New York and Hollywood – he felt safe to hint, at least, at some of the real business in his script. He had already talked to the other principal actors, those engaged to play General Mai, Akhenaten's army commander, Ramose the Grand Vizier, Panhesy the High Priest at the Temple, Huya, major-domo to Queen Tiye, and the devious courtier Ay, whose wife was Nefertiti's royal nurse. Now he spoke to the three stars – Hetty, Clive Brook and Anna Barani, the Italian-American actress who was to play Queen Tiye, mother of Akhenaten – in the great royal saloon aboard the *Omar Khayam* the evening before the first day's shooting.

'What we have to remember, because it's at the heart of the story,' he told Hetty and Clive, 'is that yours is an obsessive, unequal relationship. It starts with love all right, as children together in Thebes and afterwards in Amarna. But it soon gets into every sort of disaster. You get to hate each other! . . .'

Craig gave his grim résumé light-heartedly. But Clive Brook, flicking through the pages of his own scenario, was puzzled. 'I don't see . . . much of that here, Craig?'

'No, that's only a basic scenario, Clive.'

Clive was equally relaxed, even joky, in return. 'Goodness me, Craig, I know Akhenaten's deformed, epileptic and so on – weak and sickly as a child. But I'd understood that when he takes up with Nefertiti, when he strikes out on his own up to Amarna and becomes full Pharaoh, well, I thought things were really better for him.'

'No. Though it seems so initially. Fact is, people like that, there's never really any final improvement. They're fated from the beginning. And certainly that's the case here, because you see . . .' He turned to Anna Barani. 'You see Akhenaten never really gets out of the grip of his mother, Queen Tiye. You see how she even comes up-river after them, from Thebes, takes another palace in Amarna, just down the road from them.' Craig consulted his own personal scenario again. 'Yes . . . It's one of those fatal three-cornered relationships, Akhenaten caught in his mother's apron strings – and he doesn't *want* to get away. So, realising his incapabilities, he takes it out on his wife: punishing Nefertiti in a way he'd like to punish his mother, but doesn't dare.'

'So I get the st-st-stick?' Hetty asked brightly. 'That's not really in the scenario either.'

'That's about the size of it!' Craig leant forward, enthusiastic now. 'But there's more to it because, after all, you put up with it, and no one does that unless they somehow *like* it, see?'

'Not really.'

'Nefertiti *enjoys* the pain,' he told her sweetly. 'As I said, it's a three-cornered deal, which never works, always fatal, a cat's cradle, all held together by their vices.'

'And me?' enquired Anna. 'My vice?'

'*Power*, Anna!' He stood up, lit a cigarette, looking out on the violet light of the river, then turned to her. 'Because you're the real power, literally, behind the throne. That's why you follow the two up-river from the old court at Thebes – even before your own husband, Amenhopis III, dies. And when he does and Akhenaten becomes full Pharaoh at Amarna, it's you who tries to pull the strings – it's what you've planned all along, from the very beginning, in marrying them off as children, thinking Nefertiti's just a beautiful doll, a Syrian princess of no apparent account. You're the *dea ex machina . . .*'

'God's sake, Craig, speak English!' Hetty interjected.

But Anna understood him well enough. 'That's not in the photoplay,' she said.

Craig took no notice. 'Yes, Anna – you're the person that makes everything happen. But what you don't bargain for is Nefertiti as a grown woman, her own tough actions – and reactions. She accepts the punishment from Akhenaten, driven into all sorts of impossible corners by him. But eventually the worm turns – she takes up with Akhenaten's young half-brother Tutankhamun and has her revenge on her husband –'

'Yes, that's in the scenario,' Hetty interrupted again brightly. 'When Akhenaten becomes fre-fre-friendly with his other half-brother Smenkahare – and Nefertiti sets the snakes on him. But what I don't see, Craig, is why she doesn't do away we-with Queen Tiye instead. *She*'s caused all the trouble.'

It was a good question – and the answer certainly was not in the script. 'Simple,' Craig replied with a note of triumph. 'Akhenaten falls in *love* with his half-brother, more than his mother. So Nefertiti has to kill what he loves most.'

They were all puzzled at this. Hetty finally said, 'I don't quite get it – I thought this whole story was about a we-we-wonderful new religion up-river, doing away with all the old false gods, giving the people real love and hope when everything gets better. Instead, well, with all these de-de-deviants – it's like the Ship Café back in Hollywood on a bad night.'

'But that's the whole point of the story – exactly!' Craig was patient now, quiet. 'How we fool ourselves – because every god is false. And what matters is the truth about ourselves and the fact that we always try and hide this.'

'What – all this punishment, incest, death and sex?' Clive enquired, no longer so lighthearted.

'Well, of course – that's what we hide most! And, unless we first have an insight into people's sexual loves and hates and conflicts, there's no chance an audience can get to make sense of all the otherwise apparently crazy actions in the story. Do you see?'

They did not. But Craig was in charge. He must know what he was doing. They were all somewhat in awe of him. They had to be. *Nefertiti* looked like being the biggest, the most expensive picture ever made – bigger than *Intolerance*, bigger than *Ben Hur*.

Clive and Anna withheld any further doubts they had about this new scenario, anxious not to expose what really worried them then, which was their ability to enact some of these perverse rites. But Hetty, who found these new ideas of Craig's interesting, even titillating, wanted to know more. 'Was all this in the history books, Craig? – these incestuous ge-goings on, Akhenaten being a pansy and taking up with his half-brother, Nefertiti throwing him over then and going for the other half-brother?'

Craig laughed. 'Why, of course! And not just in the history books. You can see it all on the wall paintings, the hieroglyphics, in the royal tombs.'

Craig omitted to point out that these were his own interpretations of the lives of the three royal personages, based on much conflicting interpretations of the wall paintings which, at best, could only be made to suggest the possibility of such decadent relationships. However, given the picture he wanted to present of an ideal love and faith destroyed in Akhenaten's court by ruthless power struggles and by every sort of sexual domination and perversity, he had grasped at any hint of the bizarre or the unusual in those royal cartouches that might confirm his theme, which was really one of hate, not of love.

But he was equally keen not to alarm his cast with any over-emphasis of these depravities, so he continued now in lighter vein. 'And anyway our story is mild by comparison with the real thing. Why, many of the Pharaohs married their full sisters, even their daughters, and had children by them. So we're only touching the surface of what really went on in those days!'

Hetty felt a twinge of disappointment. So much did she trust Craig's inspirations and abilities, so entirely had she come to identify with what she already knew of Nefertiti, that she longed to discover and impersonate these further and ultimate truths of this mysterious, provocative woman, no matter how unsavoury they were.

Impersonate these ultimate truths? Why, no, she thought – *experience*, entirely submerge herself in them. That was the secret – as it had been in all her earlier successes – that she did not act her parts, for she had hardly the formal training or ability, but *lived* them, whatever the emotional challenge or cost. And in this instance she knew intuitively, as Craig had, that the part had been made for her: Nefertiti's steel-tempered will to power, her wily manoeuvrings, above all her skill in deceiving herself and betraying her friends while all the time behaving as the innocent victim – these were some of Hetty's own natural qualities. She would thus, inevitably and easily, be living the part.

What Hetty did not know, since she had seen little of Craig's private scenario, were the other parts in Nefertiti's character, which Craig had contrived for the Queen: the vicious depths she was prepared to sink to in pursuit of her aims, the hatred, misery and degradation she would incur and propagate. And Hetty, in Craig's intent, would not simply impersonate these horrors either. He would see to it that she experienced them in reality as well.

It was blue dark and moonlit with a sharp desert chill at four o'clock next morning. An hour later the sun god would rise over the forbidding mountains to the east, touching his city with the first shafts of pellucid lemon-yellow light. But already, in the tented camp, things were astir for the first day of principal photography – hundreds of shadowy figures moving to and fro by the light of brush fires, hurricane lamps and, in the recreated city of Amarna, under the glare of great Kleig lights set against silver reflectors, supplied from the two mobile generators at the railway siding across the river.

Already, in the previous days, Craig and the second unit director, with crowds of builders and carpenters masquerading as costumed extras, had filmed the final construction of the fabulous city. Now the gangs of property men, costumiers and all the other myriad technicians made ready for the first sequence with the stars and hundreds of extras – the triumphal entry of the royal party, carried in gilded, ostrich-feathered palanquins, into the great temple of Aten to dedicate the shrine. They would move from the palace, over the bridge, stopping at the Window of Appearances, then on across the vast columned plaza, before arriving at the holy of holies, mounting the steps below the great altar to the inner sanctum.

The sequence, they had calculated, would last up to eight minutes in real time – and the cameras, tracking back on top of the steel derrick, would follow every bit of the action. Johnny Seitz was on the derrick at that moment ready to start rehearsals and filming as soon as possible after first light, for this was the sequence which would have to be completed before the sun approached its meridian. Two Bell and Howell cameras, with extended magazines, had been set on top of the derrick, with a third set on the elevator, fronting on to the plaza where, at the start of the tracking movement, the elevator would sink slowly – over the crowds, right down above the heads of the royal party, as they approached the high altar. Half a dozen other cameras, together with a number of small hand-held Eyemos, were dotted about the palace, the bridge, the Royal Way, hidden behind columns and pavilions in the plaza, ready to pick up incidental crowd shots.

Assistant directors ran to and fro in the flare-lit shadows of the tented camp to the north, from the costume marquees where the hundreds of *fellahin* were being dressed, to the dressing tents of the stars and featured players, to the armoury and chariot tents, to the main production office by the wharf on the river, where Winfield Sheehan himself, as Fox's production chief, had arrived from New York the previous day to see the picture started.

Mickey Ostrovosky, with a dozen Egyptian prop men, was in charge of seeing to the fresh flowers that morning. They had arrived in hundreds of water buckets, packed in damp moss, a whole wagon-load, on the train from Cairo the previous day – lotus flowers, syringa, elaborate wreaths of jasmine and bougainvillaea, great bunches of gladioli and orchids which would decorate the streets of Amarna and hang in clustered baskets in the temple plaza and above the shrine. And now, as Mickey moved through the streets with his men in the cool desert night, arranging the fragrant bunches above doorways, littering the streets with petals, the air took on a wonderful sweetness, the scent of orange blossom seeping everywhere through the darkness.

Other assistants busied themselves, setting high-backed, gilt-embossed ebony thrones by the altar or supervising the flowing ostrich plumes for the palanquins. The whole river bank, for nearly half a mile, was alive with flickering light, yellow tinder fires and brilliant piercing carbon arcs, the shadows of some strange warrior people, preparing these magic weapons – lights, cameras, props – as if on a night before battle. Yet despite the fact that upwards of a thousand people were on the move that morning, there was a feeling of restraint and order under the waning moon.

But beneath this, and especially among the professional technicians, there was an air of tense, repressed excitement, even fear. They had hitched themselves not to a star here but to some quite unknown comet. A production of this size, so far from Hollywood or any other studios, had never been attempted before. *Ben Hur* had come nearest to it, the previous year in Rome, and that had ended in all sorts of disaster. Now their professional lives were largely in the hands of one man and one woman, sitting then at the centre of this vast web of activity, in Laura Bowen's dressing tent.

Hetty at last faced the moment she dreaded, which she had postponed until these final hours – when all her fine dark curls would be cut to the skull, that being the strict fashion of the time, and replaced in her day-to-day wear by one of Nefertiti's magnificent head-dresses or by a variety of tightly-coiled, shoulder-length wigs. Hetty saw the pairs of scissors laid out on the dressing table in front of her, like instruments of torture. She began to sweat in the chill night air, seeing the scissors rise. She closed her eyes.

The French hairdresser, a Madame Dolores from the studios in Nice, with her assistant, snipped away expertly. Craig stood beside Hetty, watching the big illuminated mirror, Hetty sitting there mute and still, eyes firmly shut. It was just after four in the morning. Craig held his breath.

Hetty, at the end of the hair-cut, with just a dark even stubble erect over her scalp, looked astonishing. She had changed utterly, but was equally striking. She was *gamine*, boyish, looking far younger, fifteen and not twenty-five. Her great oval blue eyes seemed far more prominent; her cheeks more hollow – her delicately shaped ears displaying elfin points, her whole face nude. And yet, despite this brutal cropping, there was no real air of the urchin. What before, with her rich raven curls, had been warm yet formal was now cold and barren but intensely regal.

She opened her eyes, trembling, looking at herself in the mirror. 'Wonderful!' Craig said to her, before she had a chance to speak, brushing his lips over her wounded scalp. 'I'll leave the dressers and make-up to complete the picture. See you in an hour.' Then he bent down, whispering, 'You were born for her. Remember, I told you?' She nodded, and he kissed her again before leaving. But he turned at the tent flap. 'Hey! – don't forget the scent!' he called back and she nodded once more.

Make-up came first with Chuck Stonor, all the way out from Hollywood with his myriad powders, lotions, unguents, lipsticks and eye-liners, an hour's work of infinite care – painting her eyelids with green shadow, her lips a soft raspberry, accentuating her eyebrows with kohl, her cheeks with rouge, dabbing her face and neck with a Leichner apricot powder.

The jeweller had her say then, with pendant amethyst earrings tipped with gold sun discs, ivory bracelets, a girdle and stomacher of gold plaques in the shape of tiny fish, and then the *pièce de résistance*, a magnificent deep-collared necklace, row upon row of lapis lazuli and red cornelian beads held against a filigree of gold wire, ending in a crescent just above her breasts.

Afterwards, standing at a full-length mirror, with the portrait bust of Nefertiti as a model next to it, the dresser put on her the royal gown over a thin, skin-toned elastic body stocking – material in the finest transparent linen, the colour of ripe wheat, loosely pleated over the bodice, gathered under the breasts with the girdle, then running down to her ankles, embroidered with two long panels, threads of pure gold and silver, intertwining every six inches, forming sun-bursts.

Finally the wardrobe mistress took up the magnificent headdress, eighteen inches high, tilted and flared, inset with hundreds of gold rosettes and green malachite stones, ribbed in bands of red and blue, with the royal uraeus, the sacred serpent, mounted at the brow – and placed it carefully on her shaven head.

The effect was stunning. Flaring out like a fan high above her, the headdress dropped in a sheer, unbroken line, narrowing in an inverted triangle, dead straight across her temples, her slanting cheeks, to the perfect base point of her chin.

Hetty smiled faintly as she looked at herself, comparing the vision in the mirror with the bust of Nefertiti next to it. But the others could only look at Hetty, even more striking than the wonderful bust, vividly alive, royal and beautiful beyond all imagining.

Back at her dressing table Hetty picked up the little cut-glass bottle of scent which Craig had given her in Nice. 'Nefertiti'. He'd had it specially created for her at a factory up in the hills near Grasse, asking her not to use it until the first day's filming. 'But the camera won't smell it!' she had told him. 'No, and it won't capture any of the colours in your make-up or costume – or see much of your bare scalp either. But that's not the point! *You'll* smell it, *you'll* feel the stubble, see the colours. And that's what I want – that you feel and see and smell everything, experience *everything*, just as Nefertiti herself would have done, no matter what the cost or trouble.'

She opened the bottle now, dabbing the sun-gold liquid on her wrist, bringing it to her nose. Expecting something rich, mysterious and musky, the perfume surprised her. It was a young girl's scent, delicately fresh: an initial strain of verbena, she thought, but cut with something tart, a hint of lemon – and then, at the back of her nose as she inhaled, a waft of subtle violet . . . It reminded her of something she could not quite place. What was it?

Then it came to her, a swirl of happy memories and pleasures out of the past, that same violet smell, regained now from the little bottle. Of course, it was Léonie's perfume, a scent she had always used, years before, warmed through nights in bed together, spreading from one body to another, shared indivisibly by morning.

Hetty's face, as if the bottle had released an evil genie, clouded at the memory of these old intimacies, thoughts of Léonie again, intruding once more, when for so long she had so successfully repressed them. And now she was forced to remember Dermot's words in the Semiramis Hotel once more, how Léonie and Robert had married. And the outrage of this finally struck home to her then and she was bitterly angry. 'I will wait for you . . .' Léonie had written in her last letter. Well, she hadn't. She had married Robert, and by that act had really betrayed her – their love, their schooldays, their long adolescence, their promises together. She had, as Hetty conveniently remembered it, largely forgiven Léonie for deserting her in going to Paris to see her mother that time. But this was unforgivable, this marriage – a slap in the face – because it undermined her whole earlier life, took the comfort of Léonie finally away from her, set at nought her own dominance over her.

It never crossed Hetty's mind, even at this late stage, that she, not Léonie, was responsible for the real desertion. For, just like Craig in his obsessive fantasies made flesh, she had come, not to lie about her earlier life and behaviour, but simply to deny all knowledge of it, to invent instead a succession of overlaid, alternative lives, false lives, then and now, which she lived and believed in as gospel.

The others noticed Hetty's expression of curdled disapproval. The dresser asked anxiously, 'Is it – is it not all right?'

'No. No, nothing's wrong.' Then she dismissed them curtly. 'Until I'm called, I'd like to be alone.'

When they left, Hetty gazed in the mirror, turning her head, the gleaming gold rosettes in the headdress winking in the bright light. 'I will – wait – for – you . . .' she said, spacing the words out viciously. Then she started to bunch her fingers, cracking the joints. Finally, her face now a mask of rancorous spite, she muttered the words: 'Nefertiti, great in favour, lady of grace, sweet of love, mistress of the North and South, Queen of the Two Lands, all pe-pe-powerful, le-living for ever and ever . . .'

These last stammered tones were far from suited to such regal testimony. But then they were not meant as such. Hetty, all her earlier fears and uncertainties returned, was voicing a royally vindictive curse. At this moment, just as she was about to set the final seal of power and success on her life, the ghost of Léonie had risen before her, come to taunt and plague her. And now that Léonie's implacable spirit had been so revived in this perfume about her body, Hetty could no longer ignore or repress it. Léonie, she realised, embedded thus in her very flesh, would be a constant reproach to her from then on, mocking her in this happy marriage with Robert. That was the worst thought of all – how those two, over whom for so long she had held sway, who had both loved her as she well knew, had now quite thrown her over. Hetty longed for some royal sorcery then that would annihilate space and allow her to confront Léonie with her treachery – longed somehow to revenge herself on her.

A few hours later, held aloft in the gilded palanquin, with its canopy of ostrich feathers and translucent alabaster headboard of the sun's disc, Hetty crossed the bridge with Akhenaten, and three of their daughters, stopping at the Window of Appearances; where she and the Pharaoh, alighting, took handfuls of lotus petals from huge faience vases, scattering them over the exultant crowd beneath them.

Mickey, in charge of the extras on the Royal Way at that point and dressed as one of them, stood immediately beneath Hetty, gazing up at her, apparently quite naked beneath the fine cotton gown, every curve in her figure visible and provocative behind the transparent material – the ultimate in cool suavity, arctic-blue eyes in the blazing light, bamboo-thin in wind-drifting voile, an ice maiden in these voluptuous desert airs.

'Nefertiti' – 'The beautiful woman has come.' How exactly she translated her name, Mickey thought – and how he desired her! But her face that morning more than ever confirmed the distance between them, this remote, untouchable woman, this undoubted Queen. Her expresson was more than usually set, he noticed – a faraway smile, circumspect, dilatory, almost blind somehow.

What a fine actress, he thought! – already, in this first sequence, completely living the part, scheming, thinking of the other future machinations in the plot, how she would soon come to manipulate Akhenaten and eventually destroy him.

Looking up at her face then, Mickey entirely believed in the reality of her emotion, her malign instincts and intents – convinced, too, by the veracity of everything he saw before him, the glorious royal panorama on the bridge, the costumed Egyptians milling about, the whole gilt-drenched scene thrillingly alive in the dazzling sunlight, as the petals rained about him, trodden underfoot, the perfume rising. And it seemed to him then, in the thronging excitement, that all of them, by some unexplained magic, had, indeed, returned in time three thousand years.

Then, as the royal party moved on, Mickey turned and saw the great steel camera derrick in the plaza starting to move, Johnny Seitz on top of it, his cap back to front. And he realised how he was caught, not in truth, but in an immense fantasy, a charade of Hollywood props and costumes, a dream of plaster and papier-mâché, all of it skin-deep, insubstantial as the frail zephyr breeze that drifted in from the desert, fluttering the sun-disc pennants. The whole thing was a vast conceit, a glittering contrivance, an offering, not to Aten the Sun God, but to the celluloid recording angel. And this thought, that one could dispense with corrupt reality and recreate the world in one's own image through the incorruption of make-believe, excited him even more.

A month later, far across the Mediterranean in a lurid sunset, the French Messageries Maritimes liner, the *Provençal*, left Marseilles bound for Naples, Port Said and the Far East. Robert and Léonie stood by the afterdeck rail watching the coast slip away in the indigo twilight. It had been freezing the day before in Paris that January and almost as cold for most of the train journey down. But now, in this first hint of moist southern warmth rising from the sea, propelled by a dry wind from Africa, they could take off their heavy topcoats for the first time, and breathe a wonderful softness in the air.

'Naples, Port Said, Bombay,' Léonie said. 'We could go all the way to Indo-China!'

'Egypt'll be enough . . .'

'It'll be *everything*!' She hugged him, watching a great lone sea bird hovering above the stern, gliding along, following them, like a lost spirit. Then she shivered involuntarily, as if someone had just walked over her tomb.

6

'A CTION!'
    Craig sat intently behind the lights and camera on a moored raft, on the ornamental lake behind the walls of the royal palace, its water filled with blue lotus flowers and papyrus. Hetty, in a short, tightly-curled wig and another revealing day gown, sat in the bows of a small gilded boat with Clive Brook in the stern.

It was one of Craig's new scenes, set some few years on in his version of the story, when Nefertiti continually taunts her weak and pleasure-loving husband – already, with his harems, epilepsy, drinking and feasting, prematurely aged, going to fat; the elongated skull, sensuously full lips, the deep-set shadowed eyes and generally feminine air turning him into a freak. Akhenaten started to paddle the craft past the camera.

'Right!' Craig went on talking as the camera turned. 'Now, as he paddles, Laura, you're fiddling with that papyrus leaf – yes, that's it – now you reach forward with it, start tickling him – the lips, the chin, go on! – you're provoking, *annoying* him, not playing with him, for Christ's sake! It's *malicious* and he can't prevent you – yes, that's right, Clive! Keep both hands on the paddle – then you try unsuccessfully to swat the papyrus away.'

The little boat drifted past them, Hetty tickling, taunting the lugubrious figure with unconcealed joy. It passed out of shot.

'Okay, cut!' Craig yelled. 'And print it.' He was working fast on this establishing shot, anxious to move on to the closer shots with them in the boat, when he could introduce some real venom into the proceedings.

'Right!' He talked almost aggressively to the two stars beside the lake, while the technicians prepared the next set-up, in which the little boat, tied against the camera raft, would be propelled across the water for the close shots. 'Now we have your title, Laura,' he went on, consulting his scenario. '"You make so much of your new faith, Akhenaten – a whole city built in honour of the sun – yet you've forgotten your old simple pleasures with me, how we used to swim." Okay, that's the title here. So we'll be facing you in the bows, Laura, saying this, continuing to annoy him with the papyrus before you provoke him even more, by jumping in the water, swimming away. Of course, what you're maybe hoping here, knowing he can't swim any more, is that he'll jump into the water after you and drown. Well, he does just that – but doesn't drown. We just see you struggling in the water here – the rest of the sequence, the underwater stuff, is for the tank back in Nice. Okay?'

'What about the wigs and make-up – in the water?' Clive asked.

'Hell, they'll come off, won't they?' Craig was impatient. 'It's a real struggle. You're all keyed up after that teasing with the papyrus – you know very well she's provoking you, taunting you, questioning your masculinity – so you're blind with rage, with no thought that you can't swim any more – and you *go* for her!' Craig smiled for the first time, happy in the setting-out of this impending confrontation. 'It's a real barney out there in the lake. Jesus, Clive! – this is the vital point, when you *realise* how much you hate her, yet know you can't do without her!'

Clive's sour expression, as he glanced at Hetty, confirmed all this hatred in reality. Having been so tormented by her all morning, he looked as if he could willingly strangle this bitch. Hetty, as she sat on the canvas chair, responded in kind, glowering at him. She and Clive, just as Craig had intended, had come to hate each other.

All actors, he knew, nurtured a secret animosity towards one another. And it had been his intention to unearth and provoke these jealousies and antipathies, so to lend the keener edge to this particular drama, with its alternative slave-and-master roles, its vicious power plays, its sadism and other sexual perversions. Craig had manoeuvred these factors into the players' real lives, so that on camera they would all the more realistically enact them.

Hetty thrived on her part. Clive hated the indignities of his. But he was aware that it would not always be so. The tables would soon be turned once more, as in earlier sequences they had shot, when he would take a cruel ascendancy, inflicting on Nefertiti the various and more intimate punishments the script required for her. And all this Craig had contrived as well – in these see-saw opportunities for domination and degradation the more to enhance his tale of hatred and obsession, of doomed love.

So it was that the subsequent scenes in the water, when Hetty jumped overboard and Clive joined her, were much more vicious than they might have been – the couple nearly coming to grief, though the lake was only a few feet deep, spluttering and ducking, wigs washed away, half-naked in their flimsy linens, as they struggled with each other, first mimicking a playfulness, as Craig had instructed, and then exaggerating his further instructions by really coming to grips with each other.

It was a desperate frolic, and Craig prolonged the cruelty and indignity for Hetty by insisting on several re-takes, with consequent renewed make-up and dressing, particularly in the last scene of the morning, in which the royal couple, back now on the lake shore, indulged in a slapping match, Akhenaten finally in the ascendant.

'Listen, Clive,' Craig said fiercely after the third re-take. 'It's no good – and we can't waste the time now. If you can't do the false slaps, do it for real.'

And Clive did just that, slapping Hetty hard on the cheek, repeatedly, for another two takes until Craig was satisfied and Hetty was genuinely hurt, in genuine tears.

'You *shit*,' she said to Craig quietly, but venomously, as she left the set with her dresser.

'You're welcome!' he called after her, smiling a fraction.

Mickey, watching, was appalled at Craig's cruelty. And when, as was his custom now, he brought Hetty's lunch tray to her tent, he found her with her dresser, still suffering, red-eyed, wiping the make-up from her bruised cheeks, in a bath robe, a towel turbanned round her head, sitting in front of the mirror.

He wanted to say something consolatory, but wondered if he dared. Up to now they had exchanged little more than pleasantries. Finally, thinking of the first thing that came to mind, he blurted out in his polyglot accent, half-Russian, half-French, 'Witch hazel, for bruises. It's an English lotion – my Maman always used it in St Petersburg when I was a child. Will I . . . try to get you some?'

Hetty, who until then had barely noticed him, looked up, seeing his reflection in the mirror. She was suddenly charmed. 'Why, Mickey, what a kind thought –'

'It's just,' he ran on, taking advantage of her warm response before she changed her mind, 'well, it must have been *pénible* – I was watching the whole thing. All those slaps. I was sorry . . .' He paused. He was sorry that she was married to such a brute of a husband. But he could not say this. Instead, to his astonishment, she said it for him.

'No need to be-beat about the bush, Mickey. I know what you want to say: how can I pe-pe-put up with such a man? Well, I don't know. I really don't . . .'

There was silence in the tent as she rubbed off the last of her make-up. 'You can go now, Maria.' She turned to the Italian dresser, then back to the reflection of Mickey in the mirror. 'Yes, it *was* painful . . .' She looked at this youth behind her, standing awkwardly with the lunch tray, with his tufts of damp hair sticking up like a mop, his large rather baleful eyes, his indiarubber features. 'But Craig insists on it all that way. Perfectionist, you know!' she continued ironically. 'Do pe-put the tray down.' Mickey did so. 'No, don't go,' she told him, blinking her eyes, swabbing them with iced water.

Mickey turned back. '"Perfectionist",' he said pointedly. '*Oui, mais tout de même . . .*'

Hetty shrugged her shoulders. '*Ça – ça doit être comme ça.*' They talked in French, Mickey more confident now, discussing the morning's work, before Hetty said eventually, 'The point is, Mickey, all great directors are shits – there's maybe no other way to do it, to control things, to get the real pe-pe-performances.'

'*Oui, mais* – all *husbands?*' He looked at her with great sympathy, something suddenly very adult in his eyes: a loving compassion.

'*Touché* . . . You're right. I can't explain that, right now. But what I we-wanted to say, Mickey, was – well, you're far too nice a person ever to make a great director. And that's what you want to be of course. But I tell you what – you should really be an *actor*. You'd make a great comic, with that wonderful face of yours.

No! – I've we-watched you. Really!' She swung round in her chair, confronting him squarely.

'Oh, I don't think so, Miss Bowen –'

'Yes! You should.' She gave him one of her nicest smiles, all the more telling in its sadness. 'Think about it. And do call me Laura, not Miss Bowen.'

She felt much better then. She might almost have been flirting with him. After he had left, her eyes remained on the space where he had been standing, so gauche and charming. *Distingué*, that was the word for him. And more, he was somehow so vulnerable and thus provoking. And best of all he adored her. She was entirely aware of that and had felt more than inclined just then to encourage this adoration, for with both the other men in her life, with Craig and Clive, it had been a terrible morning. She longed to call Mickey back and kiss him.

For nearly six weeks' filming now Craig had bullied and punished her, on and off the set, on camera and in his direction of her – all justified, as he had intimated, through the cruelties the script demanded from and for her. And he had laughed at her complaints: 'You're welcome!' Yes, she had finally complained, retaliated, but not truly resisted. And she did not know why, just as she had told Mickey. Logically, she argued, Craig was right: the scenario *did* demand these indignities. And she trusted his interpretations here, knowing, too, how she must live the part. But emotionally the cost of doing this was already high and getting steeper.

Off camera now, her life was in tatters. She was constantly on edge, frustrated, at a loss, almost a nervous wreck – a situation made all the worse by the fact that Craig, from the very beginning of the picture, had left her to sleep alone on King Fuad's steamer, he himself taking up permanent residence in his bedouin tent in the middle of the canvas city.

Their love-making had ceased ever since their arrival in Egypt nearly two months before. And this, too, was very much part of Craig's plan. He wanted, for her depraved role, to sharpen her tastes and frustrations in this quarter, not concerned in the least that he might be playing with fire. For, after all, Craig had never really loved her. From the beginning he had loved a fantasy woman in Hetty called Nefertiti. Craig had always really only loved his picture.

Hetty returned to the mirror, still thinking of Mickey, wanting him again in the tent with her, longing for his kindness and sympathy – anxious just as much to share in this, to return the compliment, to dispense with all this fictitious, tumultuous and hurtful a life. She longed then to live as an ordinary woman, never to have heard of Nefertiti or Laura Bowen. 'Witch hazel,' she murmured the name of the balm to herself. 'Witch hazel . . .' Then she turned away from this hateful, pretentious vision of herself as an actress in the mirror and began to sob.

Then she saw the great gold and blue headdress on the bust of Nefertiti next to the mirror, and looked into those glittering, deep, all-powerful, seductive eyes – and reminded herself how all this power was hers, too, in reality: power in life, in love – vengeance, destruction, as she willed. She had not acted her way to these strengths, she told herself once more. They were her real character, her burden. She could no longer return to the uncomplicated, innocent decencies of her old temperament. She must accept the responsibilities consequent on her present nature – the duties, the unquestioned authority, solemn judgements, just but painful retributions, the ultimate victories of a Goddess, a Queen.

'Nefertiti,' she said to herself in the mirror. 'Queen of the Two Lands, Lady of Grace, All Powerful . . .' And this time she intoned the words without the least hesitancy or stammer. She bunched her fingers together, and soon she had quite pulled herself together, resuming all her old petulant command and anger.

All was not lost yet. She was still the star of the picture. They could get by without Craig at this point, but not without her. 'Craig they can replace,' she said to the mirror. 'But not me, not half-way through the picture. Millions of dollars! – everyone depends on *me* for their future . . . Cards!' she went on quietly. 'I still have all the cards to play.' She would show these men, Clive and Craig – she would show Craig especially – she was not to be treated so. And the answer was quite simple.

She had long wanted to take one of the Arab horses, hired for the production, out on her own – some of them were still stabled on the west bank of the river – and ride forever into the sunset of the Libyan desert. Well, not quite forever. She wanted just to get away alone, with the excuse of visiting some of the ancient Pharaonic monuments west of Beni-Souef, away from the river on the edge of the desert – the ruined temple of Henen-Seten, centre of worship to the Ram God Hershef, and further west in the Fayoum oasis the decaying brick pyramid of Hawara, the tomb of Amenhotep III and the fabulous remains of the Great Labyrinth.

Well, she would do just this, soon, when she was most needed. But she would not tell anyone. Of course not! That was the whole point. She would simply dress up – disguise herself as an Arab, that was an idea! – cross the river, take one of the horses and disappear for a day or two. That would set the cat among the pigeons! – show Craig how indispensable she was. For without her, of course, the whole production would grind to a halt. The plan was all so apt and obvious. She would regain Craig's respect. And even if she did not she would certainly have her revenge on him. It was a splendid idea, for besides everything else she could go back to her old derring-do disguises again, and take to galloping horses, just as she had done all those years ago in Summer Hill with Léonie . . .

Léonie? She thought of her again now, Léonie married to Robert and the insult of all that. Well, that could wait. She had to pay Craig back first. And, besides, she could do nothing about Léonie and Robert in any case. They were thousands of miles away.

That same day Robert and Léonie arrived in Cairo. Embarking at once on one of Thomas Cook's Nile steamers, for their two-week trip to Luxor and Aswan, they had read no local papers, heard no gossip . . . were quite unaware of what lay up-river.

'"The tombs of the Valley of the Kings"!' Léonie read excitedly from her Baedeker as the boat cast off above Kasr el Nil bridge, paddles churning the water, moving upstream towards Roda island. 'Oh, Robert – Tutankhamun! Remember Howard Carter, when he first got a look inside his tomb? – "Wonderful things, wonderful things"!'

At Amarna next day, they started the sequences with Nefertiti, Akhenaten and his younger half-brother Smenkahare – at the point when Nefertiti, seeing the growing intimacy between the two men, decides to kill Smenkahare, kill what Akhenaten loves most, by setting the snakes on him, with the help of her equally malign confidant, the dwarf Puthmose, in the shape of Eddy Nolan.

The pit vipers and adders were venomous. But the scene in the royal palace gardens, in one of the little pavilions where Smenkahare is resting on a gilded day bed, was shot that morning through a large pane of glass, set across the floor of the pavilion, the snakes on one side, Smenkahare's couch on the other.

'Action!'

The handler released the snakes, pushing them out on the floor of the pavilion, where they wriggled sleepily, refusing to move. But later, when some field mice were procured and set at the bottom of the glass partition, the reptiles became entirely co-operative, slithering forward malevolently, ominously ... hungrily.

'Why, of course, Arnold! They're making that motion picture here – *Nefertiti* – some ways up-river.' Robert heard the drawling voice of the American woman, talking to her husband, on the steamer chair next to them. 'I *told* you – had it from the captain last night. We're going to stop by and take a look. Seems they've built a whole new city for it – right in the desert!'

'A motion picture?' Arnold was bored.

'Why, yes, a new Hollywood super-spectacle – with *Laura Bowen*!' She emphasised the excitement of this great name.

Léonie seemed asleep, binoculars in her lap, as Robert turned to her. His eyes were suddenly unfocused. He could barely see her, his heart was beating so furiously. Finally he managed to say, 'Léa? Did you hear?'

She opened her eyes and said quite calmly, 'Yes, I heard.' Then she looked at him, shading her eyes in the bright light. Her eyes – and her mind – were both quite clear. 'Fate?' she asked him lightly. Then she reached out and took his hand, gripping it firmly, closing her eyes again.

That evening their boat moored just downstream of the *Omar Khayam*, on the east bank of the river, below the rebuilt city of Amarna. From the foredeck, as they stood there under the awning taking a cocktail before dinner, the passengers could see the stern and Khedival flag of the royal steamer, not forty yards away. They were all agog now. The travel company, receiving permission to moor overnight, had also arranged for the passengers to visit some of the sets next morning. The Fox production manager had readily agreed. It was good publicity.

'Of course, we don't have to go,' Robert said, biting on his empty pipe. Léonie, cool and fresh in an eau-de-nil silk dress, sipped her glass of iced lime juice.

'Why not? I'm not afraid of meeting her.'

'No, it's not that –'

'But you *are*, Robert –'

'No, I'm not.'

'Well, we *won't* go visit the sets then. Honestly, doesn't really matter to me one way or another. Just I'm not going to worry about it.'

Just then there was a flurry of activity on the gangplank of the royal steamer, a group of people going aboard. Léonie lifted her binoculars. She saw Hetty almost immediately, obviously returning from the set with her dressers – saw her glance imperiously at the distant passengers before disappearing. And Léonie's heart at last began to beat much faster, seeing again this face once so loved, still vivid with all its old glamour.

She had indeed thought it fated – this astonishing conjunction on the river miles from anywhere. Would fate continue its schemes by actually bringing them together? She prayed not. Fate had an awful way of completing its schemes, she knew, and she feared this. Oh, how she feared it. For that glimpse of Hetty through the binoculars had brought back some of her old emotion, a nostalgia that pierced her heart – the clear memory of how she had once loved her and, so much worse, the knowledge that she could easily do so again.

For, of course, Léonie still loved Hetty, had never really ceased to love her – and the feeling had been re-born then. She loved her. And she loved Robert. And in an ideal world she would have loved both of them equally, concurrently, together. So that now she simply did not trust herself and longed to get as far away as possible from Hetty to avoid the occasion of sin, as it were. And, had they not both of them been stuck on board the steamer, she would have taken Robert away with her, there and then, caught a train or simply run from this awful temptation that fate seemed to be planning for her.

'All the same . . .' She turned calmly to Robert, hiding the turmoil in her heart. 'It is uncanny – coming all this way out here, just to find her moored right next to us!'

Robert, wishing that from the start Léonie had shown an obvious distaste at this proximity, had suppressed his annoyance. But now he said rather sharply, 'I just wish you weren't so matter-of-fact about it all.'

Little does he know, Léonie thought. So of course, all the more, she had to respond as if the presence of Hetty meant absolutely nothing to her. 'Oh, Robert!' she chided him, smiling. 'You mustn't be upset. Hetty can't touch us any more,' she lied. 'Why, we should be able to just go across, walk up that gangplank and meet her. It wouldn't matter!' She lied again, putting her hand on his arm. 'Robert? All that's over and done with. There's only you and me now. And, besides, there's no chance we're going to get to meet her anyway. We're only moored here for twenty-four hours – ships that pass in the night! There's absolutely nothing to it. And I tell you what!' she rounded on him enthusiastically. 'Just to make certain, we'll take off in the very opposite direction tomorrow! I was talking to the purser. Anyone who doesn't want to visit the picture sets tomorrow can ride horses out on the other side of the river – courtesy of the company! There are some wonderful old Egyptian monuments the purser told me, which tourists never see, west of Beni-Souef, out in the desert. We'll go there instead. I'd love to ride out into the desert! For ever and ever! – galloping Arab horses!'

'What old monuments? Surely they're all on the banks of the river?'

'No! The purser said – and I've been looking at my Baedeker. There's the ruined temple at Henen-Seten, to the Ram God Hershef, at the edge of the desert. And further on in the Fayoum Oasis even more fabulous things – the brick pyramid at Hawara, the tomb of Amenhotep III – and best of all the site of the Great Labyrinth! Oh, Robert – let's do that! Let's get away, as far away as possible from here tomorrow, so there'll be absolutely no chance whatsoever of meeting her!'

Robert was reassured at last. Léonie, he saw now, so obviously, strenuously, hated this proximity with Hetty – felt defiled by it, he thought. He had misjudged her. Well, of course, he agreed, they would ride out the next day, as far away as possible from Hetty, so avoiding the remotest chance that fate might bring them all together.

'You're so right,' he said to Léonie, kissing her briefly. 'I'll tell the purser then. We'll need two horses – and a dragoman – tomorrow!'

Hetty, driven beyond endurance by Craig's continued cruelty, decided to disappear that very night. She had the dark make-up already, of course – and had made all the other basic arrangements, collecting and hiding in her wardrobe a dirty turban and an old *galibeah*. Leaving the royal steamer in the darkness, she would cross the river on one of the many ferry barges or feluccas that returned to the west bank and the railway sidings there each evening. Her Arabic was quite good enough now to ask and answer at least all the basic questions. She had collected some Egyptian money as well, concealed in a little drawstring leather bag at her waist. On the far side of the river she would steal one of the Arab horses, or bribe one of the grooms. And then the masterstroke! She had also collected – it had been a relatively easy matter from the company's wardrobe department – all the sartorial items appropriate to an Arab horseman, a sheik of the desert, which she would wear under her dirty turban and *galibeah*: flowing white linen robes, soft leather boots, a crescent-shaped, jewel-encrusted dagger, a dazzling silk headdress with a silver-gilt headband.

In this perfect disguise she would ride away, free of every pain and constraint, out into the desert. As to directions – she had her Egyptian Baedeker, with its maps and routes to these legendary ruined monuments beyond the river. And, better still, she had several times inspected the large-scape map of the whole area set up in the production office. So she knew how the horses were stabled in a long tent beyond the makeshift railway station on the other side of the river, at the edge of the Nile cultivation, giving straight out on to the fields of cotton and berseem clover. A track led through these patchwork fields, beside the railway at first, before turning west towards the temple of Henen-Seten at the edge of the cultivation – and beyond that straight across the desert, for a few miles, she thought, to the Fayoum oasis. There were possible risks, she supposed. But she would take some basic food and water. And her new toy, an ebony-sheathed, ivory-topped telescopic swordstick, that declined to the length of a neat foot ruler, which she had bought from an antique shop in Cairo.

Risks, yes. For what was the point, she had thought from the very beginning, of just disappearing and lurking in some seedy local hotel or back at the Semiramis in Cairo, where they would look for her first in any case. Her plan was necessarily more elaborate. It was not only that she wished to punish Craig. She wanted just as much to break away from these celluloid fantasies, and return to something real in her life, to indulge in some free act of her own unique creation.

And besides, because of Craig, she had begun to think her reason endangered – not from her old black-outs, which had never recurred once the film had been agreed – but from a simple lack of individual effort. In the vast picture company she lay at the centre – the queen bee – her every whim immediately catered for. And that was part of the problem. She was trapped in the middle of the hive. She longed to fly – longed for some rash individual adventure, to take fate entirely in her own hands once more. And, yes, this entailed risks. But that was exactly her purpose, to test herself again, as she had done so successfully often before, against destiny – this time in the shape of something quite wonderful, she felt, waiting for her, where the green land of the Nile valley gave out, at the edge of the great desert.

Towards ten o'clock, after supper, she dismissed her servants and went below to her cabin. Here she made herself up and dressed carefully, in two layers – as *fellahin* and Arab horseman – then put a headscarf over her old turban and her ankle-length cape over all her other clothes, before taking a final look in the mirror. A little bulky. But everything else was in order. She went up on to the long foredeck, its sun-awning drawn back, and walked to and fro, as she did every evening, taking the air under the open night sky, flushed now with a low moon from somewhere over the hills to the east. She stood watching the ferry lights flicker on the placid water. It was a perfect night: warm, dry, exquisitely soft.

Two royal sentries, in white tunics and red fezes and with ancient rifles, manned the approaches on shore, standing next to a flaring brazier by the end of the gangplank. But, for over a week now, she had prepared her escape, going ashore each evening, strolling to and fro along the bank for five minutes, smoking a cigarette. So she knew already where she could change her clothes – among some scrub back from the river, hidden behind the wooden cabin that had been set up as a barrier and guard post some thirty yards downstream, on the path leading to the ferry wharf, almost opposite the tourist paddle steamer that had been moored there overnight.

She lit a cigarette, drew her headscarf more firmly about her, and walked down the gangplank. The sentries came to attention, saluting smartly. She nodded gracefully and, cape trailing in the dusty path, she moved casually away, thirty yards upstream first, then back, passing the men once more, moving south towards the cabin. She repeated the process again. On her second return downstream, glancing behind her, she saw the sentries, backs towards her, engaged in soft conversation. In an instant she was over the railing and behind the cabin in the bushes, discarding her cape and headscarf, letting out her dirty *galibeah*, and walking as fast as she dared while still mimicking the rolling gait, the casual amble, of the *fellahin*, past the tourist steamer with its sounds of laughter, making for the ferry wharf a few hundred yards away.

It was nearly midnight, with a slight desert chill in the air now, before she took the last felucca over the river, sitting huddled in the stern among a score of others like her, the great lateen sail creaking on its boom, taut against the river breeze, a vast, pale white kite against the velvet sky above her. A *fellahin* said a few words to her, something about the cold on the river, she thought. Lowering her head and wrapping the turban more firmly about her face she mutted, '*Il ham di'illah.*' As God wills. The man said nothing more.

On the far bank, leaving the felucca at the flare-lit jetty, she stayed with the other men until they had crossed the rail sidings and gradually dispersed among the huts and tents of the makeshift village. Then she set off south along the track towards the stable tent, some few hundred yards away, she thought. Leaving the flares and hurricane lamps of the huddled village behind her, she was soon in darkness. But there was enough light in the sky to show her the dust-white path, and she made easy progress.

She stopped suddenly, alarmed. There was another track, immediately to her left now, leading off into the cultivation – and coming along it she heard the rising sound of hoofbeats, some dozens of horses, a clatter in the night with the chink of bridles. The land was quite flat. There was nowhere to hide. And then she saw them, silhouetted against the paler night sky on the horizon: a group of mounted soldiers, some twenty horses, coming towards her at a sharp trot, not fifty yards away.

There was nothing for it. The troop had spotted her, cantering forward now, where they met at the T-junction. She saw the shadows of two men, in the lead, towering above her, then heard the British voice – young, tired, upper class, arrogant. 'All right, Sergeant, ask him where we can stable the horses then, where this horse boss is here.'

The sergeant, an older man with a Cockney accent, relayed the question to Hetty in kitchen Arabic. Hetty, tugging the ends of the turban even more firmly about her face, shrugged. '*Ma fische hosan Reiss heneh,*' she said. No horse boss here.

'For God's sake, Patterson,' the officer remonstrated with the sergeant, 'why *should* there be any stabling here, in the middle of bloody nowhere?'

The sergeant dismounted and grasped Hetty by the throat as if to strangle her. 'Now, you're really going to tell me, you little wog! *Fein hosan Reiss?*' he shouted at her, before pushing her on to the dirt track and prodding her with his foot. Hetty could have killed him, as she felt the ebony swordstick handle pressing into her thigh against the earth. But suddenly, seeing a chance for herself in all these events, she changed her attitude. '*Aioua, Bey!*' she shouted up from the ground, in pleading, low-toned gutturals. '*Aioua! Hosan Reiss heneh! Henak, aho, khema.*' And she pointed up the track towards where she thought the stable tent was.

'He says the horse boss *is* here, sir,' the sergeant translated for the officer. 'Up the road in a stable tent. Knew I was right, the little bastard was lying . . .' Leaving her spreadeagled on the track, the troop moved off. Hetty, picking herself up, stumbled along after them.

The horse tent was indeed there, several hundred yards further down the road. When she got there the soldiers had dismounted, tethering their horses to a rail, while the officer and sergeant, waking the grooms, were berating them in rough Arabic. 'We need fodder and stabling here for the night . . .'

The other soldiers in the troop, taking bags and baggage from their horses, were preparing to bivouac nearby. Meanwhile the Egyptian grooms, awake now, and flopping about in their *galibeahs*, had started to lead the horses into the long tent, one by one, before unsaddling them. Hetty, her features barely distinguishable in the faint light of two storm lanterns, and dressed just like the other emerging grooms, stepped in among them, moving to and fro in the mêlée of horses and people, waiting her chance to pick out a suitable beast and lead it inside.

In the half-light she saw a white Arab mare, sharply arched neck, smallish, slightly piebald over its hind-quarters, a good-looking animal, from what she could make out, still saddled over a sheep's wool saddle-cloth. It was tethered next in line but one against the rail. She stepped in smartly, untied its halter, took it by the bridle and led it away. But, instead of going through the first of the tent entrances, she took it further along to a second, where there were greater shadows – then straight past that, rounding the tent corner, when she mounted the horse and trotted away.

What a piece of luck, she thought – coming on those British soldiers. It had saved her no end of trouble. But was it luck, she wondered then? Surely it was fate? It had all been meant. Of course! Why else? Fate had obviously stacked the cards entirely on her side, she felt, as she broke into a canter, feeling the pure surge of power then in the lithe animal beneath her, finding all her old riding skills again. Leaving the tent far behind her, she galloped along the moonlit track into the night.

Craig had equally liberating activities in view that same evening, as he'd had on several other occasions since the start of the picture. He had long since stopped making love with Hetty. But – just as in Hollywood with the young girls in the Ship Café – this had not curtailed his particular appetites here. He had discovered, some time before in the great tented city, the existence of several tactful Arab bordellos, catering to every taste, including his own. And in one such bedouin tent, at the edge of the desert, he had found exactly what he fancied – better, indeed, than anything he had fed on in Hollywood – a collection of dusky bedouin child brides, girls of twelve or fourteen, early developers, with whom, for an Egyptian pound or two, he could do what he would. And now, towards midnight, in his own disguise, not unlike Hetty's, of turban and *galibeah*, he made his way swiftly, silently, between the long tented alleyways, flares and brush fires dying as the city slept.

Crouching down at the entrance of the dark tent, and paying the old woman her money, he went inside. The sagging cloth, hardly five feet above him, brushed his rough turban, the space smelling of burst cinnamon, lit by a softly flaring hurricane lamp, the desert floor covered in further sacking. At first he could see little, only the dirty cloth partition a few yards in front of him, and beyond that another fainter light.

Rounding the edge of this curtain, his eyes more accustomed to the gloom, he saw the three girls, in various attitudes of repose, in flimsy shifts, one of them asleep, lying out on cheap cushions. The old woman put her head round the partition. '*Hashishe?*' she murmured. Without looking back Craig shook his head. Two of the girls, sitting up now, gave him glazed smiles. But he wanted the first, who slept, the tallest of them, her back towards him. He pointed to her, then sat down, cross-legged, on the floor to wait.

'*Aioua.*' He nodded at the other two, confirming something obviously expected of them. They woke the third girl then who turned, and seeing Craig smiled wanly, rubbing sleep from her eyes. Unlike the other two, she had a light grey, slate-coloured skin, a high forehead, crowned with fuzzy, tightly curled short hair, like a cloche hat right round – deep almond shaped eyes, thin semitic lips, little of anything negroid in her features – she looked Ethiopian; slim, potentially proud.

Hetty dismounted some miles further on in a palm grove, with the railway on one side and an irrigation canal on the other, took her off her old turban and dirty *galibeah* – then flounced out her sheik's dress, the long fine white cotton robes, before adjusting the silken headdress and its gilded headband. There was a patch of berseem clover by the canal. She let the mare graze and drink for a few minutes while she changed, then hid the old clothes, sinking them among some reeds by the water.

It was nearly one o'clock. She could just see the hands on her wristwatch, for the moon was high by now, away to her right. The air, at its chilliest now, was glitter-bright, the mare breathing faint cotton wool fountains on the night. Too bright? – if they were already following out looking for her?

She heard a gasping, bellowing noise in the distance. Turning in the saddle, she saw sparks flying up against the dark sky, heard the rumble on the rail tracks next to her, and finally the great dark shapes of engine and carriages rounded a curve – the night express from Luxor to Cairo.

Spurring her horse, she galloped away, white robes flowing behind her, billowing out in the sharp-aired moonlight, the mare given her head now, neat hooves drumming in perfect rhythm, almost paralleling the train's wheels' clatter as it gradually drew near, creeping up behind her.

Hetty bent low over the flying mane, worried that the mare might swerve and bolt to one side or the other – over the rail tracks or into the canal. Instead the animal seemed to relish the moonlit gallop, spurred on by the engine behind her, keeping to the straight flat path, even when the engine let out a piercing whistle.

Finally, however, the train caught up with her, the engine drawing almost level. Turning briefly, Hetty saw the turbanned drivers and the sparks erupting from the golden mouth of the fire box – before, encouraging the mare to one final effort, goading it with knees and heels, she drew away from the train, Hetty felt the ecstasy of victory.

In fact, the train, approaching a curve, had slowed, brakes squealing – approaching a hazard which Hetty didn't know of.

Suddenly she saw a red lantern on a five-barred gate in front of her, looming up, not thirty yards ahead, in the shadows. A man appeared, waving his arms, as she rushed towards the gate. The train, rounding the curve now to her right, let out another shrieking whistle. Then Hetty realised. The gate was on a railway crossing, already closed for the train to pass – or for her to vault over before it did. There was no chance of pulling up in time, the mare at full gallop – she would simply be thrown into the gate, or over it, into the path of the train. She spurred the mare on.

7

Robert and Lèonie, with a mounted dragoman, set off on the same track, with hired horses, later that same morning, a faint mist over the river now, an opaque lemon-yellow dawn, before the heat gradually burned its way through and the Nile gave up its wispy shroud.

By then they were several miles south on the route to Beni-Souef, moving over the rich alluvial landscape of cotton, sugar cane and clover, men and black-shawled women out working, dotted everywhere. They paused for a few minutes at the same point where Hetty had changed her clothes earlier that morning, in the shady palm grove by the irrigation canal. Léonie, moving away from the dragoman, took off her pith helmet, kneeling by the water.

'This is all far too tame,' she whispered to Robert, scratching her legs, itching now in the unaccustomed jodhpurs. 'If we stay with this old dragoman all day, we're never going to get anywhere. Look!' She showed him the map of the area in the Baedeker. 'We're about here, this village ahead, it's Barout-el-Bakar. And here's the temple of Henen-Seten – can't be more than three or four miles, north-west across the fields, by the edge of this big canal, the Bahr Youssef – that's the one that irrigates the whole Fayoum oasis. It'll be easy to find. So let's just leave the old man! Take off on our own!'

Robert was not convinced. 'We'll get lost.'

'Nonsense. It's all quite clear on the map. Can't miss it.' Léonie, just like Hetty, was filled with a desperate urge for adventure; something seemed to drive her away from the river. 'Oh, Robert,' she went on, 'I do so want to have a good gallop, way out there!' She gestured to the west. 'Yes! – get out into the desert.' She felt impelled in this journey westwards – impelled by she knew not what.

Robert shrugged. 'All right . . .'

'Look!' Léonie said suddenly, noticing something in the reeds in front of her – Hetty's old turban and *galibeah*. 'Someone's forgotten their washing!'

Ten minutes later, spurring their horses on, they left the dragoman far behind them, waving his arms hopelessly. Léonie, flushed with excitement, turned to Robert as they took off across a track over the fields. 'I love you!' she shouted. She did. And more: in this sudden freedom from the boat and the river, this certain escape from Hetty and everything to do with her at the film set by the river, Léonie, in celebration, confirming her release from all that surging feminine temptation, wanted to make love with him.

Hetty arrived at the ruined temple of Henen-Seten. The site, on unreclaimed desert by the banks of the wide canal, was quite deserted. The crumbling stone, the vast pylons, Osirian pillars and hypostyle columns, reared up at her through the early mists, as, dismounting, she walked towards the temple down a long avenue, flanked all the way on one side by ram-headed sphinxes. These huge beasts, their eyes and sloping noses emerging from the mist, seemed to study her unkindly. They frightened the mare, they frightened Hetty.

Ahead of her now, the two pylons, one on either side of the first temple gateway, appeared. Passing between them, she entered a long colonnaded forecourt, with vast fluted, bulbous pillars, each topped by a papyrus-bud capital, covered in cartouches and hieroglyphics, supporting broken architraves, the remains of what must once have been a whole stone block roof.

Beyond lay a second smaller columned court, this time partly roofed over, so that the light was frailer, uncertain. Suddenly she turned, looking upwards, at some sound – a bird?

She started backwards, terrified. The huge deformed faces were staring at her, each of them atop fifteen-foot-high statues, the ghostly features coming clear now through the wafts of mist: faces, not of rams, but in some vague human form, with the cold gaze of kings, all in a line, a dozen horribly eroded shapes. For the stone in their lips and cheeks, ears and noses, had been rubbed away by forty centuries – they had great cracks through the eyes, twisted gaping mouths, arms crossed in front of them like crusaders' effigies.

Here, in this early dynastic temple, in these ram-headed sphinxes, these sightless human colossi – so unlike Akhenaten's loving decorations at Amarna – was all the cloudy, superstitious worship of the old Pharaonic kingdoms, offerings for immortality set against the nightmare world from the Book of the Dead – these stone supplications to the animal Gods, to Hershef, Toth, Horus and a thousand others. The threat in this temple was all the malignity of the ages, the power of the underworld, dominated by these fierce gods, where mortals lived in the shadow of every sort of dread and evil, walked at their peril.

Hetty was exhausted. Tethering the mare by some scrubby bushes, thin grazing by the canal, out of sight behind the temple, she sat down, hidden by the vast broken stone columns, eating her meagre breakfast – exhausted indeed, but infused with happiness, satisfaction. The night had gone well. She had achieved her every objective. And what a moment that had been! – vaulting the gate, and the one beyond, like a steeplechaser, barely fifty yards in front of the train. She looked up at the mare, its flanks and muzzle cooling now, as it fed on the sparse dry clover.

'You were wonderful! "Witch Hazel",' she went on. 'I'll call you "Witch Hazel".' As the sun rose behind her, shafts of light burnt away the mists and a flush of pink touched the temple, rising over it, gradually warming her as she ate. Twenty minutes later, in the first of the day's heat, she fell asleep.

Several hours later, the sun full up, a brilliant orb in the lead-blue sky, Robert and Léonie rode down the same avenue of ram-headed sphinxes – marvelling at them, not frightened, in the full blaze of noon. Stopping in the shade of the two pylons at the entrance to the temple, they tethered the horses, sat down for a minute on some stones beneath the monuments, mopping their brows.

'We made it!' Robert turned and gazed at the long cartouche with its hiero-glyphics on the pylon at his back. 'Wonder what it says?'

'"No Admittance", I should think. The Baedeker says only the Pharaoh, the high priests and chief courtiers were allowed into the temples in the old dynasties.' She turned to Robert, shading her eyes, gazing at him lovingly. 'Oh, Robert, yes – we made it! Let's find some proper shade inside and eat our lunch – then I can take these damn jodhpurs off as well.'

They walked inside the first of the colonnaded forecourts, inspecting the vast pillars briefly – then went on into the second smaller court, where they found a huge sloping block of stone, the top of some sarcophagus or altar, partly buried in the sand, half in shadow, near one of the great sightless colossi. Here they laid out their picnic lunches and their water bottles.

Léonie took off her itching boots and jodhpurs, sitting down cross-legged in just her knickers and bush shirt; opening the picnic lunch: cold delta pigeon, tomatoes, olives, unleavened bread, tepid soda water.

She lay back on the sloping stone, looking up to the top of one of the columns. Then she leapt to her feet. 'It's too damn hot!' She took her bush shirt off, naked to the waist now. 'Robert?' She looked at him invitingly.

He put his head on one side, half-smiling. 'Offend the Gods, wouldn't it?' He looked up at the row of deformed and sightless pharaohs.

'Rubbish! They were always making passionate love – I've read the books. It's even in my Baedeker . . .' She reached over, drew him to the sloping altar, put his hand to her breast, encouraging him gently, feeding on him, undressing him with her eyes, full of audacity and knowing ardour. She leant back then, slipping her knickers off in a rising fever of pleasure, an infection Robert soon caught as she pulled him to her, undoing his belt, seducing him, opening her thighs, moving his hand again, so that he found it between the smooth flesh.

'Oh, Robert – love me, *love* me! . . .'

Hetty, who earlier, inspecting the monuments, had climbed up the interior stairway to the top of this same courtyard, was hidden now beneath the rim of a papyrus-bud capital high above Robert and Léonie, looking down on the passionate scene beneath her.

She was not merely astonished. She literally could not believe her eyes – the vision of this love-making becoming clouded as her eyes glazed over, so that she started to sway, before regaining her balance. She looked up, trying to clear her eyes, blinking out over the vast desert landscapes behind the temple, west beyond the canal, then forced herself to look down again.

Yes, it was all true. It was Robert and Léonie, naked, both of them in shadow, loving each other. Hetty was outraged. Was this the sweet fate that had waited for her at the edge of the desert? But how had the two of them got there? – it was not possible – not just to Egypt, but out here, miles from anywhere, coinciding with her in this temple? No, it must be an illusion in the shimmering heat – an illusion, a bad dream, a nightmare. The two people below her were chimeras: she was seeing things – from lack of sleep and after all the night's excitements. They were mere figments of her fevered imagination in this brilliant desert light, a ghastly sexual fantasy cast on the shadows beneath her. They could *not* be real. She would test the vision. Getting up and crouching on her knees, she saw the huge chunk of cut stone, a great chip from the hypostyle capital, balanced near the edge of the architrave some yards away. Yes, she would test the reality of this vision, she thought, moving towards the stone, set almost immediately above where Robert and Léonie were lying.

At the same moment Léonie, on her back, gazing up over Robert's shoulder, suddenly started up. 'Robert!' she whispered urgently. 'Something, someone's up there – watching us. I saw . . . it looked like an Arab headdress . . . moving.'

Robert turned, leaving her for an instant, so that they both saw the little stone chips and bits of grit scattering around them. They got down at once from the altar stone, and reached for their clothes.

'See! I told you! There's someone up there!' Léonie repeated her assertion while trying to dress hurriedly.

'No,' Robert calmed her. 'Can't be. Just some loose stones in the wind. Or a bird. Look at all those doves flying in and out from the stones, lots of them, all morning . . . It's nothing.'

They were lucky in their escape. Hetty had tried to push the great stone over on to them. But it had refused to move, stuck fast, despite all her efforts.

Robert and Léonie got dressed. 'There was no one there – don't worry,' Robert reassured her.

'All the same, I don't like it. Come on, let's get out of here – give the horses some water at the canal – and get back to the steamer.'

Untethering their horses from the great pylon, they led them round the outside of the temple, clattering over a debris of broken stone, to the greeny, sun-dazzled waters of the wide Bahr Youssef canal. There, where the temple backed on to the water, they came to a sudden halt. In front of them, standing by a huge fallen column, was a white Arab mare, untethered, whinnying gently as the other horses approached it. Léonie felt the back of her neck prickle with fear. 'Oh God, Robert – I was right! There was, there *is*, someone back in there.'

Inspecting the mare, they saw the British royal arms cut into the leathers. And the inscription beneath it: 'Royal Engineers, Abassia Barracks, Cairo.'

'A British soldier – out here?' Robert wondered.

Then, poking out from the mouth of a small saddle bag, they saw something else, the remains of a cardboard picnic lunch box, not unlike their own. Inside were a few crumbs, some olive stones – and a soiled handkerchief, used as a napkin. A woman's fine silk handkerchief. Robert opened it, letting it flutter in the faint breeze off the water. He was puzzled, fingering the delicate material. 'Strange soldier, or maybe it's his girl friend's,' he said lightly. But when he looked up he saw that Léonie was gazing at something else now, over his shoulder, a look of real terror in her eyes this time.

The two bandits had seen the fine white mare tethered alone in the shade of the broken columns some twenty minutes before. They had stalked the animal down the canal bank, confirming its isolation until, a minute before, they had surprised and then untethered it, before being surprised themselves by the arrival on the scene of Robert and Léonie. The mare meanwhile had strayed out from behind the fallen columns, while the two men lay behind them, peering over.

It had not taken the thieves long to realise that these young *farangis*, quite alone, offered no threat. They would have the mare, and better still the two other horses that had just come into their reach. The older, bearded man stepped out from behind the columns, the hem of his ragged, dun-coloured *galibeah* tucked up into his waist. He held a lead-weighted night stick in one hand. His younger companion, one eye almost completely closed with bilharzia, joined him, carrying a coiled hippopotamus-hide whip.

Robert, following Léonie's glance, saw them not twenty yards away. Their intent was obvious. The older man moved sideways towards the mare. The younger approached Robert and Léonie, uncoiling his whip, flexing his arm, the wicked thongs at the end flicking up little dust storms in the sand.

Léonie shrieked. 'No! No!'

The younger horse thief, his one good eye half-closed in a leer, continued towards them, his other arm outstretched. '*Gib le, gib le hosan . . .*' he intoned in a low voice. He lifted his whip menacingly. '*Gib le . . .*' He seemed to wink at Léonie, mockingly, his good eye blinking repeatedly in the harsh light. Beads of perspiration began to drip down Léonie's forehead, clouding her vision. 'No!' she screamed again. 'No!'

Robert interceded, stepping in front of Léonie, barring the man's path. The thief raised his whip and, flicking it expertly, let the tail thongs open a flesh wound on Robert's neck, three or four livid weals. Robert gasped in pain. The thief advanced towards his horse, with a fuller smile now, hand still outstretched.

Then suddenly he stopped, seeing something over Robert's shoulder, surprise and fear in his sallow features. Robert and Léonie turned. They all gazed, astonished, at the approaching figure.

The Arab, emerging from the shadow of the temple wall in his brilliant white robes, walked easily into the dazzling light towards them. Léonie could make out little of his dark features, hidden behind the cowl of his silk headdress, as he came nearer. Nor did she take in the curious fact that the Arab's right hand, unlike his face, was smudgy white, for all she noticed was the sword he held in it, a very thin, needle-pointed run of steel, metal glittering in the light, as he held the wicked instrument out, gestured for Robert and Léonie to move aside. Passing them, he confronted the man with the whip, who used it at once, the coils shrieking viciously through the air, unleashing their venom at the Arab, but harmlessly, as the thongs caught in the billowing folds of his robe. Once more the thief let fly, but to no better effect, as the Arab sidestepped before continuing his ominous approach.

Then, suddenly, nearing his prey, the Arab took up a position that was vaguely familiar to Léonie, the side-on stance of a fencer, about to lunge with a foil – which he did just then at great speed, stamping his foot on the hard sand, so that now he was well within the compass of the whip, where it could hardly be used against him. Teasing the thief now, circling the blade tip in little provocative flourishes just beneath the chin, the Arab drove him back towards the fallen columns.

It would have been no contest, but for the older man, who joined the fray then with his lead-tipped night stick, waving it about his head, flailing his arm like a windmill, approaching the Arab, and allowing the younger thief to make his escape.

The Arab retreated for a moment, too, letting the older bandit come towards him now, scything the air with his club. The first thief, moving to the side, some way back, was able to use his whip again – and he did so, the coils snaking out, cutting the Arab about his headdress. The other thief closed with him as well, using his stick as a sword.

But the Arab parried the night stick, slashing against it left and right, the thief holding it in both hands now, attempting to use it as a mace, trying to club the Arab to death.

And again he seemed likely to succeed, before the Arab, showing a sudden fevered agility, sidestepped the blows and then, crouching down, made a rush for the thief's legs – cutting at them repeatedly, whipping the bare flesh there, opening little cuts about his ankles, so that the man bellowed out in pain, hopping about on one leg, before stumbling over.

The Arab ran at the younger man now, like a sprinter – went for him with a startling vehemence, sword flashing, circling, boring in towards his chest, where the thief, astonished and fearful at this expert swordsmanship, saw the tip of the blade coming ever closer. Swaying back now, he fell against one of the great broken columns, where the Arab stood over him, about to administer the *coup de grâce*, the needle point an inch from his throat.

The man bellowed for mercy. The Arab pushed him further to the ground with his boot, forcing him to grovel in the sand, before he stepped back and whipped the man on the soles of his bare feet with the blade. Then he gestured away towards the desert. The two thieves needed no second bidding – running, hopping, stumbling away, yelping in pain from the wounds on their feet, disappearing behind the broken columns and along the canal bank.

Robert and Léonie simply stood there, too astonished to be grateful. Robert was bleeding, with a trickle of blood running down his neck, smearing his bush shirt.

The Arab came right up to Robert then, gazing at him from behind the white cowl of his headdress. Robert, the sun in his eyes, saw little of the man's features, noticing only how the dark skin seemed to be melting somehow, the colour changing, as beads of perspiration ran down the man's face. The Arab reached out suddenly. Putting his hand to Robert's cheek above the wounds, he stroked the flesh there tenderly, almost provocatively, before lowering his fingers and taking some of the congealing blood, rubbing them together, as if testing the consistency. There was complete silence, the others puzzled by these intimate gestures, thinking them part of some bedouin ritual.

'Thicker than water! . . .'

Hetty spoke at last, the cool slightly mocking tones of her familiar voice invading the hot silence. 'It's funny,' she went on before the others had a chance to respond in any way, turning to Léonie, 'seeing you both here. Though now I come to think of it, of course you must both have been on that Nile tourist steamer, moored just next to mine. But why meet out *here*, miles from anywhere, when we could so easily have met at Amarna?' She smiled, an expression of almost cruel satisfaction crossing her features, seeing the quite startling effect her voice was having on her two old friends. But her smile meant nothing to the others. Robert and Léonie, though recognising her voice, could still not believe it was Hetty in these sheik's robes. They were speechless. 'Yes,' Hetty went on slowly, speaking to herself now. 'What fate is that? – that I should try and kill you, then save you?'

Léonie, aghast, still not taking anything in, looked at the robed figure as at a ghost. 'Hetty?'

'Who else?'

'Oh, my God, no! No, not you,' Léonie blurted out, unable to contain her horror. She put her hand to her mouth as if she was about to be sick.

'Yes, me,' Hetty went on, taking no notice of this rebuff. 'But why *here*?' she repeated the question, as might an astrologer, pondering some new star in the heavens. 'That's what puzzles me.'

Robert and Léonie remained rooted to the spot. Finally Robert said coldly, 'I don't understand. Can't you leave us alone? – you must have followed us out here.'

'Certainly not! Pure chance.' Hetty moved away then, tending the mare, stroking its nose. 'I was out here, oh, at first light, taking a break, getting away from the picture for a day – or two!' she added, all the old mischief in her voice.

Hetty took her headdress off, the better to mop her brow, displaying her sparse cropped hair, taking the silk handkerchief from the saddle-bag, trying to clear the make-up, walking back to them easily, still entirely relaxed, in command. But then, when next she spoke, her stammer, no longer kept at bay by her role as Arab sheik, returned. 'So why didn't you come and see me on the be-be-boat?' she gasped out. 'I we-was just there, right ne-next to you.'

She struggled so with her words then – her face a mass of chocolate streaks, suddenly a pathetic vulnerable child again, caught at the cake tin – that Léonie, who at first had been angry, quite appalled by her presence, began to relent a fraction towards her, offering her the ghost of a sympathetic smile.

But Robert, finding his voice and wits at last, became more icy. 'It's perfectly obvious why we didn't come and see you. After your appalling behaviour to both of us, years ago, it hardly seemed a meeting any of us would have enjoyed.'

'Still, a meeting was obviously intended!' Hetty, regaining her composure, took no notice of Robert's remarks. Instead, noticing Léonie's slight warmth towards her, she started to play on it, turning, offering her a dazzling smile. 'Obviously intended, because look, here we all are! And be-besides, why did you come out to Egypt in the first place, or at least all this way up-river, if you didn't want to see me?'

'We had no idea you were here . . .' Robert continued his sour response.

'Oh, Robert!' Hetty turned her smile on him. 'You *must* have known –'

'No, only at the last moment –'

'And as to the past,' Hetty rushed on, laughing now. 'That was all *ages* ago – childish rows, mistakes and misunderstandings, all that sort of thing. We're surely all adult enough now not to go on holding all that against each other, aren't we? Can't we just be fre-fre-friends?' She smiled again at Léonie, this time sweetly, quizzically, without guile.

Whereas Robert had obviously confirmed his vast distaste at this meeting, Léonie was almost in two minds about it now. Of course, it was a disaster – running into Hetty like this: a real slap in the face from fate, given that she had taken so much trouble to get as far away as possible from Hetty that morning. Nonetheless, her fortuitous intervention with the thieves had certainly saved their horses and possibly their lives. She should at least express some gratitude for that.

'Yes, well, thank you anyway for saving us,' she said coldly. 'They were certainly out to rob us. Even kill us,' she added grudgingly.

But it was Robert who interjected brusquely then. 'Yes, you said a minute ago – that *you'd* tried to kill us. What did you mean?'

Hetty turned one of her most disingenuous smiles on him. 'Oh, not *really* kill you! Just a thought. You see, I was up there, on top of one of those columns in the temple, when you were down below – well, being happy te-te-together. It hurt a little, seeing you both – that way – because we – were all such close friends, weren't we?' She looked at Léonie, a resonant regret in her eyes. And Léonie coloured, seeing how, from Hetty's point of view, she must have most visibly and passionately betrayed that friendship – with Robert, half an hour before on the altar in the temple.

'Now you're me-me-married, of ke-ke-course,' Hetty continued, stammering badly once more, but with the hidden intention of doing so now, seeing how this flaw had earlier touched Léonie, even against her will.

'Yes,' Robert said dully. 'Married.' The peeved note had increased. He found it difficult even to look at Hetty, this old robber in his life who had now so conveniently forgotten all her earlier thefts and betrayals.

Léonie, clearly aware of all this rising anger in Robert, followed suit. 'Yes, married – *happily.*' She paralleled her husband's coldness in her voice. But she did not entirely feel the same chilly emotion towards her old friend now. She did not want to be – no, she truly did not – but she had begun to be fascinated by this re-born vision of Hetty: the cropped hair, a Joan of Arc cut above the thin, incongruously chocolate-smeared face, the whites of her eyes dancing with drama, the lizard's tongue, darting to and fro, moistening her dry lips, the old petulant chin, but still the defenceless vulnerability in those blue eyes, so arrogant yet so hurt – this proud but pathetic do-or-die child's face, which she remembered so well, returned to her at last, pleased with herself now at the end of this, one of her most spectacular charades, which yet had saved them, which seemed only to have friendship as an end. Yes, perhaps in the eight years since she had last seen her, Hetty had become truly adult, or at least much more reasonable. Certainly she had lost none of her old extravagance or magic. But this seemed a creative characteristic now – no longer, as in the old days, almost purely destructive. What was the secret behind this happy development? Léonie longed for answers, confirmations here – found herself glancing at Hetty surreptitiously, wondering for the first time if this meeting was entirely an evil chance.

Perhaps, she thought, it had a quite different message, not evil but happy, and she had simply misread the signs, wilfully avoiding fate's true intention here. This encounter – which she had so resisted – was it, in fact, an answer to her deepest, most secret prayer? Oh yes, despite the bitterness of Hetty's earlier betrayal, despite 'getting over her' and being so happy with Robert, she *had* wanted to see Hetty again – once more, to make things up with her, at least. So that now, suddenly believing in a happy outcome, she could not resist pursuing, nurturing the meeting in some way.

Looking into Hetty's eyes, Léonie was certain she saw everything she felt in her own heart reflected there – sure confirmation that Hetty, too, felt some happy destiny was being offered. So a look of wonder, of invitation, a mood of connivance bloomed between them then. Yes, surely that had been the real purpose of their coming together, Léonie thought: that Hetty, finally recognising all her old faults and betrayals, some fate had sent her out here to make amends, so that they could all at least be friends again. Gradually Léonie's resistance to Hetty weakened.

For Hetty, too, this meeting was a happy fate, but of quite a different kind. Their coming together offered her the chance not of reconciliation but of destruction. Given the brooding, rising anger she had nurtured ever since she had heard of their marriage – a sense of outrage now vastly increased by the vision of their actual love-making – here, she felt, was a heaven-sent opportunity to take revenge on them both. She wanted Léonie again, without Robert. Yet her real aim was even more malign. She only wished for Léonie so as to separate her from Robert, for what she really wanted was to destroy their marriage. Indeed, that had been the real reason she had saved them from the two thieves, so that she could rob them of something infinitely more valuable than their horses – of their love for each other.

'Well, anyway,' Hetty said, finishing her toilet. 'Goodness me! – here we are.

Do let's leave bygones be bygones. I was going on out into the Fayoum oasis, see the Harara pyramid and maybe the remains of the Labyrinth. Just over that pa-patch of desert there, can't be more than half an hour away. Coming? Then we can all ride back again to the boats.'

'No. We really have to get back now.'

'Oh, Robert,' Léonie interrupted. 'You did say, I did tell you – how much I wanted to see the remains of the Great Labyrinth. Please . . . I know you're angry with Hetty. And so am I.' She scowled at Hetty then, pretending to a fierceness she no longer quite felt.

Robert, recognising Léonie's genuine feelings for the antiquities and reassured by her last harshness towards Hetty, weakened. 'Well, if it's only half an hour away –'

'Oh, Robert!' Léonie rushed over to him, embracing him, giving him her most passionate undivided attention, the better to snub Hetty, in the pretence that she felt nothing for her – Hetty, who stood aside and alone now, disregarded. But Hetty was quite content. If Robert had noticed nothing of Léonie's dissembling just then, she had, knowing exactly what Lèonie was up to. After all, Hetty thought, she knew Léonie, knew her secrets, really so much better than Robert.

In these machinations and subterfuges of the heart, they none of them glanced at the distant horizon to the west, where a few dark, pencil-thin dust devils were getting up, little spiralling eddies caught in some encroaching wind far out in the desert, moving slowly towards them.

It was that late winter season in Egypt when the khamseen winds blew in from the deserts, changing the whole air and climate of the country for a few weeks – wicked winds, far out in Libya, gathering up and sweeping the desert sands towards the river, swirls of fine white dust that soon became blinding, choking storms as the winds increased and the air filled with stinging motes.

The khamseen had come early that year. Though in any case, the three mounted figures, single file on the desert track, riding out towards these first intimations of it, knew nothing of this vicious climate, or its sudden furies, remarking only on the strange grey pall that had risen up then, far away on the horizon, obliterating the afternoon sun.

'Clouds!' Léonie said brightly. 'Don't say it's going to rain!'

The atmosphere was suddenly oppressive – the air at that moment being sucked away from them, towards the great feeding spirals of sand, invisible as yet, a mile in front of them. They noticed this impending force only through the rippling top sand on the dunes, wispy rising waves, running away from them, being scooped up by the vacuum ahead.

'Funny – how the sand's all blowing like that, because I can't feel any wind.' Hetty, in front, turned on her mare towards Léonie immediately behind her.

They rode on for another few minutes, the air becoming thinner, with no sound, but for the rustling and skimming over the dunes. Then the mare started to whinny, the other horses following suit, all of them suddenly anxious, starting to prance and swerve, as if refusing a jump. That was their only warning, before, rising over a dune, they saw the first great grey wall of sand, several hundred feet high, rolling towards them. Then it engulfed them, a stinging wind filled with fine white grains, choking them.

Dismounting, they turned their backs and their horses against the onslaught, as the sandstorm roared over them, the force of the wind pushing them back the way they had come, the horses' manes flicking viciously in their faces as they led the frightened animals, struggling at their bridles.

Hetty, with her cowled headdress, was best off, wrapping it about her face, avoiding the worst of the sand. 'Put your hankies round your mouth!' she yelled at the two vague figures ahead of her. 'Or take your shirts off and use them.'

There was no reply. Suddenly both figures were lost, invisible in the sand swirls, which had thickened and darkened now, giving only a few yards' visibility.

'Léonie! Robert!' Hetty screamed above the wind. 'Stick to the track. Or stop! – stop where you are!' But again there was no answer. 'Oh God,' she moaned. Still, she thought, they had been riding for less than half an hour. They couldn't be more than a mile from the big canal. Robert and Léonie would have the sense, surely, just as she had, simply to make straight on until they got back to the water, and wait for her there. Almost bent double now, the better to avoid the blistering sandpaper wind, Hetty led the mare on.

The others meanwhile, having lost Hetty – their calls back equally unanswered in the roaring wind – had waited together a minute; and then, thinking just as Hetty had done, decided to return without her, making straight for the canal.

But all of them were mistaken in their direction. The sandstorm had changed its course, the wind veering southwards. Without appreciating this and quite disoriented in any case, all three turned imperceptibly, continuing to travel with the wind, so that soon they were moving parallel with the canal, away from the oasis, going due south into the empty desert.

It was not quite empty. Half an hour later, the sandstorm abating a little, the air clearer, Hetty saw the vague dark shapes ahead of her – large, strangely crouched beasts, camels, she saw, a minute later, when she came into the impromptu desert caravanserai, stalled at that moment by the storm, herds of fat-tailed sheep and a few scraggy goats corralled in a circle of camels, twenty or so dark robed bedouins, motionless, faces almost entirely masked, shadowy figures, standing with their lances as sentinels right round the outskirts of the encampment.

The first bedouin, alarmed at Hetty's sudden approach, offered his steel-tipped lance to her. A second, sitting cross-legged a few yards from him, stood up quickly, unslinging an old rifle. Hetty stopped, uncertain, forgetting her sheik's outfit. The two men approached her slowly, menacingly.

Meanwhile Robert and Léonie, who had earlier passed invisibly within a few hundred yards of this same bedouin encampment, were now quite lost in the blinding sands, heads bowed, moving in vague circles, but ever southwards into the desert. Their useless progress came to an end, however, when, at the foot of a dune, Robert's horse, alarmed by the looming hill of sand, suddenly swerved, knocking him to the ground, trampling on his foot in the process. Giving one shout of pain, he lay there, the sand whipping round his face, into his open mouth, before Léonie rushed to him. 'Robert! Robert . . .' She brushed the sand from his lips, cradling him.

'It's all right, nothing too bad, not the whole weight of the beast – think I've just twisted my ankle!'

He was just being brave, Léonie thought. His ankle had a bad gash when she looked at it. All round them, the vicious sand-filled dragon's breath seemed set on suffocating them. And they were lost, quite lost. They should have long since reached the canal had they been travelling in the right direction. With only a trickle of water left in their canteens, without food and with Robert immobile, there was no chance of survival.

The bedouin, at first alarmed by the vision of the mysterious sheik coming at them out of the sands, were then unbelieving when they discovered the man to be a woman and a *farangi*, a foreigner, at that. But they were not thieves – far from it: part of the ancient Aneza tribe in these wastes, they had driven their flocks for centuries to and fro across the western desert, between the various oases, Siwa and the Fayoum, and from these to the Nile valley.

So it was that, when Hetty spoke to them in her kitchen Arabic – '*Etneen habib, kitabi hosan,*' pointing out into the sand storm and gesturing hopelessly – they eventually understood her message, that she had lost her two friends, out there on horses. They at once agreed to help her find them.

Hetty tried to cement their agreement by getting out her purse and offering them what Egyptian money it contained. But they looked at her askance, shocked by the idea. They would have none of it, shaking their heads, eyes to the sandy heavens, murmuring darkly. These were true men of the desert – quite untouched by civilisation. Hospitality, and every help to a stranger met with in their barren world: this was their immutable law, the vital law of survival for everyone who lived in these cruel wastes.

'*Etim, lel!*' – the dark, the night – Hetty said to them urgently, showing them her wrist-watch which they looked at uncomprehendingly, before she gestured up at the furious sky. 'We must find them *now*,' she pleaded, and they understood.

'*Aioua, Aioua!*' they told her reassuringly. But they did nothing, opening their arms, pointing to the sky. '*Ma Fische . . .*' they warbled on. It was still too black, she understood them to mean, useless to look for anyone as things were.

But twenty minutes later the skies cleared sufficiently as the worst of the storm blew over. And then half the men, nearly a dozen of them, mounting their camels, went off with Hetty, leaving the others to guard the flocks, all of them moving south with the wind at first, before each of the camels started to radiate out in different directions, zig-zagging across the vast desert, visible now for a mile or so under the cover of bruised black, sand-filled clouds.

There were no footprints to be looked for over the sand-thrashed dunes. But these bedouin, alone among all people, knew how to search for the lost in these desolate sands, riding their ships of the desert, which they used as look-out posts every so often, stopping and standing right up on the hump saddles, scanning the horizon, as they moved away from the camp in an ever-expanding circle.

Hetty, insisting on riding out with them, had taken a camel herself, following an older bedouin, their leader, she supposed, an ancient fellow, swathed in a floppy turban, with a scraggy beard, sharply aquiline nose and tiny black oval eyes, who rode immediately in front of her. But they saw nothing.

Finally, almost giving up hope in the darkening sky, from somewhere far away to their left behind a ridge of sand, Hetty heard the eerie whistle, sharp and thin, repeated like a curlew's cry in an Irish bog.

'*Aioua*,' the old man half-turned to her impassively, nodding. '*El ham di'illah.*' They had found them and Hetty's heart soared with relief. No, she had not wanted them lost or dead. Of course not! That would have been too cruel a fate. After all, she had only wanted to punish them . . .

The old man veered off to the left, over the ridge, and soon they came on them all, several camels surrounding the horses and the two figures lying on the sand beneath a dune just half a mile away: Robert and Léonie, exhausted, shriven, sand-encrusted, but alive. Hetty, dismounting quickly, knelt by Léonie in the middle of the circle of camels and bedouin.

'Léa – are you all right?'

'Fine. But Robert, his ankle, it's cut rather badly, the horse . . .'

Hetty turned to Robert sympathetically, bending down, looking at his ankle. 'I'm sorry. But I'm sure it'll be okay. We'll get you back to the bedouin camp. It's not far.'

'Thanks.' But Robert still regarded her coldly.

The bedouin helped him to his feet. Hetty turned, doing the same for Léonie. As she did so, Léonie murmured, 'Thank you – thank you, Hetty.'

It was pitch-dark by the time they got back to the camp, a dozen goat-skin tents set up, with a few smouldering fires, a stiff wind still blowing and sighing. But the sandstorm itself had gone, leaving only grit in the air, mingled with the smell of food cooking over the stone hearths.

The three strangers were royally treated. Robert had his cut tended with some sticky desert balm that smelt of honey, then roughly bandaged. Afterwards all three of them sat down, Robert on a small stool, leg outstretched, the others cross-legged, on rush mats in the chief's tent, the largest in the caravanserai, some fifteen feet long, lit by tallow flares, spread over half a dozen poles, the chief's lance stuck in the ground by the doorway.

They drank tepid goat's milk from shallow wooden bowls and ate from similar platters – beans and strips of yellowish, sweet-tasting grilled meat, a lizard they were given to understand, served in their honour – the food handed round (to their surprise, for they had not seen them before) by some of the heavily shawled but not veiled women of the camp, wrists and ankles clinking with copper rings and bracelets: small, plain women, quite expressionless.

Hetty talked as well as she could to the chief and half-dozen of his lieutenants grouped about him. But it was hard – her Nile Arabic as minimal as theirs. Instead, they largely contented themselves, each group in its own fashion and tongue, with nods of the head, smiles, guttural murmurs of appreciation, contented silence.

A problem arose only afterwards as to where they were all to sleep. The chief, standing up, beckoned Robert to a rough litter of mats and goatskin cloaks that had been prepared for him in a corner of the tent. Clapping his hands, two women appeared at the tent flap, and the chief nodded, gesturing for Hetty and Léonie to follow them out.

Robert, turning awkwardly on his foot, started to demur, as did Léonie. 'But we're married. Can't we stay together?' She addressed herself to the chief, a note of desperation in his voice. He seemed to frown. She turned to Hetty. 'Can't you explain?' Hetty shook her head. 'No idea what the word for marriage is. The bedouin obviously don't stay with their women at night. Just visit them in the harem.' She shrugged. 'The Arab custom . . .' The chief's frown deepened, thinking the foreign women were questioning his hospitality. 'I suppose we'd better do as he says,' Hetty added. 'He's getting offended.'

'All right.' Léonie turned to Robert. 'Seems we can't stay together – not their custom. Obviously we have to sleep in the harem with the women.' She went over to him, kissing him quickly, tenderly. 'I'll be all right, promise . . .'

The girls left the tent with the two women. Their own quarters, when they found them, stumbling through the blowing sparks from the fires, were on the far side of the camp, in a smaller and much lower tent, less than five foot high, so that they really had to stoop to get into and move through it. Inside, lit by a single tallow flare, the air was a sweet and sour mix of goat and honey, just like the balm used on Robert's ankle.

'Are there bees in the desert? They seem to use it for everything,' Hetty made inconsequential chatter, though the drumming of her heart belied her easy tones. Then, their eyes becoming more accustomed to the faint light, they saw the vague forms of at least half a dozen women – crouched, kneeling, lying out along the length of the low tent, the whites of their eyes visible now, all staring at them. 'Oh, God,' Hetty said. 'A real girls' dorm . . .'

The eyes followed them as they were led to the end of the low tent. Here, to their surprise, they rounded a corner where the space extended to their left, with rush mats and goat-skins on the desert floor, a bed of sorts prepared for them, beyond the flickering beams from the tallow flare.

Their suppressed excitement at being alone together took the edge off their exhaustion as they sat down gingerly on the skins, preparing themselves for some sort of sleep in the cramped, fetid space, smelling of burnt tallow, and some deep musky odour they noticed now, with which the whole tent seemed impregnated, a smell of cloves, cinnamon. Hetty struggled out of her sheik's robes, making a lower sheet out of part of them, and bundling up the rest as a pillow for them both, a shared headrest in the narrow space, the wind rattling and flapping at the tent just inches away from them.

Their eyes now quite accustomed to the frail yellow light, they looked up as they undressed, only to see all the eyes peeping at them surreptitiously round the corner of the tent pole.

'On show,' Léonie said, breathlessly, trying to hide her nervous excitement, joining Hetty, lying down as far away from her as the space allowed.

'Shush!' Hetty waved the bedouin women away with her arms, as if they were chickens, and the eyes disappeared. Then she laughed softly. 'Who would have believed it – sleeping in a harem tonight!'

'And all the more extraordinary, because remember,' Léonie murmured, 'if we hadn't met you at the temple, Robert and I, we'd have gone out alone into that sandstorm across the desert – and never been found till we were dead! Fate indeed. You saved our lives . . .'

Hetty did not reply, since for her this fate meant something quite different. Fate had given her the opportunity of saving Léonie only because Léonie was hers, had always been: fate had simply returned her property. Léonie's marriage to Robert was just a dreadful mistake which could now be corrected. That was the true meaning of all this. But did Léonie see it that way?

Hetty, testing the water, reached across in the dark, touching Léonie's gritty cheek, finding her lips, brushing them delicately. Léonie made no resistance. Hetty's confidence rose, so that she said, 'Oh, Léa, I'm just so *glad* – to be with you!' And she was, though thinking more of possessing Léonie now, taking her, dividing her from Robert. 'Of course, all that in the past,' she continued disingenuously, 'my disappearing to America with Craig. Well, I just had to, don't you see? – make a clean break. Things had got too much for me at Summer Hill. And I'm sorry. But it wasn't just childish of me, Léa. You see, I so wanted to grow up, like you always said I should. And I think I have . . . grown up,' she added, allowing the lie to bloom.

Léonie listened to these soft, familiar tones, their pillow talk renewed, excited by this confirmation of her earlier thoughts, that Hetty had indeed matured.

'I'm glad then, too,' Léonie said. 'So that now – well, we can be friends again.' There was still a foot of space between them, as they lay there chastely, talking – both, as Léonie thought, savouring these ideals of maturity and friendship, now held in common.

'Friends, I hope so . . .' Hetty sighed. 'Robert, though – he won't be friends, I'm afraid. He hates me.'

'Yes, because he loved you, as much as I did. And never . . . had you. So he's angrier. And jealous, too. But maybe that'll change.'

'It won't,' Hetty said off-handedly. 'Men are like that. They won't change. Like Craig. I've had terrible trouble – he's been so cruel . . .'

'Yes, I wondered – oh, a thousand things!' Léonie, roused now by a desperate curiosity for all Hetty's lost years, could no longer restrain her emotion. 'So often wanted to know – how you'd got on?'

'Wonderfully, to begin with. Oh yes, Craig was so exciting!' She thought to tease Léonie, make her jealous. 'Then Hollywood and everything – but it would all take *days* to tell – and I will tell. Simply, it's been *such* a life!'

'Yes, I've forgotten – you're so famous!' Léonie, ironic, did the teasing now, turning the tables.

'Oh, the fame – that's nothing. Except that being Laura Bowen – that gave me the ke-confidence at last to be *myself*,' Hetty lied. 'It's Craig and his cruelties that have ruined everything. One can't live with that – just as you couldn't live with me in the old days, when I was so beastly to you.' Léonie's heart jumped at this – one more happy confirmation of Hetty's change. 'And you?' Hetty propped herself on her elbow, looking down at Léonie, her hair and nose just visible in the shadowy flare light. 'You and Robert? I've often wondered, too – how you've got on – together?'

'I love him, Hetty,' she told her confidently. 'There's been no problem – that way.' Léonie was a fraction less confident in her last words, and Hetty noticed this.

'But you've not changed completely, have you? I mean, about what we did, le-loving each other?'

Léonie had half-expected this question and decided not to lie about it, not to Hetty at least, for it was something she had longed to speak to someone about over the years. 'No, I've not completely changed, I don't think. I still . . .' There was a sudden frustrated urgency in her voice. 'I still see faces in the street, women in cafés – and I wonder what it would be like, loving them, if I did. Such a secret. No one knows.'

Hetty felt a spasm of triumph drumming through her body. The trap had been set and Léonie was approaching the bait.

'Oh, well,' Hetty said lightly. 'That shouldn't be a problem, or a secret –'

'But it *has* to be, don't you see? Robert would be appalled. It'd be the end for us if he knew, if he found me doing anything like that.'

'Not like Craig! He wouldn't mind, with me.'

'You still have . . . the same feelings?'

'Yes,' she said tenderly. 'I do. But not *with* anyone. Not since you,' she lied once more.

She stroked Léonie's cheek again, then her lips, feeling her tongue momentarily on her finger tips, before Léonie withdrew altogether from her, hurriedly, resisting. 'No, Hetty, no, I can't! –'

But Hetty, aroused now and seeing she was only an inch away from success, persisted – drawing this other straining body to her, kissing her silently, their sandpapery faces rubbing together, as Léonie tried to struggle from the embrace, before Hetty, driven by sheer need, exasperation, frustration, goaded on by an explosive mix of deceit and desire, forced herself on Léonie, crushed herself against her, so that Léonie, her resistance snapping, suddenly gave way, responding.

Hetty drew apart then, the better to touch her elsewhere, so that she could seduce her, make love to her in the narrow space; which she started to do then, with a shivering delicacy at first, opening Léonie's shirt, touching her breasts, before reaching for her sex, flattering it, slipping her fingers down, easing her knickers off, then her own, tangling with Léonie softly, more feverishly, both of them discovering all the forgotten processes of this love in one giddy-making swoop – this shared, suppressed nature reborn in them, rubbing their moist gritty bodies together, coming apart, fondling, stroking, kissing, pushing, feeding this passionate renaissance of desire, their shadow lives touched by flame now, exploding everywhere about and inside them in an ecstasy of pent-up liberation.

Here, for long minutes on end, as the wind whipped the tent, they lost all sense, morality, maturity, became adolescent again, as they had been in those Dublin days – Léonie the willing victim once more, helpless, craving this fierce domination from Hetty, with its pain – as, lying above her then, Hetty spreadeagled her, punishing her, with love bites all over her neck and shoulders. But Léonie did not care, was quite oblivious in her pleasure – a pleasure she could not contain indefinitely, gulping for air then, twisting, arching, quite speechless at the last; when later she could only murmur, 'Hetty, oh, Hetty darling . . .'

Afterwards Léonie said, 'Robert, he mustn't know, ever.'

'He won't! Because he won't be there. You'll come back with me, won't you?'

Léonie fondled Hetty listlessly. 'Of course not,' she said. 'You know I can't. I told you – it'd be the end between Robert and me.'

'But you can't live a lie with him, Léa! – for the rest of your life.'

'It's not a lie! I love you both.'

'He won't accept that, though. You just said. So you'll always be unhappy, because you won't really have *either* of us. And sooner or later the whole thing with him, well, it'll just die,' she added, playing the devil's advocate for all she was worth. 'You're not being fair – to him or youself.'

'Maybe. But I'll just have to accept that. I can't leave him. There's no question.'

'No,' Hetty said sadly, giving the impression of accepting this – which she did not, not for an instant. Oh yes, she had loved their loving, really wanted Léonie back. But it was hardly love she felt for her. It was more sex – above all power over her, here so happily renewed – which she wanted. And that power she had not yet achieved. Not final power, not full revenge – for their betraying her and marrying. That would only come in her separating Léonie from Robert. So how could that be done? Hetty smiled in the dark. She had practically done it already, she thought.

Robert only had to know how they had made love that night for things to start breaking up between them – that was perfectly clear. And so she had prepared the evidence of this for him with her love bites, which Léonie in her passion had failed to take account of – love bites, on Léa's neck and shoulders, some on her face, which she had so enjoyed, would now be her undoing. Those fierce little teeth marks of possession – which would bloom in the night into red bruised flesh, clear evidence of their passion, would tell all when Robert saw them.

When Léonie, in her impatience to see Robert, rushed over to his tent next morning, she was quite unaware of the livid blemishes dotted over her neck and face.

But Robert, in the windy dawn light as she moved forward to kiss him, saw them clearly enough. 'What's happened – all those marks?'

'Where?' Léonie quickly put a hand to her cheek, colouring, realising now, remembering what had happened with Hetty, how she had marked her in their passion.

'There – on your neck, everywhere.'

Léonie swung her head round, tilting it downwards. 'Oh that! Just insects – some sort of awful bedbugs – in those goat-skins. We were eaten *alive* last night, in that squalid tent!' She smiled, yet was unable quite to hide her nervousness, covering the bruises with her hand, scratching them.

Hetty had joined them by now, standing next to Léonie, without her robes and headdress, neck and face open to view, the skin pure and unblemished, something of a contented, Cheshire cat smile on her face.

Robert looked from one woman to the other. Hating Hetty, and suspicious anyway of their night together in the harem, some sixth sense was at work in him now, quite against his better nature, anxious to promote and confirm his worst fears. He turned back to Léonie.

'Bedbugs, you say? Both eaten alive? But there's no mark anywhere – on Hetty.' He looked more closely at Léonie's neck, at the tiny intermittent empurpled bruises just beneath the flesh. 'Why wasn't Hetty bitten?'

'Oh, Robert! – you are being a bore,' Léonie said with joking impatience, trying to bluff her way out. 'I don't *know* why she wasn't bitten – though she said she had been, didn't you, Hetty?' She turned, desperately seeking confirmation, which Hetty thought it politic to offer.

'Yes,' she said vaguely, rubbing her untouched skin.

But the poison had taken with Robert now – so that suddenly, sure that he was being cheated, lied to, and unable to contain his frustration any longer, he became enraged, a quite unexpected fury breaking out through his normally kind and placid nature. 'You're lying! – both of you! You take me for an idiot!' he shouted at them. 'As if I can't see what you were both up to last night! Bedbugs indeed, when it was your squalid love-making. How could you, Léa? How *could* you? – on what was supposed to be our honeymoon.' He glared at her, shaking with rage. 'Well, you can have each other, if that's what you want. I never want to see you – either of you – again.'

'Robert, it's not true! I love you! –'

But already Robert was walking away from them, as fast as his leg allowed, making towards their horses. Léonie rushed after him. 'Robert! You *can't* go, don't be an idiot – it's not *true*, I love you –'

'Liar,' he interrupted. 'Liar, liar, *liar!*' He kept on repeating the word, a vicious malediction, pushing her aside roughly so that she fell to the sand, crying out, a mix of sobbing emotion, physical pain, sheer terror at this impending desertion. Hetty, who had watched all this with a faint, wise smile, rushed out to Léonie then, picking her up, consoling her. 'It's all right, Léa – it's *all right*. Just a tiff – he'll get over it . . .'

Léonie did not reply – just pushed Hetty away from her, kneeling now, doubled up with sobs, as the hazy sun rose through drifts of fine sand far above them and

Robert stumbled on towards his horse. Hetty gazed out over the wide desert panorama: the figure of Léonie, motionless, quite desolated, in front of her; Robert moving inexorably away, the distance ever widening between them, dividing them.

Hetty savoured what was perhaps her greatest, and certainly most malign, triumph. Fate indeed – at this point and for years, she reflected – had dealt her all the high cards, every one: the joker that had led to her meeting with Craig, who had made her a great star; the glittering royal card which had brought her the role of Queen Nefertiti . . . and now an ace, with which she had regained Léonie. There were many triumphs to savour. For surely it was obvious at last: fate had nothing but royal cards and aces for her.

8

ROBERT, STILL UNFORGIVING, had taken the train back to Cairo alone, leaving Léonie with Hetty on King Fuad's steamer. Léonie had pleaded with him, and – in a calmer, more philosophic mood at least – he had told her, 'Look, it's something you'll just have to work out alone. Get it out of your system. Or not get it out – and take up with Hetty again. It's no use my being with you now. I can't help you decide what's your real nature. Though God knows I've tried, all that last year in Paris . . .'

'But, Robert, it's nothing, *nothing* to divide us. I love you just as much as ever, promise . . .' She gazed at him, in so loving a manner, quite without guile, that he was forced to believe her.

'Perhaps,' he said. 'But I can't share you with Hetty.'

'I'm *not* going to go on loving her, Robert! It's *you* I want to do that with! You, you, *you*!' She looked at him challengingly. But he made no response, maintaining his cold indifference, so that she became quite abject. 'You're only punishing me now, and it's not fair, not just . . .' And she had started to sob then. 'How could you do this to me?'

'How could you have done . . . what you did . . . to me?' he replied calmly, just as unhappy as she was. She could not answer through her tears. 'I just think it better we don't see each other for a while. Give us time to think things over. Only going to make things worse, if we stay together, rub salt in the wounds . . . You have your ticket back to Paris. We'll meet there, later, at the flat. Maybe we'll both be able to think about it more clearly then. For the moment I can't think sensibly about anything. I'm just – so *angry* . . .' And he had left, without admitting how he was simply so hurt, which Léonie understood well enough, blaming herself, as she had to, and so letting him go without further argument or protestation. What else could she do? She had, after all, brought the whole tragedy on herself, and she was mortified.

Léonie, quite drained by all this emotional blood-letting, and by the oppressive, sand-filled heat brought on by the khamseen, had more or less collapsed and taken to her bed in the cabin of the royal steamer which Hetty had organised for her. There, she was tended by the film unit's Italian doctor, given sedatives and cold compresses; an electric fan blew over her bruised and tear-stained face. For Hetty, having regained her possession, this glittering trophy which was Léonie, had other fish to fry, and bones to pick, with Craig.

At first, on her return, he had been furious with her. But, filled with the success of her escapades and conquests in the desert, she had simply mocked him. 'Pe-pe-perhaps,' she told him as briskly as her stammer allowed, 'you'll be more considerate towards me now, stop pe-playing the brute behind the camera. You say you've missed two days' filming without me? Just be glad you haven't lost the whole picture! Remember, at this st-st-stage, *I'm* the pe-person they need in it, not you.' She glared at him, before striding away to her cabin, walking on air.

Craig had to accept defeat. The worm had turned. He pondered the matter. Hetty had taken up with her old girl friend again – that was what had really set her all cock-a-hoop. Well, this hardly mattered. And it would not last – if he did not want it to. Hetty's cheeky confidence and independence from him, he knew, was a passing thing. Soon, either Hetty would tire of the girl as she had before, or Léonie herself would go scuttling back to her husband.

He still held all the real cards with Hetty – her access to professional mastery in him being just one of them, for she could never make successful pictures on her own since no other director could mimic his unique hold over her, on camera or off. He had created 'Laura Bowen' – a painstaking, lengthy manipulation – professionally, emotionally, sexually. And, for as long as Hetty wanted to inhabit this invented persona, and draw the glittering dividends that accrued from it, then he was her master. He knew he would only ever lose that power over her if she decided to forsake everything in her life as Laura Bowen and return to her earlier character as Henrietta Fraser – that divided, frantically unhappy girl she had been when they had first met.

This she would never do, Craig thought. Who would wish to return to such early horrors, re-inhabit all those bitter familial hurts, enmities, divisions? – all that Hetty had suffered from in Ireland. Above all, what woman, like Hetty, whose problems all stemmed from her lack of a father, would ever willingly return to a fatherless state? He was her father now – that was his strongest suit, the essence of his hold over her. Father, brother, playmate, confidant, friend, lover, enemy – he was all things to her, he knew, but most particularly the first: wise, powerful, all-knowing, ever reliable, for good or ill, there to pick her up from the worst pitfalls and mistakes, punishing yet forgiving, but finally distant, unknowable, not ever to be fully possessed in return.

These were the cards which Craig held – one or all of which he could bring into play at any time, from now on, so regaining control of what he knew to be finally his possession: Laura Bowen.

Why, he only had to make love to her again, for example, to mimic love to her, as he had done so often before, to regain her. Yes, he thought, he would reward Hetty with that, not at once, something she would construe as a weakness, an admission of guilt or fault on his part, but later when they returned to France in a few weeks' time, for the interior work at the Victorine studios in Nice. Meanwhile, let her savour her illusions with Léonie – while he, once more, would take some final pleasures with the child brides in the black-tented bordello on the edge of the desert.

They were nearing the end of the shooting in Egypt. Only two exterior sequences remained. But they were major ones, which would require all the present *fellahin* extras together with the addition of a regiment of Khedival cavalry in Cairo, already sent up-river and encamped beyond the tented city. The first was the attack from Thebes, led by the old conservative priests, on Amarna – and the second their subsequent gory victory, when the renegade citizens of Akhenaten's royal capital are put to the sword, the city itself sacked and burnt, the apostasy of these sun-worshippers extinguished for ever.

But these epic sequences were delayed by the cloudy, hazy skies and gritty wind that had come unexpectedly with the early khamseen. Work came to a halt everywhere. Accountants all the way from America, some from Nice and others down from Cairo, loomed ominously in the production office by the river. Invoices and payrolls were mustered and computed, ledgers grimly compared, columns of figures added and subtracted, as vast debts emerged. Urgent telegrams began to move to and fro – between Amarna and Cairo, Cairo, Hollywood and the head office of the Fox Film Corporation in New York.

And it was here, in his oak-panelled office on West 56th Street, that William Fox himself, a sallow, bald-headed, aggressive man nursing a withered arm, came to inspect these same appalling debts, brought to him by his flamboyant production chief, Winfield Sheehan. Worse still, that same morning in March 1926, Sheehan had brought him the latest crop of dailies from *Nefertiti*, over eight reels of film, a month's work in Egypt, including much of the earlier perverse and unscripted footage, which Craig had intentionally delayed sending. The two men had just emerged from the small projection room next to Fox's office. And Fox, so startled by what he had just seen, was speechless with rage, unable at once to comment on these reels of uncut film, so that he tried to distract himself with lesser ills, pawing about among the *Nefertiti* production accounts lying on his huge desk beneath a tall stained-glass window.

'There's nothin', but *nothin*' . . .' Lighting a cigar, he picked up a sheet of figures at random. 'Not a goddamned thing in this production, Sheehan, that ain't a fuck-up of bullshit. Here, take a look at this,' he went on in his strident, lower-East-Side Hungarian accent. 'Twelve thousand dollars – to "palm-trees"! But that country's *full* of fuckin' palm-trees! Seen pictures of 'em, can't move for goddamned palm-trees. So what the fuck is Craig *doin*' – importing palm-trees?' he roared out in sheer disbelief.

'They didn't have any there in the desert, up-river, Bill –'

'And here, even worse,' Fox went on, turning over another sheet in the accounts, 'fourteen thousand bucks for "clover" – now someone must be right outa their mind there, Sheehan, "clover" – that's right! Bloody living in it! *Fourteen thousand dollars* for "clover". It says so. Now, what is this, Sheehan?' He tried to wave his withered arm about, so incensed had he become. 'Palm-trees? Clover? Are we in some big agricultural business out there?'

'It's the grass, the forage, Bill, from the local farmers, to feed all the horses. It's all desert country up there on the other side of the river . . .'

Fox stopped then, quite motionless, seeming to relax. '"Forage, clover" . . .' he said at last, with an ominous quietness, weighing up these mysterious words, licking his lips, seeming to taste some exotic but unpleasant foodstuff. Then he exploded, his black moustache dancing up and down as he roared out, 'I've been conned, Sheehan! No one's spending twenty-six thousand bucks of my money – on clover and palm-trees – and getting away with it! . . .'

'Yes, Bill –'

'What d'ya mean "Yes, Bill"? They've gone and done it, haven't they?'

'Yes, they have. They *had* to! Even horses have to eat, Bill –'

'And that's only the *beginning*!' Fox started to stride about the office now, his agitation rising. 'Those dailies, Sheehan, we just saw – millions of dollars, and it's all porno-graphy – *porno-graphy*! Cock-suckers, rapists, pansy boys, hoors, deviates, every one of them. Why, ya couldn't show that stuff from one end of the land here to the other, not even in *Mexico*, Sheehan. Over three million dollars already – on cock-suckers! We're ruined, Sheehan, ruined!' Fox started to dance about his office in fury. 'Get me Howard Brenon. We'll have him on the picture straightaway. And get that two-timing bastard Craig *right* outa it! And sue him, Sheehan! We'll *sue* him, the fuckin' little porno-grapher . . .'

'But he has a contract, Bill –'

'Yeah, and he's broken that contract! None of this crap was in the original outline – or the scenario – we okayed. He's made it all up as he went along! I *knew* we shoulda never let him out there alone, with all those weird dagoes and wogs, the goddamned little prick of a Paddy! Tossing himself off – on *my* money.' Fox tried to activate his withered arm again, such was his fury. 'And this was supposed to be a *family* picture, Sheehan – a great *religious* picture – with that Pharaoh an early runner for Jesus Christ. And what do we have? A picture ya couldn't even show in a sporting house – in *Mexico* . . .'

'Yes, Bill, but –'

'No fuckin' buts, Sheehan! Get on to it – get Brenon in, and a new editor, and start cutting out all that crap I wouldn't even show my worst enemy.' Fox started to scratch his crotch vigorously.

'But, Bill, if we fire Craig, we'll lose Laura as well. Remember? – we have a deal with them, as partners together on *Nefertiti* – with their company Willbow Pictures. Without Laura we couldn't even begin the interiors in France – whole picture'd be straight down the drain then.'

'Jesus,' Fox said softly. 'I'd forgotten.' Then he burst forth once more. 'The short and curlies, Sheehan!' he roared. 'They have us by them!' He started a series of little jumps then, like a jack-in-the-box, both feet off the ground at once, skipping across the thick pile carpet.

'*Yes*, Bill . . .'

Fox came to a halt. 'Well, I tell ya, Sheehan – every dog has his day. But I'll nail Craig good, one way or the other, believe me. He'll never work in Hollywood again, for *any*one, after this picture. And, as for Laura Bowen, she musta bin in the bag with him over all this, from the very start! Well, she's for the big drop *anyways* . . .'

'What do you mean, Bill?' Sheehan, who had thought he could handle all Fox's earlier bluster, was now suddenly anxious. 'Whatever Craig's done with the scenario, Laura's absolutely sensational in the picture, best thing she's ever done. Just to look at her! – why, there's a fortune to be made out of this picture, if we can just cut the crap out. So what do you mean? – she's for the drop?' Sheehan, regaining all his flamboyance, was almost aggressive now, leaning across the desk.

Fox smiled for the first time that morning. 'I'll tell you what I mean! For only fifty grand, I just bought all US rights to this new Kraut sound picture process, Sheehan – Tri-Ergo or some cockamanie thing it's called. Going to put a bomb under the whole picture business. Change everything! – a whole new breed of directors, technicians, and most of all stars, Sheehan! We're going to need stars that can *speak*, don't ya see? Not broads like Marion Davies and Laura Bowen – who talk like they had a bag of marbles in their mouths.'

Sheehan was astonished. 'But, Bill, Laura's our biggest money-spinner –'

'Yeah, in *silent* pictures! But with this new Kraut sing-song stuff she won't be! I tell ya, Sheehan, I aim to teach *both* of 'em – a *real* lesson . . .'

The khamseen passed away, the picture started up again and Léonie, physically at least, recovered. But her relationship with Hetty, living together on the *Omar Khayam* now, was cold and strained. So that Hetty, returning each evening from the sets, became frustrated with this toy she had regained but was unable now to play with. Léonie, still exhausted and vastly depressed, looked sourly on everything and everyone, and that included Hetty.

'But it really *wasn't* my fault, Léa!' Hetty told her one evening at dinner, as they ate alone in the candlelit royal salon. 'I've told you, haven't I? How could either of us have known, in the dark, that my . . . loving you that way – that Robert would come to see it all?'

Léonie, as before horrified by the memory of this love-making, made no reply. She did not, though, suspect that Hetty had bitten her with just this end in view, so that Robert would discover their passion and leave her. For she knew perfectly well that she had shared the passion that night. And now she was simply so deeply ashamed at herself, at this act of resurgent nature that had ruined her life, that she could not speak of it, could not face anything of it in herself. She thought of nothing but how she could regain Robert – and this was all she wanted to talk about with Hetty. So, instead of replying to the question, she said without a glimmer of emotion, 'The only thing I want – is to have him back.'

'But, Léa, if Robert really loved you – he wouldn't *do* this to you, treat you like that and just leave you here. He wouldn't pe-punish you – he'd *forgive* you, if he really loved you!' And then she added, most reasonably, 'Because after all it's not as if he never knew about you and me, how we . . . loved each other. So it shouldn't have been such a shock to him, when he found out we'd . . . loved each other again. Don't you see?' she said tenderly, shaking her head sadly in the soft candlelight. 'He's just being childish about it all. Really is. I've known him – really a lot longer than you! If he was grown up, well, at least he'd feel some sympathy or understanding for you. But he can't, you see, because he just wants to pe-possess you, losing both his parents and so on. That's his *real* problem. So he can't really love you – it's just jealousy and spite – *that's* what really dominates in him. Like most men,' she added for good measure.

Hetty, not only playing the devil's advocate again, was presenting much more of her own failings and feelings towards Léonie. And, at last, Léonie began to have suspicions.

'I don't believe all that,' she said evenly. And then, showing some vigour and emotion, 'Oh, I know him, too, Hetty! You forget that! And different things, things you couldn't possibly know about him at all, no matter how long you've known him before. The person, these last few years in Paris – you've never known that part of him. And, besides, it was *you* who simply wanted to possess me in the old days. Remember?' she asked acidly. 'You who always played the childish jealous thing, who wouldn't grow up.'

'Yes,' Hetty admitted, mimicking the older and wiser woman now perfectly. 'You're right, I did. But I've changed. Can't you see? And that's what's so ironic: Robert is doing what I used to do – showing his true colours at last. I don't want to own you any more, or go in for all that juvenile dressing up thing. That was only because of all the bad things I felt then. It's so obvious! I've got all that *out* of me, these last years, in my work, not bottling it up and letting it sour everything in my own life.'

This was an honest-enough appraisal of Hetty's – as far as it went. But it was not the whole story. Hetty lied by omission. She had indeed matured, in so professionally diverting these histrionic frustrations. But she had not lost her will to power, her need to dominate and control. Far from it. This urge had fattened on its appetite, become a vast and greedy thing, which bloomed in the dark, a malign flower. And as before, when she wanted to blackmail Léonie into sharing her fantasies, now she simply wanted to devour her, let loose this voracious hound, which, since Craig no longer fed it, she could not contain within the walls of her temperament.

'I only want you to be happy,' she went on. 'Like me, expressing your real self. Léa. *Our* real selves. That's all.' She was wonderfully meek in this exposition. 'Can't go on telling lies about our real nature, all our lives – that's what I've found anyway, with you the other night. I know it now. Tried to avoid it, just like you. But I can't any more.'

Again, the fair reason here, resonant in her voice, in Hetty's whole candid attitude, could not but affect Léonie. And Léonie had to admit it now: she could, she did, she had loved women – even though of course she loved Robert much more now. She had simply blinded herself to this fact, avoided the issue for so long, for the sake of Robert. She loved men and women – in the shape of Robert and Hetty at least – and could not handle this quality in her nature, as Hetty obviously had come to do. So that the tables were turned now, and it was she, not Hetty, who had the problems of immaturity here – she who might well now be accused of behaving childishly, of dissembling, of avoiding this vital issue: a point which Hetty, with her cunning sixth sense, saw at once, confirming it then, leaning forward, touching her on the arm.

'Because, Léa, you must see – it's not fair to Robert, to lie to him like that – about this, anyway, something so important in your life. After all you told me, that night in the tent – and it was so obvious anyway then – you *do* like women. You like me at any rate! And I love you, not just the love-making thing. And you can't go on having it be-both ways – being secret about that other part of you, with Robert, *and* loving him, as if you *only* loved him, only loved men. I tell you, even if we hadn't met out here, and you'd gone on like that with him, it'd all have come out one day – exploded, with some other we-woman, someone at a café or in the chorus, just like you said.'

And Léonie had to admit the truth of this. 'Yes,' she said hopelessly. 'Perhaps . . .'

'No, it's a certainty, Léa. 'Cos the one thing I do know is that, if people lie about something for a long time, like my Mama – about my father – it all leads to much worse trouble in the end. The tr-tr-truth can't hurt us, I've always told you that, told Mama, too. But she was too far gone to take any notice then. So, you see, the only way you can lose . . . is by going on lying to Robert about yourself . . .'

'And you, with Craig?' Léonie enquired. 'He doesn't mind – that other part of your nature, your expressing it?'

Hetty laughed, huge eyes dancing beneath her urchin haircut. 'Oh no. He's known about you and me all along. I told him. Entirely understanding about it – least he used to be, until recently, before he took to just playing the be-bully boy.'

'But you – you loved him, in that way, too?'

'*Yes!* Of course I did. Because I like men, too, Léa – just as much as you do – sometimes. Because, you see! – we're just the same sort of people in that way, loving men and women. Except the pe-point is – and things have rather proved it, haven't they – I think at heart we really like we-women, like each other anyway, better than any man. Don't we? So why don't we live together? Come back with me! We have a lovely villa – one of Napoleon's generals built it – right in the middle of the studios at Nice. Craig wouldn't mind. Don't you see? You could go on with your opera work in the south, at Monte Carlo maybe. Because Craig is going to work in Nice permanently now, take over the little studios there, never going to go back to Hollywood again, which we both loathe. And we're going to do another picture in Nice right after this one. So *do* come back with us, Léa!' she ran on with vast enthusiasm. 'Oh, Léa, there's so much you and I could *do* together again, make up for all my idiocies in the past, now that I'm . . . so much easier with myself and won't be-bully you and be stupid: all the things we *should* have been doing all these years, if only I hadn't behaved like such a fool. Do come!'

Just as Craig, seven years before in the Shelbourne Hotel in Dublin, had offered Hetty the promised land of Hollywood, with all its temptations of glittering self-expression and appropriate happiness, so Hetty offered the same to Léonie now. But Léonie, stunned by the offer for an instant, said nothing, so that Hetty, misinterpreting her blank expression, was forced to illuminate the vision further. 'Oh, I know,' she continued. 'You think Robert would never have you be-back, if you did that, came and lived with us for a bit. But, Léa! – that's the whole point! You mustn't crawl back to him. That'd be fatal, promise you. Because, after all, you've nothing to be ashamed of! It's you – your true nature, loving men *and* women. Your generosity. There's no guilt in that. So stop all this *pe-pleading* attitude with him. Why should you be ashamed of what's really you? – that you love him, but have, well, an affection for women too. If he won't see that . . . then he's not worth living with. And if you *do* go on living with him, and deny your true feelings, then the whole me-marriage is a fraud and a lie. You have to operate from a position of strength with him, not weakness, lies or excuses. *Then* he'll have you be-back. You'll see!'

Again it seemed a fair argument – one which, in many such emotional divisions, could well have led to a reconciliation. Léonie, by the skin of her teeth, was persuaded by it. 'All right!' she said at last. 'I'll stay here. And come back to France with you.'

Subsequently she wrote to Robert, explaining her decision – writing to him lovingly thereafter almost every day, believing, on Hetty's advice, that she was taking the correct decision by postponing her return. Which she was, in a way, for Hetty's advice was valid enough – though Léonie was unaware that Hetty intended she never succeed in implementing her proposals.

But Hetty reached the summit of her triumphs the following day, on set, in her final location scenes with Clive Brook. As Craig's script demanded, the priests of the old faith down-river at Thebes, together with the army of lower Egypt, finally take their revenge on Akhenaten, storming Amarna, sacking the golden city, setting it ablaze, erasing every image and memory of the sun god Aten and his earthly disciples.

But prior to this, seeing the hopelessness of their position, Akhenaten and Nefertiti choose death in a murder-suicide pact rather than acknowledge any public defeat in their religious and sexual obsessions.

These scenes were shot in the little gilded love pavilion, with its delicate hieroglyphics and cartouches depicting the ideal domestic happiness shared between the royal pair in their earlier lives together – the pavilion perched over the ornamental lake in the palace gardens, where the two had retreated, the army from Thebes already battering at the palace doors, storming the walls.

Hetty – dressed in all her full regalia, the magnificent blue and gold headdress, silver-threaded robes, sun-burst jewellery – gazes at Akhenaten for a long moment, lovingly, remembering the young man there, the days of hope, all the freshness of their love then, their belief in the loving sun god Aten.

Akhenaten, almost an old man now, bulbous and gross in all his increasing deformities, returns the gaze, wordlessly, something of his old fire returning to his eyes at least, before he stares down on the lake water, seeing the reflections of carnage there from the palace gates and walls, then looks back at Nefertiti, pleading now for death.

She kills him, in a murderous embrace, smothering the dagger in his stomach, before turning defiantly on the approaching soldiers, holding the dagger aloft, then driving it deep into her own breast, blood seeping through the diaphanous linen, flooding the robe, as she falls headlong into the lake, floating there among the lotus flowers, head turning in a faint smile, then sinking slowly in front of the astonished soldiers, gathering round now, afraid to touch her, save her, do anything for her – as she disappears, replaced then by a brilliant sunburst on the water, from a great carbon arc suddenly ignited over the set.

Hetty's regality, her courage, beauty and self-belief, had earlier reached an incandescent pitch, which she maintained throughout the day, in a performance that was lived through, barely acted at all. Here was Nefertiti – but Hetty, too – a woman renunciating nothing, standing by her life, every moment of it, every act, good and bad, faithful unto death. It was a sensational performance – Hetty's apotheosis. And the applause at the end of it, when Craig finally called 'Cut!' was spontaneous and unstinted.

Mickey Ostrovosky was quite bewildered by it all. What further triumphs in this art could there be for this woman who seemed now, in the role as Nefertiti, to have exhausted every emotion available to a woman?

And Léonie, too, watching from the sidelines, was equally spellbound, believing she had witnessed a final confirmation of all her hopes for Hetty, in which the evil that was in her character had finally passed over into Nefertiti, had now all been encapsulated and sealed there, dying with the Queen.

Léonie chose not to see how Hetty, in this last act, had forsaken nothing of her divided temperament – that it was just these violent contradictions, maintained and fanned in her soul, which enabled her so wonderfully to impersonate the Queen, in all her good and evil.

Instead, standing behind her at the mirror, back in her dressing tent as Hetty disrobed, wiping her make-up off, Léonie allowed herself to be drawn once more into Hetty's magic orbit, the shining lights round the mirror, a moth to flame – fluffing her short-cropped hair about for an instant, before Hetty took her hand gently and put it to her lips, smiling up at her reflection.

'Well?'

'It was – extraordinary . . .'

Léonie's fingers slipped down and she stroked Hetty's neck, before Hetty caught her hand again quickly and put it to her still damp and bloodied breast. 'It's only the beginning again, Léa – for us.'

Léonie, in a daze of light and warmth, let the intimacy continue, even when

Hetty put her hand directly on her breast, so that Léonie felt the heartbeats, strong, vibrant, before the dresser arrived in the tent.

Léonie hurriedly withdrew her hand, smeared with make-up blood. She looked at the crimson on her fingers. And something turned over in her stomach, some strange emotion, deep and happy yet tinged with horror, a feeling she did not understand.

Hetty experienced quite a different emotion just then, which she understood very well: it was a sense, finally confirmed now, of invincible power, which Léa could not resist – that of an animal toying with its prey. She had regained everything, she felt: professionally – and personally, in the shape of Léonie. She had reached the supreme moment in her life.

Hetty turned her gaze again towards Léonie in the mirror, almost exactly mimicking the sum of all this – this expression which for Léonie, as always, remained inscrutable, the central mystery of her attraction, which thus formed the hold which Hetty maintained over her, a mystery which Léonie could never decipher; if she had, she would have found as much dross as gold.

Later, in the days that followed, moving around with the cameras, the women watched the vast action sequences which would complete the picture: the initial battles on the Nile – the surprise attack by the army from Thebes coming up-river, in a collection of adapted feluccas, engaging Akhenaten's two royal barges, putting them to rout with flaming slingshots and arrows; then the long lines of soldiers disembarking on the east bank below the Royal Palace, unloading stores and armaments, commandeering Akhenaten's chariots, before storming through the city.

First they rampaged down the Royal Way, chopping down all the hanging flower baskets, ramming doors open, starting to massacre the citizens of Amarna. Then they entered the great plaza of the temple, where most of Akhenaten's priests, courtiers and nobles had retreated – bludgeoning their way through, laying about them with their short swords, desecrating the sanctuary, blood spilling everywhere on the beautiful mosaic pavements, before launching a final attack on the holy of holies at the high altar, using ladders and grappling irons, climbing up and pulling the great sun disc emblems from their niches; the white bas-reliefs of Akhenaten, Nefertiti and their children crashing down, splintering among the dead bodies of the priests, signifying final doom for Akhenaten's apostasy.

Afterwards, gasoline having been sprinkled in crucial places, the city that had taken so much of Fox's money and Leo Kuter's loving genius to build, was set alight – the pastel-coloured wooden buildings at one end of the Royal Way going first, so that soon, like a long fuse, the whole street took fire, in crackling bursts, fed by its own internal winds, creating explosive vacuums and fire storms, the painted lotus-flowered lintels above the doors smouldering and peeling at first as the heat drew near, then exploding as the fire ran on down the street; costumed extras stumbling, falling with it, before the flames caught the bridge at one end, ripping across it, a great pall of fiery smoke filling the 'Window of Appearances', then rushing on to devour and engulf the Royal Palace.

It was a holocaust of flame, mayhem, destruction – ash and sooty cinders leaping up far above the river into the bright blue dome of sky, so that soon, with the dusk, the city was reduced to red embers.

The heat on the girls' faces, as they watched from one of the half-dozen camera rostrums, was intense. Hetty was upset at this final destruction of Amarna, this end of Nefertiti's and Akhenaten's dream; it touched her, pricking tears – this violation of their love together as King and Queen in their early days, this destruction of their religious creation, both reflected now in the fiery debris all about them: the end of an age of hope in ancient Egypt, to be replaced once more by the old regime at Thebes, with a further 1,500 years of darkness, superstition, evil.

She turned to Léonie. 'An end of love, isn't it? – of what was good. You see why, don't you?' she hurried on. 'Why it's really going to be a *great* picture! Because it really *says* something – how evil always wins out, the urge to destroy! Unless we fight against it,' she added as an after-thought, her moist eyes glittering in the firelight, dazed, mad even.

Léonie nodded, thinking she understood. 'You mean – like you had to fight what was bad in you?' And Hetty nodded vigorously in return. 'But, Hetty, here it seems the other way round – the good is killed in the end. Surely people won't want to see that? – if there's no hope –'

'There's the *truth*, though. That's more important.'

'But lots of people don't like the truth, won't face it – especially not in picture palaces.'

Hetty at that moment, however, felt impelled by it. 'The truth can't hurt us, Léa! I told you. Only our fears of it, our illusions.' She touched Léonie's arm. 'Don't you see? – we're free now. From here we can go *anywhere*!'

What Hetty meant was that this brutal sacking of the city reflected the true nature of things in life for her. In short, this holocaust justified her own continued scheming and destructive behaviour. It reassured her greatly to think that people, even so powerful as Akhenaten and Nefertiti, had been unable to win over these basic imperfections in humanity – as she had been unable to do. The burning of the city, this triumph of evil, exactly paralleled her own remaining flaws, confirming the validity of all those malign parts in her own quite unreconstructed nature.

Craig, nearby, stood on top of another high rostrum with his cameraman Johnny Seitz, cap still back to front, filming these last images of destruction, the sparks and ashes of Akhenaten's dream city blowing up into the indigo sky.

Throughout these last days of shooting, Craig had watched the destruction of the city with an increasingly exultant expression, a face that matched the fires raging beneath him now – as if, as with Hetty, this end to love and beauty perfectly reflected his own deepest beliefs. He seemed to thrive on this desecration of hope, proof of his own sad philosophy that there could be no lasting happiness, that the malign and the perverse would always triumph in the end. And, in this, he and Hetty were the real sisters under the skin, not Hetty and Léonie.

Now, still immaculately dressed, his white silk shirt smudged with flying cinders, he watched this last grim action with a studied satisfaction, until the flames finally began to wane and he gripped the big megaphone, shouting 'Cut!' – then swivelled the huge cone round to the other cameras – 'Cut!' – 'Cut!' – 'And *thank you*, ladies and gentlemen, all and every one of you. Thank you, *grazie, merci, shoukran* – and that's it!'

He mopped his brow, then turned to Seitz. And suddenly, in the heat of the moment, they embraced briefly. 'Thank you, Johnny. The end, though? Why, it's hardly the beginning . . .'

Léonie glanced over at the two men, seeing this gesture of professional camaraderie, something she was quite familiar with in the world of grand opera. And something touched her then, an emotion about Craig she had never expected: a grudging admiration for his myriad skills, his single-minded dedication, his artistry, his passion to encapsulate all that was vivid and passing in real life, trapping it on these little frames of celluloid, before casting them as mere shadows on a silver screen. There was something heroic in all this, she recognised. And, though she still hated him for his wrong-doing with Hetty, she saw now how Hetty was really a secondary consideration to him. He only lived among, and loved, these flickering emblems of life, invented images quite outside reality. About people, real people, he was hollow. They were just pawns to him on his chessboard of dreams. And she said as much to Hetty later that night on the steamer, in Hetty's cabin, when they were getting dressed for the unit party. 'Just pawns.' And she continued, 'I can see now why you haven't got a future with him, because nobody has, in their real lives: only on the screen.'

But Hetty was surprised at this. 'Oh yes, he's been awful, ghastly, these last months. But that's his work, Léa – all the frightful difficulties of this location. Back in Nice . . . it'll be quite de-different. And even better when the picture's finished. Then he'll be fine – you'll see! Of *course* I've got a future with him. Just as you have with Robert. It doesn't always have to be either/or, you know. We *all* have a future – together. All four of us!'

Léonie was confused by this. She had wanted, in her ideal world, to love both Robert and Hetty, for them to reciprocate. But she had no plans whatsoever in this vague idea for Craig. She could never for an instant – as Hetty obviously did – imagine Craig becoming any sort of friend of hers.

Yet it was not only Hetty's hope that this might happen – it was Craig's, too. Now that the location work was over, it had crossed his mind that Léonie, Hetty's old lover, was an attractive woman, had something about her . . . Hetty's earlier impertinence, her cheeky independence, had continued to aggravate him mildly. Well, he would start to draw the kite string now, but in quite a different manner than he had earlier foreseen.

Hetty's real purpose, he was pretty certain, in this renewed association with Léonie, had not been so much to love the woman, but simply to use her as a means of asserting her independence against him. And more than that, for he could read her mind like a book, Hetty – to punish the woman for her marriage – had simply wanted to divide her from her husband.

Well, he could do something of the same sort to bring Hetty to heel – divide her from this old love renewed, separate her in turn from Léonie, by intimating in some manner how Hetty's love for her was only skin-deep, which of course was no more than the truth. What would serve his purposes here? Then it suddenly struck him – the livid little teeth marks he'd seen on Léonie's neck and face, when he'd met her briefly on their return from the desert. And, of course, it was clear to him then – that had been Hetty's way of taking Léonie from Robert, of showing him conclusive proof of their covert passion together that night in the tent among the bedouin women, by fixing her mark on the girl, something she had intended from the start – not as true passion, but simply as evidence of that passion. Well, if Hetty had so separated these two, he would do the same for Hetty in turn – separate her from Léonie, using the same lever, those love bites. The idea had a perfect symmetry to it, which appealed to him as much as anything.

Craig at the party that evening, with the principal actors and technicians, was at his most relaxed and genial. Released at last from months of tension, all his old boyish charm emerged again, his Celtic roguishness. And there was drink, too, for the first time on the location – crates of Gianaclis's red and white wine sent up from Cairo, so that soon there was an air of conviviality, release, truth-tellings.

Some hundred or so people were on board the *Omar Khayam* that night, milling about the open decks under the stars, trestle tables laden with cold delta pigeon and Port Said prawns – while others chatted in the huge mahogany salon with its opulent *belle époque* décor. And it was here, after supper, with Hetty engaged elsewhere, that Craig, in a white dinner jacket and red carnation, tactfully cornered Léonie, apologising for not having paid her more attention in the past weeks, his eyes wheeling over her in a gaze that was both contrite yet mischievous.

'Oh no, not at all – it didn't matter.' Léonie tried to be as distant and formal with him as she could.

'Oh yes,' Craig ran on, at his most charming. 'Just I'd not the time. And I'd wanted to . . . to sympathise with you as well, over Robert. Wanted to apologise in general. Knowing how close you were to Hetty, in the old days – well, you must have thought me – think me – a real bastard!' Léonie made as if to concur with this view, before he ran on, 'Yes, you're quite right. Obviously, why wouldn't you think that? When I took Hetty up in Ireland, I left a lot of damage behind. And I'm sorry, truly sorry. But I loved her, love her, just as much as you did – and do,' he added, coming to the point now, in quite a different tone of voice, soft and serious. So that Léonie was involuntarily drawn into his confidence then. 'You see, I wanted to help her just as much as you did then, and now . . . all that unhappiness with her mother. And her father, or rather the lack of one. And I think I have helped her. She's a lot easier these last years, expressing herself, all the things she'd bottled up. We all have to *express* ourselves these days, don't we?' He laughed nicely. 'The curse of the age! But she's done that. And she's a much better person now . . .' Yet as he said this a distinct note of doubt came into his voice, and he broke off in a dying fall, so that Léonie, intrigued, spoke for the first time.

'Better. But you're not quite sure?'

'Well, we all want that for her, don't we? Trouble is, the pressure of her work, being such a big star, it's not easy, being *always* better. In some ways she's worse because she's so successfully expressed herself – worse in her own private life, I mean, because the Laura Bowen part of her leaks into her real life. Do you get me? Being a picture star satisfies all that acting thing in her, but it gets to be quite at odds with her own true personality, gives her ideas she can't, or certainly shouldn't, act on privately, like running away into the desert the other day. She gets to mix the two things up – the public and the private person, confuses them – and that's dangerous, for herself and just as much for other people, her friends, do you see?'

'Yes, I think I do . . .'

In fact Léonie – taking this as a very fair appraisal – saw exactly what he meant. And she slightly thawed towards Craig now, acknowledging his percipience, his apparent care and concern for Hetty.

'So what we have to do,' Craig continued in a more lighthearted manner, 'is to try and see she doesn't go on confusing fantasy with fact like this. And that's been difficult for me, since making pictures with her I naturally have to *encourage* her fantasies! And it's not so easy then to get her back on an even keel after a picture's over. So I'm glad you're coming back with us, for a bit, to Nice, while you get things straight with your husband. And I'm sorry about that, by the way – all this talk of Hetty when you've suffered far more than her right now – truly sorry.'

'Yes. Yes, it was all so stupid. I want him back. Robert simply . . . misunderstood things . . .' Léonie was confused.

'Well, that's the very danger, you see.' Craig, having carefully laid the foundations and seeing this confusion, moved in for the kill. 'Like I was saying, it's this very problem of Hetty's – that's caused all the trouble, between you and Robert: her playing games, mixing fantasy with fact, so that other people are bound to suffer . . .'

'I don't quite follow. Playing games with me and Robert? What games?'

'Oh . . .' Craig paused, looking at her quizzically. 'I thought you understood. Hetty's games! – how she, well, with you and Robert, she was just playing out some drama of her own – a melodrama! – how she really just wanted to separate you, from the beginning, because she was so damned jealous over your marriage. Oh, yes,' he ran on, before Léonie, whose face had clouded, could interrupt, 'that's exactly the problem we were talking about: making a drama out of other people's lives, as if she was in a picture with them, trying to destroy them that way.'

'But Hetty . . . couldn't have been doing that – with us.' Léonie was aghast at the very idea.

''Fraid she could. I don't want to pry – but, well, why else would your husband just drop you so suddenly and disappear – on your honeymoon?' He looked at her, at his most confiding and sympathetic.

'I don't – well, as I said, Robert quite misunderstood. He must have thought that Hetty and I . . .' She stopped.

'Léonie,' he helped her. 'You've absolutely nothing to fear from me. I've known Hetty was that way, with women, for *years*. And it's never really disturbed me. I understand. So you can trust me that way. But the point is, Robert sure as hell doesn't understand – and he must have thought you and Hetty had taken up again, you know, in that way – that night you spent in the tent together.' He looked at her calmly.

'Well, yes – I think he did. But we *hadn't*!' she lied firmly.

'No, of course not. Just those bites!' Craig introduced the murder weapon tenderly. Then he laughed softly again. 'Hetty – know her of old . . .' He rubbed his neck abstractedly. 'How she likes to mark people that way. Well, that's just her problem, with you two people – little drama she had to create, when her own work wasn't going too well – wanting to wreck other people's lives . . .'

'I still don't follow.'

'Isn't it obvious? She bit you that way – just so your husband would see, just so she could separate you.' He ran on before Léonie could stop him. 'And that's what we have to help her over, the one real flaw she has left, a hangover from the old days, this destructive urge with other people. Look at the havoc it's caused between you and Robert. So it's good you'll be with us for a bit, see if we can help her over this last hurdle. I'm too close to her . . . Though frankly I wouldn't blame you, in the circumstances, if you just dropped her, the way she's behaved to you – trying to destroy your marriage – and went back to your husband straight-away. You'll make things up with him easily enough when you tell him what really happened . . .'

During this peroration, Léonie was backing away from him in horror, digesting all that he had said, seeing, sensing the truth in all this nightmare synopsis of Hetty's actions, her real motives. Now it had been spelt out to her, she could hardly but see it, for it was, indeed, the truth.

'No,' she said, shaking her head violently. 'No, no . . .'

Craig advanced on her, puzzled. 'But yes,' he said, with pained sincerity. 'It's the truth, Léonie, that's the awful thing. And you and I can help her over it, if you'll help me . . .'

But by that point Léonie had turned and fled into the crowd.

Craig savoured his victory – his charity, indeed. He felt no qualms whatsoever at his behaviour. Quite the opposite. Why, he'd done the girl a favour, returning her to her husband, giving her the evidence with which to make things up with him.

Léonie, running to her cabin then and locking the door, was quite appalled. Was Craig lying, inventing, presuming, merely deducing in all this? Possibly. But then why should he do so? As far as she could see, he had nothing to gain. He had obviously been keen to have her come back with them to Nice, to help him out with Hetty. Certainly he had not been trying to separate them again. And, besides, she had no intention of taking up with Hetty permanently. She desperately wanted Robert back, and had told Craig so. Thus he could not have seen her as a rival any more for Hetty's affections.

Had Hetty, jealous of their marriage, simply wanted to separate her from Robert? In terms of the old Hetty – childish and malicious – it made sense. She would have done just that. But the new Hetty? Perhaps there was no such person. That was just another invention of hers.

Léonie put her hand involuntarily to her shoulder, touching the little teeth bruises there beneath her blouse. Had that been Hetty's intention – from the start? Not loving passion, but destruction?

Having mulled over all the evidence, Léonie decided it must be so, just as Craig had said. She stood up, agitated, pacing the cabin, then took her purse from the wardrobe, rifling through it, finding her return tickets, checking them, with her passport, before seeing the photograph of Robert she always kept there. And that finally decided her. Robert obviously was so much more important than Hetty to her. Her sojourn on the boat this past fortnight, as well as her night with Hetty in the tent, had both been sheer folly.

Delving further into the wardrobe she got her suitcase out, starting to pack quickly. If she hurried she could catch the night express from Luxor to Cairo on the other side of the river, without having to face Hetty again. Yes, she'd do just that. Her heart thrilled with the idea of seeing Robert again, as soon as possible, of making things up with him, armed with this evidence of Craig's. Robert would understand, just as she did now.

And besides, even if Craig had invented everything, she suddenly saw how, just as in the old days, anything to do with Hetty was fraught with potential disaster – how she, in these last weeks and in the bedouin tent, had simply blinded herself to this, given in to her wiles. For that was the truth: Hetty – so admirable, brave, talented, lovely in so many ways, also carried within her, like a killing virus, the seeds of plague, of havoc. Her work thrived on and encouraged what was fantastic in her nature, drawing these obsessive fantasies from her, which in turn became dripping acid which would always corrode and destroy when set against the decencies of ordinary life. What was wonderful in her nature depended on what was malign, each feeding on, dependent upon, the other for its movement, its existence. To be with her was an enchantment. But it was a dream from which, at the cost of her sanity, her life, she had to awake.

Léonie left the boat that evening and caught the train, without seeing Hetty again.

9

HETTY, NEXT MORNING, was beside herself with rage masquerading as grief. 'Why – oh why?' she yelled at Craig.

'I've no idea.' He tried to console her.

'Did you see her last night?'

'Yes. But just to say hello to.'

Hetty started to sob. Charged with his own successes and conquests, Craig felt free to play the sympathetic father, husband, lover once more, taking Hetty in his arms.

'Don't, Hetty, don't. Things happen like that, and I'm sorry. But you can't just pick up old loves – and think they'll work all over again, as if nothing had happened meantime. It never works . . . And she must have seen that, last night. Don't blame her too much. You love in a way she can't. Remember? I told you just that years ago, in Ireland, when we first met. You have so much more of love. And she only has a little to spare. And, Hetty, I'm sorry I've been so difficult with you. Things'll be easier now, with this location shooting out of the way, I promise . . .'

But Hetty remained angry. 'Léa just disappeared, without a word,' she yelped, conveniently forgetting how she, with Craig, had done exactly the same thing to Léonie eight years before. 'And I loved her, I truly did.'

'I know you did.' Craig, holding Hetty in his arms, looked wisely over her shoulder at the mists clearing across the bronze-blue waters of the river. 'But she couldn't match you.'

Craig – the master of love with Hetty and Léonie, telling to each the story of the other's death – so that their hearts were broken and they died . . .

And he drew Hetty back then, in her silk Molyneux pyjamas, to the big double bed in her cabin, the sheets still tossed about, where she had spent the night alone. And, as the river mists cleared and the bright desert sun streamed through the cabin curtains, Craig gave her that reward he had prepared for her – earlier than he had anticipated.

He began to make love to her, tenderly, expertly, mimicking love, drawing her pyjama top open, sliding the silk across her nipples, bending down, feeding there for an instant, so that she jumped with pleasure, before responding – gently at first, shyly, in a way she never remembered doing before, without vehemence, with a feeling of awkward humility, as if learning this way of love for the first time, returning to her old true self now in a heartfelt process, where there were ends in view beyond mere pleasure. As indeed there were.

'Craig . . .' She looked at him intently. 'Now the picture's coming to an end, and there'll be quite a break after it, I'd so le-le-like a child. So want one. Can't we? Couldn't we?'

'Maybe.' Craig temporised, hoping it would never come to that.

'We'd be easier then, I'm sure we would, you and I, if there was someone else – a family,' she added urgently. With the loss of Léonie, Hetty suddenly felt the unconscious urge for some other quite dependent person. She had not really wanted a child before. Her earlier miscarriage had confirmed this and in any case her career then, and her stark ambitions, along with Craig's, had always been a prohibition. But now she wanted one – as an inviolate security, a salve to her battered pride, to confirm the reality of her marriage with Craig. 'Oh, love me that way, Craig – for that, please do . . .'

She lay back, eyes wide with longing, encouraging him now, as he slipped her silk trousers off, twisting urgently then, suddenly hungry for him, hungry for some vague future mirror image of herself, a toy, her entire possession which could never be taken from her, never betray her, so that now she allowed him full play, provoking him, as he slid over her, into her, lust beginning to rise, so that soon she felt herself sinking – sinking, goaded beyond endurance by wild spasms of joy. Here was a confirmation of all her old happy obsessions, a life renewed with Craig so that, together again, they could don the incorruption of make-believe.

So thrilled was she by this renewal with Craig that the long-delayed letter, sent to Hollywood by Mortimer Cordiner, which she finally received on their return to the Semiramis Hotel in Cairo, barely moved her at all.

'Can you imagine?' She turned to Craig, out on the balcony overlooking the river. 'Think what that old fool of a woman my mother has done: left the entire house and estate of Summer Hill . . . to the *butler*! Mortimer suggests I should buy it off him: buy my own property in effect!'

'Well, why not? You have the money. And it *is* yours, or should be –'

'Oh, what does it matter?' Hetty interrupted as she joined him on the balcony. 'Never really liked the place anyway – or want to live in Ireland.'

'Still, it's the principle – and the family.'

'But I don't *need* it! – the house, the land, my mother, Léonie, Robert . . .' She joyfully enumerated, the better to try to persuade herself how they had no effect, simply did not impinge on her. 'Don't need them . . .' She looked at him, a tender mischief in her eyes. 'As long as I have you.'

But then she looked at Craig much more seriously, intently, trying, as so often before, to plumb the unknowable depths there, seeking some confirmation of her last words.

'Oh yes, you always have me, Hetty,' he lied.

When Léonie returned to Paris a week later she had, quite apart from Craig's revelations about Hetty, some other and entirely happy evidence to offer Robert – a confirmation, she thought, of their own real love.

'I'm sorry – sorry I'm late!' she said to him breathlessly, having run all the way up the six flights of stairs to their small apartment on the top floor of the old building on the rue Saint-André-des-Arts. 'You got my telegrams?'

He nodded, not cold, but not warm either. Then she handed him the little bunch of flowers, the bouquet of early spring violets she had bought for him at the flower market in the rue de Buci at the end of the narrow street. He took them awkwardly. 'Thank you,' he murmured rather formally, holding the paper sheath as if it was a bomb. It was nearly eleven in the morning – the overnight train from Marseilles had been delayed – and he had just been about to leave for work at the *Tribune*; the smell of the freshly-ground coffee they always shared together at this time was still in the air.

Léonie embraced him wildly. 'Oh, Robert! – I'm so *glad* you haven't left yet – so glad to *see* you! You can't imagine . . .' She kissed him on the cheek, stroking his hair, flattening it sideways across his scalp, relishing the coarse touch of something missed and loved. 'So glad because I think – *think* I've some wonderful news!' She stood back from him a moment, taking off her headscarf and releasing her hair, so that it crackled with static electricity in the frosty air of a brilliant March morning, sun streaming in through the slanting skylight just above them.

Robert looked at her, overwhelmed, but still doubting. 'What?'

'I'm pregnant! Sure I am! I was due last week – and nothing happened. Oh, Robert! . . .' She came to him again, taking him in her arms, close to him, close to tears. 'And I'm so sorry about everything else. But it was all really . . . *nothing*. I'll tell you later – Craig told me all about it. Hetty was just being a bitch, she only wanted to separate us. And it was all just a brainstorm of mine, with her. Means nothing now. Because, don't you see? – I love you more than anything, anybody else in the world. And now this, I'm sure of it, a child! – that day in the temple . . . So it's all going to be okay.' She clutched him again. '*Oh*, how I've missed you!'

Robert, during all this, had slowly and invisibly thawed. Now he responded more openly, taking her in his arms, leaning over her shoulder, gazing out of the high window at the sliver of blue sky over the crazy paving rooftops, hearing the faint cries of the flower vendors echo up the street in the glittery weather. Mornings with Léonie again, he thought. Bright days in Paris once more. He held up the bunch of spring violets behind Léonie's back, sniffed them a moment, that faint odour of violets which so epitomised Léonie. It was as if, through these flowers, she had given him back the very essence of herself, so that he doubted her no longer. He felt tears pricking his eyes. 'Yes,' he said at last. 'I've missed you, too. Missed – both of you . . .'

*

Léonie was right. She was pregnant. Her child, in the following months, material-ised. But Hetty's never did. Instead of new life she conceived nothing with Craig but misfortune, the first hints of this becoming apparent nearly two months later, just as they were nearing the end of the filming at the Victorine studios in Nice.

She had always slept well enough, even in Egypt, despite the heat and tension there. But now, on her return to the more equable climate of the south of France, she found herself waking regularly at three or four in the morning, unable afterwards to find any release from this hour of the wolf; she lay feverishly, plagued by waking nightmares, delirious abstract visions, tossing about on the bed, seeking relief from the pains that had come to scorch her joints, so that by morning, with a blinding headache, she was worn out and had to miss that day's shooting at the studio.

Yet these bouts went as quickly as they came, so that Hetty thought them no more than a variation of morning sickness, which, together with the cessation of her periods, surely confirmed her pregnancy, so that she bore the discomforts with an unenquiring, almost happy fortitude.

But to the unit doctor these symptoms seemed more those of malaria than of pregnancy. So that initially, without denying the latter, he treated her for the former, with doses of quinine, which left Hetty feeling worse for a time, before her maladies suddenly disappeared and she was able to resume work, finally completing the *Nefertiti* interiors some three months after their return from Egypt.

Subsequently, Craig, moving a bed in, locked himself away more or less permanently with his assistant in the cutting room, on the other side of the lot, editing the picture to show William Fox in New York. He was well aware of Fox's displeasure at what he had already seen of the uncut film. He had expected no less. Equally he had always known that, given Fox's contract with both him and Laura jointly, Fox would never fire him in mid-picture, thus losing all his invest-ment. Of course not. He had the whip hand there. But just as certainly he knew that as soon as he completed the picture, together with the editing and titling, and delivered it to Fox, the latter would then take control of it, try to tamper with it, dictating cuts that would ruin it.

So, like Penelope at her loom, he prolonged and then dallied with the editing, often unravelling at night all that he had woven from the myriad celluloid spools during the day. He took excessive care and time over what in any case was an elaborate process – to ensure as much as anything that the final story line was watertight, that each sequence formed an immovable link with what went before and after, so that any subsequent cuts that Fox might make would make nonsense of the whole. And in this pursuit for perfection nothing else mattered; not time nor cost – nor Hetty, or even her illness.

Craig became more obsessed than ever in this final topping and tailing of the picture, which had been almost a life's work with him in any case. He was determined to complete his vision, to perfection, down to the last tiny detail. No one and nothing would stand in his way, quite sure as he was that, in the end, when Fox and the others saw it in its immaculate final form, there would be no arguments over some of the more bizarre detail: they would be bowled over by the sheer audacity, the miracle of it all, exhibit it in its entirety.

Hetty, given her earlier miscarriage and what she now expected to be another difficult pregnancy, stayed quietly in the ornate villa in the centre of the studio lot. She thought herself quite recovered, until one morning she was violently sick. Yet this, too, seemed only to confirm her pregnancy. However, one factor was missing in all this hope, which Hetty chose to ignore. Instead of gaining the slightest weight she had started to lose it steadily. While that night, and subsequently, her draining insomnia and feverish headaches returned, together with the wicked pains in her joints, so that she took to dosing herself with veronal powders, two at a time, which eased the pain, but left her unconscious until midday, when she woke in a state of numb depression – which lasted for days afterwards.

Something was seriously amiss, there was no doubt. So that the unit doctor, before he had to leave, insisted she see a specialist in Nice, a Dr Verneuil, with consulting rooms on the Promenade des Anglais overlooking the Baie des Anges. The silver-haired, somewhat aloof doctor examined Hetty thoroughly, taking blood, urine and other samples for subsequent analysis. To Hetty's impatient annoyance he gave absolutely no opinion then, deferring that until she visited him again nearly a week later.

'Well?' she asked brightly. 'Pe-pe-pregnant? I am, aren't I? I must be!'

'No, Madame. You are not pregnant.' Dr Verneuil stroked his greying moustache judiciously. His blunt reply shocked her; the blood drained from her face, all this hope so abruptly dismissed.

'Malaria then?'

'No, not malaria.' The doctor, just a fraction pleased with himself, stopped dead as if she was playing some guessing game with him.

'Well,' Hetty continued almost aggressively. 'What then?'

'You have syphilis, Madame.'

He was so entirely matter-of-fact that the news hit all the more violently. She felt dizzy suddenly, her vision clouding, shaking. For the first time, after all her recent triumphs, which had seemed to set her so securely on a pinnacle of life, she sensed she had reached some turning point, felt a vague intimation of descent, the barest hint of future calamity.

But she put these thoughts from her mind, seeking to avoid the whole issue and its implications in any way she could. The doctor had turned to the window, looking at the light glinting on the waves out in the bay, beneath a cloudless summer sky. Hetty followed his gaze abstractedly, as if he were indicating that the disease was hardly important, like a cold – that it had come to her from the elements out there, blown on the wind, and would as quickly disappear.

'Syphilis?' She came to her senses at last. 'Be-be-but it can't be! I've only ever be-be-been with my husband.'

'Indeed?' The doctor looked at her distantly, as if she had just made some banal comment on the weather. 'Then you have contracted it from him, Madame. Does he know?'

'No. I mean, I don't know. Should he know?'

'There are usually clear signs, in both parties – though not invariably.'

'You mean, he could have known – and didn't tell me?'

'Ah, there I cannot help you. I have no idea. You would have to make enquiries there yourself,' he added delicately, turning again to the window.

Hetty was thunderstruck. 'But he *might* not have known?' she persisted.

'It's possible. Or he may not as yet have recognised the signs. Or have milder symptoms. In any case he should be told. You should both of you seek appropriate treatment at once.'

'Appropriate treatment?'

'Yes.' The doctor spoke more enthusiastically now. 'A full course of it. Not mercury luckily, which is no real cure at all. We have Salvarsan now – the "magic bullet" – a dozen weekly injections to start with, and perhaps intra-muscular bismuth then, for a year or so, depending on how the infection develops. It can change its character, you see, Madame – primary, secondary, tertiary syphilis. There are stages, variations,' he added neatly. 'You are at the primary stage – and one would hope to stop it there . . .' He left the sentence hanging in the air.

'And if not? These headaches, these awful pains in my joints, the nausea, so that I can hardly we-work as it is – it would get we-worse? So that I couldn't we-work at all?'

'Oh, I would hope not.' Again the doctor's gaze seemed distracted by something outside the window. A fleck of cloud, Hetty saw, no bigger than a man's hand, had come to perch over the bay. 'Salvarsan,' the doctor continued, 'has proved effective, in most cases, in . . .' He paused, looking for the right word for the first time in their consultation. 'In subduing the symptoms, Madame.'

But Hetty caught the real gist here. 'So that I might never be cured, you mean?'

'No. I do not mean that. Simply – it's impossible to say, to speak of a total cure as yet. This new drug has not been in use long enough. What we do know is that it can entirely suppress the symptoms. On the other hand we know that the bacterium can lie quite dormant for years, in any case. So it's a matter . . . of time, Madame,' he finished ambiguously.

'A time-bomb, you mean?' The doctor ignored this grim sally. 'And children?' Hetty went on. 'I could never have children?'

'You could, biologically speaking – unless there was some other venereal infection, affecting the fallopian tubes for example. But you would be most ill-advised to do so, whatever the case. There would be very real risks for you and possible complications for the child.'

Hetty at this news bowed her head. She had started to sweat, to shake, almost to cry. Dr Verneuil, seeing this, took her in hand. 'Come, Madame, there is little point in our going into further details at the moment. You must not over-concern yourself there. The important thing is that you start the treatment at once. Will you be staying down here on the coast for some time?'

He stood up, a trifle more considerate now, coming towards Hetty, speaking to her as if she were a wilting flower and not a beautiful woman of twenty-seven, at the height of her powers – a woman, he had naturally omitted to tell her, suffering a painful and debilitating disease, which was likely to develop even more painfully, where there was no certainty at all of any cure. Indeed Salvarsan, as he knew, with its arsenic base, was toxic, so that this cure, if the course had to be prolonged, could be worse than the disease, resulting in agonising side-effects, even death. None of this Dr Verneuil told her. It had been sufficient simply to break the ice. She would face troubles enough in any case over this disease in the future.

Hetty, driving back to the villa that morning, typically decided there were only two ways of dealing with the problem: either shoot the man or accept her condition. Equally typically she decided more or less on the first course. The problem was that, with Craig incarcerated in the cutting rooms, she rarely saw him these days. Finally she had to beard him in his lair, late that night, when the editor and his assistants had gone home.

She found him, in the stuffy heat of the cutting rooms, dishevelled, sweating in a striped fishing vest, an alchemist once more, now in the final throes of turning dross to gold, bent over a chattering moviola machine at one end of the long room, with high shelves down each side filled with hundreds of numbered cans of film. A long table in the middle held great open wire spools linked together with slack trails of celluloid. Further down, above the cutting bench, dozens of title and leader strips, clipped to the wall, fell in profusion.

He looked up unwillingly, stopping the machine, as she closed the door. 'Christ, honey, I'm pretty busy.'

'I know you are.' She smiled, brushing her short-cropped hair, which was growing again now, an inch or so above the scalp, but still giving her the air of a bright but in this instance a malicious street urchin.

Craig returned to the moviola, setting it chattering again, peering through a lens, as the film sped past beneath him, snapping through the gate. 'Hey, this is the sequence near the end, in the little love pavilion. My God, it's quite something – you're really good . . .' He didn't look up, preferring the image of Hetty to the reality.

'Yes, I know. I saw the dailies –'

'Nothing like when it's all cut together, though. Here, want to take a look?'

'I saw the specialist today.' Hetty was quite calm.

'Why, yes.' He looked up at last. 'Did he confirm it – the pregnancy?'

'No.'

He gazed at her. 'Oh . . . Just malaria, after all?'

'No, Craig . . .' She paused and he returned to his vision of the little love pavilion. 'You know, you must have known,' she continued evenly, 'that it wasn't malaria, that I wasn't pregnant. It's syphilis.' The moviola had started to clatter away again, so that Hetty shouted now. '*Syphilis* – did you hear me?'

He stopped the machine. 'Yes, I heard you.' He stood up, took a handkerchief out and wiped his brow, then looked at her, his face still damp, without expression. 'Hell, that's bad, Hetty. But what do you mean I knew? I'd no idea.' He looked at her now, without any condemnation, just with genuine puzzlement. 'Who?' he asked her then. 'Who was it?'

Then she erupted. But it seemed to her, as she experienced the sudden anger, to be something quite different – a gradual explosion, as if in slow motion, expanding in waves to fill the long room. '*You*, Craig! – you shit, because I've slept with no one else. *You!* – and you must have it too – you gave it me!'

Her voice rose, before he interrupted her. 'That's nonsense, Hetty. I don't have syphilis. I'd know if I had, wouldn't I?'

'Just hasn't shown itself with you, that's all – can't have de-de-done. But *I* have it.' Hetty went for him then, hammering at him with her fists, before he warded her off. 'And I can't really ever have children now – you've ruined my life – *and* I won't be able to work.'

He stood back from her, holding her at arm's length. 'Now listen, honey, calm down. Can't be that bad –'

'Of *course* it's that bad –'

'And there's a cure these days –'

'Yes, injections – months of them, pe-possibly years of treatment, the doctor said. And maybe I'll *never* recover.'

'That's crazy, Hetty. Lots of people get the clap – and recover.'

'It's *not* clap, it's syphilis you've given me! Just look at you, you shit! You've your whole life round you, here, right now, in all this film. But I'll have nothing – won't be able to work, stuck in bed with these aching joints, sick headaches, vomiting. You lying creep. God, how I hate you – your saying how everything was going to be better when we got back to Nice. Instead I can't have children now, never make love again, probably never we-work, ride horses – all that, just gone. The future we had, like you said that morning in Egypt: you and me and – children. And pictures at the Victorine here, when I thought we were both back on the rails. You've killed all that future! And I never want to see you again.'

In default of killing him then, she thought to destroy what meant most to him, in all the cans of film. She turned, throwing herself at the shelves, flinging the cans to the floor, the film reeling out. Then she moved to the big open spools on the central bench, doing the same there, so that before Craig finally got control of her the room was awash in loose film, filled with piles of snaking celluloid, crackling underfoot.

'That's mostly old outcuts anyway,' he said, getting a grip on her. 'But just tell me now – who? *Who* was it you were sleeping with?'

'*No* one. But you, you bastard!' she screamed, before breaking down in convulsive sobs, kneeling on the floor among the serpentine reels of film, crunching it up in her fingers, trying to destroy these images of herself in an impotent frenzy.

Craig looked at her without sympathy. He had consoled her before, many times. But now he made no effort to comfort her. 'You can destroy yourself, Hetty. Or try and destroy me. But you can't kill the real thing in both of us. That's on film now in *Nefertiti*. And it's indestructible, live on long after you and I are gone.

Besides, there's a cure for syphilis – if you want it. We're not living in the Middle Ages. You'll get better.'

Well, yes, he thought, she would get better. But something, at last, had finally snapped between them. Something told him this was the beginning of the end of his relationship with Hetty. Timely, perhaps, in that now he had almost completed his long drama with her. All that he had ever really wanted of her lay securely embalmed in the film cans all round him now, in the master print spools of *Nefertiti*, locked in a huge fire-proof safe in the next room.

The culmination of her professional life, everything he had taught her, manipulated and drawn from her, in eight years together, lay there inviolate, captured indefinitely, in long strips of celluloid. So that, even if he lost her, in reality, what did that matter? He would always possess her – at her most perfect, in *Nefertiti*. That was what pictures were, after all – little bits of time, people trapped for ever by a camera, rescued from oblivion, whom other people would never ever forget.

'Listen,' he told her coldly, the image of father, lover, friend melting from his face. 'What happens between us now doesn't matter any longer. Did it ever really matter? What did we amount to anyway? – that wasn't meant for all this.' He gestured round the cans of film. 'You and I and our problems, mistakes, whatever . . .' He smiled shortly. 'Nothing more than a whistle in the dark . . . But there!' He turned again, looking triumphantly round the cutting room. '*There*, in those cans of film – that's where we really live! That's where our life together begins and ends, where we'll be saved or damned. In *Nefertiti*. For the rest, well, I'm sorry.'

But he was not really, as he offered her this brief apology, a final distant smile from the dandy man with the rogue good looks, his face filled for an instant with all that had made him wonderful to Hetty: power and dreams – the gift of bridging them, in art, in celebration; of giving chaos form, rescuing the passing minute, that magic touch of resurrection. 'I'm leaving for New York in a few days. Show the picture to Fox. That's all that matters now – for you and me.' Then he was walking out the door.

'No, no! . . .' At the last moment Hetty wanted him back. Yet that intensely real but still unknowable image of Craig had gone. And she knew then how she wanted him again, at whatever cost, still wanted Craig – for what she could never possess in him.

It was not until later that evening, going to bed on the couch he had set up in the next room, that Craig, inspecting himself carefully, saw the tiny, slightly pitted white circles on the underside of his penis – quite painless, which was why he had not noticed them before, but none the less evidence of exactly what Hetty had accused him of.

'Jesus . . .' he murmured. 'Those damn bedouin children. Christ!' he added. Should he tell Hetty? What difference would it make, other than to make matters worse – make their parting more difficult, more acrimonious?

*

In New York ten days later, when William Fox saw Craig's six-and-a-half-hour version of *Nefertiti*, he started by firing everyone in his company who had ever had anything to do with the picture, burning up the Western Union wires between his office and Hollywood, until wiser counsels prevailed.

'Look, we can get Brenon to re-shoot what we need changed, on the Hollywood lot. Then cut it by half – and more,' Winfield Sheehan told him.

Fox still trembled with fury in his vast and gloomy office. 'Okay – as long as Craig has nothing to do with it. *Nothing!*' Fox had refused to meet Craig. 'I'll ruin him, though,' he went on now. 'He'll never work again in Hollywood. I'll talk with Zukor even, and Sam. Never work again, *never!* And from now on it'll be comedies, Sheehan, melodramas, gangster pictures with us – anything – but no more epics, Sheehan, *ever.*'

News of the *Nefertiti* disaster spread quickly in Hollywood. And Fox was as good as his word. Swallowing his pride, he talked with the other studio bosses. Secretly delighted at his epic setback, they were nonetheless warned now and fearful, too, of Craig's wild extravagances – and, having always mistrusted his cultured European airs and graces anyway, they were pleased to blackball him.

Howard Brenon re-shot many of the scenes, with Clive Brook and some of the other principals. Afterwards a posse of craven editors was put to work on the picture, delving into mountains of celluloid, cutting it to pieces, reducing Craig's masterpiece – for it was that – by more than half, to a banal tale of blood and thunder in ancient Egypt, in which all the cleverly worked psychology in the script, the religious and sexual deviations, the subtle performances, all the obsessions and perverse nuances in the characters, were brutally removed, making nonsense of Craig's original story, turning what had been an artistic epic into an almost incoherent tale of banal mischief on the Nile.

Craig, back at the Wolf's Lair in Hollywood, sacked by Fox and knowing of all this desecration going on down in the Fox studios, fought back vigorously. He instigated legal proceedings against the company, charging them first with unjustified dismissal, then with breaking clauses carefully inserted in his contract which had stipulated that he be consulted over all post-production work on the picture.

Fox counter-sued, charging Craig with gross professional negligence, together with other assorted legal euphemisms covering his various delays and extravagances. Craig employed the best attorneys. It would be a long and costly business, he realised. But then he had the money, plenty of it – over a million dollars cash in WillBow Pictures, his joint company with Hetty, in which his and nearly all her huge earnings over the last few years had been deposited.

Their joint signatures were required to withdraw on this account. But Craig, in his good times with Hetty before leaving for Egypt, had signed a dozen open cheques with her, so that various impending bills in America could be met by the company secretary in Los Angeles while they were away.

Craig used these cheques now, first to transfer half a million dollars into a separate checking account for himself, then to pay the attorneys, then to spend much larger sums in setting up his next picture at the Victorine Studios, a co-production with Gaumont in Paris. For Craig, now increasingly blinding himself to the realities of every situation, saw the *Nefertiti* reception as nothing more than a temporary setback. He would be vindicated there and was perfectly confident of his future, in Europe now, if not in Hollywood. He had long wanted to be finished with Hollywood in any case, so that being blackballed there meant very little to him.

And, besides, he still had a phenomenal record of commercial successes behind him, and a reputation quite unblemished as far as the European producers and exhibitors were concerned; his pictures had always done more than good business in Europe, and they still therefore held him in considerable esteem. Craig had made them a great deal of money over the years and would have no difficulty now in making his own way with them as an independent producer in the picture business outside Hollywood, starting with this first adventure epic, *The Lost Valley* – a tale of an English mining surveyor, journeying alone in the high Atlas mountains of Morocco, coming on a hidden valley there, finding a group of missionaries, together with attendant nuns, attempting to convert and educate the infidel.

Hetty had earlier been set to play one of the young nuns, falling in love with the Englishman, breaking her vows, running away with him – into all sorts of amorous and dramatic disasters. The picture, with its costly locations in the Atlas, had been budgeted at nearly $400,000, and close to half of this was to be supplied by WillBow Pictures. Craig, in Hollywood, had already delved into his capital to pay his attorneys. Now, setting up *The Lost Valley* he went deeper still into it – as well as committing most of the rest of the capital to future co-productions with Gaumont. So that by the autumn of 1927, without Hetty's knowing, the uncommitted money left available to both of them in WillBow Pictures had been reduced, by their standards, almost to a pittance.

These had not been Craig's only activities during his six months back in America. Driving down to Hollywood one summer morning soon after returning he had stopped his Pierce-Arrow at a favourite old picnic spot, hidden by a grove of shady pepper trees right on the edge of Hollywood Lake – stopped because he had been astonished to see half the pepper trees felled, the site levelled and a collection of builders' trucks grinding up the earth, unloading scaffolding, bricks, cement, with other men out and about with theodolites surveying the whole ruined area.

'What's up? What's happening?' Craig had walked over to one of the surveyors.

'What's it look like? New development. New apartment block. Lakeside Court.'

'But, why, you can't! It's a beauty spot.'

'Can't?' The young man was impatient, laconic. 'Well, you go tell that to the boss. He's here right now in fact. That big limousine over there. Mr Borzsony.'

Craig, furious, had walked over to the car parked under one of the last of the pepper trees. He thought it empty at first until he saw something move under a huge mohair travelling rug laid out along the back seat. 'Mr Borzsony?'

The rug moved once more, thrusting, wriggling. And then, like a butterfly emerging slowly from a chrysalis, a girl's face emerged, eyes full of sleep, followed by a neck, then a hand reaching to close the collar of her dress shyly. Finally the whole torso came clear of the rug, sitting up, and Craig saw the full beauty of a young woman, hardly twenty, he thought, the sharply chiselled features, long chin, fine nose, hollowed cheeks, waking now, at first embarrassed, then interested, thin wide blue eyes blinking at him.

'No, it's *Miss* Borzsony. Sorry, I flaked out again. Out late last night – you know . . .' She smiled vaguely. But it was the voice that immediately struck Craig, much more than the pretty face – surprising tones from someone so young: it was dark, fluent, mellow, knowing, the sounds linked together like a rich sigh. It was sexy. Educated, East Coast – some posh girls' school in New England, Craig thought. But with a timbre all its own: autumnal, dream-filled. 'My father's over there, I guess, with the foreman.' She stretched forward, still half-asleep, reaching out towards the window, a long, thin-fingered, sun-browned hand resting on the glass, as she inspected Craig carefully. 'And who are you, may one ask? . . .' Yes, Craig thought again, that extraordinary voice, resonant, full of old music. 'The architect?'

'No. I'm Craig St John Williamson – I make pictures and I'm goddamned furious with your father, ruining this place. Used to picnic here in the old days . . .' Craig gestured about him. 'This was *beautiful* last time I was here.'

The girl leant right forward now, peeking her head out of the window. 'Yes,' she said appraisingly, 'I bet it was.' Her gaze returned to Craig. 'Well, you go over and give him hell then – Mr Craig St John Williamson who makes pictures. And tell him I was due riding at the Country Club half an hour ago.'

'Yes, I'll do just that,' Craig moved away.

'Or wait!' she called after him. 'I've a better idea. Is that yours over there – that Pierce-Arrow? Yes, well, maybe *you* could take me to the Country Club instead?'

Craig looked back at her, the long triangular face leaning out of the window, the fine pointed chin resting on her hand, eyeing him nicely, reasonably. Apart from her voice there did not seem anything terribly special about her – the clear, washed-blue eyes under a swathe of corn-blonde hair, not cropped in the current fashion, but long, flowing untended. She was simply . . . pretty.

But at just that moment a breeze off the water raked the blonde strands across her eyes and nose, her mouth. And for some reason this silk-gold curtain, like a gauze front drop lowered against a theatrical set, suddenly entirely altered Craig's perception of her, enhancing the features, highlighting them dramatically, transforming her whole personality. This new view of her excited him – caught his heart strangely, as she let the hair tickle her, doing absolutely nothing about it, not moving a muscle, a still centre amidst the clatter and destruction going on all round them. So that for Craig, too, the world stopped as he gazed at her.

She spoke again, waking him. 'Well, will you – take me?'

'Why yes, of course, Miss Borzsony.'

'Duna Börzsöny,' she said, stepping out of the Dodge. She had on a summer frock, showing long fine legs, as she walked confidently towards him over the ruined site where he and Hetty had once picnicked.

'Interesting name . . .'

'Hungarian. With two little dots over both of the o's.' She cleared her hair away and smiled. They shook hands in the middle of all the disruption – and he took her.

For Craig, just as with Hetty eight years before, Duna in the following months became an obsessive necessity, something offered out of the blue by the gods, a destiny, a happy fate – a woman to love, to mould, someone with whom to renew his old dream of true romance; someone quite untutored with whom to further all his professional dreams; a new photograph in his select album of wondrous women, unmarked, whom he would remake in his own images. And, just as with Hetty, he did everything with and for her from then on, in the way of advancing their personal and professional relationship – teaching her, grooming her, flirting with her, arranging screen tests – doing everything in short except make love with her. It was part of his usual initial way with his conquests, of course – part of the trap, the enticing poison flower he always laid out for these women. But in this instance there was another reason for his restraint – his syphilis.

He had to visit discreet clinics, in Los Angeles and New York, undergoing treatment similar to Hetty's, though for what in his case turned out to be a much less severe infection. He told Hetty nothing of this. He barely corresponded with her in a personal vein at all, merely dictating letters to her about his *Nefertiti* battles – and her new role in *The Lost Valley*.

He told her nothing of how he had spent, or committed, most of their joint capital in WillBow Pictures, nearly two-thirds of which had been Hetty's money in the first place. He told her nothing of Duna Börzsöny either. What was there to say? – other than what Duna herself had said that morning as they drove away from the ruined site: 'Can't stand in the way of progress, Mr Craig St John Williamson who makes pictures!'

Hetty, in these months apart, wrote to him more regularly and personally. She ate no humble pie, yet was conciliatory. Recovering her pride, she nonetheless wanted to make things up with him – believing that she had, perhaps, over-reacted that night in the Victorine cutting rooms. They had after all – albeit in very different ways – both been unfaithful during their marriage. Her infection had come about simply in the nature of their separate desires – she had slept with women, if not with any other man, while he, no doubt, had made love with other women. Yet it might have been the other way round. So, regretting her initial outburst, she took steps to repair the damage.

For, even if she had lost him personally, she wanted him still for his professional support. She, like Craig, was aware that without him behind the camera she might well make a ham fist of the whole motion picture business – in choice of stories, scripts, costumes, performance, everything.

She needed him again for all that, since despite her setbacks she still had, she knew, one tremendous card left to play in her life. She remained a great star. Her continuing fan mail confirmed this – as did the experience of her immediate surroundings in Nice. She could not walk down the Promenade des Anglais or take tea at the Negresco without being almost immediately recognised, pestered, sometimes mobbed. And her last Hollywood picture with Craig, *Gold Dust*, a costume drama set during the California gold rush, just released in Europe, was doing record business.

So that now above everything she wished to maintain this pre-eminent position in the picture palaces of the world. Her talent, she knew – whatever else happened to her – must remain her saving grace. And that particular talent, of course, lying as it did in her astonishing mix of beauty and athleticism, was what was most threatened by her disease.

So she took to Dr Verneuil's cure religiously, suffering it with quite untypical patience – the continued tests and intimate examinations, the Salvarsan injections, the subsequent bismuth salts treatment. It was a painful business, these weekly visits to his surgery on the Promenade. But the treatment seemed to work. The symptoms disappeared – and, most crucially, did not return when the course of Salvarsan was completed three months later. So that by the autumn of that year, 1927, buoyed up in any case by the balmy southern airs, she thought her recovery complete.

Her dark beauty, apart from the slightest hint of pain wrinkles to either side of her eyes and mouth, was unimpaired. Her body had regained most of its old snap and vigour, so that she felt able to take up riding again at the local Cercle Hippique, often hacking out with Mickey Ostrovosky, returned to his family home now, on the hills behind Nice. Then, in order to test her mettle properly, she started fencing again, at the Foils Club in the rue Gambetta. Here she soon astonished several of her male partners.

So that at a dinner party in October with the Ostrovoskys, she was able to respond to the toast they made to her in full consciousness of health and life regained.

'Th-th-thank you, all of you, ve-ve-very much!' Yes, she was happy again. Her cure seemed complete, except for her stammer.

And it was then, in that same autumn of 1927, that the sound revolution in pictures began to explode everywhere in Hollywood. Months earlier it had first started to spread like a slow fuse towards a tinder-dry forest. Fox and Warner Brothers, both well-advanced in the development of their own differing sound systems, were in the vanguard of the incendiarists. Warners, indeed, had already embarked on a semi-sound picture, with *The Jazz Singer*, shortly to be released. But Zukor, Laemmle, Goldwyn and the other big studio bosses, already committed to a whole programme of silent pictures for the coming year, were, for the most part, firmly in the camp of firefighters. However, their technical advisers warned them that it was only a matter of time before sound took over everywhere. Sound was the coming thing, they said. There was no way of beating Fox and Warners. They would have to join them.

Craig, greatly taken by all this news in Hollywood and excited by the dramatic possibilities of dialogue, was anxious from the beginning to work with this new sound process. So that when he arrived in Paris that December, just after the sensational release of *The Jazz Singer*, he at once suggested to Gaumont that they film the interiors at least of their new picture in sound. Gaumont agreed.

There was only one flaw in this idea, which Craig had recognised from the beginning: Hetty's stammer. At the very least, he thought, she would have some difficulty in adapting to this new sound process. Quite possibly she would not be able to handle it at all. What then? Should he sacrifice the new sound system – or Hetty? He delayed the decision. She could have voice training, speech therapy, he would test her at the microphone – they would see how it went.

Yet Craig was aware of another factor in all this, which he kept at the very back of his mind. With *Nefertiti* completed, and after their blazing row, he had clearly sensed an end of things with Hetty. Despite her conciliatory letters their personal relationship was doomed, he thought. She would never truly forgive him – he made the convenient argument here – because in truth he was tired of her. And besides he had taken up with Duna. So that perhaps the arrival of sound had come at an opportune moment. It would allow him to make a final break with Hetty professionally, since she might never adapt to the new system, while he had every intention of continuing with it. Sound, without its being in any way his fault, might offer him what at heart he really wanted: a cast-iron excuse to drop Hetty completely.

And if that happened, well, they would have to look for another star in *The Lost Valley* – Louise Brooks or even Garbo? Or find someone new altogether? Why, of course – and in fact he had thought of this almost from the start: Duna Börzsöny, now already taking small parts in Hollywood, in some of Mickey Neilan's and Raoul Walsh's pictures, under her new name of Diana Belleville. He was a star-maker, after all – and what he had done for Hetty he could equally well do with this woman.

And really, when you thought about it, he continued the convincing argument with himself, that was how it had always been in the motion picture business. New processes, new people. Just as Duna had said – you couldn't stand in the way of progress. Things had always changed overnight in pictures. A chauffeur one day, a director the next – like Mickey Neilan. The cowboy, or the blonde in the drugstore, stars overnight. You could never put a stay on the crazy momentum of the picture business. It had its own unstoppable energies and directions, fuelled in the end by capricious audiences, the fans who paid for it all, driving the industry ever onwards towards new faces, new techniques. He had not invented this new sound process. It was not his fault. You had to ride with change. And so would Hetty.

And so she did – or tried. As soon as Craig wrote confirming the news of the sound revolution (of which, in any case, she had heard ominous rumours at the Victorine) she at once engaged the services of a Miss Dorothea Cave, a retired English actress living in Nice who, rather failing in her earlier career on the boards, had become instead, among the theatrical and operatic community on the Côte d'Azur, something of a specialist in diction, accents, a voice coach generally.

Miss Cave, who turned out to be Scottish, with a startling shock of fuzzy red hair, attended the villa two or three times a week – and, over many hours and sessions, Hetty's stammer improved to the point of being practically undetectable, a mere attractive hesitancy over some few words.

And even this disappeared when, in the spring of 1928, Craig arrived in Nice with the new dialogue script of *The Lost Valley* and Hetty got to work on the actual lines which she would have to deliver in the coming voice tests. However, if her stammer seemed quite cured, Hetty, to her fury and frustration, was now presented with a quite different problem: remembering the lines.

Though in fact rarely longer than a few sentences, they seemed to her great mountainous blocks of recalcitrant, ever-disappearing words, which she tried to hold in her mind, feverishly grappling with them, like great slippery fish, only to have them quite elude her when she came to the point of delivering them. She began to panic at this inability to remember, and the panic made remembering more difficult still. However, as Craig told her, when the time came they would write the words up for her on a blackboard next to the camera. It would be all right on the night.

In the stuffy little covered stage at the Victorine studios a month later Hetty, dressed in the all-enclosing habit of a young nun, took the first of her costume and make-up tests for her role in *The Lost Valley*. But much more vitally it was also to be her first voice test as well, since Craig thought she would find the dialogue easier if she were fully dressed and made up for the part, so that she could really believe in it all. And he might have been right but for the furious oven-like heat in the studio, which Hetty's heavy costume and make-up made all the more difficult to bear.

The stage, with a bright summer sun beating down for several hours already, was hot enough in any case. But now it was worse, in that with silent pictures it had always been largely open to the sky, but was now entirely closed, darkened, sealed from every outside sound, so that the heat had become intense.

Hetty, nervous already in this fevered cavernous atmosphere and at a loss without the traditional mood music which Craig had always worked with before, was even more startled, scorched, when the unusually bright stage lights burst upon her and the cameraman began to adjust them – on her face, then over the makeshift set which had been got up as the mother superior's office at the mission.

Now, as the lights played over her, she was sweating profusely under her habit, the make-up beginning to run on her face, half-hidden by the white cowl. The perfume rising all about her was almost overpowering now as well – the little magic phial of *Nefertiti* scent which, as a good-luck charm, she had dabbed over her throat and face before dressing. Craig, she had hoped, might have noticed it. But he had not. And now she felt like a tart, not a nun. She wanted to change everything, go back to her dressing room, start again.

But Craig was waiting to go on a first take – Craig sitting there, invisible now as he never had been in silent shooting, no help to her at all, somewhere in front of her not next to the camera which, even more unnervingly, was equally invisible – entirely set apart, sealed up in some sort of cubicle with a glass window in front. With the heat and all that was quite new to her in this sound filming, she felt a surge of panic rising in her, like nausea, trying to escape her gut – about to explode out among all the technicians and disgrace her.

With an effort of sheer will she beat the nausea back. For now there was the most important thing of all to attend to: the microphone. Where was it? She glanced wildly about. Yes, there it was, right in front – a large black honeycombed lozenge below her, attached to the side of the desk, facing the hard chair she was to sit on while talking to the mother superior – she was to sit absolutely still, Craig had told her, facing this dark evil thing, this gorgon's eye, a wicked presence which she must somehow outface, which would form her nemesis or resurrection.

That was the microphone. And then there was the blackboard with her lines. Where was that? Again, she glanced around in panic. Yes, there – to the other side of the great black camera cubicle. But in the dazzle of these new strong lights, biting at her all round from out of the darkness, she could barely make out a word of the chalked dialogue.

'Craig! I can't see the lines properly. The lights are blinding me –'

'That's okay, honey. You'll remember them – or see them on the take when everyone's stopped moving and we're all settled. Right, are we all done?' Craig called round the sound stage. 'Okay, Hetty, your first position behind the flat . . .'

She rose unsteadily, going behind the wooden flat, and waited, breathing deeply, trying to compose herself. First, the lines . . . the lines. What were they? She'd have to remember them, for she couldn't see them now on the blackboard. But it was no use. She couldn't remember a word. She said a silent prayer then – not that she remember the lines, for she was certain now that she wouldn't, but that everyone in the studio – the technicians, Craig – would forgive her for making such a fool of herself, for wasting their time. 'Please, God,' she murmured, 'forgive me, I don't think I'm really able for this life any more . . .'

And then, with this prayer, out of the blue, her lines returned to her. Of course! There was Craig's cue first, 'Yes, Sister Martha, you asked to see me. What was it you wanted?' – and her reply 'Mother Superior, I have been anxious. *I am not sure if I am made for this life . . .*' They were almost the same words as her prayer. And then they went on – it was easy now – 'I mean, I want to help others – very much. But in the world outside our mission. I want to help in the *real* world.' Now that she remembered the lines, all would be well. Her stammer had quite disappeared, after all. It was remembering the lines, those awkward bloody lines – that had been the great difficulty. And now she knew them! God or someone had given them back to her at the last instant.

'Action!' Craig called from inside the set. And suddenly, with that old familiar voice and call, it seemed to Hetty that all indeed was well now – that old call to attack, which she had missed, but which gave her a vital thrill of reassurance, reminding her of her power, her beauty, her skills in this business. She opened the door into the set and walked confidently into the light, acting now, transformed from her real self. She took her chair in front of the desk, sitting quite still, not looking at the evil eye of the microphone, but straight towards the glass wall where the camera was. She still could not see the words on the blackboard. But it did not matter. She knew the lines now.

'Yes, Sister Martha, you asked to see me.' She heard Craig's cue from somewhere in front of her. 'What was it you wanted?'

'Me-me-me-Mother Superior, I have be-be-been anxious. I am not sure I have be-be-been made for this le-le-life . . .'

She could not believe it. The lines were there – but the stammer had returned. The vital consonants had seized up, bad as ever. The heat was stifling, beginning to overwhelm her. It was torture. It was disaster.

'Cut!' Craig shouted.

She repeated the scene. She did it nearly a dozen times again – relaxing half-way through for a break, cooling her face and throat with iced water, even trying quite different parts of the script. But it made hardly any difference. It was all torture. It was all a disaster.

'I don't understand it,' she sobbed to Craig later in her dressing room. 'It was re-re-remembering the lines I was we-we-worried about. Not the st-st-stammer. And I prayed for the lines to ke-ke-come back, and they did. But then my old ve-ve-voice came back as well and ruined everything . . .'

Craig considered matters. Then he sighed. 'But maybe that's the whole thing, Hetty. That old voice – that stammer – *is* your real voice. And all these weeks we've all been trying to make you into something you aren't. You're a great *silent* star. But not for the talkies. That's all it boils down to in the end. Nothing to be ashamed about. Besides, the talkies probably won't last,' he tried to console her, lying. 'Just a nine-day wonder.'

Hetty did not believe him. And now, in face of this disaster, she wanted, needed, him more than ever. But he wasn't there. He disappeared from her dressing room then – just as he disappeared from the villa the following day, returning to Paris to confer with Gaumont, showing them the voice and costume test on Hetty.

'Well . . .' They were cautious with him. 'Perfect, of course – perfect in every way – except for the voice. But we have to make the picture in sound now, Craig. We're committed to it, everyone is. We'll have to . . . look for someone else. It's tough, she being your wife – and such a great talent, such a great silent star. But that stammer, well . . .' They shook their heads, commiserating with him.

'No, no, you're right,' Craig said. 'Wife or no, she simply can't do it. We'll have to get someone else. There's Louise Brooks perhaps. Or we'll test others. And maybe there's this new American girl, Diana Belleville. She's sensational. I've got some reels of her latest picture with me. Think she'd play the nun perfectly. Naive yet knowing. Just like Sister Martha. And, as for sound, well, she's got this quite extraordinary voice – you'll hear it: sexy, absolutely wonderful . . .'

Craig called Hetty with the news – that they'd have to look for someone else in the part. He'd been wrong. It seemed there was no turning back with the talkies now: Gaumont was quite committed to doing *The Lost Valley* in sound. Every picture was going to be in sound, from now on. He was sorry . . . terribly sorry, but there was nothing he could do . . .

Hetty was stunned at the news, which soon spread around the Victorine studios like wild fire. Everyone, initially, commiserated with her. But thereafter most people seemed to avoid her when she walked round the lot, or saw her in the café-restaurant – making way for her, giving her space, as if she carried some fatal infection.

Hetty was reminded of something in this behaviour. What was it? Then it came back to her – the incident years before, as a child out at the harvesting at Summer Hill, when Snipe, the maimed fortune-teller, had seen her as a secret princess in the tea-leaves. And all the crone-ish old tea ladies had been astonished then, gazing at her fearfully, making way for her in awe as she had rushed from the circle. But this time, she realised, it was failure which made the technicians avoid her, a failure which, they thought, might infect their own careers – a failure which made her a pariah now and not a princess. And failure stalked her then, increasing its hold over her now at every step.

A few days after Craig had called she woke at four in the morning, a dull pain in her back, with a feverish headache. Her syphilis, merely dormant, had returned. And several days later, due to a mistake by a new typist in Hollywood, a letter arrived, from the WillBow company secretary in Hollywood – a copy of one sent to Craig in Paris – informing them both that funds in the company had sunk to below $25,000 and would have to be immediately replenished if the account was to be drawn on again over *The Lost Valley*.

Hetty was dumbfounded. Money, at least the want of it, was something which had never crossed her mind in years. It had been a fact of life, like air and water. And she had always trusted Craig with it for the simple reason that she knew how little it had ever mattered to him too – talking of it only in vast sums, half a million or more, the entire budget for a picture. Now this. Craig, she saw then, had withdrawn all the money – mostly hers – in their joint company without telling her. But much worse than that he had been financing *The Lost Valley* with it, a picture she had now been cast out of. It was unbelievable. Craig, who had first given her syphilis, then dropped her personally, then professionally, had now almost bankrupted her.

But worst of all – truly worst of all, like the touch of death – was the sudden loss of power she sensed in all this. Money she could do without – losing Summer Hill, Léonie, Craig, even her health. But power was quite another matter. She could not live without that: the power she had possessed, groomed and refined for years, so that it was instinct now, never performance – a confidence that stemmed not from great houses, from love or money but from her own sheer force of will, character, talent. All this most vital flow, the fountainhead of her life, was suddenly draining away from her. She no longer possessed that quality which was essential to her – of inevitable dominance, which had brought her such success, enabled her to overcome every setback. All this had been taken from her now, like wings clipped from a bird, leaving her earthbound, utterly vulnerable, fallible, fearful.

Now at last the full enormity of what she had lost in the last month dawned on her. Each item in her once brilliant portfolio, all her wonderful shares in the world, stared her in the face then as quite worthless certificates: Summer Hill, Léonie, Craig's love, the possibility of children, her career, money, health – these were gone, but above all power: that sovereign wand, aura of invincibility, that cloth of gold had been stripped from her.

Yet even then, suffering the full horror of this realisation, she tried to blind herself to it. It couldn't be true. Craig, for so long needed – as father, lover, friend – could not so betray her, could not be such a monster. It was a temporary aberration on his part. They would come together again. Even then, she could not find it in her heart to condemn him outright. Even then, in the face of all this appalling behaviour, she loved him.

He was still in Paris. She tried to reach him there on the telephone. But each time his new secretary told her he was out. She tried to call the WillBow company secretary, trans-Atlantic, but there were long delays. She called Micky Ostrovosky. But he had gone to Monte Carlo for the weekend.

Sitting at her bureau then, in the big salon of the villa, twilight coming on, as she gazed out at the line of waving palm trees running down the drive to the studio gates, she started to weep. And now, for the first time in her life, she found no reserves, nothing to halt the flow of tears as the soft, velvet-warm evening descended all round her, sitting there alone, a sick headache coming on, joints beginning to burn, so that first she reached for a packet of veronal powders, then a bottle of Italian grappa, something she had never touched before, washing down the powders with big gulps of the fiery liquid.

Soon she was unconscious, unaware of everything, lying on the sofa – unaware then, as she had been until a few minutes before, how in the space of a few months the tables had finally turned on her – how she had fallen from the pinnacle of every kind of success, and was headed downwards now towards the depths.

Craig himself, of course, was the key to the whole matter. And, when he returned from Paris and they finally met, he played a wily game, allowing her no leverage with him, pretending shame in some matters, none in others – the whole a ploy to be finally rid of her. For his secret use of their joint funds he made no apologies whatsoever.

'Why, listen, honey,' he told her that afternoon at the villa. 'The accountants have all the figures: exactly what was your money, and mine, in WillBow Pictures. And you can have your share back, every cent, if that's what you want, in six months or so when this picture goes out on release. But you ought to see the point. WillBow is a motion picture *production* company, not an investment trust for either of us – there to make *other* pictures, not just *Nefertiti* – to show a profit over the years for both of us, as it has, as it surely will. But you can take all your money out of it if you want –'

'For Chrissakes, Craig – a company to make pictures with *me* in them. Not some other be-be-bloody woman. Not this Diana Be-be-Belleville or whoever it is you've got for it.' Hetty flushed then with anger. She had heard rumours of Craig's liaison with this up-and-coming picture actress, heard how she was almost a certainty now for the role of the young nun in *The Lost Valley*.

'We've been through all that, Hetty. The voice test. Talkies. They're not for you.'

'Okay.' Hetty climbed down. 'But *you* – you and I? Aren't we – something else? Nothing to do with WillBow Pe-Pictures? What about us, Craig?' She smiled, an expression that was both meek and passionate, staring at him intently. But Craig turned away from her, gazing out at the palm trees from the bay window of the big salon.

'Honey, you and I have gone . . . our different ways.' He spoke abstractedly, pondering the swaying palm trees, their leaves crackling drily in the moist autumn wind that had come to blow over the coast.

'Craig, I've gone nowhere! Just been here. We-we-waiting for you,' she said evenly, retaining her calm with an effort.

'Well, that's as may be. But . . . I've gone. How could I not? – given what's happened.' He turned then, walking over to the drinks table, helping himself to a scotch. His slight limp, she noticed, had returned. It always did with the first sign of damp in the weather. She knew so much about him, everything, like a well-thumbed scrapbook. And yet she really did not know him at all. Now she made one last effort to know him, to show herself, to commit herself to him, to touch his heart somehow. She went up to him, holding him gently by the shoulders, speaking softly.

'Craig, it's just not pe-pe-possible,' she told him. 'That all this, all of us, in eight, nine years – that it just "goes" like that. It can't. It doesn't.'

'It's perfectly possible, honey.' He let her hold him but made no gesture in return. 'I like you, admire you, you're a wonderful actress . . . wonderful times. But times change. And, worst of all, I changed them.' He released himself then, sipping his drink, turning away. Then suddenly he turned again, facing her, serious now, talking urgently for the first time. 'Why, how could you go on loving, living with, someone who's brought you such pain, this syphilis – someone who's taken up with another woman? It's nonsense. Makes no sense, don't you see?'

'I can bear it. Even her.' Hetty played her last cards. 'If we went on together – in some fashion.'

He shook his head. 'You couldn't, Hetty. You'd be denying everything that's good in you, everything that's simply . . . you. Your confidence, vitality, your *brain*. You'd never be any good at playing second fiddle.'

'I might surprise you. Maybe second fiddle could turn out to be my forte . . .'

'No, Hetty. Your music, one way or another, has to be the best. Just going to have to be with a different orchestra. I don't know where, or when, or who'll write the score, who'll conduct. But it can't be me. I'm no use to you any more. How could I be? – failing you so? But at least remember – we'll always have *Nefertiti*. And that was the very best of us. No doubt. Even in the cut version, even how they mangled it, they couldn't destroy you at least. You're sensational. You'll see. They're releasing it soon. And one day – I still have a full print of my own here at the Victorine – they'll show the whole picture, just as I wanted it – and then, why, we'll remember each other even better!'

So it was – neat as ever, with such fine words, truths and outright lies – that Craig finally dropped Hetty. And when he left the following day, looking for locations in Morocco, Hetty, having played all her most treasured cards with him, did not weep. She showed no emotion at all – simply because she had no decent emotions left, only bitter and destructive ones. She had, she saw now, been finally and completely betrayed by this man whom she had loved, who had meant everything to her.

So, with only those seeds of havoc which Léonie had so well identified in her, she set out then, covertly, tactfully as she thought, to take revenge on life. It would be a punishment which, since it was purely spiteful and vindictive, she came to inflict much more on herself than on anyone else.

10

Y ET TO BEGIN with Hetty's descent was not clearly visible as that. It ran in
dramatic fits and starts, like a faulty elevator, where there were sudden,
startling recoveries, glorious upward flights, followed by steep, stomach-turning
drops, juddering halts, reprieves, dramatic ascents, further declines. In this way
her fall was even more spectacular than her rise. Initially, for the next month at
least, she kept a reasonably even keel, with most of her wits about her, as she
started a series of losing battles – with Craig, with WillBow Pictures, with assorted
doctors, agents, producers, directors, attorneys, above all with herself.

Moving out of the Victorine, staying with the Ostrovoskys in their villa outside
Nice, she soon discovered she had no case against Craig financially. She herself
had signed the cheques with which he had partly financed *The Lost Valley*. And
that was that. Meanwhile she had only some thirty thousand dollars in her own
personal account. However, the dollar at that point was ridiculously high against
the franc – and this was more than sufficient for her to live on, if on a somewhat
reduced scale.

She met various picture producers and directors – in Paris, Berlin, London.
Socially, at least, they were pleased to see her – and even more happy to be seen
with her. They wined and dined her, at the Adlon, the Crillon, Claridge's, picking
up all her bills. For *Nefertiti* was about to be released and a vast worldwide publicity
campaign had already been launched by Fox – her astonishingly chiselled, regal
face, beneath the dramatic gold and blue Nefertiti headdress, already going up on
European billboards, the same regal features appearing in all the picture magazines
and popular newspapers. But sound was definitely the coming thing – and these
producers merely dallied with her. They saw, they heard, all too well how her
stammer now disqualified her – her stammer, which had returned now with a
vengeance. They had no real work for her.

She took on a new agent, a balding middle-aged American in Paris, a nice but
essentially useless man. She stayed in Paris at the Crillon, conferring in her suite
with this Bernie Franklin, who then busied himself on her behalf, but to no avail.

However, anxious to save on expensive hotel bills and drawn by the vibrant Paris social scene, she subsequently rented an apartment, small but rather grand, painted all in stark white, with mirrors, and furnished in the latest art déco style, on the Ile Saint-Louis, the second floor of an old town house on the Quai d'Orléans, with a spectacular balcony view looking straight out over the river and the spires of Notre-Dame.

Here, with her fame and through her contacts in the French picture business, she was soon taken up and fêted by the smart social and literary sets, both French and expatriate, dining with Cocteau and Colette at the Grand Véfour, at Maxim's with René Clair, the new white hope of French pictures, whose *Italian Straw Hat* had just opened to great acclaim in the boulevard cinemas.

But more often she took casual suppers, sausages and steins of lager at the Brasserie Lipp, with new American friends living in or visiting Paris then – Hemingway, the poet Archibald MacLeish and his pretty wife, the boxer Gene Tunney – going on afterwards to fashionable theatres and night clubs: to see Josephine Baker, sensationally dark and nude in *La Revue Nègre*; to hear Mistinguett at Les Ambassadeurs, the cocky new singer Chevalier at the Olympia Music Hall – or sometimes, from the sublime to the ridiculous, visiting the Folies-Bergère up town, then the Boeuf sur le Toit, with onion soup at Les Halles at four in the morning before a last *café-cognac* back at her apartment.

Hetty knew, of course, that Robert and Léonie were living in Paris then – knew their address, too, not far from her, over the river on the rue Saint-André-des-Arts. At first, quite taken up with her new social life, she did not think of them. Yet, although she repressed the fact, they were never far beneath the surface of her thoughts. They had in fact a powerful existence for her still, in shadow, a life invisible but not forgotten. So that although, when she did come to think of them, she had no intention of making any direct approach, she was left feeling a curiosity which she was not able to repress.

So she took to passing along the narrow rue Saint-André-des-Arts, on her way from the Ile Saint-Louis to the Deux Magots or the Brasserie Lipp, in a headscarf and dark glasses, glancing over at their doorway, sometimes stopping at a café almost opposite, watching, waiting. And one afternoon she was rewarded – and astonished.

Léonie, looking radiant in a summer frock, emerged from the door with a perambulator – a beautiful dark-haired girl, a year old, she thought, sitting up, madly waving a rattle. She followed them across the Boulevard Saint-Germain, up to the Luxembourg Gardens, walking some way behind, past the ornate terrace statuary, until they stopped among a crowd of other children out with their mothers and nannies, spellbound, watching the marionette theatre, the hunchback Polichinelle – tipsy, talkative, quarrelsome – beating his wife with a large stick to the joyfully alarmed cries of all the children.

Hetty, moving tactfully forward, finally got a better view of Léonie and her daughter: Léonie, so happily the natural mother now, had the child in her arms, holding her up to the spectacle. Hetty was quite stricken by the sight, this woman, whom she had loved, who had betrayed her, so happy now, fulfilled – with a child, as she had so much wanted for herself. The vision horrified her. She could not bear the thought, the sight of it all, turning away then and running from the happy throng. So that afterwards she took all the more vehemently to her frenzied social life, hoping to blot out every memory of that terrible vision at the marionette theatre, and the unutterable sense of loss she had felt.

And for Hetty, initially and at least on the surface, these increasingly chaotic, hectic times were happy – happy in that her starved vanity was now so regularly fed, her self-esteem repaired. For most came to adore – or just enjoy and toady – this vivacious, so original a woman, with such a surprising mix of gifts: Irish, Jewish, American all at once, who yet spoke perfect French, and who more surprisingly still, as they had to remind themselves, was a great picture star, talked of in the same breath as Garbo or Gloria Swanson, a woman out of all that Hollywood vulgarity, who yet so obviously was not vulgar herself. Far from it. Just like her dramatically looming presence as Nefertiti going up on billboards all over Paris just then, she had the manners, the hauteur, the whole natural air and breeding of a Queen.

And yet, among these new friends, how often, how splendidly, she climbed down from this pedestal! They loved her even more for that – dancing the can-can or taking two walking sticks and engaging in mock duels at a party, displaying a lovely wit, sometimes lacerating, even coarse, with a mind that could be equally refined or down to earth. Hetty, among these new friends, became profligate with her talents, wasting them, casting them out, words upon the water – all these conflicting dramas in her soul which before had been used to great purpose, absorbed and fixed, in art, on celluloid.

Now, though she could not admit it for an instant, thinking instead how she was regaining herself, she was steadily overdrawing her account, living on borrowed time – on her wits, her nerves, her over-bright looks, her reputation. Now, beneath the surface of her fevered gaiety, there was a festering guilt at her wasteful life, a deep unhappiness. And it was these repressed feelings more than anything else which gave her this brilliant social attack now, this brio – in words, gesture, thoughts. Her friends mistook her irresponsible *éclat* as central to her real nature. But it was simply the product of her secret despair, her sense of betrayal, by all that she had known, by everyone she had loved, in all her previous worlds.

So, trying to forget this, in a whirl of ever more heady parties, chatter, drinking, she launched herself, devil-may-care, on the wild *zeitgeist* of the times, which by that autumn of 1928 in Paris had reached a crescendo of insensate bravado.

This *beau monde* of the city – the shallow, the aristocratic, the genuinely celebrated – did nothing to help her, since they were unaware of her problems, entirely overlaid as they were by what seemed to them a wonderfully genuine *bel esprit*. And this they lapped up, savouring her bewildering mix of wild Irish spirit, Jewish languor, American openness and practicality. They loved her *bons mots*, bizarre Irish twists of thought and turns of phrase, translated into a perfect, if stammering, French. And some of the men were equally tempted by her rash and wind-blown beauty now, by features that were getting thinner, more chiselled, in a way more desperate and so more appealing, with her illness. Or the men were taken by her sly invitations in other moods, her sex, which she promoted now and then towards them, but only as an impossible ideal, a Holy Grail, always finally withheld.

Hetty walked all sorts of tightropes then, a dazzling high-wire act, which her new friends applauded, quite unaware that she was really a rank amateur in these social routs, that this hair-raising approach of hers was a forced performance, so much a lesser part of her nature, the result simply of growing secret despairs which she would not confront.

A few came to know this, though, becoming real friends, among a group of women she came to meet – writers, artists, poets, Amazons of a quite declared sort – who were living in Paris. Initially she had met Gertrude Stein and her companion Alice B. Toklas – and through them a circle of other women friends: the American balletomane and bizarre film director Loie Fuller, the booksellers Sylvia Beach and Adrienne Monnier, the English writer – all the rage then among these women – Djuna Barnes. Above all she met the doyenne of this left bank American artistic set, Natalie Barney.

A friendship ensued here which became close. Miss Barney was not deceived by Hetty's frenetic clamour and social high-jinks – soon sensing the deep unhappiness which lay behind this façade: a surmise which proved entirely correct when Hetty came to explain all that had happened to her in the last year.

And here, with Natalie and her circle, in this gracious and quite open lesbian *milieu*, Hetty found some solace, spiritually, then sexually, involving herself in a number of *tendresses* with Natalie's younger friends and acquaintances, some of which became mild or passionate *affaires*, for a night or for longer engagements, which she pursued vehemently, tasting all sorts of sweet revenge against Craig, against Léonie – and even sweeter, forgotten pleasures, re-animated only so briefly with Léonie in the bedouin tent, but now indulged more continuously and so much more comfortably: a pleasure, she was happy to confirm, still part of her real nature, perhaps the truest part, she felt, in a nature so deeply wounded in every other way.

Yes, there was great happiness for her then in this simple release of a pent-up sexual energy, a loving and a vast need satisfied, which she had so missed, which she could no longer share with men. Above all, naked in these women's arms, she could forget the stigmata of her disease, her syphilis, dormant now again after the last Salvarsan cure, but which she knew was likely to recur at any time. She could forget the disease and its infection, for she did not make love with women in that way, a manner in which, with men, she no longer dared pursue. And besides, with women, she soon confirmed, as she had discovered years before with Léonie in Dublin, love-making was so much longer and better a thing than it had ever been with men.

So, in such loving, throughout wild and tender nights, she found a respite from her social mania, found a liberating contentment. However, in every other sphere of her life she continued to live on frantic tenterhooks, swaying dangerously on her various high wires, always hovering over an abyss.

One such pitfall was drink. As the summer went by, and it seemed more and more that there was no future for her in motion pictures, she took to drink as a stay against admitting this failure. To begin with she drank only socially – reasonably at first, but then overmuch. So that soon, suffering hangovers, she started taking nips of spirit or mugs of champagne with orange at midday or in the afternoons, as a hair of the dog. Then, on the rare nights when she was alone in her apartment, she took to these bottles more vehemently, when she could not sleep or her pains came back, thumbing giddily through old scrapbooks of reviews and production stills from her great pictures.

She never really came to like the taste of drink. But she came to crave first the euphoric release it brought – the illusion of power, dominance, success once more – and then, before she had time to realise how baseless these feelings were, the complete oblivion the alcohol gave her. So that by the autumn, though not a full-time alcoholic, she had started a promising career in the business.

She had, too, among some of her circle, taken to puffing marijuana weeds – some of Cocteau's friends had introduced her to them. But she thought nothing of it – just as she thought nothing of her now considerable drinking. She worried only over the hangovers. But, since these were readily curable with another *coup* of cold champagne or a sharp vodka, she soon ceased to worry about these hangovers too. She was still young enough easily to recover from her excesses, while yet maintaining them.

And then, quite realistically, her circumstances took a turn for the better – and the elevator of her life leapt upwards. *Nefertiti* was finally released – first at Graumann's Theater in Hollywood, then in New York just after Labor Day. Hetty, though she was asked, pointedly refused to attend the Hollywood première – as evidence of her displeasure at this mangled version of the picture. Yet even in its truncated 2½-hour version, some of its glories remained intact, in the huge set-pieces, the battles, and particularly in Hetty's performance in which her regality, together with all her other brilliantly characterised ploys and wiles and final tragedy, overshadowed everything else in the production. Most critics were wild about her, at least, and the public flocked to see the picture. With all this clamour and acclaim Hetty sensed a recovery in the air – the more so a week later when the gilt-edged invitation arrived from London.

Nefertiti was due to open there with a European première at the Empire, Leicester Square – a special charity showing for the British Legion in the presence of the young Prince of Wales as royal patron, in mid-October. And Hetty had received what amounted to a royal command to attend. Craig would not be there. He had already started location work in the wilds of Morocco. Hetty was charmed by the invitation, by the whole idea of renewed public view once more, a fresh start to her career perhaps as well – excited by the idea, too, of meeting the glamorous young Prince.

A suite had been booked for her at the Savoy Hotel. She travelled with her maid, the hairless Mr Franklin and a train of baggage filled with the latest fashionable clothes, for she thought to spend some weeks in London, seeing how the land lay as regards future possible work.

Arriving at Dover after a choppy crossing, they took the boat train to Victoria Station, where to her joy she saw some hundreds – perhaps thousands, she thought – of her fans milling round, cheering and waving madly, beyond the platform barrier as she stepped down on to a red carpet.

The staid, top-hatted station-master greeted her and the head of the Fox Picture Corporation in London came forward, an aggressive, overweight little man in a quite unsuitably loud check suit and bow tie, planting a wet kiss on her cheek, before his chichi, bijou wife presented her with a great bouquet of hothouse red roses.

Hetty stood there for a long moment in her new polka dot Chanel suit and huge cloche felt hat with a dramatically upturned brim, gracefully acknowledging the cheers. Then, taken by this fizzy warmth in the air, and seeing how the drama there might be accentuated, she suddenly removed the big hat, discarding it, as something foreign to her true wild nature, that swashbuckling dare-devil which her fans knew and loved her for – flouncing her dark curls out, eyes flashing, as if she were about to embark on a duel. And in that moment the whole platform seemed to explode, the hurrahs and cheers and blown kisses redoubled.

Hetty smiled wonderfully, sniffing the roses, lifting her huge blue eyes to the crowds, basking in the limelight once more, quite ignoring how this feeling and most of her vivacity, the sparkle in her eyes, the colour in her cheeks, all this suddenly-renewed beauty and confidence, was largely the result of a steady medicinal intake of brandy on the rough Channel crossing, and of the subsequent downing of several large gins on the boat train. She quite put the idea of any such unnatural stimulus from her mind. It was her public, her fans, who had so renewed her spirit. She was herself again. She had found her true position once more. Life was just about to begin all over again for her.

She met the Prince the following evening at the theatre, first in line among others connected with the production, curtsying to him very formally, hardly daring to look at him – then following his retinue of guests, up the grand staircase to an open-topped royal box of sorts that had been set up at the centre of the circle, half a dozen armchair-like seats, specially arranged there for the royal party.

She was to have sat immediately behind this plush corral, with the Fox executives and her hairless agent. But, after the Prince had self-deprecatingly acknowledged the cheers on his arrival, as the spotlights coursed over the royal party, he stood up, turned and gestured for Hetty to join him. There was a spare seat with them, he intimated; the audience, unable to see Hetty, held its breath, wondering what might have gone amiss in the arrangements.

Then, coming forward down the dark aisle, before another spotlight suddenly caught her, Hetty joined the Prince, standing next to him at the front of the circle in the blinding limelight. Then the house erupted, roaring its approval at this unexpected conjunction, the sight of a Prince and a Queen together, both now fulfilling every possible fantasy they might have – a real Prince of the blood royal, linked with something equally unobtainable, a great Hollywood picture star, the two of them standing there, heavenly emblems come to earth, a perfect match, the

Prince in tails and white tie, small, neat, charming, outrageously handsome under a thatch of straw hair; Hetty, with amethyst pendant earrings, dressed in a spectacular evening dress, low-waisted, with a scalloped hemline dipping at the back, in fine white tulle, covered in gold and over patterned silver sequins that glittered now in the spotlights. The applause increased. But Hetty knew well what her response must be. She refused the plaudits, curtsying briefly to the Prince, then looking up at him, seeing his face clearly now, staring at him, smiling hesitantly, before preparing to turn away and take a back seat.

Their eyes met – for now he was staring at her, surprised, yet unflinching. He had the same sort of Wedgwood-blue eyes, Hetty thought, as her own, glittering in the light. And there was something else similar in his features – the line of his chin, his nose, the set of his eyes. What was it? She had seen these same expressions, or something very like them, somewhere, in someone, before. The rebellious air, yet the delicate charm, an attractive hesitancy about him as well, the vulnerability – a sadness too, in the whole expression, which she felt she remembered in someone she had known.

Finally, unlocking herself from the Prince's gaze, she took a seat next to him. The Prince remained standing a few moments longer as the lights faded, a quizzical expression on his face. He, too, had suddenly been struck by something in Hetty – those piercing blue eyes, the pointed chin . . . Who, what, was it, he wondered? She reminded him of himself in some uncanny way. There was the same sadness behind their public façades, a vulnerability – all that he had so clearly sensed in that hesitant smile of hers; all that for so long he had had to repress in himself. The whole sudden confrontation just then had some quite unexplained magic to it. He determined to see more of her, to try to discover the source, the meaning behind this extraordinary sense of affinity he felt with her.

Meeting her properly was not difficult. With the royal party, which included his younger brother George, his equerry Captain Hamilton and several older women, Hetty went on afterwards for dinner and dancing at the Prince's regular night spot, the Embassy Club, a long basement room, mirrors everywhere, with swing glass doors leading from the restaurant to the crowded dance floor.

Here, with small tables edging right out on to the open space, they took seats at another much larger table, always reserved for the Prince, against one wall, opposite the orchestra set up on a balcony at the far end of the smoky, mirror-glittering room. Luigi, the head waiter, ministered with appropriate regality – pâté de foie gras, devilled lobster and jeroboams of Möet champagne. And, very soon after supper, the Prince was dancing with Hetty – first a vibrant foxtrot, then a quickstep, and later, his third consecutive dance with her, a waltz.

'Pe-pe-perhaps, Sir,' she said apologetically, glancing over at the other, older ladies in the Prince's party, 'I impose. The others? . . .'

'Certainly not. I'm imposing, if anyone is. Besides, I assure you, my women friends – they will be only too pleased that I dance with someone nearer my own age!'

He smiled, the very slightly hooded eyes narrowing – holding her not too close nor yet too distantly, swinging round in perfect step with the music, as if they had been dancing thus for years. There was nothing the slightest bit shy or risqué in his attitude, his remarks, Hetty thought. He could not dissemble – that was her first and clearest impression of him. His whole attitude – if it was not forthright, almost rebellious – was naive, willing, simple, utterly straightforward. And so his absolutely magnetic charm – and there was no doubt about that – was something that Hetty could entirely believe in. It was not assumed. It was him.

'I see . . .' Hetty smiled, with a touch of mischief, tightening her grip on his shoulder just a fraction. 'I should have thought – every young we-we-woman in England . . .' She left the idea hanging delicately in the air.

'Indeed.' He came back then with the same amused irony. 'Quite so. That's not the problem – but that there are so few such young women in England – like you!' Hetty demurred, bowing her head. 'No, no,' he ran on. 'I can tell you honestly – few so young in spirit, yet somehow so . . . mature. Regal indeed! But of course I shouldn't be surprised. One saw all that in your performance tonight, as Queen Nefertiti – sensational! You couldn't have played her like that, so convincingly, without having some of exactly the same qualities yourself! Captivating!'

'Thank you.' Hetty, on her best behaviour and having only drunk a very little that evening, coloured quite naturally.

'You surprise me in so many ways,' the Prince went on. 'For of course – I was certain – you were American!'

'No, English –'

'But that slight accent, a touch of something else – Ireland?'

'Well, yes, originally.' Hetty tried to make the least of her origins. But the Prince insisted.

'Irish, indeed! What part?'

'Oh, my family – we le-le-lived at Summer Hill, a house in the south there. My fe-fe-father, no, my grandfather rather, Sir Desmond – I never knew him – le-le-lived there. But I left years ago, le-living in Hollywood. I married the motion picture director there, Craig St John Williamson, who made *Nefertiti* –'

'Of course, of course – I knew you were married!' The Prince broke happily into this stumbling and embarrassed personal history, unable to hide what seemed to Hetty to be clear relief at her married status. 'I know a little of your public career, of course. Your last picture – *Gold Dust*, wasn't it? – we all so enjoyed that at York House earlier this year. But I'd no idea of all this *other* background, so close to home, as it were! Shall you be staying in London – then visiting home in Ireland?'

'Yes . . .' Hetty was beginning to tread on thin ice. 'Yes, I expect to be here for several weeks, I think. There are pe-pe-possible pictures to talk about. But Ireland – I don't think so . . .' She smiled vaguely, hoping to drop this whole difficult topic of her homeland.

'Oh, why? I've often wanted to visit. But can't, of course. Wonderful countryside, wonderful riding – everyone tells me. Why?'

'Well, the house, I believe, is falling down. It's no longer in the family. I live in

Pe-Paris now. And Nice, in the hills outside. I expect you know the area. Nice is really much nicer . . . than Ireland!'

But the Prince, anxiously trying to identify some reasons for his strong emotions, his sense of affinity with this woman earlier that evening in the theatre, was not to be diverted from his enquiries as to her background.

'Indeed . . . But your own family, in Ireland? – surely you shall want to see them?'

Hetty felt herself on very thin ice indeed now. She could not admit to the Prince that her mother – as far as the British were concerned – was the infamous Irish republican and revolutionary, friend to the arch-demon De Valera, sentenced to death with the other leaders after the treacherous Easter rebellion only thirteen years before, and still a well-known name in some quarters.

'Oh, I don't see my me-me-mother. We rather fell out. She lives in Dublin, involved in all sorts of good works. And as for my fe-fe-father . . .' She paused. 'Well, he died, he was killed long ago, when I was tiny, on the West Indian island where we lived first – killed by a te-tribe of marauding se-savages, can you imagine! I can just remember it,' she ran on, intent now on making an amusing story out of it all. 'There was a stockade of mattresses on the verandah and fe-fe-flaming arrows and cutlasses and guns going off left, right and centre! An extraordinary fe-fracas!'

So Hetty made a joke of her parentage, her own past – hoping thus to dismiss the whole awkward topic. But this only served to increase the Prince's curiosity, increase his sympathy for her as well.

'My goodness me!' He was genuinely astonished. 'I'm very sorry. But what a tale – more dramatic than your pictures.'

'I suppose so . . .'

'I *am* sorry. How very unfortunate – so to lose, and fall out with, your parents. A father gone so early in life . . .'

The Prince looked at her with something more than sympathy now, with an intense, piercing gaze, as if by such a look he could somehow divine all her secrets without further enquiry.

But he could not, so that finally, seeing Hetty's embarrassment, he mumbled, 'Forgive me for prying like this, about your family. But let me explain – something quite strange, you see – because earlier this evening in the theatre, when I first saw you properly, I had the distinct impression that we'd met before somewhere. Long ago perhaps? Something familiar about your – face, yes . . .'

At this admission Hetty felt the back of her neck prickle. So that, without any restraint now, she said, 'Yes, that's very strange, for I fe-felt just the same myself when we met this evening, in those lights – that I'd met you somewhere before!'

The Prince was wonderfully pleased with this. 'Well, perhaps we *were* together in some previous existence, before either of us was born. And so we may renew the acquaintance, properly now, in reality! If you're here for a few weeks, perhaps you might care to dine with me at York House, or come beagling with us at Lord Carrington's place next weekend? I'd be very pleased.'

'I'd be honoured, Sir . . .'

'Come!' He seemed to take her a little more firmly in his grip. 'Not "Sir" – Edward, please. And perhaps we can forget the "honour" business too. After all, with our previous incarnation together, we must really know each other very well already!'

And that was true, Hetty felt. She had never got on so well, so quickly, with a man – not even with Craig. Of course he was royal, heir to the throne, and so charming – the most glamorous young man in England, no doubt. These were not the reasons for her attraction, however, which was so much more due to that mysterious affinity they had talked about – the sense somehow that he was brother to her, or father even, that all-powerful kindred figure she had so lacked and longed for all her life.

But meanwhile they laughed uproariously at other things and danced the rumba.

For the Prince was quite captivated by her, as well – for a lot of other perfectly obvious reasons: her spirit, beauty, her sharp wit and a mind in which, for him, there was nothing clammy or too intellectual. It was a *coup de foudre* of sorts, made all the easier by the fact that his great but unrequited love for Mrs Dudley Ward had, at that point, come to something of a full stop. She had gone away for several weeks, visiting relatives in Yorkshire. And of course in any case, as he knew so well, so sadly, she would have done nothing but tactfully encourage any steps he might take with other younger women – unmarried women, of course. But then that was another of his problems in love. He could not somehow ever get on with unmarried women. So, in the circumstances, he decided he should, and could, get on very well with Hetty.

When they left the Embassy Club early that morning, press photographers were outside. And later that day the early editions featured the Prince and his new friend. Hetty glanced at the papers in bed at the Savoy. At first the whole thing seemed unbelievable. But then, thinking it over, remembering the extraordinary sense of familiarity she had felt with him from the very beginning, it all seemed entirely natural.

Hetty went beagling that weekend with the Prince and some of his friends, house guests at Lord Carrington's place outside Aylesbury – sloshing through the muddy fields in shafts of rainy autumn light, eating late blackberries, sipping cocktails that evening, attending the local parish church next morning. Their friendship bloomed. And the following week Hetty dined alone with the Prince at York House, not in the chilly ground floor dining salon, but upstairs quite informally in his drawing room, decorated everywhere with huge maps of the world, a round table set up by the fire, a simple meal – for unlike his grandfather the Prince was no great eater: soup, grilled lamb chops, a good claret.

The Prince was entirely relaxed with Hetty now – both of them, secure and confident, behaving as old friends. The Prince poured the claret, taking the bottle from his major-domo Finch, who left then, flourishing the wine napkin casually over his shoulder as he went. Hetty loved the informality of it all – the soft lamplight, the shadows running away into the old rambling room, filled with Victorian furniture.

'Your health, Hetty!' The Prince raised his glass. And Hetty hers. But she barely sipped. She had quite stopped drinking. She had no need of that now. She was no longer a failure. She was, in one way, sitting here alone with the Prince, the most successful woman in England. She glanced round, looking at the maps of the world everywhere, looming out from the walls, the Empire, over half the globe, it seemed, coloured red. What were motion pictures, all that fantasy? – when this person, and all this fabulous reality, lay at her feet?

Gradually that evening, as they dined and later sitting opposite each other by the fireside, with her stammer almost disappearing in the extraordinary ease she felt with him, she told the Prince of her life – its beginnings, all the passions and alarms then, in Domenica and Summer Hill as a child, the loss of her father, the frightful rows with her mother. Léonie, too, was described – though not the full depth of their relationship. And so was Craig. Though here she felt quite free to tell him almost all the worst, everything Craig had done – apart from the disease he had given her – how they had finally separated.

The Prince nodded sadly. 'Indeed, how often it turns out that way. A first marriage . . . If we could only *start* with a second. How much better things might work out!'

And the thought crossed the Prince's mind then: here, here right in front of him, was just the sort of woman he would have wanted to marry – if she were not married already, of course, and if he were not born to be King. And yet he had often wondered about that role . . .

With his lack of stuffy attitude he enjoyed most of his official work as Prince of Wales. But he had come to dread the idea of the throne – the crushing responsibilities, above all the strait-jacket of formalities and ceremonials he would have to take on then, forsaking all his own happy and informal life, which he had come to depend on – to the point of retaining his sanity, as he thought. In his heart of hearts he felt he would be a failure as King. While his younger brother Bertie, so much less restless – steadier, quieter, above all more patient and dogged – would be ideal in that role. Fate had cruelly produced them in the wrong order. And the idea of necessary marriage to some other royal or aristocratic woman – to any of the women he had already met in that line – was abhorrent. But with Hetty, for example . . . Goodness! he thought – how very different life would be then. He smiled at her, thinking these things.

'The awful trouble,' he went on, breaking the silence. 'The way marriage is – we really only have one chance at it. Just like a stupid cricket match, when you're so easily out first ball – and have to spend the rest of your life locked up in the pavilion, as it were!'

Hetty agreed. 'But there is divorce, of course,' she added.

'For you, perhaps. Never for me.'

'No. No, of course not.' They gazed at each other, something passing in the air between them which was more than simple friendship, understanding – a whiff of physical tenderness, the vague smoke of desire. 'You'll have to be absolutely sure – the first time then!' Hetty continued, lightening the atmosphere.

'Yes. But my parents, so many people, want me married off at once, already – willy-nilly, packed up, tickety-boo, out of harm's way . . .'

The Prince galloped through these marital imperatives and they laughed outright at the nonsense of it all, as he eased his legs towards the fire. A sudden wind rattled at the windows beyond the heavy drapes. Hetty turned as if it were a ghost.

'Autumn storms,' the Prince remarked. But when Hetty turned back she found him staring at her, not at the windows.

'Well, of course, you must re-resist being so packed up and put away.'

'Oh, I have! I will . . .'

'A fatal curb. I found it myself with my own Me-Mama, wishing all sorts of ridiculous restrictions on me. One absolutely must be one's own pe-person first – if one's to be any real good to anyone else.'

'Of course. But in my position,' he laughed shortly, 'that's not so easy. I'm not my own property, you see – that's the frightful bind. "House of Windsor, the Nation, the Empire . . ."' He intoned the words lugubriously. 'They all have first call on me.'

'Yes!' Hetty leant forward eagerly now, passionate about something. 'Of course. But not yet. Not entirely. *Not yet!*' She smiled at him – forceful, bright and energetic suddenly, her eyes blazing with dictatorial purpose. Then, equally suddenly, she leant right back on the sofa, hands behind her head, gazing vacantly up at the ceiling. 'Not me-married yet, nor King . . .' She too, in turn, intoned the words mock-mournfully.

'No, indeed.' The Prince got briskly to his feet, as if infected with the energy which Hetty had just then shown to him. He glanced at Hetty, in sudden repose now, lying almost horizontally beneath him – long legs stretched straight out, in sheer grey silk stockings, a pale lilac silk dress riding up slightly over her knees, to a low-belted waist, a lower neckline circled by a single string of creamy pearls, a bloused bodice loosely moulding the shapes of her small pointed breasts. Then, turning away abruptly, the Prince started to busy himself, but aimlessly – looking for a cigarette, then a lighter, kicking the coals with his foot, while Hetty remained there, lost in thought, staring upwards. The Prince finally managed to light his cigarette.

'Shall we dance tonight? The Embassy? Or I have a few records here.' He gazed down on her again, drawing deeply on the cigarette.

'Why not both?' Hetty, without moving, looked up at him. Then, with a sudden spring, she sat forward, brisk and bright once more, keen to promote the Prince's busy new mood, anxious too that he should not think she was being in any way over-familiar with him.

So they danced – to the sounds of the Prince's new electric gramophone: a selection of vivid Scottish dances which happened to be on the turntable – increasingly frantic, far from the proper steps or order, romping about helter-skelter, charging over the great Aubusson carpet, in and out between the heavy chairs and tables, reeling from light to shadow, swinging under the great maps of the Empire: an ever-more frenzied dance, laughing and shrieking as they fell over and into things, picking each other up, jumping round the room like young animals – until finally the music stopped and they fell into each other's arms, congratulating themselves, enchanted, exhausted, tears of laughter in their eyes.

Then suddenly, drawing apart for an instant, looking at each other in amazement, they kissed.

'Oh my, oh my! . . .' was all Hetty could say, drawing breath, astonished at the end of the embrace – before she moved away from him, putting fingers to both cheeks in happy amazement. 'I see what you mean now – about being out first ball and locked up in the pavilion for the rest of your life!' Then she sighed, turning from him a little despondently.

But he reached for her, gently turning her back towards him. 'Not yet, remember.' He spoke softly, but then suddenly with great brio. '*Not yet!*' And he took her hand then, leading her off to the Embassy Club, both of them imagining themselves as happy as they had ever been in their lives.

Hetty stayed on at the Savoy and in the next few weeks their affair grew in every sort of intimacy, except one. They did not make love. The Prince might have wished it – he did at times. But something – the sense of old innocent friendship with this woman as much as anything – drew him back. As, for Hetty, there was another much more obvious reason for withholding herself.

And yet this enforced restraint did not really cramp their style. They made endless virtues out of the necessity, suspended in what they felt was a delicious balance to their affair, veering towards an even more delicious precipice, over which they might one day launch themselves. And, besides these happy prohibitions, the Prince had come to feel a great respect for Hetty, so spirited and outspoken in one way, wise and calm in another, a mix of sister and potential mistress for him – a variety of conflicting images, none of which he wanted to sully. More and more he saw Hetty not as a passing fancy, but as someone with whom he hoped to have a long relationship, one that might release him from his awful heartache with Mrs Dudley Ward, save him from his consequent restlessness and frustrations there, save him from himself.

So, if not with sex, they satisfied themselves with everything else to hand – and there was much of that: beagling again, theatres, night clubs, uproarious private cinema shows of some of Hetty's old pictures at York House, large or intimate dinner parties, a trip to Brighton, the Prince driving incognito in his open-roofed DeLage tourer.

And it was on this journey, a touch of overnight frost chilling the bright Sunday morning air, the wind bringing tears to their eyes, speeding down the Brighton road at sixty miles an hour, that the Prince turned to Hetty, touching her hand.

'Know something, Laura?' he said lightly. 'If things were different, I'd marry you tomorrow. Would you?'

'Oh yes. Yes, I would!' She laughed, keeping her eyes on the road ahead, thinking the Prince was joking. Then she turned and looked at him – as he turned to her in the same instant – and she saw how serious he had been. And she was sad then, as he was, both of them looking back at the empty road.

'Never mind,' he roused himself, bright once more. 'We'll see each other, won't we? From now on, whatever happens, one way or another – though of course we'll have to be more discreet. In Paris, London, Nice. Won't we?' He looked round at her, anxious again, the small fair face suddenly vulnerable, childlike.

'Yes.'

'Promise?'

'Yes. Yes, Edward – yes!'

Later they dug out the caretaker of the Brighton Pavilion – an astonished functionary, for it was a Sunday morning – who opened the building up for the Prince. And they walked alone through its fantastic eastern rooms, an exotic caravanserai, decorated in every sort of elaborate arabesque and gaudy colour, admiring the set-pieces, the gilded plaster palm columns, with their leaf capitals rising to a blue-domed heaven high above, a fabulous dream of a thousand and one nights here set down by the raw English briny.

'George IV, when he was Prince Regent,' the Prince commented, moving his eyes round the whole glittering extravaganza. 'What a scallywag – and all just for his mistress!'

'She did better than his wife!'

'Mistresses usually do . . .'

They laughed and wandered on silently, arm in arm, thinking now of all sorts of possibilities and compromises which might sustain their future together.

In an office looking out over the royal mews at Buckingham Palace Lord Stamford-ham, King George's Private Secretary, glanced once more through the rising stack of popular newspapers which had been collected for him during the past weeks – containing photographs of the Prince with Miss Laura Bowen, gossipy articles linking them together, references and surmises which had already upset both the King and Queen Mary. But the King and Queen had simply been put out by the Prince's indiscreet association with a woman whom they took to be a vulgar Hollywood picture star – and a married woman at that, as all the Prince's women so unfortunately were.

Arthur Stamfordham, however, was horrified by a quite different aspect to the relationship. A man in his seventies now, he had been one of Queen Victoria's equerries and had afterwards worked closely with Lord Knollys, Private Secretary to King Edward VII. So Stamfordham had known Edward well, both as King and before that as Prince of Wales – and now, with Knollys himself dead five years before, Stamfordham, alone among courtiers, was privy to some most dangerous secrets.

Rising from his desk then, he opened a safe in the corner, and with further private keys unlocked a drawer inside. Taking a sealed envelope from it he returned to his desk. Inside the envelope was a hand-written memorandum from Knollys which the latter had entrusted to him, a résumé of several meetings which Knollys had had with Edward, as Prince of Wales, in 1899, when the Prince, on his Private Secretary's stern advice, had eventually and unwillingly agreed never to see again, or correspond with, a certain Irish woman – a Miss Frances Cordiner from Summer Hill in County Kilkenny – with whom the Prince for several years had been on most intimate terms.

The relationship had come to a disastrous head between the two of them, the memorandum continued, as a result of Miss Cordiner's giving birth, in the summer of 1899 in America, to a child, a girl called Henrietta. The Prince had been the father. The woman had subsequently written to the Prince – most indelicate letters which had long since been destroyed – not asking for any financial support, for she had means of her own, but that, to her at least, the Prince should acknowledge his paternity, something quite out of the question, of course. So that subsequently the Prince had cut off all contact with Miss Cordiner. Eventually the woman had ceased to write – and there, quite buried, the matter had rested for nearly thirty years.

But now Lord Stamfordham, remembering very well this ancient liaison and its disastrous results, and having read the popular newspapers over the last few weeks, had that morning suddenly been struck by a brief reference in the social column of the *Tatler* – a note to the effect that Miss Laura Bowen was in reality, and originally, a Miss Henrietta Cordiner, born in 1900 in America, but been brought up in Ireland at the Cordiner family seat of Summer Hill in County Kilkenny. A glance at Burke's Irish Landed Gentry in his office had confirmed the birth of just such a girl, on that date, to a Mrs Frances Fraser, daughter of Desmond and Sarah Cordiner, whom Lord Stamfordham already knew to be the woman's parents.

What followed was all too clear to him. Laura Bowen – this Henrietta Cordiner – was without doubt Edward VII's illegitimate daughter. So that this King's grandson, the present Prince of Wales, was now consorting, and probably indulging in every sort of intimacy with, his aunt. And, almost as bad, Lord Stamfordham suddenly realised, Henrietta Cordiner's mother, this Mrs Frances Fraser, must be none other than the woman who had later become the vicious Irish Republican and revolutionary, a traitor, sentenced to death for her part in the Easter Rebellion of 1916, a fact that the newspapers had so far luckily not yet discovered.

It was all too clear to Stamfordham. If the press were to learn any hint of these familial, sexual or political antecedents, so directly involving the Prince's current friend, there would be a furore of such magnitude as would likely provoke a constitutional crisis and possibly topple the very monarchy itself. The Prince's relationship with this young woman would have to be stopped at once – at any cost.

Lord Stamfordham had asked for a personal meeting with the Prince immediately. And the following morning he was with him, upstairs in his drawing room at York House. At first Stamfordham had hoped not to bring up the matter of Laura Bowen's real provenance, persuading him by other means. So he had started on a line of realistic advice: that Miss Laura Bowen was not a suitable companion for him – simply because she was a motion picture star of such fame herself, and married to boot. Thus there could not but be unsuitable 'talk' whenever they were seen in public together, which must inevitably bring himself and the monarchy into disrepute.

'I am obliged to you, Arthur, for your concern,' the Prince responded nicely. 'And indeed, you're quite right. Given her fame, I have perhaps been too "public" with her. Be assured, I will be very much more discreet with her from now on. Not seen in public . . . Though in any case she returns to France soon . . .'

The Prince stood up and gazed a little sadly from the window at the last leaves blowing from the trees all down the Mall, the beginning of winter. Then he smiled at something. 'So, indeed, I shall see her there, where people are more discreet in such matters . . .'

Lord Stamfordham also rose to his feet. 'I think, Sir, you misunderstand me. You must cease to see her altogether and completely. You would, I assure you, be very well advised.'

The Prince turned from the window, a little annoyed, though still perfectly polite. 'Indeed, Arthur, and I'm sure it's good advice – you have never offered me or my family anything less. And I take your point entirely. I must handle the thing quite out of the public eye. But that I should not see Miss Bowen *at all* is surely a quite unwarranted imposition. I am a grown man, neither married yet, nor King. I may surely, if it's handled with suitable decorum, see whom I please.'

The Prince began to fidget, lighting a cigarette, turning towards the door – hoping, intimating, that perhaps the interview might now be over.

Lord Stamfordham saw he had no alternative. 'Sir, you must believe that I should never normally have questioned your right to see whom you please – within the limits of the decorum you mention. But in this instance, with Miss Bowen, there is more to it, much more, and I shall have to tell you now, in the strictest confidence of course. But the reason that you must break entirely with Miss Bowen is that she is the daughter – the illegitimate daughter – of your grandfather, King Edward VII.'

The Prince, who had been moving towards the door, stopped as if he had been hit. He turned, taking the cigarette from his mouth. All the engaging bright sharpness in his face disappeared – all his charm, his natural brio, which this love affair had so increased recently, disintegrated.

'What? . . .' He was stunned.

'Yes –'

'You cannot be serious.'

'Sir, to think that I should ever have brought such a topic up if I were not –'

'I'm sorry, Arthur. Of course . . .' The Prince, ashen-faced now, became extremely agitated, pacing to and fro. 'You mean . . .' He seemed to be counting things in his mind. 'That Miss Bowen – is my aunt?'

'Yes. But her real name, as you probably already know, is Henrietta Cordiner, from Summer Hill in Ireland –'

'Yes, I knew.'

'It was her mother, then Miss Frances Cordiner, with whom your grandfather had this – intimacy . . .'

'You're sure?'

'There is no doubt. I have Lord Knollys's personal memorandum on the whole matter here with me – he was much involved with it at the time. You should read it. It will confirm everything.'

Lord Stamfordham handed the memorandum to the Prince, who read it through quickly. But, thinking of something else as he did so, his eyes soon clouded over. Now he saw the reason for that marvellous sense of ease and familiarity he had felt with Hetty – that surge of natural affinity that had so lifted his heart in her presence, as if they had been related in some way. As indeed they were. He was her nephew.

And yet he had come to love her for all those other quite ordinary reasons for which one might come to love a woman; she had become an adored friend and companion – already, in only a few weeks, supplanting his unhappy love for Mrs Dudley Ward. And now, as he saw equally clearly, he would have to lose all this, that love, give it up at once and completely – lose that excitement, too, and all the possibilities that had waited for them in London, Paris, Nice. A whole happy future was suddenly being destroyed in front of his eyes, as he read through the memorandum. Fate, he thought, could not have played a crueller trick on anyone.

The Prince was quite desolated. But, despite his rebellious nature, he saw how impossibly dangerous and inappropriate it would be to continue the relationship. He had no alternative but to cut off every contact and connection with Hetty immediately.

At first, when the Prince did not call her – as he did every morning at the Savoy – Hetty put this down to some sudden unexpected official business, or absence from London. And then, too, when she could never get through to him at York House, she thought the Prince's secretaries were just being difficult. She sent short notes to him then, by hand. But there was no answer. On two successive evenings, she went with her agent, Bernie Franklin, to the Embassy Club. But the Prince was not there. They had difficulty getting a table. And a group of the Prince's friends, present on the second occasion – people she had met with him – clearly wished not to meet her again. She was being snubbed. By the end of the week it was perfectly clear: the Prince had dropped her.

To her agent the reason for all this was obvious. 'Honey, you gotta see it: you – a Hollywood picture star and married, with the heir to the goddamned British throne – the whole thing was going to run against the grain here from the very start. It stands to reason!'

But for Hetty it did not. This could not be the reason, for she and the Prince, recognising this very problem, had so clearly agreed that they would go on seeing each other, much more discreetly, whatever happened.

Hetty had no answer as she gazed out over the chilly, windswept Thames from her expensive river suite at the Savoy, no longer paid for by the Fox Picture Corporation. No answer whatsoever, except – and it was there for her in abundance – drink. In face of this appalling turn of events, this sudden brutal ending to something which she knew to have been wonderfully happy for both of them, she took to the bottle once more, hovering over the telephone in her suite, waiting for it to ring, or drunkenly badgering the operator downstairs, attempting to get through to York House, where they no longer accepted her calls, putting the receiver down as soon as they heard her slurred voice.

And it was then, in this mood of bitter alcoholic despair, that she suddenly thought of her cousins in London, Mortimer Cordiner and his son Dermot: Dermot, whom she had last seen in Cairo nearly eighteen months before. He must still be in the Army, she imagined, back in England now, in London even, perhaps living at his father's old house in Wilton Place – an address she knew well, number 16, having visited the place and written to Dermot there so often when, as a girl years before at Summer Hill, she had had such a crush on him. Suddenly she felt she needed someone like him – someone of her family. Yes, she needed Dermot. Swaying with drink, and putting a flask in her handbag, she took a cab there straightaway that afternoon.

When they turned off Knightsbridge she saw the house at once, half-way down on the right. It had a big 'FOR SALE' sign outside. Dismissing the cab, she knocked at the door, peering through the downstairs windows. The curtains were half-drawn. A chill bitter wind blew at her ankles, the grey December sky lowering everywhere over the city. But perhaps someone was still there? Perhaps there was a back entrance.

Rounding the first corner, she came into a narrow mews behind, with garage doorways along one side. Establishing what she thought to be the back entrance to number 16, she tried the door there. It was not locked. She stepped into an empty coachhouse. Beyond was another smaller door leading into an overgrown garden. It was the same untended house. She stumbled up between the ruined flower beds and bushes, rustling in the cold wind, until she came to some steps leading to a french window. The windows were locked and curtained. But other steps, she saw, led down to a small basement area. Descending, she found a window, which opened when she pushed the sash. Climbing inside, moving through a dark dank scullery into the kitchen, she saw some shadowy steps leading upstairs. Stumbling drunkenly up them, she eventually found herself in the hall, with reception rooms to either side. Peering into the first open doorway, she was confronted with a shabby and desolate scene – the grey winter light illuminating piles of old newspapers, dry leaves and torn curtain blinds littering the floor; mice droppings, old bottles, broken tea-chests, wallpaper peeling everywhere, the blackened grate clogged with filth, soot covering the hearth, a smell of musty damp everywhere.

Had Mortimer and Dermot ever lived here? The window suddenly rattled, a bitter wind from a broken pane sweeping into the room, scattering the dead leaves towards her, covering her feet like a drift of snow, as she stood there, trembling in the chill, like Rip Van Winkle, aghast at the change in the place – this return to a house she remembered in all its warmth and vivacity. But perhaps it was the wrong house?

She fingered through one of the broken tea-chests. It was filled with old Hansard parliamentary reports. Mortimer, of course, had been an MP at Westminster. And then, certain confirmation that this had been his house, too, that Dermot had lived here, she found an old envelope stuck into the side of the tea-chest, the address written in a youthful hand she knew well. It was her own – one of the many letters, this one forgotten here, which she had written to Dermot years before. Kneeling down, she read it in the waning light. It was headed Summer Hill, the date May 1911. 'Dear Uncle Dermot, It was so bad to have you go. But I am fairly happy, going out and about on my own now, down by the river. At least I was this morning when I saw those otters we discovered together before you left. They're still there! In that hide beneath the willow. And the big one, the dog otter – Mr Mullins we called him, remember? – he was there, just for a moment, poking his nose out and washing his whiskers after some big fishy breakfast! I do wish you had been there to see him . . .'

But her eyes had begun to cloud over and she could read no more – starting to cry, her whole body shaking, before she fell forward, tearing at the dirty floor-boards with her nails, breaking them, spreadeagled there, starting to grovel in the dust and debris, her face smeared in soot, weeping uncontrollably now as unhappiness overwhelmed her.

Neighbours next door, hearing these piercing wails, called the police, who found her there some time later – a drunken, hysterical woman, whom they took to be a tramp at first, putting her into the police car and taking her down to Chelsea Station. Here, identifying her as Laura Bowen, the great picture star, they were astonished, bringing no charges, taking her back to the Savoy.

But one of the constables, in the way of making a pound or two on the side out of such mishaps and misdemeanours involving celebrities, later called the *Daily Mail*, so that news of Miss Bowen's strange escapade in Knightsbridge appeared in the paper next morning. The Prince, reading the same paper at breakfast, saw the item. He bowed his head, closed his eyes, in agony.

11

DERMOT HAD INDEED been living at the house in Wilton Place until some six months before, using it as his London base, home on leave from overseas, or more recently – having been appointed to the staff at Sandhurst, lecturing there on military tactics – as a weekend retreat.

But, since his father Mortimer, now in his seventies, had retired several years before to the family home at Islandbridge just outside Dublin, the house in London had been too big, too isolating an encumbrance in a life which, for Dermot, was already – though he rarely admitted it – lonely enough. His father had readily agreed that it be put up for sale and Dermot himself had just taken a small bachelor flat down the road in South Kensington which, together with his similarly austere accommodation at Sandhurst, entirely sufficed for his few domestic needs.

However, at that point, he was not in England at all. Three months' accumulated leave was due to him and he had returned to Dublin the week before, to stay with his father at Islandbridge. Apart from taking a holiday and seeing Mortimer, there were impending problems of all sorts now to do with Summer Hill, with which Mortimer was getting too old and infirm to deal with properly.

Dermot, on the other hand, in his early fifties, with his vigorous outdoor life, had aged only a little. Slim and neat as ever, with a clipped moustache, spruce hair, greying slightly, still parted severely in the middle, he remained a handsome man, albeit in the traditional military manner. There was a calm assurance about him, a kindly confidence in his sharp blue Cordiner eyes. His long military career had not hardened or soured him. Lucky to survive the Great War, he had made a success of all he had put his hand to since – recently promoted to full Colonel, he still loved the army life, the activity and companionship there, and now this lecturing to young officers at Sandhurst.

Yet at heart he remained a lonely man. So that the house at Islandbridge, and the Cordiner family seat at Summer Hill, too, had come to mean more to him than ever, as homes which he wished to preserve if he could. He was quite set on maintaining this brick and mortar, at least, in his Irish background, as a stay and occupation against his isolation in part, but much more with the idea that one day some other Cordiner – Hetty's children perhaps, or other cousins in the far-flung family, or even Robert and Léonie – might take these houses over, particularly Summer Hill.

And there was the very problem about which he had now to talk to his father. Frances, some years before, had left the whole place to the butler, Pat Kennedy. And Pat would have certainly sold everything up long before had not Dermot and Mortimer taken a seven-year lease on the house and lands, a lease that was due for renewal in a month's time.

Dermot spoke to his father now in the bow-windowed drawing room, curtained against the chilly December night, the river murmuring over the weir just beyond the lawn, the faint sound of engines chuffing in and out of Kingsbridge station a mile away, the two men taking sherry in the lamplight by the fire, before Mrs O'Hanlon, the housekeeper, called them to supper.

'So what's the latest position?'

'There's no doubt – Pat Kennedy will sell up as soon as our present lease expires. Married now, you know, with children. The wife wants him to buy a farm near her own people in Tipperary. He certainly won't want us to renew the lease.' Mortimer, stooped and patriarchal in a chintz armchair, sipped his sherry through his still formidable whiskers. 'And, besides, I've no mind to go on kow-towing to that avaricious blackguard Pat Kennedy – or his crooked land agent Cassidy – submitting to what amounts to blackmail, since they both know very well how much we want to keep the place in the family. It'd be different if we had any real income now from the lands. But of course the Land Commission has taken well over the half of it. And there's little enough coming in from what's left in the present agricultural decline. Fifteen shillings an acre at best, when we got two or three pounds there during the war.'

'How many acres do we still have?'

'A thousand odd. Outside the demesne.'

'And the price, at auction, if we had to buy the house and demesne alone?'

'Difficult to say. The house is in bad shape. But the pictures and furniture are worth a bit. Forty, fifty thousand?'

'But, Papa – we can't just let the whole place go, to some timber merchant or institution.'

'May have to. Where's the fifty thousand? And even if we did manage to buy it – what about the running costs? And all the repairs? And the gardens have gone to seed completely. Last time I was down there, this summer, the whole place was sheer jungle – only Aunt Emily really in her element, having a splendid time with her pictures of it! . . .'

'Unless we wrote to Hetty again? . . .' Dermot wondered. 'She'd have more than enough money to buy the place outright.'

'No reply to your last letter! So why should there be now? Tragedy . . . She obviously still loathes the place, the whole idea of Ireland . . .'

'And then, of course, there's the other problem. Hetty and the present Prince of Wales gallivanting about – in all the papers. What should we do about that? Hetty is his aunt, of course. Delicate – to put it mildly.'

'Indeed . . .' He drained his sherry, a little of the old fire returning to his voice. 'Absolute . . .' He shook his head in wonder at the whole thing. 'But what can we do? We can't tell her, at least not while Frances is alive – which may not be long, I grant you. She's pretty poorly by all accounts up in that damp, cat-infested little bungalow in Rathgar Road. Involved in good works for everyone but herself. Probably do for Frances altogether if Hetty were told – since she'd more than likely go for her mother and try and have it all out with her. Anyway, it's my opinion that someone at Court – old Lord Stamfordham for example, who's still alive – knows all about who Hetty is, and will put a stop to her goings-on with the Prince. Besides . . .' Mortimer touched his beard ruminatively. 'Would it really do Hetty any good – telling her now? Years ago, yes. But now?'

'Yes! Yes, Papa – that's the whole point! I'm *sure* it would.' Dermot paced the room restlessly – suddenly touched by his early memories of Hetty, when they had first met, the bruised and unhappy little girl, malicious, withdrawn, whom he had taken in hand twenty years before, showing her all the miracles of life and landscape around Summer Hill, going down to the river bank with her and about the estate, looking for kingfishers, otters, rare wildflowers – teaching her to know and name all these wonders, and so possess them truly – astonished by this wild girl, his heart going out to her, the old King's daughter, yet so dispossessed herself then in every way, being deceived and punished, made an outcast by her mother for her own indiscretions.

So that now, suddenly, apart from saving Summer Hill, he wished passionately that he could save Hetty with it, for it. 'Yes! She should be told.' Dermot turned to his father. 'Because that's the *real* reason for all her hurts, you know, Papa, all her subsequent unhappiness and stupidities – that running off to America and so on, for her hatred of Frances, for Summer Hill, for everything in Ireland. It's because of all the lies she was told then. I'm certain, if she were told the truth now, she'd be a lot easier as a person, perhaps even take up with Summer Hill again. It might change everything for her. She might even buy Summer Hill back for the family.'

'Possibly. But *how* tell her? Where? When? She lives in France now, doesn't she? And our lease comes up with Pat in a few weeks' time.'

'There must be a way . . .' Dermot thought out loud, sitting down again. '*Must* be. Can't see the whole place go . . .'

His father commiserated with him. 'I know how you feel about the place. I feel the same. But this may be the one battle neither of us has the reserves for.' Both of them gazed into the dancing firelight. Mortimer tried to bring some cheer into the sad mood then. 'Let's have another sherry. Rather good, had it from Findlaters. Perhaps we should get a case in for Christmas?'

*

At that same moment, having returned to Paris, Hetty was taking to stronger drink alone in her apartment – already half-way through a bottle of vodka. Since her return there she had rarely been sober. At first, as Christmas approached, she had launched herself on a series of visits and seasonal parties with her friends, reputable and less so. But quite soon the former found her continual drinking tiresome, her earlier wit and vivacity, once sharpened by alcohol, now quite drowned in it – her beauty dissolving, the chiselled features aerating in a blotched and puffy skin. They tactfully avoided her in public and made excuses when she called. Her louche acquaintances started by encouraging these excesses, in *boîtes*, restaurants or cafés. But soon even they tired of picking up her bills, the mess she made, carrying her out into taxis and seeing her home.

So that now, locking herself away from her maid in her bedroom, Hetty drank alone, often through the night, gazing glassy-eyed through old scrapbooks of her Hollywood pictures, lying senseless in bed most of the day, until the returning pains in her joints roused her in the afternoon and she took to drink once more – to cure the hangover, kill the aches.

Her maid had warned Bernie Franklin. And twice, almost forcing himself into her bedroom, he had tried to reason with her. But she was quite beyond reason. Her life, she intimated drunkenly, was coming to an end. Mr Franklin, having witnessed just such emotional or professional setbacks and consequent alcoholic excess among picture stars in his old Hollywood days, feared this might literally prove to be the case – that she aimed to kill herself.

Well, he certainly was not going to have this great picture star – *Nefertiti* was due to have its French première in a few weeks' time – die on his books. He called the American hospital at Neuilly. A young doctor came to the apartment that same evening. He was probably only just in time. Tapping some secret supply – for the maid had already by then thrown out all the drink – Hetty had consumed a half-bottle of brandy that afternoon and was unconscious on the floor when the doctor and Bernie Franklin broke into the room. Her pulse was faint, breathing weak but stertorous, pupils dilated. They brought her in an ambulance straightaway to the hospital.

Here, in the next ten days, with careful nursing and constant supervision, Hetty made a surprising recovery. Her real friends visited her, Natalie Barney, other women, some of the men she knew in Paris. Hetty seemed quite calm now. They complimented her, her good sense on admitting herself to the hospital, they commiserated with her generally – the pressures of her work . . .

They lied to her tactfully, noticing too, but equally failing to remark on it, the deadness in her voice and expression, a chilling vacancy there. She was physically better, they saw, but her mind was no longer that bright thing, full of wit and brio. Behind the big blue eyes there was a void, a brain quite stunned, it seemed, without thought.

Yet Hetty did have thoughts – or one at least – which she nurtured secretly. She had put herself on her best behaviour here since she was determined, at the first opportunity, having allayed everyone's fears, to escape the hospital and resume her deadly life.

It was not that she wanted to kill herself, to kill Henrietta Cordiner. Franklin was wrong there. This vehement drinking, the ever-increasing oblivion it brought, was simply an unconscious means of killing that other overlaid persona of Laura Bowen, an invented character who had betrayed her, that fictional woman with whom the Prince of Wales had fallen in love – and, discovering the hollowness there, had dropped.

Without admitting it – for she could not face the stupidities of her life consequent on this long-assumed role, the cruelties and betrayals she had imposed on Léonie and her own family through it – Hetty desperately wanted to be rid of this other woman now, this false personality, the fatal carapace she had taken on over the years with Craig.

So that now, in this suicidal behaviour, she was acting out the last rites appropriate, as she saw it, to a failed picture star, believing that when she had taken this role to its ultimate depths she would emerge then into a new and proper self, the person she really was, indeed had once been.

This she felt intuitively, the pain expressing itself in drink, the only means of repressing the guilt for all those wrong turnings made long ago. She felt obscurely that, in order to live again, she must first die, must kill that other woman in her, continue to the end of the night, before emerging into a new dawn.

She was right in all these intuitions. But she quite lacked the support and reason then to see how, in the alcoholic means she took towards this happy transformation, she faced literal not metaphorical death.

Of course, as Franklin had warned them and the staff knew well themselves, such ideas of escape were an expected reaction in some of these alcoholic cases. So the nurses kept a constant eye on Hetty in her private room at the clinic, whose windows, though not barred, could only be opened a mere six inches.

However, as she improved, Hetty pointed out that she ought to take some exercise. And so she did, always with a nurse in tow, through the walled garden behind the hospital. And as she walked, in her greatcoat and muffler she inspected the high walls covertly. Recovering as she had, she was sure she had not lost all of her old athleticism. Indeed, it would be a simple matter, she thought – when she saw the low-roofed potting shed, set right against the wall at the far end of the garden . . .

And so it was. Jumping on to the roof here one morning a week later, she easily scaled the remaining four or five feet of wall, before dropping down into a narrow lane on the far side. In a minute she was out on the main road back to Paris – and minutes later she found a cab, directing it straight to the Crillon Hotel.

Here the management, assuming she had come to stay again for the première of *Nefertiti*, welcomed her most graciously, offering her a large suite overlooking the Place de la Concorde. Hetty explained, with a winning smile, how she had arrived early – her entourage, with her luggage, were due later – and could they meanwhile send some iced Veuve Clicquot up to her rooms straightaway?

Several hours later, a hectic party was under way in the suite, attended by her least reputable Parisian friends, drinking fiercely. Later, far gone in drink, when the party had dissipated itself, she made love with one of the men in her bedroom, opening her legs to him vehemently, a vicious love-making; she cared not one whit for any possible infection she might give him, pleased indeed to take such revenge, on Laura Bowen's part, against all men.

A few days later Hetty, having returned to her own apartment, had sobered up once more. Bernie Franklin had seen to it. The Paris première of *Nefertiti*, to which Hetty had of course been invited and was expected, was due to take place at the end of the week. So he had temporarily moved into her apartment, together with a nurse, round the clock, to ensure she took no more drink. They thought themselves entirely successful. Hetty appeared quite sober when she and Franklin set out that Friday night for the Elysée Cinema next to the Rond-Point – to a glittering occasion with a specially-invited audience of the smartest Parisians. Cars were lined half-way up the avenue when they arrived, spotlights picking Hetty out as she stopped on to the pavement. She looked sensational in a superb evening creation by Worth – a black lace dress, with a skin-coloured silk underdress, low square neckline, inset with squares of shimmering satin, a curved hemline dropping to sequinned handkerchief points at the sides and back.

But again Hetty had managed to deceive her overseers. Some time before, she had hidden a bottle of vodka in the lavatory cistern of the apartment. She had drunk a third of it before leaving that evening, then decanted most of the rest into a flask which she carried with her in her purse, gulping this down in the ladies' room at the theatre before the performance, and finishing the flask off there again after the show, just before she was due on stage to receive the plaudits of the audience and to make a brief speech.

Bernie Franklin, smelling nothing on her breath, held her arm as they stood in the wings, before the head of the Fox Picture Corporation in Paris led her out into the dazzling spotlights. She acknowledged the applause in a glazed but steady fashion. Taking the microphone stand then, she leant forward, stumbling a fraction.

'Mesdames et Messieurs,' she started in her perfect French, smiling wanly. 'Je vous remercie beaucoup, mille fois . . .' Then she paused, beginning to sway much more obviously now, before seeming to recover herself again. Then, quite suddenly and spectacularly, she was sick – a jet of liquid spurting out over the orchestra pit. The conductor took cover from the spray, as if from an exploding fire hydrant. Hetty was on her knees, her gown quite soiled, grovelling against the footlights, moaning piteously, 'Oh God, oh God . . . I want to go back to the cosy-warm.'

The spotlights were cut as Hetty was carried off. The orchestra, attempting to cover the disaster, started up with a sudden, ragged *Merry Widow* waltz – more a funeral dirge for Hetty as she was set down, like a sodden corpse, in the wings.

*

Pat Kennedy, in his wealth, had purchased a small Ford motor. He kept it in one of the old coachhouses, or what was left of these, giving out on to the stable yard, littered with domestic rubbish now, the cobbles encrusted with moss, a thick carpet of ragwort and lesser weeds: a moist green rug spreading voraciously everywhere, climbing the yard walls, giving the place the air of some green-glazed jungle grotto, inexplicably filled with the detritus of hideous civilisation.

Manoeuvring the car out from the smashed coachhouse doors he carefully navigated it round a tip of broken stout bottles, another of old tin cans, before circling a suppurating old manure heap, passing under the crumbling yard arch-way and down the front drive. The main avenue was almost entirely grassed over, the route only just discernible, a passage made the more difficult by several huge beech trees which had fallen across it, necessitating detours out into the demesne and back. The front gates, with their Georgian pillars and pineapple tops, had been closed and padlocked since one of the pillars had fallen over two years before. So that now, turning off into the demesne again, he left the estate via a jagged entrance broken into the high wall a hundred yards further on.

But Pat Kennedy noticed none of this seedy decay and destruction. He lived here, was too familiar with it, completely unconcerned about it in any case. It was only the farm land that interested him here, not the house and grounds – a house that sat there then on the hill behind him all tattered and torn in the pale December light.

After the disastrous fire ten years before, Lady Cordiner's little study-boudoir at the north end of the Georgian house had never been properly restored; nor had the fire-gutted Victorian servants' wing next to it. Both had simply been patched up with unsuitable brick and weatherboard, which in turn had started to crumble and rot.

In the main house itself several of the tall sash windows on the ground floor had broken clean away from their casements, had been replaced with blind brick, while far above some of the tall chimneys had crashed down on the roof, cannonading into the balustrades, falling overboard together, forming piles of blackened masonry, fluted columns and cornices, lying embedded in grassy hillocks on the lawn beneath.

The roof, holed in several places, had been covered with tarpaulins which flapped now over the gable ends, ominous black triangles, like the wings of monstrous pre-historic birds nesting there. The great porch was fouled with dark rain smears and lichen, while Lady Cordiner's meticulously-kept pleasure garden beyond was now a field of tall rank winter grass and weeds, only the broken astrolabe visible, poking up at the centre, a vision of science and reason quite destroyed everywhere else at Summer Hill.

Higher up, to the west, the ascending lawn terraces and stone steps had become virtually invisible. Here, nearer the real woods, this area was almost a wood itself now, filled with thorn bushes, thick bramble, and vast sprouting clumps of elder, which had spread everywhere, choking the old willow-and-rock garden and almost smothering the trunks of the great trees themselves, the cedars, Spanish chestnuts, the Canadian maple.

In summer all this surging growth, rising up round the house, made it practically invisible from any distance. But now, in bare mid-winter, Summer Hill was seen as the wreck of a great ship, driven far inland by some huge tidal wave, foundering in a jungle of ivy, dead nettles, dry thistle, rotting trees.

'No. I won't lease it again to the Cordiners.' Pat Kennedy, arriving in Kilkenny for his appointment, spoke to Mr Cassidy, the auctioneer and land agent, in his musty office. 'I want it sold up, the whole place – house, demesne, farm lands. I have my eye on this farm in Tipperary, near the wife's people . . .'

'Indeed – I'll sell it surely,' Mr Cassidy, slightly hunch-backed, with long strands of wispy hair right round the nape of his neck and a bald crown to his egg-shaped head, had the air of a long-spoiled priest. He leant forward eagerly now, hands shaped as if in prayer, his little eyes glinting at the prospect of the vast commissions here. 'And you'd be well advised, Mr Kennedy – well advised and no mistake. With agriculture the way it is today there's no real money in leasing. But an outright sale – now, that's a different matter altogether. People'll always want to *buy* land here, whatever the other circumstances.'

Pat Kennedy agreed. 'And what would you estimate it all at, Mr Cassidy?'

'Oh, £25,000 or so for the land certainly. And the same or more for the house and demesne. In or about £60,000, Mr Kennedy. So we'll put it all up for auction then, in a month or so, just as soon as I get the par-tik-ulers printed and out. Say in February or March?'

'Right, Mr Cassidy. And you'll let Mr Cordiner know in Dublin.'

'I will indeed!' Mr Cassidy stood up, came round from his desk and shook Pat Kennedy warmly by the hand. 'Ah, sure,' he reassured him. 'Isn't that the best thing to do with the oul' place altogether. Going to rack and ruin as it is. And who'd miss it anyway? Thim big houses of the English over here – no place in Ireland for them now. Hand of the oppressor. Pity the lads didn't burn more of them in the bad times. And then, besides, ye tell me the roof is almost off it already. So ye have a right to sell it now – before the whole place falls down about your ears. And I've a mind who'll buy it, too – the house and demesne, I mean. There's a big timber merchant in Waterford. He'll go for it! Sure, look at all the fine timber about the place. And there's another builder fellow I know who'd take the good stone outa the house as well. Ah, sure there'll be nothing go to waste at the heel of the hunt, Mr Kennedy – nothing! – like a pig at the butchers! *Nothing!*'

Hetty, after the fiasco at the première in Paris, made one last realistic attempt to save herself. She decided, in one of her drunken but more active moments, to visit Léonie at her apartment on the rue Saint-André-des-Arts, and perhaps make things up with her. But, when she got there one chilling afternoon just after Christmas, the concierge told her Léonie had left – for London.

'Londres?'

'Oui, Madame – pour Londres.'

They had all gone there, the old woman went on, aggressively, when Hetty questioned her, not just for a visit, but to live there. Yes, Monsieur Grant had taken up a new position – with the *Times* newspaper, she added dismissively.

Hetty swayed about the street afterwards, drank hot rum in a nearby café and later was nearly run over by a taxi crossing the Boulevard Saint-Michel. Again, as with Mortimer and Dermot in the house in London, her old friends no longer existed – in fact or fancy. They had betrayed her – family and friends – all of them. They had betrayed Laura Bowen, at least. And so, with even more self-destructive energy, she resumed her murderous pursuit of that woman in herself.

Her descent became entirely uncontrolled now. As she made abrupt forays in and out of the clinic at Neuilly, her health seriously deteriorated. Her syphilis, exacerbated by the alcohol, returned to plague her more fiercely. And then, though the fact hardly impinged on her now, her money ran out altogether, large bills could not be met, her credit was withdrawn and claimants everywhere initiated bankruptcy proceedings against her. Craig, still on location in the wilds of Morocco, could not be reached for any help. A few of her friends in Paris did what they could. But Hetty's state was such as to make them quite impotent.

News of her impending bankruptcy and her condition generally appeared in the popular newspapers, whose reporters, after the sensational events in the Elysée Cinema, had come to haunt the clinic or her apartment on the Ile Saint-Louis. They were there on the day that Hetty was ejected by the Paris bailiffs, and returned in an ambulance to the hospital at Neuilly. A number of papers next morning featured this dramatic event on their front pages, including the *Daily Mail*, one of their Paris reporters having been assigned to cover the decline and fall of this once-great picture star.

Hetty, in the weeks after Christmas, had become maniacal in her drinking, alternating between bouts of extreme excitement and fury, a sustained frenzy, when she barely slept or ate, pacing the apartment, shouting, laughing, throwing things about, then suffering sudden black-outs of the sort that had overwhelmed her in Hollywood. So that, when she arrived in the clinic again that day in the new year, she had moved to a further stage in her malady: the blue devils, *delirium tremens* – her body shaking all over, making constant purposeless movements, hallucinating, screaming, as she gazed at the terrifying visions materialising all about her in her room, the furniture distorting itself into weird shapes, so that she wrenched her head upwards – only to be confronted by monstrous toads and snakes squirming and crawling all over the ceiling. And, when the doctor arrived in the room, she saw him as hooded and malign, the figure of a hangman come for her execution, so that she leapt off the bed at him, struggling fiercely before they held her down, trying to sedate her.

Failing in this, for she fought so violently, they finally managed to strap her to the bed. Eventually she ceased to struggle; her breathing became quite faint, her eyes stared glassily upwards. Undoing the straps then, they administered what drugs they dared and watched over her.

'Fifty-fifty,' the doctor told Franklin that evening. 'There's inflammation of the lungs. If she develops pneumonia, as quite often happens at this stage of alcoholism, it's usually fatal.'

One who read of Hetty's predicament then – he saw the paragraph in the *Dublin Evening Mail* that same day – was Dermot Cordiner. He showed the Reuter's news item to his father that evening: 'Miss Lauren Bowen, the Hollywood picture star, was yesterday evicted from her Paris home for non-payment of rent. Bankruptcy proceedings have been instituted against her. Subsequently, in a state of collapse, she was removed by ambulance to the American hospital . . . Miss Bowen, until recently a close companion of the Prince of Wales . . .'

'So you see, Papa – you were right. Someone at court has obviously told the Prince who she really is, and he's dropped her. And now she's no money and taken to the bottle by the looks of it. Simply can't let it go on like this. I'll have to go over to Paris, bring her home . . .'

His father agreed. 'That makes two of them,' he said. 'Mother and daughter, both on their beam ends. News has it Frances won't last the winter. She's very low. Bronchitis, pneumonia –'

Dermot was suddenly impatient. 'Papa – so you see now, don't you? – this whole thing is nonsense, gone on far too long. Hetty will have to be told who she is. Perhaps that's the only way to cure her, save her from the same fate as her Mama. I'll tell her . . .'

His father sighed. 'Yes, perhaps you're right.' He sipped his sherry. 'Lies . . . I used to tell Frances in the old days – the truth is the one thing that can't really hurt us.'

Dermot snorted. 'Of course! So what have you and I been doing all these years?' He almost stamped his foot in frustration. '*Why* didn't we tell Hetty long before – so that she might have avoided all this? – this stupidity, this tragedy? I blame myself!'

'No, you shouldn't. We were both of us strictly bound by Frances's confidences in the matter, remember? She asked us never to tell Hetty. Have to remember, too – though it's easy to forget – how Frances was once so much a happy part of our lives, when she was such a different person, before all that ranting political bitterness overtook her.'

'You needn't remind me – I was to have married her!'

'So, we both of us had – must still have – a loyalty towards her, despite the appalling way she's behaved, towards Hetty, over Summer Hill . . .'

'Of course. But, if telling Hetty might save her now, then I'm quite prepared to break that loyalty, Papa.'

Mortimer nodded. 'Yes,' he agreed. 'You're right. The greater good . . .'

'I'll take the mail boat tomorrow then. Should be in Paris the day after.'

Another who read of Hetty's condition was Robert, now working in London as a junior parliamentary reporter with *The Times*. Seeing all along that, as an Englishman, there was no real future for him with the Paris *Tribune*, he, together with Dermot (who had known the editor Geoffrey Dawson well, when Dawson had been private secretary to Lord Milner in South Africa thirty years before), had tactfully lobbied for a position at Printing House Square for some time.

Attending an interview in London the previous autumn, he had been successful, offered work in the press gallery of the House, covering the less important debates, but with a clear intimation from the editor himself of better things to come. Dawson had been impressed by Robert's political acumen, his sober style and general bearing – a true *Times* man in the making, he thought, offering him what was, for that paper, the handsome sum of £650 per annum to start with.

With a first month's salary in hand, together with financial help from Léonie's father in Paris (so that, in Léonie's liberated canon, they could both contribute to their accommodation), they had taken a leasehold on a large, pleasant top floor flat in a Victorian terrace house in Denning Road, Hampstead, just down from the underground station, with views over a pretty back garden, bounded by a row of tall poplars, then a vision of London down the hill beyond – a pearly shimmer in the distance that morning, mists clearing in the bright January sunlight, as Robert read the papers over breakfast, while Léonie tried to feed their child Olivia, fretful and difficult, strapped into her high chair across the table from him.

Opening the *Daily Mail* he had seen this most recent news about Hetty on the front page. Now he tried to read it aloud. But Olivia, refusing her food, had started to whine and squeal, so that eventually he had to hold the paper out in front of Léonie.

'Well?' she asked, harrassed herself now. 'What can one expect? In and out of the papers for months, up to one sort of nonsense or another – oh, do sit *still*, Olivia! . . .'

Robert wiped some crumbs from his chin, sipped at his coffee. 'Yes, but she's seriously ill now – and bankrupt. And that letter we had from Dermot the other day, about Pat Kennedy selling up Summer Hill.'

'What's the connection?'

'Well, for one, Hetty might have bought the place. She must have had oodles of money.'

'Spent it all on high living. Picture stars do, you know.'

'She's hardly that any more. They're all sound pictures now. And, with her stammer, she must be finished in all that world.'

'Well, serves her right, for going into it in the first place. I always told her – how it wasn't her.'

'Why have you got such a down on Hetty? Oh, I know – all that Egyptian business. But that's all over. And now, when she's penniless and ill – shouldn't one try and help? Can one just drop someone, someone one was close to, just because one's had trouble with them in the past?'

Léonie turned to him, wide-eyed, astonished. 'But, Robert! – that's exactly what

I used to say to *you*, when you were so dismissive of Hetty, in Paris, years ago! How have you so changed your mind about her?'

'I haven't. Still think she's behaved . . . very stupidly. But now it's different, when she's so obviously lost. You, who were her greatest friend after all – why are you so unconcerned about her now?'

'Oh, Robert, can't you remember? What happened between us in Egypt?' She turned away, as if her face might betray her in something. 'Well, I don't want anything like that ever to happen again, *ever* – and ruin our lives, you and me, as it very nearly did then. So it's obvious, isn't it? – why I'm not too keen on her. Oh, for goodness' sake – do sit *still* a moment, Olivia!' She wiped the child's mouth and chin. 'Anyway, about Summer Hill . . .' Wanting to change the subject, she turned to Robert. 'There's nothing we can do.' Looking at him properly now, she saw how serious he was, a sad tense face gazing out of the kitchen window on to the garden, lost in thought. 'Robert?' He turned vaguely towards her. 'You *know* there's nothing we can do.'

Robert stood up, going to the window, staring out at the tall poplars. A light frost silvered their delicate branches, the sunlight melting the mists far below, domes and spires in the city gradually emerging. Léonie took Olivia out of the high chair, holding her up in her arms – cuddling, trying to comfort her, joining Robert at the window. 'Oh, that damned house, Robert! I wish you weren't so sad about it. But you – we – we'll have just to accept the loss. We have our *own* place now – here.'

'Yes. But you still have your home in Paris. And Summer Hill was, is, my home,' he answered her rather shortly. 'I'd like to be able to do something about it, obviously.'

'I'm sorry,' Léonie relented. 'It's just that Summer Hill is all tied up with *Hetty* – for both of us. You loved her, I loved her – and it's *gone*, all that, thank God, because it nearly killed us both. So why can't we let the bricks and mortar go, too, of all that past – now that we have all this, *here* in London?'

She came closer to him, Olivia in her arms, the child pressed between them, as she put her other arm round Robert, so that the three were joined in a mild familial embrace. 'We're *us* now, aren't we? And happy. And we can live *without* all that past!'

Robert responded, smiling faintly, stroking Olivia's dark hair. 'Yes. Yes, of course.' But then, gazing over Léonie's shoulder, he returned to his view of the distant city, the rising mists. So that Léonie, despite his warmth and attention just then, knew he was still really thinking of Summer Hill.

'There's always so much there for you, in Summer Hill, isn't there?' She moved away from him, trying to catch his attention again. 'That's the trouble, isn't it?'

'Hardly a "trouble" . . .' He didn't look at her. 'Bit more than that. It's the total disappearance of it.'

'But it's Hetty, too, in some way. Isn't it?' she asked, unable quite to hide the touch of anxiety in her voice. 'So mixed up in the place for you, loving her then –'

'Oh, Léa, no more than a crush.'

She laughed then, sardonically. 'That's exactly what I thought with Hetty first. And look what happened!'

'Well, I don't think I –'

'Things like that, when you're young – first love and so on – why, it can mark you for ever.' She stared at him, suddenly aware, aghast, at how rash this statement might appear to him, applying, as it did, so much more to her than to Robert. But he did not seem to notice.

'That's just operatic of you, Léa. It hasn't marked me,' he went on simply. Yet somehow she felt he might be lying. 'You know very well what I've always thought of Hetty's behaviour.' He had turned to her now, raising his voice over the renewed hullabaloo from the child. 'But now that she's ill with no money – wouldn't you want to help? Just objectively – as a friend?'

'How can either of us ever be objective about Hetty?'

'I can. I thought we both were – have been – ever since that Egyptian business.'

'I wouldn't *dare* help her, Robert. I mean – face to face. Like a bad penny turning up again.'

'That's . . .' Robert hesitated. 'That's nonsense. We've got over all that.'

'We thought just that before – before we went to Egypt.'

Robert turned decisively towards her now. 'Anyway, my real worries are about Summer Hill – if I could do something . . .' Lighting his pipe, he resumed his gaze out of the window.

He seemed, Léonie thought, in this last statement to have quite dismissed Hetty from his mind. And yet still she refused to believe this – did not really believe in his 'objectivity' about Hetty. It worried her. Had she got over all this business with Hetty – and Robert had not? She, after all, had loved and made up her final account with Hetty in Egypt. But Robert had never successfully expressed his love towards her. Did something of this desire still lurk in his heart, repressed, but re-awakened now in this news of her desperate condition?

So that perhaps Robert's anxiety to preserve Summer Hill was linked with this same hidden love he still felt for Hetty, which continued to frustrate him, which he still wanted to offer her, by saving her in some way now? If this were so she could hardly blame him. Yet the idea posed a threat to her. Léonie had felt it then, the little tremors of insecurity as they had talked – that image of Hetty, come to loom over them once more, as those great cinema posters had done, years before in Paris – so that Léonie longed tactfully to dissuade Robert from having anything to do with Summer Hill now, so to avoid, in that great house, the occasion of sin.

Let the house go, she felt – every last stone of it, levelled to the ground, so that there would be nothing, no evidence or memory, of her love for that woman. Let not one jot remain, she thought, of all that had encompassed that misguided past of hers, when she had loved Hetty, not Robert – whom she so loved now. Let nothing come to disrupt that love again, she prayed.

So it was that Léonie's real reason for wanting an end to Summer Hill, which she could not admit, was that this most recent news of Hetty and the house had renewed her guilt about everything that had happened there. Memories of Hetty, their happiness at Summer Hill, and her subsequent abrupt departure from Hetty in Egypt, crowded back on her now, memories which she had long suppressed in her new content with Robert.

And then, too, what Léonie most feared in all this, equally unadmitted, was something different again. She was not so much disturbed by the possibility of Robert's expressing any great emotion towards Hetty now, but more by the fear, if they met, that *she* might come to do exactly this herself – deeply touched, as she was in her heart of hearts, by Hetty's awful predicament now.

Léonie, in short, feared a resurgence of her old nature, that other nature, in loving women. The past was never really dead, nor one's real nature, she suspected. Both could be buried. One could hold them down successfully for years, as she had done, like suffocating a sweet enemy with a pillow. But the body could go on breathing – she saw that now – could rise up one fine day, come to haunt and destroy again, a ghost at noon. Léonie wanted none of this, was terrified of such spectres. If, even after marrying Robert, she had succumbed once to Hetty, as she had in Egypt, might she not do so once more – if they ever met again? So she prayed for an end to the house, as the site of what she took now to be her own original sin.

Thus for both of them Summer HIll, though for so long unvisited, intangible, remained a secret wound, from which the blood, like stigmata, could suddenly flow again – a place loved and hated: for both, a fiercely radiant emblem, obscured by the years, yet which nonetheless retained the power of resurrection or destruction. The news that morning in the *Daily Mail*, together with Dermot's letter about the impending sale the week before, had uncovered fears and hopes in both of them which they could not fully speak of, nor yet deny. The great house, decaying on that distant hill, reached out to them then, like a mirage hovering over the London mists, touching them deeply, strangely.

Robert finally turned to Lèonie. 'I shall have to go over to Dublin, and see Dermot. It's the least I can do.'

Léonie drew the child closer to her breast, as if trying to muffle the spasm of fear she felt.

Hetty, contracting pneumonia as the doctor had forecast, hovered between life and death for over a week. Dermot, arriving in Paris, saw her at once. Sedated, partly comatose, sometimes delirious now, she drifted in and out of consciousness without recognising him. Taking rooms nearby in Neuilly, he visited her for most of every day, watching over her – sitting on a chair near her bed, reading *The Times* or a detective novel, an electric fire warming the room against the chill dark winter days that gripped the city, rain battering on the windows at first, replaced by frost, and by the end of the week a heavy snowfall which encrusted the edges of the glass, brightly illuminating the room as he gazed at her pale face, lying flat without a pillow, her small pointed chin poking down over the sheet.

He was horrified at the changes wrought here in the eighteen months since he had last seen her – the pencil-thin body, the face emaciated, wrinkled with pain, crow's feet running away to either side of the lifeless blue eyes, whenever they opened momentarily, staring upwards blankly, only to close again – like a marionette dying on the threads.

Was this the same girl with whom he had roamed the land and discovered otters long ago at Summer Hill? Hetty Cordiner, most lovely, wild – and most hurt then, yes, but not like this. He found it difficult to contemplate the change – this vivid past and deathly present of someone for whom he had felt such affection, in herself, through all the letters she had written to him then, letters which he had brought with him from Dublin, kept all these years at Islandbridge, unearthed before leaving, taking them as a talisman of all that happy past, an emblem of some vague hope for the future.

'You see,' the doctor told him the following morning, 'since you are her family, I have to tell you that, quite apart from her alcoholism and pneumonia, she has tertiary syphilis too. *Tabes dorsalis* affects the spinal joints, the digestive muscles, which is why she can hardly take any food. I'm afraid you must be prepared for the worst. There's very little hope – if she lasts the day, even.'

And Dermot thought of this new aspect when he sat with her later – betrayed, even in that deepest part of her, by Craig Williamson, no doubt – the whole disaster of her life with that picture director, that wrong turning, inspired by her mother's lies and coldness, taken long ago. He gazed at her, seeing the damp toss of dark curls falling around the pinched skull, skin set tight against the forehead, a froth of hair like a hat that was far too large for her now, the only remnant of her former glory – raven-dark curls just like her uncle Henry's and her mother's too, both of whom he had so loved – and, now, these same dark curls, the only thing left intact and still beautiful of this family in the wreck and disaster of the years.

He stood up, touching a lock of her hair as she slept. As she lived? As she died? Yes, she was dying, just then – he sensed it, clearly, unable to hear her breathing, even in the utter stillness of the room, as the snow fell in dark drifts outside. She was slipping away from everything. But she must not, she could not die – this last emblem of a family that had meant so much to him; this woman he loved now as well. She must survive, else there would be nothing left of Summer Hill, for Summer Hill, nothing of all that miraculous past, no future.

What could he do? He was not religious. He never prayed. Instead, on an impulse, taking out the envelope of her old letters he started to read aloud from one of them, as he might have read a fairy tale to a child, an account that Hetty had written years before, of her adventures in search of an old badger in Cooper's Wood, on a rise beyond the great house.

'. . . and you know how we suddenly saw him, in the woody dell, snuffling about in the dry leaves that evening? – the big daddy one we called Arthur – well, I didn't see him again until I more or less camped out and stayed there almost into the dark yesterday night – and there were the snufflings and scratching again and I saw Arthur, the huge one, and then the *two* others with him, *much* smaller! His children, I suppose! Or grandchildren. And there they were, *so* near me, until something frightened them and they loped back in that funny bouncy way they have, like waves running, pitter-patter, pushing and shoving each other, back into their set, back into the cosy-warm! . . .'

As he read, the snow fell in lesser drifts outside, shafts of light breaking through from the west, illuminating Hetty's face. And then, almost at the end of his reading, she opened her eyes, turned her head a fraction, seemed to smile, seemed to recognise him.

She had been dreaming, an extraordinary, wonderfully calming dream. She was floating, rising in the room, suffused in brilliant light, suspended in a drift of warm snowflakes, floating above herself, that was the miracle – hovering beneath a transparent ceiling, with a vast blue sky far above her, as she looked down on her own real dying body stretched out on the bed way beneath her. But how could she be in two places at once? – how feel this incredible lightness of spirit, an exhilaration she had never known before, of total warmth, relaxation, a freedom from all pain, floating off high above her old corrupt self, there fading away in the bed below her, drifting upwards among the snowflakes into the glassy blue dome, from where she never wished to come to earth again, so great was her joy, being beckoned, pulled somewhere, into the glorious sky above her, towards some ultimate wonder and release?

Then she heard the voice – well-remembered, yet surprising – and saw the figure of a man, on a chair. She was looking straight down on him: his voice tugging at her, as she tried to resist the pull of it, but somehow could not – unable to resist some other magic here, a voice from the past, her childhood, from a distant country she had known well in some other almost equally happy dream long ago. Again she tried to pull herself away, to float upwards again, but some stronger force, emanating from the man, pulled her downwards and her warm, free floating dream collapsed and suddenly she found herself one with her own real body again and heard the words now – '. . . as they loped back in that funny bouncy way they have . . . like waves running, pitter-patter, pushing and shoving each other . . .'

She opened her eyes then, blinking in what seemed an almost equally blinding light flooding in from the window which illuminated the figure in the chair. She recognised him.

'Dermot?' she whispered weakly.

He stood up, coming towards her, smiling. He had something in his hand. It was the snow-dome, she thought, the little crystal ball with the ivory model of Summer Hill inside. Becoming tiny, it must have been in this, she thought, that she had been floating a minute before. But now, like Alice after the magic potion had worn off, she had resumed her true proportions. She tried to reach out for the little globe but her arms would not move. Yet she suddenly wanted the snow-dome, wanted it desperately then. It was hers. She would stay here, in her own real body, to have that thing, that crystal emblem of Summer Hill, more necessary to her then than anything else on earth.

'It was so extraordinary!' she told Dermot a week later, as she began her slow recovery. 'Because, when you came towards me, I was certain you had that old snow-dome of Summer Hill in your hand, not one of my letters. You see, I'd been floating about in it! – just before that – absolutely! – high above my real self, the snowflakes lapping all over me. How can you explain it?'

She tried to push herself up in the bed, then relapsed. Dermot helped her with the pillows. 'I can't. Unless it was some need, something you wanted very strongly then –'

'Oh yes, it was! It was! I *wanted* it, terribly.'

'Well, then – that was it. Something meant. You wanted Summer Hill. After all, I was reading about it, Cooper's Wood, the badgers there, years ago . . .'

'Yes, I suppose so. But I've not really thought about the place – in years.'

'Perhaps you've just been repressing your thoughts about it – all these years!' he said lightly.

'Perhaps. It's all very strange.' She seemed tired then, with the exertion of talking. Dermot stood up.

'Try and sleep, Hetty. I'll come again this evening.'

She put out her hand to him weakly. 'Yes, Dermot, do – please. It's so funny – that snow-dome dream, and coming down to earth again – as if I'd returned from some long journey – then suddenly seeing the actual snow-dome and thinking I was back at Summer Hill again . . .'

'Well, perhaps that's what you want – to be there again – in reality?' He looked at her closely.

'Yes,' she said vaguely, drowsy now. 'Yes, it must be that. Oh, Dermot – let's go back and look for the badgers in Cooper's Wood again! . . .'

She dropped off to sleep then, and Dermot left her – with another letter inside his pocket, one from his father which had arrived that morning, enclosing the catalogue which Mortimer had obtained, filled with all Mr Cassidy's 'particulars' on the forthcoming auction of the house, demesne and farm lands at Summer Hill. He could not tell Hetty about this – it would jeopardise, indeed perhaps prevent, her recovery. Yet now, more than ever, Dermot knew that he must somehow save the place, save it for her. For it was in this house, he sensed then, in the re-possession of it and in knowing who she really was – though he could not tell her that yet either – that Hetty's real cure would lie. Years before, at the very outbreak of the Great War, he had told her more or less the same thing, when she had so doubted her future there, hating the place, the two of them looking down on the house in the August sunshine – how Summer Hill really had so much beauty and promise in it, for her, for every-one. And now, when he next saw her again at the clinic, he repeated the gist of this.

'Yes, I'm sure it's the house you need, Hetty. That's the key to it all – if you can go back there, live there, your own birthright after all – then you'll recover properly, be happy. Mortimer and I can visit. I can help you fix things up – it's in a bit of a state now by all accounts. But Aunt Emily still lives there. And Robert and Léonie can come over. And life can be really good, really wonderful again, for all of us!'

'Robert and Léonie?' Hetty's face clouded. 'I've so fallen out with them, though, been so stupid . . . And what about Mama?'

'She's not well. Lives in Dublin now, you know – and not expected to live much longer. I don't think there'll be problems there – except that you should try and make things up with her . . .'

Hetty was close to tears now. 'But, Dermot, there's *far* too much for me to make up for, isn't there –'

'No –'

'How could I ever *begin* to make things up? I've been so stupid. I've fallen out with *every*one, so badly . . .'

'You've only really fallen out with yourself, Hetty, all these years. Don't you see?' He reached over, touching her hand. 'And you'll find your own true self again, when you go home. I promise you.'

She clutched his hand weakly in return, breathing faster now. 'Will I, Dermot, will I?'

He gazed at her, staring into her moist blue eyes, life beginning to return there. 'Yes, you will, I promise.'

It was a promise he knew he would have to make good at any cost – the cost of Hetty's life, her future. For she, too, now, at his persuasion, had come to believe that in this house lay her resurrection. But there was only one problem. And the horror of it struck him then: that he had identified the cure for Hetty – this magic elixir of a house that would end all the pain of the years for this family – yet the potion itself, available to them all for centuries on the hill, was about to be snatched from their hands forever.

12

ANOTHER WHO READ of Hetty's headlong decline in the *Daily Mail* during those winter months was the Prince of Wales. He was horrified. It was all a sheer tragedy. And he felt himself responsible for it. He had dropped her, perforce – but most cruelly. What more understandable – since she was obviously quite unaware of the reasons for his abrupt dismissal – than that she should take to drink? Now she was ill and bankrupt as well.

He would have to do something for her – on his own behalf, but just as much on his grandfather's account, he felt, the old King, who as Prince of Wales had been initially responsible for the whole calamity and had subsequently done nothing about it. He must therefore try to make up for that appalling lapse, too.

He met with Godfrey Thomas, his Private Secretary, immediately after breakfast one morning in January. 'I shall need the release of some funds, Godfrey – some considerable funds. From the Duchy of Cornwall account, I imagine,' he added brusquely.

'Yes, Sir. Some hundreds of pounds?'

'Some thousands, I imagine . . .' His Secretary looked up, surprised. 'What is there available on hand, in cash, immediately?'

'I'm afraid it's not likely to be –'

'I shall need about £50,000,' the Prince interrupted him. He had already decided on a figure commensurate with what he took to be the gravity of his grandfather's fault and his own behaviour. 'If the sum is not available – then things must be sold.'

Godfrey Thomas failed to conceal his astonishment. 'Sir! – that's a considerable sum. If we are to sell from the Duchy estates on such a scale, others may have to be involved –'

'That's quite all right, Godfrey. I shall be seeing Lord Stamfordham this morning. It's a matter of some urgency . . .'

The Prince, in this instance, went round to Buckingham Palace to see the old man, bringing him up to date on the matter of Laura Bowen, explaining his new intentions there.

'But, Sir, such a vast sum – there is no need. It is not as if you –'

'Arthur, I have to say – in the light of that secret memorandum you showed me – that there is *every* need. It is the very least I can do in the circumstances. My grandfather appears to have behaved appallingly in the matter.'

'He had no alternative, Sir – as you had none.'

'I can't agree. He could have acknowledged his parentage, tactfully, in some manner at least, to Mrs Fraser. So to deny his own daughter in that way – it was shabby to a degree. Because we are royal cannot mean we may simply brush such things under the carpet, as if they'd never occurred. Why, the matter could have been dealt with confidentially years ago, and the whole problem avoided with this Mrs Fraser, long before she became an Irish republican or whatever. Yet here am I, having had to drop Miss Bowen quite against my will, to her great distress, and all entirely on account of my grandfather's, or his advisers', moral cowardice. Well, I shall not be party to the same grubby behaviour.'

The Prince, fuming now, was in his most rebellious mood. 'Yes, remember, I dropped her *most* unwillingly, Arthur! And now, as you can see for yourself' – he flourished the front page of the *Daily Mail* – 'the pickle she is in, as a result of this. Ill and bankrupt! Vast debts apparently – ejected from her Paris home, and so without even a place to live now. I must make amends, on my grandfather's behalf as much as my own – in any way I can. I insist on it,' he added coldly.

'But £50,000, Sir – it is a vast sum –'

'Restitution must be made in line with the gravity of the original offence, Arthur. And I hope you will facilitate any financial arrangements necessary to secure the sum. If, on the other hand, you feel you cannot support me in this, well then, I shall clearly have no alternative but to bring the whole matter up – the *truth* of this whole ghastly, underhand business – with my parents, who of course, as you've told me, are quite unaware of who Miss Bowen really is: Miss Bowen, Hollywood *femme fatale* – in fact step-sister to the King, my father. He will be pleased to hear that, no doubt . . .'

The Prince, with what he felt to be this entirely justified blackmail, believed he had won his point resoundingly.

But Lord Stamfordham, canny and persistent, and still determined to forestall these ridiculous plans of the Prince's, had another card to play. 'Sir, there is one point you may have overlooked. Miss Bowen, as I see, is now a declared bankrupt, with very considerable debts by all accounts. Thus any such monies paid to her would immediately be forfeit. So that your purpose here, as I understand it – to effect a rehabilitation for the woman – would not be realised. She would receive very little, if any, of the money. Her creditors would receive it.'

The Prince admitted this point grudgingly. 'Well, then, I shall make some gift in kind.'

'The same would apply. Any such gift, coming into her legal possession now, could – and almost certainly would – be sold off to pay her debts.'

'Indeed, well . . . I am sure there must be some way round that problem. I shall speak to my own solicitors and let you know. Meanwhile I am determined on this course. Miss Bowen – my aunt – cannot be left to languish, penniless, in some hospital ward in Paris, or on the streets. I shall do *something* for her, Arthur – you may depend upon it.'

The Prince at once contacted a close personal friend of his, Montagu Bennington, a senior partner in the firm of Bennington and Peabody, solicitors, at Lincoln's Inn, asking if he could come and see him at the earliest opportunity. Mr Bennington arrived later that afternoon, when the Prince explained the whole situation to him.

'Lord Stamfordham is right, of course. Any monies you paid, or any outright gift, could be forefeit.'

'Is there no other way I could contrive it?'

'Well, really only in one way as I see it. You would have to retain the freehold, as it were, in any gift you made her – just as with Grace and Favour residences belonging to the Crown. A house, for example – might you consider giving her that? At least she would have a place to live, to recover herself in.'

'Indeed . . .'

'You have many such houses, I imagine, in your gift, here in London, or the country, from your Duchy of Cornwall estates.'

'Yes, indeed – I have. An excellent idea. The problem, though, is that I have to make the gift, and secure her future, anonymously, so that nothing could be traced back to me. I'm afraid . . . it has to be that way.'

'Well, that can be arranged, too. You may *buy* a house for her, the deeds retained by you, but under another name or by some holding company. I can easily arrange all that through my office, so Miss Bowen will never know who her benefactor is. The house can be given her from an "admirer" – what more natural? She must have many such, distressed by her present condition – the place to be given her without any legal possession, so that her creditors couldn't touch it.'

'Good, Montagu. Excellent. But a house – where? Not in England, perhaps – too close to home.'

'In France then? Or in Ireland, where you tell me she comes from.'

'Yes, yes . . .'

'Let me have some enquiries made of her, Sir. I have a good man – really excellent, entirely discreet – in a firm of private investigators in Jermyn Street. I can have him find out exactly what her present circumstances are, where she might best want to live. Then we can arrange to buy her what she wants there.'

'Excellent, Montagu, excellent! . . . I am most obliged to you.'

'Not at all. Anything I can do – it would be a pleasure. I'll be in touch with you.'

'Really most kind. I only wish . . .' The Prince paused, a sadness suddenly overwhelming him, clouding his bright good looks. 'Only wish – it didn't all have to be anonymous . . .'

His friend, half-way towards the door, turned back. 'I understand entirely.' Montagu Bennington, of course, had read all about the Prince's association with Miss Laura Bowen – and, knowing him well, realised too – seeing it all confirmed in the Prince's sad expression – how he had so obviously loved this woman and been forced to drop her, of course. Not knowing the real reasons, he simply assumed the obvious: that the heir to the throne could not for long be mixed up with a married, and now alcoholic and bankrupt, Hollywood picture star. But Montagu Bennington would never for a moment presume on his friendship with the Prince, by bringing such a topic up, so that all he did now, by way of terminating his part in their interview, was to repeat himself. 'I understand it all completely.'

The Prince, when his friend had left, went to the window, gazing down the lines of frozen trees. 'How I wish you did understand it all,' he said to himself. Then, turning back to his desk, he added, 'And, even more – if she could . . .'

Aunt Emily, standing by an easel at her bedroom window, looked out at the huge crowd assembled for the auction in front of Summer Hill. They stood packed together or in straying groups on the outskirts, several hundreds of them, beneath a blustery March sky – people from all over the country and further afield, rough mountainy men from the hills across the valley, local farmers, great and small, some few Ascendancy landowners, in gaiters and bowler hats, with their stewards; priests, gombeen men, and some professional-looking gents in dark suits and unsuitable town shoes, together with a large assortment of hangers-on and gawpers, come for the sport or to service the multitude – with porter, sweets and oranges: a gaggle of tinkers in damp plaid shawls purveying the latter; their barefoot children pressing in and out between the crush, threatening the mountainy men with this exotic fruit, when they were not trying to lift the wallets from the back-pockets of more substantial prey – portly farmers, big men of the county, who pushed them aside, making for the bar tent, a dank, rain-smeared marquee, filled with barrels of porter and crates of Jameson by courtesy of a shrewd Thomastown publican, set up on the trampled grass in the middle of Lady Cordiner's old pleasure garden, beyond the astrolabe, which stood above the crowd now, a desolate thing, rusty circles of iron, which some thought to be a piece of old agricultural equipment, part of the later sale of such things from the Summer Hill farm. Despite the chilly, unsettled weather there was an air of high festivity and happy expectation everywhere, a holiday mood, with vivid chatter, oaths, backslapping and gossip, wily groups whispering over the sale catalogue, weighing up lots like horses on a point-to-point card.

Aunt Emily's big studio-bedroom, with its trompe l'oeil murals of the old Residenz Theater in Munich, had sometime before been tagged and docketed by Mr Cassidy's men – most of the furniture, as everywhere else in the house, numbered with sticky labels, due to be auctioned in the latter part of the sale. She herself, though, had steadfastly refused to vacate the house or indeed leave her room. Quite unperturbed, believing that all this auction was a nonsense and the house would never be sold out of the family, she had locked herself into the bedroom with a supply of oatmeal biscuits, and was set now, as always, on commemorating events – in this instance the whole pulsating scene outside her window: the push and shove of farmers in their bowlers, the shawly travelling people and their impudent children, all this boisterous avaricious congregation come to inspect and devour the carcase of a house where she had spent all her life – a scene lit then by a brilliant sun-shaft which had rushed across the valley from Mount Brandon, illuminating everything in a flush of early-spring light, before the chill wind brought dark clouds scurrying back over the landscape, together with a sudden battering rain squall, driving the crowd to every meagre cover.

As they dispersed then, leaving some of the trodden lawns free, Aunt Emily saw a few first daffodils pushing up from the undergrowth on the lawn terraces to her right. Dabbing her brush in yellow watercolour, she started to sketch in these golden heads on her drawing. But, by the time she raised her eyes again, the shower was over and the crowds, returning, had trampled the little patch of gold into the muddy ground.

She heard the heavy stamp of boots outside on the landing then, unwanted visitors roaming the great house. Her door-handle turned. 'Oh no! You won't get in here, me hearties – you brazen lot of jackals and buzzards.' She picked up a sharp-tipped shooting stick she had with her and advanced with it menacingly, shaking it at the locked door. She had much the air of a pirate then, too – a large red handkerchief as a bandeau round her head, wisps of white hair flying all about outside it, a wicked and yet somehow amused glint in her still-clear blue Cordiner eyes. In her mid-seventies she was a formidable old party, barely one whit less intent, intense, bizarre and cantankerous than thirty years before.

Dermot, surrounded by strangers, stood in the great hall, filled with numbered furniture and with a debris of fallen plaster, the room never properly restored since the Black and Tans had desecrated it. Some of Cassidy's men were there, sitting at a trestle table, noting financial bona fides, letters of credit and such like, from intending bidders unknown to them. Cassidy himself was outside on the porch steps with several other assistants, fussing round his auctioneer's desk, set up high on one of the Summer Hill mahogany tables, getting ready to face the assembly.

Pat Kennedy was nowhere to be seen. Believing that some, at least, of the Cordiner family were likely to be there, and not at all in good odour either with most of the locals now, he had absented himself from the proceedings and was down in one of the basement still rooms at that point, entertaining a few close friends over a bottle of Jameson's.

Dermot, ten days before, when Hetty after nearly six weeks at the clinic in Neuilly had recovered sufficiently, had taken her back with him to convalesce at his father's house in Dublin. At that point he had, finally, to explain to her how Summer Hill was about to be sold. But by then, too, their house in London had found a purchaser for the long leasehold, paying some £11,000; and a further £15,000 had been realised, between him and his father, by selling stock, through bank loans and mortgages – so that, as he had told Hetty, he hoped to be able to buy the house and demesne at Summer Hill at least, so fulfilling his promise to her. Thus he had with him now a letter of credit from the Bank of Ireland for some £26,000. He prayed it might be sufficient. Taking a last look round the ruined hall, he moved outside among the crowd, pushing himself into a circle of big booted farmers some few yards in front of Mr Cassidy's desk on the porch steps.

A minute later Cassidy, ascending the dais, rapped his gavel on the desk. 'Good morning, ladies . . .' He looked round, there were few such to be seen. 'And *gint*lemen!' He beamed slyly. 'I have here! . . .' He flourished the sale catalogue aloft. 'A sale, by order of Mr Patrick Kennedy – the house and demesne of Summer Hill in the County of Kilkenny, together with all the contents of said house, and of all other farm lands, farm equipment, dwellings and all other rights apertaining to the said estate of Summer Hill in the County of Kilkenny. In short, gintlemen, opportunities of a lifetime!' He looked about him, up at the crumbling portico and façade of the house. 'Five hundred years of history – the sale of the sintury! The lands will be first under the hammer – and some of the finest land in Ireland it is – all noted and itemised in yer copy of the par-tik-ulars: in all one thousand, one hundred and nine Irish statute acres, including, in the main, some of the best of agricultural land, together with assorted woodlands, wetlands, orchards, kitchen and market gardens, river inches, fishing rights, pleasure gardens – ye can see them all about ye!' He glanced over the ruined terraces and herbaceous borders. 'And sundry other parcels. The whole divided into forty-three lots, as per the par-tik-ulers in that first part of the catalogue. Now ye've all seen the lands concerned – I hope – and I want no mistakes as to yer intentions!' He leered out at his audience, continuing his mix of cajolery and threats towards them. 'Gi' me yer bids loud and clear, so there'll be no misunderstandings. And the last man in at the drop of the hammer – has it! Now, then – lot number one: 33 statute acres, the four inch fields on the river Nore, to the north of Cloone village. What am I bid?'

Silence. The crowd, hushed now, was quite still. No one wanted to make a first move. Cassidy, knowing this, addressed himself to one of his plants in the crowd. The man raised his hand. 'Good for you, sir! Put me in there with a bid – good man yerself – £400 – I have £400. £410!' He looked at another and this time entirely imaginary figure. '£420, £430 I have . . .'

Finally a real farmer made a genuine bid. '£440 . . .' The auction was under-way. The weather outside continued bitter and squally.

Later that morning, the tenanted farms and other outlying lands having been dispensed with, they came to the sale of the house and demesne itself. There had been a ten-minute break during which Cassidy had refreshed himself with a large glass of Jameson's with Pat Kennedy in the basement still-room. Now, mounting the dais again and blowing his nose vigorously, he set about promoting the central drama of the day. Straightening his hunch-back, raising his hands, prophet-like, he called for quiet. Then, starting slowly, in a low key, he began his encomium – the pace, the drama in his voice, mounting as he spoke, enumerating all the virtues in the great pile which towered above him.

'And now, gintlemen – the crowning glory, the centre-piece of all our deliberations here today . . .' He lifted his arms up, turning, gesturing to the old stone. 'The house of Summer Hill . . .' He paused for effect, shaking his head, as if in wonder at the vision looming over him. 'One of the greatest Georgian mansions in Ireland, I'll say – without fear of contradiction.' He glowered at his audience an instant. 'Built by Mr David Bindon the great arkie-tect at the height and breadth of his powers. Ye have all the par-tik-ulers in yer hands: three stories over a basement, three wings, eight reception rooms, twenty bedrooms, thirty-two other sundry rooms – smoking rooms, billiard rooms, gun rooms, morning, afternoon and evening rooms!' – he essayed another bad joke. 'And further quarters galore: servants' rooms, laundries, sculleries, kitchens – old and new – pantries, larders and still-rooms, game rooms, rooms without let or hindrance *ad infinitum*! – inything and everything ye could ask for – together with sundry other outbuildings: stable yards, twenty loose boxes – enough to keep a string of horses! – lofts, haggards, corn stores, kitchen and market gardens. And then the very fine demesne itself: 173 Irish statute acres, filled with the best of mature timber, with a two-mile frontage on the river Nore, to include salmon trapping, and all fishing rights . . .

'And I needn't tell ye –' He paused, blew his nose, coming to his peroration. 'Though there is some very slight dilapidation here and there in the house – nothing ye'd notice – an opportunity like this comes only once in a lifetime. This is no mere gintleman's residence I'm offering here this morning – but a palace, a veritable palace, a home fit for a King! And I have a bid with me already – £23,000!' He smiled ogreishly about.

Dermot's face fell. That was almost all his money on the reserve price.

'£24,000!' Cassidy shouted, pointing at a tall cadaverous figure in a dirty trenchcoat in the middle of the crowd. It was Mr Oliver Mulcahy, the big timber merchant from Waterford, who with his friend Seamus Mulligan, the building contractor, had decided to collaborate in buying the whole place together, so that they could then, at their leisure, gut the house and estate of all its fine stone and timber.

Dermot joined the bidding, raising his hand.

'£24,500,' Cassidy shouted, perspiring now after his whiskey, excited himself at the very idea of dealing in such sums, on which he would take a handsome commission.

'£25,000.' The timber merchant nodded. '£25,500,' Dermot responded again. '£26,000,' Mr Mulcahy increased it. '£26,600,' Dermot raised his hand for the last time. He could go no further.

'£27,000 I have . . . £27,500!' Mulcahy had nodded again. '£28,000 then.' Cassidy looked round the crowd expectantly, taking up his gavel. Suddenly someone caught his eye. 'Yes! – at the back there, you, Sir!' A small, innocuous-looking man at the edge of the crush had raised his hand – a city gent in a dark greatcoat, bowler and wing collar, with town shoes covered in mud, carrying a brief-case. People craned their necks round, trying to identify him among the bobbing heads. '£29,000 bid,' the man said in a calm Dublin accent.

'£29,000 I have!' Cassidy roared his approval. But immediately he bent down to his assistant, asking sotto voce, 'Who's that fella?'

'Mulrooney – solicitors from Dublin, Mulrooney and Owen – he's more than all right. Showed a banker's draft for up to £75,000.' Cassidy returned to business. 'And thank *you*, Sir. £29,000 I have. It's against you, Mr Mulcahy?' Mulcahy nodded once more.

£30,000, 31, 32, 33, 34 . . .' Cassidy swung his gaze rapidly between the two bidders. '£35,000 then. Any more? Yes, Mr Mulcahy! £36,000, 37, 38, 39 – £40,000 I have. Against you, Mr Mulcahy.' Mr Mulcahy nodded. '£41,000.' Cassidy turned to the little man in the dark coat. 'Against you, Sir?' The man nodded, a mild, barely perceptible assent, as if the sum involved was a mere pittance. '£42,000 then – 43, 44, 45 – £46,000 I have. Against you again, Mr Mulcahy.' But Mulcahy shook his head, disgusted.

'Very well then,' Cassidy roared. 'I have it – at £46,000 – for this whole magnificent edifice and pertaining demesne. Do I have any more?' He lifted the gavel. The crowd was absolutely still, but for the cries of a few tinker children playing in the ruined grotto on the high lawn. 'Going, going, *gone*! Sold to the gintleman at the back there in the black coat. Mr Mulrooney it is, Sir, isn't it?'

There was a flurry of animated chatter then, heads craned round once more to see who this stranger was in the wing collar and bowler. But the man had disappeared in the crush and was nowhere to be seen. Dermot, also trying to identify him, sighed, finally moving away, biting his lip, looking up at the great house, as a flash of sunlight struck it now – and suddenly he saw the figure of Aunt Emily, spotlit for a moment, standing in the window of her bedroom, motionless, like a ghost. And yet she was smiling, Dermot saw to his astonishment. A happy ghost . . . The poor mad woman, he thought. What had she to smile about? The great house was gone.

Six hundred years of Cordiner history in Ireland, twenty generations of the same family on this hill – first in an old Norman keep at the bridge, then a buttressed castle on the steep side of the hill, finally a lovely Georgian house. All this – and the future, too – Hetty's, Aunt Emily's, his own, all had gone at the drop of a hammer.

Whereas the house and estate had survived the physical attacks and depredations, the familial passions and alarms of centuries, a little blow from a hammer had finally done for it all – in the hands of Cassidy, one of the gombeen men supreme come to power in this new Republic, someone who did not give a tinker's curse for the place: sold to another of his kind, as Dermot thought, some anonymous Dublin city slicker, probably bidding on behalf of a religious institution, who would draw all the warmth and life from the place, turn it over into some cold and ghastly convent or college for the priests. God forgive them all, Dermot thought. Then he changed his mind – God damn them for their meagre souls. He hoped never to see the man with the briefcase and bowler ever again.

And yet, attending the afternoon sale of the house's contents, Dermot did see him again – constantly hovering in the background just as before, making his calm, ever-increasing bids, hammering in the loss that Dermot already felt, buying up nearly all the best items: the Irish Georgian effects – the Chippendale and Sheraton furniture, the silver cutlery, candlesticks and épergnes, the Flemish tapestry in the hall, the better oil paintings, the Cordiner family portraits, the myriad sporting prints, the books and much else – each time outbidding all rivals; including Dermot who, with his money still intact, had tried to secure anything else he could, managing to end up with some few of the lesser pieces, but including at least what in a way he most valued, the contents of Henry's old work rooms on the top floor, and all his equipment there, the butterfly collections and the menagerie of stuffed animals, together with most of the furniture in Aunt Emily's room and a variety of other small mementoes which he would pass on to Hetty, after keeping a few for himself.

Dermot was heartbroken. Moving out of the great hall he stopped by the tall window next to the door, gazing at the tiny inset of coloured glass there showing the Cordiner arms, the great yellow-eyed eagle on top of the visored helmet with the legend beneath – 'Fortune Favours the Brave'.

What a mockery the family motto seemed to him then. The Cordiners had come to the end of the line in this house – through a mix of latter-day arrogance, insensitivity, mismanagement and sheer spite, not bravery. The great fortune had been dissipated by selfish obsession – for all the wrong things. Above all, he thought, in the shape of old Lady Cordiner and Frances, they had, with whatever excuse, promoted pain and not love in this place, and that had really been Summer Hill's undoing. This house, as he knew so well himself, was a warm thing, full of promise. And if you loved it, and the people in it, as he had – if you could love it room by room, every nook and cranny, as he did – then it would have survived, would have avoided its complete physical change or destruction, which was all that awaited it now.

Outside, standing on the porch steps in the late afternoon, he saw how the day had cleared at last, with a stormy sunset, the valley strewn with vivid colours, hints of spring green everywhere, glistening after the rain, budding yellows, patches of white narcissi and golden daffodils, the mountains, Brandon and Leinster away to the east, bathed in a pale-blue evening light. And the light from the west as he turned, clear and rose-tinted, shone on the great façade of the house, gently firing the stone, touching the windows with a soft glitter. So that once more, as he left it, the house was full of warmth and promise. He stood there, as the departing crowd pushed and shoved about him, gazing up and around, trying to imprint this happy vision on his mind, to keep it there as a last treasure. Then someone touched him on the shoulder. Turning, he was astonished to see the little city gent in the greatcoat and wing collar. He had taken off his bowler, deprecatingly.

'Colonel . . . Cordiner?' he asked diffidently. Dermot, too surprised to make reply, barely nodded. 'I'm Mr Mulrooney – um, from Mulrooney and Owen, solicitors in Dublin . . .' The voice, with its genteel Dublin tones, was so mild and other-worldly, frail, full of dying falls. And now, in the silence, it seemed to have given out altogether.

'Yes?' Dermot finally asked.

'I wonder . . . I wonder if you could spare me a little of your time? – er, I have some news . . . some matters concerning this house and . . . Miss Laura Bowen. I understand she is a cousin of yours?'

'Yes.'

'Good. Yes, quite so. I'd be very grateful if . . . if you could, if I could – talk with you for . . . a half-hour . . . confidentially.' He glanced round him anxiously. 'I'm staying at the Club House in Kilkenny. Perhaps? . . . I have a car round by the yard. If you'd like to come with me? – I could give you a lift?' The man smiled, a wan ghost of a smile. He had, Dermot thought, the appropriate air of an undertaker. But he followed him.

'I don't think I entirely understand you, Mr Mulrooney . . .?' In truth Dermot had been quite unable to believe his ears. Steadying himself now, he lifted his whisky-soda, which Mr Mulrooney, with a lot of nervous footling, had finally managed to order for them both, the two men sitting on the edge of shabby chintz chairs in the residents' lounge upstairs in the Club House Hotel. 'You were instructed to buy Summer Hill, its contents and demesne – on behalf of an anonymous "admirer" of Miss Lauren Bowen?'

'Quite so, Colonel Cordiner, quite so.' Mr Mulrooney sipped his whisky, then eased a pointed corner of his wing-collar away from an old spot on his neck that had been rubbed there over the years. 'And since, as I understand it, Miss Bowen is, er, indisposed at the minute, I took the opportunity . . . the chance of approaching you, as her nearest relative in the matter. I hope you'll forgive me . . .' Again the ever-diffident, apologetic hesitancy of the man, Dermot thought – as if he were commiserating with him after a funeral, and was not, as he seemed to be, the herald of some miraculous birth. 'Yes, Colonel, I was so instructed, by . . . by my client – my clients, I should say,' he corrected himself quickly. 'And I believe I have fulfilled my commission – rather advantageously, perhaps . . .' He allowed himself this tiny congratulation. 'Though the house is not perhaps in the best repair –'

'To put it mildly.'

'Nonetheless –'

Dermot pulled himself together. 'I'm sorry, Mr Mulrooney. Of course . . . it's just that I can't quite take it all in. It's a most generous gift, quite incredible . . .'

'Yes,' Mr Mulrooney assented neatly, with a brief smile. 'There is one point, however. It is not an actual *gift*, Colonel Cordiner.'

'I see.' Dermot did not quite see.

'You will be aware – perhaps? – that, um, Miss Bowen, as of now, is an undischarged bankrupt?'

'Yes – yes, of course.'

'Ah! – there is the point, Colonel Cordiner!' Mr Mulrooney, raising a finger, came to genuine life for a moment, a real smile flooding his wan features, clearly delighted with himself. 'Thus any such outright gift could be forfeit to her creditors.

So it is my clients' wish, in the meanwhile, to allow Miss Bowen full occupancy and use of the said house, its contents, and demesne, while retaining the title deeds in their possession . . .'

'I see.'

'Indeed . . .'

There was silence in the lamplit room. A dog barked in the street. The fire crackled and Mr Mulrooney essayed a further smile. 'So, Colonel, tomorrow, at the end of the sale of contents, I shall be meeting Mr Patrick Kennedy's solicitors in Kilkenny and making arrangements for the transfer of those deeds, which will then be held in fee-simple by my clients. And after that, in return, I will give you a deed of legal occupancy, made out in Miss Laura Bowen's name, and all we shall need then is her signature to the agreement, which will complete matters . . .'

Mr Mulrooney raised his glass – almost in a toast, before thinking better of it.

'That all seems very fair – more than fair, Mr Mulrooney. There is one point, though – may Miss Bowen never know who her benefactor is?'

Mr Mulrooney fiddled with his glass, seeming to regret his near-celebration a moment before. 'Ah . . . that is, er, quite beyond my brief, Colonel. I am not dealing with any individual in this matter – merely representing . . . legal offices, elsewhere. So I may tell you, in all honesty, that I have absolutely no idea who this benefactor is . . . or might be . . .' He offered another of his wan smiles, becoming almost spendthrift with them now. 'No idea at *all*,' he added, emphasising a word for the first time, obviously charmed by the neatness of this whole legal conceit, this so-perfectly-closed circle into which no one could ever break.

And indeed Dermot remained entirely at a loss – until just then, easing himself in his chair, his glance fell on one of the Spy cartoons by the fireplace. Part of a long row, it was no more conspicuous than all the rest. But it was immediately clear who it portrayed – the great beard, the aggressive Hanoverian features beneath a grey topper, a portly figure in a morning suit, the suggestion of horses and racing, in the background: it was the old Prince of Wales, some time in the late nineties.

And it came to Dermot then, in a sudden intuitive flash, that this gift of Summer Hill was in some way his, a recompense of sorts – his, through his grandson, perhaps, the present Prince of Wales. Of course! The gift of an 'admirer' . . . Two admirers. Who had admired Frances more – those long years ago when they had all lived at Wilton Place in London? And who since, most recently, had so obviously admired Hetty – and had had to abandon her?

Dermot was almost certain of it – as if the two royal figures were in the room with him then, nodding agreement: the house miraculously returned in all its warmth and promise.

Summer Hill, despite Frances's earlier folly in giving it over to Pat Kennedy, was in Cordiner hands once more. And yet Frances herself remained, if only just:

perpetrator of this and other madnesses, but for reasons which Dermot, at least, understood. She had been betrayed, abandoned, exiled – her youth destroyed by Lady Cordiner and the old Prince. And besides, whatever she had done since, one had to take the total life into account. And, if you loved someone, as he had, you loved the whole person, good and bad. And if the faults had come to so outweigh the virtues in that person, so the more must one try and maintain that original act of faith, in loving her. He would have to see Frances now, tell her what had happened over Summer Hill, offer her these last rites of affection. And so would Hetty.

Hetty, if all the ghosts of her past were to be finally laid, if she was truly to start her life anew at Summer Hill, would have to see her too.

Having told her, to her sheer astonishment and delight, how Summer Hill had been regained at the hands of some admirer, he went on to say how this was the moment to make things up with her mother. At first, though she did not refuse outright, there was antagonism everywhere in her face.

'Hetty, she's dying,' he told her bluntly. 'I know how cold and cruel she's been to you. But, unless you can forgive those who've hurt you most, you'll never be able to forgive yourself. Don't you see? Unless you meet, you'll go through the rest of your life regretting it, hating yourself, a secret wound that'll never heal. And it'll poison you, undermine every other happiness you may have. You really have to see her, for yourself as much as for her. Don't you see?'

Hetty, listening intently to this man she so trusted, eventually did see.

Dermot knocked on the bungalow door in Rathgar a few days later. It was opened by a fraught, dishevelled woman – quite young, with a toss of untidy red hair, in a long yellow crochet-work cardigan and wellington boots: a Mrs McDaid, Frances's housekeeper, widow of a Citizen Army insurgent killed at the Easter rebellion, his father had told him, killed accidentally by his own side in the General Post Office – one of any number of Republican friends and sympathisers who had ministered to Frances since her arrival in Dublin, and especially in these last years of her illness.

Once inside the narrow, damp-stained hall, sacks of coal stacked along one side, Dermot and Hetty were immediately assailed by the rank odour of cats – a smell of urine (which perhaps explained Mrs McDaid's rubber boots, Dermot thought) and old fur, mixed with the acrid fumes of a badly-drawing coal fire coming from a small sitting room immediately to their right.

Moving through the doorway here, taking their coats off, they started to choke in the foul and sulphurous air, lying in streaky layers, partly obscuring the chaos of the room: a haphazard collection of further half-completed crochet-work cardigans, holy pictures and framed Republican manifestoes, poems and stirring political declarations which covered the walls; yellowing, mildewed piles of Gaelic newspapers with other rebelly and religious mementoes that littered the furniture or had found a home among old blankets on the floor where some great cats lay cushioned, sharing in this warm-moist, festering debris, heads sunk well below the smoky air, and thus impervious to the fumes.

'Surely this isn't good for Mrs Fraser – with her bronchitis?' Dermot gestured through the fog at Mrs McDaid.

'Indeed – an' isn't that just what the doctor's bin telling her Ladyship this long time, and she not takin' divil a bit of notice of him?' Mrs McDaid spoke with an excitable smile. 'How and so ever, she's bein' moved outa here this afternoon, to the nuns in Leeson Street. So ye're only just in time to see her.'

'I'd better see her first?' He turned to Hetty, who nodded.

The woman led Dermot into a much less smoky but no less chaotic bedroom at the back. Frances lay propped up in a narrow iron bedstead surrounded by other cats, a more favoured brood, the animals asleep, Frances gazing vacantly at three sizeable pictures on the wall opposite: a vivid oleograph of the Christ King crowned with dripping thorns, bleeding heart bared, together with two quite contrary portrait photographs, stuffy and retouched, without blemish, formal to a degree – one of Pope Benedict XI, the other of Frances's friend and comrade-in-arms Eamon de Valera. On her bedside table was a plaster statuette, in garish blue and gold, of the Virgin holding her arms out – in a blessing, a supplication or sheer resignation, Dermot could not decide. The Virgin's piteous features, though, could not be misinterpreted – not unlike Frances's own expression a few feet away.

'Frances?' Dermot drew a kitchen chair towards the bed. 'It's me – Dermot.' Silence. 'I hear you're going to the hospital tomorrow. That's marvellous. Should have gone . . . much earlier,' he added diffidently.

Frances wheezed by way of reply, then started a racking cough, her whole frail body heaving in the bed for half a minute, before she eventually turned her face towards him.

He was astonished, appalled by the drawn, heavily-wrinkled, emaciated features, the toss of skimpy withered grey hair – the desperate toll that age and illness had taken here. Age? But she was only in her mid-fifties, Dermot had to remind himself. The clear blue Cordiner eyes, however, had survived largely intact in the wreck of the years.

He had to turn away an instant – gathering, controlling himself, so hurt was he by this ruined vision, this ghost of times past, when her beauty had only been equalled by her spirit, both radiant.

'Yes,' she wheezed at last, mucus starting to drip from her nose. 'Hospital – the good Sisters of the Sacred Heart. But I doubt it . . .' Her voice was thin, ethereal, without any timbre to it. 'I shan't leave here alive.'

'Francie! . . .' he said, moved almost beyond endurance, a lump rising in his throat, with that endearment he and her brother Henry had used all those years ago, the three of them, happy together at Summer Hill. 'Francie, of course you will.'

'No. And why should I?' A spasm of coughing took her again. 'You can see,' she went on at last, eyes filled with tears from her exertions, 'I've had everything I want – of this small life . . .' She looked at the statue of the Virgin then before closing her eyes, seeming to sleep.

Dermot took out the little present he had bought at Summer Hill for her – one of the dozen or so of old Lady Cordiner's Baccarat paperweights: a lovely oval crystal with a great, black-hearted scarlet poppy embedded in the glass. 'I brought this for you – from Summer Hill.'

At the naming of the house Frances opened her eyes and gazed at the crystal globe – eyes soon filled with an emotion which Dermot could not quite decipher, a mix of hatred and yet of longing, he thought. He reached out with the paperweight, putting it on the stained coverlet near her desperately thin, blue-veined hands. But she made no move towards it, closing her eyes once more. The glass lay there, next to a big tabby cat, who equally ignored it.

'I've just come up from Summer Hill,' Dermot went on. 'I was there a few days ago.' Frances opened her eyes. But again she made no comment. 'Hetty,' Dermot continued gently. 'You remember? – Hetty, your daughter . . .' She closed her eyes at once. 'Well, some friend of hers – he's bought the whole place back for her, from Pat Kennedy.'

At this news, and at last, Frances, opening her eyes again, spoke with stiff clarity, a glimmer of passion. 'But it *couldn't* be hers. I gave it all to Pat – long ago.' Her blue eyes were sharp then – as Dermot mostly remembered them: sharp with frustration, anger.

'Yes, but we've managed to buy it back. For Hetty – and for you, too. For all of us – Cordiners.'

The family name hung in the rank, stuffy air, isolated in the silence.

'Not for me,' Frances said at last. 'My name – is Fraser. And you should not have bought it back. I'd left it – for Pat, for Ireland, for the Irish.'

'But *we* are Irish, Francie – you and I and Hetty – just as much as Pat Kennedy.' Dermot spoke with a touch of acerbity. 'And Hetty – she's here now to see you.'

Dermot stood up quickly to fetch her. But when he turned he was surprised to see Hetty standing there in the doorway already, quite still, suddenly materialised there, softly as a ghost. Indeed Hetty, after all her illnesses, was almost as ethereal a figure as her mother – tall and thin in a green velvet jacket, lace blouse, long oatmeal skirt, gazing at Frances who, looking up then, recognised her quite clearly.

Dermot, standing between them, glanced at their two expressions. At first, with Frances, there was a dull glower, a dismissive bitter curl to her lips – while Hetty's face, which before had been calm, devoid of any emotion, now reflected her mother's angry distaste. And then, in a moment, having locked horns in this way, exchanged this wordless fury, both their expressions changed to one of supreme disinterest. It was as if two bitter enemies had had the misfortune to bump into each other at a street corner, and having confirmed their antagonism were about to move apart, going their separate ways. And indeed, in the next moment, Frances turned away, facing the wall, while Hetty started to fiddle with her feet, about to move out the door.

But at that moment a big tabby-cat stirred on the coverlet and the crystal paperweight, lying in the folds, fell to the floor, splintering.

The dumb, cold mood was broken.

Hetty, coming forward, picked up the broken crystal, while Frances, alarmed by the crash, turned her head towards her daughter, close to her now, kneeling by the bed. Hetty held up part of the broken paperweight. 'Bit smashed. But not too badly. Perhaps we can get it re-re-repaired,' she added, her expression softening as she looked at the broken paperweight more carefully – the poppy still intact in one half. Of course, she remembered it now – that blazing scarlet flower with its dark heart held in the glittering crystal: it was one of her grandmother's paperweights which Frances had stolen years before at Summer Hill, as Aunt Emily had told her – and which Hetty, with Léonie, had discovered in the chimney flue: one among dozens of such little objets d'art which her mother had taken in enmity then, in hatred for old Lady Cordiner.

Frances, too, suddenly seemed revived by this vision of the broken paperweight. 'Yes – yes, perhaps we can get it repaired.' Then, in a strangely confiding, almost pleasant voice, she quite changed tack. 'Did you find it in the chimney flue, in the primrose room, my old bedroom, where I used to hide all those little things?' Hetty, not wishing to break this intimate flow of talk, nodded. 'Good . . . Well, we'll keep them all ourselves now.' Hetty nodded once more, happy to collaborate in this imagined conspiracy of her mother's. Then Frances's tone changed again. A look of deep hatred crossed her face and she said with startling anger, 'Whatever you do – don't give it back to Mama – *any* of those little paperweights and things. Never give it back! – to that monstrous old woman, with her pryings and hatreds . . . and killings. It was she who killed Henry, you know, my dear brother . . . So have *nothing* to do with her, *ever.*'

Her voice was cruel and vehement now – just as Hetty remembered it from the old days, when she had so often punished her in just the same tones. But now, in these wanderings, Frances was attacking her own long-dead mother instead. And Hetty was pleased, happy indeed, at this renewal of her own mother's old spirit. For what she had never been able to understand or bear in Frances's latter life was her sudden conversions – to the Catholic faith, to Gaelic ideals, to good works, all her meek and mild renunciations of that previously vibrant spirit, which she thought to be sheer hypocrisy on her part. But now her mother had clearly regained some of that earlier vivacity and ardour which had so characterised what Hetty had always believed to be her real temperament. Now there was a cutting edge to her heart once more, the grandeur of real emotion.

'No, Mama, I won't give any of them back – ever!'

Through these old secrets revived and shared now, the two women suddenly found themselves on easier terms – a secret resurrected from her mother's youth at Summer Hill long before she was born, and confided in her now, so that she and her mother, for the first time in their lives, found themselves on the same side of things, against the world, against others, miscreants both, companions-in-arms in this conspiracy, a solidarity between them which had never remotely existed before; and all created over the memory, the remains, of a broken paperweight.

Hetty, encouraged by this birth of trust between them, was no longer so appalled by the cold and frowsty bedroom – its fearful air of barren nationalism and opiate religion – reflected in the bleeding hearts, lifeless photographs and arid political manifestoes that littered the room. These images faded for Hetty, as she saw her mother revived by this angry intrigue – no longer overwhelmed, deadened, by that timidity of intellect which had taken and crushed her more than a decade before.

Hetty drew up a chair, sitting close to her mother.

The two women gazed at each other in the silence. Now, in this clear regard, they were no longer such strangers. Instead, sharing a complicity over the paperweight, their own long antagonisms had been subsumed in a greater one – against that third figure who stood in the room with them then, the malevolent spirit of old Lady Cordiner who had set in motion this long trail of familial pain and cruelty, and against whom now their own mutual hatreds, dissolving, were redirected. They found some forgiveness for each other solely in this unforgiving of a long-dead woman, mother and grandmother to them. They were reconciled then as conspirators, both their true natures coincided at last, brought together by this whiff of danger, of secrets shared.

Frances moved her lips then, as if about to continue with these intimacies. But instead a frightful spasm of coughing took her and she started to heave to and fro in the bed. Eventually, recovering herself, she fell back suddenly on the pillows, exhausted, eyes gazing upwards, remaining absolutely still.

Hetty reached forward, taking her mother's hand on the sheet. Without her noticing it, the inside of her own middle finger was bleeding, cut by a small splinter from the paperweight, still embedded in her flesh. So that, after she had held her mother's hand for a minute, and still unaware of the cut, the blood began to seep out, a trickle of scarlet falling down Frances's hand – increasing as Hetty took a firmer grip, gazing at her mother all the while, neither of them needing to speak, as Hetty felt, words unnecessary in this vague reconciliation.

Later, when Hetty tried to move her hand, she found her mother's fingers had stiffened in hers. As she released herself, Frances's hand fell limply on the sheet, a red-smeared claw, without life. Hetty, seeing the blood on her mother's hand, thought this was somehow connected with her death. Then, looking at her own palm, she saw the small wound and realised what had happened. The splinter, still embedded there, had cut her mother's hand as well – their blood mixing in the end, as it had at the very beginning, the flow coursing together, uniting them at the last – in birth, death, resurrection. Frances was gone and Hetty thus reborn.

The funeral a few days later was an enormous affair – the largest seen in Dublin since the death of Daniel O'Connell, the Liberator, nearly a hundred years before. After a Requiem Mass in the local church and a subsequent lying-in-state for two days in the City Hall, some quarter of a million people – mostly the poor of the city, the hungry, the cold, the dispossessed, to whom Frances, with her bags of coal and crochet-work cardigans, had so ministered in her last years – turned out to honour her.

They lined all the streets of the three-mile route to Glasnevin cemetery, packed five and ten deep to either side, heads bowed, reciting their rosaries, paying their last respects to this martyr in their cause. It was a tremendous occasion – a mourning, yet a celebration, too; the latter element encouraged by the quite unseasonable April weather, the warm bright day that had flooded over the city almost since first light: a day, as Hetty remembered it, almost exactly similar, green-budding and soft, to that Easter Monday in 1916 when the rebellion had broken out, when she and Léonie had been at the Shelbourne Hotel and had later been trapped with her mother and the other insurgents in the long and bloody battle for Stephen's Green.

Now, following the tricolour-draped coffin in the creeping hearse, with its marching honour guard of young Fianna scouts, Hetty was no longer trapped by her mother, by that bitter intractable enmity that had soured all her early life, every part of their subsequent relationship. She was freed from her and from all the pain in her own disastrous years, as a child, in marriage, as a picture star.

Now, she thought, finally recovered and come to her senses, she could take up her own real life, before her then in the balmy, summer-like air – a future indefinite, a blank page, a life of unknown adventure. And so her heart was strangely light that morning, a knot of half-fearful excitement turning in the pit of her stomach, that sensuous expectation of youth returned, when there is certain knowledge of a void to be thrillingly filled – as she sat back in the car, veiled, in black, her two cousins on either side of her in dark frock-coats, top hats on their knees.

'What a turn-out,' Dermot remarked, rather shamefaced, for all three of them, seeing this vast crowd of mourners, felt somewhat guilty now at their earlier condemnations of Frances's passionate republicanism. Lost to them, she had given her life, literally, to these other far more needy Irish people.

'Yes . . . Frances would have been appalled at the show of it all, the grand clerics and dignitaries,' Mortimer commented.

'Another part of her would have loved it, though,' Hetty said. 'That older part of her . . .'

'Yes – that spirited part – slapping Appleton the head gardener in the face and all that. The part she lost . . .' Dermot added, a touch of regret in his voice.

'But she didn't lose it!' Hetty came back, turning to both men, bright-eyed, eager herself once more. 'She was angry and spirited as ever at the end, against *her* Mama. That was what was so wonderful. She *found* all her old self at the end!'

The two men looked at Hetty curiously. They had learnt of Hetty's reconciliation with her mother through the medium of the paperweight. But they had not realised how, in this event, Frances in the end had been reconciled with her own true nature as well.

Arriving at the Republican Plot at Glasnevin Cemetery, a small, ageing, white-haired man who yet still retained the air of a courtly flyweight boxer – Pedar O'Hegarty who had first recruited Frances into the Irish Republican Brotherhood nearly twenty-five years before – gave a short funeral oration.

'. . . She came of the grandest station. In her youth she had every ease that money and civilisation can bring . . . She had besides, in herself, great beauty, intellect, wit, a lovely energy for all the distractions of her circle – riding to hounds, music, theatre, dancing. Withal, in that world of her class, she had a future of the greatest privilege, wealth and position. The world lay at her feet . . . Yet she threw it all aside, every worldly prize, to devote herself first to the cause of nationhood – this free Republic, which is her creation, along with those other great Irish patriots whom she is now about to join – and then, in the long years of her own illness, giving what was left of her life, without stint or thought for herself, to those in this city who had less than nothing: the poor, the destitute, the old, the hungry, the uncared-for.

'With these two great visions – the greatest we can know on this earth – of freedom and charity, she brought life, political and material, first to a nation, then to many of its citizens . . . It was a blazing life, in Stephen's Green that Easter week, followed by an equally passionate generosity in all those smaller consolations which she offered to the people of Dublin . . .

'She gave herself utterly, without compromise, to both causes. For her there were no complexities or indecisions, no half-measures or regrets. Hers was an angry passion – for the *right*, and no sacrifice was too great to achieve this end . . . Losing her life, she found it. In suffering she drew happiness. In battle she made peace. So, in death, she has true immortality . . .'

Standing by the graveside, Hetty felt the tears pricking her eyes behind her veil. As O'Hegarty had confirmed it now, the matter seemed beyond dispute: how wrong she had been about her mother, blinding herself, through her own obsessive self-will, to her virtues – and worse still refusing to acknowledge the validity of her mother's latter purposes, the different roads she had taken towards her own salvation. Hetty saw all this at last. Indeed, that was the final message from her mother as they lowered her away into the ground: how she herself would now have to take a quite different route towards the same end.

Oh yes, her mother had returned to some of her old spirited ways at the end. But that was no more than a deathbed conversion, a last acknowledgement of her earlier glowing but flawed nature. One could not, as her mother had discovered long before, sustain a whole life on such false premises. Nor, Hetty saw, could she. The vainglory she had espoused in Hollywood – rampant ambition, will to power, the need to hurt, dominate, betray – why, these had been exactly her mother's old failings, too, and her grandmother's before her. It ran in the family. And she had lived just such a life herself – taken to the brink of death by it, much sooner than the other two. It was all too clear: she must adapt or perish.

And yet . . . Now that she was growing stronger, her taste for life reviving, Hetty saw her predicament in any such adaptation. She could not become a saint, a martyr, like her mother, could not renounce all her true characteristics, each and every one – for there was the hypocrisy.

How then, in what manner of compromise, was she to survive and yet advance? She had lost her career, her marriage, and had nearly died. But through Dermot's intervention she had recovered her health, her family home, and she was not yet thirty. Was she to renounce every other possible sweetness in life? – so tempting then in the balmy spring air standing above her mother's grave. And yet in embarking on that adventure, in tasting that sweetness, had she the self-discipline, above all the new character to savour it without lapsing again – which, if she did, would bring her to the same yawning pit long before her time?

BOOK FIVE

1

D ERMOT DROVE DOWN to Summer Hill with Hetty a week later. Though not
entirely recovered – she was still thin, weak on her feet and suffered the
sporadic backache and violent stomach cramps of her syphilis – she had insisted
on it, wonderfully excited by the prospect of returning home after nearly twelve
years, of coming, however conditionally, into her inheritance.

Dermot, as yet, had told her nothing of his intuitions as to the identity of her
'admirer' – and now, that bright April morning in 1929, as the car drove up the
unkept, grassed-over avenue swerving round the fallen trees, Hetty wondered out
loud again.

'Who? – who could it have been? Giving – giving back – all this?'

She gazed around the ruined demesne as the car climbed the slope. Some of
the chestnut trees, lower down by the river gorge, were just in bud. Clumps of
daffodils, forcing their way up through the rough, thistle-filled pasture, showed as
patches of vivid yellow in the winter grass. Across the valley the mountains had a
soft blue, almost summery sheen to them in the mild light.

'Who?' she asked again, turning to Dermot at the wheel of his father's old
Daimler.

Dermot shook his head. It was not the moment for any such revelations. Later,
when Hetty was settled here – there would be time then. Meanwhile he was almost
as excited as she when, as they reached the brow of the hill, the house finally came
into view.

The rooks in the broken chimneys, alarmed by the engine, suddenly spiralled
into the sky, climbing over the half-circle of trees behind the house, cawing
raucously, their cries filling the air, an anthem of homecoming.

Hetty gasped with pleasure. 'The rooks! Hear them? They *are* Summer Hill,
aren't they?' She watched, wide-eyed, as they tossed and turned beneath an arc of
blue sky and puffy white cloud.

Then, careering up the moss-soft drive, rounding the old formal pleasure
gardens, stopping on the muddy, potholed gravel in front of the house, they were
there. Dermot turned off the engine. There was silence.

'Home,' Dermot said simply, turning to her with a brief smile, reaching quickly for his pipe and matches in his tweed jacket. But before he could get to them Hetty leant across quickly and kissed him on the cheek, feeling the rub of his small moustache an instant, the vague odour of pipe tobacco. Then, involuntarily, she repeated the kiss. 'Thank you,' she said just as simply, leaning away, gazing at him.

This was the man who, nearly twenty years before, had really introduced her to Summer Hill, the wild landscape, this great kingdom – naming all the parts of it for her, so that she had come truly to possess it – the man who, despite the malign humours of her mother, the dooms she had cast over all her childhood here, had brought her to love the place, to love him too, before everything had changed in 1914: Dermot, for whom she had pined at the French convent school, whom she had thought lost in the Great War, before she herself had been lost, deserting Léonie, family, friends, home, lost in the imbecilities of her marriage, her wastrel career in the motion picture business, those disastrous years which had led to her downfall.

She gazed at him in silence, as at last he found his pipe. She opened the car window, and the drifting odour of an Irish spring came to her then, a damp mossy fragrance, moist with rot, and warm with growth, mixed with a hint of turf smoke from somewhere – a fragrance, sweet and sour, which had been the air of her whole universe once. So that now it was as if, as well as her life, Dermot had given her back even her childhood, returned her to all the innocence and beginnings there.

She loved this man again, as she had years before as a child. And there was the problem. Would he now, as then, prove unpossessible – now as then remain somehow just outside her orbit, the light of her adoration – fond and affectionate towards her, yet somehow distant, always leaving? Could she ever change that? Her kisses just then had changed nothing. She breathed deeply, inhaling the fresh soft air. She wished she could tell him how much she loved him, so far beyond simple fondness and affection. But she could not. Yet words were all she had to express her feelings for him.

'You know, Dermot,' she said intently, still gazing at him. 'It doesn't matter who it really was who gave the place back to me, to *us*. As far as I'm concerned, it was you . . .' She risked a last physical gesture, touching him on the sleeve.

Dermot bit his lip, thought to speak, but said nothing. What could he say? He saw Hetty's love, recognised it exactly for what it was, a woman's bright passion for a man, frustrated. He loved her too, just as he had her mother years before. But he knew that it was a familial love he felt for Hetty, a vast tenderness without desire, an intense concern, filled with every emotion – every hope except that of physical possession.

Her mother was dead. Yet here was Hetty, back from the grave almost, waiting to start her life anew. And, were it not for his nature, she might have started it again with him. He realised that. That was the message in her eyes. Looking at her then – her thin features radiant in the April light – he saw how Frances, betrayed by the old Prince and for lack of just this familial love, had fallen headlong into a career of bitter violence, destroying herself. Would Hetty, though restored to life, come to find just the same sort of betrayal in him, for his inability to respond to her – in that way of desire? It was this thought that made him restrain the kiss he longed to reciprocate with, fearing that she might misinterpret it. They got out and walked towards the house.

A small, rather stout woman in a white apron, with a taller man behind, had appeared on the porch steps.

'A surprise for you,' Dermot said to Hetty quietly. 'I asked them to come here for a bit, as housekeeper and general handyman, until you get yourself settled. Remember? – recognise her?'

Hetty paused at the bottom of the steps, looking at the woman in the apron, a flush of dark, greying hair above a round sweet face, with dimples still there, embedded in her ample cheeks. Suddenly Hetty recognised her.

'Eileen, Elly? – I don't believe it – Oh, Elly!' She rushed up the steps, embracing the woman. 'How on earth? – how did you come?'

'Ah, sure, didn't I come straight up the front avenue, or what's left of it – me and Jack here, me husband, Jack Welsh, from beyant Cloone.'

'And will you stay? – is it true? – really stay?'

'Indeed why not? Sure there was no problem, once that divil Pat was out of the way. And our own children, aren't they all grown up now and we have time on our hands. Of course we'll stay! Once Mr Dermot here asked us and we knew you were coming back, sure there was no question. And isn't it the greatest thing ever? – to see you here again –'

'Yes, yes!' Hetty had tears in her eyes. 'You, though – I never thought – you back here!'

'Why wouldn't I be back here? – an' I with you from the very beginning, out on that island with all them savages! And I'd have been here all along, but for Pat Kennedy and all the other . . . disturbances . . . And but for Jack.' She turned and smiled at her husband. 'Ye remember Jack? – Jack, up in the garden here?'

Hetty turned, shaking the man's hand. 'Yes . . .' She was hesitant, not really remembering him – a stoutish man in his fifties, strong-looking, with the clearest blue countryman's eyes and reddish cheeks.

'Oh, indeed, I remember you, Miss, Mrs . . .' he corrected himself, not sure how to address her.

'Miss *Cordiner*,' Hetty suddenly and resolutely said. For it was at that very moment – in this meeting with Elly, her old nurse, which finally confirmed her homecoming – that she took the final decision to throw over everything of her past life, resuming neither her married, stage nor Fraser name, but taking on that of her original family. 'Henrietta – Hetty – Cordiner.' She would have that as her name now – and for the rest of her life.

'Indeed,' Jack said, easier now. 'Indeed, Miss – and you up in the oul' walled garden, with Mickey, the under gardener then, remember him? – with that crab apple tree yonder that belonged to the childer here –'

'Yes! I remember! The magic apples – the apples of life!' She remembered how she had taken them for Robert, intent on saving his life, when he had whooping cough, and how her mother had cuffed and slapped her when she found her crouching outside Robert's sickroom door with the apples in the fold of her nightdress.

'The magic apples – and the jam!' Elly came in then, laughing hugely. 'Ye remember the jam-making, Miss? – in the big kitchen below? You and Mrs Molloy – God rest her soul – you were never out of the place in the old days, making greengage jam, I remember it well –'

'Yes, yes – so do I!' And Hetty did – the lovely greeny-yellow fluid, translucent, sugary, dripping from the long wooden spoon over the preserving pan on the great black range, the sticky labels, her neat copperplate writing on the warm jars. The past – her whole childhood at Summer Hill, the joy and the pain there, all the drama which she had repressed or forgotten – was pricked into life for Hetty by these cues from Elly and Jack. These haphazard memorials of crab apples and greengage jam, unearthed from the years, became the emblems now of Hetty's resurrection, spirits disinterred from an autumn twenty years before, miraculously reborn, blossoming on the air of that mild April morning.

Just then a third figure poked her head round the dilapidated hall door – a scrawny beanpole with a quite unruly toss of white hair blowing out from beneath a floppy corduroy hat, wearing a long brown Aran knit cardigan. It was Aunt Emily. Hetty rushed forward to embrace her.

'Aunt! – how wonderful!' She clasped her great-aunt, almost squeezing the life out of her, so that the old lady, eventually disengaging herself, was breathless and more than usually huffy.

'Well,' she said recovering herself with a splutter. 'You're back . . .' She spoke in that harsh slight brogue that Hetty remembered so well, spoke as if Hetty had only been away for a week or two. 'Knew you would be. Had enough of the world, eh? Not surprised. All an imbecility, *tout court*. Heard you were married, too – enough of that, as well?' She looked at Hetty, a dismissive glint in her still-bright eyes. 'Can't say I didn't tell you. Men . . .' Her lined face curdled in deep displeasure. 'Worthless lot, from start to finish.'

'Oh, Aunt, not *all* men. Look at Dermot – and Jack!' She turned back to the others.

'*Excuse* yourself, girl. That's quite different. They're family.'

They all went inside then, through the ruined hall, filled with tea-chests and scattered furniture from the auction, passing beneath the forest of great pillars, beside the tattered Flemish tapestry, down a littered corridor – through the green baize door leading to the servants' quarters: a door which clunked shut behind Hetty in a most satisfying way, the sound risen from her past when, on the run from her mother, she moved across this clear frontier between pain and happiness, from the cold maternal dangers in the front of the house to the warmth, the peace, fun and security of Mrs Molloy's jam-filled kingdom at the back.

Here, in the old servants' quarters where the Kennedys had lived, the Welshs had cleaned up most of the squalor which they had left behind, making over the housekeeper's parlour into a temporary drawing and dining room for Hetty, with a bedroom, within calling distance in which had been the butler's pantry, where Hetty could settle herself and convalesce until the rest of the house was set in some kind of order.

Aunt Emily would not take lunch with them – a hot lunch of roast mutton and a few early vegetables which Elly had prepared. 'Have to finish a drawing,' she told them brusquely. 'That rogue Cassidy – out there on the front steps at the sale and all the jackals he had round him. Doing a series of them . . .'

'Yes, I saw you at your bedroom window,' Dermot remarked. 'Just after the hammer fell, looking pleased as punch. But how were you so certain the place wouldn't be sold out of the family?'

'Out of the *family*?' Aunt Emily looked genuinely puzzled. 'Oh, there was no question. I had a jinx out on that fellow Cassidy from the very beginning. And then, besides, when I was doing the first drawing of it all, that morning, with the vultures out all over the old pleasure gardens, didn't I see Hetty herself out there as well, clear as day, raising her paw, standing by the old astrolabe. Knew the place was coming back into the family then.'

Hetty was astonished. 'But, Aunt, how could you have seen me out there? I was in Dublin –'

'Excuse yourself, girl! I told you once – people are exactly where *you* want them in drawings. That's the whole point,' she went on in her slight brogue. 'I'm in charge when I draw. *I* make the running – not the buzzards and gombeen men.' And she stamped out of the room, rattling her stick against the dining room chair-legs as she went.

As they sat down to lunch Hetty looked round the bare, damp-stained walls. There was just one picture, a Landseer reproduction of 'The Stag at Bay' which the Welshs had rescued from somewhere as temporary decoration, hanging over the small mantelpiece. The horsehair stuffing was coming from one of the leather armchairs. The table they sat at, a mahogany dining table, was deeply scarred at one end, cut by bayonet marks, last used as a table in their armoury by the Black and Tans during their occupation of Summer Hill.

'Oh dear – where does one start?' Hetty, eyes returning, looked across at Dermot now.

'At the beginning . . .' He glanced back at her, struggling with a fatty piece on his chop. Hetty, leaving her meat, only tinkered with the vegetables. 'There's plenty of time. Do it up how you want, room by room. I estimate, between Mulrooney and myself, we must have bought back about half or two thirds of all the better furniture, pictures and things. So you can start out from scratch, painting the rooms, rearranging them, how you want. It's *yours*, Hetty.'

'Yes . . .' Hetty ran her hand nervously over the bayonet gashes in the table. 'But the damp and all the be-building repairs – the windows, the roof, the chimneys. All that we-would have to be done first, before there was any pe-painting or rearranging of the furniture.'

'Yes, well, we're going to get a few of the old estate workers back from the village – and Hoyne, the builder from Thomastown, to do the major repairs. I've talked to Jack about it. He's going to organise all that.'

'But the money. I'm bankrupt – haven't got a pe-pe-penny . . .'

'Yes. But with the money that was left after the purchase of the house and contents – some £20,000 I gather – Mr Mulrooney has given me that to hold in trust for you. So that can go towards the building repairs – if you agree. Then my Papa and I will invest a further £10,000 on your behalf – and you will have the income from that, not much, something under £1,000 a year, for the household running expenses. So all in all there'll be enough to see you started out again here.'

'Oh, Dermot, all that's too much – and too kind of you be-both. But started out on *what*, exactly?' For the first time since her recovery she looked at him almost desperately, the lines of worry and incapacity drawn again on her face, as she raked a thin hand through her prematurely greying curls.

'On change, Hetty. That's the main thing. You have to change your life,' he told her plainly. And seeing her haggard features again he went on even more bluntly. 'You've seen what'll happen if you don't – all that nonsense in Paris. The drinking and so on. Next time . . . it'll kill you.'

'Oh yes, I see that – all too well. And be-but for you I'd be dead already . . .' She gazed at him, head to one side, as if, at this angle, she might somehow wriggle her way into his heart. 'But *how* do I change my life?'

'Well, running Summer Hill, for a start. That's the whole point, isn't it? The house is back in the family now. And you must take responsibility for it. Why, there's some income to be made, too. Some of the trees in the demesne, dead or dying, they can be sold. Farm or rent out the 50-acre water meadows over the river – they're still part of the estate. The salmon traps by the bridge, the fishing rights – we still have them. Some money there. Get the vegetable garden going again, as a market garden perhaps. All that, Hetty, in time, when you're perfectly well again . . .'

He smiled at her, one of his short, quick, shy smiles.

'But you'll help me, Dermot? I ke-ke-can't do it all on my own.'

'Of course! I'll be over as often as I can, any leave I get –'

'But, Dermot, you're not leaving *yet*?'

He nodded. 'I have to, Hetty. Tomorrow on the mail boat from Dublin. I was due back at Sandhurst earlier this week, in fact –'

'But, Dermot . . .' She felt her face about to break into tears. Oh God, she thought, it was just as she'd feared, the same old thing: Dermot always leaving – never there, never permanent.

He reached over, taking her hand, secretly stricken himself. 'But I'll be back in the summer. And listen! – I'm trying to arrange to have the telephone put in, so that you can phone – long distance, to England even! So that I can telephone you as well. And I'll write. We'll both write. Give you all the advice and help you need.'

'But Dermot? . . .' She had considered posing this question all morning. And now, in desperation at his leaving, she finally plucked up courage to ask it. 'Dermot, how can I manage all this huge place – by myself? Ke-ke-couldn't you live here, a bit, yourself? Live here with me?' she added abruptly, in a startled tone, fearful of her audacity in finally putting her cards on the table.

'Hetty . . .' Dermot, who had feared just this same question all morning himself, looked away.

'Yes!' Hetty interrupted, allowing him no time for a refusal before she had completed her happy theory. 'Live here together. It'd be easy! Near your father in Dublin. Or just down on the train to the Waterford boat – for Sandhurst.'

'Hetty, I can't. I have a full-time job at Sandhurst. And I could hardly cross to and fro every weekend!' He tried to make light of it all.

'Well, give up the Army then! And we could run the place together here – what's left of the estate, the market garden, the fishing rights . . .' She looked at him – not pleading, but wide-eyed, with all the clearest evidence, the imperatives of love.

Dermot sighed. 'I'm not really much good at estate management, market gardening . . .' He realised at once how lame this excuse must sound – as Hetty certainly did.

'Oh, damn the market gardening!' she cried. 'That wasn't the real point. De-de-don't you see?' She paused, looking across at Dermot, who had turned away again, as if to avoid some expected blow. 'Don't you *see* – I love you, Dermot. That's why I'd like you here.'

The die was finally cast. There was silence.

'Hetty,' Dermot said at last. 'I have much the same feeling for you –'

'Well, why not then?' She beamed in sudden hope.

'But not exactly the same feelings perhaps . . .'

'What then? You don't really like we-women, in that way?' She rushed on. 'You like men, don't you? I've thought that . . . the only explanation for your never marrying.'

Dermot avoided this issue. 'It's more . . . a familial love I feel for you, Hetty. I'd be no good in loving you – that way, in the expected ways.'

But Hetty was not to be discouraged by this, taking it quite in her stride. 'Well, that would hardly matter. With my problem – my "social disease" as they so politely put it – I can't now expect to love people, in *that* way, either!' Hetty was bright again, believing that Dermot thought that sex was the only real obstacle between their coming together.

'It's not only that –'

'No!' Again she pre-empted him. 'I know you prefer men. But there's nothing wrong in that, absolutely not, not as far as I'm concerned. Lots of people in Hollywood were just like that – friends of mine, too,' she ran on, even more enthusiastically now. 'So that wouldn't be any problem between us. One can love men *and* women surely? I certainly have. Loving one doesn't have to exclude the other. The *loving* is surely the same, isn't it – whether it's for a man or a woman. And that's what counts, doesn't it? – the feelings, not the goings-on.'

'Yes, perhaps. Ideally. But situations, and the people involved, aren't always ideal. People, in the event, will rarely put up with that sort of loving – concurrently.'

'But I could. I'm sure I could – with you.' She looked at him, a crowd of different expressions crossing her once-more mobile face, a sense of mischief alive in her great blue eyes, compassion in her smile, the actress at large in her again, but expressing things truly felt now.

And Dermot, just as he had been with Frances thirty years before – when she had so consoled him and understood his feelings for her brother Henry after his death – was warmed, amazed by Hetty's almost identical response here. He saw, too, that just as he had once offered Frances marriage – both of them accepting these same conditions consequent on his nature – so, too, he might have embarked with Hetty, under the same equally understood conditions and handicaps.

And once more he was tempted for a moment – just as he had been with Frances all those years ago: to give up this aberration of his, as he saw it, this loving men, a covert passion which he had fed, yet which had haunted him for most of his life. Perhaps with Hetty and even at this late stage, he might cure himself of this sweet disease, find that it was not an indelible part of his nature. Perhaps, as he had helped her, she, in turn, might have the key which would release his spirit, his body, into normality.

He gazed at her: so sympathetic, vulnerable, so much more beautiful now that all her old arrogance and vanity, that fearful dominant regard, had slipped from her features. Oh yes, objectively, there was so much to love in her now, just as there had been long ago in her mother. But to live with her, to marry as he supposed, and thus be responsible for all her daily life and humours, her future? It was possible. But the risks were enormous. What if he failed – and he well might – to satisfy her, even in this sexless loving? And could there ever be such a thing for so attractive a woman as Hetty, who at thirty might one day be cured of her disease – her syphilis – and want that one thing which he could never give her.

As for himself – the leopard who changes his spots, he thought, has no more protection in the jungle. Camouflage gone, the animal, instead of living its nature, must fight every day for survival. Dermot decided then the risks were too great with Hetty and retreated back into the protection of his aberration.

'Well?' Hetty asked again. 'Couldn't I share – in your love?'

'Hetty, you've become wonderfully understanding – and *good*. But that's the whole point. You're recovering, you're already changing – from all that old earlier life that let you down. And you're only thirty. You've a chance to begin all over again. The disease can surely be cured – you're seeing that French doctor in Dublin regularly about it. And there's no reason, in time, that you shouldn't take up with someone else. I'm nearly fifty-five!' he added lightly.

Hetty was crestfallen, shaking her head, wounded. 'As if that me-me-mattered – your age. As if age mattered in loving either. You're just avoiding the issue – be-bringing that up.'

'No, honestly, I don't think I am –'

'You just don't want to live with me,' she said rather piteously. 'When you know you could, because there *wouldn't* be any demands – and you said you *did* fe-feel for me . . .'

Hetty's whole expression had changed. She was heartbroken. But Dermot remained calm. He had to.

'No demands you say, Hetty. No, not now. But do you really believe, at your age, that you're *never* going to make any demands, ever again? No demands now, in your illness, convalescence. But when you're really better – you'll know you are, because then there'll be things you *want* again, badly want –'

'You! I'll want *you* . . .'

'I'll always be there. Promise you.'

'But not here.'

'Not immediately. But when I retire – when Papa goes – I'd always hoped, perhaps, to come back and live here, not Islandbridge. The house is big enough! And I'd be with you then, Hetty. But meanwhile there is another point: my life *now*. You see, I still love the Army very much. That's what I've offered to life. And I get a marvellous return. And I want to keep that exchange going a bit longer. I'm sure you'll find something of the same sort to fill your life with – not the cinema, not *people*, but some other passion. We have to have other things besides people in our lives – something non-human to live with, to *change* our lives with.'

'But how? *What* can I change my le-life with? Not by just sitting here for years, doing up and tinkering with Summer Hill. I'm no more interior decorator – or market gardener – than you are.'

'You'll find something – you'll see. It'll come out of the blue one day, when you've quite recovered. And there's the real point of it all, Hetty – we can only ever change our lives *ourselves*. Other people can be stepping stones. Only you can get to the other bank . . .'

'No, no . . .' Hetty tried to hide her tears, turning away from him – until she saw a furry shape, pushing its way round the door, peering into the parlour. It was a cat, black and fat, with a white bib. 'Pussy, pussy,' Hetty said between her tears, beckoning it – and the cat, tail suddenly erect, came trotting over to her. Turning back to Dermot, still seeing him only as a cloudy shape, she took the piece of gristle from his plate and handed it down to the animal which, reaching up, clutched at it, squirrel-like, before devouring it.

'You see,' Dermot said. 'You've already got company, a new friend . . .' As he spoke, he remembered an almost identical incident, with an almost similar cat, in the crowded saloon bar at the Bear Hotel in Salisbury more than thirty years before when, as he lunched with Frances, she had leant forward to his plate, in just the same manner, offering that other earlier cat a similar piece of gristle. Strange continuities . . .

But that was exactly how it should be, he suddenly thought. The black cat then, and its repetition here – this was surely a perfect omen. That was precisely what all his efforts over Summer Hill had been about – the continuity of family in these three Cordiner women: the first two had ruined or squandered their inheritance and gone, but he hoped this third would in time manage to rebuild herself and the family's fortunes.

And surely Hetty, freed from these two bitter and unhappy women at last, and returned to the soft airs of her country and her home, would do just that – would now truly recover, reanimate all those older and happier Cordiner traditions, when Summer Hill would finally be warmed again, the promise reawakened.

Dermot's was the romantic attitude. And that was the 'passion' – Summer Hill the thing 'out of the blue' – which, though he had not wanted to insist on it, he hoped would come to Hetty, which would fill her life while at the same time giving life back to the great house. That was the non-human pursuit which he had forecast for her, which he hoped she would marry – not him.

A little more understanding of the human heart might have made him see it more realistically. But Dermot – wounded so often before by his nature – had come to love and understand solid brick and mortar better than he did the perverse eruptions, the splendours and miseries of the heart. He did not quite see that Hetty, though longing to change, was no recluse – was not temperamentally built to change her life purely by falling in love with a house. Rather this was Dermot's very nature – a long obsession with renewing old Cordiner certainties and traditions, in the shape of Hetty, a form, he hoped, now undevilled and untinged by aberration.

Dermot pined for an immutable order of brick and mortar, which posed no threat – as women invariably did. So for him this renewal of Summer Hill could not include marriage or any other serious emotional involvement with Hetty. What he wanted of the house was an emblem of restored familial honour, behind which he could the more securely hide his real nature. Hetty would change the house, bring it to order again, when he – indistinguishable once more against this renewed lustre and propriety – could be confirmed in his camouflage. Dermot in this way probably needed Summer Hill more than Hetty – for, though frightened of nothing else, he was horrified by the anarchy which his nature implied, and so had been equally dismayed by the deviations of the lives of both Frances and Hetty, which had resulted in the fall of Summer Hill. Thus to restore the house was to still all such disruption – his own, his family's, the world's.

Only the vaguest intimations of all this occurred to Dermot as he drove away from Summer Hill later that afternoon. He had always lived in action, not in thought – least of all thoughts of this kind, which he had successfully repressed over the years. Dermot, as well as being a romantic, was an honourable man.

Hetty, standing on the porch steps, watched his car disappear down the drive, the rooks screaming again in the late-afternoon light, the great flank of Mount Brandon touched with pale-blue tints of evening, silence descending everywhere as the sound of the engine died away and the birds settled.

Very tired, she knelt on the stone steps, hands flopped in her lap, palms outward as if still waiting for the gift denied her in Dermot, head bowed, kneeling in the dying light, quite immobile, too exhausted even to cry. Elly found her ten minutes later, still crouching there, her cheek touched by the crimson rays of sunset.

'Miss, ye *mustn't* be out here like that in the chill. I've some tea made in the kitchen – jam and a fruit cake I baked . . .'

Elly helped her up. But Hetty could hardly move with weariness. 'Ah, ye'll be all right.' She moved her forward. 'Didn't I know ye'd be tired after all your travels and sickness. So didn't Jack find this old wheelchair up in the attics – and ye can use that!'

Hetty saw the chair in the hall doorway then – the same chair that she and Léonie had used after their accidents years before. She smiled weakly now.

'Why, Elly! – That was Léonie's! Léa's chair.'

Hetty looked round at the shadows seeping forward everywhere, down the ruined lawn terraces, over the potholed gravel, up the porch steps, where a last shaft of sunset light caught the wheelchair now, illuminating it, touching the wickerwork with a faint gold. Then, helped forward by Elly, she collapsed into it. Léonie, she thought – Léa, beloved Léonie . . . And all the terrible wrong she had done her. She had come home. And yet she was only at the very beginning of things. It wasn't just the house that had to be repaired – that was almost the least of it, she thought. There was so much else to repair – to atone for – with people.

Jack came into the hall, carrying an oil lamp in his hand. The so-remembered smell of paraffin suddenly filled Hetty's nostrils, the soft light illuminating the torn Flemish tapestry as they passed it, Hetty gazing up at the royal hunt it depicted, stories of mediaeval kings and queens, a world of violent grandeur. And Hetty thought herself well finished with all that then – that world of arrogance, power, vanity and obsessive self-will where she had lived too long.

She turned the other way, looking up at Elly. 'Yes, Elly,' she said, 'we'll have tea – and jam and fruit cake, won't we?'

Elly nodded, as the lamplit procession made its way out of the hall, along the corridor, and through the green baize door, which thunked behind them, leaving the hall in darkness but for a faint coloured glow, illuminating the little pane of stained glass in the big window – the Cordiner coat of arms, the spreadeagle on the visored helmet: 'Fortune Favours the Brave'.

2

For nearly three months Robert had been totally occupied, to and fro between London and Paris – covering the new Anglo-French trade and tariff agreements – and had thus been quite unable to travel to Ireland, as he had earlier intended.

Now, however, the conference over, he had been given a few days' leave as recompense for his extra efforts. Meanwhile, too, Dermot, back at Sandhurst, had come up to London for the weekend to his South Kensington flat where Robert had met him alone, hearing all the news – first of Frances's death and then of Summer Hill and its conditional repossession by Hetty. This had astonished and pleased him – though Dermot had not mentioned his theory as to the identity of her benefactor. 'Hetty's always been lucky in her admirers,' was all he said tactfully.

'Why don't you and Léa – and the child – go over and see Hetty?' he had gone on to say then, feeling rather guilty for having deserted her himself and hoping for just such a meeting in any case, seeing it as very much part of the whole renewal of things – at Summer Hill and for Hetty: a renewal of friendship between these three old friends, whom he knew to have so fallen out over the years. Such a reconciliation would put the seal on his success in re-establishing the house and Hetty herself.

'I'd very much wanted to go over, when I heard the house was to be sold. I was pretty upset – about the house.'

'And Hetty?' Dermot asked with even more tact.

'Less so, I have to admit.'

'Of course, she behaved very badly . . .'

'More to Léonie than to me.'

'Yes, they'd been such close friends . . .' Dermot left the real nature of their friendship, which he had long suspected and which Hetty had more or less confirmed for him the week before, hanging awkwardly in the air for an instant. He was glad that friendship was over – one more disruptive emotion. 'At the same time,' he hurried on, 'it'd be nice if one . . . could make things up now.'

'Yes.' Robert was almost eager. 'Though Léonie isn't so inclined.'

Dermot nodded. 'And you, you've had your difficulties with Hetty, as well. Not easy. All the same, settled now yourself – perhaps it'd be the moment? And you see!' he had turned to Robert enthusiastically. 'Hetty's quite changed now, setting out on a new life, with none of that old petulance and cruelty, that domineering need to fight and win all the time. You wouldn't recognise her! And I'm sure she'd like to see you, know she had your support – for this new life she's setting up for herself at Summer Hill. You know, she's often told me, since her recovery, how *bad* she feels about the way she behaved to you and Léonie. She really wants to make things up with you now, with both of you. I know she does. So why don't you go? And perhaps Léonie might come to think better of her as well – in time. I hope so. Because you see, Robert, now the house is back in the family again, that's really what Summer Hill must be all about in the future: a place for *all* of you – especially you, so much a part of the family – to visit, live in, whatever. And little Olivia, too! Can't waste it – with just Hetty there in the huge place all on her own.'

Robert, in the light of Dermot's obvious sincerity and enthusiasm, had been largely convinced by these reflections and suggestions. Léonie, when he told her of all this back in Hampstead, had not been convinced.

'The leopard doesn't change its spots,' she said abruptly, on hearing how Hetty had altered, how much she wanted to make things up with them both now.

'Dermot said for us all to go over. Won't you?'

'No, no –'

'Oh, Léa, if Hetty's changed –'

'She hasn't, I bet! It's another of her acts. She did just the same thing to us both in Egypt, don't you remember? – when we met her in that temple with the horses: being nice as anything and pretending she'd quite changed and how she was *so sorry* for what she'd done –'

'But she's not an actress any more –'

'And you think, just because she's no longer an actress, that means she's stopped acting *herself*? That's nonsense! I know her – better than you. Why, acting is the heart of her nature – and people can't ever really give *that* up! They'd be dead if they did.'

'But that's just it! Her old nature very nearly did kill her. Dermot told me all about what happened to her in Paris, her vast debts, her alcoholism, pneumonia, in the hospital there. She's bound to change now. Or die.'

'Well, I can't help that. I tried to help her, so *much*, in the old days. And you know what happened – it nearly killed *me*. So I'm not going to start on any of that again.'

'Yes, I see all that, Léa. And I was hurt, almost as much. But she's *family* to me. Can't you see that? Practically my sister. And Summer Hill my home. So my going over there won't have anything to do with what happened later between all of us – the rows and betrayals. Only about now, the *future*.'

'Well, maybe you can forgive and forget that easily. I can't.'

'Léa, you're being unreasonable. I only want to see the house – not dig up any rotten old emotions in it.'

'You're being naive.' She was bitterly sardonic.

'No. Just realistic.'

'About such old emotions? They never really die – I told you, when we last talked about Hetty.'

'That's what worries me, Léa – with you. Those old emotions – they've dug in so deep, rotting away. Get them out into the air – and they'll disappear.'

She had snorted at this. 'That's how old emotions *bloom* again, you idiot! – in the air.'

'You know what I mean –'

'Oh yes, I know what you mean: *you* don't know what you mean. You don't know what you're really saying!'

They were fighting now, for the first time since the events in Egypt. So that Robert, suddenly aghast, decided to curtail the whole argument, though his tone remained nonetheless abrupt, bruised. 'I'm sorry, Léa – if you feel like that. Let's drop it. I have to go to Ireland. I want to go to Summer Hill. I've every perfectly good reason to go – and I'm going.'

Robert, if he was to make use of his short leave, had to take it at once. So he caught the boat train to Fishguard that same afternoon, without having time to warn Hetty of his arrival, quite preoccupied instead by Léa's latest reactions to Hetty's return, thinking of them on the long train journey to Wales. He had been shocked by this re-emergence, after so long, of Léa's bitter enmity towards her old friend – a feeling he had thought quite dead in her, dissolved in the renewal of their own close marriage and her happy absorption with the child. It simply was not like Léa – so open, warm, forgiving, realistic in her American way – that she should still harbour this striking animosity. Was it fear of a return to her own old nature, in loving women? Perhaps. Yet in any case that wasn't the point in this instance, as he had so clearly told her. What really mattered to him in all this was the survival of his home, his 'family' in the shape of Hetty, together with Dermot and Mortimer, and his need to see how things stood now at Summer Hill.

Had she completely forgotten that he was without parents, orphaned years before in Domenica, and how therefore he, at least, had naturally always loved Summer Hill, had been desolated at the news of its impending sale and was now, equally naturally, overjoyed at its astonishing return to the family – which included him?

Yes, she had forgotten. Or, worse still, she had wilfully blinded herself to all these other facts, so obsessed had she become again with her own old problems over Hetty, when she should have had the courage and the charity – which she showed in every other matter – to face up to her bad feelings over Hetty, dismiss them as the chimeras they were, and support him in all this renewal.

Instead, self-indulgently taking the scabs off old sores, she seemed intent only on running Hetty down, taking no account whatsoever of her vast distress – her near-death, in the first instance – and then giving her not an ounce of credit for her subsequent strengths, her fortitude in recovery, her determination to turn over a new leaf, above all her heartfelt wish, as Dermot had described it, to make amends with them both for her earlier appalling behaviour.

It was all so uncharacteristic of Léa. And, whatever she felt about Hetty, the fact that Léa saw none of his own quite separate feelings in the matter hurt him most of all. After all, in her earlier trouble with Hetty, after she had returned to him from Egypt, he had seen her point of view, consoled, understood, forgiven her. Whereas now, in a matter quite without such blazing emotional overtones, one simply of familial concern, Léa had offered him no help or understanding at all. He felt deeply hurt by this, feeling another clear division between them – a horrifying sense of real absence from her, loneliness, as he gazed out of the carriage window into the dark night.

After Robert had left, Léonie consoled herself with the child, playing with Olivia on the hearthrug by the fire until long past her bedtime.

'He doesn't see, you see,' she whispered to the uncomprehending little girl, as she dangled Thompson, the teddy bear, in front of her daughter. 'He has *no* idea – and I can't tell him,' she went on, handing the bear to Olivia, who took him up vigorously, crushing him to her cheek. Léonie, kneeling on the hearthrug, watching her daughter, but thinking of Robert and Hetty, could make no sense of her conflicting emotions, shared between both of them once more. Now, with Robert's departure for Summer Hill, all her old feelings for Hetty, which she had repressed for so long, came to the boil again.

Before, when Hetty had been so besotted with Craig Williamson, a distant frivolous picture star in Hollywood, she had posed no threat to her. At first, though desperately wanted, Hetty had simply been unobtainable. Then, loving Robert, she was unwanted, almost forgotten. Afterwards there had been the shocking mischance of their meeting in Egypt, all her old feelings for Hetty disastrously renewed. And that, she had been certain, was the final meeting, the ultimate lesson. Making things up with Robert, she was determined they should never meet again, that Hetty would never again threaten their marriage.

But now, with Hetty's fall from Hollywood, rather than just disappearing into anonymity, she had tumbled headlong into their own domestic orbit once more. Having almost wished her dead and Summer Hill destroyed or sold, Léa had instead come to see Hetty not only recovered but in possession of Summer Hill again, so giving life to all the ghosts of their past together there, revivifying their love, which as long as Hetty had remained untrue to herself in another world, pursuing her false life in pictures, she had been able to repress.

Now the past lived, as Hetty did – Hetty who by all accounts had finally gained her real self, that mix of courage, candour, vivacity and deep feeling which she had always known lay at the heart of her character. Hetty had come into this true inheritance at last, in temperament and materially, so realising all her greatest hopes – which were now fears. Fallen to earth in this true spirit, Léonie thought she could not rest until she had seen Hetty again, confirmed this magic transformation, shared in it. Yet if she saw her she knew not what disasters might ensue. 'I will wait for you,' she had written to Hetty twelve years before when she had first gone to America. And here Hetty was, waiting for her: she, who until a few hours ago, had been so completely and happily married to Robert.

No wonder she could not explain to him her bitter animosity towards Hetty. How – admitting it finally – could one tell one's husband that you loved someone else so much you had to pretend just the opposite, that you *hated* that other person? And yet even that wasn't true, Léonie realised. The violent turmoil in her heart just then made one thing clear to her at least. She loved and hated Hetty equally – wished her dead, yet longed to be with her. How explain such a mix of wicked and tender emotions to anyone?

'So you see,' she said softly to her daughter, words breaking into her thoughts, 'what can I do – loving them both like this?'

Olivia, responding to what for her were just sweet sounds from her mother, thrust the teddy bear at her. But Léonie, just like Robert then on the train, was not to be consoled. Instead she too felt a frightful loneliness, an absence from the two people who, once again she knew now, meant most to her in her life.

Robert, arriving at Thomastown station next morning, found Matty, old Joe Newman's son, whom he had known vaguely as a boy years before – now running the station taxi service, no longer in the shape of a hackney trap but a battered Austin motor. Happy in this continuity of things, in a countryside he had not been in for nearly ten years, he took the taxi straight to Summer Hill, basking in these renewed visions, memories confirmed in a landscape hardly changed at all, he thought, as he drove south, along the twisting river valley road towards Cloone.

Everything seemed more wild and unkempt since he had lived there – the margins and potholes of the road, the landscape: that was the only difference. Or perhaps it was just the brilliant growth of spring which gave this impression – the tall hedgerows ablaze with hawthorn blossom, the budding chestnuts in the village square as he entered seeming vast now, with an almost exotic abundance, spilling right over the railings, huge branches almost smothering the little shops all round. Ireland, in the intervening years, in its new guise as a Free State, had quite gone to seed and run wild, he felt – a world being smothered by moss and dead leaves, disappearing behind tangled briars and great raggedy trees, overwhelmed in drifts of hawthorn blossom, an enchanted kingdom, a lost estate.

With the fine breezy weather, and since he only had an overnight bag, he left the taxi in the village, deciding to walk along the river avenue, then up the hill by the back way to Summer Hill. A minute later, passing through the lower gates, he moved into the shadows of the demesne under the heavy trees, the canopy of great beeches that lined the river gorge here – the salmon traps and the water, high after spring rains, a sun-dappled flow to his left. After a mile, coming to the stone boathouse, he turned right up the steeply-winding track through the birch plantations, emerging a few minutes later on top of the gorge. The house was suddenly above him, a shimmer of stone set against its semi-circle of budding trees, fired by the sun.

His heart beat faster as he neared it along the old beech walk, hidden by these trees – wood pigeons above him, alarmed by his steps making sudden wing-cracking bolts into the sky, pheasants squawking in the undergrowth, a cuckoo calling repeatedly nearby. Home . . .

Crossing the ruined pleasure gardens, he made for the great portico, the battered hall door partly open, welcoming him. But when he pushed inside the whole house seemed deserted. He gazed about at the debris of tea-chests, fallen stucco, furniture piled haphazardly everywhere, still with the auctioneer's labels on them.

'Hetty?' he called out. But there was no answer – no voice but his in the loud spring.

Standing there a minute on the threshold, he breathed the air wafting in behind him, mixed now with the smell of damp and decay from the ruined hall. Turning back, he threw open both sides of the great door, so that the warmer breeze outside rushed in, obliterating the musty climate inside, flowing up the stairs and along the landings, through open doorways, a zephyr of renaissance, flushing the house with its fragrance.

Robert, looking for Hetty, followed the wind up the stairs, the broken glass pendants in the huge Waterford chandelier tinkling in the sudden disturbance. Reaching the first floor he walked round the stairwell balustrade, then down a first long bedroom corridor, back along the second, poking his nose into open doorways, inspecting the cluttered, mouldering rooms, yet light-hearted, walking the marches of his home in his search for Hetty.

Finally, taking the narrow staircase up to the top floor, he found himself opposite Henry's suite of old workrooms. The door was ajar. Pushing it open, he seemed to have arrived in some tropic jungle – long arms of ivy and Virginia creeper, with the thorny briars of a climbing rose, which years before as tendrils had crept through a broken window-pane, had now expanded vastly about the old rooms, half-filling the space, smothering the work bench by the window, throttling Henry's old bunsen burner, his bell jars and retorts, the glass long since smashed in the ivy's slow grip, before the foliage had swelled onwards, falling to the floor, cocooning the stuffed crocodile, so that the beast looked all the more dangerous, its wicked eyes and snout poking up through the greenery as if from some Nile swamp – until finally, in slimmer tendrils, the vegetation ran out, garlanding the old horsehair sofa by the door with sprigs and buds, as if the seat had been part of a stage set, prepared for some bucolic revels.

'Hetty?' Robert, doubting she was here, looked about him, stepping gingerly through the foliage.

Hetty, who that morning, as on previous days, had been moving up through the house making inventories and taking notes of what might be done in the way of repairs and decorating, was in the next room, the little museum with its glass display cases of Henry's butterflies and stuffed animals. Hidden behind these cases, she heard the briars rustle in the next room. Then, beyond the open doorway, she thought she saw Robert caught in a shaft of sunlight, his figure refracted, distorted in the glass, confirming what was obviously an illusion. The figure turned, retreated, disappeared, so that she was certain now of its unreality. Then she heard the oath.

'Damn it!'

Robert had tripped in the tangled network of creeper. Rushing into the room, Hetty found him spreadeagled on the mass of vegetation, next to the crocodile's snout, the searching knight-errant come to grief in a most undignified manner.

'Robert!' she screamed, as she helped him up, embracing him before he had a chance to resist. They stood there, together, Hetty in a pair of old slacks and floppy pullover, Robert garlanded like a wood demon with ivy leaves and bits of creeper. 'What *are* you doing here?'

'Here?' he asked vaguely, a little stunned, picking a thorn from his hand. 'Yes, here,' he answered himself awkwardly. 'Sorry I didn't have time to let you know –'

'Oh, that's nothing. Just, I meant – up *here*.' She looked at him, perplexed.

'Well, I couldn't see you anywhere else. So I came up to the top –'

'No – it's just that before I saw you, I'd been *thinking* of you – in there by the old porcupine!'

'Yes?'

'Yes! All those sharp quills . . . reminded me of you in the old days.' She laughed, but quite without any of her old cruelty. 'You were so unapproachable then.'

'Oh, was I?' He had remembered rather the opposite – how he had so longed to approach Hetty.

'Yes. But I was such a little bitch then, teasing and getting at you all the time. No wonder you had sharp quills!'

She looked at him with an elation which her fragile body seemed barely able to contain. She was so changed, Robert saw at once. Nothing of the regal, arrogant picture star remained. The imperious vanity, the lines of spite, the fevered dominance – all this had dissolved, to be replaced by a haunting finesse. Her face had undergone a complete distillation, each feature refined, the skin paler, almost translucent, nose straighter and thinner, chin and cheek-bones more prominent beneath a toss of faintly greying hair – and yet, in all, more beautiful, he thought.

'Yes, so strange to see you up here again,' Hetty ran on breathlessly. 'Just look at the place! Talk about going to seed. And yet beneath nothing's really changed at all – all held in aspic – by the ivy!'

Hetty wandered about, stepping carefully over the matted floor of vegetation. 'Look! – even that old snake skeleton in the tea-chest!' She had moved over to the box by the fireplace. 'How you used to tease *me* with it – when we used the place as a secret den.'

'Yes –'

'Where Mama couldn't get at us – and I could take off those frightful ticklish Irish clothes she made me wear.'

'Oh yes . . .' Robert could barely take in all these enthusiastic memories of Hetty's.

Seeing this, she apologised. 'It's just, coming up here for the first time today, I'd been thinking of all these things we did here – and then that *you* should appear at the same moment. Something must be meant!' She laughed easily, rattling the snake skeleton for a moment, then letting it fall back into the tea-chest, closing the lid firmly.

Later, after Robert had seen Aunt Emily and had an astonished meeting with Elly in the kitchen, he and Hetty had lunch alone in the housekeeper's old parlour, when Hetty, in a rush of news, brought him up to date on all her affairs. Robert was more guarded, particularly when Hetty enquired of Léonie.

'She's well,' he said, saying no more, so that Hetty looked at him quizzically.

'Oh, Robert, don't worry, I only asked. Nothing like that is ever going to happen between us again. All that's changed, in me at least. Truly. Quite another sort of life for me here, don't quite know what yet. But *nothing* of that old life. Yet you seem somehow sad – about her?'

'No.' He brushed the idea aside. Hetty had lost none of her old intuitiveness, he realised, in all her changes. But Hetty sensed that something was amiss between them, and thought she knew what. 'Of course, she didn't want to come over, because of me . . .'

'Yes,' Robert admitted. 'She still feels –'

'Naturally. How's she to know there's anything different in me? But I *have* changed, I have to –'

'Yes, I told Léa that – you were so ill . . .' Knowing of her alcoholism and pneumonia, if not her syphilis, Robert was tactful. Hetty was much more forth-coming.

'My actual illnesses were the least of it! I wasn't really infected by anything except myself. It all came from the crazy way I was living: the picture business, that brute Williamson, my drinking. But I *chose* to live that way. So the real change has to be up here.' She tapped her head.

After lunch, in the bright weather, they took a turn outside, walking up through the long grass of the old terraced lawns – the great exotic trees, the Canadian maple, the Wellingtonia and the cedar towering above them. Hetty, needing support over the matted carpet, took Robert's arm.

They passed the grotto, some of its white limestone boulders just visible, its waterfall now entirely hidden behind a tangle of nettle and ivy. The domed stone dovecote came into sight, though the doorway and all the lower brickwork were hidden by impenetrable clumps of elder.

'The awful row we had in there,' Hetty remarked. 'When you frightened away my pet dove!'

'Yes . . . You weren't alone, in being difficult.'

Pushing on through a thicker tangle, they came to the line of old wire cages against the kitchen garden wall where Henry had kept his menagerie of snakes and wild animals years before, now almost entirely obliterated. Something stirred in the dank undergrowth – a pheasant or a blackbird – but enough to make Hetty start, gripping Robert's arm more firmly, shivering.

'I never liked this place,' she said. 'Remember how we always kept well clear of it? – after Mickey Joe told us how the snakes got Uncle Henry up here –'

'Yes, and we didn't believe him, because Elly had told us there were no snakes in Ireland. St Patrick had booted them all out –'

'But Elly knew perfectly well he'd been killed by them – just covering up. Everyone covering up everything then. I *hated* that worst of all. Not telling the truth.' She paused, reflecting. 'But then I took just the same line myself later: avoiding the truth. Runs in the family. Oh dear, what a mess we Cordiners always get ourselves into – and now this.' She surveyed the decaying scene. 'A total mess.'

'Well –'

'And all to be put in some kind of order.'

'By degrees . . .'

'You're just like Dermot, saying that!'

But Hetty did not underline the problems ahead of her, as she had with Dermot. Robert was not needed with the same kind of rash emotion. He was more brother to her once more, and so a confidant in quite different, older intimacies.

Passing on into the walled kitchen garden they were confronted by a wilderness, the tall apple and plum trees run riot above a jungle of swaying grass, the once-neat paths now rivers of weed, the old strict vegetable rows, raspberry canes and gooseberry bushes submerged beneath a tide of weeds.

Finally, walking over a scented patch where the old herb border had been, their feet releasing a faint odour of thyme and sage, they came into the smaller walled garden, the children's garden which generations of Cordiner offspring had planted out, and where only the crab apple tree, wizened and raggedy, its furthest branches crackling in the wind high up, still survived, one branch fallen, with several of last year's minute yellow apples still attached to it.

'The magic apples,' Hetty said. 'Remember? When you were so ill with that awful whooping cough and I thought they were the cure – Mickey Joe told me – and I tried to smuggle them up to you, before Mama caught me by the scruff of the neck . . .!'

'Only just. I remember the dark room and the awful smell of camphor oil. And, of course, your Mama . . . not that row, but all the other fearful rows you had with her –'

'Yes. Because of my Papa mostly – his not being my real Papa . . .' She turned to him. 'There was all that too. Remember?'

'Never forgotten. Does it still . . . worry you?'

'Yes, I think it does – because I'm sure he was someone else. And I've no idea who . . . But then it was much worse for you, knowing but *losing* both your parents. And I was such a selfish, unfeeling prig, taking so little account of all that. Robert, I am so sorry.' She gripped his arm more firmly still. 'All that past, when there was just us – and things only you and I shared. And I wrecked so much of that, for you, for both of us – things that could have been so precious then – and now.

I wish I could make up for it all – the cruelties, towards you and Léa. Just awful.' She bowed her head at the memory. 'But I am going to *try* and make up for it all. And none of those old emotional ne-nonsenses is ever going to come between you and me again. Robert?' She looked at him, calmly, gravely.

'Yes,' he said. 'I believe you.'

She took his arm again, looking up at him. 'I'm so happy – because you're the person I'm really closest to. I never really stammered with you then, remember? You were the only one. That's how close we were. And I've not really been st-st-stammering with you now, have I?'

They laughed. 'No.'

A bumblebee droned heavily past them, climbing steeply over the high wall. Pigeons murmured in the woods beyond. But the two of them in the hot sunshine, hidden in the secret garden where there was no wind, were no longer part of that other, outer, present world. Instead, drifting back, they were almost children again.

They really had so much more in common with each other than with anyone else – more to remember, more to offer each other now. Robert felt this, so did Hetty, without need of further words. Their arms linked together, without the least embarrassment or tension, said it all. And nothing would have breached this sibling innocence, if Robert had not taken one of the yellow crab apples from the fallen branch beside him, biting into it briefly, before offering it to Hetty. 'Nice. Not as bitter – like they used to be. Try it?'

Hetty, offered the apple, suddenly changed her expression, frowning, downcast. But she took it, biting into it heedlessly where Robert's teeth had been. Then she started to cry.

'What's the matter?'

'Nothing, only . . .' She turned away, her whole frail body shaking with emotion.

She was so piteous a figure that Robert, moving toward her, could not but more openly console her. He took her arm. 'Hetty, what *is* it?' Before he really knew what he was doing, he had taken her in his arms. In another moment, when she responded, he was kissing her, feeling the smoothness, then the slithery damp of her tear-stained face, and then neither of them could restrain this – for Robert – so-long unrequited and repressed emotion, to which Hetty now, for the first time in all their years, responded, fully, warmly, joyously.

Afterwards, both shaken to the depths, they looked at each other.

'Oh God,' Hetty said, her face, like Robert's, a mixture of amazement and horror. This was the last thing they had wanted or expected. And now that it had happened their childhood dissolved, innocent memories shattered. Now, in this admission of love, they were quite new people to each other. And both, though enraptured by the change, were appalled by its implications. So that at first they tried to pretend that nothing of importance had occurred, not speaking of it. But this was a useless ploy. There was so much at stake now in these restless emotions they knew they could not be held down indefinitely. They had to speak of them.

After dinner, when Aunt Emily had gone upstairs, with a fire in the half-refurbished drawing room, Hetty turned the zoetrope, the old peepshow machine rescued in the auction, gazing through the spinning slats as the little dog laughed to see such fun and the cow jumped over the moon. Then, putting her hand to the wheel, she brought it to a sudden stop.

'What do we do?' But, before Robert had a chance to reply, she answered her own question. 'You can't stay here with me – though God knows that's what I'd love, the most pe-pe-perfect thing – do up the house together. *Our* house, after all.'

'Yes . . . And, no, I can't stay. There's Léa and Olivia,' he went on, downcast.

'There's no use feeling guilty about it. But I do.' She glanced up at him quickly, looking for some sort of confirmation or denial.

'Yes,' was all he said, equally ambiguously.

'Oh, Robert, you liked me so much – in the old days, and I knew it, and I was so cold to you. Well, I suppose that's just another change in me. I like – I love you now. Don't I? I do.'

'And Léonie?'

'Loving her – that was all part of my past, going down dead ends. The need to win – with everything and anybody, it didn't matter who or what. Léonie wasn't really me.'

'I love her, though.'

'Of course.' She sighed, turning the wheel again, the fantastic, potent, inexplicable life inside set in motion once more. 'Loving two people? – I've known that well enough. Or is it?' She looked up at him carefully. 'Perhaps it was just a fit we both had up there in the children's garden. Thinking of the past, all those old feelings. Just a fit?' she asked, hoping Robert might confirm this so that they could then forget about the whole thing – yet at the same time longing for him to say it had not been; that the whole thing had been wonderfully real. The fire crackled in the silence – Hetty's new friend, the black cat called Ethel, curled up by the fender.

Robert saw the same chance as Hetty. He could easily deny his feelings, and hers, dismiss the whole thing as just a fit, a mere physical consolation, an explosion consequent on all the renewed emotions from their shared past. What more natural than that they should have been momentarily overcome by these old feelings?

But he could not deny his feelings. And he did not want to. Something vital had come into his life then, in Hetty's arms up in the little garden. Something he had longed for all those years ago, had now been achieved, reciprocated, so that he felt transformed, fulfilled. All his anguish in loving Hetty then had now been justified, his suit returned, his life made good. The past, seemingly so completely lost, had now been astonishingly regained. One could not pretend such a transformation had never happened.

'No,' he said. 'It wasn't a fit. And you're right: loving two people. I feel that – for you. And Léa.'

He turned away. Hetty relaxed. 'Well, there's no point getting into the de-de-dumps about it. It's one of the best things that's ever happened to me. This feeling I have for you – makes me the person I know I always ought to have been, going the proper way at last, with *you*, which is what I should have done all those years ago. Yes! – married you! And it's extraordinary, because I wasn't just a cold prig to you then, I *hated* you! Getting in the way between me and Léa, here at Summer Hill, and then when you finally married her, I was absolutely beside myself in hating you! Yet now there's this love of you. Was it there all along, hidden in what was my *real* nature? Is that how one can love and hate someone at the same time? – because the feelings come from two quite separate parts of our nature, the good and bad? – the bad part which we don't know about, or won't admit to, as I certainly didn't. Do you think that's how it is, so that, when we have a terrible, unreasonably strong hatred for someone, it can sometimes be that we love them just as fiercely?'

As she was speaking Robert suddenly thought of Léonie. And it came to him in a flash. Yes, of course, what Hetty had said was true – for Léonie as well. Because this was just how Léonie was behaving. This explained her bitter animosity towards Hetty. She hated her violently because she secretly loved her just as much. So that now he said, with full conviction, 'Yes, I'm sure you're right. That can happen – exactly.'

But he could not tell Hetty of this new thought about Léonie. The whole idea was too undermining already – this clear intuition he had now that Léa's hatred of Hetty was something from the worst part of her nature, and that at heart Léonie still loved her – as he did now. Oh God, he thought. Where were their bright promises, made but a few hours before, of appropriate, sensible life – all three of them, separately and together? He and Hetty might have saved themselves, escaped their predicament, simply by his departure, his absence on the following day. But if, on his return to London, he confirmed how Léonie had been repressing just the same sort of passionate feelings for Hetty, what hope was there for his marriage? It would be based on a lie.

Had it, in fact, and despite all Léonie's earlier avowals, been a lie all along? Was Léa quite incapable of changing her real nature – as Hetty had done, was doing? Or was it, with Léa, as Hetty had suggested, simply a matter of her loving two people, just as he loved both women, a division in himself, similar to Léa's, which he had only just discovered.

In which case, like musical chairs, only Hetty in her new reformation, loving him alone, was going to be left out. Or a further horror – compounded by his feelings then over Léa's insensitivities about his coming over to Summer Hill: did he now, or would he come to, care more for Hetty than for his wife? The idea of his having married Hetty, which she had just suggested, had been so exactly his own wish years before, when they might both of them have taken over Summer Hill. And now that the idea had been given shape again, entirely at Hetty's instigation, it renewed for him a remote vision – that this might still be possible, creating a stark, unreasonable longing in his heart. If this could happen, then at last he and Hetty could finally still all their old agonies – her loss of a father, his loss of both parents, their general sense of disruption and homelessness.

They could set up a true life for themselves – Hetty had just suggested, well-nigh offered, as much, at Summer Hill, a life which they had carelessly mislaid but which had been their destiny from the very start, since they had first come together as children in Domenica.

This, exactly this, had once been his vision. And now Hetty, so temptingly, had put it just within his grasp again. How might he and Léonie survive together with this vision, this itch, at the back of his mind now? For of course, and he had to admit it then, that had always been his secret ambition, to *possess* Summer Hill, with Hetty.

But then again, he thought, it was all nonsense. He could never desert Léa and Olivia. And yet, and yet . . . Conflicting thoughts stormed about his brain. And, instead of finding all such disruptive emotions over and done with at last, Robert saw then how all three of them were more deeply embedded than ever in potential disaster.

'Yes,' he said at last, 'loving two people. But just as much this house. When you said we'd do it up together, how much I'd have liked to do just that! You know how I love the place.'

'Yes.'

'And if we had married –'

'Don't –'

'How that's exactly what we could have been doing together now.'

'No – don't make it a torture.' Hetty, on the brink of tears, turned away, trying to compose herself, succeeding. Then she turned back to him. 'If my loving you comes from the good part of me, then I can't change it. But I'm not imposing it!' She tried to make light of this promise, but failed. 'And it certainly mustn't come between you and Léa . . .'

'No –'

'Because you and she – that's far more important, with Olivia. And Léa loves you. Of course she does, because she changed long ago – as I have now – to that ordinary, happier kind of loving! And I had the chance of that with you years ago – and threw it away. So I've no expectations. And there's nothing – absolutely nothing – for you to feel bad about. It's just nice that we've found this thing now, between ourselves. And Léa need never know. Go back. And love her.'

'Not all that easy . . .'

Hetty had wanted him to say this, yet she could not openly encourage this attitude in him for a moment. 'Why not? You're just being an old pessimist! It's *nice* – loving people. Shouldn't be stuck in the de-de-dumps about it. There's always a reasonable way out in these things. God, it's hot in here!'

She stood up, moving towards one of the long curtained windows, pulling them aside to let some air in. But she was confronted by a completely bricked-up space – where one of the windows had rotted and collapsed and had then been repaired in this harsh way. Hetty, hammering on the cold wall then, could contain herself no longer. She started to cry. Robert took her in his arms once more.

*

In London that same evening Léonie, having thought of little else since Robert's departure, had decided on a complete about-turn over Hetty. When Olivia was in bed that evening she sat down to write a letter to Hetty on Robert's typewriter, keeping a carbon for him.

She had been such a fool, she thought, hating Hetty, when she was really . . . just fond of her. Yes, on reflection, it was simply that: affection, not love. That had been a brainstorm, she felt, the previous night – feeling all those impossible, passionate emotions for her. In the clear light of day she saw it differently. And it was time now that she rid herself of this nonsense in her soul about Hetty – time she set things on an even keel again, promoted a friendly relationship with her, at least, showing goodwill in all Hetty's renewals.

She had nothing to lose. She need not see Hetty, after all. Distance lay between them. And there was safety in that. But she must show willing towards her now, for she saw clearly how she had angered Robert by her fierce reactions towards Hetty – and more still how she had upset him by her stupid insensitivities about his going to Summer Hill, so blinded had she been over Hetty. It was time to mend her fences here. Her marriage was at risk, the child. There was no question. She could show Robert, in the carbon, how she had seen the light, recanted, and was now to be just as reasonably and charitably concerned over Hetty as he so obviously was. Nothing emotional, just care and concern, which she ought to have shown in the first place and so avoided this quite needless row with Robert. Robert, who was so dear to her – so attached to her, trusting, so forgiving: Robert – who would never love anyone else.

'Dear Hetty,' she began. 'Sorry not to have come over with Robert. But Olivia's been a bit difficult lately. This is just a note to say how sad I was to hear of all your awful illnesses and problems and how *pleased* I am that you are back at Summer Hill and how I so much hope that everything's going to work out for you now . . .'

So Léonie lied to herself, once more repressing her real feelings about Hetty – to save herself and her marriage – while Hetty and Robert, at just the same moment, expressed exactly what they felt for each other by the blocked-up window, Robert knowing full well that what they were doing might well come to destroy his marriage.

Only Hetty, after Robert had left the following morning, viewed this new situation with any equanimity. Upset at his departure – this brief taste of loving him had left her with an anguished longing for what could never be – she was happy, at least in that she had made things up with him so convincingly, happy in almost entirely regaining her true self, along with Robert, Elly, Dermot and the house itself. Only Léa remained outside this orbit of happy change and renewal: Léa, and the identity of that 'admirer' who had returned Summer Hill to her – and beyond these, of course, the greatest mystery, which had hurt and haunted her all her life, of who her real father was.

But surely, settled again in Summer Hill – surely, in this new lease of every kind of life, she would come to answers for these matters? – above all make that final identification about her father which would set the seal on her renaissance, give her complete peace at last.

A first step to this end, of course, would be to look through her mother's effects and papers. Several large boxes of these had arrived from Frances's bungalow in Dublin. And there must besides, Hetty knew, be other older, possibly more relevant papers strewn or hidden about the house: in the old safe, for example, set in the wall of her mother's, and grandmother's, office-boudoir beyond the drawing-room. The keys to this had long since disappeared. But the local blacksmith could soon fix that. So, immediately after Robert had left that morning, she asked Jack Welsh to have the man come up from his smithy in the village.

Waiting for him that afternoon, tense and expectant, she calmed her nerves at the old Blüthner grand piano, bought back at the auction and still preserved in the drawing room, sitting down, starting to pick out a tune. It was nothing from *Madame Butterfly* that came to mind. That, along with all her cruel and foolish passion for Léonie, was long gone.

Instead she found herself playing quite a different melody as the spring afternoon waned and tinges of yellow and gold crept into the sky. She had no idea why the tune had come to mind – half the loss of Robert, half pleasure in this wonderful renewal with him, the memory of their embraces? However it was, the old Scottish melody, 'The Skye Boat Song', ran from her mind then and out over the keys in a delicate thrill of sound. So that soon – while waiting for the blacksmith and perhaps at last an answer to this great mystery of her life – she was humming and then singing this lament for a lost prince, for a king over the water.

Speed bonny boat, like a bird on the wing,
'Onward,' the sailors cry.
Carry the lad that's born to be King
Over the sea to Skye . . .

A few minutes later there was a knock on the door. It was Jack Welsh. 'Mick Duggan is here, Miss Cordiner – with all the tools, to open the oul' safe.'

3

THE BLACKSMITH HAMMERED and chiselled away at the safe for half an hour making little impression on it, while Hetty looked on in a rising fever of anticipation. But eventually, under the rough pressure of crowbar and jemmy, the door gave way and Hetty rushed forward, peering into the dark cavity.

There was nothing inside. The safe was absolutely empty.

Hetty was stricken. The blacksmith, as though this new châtelaine at Summer Hill were half-witted, offered judicious consolation. 'Ah, an' sure it's the *banks* people do be putting their money into these days, Miss Cordiner . . .'

For the second time in her life – like the hoard of sweets she and Léonie had found in old General Morton's safe in his house up-river – an expected cache had mocked her, yielding nothing. Nor did her mother's papers which had been sent down from Dublin reveal any clues when she went through them. There were some old ledgers, stock certificates, solicitor's letters, other bits and pieces without any value or interest. Hetty had not really expected anything here, for Frances in her will had left everything of any real value in the bungalow to her Republican friends. Even the photograph of her supposed father, Bruce Fraser, which she remembered seeing years before, had disappeared when Hetty, in the following days, had thoroughly searched the other rooms, attics, drawers and cabinets of Summer Hill.

True, she found some things of interest – a collection of old newspapers in an attic trunk marked 'Captain B. R. C. Fraser, Fraser Hall, Domenica, W. Indies' – copies of the *New York Post* describing the Carib attack on their house on the island, an old Webley service revolver still in its holster with two rusty shells in the attached pouch – an object which stirred some memory in her which Hetty could not quite identify, giving her a feeling of unease – together with title deeds and a lot of legal correspondence to do with Bruce Fraser's estate and Frances's subsequent sale of Fraser Hall. There was nothing else – no real letters, nothing intimate or revealing.

Well, of course, she had been foolish to expect anything of this sort. Her mother would long before have destroyed any such evidence, taking every care to hide the truth about who her real father was. So Hetty resigned herself again to living without answers.

But, at the end of the week, in a corner of one of the attics – and entirely out of the blue, as Dermot had suggested – Hetty found another and different answer to her frustrations about the past, and more importantly a quite unexpected key to her future.

It was one of Combridge's artist's sketchbooks, in a chest with some of her old toys and children's books – a cartridge-paper sketchbook which Dermot had given her as a child, just before he had gone away, leaving her heartbroken. In it, as a solace, Aunt Emily had encouraged her to write the story of 'The Magic Jaunting Car', of the man in the Norfolk jacket with the little girl in pigtails – and their adventures with the pony and sidecar, travelling down the railway line, floating over the ocean to the island where the Gobblies lived, prey to the fierce Marshmallows, those blobby, evil, one-eyed beasts, coming out at evening from the mists, the noisome stagnant pools, doing battle with the knight errant in the Norfolk jacket and the little girl, when evil was put down and virtue finally triumphant.

Taking the sketchbook with her into the proper light of the study-boudoir which she had now made over into her own workroom, Hetty gazed through the pages, enchanted now by Aunt Emily's vividly-coloured pen and ink illustrations on one side, her own text in a childish hand on the other.

Had she really been able to invent all that? Well, some of it at least, if largely at Aunt Emily's prompting. The whole thing so sparkled with wit, invention, colour: this magic world, hidden for so long, preserved in the pages, and released from them now, leaping forth mint-fresh, exciting, disturbingly potent, telling Hetty something which she could not at once quite interpret.

Then it came to her. Of course! Here, in her present reclusive circumstances, was the obvious manner of expressing herself – by writing, inventing in this way again. But instead of a child's book she would do one for grown-ups. Why, it was a perfect idea, she thought, rushing upstairs to tell Aunt Emily about it at once.

'Aunt – I've thought of something really good.' She showed her the old sketchbook. 'I'm going to try and write something, like we did here, but not for children.' As she leant over her great-aunt's shoulder, they looked through the sketchbook together, commenting, laughing over it.

'Indeed, why not?' Aunt Emily said eventually.

'Of course, it was all really you – in that be-be-book.'

'Oh no. I just did the drawings. You had the ideas, I remember. That fat old pony with its ears through the straw hat for a start – *you* called him "Awful". So of course you can write. Best thing ever books – and drawings and paintings. I've hundreds of old sketchbooks here.' She gestured round at a pile of them in a corner. '*You're* in charge, you see, with books and drawings and the like, not the other imbeciles . . .'

'Yes, of course. Like motion pictures . . .' Hetty spoke more to herself then, gazing round at the high theatricality of the room, remembering her own similar power in acting, how it was she, when the cameras rolled, who imposed the initial order on the celluloid. If she had done that so well once in the crowded picture studios, she could surely do the same again, alone, on paper.

'But what'll I write about?' she mused. 'You do all your drawings – from what's *real*.'

'Excuse yourself, girl!' Aunt Emily was huffy. 'That's only the *start* of it all in my drawings. It's the invention that counts. After I've got the background in I've no interest at all in *reality*. That's a mug's game, just painting what you *see*. The last thing you want to bother about – reality . . .' She curled her lips in vast distaste.

So it was that Hetty started writing for grown-ups – taking as theme and background her own life, the story of her childhood in Domenica, growing up with Robert in that island paradise: the pellucid, dew-drenched mornings in the old citrus groves, the dazzling rainbows spotlit against the plum-bruised skies over the thunderstruck mountains, the fantastic lemon and crimson sunsets, the great python in the Emerald Pool, the voodoo ceremonies with Cook and Big Jules the sailor behind the laundry, the dismembered chicken in the flare light, the drunken father, the hurdy-gurdy music machines in the hall, the battle with the Caribs, the hurricane . . .

It would be the tale of a girl cast out of this strange Eden, with her orphaned friend – exiled to a cold and fearful house in Ireland, the years of pain there, with her cruel Mama and wicked grandmother, locked away in the Gothic wing of the house: the meeting with the man in the Norfolk jacket, and her consequent joys in discovering the world outside the house with him, running free and wild, looking for otters and kingfishers, before his sudden, awful disappearance in the war. Then her years at the convent school in Normandy, the meeting there with that other person, the girl who was to dominate her subsequent life . . .

My goodness, Hetty thought, there was no lack of interesting background. All that was needed was an invented foreground – the drama, conflict, dialogue. And that would come. After all, she had read or acted through scores of every sort of dramatic motion picture photoplays. She knew what was required there. It would be a novel – perhaps a series of novels, in which she would delve through all her past, feeling intuitively how in this way she might finally take the sting out of it, by mapping all its fears and wonders, so capturing the imaginative truths of her life, as consolation for all its folly and loss in reality, a balm in such fiction for all that had wounded and defeated her in daily life, a redemption for all the wounds she had imposed on herself and others.

Above all, perhaps, she might in this writing achieve what she had quite failed to do in looking into the safe and through her mother's papers – might, in these fictional recreations, come to some peace, make terms with that ultimate loss, that deepest intuition of hers that she had another and quite different father.

So she sat down that same morning – just as the builders from Thomastown arrived to start on the major repairs to the house – opening a fresh sketchbook which Aunt Emily had given her, considering how she might best begin.

What would she call the book? She remembered the rippling play of light and shadow, the endless sea glitter, the crystal drifts, the prisms of colour slanting off the Atlantic waters below the cliff in front of Fraser Hall: iridescent green and blue and deeper purple. Yes, she might well call these first adventures *Aquamarine.*

And then, as she thought of her early life on the island, basking in those ever-changing colours, the first paragraph, after half an hour's work, came to her fairly easily:

> Running through the coral-walled garden, she stopped to pick a little hard green lime, sticking her nails into it, scoring the skin deeply, putting it to her face. Immediately the sharp, tart smell fizzed up her nose. She loved this limey essence of the island. Taking the fruit, she danced on across the lawn, dipping her nose into various flowers – roses, orchids, heliconias – comparing the flavours, darting from one to the next, savouring each bloom, just as the humming birds were doing. But soon, sated and confused by the different odours, she ran on around the house to her look-out point, a raised flat rock on the cliff above the cove, a crow's nest high above the bay, where she could wait for the first sight, the twirl of dark chocolate smoke on the horizon, which heralded the arrival of the weekly packet steamer . . .

As she wrote, correcting, changing, becoming completely absorbed in the work, she smelt the tart odour of limes invading the air around her once more, felt herself sitting on that same rock, as if on the bowsprit of a ship held far out over the ocean, the waves rolling towards her, so that she seemed to be moving herself, pushing away from the island, a strange sinking feeling in the pit of her stomach. As she wrote, testing this alchemy of invention, adventuring into these miraculous caves of the imagination, the temporal scene before her faded and she found herself launched forth, as over the waves, into a magic restoration.

Robert, returning to Hampstead, found no such inspiration. For the first time with Léa he was forced to live an outright lie with her and it hurt him deeply – the sense of betraying her, made all the worse when he saw the carbon of her letter to Hetty: Léa was rediscovering a true perspective over Hetty at last, while he was cheating her, just at the very point when she had seen this light and was being so particularly loving to him.

'Oh, Robert, I made such a fool of myself before you left,' she had started out straightaway, standing in the hall. 'About Hetty, about your going over to Summer Hill. Forgive me. I was just frightened about the past.' She had kissed him sweetly as Olivia clawed at his trousers, reaching up, insisting on her own embraces. But Robert was depressed.

'So, how did it go? How was she?' Léonie asked later when Olivia was in bed. And Robert told her everything that happened, except the most important thing. Later, when they were in bed themselves, she wanted him and they made love together, and Robert, trying to forget his feelings for Hetty, almost punished Léa in his love-making – bringing an anguished, unaccustomed vigour to it all, to which Léonie responded just as vigorously, trying in her case to expunge all memory of her brainstorm a few evenings before: the thought that she might still love Hetty.

Later still, just before dawn, Robert had a dream. He and Hetty and Léonie were at some party in a huge house of endless rooms. Both women had left him and he was searching frantically for them, through room after room filled with strangers.

'Léa? Hetty?' He was running, shouting out for them both desperately now. Then he woke with a start. Léa was awake beside him in the half-light of dawn.

'Yes, I'm *here*,' she reassured him. 'What's the matter? – your calling out for me and Hetty like that? *I'm* here!'

God, he thought, am I to betray myself like this, even in my dreams?

Meanwhile Hetty got over Robert's absence more readily – by turning her thoughts of him into fiction, starting to commemorate him there, as the companion in her story, so that she could hold him in these pages, if not in her arms. So the novel flourished each morning in the little office-boudoir, while the builders got about their restoration on the roof, tugging rotten rafters out, renewing slates, rebuilding balustrades and chimneys. Jack and Elly began to sort out the furniture, while men from the village, stripping the tattered wallpaper and plaster, set up ladders in the reception rooms prior to redecorating them. A man came down from Dublin to see what he could do about repairing the delicate Italian stucco work, the bas-reliefs of cherubs and cornucopias and gilded harps. Aunt Emily sallied forth with her easel into the overgrown, daisy-filled gardens, where some half-dozen other local men, glad of the casual labour, were attacking the overgrown wilderness there, the briars, nettle and elder, with scythes and saws.

Hetty continued to visit her doctor in Dublin, Dr Langlois, and, on his insistence that she take up some form of regular physical exercise, began some gentle horse-riding, with a quiet mare called Buttercup, purchased from a livery stable near Thomastown, moving about, rediscovering, inspecting the ruined demesne. So, too, gathering strength in the spring days that followed, and largely due to the enthusiastic suggestion of Major Ashley who came to visit, she thought she might well repair her reflexes with some fencing, getting out Henry's old foils and laying the marked hessian carpet again across the hall. Here, once a week or so, she and the Major indulged in some mild bouts, with masks and padded vests – the Major, still spry, glorying in these renewed jousts, much laughter between them, so that Hetty, taking to this old sport and aiming to maintain her fitness when he was not there, had a big leather punch-bag set up in the hall, hanging it from the first-floor balustrade. She lunged and parried at the swinging leather for ten minutes each morning, before settling down to work on her book.

The whole house became a hive of activity, life renewed, inside and out, in the warm spring weather. Hetty finished the first chapter by the end of May, reading it aloud to Aunt Emily on the porch one afternoon.

She came to the final paragraph, where the women and children, left alone in the coral-walled house on the cliff-top after the battle with the anaconda at the Emerald Pool, decide they must leave at once for the capital before the August storms set in.

Almost as soon as her Mama had finished speaking they heard the first faint thunder, a long gathering rumble out over the bay, which ten minutes later had moved over the house, in withering explosions and spits of blue lightning. Afterwards the rain fell in solid curtains. During the night a fierce wind came which lasted for days, the sea rising in vast breakers, dashing up over the cliff beneath the house, rattling the green storm shutters, every room tight shut now against these searing gales. The packet from Roseau was cancelled. All of them were marooned then, as the wind and rain shook every fibre of the house, so that it seemed to lurch and fall in the great storm like a ship at sea about to founder.

'Not bad,' Aunt Emily said grudgingly at the end. 'You've got the girl – it's you I suppose. And those awful women – and the feel of the whole place – pretty well. I can see it, almost as good as a painting . . .'

Hetty, with this faint praise, felt a thrill of pleasure. Everything was coming right. Her world was being put together again, bit by bit, inside and all about her; all the failures of the past banished in this restoration of the house and in this bright pure light of her imagination. 'I'm glad you like it. Really so happy!' She leant across, touching her great-aunt's hand.

Just then, in the silence, they heard a car coming up the avenue. A minute later it drew up by the porch. Hetty, remembering her bankruptcy, thought the casually-dressed stranger who stepped out then must have come about her debts, since he addressed her at once as 'Miss Laura Bowen'.

'Yes?'

He was American – baby-faced yet cumbersome, overweight, in ill-fitting clothes, with a loose necktie and fedora hat tilted back, which he took off now, displaying an almost shaven head, hollow eyes that had dark circles round them, giving him a theatrical air somehow, the eyes staring out from their dark rounds, like a clown's face, only half-made up. The effect was almost comic, yet inquisitorial, vaguely sinister.

The man hitched up his baggy trousers – a further clownish effect – his stomach bursting out over his belt. Yes, Hetty thought, there was something both farcical and dangerous about him. Could the man have to do with her financial affairs in America? He reminded her of Fatty Arbuckle. And this memory of the doomed comic with his disastrous taste for young girls at once triggered an unease in her, a feeling immediately strengthened when the man introduced himself.

'I'm Carlo – Charlie – Mariani, detective, Los Angeles Police Department.' He produced a card identifying himself as such. 'Could I talk with you privately for a few minutes?'

At first Hetty had no idea what this might mean, until they were both alone in the drawing room and the man continued very evenly, while gazing at her all the while with his deep-set, questing eyes. 'We've been investigating the murder of

William Desmond Taylor some years back, in Beverly Hills. Could I ask you a few questions on this – I believe you knew him: you and your husband, Craig St John Williamson?'

At the mention of Taylor's name, Hetty froze inside, something deeply hidden in her past striking back at her now which she could not immediately identify. But something quite fearful, so that she knew she must at all costs maintain her composure with this herald of danger, which she did almost at once by resuming some of her histrionic skills.

'No, I never knew him,' she said off-handedly.

'Oh.' The detective was not in the least put out.

'My husband – we're separated – he may have known him, be-before we married. Directors together in Hollywood.'

'Yes. Yes . . . They were on pretty bad terms, I gather.'

'Were they?' Hetty shrugged, getting into her role now. 'I've no idea.' She was lying now, for she remembered it all then: Craig's bitter antagonism towards Taylor for stealing his Huck Finn picture; the row they had had over this at the Hollywood studio that morning soon after she and Craig had arrived there after the war. 'As I say, I never met the man. You'd need to talk to Mr Williamson about that.'

'Yes, yes . . .' The man had wandered over to the piano, admiring a vase of narcissi there.

'I can't see why you've come all this way just to see me about this.'

'Oh, just a few points – I have to see if I can tidy up.' He fondled one of the narcissus cups in his powerful hands. 'Wonderful flowers you have in this part of the world – never see the like of them out on the coast, Miss Bowen!'

'Yes, wonderful.'

'I'm sorry you left the motion picture business. I was a great fan of yours!'

'Thank you.' Hetty was impatient now – her role demanded that. 'But Taylor died years ago, didn't he? Four, five years ago?'

'Oh, yes.' Mr Mariani smiled, his clown's face lighting up – apart from the dark orbs, which retained all their ominous gravity.

'And wasn't it – I seem to remember – something to do with the Minters? Mary Miles and her mother? I remember all the gossip. Weren't they supposed to have been in his be-bungalow that night?'

'Bungalow?' Mr Mariani asked nicely. 'You knew Taylor lived in a bungalow?'

'Well, I heard he did – saw it in the papers, the photographs.'

'Of course . . .'

Hetty still showed no sign of fluster. But her heart was beating wildly now, as memories flooded back to her, so that she hoped to keep her distance then as Mariani approached. She stood up, moving easily towards the window, while he stopped by the fireplace, looking after her intently. 'Yes, the Minters,' he went on easily. 'But there was no proof, no final proof.'

'So?' Hetty turned back to him. 'I don't see how I can help you. If you couldn't pe-pin anything on anyone – surely the case must have been closed?'

'Well, it *was* closed, Miss Bowen. Until a month ago, when a hand gun turned up in Hollywood Lake. They were emptying it, dredging the shoreline for some new apartment development. A Smith and Wesson .38. We checked the serial number. They still had the records at the Hollywood police station – you know how fussy they used to be about guns there in the old days. The gun had been licensed out to your husband. And the shells that killed Taylor came from the same gun . . .'

Mr Mariani smiled faintly. Hetty was dumbstruck for a moment. But again she recovered herself. 'Well, you'd better ask my husband about that.'

Mr Mariani sighed. 'I have, Miss Bowen. I met with him last week in France. Told me the revolver had been stolen, about six months before Taylor's death, from a drawer in his bureau. One of your servants, he thought, maybe. Or a party guest. And that's what I wanted to ask you – the servants – who did you have up in the Wolf's Lair just then? Can you remember?'

'Barely. We had a Chinese cook and his wife – a Mr Chen. And half a dozen others, inside and in the gardens – they came and went. But they're not very likely candidates, Mr Mariani.'

'No.'

'More likely a party guest. There were a lot of them, when we first lived up there. Some total strangers, too. Anyone could have taken the gun.'

'Indeed. And you yourself, Miss Bowen – I have to check out everyone who was living up at the Wolf's Lair then – what were you doing, on the night of the murder? Can you remember at all?' Mariani, still gazing at her carefully, took out a notebook and pencil.

Hetty laughed. 'No, of course I can't remember. But I guess we were both at home, Craig and I. Because we very rarely went out evenings – when we were both at the studios all day.'

'Of course.' Mr Mariani consulted some earlier pages in his notebook. 'Except – I have a record here, from the Fox studios. In those weeks before and after Taylor's death – nearly six weeks in fact – you weren't working at the studios. You were indisposed, as I understand it.'

'Or between pictures? I don't remember. You may be right. But, whether I was working or not, we always stayed in evenings anyway. Didn't have much to do with the social goings-on in the valley, Mr Mariani.' She gazed at him, regaining some of her old imperious hauteur. 'So you can take it – yes, we were in the house, *all* that evening.'

'I see, Miss Bowen.' Mr Mariani made a note of this in his book. 'Well, maybe that clears everything up, doesn't it?' He gazed at her in a way that suggested rather the opposite. 'And now we're back to square one again. Like looking for the proverbial needle in a haystack, isn't it?' He smiled knowingly, getting ready to leave, gazing at her intently once more. 'A needle in a haystack . . . A shame you gave up the picture business, Miss Bowen. I was crazy about you – in *Nefertiti*.'

'Thank you.'

Mariani, at the doorway now, fiddling with his fedora, suddenly turned back to her. 'Oh, by the way, that reminds me, *Nefertiti* – extraordinary coincidence, wasn't it? – how Taylor was all set to make that same Egyptian story. Bungalow was full of notes and drawings about it, photoplays we found afterwards. Funny coincidence, two directors – Taylor and your husband – having just the same idea at the same time. But of course it was Miss Minter Taylor had in mind to play the Queen. Lousy casting, Miss Bowen. She could never have played it the way you did – that ruthless lady!' He smiled a last time, the dark-circled eyes full of irony, knowledge, some sure appreciation, as it seemed, of the truth in the whole Taylor situation. 'We'll be in touch, Miss Bowen, if there's anything else,' he added finally, rather emphasising the provisional tone, before closing the door.

After he had gone Hetty paced the drawing room in something of a frenzy. Here was something which, above all else in her life, she had completely repressed: the business with Taylor. At the time, suffering those recurrent epileptic fits, complete black-outs, when she forgot everything that had happened immediately beforehand, the whole thing had been entirely vague to her. But something had gone very wrong in Taylor's house that night, there was no doubt about that, and she had thought herself somehow involved. Dressed as a man, she'd been to a fancy dress party there – wasn't that it? – and there'd been some sort of awful row, between the Minters and Taylor. But her involvement, she'd thought then, had simply been part of those nightmare fits, a fantasy, a bad dream of the times, which she had completely forgotten afterwards.

But now, at Mariani's enquiries and promptings, most of the reality of that evening had come back to her. She had not gone to any fancy dress party at Taylor's bungalow. She had taken that same revolver of Craig's and driven down to Beverly Hills alone, not in fancy dress but *disguised* as a man. She remembered waiting outside the bungalow, seeing the lights on in the front room, the sound of raised voices, arguing – then going round to the back and coming in through the kitchen, seeing the Minters through a curtain in the front room, Mrs Minter threatening Taylor with another gun. She remembered all that now, before the shot had gone off. Then nothing. She'd blacked out and the next she knew she was back at the Wolf's Lair with Craig and little Eddy Nolan.

The papers then had been carefully vague about motives and suspects in the killing. But the Hollywood gossip had been entirely to the point. Everyone came to know how Mary Minter and her mother had both been at the bungalow that same evening: Mrs Minter surprising her daughter there, and killing Taylor for his affair and drug peddling with her.

But now, with all that time unearthed again by Mariani, Hetty had to face the fact that she, and not Mrs Minter, might well have killed Taylor. She certainly must have had something of that intention, taking Craig's gun with her. And her motive was clear enough – that had all come back to her in Mariani's remark about how Taylor as well had been preparing to make *Nefertiti*. She had been determined to stop him doing just this, obsessed as she had been for months with playing the Queen. And then there'd been that last knowing look of Mariani's, his remark about her being so ruthless a lady in her role as Nefertiti. And in reality, too, he'd implied. It was clear – he suspected her of the murder.

But was it true? Was it possible? All her new-found contentment disappeared. Evil shadows sprang up from the past, infecting her thoughts, putting her off every kind of balance – that so hard-won equilibrium which she had achieved in these last months – confronted now with the fact that, quite apart from all her other old faults and cruelties, she might well be an assassin, a killer. One person alone might confirm this or allay her fears: Craig himself, whom she thought she loathed above all people.

A week later Craig, as if sensing from afar this vast alarm of Hetty's, turned up in a hired car at Summer Hill. Hetty was fencing in the hall that morning when he arrived, lunging at the punch-bag. In any other circumstances she would have shown him the door at once. But now she did not do this. Instead, after Elly had let him in, she viewed him coldly in the hall.

'Hi! . . .' He stood there, in a soft Donegal tweed jacket and flannels, well-dressed as ever, quite unabashed, even the hint of a smile crossing his still-boyish good looks, tints of grey at the temples creeping over his darkly-brilliantined hair. 'How are you? Glad to see you back with the foil!' He seemed particularly pleased over this. 'Quite recovered?'

'Recovering. No thanks to you.' Hetty glared at him, so angry that she could barely restrain herself from throwing him out. But she had to keep control. And Craig sensed this clearly.

'I know . . .' He took off his tweed cap, fiddling with it humbly. 'You'd like to boot me out of here. And I deserve it. I'm sorry. Truly.'

She made not the slightest effort to forgive him. 'Why did you come?'

He walked away, gazing round the pillared hall, fingering objects, as if this huge space might form an ideal setting for some epic motion picture he was preparing. He turned back to her. 'Oh, several things – when I heard you were settled back here. I thought we should meet anyway – talk about our finances. I guess you want a divorce?' He smiled. 'And what about that gumshoe Mariani . . . I expect you've had a visit from him?' He looked at her easily.

'Yes. He did come to see me. You'd better come into the drawing room.'

Ten minutes later, having described her meeting with the detective, Craig said quite simply, 'Well, they can't touch us. Not a shred of evidence – other than that revolver – to link us with the slaying. And, as I told Mariani, some party guest stole the gun at the Wolf's Lair some months before.'

Against her increasing agitation, he looked at her calmly. 'Yes, but me – what about *me*? Because I remember me-most of what happened now. I *was* down at Taylor's house that night, with your gun, and there was a shot, just before I blacked out. Did I kill him? And how did I get out of the place?'

Craig, drawing on a cigarette, waited a moment before replying. 'Yes, honey, I know you were down at Taylor's place. Me and Eddy Nolan – we followed you –

found you in the passageway, behind the curtain there. You'd blacked out, one of your fits. So we picked you up and got you out of the place – *quick*!'

'But did I *kill* him?' Hetty's face was a mask of anguish.

'No, honey. That's what you had in mind maybe. But it was Mrs Minter who shot him. Everyone knows that she was there before you with a gun –'

'Yes!' Hetty was suddenly bright again, for the first time in a week. 'I remember seeing her, from the curtain, threatening Taylor with it just before I blacked out.'

'Of course! She'd been gunning for Taylor for months, ever since she'd found out he was having a heavy affair with Mary, as well as giving her snow and decks of coke. And there were half a dozen others in Hollywood then who'd have done just the same for Taylor. He was the worst, peddling drugs to all those little girls, debauching them – Mabel Normand, Mary Miles, there were dozens of them. He got exactly what was coming to him.'

'You *are* telling me the truth, Craig?' She addressed him by name for the first time. 'You know I couldn't live with the idea –'

'Of *course* I am, honey. Why, that revolver of mine – none of the shells had been fired. I checked, before I threw it away in the lake.'

'So what's this Mariani up to – saying the bullet that killed Taylor came from the same gun?'

'Trying to set us up, that's all. You see, we were suspects, once we'd started out on *Nefertiti*, since they'd found all those notes and photoplays about the same story in Taylor's bungalow. Then, when they found my gun in the lake, they guessed it might have been the murder weapon. Well, the serial number was maybe there, under the rust. But they couldn't possibly have matched the bullet with the same gun after it'd been in the water all that time. They're just trying to close the case, that's all – since they never managed to pin it on Mrs Minter. But everyone knows it was her.'

'You're sure? Because I have to know – and I'd never have let you in here today, not for a moment, but for this Taylor business cropping up with that detective.'

For the first time Hetty forgot her antagonism against Craig as he approached her now, allowing him to put an arm on her shoulder for an instant. 'Laura, you just believe me. That's all you got to do . . .' His tone had quite changed, lulling yet imperative. Hetty relaxed.

But Craig did not press his suit – his various suits, for such they were. He was happy the way this first hurdle had been taken. He was a step nearer getting Hetty back, to dominating her once more, to working with her again and eventually, perhaps, achieving what he had longed for all his life: a great house in Ireland, when he could at last take revenge on his own banal upbringing in this land, the mean streets of Cork, the cold threadbare rooms above the shop, the penny-pinching grocer who had been his father. Here, at Summer Hill, he would come into his true inheritance.

But Craig had another even more important card to play with Hetty now – one which he had kept up his sleeve for years, since he had never been quite certain of its value. Now he thought he was sure. And, in playing it with her, he would win her back. He turned from the window, standing quite still, silhouetted against the light, jangling some loose change in his pocket. Then the sound stopped.

'Forget all about Taylor, Laura. Because I've got something much more important for you to think about.' He took a small glittering object from his pocket, holding it up, walking slowly towards her across the length of the room. Hetty remembered just the same dramatically-charged approach years before in their bedroom at the Wolf's Lair when he had first brought her the portrait bust of Nefertiti.

'What? What is it?'

'Your father, Laura. It must be. Look on the back.'

He handed her the little brooch watch with its diamond-studded clip which he had found in the rubble after the fire at Summer Hill and kept all these years.

Hetty, not yet following anything, turned the watch over.

'You see,' he said. '"Frances – from Alix and Edward. Sandringham, Xmas, 1898."'

'So?' Hetty was still quite bemused.

'Your mother, Laura. And Edward, the old Prince of Wales. *That's* where you came from.'

Hetty felt the back of her neck prickle. 'How?'

'You never knew? – how they must have been pretty close friends, for him to have given her that.'

'No, never. No idea they even knew each other.'

For Hetty, receiving this gradual information was like unwrapping a fascinatingly-shaped present when the final gift was not yet visible. A strange thrill coursed through her. She felt herself shaking.

'Well, they *must* have known each other. And more than just a little, if she'd been asked to stay with them over Christmas. Besides, have you never looked at yourself? Here, look at this.' He took out a portrait photograph of the old Prince of Wales in the 1890s, torn from a copy of the *Illustrated London News* in Hollywood years before, handing it to her. 'See the resemblance?'

Hetty gazed at it. 'No. No, I don't.'

Craig laughed. 'I've been looking at faces very closely all my life. It's my business! It's there, I can tell you. Shape of the eyes, run of the eyebrows, the forehead . . .'

'It couldn't be!' Hetty decided not to tempt fate by opening the package any further. 'Me-me-must have been some quite different Frances he gave it to. Where did you find the watch?'

'Here. Found it right here, in the rubble after that fire, the day I came to see you and we went off to Dublin together. It's your mother's watch, no doubt about that.'

'Well, maybe. But that's no real proof. They could have been just friends. My Mama did the London season after all when she was a young we-we-woman.'

'Okay: the watch and the looks – maybe both just circumstantial evidence. But there's one more thing . . .' He had come close to her now, gazing at her intently. 'Which pretty well convinced me of it – when I read about it in the social columns last year: all that business between you and the *present* Prince of Wales . . .' At mention of this Hetty started again, as if, with this hint, the final wrapping on the gift was about to be discarded. *'Why* did he drop you?' Craig continued firmly.

But still Hetty would not take the final step. 'Oh, because I was a pe-picture star. And a bankrupt drunk as well,' she continued, lying now, for she had never been remotely drunk with him and money had been absolutely no object between them in any case.

'You don't think there was any other reason?' Craig asked lightly. 'Like maybe someone at Court told him, or he found out, that you were his *aunt?*'

'Me? His *aunt?*' She laughed, thinking then how it must all be nonsense, that Craig had gone too far.

'Yes, illegitimately, of course. But the same thing. And that's why he dropped you. A real skeleton in the closet. Just think of it! – if the papers had gotten hold of that: the glamorous young Prince carrying on with his *aunt!* So you see, it fits, doesn't it? – the watch, the looks, the Prince dropping you like that . . .'

Hetty, feeling herself sway, sat down on the sofa. Her head was swimming. Because she saw now how it might well all fit. And certainly it at last explained how the Prince, when they had been so close and happy, had suddenly and brutally cut her off.

Then another distant memory came to her, filling in one more bit of the puzzle. She remembered Snipe, the maimed fortune-teller out at the harvesting years before in Summer Hill, and how he had clearly seen her as a princess in the tea-leaves. She had a sudden feeling that Craig must be right – so that the shock mixed with relief was intense, as the gift was finally unwrapped and displayed before her.

'There's no real doubt in my mind, Laura. This explains it – your mother's hiding everything from you about your father. Because you're not a Cordiner or a Fraser, nor even Laura Bowen. Your father was Edward VII – you're his daughter, daughter of the old King.'

He turned away, jangling the coins in his pocket once more.

'Yes . . .' Hetty said more to herself. 'Me-me-maybe I am.'

Craig, at the window again, turned back to her, smiling. 'Changes everything, doesn't it?'

'Yes, I suppose it does.'

Craig, she felt then, had brought her another gift, greater than Nefertiti, greater than any she had ever received before. It seemed he'd confirmed her birthright, brought her finally home again. And yet, because the gift had come from him, it was somehow poisoned. She felt that just as strongly. For Craig personified everything she most hated, a whole way of life which he had imposed on her, cruelly and almost fatally – nightmare years from which she had now recovered. She might accept his consoling evidence over Taylor and his other astonishing deductions about her real father. But she could never have anything more to do with him again.

Craig had a quite opposite aim in mind. His last picture, *The Lost Valley*, with his new girl-friend Duna Börzony, had not done well. Always a great pictorial director, he had not yet successfully adapted to sound filming, where the dialogue, which had always to be shot in close-ups, gave no play to his real gifts, which were for the depth of crowd scenes, great perspectives, subtle lighting, elaborate props and scenery. Now, with the camera immobile in a sound-proof cubicle, his hands, his eyes, were tied. And all the money he had invested in *The Lost Valley* – mostly Hetty's share in WillBow Pictures – had not been returned. He, like Hetty, was now bankrupt, living on fees, advanced in cash by his producers in France, while trying to set up another picture there. But not with Duna Börzony who had left him for another man some months before. His future had looked bleak, until he had met a new producer with his own independent production company in Hollywood – Howard Hughes, a young multi-millionaire, who had just completed *Hell's Angels*, a tremendous flying picture with Jean Harlow, and who was now anxious to invest in another equally grandiose project.

Craig had met with Hughes in Hollywood. They had talked. Craig had a particular picture in mind. Hughes had liked *Nefertiti*, liked Craig as well – two men, rebels outside the Hollywood system. Laura Bowen had been the key to Craig's idea, and Hughes had immediately agreed. After all, Laura Bowen was still remembered everywhere. She had been a great silent picture star, along with Pickford, Garbo, Harlow. *Nefertiti* was still doing the rounds, making money all over the world. So that Craig, after his failure with Duna Börzony, saw the opportunity now to resuscitate his career, just as he had done before – with Hetty. And surely, with these consolations over Taylor and this vital information about her father which he had brought her, she might well be persuaded?

He broached the topic very gently at lunch. 'Had you ever thought . . . of pictures again? I mean, maybe only as the means of getting rid of all these debts we have?'

'Your debts, not mine,' she told him shortly.

'My debts, yes, and I'm sorry. But, hell, Laura, I've spent the money making pictures, not living in the Ritz.'

'You said *The Lost Valley* would pe-pe-pay all those debts back.'

'And it *will*, in time. It'll be in profit soon. But I meant a much bigger picture, Laura. Where there'd be *real* profit – for us both. I have a producer now, young millionaire quite outside the system, Howard Hughes, just finished a great picture with Jean Harlow. Got a lot of money he wants to invest. In me – and you. Something really big . . .' He gazed over at Hetty. There might, he thought, have been just a flicker of interest in those blue eyes. 'Yes, a big picture, with all the finance we want, where I could get you all your money back – profits later maybe, but a guaranteed salary anyway – which would more than pay off all your debts. That's the point. You had $10,000 a week on *Nefertiti* as I remember. Well, this guy Hughes would pay you that as a *minimum* now. On a sixteen-week schedule, say, that would be close on 200,000 bucks. Cover your debts four times over. And, even if you never did another picture, you'd have $150,000 or so to put in the bank here – put it towards running this place.'

Hetty, watching him equally carefully, let him run on. It was all nonsense, of course, but the idea of all that money, for Summer Hill, did vaguely tempt her. At one fell swoop she could put all her financial worries behind her, pay Mortimer and Dermot back, set the house in real order, be secure financially for the rest of her life. But it *was* all nonsense, of course, for there was one point at least which Craig had taken no account of.

'Look at me, Craig! Doesn't your pre-pre-producer friend know what I *look* like now? As if I'd been dragged through a ma-ma-mangle. And I have. No resemblance to that other we-woman, Laura Bowen, who played Nefertiti . . .'

'Yes, I told Howard that,' Craig came in brightly. 'Told him how you weren't the same, how you'd gone through a pretty rough time recently. But that's exactly the whole point of the story we're going to do, Laura! This woman in it goes through a pretty bad time as well. Worse than you in the end. So for a lot of the time she *has* to look like you do now!'

Hetty, at this continuously-proffered mystery, could no longer restrain her curiosity. 'What? – who is she?'

'Joan of Arc,' Craig said simply.

And Hetty, just as she had when Craig had first suggested Nefertiti to her, bringing her that portrait bust from the darkness into the light of their bedroom, felt a thrill rising in her, which she wanted to repress, but could not.

But, thinking of something, she finally did resist it. 'Joan of Arc? But that Swede – Dreyer, wasn't he? – he made that picture only two or three years ago, I remember. You can't do it again – so soon.'

'A Dane, not a Swede. And of course I can make it again. Carl's version was only the trial and execution – done as a silent, a small-scale picture. Shot largely in close-ups, with only a limited exhibition, cinema clubs and so on. This'll be in sound, starting from the beginning – the wars against the British, the storming of Orleans, you dressed up as a man like Joan herself, the riding, the sword play – and you can do all that again. I've seen you. A popular epic, honey! The whole works, Laura. Like *Nefertiti*. And filmed in France, not back in that dreary Hollywood. Don't you see? Okay, forget it all between you and me personally. I don't expect anything there. I behaved like a shit. I know that. But this'd be just a professional relationship, to recoup our losses *and* make a great picture. You know I can do that, too, don't you?'

Hetty, glimmers of all that old exciting life coming alive in her again, nodded. 'Oh yes – I know you could do it . . .'

'We can do it, honey. Only *we* can do it – just like only *both* of us could have done *Nefertiti*. Because, don't you see? – this is a story about suffering, like you've suffered. Not scheming vengeance. But sainthood. And just as only you could have played Nefertiti, only you can do Joan now. You've just lived through something like she did. I've got a draft photoplay with me. Just look at it at least.'

Hetty looked at him instead – the devil tempting her again. But again she resisted. 'And my stammer? Wah-wah-what about that? Remember the test at the Victorine?'

'That was my fault much more than yours. I rushed it. If I'd been more patient with you, it'd have been okay. This time we'd get it right. Promise.'

And looking at him, his face lit up with all that old surging confidence, she had to believe him. The whole thing *was* possible. Certainly she felt much better physically, what with the horse riding and fencing. And her syphilis had indeed once more responded to the Salvarsan treatment which Dr Langlois was giving her. The violent aches and stomach cramps had disappeared. Perhaps, as Dermot had suggested, she was going to be cured. Or at least the disease was once more entirely dormant.

Why not? Why not at least consider the idea? As Craig had said it would be purely a professional relationship. She needn't forgive him his earlier behaviour. But surely she was composed, wise and sure enough of herself now, just to collaborate with him, drawing on his undoubted professional gifts which, as in the past, had drawn such magic from her.

'Well,' she said. 'No promises. Leave me the photoplay. I'll consider it.'

'I'll be back – at the end of the week! . . .'

Craig left that afternoon, thinking how almost certainly he'd hooked Laura again.

Hetty, when he had gone, considered these extraordinary results of his visit. Change of all sorts – way back before she was born and in the future – was in the air. And she was suddenly revivified by it all. Instead of settling down to a reclusive, semi-invalid life at Summer Hill, it seemed she might be about to embark on the great world again: a woman with a future – and a father. She would move forward not in her old false persona, of course, but as the new and responsible person she now was, and therefore as quite another sort of actress, too.

Then, as well, and much more importantly, she was embarking on a startlingly fresh character in reality – as the old King's daughter. Was it true? She looked at the portrait photograph which Craig had left behind, holding it up to a mirror, gazing at it. Yes, she thought, there might be some resemblance. But how on earth had it all come about? – when her mother had been a débutante at the London season in the 1890s? But, checking the dates here, they did not fit. She had been born in May 1899, in New York – and therefore must have been conceived the previous August. Her mother, by that date, had long since finished her London season – had been living in London with Mortimer and Dermot before going out as a nurse to the Boer War. So it was then – and there in London – that she must have been conceived. But the Prince had lived just down the road at Marlborough House, so that was quite possible. She would ask Mortimer about it when she next went to Dublin for her medical treatment – for surely he, if anyone, would know of her mother's associations then?

However, a few days later, she received another unexpected visit – from a small man, in a slouch hat and wearing a rather shabby trenchcoat despite the warm weather, who had driven up to the yard entrance, knocking on the kitchen door, before Elly had brought him into the drawing room.

'Yes?'

'Ah, Miss Cordiner – I'm sorry to trouble you. Detective Sergeant O'Reilly, from the Kilkenny barracks.' The man had a soft brogue. He stood there awkwardly in the great room.

'Sit down, Sergeant. What is it?'

He remained standing. 'It's just – I've been asked to make enquiries, from police headquarters in Dublin, Ma'am . . .' He opened a notebook. 'An American, a Mr Marian. I wonder did he come to see you here, about ten days ago?'

Hetty's heart started to thump, so that once more she immediately resumed a role, detached, distant to begin with. 'Yes. A Mr *Mariani* I think he was called.'

'Ah yes, Mr Mariani . . .' Mr O'Reilly made a correction in his book. 'Do you remember – anything about him, Miss Cordiner?'

'How do you mean?'

'Did he – did he identify himself to you?'

Hetty could not lie here. 'Yes – as a detective, from the Los Angeles Police Department. He showed me a card in his wallet saying so.'

'Ah, good, quite so . . .' O'Reilly made a note of this. 'Did he issue any threats? Was there anything missing from about the house after he left?'

Hetty was astonished. 'No, nothing. Why? Why would he take anything here, if he was a detective?'

'Ah, well, now that's the whole thing, d'ye see, Miss Cordiner. He wasn't a detective. He had an accident, like, in the oul' car he hired in Dublin. They found that wallet on him – and the police card – and your own address down here. So the Dublin police sent a telegram to Los Angeles informing them. But they had no one on their force of that name, nobody at all. And never had. So the fellow was an impostor, Miss Cordiner, and that's why we had to check up with you, in case he'd thieved anything here or issued any threats, like.'

'An impostor?' Hetty was suddenly shaking – not with fear now, but with rage.

'Indeed. That's what he was.'

'Was?'

'Oh yes. The car he was in ran into the back of a cart on the Naas road, a terrible mess be all accounts –'

'But he must have come from somewhere in America?'

O'Reilly consulted his notebook again. 'No, Ma'am. I have it here. He had another address on him. Headquarters are investigating it now. He lived in Paris. Some class of an actor,' O'Reilly added dismissively, before realising his gaffe, looking up at Hetty. 'Well, now, I didn't mean that derogatively, Miss Cordiner – I meant he was nothing like the class of an actress you are yourself . . .'

But Hetty, her mind crowded out with astonished rage, did not take the compliment. Of course, she thought. Baby-faced Mr Mariani: she'd felt there had been something theatrical about him from the start – a made-up character, disguised, with those hollow eyes ringed with dark circles, the shaven head, the little moustache, the baggy trousers. But Craig had made him up. Mariani had been his production – another of Craig's lying ploys.

And, then, she saw how Craig's whole visit had been a ploy of some kind. So that everything had been untrue about it – not just Mariani, but Craig's consolations about Taylor and his idea that the old King had been her father. Craig's behaviour had been a malicious, evil charade from start to finish. And all her happy release in knowing who her real father was had gone now. That was the worst thing – that Craig had lied to her, betrayed her over this most important thing in her life.

She was astonished at the fury she felt then – an anger against Craig, which did not subside after O'Reilly had left, but became the more intense the longer she thought about it. She saw it all now: how Craig had done this simply to ingratiate himself with her again, to secure her agreement to return to pictures as St Joan – for of course, as she had said to him, she would never have let him in the door if it had not been for Mariani's arrival the week before.

Yet how could anyone have been such a savage as to impose this pain on her, in the shape of that phoney emissary, then turn up himself to capitalise on her fears, before going on to tell such lies about her father? Since he knew how she would always feel about her empty background here, this was unbelievable cruelty, Hetty thought, beside herself with rage.

Craig returned to Summer Hill that Friday morning while she was exercising with the foil, chaffing and parrying the big leather punch-bag in the hall.

'Hi!' he said again, coming in, closing the door, watching her lunge. 'Getting in shape for St Joan? How did you like the photoplay?'

Hetty paused, dropping the point of the foil. 'You shit,' was all she said, not even turning towards him. 'Mariani,' she went on with chilling emphasis, 'was a fraud. A lie, just like everything else you told me . . .'

Craig coloured, looked grim for an instant, but regained his composure at once. 'What do you mean?'

'I mean your Mariani was some bit-part actor in Paris you set up to come here and torment me, so you could get me back into pictures. *That's* what I mean.'

'That's crazy, honey –'

'No, it's not. Mariani died in some car accident here ten days ago. A detective came out from Kilkenny and told me so – Mariani was nothing to do with the Los Angeles police.'

Craig had begun to walk towards her now across the great hall. 'That's nonsense, Laura – the guy from Kilkenny must have been the fraud. Did you see his card?'

'Didn't need to. The man was real. I checked. And everything you told me was a lie: about my father being the old King, everything.'

At last she turned to face him, looking at him, shaking her head in amazement, the volcanic anger she had felt in the last few days beginning to erupt.

Craig continued his progress towards her, aiming to console her, allay her fears, then control her again with that old fierce chemistry of his.

'Look, honey, you just *believe* me . . .' His eyes never left hers, full of blazing intent. 'The guy from Kilkenny was lying . . .' He took another step towards her.

'No! Get away! *You're* the liar, everything you told me.'

But still he approached her, so that she lifted the foil simply to make him keep his distance. But he took the buttoned blade easily in his hand, pushing it gently aside. 'No, honey, no. You just listen to me . . .' His voice was slow, hypnotic.

But Hetty was not to be enslaved this time. Raising the foil, she struck him on the arm with it. But the blade slid along the shoulder of his tweed jacket and opened a weal on his neck. Gasping in pain, he put a hand to the wound, before launching himself forward, trying to disarm her.

Hetty struck from the side again, this time on the brow, so that enraged he lunged at her once more. But this time Hetty had the foil straight at him, so that he rushed blindly on to the button point, the blade buckling against a rib, before the rusty button snapped off – and the sharp steel pierced his shirt over his heart and went deep into the flesh behind.

Crying out in agony, he tried to pull the foil from his chest, before falling to the floor. Hetty, standing above him, pulled the blade out herself. Then she called out 'Jack? Elly? Quickly!'

Her tone was one of command, not panic or fear. In those manic instants of the fighting she had quite lost herself, thrown away all her good resolutions, all the happy changes in her months of recovery, regaining her old character: bitter, raging, dominant – as she stood over Craig's body, triumphant for a long moment in this vengeance.

Then, nervelessly, she dropped the foil, letting it clatter over the marble flagstones, standing quite still, head bowed, vacant-eyed, placid.

The doctor came and Craig was taken to the county hospital in Kilkenny. Later that day Detective Sergeant O'Reilly, with another officer, paid a second visit to Summer Hill.

'I'm sorry for your trouble, Miss Cordiner . . .' He was diffident, humble as before. 'But I'm afraid you'll have to come with us to the barracks. A few questions . . . The matter of your husband.'

'Is he dead?' Hetty was still entirely calm, resigned, had entered a nightmare, where all was lost and where there was nothing she could do to retrieve the situation.

O'Reilly did not reply. Instead he led her gently away down the porch steps and on to the gravel, where the builders on the roof and the casual labourers clearing the lawn terraces looked down dumbly on the little procession. Elly was in tears on the front steps, but Aunt Emily wasn't standing beside her as Hetty was helped into the car.

'Men . . .' Aunt Emily said, scowling at the motor wheeling round the old pleasure garden, disappearing down the avenue into the bright summer light.

4

LÉONIE CAME FORWARD to the wire grille separating visitors from prisoners in the grim room at Mountjoy Jail in Dublin. She had not attended Hetty's trial a month previously, though all the others had been there – Robert, Dermot and Mortimer, who had organised Hetty's defence. But now Léonie, leaving Olivia with Robert, had come over to Dublin, seeing her old friend for the first time since the events in Egypt nearly six years before.

Taking a hard chair, she watched anxiously as the group of women prisoners were admitted to the space beyond the partition. At first she could not see Hetty, who was standing in the background, uncertain where to go. A wardress led her forward, pointing out her seat, her visitor. And when Léonie did see her then she barely recognised her: the vague, emaciated figure in a coarse, ill-fitting grey flannel dress almost down to her ankles, the wan features, short-cropped greying hair, the whole impression quite colourless.

This was not the glowing woman Robert had told her about, the woman who had rediscovered herself, in beauty and true character – with whom she had so feared to fall in love again. This was someone, she saw at once, quite broken in spirit, a lost soul, and Léonie's heart went out to her, not with love but with a sudden overwhelming pity.

'Hetty!' Léonie reached forward impulsively, only to knock her hand sharply against the grille. Hetty did not reply, just looked at her with a frown, vaguely puzzled about something quite unimportant in her vision. 'Hetty! It's me, Léonie . . .'

'Oh . . .' Still the quite vacant look.

'Are you all right? You got my letter? I'm sorry I couldn't get over before.'

'Yes. Yes. I'm all right. I suppose . . .' Hetty spoke slowly, the words unfelt, unconnected. There was no real response – as if, with the grey of her clothes and skin, all the spirit had been washed out of her as well. And Léonie was stricken by the idea that Hetty, though physically alive, was dead in every other way. So that she wanted to revive her now – reach forward through the wire and warm her somehow, rub her hands, bring her back to life.

There was silence between them; the long room loud with country brogues and raucous Dublin tones as the other prisoners chattered with their visitors. Léonie had to raise her voice when she next spoke. 'Did you get my letter?'

'Did I? A letter? I think so . . .'

Oh God, Léonie thought: she doesn't know me, remembers nothing. She's lost her mind. So that again she took the initiative, more forcefully this time. 'Hetty, it's been so awful for you. I do feel – I wish I could touch . . .' Moving her hand forward, but finding the barrier once more, she turned away, tears beginning to prick behind her eyes. Then, regaining her composure, she decided on a different, consolatory line. 'Craig – he must have behaved terribly that day at Summer Hill . . .' Her voice trailed away unconvincingly, for Léonie had no real evidence for saying this.

Hetty had said nothing, to anyone, either before or at her trial, about the Taylor business, or spoken of Mariani from Los Angeles nor told of how Craig had led her on and lied to her about her father. From the moment she had killed Craig she had been indifferent to her fate, already in that vague, unresponsive state which had now almost overwhelmed her.

So that her defence had had to rest on her husband's many earlier cruelties towards her, in Egypt and the south of France, when he had punished and lied to her, bankrupted her, then taken up with another woman before finally abandoning her. In France murder as a consequence of such repeated betrayals of fidelity might well have been viewed as a *crime passionel*, with the lightest of sentences or possible acquittal. In Ireland no such worldly attitudes obtained.

However, Hetty's senior counsel, an old friend of Mortimer's, a Mr Archie O'Grady, with several crucial witnesses brought from overseas, had pointedly and very successfully illuminated Craig's long provocations, the general appalling stress he had imposed on his wife, resulting in her bankruptcy, alcoholism and near-fatal illness. Then, too, in Hetty's favour and hovering radiantly above the whole sensational trial, there was the halo of her illustrious mother – heroine of Easter Week, Republican martyr, saint of the Dublin poor, only recently interred among Ireland's greatest patriots at Glasnevin cemetery.

The court, disposed towards leniency in any case, and covertly taking this last matter into account had, on Archie O'Grady's initial plea, reduced the charge to one of manslaughter (the foil wound had been a complete accident), eventually sentencing Hetty to a minimum term of five years' imprisonment. So that Léonie, remembering this, and for lack of anything better to say, thought to console Hetty with this fact.

'Anyway, Hetty, it won't be too long before you're out, Mortimer said. With good conduct, you'll be out in two or three years – even less perhaps, on parole . . .'

'Good conduct?' Hetty was puzzled.

'Yes, of course.'

'Oh, there'll be no problem about that.' Hetty at last put a coherent sentence together, so that Léonie was encouraged.

'Yes, of course –'

'No problem at all!' Hetty was almost bright now. 'The nuns are very strict here. We even have to bath in our shifts – just like I had to . . . do years ago, at a convent school in France. With someone? . . .' Hetty's voice trailed away. She was puzzled again, gazing round the crowded room now, as if trying to locate that person.

'Hetty! It was me – *me*! I was with you then – at the school in Normandy. The Château de Héricourt – remember?' Léonie asked desperately. Hetty's blank gaze returned to her.

'You?' She was not put out, just genuinely mystified, gazing at Léonie for a long moment before turning away, distracted by some other thought, starting to crack her finger joints, clasping and unclasping her hands nervously. At this point Léonie could barely restrain her tears and had to turn away.

'I couldn't believe it,' Léonie told Mortimer that same October afternoon at his house at Islandbridge, where she was staying. Dermot was there as well, over on leave from Sandhurst. 'She didn't really know me at all.'

All three were in the pretty, bow-windowed drawing room, looking over the darkening lawn covered in swirling drifts of autumn leaves, the river running high over the weir beyond, squalls of rain thrashing against the glass. The mood among them paralleled the sad weather.

'Sometimes she's better,' Mortimer murmured through his whiskers, trying to make the best of things. 'Depends on her mood . . .'

Dermot stood up, offering Léonie more tea. But, before he had time to pour it, Léonie had burst forth once more. 'I really can't *believe* the whole thing – when everyone said she was so improved: then killing Williamson like that.'

'Could have been so much worse.' Dermot tried to console her. 'Charge reduced to manslaughter –'

'Of course! But why that sort of violence in the first place?'

Neither of the men replied at once. Then Mortimer said, 'Like mother, like daughter . . .' He sipped his tea. 'One has to remember that, perhaps. Frances had just the same sort of violence in her.'

'Yes,' Dermot broke in, 'and one assumes there must have been some terrible provocation that day Williamson turned up at Summer Hill.'

'Okay. But why can we only *assume* that? Why did Hetty never tell the court – or any of us, at least – what exactly happened that day, what the provocation was?'

'Oh, just all Williamson's cruelties towards her, as the defence showed. And, when Hetty saw him again, she lost her head.'

'But if that's the case why didn't she kill him the *first* time he showed up at Summer Hill? After all, he'd been there several days beforehand, hadn't he? Why didn't she kill him then?'

The men had no answer to this. 'Who can tell?' Dermot said eventually.

'But that's the whole point!' Léonie burst out again. '*Why* can't Hetty tell us?

Privately, at least. When she saw you both – or me this afternoon. Why is she like a zombie, ever since it all happened?'

'She's trying to forget the whole thing, that's why.' Dermot attempted to speak with some consoling authority now. 'I talked to her doctor about it all. This French chap, Dr Langlois. He's some sort of . . . "psychoanalyst" he calls himself. As well as a doctor. So that she can survive, he says. In order to live with what she's done, she's burying everything that happened that day with Williamson – killing him, then the trial, being in prison, everything. Sometimes happens, he says – people like Hetty, imaginative . . . They blot it all out, pretend the whole thing never happened –'

'All right. But what do we *do*?' Léonie almost shouted. 'We can't just let her stew there, getting crazier every day.'

'No,' Dermot responded, in his optimistic mode once more. 'Said just that to Dr Langlois. And he's going to see her, on a regular basis – if the authorities allow it, and I think they will. Talk to her. That's what he does. This psychoanalytic stuff. That's what it's all about, apparently. Talking about the past, dreams and so on, so he told me –'

'I *do* know what psychoanalysis is all about.'

'Yes, well – that's the point: to try to get her to confront reality, he says. So . . .' Dermot gestured vaguely, rather losing his optimism. 'That's really all we can do.'

Léonie slumped dejectedly. 'Oh God, it's just – I wish *I* could do something . . .' She looked up suddenly. 'Because *I'm* her past, more than anybody really.'

Mortimer glanced at Dermot an instant before turning to her. 'Yes, of course you are, Léa. So let's hope you can see her as often as . . . as you can get over . . .'

When Léonie had gone to bed that night, the two men talked, taking port together in the storm-buffeted house.

'Léa was right, of course,' Mortimer gazed into the ruby depths of his glass. 'She'd be more help to Hetty than this psycho – what is it? – chap.'

'Yes. They were close – years ago.'

'They were in love.' Mortimer, remembering all the emotional turmoil he had been indirectly part of then, corrected his son rather bluntly. 'That spectacular business when they had my flat here, and Frances found out they were up to something "unsuitable" together before they ran off with that theatrical troupe. That's obviously why Léa is rather more than just upset by the whole thing.'

'Yes . . .' Dermot turned away, dropping this topic of improper love. 'Though their relationship can't have anything to do with her killing Williamson.'

'No. All the same, you and I know, at least, that something spectacular must have happened again with Hetty that week when Williamson visited her. Frances's little brooch watch from Sandringham. And that photograph you found on her desk when you went down there after she'd been arrested – of the old Prince of Wales. She must have found the stuff about the house somewhere, found out she was his daughter.'

'Yes. But is that linked with her killing Williamson? And why did she never mention finding the watch and so on to any of us?'

'Simply because she's buried it all, like this French chap says.'

'And yet . . .' Dermot was thinking along another line now. 'As Léa said, why didn't she kill Williamson the *first* time they met?'

'Something changed her opinion about him – between the first and second meetings. That's why.' Mortimer spoke emphatically, pleased to resume his old courtroom attitudes.

'Yes. But *what* changed her opinion?'

Mortimer shrugged. 'Who knows? And we may never know now.'

Dermot drummed his fingers on the chintz arm of the chair. 'The old King,' he said impatiently. 'Something to do with her finding out about him, I'm sure. All Hetty's problems go back to him, her not knowing. We should have told her the truth years ago – and none of this would have happened.'

Mortimer grunted. 'Perhaps just the opposite. Perhaps she killed Williamson *because* she found out who her real father was. Unhinged by it in some way. Some things are better hid, Dermot – forever.' .

'I still think all this would have been avoided if Frances had been honest with Hetty, years ago.'

'Sins of the mother . . .'

'Exactly.'

'And what of Summer Hill?'

Dermot shrugged. 'Back to where we started. Place will collapse again.'

'But it mustn't.' The old man was decisive. 'You've put so much effort –'

'I can't look after it now, though – not with this Sandhurst job. And I may be posted to India. There's the hint of a brigade command there . . .'

The two men sipped their port without further words, hearing the storm rattling the windows, rushing up from the south – sweeping up the Nore valley as they imagined it, over Summer Hill and the demesne which they both loved, a place which seemed barren to them once more, all the promise they had nurtured there, first with Frances, then with Hetty, destroyed again.

Then Mortimer, still set on finding some hope in the whole disastrous business, said suddenly, 'Robert. Robert and Léonie – and the child. Had you thought of them? He loves the place.'

'Yes, but his work in London –'

'Of course. But he could come over regularly, keep an eye on it. And holidays there with the child. Why not give him the authority at Summer Hill, while Hetty's . . . away. I'm sure he'd jump at the idea.'

'Maybe.' Dermot considered the point. Then he nodded. 'Why not?'

Mortimer smiled, fluffed his beard, licked his lips judiciously. 'Why not indeed?' He lifted his empty glass. 'Shall we have a last one? This Taylor's Imperial – rather good. No? Got it from Findlater's last week. Think I'll get a case in for Christmas . . .'

*

Léonie, when she returned to London, repeated to Robert, in the same vehement tones, almost exactly what she had said to the two men.

'Yes,' Robert said. 'Hetty was in that same unresponsive way, more or less, when I saw her, too.'

In this he lied. For Hetty had been only intermittently vague when he had seen her – and certainly she had recognised him. She had said to him, 'Oh, the children's garden, Robert . . . And now all this. What a rotten, stupid thing to do – when there was so much we might have done.' And she had looked at him intently, entirely aware, almost passionate. Had she meant things all three of them might have done, Léonie included, with Mortimer and Dermot? Robert thought not, because just then she had reached forward, trying to grasp his hand, before finding the painful barrier of the wire grille.

'But what can any of us do about it now anyway?' he continued with Léonie. 'The whole thing . . . hardly bears thinking about.'

'But that's just the point! We *have* to think about it. Can't let her go quite mad there,' she added loudly.

Robert was surprised at the passion in her voice. 'You've rather changed your feelings about her, haven't you?' he asked cautiously.

'Yes. How could I not?' She was defiant.

'Well – just before, when she was in almost as much trouble as she is now, you couldn't bear the thought of her, of helping her.'

'Seeing her – it changes things.' Léonie turned away.

'Yes. Yes, it does . . .'

The thought came to Robert then: did they both love the same woman once more – just as they had all those years ago at Summer Hill? Well, if so, it hardly mattered. Hetty was quite beyond the reach of both of them now, untouchable, existing only as a wraith. But then, he thought, perhaps loving a ghost could become just as disruptive a passion as any other.

Dermot visited them a week later, pleased to dandle his god-daughter Olivia on his knee before supper. After the meal he said to them, 'Papa and I have been talking. Now that Hetty's away, would you like to take over the running of Summer Hill? Be responsible for it – whenever you can get over, I mean – and for holidays and things.'

Robert was astonished – this dream, this longed-for possession, offered to him now, albeit temporarily. He looked over at Léonie before replying. She said nothing. Her answer lay in her smile.

'Yes,' Robert said. 'Yes, I suppose –'

'Good, good.' Dermot leant forward enthusiastically. 'Olivia would love it, I'm sure. Jack Welsh has got the old pony and trap out again. And there's the river, fishing and everything –'

'Yes.' Léonie interrupted, equally enthusiastic now. 'Olivia'll love it.'

But Léonie's enthusiasm was due in part to her entirely unadmitted feeling then that, at Summer Hill, as well as having readier access to Hetty, she would be living in her aura – that passionate spirit, now lost again, but which might yet in some way be regained, returned to her. Robert, equally repressing the fact, felt almost the same thing: Hetty, not dead but sleeping; Summer Hill – an advance position from which he might better rescue her.

Hetty in her present incarceration had come to haunt them both again – just as she had years before when they lived in Paris. But now there was a difference. Then, after her callous betrayals, they had neither of them wanted her. Now, in this tragedy of her finding and so falling from grace, they both did. Both of them hoped to save her – save her sanity, her future in a world in which she had come down from her pinnacle as cold goddess to their own warm, fallible, mortal level. Ideas only of charity, of objective concern, motivated them, as they thought – hoping to restore Hetty to a free and unencumbered life, to that stance of right true character she had herself regained before meeting Craig again.

In truth, they also hoped to restore her to this spirit so that they might once more love her in some manner, a feeling they could not admit to for a moment, since once again now, as after their divisions in Egypt, they had come to love only each other. Robert, after Hetty's mental paralysis, had found it easy to repress his re-awakened desire for her, which appeared almost obscene then, like thoughts of seducing a child. And Léonie, too, had come quite to disregard that brainstorm of emotion for Hetty which had overwhelmed her six months before.

Now, by going over to Summer Hill from time to time, by simply concerning themselves with the place while Hetty was away, they thought themselves involved only in good works, as neighbours might tend a vacant plot of ground in winter, so to ensure spring growth for the absent owner; neighbours expecting nothing more than traditionally temperate growths there – daffodils, narcissi – but harbouring the vaguest, secret hope that some much more exotic flowers might bloom from the cold earth.

Hetty lay on the cell bed staring up at the ceiling. Her vagaries had changed so much for the worse that she had been moved a month before to the women's section of the criminal lunatic asylum in Dundrum, a village suburb on the south side of the city in the shade of the Dublin mountains. Dr Langlois, disappointed again in his efforts, turned away from the bunk, opening his attaché case.

A small neat man in his mid-thirties, compact and muscular, with tortoise-shell spectacles, he had delicate features and a noticeably fresh-complexioned skin, both at odds with a shock of unruly hair, thick and dark and crinkly, that leapt straight up from his scalp, giving him the air of someone permanently startled – for which he then apologised with his eyes, which were mild and kind, almost childish.

There appeared to be two quite separate people in Pierre Langlois: in his hirsute body there was a thrusting, self-confident character, limbs aggressively poised over the main chance. But, in his pale skin, the finesse of his mild blue eyes and delicate features, there was a mood of the artist, the contemplative. He was like a double-headed coin: Caesar on one side, Christ on the other.

He had qualified in Paris, specialising in venereal diseases. But, with an increasing interest in psychoanalysis, he had gone on to study the subject in Vienna, under a Dr Fischer, a friend and colleague of Dr Freud's. Some years later Dr Langlois had come to Dublin at the invitation of an Irish doctor, much taken with the same movement, a Dr Harry Craig with a practice in Fitzwilliam Square, whom Langlois had met at a conference of the International Psychoanalytic Association in Vienna.

Pierre's mother had been English, originally a nurse who had married his father, also a doctor, when he had been posted – in effect exiled – as a junior physician at the French Hospital in London, forced there by the gentile French medical establishment as a result of his so favouring Dreyfus during the scandal and subsequent trial of that officer in Paris thirty-five years before.

So Pierre spoke English almost perfectly. His father was dead. His son had not got on with him – familial disagreements largely, which culminated in his refusing to join his father's practice in Paris. Six months later his father had suffered a stroke. His mother had been taken ten years before in the influenza epidemic in Paris. Medicine in France thereafter had not greatly appealed to Pierre – particularly since it offered little scope in what had become his main interest, psychoanalysis.

Fresh fields, pastures new, Pierre had thought. And, besides, he believed English was the coming language in both medicine and psychiatry – and thought he should capitalise on his natural gift in that tongue. So he had taken up Dr Craig's invitation gratefully.

Subsequently, while working under Dr Craig, who was an old friend of Mortimer's, he had been given the task of treating Miss Cordiner – or Laura Bowen as he knew her better. Indeed, he was something of an admirer of hers, having seen most of her pictures as they had appeared in France, so that the chance of dealing with her problems – first medical and now psychological – had appealed to him.

Hetty would have been allowed books and writing materials had she wished them. But she was beyond all that now, so that her cell contained only the very fewest personal effects and was without any decoration whatsoever. For Hetty, if she had a life at all, lived it only somewhere deep within her soul – a closed mind, which Dr Langlois, with little success, had been trying to prise open for some time.

But today, with first hints of spring, a few light fluffy clouds passing across the blue space of the tiny window giving out on to the mountains, Dr Langlois had decided to take a quite different line with Henrietta. Opening out half a dozen travel posters which he had taken from his attaché case, he started to decorate the cell with them. They were French and German State Tourist posters, which he had obtained from Hewett's travel agency in Dublin, beautiful things, strikingly designed, vividly coloured: a skier leaping into the blue above the French Alps; an onion-domed Baroque church set against the other side of the same dazzling snow-peaked mountains; a gingerbread hostelry in the midst of the Black Forest; Mad Ludwig's Gothic fantasy castle set high on its crag above the pellucid blue waters of the Bavarian lake. Soon most of the walls were covered by these romantic visions, an air of dramatic liberation invading the cramped grey space of the cell.

It might have seemed a cruelty so to impose these dreams of escape on someone who had no chance whatsoever of indulging in them. But this was exactly Dr Langlois's intention. Having failed to elicit a response from Hetty by any conventional psychoanalytic approach, he had thought to introduce these posters as a shock treatment – a sort of cinema show as he viewed it, which, promoting these romantic visions of all the happy drama in the world, might tempt some reaction from his patient.

At first, as he hung the posters, Hetty had taken no notice. But when he came to pin up the last of them, Ludwig's castle on the crag, he saw her sudden agitation – eyes flickering as she pressed forward, half-sitting up, seeming to understand something at last in this mountain view and becoming rapidly more alarmed by what she saw.

'Yes?' he asked quietly, standing quite still at the far end of the cell like a fisherman giving the hook free play, waiting for the fish to take it firmly before striking. 'You see something . . . here?' He gestured to the fairy-tale castle.

'I . . . I le-le-lived there.' Hetty's face was angry now as she leant further forward, stabbing the air with her hand. 'Hateful . . . horrible.' She turned away, slumping back in the bed. 'Horrible, horrible . . .' she murmured, facing the wall now.

'Why? Why horrible?' Dr Langlois advanced, taking a chair by her bed. He was happy at his success here. Henrietta had not managed such a definite response in weeks. But why had this particular poster drawn it forth? Hetty cracked her finger joints in feverish annoyance, humped up, writhing in a foetal position. She made no reply.

'When did you live there, Henrietta?'

'Laura Bowen – lived – there . . .' She spoke slowly, in harsh, unnatural tones, like a medium in the voice of another woman.

Dr Langlois tried to remember a Laura Bowen motion picture with such a fairy-tale castle in it, but could not. She was fantasising, he thought. But at least she was voicing the fantasy, speaking whole sentences now. That was something. 'When did Laura Bowen live there? *When?*' Hetty, her back towards him, continued her writhing, hunching her knees up, then down, seemingly in pain, as if struggling to force a birth. 'A castle, looking over a lake,' Dr Langlois continued. 'But where? *Where?*'

'A lodge,' Hetty replied, in that same harsh tone of another woman, Laura Bowen. 'A hunting lodge. Looking over a lake. But it was all phoney!' She screamed then. And then, just as suddenly, she sprang round in the bed, reaching out with her arms and pummelling the doctor with her fists. '*Why?*' she shouted. 'Why have you – why torture me – with *that?*'

Dr Langlois resisted her blows, while still allowing her the satisfaction, the release of hitting him about the chest. He knew well of this violent reaction. It was usually a good sign. He had experienced it several times before in sessions with other patients – how, at a certain point, a real nerve touched, the patient may literally attack the analyst, so signalling the release of some nightmare pressure, a dark secret, a long-festering mental boil, now lanced, signifying the beginning –

or sometimes the end – of a cure. Yet he remained quite mystified as to why this Bavarian castle should so evoke this violent response. He was not left in doubt much longer.

'But why?' he asked, warding off her blows. '*Why* is it a torture, Henrietta?'

'Craig!' she screamed at him. 'Craig Williamson – we lived there, in Hollywood. The man I killed.' And then, just as suddenly as she had started the attack, she stopped it, dropping her arms, blinking, as if waking from a deep sleep, looking round her, dazed.

Dr Langlois smiled faintly. At last, he thought: reality. A clear, fierce, first admission of the real world which she had buried for months. She and her husband Craig Williamson – they must have lived in some sort of Hollywood imitation of a Bavarian hunting lodge, he thought. But he could not let the moment slip. 'So, you lived in a place like that –'

'Put it away – away – the picture,' Hetty interrupted him, not looking at him or at the poster, but calm, insistent.

Dr Langlois did nothing. To remove the poster might be to let her sink back into her mute world. 'It's only a picture, Henrietta. If you face it, it won't hurt you –'

'No,' she said urgently. 'I won't – no.' She shook her head vehemently.

'But you *have* faced it – already. And you got rid of the hurt, didn't you? – here, with me. Here, look.' He reached forward and took her arm, placing her hand on his chest. 'Here – the pain is in here now, with me, not with you. I have it – see?' He kept her hand over his heartbeat. 'It's here – and it's gone. Because I've thrown it away, too. I don't need it either.' He looked at her easily, then dropped her hand. 'There, it's all gone. Disappeared.' Hetty, at this, finally turned her head and faced him.

'Is it? Really gone?'

'Yes.'

Hetty looked at him clearly for the first time in months, her vacancy dissolving, a puzzled but intelligent look on her face. 'Your hair,' she said at last. 'It stands up, doesn't it? Straight up – as if you had an electric shock. Funny . . .' She reached forward, running her fingers over his hair with the entirely unselfconscious gestures of a young child. Then, retreating, she gazed over his scalp in wonder, like someone viewing the Alps for the first time.

'Yes,' he said brightly. 'My hair – it goes straight up. Just like an electric shock. That's where the pain went out.'

Dr Langlois – he took it from his witty English mother – had an inventive humour. And he was lighthearted then in any case. Not only had Hetty seen him properly at last but she had looked at him, made comments, exactly as a young child would, quite uninhibited and naturally curious – exploring the physical attributes of a visiting uncle. She had, in this reawakening, even lost her stammer. It all added up, he felt. She was coming back into the reality of her childhood, not her maturity. And this was something he could put to good use in his future conversations with her. For it was in childhood, as he well knew, that such traumas and repressions had their origins. He would develop, open up, this distant country. Hetty was more or less a child again – returned, hovering over a violent land, which was yet the only place where she might find a cure.

When Robert, Léonie and Olivia came to Summer Hill on those earlier occasions they gloried in the place: Olivia, nearly eight, revelling in all that was new and wild; the other two remembering old emotions between them there, initial covert affections out on the river or on the croquet lawn – affections which had bloomed elsewhere, in love and marriage, which had withered in dispute several times, but which now, to their surprise, they found wonderfully revived and cemented at Summer Hill.

So that the June airs of their first holiday there together seemed to gild the lily of their content, zephyr breezes through the chestnuts increasing their ardour for the place and for each other. The great house, smelling of new paint and re-newed plaster, doors and windows open to the weather, dazzled in the summer light – the old timbers cooling later when they sometimes took supper alone out on the porch, the house unbending with slow creaks and murmurs behind them.

The midsummer twilights lasted forever, as they sat without lamps on the steps, watching and waiting, silent or talking, until stars pricked the gloaming. Then, as they took candles for bed, the moths badgered the flames before the lights were doused. To their happy astonishment they found they had come into a new country of the heart at Summer Hill – two unique emigrants, for whom the house was a tender empire all round them, peopled only by benevolent spirits. Their love, which had been so fraught and divided a few months before, was nurtured here and mended.

Olivia, released into proper country for the first time, roamed free beyond all cars and streets and tall red buses – her fall of dark hair bobbing and flying as she ran into every distance: down to the salmon traps by the bridge which Jack Welsh had got working again, or standing on the look-out post with him over the river waiting for a run, seeing the fish trapped once more in a tremendous flurry by the opportunity netting; limpid dawns with her father tucked in a hide spying for otters, or out with him in the midge-veiled evenings as he waded for trout over the shallow water. Olivia was living just as Hetty had, years before at Summer Hill, but sharing it all with a father.

Sometimes, thinking of Hetty in her prison cell, Robert's thoughts ran along these lines: Hetty, then as now, lost to this world of fathers and daughters – when a moment's passion and sadness for her struck at him, so that he tried not to think of Hetty at all afterwards, both to avoid this sickening resurgent emotion and because, though she was lost to him in prison, he would also lose Summer Hill on the day of her return. If she returned? Or might she, with her lunacy, be incarcerated indefinitely? Here was a worse thought which he suppressed – for, if this proved to be the case, then he and Léonie might in some manner come into Summer Hill as a permanency. And he secretly longed for that.

Léonie on the other hand, at least during those early holidays, was more open in her feelings about Hetty. While still firmly maintaining her charitable approach, she visited her every time they came over, finding her improved on the first occasion, but astonished at the form this had taken. Hetty seemed a child again. She talked now, more or less. She responded, but with the confused stops and starts, the bizarre logic, of childhood, in the voice and manner of someone Léonie had never known. She spoke, apropros of nothing, of her early years on the island of Domenica, of a time when only Robert had really known her.

'The island,' she had said wondrously, 'rising out of the sea from all that fluffy cotton wool mist in the mornings . . . Then the air so sharp and clear, running through the lime groves. Robert – and those rainbows . . .' She had looked at Léonie so happily then, wanting her to understand it all, and disappointed when she did not – seeming to remember nothing of their own subsequent life together at the convent school, the loving days in Dublin, the magic of Fonsy O'Grady's theatrical troupe. And this hurt Léonie to the point of jealousy almost, realising how only Robert could join her along these paths of island memory.

So that on her return to Summer Hill she barely mentioned the substance of Hetty's talk, simply telling Robert rather abruptly that he ought to go and see Hetty instead, since she spoke of nothing but Domenica, the life she had shared with him there all those years before. But Robert was unwilling.

'Oh, Léa, I can't. There's so much to do here. And Hetty'd want me to get on with that, rather than chattering about our childhood. It's *now* we have to think about – both of us.'

And indeed Robert had much to think about and execute in this direction. On Dermot's authority, through Mr Mulrooney the solicitor in Dublin still acting on behalf of Hetty's unknown admirer, Robert had taken up on all the repairs and renovations of the house where Hetty had so suddenly left off, putting these suspended effects in hand again. For he had financial control now as well, over the various budgets for household expenses and the major repairs. And he greatly enjoyed exercising this power over a house which, though not his or his inheritance, he more and more regarded as his birthright, his home.

At first he quite accepted the temporary nature of this possession. But, as the months of Hetty's imprisonment drew on, visiting Summer Hill over long weekends, Christmas, spring and summer holidays, Robert came to forget how he was tenant here, not freeholder. Léonie, too, came vaguely to assume the role of châtelaine. This was natural, they thought – when they thought about it at all. For it was so obvious: without their practical concern over the place, their ever more frequent visits, the house would have lapsed again, decayed, lost without a purpose. It was almost inevitable, given their own growing ease and content about the house, that they should gradually come to play the part of owners, not of visitors.

They saw how Summer Hill, with its aura of grace and tradition, its spacious air and setting, had cemented their marriage, given it a real foundation, which the little flat in Hampstead had somehow not quite done. And so, in the nicest possible way, they gradually took to forgetting Hetty – unconsciously seeing how their content depended on her continued imprisonment – feeling too, in the same unconscious manner, how that happiness could be shattered by Hetty's recovery and return, when they would both once more have to confront their buried emotions for her. So, for the same reasons, they no longer had quite the same firm thoughts of saving Hetty. Rather they came to hope vaguely for her continued childish incapacity. Their happy cat's cradle at Summer Hill, seemingly so firmly held between them, was in fact a delicate thing, depending for its stability on the absence of that third hand, Hetty's, which would immediately disrupt the strings.

But Hetty, under Dr Langlois's clever intuitions, his sympathetic but insistent enquiries, was not to be so innocently childish forever. As the months went by, turning into years, feeling for her secret wounds, he found them, one by one – exposing them, often explosively, painfully, when the long-suppressed corruptions burst forth, exhausting Hetty, but bringing her one step nearer to recovery. Through these tender probings she was not to be held in limbo indefinitely.

'But who, Henrietta? Who was it you saw upstairs that night at Fraser Hall coming out of your Mama's bedroom?' Hetty shook her head, refusing all reply. '*Who?*' Again, the ever-gentle insistence.

'A man,' Hetty said finally, almost petulantly.

'A man. Good, Henrietta. What was he doing – what was happening?'

'A row. A terrible row, in their bedroom . . .'

'And what sort of row?'

'I . . . I didn't see. But Mama ran down the landing with no clothes on – down to Elly's room where they slammed the door and he tried to break it open. The man, he'd been drinking. Rum. Always drinking rum.'

'Il était soûl?'

'Oui, il était ivre mort.'

Sometimes, knowing how her French was almost as good as her English and as a means of perhaps plumbing deeper depths in her, Dr Langlois would suddenly break into his own language.

'But who was he, this man? He cannot have been some stranger in your Mama's bedroom –'

'He was – he was,' she interrupted loudly. 'He – he was re-raping her.'

'But *who?* You must have known.' Hetty shook her head once more, dead to all his entreaties. 'Who? Who?' Dr Langlois, stopping his slow pacing of the cell, sat down now, facing Hetty.

'My fe-father,' Hetty said at last. And then she shouted, coming alive with fiery anger. 'But he *wasn't* my father! Never, ever.' And now she was shouting, weeping almost, about to attack the doctor once more – her screams reverberating about the cramped space.

Well, there it was of course, Dr Langlois thought: the loss of her father, who he knew had been killed on the island when Hetty was six or seven, so that she had, for this loss, to denigrate him subsequently, make him out to be a drunk and a rapist, a monster for betraying her with his death. So, too, because of this, she had eventually come to see him not as her father at all, which had created all the later patterns in her life, as he had learnt or guessed from her in the last months; her frantic search for a father and her consequent failures with men when they did not live up to that paternal image. It was so frequent a reason for a wounded psyche, one he had met with often before in his patients, that he was almost disappointed that such a commonplace neurosis should be Hetty's.

'So,' he asked her, as if talking to a child again. 'This man – Mr Fraser it must have been – was not your father, Henrietta?'

'No.' She was sullen now, head bowed, leaving her tear-streaks untouched.

'Who do you think was, then?' She shook her head. 'No ideas at all?'

'The old King,' Hetty said at last, almost off-handedly.

'Who?'

'Edward – Edward VII, King of England.'

Dr Langlois was properly disappointed now. After nearly two years in prison, Henrietta had been improving recently, getting out of her childish stages. Now, in a typical regression to childhood, she was fantasising again. So that, when he next saw Mortimer and Dermot at Islandbridge, as he did from time to time to give them news of Henrietta's progress, he had no very favourable report to offer.

'I had thought she was getting better,' he told them that summer evening in the drawing room, the river invisible behind the heavy shroud of trees. 'More reality in her mind, more coherence in her ideas, her speech. But now – inventions again, sheer fabrications.' Dr Langlois had moved to the window. He turned, gesturing hopelessly. 'For example, when I saw her last, she told me – she believes her father was the old King of England, Edouard VII.' He was about to turn away again when he noticed a look of triumph on Dermot's face. And what he heard him say then kept him rooted to the spot.

'Well, doctor, that's precisely the truth. The old King *was* Hetty's father. Her mother never told her. It was the main reason for Hetty's hatred of her, I'm sure – suspected she was always lying to her. And she was. But we knew. Both my father and I – we were both very close to Hetty's mother when she was young. And perhaps we should have told you before. But there were – there still are – problems.' He glanced at his father. 'However, now that Hetty has told you, you ought to know the whole truth.' Dermot proceeded to tell Dr Langlois of Frances's liaison with Edward, Prince of Wales – a story which Mortimer had to confirm in every detail.

'So, Henrietta was speaking the truth.' Dr Langlois, having been astonished, had a defeated air about him now.

'Yes, absolutely.'

'She *is* improving then. But how could I? – I was so sure. Such a common fantasy: a girl's traditional father image – a King. Or the Prince of Wales . . .'

'Well, Hetty had both in a way.' Dermot broke in with some satisfaction. 'Her Papa *was* the old King. And, as you probably know from the papers, Hetty herself had a close relationship with the present Prince of Wales.'

'Yes, I remember reading of that –'

'So, you see, that's part of her problem too: the Prince had to cut her – when someone at Court, obviously, told him she was his *aunt* . . .'

Dr Langlois shook his head, astonished once more. 'Yes, of course. But the point is she has told me of this at last. And I didn't believe her. What a fool . . . She is improving. I am failing.'

'Oh, I wouldn't say that, doctor. Anyone would have thought that a complete fairy-tale.'

'Does her particular friend know this? – Robert, who she talks so often of, their life on the island together. A sort of brother to her.'

'No, he doesn't know,' Mortimer said. 'He's married to Léonie now. They look after her home at Summer Hill. Léonie was an even greater friend of Hetty's, later . . .'

'She has not spoken much of this Léonie. Though I know she comes to visit her.'

'An American woman. They were very close,' Mortimer went on. 'When they were younger. In fact – they loved each other,' he added, determined not to beat about the bush.

'I am surprised, then, that Henrietta has not spoken of her. But perhaps it will come. We are barely out of her childhood at the moment. But, if neither of them knows, how the old King was her father, they should be told, if they are to help her, now and when she is released. It would help when they visit her – for them to confirm this reality about her father. Because that's the heart of all her problems: never knowing. And Henrietta in my opinion will never completely recover *until* she knows these truths, everything that was hidden from her. Only then does she have any good chance of facing reality, of properly taking her life. It is all these lies, more than anything, which have put her in the state she is in.' He looked at the two men somewhat critically through his tortoise-shell spectacles.

'Indeed,' Dermot said. 'That's always been my opinion, too. But there have been many difficulties over the years in telling her the truth. Most particularly her mother, not to mention Hetty's own often rather unbalanced state . . .'

'Well . . .' Dr Langlois spread his hands in a Gallic gesture. 'It's as you wish. But if Henrietta is to be cured the truth should be the first, the only, consideration here.'

'I'll tell Robert and Léonie then,' Dermot said with military precision. 'When next I see them.'

Dr Langlois, when he left, was incredulous at these revelations. He had begun to think Hetty's problems commonplace. Just the opposite. It was obvious now that he had only touched the surface of her many traumas. Her mother had lied about everything important to her. Without her knowing, her father had been the King of England. She and her girl-friend Léonie had been lovers, it seemed. She had had some sort of very possibly intimate relationship with her nephew, the present Prince of Wales. She had murdered her husband for some not entirely explained reason. Good God, he thought, a commonplace neurosis . . . After nearly two years he had hardly begun to plumb her depths.

This, for Henrietta, was parental deprivation and betrayal on the grand scale – mixed with subsequent sexual aberrations, combinations both within and outside her family, that he could hardly have dreamt of. No wonder she had so searched for a father figure. No wonder she had so successfully impersonated the revengeful, murderous Queen in *Nefertiti*. It was not surprising that she should have come to kill her husband in reality.

Yet, for all these appalling mental bruises and sexual bizarreries, he saw how, in Hetty's calmer moments at Dundrum, there was a firm shadow of sanity in her, a reasonable person, trying desperately to overcome these huge handicaps and escape back into reality. Indeed, he had known something of just this other woman in her earlier visits to him in Dublin over her venereal disease. And now, with this new information, he felt touched by Hetty. Her suffering to some extent at last explained – why had these men so long delayed the explanation? – drew a new and personal response from him. She had been badly misused by her family – as of course most of the patients he saw had been. Yet this woman had obviously once had such courage, gifts, beauty and spirit that her tragedy seemed the worse, so that he was all the more determined to restore these virtues to her. Henrietta was no longer just a professional challenge to him.

5

'**B**UT WOULD IT really have made any difference to Hetty?' Léonie asked disingenuously, talking to Robert in their flat the morning after Dermot had told them of Hetty's real father. 'People are what they are – whether they know who their father is or not.'

'Would have made all the difference to Hetty. It's incredible. Astonishing no one ever told her – or us.'

'But Dermot said how Frances came to forget, to deny everything about the old Prince. And now it's so clear – Frances's life, all that violence – against the British, against the *Crown*.'

'And Hetty's violence too . . .' They sat in the kitchen after breakfast, Olivia away at her school down the road in Belsize Park.

'Does it change anything, though, for us?' Léonie wondered aloud.

'I can still hardly take it all in. I don't know. Just feel . . . *angry*. So much of Hetty's life wasted, ruined, and all probably because of this. I remember . . . so wanting to help her, in the old days, about her father.'

'Me too. Always her great theme. The tears she went through. But she wouldn't have been the person she is, then or now, but for the lies. That's what made her – good and bad. Anyway, it doesn't really change anything. She's still there, the same person, locked up.'

Despite all these theories and denials, however, this news had changed their view of Hetty.

For Léonie, the knowledge of who Hetty's real father was had given her a full definition of her at last, as if someone had finally drawn the missing head of a mysterious character in a game of Consequences.

It completed Léonie's view of her after so long, filled in vital gaps, explained so much. It brought to Léonie a whole new person, someone she had never met, and wanted to meet now – just as she had so wanted to meet her before, on hearing how Hetty had regained her true self. Hetty, chameleon-like, had transformed herself once again for Léonie.

And all that Léonie felt in this manner Robert felt as well. He saw how, years before and more recently, he had only loved a part of Hetty. Now there was a final reality to be discovered, to be seen in her, a full extraordinary photograph come clear into the light, which again attracted and repelled him.

Though unable to admit it to each other they both now wanted to see Hetty again. Admitting only to a natural curiosity in all this, their knowledge of who her real father was had stirred up embers of their old fascination and love for her, as the startling discovery of a masterpiece under a cleaned canvas, signed and entirely authenticated, will send people scurrying to view again a favourite but neglected picture in a gallery.

'So, your Papa ... was the old King ...' Léonie said diffidently, trying to catch Hetty's attention as she walked ahead of her, preoccupied, the two of them strolling the narrow prison gardens of the women's wing in Dundrum prison. Half a dozen other inmates wandered in the high-walled space, safer lunatics, yet none the less disturbed, sometimes grotesque figures: one jumping repeatedly back and forth over a minute hillock, shouting 'Hannibal! Hannibal!' – another down on all fours meticulously shredding and chewing individual leaves from a pile which had blown into the garden from a row of chestnut trees beyond the walls. The sun that autumn afternoon was low in the October sky, so that it cast a long shadow across the exercise yard, leaving only one side of it in light, as the two women stood together, backs to the wall, heads raised, quite motionless, gazing into the sun, like fire-worshippers longing to be consumed in these faint and temperate autumn beams. Léonie had special permission to see her friend in this way, Hetty's patriot mother casting privileges on her daughter from beyond the grave.

'My Papa? – the old King?' She was entirely unconcerned.

'Yes. Dermot told us.'

'Oh. I thought you knew already ...' Hetty had stopped and was gazing up at the Dublin mountains.

'No, of course we didn't know.' Léonie looked at Hetty, who was still absorbed in the mountains. Hetty spoke now in a less childish way. But there was still some strange vacancy, a hole deep inside her. Though she clearly recognised her – even called her by her name now and then – her whole attitude towards her was one of dealing with a kind stranger, someone recently met. She still wasn't *there* for her, Léonie knew, as a person in memory. Their earlier life together didn't seem to figure at all in Hetty's mind. And Léonie found this unnerving. Worse, it was like the chill of death – this complete erasure of their shared past, all that they had done, all that they had felt for each other. But perhaps these meagre responses were better than nothing. Perhaps at any moment something would jog Hetty's memories of her back into life, Léonie hoped.

So to this end she said then, 'It's funny, you know – it kind of dominated all your life in the old days. Your not knowing, about your father.'

'Did it? Yes ...' Hetty turned from the hills but did not look at Léonie, still preoccupied. They walked forward. But another young woman – hawk-nosed with some old wound running in a scar across one eye, twitching her shoulders uncontrollably – was on a collision course towards them. It was clear she would give no ground – and Hetty did not seem to see her. At the last moment Léonie took Hetty's arm and pulled her out of the way.

'Yes,' Léonie went on. 'Don't you remember? – in Dublin, at Mortimer's flat, those evenings, when you used to get into such weeps about it!'

'No?' Hetty was genuinely astonished.

'Yes!' Léonie continued rather desperately. 'And at Summer Hill – I remember one morning – you were in the old wheelchair when the postman came up the avenue –'

'A whe-*wheel* chair?'

'Yes. After your accident with Robert down those awful caves!'

'Robert!' Hetty suddenly came alive, beaming, as if she had at last identified her earlier preoccupation. 'Oh yes, I remember Robert. On the island. And Robert – in the children's garden at Summer Hill. That was we-wonderful . . .' She nursed the memory, turning away.

'What was wonderful?'

'You know – the little garden with the old crab apple tree – the magic apples of le-life that I wanted to cure him with. And then – we so made things up there! Oh, that was really happy, kissing there. You see, I knew he always loved me. But I'd been such a beast to him – I've been talking about all that with Dr Langlois – and then we made it all up so wonderfully!'

'When?' Léonie tried to hide her sudden agitation.

'When? Oh, when he last came to see me there. When was it? Sometime – lately, wasn't it?' She rushed on, seeming in full sane spate now. 'I'd been so awful to him. But then I loved him too. So much, in the garden . . .' Her voice trailed away as she walked on ahead, counting out something on her fingers now, muttering. Then Léonie saw she was pulling petals from an imaginary flower. '"He loves me, he loves me not. He loves me, he loves me not" . . .' Hetty suddenly turned to her. 'Wh-*why* doesn't he come and see me?' she asked pitifully, agitated, cracking her finger joints. 'It's been so long, hasn't it?' She spoke to Léonie, as if she were a confiding mother. 'Wh-why has he gone away from me?'

Léonie so wanted to think these words the ramblings of a mad woman, among the other obviously mad women about them. And at first she thought just this, until Hetty came to her then, touching her arm delicately, with the hesitant gesture. 'Do ask him. Oh, do!'

Hetty seemed so sane and open in her request, then, that Léonie felt she had spoken the truth about her extraordinary coming together with Robert. And she was suddenly stricken by the hurt that overwhelmed her. Why had Robert never told her?

*

'It was nothing,' Robert told her later, at Summer Hill. 'She was exaggerating completely. Madness. Nothing at all – that thing in the children's garden.'

'What "thing"?'

Robert sighed. 'Just old affection, goodness me! When she was so happy and restored in herself that first time I came over – I kissed her. Just an impulse. What's so surprising about that? – Good God! And now she's built it all up, poor woman – locked in there with all those other mad women, inventing things with men.'

Robert hated the lie, all the more so for knowing how reasonable it must sound. And indeed at that moment – because she so wanted to – Léonie did believe him. 'It's funny though . . .' She was pensive. 'When everyone said she was getting so much better.'

'Doesn't look like it.'

'No. Well, you really had better go and see her. Even if she's only pining for you in her crazy imagination.'

'Yes.' Robert, as a result of this revelation, was now not at all anxious to see Hetty. To do so, and because of these lies, he felt he might find himself in ever deeper waters. But this was true already. For Léonie, almost immediately, did not entirely believe him. Robert, she thought, with his restraint and formality in such matters, was the last person to kiss people impulsively – unless he loved them. And, if he had done this with Hetty, then she knew it must have been more than just friendly attention.

For the first time her image of Robert as the entirely faithful husband was dented. A small, cold sliver of doubt about him came into her heart then. While for Hetty – well, now there was something else in her feelings about her. She felt betrayed again by her in some way – and this because of Robert. She had a firm intuition of it: Hetty and Robert had found some special bond at last in the children's garden, achieved an intimacy there of some sort from which she was excluded.

When Robert, to maintain face, finally did go and see Hetty during that Christmas holiday, visiting her in the Governor's parlour with a smouldering coal fire beneath a large oleograph of the Christ Crucified, she was almost passionately forthcoming towards him, embracing him.

'Hetty –' She had nearly smothered him.

'At last – you've come. I've so missed you!' She stood away, both arms on his shoulders the better to see him, to hold him more firmly in her gaze, which seemed quite balanced now, without vacancy. 'I – I've be-been waiting for you. So me-much!' Her sanity shone out in her stumbling words. She cradled him with her eyes. 'You've no idea how much better it makes me feel – your coming . . .'

Her eyes sparkled – with tears perhaps, Robert thought. Yet all he could find to say was, 'Yes. Yes . . .'

But she noticed nothing empty in his tone, running on. 'Oh, when I'm out of here, *out* – why, then we can take up again, just where we left off – in the children's garden. We will, won't we?'

Her smile was so reasonable, as though she were speaking to her husband and such an expectation was the most natural thing in the world. And it was then that Robert realised that she was still quite mad – that she had entirely repressed the fact, which had formed such a block after their earlier coming together in the children's garden, that he was married to Léonie.

'Hetty,' he said as gently as he could. 'Of course we'll see each other. But Léa – I'm with her, you know. Married. Remember?'

'Léa?' she asked curiously.

'Of course – Léonie.'

Hetty seemed to rummage then in some dark basement of her mind, among long-forgotten things, picking them over in the dust before finding an object all tattered and torn, of no use whatsoever to her now. 'Oh, her,' she said, discarding the dull relic.

'And Olivia. Remember?'

'Who?'

'The – our child.' He tried to smile.

'Well, of course.' Hetty was almost bright again, before she hesitated. 'But we can't have children. I've se-something wrong with me . . .' She sighed, hurt by her inability to remember what was wrong here, before turning back to him. 'But we'll have each other. And Summer Hill.'

Then she embraced him again, while Robert stood in her arms, unresisting but quite unresponsive, so that she withdrew, first in sadness, then in tears. 'But wh-why?' she said at last. 'Why is there no more fe-fe-feeling for me? When you fe-felt so much before, in the children's garden?'

She shook her head in anguish – a feeling which Robert shared but gave no indication of, standing there mute, quite overcome with guilt, watching her cry, before a wardress, entering the parlour, took Hetty away, when Robert found himself alone for a moment staring at the vivid bleeding oleograph of the crucified Christ.

From then on, with this guilt, Robert started to nibble away at his marriage to Léonie. At first he was merely increasingly distant with her, as a means of hiding his feelings, repressing the whole substance of his last meeting with Hetty. But soon the sore of his deceit with both of them began to fester beneath the skin of his life – starting to erupt in little poisonous explosions.

He became short-tempered, irascible with Léonie, his old inner calm disrupted. Indeed, he thought – it was just that disruptive passion for a ghost that had now come to him. For he had to recognise it, he loved Hetty once more – and yet had so betrayed her at their last meeting. And betrayed Léonie as well, with his lies to her. Two entirely guilty loves now which, like opposing chemical elements forced together, set up an explosive turmoil, seeking release from the sealed confines of his soul.

At times, the pressure becoming almost unbearable, he thought to tell Léonie, to bring it all out into the open, to take his chances with her. But he could never finally bring himself to do this, fearing the loss of everything dear to him in her and Olivia. Instead, he began a fatal undermining of his marriage, transferring his own guilts, in shabby bits and pieces, on to Léonie, starting to blame and find fault with her over failings which were his own.

Yet Léonie, as regards Hetty, was not faultless either. So that, as a result of this distancing, these pressures that built up between them in the following months, Robert's guilts did indeed take root in her. For she, too, like Robert, still nurtured secret feelings for Hetty. While Robert was trying to repress his love for Hetty, Léonie had an unconscious hope that she might regain with her what they had once shared.

So Robert and Léonie were not so much at cross purposes in this matter. Rather they were both on the same path: one seeking surreptitious retreat down it, the other poised for an equally secret advance. They became in these covert manoeuvres confused figures to each other, alternating between performer and spectator, watching a shadow play with hands behind a lit screen, where simple fingers create demons, promoting nightmare dramas from a secret text hidden in the flesh and bone beyond the curtain. They started, turn about, as audience and shadow-master, to torture each other – never quite understanding how they had brought each other into this chamber of horrors.

Léonie asked him one day a few months later at Summer Hill why he never saw Hetty now at all. And he had responded sharply, 'Why me? It's you she loved. As you loved her,' he added accusingly.

'Robert, that's all over and done with years ago.' She looked at him, believing the surprise she felt to be quite genuine.

'It's never over – those sorts of emotions. You said so once. You should go and see her, not me.'

'Oh, Robert.' She leant forward in the deck-chair on the sunny porch. 'What's the matter? These last months – you're so difficult. Nervy. Is it the work?' She took a convenient side-track away from what she sensed might be his real problem. And Robert took the same opportunity to follow her down it.

'Yes. I'm so tired of *The Times*. That dreary sub-editor's room upstairs. Every time I go into it – I can hardly face them all, at the long table, all dry as dust.'

'Well, move then! That man in the *Express* said they'd take you – said how much Beaverbrook liked your articles.'

'Maybe. But travel, right away somewhere – that's what I need. Then you can see Hetty without let or hindrance,' he went on acidly.

'I don't understand, darling . . .' Léonie was truly upset, alarmed.

'What's the point of pretending?' he asked wearily. 'You have this thing about Hetty. Always going up and seeing her –'

'But I don't! Haven't been for ages –'

'Then you *want* to and you're hiding it. And that's what makes me nervous.'

'It's not true! There's no "thing" between us now. None at all. Just the opposite.

She hardly recognises me. It's you who had those goings-on with her, not me. In the children's garden!' She had raised her voice now. 'And you're the one who's pretending – that "impulsive kiss" you told me about. I bet! It's you two who have some secret goings-on between you now, not me.'

Soon they were fighting – just as they were both lying, for both had a hidden 'thing' about Hetty. And Léonie was unable to make any honest reckoning with herself or with him over her feelings for Hetty – and yet felt more and more helpless in the face of Robert's withdrawal from her.

Finally, in desperation, looking into her heart of hearts, she wondered if there might be some truth in what Robert had said. Did she still harbour any such emotion for Hetty? She had done, she knew, with that brainstorm over her nearly three years before. But now? She could identify nothing here – nothing but the dead coals of a fire, quite burnt out. Were there hidden embers? Perhaps. She was not going to finger through the ashes. But what if she at least spoke openly to Robert of this possibility, making such admission simply as a means of achieving a reconciliation with him? No. Such an admission, she felt, might well sink their boat in open sea. As it was, with both their ditherings and navigational deceits, their boat was heading for the rocks in any case.

Robert soon after this responded to Beaverbrook's overtures and took a position as roving political correspondent with the *Express*. With his particular knowledge of France and Germany he was soon ferrying between London, Paris and Berlin, covering – in a much freer way for the *Express* – the increasing tensions between these three capitals, a situation now exacerbated by the advent of Hitler as German Chancellor in the spring of 1933 – triangular tensions in Europe which came exactly to parallel those which grew in him, in his frustrated inability to sort out his own emotions between the two women who, like persistent tides undermining a cliff, had come to eat away at his own life.

Hetty lapsed badly after Robert's visit. When Dr Langlois saw her next she had gone right back into her wan vacancy and despair. And the reason soon became obvious.

'But your friend Robert,' Dr Langlois said, 'he is married, with a family. It is unreal of you – to have this . . . so strong feeling for him.'

'*Who* am I to feel for then?' she asked bitterly. 'Must fe-feel for someone . . . And him – I feel for *him*.' She was petulantly childish now. Yet Dr Langlois had to concede her point.

'But of course . . .' Yet having said this he felt at a momentary loss. For whom indeed could she properly feel, incarcerated in this asylum? 'But you must first feel for yourself, Henrietta – realistically,' he went on, finding an appropriate way out. 'You must feel well about *yourself*. And distant people cannot really help you in that.'

'Oh, but they can! Here.' She tapped her head. 'I think about him here. And wha-what a help that is.'

Again Dr Langlois had no ready answer. It was a fair point, if one were completely balanced. So that he said then, by way of diversion really, 'Why do you not think of Léonie? You have other friends. And she was a great friend, I know. And comes to see you much more often than Robert does.'

Hetty was puzzled. 'But Léonie . . .' She dried up.

'Yes?'

'Why, she's a *woman*,' Hetty had a startled look now – a child caught with her hand in a sweet jar.

'Yes?' Dr Langlois said evenly.

'I can't think of a woman in the same way.' Hetty turned her face to the cell window. There was the finger-cracking again. Dr Langlois saw how, inadvertently almost, he had raised this repressed trauma in Hetty's life – her love of women.

'Why can't you think of a woman in that same way?'

'It's – it's disgusting!'

'Is it? Why is it?' Hetty shook her head violently. 'It's not disgusting – if you face it,' Dr Langlois went on. 'Only hiding it makes it disgusting. Don't you see?' Still Hetty refused any response. 'One can love men and women, Henrietta – if that is how you really feel. And you have, have you not? – loved both?'

'No! No!' she shouted, turning to him.

He smiled a fraction. 'But of course you have. Why not? – if it is natural to you. What is *not* natural is to hide from it. You are trying to love Robert too much, so that you may pretend that you don't love your old friend Léonie at all. But admit them both, Henrietta, love them, think of them both, *reasonably* . . .'

She looked into his eyes at last. 'Yes?'

He nodded. 'Yes . . .'

Hetty was relieved, a clarity coming into her own eyes then, as if she had suddenly seen an old and well-loved landmark coming into view at last after a long and perilous journey.

'Léonie,' she said. 'So loved –' She clapped her hand to her mouth as if she had said something obscene.

But Hetty was recovering. At first, though, there was a great block over Léonie which Dr Langlois at once started to try to clear. It took him months. Hetty had forgotten Léonie, put her right out of mind, simply because, once again but more thoroughly, she needed to repress the terrible guilt she felt over her earlier behaviour towards her, all her betrayals: leaving her without a word for Hollywood, seducing her so as to take her from Robert in Egypt. Now, under Dr Langlois's careful probings, she had to face, to admit, these betrayals all over again. But now, in her unbalanced state, the guilt lay at a much deeper level. It was a long excavation.

'So,' Dr Langlois said one squally spring day, 'you were in Egypt, with Léonie. And Robert – when you were making *Nefertiti*?'

'Yes. They visited . . . the location,' she said quite reasonably. Then silence. The rain battered on the cell window.

'Of course. They would visit. You were old friends.' Dr Langlois eased himself on the hard chair. 'Except, as you've told me – how originally you went to America without telling Léonie. So she cannot have been too pleased to see you in Egypt . . .'

'No. But she was – later . . .' Hetty spoke with a small note of triumph.

'Later, she was friendly to you?'

'Yes.'

'How?'

But Hetty closed up then, quite unable to face the facts of what had happened 'later'. She gazed vacantly out at the rain. So that Dr Langlois, seeing these usual signs of a complete refusal to respond, took a stab in the dark. 'You met later out there, alone. You made things up. You loved her again –'

'No, no –'

'Yes, Henrietta. You made love with her – you loved her again.' Hetty shook her head. 'But she was "friendly" to you, you admitted that. What *made* her so suddenly friendly to you again?' he ran on, insisting. Still she shook her head. 'And if she was friendly, then it must have been because she liked you once more. And if that was the case, you loved each other again, didn't you?'

Hetty had started to weep now. 'No, no!' she said desperately.

'Yes, Henrietta.'

'All right!' she suddenly screamed like a cornered animal. 'Yes, yes, *yes!*' Then she broke down helplessly.

'So . . .' Dr Langlois had calmed her slightly after a minute or so. 'You made it up. But what about Robert? He was out there too.'

'Of course,' she gasped between her sobs. 'And that was what was so awful. I – I made love to her really only for that re-reason. To get her away from him. No, it was so awful . . .' She shook her head violently again, trying to push the memory away, to repress it once more.

'Face it, Henrietta. *Face it!*' he told her urgently. 'Keep it there. Don't bury it again. Here . . .' He took her hand and placed it on his head, on his wiry stand of hair. 'Put it all away here, let it escape.'

Keeping her hand there for a minute, Dr Langlois saw her relax, just as she had done on that first occasion with him, through this same emblematic transference, as the pain drained away from her and into him.

So that, when Léonie next came to see her, while Robert, after the last in a series of quarrels, had gone away for a month to Europe, the air was quite changed between the two women. Hetty entirely recognised Léonie now, was sane and confident about her once more.

Léonie was astonished and charmed by the transformation. Here indeed was the return of right, true character in Hetty, which she had heard about before her imprisonment. Here was the woman she had so longed to meet – the masterpiece restored. They, too, met in the Governor's parlour. But it was almost spring, not winter, and the crucified Christ seemed a wan and unthreatening figure over the empty grate.

'Léa, dearest, it's such ages . . .' Hetty gazed at her friend, having embraced her gently. 'Such a foolishness, all this time, about you. Not – not knowing you. But I'm so much better now, with Dr Langlois. Now I can see you properly. I *know* you! Oh, for so long . . .' She shook her despondently. But then she suddenly brightened. 'Yes, now I *know* you!' And she laughed outright.

'Yes. These last years – the coldness – I didn't quite understand . . .' Léonie was tactful.

'Of course not!' Hetty stood up and wandered round the room. 'I didn't myself. But now – it's going to be all right. With us.' She turned to her intently. 'And, when I'm out, we can be proper friends again, can't we?'

'Well, of course . . .' Léonie temporised, still somewhat distant, still trying to suppress her joy at this turn of events – trying to hold down the swarm of sudden emotions re-born for Hetty then, feelings she had for so long repressed. But they bloomed in the spring light streaming into the room, an irrespressible harbinger of renewal, which warmed all her old thoughts for Hetty, so that she said, 'Why, of course, Hetty. But we can be friends like that *now*, too.'

And something impelled her then – the last rows with Robert, the sense of how some long emptiness might soon be filled, a streak of her real nature rising into the glittering light – to move towards Hetty. She kissed her.

Later they talked. 'Oh, Robert,' Léonie said. 'It's not been easy. It's – it's gone bad. I don't quite know why.'

'Why? You must *feel* why?'

'Rows. And things . . .'

'About me?' Hetty asked sadly.

'Sometimes.'

'My fault, too. I had such a thing about him – he must have told you, when he came to see me here, and before at Summer Hill.'

'No. No, he didn't. But I thought – something was going on.'

'Well, it was. When he first came back to see me at Summer Hill, I sort of – well, I fell for him. The past and everything. It caught up with us. Then it all became a me-mad obsession. He did – for me – here in prison. But Dr Langlois has put all that away. I'm clear, I'm in control of it. It's all *raisonnable* now – that's his great word!' She laughed and Léonie believed her. 'Oh, Léonie, it's so good to have made things up again. And I'll tell Robert when he gets be-back, when he comes to see me again – that I'm over all that nonsense for him. And then you and he'll be fine together again. You'll see! – You will be, because it's all going to be *reasonable* from now on.'

Hetty's blue eyes were locked in Léonie's. And something quite unreasonable passed btween them then – old nature, old times, old emotion – all reborn: a flood which they could not resist, which they hoped only might support and not drown them. But they did not speak a word of it in the long silence – this love between them flowing again in the spring light.

One by one Hetty's fears and phobias were brought to the surface, admitted, released – until she and Dr Langlois came to that day nearly three years before when Craig had first arrived at Summer Hill.

'How could you have let your husband in? You told me how you hated him for all he'd done to you.'

'Another man – had come the week before . . .' She described the visit of the bogus detective Mariani. 'But Craig had set him up, just so I'd do another picture with him, *Joan of Arc* . . .'

'I'd like to have seen you in that . . . But how would this Mariani have helped towards that?'

Still there was the remnants of refusal in Hetty's face. 'That's – that's a de-different story . . .'

'Well?' Dr Langlois said conversationally. They were much easier, calmer together now.

'Another murder – in Hollywood. A director called Taylor. I thought – I still think – I killed him . . .' Hetty told Dr Langlois of the incident years before in Taylor's bungalow. 'So you see,' she went on, 'Craig sent this Mariani to scare me, so he could turn up later and console me by telling me I *hadn't* killed Taylor – and get me to work on this new picture with him. And that's why I let him in, so he could tell me all this, that of course I *hadn't* killed Taylor – which is exactly what he did!'

She continued her tale of all that had happened that week at Summer Hill: how she had discovered Mariani was an impostor, seeing then how Craig had lied about the detective, about her not killing Taylor, about who her real father was. All lies – all the most terrible, despicable, hurtful lies. So that when he had turned up again – well, she had killed him.

'I see . . .' Dr Langlois sighed. He had the truth now at last, as the court at her trial never had.

'So you see how, don't you? I *must* have killed Taylor – and the old King wasn't my father. That's what I had to believe afterwards.' Hetty bowed her head, vacant again, seeming not to care one way or the other about the implications of these truths for her.

But Dr Langlois, watching this stark depression overwhelm her, saw full well how Hetty had another and perhaps greater problem on her hands now. He fidgeted a moment, uncertain how to proceed. 'Well, we know the King *was* your father. That part was true.' He offered her this consolation.

'Yes, but I killed Taylor. I must have done. And se-se-certainly Craig. I killed be-both of them.' She was quite dulled now, careless, hopeless in her response. Her stammer had come back badly once more.

Hetty had been stricken by these final admissions of the last weeks, which she had come to face without hiding from them, without taking refuge in her earlier imbalance. Now she had nowhere to retreat to. Now, in her sanity, she saw how she was a double assassin.

Yes, Dr Langlois thought, as far as plain balance went, she was almost cured.

And there was just the problem – another task they had to face, just as difficult: Hetty's cure-in-life. She had come to admit the worst, to face it. But this had left her, as he had seen in these last weeks, quite drained, hopeless. Finally admitting everything, she had now to face the open guilt for these acts – acts which were real, not fantasies. How was she to carry this burden with her into freedom, when she was released, as she might well be, at the end of the year?

What use curing someone, dispelling their traumas, all those dark deep-sea repressions, only to leave them beached, immobile, manically depressed, prey to marauding reality? To leave Hetty like this would be to have her regress at the first pressure, taking on the camouflage of fantasy and madness again, to slip back into those murky depths where she would no longer have to confront these terrible facts.

Henrietta now had to live with cold truth. And that, left alone in her present state, could be just as much a threat as her madness had been. She would not survive in the real world outside. Dr Langlois was certain of that – not without watching, care, above all company. Of course, as he had come to see, that had been Henrietta's problem all along: she was simply unable to live alone.

But even these were not to be the worst of Hetty's problems. Robert, taken abroad by his work, stayed away from London and Summer Hill more often in the ensuing months of 1935. So that Léonie, coming over on her own with Olivia, had indeed more frequent opportunities to see Hetty without let or hindrance.

These first meetings, on the surface at least, seemed only to cement their friendship. But that did not last. Soon they came, if they could in no way speak about it, to admit their love in a variety of other covert ways: a brief touch, a happy gaze, the joy and hurt at meeting and departure – those irrepressible marks of the heart coming clear into the light without words.

Léonie, so aware of the fire, kept her distance from it, yet could not turn away from its warmth – a temptation encouraged by Robert's cold silence and increasing absences. Hetty likewise – seeing all the dangers, how she might once again disrupt Léonie's marriage in this renewed *tendresse* – took a firm rein on these emotions, quite determined that the horse should not bolt. Yet she too, equally aware that she was saddled on a dangerously exciting beast, did not dismount. Both women in their separate ways were playing with fire.

Yet, even so, things might have been saved if Hetty, one day in midsummer and feeling so depressed, had not written to Léonie while Robert was still away in Berlin – a mild enough letter, speaking of this and that, of her depression, but ending with a rash postscript. 'I can't tell you, Léa, what it means to me in these awful dumps to have you again – thinking of you.'

This, too, would have brought about nothing if Robert, finishing with the Berlin conference early and travelling over to Summer Hill unexpectedly, had not taken the post first the following morning and seen the envelope from Hetty with its Dundrum postmark and had afterwards enquired about its contents. Léonie had no alternative but to show it to him.

'So,' he said shortly when he had read it. 'Just as I said. You and Hetty – all the old business again. All the while I've been away.'

'No.' Léonie tried to bring some conviction into her voice.

'But of course!' He was sardonic. 'As I said – the leopard not changing its spots!' There was a harsh, unreal triumph in his voice. 'Well, so be it. But don't expect me to tag along with your life any longer. We went through all this before in Paris – after Egypt. And I'm not going through it again. You have her. But not me.'

Listening to this, Léonie bowed her head, paralysed. Once before, indeed, in Egypt, she had protested how this was not true, how she loved only him. And he had believed her and they had made things up. But he would not believe her again. For what could she truthfully protest now? – that she loved both of them, then as now, and that for Robert it was the same, she was sure, except that he would not admit it, his old morality keeping him in a straitjacket – so that rather than relax these strictures he would sooner lose both of them, because he could not share love in this way, as she would so willingly have done. Léonie sensed all this clearly, but was afraid to talk of it directly, thinking this would only incense him further.

'You've not seen the whole thing, Robert,' was all she said.

'I see it too well. This last year everything, growing between you and Hetty again. Besides, it's all there in the letter, in black and white.'

'The letter, the postscript, only says the half of it. The other half is *you*.'

'The other third, you mean, if I'm in the equation at all. And I don't want to be, in any case,' he added sagely, a man supposedly free of all this messy emotion.

'If only you realised how you *are* in it, so lovingly – how all three of us are part of the same thing.'

'Three's a crowd, Léa. It's lucky I'm going to Abyssinia,' he went on curtly, 'to cover this fascist war.'

Léonie, quite desolated, was left alone in Summer Hill. And when next she saw Hetty she could not refrain from telling her a little of these events with Robert. Who else could she speak to? – of something that had come to tear her heart out. She did not want Hetty's sympathy, just her response as confidante, for Hetty was that third in the magic equation.

Had Hetty been less depressed, had she been free and stronger, she would certainly have taken on this role, listened to, consoled, her friend – and more perhaps. But as it was, imprisoned still in every sense, behind walls and with her own guilts over Taylor and Craig still fresh, it was she who really needed help even more than Léonie. So that her reaction on hearing this news was to dismount that wild horse at once, to stumble away from Léonie, taking with her a further burden – this time of intolerable guilt.

'Oh God,' she said towards the end of their short meeting, agitated again, cracking her finger joints. 'I can't – I can't bear it. Because it's all my fault again. And I truly didn't mean it this time –'

'But it's *not*, Hetty!' Léonie was suffering agonies at this unexpected reaction. 'Not at all. No one's to blame. Who's to *blame* – for loving.'

Hetty shook her head violently, turning away. 'Of course there's blame – *me*! Without me, this would never have happened –'

'And me! –'

'No,' Hetty almost shouted. 'I'm the outsider. Had no right to this – loving you again. And you must make it up with Robert, as soon as you can –'

'What's the use? He won't believe me any more. And, besides, why should he?' Léonie was brutal in her truth-telling now. 'It's true. I love you and him – both of you.'

But Hetty could face none of this. All she saw then was that once more she had destroyed Léonie's – and Robert's – marriage, their lives, the life of their child. She in her madness – for she must in some way still be mad, she thought, so to let this love for Léonie escape into the open – had betrayed these two friends once more, ruined their lives and so again ruined herself.

The scalding meeting ended in tears. Hetty rushed from the room. Léonie was left alone – totally thereafter, for Hetty refused to see her again at Dundrum and Robert was somewhere far up-country in Abyssinia, where she heard nothing from him and could not reach him.

Dr Langlois, in the months after this terrible meeting, had to start with Hetty almost all over again. Her despondency, though she was sane – at least for as long as she saw him every week – seemed fathomless. And soon Dr Langlois learnt the reasons for it. Indeed, he thought, hearing Hetty describe her last meeting with Léonie: 'The heart has its reasons, which reason knows nothing of.'

Hetty, though he believed her when she told him how hard she had tried to prevent it, had fallen back into her old nature with her girl-friend. As Léonie must have done, too. And yet of course, with the men in their lives, this, though the deepest part perhaps, was only one aspect of their natures. These two women had struggled for years – in sharing their affection between men and women: two who could not determine love by gender; women who simply loved. What more natural? What better? But of course the world would not accept that – and they were forced to repress that nature – with all the consequent disasters.

But it was precisely his job to confront just such *bizarreries du coeur*, to disentangle them, let his patients live with them – however deep and grievous the wounds imposed by others had been. There was nothing in life, no psychological horror or aberration, which could not, he thought, be brought to light and dispelled. For these were the world's impositions, misguided men and women punishing others, refusing to see how their strictures were more aberrant still. And to clear all this brutal undergrowth – this was the promise of the new science of the mind. And he would fulfil this promise with Henrietta, from her imprisonment and beyond into freedom if necessary, for she was to be released before the end of the year.

So, in the succeeding summer and autumn months, he talked to her week by week, and sometimes more often – digging, listening, questioning, consoling or sometimes more forcibly trying to get her to see the innate philosophy of human life, what was tragic and joyful at the same moment – which was exactly Hetty's predicament in that she could not face the dichotomy.

He told her one day, as hints of autumn crept over the faded chestnut trees beyond the prison walls, purple-cloud shadows sweeping over the mountains above them, 'Your friend Léonie was right, from what I can gather. You cannot blame people – for loving, Henrietta. And there can be, there often is, pain for others involved.'

'But *that* is the be-be-blame then. *Me.*' She sat on the cell bed, hunched up, arms fiercely wrapped about her, as if she were freezing. But the room was warm, almost muggy, in the hot afternoon sun. She stood up quickly, fanning herself, seeming to change her suffering from cold to warmth in an instant. She was almost feverish now. 'One mustn't hurt people. Everything, as long as you don't do that. And look what I've done.'

'Yes. And that's a fine "rule of thumb" as you English say, Henrietta. But none of us is actually made that way. Nature is not subject, I'm afraid, to such morality. We are thinking animals. There is the division. The problem. Try our best not to hurt, of course. But in the end we remain . . . animal. And we have to accept – or painfully learn – this. That gulf, that flaw in all our lives. Accept it, when we have to – and not blame yourself or others for it. And Léonie's husband Robert, from what you tell me – he especially will have to realise this. We never stop growing up, you know – doing battle with our nature. Blame . . .' He waved his hands dismissively. 'In these matters of the heart there cannot be blame, for there is no law.'

He looked up at Hetty, standing by the cell window now, gazing out at the cloud shadows sweeping over the yellow gorse on the hills – and saw the animal longing in her gaze then, a bird that would fly. There, outside the window, was the freedom she longed for but most feared. For she, like him, knew how she would drown in life alone.

He felt stricken by her predicament – her closest friends both gone, her cousin Dermot away in India; husband, lovers, friends, family, parents – all that makes for stepping stones in life disappeared in the flood. Hetty could see across the water once more. But there was no one to take her over to the other side.

Yet he had to say it then, how she must move forward somehow, into that life beyond the cell window. 'In a month or two,' he said almost desperately. 'We've heard the news – you'll be free, Hetty. You'll find it easier –'

She turned to him then suddenly. 'You – you called me Hetty. You've never called me that before.' Seeing his puzzled face, myopic eyes enlarged behind the tortoise-shell spectacles, his shock of unruly hair seemed all the more rampant, giving him a really farouche air. So that she had to smile. Then she laughed. 'That's nice – that's wonderful! "Hetty" . . .' She tested her name against him, enjoying the informality of it, the intimacy which it implied. Taking his spectacles off, wiping his face in the muggy air, Dr Langlois laughed as well.

Hetty, he saw, in these last turmoil-filled months of analysis, had been brought to life again not by any of his psychoanalytic probings but by an inadvertent human word, a diminution of her own name, which he had heard her friends call her. Her nature had at last been touched by this – quite by mistake, he thought. But it was no mistake. Dr Langlois had lapsed into the personal with Hetty, his professional objectivity towards her beginning to crack.

Hetty walked over to him. She put her hand on his crinkly hair. 'No,' she said after a few seconds. 'I de-de-don't think I need that sort of release any more. Somehow, you've done it all – just then, calling me like that.' She brushed the prickly strands. 'It's just nice – to touch your hair.'

When Hetty was released a few months later, it was Dr Langlois who drove her down to Summer Hill in his new Wolseley motor. But now she called him Pierre. It was December when they drove through Naas and Carlow towards the great house. In the early twilight the cold turned to snow, a few light flakes, spiralling into the windscreen, the wipers nudging them aside. Soon the leafless roadside trees, caught in the headlights, had gathered a carapace of astonishing white as they sped into the night. She touched his arm now and then, for comfort, against the huge dark outside.

They flew down the trail between the pines, one ahead of the other, skis hissing over the snow, the pass of trees ringing in their ears. The sun had dipped over the Col Marmontan to the west and it was almost dark as they came out into the open, moving through orchards and hillside farms now, a silver-and-red-streaked aura in the sky above them, with the cold creeping in everywhere. But they were still warm, the inn less than a mile away, the lights of the village of Marmontan twinkling here and there between the pines as they rushed down the valley.

Later, at the bar of the logwood inn with its fine trophies of chamois horns set round the polished wooden walls, they sipped hot chocolate in the sudden dark, their faces glazed with heat and sunburn.

Hetty touched his peeling nose. 'You'll need some more cream . . .' She kept her finger there, before taking a minute piece of skin off, gazing at it. 'They say we shed our skin completely, every seven years,' she said. 'Become new people.'

Pierre put his glasses on. He needed them only to read. He read Hetty then. 'Yes – yes, something like that. Every seven years!'

But Hetty had changed in far less time than that: in barely three months since that day when he had brought her back to Summer Hill, when he had spent Christmas with her. Then they had come on six weeks later, he taking leave from his practice, for this skiing holiday at Marmontan in the high Savoy. He looked at the change now – her own sun-frazzled face, the blue eyes heightened against the silver-brown skin, the lines still there, small crow's feet running away from eyes and mouth, but only as archaeological remains, already softening in the growth of new life which she had found with him.

Later, at the far end of the big wood-floored room, scarred from hob-nailed boots, they sat over a red-checked tablecloth, eating cuts of venison in a chestnut sauce. And she said, 'You like that new wine – so have some. Don't be stupid. I need only smell it! The wine breath . . .'

'I don't suppose it would hurt you.'

'No. Probably not. But why tempt fate? – with all this.' She cradled her arms on the table, head down, then to one side, gazing at him. And her way of looking at him now was only the repetition of a common gesture she made towards him, confirmation of a happy certainty and fidelity between them.

'Such a day! . . .' she said.

'Such a two days.'

They had left the village early the previous morning, climbing the slopes with rucksacks, sealskins attached to the bottom of their skis, towards the higher passes, making long runs there over the untracked snow – marked only by the spoor of hares and foxes in the high world at the edge of the treeline, moving from one peak to another across country, sleeping the night in an empty woodcutter's hut on a mattress filled with beech leaves, leaving a few francs for the wood they burnt in the open grate, grilling cuts of venison, warming the bread, before travelling back next day, their own tracks still in the snow, without any others, making great glacier runs, smooth and straight and seemingly forever over the bright slopes in the winter sun. They had barely spoken in all this exaltation. And now, in their fatigue, it was the same – only a shorthand on these wonders available to them.

'Oh, such days,' Hetty said, sniffing the carafe of new wine. '*All* such days.'

'Yes.'

Later that night they lay together under a feather quilt in the big bed upstairs, a window partly open to the starry night, star bright without a moon, skin to skin. It had not been easy, the first time – making love. Hetty, for her disease alone, had not wanted it. But her syphilis had been long dormant now. And Pierre took the risk in any case. Now they made love easily. She said afterwards, '"When the day breaks, and the shadows flee away."' And soon it was morning, glitter-cold and bright, when the maid came in to light the big porcelain stove, bringing them breakfast afterwards, the fire crackling and the room smelling of coffee and burnt pine.

Hetty reached out, touching his hand on the coffee pot. 'I didn't dream again last night, did I? – a nightmare or anything? You didn't hear anything?'

'No. And not any night here. I told you.'

At first, when they had slept together, a month before at his flat in Fitzwilliam Square, there had been nightmares, a continuation of those she had had in prison and later, on her own in Summer Hill: fearful dreams, of running, but not running, of being caught, pursuing Léonie or Robert, or being pursued by them, monstrous visions of Craig. But, for as long as she had slept with Pierre, in these last weeks, they had not returned. As long as she was with him, she was free.

Pierre finished his coffee. Then, with a gesture of formal decision, he wiped his mouth and put on his spectacles. 'Will you – will you, do you think, marry me?'

His voice was calm enough. But with his hair on end, tousled with the night, he had such a more-than-usually startled look that Hetty had to laugh. She laughed outright. 'But would you have me?' she asked eventually.

'Oh yes,' he said more cheerfully. 'I don't see why not.' He pondered the idea with Gallic thoroughness, as if trying to find a flaw, any at all, in the proposition. 'No, I can't see why not.'

'Who's to object?' Hetty said. But the joke did not quite work, so that they clasped each other suddenly, in a moment's sadness, as the fire roared in the tall stove, hugging each other. But then Hetty brightened. 'My!' she gasped. 'What a cosy warm this is!'

Two days later they took the train back to Paris and from there they returned to Summer Hill.

6

T HE STARTING FLAG dropped and the crowd started to bay almost at once. The half-dozen hunters, jockeys crouched over their necks, thundered away between the gorse bushes, over the first of the hedges, before they were lost to sight in a dip of the hill. Hetty and Pierre, surrounded by some hundreds of other vociferous and rather bibulous locals, rushed across the track and up the slope to where they had a vantage point over the circular course: nearly three miles, marked by yellow flags, running away through rough pasture, over banks, fences, ditches, and hedges, behind coppices of elm – all in the lea of Mount Brandon across the river from Summer Hill.

It was the high season for point-to-point racing in Ireland. So it was a bitterly cold and rainy March afternoon. They shivered in their hats and mackintoshes as they shouted, Pierre watching the disappearing colours of the jockeys as the horses stretched out in a line now, the bright golds, reds and blues of the racing pullovers strung over the sodden grey landscape like a vivid beaded necklace.

'Come on, Nickelodeon!' Pierre shouted. He had backed this grey mare, ten shillings on, to win. But at ten to one it was almost the rank outsider. 'How is she doing?' he asked Hetty, who had the binoculars.

'It's nowhere,' she told him happily. 'It's last! My horse is second,' she added with sweet malice.

'Here, let me see – give me the glasses!' She handed them over. '*Mon Dieu!* It *is* last.' The horses were making a gradual circle now, disappearing behind slopes and spinneys, before re-emerging. 'And your horse, Mooncoin, is third. Come on, Nickelodeon,' he shouted despairingly. Hetty took the glasses back.

'No hope, Pierre. I told you – an old mare.'

The horses disappeared again for half a minute. But, turning into the home stretch, when they came in sight once more, Hetty saw there were only three horses left in the race. At the last hedge before a ditch, Nickelodeon, to her astonishment, was leading, with Mooncoin nowhere. Then the mare, tiring, stumbled on the far side, landing awkwardly – and the other two horses passed her. But, recovering wonderfully, Nickelodeon made ground in the last few furlongs, overtook the second horse and was only beaten to the post by a length.

'See, I told you!' Hetty said, breathless with excitement and happy now at Pierre's justified choice of a nag. 'If only you'd backed it *both* ways. Then you'd have had your money back – and some winnings!' She tore up her own betting slip.

'Each way? – I don't understand you.'

'Yes – you back it to win, or for a place, second or third. You don't have to go for bust on every race, like I told you.'

'"Go for bust"?'

'Yes – I mean risk everything on a win.'

'Well, why not?' he asked, putting his spectacles on, looking at her.

'Because a clever gambler hedges his bets . . .'

'"Hedges his bets"?'

'Yes, you idiot! That means you do things *both* ways, to cover possible losses.'

'Oh? Why should I do that?'

'It's safer, that's why. You can get to keep your money that way.'

'I'd prefer to "go for bust".' He smiled, taking his glasses off, blurred with raindrops now, and then his tweed cap which had come to perch dangerously on top of his unruly hair.

He looked naked. Hetty could have kissed him. Instead she said tenderly, chanting her mocking tones, humbled by her feelings for this humble man, 'Well, all right. But you can tear your betting ticket up now as well.'

Responding suddenly, he tore it with a dramatic flourish, then threw the pieces in the air, laughing, as the tiny bits of coloured cardboard span away like confetti in the squally wind.

Across the river they could see the bare winter trees around Summer Hill, the house itself, with an inviting curl of smoke rising from a chimney, visible behind.

'It'll be dark soon.' Hetty shivered in her mackintosh. 'Only one more race anyway. Teatime? There's fruit cake. Elly made it specially for you – and strong tea,' she added with exaggerated relish. 'Strong enough to trot a mouse across . . .'

'What? A mouse in the tea? What is –'

'Just an expression. Irish . . .'

She took his arm and they went back to the car. It stuck in the muddy gateway as they were leaving. But a big carthorse was on hand for just such eventualities, pulling them out with ropes.

'Ireland, indeed,' Pierre said, rather morose behind the wheel. It had started to rain in earnest now. 'Strange being pulled by a horse – in my new Wolseley . . .'

'It's wonderful,' Hetty said as they moved sluggishly forward.

'Yes. Yes, I suppose it is.'

And it was, for both of them in the ensuing months, when spring and summer came – great deep drifts of daffodils spreading over the lawn, followed by the high green of the chestnuts in early June round the edge of the demesne.

Hetty recovered herself once more at Summer Hill. Pierre came down from

Dublin every weekend. Elly and Jack Welsh took to him – seeing not only how he was Hetty's cure, but now her friend – and more than that perhaps. They had separate bedrooms, for propriety – Pierre along the landing from Hetty's primrose room. But late at night he came to her, leaving at dawn, before Elly brought Hetty a cup of tea at eight.

Aunt Emily still occupied her bedroom-studio. But at over seventy she was finally frail. Age, stalking her in the last years, had suddenly taken her by surprise, bowing her head, withering her neck and leg muscles, so that she stayed indoors mostly, working at her immemorial sketchbooks, drawing and painting from the memory of things. Sometimes, on a fine day, she would go out in the wicker wheelchair, Hetty pushing her down the avenue and back.

'So,' Aunt Emily said one brilliant June morning. 'You've taken up with men again. I'd have thought you'd have learnt your lesson there.' She was grumpy, sitting under a patchwork quilt rug.

'Yes. But not men. A man. Pierre.'

Aunt Emily sighed. 'All the same. There's no teaching you, is there?'

'Yes, there is! I've learnt. Pierre is a good man.'

'Oh, they all make themselves out to be that. Clever that way, you know. But just look at you – with men. Taken in by every one of them.'

Hetty laughed. 'No, Aunt Emily. One can be lucky, you know. At last.'

Aunt Emily humphed. 'Here – stop here. Give me the sketchbook.' She raised a gnarled, arthritic hand from beneath the rug. Hetty handed her the Combridge's sketchbook and a big carpenter's pencil. Aunt Emily put the pad on her lap, holding the pencil awkwardly. But she could still move it about the paper deftly, almost at once finding the essence of the sketch, filling in the rough outlines, as Hetty watched over her shoulder.

'What is it, Aunt Emily? What are you looking at? There's nothing there.'

They had stopped at the first of the white gates, near the house, with tall chestnut trees to either side. Aunt Emily had drawn one of the trees. And now she was sketching something in the branches. Soon Hetty saw what it was – a tree house high up among the leaves, with a little pagoda roof, all in the Chinese manner. And inside it, soon emerging, Hetty saw two figures – a man and a woman. One was obviously her, the other, with a shock of dark hair sticking up like a crop of bad thatch, was Pierre.

'What is it? Why are we up there?'

'Excuse yourself, girl. Men . . . It's all a childish game, don't you see? Playing houses.'

'But why is it a *Chinese* house?'

'Oh, it's *fun* – while it lasts.'

For Léonie and Robert meanwhile things had not lasted. They had come to the beginning of the end. Robert had spent months away reporting Mussolini's war in

Abyssinia and when he returned to London late the previous year he and Léonie had not managed to make things up. Léonie had tried – vaguely. But she was depressed and bitter over many things: his lack of communication with her ('How could I? – there were no posts out of Addis Ababa'), but for a few messages passed on to her and Olivia from the *Express* newsroom – while her break-up with Hetty continued to hurt, to obsess her.

She felt deeply that both Robert and Hetty had let her down. She was sullen, unforthcoming, on Robert's return. What was the use of explaining things to him, she thought? He had gone from her, in body, but much more in spirit. What was there to explain that wouldn't appear either self-justificatory or give him further ammunition against her?

Nonetheless she was honest enough and still at that point just sufficiently anxious to make things up with him, to tell him how her relationship with Hetty had come to an end.

He seemed unconcerned. 'Well, it was all a crazy thing from the beginning. I'm not surprised.'

'It came to an end because she didn't want to break things up between you and me,' she said dully.

'No doubt. But you love her. You love women. What use is that – for our marriage?'

'You loved her, too.'

He shrugged. 'A long time ago.'

'In Summer Hill as well, last year. She told me.'

He poured some more coffee. They were having breakfast. Olivia, at a boarding school now in Kent, was not with them – due back for the Christmas holidays in a few days' time. 'Summer Hill,' he said, sipping his coffee. 'Yes. But that was impulsive. I told you. A passing thing. And it's not my nature, to love *men*. That's the crucial difference.'

'I wouldn't have minded, if that were the case.'

'No. But that's the whole point. We're built differently. And I do mind. Anyway . . .' He remained aloof. 'There's Olivia. I'll pick her up in Maidstone. There's Christmas. Let's make the best of it.'

There was silence until Léonie said, 'Robert, what is it that's got into you? You were never really like this. Okay, we have these differences. But for you to be so *cold*, impersonal, unconcerned.'

He stood up, draining his cup. 'The war, maybe. Ethiopians strung up with piano wire in the main square in Addis. Or flung from aeroplanes, alive, and finding them spattered about in the valleys.'

'Yes, but to be so hard as this, now that you're home –'

'Well –'

'It's so much not you!' She was her old concerned self again for a moment. 'This time last year – we were happy, going to Summer Hill for Christmas . . .'

He turned to her bitterly. 'I loved Summer Hill. That was my home. Don't you see?'

'Well, yes, I *do* see. But we both knew Hetty was going to be free one day, that she'd take over again there. And if only you'd been a bit more understanding about all of us . . .' Léonie had started to shake with suppressed anger. 'You wouldn't have lost Summer Hill. And nor would I. And I love it, too.'

'Well . . .' Robert had no real answer.

And this was exactly what made him hard. He had lost Summer Hill because of his own intransigent attitude – a fine nature become bitter and self-righteous because of his inability to share Léonie with Hetty. Had he been able to yield on this, the prize would have been Summer Hill – and the two women. But to these ends he could not sacrifice what he saw as a paramount morality. And so he had to be hard – to defend the stockade he had set up to protect himself against his own, and the other two women's, marauding nature.

So, too, the real reason for Léonie's lack of ardour in regaining him – her creeping dislike for him indeed – was that she saw all this in quite a different way: how for the sake of dull principle, as she viewed it, he had wrecked their marriage, lost them both Summer Hill and Hetty as well. And, since she was angry then at his inability to admit anything of this, she told him as much.

'You know the *real* reason for your coldness, Robert? It's not the war, or my loving Hetty – but simply that you can't relax, over your real nature, or mine, for we *both* love Hetty. If you could just stop playing dog-in-the-manger – you could have Summer Hill. And me. And her. Your principles are killing you.'

He left for the *Express* office without another word.

And Léonie was able to confirm her thoughts on Robert then. It had not been Hetty who had destroyed their marriage. It had been Robert with his unyielding nature. What Robert had as a strength in his character, Léonie could only see as weakness. It was something which he must always have possessed, she thought. Before, she had seen this only as a rather stuffy European sense of duty, something which had amused her, even endeared him to her. But, now that it had so destroyed things between them all, she could only abhor this in him. It was not now a sense of honour which he harboured, as she had earlier seen it. It was a façade, hiding an essential immaturity, an inability to adapt, sheer jealous childishness. Whereas she at last fully admitted her own divided nature, and was prepared to face and grow with it, Robert, the child, could not do this.

Robert's charm, balance and good sense had been destroyed, she thought, by this fatal weakness, this intransigence in his soul preventing him from seeing the real nature of living, loving and giving. So, after he had left that morning, she believed she might better survive without him – better swim alone than sink with a wounded man, pulling her down.

Yet Léonie in all this failed to see the truth, just as Robert had. Anger, hurt and high emotion had blinded them. For they were both of them, in their opposing attitudes, entirely true to their natures. Robert's beliefs were not a weakness. They were the product of his old-fashioned Victorian background and a temperament that happened to match this. And so were Léonie's beliefs – moulded by her father's always very liberal ethics, her own sexual characteristics, her modern and relaxed view of things. Robert would and could not for a moment give substance to the animal in him, to what he saw as aberrant. Léonie could not accept this denial in him of what to her was entirely natural. They both remained, according to their lights, honourable people. Their incompatibility lay in their strengths, not in their weaknesses.

So that their separation, when it came a few months later, was all the more tragic – two people who, through their hurt, could no longer see the virtues in each other. And perhaps it was hearing of Hetty's marriage to Pierre in that summer of 1937 which brought about the final rupture between them.

Hetty and Pierre were married in France at a civil ceremony outside Paris, at the Mairie of the village of Saint-Germain-en-Laye, where Pierre had relations, cousins of his, who lived in a small *manoir* there. Hetty had told only her most immediate circle of her plans. But some of the French press got wind of the event the day before the wedding, and a paragraph on it came through on the tape from Agence-France-Presse to the *Express* newsroom in London where Robert, checking through that day's news from France, spotted the item: 'Mlle. Henrietta Cordiner, qui était autrefois la vedette fabuleuse Hollywoodienne Laura Bowen, fut mariée hier à Docteur Pierre Langlois, à Saint-German-en-Laye . . .'

He told Léonie when he saw her that night. She barely responded. She had been busy arranging their summer holiday. She and Olivia were going to Paris first for a few days, visiting her father who still lived in the old house in Passy, before all three of them went on for a month to the seaside, where they had rented a villa near Carteret in Normandy. Robert, who had conferences and interviews throughout most of the summer, in Paris, Rome and Berlin, was to join them there as and when he could.

'So,' Robert continued rather sourly that evening, 'you won't have to worry about Hetty any more . . .' Again Léonie made no real reply. And they left it at that.

But Léonie no longer saw the pretty gingerbread villa above the cliffs over the beach which they had rented once before; she could not remember the details of picking Olivia up the following day from the school in Kent – had no mind for all the other business of tickets and travel. She saw only Hetty – a sudden sharp vision: the slant of blue eyes, the particular smile, shy yet audacious, the run of lips, a face she had kissed. All this now quite lost to her. Then she saw Robert standing in the kitchen doorway, a hint of triumph on his face. And she thought afterwards, journeying to Paris with Olivia, how it was just then, as he stood in the kitchen doorway, that she had ceased to love him.

Hetty meanwhile crossed over the Channel on that same day, but in the opposite direction, returning with Pierre to Summer Hill, while Robert a day later took the train to Berlin – and the day after Léonie and the other two made the journey north-west to Carteret. Each of them travelled in a quite different direction, all three of their lives now irretrievably broken and separate.

And, because this was so painful a thought to them, they took care not to think about it. Léonie exhausted herself in holiday activities with Olivia and Ben Straus, her father. Robert pursued his featured news stories throughout Europe that summer with incessant attack – while Hetty buried any thoughts she had of the other two by throwing herself, with Pierre's active help and money, into the life of Summer Hill, once more starting to redecorate and repair all that she had had to abandon there six years before. A proper bathroom was at last installed and electric light finally brought to the house, by means of a windcharger, a tall metal pylon set on top of the hill beyond the orchard, a sinister whirring device as she thought it, so that she was secretly pleased when it broke down, as it quite often did, and they had to return to oil and candlelight.

These frenetic activities successfully held the past at bay for all three of them. And then, as the months went by, they began to bury it, like the ruins of a lost city, which started to sink below ground, overlaid by layer upon layer of current life, the detritus of time, expunging the memory of that once-fabulous civilisation all three had shared in. The past, which had indeed been merely sleeping between them all, now seemed quite dead.

But, as an archaeologist can see in the vague ridges of a grassy hillock the lines of old walls and buildings far beneath, there emerged a vibrancy sometimes, emanating from somewhere, which brought the three of them back to each other when they least expected it.

At odd moments in the following months, years, they were linked in this way – a sudden spirit arriving in a room or from an open sky, making its presence felt as a spine-pricking air wafting through a closed door or an odour of violets in midwinter, which would immediately bring one or other of them together again, in that sealed room or frozen solstice of the year. The ghosts of their former selves walked, meeting across the ether, each wraith identifying the other in their old manner.

One autumn evening, when the windcharger had failed again, Hetty was lighting a tall oil standard lamp in the airless drawing room at Summer Hill. Her eye caught by some movement, she looked over at the small drum table some distance from her. On it the zoetrope, the magic wheel of life, was moving slowly, the strip of coloured paper inside beginning to animate the cow jumping over the moon. And then she thought of Léonie.

The memory was startlingly clear, though she had quite forgotten about it in the intervening years. She and Léonie had been sitting there, next to the same small drum table, years before, Léonie reading *Middlemarch* to her, while she sat in the wheelchair after her accident in the caves, spinning the same wheel of life, repelled, yet attracted by the moving images, which had seemed to beckon her, away from Léonie, her future staring at her somehow in that wilful machine.

Robert, walking alone one evening along the Unter den Linden in Berlin, was suddenly assailed not by the smell of lime trees in blossom, but by an odour of violets, almost sickly-sweet, so that he hurried on, as if pursued by some horror.

Léonie, standing on the porch of the villa above the beach at Carteret in the dazzling sunlight on the last day of the holiday, suddenly thought she heard a voice behind her, so that she swung round. The voice said, 'Hello! What on earth are you doing here?' The tones were unmistakable. It was Hetty's voice; Hetty, inside the villa soon to emerge and welcome her on the porch, as if they were about to begin everything again.

All three of them immediately re-buried these vivid intimations of each other, like undertakers returning to a grave, secretly at night, determined now to do the job properly, to hammer longer nails into the coffin of their past, prevent any further release of these tormented spirits.

Dermot returned from India on leave that December in 1937, staying first with his father at Islandbridge, before both of them came down to Summer Hill for Christmas. Mortimer, at eighty-four, with painful arthritis and a touch of gout, was a little feeble, so that he, rather than Aunt Emily, sometimes used the wheelchair in the house and down the front drive. But his mind – and his great beard – were both as stately as ever.

All five of them celebrated Christmas with dinner in the great dining room. Though Aunt Emily, her moods ever more bizarre, insisted she ate separately, having a small round table to herself, set next to Hetty, sitting there with her back turned to the company, apparently intent only on her private *dégustation*, but in fact, like a nosey-parker in a café, eavesdropping sharply on everything that passed at the main table.

The dining room had at last been redecorated, a dozen Cordiner ancestors cleaned in their portraits. These gallants, more gallant still in the flickering light from the great candelabra on either sideboard, seemed poised to launch themselves from their wire trapezes hanging from the picture rails. The ceiling bas-reliefs, already gilt, were yet more golden: risen angels, swaying vines, soaring strings – all starting to sail across the oval blue which was their usually windless empyrean, seemingly stirred now by the candle flames far below them. What was shadowy and inanimate on the walls and ceiling came to life in rising waves of light, breathing motion into this lifeless art, returning the room to all its old familial vivacity – bonds of blood, elegance and wit, a calm certainty in the order of some heavenly host.

Elly had done a splendid turkey and a flaming plum pudding; and, when this last arrived, Pierre had raised his glass to her, proposing a toast. Elly, in her long white apron, blushed.

Later, when port and nuts were passed round and some crackers pulled, Mortimer, in a funny paper hat, turned to Hetty. 'Thank God women don't have to leave the room these days, least not with us . . .' He gazed at her. Hetty, in a dark, loose-flowing Paisley dress, with her amethyst pendant earrings, looked back at him fondly. 'Without you, Hetty, none of us would be here now.' He raised his glass to her. 'To your return to Summer Hill – to your most happy and welcome return . . .' Then, gesturing his glass towards the portraits, he added, 'Among your ancestors.'

And it seemed that these Cordiner grandees responded to the toast, drawing life from the flowering light, the wine's breath; that the presence of these five people raising their glasses – for even Aunt Emily joined in this toast – had revivified them in their gleaming colours, their white cravats, stiff gilded coats and breeches, wigs and rouged cheeks.

Mortimer, encouraged by the port, went on. 'I remember a great dinner party here at this same table – oh, it must be forty years ago now, with your grandmother, Hetty – old Sir Desmond and Sarah, Henry, Eustace, your mother Frances – and Humphrey Saunders, that theatrical rogue who was such a friend to us all. And Bunty and Austin . . .' He seemed to half-raise his glass as he spoke, acknowledging if not toasting the memory of all these Cordiners dead and gone, while the table remained silent. 'All the women left the room, of course, with the port, and we started to talk of Home Rule . . .' Mortimer smiled, then cleared his throat. 'Or rather I must have started it. None of the men – except Humphrey of course – had the least idea of what was upon them in Ireland – that Home Rule was inevitable and would come soon or else come violently. I told them so. And it did both . . .' He looked about him with as much awe as his patrician features allowed. 'So that I never thought to sit here again like this – among Cordiners. With all those other Cordiners.' He tipped his glass in their direction. 'Yet here we are!' He brightened. 'By the grace of God – for whom I can't say I've ever had an over-abundance of time. Nonetheless, he must have had a hand in this. But may I say, if I be not struck down in the saying, that the bigger hand is yours, Hetty, and you with Pierre.' He turned to the doctor, then back to Hetty. 'Let me honour your fortitude, in survival – and simply your being here this Christmas, and many more to come.'

They drank her health.

'Th-th-thank you . . .' Hetty was nervous. 'Thank you all. I se-se-survived only because of all of you here, no other reason.'

And then, having raised her glass to them in return, Hetty, quite inadvertently it seemed, raised her glass once more, offering the traditional Christmas toast. 'To absent friends,' she said.

One of the candles started to gutter and complete silence returned. Silence, for there was nothing anyone cared to say about these absent friends – and enemies – dead or alive, or in the family portraits, all of whom, taking their cue, spirited themselves into the room then, invading the silence, like latecomers gate-crashing the feast, the welcome and unwelcome together, seeking their rights, to share in this living toast, to answer it in their own coin; to reprimand the present company, to plead their case, to justify, explain, redeem or just to express their love again, of all that they had once loved in this great house – speaking from whatever distance or tomb they occupied, calling voicelessly from afar or from the Cordiner vault in the little family church over the river, actors in a passionate dumb crambo condemned to wander forever, seeking their true theatre, which was here at Summer Hill, among these other living Cordiners.

The following evening, on Boxing Day, Hetty, renewing the old custom at Summer Hill, had invited Jack and Elly, together with the new maid Bridget and the half-dozen other people of the village who were now working again on the estate, with their families, to take their presents from the tall Christmas tree set up in the great hall. She and Dermot, with a step-ladder, had been preparing the tree for the last half-hour. And now, half-way up the steps, Dermot started to light the candles one by one about the tall fir. Soon, the candles all lit, the hall began to smell of warmed pine and burnt wax, a smell that Hetty so remembered from her childhood here. So that when Dermot came down from the ladder she took his hand involuntarily.

'What?' he asked.

'Just all this! Can't believe it. All . . . How much! – returned to me.'

'But it's yours, Hetty. Always had been.'

'No. I lost it all. You know very well. All this: the gift of some "admirer".'

'Yes . . .'

'Some rich fan. But who, Dermot? Who, I've often wondered. Do you think Mr Mulrooney could ever be got to tell?'

'No.' Then Dermot, deciding on something, changed his tack. 'But I've had my ideas – and why shouldn't you know them now? Now that you're settled.'

'Oh, do tell!' Hetty was all enthusiasm.

'I – I can only think it must have been your friend David, seven or eight years ago, when he was Prince of Wales – before the abdication.'

Hetty's face clouded suddenly. 'David? But why?'

'Making amends. For his grandfather. And his behaviour to you.'

Hetty's face, lit by the myriad flickering candles, was ghostly bright now, a mix of awe and hurt. 'You *think* so?' The candles stirred in some faint breath coming down the stairway.

'I can't think who else. He would have had the motive, above all the need – once he'd been told who you were, as somebody must have done – remembering how he'd had to treat you then, dropping you completely. And with his impulsive nature – it's just the sort of gesture he'd have made. I feel it.' He looked at Hetty. Head bowed, she was agitated, cracking her finger joints. 'But you mustn't get all fraught about it, Hetty.' He put his hand on hers.

'No, I'm not. It's just all that re-re-royal business. I still haven't really come to terms with it – be-be-being the old King's daughter.'

'Well, that's true. There's no doubt –'

'And now this, that his grandson – poor David – might have given me back all this.'

Dermot, using the last of his Swan Vestas, lit his pipe, letting a curl of rich smoke drift in the air. 'The past sometimes has a way of settling its bad debts, Hetty, of paying for old wrongs. Sometimes. And I think that's what's happened for you. Goodness me!' He swung his pipe in the air. 'All those years ago, when you and I first met – that day you sent me over the weir in the boat, remember? – you were such a put-upon child, all those lies . . . Your Mama's hurt – so that she hurt you. Remember that so well – and wondering if anything would ever come right for you.'

'And it didn't – went from bad to worse.'

'Yes! But that's just what I mean. There was Pierre at the end. And all this.' He gestured round the great hall. 'All this, waiting for you. A reward. Sometimes things do end well, you know. And you, and the child I knew – no one could have deserved it more.'

They heard the others moving in the drawing room and the footsteps of the estate workers coming along the passageway behind them. Hetty kissed Dermot quickly on the cheek. 'Thank you. But you're my best reward.'

Dermot turned, almost embarrassed, fearing he had said too much. And Hetty thought then – loving Dermot in that old familial way at last, which she could not do before – how her life was filled with every sort of love.

Yet something still irked her, stirred in the very corner of her mind, an itch, a loss. She knew what it was, but refused to touch the dead pain lest she might re-awaken it. She was complete in every way at Summer Hill that Christmas – but for the lack of those two others, her contemporaries, who had made up all her young life in the great house. And these two she had lost, irretrievably. But they lived, she knew. They were alive somewhere at that very moment – just as they lay dead in that sealed cupboard of her mind – as in a hidden sarcophagus, embalmed, surrounded by the grave-gifts they had all shared in a previous life together, funerary emblems, cartouches, mysterious hieroglyphics – all the texts of a lost language whose Rosetta stone had been smashed and buried as well.

The company arrived in the hall. Dermot put away the stepladder. Hetty stood alone by the sparkling Christmas tree, a tall frail figure in a quiet dress, amethyst pendants motionless at her ears, the parcelled presents lapping round her feet in brightly coloured waves: the châtelaine resurrected, who would now dispense these gifts, supported by everyone and everything that was most dear to her. And yet, standing there alone, before Pierre joined her, she had the air of someone quite lost.

Robert and Léonie had separated. Robert's political commentaries for the *Express*, featured on the leader page now, had brought him more money as well as prominence, so that he had the income to set himself up in a small top floor flat in John Street, up from High Holborn, not far from the *Express* building in Fleet Street. Léonie retained the pretty top floor flat in Hampstead, while Olivia, now nearly fourteen, remained at the boarding school in Kent, returning sometimes at weekends to Hampstead, where Robert, when he was not abroad, saw her.

But he was in Europe much of the time now, reporting on the ever-increasing political tensions consequent on Hitler's aggressive policies – his open demands for the Sudetenland, his covert intent to annexe Austria, his harrying of the Jews in Germany. So that although Robert saw as much of Olivia as he could when he was home, and sent her postcards from everywhere he went, he saw little enough of Léonie. However, that Christmas at least, they were all together in Paris with Léonie's father at the house in Passy.

Ben Straus had aged well. At nearly seventy-five his hair had barely thinned, was all a rich silver now, and he still possessed his old mix of wit, bustling American ease, above all his liberal man-of-the-world stance. He had continued working part-time for the American Marine Insurance and Salvage Company in the Avenue de l'Opéra until only the year before. And now he spent his leisure strolling the city he loved so much, taking a cab or the air on the open deck of the number 63 bus down the Avenue Henri Martin, going to the Café de la Paix or the Crillon bar next to his embassy, passing the time with his old cronies.

If Olivia was confused and hurt over her parents' behaviour and problems, Ben Straus understood most of it. And Léonie had filled in some, if not all, of the obscurer details. She did not tell him how she had wished that all three of them, she and Robert and Hetty, could have shared Summer Hill together. She told him nothing of her hopes here and of how Robert had destroyed them. She hid these longings from him, for she could not face them in herself.

Instead she said how they had come apart in dribs and drabs – Robert's work taking him abroad so often, an incompatibility of character – how they could no longer supply anything of each other's needs. And her father accepted this, if not entirely. For he sensed there was another reason, and that that was Hetty. He knew well how his daughter had loved her, and supposed she might still in some manner. And that here, perhaps, was the greater reason for things having come apart between her and Robert. But he said nothing of this, only consoled her as he could.

'Things, well, they get to be like that between people,' he told her on Christmas Eve, as they sat alone together in the small upstairs salon, after Robert had taken Olivia out to the Cirque d'Hiver, the two of them sipping flutes of Veuve Clicquot. 'There's little to be done about it. And, once it gets beyond a certain point, there's no retrieving the situation. Though people often kid themselves they can. Only start out to save the marriage – when it's already dead.' He smiled faintly. 'Glad at least you haven't done that. A clean enough break. And don't feel blame. Because there's little point in that either. It's the fate of people – to complicate their lives. And few can get to untangle it afterwards.'

'Yes. But I'd like to have done just that. Because it *could* have been set straight.' Léonie spoke with barely suppressed passion.

'Of course! We Americans, we believe in that more than most. Setting everything to rights! And you can sometimes do that with a wrecked ship. But, if it's a marriage, well, you usually can't – and there's no insurance policy that'll cover it.'

'I still think Robert and I could've stayed together, if – if he hadn't been so *stiff*, unyielding about things . . .'

'What things?' he asked gently.

'Oh, so many things.'

Ben Straus played with the stem of his glass. He thought he knew what these things were, but could not say so directly. 'Yes . . .' he said. Then, changing tone and tack, he asked brightly, 'And Hetty? Do you have any news of her?'

Léonie responded in the same casual tone, but it was not easy. 'No, nothing on what I last told you. She's cut off everything completely, with us, me and Robert – living with some Frenchman at Summer Hill, like I said.'

Ben Straus shook his head, making nothing of this response, staring into the champagne bubbles. 'Extraordinary girl. Quite extraordinary. Always saw it in her, that mix of Jewish and Irish – the magic people . . . But dangerous, volcanic. Lucky there aren't too many of them around!'

'Yes,' Léonie said dully, head bowed, before she stood up and walked to the curtained window. Her father knew she was trying to hide some emotion, tears even – and knew almost for a certainty then what must have taken her and Robert apart. But he left it at that.

'So, what will you do now?' he asked, bright once more, much in his old get-up-and-go mode. 'Ever thought of taking up the singing again? Your voice – it's still lovely.' He smiled at her, loving this hurt daughter of his more than ever.

'Too old – and too late.'

'Oh no! It's never that. That's nonsense, Léa, from us Strauses. At thirty-eight, why, things need only be starting for you.'

'What things?'

He leant over and touched her hand. 'You know something, I was all of thirty-eight and more before I married your mother.'

'But I'm a woman.'

'So? That's no bar. There are other fish in the sea.'

He smiled again, raising his glass. But it was quite a few moments before Léonie finally raised hers, and then with little conviction.

At Summer Hill, after the presents had been given out and the estate families had gone home, the others gathered round the tree, Dermot up on the step-ladder again, extinguishing the higher candles, snubbing out the little dancing flames one by one.

'Well – *voilà un Noël!*' Pierre said.

'And the next – and the next!' Hetty said with vast enthusiasm. 'We'll meet here every year like this – won't we?'

'Yes, I hope so,' Dermot called out, licking a sooty finger, extinguishing a top candle, before climbing down to them. 'Except my brigade's being called back from Delhi –'

'Well, that's even better! So you'll be much closer to home anyway.'

'Yes. But it's because they really need the troops back here at home – Auchinleck, our C-in-C in Delhi, told me privately.'

'So what? What does that mean?' Hetty asked.

'Hitler,' Pierre put in quickly, snuffing out one of the lower candles. 'War,' he added abruptly.

'But I thought we – I mean the British – we weren't going to have any trouble with that little moustache. Everyone, Chamberlain, says so.'

Mortimer humphed in his wheelchair. 'All the fools and the appeasers say so. Dawson of *The Times* and his fatuous cronies. But the more we kow-tow to that little moustache the more trouble we'll have from him.'

'Exactly,' Pierre said. 'Though the French, we think we can hold him on the line – the Maginot line.'

'Possibly,' Dermot wiped his fingers. 'But in my view the French Army won't hold him there at all. Because he won't come that way. Hitler's armoured divisions will go straight through – right to the north, through the Low Countries.'

'But that's Holland, Belgium,' Hetty said.

'Oh, the Germans will eat them as a snack – for breakfast,' Dermot, quite unusually for him, was terse, his wit mordant.

The company was silent.

Hetty, wanting to break the suddenly-glum mood, said, 'I know! Let's sing some songs, a few rousing carols and things – "Good King Wenceslas" – we've not played a thing on the pe-piano here, not for years! And it's still Christmas!'

They went into the drawing room, where Pierre opened the whole lid of the old Blüthner grand for Hetty, taking out a pile of music which had been stored there, lying over the strings, and putting it out for her on the music stand.

'There,' he told her. '"Oodles" of music for you. The right Irish expression?'

'Oh, I can play it all from memory.'

Some books of music fell from the stand before Hetty could start. So that when she finally looked up she suddenly saw a score of Puccini's confronting her: *Madame Butterfly* – the same score which she and Léonie had used, guying all that emotion, years before at Summer Hill. She stared at the prelude. The music came back to her. The sweet, plangent notes struck in her heart. The past was in front of her once more in all its loss. And the future was suddenly indefinite.

Upstairs Aunt Emily, by an oil lamp – for she refused to use the electric light – was at work on a drawing. It was another of her vivid natural history pictures taken from memory from about the demesne. It showed a dead rabbit lying on the snow, brilliant meringue folds running down the lawn to the river gorge, with the bare winter trees and house in the background. The rabbit, its bloody entrails splashed in the immediate foreground, red against white, was being devoured by black crows.

Downstairs she heard the faint music and voices. '"Good King Wenceslas looked out, on the feast of Stephen. When the snow lay all about, deep and crisp and even" . . .'

7

After Christmas Robert took Olivia back with him to London while Léonie stayed on in Paris with her father until the new year; he had suggested she might come with him to a dinner party celebration with Ambassador Bullitt at the American Embassy on New Year's Eve. So that it was not until early in that January of 1938 that Léonie finally returned home. Despite all the festivities, she remained low in spirits. So much had ended for her and the new year promised nothing. To cheer her up, Ben Straus had bought her a return trip to London on the Dunkirk-Dover night ferry.

'I couldn't reserve you a bunk. Booked up. But they told me you'd be almost sure to get one on board – cancellations, or a little money to the conductor. Anyway, it's all first class, so you'll be *comfortable*.'

He came with her to the Gare du Nord, kissing her at the entrance to the green and cream Pullman carriage; the big engine letting off steam, mushrooms of smoke spiralling up into the freezing air.

'Yes, comfortable . . .' He repeated the thought idly. 'Because in the end, when things go adrift in one's life – there's always a solace in comfort. The little things – Veuve Clicquot, first class sleepers . . .' He smiled and they embraced again. 'You'll see,' he told her as she climbed on board. 'Next time we meet, when I get over to London with the better weather, you'll be a different person. Know you will. We Strauses – we're never down for long!'

He prayed she would meet some other man. He was not the least censorious of what he had long before recognised as his daughter's divided sexuality and, for the most part, he had always liked and admired Hetty. But there was no doubt that Hetty had finally been a disaster for Léonie, and that she had been the real reason for the break-up of his daughter's marriage. And, since he loved Léonie more than anyone, he said to her then, as a last word, 'Seriously, though, bound to be other fish in the sea . . .'

Buffers clanked. The long train stirred minutely. Latecomers shouted and rushed along the platform. A signal turned from red to green out in the bitter night. A whistle shrieked and in a minute the train started to move. Léonie waved to her father for as long as she could see the crown of his silver head on the disappearing platform. Then she turned into the dark corridor, unable to restrain her tears.

There were no sleeping compartments available. She might possibly share one of the double compartments, the conductor told her. But, in her present mood, she did not want this. She had a seat, though, a veritable armchair in heavy maroon plush, once she had mopped her eyes and tidied herself in the Ladies. She had a copy of that evening's *Paris-Soir* and a fashion magazine, too. But she could not concentrate on either. She was depressed at leaving her father. And the chic advertisements in *Elle* depressed her further. She felt frumpy, fat and sad. She had put on weight in these last months, eating too much, especially chocolates, as some sort of recompense, she supposed, for her various losses. And now she felt hungry again. She would take dinner at the first sitting.

Arriving in the dining car, she saw the soft pools of light from the coloured scalloped shades over little silver table lamps, set on every gleaming white tablecloth. The head waiter brought her to a table for two right at the end of the car.

'*Si vous voulez partager?*'

No, she did not mind sharing – not the meal at least.

Another woman was already sitting there. Léonie could not see her head, hidden by the lampshade. But her hands were visible, embroidering or repairing a sequined Victorian envelope purse, a needle being thrust deftly to and fro under the light. An older woman, Léonie thought, who might not care for company.

'*Si cela est égal à Madame?*'

Léonie spoke to the hands, assuming they were French. And then, to one side of the coloured *art décoratif* lampshade, the woman's face appeared, sharply triangular, pastel-coloured, brown and rose, the red-tinged hair, parted exactly in the middle, sweeping straight down past wide brown eyes behind glasses, a competent but withdrawn, preoccupied look.

'*Non, pas du tout,*' the woman said. '*Soyez la bienvenue.*'

Léonie, sitting down, was surprised. Far from being old the woman was about her age: a pretty mouth that turned down slightly on each side, eyes that slanted upwards in balance, it seemed, giving her face a strange symmetry, a vaguely oriental air. Yet she must certainly be French, Léonie thought. Her clothes confirmed that. She was beautifully dressed in a three-quarter-length cotton gaberdine coat with patch pockets and a wide roll collar over a high-collared shirt, striped in red and white, an ivory cameo brooch at the top stud. A low-crowned wide-brimmed stiff felt hat with a bow trim lay on the table beside her. She put it beneath the table, allowing Léonie more space, then passed her the menu.

Léonie gazed at the choice for a minute before peeping over the top of the card at the other woman, now entirely absorbed in her needlework once more.

She was smallish – rather her own build, Léonie thought. But she had not let her body run to an inch of fat. Léonie saw that, too – the sharply-narrowing waist, hugged by the candy-striped shirt, behind the open coat. And Léonie envied her that – but even more her complexion and her hair. Her cheeks in the soft light had a peachy opalescence, which was not from the lamp or any make-up – simply a bloom of youth retained, the skin everywhere absolutely unflawed. And her hair was that perfect wavy brown colour, ripening into red, ending in a flutter of curls about the nape, under the ears – again nature's work, not that of any hairdresser with curling tongs or tints. That was obvious. Only her nose might have been criticised. It was very straight and pointed, but ended too soon – abruptly, in a sudden *retroussé* – as if the designer had lost his nerve at the last minute in this otherwise heady creation.

She might have been a mannequin, Léonie thought, in her chic clothes, with her upright carriage. Yet she was surely too small, and perhaps too old – and somehow too distant, formal, even severe. So that Léonie feared to open any conversation with her. 'Do Not Disturb,' the woman seemed to say, totally absorbed in her sewing.

And indeed they might never have spoken if another waiter, assuming they were together, had not arrived at their table with his note-pad.

'*Mesdames? Vous avez choisi?*'

He looked expectantly at them each in turn – and the two women regarded each other an instant. Léonie forced a smile. '*Nous . . . nous ne sommes pas ensemble.*' She offered the menu back to the woman. '*Madame – elle était ici d'abord.*'

'*Non, non – je vous en prie.*' The woman, refusing the menu with a delicate gesture, offered Léonie first choice.

'*Non, pas du tout.*' Léonie in turn tried to hand it back. The waiter, confused now, was becoming impatient. Léonie was nervous, in a panic almost. 'Oh God,' she said. 'I don't know . . .' The waiter fidgeted. She scanned the menu furiously.

'Try the veal escalope.' She heard the voice opposite. 'I've had it before on this train and it's good. They do it without too much batter.'

'Oh, thank you.' She turned to the waiter. 'The veal, please.' She spoke in English now herself, before looking back at the woman, astonished. 'I'd . . . I'd no idea you were English.'

The woman smiled for the first time, then nodded, so that her curls danced. 'Yes, English. Or half so.' She left the other half open. 'And I thought you must be French, too.'

'No, well I . . . I've lived in France a lot, went to school here. But I'm actually American.'

'Of course – there's that slight intonation. I couldn't spot it at once.'

The woman's tone was outgoing and direct. But Léonie felt she was not really seeing her, was looking through and not at her – her calm grey eyes unfocused, vague. But then she took her glasses off and the effect was startlingly different. 'Sorry,' she said. 'I hadn't quite seen you. I've been so tied up with this sewing. Forgive me. I can't see anything much beyond my nose with them on!'

She looked at Léonie properly then for the first time. 'I'm Jennifer Bryden.'

'Léonie – Léonie Straus.' Léonie wondered immediately afterwards why she had given her maiden, not her married, name.

With the crush of people and the steaming dishes, it was becoming warm in the dining car – so that Jennifer had to take off her coat half-way through the meal. Léonie saw the vague imprint of her breasts through the striped shirt, as she moved her arm across the table, pouring from the bottle of hock they had decided to share.

Léonie raised her glass. 'How nice to have some company on these trips,' she said casually, trying not to notice how her heart had started to thump.

By the time their dessert arrived they had become only a little better acquainted. Despite the relaxed mood in the dining car, the touch of alcohol, their exchanges remained strangely stilted, formal. Something – something wary and unspoken – seemed to prevent them falling into any true ease of communication. And yet, as Léonie felt, it was not any coldness between them. Rather the opposite. Perhaps it was the heat of the dining car which kept them at such an arm's length, which made them both stick to banalities in their conversation: talk of the weather, the Christmas holiday, the Paris fashions, together with the briefest exposure of their separate backgrounds.

It seemed as if they did not want to know – at all costs must not know – too much about each other; that they should strictly maintain their role as polite strangers, forced together at a dining car table, who would very soon go their separate ways. Léonie was perplexed by this barrier, for it was obvious that they had much in common – a natural fluency in French and English, a life spent moving between the two countries, an intimate knowledge of Paris and London, same age, same sex, an interest in clothes, even in sewing, for Léonie remarked on Jennifer's skills here, wishing she had more time for it herself.

And yet they persisted, both of them, in talking only of formal commonplaces. Léonie gave only the scantest details of her life – how her father lived in Paris, had been an attorney in marine insurance, that she was married to a British journalist, had a daughter of fourteen, lived in Hampstead. While Jennifer, in her résumé, was equally restrained and far more mysterious. Her mother was French, worked in some capacity for a Paris couturier, her father lived somewhere near London – the 'home counties' – a retired Army man, while she herself was a secretary in Whitehall and had a flat somewhere off the Edgware Road.

She did not explain the very disparate backgrounds of her parents, or why they lived apart. Nor did she enlarge on her job in Whitehall. So that Léonie, a little frustrated at this constraint, thought to lighten the mood and prosper some greater friendliness by saying brightly, 'Oh, Whitehall! What do you do? Something exciting or dreary?'

Jennifer sipped her coffee guardedly. 'Nothing – nothing really. At one of the Ministries. Just typing, letters and things.'

But Léonie, smiling now, was not to be deterred in her lighthearted mood. 'I suppose you think I'd tell my journalist husband! Well, I won't. Because he and I are separated, I'm afraid.'

Jennifer looked up, concerned at once, though only formally, it seemed. 'I'm sorry . . .' She looked at her. But it was not a warm look, Léonie saw. Jennifer seemed agitated by something in her last statement.

'Well, yes, it was . . . all rather tough.' Léonie avoided any suggestion of the crestfallen. 'Are you happily married? I hope so!' she added brightly.

'No. No I'm not – married, I mean.'

'Oh, should I be sorry?' Léonie was confused. 'No, I mean – did you, were you, did you want to be? . . .' She left all these possible permutations hanging on the close air. A man at the table behind had started a cigar, the smoke drifting over their heads.

Jennifer started to cough. 'No, no . . .' she spluttered. Her face, her eyes, were more than ever alarmed now. She was shaking with mild paroxysms – from the effects of the smoke, Léonie supposed. 'No, I'm not married,' she added with finality, a cold aggrieved look masking her warm features, as if Léonic had verged on the impertinent with these enquiries.

'I'm sorry. I didn't mean to pry –'

'No, no. It's just – I can't stand the smoke any more.'

They had settled the bill. They both stood up. Jennifer held out her hand, offering a formal goodbye. But a group of people for the second sitting were pushing behind them, so that they had to walk the length of the dining car together, before they could stop at the junction of the two carriages, both of them swaying over the jolting couplings in the half-dark, Jennifer still coughing, a handkerchief over her mouth. At last she held out her hand again. 'Well, goodbye. I hope you have a good night.' She seemed so anxious to escape. But another coughing fit took her then.

'Are you all right?' Léonie asked, putting her hand out, steadying the other woman over the swaying junction.

'Yes – yes. Fine, thank you. I'm this way.' She gestured towards the engine where the wagons-lit were.

'Lucky you,' Léonie said. 'I couldn't get a sleeping compartment, all booked up . . .'

Jennifer, who had turned away, half-opening the door into the next carriage, turned back.

'Oh dear . . .' Her voice was resigned. 'You could share my compartment. I've one all to myself.' Her tone was filled with such an air of defeat that Léonie said at once, 'Of course not! I've got a perfectly comfy armchair – the other way. Sleep like a log in any case – after all that hock! Goodbye.'

She had half-turned, leaving Jennifer, before she felt a hand on her shoulder and heard the suddenly urgent voice.

'No! No, I meant – I'm sorry – I meant, *please* share my compartment. There's plenty of room.' She touched her shoulder again, a gesture in which there was a whole surge of informality, of need. 'Please, it's this way. Just up here.'

Together this time, they opened the door into the next carriage, moving into the smooth-carpeted, tactfully-lit calm of the wagon-lit carriage.

The moment they were inside the compartment and she had locked the door, Jennifer embraced her – delicately, urgently, apologetically. 'Oh, you poor thing . . .' She kissed her on one cheek. 'I'd no idea, not having a berth . . .' Then on the other. 'Just one of those stuffy armchairs . . .' She kissed her on the nose.

So formal in her speech, distant in attitude a few minutes before, she had now run to the opposite extreme, was utterly informal – childish almost, in her excited tumbling words, her nervous, unresolved movements, fondling Léonie's ears with her lips, standing away a fraction, gazing at her happily, sadly, her grey eyes dancing with concern, ardour.

Léonie for a moment pretended not to know what to make of this sudden onslaught of passion. Yet from the start she had made no attempt to resist it, so that she saw then how something had snapped between them the moment they had entered the compartment, saw how willing a partner she was – had been all along in this meeting – in this now equally irrepressible, unquestioning feeling she had for Jennifer. Embracing her, kissing her in return, she sensed a great well of long-suppressed physical desire rising in her, for this total stranger, who was holding her, facing her, chin slightly tilted, lips apart, speaking to her again in that startlingly different voice, soft, capricious, yet almost desperate, stammering: 'Oh, I can't . . . can't tell you how awful I felt, all the time at dinner, being so cold to you, because I *knew*, I just knew –'

'Yes, yes!' Léonie put her fingers to Jennifer's lips. 'But don't. It doesn't matter now . . .'

The dross, the hurt and pain of the last months – the last years, indeed – started to drop away from Léonie then, like weights, and she seemed to levitate with joy, felt herself rocketing upwards in the compartment, stomach churning, head swimming about the ceiling, so that she was surprised at her own tears, unaware of them until she felt them trickling down her cheeks. Jennifer, hugging her once more, brushed the tears away with her nose, and they stood apart again, holding each other at arms' length. Then Léonie laughed. But her mouth was strangely dry, her throat constricted, so that the laugh emerged as more of a cackle. She reached out for Jennifer, about to hug her once more.

'No, let me –' Jennifer struggled out of her cotton gaberdine, then tugged at her cameo brooch, hurriedly opening her shirt all the way down the front – 'These buttons – they're so twisty!' – climbing out of her pleated beige wool skirt, standing there in a silk petticoat with a low neckline, a tie belt at the waist, her hand on the bow.

But, before she could pull it, Léonie, reaching forward pulled it for her, and the petticoat flowed freely out about her waist. Lifting it by the hem, Léonie drew it right up over her small breasts, her head, knelt down, head against her chin, her neck, running her lips between her breasts, over her stomach, clasping her round the middle, nibbling at the elastic rim of her knickers.

Then suddenly they both seemed furious with each other – in their delay, delight, the urgency of their desire. So that Jennifer tugged at Léonie's clothes in frustration – pulling at her collar, the shoulders of her navy cardigan, as she knelt in front of her. Léonie, standing up, made a huge effort to be calm. 'Here – they're here – the buttons.' She brought Jennifer's hand to the top of her blouse. 'They all unbutton . . . quite easily!'

Jennifer, making an equal effort to control herself, undid them one by one down to the waist. Léonie, releasing the belt, stepped out of her skirt and took off her blouse, standing there in her black satin petticoat, garters and silk stockings. Jennifer took her then, arms linked round her waist, pulling at the crinkly satin, lifting it over her behind, finding it caught between them then, so that Léonie moved away and, crossing her arms, herself lifted it off.

They hugged each other, finding their skin together for the first time, a velvet burning all the way down to their waist, standing half-naked together in their knickers, suspenders, garters, silk stockings – swaying suddenly as the train rushed over a curve of points, so that they fell on to the bunk in a fever, writhing and twisting, pushing and pulling, tearing, tugging and arching.

It was making love to a stranger, Léonie thought. And it was intoxicating – just because this woman was so entirely unknown, so that she felt quite without any inhibitions, her appetite correspondingly increased, so that she was almost brutal in her desire. For she was a stranger to herself now as well, liberated, a dare-devil adventurer. A feeling of sheer irresponsible abandon swept over her: there was no past or future, in either body caressed; no questions, fears or obligations, no dross of yesterday or tomorrow – as she discovered this woman, nameless almost, sweeping into virgin country, reaching a hand down her smooth flank, stroking it, then moving inside her thigh, caressing the smoother skin there, until she touched her sex and Jennifer shuddered an instant, arching away, then back, offering, opening herself to Léonie's hand.

Jennifer touched her in the same place, supple questing fingers – and Léonie felt that choking sensation again as her stomach rose and churned before she killed the feeling by giving, thrusting herself vehemently at her: the start of a pulsing rapture in their love making now, when time disappeared, as she felt the bolts of pleasure, striking her, one after the other, a near-painful ecstasy, as Jennifer discovered her – bolts that came like lightning now, a sharp searing joy, remembered and regained from a lost time, her old nature re-affirmed in rising spurts, a gulping famished bliss, as of two strangers, dying of thirst, met at the same water-filled oasis.

'Oh God!' Léonie almost shouted, towards the end, as Jennifer so held and felt, touched and moved with her, then lifted herself above her, hands to either side on the berth, arching over her, moving to and fro, before Léonie hugged her down on to her, taking her breasts, widening her legs. 'Oh God!' she breathed, violently, on the edge of an abyss, gulping thin air.

Léonie seemed to black out for several moments, as the berth tilted and spun and she saw Jennifer arching and shuddering above her, curls dancing, eyes shut tight, her face a creased mask, almost of pain, before suddenly everything flowed and rushed between them and they fell together, half laughing, half crying, in a tumbling flurry of intertwined arms and legs, heads and clenching toes.

Later, as a tired calm descended on them, Léonie saw all the reasons for Jennifer's earlier formality and restraint – how she had wanted her almost from the beginning, when she had somehow sensed their similar natures, but had bitten this knowledge back, withheld herself in the dining car, been brief, even brusque, fearing to involve them both; until, seeing the end of this chance-in-a-lifetime meeting over the swaying carriage junction, she had dived in recklessly, asking her to share the compartment, rescuing their joint needs at the last moment.

'Thank you,' Léonie whispered, touching the lobe of her ear with her tongue, 'for finding me.' Jennifer turned on the pillow then. 'You see . . .' Léonie was about to start again. But, this time, it was Jennifer who reached out, putting a finger to her lips, shaking her head in loving astonishment. 'No, no need to talk,' was all she said. 'Each other – we found each other.'

They slept then, oblivious to the vague noise as the train pushed on board ship, slept in each other's arms, the sleep of the just in their true nature. But Léonie woke later in the early dawn, feeling the boat swaying beneath her and, seeing the other woman next to her in the vague light, thought for a moment that something terrible had happened to her.

Where was she? Who was this person? – gently asleep beside her, the long curls twisted round, falling across her cheek, the small, half-bared breast lying over the sheet, the sweet smell of warm linen, and of something else . . .

Then, as she came to her senses, it all returned to her. Jennifer. Jennifer Bryden. Léonie tried to cling to the mundane name – like a life raft, something just out of reach, unpossessed. For the name and all that lay behind it in the workaday world had meant nothing to either of them last night. They had lived in a different country then, under all sorts of aliases.

Oh, the sheer release, the joy of it . . . And yet it all frightened Léonie now. Their love-making, thinking of it, seemed too vehement, too abandoned ever to be a part of the real world. It was a temporary fever, a moon flower, that bloomed and died in a night, an extravagant creation dependent on their being, remaining, strangers.

Léonie remembered how Jennifer had put her fingers to her lips. 'No need to talk,' she had said. And Léonie was terrified then, for that was what Jennifer must have meant. It was, it would be, all over by dawn. That was the unstated agreement. Ships that pass in the night. And she longed to wake Jennifer then – to promote reality between them, to talk and talk and talk – for she longed for a future with this woman now. Yet here she was gone away from her, fast asleep, already forgetting her, the widely-spaced, slanting eyes now blind.

She need not have worried. When Jennifer woke half an hour later, just before they docked at Dover, she reached out for her quickly, touching her cheek, taking her hand, kissing it. 'Léonie . . .' She was quietly astonished. 'You're still here. I thought – thought you mightn't be. That you'd have left, without saying anything . . .'

'No.' Léonie was almost shocked. 'No, of course not. I'd never do that.' The two women gazed at each other gratefully in the cold morning light.

A thin fall of moist snow slanted across the docks as the train left for London. They had breakfast in the dining car. The waiter asked if they were together. They nodded, smiling.

No, neither of them need have worried. In this *coup de foudre*, somehow knowing intuitively that they were meant for each other, they had simply reversed the usual processes of loving. From then on, having first come together with such unthinking fever, they worked backwards – gradually, carefully, like explorers – into all the other usually undiscovered tributaries of blind passion: the deeds of association, the revealing texts of domestic enquiry, the set books of care beyond intimacy, friendship.

'You want to know what I do in Whitehall? – something *terribly* secret!' Jennifer stood by the tall first-floor window of her flat in Connaught Square, just off the Edgware Road. Léonie gazed at her, as Jennifer gazed out of the window – seeing her in profile, exploring a face that was still new to her, noticing how the point of the chin rose a fraction, as if to parallel the tip of her nose. Another discovered symmetry in the geography, new bearings in the map of love.

Léonie sat on the sofa, stroking Brewster, an ageing corpulent springer spaniel belonging to Mrs Ogilvy, a rich widow wintering in Monaco, from whom Jennifer rented the flat, and looked after the rest of the house while she was abroad.

It was a week later, a Sunday afternoon, under a frozen sky. Snow had fallen thickly for three days, drenching the plane trees in the square with a heavy powder. Some branches had fallen. People walked the half-cleared pavements along narrow trenches, dodging little Matterhorns. 'But it isn't really, the job – just letters and things, in French, for the War Office.'

Jennifer, in a plain beige skirt, patchwork-quilted waistcoat and bright red stockings, came over and sat beside Léonie for a moment, ruffling her hair. 'But *do* come and look. Some boys in the square, behind the bushes, getting snowballs off at the old dears and major-generals! A bit cruel, I know – but funny.'

Léonie went with her to the window, gazing down at the sporadic ambushes – some elderly pedestrians all in a rage, ducking the powdery cannonades. With their faces glued to the chilly window, two of the small panes in front of them were soon clouded over by their warm breath. Jennifer drew some letters with her finger on the glass. 'EMIA'T EJ'

Léonie was mystified. 'It's a secret code,' Jennifer told her gravely.

'Oh, what does it mean? Do tell!'

'Read the letters backwards, you ninny!'

Léonie was momentarily surprised at their childishness, for they were both of an age – she at thirty-eight, Jennifer a year younger – when maturity might have tempered, even prohibited, such juvenile responses. Instead she saw how this surge of loving had released a whole lost innocence in them, youthful conceits – flooding their adult reserve, promoting these games, floating them out on a second childhood.

'ISSUA IOM,' Léonie, after some hesitation and several corrections, wrote her message on the window-pane. They laughed and hugged, before Jennifer put some more coal on the small grate behind them. 'You're pretty quick and clever with words though – writing backwards straightaway.'

'Ah, the War Office – codes and things,' Jennifer joked.

Léonie looked at this woman, the flow of tawny-red curls fallen right over her face, glinting in the firelight – incredulous at her new possession: neat, so accomplished, contained, someone who knew who she was and yet was hers. Here, Léonie was sure, they would neither of them have to search furiously for an identity, dress up and swap clothes, as she and Hetty had done. Jennifer was already so entirely herself – dressed or undressed.

'Oh, so it *is* exciting work that you do.'

'No. It's deadly dull.' Jennifer stood up from the fender. 'Come on, before it's too dark. Brewster needs a walk. And after we can go and eat at that little Italian place on the Edgware Road.'

'I'm sorry – all that about your friend Hetty . . .' Jennifer, gazing down, picked at her spaghetti.

'Yes, well, it's all over now anyway. And Robert, too.'

'A sort of whole family to you really – Hetty and Robert, with those two other Cordiner cousins, all those servants, that huge house.'

'Yes . . .' Léonie for a moment considered the world she had lost. 'But I still have my own Papa. And now . . . you.'

Jennifer looked up at her suddenly. 'I was to have married – oh, ten years ago. The son of a great friend of my mother's. Frenchman. But when he sort of realised, about me, well, it was nonsense. He became flustered – and chilly.'

'Yes, I did wonder.' Léonie's lips opened in a half-smile. 'You're, well, obviously so . . . "marriageable" – is that the word?'

'And another older man at the War Office . . . I liked him very *much*. And he liked me. But he was married, of course . . .'

'*Would* you have married though, if he'd been free?' Léonie asked, a trifle anxiously.

Jennifer sighed. 'Yes. And no. Don't really know.' She put on her glasses as if the better to consider the problem, then took them off again. 'He was so tremendously kind, understanding. I might have done, a sort of companionship marriage. But that wouldn't have been fair – because he wouldn't have entirely wanted that, I'm sure . . . Anyway, then I met Mary. Not at all plain, like the name. Very startling looking, dramatic. Long golden tresses, like Rapunzel. Worked in the Zoo here of all places. But that came to an end, last autumn. She wanted to go out and live in Kenya, Uganda – study, deal with the animals there, the baboons up the Ruwenzori mountains, and so on. Wanted me to come out with her. I couldn't.'

'Because you didn't want to?'

'Oh yes, I did, as far as she was concerned. Just, I knew Africa wouldn't work for me – out there in the colonies, all that Happy Valley crowd. I just wouldn't have felt *responsible*, do you know what I mean? I'm something of a home-lover, too,' she added a little ruefully. 'Spent such a time getting the flat right here –'

'It's lovely, those Liberty fabrics – and your sewing! I *like* your being a home-lover!'

'And London,' Jennifer rushed on enthusiastically. 'I *love* the winter walks in the parks, round Regent's Park. And Paris – my Mama, and the shops there. And the Opera! How could I have lived in Kenya?'

'I used to sing at the Opera there years ago.' Jennifer was astonished. 'Yes, I was trained as a singer.'

They took coffee. 'Next weekend,' Léonie said, 'come up to Hampstead – and we can go for a long walk on the Heath!'

'I'd love to!'

Jennifer came up to the Hampstead flat with Brewster next Sunday morning, and they all walked up to the Round Pond next to the Heath. The snow had been replaced by a sharp frost for most of that week and the shallow pond was frozen solid. Children in bobble hats and red mufflers, taking long slides over the ice, laughed and shrieked. A few adults were majestically skating. They watched the animated scene, the figures waltzing and sliding under a freezing grey sky.

'Come on!' Léonie, stepping out on to the ice, beckoned her. Jennifer, in a long green woollen coat and even longer striped college scarf, stood on the edge, nervous. Léonie went back, holding out her arms. 'Come on, I won't let you fall!' Jennifer put a foot on the ice, gingerly, holding on to Léonie's shoulder.

'It's just . . . I'm not so . . . athletic as you . . .' She put her other foot on the ice and, with Léonie holding her arm, they paraded very gently, Jennifer making tiny slithering steps, out towards the middle.

'You home-lover, you!' Léonie told her. 'I can see why you wouldn't have been much good storming up mountains looking for baboons in Uganda . . .'

Jennifer stopped, her peach complexion reddening now in the cold, breathing fast, the chilling frost bringing tears to her eyes. 'You are an awful tease, Léa.' She looked at her weakly. The same tears of cold had also come into Léonie's eyes. She took out a handkerchief, holding Jennifer with one hand, while she dabbed her face with the other, then wiped her own cheeks.

'No, not really a tease, Jenny. It's just . . . that I'm teasing because I can't . . .'

'What?'

'Because I so want to kiss you! Come on, we'll go for a walk round the Heath . . .'

Far down the Heath, where there was no one about, they ran to keep warm beneath the frozen beech glades near Kenwood House, digging up snowy sticks and throwing them for Brewster. But the old dog made a mere pretence of chasing them – ambling a few yards before turning back, sitting firmly down on the snow and looking at them with infinite regret.

'And Olivia?' Jennifer asked, when they had slowed to a walk. They had been talking of Léonie's affairs.

'Well, she likes the boarding school in Kent. And I like to think she hasn't been hurt too much by all . . . this separation business. She's very quiet and resilient. But she must have been.'

'Better the separation than tensions and rows.'

'So one would like to think.'

'I'm sure it is. Which is why my parents live apart. Mama still sometimes does work for Coco Chanel.'

'Why didn't it last – between her and your father?'

'Oh, Daddy met her years ago in Paris – he was at the Legation there, junior military attaché. "Love at first sight" business. But it didn't work out when they got older. He was too British and she just the opposite . . .'

They walked on to the edge of the empty lake in the lea of the great house. It was chilling cold, but they did not mind, watching a group of mallard standing motionless far out on the ice.

'Anything's better than rows and tensions,' Jennifer said. 'Your living with Robert – it simply couldn't have been you.'

'More, it simply wasn't *him*, I'm afraid. Couldn't accept – me and Hetty. And he loved her too, after all. But *she* couldn't be doing with me in the end anyway. So it didn't much matter . . .' Léonie turned impatiently away from the lake. 'Better get back and have that hot lunch.' But Jennifer stayed where she was by the edge of the frozen water. 'What's the matter?'

'Just – all these separations and leavings.'

Léonie walked slowly back to her, fiddling with a snowy twig. 'We needn't have them. We *won't*,' she added very firmly. 'I've had all and enough of that. But not this time, not with you. I'm not going to lose my life with you, Jenny. So let's be open and honest – and I'm not going to be ashamed of anything – so you'll meet Olivia and Robert and my Papa and anybody else in my life. I'm not going to lose this chance with you, ever.' She kissed her then, a kiss full of purpose, a kiss with a future.

'Me too,' Jennifer said.

As they walked back, the sun emerged strangely as a pearly halo through the clouds, casting their pale shadows ahead of them on the snow. 'You see!' Léonie said. 'A future! . . .'

In the ensuing months they were as good as their word. They usually spent only weekend nights together, at one or other's flat, and went out mostly then, too. They tended to save each other up for weekends. They went to the Everyman cinema in Hampstead or the Academy in Oxford Street. Carné's *Quai des Brumes* and Eisenstein's *Battleship Potemkin* made them feel sad and serious. But, listening to the Savoy Orpheans on Jennifer's wireless, they danced the tango; and had a sweet martini round the corner afterwards at the Duke of Kendal pub.

They visited Keats's house in Hampstead one day in March when the first warm hint of spring was in the sun, tiny buds on the cherry trees down Frognal.

'Look – in his own writing! Part of his "Ode to a Nightingale"!' Jennifer gazed into the glass case. She read out the fragment.

'. . . "the viewless wings of Poesy,
Though the dull brain perplexes and retards:
Already with thee! tender is the night" . . .'

The next weekend they persuaded Brewster on to a Green Line bus, out to the beech glades near Aylesbury, an ancient forest, bluebell heads nudging up through the leaf mould. Kew Gardens offered them more exotic spring blooms a few weeks later.

Once, for no reason, they gave a grand tea party for themselves, with Mrs Ogilvy's best Spode china. Jennifer made cucumber and sardine sandwiches and a sponge cake with cream and raspberry filling. Brewster, taking vaguely ill on the remnants later, was excused his walk that evening.

Sometimes, in placid diminuendo, they stayed in most of the weekend, one or other of them writing letters, reading, sewing. Or both of them making love.

Through these idle or intense preoccupations, their lives had come to a balance: a caring give and take, making or not making love, Jennifer standing vacantly at a window, spellbound by some lines in Keats's hand, long red knitted stockings on the white bedspread, Léonie allowing herself the one cigarette of the evening, before dragging Brewster to his unwilling duty in the square. Trips to the local Odeon, sausages and chips, a shared bedsitter, an Ascot heater spuming water. Diminuendo and crescendo. A London romance.

It was an attraction of equals and opposites, where neither was the lesser or greater: Jennifer the frustrated home-lover; Léonie the wounded explorer. They met now in the middle of their lives together, fulfilling longed-for needs in the other: Léonie so wanting this balanced companionship, never discovering it with Hetty – but finding such an anchor in Jennifer. While Jennifer at last possessed in Léonie a vital spice in her domestic adventures.

They did not advertise the nature of their relationship – nor yet make efforts to hide it. A life which soon became so natural and happy for them radiated an ease towards others. Except for Robert.

He met Jennifer one weekend at the Hampstead flat. He was distant. But that was his usual attitude towards Léonie now. And seeing almost at once the nature of their friendship made him no more or less so. He was, perhaps, secretly pleased to confirm his opinions about Léonie once more, how he could never have led a real life, or made things up with her. He left immediately after tea – to catch the night ferry to Ostend, going on to Berlin and Prague. He had an article to do, with a series of interviews, he hoped, on Hitler's latest plans to annexe the Sudetenland.

Afterwards Jennifer said, 'It's funny, because he doesn't seem the sort of person who'd make a fuss – over all the things he did. Seems so gentle.'

'Yes. He is. He was. Just, there's some poison – that's got into him. Oh, a self-righteousness. Nice, gentle people – they can fall ill that way, sooner maybe than others.'

'Other women – do you think? With all that travelling?'

Léonie shrugged. 'I doubt it. That's part of his self-righteousness. He doesn't want to risk being proved wrong over me – because I'm not really so very different from many women.'

Olivia came home for the spring holidays from Kent: rapidly growing, slightly gauche in pigtails, beautifully dark, nervous, trying to find herself in all sorts of covert ways. She had, with the pressures of the last years, developed something of a stammer. At first things were a little awkward between all three of them. But Brewster marvellously eased matters, making a beeline for Olivia, resting his head on her lap, gazing up at her lovingly, wagging his tail.

'He is a sw-sweet dog!' Olivia stroked him. 'I suppose he really only wants me to take him for a we-walk.'

'Oh no, he doesn't. He *hates* walks!' Jennifer told her. 'He's the soppiest, laziest old dog ever. All he wants is a cuddle and then for you to *stop* us taking him out!'

Olivia quite took to Jennifer. Unaware of the real nature of her mother's relationship with Jenny, she came to regard her as a sophisticated, interesting aunt. 'Such smart clothes she wears,' she remarked to her mother. 'I do rather envy her.'

'Yes, so do I – sometimes.'

Léonie, though far less frumpy now, had not quite the same delicate figure.

'I bet she's pretty in a bathing suit,' Olivia went on.

'Yes, I should think so. But we'll see anyway – I've made arrangements, like last year. We'll all spend part of the summer together, at that seaside villa in Normandy.'

Ben Straus arrived for a holiday in London, staying at the Hampstead flat, early in May. Léonie had dinner with him alone on the first evening.

'So who's this great new friend of yours?' he asked expectantly.

'You had my letters –'

'Yes, but you didn't say exactly –'

'Jennifer – Jenny Bryden. I hope you'll meet her tomorrow.' Her father was put out – only for an instant, but Léonie noticed it. 'Oh, I didn't tell you all the details in the letters, Papa – wanted you to see me, and her, first. I'm afraid . . . it's not a man!' She looked at him, smiling a little wanly. 'But it's even better!' she rushed on. 'I'm really so happy.'

He gazed at her. 'Yes, I can see that. All the depression gone entirely. Lost weight, too. I've not seen you looking so good in years.'

'It's true! It's – she's changed my life. Couldn't be better. And all because of you!' Her father looked doubtful again. 'Because I'd never have met her, if you hadn't given me that first class ticket back on the night ferry. I've never ever had a better present.' She kissed him on her way to the kitchen.

The following evening, when he met her, he had to agree with his daughter's luck in meeting Jennifer. As they sipped drinks together before supper in the Connaught Square flat he saw everything: the gleaming reddish hair in the lamplight, the delicate lively eyes, faint blue, widely parted, slanted, the small mouth, full lips, the perfect symmetry, the neatness everywhere, the Paisley blouse and skirt and bright red stockings – above all the obvious happiness of the two women together.

He raised his glass to his daughter's new friend.

Good God, he thought afterwards – what could it possibly matter? People surely had a right to love in any combination of gender. They could fail or succeed in one permutation just as much as another. But at least it was blindingly clear here for the moment – the success of this arrangement. His daughter was transformed. That was what counted. Nothing lasted forever.

He stroked Brewster, who had come to him lovingly, chin nuzzling his knee, paying him almost unbridled attention, huge liquid eyes filled with a worried, hopeful emotion.

'Your dog – he seems to have taken quite a shine to me!'

'Get down, Brewster! Do push him down, Mr Straus. It's entirely feigned. He courts every stranger, in the hopes of enlisting support against his evening walk . . .'

Ben Straus decided he liked a relationship which included such a percipient, right-thinking dog.

8

AT SUMMER HILL meanwhile Hetty and Pierre lived a life of equal content. The house and gardens had now been restored to something, at least, of their former splendour. Even the many unused, dust-sheeted bedrooms and reception rooms did not depress. Summer Hill had a heart to it again, a body without the tensions, or suffering the prohibitions of old, so that the house came into its own once more, breathing freely in the summer sun.

But even in this remote rural paradise by the river, circled by rooks and water, where growth, decay and the weather were the only dictates, the war clouds in Europe could not be kept at bay forever. Other dictators would now have their say over the chestnut-shrouded house, as the buttercups faded and the climate dipped to stormy, then fell beyond the measurements of the barometer. In late September 1938 the stockade of Summer Hill which enclosed their happiness began to tremble.

The postman brought the letter from Paris. Pierre showed it to Hetty on the porch as they took coffee after lunch – a letter from the Medical Adjutant General at the French Ministry of War.

'The French Army – about to be mobilised?' Hetty was calm enough at this idea, though not at the next. 'But why *you?*'

'I'm on the reserve – of the Army Medical Corps, Hetty, that's why. I'm still a French citizen, you know.'

'Yes, but there isn't going to be a war. Chamberlain, Daladier – they've all said so.'

'Wishful thinking, I'm afraid. Chamberlain – "J'aime Berlin" we call him – and Daladier . . .' Pierre scoffed. 'Both of them just postponing the inevitable. Hitler has Austria, he's as good as taken the Sudetenland, Prague. Next he'll turn on Poland, France, the rest. I'll have to go back to Paris –'

'But, Pierre! –'

'Even if the Army hadn't been mobilised, Hetty, I'd have to go. I'm French. I couldn't stand apart and see France go down.' He stood up from the wicker chair, taking the letter, draining his coffee, looking out over the landscape – autumn tints, browns and reds and golds creeping over the valley.

'But if all of us – the French and the British – if we make a show of pe-power, as Daladier's doing now, Hitler'll climb down.'

Pierre shook his head. 'Chamberlain won't make any show. And Daladier'll climb down, not Hitler. Daladier will always compromise, I know it. Hitler never will. I'll have to go over to Paris more or less at once.'

'I'll come with you of course.'

He turned to her. 'If there is a war, Hetty, you'll have to stay here.'

'No. No, I won't.' Hetty was suddenly her old vehement self again, dictatorial, imperious. 'Let's not even start to argue about that – because I *won't*. I won't be apart from you. Or from France for that matter. There's no question.' She looked at him steadily. He said nothing. 'I'll tell Elly,' she went on, 'to get some clothes and things ready.'

Pierre, with a gesture of resignation, let the letter drop. A breeze took it and it sideslipped like a leaf down the porch steps, blowing with the other falling leaves over the gravel.

Hetty took Pierre's arm and together they walked up the lawn terraces, past the maple tree, the big cedar, to the little limestone grotto with its waterfall, now all restored. The water murmured in their ears as they turned round, gazing back at the placid vision below them, the house with its brilliant red creeper gleaming in the sun, the purple hills way across the valley, the murmur of the hidden river, the stillness of an autumn day.

'Such peace,' Hetty said, gripping his arm tighter. 'Neither of us . . . can let anyone destroy it.'

On just such a day, almost to the month, twenty-four years before, Hetty had stood at this same spot with Dermot gazing down at the house: August 1914, a few days before he had left for the Great War. She remembered the moment: Dermot puffing his pipe, blowing smoke rings over her, trying to cheer her up, saying – after all the rows with her mother, when she had come to so hate Summer Hill – how the house was really so full of peace and promise, how they could all be unimaginably happy there in the future. Now, through Dermot, through Pierre, that promise had been fulfilled. Lost before to her, through her own stupidities, this time she was not going to lose it.

A week later, at the end of September, after his meeting with Hitler in Munich, Chamberlain returned to Croydon airport with a piece of paper. It was 'Peace in our time'. By then Hetty and Pierre were in Paris, staying temporarily at the Hotel Rond Point just off the Champs-Elysées. From their bedroom balcony they watched the vast crowds, ten deep on either side of the great boulevard, welcoming Daladier home from Le Bourget to the War Office. He, too, had been with Hitler in Munich – and, just as Pierre forecast, had compromised. For France, as for England, it was peace with dishonour. Having promised to go to war over Hitler's rape of Czechoslovakia, Daladier had done no such thing. Prague had been thrown to the wolf.

But Hetty, taken by the joyous surge all about her in the city, saw it differently. 'Look!' she said. 'It's peace. It must be!'

Pierre sighed. 'Daladier's Munich accord is nothing but a diplomatic Sedan –'

'Oh, do stop spouting history at me! –'

'A disastrous climb-down then,' he said irritably. 'Daladier's delivered us over to Hitler all in a neat parcel. And we won't see that. Just look at them out there on the streets, women and children crying for joy. And where are the others, the men? Do you notice? So few of them. Because they've drafted every man under sixty, half a million Frenchmen under arms, up to the Franco-German border – where I have to go tomorrow.'

'But isn't that exactly the point? Hitler won't fight France – or Britain – now. Not with all this show of force.'

Pierre laughed. '"Force"? France is a second-rate military power now. They're all up there on the border just "twiddling their thumbs" as you say. They're not a fighting force. Their heart isn't in it. You can see that, out there, all those wives, women and children. The political issues are all far too confusing for any of them to feel any anger or threat. The men don't know what they're *doing* up there on the border! They won't *fight*. They want peace. Everyone wants peace, which is fine. Except you have to be *really* prepared to fight for peace. And none of us is. Which means war – sooner or later.'

In London Léonie and Jennifer heard Chamberlain's thin voice on the wireless: 'Today I have met with Herr Hitler . . .'

'Well, that's that all over at least,' Léonie said joyously. 'All those elaborate preparations for air raids last week, the sirens . . . We can sleep easy at nights.'

But Jennifer was not so reassured. 'At the War Office . . .' she said.

'What?'

'Some people are not at all certain.'

'Well, that stupid little moustache of a Hitler isn't going to bomb London tonight anyway. "Peace in our time"! We should celebrate. Let's go – let's have a splurge at Kettners!'

Brewster, asleep on the carpet, stirred at these lively tones, then whined unaccountably, some canine nightmare oppressing him.

These celebrations, many in Paris and London thought subsequently, had been entirely appropriate. There was no war that month, or the next – and the coming season of Christmas goodwill would surely set the seal of the peace. 'You see!' Hetty spoke in French. 'All that Munich business – just a war scare.'

It was mid-December. She looked down the dining room table of the furnished apartment they had taken in a modern block on the Avenue Mozart in Passy. Pierre had returned the previous week from the Army medical headquarters at a hospital near Lille. Most of the French forces on the border there had been stood down as well, returning home. Hetty and Pierre were entertaining an old and close friend of Pierre's from his medical student days in Paris, a Dr André Vonot, and Eve his wife.

Pierre, as usual on this topic – and becoming generally depressed by the continued political cowardice of the French and the British – disagreed with Hetty. 'We've compromised with Hitler to such an extent that even his greed is temporarily satisfied. Now it's the lull before the storm. I went over the border a few weeks ago to see a friend of mine in Osnabrück – a German doctor I know there, met him when I was studying in Vienna. He takes the worst possible view of things. Clearing out of Germany altogether, can't practise any more of course, because he's a Jew,' Pierre ran on before he could stop himself.

Dr Vonot looked at Pierre an instant, something wary, protective in his expression. Hetty noticed it, this worried look – so directed at Pierre. She asked him about it after the guests had left.

'Yes.' Pierre was resigned. 'He was thinking of me. Because I'm Jewish – half-Jewish – as well.'

'You?' Hetty was more mystified than astonished.

'I should have told you about it before.' Then, in his frustration, he turned to her. 'Can't you see?' He took off his spectacles, then ran a hand through his thick spiky-dark hair, before moving to the bedroom window, drawing the blinds.

'But your name is Langlois?'

'My real name if Neymann. Jewish family, settled here years ago from Alsace. But my father changed the name – after the Dreyfus trial, when he couldn't get any preferment in medicine here. That's why he went to London to the French hospital. Afterwards he changed his name to Langlois – the most *petit bourgeois* name he could think of – when he came back to France, starting up afresh.'

'But why didn't you tell me before?' Now Hetty was truly surprised. 'Nothing to be ashamed of. Just the opposite – I'm half-Jewish after all. We're both Jewish that way!'

'No. Nothing to be ashamed of. Except the fact that I've always been ashamed of my father for changing the name in the first place. And Vonot knows I'm Jewish. Known since we were students together. That's why he looked at me. He was worried for me, I suppose.'

'But the Jews aren't being persecuted in France now.'

Pierre turned from the window abruptly. 'Oh, you don't know. They were, they are – and they certainly will be if Hitler gets his hands on France.'

'Pierre, darling, he *won't* get his hands on France! You're far too pessimistic about the whole situation. You must get out of yourself a bit.' She stood up from the bed, kissed him, then ruffled his hair. 'Of course, I should have seen it! . . . But your skin is so pale.'

'My mother's. Pale as snow.'

'How *good* you're half-Jewish! Brother and sister under the skin! Always felt we were.' He took off his spectacles again, scratched his nose, gazing at the delighted, optimistic Hetty. 'So don't go on anticipating war. It's nearly Christmas. Come and we'll do nice things – go to the Cirque d'Hiver, see Chevalier at the Casino, have a treat at Maxims!' Hetty was determined to float Pierre off these shoals of discontent.

'But I thought you didn't want to go to any of those smart places, from your old days here. Might be recognised. The old Laura Bowen . . . which is why we took this quiet place in Passy.'

'Yes, I did think just that, to get as far away as possible from all those old dives of mine on the left bank. But I'm cured of all that now. And no one's going to recognise me as Laura Bowen now – an old hag of nearly forty!'

'Far from it, Hetty, far from it . . .'

They went to bed then, and they were happy.

Pierre, though released from the front, was still retained on the active service reserve. He had to remain in France. However, he was given a week's leave over Christmas and both of them returned to Summer Hill, spending the holiday there, as on the previous year, with Aunt Emily, Mortimer and Dermot.

Dermot, returned from India six months before, at nearly sixty-five, was just too old to be appointed to an active service command. Instead, with a promotion to Major-General, he was put in charge of Home Defence – the Territorials and a mooted Home Guard – for south-east England. His temporary command headquarters outside Maidstone in Kent had taken over a defunct girl's school. 'We'll be fighting them with hockey sticks,' he told the assembled company over Christmas dinner. He, like Pierre, was in no doubt that war would come, and soon at that. His father Mortimer, frail now, agreed. 'Churchill,' he said, 'knew him a bit in the old days at Westminster. An awful rogue in some ways. But the only one of them with any guts, only one who'd give Herr Hitler a real clip over the ear. And where is he? Building garden walls somewhere down in Kent!'

Only Hetty remained resolutely hopeful. 'You're all just a lot of warmongers,' she told them, rather hurt. Not wishing further to offend or depress her, they kept off the topic, in her presence at least, for the rest of the holiday. Privately they were blunt.

'Peace – until he addresses the Reichstag?'

'Till he can get the rest of his Axis war crew into the fighting line?'

'Till the Balkan wheat harvest is in? . . .'

Hetty and Pierre returned to Paris immediately after Christmas. Pierre, who by this time had had to relinquish his medical partnership with Dr Craig in Fitzwilliam Square in Dublin, resumed his negligible duties with the Army Medical Corps. But soon he, too, was stood down from active service. However, he remained on the reserve and had to stay in France. Anxious to continue with his medical work, he took up his practice again, joining his old friend Dr Vonot who had a private clinic and dispensary on the Avenue Foch, not too far from the Avenue Mozart.

Hetty in the following months, as the cherry flowered in the Bois de Boulogne, moved between the apartment in Paris and Summer Hill. She came to enjoy this alternating change of scene: Summer Hill, but above all Paris again, where she spent most of her time, in the comfortable modern apartment in Passy where there were no memories – so different a Paris from the one she had known, and ruined for herself, ten years before: a city always loved, but so lost to her then, in which she now lived soberly, happily, gradually coaxing Pierre out of his depression as the spring burst over the city.

She took him to Serge Lifar's 'Ballets Russes de Diaghilev' exhibition at the Louvre, to the Théâtre-Français revival of *Cyrano de Bergerac* with Bérard's fantastic Gothic costumes and décor, persuaded him to Maxims, to dinner in the Bois de Boulogne – took him here, there and everywhere, discovering the city anew with him, without that overwhelming vanity, that idiocy, arrogance, that stammering fury of heart: free now of all that had nearly killed her, with the man she loved who had given her this new life.

She had as well, while Pierre was out of work, another more intense and private pursuit. With Pierre's encouragement, at Summer Hill, and now in Paris, she had taken up her autobiographical novel again, *Aquamarine*, which she had started and dropped nearly ten years before. She continued with it now, remembering her past once more – the years in Domenica, the deadly hurricane, coming to the great house in Ireland, the shadows, the cold terrors there, her stammer, her punishing Mama, the magic apples, the old witch hidden in the Gothic wing: she remembered it all, and wrote with some fluency, until she came to that part of the story where the girl Alice, sent to the convent school in France, meets Sarah, embarking on a friendship which would dominate all her young life.

But there, having completed a few paragraphs, Hetty stopped. To write of Sarah was to remember Léonie – every emotion, every detail of their first experiences together at the convent school in Normandy. And this Hetty felt quite unable to face. She was surprised, upset – for surely she had recovered from Léonie, had confronted, with Pierre, all the hurt and damage she had done there?

But now, with this literary impasse, she wondered if, in her heart of hearts, she had really recovered from Léonie at all. Remembering the adventure of the holy relic in the convent chapel, the trout-fishing with a bent pin, the mysterious emotion she had felt in placing the snail on Léonie's forehead – in writing of all this the past returned and struck her viciously once more.

She had, she saw then, not only so hurt and lost Léonie, she had thrown away her own youth as well, debased the unique emotions there, sabotaged that unrepeatable adventure which they had shared, sullied everything they had experienced, hoped for and found together – all the mystery, beauty and imagination which life had offered them then.

She had betrayed more than human flesh, she saw. She had broken with the spirit of existence itself. And so, in writing of these early years with Léonie, which should have been a comemmoration of happiness, she saw only her responsibility in a terrifying loss – the gift of faith, so that she had dropped the pen halfway down the page. Such fictional atonement could only be a pale shadow of what was required here. And what was that? She had no idea – but that such atonement would have to equal what she had destroyed: the spirit of life itself.

'How can I ever really make it up to her?' she asked Pierre when she had explained the whole matter to him that evening. 'All those early things she gave me, that we had together, that I killed – in her and me.'

Pierre, worried at this turn of events in someone he had thought long cured, had no ready answer, seeing how, in this area of supposed sin and redemption into which Hetty had moved, science had no reach or cure. So he fell back on vague proverbial wisdom. 'You can't make up for things that happened that far back, Hetty – first love and such like – unless perhaps through your writing, which is exactly why I suggested you take up the book again.'

'Yes, but I can't face it – all those early days, now I'm remembering then, and knowing how I treated her later.'

Pierre made a vague gesture. 'Well, drop it then. Accept the fact that none of us can make up for the past that far back.'

'Yes, but I so *want* to make it up to her – now that I'm quite better.'

'But you can't . . .'

'No.'

'Why can't you?' Hetty shrugged despondently. 'You can't face the complete dissolution of the past,' he went on. 'Few people can. And psycho-analysis isn't much help. It can disentangle – clear the fears and horrors there. But it can't set the past right. God, if you like . . .' He smiled. 'Or art. But if you can't do it in your story, Hetty – what other way is there?'

'There *ought* to be some other way. There's still this huge gap in my life, about Léonie, I see it now. Of things – undone.' Hetty was more downcast still.

And now it was Pierre's turn to coax her out of her depression. 'Well, drop the book for the moment. Because I've got a surprise for you this time. One of André's patients – I've been dealing with her, too, she's a hypochondriac – the Comtesse Etienne de Beaumont, she's giving a *bal costumé*. And she's asked all of us, all four. What about that?'

'Where?' Hetty was doubtful, seeing in this something frivolous, a temptation, something out of her old louche Parisian life.

'At one of the Versailles pavilions, Madame de Mury's. And you needn't worry. It's all awfully proper. The *ancien régime*, Comte de Paris, Maurice de Rothschild. None of your old friends from the left bank! . . . And all of us to be dressed as characters from the plays or the period of Racine. And each partner to be dressed in complete opposition to the other!'

With the arrival of the better weather, Paris celebrated peace all the more vigorously, in manic fits of gaiety, the city en fête all that summer – music and dancing everywhere. Lady Mendl gave an international garden party for 750 guests and three elephants, all of which refused to be ridden. Mrs Louise Macy hired the empty Hôtel Salé for the night, installing temporary furniture and plumbing with a mobile kitchen. But greatest of all the receptions was the de Beaumont costume ball at Versailles.

It was held early in July – an aristocratic *fête champêtre* at first as the several hundred guests took a buffet supper on the lawn surrounding the lovely pavilion which Louis XIV had built for his mistress, milling about in costumes of every conceivable extravagance, wit and splendour, before going inside the long marble-floored *salon*, now cleared and made over as a ballroom, lit by some thousands of candles in silver sconces and candelabra, a Paris chamber orchestra at one end, harpsichords, violincellos and little tambourines playing minuets, sarabands, gavottes, pavanes and quadrilles.

Marie-Louise Bosquet went attired as La Vallière, with a pale chiffon mask painted in the likeness of the nun that she was to become. Maurice de Rothschild was the Ottoman Bajazet, wearing the famous Rothschild diamonds in his turban, the family's Cellini jewels across his sash. Hetty and Pierre, dressed more soberly in Grecian robes, went as the lucky lovers Iphigenia and Achilles, an appropriate mix of the noble and the chivalrous.

The air was heavy with the scent of orange blossom and crushed bay leaves from the miniature trees set up at intervals along the gilded walls, the *salon* filled with the sound of the delicately fingered music as the bewigged and doll-like figures made their stiff peregrinations about the marble floor. They were like automata – the men retreating, advancing, arms held high to the proffered hands of the women, linking, turning in the stately dance.

'Strange,' Pierre said to Hetty from the sidelines. 'The essential immobility of everyone. Straitjackets. Blind. Mad.'

But Hetty loved the formal drama of the ball – the wild contradictions of time and place and costume reawakening something in her histrionic soul. 'It's all a *jeu d'esprit*,' she told him. 'There has to be that in life, you know – as well as reality,' she added sweetly.

But that was exactly the trouble, Pierre thought. There was neither here, because there was no life at all in these dancers. They were people on strings, erect but dead behind their wild disguises, Meissen figurines moving through a flood of archaic golden light. The effect was eerie: an arcadian shepherdess circling a lascivious Ottoman prince; a masked nun in a saraband with a cardinal-archbishop. Bérénice with her flaming hair, turning, ever turning, only just at arm's length from the chilly figure of Death. Phèdre herself, the epitome of human agony in a torn Grecian robe, dancing with the court jester.

Here, in the clockwork movement of these bizarre conjunctions, there was a perfect order, but no rhyme or reason. These dancers fled away, retreating into chaos. And time was not reclaimed by those who would not seize the day or set one finger out to save the future.

9

THERE HAD BEEN no sirens that night in the area, so that the first in a stick of bombs fell quite unexpectedly behind the Cumberland Hotel not a quarter-mile away from Connaught Square.

Léonie woke with a frantic start. Beyond the black-out curtains the bedroom window rattled from the blast, as the other bombs fell in quick succession, moving away from them along Oxford Street. She clutched at Jenny, awake beside her now. 'It's all right,' she reassured her. 'When you *hear* the explosion you're not going to get hit –'

'That's nonsense! –'

'And anyway that must have been a mistake. They're bombing the City now, the East End, or the docks.'

'We should have been in the shelter – or Hampstead.'

'I'm only frightened of one thing – being buried alive. Besides, we can't sleep together in the shelter – and, I've told you, it's so much easier for me to get to work in Whitehall from here. Léa, it's just a matter of *controlling* yourself.' She touched Léonie's shoulder and they lay back together as the bombing disappeared in a sharp thunder down-river over the docks.

But Léonie could not sleep. It was true – Connaught Square was much nearer to Jenny's office in Whitehall than Hampstead. When the buses were re-routed, as they often were now, taking long detours round the blocked streets, Jenny could safely walk straight down to Whitehall, across Hyde and Green Parks, in half an hour. She was a great walker. And sometimes, too, she kept odd hours at the War Office, working at weekends, or going out early and returning late, when public transport had stopped, so that being able to walk to work was all the more important to her.

Léonie, returning to Hampstead by tube, had made the first part of this journey with her on many Monday mornings beneath the silver barrage balloons, walking along the sandbagged streets, glass crepitating beneath their feet from blasted houses, the air full of greasy dust, floating motes of ash, snowflakes of plaster, the debris of disaster settling in their hair, aggravating their eyes, itching the skin, so that she and Jenny, along with other women, often wore turbans now, putting on any extra lipstick and face lotions they had against the insidious dust and grit.

But in Hampstead, which had hardly been bombed at all there was none of this. The streets and houses were still intact on the high hill in the spring weather of 1941. How she wished Jenny would come and live with her and her father, whom she looked after now, in Hampstead. Oh God, she prayed silently – *do* have her come up and live with me and Papa safely, and not this living apart, my coming down here just at weekends. Let her live with me so that, if we are killed, we'll be killed together.

When the blitz had begun on London the previous August in 1940, people took it almost as a relief from the tensions of the long phoney war. They had not expected such intensive bombing to last. Yet now, over six months later, the bombs continuing to fall almost every night, the self-control and good humour of the populace had increased, not diminished. It was phenomenal.

And Léonie, too, who had become a fire-watcher in Hampstead, was normally part of this impeccable British self-control – except in so far as Jenny was concerned. Personally, at least, she had little else to worry about. Olivia's school in Kent had been evacuated to a country mansion near Cirencester in Gloucestershire. Her father, putting the house in Passy under wraps with a French caretaker, had left Paris just before the Germans moved into the city the previous June. Robert, too, covering these climactic events for the *Express* – the German Panzer *blitzkrieg* through the Low Countries, the fall of France, the British Expeditionary Force's retreat to Dunkirk, the Nazi occupation of Paris – was now back in London, still in his Holborn flat, as safe as anyone could be in the increasingly broken city.

Léonie saw him rarely: a visit together to see Olivia at an inn in Cirencester on one of her half-term breaks, odd London meetings when the telephone wires were cut to discuss their daughter's affairs. But otherwise they remained apart – and distant together, preoccupied in their own worlds. Robert was vastly stimulated, engrossed in his work. Some people had come to flourish in the war, Léonie realised. There were many whom this climate of danger suited, who took to the razed streets at dawn or walked the nightly black-out of the city like excited explorers adventuring into undiscovered territory. Robert was one. Jenny another.

Yet Léonie was not so sure of things in herself – not so certain, as an American non-combatant, of her part in this war at all. Certainly she was not excited by it, like Robert – nor so icily self-confident and fearless like Jenny. She feared the war, not so much for herself but for Jenny, who was so much more involved in, and exposed to, it in the city centre. She had put so much of her life into Jenny in these last years – relied on her so completely in return – that she had little heart left over to maintain her own sense of self-preservation. Her real fear was that, without her friend, she would be nothing.

So that at night, up in Hampstead when she heard the bombs falling all over the city below her and saw the fires raging in the lurid sky, she lived in tremulous fear, until she could confirm Jenny's safety the following morning. They telephoned each other as often as the connections allowed. And when the telephones were out she usually travelled down to Connaught Square during the day to see that the house was still in one piece.

Léonie lived on tenterhooks, impotent, unable to do anything which would stop these raids which on weekdays so threatened her sanity, longing above all that Jenny would come and live with them out of harm's way in Hampstead.

Hetty and Pierre meanwhile had stayed in Paris. Hetty initially, on the outbreak of war in September 1939, had refused all Pierre's pleas that she return to the safety of Summer Hill. And she did the same, when she might still have escaped the chaos of the city in face of the German advance, in June of the following year. Hetty, too, with her Irish passport, was a non-combatant – and she made much of this to Pierre.

'Ireland's neutral,' she told him forcefully. 'Quite a few people over there are even pro-German! "England's difficulty – Ireland's opportunity." So the Nazis won't – they *can't* – touch me here. I'm staying – with you.'

Hetty, like Léonie with Jenny, depended for her very life on Pierre. She, too, had invested everything in her companion. She, too, would survive the war with him or not at all. But unlike Léonie she lived with Pierre all the time, and so had a blinding sense of self-preservation – as long as that included their both being preserved together, in the same place. Without him, she knew, all the chasms in her life would open again. And so that was her only fear – that they should ever, in any way, be separated. Dying together, if it came to that, would be relatively easy. Living apart, so that he was lost to her, by distance or in dying alone – that would be the only death for her. She had seen that clearly when he had been away from her in the first months of the war.

Pierre had been at that time with the French Army, along the Maginot Line. But the Germans, just as Dermot had forecast, had run their Panzer divisions well north of the line through the Low Countries. In the subsequent collapse of France, the signing of an armistice with Germany in 1940 and the appointment of Pétain as Prime Minister with his supposedly independent administration at Vichy, Pierre was released as a medical officer from an army that no longer existed, resuming his partnership with his friend Dr Vonot on the Avenue Foch.

Pierre, like so many others in that June of 1940, had thought to escape the city with Hetty before the Germans arrived, going south – and thence perhaps over the Pyrenees, getting back to England, and joining the Free French there with de Gaulle. But André Vonot had suggested otherwise.

In the silence of their consulting rooms, late one evening in early June, when the daily panic outside on the streets with the vast exodus of people fighting to get south had subsided, he had said to Pierre, 'With this practice on the Avenue Foch – and all our right-wing "clientele" – we might serve France better by staying put, here at the centre of things, when the Germans take over the city.'

Pierre was appalled. 'You can't be serious! Stay here just to minister to those

French traitors. I hate them! – the cowards, turncoats. That's one reason why I want to get out of France and back to London – so as I can see those people finished with –'

'Yes, Pierre.' Dr Vonot stood up quickly. 'Exactly my own feelings. But think of it another way. When the German high command arrives in Paris, the senior officers – some of them are bound to come to us for consultation. If we play our cards properly, pretend we're turncoats, too, we'll be in a position to learn from these Germans. Their troop movements, dispositions, other goings-on in Paris. It could be vital.'

Pierre was not clear about this. 'What good will that do *us*, you and I –'

'*Others*, Pierre, in London. And in France. They'll want to know.'

'What others? Who? France has collapsed – totally. There are no others.'

'But there *will* be others – soon. There'll be a resistance. There's one already. Me.' He looked at Pierre carefully.

'I *see* . . .' Pierre nodded. Then, after a long moment, he said, 'Yes. Well then, there's me too. I'll stay.'

'Good. But say nothing of this – to anybody. Not even our wives. Nobody must know, except us. Safer that way. Agreed?'

Pierre nodded again.

In the summer of 1941, when Léonie wanted to visit Olivia for her half-term in Gloucestershire, Jenny offered to stay in Hampstead and take care of her father while she was away. 'And I'll be safe up on the hill, too.' She smiled. 'So you won't have to worry about me when you're gone!'

When Léonie left Olivia after the long weekend in the country she caught an afternoon train back from Kemble junction. But the train was endlessly delayed – first by military transports, then by another train detailed outside Reading and finally by that night's bombing, when the Luftwaffe chose the north Paddington area again as their target, so that Léonie's train stopped short at Southall station in the London suburbs at three in the morning, and it was not until dawn that she arrived in Hampstead.

At once she realised there had been a raid somewhere in the area. The High Street was alive with emergency traffic – fire engines and ambulances, bells ringing, streaming up the hill and turning into Willoughby Road some way below her. Over the rooftops a pall of thick black smoke rose into the crystal air of the summer dawn, bits of charred paper and soot spiralling about, an acrid smell of gas, scorched paint and burning wood everywhere.

She went down the High Street, turned left into Flask Walk, running fiercely towards her house in Denning Road. But at the end of the Walk she had to stop. The junction here, which led down towards her street, had entirely disappeared, replaced by a crater, a sheet of yellow flame leaping upwards from a broken gas main; the whole area was roped off, so that Léonie had to turn away.

Retreating back to the High Street, she tore on down the hill, turning left again, taking another route home. But here, in Willoughby Road, there was worse chaos – numbed victims picking their way between fallen rubble and household debris. She pushed through the scurrying crowd of ambulance and firemen, police, ARP wardens, first aid and rescue workers, moving between dazed groups of civilians, in blankets or pyjamas, sitting on the pavement, some still bleeding, others being bandaged, given cups of tea, or taken off in ambulances.

But the really wounded – and the dead, she saw – were being carried out on stretchers from behind another rope barrier which led into her street. There was a stench in the air here – of broken drains, sewer pipes, a smell of suppurating corruption.

Léonie ran on desperately through the crowd, getting right up to another rope barrier. Beyond her the entrance to Denning Road where she lived was partly blocked by smoking rubble, some houses with their windows blown out along either side. But, further, almost two houses had simply disappeared – leaving a great gap in the Victorian terrace – with their back gardens exposed, giving a view clear out over the Heath.

These flattened houses lay to the end of the street where she lived. But from this distance she could not make out if her own house was still standing or not. Running furiously now, she made a second detour, via Pilgrim's Lane, coming back to the south side of Denning Road. But here was another rope and a policeman. She tried to pass.

'Sorry, Miss. No entry. None of the houses is safe. It's been a dirty night here. There may be more time bombs in some of 'em.'

'But I must! My father, my friend – they live, I live, halfway along!'

But now, from this new vantage point as she spoke, Léonie saw the familiar porch, the steps, the hall door of her own house – all intact. She felt a surge of relief. It took her an instant to realise that only the far side of the house was still there.

The building had been cut sheer down the middle, the inside exposed like a doll's house neatly sliced open by a huge knife. She looked up at the top floor where their flat was. Her bedroom was still there. But something was blinding her. She moved aside. It was the big dressing table mirror, she saw then – the one she'd bought at Heal's last year – glittering in the rising sun.

The mirror seemed to have been smashed in half. But why was it moving about like a semaphore mirror – glinting malevolently in the rising sun? Stepping back she finally saw what had happened. The mirror was suspended on a swaying floor joist sticking right over the empty space which had been the other half of the house. And next to it now she saw half her bedroom carpet lurching out into the void, moving gently in a spume of dirty smoke rising from the basement area.

Léonie looked across to the bathroom, where her eye was caught by a tall white shape. Then she saw it was the bath tub itself, but upended against the interior wall, standing vertically, its four clawed feet facing out into the air.

'Your father, Miss?' The policeman had continued talking. 'Well, they've all been evacuated from those houses or – removed . . . You can't go in yourself. Go round to the first aid people in Willoughby Road. They'll know, give you all the names . . .'

Léonie rushed back to the ambulances and first aid post in Willoughby Road, finding a first aid post in a caravan. The door was partly open. Inside a doctor was bandaging a man's torso, the partly mummified figure groaning. A nurse pushed by her.

'My father – and a friend – they were in one of those bombed houses,' she said to the woman as she passed.

'Not here – this is only for the worst cases. Ask Sister – down there, the other first aid post.' She gestured back down the street. Running up and down the street then, Léonie looked at the faces of the stunned civilians, some sipping tea from the mobile canteen, others smoking, their hands shaking, eyes quite blank. Léonie recognised a neighbour of hers, a Mrs Cowdrey, who lived two doors up, sitting there, a blanket round her shoulders. 'Mrs Cowdrey?' She looked up but said nothing. 'Mrs Cowdrey – it's me, Léonie. Did you – did you see my father, or my friend, a woman with reddish hair? Half our house, the whole side of it has gone.'

Mrs Cowdrey shook her head vaguely. The man sitting next to her said, 'All her house went. Lucky she lived in the basement – they just dug her out.' Léonie knew what she had to do then.

A few minutes later, having run right round behind Denning Road on the Heath side, she was climbing over the rubble of her own back garden, dodging a fallen poplar tree, stumbling across the smoking debris scattered over the lawn, making her way towards the garden entrance to the house. This door, to one side, leading into the ground and first floor flat where the Morsebys lived, was still more or less intact. And so was most of their drawing room inside, and the hall, and the flight of stairs leading up to their own hall door. On the way up she found an ARP warden's helmet.

At the top, pushing open the remains of the shattered door, she stepped straight out into bright sunshine, pulling herself back at the last moment, gasping. Only half their hall corridor remained, floorboards still running along one side against the wall, but the other half was empty space, smoke drifting up, dark spumes in the crystal light, from the basement area.

Very gingerly, hands clutching the wall, she moved along this perilous bridge towards the first bedroom door on her left, where her father slept. The door was wide open. And since this bedroom was on the intact side of the house the room seemed largely unscathed. The blast had tipped the furniture and a chest of drawers over, scattering her father's clothes everywhere. But his bed on the far side was still in one piece – and empty. Her father was not there.

Moving on along the swaying floorboards of the corridor she passed the small kitchen and dining room, both damaged, but both empty, then rounded the corner and saw the drawing room in full view ahead of her. There was no door here now at all. It had been blasted clean away. And half the room itself had gone as well, but down the middle, the rest of it a mess of smashed debris and charred furniture.

Beyond it lay her bedroom, the door gone here as well, so that she could see straight into it. Crossing the remains of the drawing room she stood at the threshold. There, to one side by the wall, was her white divan bed, the coverlet all a rumpled mess, smeared, and filthy, but otherwise undamaged, just as her father's bed had been.

Beyond lay the bathroom, the door quite disappeared here too. Hugging the one firm wall, she moved along it into the bathroom. The tiles and washbasin were smashed, the lavatory cistern leaning out into space, and the bath tub itself upended against the firm wall to one side. But the bathroom was quite empty, too.

The whole top flat, or what was left of it, was empty. Above all the two beds where her father and Jenny must have been sleeping when the bomb had fallen were quite intact. And there had been the ARP helmet on the hall stairs . . . They had been saved, miraculously saved – both of their beds against the walls on the side of the house that had survived the bombing. Then, just as she was about to turn and leave, she noticed something on the bathroom floor, a red stain, a pool of liquid, oozing over the remains of the white tiling. It had come from beneath the rim of the upended bath tub. Léonie thought it nothing at first, the water reddened by soil, she imagined, which had come up through the pipes from a broken water main.

Then she started to tremble.

It was too thick for water, the liquid congealing round a mess of glass splinters, broken tiles, familiar cosmetics, old sponges, toothbrushes lying on the floor. She dipped the tip of her shoe in it. It was sticky.

She felt dizzy then. She was dreaming, living out of time now as she moved forward, putting her hand out, grasping one of the upper foot claws of the tub, pulling at it.

A moment later the tub reeled forward and then, gathering momentum, spun outwards, crashing down on the remaining floorboards, where it lay for an instant exposing its contents, before it slipped away over the edge of the broken joists into space, falling out into the sunny morning air, landing with a crash on the rubble beneath.

But in that instant Léonie saw everything – the naked, mangled, bloodied remains of her friend Jenny, entombed in the white enamel tub.

Robert was away, reporting out of Cairo on the Eighth Army's campaign against Rommel in the Western Desert. So he had no immediate knowledge of this appalling tragedy, or of Léonie's stunned reactions to it and her subsequent stay at the New End Hospital in Hampstead, suffering acute shock. There was only her father as immediate consolation – and Olivia who came up to see her for the day.

Ben Straus had survived with a nasty gash and some other minor cuts and bruises. He had gone to bed that evening after Jenny had told him she was taking a bath and had been asleep when the bombing, quite unexpectedly and without any sirens, had started – a whole stick of bombs from some Luftwaffe pilot off-course or, possibly hit by ack-ack fire on the Heath, intent simply on dumping his load anywhere. Stumbling out of bed, Ben Straus had luckily been crouching down, near the inside wall, looking for his dressing gown when the second or third in a series of bombs had exploded, slicing off one side of the house. The blast had hurled him against the wall so that he had been knocked unconscious, lying there for an hour or more before an ARP warden had found him, rescuing him. But the same man had seen nothing of Jenny, hidden in the bath tub.

Now, a week later, recovered and staying with a family temporarily across the High Street, he could say little to Léonie – except, as he did on his first visit to her in hospital, 'I only wish it had been me, dear Léa . . .' And she had looked up at him blankly, saying nothing.

All she could think of was the hideous irony, the malign fate of Jenny being up in Hampstead that weekend, a safety which she had longed for but which instead had resulted in her death.

And Léonie felt responsible for this. So that a sliver of ice grew in her heart, soon becoming a glacier. A cold passion for retribution, or for sacrifice of some sort, came to her then. She was part of the war now, with a vengeance. And the only thing she felt which might release her own vast hurt and guilt would be to punish the Germans somehow, punish fate for its cruelty, punish herself.

By the end of her few days in hospital Léonie had become a different person – hard, bitter, cold. Without Jenny her own life meant nothing. At first, in bed, she had thought simply of killing herself. But then, as she recovered her senses, she changed her mind. She would maintain her life now, but for one reason alone – that she might in some way make amends for Jenny's death.

It was Robert, when Léonie left hospital at the end of the week, who ensured their immediate survival in London. Ben Straus, through the *Express* office, had managed to get a cable through to him in Cairo, giving him the news. And he had replied almost at once, saying they should both move into his empty flat in John Street near High Holborn.

And it was from here, almost immediately after they had moved in, that Léonie went across London one morning on her own to Jenny's flat in Connaught Square. Jenny's father in Camberley had been in touch with her after the funeral – she had been buried in the local churchyard there – offering Léonie what consolation he could and suggesting that she might like to go to the flat herself and take any small mementoes she wished.

Léonie still had the key of the house which, apart from Jenny, had been unoccupied since the start of the blitz, when Mrs Ogilvy had removed herself, with Brewster, to her daughter's house in Yorkshire. Walking into the familiar square where the plane trees were full-leaved in the summer light, Léonie's heart ached. She wondered if she could face it all. But she would, she *must* . . . Jenny would want that. 'It's only a matter of *controlling* yourself, Léa . . .' Jenny's confident voice came back as she walked round the square, the railings all gone, where Brewster had exercised so unwillingly. And she could hardly bear the memories, so that when she came to the sandbagged steps leading up to the front door she was almost in tears.

She wiped her nose. The milkman was coming towards her. Léonie knew him from her own frequent visits to Jenny, leaving with her on those early Monday mornings.

'Mornin', Miss,' he called out brightly. 'Another dirty night ... Glad to see you're still in one piece. And Miss Bryden?'

Léonie could say nothing. Shaking her head, putting her key in the door, she rushed inside. And now she cried – all the way up the darkened stairs, until she got to the door of Jenny's flat, bursting it open.

She pulled herself up, quite horrified. A man was standing by the window where the black-out curtain had been drawn apart – next to Jenny's bureau, which was open, papers scattered about, which he had obviously just been going through. A burglar. Léonie stood rooted to the spot.

A burglar? He seemed far too well dressed for that – a small, neat man in his early forties, fastidious-looking, with a tiny moustache and sleek black hair, wearing a sharply-cut brown suit and expensive dimpled leather brogues, almost a dandy.

Léonie was speechless. But the man was not at all put out by this discovery of his presence in the flat. More surprising still, for Léonie had never seen him before in her life, he knew who she was – calling her by her married name then, which she had not used in years.

'I'm sorry – Mrs Grant, isn't it?' He dropped the folder he had been looking at, came towards her, taking a white silk handkerchief from his breast pocket, offering it hesitantly. Léonie refused it. 'Your great friend Jenny – what a blow. What a blow for all of us.' The man used the handkerchief himself now for an instant absent-mindedly, dabbing his nose.

Léonie stirred at last. 'Who? What? – "All of us"?'

'I'm sorry ...' The man smiled a fraction in the half-light, before turning and opening the other black-out curtain so that the room was flooded in sunlight. 'I'm Swanning, the War Office, Jenny's department. I've been in touch with Colonel Bryden, of course, who knows all about it – my being here, I mean.' He gestured towards the bureau. 'Just in case, to check Jenny didn't leave any War Office papers here.' His tone was clipped, but soft. There was something sensitive about him, and yet dynamic.

'I see.' Léonie was a little more at ease, wiping her own nose, recovering. 'But how did you know my name?'

Swanning smiled quickly again. 'Oh, Jenny told us about you, Mrs Grant.'

Léonie was annoyed as much as surprised. 'Did she? Why?'

'A close friend ... We're a small department. You met each other in Paris, I believe?'

'No.' Léonie was abrupt. 'On the train from Paris actually. The night ferry.'

'Of course.' He wiped his neat hands on the silk hanky. 'You've both spent a lot of time in Paris.'

'No.' Léonie was pleased to contradict him again. 'We were never there together.'

'I meant separately. She said – how your father lived there –'

'I was born and brought up in Paris, Mr Swanning,' she told him abruptly.

'Of course –'

'But why should Jenny have told you all this? What's it to do with you?'

Swanning, looking at her carefully, made an apologetic gesture. 'I'm sorry. It must seem like prying. It's just – that Jenny always spoke of you so highly. I was going to write to you – when you got out of hospital,' he rushed on.

'About what?'

He seemed surprised. 'About the possibility of our meeting. At my office – if, if you could spare the time.'

'Yes. But *why?*' Léonie was increasingly impatient.

'Well, I'd wondered if – if you might consider doing something with us for the war effort.' He turned, looking out at the blitzed view – the sandbags, a fallen plane tree in the square, a shattered house on the other side, the silver barrage balloons floating over Hyde Park in the pale summer sky. 'You see . . .' He turned to her, picking up a framed photograph from the bureau, so that Léonie glowered at him and he put it down again. 'You see, we can't just let the Germans go on killing innocent people like this. We've all got to help stop it.' He looked at Léonie. There was silence.

'Yes,' Léonie said at last, but without interest. Then she added, but with no more enthusiasm, 'Yes, I'd like to help.'

'Good. Very good.' Swanning took no notice of her dulled response. 'I thought you might. When would suit you to meet me more formally – next week?'

'As soon as possible. Tomorrow?'

He seemed slightly put out by this eagerness. 'I'm afraid . . . I'm away tomorrow. Would next week suit? Friday, ten o'clock? Here's my card. We're at the Victoria Hotel for the moment, the Quartermaster-General's H.Q. in Northumberland Avenue. Ask for me with the commissionaire. He'll show you straight up.'

After Swanning had gone Léonie picked up the photograph he had been looking at. There were two separate photographs, joined together in the same frame – both taken at the same time several years before, in the beech glades near Aylesbury when she and Jenny had gone out there with Brewster on the Green Line bus. Léonie pulled out the one of Jenny, sitting against the bole of a huge trunk with Brewster. She left the other happy vision of herself, in the same position, behind.

'It's a matter, Mrs Grant, of causing maximum discomfort and inconvenience for the Germans in France . . .' Mr Swanning spoke in an off-hand way, as if these Germans were unwelcome guests in an hotel and Léonie was simply to help in persuading them to leave.

'Discomfort, inconvenience – I see,' she said with some irony. Swanning was gazing absent-mindedly up at the ceiling.

'Well,' he pulled himself together. 'I meant sabotage, physical disruption of every sort – trains, factories and so on. That's what our work is all about. And the Germans don't like it. They react savagely, brutally.' He looked at her carefully.

'That would suit me fine,' she replied immediately.

This seemed to bother Swanning. But he continued with his initial résumé. 'There are a number of French resistance groups involved in just this sort of sabotage at the moment – but with too much uncoordinated enthusiasm, I'm bound to say. It's our aim to help them – actively on the ground, as well as supply them with arms, ammunition and so on. So we're going to need people over here – French people, or people like yourself who can pass entirely for French – to help us in this. How would you like to go to France?'

He stood up from the plain table with just a green folder on it, offering Léonie a cigarette. Apart from a notice about air raid precautions, the room was quite bare, high up in the Victoria Hotel, all the windows shuttered, just a naked light bulb illuminating what had once been a single bedroom, a dusty washbasin in one corner.

Léonie refused the cigarette. She was quite calm already, icy calm. 'I don't know whether you're aware of it, Mr Swanning, but all the Channel boats have stopped . . .'

'Ah, yes . . . But there are other ways of going to France – other than by the night ferry, Mrs Grant.'

'The War Office can send people to France?'

Mr Swanning was shocked. 'Goodness me, no! Far too proper an organisation. Just accept that we could get you to France, if you were absolutely sure that this was something you'd be prepared to risk. This would be dangerous work – and entirely voluntary.'

'Who is "we"? I thought you – you and Jenny – worked for the War Office.'

'Another and quite separate department of it, Mrs Grant. But just accept that we could get you there. Would you go?'

'Yes.' Léonie responded at once. 'I'd be quite prepared to go.'

Again this immediate agreement seemed to worry Mr Swanning. 'Why, Mrs Grant?' He looked at her closely.

'Why have you asked me here, suggested I go – if you didn't think I would?'

'I just wonder about . . . your motives.'

'Well, the Germans obviously – as you said the other day – killing innocent people. Jenny . . . I wouldn't mind dying, the way she did.'

Swanning looked even more worried now. 'This work is about living not dying. We'd want you to *live*, Mrs Grant. That would be the whole purpose of the work. This could be no personal vendetta against the Nazis, or gone into with any idea of self-sacrifice –'

'No,' Léonie interrupted him. 'I just meant I was quite prepared to face the risks. You said the work was dangerous. If that includes dying, well, I'm prepared for that, too.'

'The risks are very real. We've already lost quite a few of our agents and wireless operators over there. And by lost I mean almost certainly dead – and cruelly tortured by the Gestapo before that –'

'Shall we talk about the work involved, Mr Swanning, not the risks,' she told him brusquely.

'Yes, of course.' He was almost apologetic. 'You would have to be trained for what we have in mind, several months at least, before being sent into the field.'

Again Léonie was impatient. 'Yes – but what kind of work, and where in France?'

Mr Swanning sighed, leaning forward. 'I don't want to go into details now. I want you to think about the general idea very carefully, before committing yourself. As I've told you, this is entirely voluntary –'

'But I've *said* – I'm quite prepared to go.'

'You have a daughter, Mrs Grant.'

'She's at boarding school, safely in the west country. And, if anything happened to me, my husband would be there to look after her.'

'Yes, your husband – Robert Grant, the *Express* war correspondent –'

'We've been separated – nearly four years.'

'Yes, we knew that. I'm sorry . . .'

Léonie was surprised how much he knew about her. 'But, you can see, there's nothing to stop me in that direction.'

'All the same, give yourself a week, be quite sure.' He stood up. 'Get in touch with me again. Here's my card.'

'You've already given me your card.'

'Another card.' He handed it over to her. It gave quite a different name and address. 'Capt. Selwyn Jepson, Ministry of Pensions, Sanctuary Buildings, Northumberland Avenue, W.C.'

Léonie looked at it. 'My, is that your *real* name this time?'

'Yes.'

'What a lot of cloak and dagger . . .'

'Yes, Mrs Grant. That's exactly it. And I have to tell you that's the very basis of all the work we do. So you will remember, won't you? – "Careless talk costs lives." In our business – literally and most painfully. You must mention nothing of our meeting – to *anyone*.' Captain Jepson had quite lost his vagueness now, was direct, steely.

'Of course. I can keep secrets.' She stood up and Jepson went with her to the door, before she turned to him. 'All the same, you must have been very sure of me, to ask me here and tell me all this secret stuff in the first place.'

'Jenny was very sure of you, Mrs Grant.' He looked at her now in his old vague sensitive way. 'And Jenny was one of the mainstays of our organisation.'

'*Was* she? How? What did she –'

He put a hand on her shoulder, then took it away almost at once, embarrassed. 'Not just now. *Think* about it all first.'

'I *have* thought about it, believe me. I'll be in touch with you. Goodbye.'

He opened the door for her. 'Well, Mrs Grant – *au revoir* perhaps, rather than goodbye.'

Returning to his desk, he opened the dark green folder, making a note at the end of a long typed memorandum, which included a great deal of personal information on Léonie – her family background and much else – which had been supplied to him during the past ten days by MI5.

'As far as I can tell at this juncture,' he wrote, 'Mrs Grant would in many ways be an ideal recruit for us. Her French is practically flawless, as is her knowledge of Paris and much of Normandy – two of our main target areas. There seems a steely purpose in her temperament – to the point of truculence almost. And here is one of her problems. I fear that perhaps her motives in so readily accepting our offer to join us (in the main, I am sure, due to the death of her – and our – close friend Jenny) may lead her into a quite unwanted mode of impetuous self-sacrifice, of personal revenge indeed, in any work she might do for us.

'The other problem is her age. At 42 she may be too old for the rigours of training, not to mention the physical requirements and dangers of life in the field. However, she certainly looks fit enough – and I believe her other merits outweigh these possible disadvantages. I shall be seeing her again, I am sure, and will make a final recommendation then.

'Meanwhile, it is my feeling that she would make a first-class agent. She sees the alternatives, yet the *heart* in every matter. Above all she has the *intelligence*, in every sense, which is so essential in this work. On the other hand, as I have suggested, she is a woman of very strong emotions, not always kept under control. There is a core of explosive personal venom in her which she must suppress, or redirect towards the common ends of our work. In short, she must temper this emotional imprudence, become more self-aware, objective, cold, calculating, more concerned with her own preservation. If she can achieve this I believe she would confirm all Jenny's high recommendations of her.'

He put the memorandum into a TOP SECRET manila envelope, addressing it to a Colonel Maurice Buckmaster, at premises in Baker Street.

10

'So, Mrs Grant, you have thought about it. And so have I. You are quite certain about it all. And I think I am as well.'

Captain Jepson smiled his vague smile, then offered her a cigarette. The mood between them was easier now – a week later, in Jepson's equally austere, unused room in the Ministry of Pensions. 'Now we can start on the details. You'll have to enrol first as an officer in FANY. It's necessary under international law –'

'FANY?'

'Yes. First Aid Nurses Yeomanry. A fine body of women – they run ambulance units, work in forces canteens, act as chauffeurs for senior officers –'

'But that's not the sort of work I expected –'

He raised his hand. 'No, no, of course not. Just a necessary, indeed an excellent, cover while you're in training here. You'll be commissioned as a subaltern – you'll even get to wear a red "raspberry" on your shoulder strap! Once we get through with that I'll take you to our HQ, introduce you to the man in charge of all these operations.'

'Some other room tucked away here?'

'Oh no. We have quite separate premises – just north of Oxford Street.'

'Where Jenny worked?' He nodded. 'But I thought she was in Whitehall all the time.'

'No. She was closer – to home . . .'

'What did she do? You said you'd tell me.'

'She would have been doing just what we hope you may do – an agent in the field. She very much wanted to. But her short sight prevented her. She worked on codes with us, Léonie. Codes – and clothes . . .'

'Clothes?'

'Yes. French clothes. And all the many accessories. Everyone we drop into France has to be kitted out in exactly the current manner over there. Right labels, stitching, linings, buttons, clothes coupons, and so on. Women's jackets, for example, are eight or ten inches longer over there now than here.'

'I see. Of course . . . Clothes, all Jenny's sewing and so on. All her experience with her mother working for Chanel.'

'Exactly.'

And codes, too, Léonie thought – seeing then how Jenny could so easily write 'Je t'aime' backwards on the clouded window-pane. Their life together returned to her, heart-rendingly. But she would make up for that loss, she thought with a bitter certainty, in one way or another. 'But "dropped" into France?' she asked.

'Parachute, Léonie. I told you – we can't send agents in on the night ferry now. That'll be part of your training, too. At Ringway, Manchester. They say it's wonderful – floating down in the blue . . .'

He smiled, his nice vague smile.

A week later, enrolled in FANY and wearing a smart new uniform, Léonie was taken by Jepson not to Baker Street but to a luxurious private apartment nearby at Orchard Court in Portman Square. Here she met Maurice Buckmaster, a willowy, sparse-haired, pipe-smoking Colonel, out of uniform now, with a notably melliflu-ous voice quite at odds with his austere, sharp-eyed military bearing. He treated Léonie as an equal, from the moment she sat down on a deep-cushioned sofa in the drawing room.

'Léonie . . . Léonie Grant.' He looked at her appraisingly then continued in French from then on. 'Good to have you with us – in Special Operations Executive – more usually known as "the Firm", "the Racket", "the Org" – and sometimes, indeed, as the "Stately 'Omes of England"!'

He laughed, tipping his chin up in the air and lighting his pipe. Léonie was surprised at this sudden jocularity. The Colonel continued more soberly: 'Forgive me, but absolute trust, confidence, mutual understanding is, must be the basis between all of us at HQ and anyone we send into the field. We're equals here. No standing on ceremony. Everything, at Orchard Court at least, in the open.' His eyes twinkled. 'A cup of coffee, Léonie? Selwyn, would you do the honours? It's in the kitchen. We have some *real* coffee – sent over by our man in New York. Now where was I?'

'Confidence, Colonel.'

'Ah, yes – absolute mutual trust and confidence. We depend on you, as you do on us. That's the first thing to realise. Without this feeling of close partnership the whole enterprise collapses. And the second thing to remember, Léonie – if and when you succeed in this training and go into the field – is that your life, the life of your contacts, comrades, will always lie on the tip of your tongue, on your *silence*. "Upon these two commandments hang all the law and the prophets!"' He laughed uproariously again.

'And – what else, Colonel?'

'Yes, indeed . . .' He leant forward briskly in his armchair by the marble fireplace, then paused, setting a flame to his pipe once more, puffing vigorously. 'A hundred

and one things, which you'll come upon in your training. But, first, your name . . .'
He took another match to the recalcitrant pipe.

'A name?' Léonie asked in the silence.

'Yes,' he said at last, now garlanded in smoke. 'From now on, and through each stage of your training, you will have a different name, a French Christian name only, and you will be known by no other, so to make it the more difficult for other agents, or nosy outsiders, to keep track of you. May I offer you the name "Lise" to begin with?' he said with a touch of irony, the mock knight-errant.

'If you like.'

'Excellent, Lise. This will only be the nursery slopes of your aliases. The Everest, if you complete your training satisfactorily, will be the name you take up before you actually go into the field. Not only a new name but a whole new identity, as a French citizen, living – who has *always* lived – in France. And before you leave you will have to know everything, but *everything*, about an entirely imaginary person, who will be *you*. You'll have to eat, sleep and dream this person – at the cost of your life, if you slip up on the picture.' The Colonel was entirely serious now. 'That's really the third law, Lise: an absolute belief in this mysterious other person whom you will inhabit when the time comes.'

'Like being an actress?'

'Yes. But dramatist as well. You'll have to write the text here, too, as you go along.'

'I think I could do that well enough.' Léonie remembered her years with Hetty, playing just such games, swapping clothes, roles, getting in and out of new characters almost every day.

The Colonel nodded, but then was gently dampening. 'Indeed, Lise, I hope so. Your audience and the critics, will be made up of the Gestapo or their French lackeys. And the subsequent notices – quite possibly death notices.'

'Yes, of course.'

There was a moment's chilly silence, until Jepson returned with the coffee.

'Ah, Selwyn! – *real* coffee. You can always rely on that here as well as in Orchard Court, Lise.' And again there was the soothing, confident laugh.

Ben Straus was pleased though surprised when Léonie joined the Nursing Yeomanry. It would get her out of herself, he thought, occupy her after the brutal shock, the tragedy of Jenny's death. Yet he was taken aback by the speed with which she had started on this fresh war work – surprised, too, by a whole new air of cold decisiveness now in her character. He had expected a dumb depression, for he had seen just this in her before, for months on end, when her life with Hetty and Robert had come apart. Instead, almost as soon as she had left hospital, there was this hard streak in her, a ruthless intent which he did not understand.

After all, she was only going to drive ambulances in England, work in canteens or as a chauffeur – mild enough war work. Yet here she was behaving like a combatant about to go into the front line. It disturbed him so that, when she told him she was going to be away for a month or more at a FANY training course, somewhere in the country, he could no longer restrain some of his feelings.

'I thought they'd train you here in London? You have an address for this place? So we can keep in touch?'

'No, no. I don't. I'll be moving around, different places, all over the country apparently. And that's what really worries me – you. I don't think I'm going to be able to get back to London at all, even weekends.'

'Oh, I'll be fine. The bombing's stopped by and large right now. And I can manage the stairs here, not in my dotage yet, you know. And I've all these new friends over here now at the Embassy in Grosvenor Square. It's you I'm worried about, Léa. You've gotten so . . . preoccupied, hard, lately. Not like you. Oh, I know it's one way of dealing with tragedy –'

'Yes. Yes, it is,' was all she could say.

'But this going away, to some unknown address, Léa. You're not doing anything stupid?'

Wearing her smart new uniform, she turned to him from the window, smoothing the lapels out, brushing down the skirt. 'No, Papa. Not stupid. Just necessary.'

She stood against the light streaming into the Holborn flat. She had almost entirely lost her slight plumpness, he noticed. That soft mellowness had quite disappeared, the friendly, candid air. It seemed as if the warm heart had been torn from his daughter and replaced by a cold pump. She was harsh and military as she stood there in her uniform. Léa, his dear daughter, had grown away from him – embarked on something he knew nothing of. For he knew with some certainty that she was lying to him about going off on some innocent nurses' training course in the country.

'Well, you're no fool, Léa . . .' He came to her, touching her cheek an instant. 'You'll know what you're doing. But I hope – I know you're up to something out of the ordinary, probably dangerous, not just driving superannuated colonels round the parade ground – I hope you're not thinking of doing something rash, because of Jenny.'

She turned to the window. A taxi crawled along High Holborn – making a complete circle round an old bomb crater, before returning the way it had come.

Did she know what she was doing? Was she really prepared to go to France – to shoot and kill and very possibly die herself – simply on behalf of Jenny?

Did she owe Jenny her own death?

No, it wasn't that. It had been – initially, when she'd first met Selwyn Jepson. But she saw clearly that she owed Jenny, owed everyone, her life, not her death – just as Jepson had told her afterwards. Her hardness was for that now. She would survive this work, this war. Certain before that she could not live without Jenny, she saw now how the only way to do this was to survive for her – and to fulfil what Jenny had not been able to do because of her short sight: go to France for the same organisation as she had worked for. This way, at least, she would remain with Jenny in a sense – linked with her, not through death but in this future life.

This way, however tenuously, she would keep faith with her, preserve their love.

She turned back to her father then. 'No,' she said. 'It *was* that feeling, that I didn't want to live, wanted to die like her, just in any violent old way in the war, it didn't matter. But now it's different. I want to live for her – and you. And Olivia.' She looked at her father. 'But I can't live any more just twiddling my thumbs in London. I have to do something – as Jenny did.'

'Which I bet wasn't driving decrepit old colonels about . . .'

'No. But I can't tell you what, exactly –'

'No. You don't have to. I can guess – something secret, and therefore dangerous. So – I just hope you don't see this work as a simple way out.'

'A way back, Papa – I hope. For me, to her – to all of you.'

With half a dozen other girls Léonie, as Lise, started her first month's training at Wanborough Manor, a rebuilt Tudor country house in a heavily-guarded estate outside Guildford in Surrey. The place was as comfortable and well-appointed as Orchard Court – antique furnishings downstairs, large chintzy bedrooms, special rations, a French chef, tennis courts and a swimming pool among the pines. The mood was one of a pre-war country house party.

They were not told, of course, but this luxury was intentional – intended to get them all at their most relaxed, the better to put them off their guard, so that the training officers and NCOs, under the elegant Major Roger de Wesselow, might spot any character faults, lapses, gauge their true spirit and outlook.

Léonie came through with flying colours in this respect. Unlike some of the other girls from suburban backgrounds, she, with her long experience of just such elegant living, in Paris and at Summer Hill, found nothing tempting or extraordinary in this mode of existence.

Nor – soon getting back into the way of her circus experience with Fonsy O'Grady's troupe in Ireland years before – did she find much difficulty over the initial physical training – or in the various tumbles and painful falls which she had to undergo in her unarmed combat course.

So, too, the evening indoor games – played to sharpen their wits and memory as when they were given a quick glance at a laden tray and had to itemise all the objects on it afterwards – posed no problems for her. And the charades, which she had indulged in so many times – publicly and privately, with Hetty – were almost too easy: these theatricals designed to prepare the girls for the new identities which they would have to assume in the field.

French was spoken at all times. And Léonie thought her grasp here was as good as any, until Major de Wesselow remarked on her slight American intonation in some words.

'You must remember,' he told her in his own perfect French. 'Some of the Gestapo are the world's best interrogators. And certainly all the ones you meet, if you have that misfortune, will speak and understand French like natives.' The shadow of the Gestapo was never far from the Major's presentations and lectures. This, too, was intentional. Fear, he knew well, was a great aid to self-preservation.

All mail sent or received was censored. And telephone calls either way were strictly forbidden. But here, like the other girls, Léonie was able to keep in touch with her father via letters written on a number of differently-headed sheets of Army notepaper, addressed from various barracks and military depots throughout the country, and posted from there, so that relations and husbands might be reassured as to the girls' well-being and whereabouts.

In the other training activities Léonie was less adept. Morse code she found difficult. Hand grenades and explosives alarmed her far more than they might any enemy. So, too, the use of weapons – Tommy guns, rifles, revolvers – was something she did not take to easily. She handled these violent lengths of metal clumsily, afraid of them, afraid of her ability to control them.

The Major watched her one day at the indoor shooting range in a barn behind the house. Her first four shots from the Beretta automatic had all gone wide, outside the circle. She paused, in frustration.

'Two hands, yes, but hold it more *firmly*, Lise! And you really have to *look* at the target, not turn away at the last moment.'

'I wish I could use a foil – I used to fence a lot . . .'

'Indeed . . . But I fear the days of the Three Musketeers are over in France, my dear.'

'Or a knife. Couldn't I just use a knife to kill them?' She was entirely serious. And the Major saw this.

'Yes,' he said. 'In certain circumstances. And you will have training in that later, if you pass on from here. But, for the moment, let us concern ourselves with your just *shooting* your enemies, Lise . . .'

The Major watched her. She raised the Beretta again. And this time, with a vehement look in her eyes, clutching the automatic fiercely and without turning away when she fired, she let off the remaining bullets, two of them finding the circle. The Major congratulated her. 'Well done,' he said. 'Two Germans down the hatch.' She would just about pass the initial course, he thought. More likely to wound, rather than kill, in her small arms ability. On the other hand her intelligence work, her memory, her impromptu charades, her gift of taking on new identities, her quick-thinking responses under questioning – all this was superb.

In the far north of Scotland, where she went for a second month, after a week back with her father in London, Léonie's training was far more rigorous. They were camped in a small, partly-ruined farmhouse at the end of some five miles of tortuous, bumpy tracks, way out on the wildest part of the Inverness coast.

The food consisted largely of herrings, stale bread and weak tea. The broken windows rattled in the autumn storms. It was wet – and cold, especially at five in the morning when they set out on their daily treks and training sessions over the bare mountains rising steeply up behind the farmhouse.

Here, throughout the autumn, the girls were put through an entire commando course at the hands of various instructors, both military and civilian, experts in small arms fire, rock-climbing, map-reading, judo, close-armed combat, sabotage – involving mock attacks with live ammunition, the use of explosives of all kinds. Even a royal gamekeeper from Balmoral had been engaged to teach them how to stalk, to avoid being stalked, how to live off the land.

Léonie, under the new name of Céline, was twelve years older than the next oldest girl, and did not bear up well to this punishing regime. The forty-eight-hour treks over the stormy hills, sleeping rough at nights, getting lost in the freezing mists, falling into ice-cold burns, climbing almost-sheer rock faces, live ammunition whistling over her head as she crawled across a sodden bog – all this, despite her very best efforts, very nearly undid her.

And her instructors noted these disabilities in their reports. So that when, after six weeks, she returned to London, Colonel Buckmaster, having read the reports, spoke to her in Orchard Court.

'So . . .' He looked up from the papers. 'It seems the hard life is not quite your forte, Céline!' There was still the musical voice, the laughter there. But a note of regret now as well.

'I didn't do too badly, surely?' She knew from his tone that he was going to turn her down.

'No. Indeed not. For someone your age – if you'll forgive me – you did remarkably well. It's just that, in France – this is rough work, Céline. No two ways about it . . .' He glanced back at his papers. It was a cold, depressing November day. Léonie felt the chill of failure then, as well as of climate. He had not offered her any coffee either. But she was not to be put down. She was not out of it all yet.

'But I did well in the close-armed combat, didn't I?' She referred here to her vicious exercises with a short-bladed knife, first against a suspended sack of straw, then against a rather surprised young man, a commando NCO. Her fencing experience with Hetty had served her well in this.

'Yes, I see that. Full marks! –'

'And surely this work in France won't be all physical. Won't it be just as much *intelligence* work? Walking the streets, sitting in cafés, eyes and ears open, taking trains and buses, knowing the routes and timetables and so on. And not being *noticed*, living the part. Isn't that so?'

'Yes, quite so – when the work is going well. But if it doesn't – as will quite likely be the case – then you have to be entirely competent in the other, more violent aspects of the job.'

'Well, I'm obviously better at the first part. But I can do both. And, besides, my age may be a disadvantage for sabotage work. But in another way it's an advantage. The Germans won't expect someone my age to be a British agent!'

'Possibly, yes –'

'And then, couldn't you give me – won't you need people in *Paris*, not in the country? Because Paris I know like the back of my hand.'

'Yes, that's possible . . .'

'Please, Colonel – you know I so want to do this, to go to France.' She looked at him, without pleading, without any expression of bravado, totally controlled, sincere.

The Colonel, seeing all this – this calm passion – suddenly knew he must take a chance on this woman. On physical grounds he ought to have turned her down. But she had so many other gifts – of imagination, adaptability, quick verbal response – all so ideally suited to some of the work involved, that he knew he could not let them go to waste. And, besides, she was right – there was, he thought, likely to be most vital work required in Paris . . .

'All right,' he said finally. 'I take your points. What name would you like – for the last part of your training – the "finishing school"? Michèle?' She nodded. 'Right, Michèle. Now what about a cup of real coffee before you go?' She smiled for the first time in weeks.

Léonie woke with a violent start, the torch light directly in her eyes, before two shadowy figures in trench-coats pulled her up from the bed and pushed her violently out of the room, rushing her down the stairs, taking her at a run down to a bare, cold, cell-like room in the basement.

A plain table was set in the middle, chairs to either side, with another much brighter light shining straight into her eyes. The two men sat opposite. She was still half-asleep. The first man, quite invisible now behind the light, started to question her aggressively in French.

'Name?'

'Yvonne . . .' She hesitated, wiping the sleep out of her eyes. 'Yvonne de Sertigny.'

'Your father?'

'Jean de Sertigny. And my mother was called Claudine –'

'We didn't ask you about your mother.' His tone was vicious, spiteful. 'What does your father do?'

'He's dead –'

'How, when did he die?'

'Killed. He was a Captain in the 54th Regiment of Infantry. Killed just a year before the armistice at Verdun – in the Great War.'

'And your mother? – what did she do?' The questions, switching suddenly and irrationally, came staccato from both men now.

'My mother disappeared –'

'I asked what she *did*?'

Léonie shook her head in confusion. 'She – she didn't do anything. She was just married –'

'How did she disappear? When?'

'On the route south from Paris, in June 1940. We were just outside Rambouillet, all the crowds on the roads. I think – she was killed, in the strafing.'

'Where were you brought up as a child?'

Léonie hesitated again, wiping her eyes. 'We lived – number 12 – no it was 14 – rue du Dragon, eighth *arrondissement*. An old *hôtel particulier*. A big ground floor apartment, through the arched doorway, right at the far end of the courtyard. There was a little bell over the side-door, the servants' entrance – and we used to eat sometimes at the Restaurant du Dragon, just a little way up –'

'The Chinese restaurant?'

'No, of course not. It's French – just a bourgeois family restaurant – Madame Galliard runs it.'

'And when you lost your mother outside Rambouillet – what happened then?'

'I came back to our apartment in Passy. Number 27, Avenue Henri Martin, just up from the Cimetière de Passy.'

'Not married? Why is that? – a woman like you.'

'My fiancé, Richard Bouvrier, a Captain in the Fifth Armoured Division – he was killed on – on 29 May, 1940, near Lille, during the Panzer *blitzkrieg* there.'

'Convenient, isn't it, Mademoiselle de Sertigny – your father and your fiancé both dead, your mother "disappeared" ...'

Léonie shrugged. 'I don't know what you mean "convenient" ... It's a tragedy. The war. Two wars.' She glowered at the two men beyond the bright light.

'What did your mother do – between the two wars?'

'Nothing. I told you. She was a widow. She bought our apartment on the Avenue Henri Martin – and lived there. With me. I looked after her.'

'Is that *all* you did?' The question was derisive.

'No, I taught the piano, and singing, privately, in the apartment. I'm a music teacher. You've seen my Carte d'Identité.'

'And your grandparents? Who were they? Where did they live?'

'My mother's parents, the de Bellays, came from Chambrais near Lisieux –'

'And your father's father?'

'The de Sertignys – they lived in the Château de Courcy, just south of Coutance in the Cotentin peninsula. My great-grandfather bought it in –'

'Where was your fiancé educated?'

'Here, in Paris. The Lycée Henri Quatre.'

'He was clever then?'

'Yes.'

'Why did he join the army, when he could have gone on to one of the *Ecoles Supérieures*?'

'He disliked ... bureaucracy. He wanted something in the open air.'

'What was your grandfather's château like?'

'Small, in the Louis XIII style, two turrets at either end. There was an old dry moat, the ruins of an Abbey just behind it. Mama and I used to come up on the train for summer holidays there – the branch line that runs south of Bayeux, up to Carentan –'

'We don't want to know about your summer holidays. Where were you at school?'

'At the Ecole Sainte-Mathilde, near Bayeux, at the Château de Héricourt. It was a convent. The nuns were *soeurs sécularisées.*'

'An expensive establishment, in another château . . .'

'Yes. The school no longer exists. Closed years ago.'

'All these châteaux, Mademoiselle de Sertigny – *la vie grand luxe*. Châteaux and apartments in the *seizième*. Well, we'll soon take you down a peg or two from all that.' The man stood up. 'Your *Carte d'Identité*,' he shouted now, coming round to her side of the table, laying her *Carte* in front of her. Léonie looked at in the bright light. 'It's out of order,' the man continued grimly.

'Out of order?' Léonie felt herself tremble with fear.

'And you cannot see it yourself?'

'No.'

'Your hair, Mademoiselle. Black, it says here. But your hair is obviously brown . . .'

'Oh, I had it dyed,' Léonie said immediately and quite evenly.

'And your photograph – it shows you wearing spectacles. Yet you have none on. And none with you.'

'I only wear them for reading,' she retorted equally quickly. 'But they broke, just the other day.'

The bitter, brutal interrogation dragged on for another thirty minutes – in the cold little basement still-room at Beaulieu Manor, before Léonie was finally released and returned to her comfortable bedroom in the huge house in the New Forest.

'So, Yvonne – flying colours, on all your finishing school reports.' Colonel Buckmaster congratulated her as she entered the drawing room of Orchard Court a week later. For the first time she saw him in uniform – both of them in uniform, standing at the doorway, exchanging smiles.

'Thank you, Colonel. A month's parlour games in the New Forest . . .' she added a little ruefully.

'Your forte, Yvonne – as I well knew!' The pipe was not in evidence today. He was brisk, pleased. 'And it's the most vital part of the training. All these psychological games, taking on an entire new life – every detail, every *potential* detail, living it, dreaming it, day and night. Not easy. But the reports –' He moved over to the marble mantelpiece, picking up a folder there. 'Superb – by and large.'

'By and large?' They sat down.

'Difficult to fault you. Except that you had a tendency in the interrogations to be a little *too* forthcoming, inventive. Watch that. Remember, you're a woman of the French upper classes, of the *seizième*, the *ancien régime*. They would not be so forthcoming, more *de haut en bas*!'

'Yes.'

'On the other hand your hesitancies – they were fine.' He opened the file. 'Forgetting the number of your old apartment in the rue du Dragon – and contradicting them about the Chinese restaurant. Very quick of you!'

'Who *were* those men?'

'Clever, weren't they?' He smiled.

'Especially about the *Carte d'Identité*. The wrong hair and no glasses. That nearly threw me completely.'

'As was intended. But your responses were just the ticket.'

'Thank God! I certainly don't want to wear glasses and dye my hair . . .'

The Colonel looked up at her searchingly now. 'That is exactly what you're going to have to do, Yvonne – on your first mission, after you complete the parachute course at Manchester.'

'Oh, no –'

'Yes, Yvonne. Because we're sending you to the same *quartier* where you lived in Paris – Passy, the *seizième*. And although you've only been back there to your father's house irregularly over the years, it's just possible a concierge or someone might recognise you – on the street or in a café. And then, of course, Yvonne de Sertigny herself had brown hair – and wore spectacles . . .'

'Yes, but *Passy?*'

He nodded. 'It's vital work. There's a French resistance network operating there. One of the most important we have connections with in France . . .' The Colonel paused. And now he took his pipe out and started to fiddle with it.

'And?'

'We believe it's been penetrated by the Germans. Various suspicions. They transmit on the usual short-wave circuits, from various parts of the western suburbs and further out. But several times in the last month or so, the WT operator's call-sign – his "fingerprint" – has struck us, not as incorrect, but "smudged".'

'But if he was under any sort of duress there'd be the other signal – the intentional mistake in the message itself.'

'Yes. And there's never been that. Which makes us think that either the WT operator has been turned, or that the network recruited a French traitor from the word go.'

'But you've no other direct evidence?'

'Well, we may have, I'm afraid. We've sent two of our agents from Normandy into Paris in the last two months, to contact the head of this circle to check on his WT operator. The idea was to get him to transmit some false information, which, if he was a double agent, would get back to the Germans, of course – which they'd act on and which we'd know about then, proving the operator was a traitor.'

'And did the information get back to the Germans?'

'No. It didn't. Because both our agents, either before they got to Paris, or as soon as they arrived there, got picked up by the Gestapo.'

'Who in the Paris network knew they were arriving?'

'No one. No one from this Passy circle anyway – as far as we know. So it may be just coincidence they were both picked up. On the other hand we can't rely on that. The head of this Passy circle – code-named Michel – may have betrayed them. Or French resistance groups in Normandy, where they went in, via Gisors, part of the Centurie network. Some of these French resistance networks are not at all secure.'

'You mean this man Michel may be a double-agent as well?'

'It's possible. And that's exactly what we want you to check out: him and the WT operator, code-named Louis. They may be working this together. And your job will be to contact Michel without his having any idea that you're with us. And, having contacted him, stay with him, find out all you can, above all try and join his resistance group. We have to be sure of this network, one way or the other. Because the information we're getting from them is grade A stuff. But this could well be a ploy, their offering us genuine information, so as to trap more and more French resisters as well as our own SOE agents, before they entirely bust the circle.'

'Fine. But there's the problem, isn't there? – if I contact this man as Michel he'll know at once I'm an agent myself, with SOE or a French group . . .'

'Yes, but we've been doing some work on our own over there, Yvonne. We now know who Michel is. We have his real name and his business address in Paris. You'll be able to contact him quite openly and directly there.'

'Who is he?'

The Colonel demurred. 'It'll all be in your operation instructions. When you get them, read them here, memorise it all, after the parachute course at Ringway. What I want to impress on you now is that this is important – and dangerous, of course. Because, if one or other of these two men are working for the Germans, and for a moment suspect that you're with us, you'll go the way of the other two agents we sent in. Because they'll do anything to maintain the fiction of their running a genuine resistance circle. And we'll be none the wiser. So we have to know.' He stood up, opening Léonie's finishing school file. 'I'll see you again, of course, before you leave. But you're happy about Yvonne de Sertigny?'

'Yes. Yes, I'm her all right, top to toe. Apart from the hair and glasses . . .'

'The relations, your fiancé – the addresses are all covered – because they're nearly all true in fact. And your Passy address, where you live now, well, it's as clear as we can get it. The apartment's been unoccupied since June 1940, as you know – ever since Madame de Sertigny got out of France and came over to London. You're her daughter of course . . .'

'Of course. Yvonne de Sertigny – who died in the Luftwaffe strafing on the road near Rambouillet.'

The Colonel nodded. 'But you are her – reincarnate.'

'I hope so.'

'Oh yes, Yvonne. You *are*. That's your great gift. Yvonne de Sertigny, to the manner born . . .'

'I sometimes think it might have been easier if I'd taken over some completely fictional identity.'

'Perhaps. But how could we have turned down the chances offered here? You know the whole *real* story of your mother Madame de Sertigny – to put it mildly.'

'Yes, indeed. And the whole family. By heart. Spent days with the old lady . . .'

'And, remember, she's totally secure here in London. Under surveillance day and night – not that she isn't entirely on our side anyway, what with losing her daughter that way to the Luftwaffe.'

'Yes – I'm not worried about her. It's the others in the apartment block.'

'I know. But that chance was too good to miss as well – a "safe house" right at the centre of things, which if all goes well we can use indefinitely.'

'The neighbours, though –'

'Your immediate neighbours, on that third floor of the building, have gone. Two of them to Vichy, the other man died. Those three apartments have been sold to new owners. They won't know you. And the other occupants downstairs won't know which apartment you're going to – because you'll be using the lift. The only problem is Madame de Sertigny's brother-in-law –'

'And the concierge.'

'Yes . . .' The Colonel paused. Then he stood up briskly, confidently. 'As for Edouard de Sertigny living in the château in Normandy – well, Madame assures us he never comes to the apartment in Paris, which of course is no guarantee that he won't.'

'No.'

'But, if he does, then you show him Madame's ring, which you'll be wearing. And tell him the story we've prepared. Her brother-in-law is a patriot, we know that. And he knows Madame de Sertigny escaped to England – and that Yvonne died. If you do meet him, he'll put two and two together – and say nothing. No, the only real problem may be the concierge, Madame Bonnot – quite a different breed. Likely to be nosy – and quite possibly a collaborator, at least with the local gendarmes. On the other hand, you have all the right keys – and she's new. She won't know what the real Yvonne de Sertigny looked like. However, if she does show any suspicions, asks questions, then you'll have to take steps accordingly. The mission is too important not to . . .' He did not elaborate on what these steps might be. But Léonie knew exactly what he meant.

11

THE WAR HAD not touched Summer Hill. Only nature – and the absence of those who loved it had done that. Ivy gripped the stones. Lichen climbed the porch columns. Elder, nettle and briar sprouted round the walls. Moss grew in thickening carpets up the terrace steps and made little rugs over the cobbles in the back-yard.

The tentacles of voracious Irish nature, no longer held at bay, began to rise and feed once more, creeping over the house and demesne, strangling and flourishing. The war, diminishing human life in the house, gave it another – a creeping vegetable animation, which soon held the place in a green calm, the great house adrift in a sea deep jungle, so that there was something eerie in this wilderness and the village boys thought twice about raiding the old orchards, hesitating at the walls, fearful of being set upon or lost in this enchanted kingdom.

The house itself, at least, was not empty. Aunt Emily survived with her sketch-books, coloured inks and oatcake biscuits in the studio-bedroom. Elly and the young maid Biddy looked after her, while Jack Welsh maintained the fires and logs in winter and swept the chimney flues in summer. John Hennessy's son Michael, from the grocer's shop in Thomastown, now that there was no petrol, had got his father's old horse-drawn van out again and rattled down the high lane every Friday with the groceries. The wind-charger had broken down completely. Spare parts, in the 'Emergency' as the war was mildly termed in neutral Ireland, were unavailable. They lived by oil- and candle-light again.

The house survived, in itself and in the memory of those others overseas – Dermot, Hetty, Pierre, Robert, even Léonie. And yet, in the potent damp-dry air of the rooms, against the unchanging décor of generations, there was still a sense of performance postponed, some few pages lost in the text of a play that would surely be resumed. For Summer Hill maintained its own secret life, a murmur beneath the dust-sheets, the stir and vague rumour of spirits past, an invitation for those to come, who would some day return, at curtain up, as audience and players, taking their seats and cues, giving voice and laughter, part once more of the house's immemorial drama.

Summer Hill did not readily give up its ghosts – either the dead or the living. Mortimer had died the previous autumn and his funeral had been held there with Dermot and Mortimer's many friends down from Dublin: Mortimer, returned at last to the family home, lying in quiet state in the great hall for a September morning, a day filled with showery golden colour, before the horse-drawn hearse took him down the back avenue and all the way along the river, to the Cordiner family vault in the little church across the valley. The house waited, faithful in life, in death.

'So, you've memorised your operational instructions?'

'Every bit. "Operation: Café Noir. Name in the field: Yvonne. Destination: Paris. Date: 16 March."'

'Good,' the Colonel said, sitting across from her in Orchard Court. 'So then,' he continued, 'let us see, let me play the ogreish examiner!'

He opened the operations file at random. Then suddenly, his jocularity over, he was serious in his ecclesiastic manner. 'When you need to send secure messages to us in Baker Street, or if you have any difficulty with Michel after you've contacted him – what then?'

'I contact our SOE circle for the Seine-et-Oise region. Their courier, Louise, comes to Paris every Tuesday, goes to the Café le Prince outside the La Muette métro station between twleve and one o'clock. She always sits inside, at any of the vacant tables to the left, reading a copy of *Le Matin*. I identify myself as Yvonne from London by taking the *last* cigarette from a packet, then putting the empty packet on the table and saying, "What are the trains from Versailles running like today?"'

'Fine.' The Colonel turned to another page, then spoke enthusiastically. 'At what point do you identify yourself to Michel, as an SOE agent?'

'Not initially at all, of course,' Léonie was very prompt. 'Having made the appropriate professional contact with him I'm then to try and join his French network, get his WT operator to transmit particular information to Baker Street which, if he's a double-agent, will get back to the Germans, who will act on it, proving –'

'Fine. What if you fail in this – and yet come to know or suspect that Michel himself is a traitor?'

'Break all contact with him and his network. Contact Louise –'

'Yes – yes, indeed. Get out quick.' The Colonel put the file down. 'Because of course we've lost two agents already, Yvonne – quite possibly in this spider's trap. You'll be going in via Beauvais, the French resistance network there will look after you initially. But, even so, say the *least* when you arrive to any of these French people. This is vital. Trust no one in your reception committee especially, because it may be one of them who's working for the Germans, not anyone in Michel's circle in Paris. All right?'

'Yes.'

Suddenly, without dropping his gaze, the Colonel switched track completely. 'Where do you live – as far as Michel is concerned?'

'In Normandy – near the Château de Balleroy, the manor there. But I'm up in Paris, staying at the Hotel Meurice, on the Rue de Rivoli.'

'Indeed you are. Because you'll take a room there initially to establish your rich and aristocratic bona fides with Michel who, unless and until you become quite certain about him, is not to know of your "safe house" in Madame de Sertigny's apartment on the Avenue Henri Martin. We have to preserve this safe house at all costs, both for yourself – and for others coming after you. You have your money? The Meurice isn't cheap and you should take a decent room there.'

Léonie nodded, patting the money belt round her waist. 'Two hundred thousand francs . . .'

'About £1,200, Yvonne. Because, remember, you're *rich*. You're part of the *ancien régime*, you favour Pétain. The Germans by and large for you are a "good thing" in France – you're almost, but not quite, a collaborator yourself. All this is very much part of your general cover, so don't forget it. Additional funds are always available through Louise at the Café le Prince. Though of course, if you meet her regularly, you'll have to change the rendezvous each time.'

He paused, lighting his pipe. 'So, now – to the details. I can't say I think much of your parachuting reports from Ringway . . .'

'I didn't break my leg.'

'Very nearly did, by all accounts. However, on this occasion, it won't matter. We're sending you in by Lysander tonight, or tomorrow night, while the moon is full. A landing somewhere near Beauvais, I gather, because we've some urgent and breakable medical equipment going in as well – and one of our SOE men to take out. And talking of medical equipment . . .' The Colonel stood up, going to the mantelpiece, picking up a number of small French aspirin bottles, returning with them, commenting on each as he handed them to Léonie.

'Some medicinal aids for you. Remember what each bottle contains – this is vital, too. Literally! They are clearly marked by the little numbers in each corner here. One: these will give you very nasty stomach pains – and all that goes with it – for twenty-four hours. Not very pleasant. But it will fool any doctor – which of course is exactly what you'll need to do when you make your first contact with Michel in Passy. Clear?'

'Yes.'

'The pills in this box – number two – have just the opposite effect: stimulants – keep you going like a Derby winner for twenty-four hours. These, number three, are knock-out pills. One in a cup of coffee or a glass of wine – and the person won't know what's hit them, unconscious for up to six hours, with no after-effects. Finally this single pill . . .' He held up a brown sphere the size of a pea. 'Your "L" pill, Yvonne. Stands for lethal. And it is. If you get in a jam, you'll be out of it – permanently. Takes about five seconds. I can't tell you whether it's painful or not. But it's likely to be much less painful than the attentions of the Gestapo. Always keep it with you, the hem of a dress or some such . . .'

He handed it to her. But she did not take it. 'I won't need that.' She was matter of fact.

'You should.'

'I must?'

'Well, no, because you can throw it away when you leave here, and I'll be none the wiser. But you *should.*' He looked at her evenly.

'You don't trust me to resist – interrogation?'

'Not a question of trust, Yvonne. We know – you know – that very few people with the Gestapo, under torture, can keep their mouths shut for more than twelve hours, twenty-four at the most. Just enough time for their colleagues in the network to get well out of the area. The pill is for that – if, or before, it gets unbearable.'

'You're not like Captain Jepson, are you?' She looked up at him, almost angry. 'Think I need that pill for some sort of glorious self-sacrifice – because of Jenny?'

The Colonel was taken aback for a moment. He knew of just this possibility from Jepson's original report on her. 'No, I don't think that. How do you know – that Jepson thought that?'

'Because I thought it myself, when I first talked to him – and I know he sensed it. And I did have something just like that in mind. But not any longer.' Léonie stood up and went over to the window, lighting a cigarette, one of the few she allowed herself each day, just as she had when she and Jenny had been together. Memories flooded back as she gazed out on the blustery March weather, the plane trees in Portman Square so like those in Connaught Square. Her breath clouded the window-pane as she stood there – just as it had when there was peace and Jenny lived and had written 'Je t'aime' backwards on the glass.

The Colonel sensed her thoughts. 'You were very close to Jenny. I know that. Closer than any of us here at the Firm. But, believe me, she was such a great friend to all of us here, too. I miss her particularly. So I know your feelings. And I understand that original feeling of yours as well.'

Léonie turned. The Colonel, by the mantelpiece, looked across at her, a clear sympathy in his gaze. 'Thank you,' she said. 'Yes, I've felt that understanding in you, Colonel, and in all the others ever since I came to Orchard Court, to Baker Street, which is why I won't need that pill. I want to live now – for you, the others – just as much as for Jenny.'

'Yes . . . Good.' The Colonel lit his pipe, at a loss for a moment. 'Well, on a more cheerful note.' He reached into his pocket, producing a silver powder compact, from Cartier in Paris. 'A much happier going-away present, Yvonne. With love from the French Section.' Léonie admired it, opening it, glancing in the mirror. 'Ideal for seeing behind you, too,' he added dryly.

'You think of everything, Colonel.'

'Of course! And now your clothes – let me have a look at you.'

Léonie came forward, parading, turning round like a mannequin. She was wearing a superbly-tailored grey woollen coat and skirt, the hem of the coat low beneath her waist in the current French fashion.

'Everything been checked?'

'Every stitch. It's all from Paris – chose it myself. The stuff only came out a month ago. French dressmaker's labels, everything. All from Molyneux in the rue Royale, Colonel. Even the knickers . . .'

The Colonel nodded appraisingly, with the hint of a smile. 'You've thought of everything, too.'

'Of course,' she said neatly.

'Yes, I think that's just the ticket!' He stood back, admiring her. 'Yvonne de Sertigny – from the Manoir de Balleroy, the Hotel Meurice and the *seizième* . . . And of course you'll have all Yvonne's real clothes and her other knick-knacks once you get to the apartment. She's almost exactly your size . . .' He had a serious air as he gazed at her. Then he brightened once more. 'And your new hair – and your glasses. You mustn't worry about that. You look *most* becoming, with both . . .'

Léonie doubted him. She had seen herself this way in a full-length mirror. As far as her new role went, her hair, now dyed brown, did indeed go very well with her tortoiseshell spectacles – giving her a distinguished, more mature air, an almost middle-aged hauteur. On the other hand, these props and changes, together with the lines of pain and sadness that had creased her face in the last nine months, suggested to Léonie all too clearly how her youth was over.

'Anything else, Yvonne?'

'One thing, Colonel . . .' She produced a number of postcards from her bag. 'I've written to Olivia, my daughter – ten of these. I've told her I'm being sent to Scotland for several months – on special war work. Could you have them posted from there, every week or so, so that she knows I'm all right? To the school in Gloucestershire, then the Holborn flat?'

'Of course. And we'll see that she's fine in any case. And your father. As you know we have several FANY liaison officers for doing just that.'

'Yes, I know. And if anything should happen to me, more permanently –'

'They'll both be taken care of, in *every* way. I can promise you. But, Yvonne, that won't happen. You'll be back. You're too good to lose.' They stood up, shook hands. '*Bonne chance – et au revoir*, Yvonne!'

She turned back at the doorway. 'Oh, by the way, Colonel – why is the operation called "Café Noir"?'

'In your honour, Yvonne. As an American – and because you were always so appreciative of our American coffee here.'

Dipping through layers of silvery cloud beneath the large moon, the Lysander circled several times over the landing zone, before the pilot, coming right down to 400 feet, finally saw the 'All Clear' code, a flashing morse from a strong beam, and then the half-dozen flares in a line, with another smoky reddish flare set out at an angle beyond them, giving the wind direction. Rising up then, and banking very sharply so that Léonie's stomach turned a somersault, the little plane swung right round, flew on for half a minute, then turned again and dipped equally sharply, before the pilot, cutting the engine, glided over some trees, then hit the frozen pasture with a thump, running on for a hundred yards before turning and taxiing to a halt near the woods at the top of the field.

Everything happened very quickly then. Léonie almost fell out of the plane, seeing the men running towards her in the half-dark, moonlight glittering on the frosty earth, hearing the sound of voices, shouted commands in French, urgent messages.

A small, broad man loomed in front of her as she ran from the slipstream of the roaring propeller. '*Bonjour, Madame. Je suis Marc – venez, venez vite!*' Another taller figure rushed past her, climbing into the seat next to the pilot which she had just left. Several others in the French reception committee were already lugging boxes of medical equipment away from the plane, running with them towards the trees – before Marc, tugging at her arm, pulled Léonie away in the same direction. She heard the plane door slam behind her – the engines roar as the Lysander took off again, rising steeply before disappearing into the moonlit, cloud-mottled sky.

Less than four minutes had passed since they had landed. And now, the flares doused and the others in the reception committee having joined them from all over the field, they took cover in the wood, crouching down in the frozen undergrowth. There was dead silence before a dog barked not far away.

'*Ça va?*' The man in the leather jacket, lying right next to her, asked.

'*Oui. Ça va.*' Léonie barely felt the cold in her fur-lined boots and thick zippered flying suit – the pockets stuffed with emergency equipment: iron rations, maps, a compass, a collapsible spade, flask of cognac, a six-inch sheath knife, the Beretta 9 millimetre automatic.

'There's an Abwehr Field Security patrol out tonight – between here and Beauvais. So we're going to take you out in the opposite direction, to Gisors, a forest near there – a forester's hut for the night. It's safer.'

Léonie was at once on her guard with this mention of Gisors. 'Safer? But I'm to come in by Beauvais. It was all fixed.'

'I know. But we can't risk it tonight. And this other way is fine. We've used this forester and his hut quite often before. You can get a train from Gisors instead of Beauvais in the morning. There's no problem. Several of your other agents have gone this way.'

Indeed, Léonie thought – but she could do nothing about this now. Marc was in charge.

After ten minutes lying in the undergrowth, hearing no further sounds, the dozen men in the reception committee dispersed silently with their guns and the medical equipment, leaving just Marc and another man to accompany Léonie. They led her, unerringly, south-east in the shadowy, quicksilver light – across rough pasture, along wild lanes, skirting apple orchards, through ever-thickening woods and then into a deep forest. An hour later, at the end of the track, a logger's hut came in view in a wide moonlit clearing and Marc introduced her to a tall, burly figure in a huntsman's cap, wearing gaiters.

'*Voici Claude.*'

'*Excusez moi.* But it is safer for you not to be in my hut.' The man spoke in a broad Norman patois. 'I have left everything – food, some blankets – in the wood store, here.' He pointed to a low wooden building, open on either side, at the edge of the trees some fifty yards away. They walked over to it, and Claude with a torch showed her a hidden nook completely surrounded by a huge pile of stacked logs. There was some hay, blankets, food.

'*Excusez moi, Madame . . .*' Claude gestured again, apologetically. 'It's not too comfortable. But it's safer . . .' He seemed to want to insist on this idea of safety, which puzzled Léonie, for surely in these deep woods his forester's hut would be as safe a place as the log store?

Marc was behind her. 'Your other arrangements,' he said. 'For the morning.' Claude was next to them. Léonie had to avoid talking in front of him. She moved out into the moonlit clearing. Marc followed her. And so did Claude, before he saw their confidential purpose and stopped, leaving them alone, rather unwillingly, Léonie thought.

'Your train from Gisors,' Marc asked. 'Which way are you going?'

'North. To the coast.' Léonie lied. Then, half-turning, she saw Claude in the background watching them.

'Fine. There are trains quite often. But be careful. They're full of German officers, going up to the coastal defences, the Atlantic wall.'

'Of course.'

'A man will take you to the station –'

'One of your men?'

'No, from the Gisors network. But we know him. I told you, he's taken quite a few of your people out through Gisors already. At first light walk down the track here, past the forester's hut, then straight on for a kilometre or so, until you get to the wooden barrier on the main road. Wait in the trees there, hidden. Then, if all's clear, sometime between seven and eight, this man will pick you up – in an old black Peugeot breakdown truck – he runs a garage in Gisors, so he has petrol. And you'll bury your flying suit carefully, won't you?'

'Naturally.'

'Because Claude is a vital link for you people coming in via this sector – when we can't take you in through Beauvais.'

'Yes, I understand.' Léonie understood all too well. As Colonel Buckmaster had told her – at least three SOE agents, including the two who had been sent to investigate Michel's circle in Paris, had come in this way, via Gisors, and had subsequently been picked up almost at once by the Gestapo, either on the train to Paris, it was thought, or soon after they arrived in the capital.

'*Alors, au revoir, Madame. Et bonne chance.*'

'*Merci. Merci beaucoup.*' They shook hands firmly. Marc she felt confident about. But when he left she turned and saw Claude still watching her at the edge of the clearing. Seeing him now, vaguely silhouetted in the moonlight, something struck her about him which made her uneasy. What was it? Of course – it was his gaiters, the tightly-sheathed leggings all the way up to his knees – gaiters which, in the shadowy light, looked just like Nazi jackboots.

Perhaps it was all nonsense. But this image, together with the man's exaggerated concern for her safety and the feeling she had had of his wanting to eavesdrop on her conversation with Marc, made Lèonie decide there and then not to spend the night in the log store – to get away from the place as soon as she could without his knowing.

But get away – out of the frying pan, into the fire? There were problems. Claude, for example, might be entirely loyal – and the man giving her a lift in the Peugeot breakdown truck could be the traitor, delivering her not to the station, but to the Gendarmerie or the Gestapo in Gisors. Then, too, if she left the log store secretly now, got to the road, hid there, but did not take the lift in the breakdown van – how was she ever to get to the train in Gisors? With all her smart clothes under the flying suit she was obviously no country woman. She would stand out like a sore thumb, either walking into Gisors or hitching a lift later in the morning. Besides, taking a chance lift could be suicidal. With the lack of petrol, nearly all the vehicles on the roads these days, she knew, were run by the Germans or the Gendarmerie. On her own, out in the country, she would be easy meat for any of these patrols.

Then she saw a way out. There were risks. But there would be those however she handled it. And at least, with this plan, she might kill two birds – get to Gisors station undetected and possibly find out who was the traitor in the Gisors resistance network.

Ten minutes later, just after two o'clock, she crept out from the back of the log store into the woods, then made a big half-circle round the clearing until she came to the logging track on the other side, making off down it in the chilly half-light, for the moon was on the wane now below the trees.

An hour later she struck the road, quite suddenly, the wooden barrier looming up in front of her. Finding a hiding place in the undergrowth, she settled down to wait – shivering in the cold, dozing for odd moments through the rest of the night.

Dawn came just after seven – the low sun, quite hidden by the tall trees everywhere, only illuminating a long path of sky above the straight road, gradually rising then over the woods, touching the frosty tarmac with glittering diamond points, a pale-blue sky emerging far above her. It would be a fine, tingling-sharp day.

She had buried her flying suit back in the forest. Now, in her elegant clothes, with her suitcase, she got out her new compact – tidied her face, combed her hair, put on her spectacles, checked everything in her handbag: Carte d'Identité, clothes and food coupons, pills . . . She was ready.

A farm labourer on a bicycle and two cars passed her in the half-hour she waited. The second car was the black Peugeot breakdown truck. It slowed as it approached along the straight road, then stopped just beyond the wooden barrier into the forest. A man got out, checking the back wheel as if for a puncture, looking up and down the road as he did so. Léonie did the same. There was no sign of traffic in either direction. Running out, she jumped into the other front seat of the truck, as the man joined her.

'*Bonjour, Mam'selle! Je suis Albert.*' He plunged the gear forward and the truck gathered speed down the road. He smiled at her. He was youngish, early thirties, good-looking, with an open face, blue eyes, fair hair – and surprisingly well-dressed for a garage man, in a new sports jacket and tie. 'All went well on your drop – I hope? Didn't break your ankle or anything!' He was easy, jokey and quite without any of Claude's suspicious airs.

'No, all isn't well.' Léonie put her plan into operation at once. 'The drop went all right. But I have to tell you – from the chief of the Beauvais network – you are not to take me to the station at Gisors. They've had word. The Gestapo are planning a big check there today. You're to take me to Gournay, up the line, or to Chaumont below Gisors.'

The man's happy features clouded. 'But, Mam'selle, I've just left Gisors – indeed I was at the station there only an hour ago, with a taxi fare. I spoke to one of our network people who works in the ticket office. There's nothing on in the station – and nothing planned for today. I assure you, I'd be one of the first to know if there was. There's a train to Paris at 10.15.'

'Fine. But I have to catch it either up or down the line, not at Gisors. Besides, it's not much further from here – to Gournay or Chaumont.' This insistence on a change of plan clearly worried the smart young man. Léonie saw his deep concern for an instant in his pale-blue eyes. 'Gournay or Chaumont,' she said with finality. 'I must insist.'

The man was equally determined, shaking his head. He would not contemplate any change of destination, despite Léonie's apparent orders, from the head of another network, to change it. 'I can't – look at the petrol gauge, Mam'selle. Nearly empty. Only enough to get back to Gisors. And, besides, I can't risk travel outside the Gisors area. The check-points: if they ask me what I'm doing in Gournay or Chaumont – I've no cover, no clients in those towns. This morning, for example, if we're stopped on this road – I've got cover behind me: a farmer who will vouch for the fact I've been trying to repair his old tractor.'

They drove on to Gisors. His excuses sounded reasonable enough, Léonie thought. Yet she was pretty certain they were false excuses. She had seen the spare can of petrol in the back of the truck. And it was perfectly clear from the map of the area she had looked at earlier that both Gournay and Chaumont, only ten miles north or south, were very much in the Gisors area. He would be sure to have some clients, at least, in and around both of these villages.

It was clear that he was absolutely determined to take her to the station at Gisors. And there could surely be only one reason for this, Léonie thought. In order to maintain his role as a double-agent with the Germans, and to trap future British agents in the same manner, Albert himself would never be directly involved in any trap. Having warned the Gestapo in advance, he would simply take her to the station – which would have to be Gisors station – where they would be waiting for her, at the entrance, easily identifying her as she stepped out of the breakdown truck. The Gestapo would then pick her up at the ticket barrier, or more likely follow her to Paris, to see what contacts she made there, before they took her, along with anyone else she might have met there clandestinely. This, indeed, must have been how the other two SOE agents had been picked up so quickly. What was essential now, Léonie saw, was to get to Gisors – the centre, not the station – then drop this suspicious blue-eyed garagiste.

'A coffee? Something to eat? – I'm absolutely famished,' she asked him as they came into the outskirts of Gisors.

'You can have something at the station. There's a buffet there.'

'I can't wait – I'm dying – to get to the lavatory.'

They stopped in the main square of Gisors. There was a café on the corner. Albert did not move.

'Won't you come, too? It'll look better, if I'm not alone. We have plenty of time – and there are a few things about the trains I want to ask you.' Léonie held her breath. He remained unwilling. 'Please.' She gave him her nicest smile. Finally he agreed.

When she got back from the lavatory she had the knock-out pill hidden in her hand. There was no real coffee, just a chicory extract, with a roll of hard bread. They sat at a table by the steamed-up window, a crowd over by the zinc bar lowering nips of Calvados and cheap *rouge*. Albert fiddled with his spoon impatiently – there was no sugar – his cup in front of him, looking straight down on it.

Léonie wiped the clouded window. 'Which way is the station?'

'Left, at the bottom of the square.' He did not look out.

'Which way?' Léonie cleared his side for him and now at last he peered out.

'There,' he said, pointing. 'Just a few minutes' drive.'

Léonie's right hand was already lying on the table, over by his cup. As they both peered out of the window she slipped the pill into it.

Then she groaned. 'Oh God, this diarrhoea again. Stomach's been upset. Excuse me a minute.' She stood up and made for the lavatory once more.

'Don't be too long,' he called after her, looking at his watch. Then, just before she got to the door of the *lavabo*, she glanced back and saw him drain his small cup of ersatz coffee in one gulp.

When she came out his head was slumped in his arms – but quite comfortably over the table, as if he were asleep, so that no one had yet taken any notice of him. She left the café and walked away, hurrying towards the station.

Along the road and outside the station there was quite a crowd of other people making for the booking hall – and a few hangers-on standing by the entrance, among them two men to either side, obviously Gestapo who, rather than looking at the passengers passing them, were gazing out on the road, waiting for some other arrival – someone getting out of a black Peugeot breakdown truck, Léonie was sure.

She walked past the two men, quite unconcerned, going on to the booking office. But instead of buying a ticket to Paris she took one to Gournay, on a train out of Gisors in the other direction, north, leaving before the Paris train.

She crossed over to the other platform. Ten minutes later the Gournay train pulled in and she took a seat – a seat offered her very readily in a reserved compartment full of Wehrmacht officers.

They helped her with her suitcase, putting it up on the rack. 'Why, it's heavy enough to have a radio transmitter in it!' a young Oberleutnant joked in bad French, before offering her a cigarette as she sat down next to him – pleased, as they all were, to have the company of this attractive and distinguished-looking woman.

A few minutes later the Paris train arrived on the other line, just across the tracks from her. Almost at once she saw a disturbance. The two Gestapo men, accompanied by the guard and ticket collector, were going through every compartment, checking each passenger. Then she heard the shouts – 'Out! All out!' – as everyone was made to disembark from the train. This was going to be a most thorough check, luggage and everything else. Her own train pulled away a moment later without being checked at all.

It was clear what had happened. The Gestapo at the entrance, failing to see the breakdown truck arrive at the station, but assuming the British agent they had been warned to expect had arrived there in some other way, had decided to check everyone on the Paris train, leaving the earlier train, the one going north filled with Wehrmacht officers, alone.

Léonie was pretty certain she had the answer then. Albert was the double agent – not, she thought, someone in Michel's circle in Paris. Her work had started well. She would get a message as soon as possible, via Louise in Paris, about Albert. The Normandy networks would use him no longer. No one would deal with Albert much longer, she thought, except the undertakers and the local curé. She looked forward to Paris now with an easier heart, arriving there that same day without incident, having changed trains at Gournay and taken a later train back to Paris in the afternoon.

Dr André Vonnot prodded about over her naked stomach in his consulting rooms on the Avenue Foch. 'Nothing much wrong, as far as I can see, Mademoiselle. Not appendicitis. A virus of some sort.'

He moved out of the cubicle in his white coat. Léonie had taken the pill for this stomach upset the previous night, having made an appointment with Dr Vonnot from the Hotel Meurice a few days earlier.

'It's just – I feel so dreadful.' And she looked it, too, as she got up, dressing herself behind the curtain, before emerging into the bright first floor room looking over the narrow gardens to one side of the Avenue.

'It's a bug going round, Mademoiselle de Sertigny. The food these days,' he told her easily, at his desk. 'And there's not much I can prescribe for it either, with so few drugs available now. Best cure is just rest in bed – not to eat for twenty-four hours, and then only some toast. And come back and see me in a day or so. You're staying at the Hotel Meurice?'

'Yes – just up from the country for a week, from Normandy. I have a place there.'

'Fine. Well, come and see me in a day or two.'

Their eyes met. He gazed at her appraisingly, and she liked the look of him, too – this tallish man, with a firm open face, a hint of laughter in his brown eyes. Dr Vonnot – Michel, chief of the Passy network – seemed a most unlikely traitor. But one could never tell. She would have to put him to the test.

'Dr Vonnot,' she said at the end of their second consultation a few days later. 'I wonder if you'd mind giving me some advice on another matter . . .'

'Of course, Mademoiselle.'

'Not medical. But I believe I can trust you – and there's no one at home I can trust.'

'I hope so, Mademoiselle.'

'Last week, before I came up from the château, a man arrived, some time in the night – I found him in one of the stables at dawn before I went riding: a British officer, a pilot – shot down somewhere in the area . . .' She looked at him. His expression had not changed.

'And?' he said evenly.

'I wondered – wondered what I should do with him?'

'Mademoiselle, you should have reported him at once to the local *Gendarmerie*. You have put yourself at great risk,' he added firmly.

'Yes – but I couldn't hand him straight over to the Germans.' She looked at him carefully. 'And see,' she went on. 'Now I've put myself in your hands.'

'Mademoiselle, I am a doctor. Anything you say in this room remains entirely between you and me. No one else. But my advice is that you should report him immediately you get home.'

'I can't do that. I hate Pétain – and the other collaborators. I hate the Germans. I couldn't possibly hand this man over – one of our allies after all.'

'That must be your decision. But, as I say, you should do so. Have you told anyone about him?'

'I've told no one.'

'Nonetheless, you've not only put yourself at risk – Mademoiselle – but also your servants, friends and neighbours. If the authorities find out that you've been harbouring this airman, they'll round up all of you, with the gravest consequences. You should get him out of your house at once.'

Dr Vonnot stood up. The consultation was clearly over. But Léonie was entirely satisfied. She had put her cards on the table – making it abundantly clear to the doctor that, not only was she a staunch French patriot, but she was also aiding and abetting a British airman.

If Dr Vonnot was working with the Germans, then the Gestapo would be coming for her at the Hotel Meurice that night. She would not be there, of course – she had checked out that morning. But she would know if they had called, by telephoning the hotel and asking for any messages. If the Gestapo had been there, the management would make this clear, one way or the other, either by hinting at their visit if they were patriots, or by enquiring as to her whereabouts now if they were not, for she had given the hotel an entirely false address in Normandy. Dr Vonnot would clearly be the informer then. But if no one turned up looking for her at the Meurice, then he – and she – would be in the clear.

Moving into the apartment on the Avenue Henri Martin without incident that same day, she let a week pass, telephoning the Meurice several times for messages. There was none – and not the slightest hint of any enquiries made of her. Finally, at the end of the week, to be quite sure, she put her head in the lion's mouth – going down to the Meurice in person, making the same enquiries at the reception desk. They were polite – there had been no messages or enquiries for her whatsoever.

Without making an appointment, simply going to the Avenue Foch and waiting for him, she finally saw Dr Vonnot again. He was not entirely pleased to see her.

'Dr Vonnot, I must apologise – but I had to be sure.'

The doctor, for the first time, looked startled. 'I don't understand? . . .'

'I'm not Mademoiselle de Sertigny – someone quite different, from London. May I explain everything?' She had lowered her voice from the beginning. Now she looked round at the walls, the door.

'I don't understand. I've no idea what you –'

'May I tell you *everything*? Are we – safe here?' she interrupted him, before she uttered the single word 'Michel' very quietly.

He gazed at her for an instant. There was no alarm on his features, which neither admitted nor denied this last appellation. 'I'm listening, Mademoiselle,' he said. Then he added, 'And, yes, it's entirely safe here. As I said before, as my patient anything you tell me in this room is entirely between us.'

'So you see,' Léonie said, having told him who she really was and coming to the end of her account of what had happened to her in the past ten days in France, 'it seems the double agent is Albert in Gisors – and possibly your WT operator here. As I've said, his call sign has appeared smudged in London.'

Dr Vonnot shook his head, gesturing dismissively. 'Simply the hurry he was in, to get off the air. We've had to transmit from dozens of different places these last months. The German detector vans are much more numerous now, patrolling everywhere. And, besides, our WT operator is completely reliable – I'm in no doubt. I've known him for years, since long before the war. It can only have been this Albert in Gisors who trapped the other two agents you sent in. Your story about him all fits. I'll get word to the Beauvais network at once. They'll deal with him. Meanwhile – thank you . . .' He stood up, coming round his desk towards her. 'Mademoiselle de Sertigny.'

'Yvonne.' She took his hand.

'You played your cards well.' He smiled. 'That château in Normandy, the British airman . . . I quite believed it all. I hope you can equally convince your chiefs in London that this Passy circle is entirely secure.'

'Yes – at once.'

'We need all the help we can get from London – particularly here at the medical practice. We treat the wounded from a number of other resistance networks in the Paris region. Need morphine, syringes, proper bandages and so on. Urgently.'

'"We"?'

'Yes, I've a partner, downstairs.'

'Oh yes, the other name plate I saw: Dr Langlois.' The common French name had meant nothing to Léonie then and no more now.

'Yes . . .' He looked at her pointedly. 'Though of course you don't know that name – or mine. You've never seen or heard of either of us in your life.'

'Of course.'

'You'll be staying on in Paris?'

'Yes.'

'With your own SOE circle over here?'

'I don't know yet. I have a "safe house" – not far away from here, in fact. But I'm to collaborate with you, if you need anything, until I get further instructions from London.'

'Good. I'm glad of that. You can contact me here any time, of course, simply as my patient. And if I need you?'

'There,' Léonie said, pointing at the window looking out over the Avenue Foch. 'Stick a white envelope on the glass there. I'll pass by most days, and come straight in, if I see it.'

'Excellent. So you'll tell them in London at once then – that all's well with the Passy circle?'

'Absolutely.' She left, returning to the apartment on the Avenue Henri Martin.

Furnished in the heavy Louis Quinze style, it was a large, gloomy place on the fourth floor – made all the more gloomy by the fact that it had been shuttered up when she arrived and she had to keep it so, in order not to call attention to her occupation there. There were three bedrooms and a heavily ornate salon in front, divided in two by sliding doors giving on to a dining room, a kitchen beyond that leading to a small servant's bedroom, with narrow back-stairs running down to the ground floor and basement cellars, with an exit leading out behind the apartment block, giving on to the cemetery – an ideal escape route which old Madame de Sertigny had told them about in London.

Léonie lived in permanent shadow now, creeping about under the yellow light from chandeliers through the untidy rooms – hurriedly abandoned by the two women nearly three years before, in June 1940, when they had joined the hordes of panic-stricken Parisians rushing southwards.

The whole apartment had the musty, decayed air of a vault, where very little had been touched or moved or cleaned since that summer day in 1940. The contents of half-packed bags and suitcases, clothes – papers, silver, knick-knacks of all sorts – were still strewn in corners covered in dust. The heavy gilded furniture was draped in cobwebs. Drawers and cupboard doors in the bedrooms had been pulled open, shoes and clothes scattered about, silk lingerie tossed over the beds, bottles, cosmetics and lotions lying on the carpets.

Yet the gas and electricity had not been turned off, nor had the place been entirely unoccupied since 1940, as Léonie soon discovered. The spare bedroom at the back, not used by the two women, was more or less entirely in order, clean sheets on the divan and a pile of newspapers on the floor. Léonie had inspected the dates carefully. There was an intermittent regularity about these. The newspapers showed a sequence of visits to the apartment over the previous year or so: every eight or ten weeks, for two or three days. The last newspapers were dated three weeks before, in early March. At this rate, if Madame's brother-in-law Edouard de Sertigny maintained his regular habits, he would be due here again some time in mid-May – to pay the apartment bills, see his friends or whatever in Paris. So she had a minimum of six weeks, she thought, before he arrived again.

Meanwhile Léonie took over Yvonne's bedroom, where there were all the clothes and shoes and hats she needed – only a little too big for her, which she took in or adapted, not even needing the sewing kit she had brought with her, soon finding all that, and more, in the eerie apartment where the two women had spent fifteen years of their life together before abandoning everything, not only their possessions but in Yvonne's case her career.

Lifting the lid of the Pleyel grand piano in the salon one morning, Léonie found a book of pencilled-in scales on the stand, no doubt used by Yvonne in a last lesson with one of her pupils. Behind, lying on the strings, were stacks of music books: Saint-Saëns, Fauré, Mozart, Chopin, together with a number of piano parts from operas – including *Madame Butterfly*.

This discovery came as a shock to Léonie. Seeing Puccini's well-remembered music in front of her, she felt a sudden echo of Hetty – her voice, her spirit, present again in the claustrophobic salon: a voice of youth and old love clear on the musty air, in the passionate duets they had shared together years before from this opera. '*Te voglio bene . . .*' Léonie fingered the notes of the music noiselessly on the keys in front of her . . .

What had happened to Hetty?

She realised then why she so rarely thought about her. Dermot had told her, some years before in England, how Hetty and her husband no longer lived in Summer Hill, how they had left the house in 1939, settling in France somewhere; with the arrival of the Germans in 1940, everyone at home had lost touch with them. And that was one reason why Léonie did not think about her. It was difficult to think of someone who had so entirely disappeared into the murderous gulf of war, who was quite lost, imprisoned perhaps, or even dead. Hetty had gone from her life beyond any possible redemption. Léonie closed the piano quietly and forgot about her once more. She had other things to think about. And besides it was Jenny, not Hetty, with whom she must now keep faith.

She had contacted Louise, the SOE courier in the café by La Muette. A message was sent to Baker Street, and the Passy circle had been entirely cleared. In return, via Louise a week later, Léonie had received instructions from London to maintain the 'safe house' on the Avenue Henri Martin for other SOE agents in Paris or those who might arrive there in the future. She was as well to act as courier between Michel's Passy circle and Louise's SOE network outside the city, principally to help Michel get his messages through to London, something which he was finding more and more difficult with detector vans increasing everywhere in the capital.

So it was, in the ensuing weeks, that Léonie came to see Dr Vonnot quite regularly, watching for the white envelope in his window as she passed up the Avenue Foch each day. So, too, as part of her instructions from London, she told Dr Vonnot the address of her 'safe house' in the Avenue Henri Martin. The apartment was never to be used for radio transmissions, and only Michel in the Passy network was to know of its existence. But Colonel Buckmaster, recognising this now-secure and vital Passy circle again, was anxious to give Michel as much support as possible – and the use of this 'safe house' in emergencies was intended as a major token of this endeavour.

The apartment was, of course, ideally suited to all their needs – since it could be left or entered, undetected, from the rear, by walking through the Cimetière de Passy, climbing a wall at the end, then in by the back entrance to the apartment block and up the servants' stairs – a route which avoided the concierge's office entirely. Léonie was pleased with herself and her work. Only the possible sudden arrival of Edouard de Sertigny gave her qualms.

12

F OOD WAS SCARCE in Paris – and meat was a great luxury, not always available even on the black market. But Hetty, in league with the local butcher, the café proprietor and one of his trusted customers who had a cousin with a farm to the west of Paris, had taken shares in a whole live pig, which had been led to the outer suburbs and then, surreptitiously and with considerable difficulty, moved across town concealed in a vélo-taxi and then a horse-drawn van to the *boucherie* where it had met its fate and been quartered.

So that on that warm spring evening, in their apartment on the Avenue Mozart, Hetty, knowing this was one dish which could not be spoilt by the irregular gas supply, had made a splendid Cassoulet de Toulouse – with ribs of pork, white haricot beans, some precious Toulouse sausage, garlic and a *bouquet garni* – which she and Pierre, together with André Vonnot and his wife Eve, ate that evening, celebrating Pierre's forty-fifth birthday with a bottle of Gevrey-Chambertin and a box of Turkish Delight both preserved from before the war.

Afterwards they danced to some popular songs on the gramophone – Jean Sablon's 'Je tire ma révérence' and Léo Marjane's 'Je suis seule ce soir'.

Hetty, holding Pierre firmly for he was an inept dancer, whispered mischievously in his ear, 'I'm not alone . . .'

'Shouldn't be playing that woman's songs at all – something of a collaborator herself, singing for all those Nazi officers in the cabarets.'

'Oh, Pierre! It's your birthday! *Some* pleasure – before you have to go out again. Why did you have to have a surgery this evening of all evenings – on your be-birthday?'

'I'm sorry –'

'And the curfew, it worries me.'

'Doesn't apply to me. But I'll be back before that in any case.'

'This be-bloody war.'

'Yes.' The record stopped. Pierre took off his glasses, rubbed the lenses, looking abstracted, hair on end. 'Yes – just that.'

Ten minutes later, putting his jacket on, he started to leave the apartment, talking alone with André in the hall for a minute.

'Look after Hetty, won't you? – if I'm not back. I'll stay overnight if I'm delayed – won't risk the curfew.'

'What do you have tonight?' André whispered.

'Bullet wounds, I gather. Someone from the Montrouge network. I don't know when they'll bring him in – if they manage to get him up to me at all.'

'There's some morphine in my chest upstairs.'

'I still have some from the last lot we got – that drop near Beauvais.'

Hetty arrived, fetching a scarf for Pierre. 'Must wrap up.'

'It's not cold. Windows are open.'

'Still . . .' She looked at him, with longing. He kissed her and left.

'Come on then, Hetty,' André said. 'Now at last you can dance with *me*!' He dragged her back to the drawing room, put a record on, then did a tango with her, holding her close, making exaggerated steps to and fro, bending right over her, pulling back, holding their arms dramatically high, ogling her like a café gigolo.

'See!' he told her. 'Rudolph Valentino . . .'

'You're better, André! I danced with him years ago.'

The three of them laughed uproariously.

Leaving the apartment block, Pierre heard the music faintly from the open window above him. 'Je suis seule ce soir . . .' The traitorous Léo Marjane, he thought – and people like her. They were never alone. They had friends everywhere in Paris.

Behind him, some fifty yards down the avenue, two figures stood in the shadow of a doorway. One, a sullen little man, was a neighbour of Pierre's living in the same block – the other a member of the hated French *milice*.

'There! – there he goes,' the smaller man said. 'The dirty Jew! You see if I'm not right.'

The second man, saying nothing, stepped from the shadows, following Pierre. As he did so he signalled to a black Citroën some way behind at the kerb, which drew away quietly, following him.

Hetty was upset when Pierre failed to return that night. But André reassured her. Even though, as a doctor, he was immune from the curfew regulations, he had obviously decided not to risk travel during it and had stayed the night on the couch in his consulting rooms.

'Why didn't he answer the 'phone then? – when we rang.'

'Busy with a patient, maybe – the receptionist doesn't come in in the evening. Or maybe he'd just left the room. Don't worry – Eve and I will stay here the night. And I'll go round to the Avenue Foch first thing tomorrow.'

But when André got there early next morning he discovered Pierre was not in his own rooms. Nor had he been there the previous night. He would have cleaned up all his surgical equipment. But there were no swabs or dirty bandages in the secret disposal bin they kept for such clandestine medical work. Pierre had never seen the wounded man from Montrouge – had never arrived in his rooms at all.

He must have been picked up en route to the Avenue Foch – by the French police – or the Gestapo. And there could surely be only one reason: they suspected or had evidence that he was with the resistance. As his partner he was at risk now, too – and so were Eve and Hetty. It was the last thing he wanted – to break, to go to ground. But he would have to – until he found out exactly what had happened to Pierre. If the Gestapo had taken him, well, it meant he had twelve hours or so to get clear. And of course he would have to take Eve and Hetty with him.

He had a contingency plan for just such a turn of events: a retreat to Yvonne's safe house on the Avenue Henri Martin. He returned to Hetty's apartment at once.

Hetty and Eve, knowing nothing of André's resistance activities with Pierre, were astonished at André's urgent directions that they must all leave at once for another apartment nearby. 'I can't explain now,' he told them. 'Later, when we get there.'

When they reached the apartment block on the Avenue Henri Martin, they entered it separately, at five-minute intervals, taking the lift up to the fourth floor. André had his own key. The place was deserted when they got inside. Léonie was out.

'What in God's name is happening?' Eve demanded. André, turning on the chandelier in the big salon, explained. The two women were even more astonished and upset.

'Not that I don't agree with what you've both been doing. But surely you could have taken us into your confidence?'

'You least of all –'

'But wha-what about Pe-Pierre?' Hetty interrupted, not concerned with this deception. She was shaking with anxiety and her stammer had returned.

'We have a contact inside the Deuxième Bureau on the Quai des Orfèvres. He'll be able to tell us if Pierre was taken by the French police. And, if he wasn't, he can usually get information on who's been arrested by the Gestapo from their headquarters on the Avenue Foch. I'll go and see him now.' He got up. 'You two stay here. I'll be back by midday, or sooner.'

'What, are we just to stay cooped up here indefinitely?' Eve demanded again.

'Who owns it? Who lives here?' Hetty asked, pacing the dusty salon nervously.

'I told you – it's a "safe house", presently being used by a British agent in Paris. She's out this morning.'

'Who is she?'

'You don't need to know –'

'What's her name?'

'No idea what her real name is. She has a code-name here. And you don't need to know that either – the less you know the better. If she's back before I am, just explain what's happened. And, remember, she's here to help – if the Gestapo are looking for us – help us all get out of Paris, which is what we'll have to do at once.'

Hetty, wild with worry now, almost shouted. 'I'm not leaving Pe-Paris. Not until I know what's happened to Pe-Pierre. And I'll go down myself to the Quai des Orfèvres or the Gestapo headquarters and find out what's happened to him. They can't touch me – I've an Irish passport, a neutral country!'

André sighed. 'They *will* touch you, and worse – neutral passport or not – if they think they can get anything out of you about Pierre. The Gestapo don't abide by the rules of the Geneva Convention. So just wait here. I'm sure I'll have news of Pierre when I get back.'

After he had left, Hetty, unable to sit still, paced the salon in a barely suppressed frenzy of agitation. She moved through the bedrooms, finding Léonie's night clothes on the divan in Yvonne's room – seeing the vague shape of her head on the pillow, putting her head down on it, sniffing. There was a faint yet somehow familiar smell of violets coming from the pillow and sheets – a perfume remembered from somewhere or someone. But she could not place it. She picked up a novel on the bedside table which the woman had been reading, with her name in it, 'Yvonne de Sertigny' – one of the 'Claudine' novels by Colette. *Claudine in Paris*. Flicking through the pages, she found a book marker half-way through, and glanced at the first paragraph there.

Strange, she thought – a British agent with a taste for Colette, for these amorous goings-on between Claudine and her girl friend in the Paris of the Belle Epoque. These sensuous feminine images, and the memories they brought, upset her now and she slammed the book shut. It was Pierre she wanted – Pierre, only him. She returned to the salon almost in tears. Eve tried to comfort her.

André returned just after midday. He was not happy. But things could have been much worse, as he explained to Hetty. 'Pierre was picked up by the local *milice* last night. But nothing to do with the resistance. Because he's a Jew . . .'

'A *Jew*?' Hetty was breathing hard.

'Yes. We should have thought of that. Someone informed on him. One of his patients. Or a neighbour in his apartment block.'

'Where – where is he?'

'A camp at Drancy, outside Paris, near le Bourget.'

'But that's terrible! –'

'It may not be. We can probably get him released.'

'What happens – at this camp?'

André had confirmed what happened there from his contact – whenever they had sufficient numbers, every week or so, they took these French Jews off in cattle trucks to forced labour camps in Germany. They did not come back. But he would not tell Hetty this. 'They hold them there – interviewing them. Some they release. Some are sent to prisons in France –'

'That's not true, André! They take them off to Germany, one of those labour camps –'

'No. It's not certain.'

'I am! I have to get to him – at Drancy.'

'No, Hetty! You stay here. The last thing you should do is to go out to Drancy now – or back to your own apartment. Because they may be waiting for you there. You're his wife, and partly Jewish, too, remember. And the Gestapo won't worry a damn about your neutral Irish passport – they'll just take you as well. So stay here till I find out how the land lies. There's a good chance, with my contacts, I may be able to get him out of Drancy myself. Now I have to get back to the surgery. They'll wonder where I am –'

Eve interrupted him, with her own urgency now. 'If you and I are in the clear, André, I should get back to our place, too. The cleaning woman's there this morning. She'll be worried – seeing we've not been at home last night, and no sign of us this morning. She may call the police.'

'Yes. Do that. And bring back some food while you're at it. Seems to be none here.' He turned to Hetty. 'I'll be back this evening – or sooner. Just stay put. You'll be perfectly safe here.' With this last reassurance they left Hetty alone in the apartment.

It was Tuesday, the day for Léonie's weekly meeting with Louise. They changed their meeting place every week now, choosing a different café, metro station or shop. Today she was to meet her at the Café des Roses on the Place de Passy. She had been out all morning and now, as she approached the café, she checked everything – stopping at shop windows, watching the view behind her reflected in the glass, doubling back along the crowded pavements, crossing and re-crossing the road, to see if she was being followed, to drop any possible tail.

Eventually she entered the café, took a table and waited. Louise arrived late. But what business they had was soon completed and Léonie, to her relief, was able to get away early. She was hungry, but had managed to buy half a Camembert cheese earlier. It was hot and she had been walking all morning. Today, at least, she really looked forward to lunch in the cool of the shuttered apartment.

So perhaps, after she left Louise, she was not so thorough in her manoeuvres about the streets as she might have been. The man who had been standing at the bar of the Café des Roses with a friend all the while during her meeting with Louise had little difficulty in following her back to the apartment block on the Avenue Henri Martin.

Waiting in the hall after Léonie had taken the lift up, he watched its progress as the counter-weight descended, then stopped. The woman had left it on the fourth floor. He was well accustomed to judging such matters, out on many such stalking missions about the city. Though he had no air of this whatsoever, he was a Gestapo officer.

Several days before, he had been informed by a Gestapo colleague stationed in the Seine-et-Oise region about a woman suspected of being a courier with one of the resistance networks there – a woman who travelled up to Paris every week, who met another woman then in one of the cafés near La Muette. This colleague, having followed the first woman up on the train that morning, had identified the second woman for him in the Café des Roses. He was to follow her, see where she lived in Paris.

Now he had done just that and it would be up to his superiors to decide what action should be taken. He hurried away to the Gestapo headquarters in the Avenue Foch. They would want to pick her up at once, he thought, while she was back at her apartment – having lunch. He had seen the Camembert in her string bag.

Léonie, who, every time she left the apartment, dusted the door handle with powder from her compact, knew someone had tried to enter the place that morning – someone who might well be inside waiting for her at that moment. Dr Vonnot – or Edouard de Sertigny? Or someone even less welcome?

Alerted at once, she went back along the corridor to the servant's entrance. Using her other key in the oiled lock, she went into the kitchen, took her Beretta automatic which she kept hidden there, before tip-toeing silently along the corridor towards the salon.

Peering round the open doorway she saw a woman, a total stranger, back towards her, sitting beneath the yellow light from the chandelier – no face, just a toss of greying hair, head bent forward in her hands, shoulders throbbing, as if the woman was trying to contain some intolerable emotion. The gun was unnecessary. Léonie stepped into the salon.

'Who . . . who are you?' she asked gently.

Hetty nearly jumped out of her skin.

They recognised each other at once – but then immediately refused to believe the evidence of their eyes. Hetty gazed at the figure in the doorway.

'Léa? But it can't be . . .'

'Hetty?' Léonie was equally uncertain. She came forward. The two women faced each other under the jaundiced light from the chandelier, at last having to recognise the truth of their vision.

Hetty finally broke the silence – but was still so stunned that the words she found seemed irrelevant. '*Now* I know – that scent on the pillow, violets – it was always yours.' She wiped her eyes and tried to smile, but could not. 'How could you be . . . the British agent?' she demanded instead, annoyed, as if this was some cheap deceit on Léonie's part.

'How could you be *here*?' Lèonie was equally put out, almost curt. Each woman, still unable to come to grips with the other's presence, spoke now in tones which suggested some possible outrage or betrayal in this meeting, as if life, in contriving it, had played one more disagreeable trick on them. And this wary, indignant tone persisted as they sat down, keeping their distance, starting out on their long explanations.

Léonie felt she should withhold herself, the details of her work at least. She would need confirmation from Dr Vonnot for all that Hetty began to tell her now. But Hetty became more animated in the telling.

'It's true,' she said to Léonie again. 'It's all *true*! I've known André for years. Though I only understood this morning that he was in the resistance, when we got over here. And now to meet you!' Hetty, becoming accustomed to the reality of her old friend, could no longer restrain the growing warmth she felt towards her. 'Oh, Léa, it's wonderful! If only it weren't for Pierre. I don't know what to do . . .'

Léonie saw her pain and despair. She recognised the feeling. It had been her own, when Jenny had gone. And now, seeing Hetty's agony, she warmed slightly towards her. 'I'm sorry about Pierre. I know how you feel. I lost someone in the war, killed in the blitz in London . . .' She paused, as if weighing some hard decision. Then she continued hurriedly. 'The woman I lived with, after I left Robert. Jenny,' she added with abrupt finality, fearing she had said too much, that Hetty might be unsympathetic towards the idea of this other woman, this later passion.

But Hetty was not. In seeing Léonie again – beginning to savour the reality of this once-so-loved woman – she began to change her mind about such love, the loves of Claudine, and of Léonie. It no longer upset her. She did not feel at all betrayed by Léonie. She felt instead – she was unable to deny it – a tenderness towards her, an envy even, for this constancy in her nature.

'Jenny?' she asked gently, with all these feelings in her eyes. 'Who was she – what happened?'

So Léonie explained about Jenny, suddenly unburdening herself, telling Hetty everything, feeling that here, in her old friend, was the one person who would understand all her agonies at this loss.

'Oh, Léa, I'm so sorry,' Hetty said at the end. 'I wish I could help.' She longed for more than this. 'I wish I could make it up to you somehow. For her. For me as well. I still feel so bad about the way I behaved, years ago, to you, and when we last met in Dublin, that awful prison. I was so dismissive, so cold. Sick perhaps. But not that sick. I just couldn't face the idea of my being responsible for you and Robert coming apart again –'

'We'd have come apart anyway –'

'No! It was me – just like that first time in Egypt . . .' She shook her head in pain at the memory. 'If only I hadn't tangled up both your lives. All those crazy, destructive feelings I had before I found Pierre. And I so regret it. I just *wish* I could make it up to you,' she added with a force that surprised Léonie.

'You don't have to feel that any more – and certainly not about Jenny. You had nothing to do with her. Besides, it's not me but Pierre you have to worry about now.'

'Oh, I'll get him out of that camp – I've quite made up my mind about that – one way or another.' She paused, her confidence subsiding for an instant, before she resuscitated it. 'And, if I can't, then I'll join him there, go where he goes, some forced labour camp or whatever. I'm not going to leave him – I'd be nothing without him . . .'

Léonie nodded. 'I felt exactly the same about Jenny. But don't be a martyr – I learnt that too. Live for Pierre, don't die for him.'

'Die? Why should I die? They've no idea Pierre's in the resistance – just that he's a Jew. As I am, partly. And it's only a labour camp they send them to. Anyway, I'm going to stay with him. I owe him – I owe you – a life.'

'Not me, Hetty.' Léonie was touched by these admissions of Hetty's – this concern for a past between them which was quite dead for her.

She looked at Hetty – transformed once more. Hetty, despite the repeated disasters of the years, had found that grace again, that true character which was transcendant in her now. Hetty possessed again all those qualities which Léonie had loved in her years before, a radiant spirit, all those destructive emotions she had spoken of, quite sunk away.

And Léonie suddenly sensed that her past with Hetty was not dead. She felt a vague tenderness towards her. 'No, you don't owe me anything,' she said. 'What's done is done between us, good and bad, years ago. That account's closed. You owe Pierre all these things now. With me, Hetty – we can just be friends, when the war is over . . .' She stood up hurriedly, turning away, thinking she might have said too much.

'Oh, Léa! If that could happen – I'd be so happy!' Hetty was enchanted by this token of forgiveness. And suddenly, in her despair over Pierre, she longed for consolation. She stood up, went to Léonie through the gloom, and put a hand on her shoulder. Then, before she knew quite what she was doing, she had kissed her, and Léonie had responded, kissing her with a moment's sudden passion in return.

They broke apart, both shocked at this old love of theirs come to life for an instant, that shared nature which Hetty had thought quite dead in her, rising like a genie from the lamp, so that they both tried to deny it at once.

'I'm sorry . . .' Hetty said limply. Léonie took the initiative. 'Listen,' she said breathlessly. 'I have to go out. I've an appointment I can't miss, down on the left bank. I'll be back – this afternoon.'

'Do stay!'

'I can't!'

She hurried out of the apartment, taking the kitchen entrance so that she could hide the automatic there. And it was she who felt she owed something to Hetty then, she who had let her down. She had no appointment. It was simply that she had not trusted herself to stay another minute in the apartment alone with Hetty.

Half-way down the narrow servant's stairs, Léonie heard the clump of boots running up the marble staircase just beyond the dividing wall. On each floor there was a small connecting door leading out on to the main staircase. Opening one of these a fraction she glimpsed a Swastika armband, jackboots, the black uniforms of several SS officers with a Field Security Patrol – rounding the balustrade, making for the top floor. There was little doubt where they were going – to the de Sertignys' apartment. Someone had betrayed them. The 'safe house' had been discovered.

Hidden behind the door, Léonie hesitated. If she had brought her automatic with her she would have run back upstairs and tried to fight it out with them – just to try and save Hetty, for she was stricken now at her fate. Perhaps she should return as she was, unarmed? – expose herself as the woman they were looking for, and hope to get Hetty released. But the Gestapo would never believe Hetty had no part in the business. Both of them would be simply taken then. Léonie remained horrified at this desertion. But she saw she had no alternative. She had to get away herself, to warn the others, André and Eve, not to return there. They were due back at the apartment later that afternoon; the Gestapo would certainly be waiting for them. And if they took André the whole Passy network would very likely be betrayed.

She knew she had no choice. She must get away as quickly as possible. Moving silently down the rest of the narrow stairs, she turned the last corner – only to be confronted by the concierge, Madame Bonnot, her back against the small door, blocking her escape out the rear entrance. It was clear to Léonie what the woman was about: it was she who had betrayed them, so that seeing the Gestapo rushing up the main staircase, and knowing of this hidden servant's exit, she had thought to take the chance of catching some prize for the Gestapo herself. And though she must have been in her fifties, she was far from frail – a big woman, weighty in all the right places.

But Léonie did not hesitate. Hurling herself down the last flight of steps she threw herself at Madame Bonnot, first clapping a hand over her mouth and pulling her from the doorway, then locking her right arm in a fierce grip round the back of the woman's neck, smelling her garlic-filled breath for an instant, before she swung her right round, increasing her hold on the woman's windpipe now as she drew the woman towards her.

Madame Bonnot fought furiously, grunting and gasping, trying to cry out. But Léonie, all her unarmed combat training coming into play now and spurred on by the guilt she felt in so abandoning Hetty to her fate, was far more skilled and vicious. Almost unaware of the strength she was exerting, she held Madame Bonnot from behind, one hand over her mouth, the edge of her wrist on her throat, in an ever-tightening embrace. Suddenly it was all over. The concierge lay at her feet, silent and quite still. Léonie escaped out from the back of the apartment block then, over the wall and into the cemetery, before getting clear away from the area into the busy Trocadéro.

She called André at once from a café, giving him the news. 'So you must warn Eve, at once,' she added. 'Not to go back there –'

'Yes, she hasn't left our place. I spoke to her a few minutes ago. You meet me there, too. All three of us – we'll have to get straight out of Paris, go to ground. Hetty has no training in this business – she won't last long with the Gestapo. We've probably only got an hour or two before they know all about us.'

– 873 –

'So, Mademoiselle, you refuse even to admit your real name – quite apart from your code-name, of course. Or the names of the others in your network,' he added as if this was a matter of lesser importance.

Standartenfuehrer Helmuth Knocken, Chief of the Paris SS, looked across his desk on an upper floor of his headquarters in the Avenue Foch. Hetty sat opposite. They were alone. The Colonel's French was cultivated. So were his pale features. He had a generally benign and civilised air. Standing up, he offered her a cigarette, which, sitting bolt upright in a high-backed chair, she did not even look at.

'Well, it hardly matters,' he went on lightly, moving over to the window. It was cool at last after the unseasonable heat of the day. He returned to his desk, picking over some papers, which the Gestapo had found earlier in the apartment. 'It's perfectly clear – you are Yvonne de Sertigny. These papers, letters of yours, this book with your name on it: "Yvonne de Sertigny" – you live in the apartment. I wonder why you won't admit it . . .'

'Yes, yes – I'm Yvonne de Sertigny,' Hetty said at last.

She had not wanted to admit this too quickly. But once the Colonel had given her this identity, which she knew now to have been Léonie's alias in France, she had thought immediately to adopt it as her own, to take Léonie's place. It was obvious – the man had played into her hands: in this way she could protect Léonie, as well as André and Eve. In her role as Yvonne de Sertigny she could protect them all, including Pierre. And that was the most important thing: now that she was Yvonne de Sertigny, branded as a member of the French resistance, they would never know her as Pierre's wife. And since he was only being detained for being a Jew – well, if she survived in the Avenue Foch, they might survive together, for she would very likely be sent to Drancy as well, before being deported with him to some labour camp in Germany.

Yes, there was a chance they might meet up in this way. But for this to come about, for her to see Pierre again, she must say nothing of the others. She must resist everything, whatever they might have in store for her – since to give them Léonie's or André's name would almost certainly result in their taking Pierre on a much more serious charge, not simply being a Jew but as a member of the resistance. Either André or Léonie might break under torture, admitting this. Would she break herself? If she did, it would almost certainly cause the deaths of Pierre and Léonie, the two people who meant most to her in life. Her own death, by comparison, was much easier to contemplate. For them to survive, she was quite prepared to die. After all, as she had told Léonie only that morning, she owed them both a life.

'Good! – Mademoiselle de Sertigny.' The Colonel was pleased at this final admission of hers. 'I can't think why you should want to deny your real name, at least.' He fingered through Yvonne's papers again, picking up the 'Claudine' novel. 'An admirer of Colette, I see. Excellent!' Then he picked up the Beretta automatic. 'Which brings me to this – and your other, your clandestine, identity.' He flourished the automatic an instant. 'You are part of a French resistance network, of course . . .'

Hetty said nothing. The Colonel gazed over the gardens again. Then his attitude changed. He was not harsh, simply more serious, concerned, a note of regret almost in his voice. 'Mademoiselle de Sertigny – it's also perfectly obvious: you were waiting in your apartment today for another member of your circle. We know that for certain. One of our officers followed this woman, to your apartment. You met her there. She clearly left just before my colleagues arrived – we found the concierge . . .' He took up a fountain pen and fiddled with it. 'We must know who that woman is. And the names of the others in your circle. Will you tell me?'

Hetty remained silent.

'No, I suppose not. Part of your job, as you see it. But, I have to tell you, we *will* find out, either from you, or from your colleagues, when they return to the apartment. It's a "safe house" obviously. And some of your friends won't know we've been there – and we're watching it, of course.'

He gazed at Hetty intently then, before she finally spoke, equally even and polite in her reply. 'Yes, no doubt you are watching the apartment. Part of *your* job. So perhaps you will find out who these people are. But not from me.'

'Indeed.' The Colonel was brisk now, as if they had at last concluded some mutually satisfactory agreement. 'Well, we shall see. I simply thought to save you . . . trouble, if you told me now. I give all resistance people this opportunity when I first interview them. However, you will appreciate . . .' He seemed genuinely apologetic now. 'I'm a busy man. I don't have time to conduct every interrogation here. But my colleagues in the Gestapo, under Hauptsturmfuehrer Puetz in the basement, though equally busy, I believe are not so considerate – or patient. Well? What is the name of your friend, the woman who came to see you this morning?'

He waited, in case Hetty should say anything. She did not. He picked up the telephone. Hetty was taken away a minute later, downstairs to the basement.

The Passy circle went to ground. André and Eve, together with Léonie, had escaped the city that same afternoon – Léonie and Eve taking separate trains south from the Gare de Lyon, André moving in the same direction, by local trains at first, before taking an express on the main line to Clermont-Ferrand. Late that night they all met at a farmhouse, way up in the hills of the wild country, to the north-east of Clermont-Ferrand. Here, taken in care by the chief of the local resistance, they would lie low, before André regrouped elsewhere in France, while Léonie would try to contact Baker Street, tell them the news and wait for further instructions.

But Léonie had no thoughts for any such future resistance schemes that night as they ate some coarse bread and ham, by the light of an oil lamp in the farmer's kitchen. Thinking of Hetty, then speaking of her, she could barely eat at all.

'You did the only thing you could,' André told her once more. 'You can't blame yourself.' Then, perhaps a little tactlessly, he was rather more blunt with the truth. 'Hetty knows very little about our circle, almost nothing. But, if the Gestapo had taken you, then they would very likely have had me – and the lives of *dozens* of others would have been at risk.'

'You don't seem to understand – Hetty, she's a great friend of mine.'

'Yes, I do understand that. But she's just as much a friend of ours, Yvonne. I promise you. We feel just the same about her.'

'But what will *happen* to her?' Léonie, though she was certain of the answer, could not stop herself from voicing her concern, her agony at Hetty's likely fate.

André said quickly, 'You mustn't torture yourself –' He stopped, aware of his gaffe. There was silence.

Before Hauptsturmfuehrer Puetz started to interrogate Hetty that night at the Avenue Foch, his men took rubber truncheons to her face, threw her to the floor, drove boots into her kidneys, so that soon one of her eyes was closed, blood streamed down her forehead and her lips had become ugly swollen lumps. Each time they dragged her to her feet, they knocked her down again, as if to some juvenile formula.

And indeed all this was the usual practice – the preamble to most Gestapo interrogations: break the prisoner's nerve at once, hurt, daze and humiliate them with these violent tactics, knock them off balance, physically and mentally, so that when the actual questioning began their victim would be at a total disadvantage. Prisoners rarely regained their nerve after such a violently capricious introduction. Finally, they dragged Hetty, bruised and bleeding, to a chair and sat her down against a bright light.

Captain Puetz, in a grey uniform, black riding breeches and top boots, arrived in the room then, to take charge of the proceedings. A pedantically fussy little man, he spoke to Hetty in much less certain French, referring back to a memorandum on his desk all the while he addressed her, as if from the text of a play where he was uncertain of the lines. Yet what he apparently lacked in memory, he made up for in volume. He increasingly harangued, he shouted, he *snorted* at Hetty in a nasal voice. There was not even the sense of a ham actor here, but of someone much further adrift from reality in these fantastic histrionics. The man was quite unreal and yet had not the least inkling of this.

'So, Mademoiselle de Sertigny, my colleague, Standartenfuehrer Knochen, managed to get nothing from you, I see.' He spoke dismissively of the senior SS officer in overall charge of operations at the Avenue Foch. 'Be assured that we in the Gestapo will not be so superficial in our enquiries. The name of the woman you met earlier today – who was she? And the others in your group. What are their names?' He gave a final snort, resting his case.

Hetty, though her lip was bleeding and badly swollen, knew she could still speak. But she said nothing. However, she could not prevent herself from shaking, with shock and pain – and fear.

The Captain noticed her shaking. 'Cold, Mademoiselle?' Then, maintaining his bad French, he spoke to one of his men standing by the door. 'Obersturmfuehrer, be so kind as to get something to warm Mademoiselle de Sertigny.'

The Lieutenant left the room, and went to the end of the corridor. There he prepared a blow-lamp, igniting thc methylated spirits first, allowing the burner to warm, then pumping the pressure up before opening the nozzle and setting a match to it. A blueish flame jetted out with a roar. Captain Puetz interrupted his work a few minutes later.

'No, you idiot! What are you trying to do? – burn her alive before we've had a word out of her? By *degrees*, Lieutenant. The matches first. The blow-lamp is a last resort, you incompetent fool . . .'

In the days that followed at the Avenue Foch they questioned Hetty, stupidly and aimlessly for the most part, about clandestine matters of which she had absolutely no knowledge – so that, unable to reply, they increasingly assumed she was hiding vital information and tortured her progressively more brutally. They stuck sharpened matches up her nails, lighting the phosphorus at the other end. They dipped her, head first, repeatedly, into a tub of ice-cold water, pulling her out each time only at the very last moment, nearly asphyxiated, before applying artificial respiration – leaving her then, in her soaking clothes, overnight in a cell. Electrodes were attached to her feet, her ear-lobes, finally her nipples, before the current was turned on. They handcuffed her wrists behind her back, slipped a hook into the cuffs, then dragged her up by a pulley, leaving her suspended until her arms were almost dislocated and she fainted. Finally the blow-lamp . . . It had started to sear the skin off her forearm before she fainted again.

She was unconscious for increasingly long periods. But each time she woke, floundering about through curtains of livid pain, she always discovered a vision of Pierre, or of Léonie and the others – seeing them clearly, in some remembered happy site or circumstance, a spring morning over coffee with Pierre, before he left for work, at the window of the apartment in the Avenue Mozart, an autumn day years before up in the orchards of Summer Hill with Léonie.

So that when the next obscenity faced her, a repetition of the cold tub or the pulleys, she kept these visions firmly in mind, expelling every other thought; soon, finding some knack in this, her own spirit seemed to leave her, joining these others, leaving only her empty, tortured body behind.

Just as years before, at the American hospital in Neuilly, with Dermot watching over her, when she was dying and had felt herself rise up out of her own body, floating about the ceiling, looking down on herself and Dermot, so now she found the same strange release – floating away from herself, as the pain overwhelmed her, so that even her fearful shrieks seemed to her then the cries of another woman.

This transference, this stepping into a quite different dimension, other lives, into the lives of her friends – like an actress completely taking over, inhabiting a new role – probably saved her, for the pain was blotted out, was suffered by a former and now discarded person.

The only thing that nearly undid her was the pain of others. One evening, while not being tortured herself, she was forced instead to listen to the muffled screams of someone, a man being tortured in the next room. Captain Puetz stood over her. 'Your *husband*,' he told her. 'Oh yes, we found out. Not "mademoiselle" at all. You're married. We picked up your husband the other day!'

She listened to the appalling screams. Was it Pierre? She could not decide. Yes! – No, they were bluffing. But *was* it? Could it be?

'*Now* will you give me those names?'

She very nearly told him then. Until she thought – if it really were Pierre they would have tortured him in front of her, not in the next room. She told them nothing.

After a week of this Colonel Knochen spoke to Puetz. 'No one ever showed up or returned to her apartment. It is just possible this woman has nothing to do with the resistance – and that the other woman was just a friend of hers.'

Hauptsturmfuehrer Puetz snorted. 'Innocent? – of course not! Anyone we arrest must be involved in *some* subversive activity. It's just a matter of time with this woman – before we find out what it is.'

'In time, Captain, she will simply die . . .'

'What matter is that?'

'You will still have found out nothing.'

'We should continue our interrogation. And, if we discover nothing, then simply . . . get rid of her, like all the rest.'

The Colonel gazed at the little man. How cocksure, how ignorant he was. He would go on torturing this woman just on the off-chance that she might know something – and the woman would be dead, when Puetz still would not admit that she had nothing to tell them at all, that she was, indeed, probably innocent. It was all so clumsy and unintelligent an approach. The Colonel was suddenly, if silently, furious with Puetz. At the best of times he hated dealing and compromising with these Gestapo thugs, drawn from the lowest riff-raff all over Germany. But now he would put his foot down, certain that in this instance Puetz was wasting everyone's time. He would show his authority in the matter.

'No, Hauptsturmfuehrer – this is not an abattoir. And to kill *everyone* we interrogate is simply an admission of defeat. Headquarters in Berlin will not like that, when they see the monthly figures – nothing but invariable deaths in the Avenue Foch. And, besides, this woman is not worth any more of your time. Send her to the camp at Le Bourget, have her deported, along with all the other . . . undesirables . . . up there.'

Captain Puetz, seeing some sense in this, agreed. He had, indeed, other pressing work – a number of new prisoners to deal with. And it was a point – a few, at least, of these French resisters should be numbered among the living when they left the Avenue Foch. Berlin might complain of the continual imbalance in the figures sent to them every month, possibly suspect him of getting too casual in his work – if the figures were all in the red, so to speak. They were fussy over little things like that in Berlin, figures . . . None the less, when next he had occasion to send a memorandum to Colonel Eichmann at Prinz Albrecht Strasse, he would insinuate his doubts about Colonel Knochen. There was something not entirely reliable about him . . .

Hetty was sent to Drancy. It was a makeshift transit camp, part of what had originally been a public housing development on the outskirts of Paris – a collection of grim four-storey apartment blocks, huts and desolate open spaces hidden from the general view, yet conveniently near the main railhead east at the station of le Bourget. Now it was filled largely with French Jews. And, since it was so obviously a transit camp, without any proper facilities, most took heart from the frightful privations and discomforts here, which could not be other than temporary, and so were the more encouraged in their belief that they were about to be sent to appropriately equipped and staffed labour or resettlement camps in Germany, or even the Tyrol perhaps – on decent trains, they assumed, which they had never actually seen, but which arrived for them every week at sidings near the station half a mile away.

However, there had been no transports out for nearly three weeks, so that the camp was filled way beyond capacity, with nearly four thousand deportees in a space built for 1,200 – men, women, and many young Jewish children, orphaned or taken from their parents – crammed together in the bleak open spaces behind the barbed wire. A few optimistic people milled about feverishly, expectantly by the gates, suitcases packed and ready to return home, certain there had been some mistake in their arrest which would at any moment be rectified. Others, wiser and more numerous, slumped on the ground or against walls, careless of their meagre belongings, with the vacant, hollow-eyed expression of people quite aware that a hideous nemesis had overtaken them, against which there was no appeal, which had already condemned them to some nameless fate.

The conditions, exacerbated by the very hot weather that summer, were quite appalling when Hetty arrived there, more dead than alive, pushed off the back of a truck, among a dozen others, like so much garbage. The deportees were packed twenty or thirty to each small room, where there were wooden bunk beds for only a dozen. There was no food, apart from a thin cabbage soup and some stale bread once a day, together with what the prisoners had managed to bring with them. And the only water came from four street hydrants dotted around the camp, some close to the overflowing cesspits and latrines already infected, so that dozens of people, contending for the few straw-filled mattresses, laid out in the rooms and long corridors, were ill or dying with typhoid, dysentery and enteric fever.

The camp, too, was infested with vermin, lice and fleas – so that infection spread like wildfire. In both the men's and women's blocks suicides were a daily occurrence, several or more people slashing their wrists or throwing themselves from the rooftops. Worst of all were the mothers who, suspecting the worst possible fate for themselves and their children in Germany, flung their offspring from these same roofs before following after them. Early every morning a special squad of prisoners took the dead away in handcarts. The place was an inferno – of sickly odours, illness, death. And yet for Hetty, after her days and nights of torture in the Avenue Foch, the camp seemed almost a happy release.

Soon discovering that there had been no transports out of the camp since Pierre had been arrested she would have been happier still – if she could have found him. But among the thousands of people there was no sign of him. And then, worse still, on the second morning, having struggled about the camp all the previous day searching for him, she fell ill herself, overcome with fearful stomach cramps, back pains, a raging headache. She thought at first these must be due to the Gestapo's attentions or the result of some infection in the camp. Then she recognised the symptoms. Of course, it must be her syphilis. Long dormant through the good years with Pierre, it had returned with a vengeance.

She was furious at this turn of fate. She had survived everything in these last years, even the Gestapo. Was her far-distant past to catch up with her once more, all her old mistakes and stupidities, paying her out one last time? For it was perfectly clear to her from what she had already seen and heard: there were only two future alternatives here. You either left the camp eastwards, on the transports, or were carried out dead on a handcart.

No longer able to move, she lay flat out on the floor at the end of a long corridor in one of the women's blocks, among scores of others in the same or worse condition – pregnant women, a cripple who had just miscarried, a paralysed woman screaming on a stretcher, old women, blind or deaf; women dead or dying. This, surely, was the end, Hetty thought. She had survived the Gestapo, survived so much before that, only to fall victim of her own inherent faults of character. She supposed it was fair, being finally paid out like this for her idiocies, all the arrogance and crass ambition of her earlier life, which had led to her marrying Craig, who had given her this disease . . .

She had done her best to atone for all this in the latter years. Above all, against the worst the Gestapo could do, she had kept faith with her friends. She had not betrayed them. And so, too, she had finally made it up to them – Pierre and Léonie. The life she owed them would be theirs soon. Her own life was not now to emerge, by some final act of bravery or renunciation, on any further brighter course. She was beyond everything then – had had that portion allotted to her of fine, bright things. She closed her eyes, not expecting to open them again.

Someone woke her, a dark-haired youngish woman, toughly built, fat, with a small pug face, but with tender gazing eyes. 'I'm Rosa,' she said, bending down, wiping the sweat from Hetty's brow with a soiled handkerchief, offering her a little water in a tin mug. 'Drink it,' she said. 'It's been boiled.'

Hetty, struggling to consciousness, tried to sit up, but could not until the woman lifted her head very gently with one arm, giving her the mug with the other. She managed to take a sip, then some more, feeling slightly better after a few minutes

– as much from the tenderness of this huge woman with the small nut-brown face as anything else.

She managed to finish the water. Rosa wiped her face again, gently avoiding the awful cuts and bruises. 'Gestapo?' she asked. Hetty nodded. Rosa shook her head, unbelieving. 'In the resistance?' Hetty did not reply. 'You must have been. The brutes don't go that far even with us Jews – I was just a schoolteacher. There's a doctor in the camp. He tries to see some of the worst cases. I'll see if I can get him to come –'

Hetty's heart leapt. 'Oh, please – please do!' she told her. Was it Pierre? Could it be?

Hours later, in the fetid afternoon heat, with people groaning all round her, Hetty saw a figure coming through the door at the far end of the corridor. He bent down, examining someone on the floor. The doctor! But was it Pierre? Her eyes were blurred, and the man was too far away for her to identify him.

Gradually, tending one person after another, he drew nearer. Yes! It must be him. Then, equally sure, she knew it was not. Like a mirage the figure hovered in her fevered vision, appearing, disappearing, bringing hope, then despair. So that she was driven wild with frustration as she waited.

Finally, after what seemed hours, she saw the shock of thick hair, the spectacles, the green shirt, all tattered now, which he had been wearing that evening on his birthday ten days before.

It was Pierre.

She wanted to shout out for him then, to roar her head off with joy. But even if her swollen lips, her cracked voice, would have allowed this, she dared not. There were sure to be *agents provocateurs* about the camp – and no one must know they were married.

It was another ten minutes before he got to her at the end of the corridor – and when he saw her he could not restrain his shout.

'Hetty!'

She at once put a finger to her lips as he rushed over to her. 'No, not Hetty – pretend you don't know me – no one must know I'm your wife.'

He saw her burnt arm then, the cuts and bruises all over her face, how aged and hurt she was with the pain of the past ten days. 'Hetty, what? . . . what's happened?' He was appalled. 'What have they done to you?' He wanted to do everything, anything for her. But again she restrained him.

'*Whisper*, Pierre darling. And don't do anything unusual. I'm just a stranger. Bend down, whisper, and I'll tell you everything.'

He bent down – and whispered then. 'I can't believe it . . .' Then, despite her warnings, he kissed her.

'So you see,' she told him later. 'I'm "Yvonne de Sertigny" – they think I'm with the resistance. And you're just here because you're a Jew. So no one must know we're married.' He nodded. 'Not for the moment anyway, while we're still in the camp here. If they discover we're married they'll take both of us back for more interrogation. When we get to the camp in Germany, well, it certainly can't be as bad as this. Things'll be easier there. They won't care if we're married then. You'll see! This is hell – but, once we're out of it, we can be properly together again – working some potato patch, or whatever it is, in Germany . . .'

The transports finally arrived a week later. Hetty, under Pierre's attentions, and with the food, drugs and bandages he had managed to obtain from the thriving black market about the camp, had improved considerably. But most of all she was better for seeing him alive and being with him. Early one broiling afternoon, lined up in columns, some 1,200 deportees, including Hetty, Pierre and some hundreds of unaccompanied children, were led out of the camp by French police and taken to the marshalling yards at le Bourget.

Here, to the surprise of many, instead of passenger carriages, a long line of cattle trucks awaited them. The police herded them on board like the beasts the wagons were intended for – eighty or ninety people crushed together into each airless, windowless truck, including a dozen or so of the children, carefully inserted into each wagon, so that onlookers, any local inhabitants or railway officials, would believe they were travelling with their parents. Inside there was nothing but dirty straw to ease them, no water, and barely any ventilation or sanitary facilities. And here they were left to roast under the hot afternoon sun for nearly three hours before the train finally left just after six o'clock.

But again Hetty, with Rosa who had become her friend now, did not complain. Nor did the others in the wagon. It was just a temporary discomfort, many of them agreed, like the camp at Drancy. They soon regained their earlier optimism, even a sense of humour. 'You know what French trains are like these days! . . .' 'The decent trains have all been commandeered by the Wehrmacht . . .' 'They've all been bombed by the allies!' 'At least there's straw and a slop-pail!' Germany was only an overnight trip, they continued more seriously. And things were much more efficient there, at least – everyone knew that. They'd be transferred to a proper passenger train, or would have arrived at the labour camp by then, perhaps in the Tyrol, where there'd be space and air and it would be clean. Everyone knew how things like railways and camps of any kind were much better run in Germany.

'You fools!' one older Jewish woman shouted. 'They mean to kill us! – machine-gun us all as soon as we get off the train – at some rail siding or in the middle of the woods.' No one else agreed. They told her to shut up. Someone opened a bottle of wine they had managed to bring with them, while others started to share out their meagre provisions – tins of sardines, some cheese, even some sweet biscuits – so that soon there was almost a picnic atmosphere in the truck.

Hetty, having experienced the Gestapo at close quarters, was tempted to believe the old woman for a moment. Yet she vigorously repressed the thought. This cattle truck, like the camp at Drancy, was a simply temporary aberration. Above all, Pierre was on the same transport – that was the great thing. She had been terrified of being separated from him. But, no, he was with her. He had been walking twenty yards ahead of her in the column to the station. She had seen him pushed into one of the first cattle trucks. He was there, with her, a few wagons up towards the engine, and she was happy.

It had all worked out, just as she had planned and hoped. She had been given a reprieve. She could change her life once more – for surely the worst that could happen to them now would be an interlude, grim enough no doubt, digging potatoes or some such, until the war ended in victory for the allies, as it obviously would. With her new friend Rosa, the tough, quick-thinking Rosa who had forcibly commandeered a corner of the truck, she settled down in the straw, counting her blessings.

The journey was a nightmare.

The pitch-black interior of the truck, with everyone so tightly crushed together that many had to stand bolt upright, soon became intolerable. It was dark, airless, increasingly hot. The picnic mood vanished completely, along with every previous optimism, as the slop-pail, soon filled to overflowing, tipped over and people began to relieve themselves where they stood.

The air stank. The children whimpered, then began to cry. People started to quarrel for space, some to fight. They shouted then, trying to attract the attention of the guards, hopelessly. There was no water and soon all the food and drink they had brought with them was gone. A woman, a cultivated Jewess, who had taken charge of two attractive boys on their own, disciplined them gently. 'You mustn't complain – you're disturbing the others . . .' and Rosa tried to comfort Hetty. 'Never mind,' she told her next morning. 'It can't be far now. They'll let us out soon – must be in Germany. We'll soon be at the camp.'

They were indeed in Germany by then. And the train did stop, but only to take on coal and water for the engine. No one was let out. And in the silence Hetty heard the cries rising from all down the train, taken up by one truck from another, carried on the stinking air – cries which had only a vague tone of protest to them now, which seemed to Hetty much more like a keening over some vast funeral cortège.

They travelled on for nearly another two days. By the time they finally stopped two elderly Jews in Hetty's wagon had died, and she had long before ceased to count her blessings. Instead, numb with cramp, filthy dirty and almost suffocating in a space that was now layered inches deep in excrement, she saw the bright lights sweeping through the chinks in the wood as the train pulled to a halt and the doors were finally opened.

'Raus! Schnell! Los – los!'

She heard the guttural orders barked in German. Tumbling out of the wagon with Rosa she felt the cool night air on her face like a balm, breathing it in deeply. The feeling of release was unbelievable. The other deportees were gathering now, from all the trucks, on a long wooden platform, brightly lit from floodlights on tall pylons, surrounded by SS guards with snarling Alsatian dogs.

Yet the dogs did not bark, nor did the guards shout again. There was an air everywhere of thankful release, of calm and good order as the deportees were made to form up in long lines down the platform. The only stir was caused when people tried to take their luggage with them from the wagons.

'No,' Hetty, who had no luggage herself, heard an SS officer say to an elderly couple behind her. 'You don't have to carry your own luggage here. We have porters for that,' he continued agreeably. 'Just make sure you can identify your bags afterwards, at the luggage bureau in the camp – after you've had your decontamination and hot shower bath.'

The old Jewish couple, almost at the point of total exhaustion, were grateful for this, setting down their threadbare bags, patting them gently, settling the labels neatly, making a studious effort to memorise these objects already so familiar to them. Hetty, too, was heartened by this consideration on the officer's part. Things could not be too bad here at all.

She was surprised only when she saw the 'porters' – rake-thin men, hollow-eyed and -cheeked, the skin drum-tight everywhere, with shaven skulls in striped pyjamas, moving like wraiths among the crowds, stumbling up into the wagons, pulling out what luggage there was. Porters? They were more like victims – victims of some punishment, she supposed, the unlucky ones who had been caught stealing potatoes or some such. They were strangely silent, too, she noticed, saying absolutely nothing when asked, as they were, where the train had arrived.

Still, she had no time to worry about them. She must find Pierre. Stumbling up the platform towards Pierre's truck she suddenly saw him, the shock of dark hair sticking up against the bright floodlights, as he helped an old woman down from the truck. He was alive and well, though as filthy and bedraggled as she was. She longed to embrace him, but did not dare. Instead they exchanged a few whispered words.

'All right?' he asked.

'Just about. It was *awful* – where on earth are we?'

'Poland. One of those porters – I heard him speaking Polish.'

'But *where*?'

'Some place called Oswieckiem, I heard someone say.'

'It can't be too bad. I heard one of the SS officers say we were all to have a hot shower bath. And they're even carrying our luggage –'

Rosa had come up behind them then as they were interrupted with more commands. The line down the platform, finally formed, was now moving forward slowly towards the head of the ramp, where a group of SS officers were standing under a floodlight. And beyond them, to her relief and astonishment, Hetty saw a line of military trucks drawn up, but each of them with a large red cross emblazoned on the side.

'Look – the Red Cross!' she said to Pierre, just ahead of her now in the line. 'We can't be in any danger here.'

The column moved slowly forward. And soon, nearing the head of the platform, Hetty saw who the Red Cross trucks were for. All the elderly, the infirm, the ill and all the children among the deportees, separated from the others by an SS officer as they reached the head of the line, were being helped on board the trucks and taken away.

'God! I hope we can get on one of those trucks!' Hetty told Rosa. 'I can hardly walk.'

'Oh, I couldn't bear to be cooped up again,' Rosa said. 'Can't we walk? – with the others.'

She gestured towards a much smaller contingent of younger, able-bodied people, now being formed up in another line beyond the SS officers.

'Oh, Rosa, let's not. I'm really finished. Let's take the Red Cross trucks. I can very well pretend I'm old and doddery. At least, if Pierre goes in the trucks, I will. I do hope he does.'

'All right, if you want.'

They were nearly at the head of the line where the column was being divided, with Pierre just in front of them. When his turn came to confront the officer he was waved aside to the left at once, away from the Red Cross trucks. And Hetty had to change her mind then. 'All right, let's not. We'll pretend we're fit as fiddles. We'll walk with Pierre.'

Hetty, when she and Rosa faced the officer, braced herself purposefully, smiling confidently. The officer gazed at them for a moment, then waved them aside, to the left, with Pierre.

But, just before they moved off, Hetty saw the cultivated Jewish woman, with her two young boys still in her care, who had all been ahead of them, all being helped up into the back of a Red Cross truck before it drove sharply away. She waved at the two boys. One of them took out a handkerchief to wave back at her, smiling broadly.

The officer, noticing Hetty's gesture, attempted a brief smile himself. 'Don't worry,' he told her in passable French. 'You'll see them again, when they've had their shower bath.'

'Oh, they're nothing to do with me,' Hetty said quickly. 'Just friends I met on the train.'

She was suddenly comforted by this last phrase, the casual, everyday words, as if all of them, setting off on a vacation and having come through an expectedly difficult journey, were now at last entering the holiday camp.

Fifteen minutes later, with Pierre and Rosa, she was walking off into the cool night, away from the ramp, flanked by soldiers, along a track among trees. There were fewer than a hundred of them now remaining, separated from the many hundreds more who had gone off in the Red Cross trucks. Again Hetty breathed the cool night air and was thankful. Though she was still exhausted and aching everywhere, still wishing she had gone in one of the trucks. They would have had their hot shower baths that much sooner. She longed, above all else at that moment, for a hot shower.

A young soldier, marching ahead of her, dropped back and said to her in bad French, 'I'll give you a cigarette – if you let me screw you.'

'*One* cigarette?' She turned to Rosa. 'That's a pretty poor rate. Or else cigarettes must be priceless around here.' She turned back to the soldier. 'No, thanks. But where are we going?'

'Labour camp. But you'll be all right. Don't worry. Two cigarettes?' Hetty shook her head and the soldier moved on ahead of them.

'It's strange,' Hetty said after another ten minutes' walk, as they came out of the trees, seeing a bare flat expanse of land ahead of them, illuminated by distant flood and search lights, set at intervals round what was obviously a huge perimeter fence. 'It's only two o'clock, so it can't be the dawn. But look – that red haze on the horizon, to the right, over the camp there.'

The two women observed this strange phenomenon which, as they drew nearer, materialised not only as a red glow, but as several smoky cones of fire, spiralling upwards, a ruddy apocalyptic vision against the clear night sky.

'Factories, I suppose,' Rosa told her. 'Furnaces. Working all night. Where we'll be working, I suppose.'

'Pity. Fields and gardens – I'd hoped we'd be doing something like that . . .'

Then, as they approached the floodlit perimeter fence, with a sentry block and high-arched gateway in the middle, a drift of air passed over their heads, a sudden sweetish smell in a change of wind that was gone in a moment. But as it passed their nostrils the message it left was unmistakable.

'*Meat?*' Rosa said in astonishment. 'Who could be roasting meat at this time of night?'

'Why not?' Hetty smiled. 'Food! We've not eaten for days – and they've got to *feed* us here, at least, haven't they? – if they expect us to work. Red Cross probably insisted we got something hot to eat, when we arrive . . .'

They came to the arched gateway. Above it, picked out in iron letters in a semi-circle round the arch, was the legend: 'ARBEIT MACHT FREI'.

'What does it mean?'

Rosa, the schoolteacher, looked at it. '"Work – work gives you freedom", I think.'

'Oh good,' Hetty said. 'Thank God we're here, in some proper camp at last. After the hell of Drancy and that terrible train journey this place is bound to be better – all round.'

'Yes,' Rosa said, as the column entered the gates and disappeared into the vast camp.

13

'Wwat *would* have happened to Hetty, though – in one of those camps?' Olivia spoke to her father on the porch after lunch at Summer Hill. It was a glorious summer afternoon in 1945. Robert, back from the war – back a few months before from Dachau where, as one of the allied journalists present, he had seen exactly what had happened in these camps – did not reply at once. 'Did no one survive, Dermot?' She turned to her cousin, in another wicker chair – Dermot, retired at last from the Army, over at Summer Hill and living there now.

'I really . . . don't know exactly . . .' He prevaricated. Olivia was only nineteen. Surely, he thought, she might be spared the details of these horrors, which he, like Robert, now knew all about.

Olivia impatiently ran a hand through her thick, glossy-dark hair and turned back to her father. 'Well, somebody must know what happened to Hetty and –'

'Some people survived, *yes*,' her father spoke at last, almost brusquely. 'But very few. Most that weren't – incinerated – were driven out of the camps just before the allies arrived and taken on forced marches, in the freezing snow, and most of them died, too.'

'So, Hetty . . . went that way?' Olivia's curiosity would not be denied. 'And what about Pierre, her husband – the same thing?'

'Possibly –'

'Or were they just burnt?'

'I – we simply don't know, Olivia,' he said impatiently.

'Or could they have *survived*?'

Robert, frustrated, stood up. 'No. No chance. The camps were opened up several months ago. Only a very few – a few thousand among *millions* – got out alive. And neither Hetty nor Pierre was amongst them. If they had been, they'd have turned up somewhere by now. So let's leave it at that, shall we? They're both . . . dead.' He moved to the edge of the porch, looking over the potholed, weed-covered gravel surround – Lady Cordiner's elaborate pleasure garden beyond, which Hetty and Pierre had so painstakingly restored before the war, now quite gone to seed again.

'All right,' Olivia said, a little put down. 'I didn't want to make a thing of it. And it is absolutely *awful* about Hetty and Pierre – terrible and sad, even though I never met Pierre and hardly remember her at all. But the thing is Mummy won't talk about it at all. And I'd like to know. After all, it is their house we're living in now.' Shading her dark eyes against a sudden burst of sunlight, she stood up and joined her father.

'I'm sorry,' Robert told her. 'It's just the whole concentration – no, *extermination* – camp thing is, well, it's all so horrifying I haven't really taken it in yet.' He shook his head. 'It simply wasn't believable. Dachau when I saw it – the gas chambers, the ovens, these huge crematoria – it just didn't make any sense at first. One of the American officers told me, when he first saw all these ovens, he thought for a moment they might have been *bread* ovens, couldn't understand why they needed so many bread ovens, especially since the few survivors obviously hadn't eatn properly in years, sheer skeletons. So, let's not dwell on it now, that's all. It'll take years to make sense of it, if we ever do.' He turned back. 'More coffee, Dermot?'

'But Mummy – what are we to do about her?' Olivia followed her father.

'All we can – all we have been doing. The doctor in London said rest. And that's exactly what she's getting here. She was recovering, too – forgetting, until she saw all those newspaper and newsreel reports on the camps.' He spoke more to himself than to the others. Pouring Dermot more coffee, he looked up at Olivia. 'You see, for her it's all so much worse – Hetty taking her place in that Paris flat, when the Gestapo arrived. If it hadn't been for Hetty, Mummy would almost certainly have ended up in one of those camps. That's the problem for her now. And, when she saw what the camps were like, what really happened there – well, it sort of sent her over the edge. Shock, depression.'

'Yes,' Olivia considered it all. 'Hetty saved her life then, didn't she?' Robert said nothing. 'And saying nothing to the Germans when they tortured her – as those French people told you. That was so brave. Will they give Hetty a medal, like Mummy's getting? – they do, don't they, even after they're dead, sometimes?'

'I don't think so. Hetty's reward . . . will simply have to be here.' He gazed across the lush valley towards the purple shoulders of Mount Brandon. 'That's what she and Pierre would have wanted – to keep this place going, set in some order again, which is why we've come back to live here. Hetty was very fond of Summer Hill.'

'Yes. Like we all are –'

'Go up and see if Mummy wants anything. She may be asleep, but just see.'

Olivia, in a pair of old slacks and a tattered blue pullover, stretched her arms high above her head, arching her back, yawning. 'God, I'm still so tired after that awful journey over. But I'm so glad to be here. Because I loved it here – remember? – when we lived here before. Can we get the swing going again, up on the big maple?'

'Yes, if you can get near the tree with all those briars . . . But aren't you a bit old for swinging?'

'Certainly not! And the river,' she rushed on excitedly. 'We'll get the boat out again, won't we? It's still there, in the boat house, I saw it this morning. And go for trips on it like we used to do. And the otters! You will come with me – and Dermot – on the river? Because I'm so glad to be back, and having a whole summer here before I go to Trinity . . .' Olivia rushed on, a child again in her enthusiasm for this return, to this place where she had been happy as a child, which she had thought entirely lost to her, a world now regained. 'I really *do*! – like it all so much better over here than dreary England. Simply couldn't stand any more of that powdered egg and margarine and *spam*. All the fresh eggs and bacon and *butter* we had this morning for breakfast – couldn't believe it. So you will come and do things, before you go back, Daddy? – like we used to do, on the river and things.'

'Yes. And I've talked to Jack Welsh – we'll get the pony and trap out and going again. Have to. Pierre's old Wolseley is still in the coach-house. But not a drop of petrol for it anywhere.'

'I wish you weren't going away again so soon. And why *Germany*, when you've only just come back from the horrible place?'

'Paper wants some articles: "The Post-War Scene" . . . But you'll be here with Mummy – and Dermot and Aunt Emily and Elly and Jack. Almost a whole household again, as it used to be . . . And I'll be back soon enough. Do go up and see if Mummy's all right.'

'And that's be-best of all . . . ' Olivia had stopped by the hall door, half-turning, her slight stammer returned for an instant. 'Us three together again, isn't it?' She made a move towards him, head to one side, quizzical, half-smiling, hesitating, running her hand through her hair again in a nervous gesture.

'Yes,' Robert said lightly. 'That's best of all.' Olivia turned then, doing a small skip, as she disappeared through the doors.

'Yes . . .' Robert turned to Dermot after she had gone. 'I never thought it would turn out like this. Back here – with Léa, again.' He sat down, gazing into his cup. 'And it wouldn't have happened, but for Hetty going like that . . .'

Dermot nodded. '"An ill wind" . . .'

'Léa always had such hidden steel in her, over things – with Hetty when they were young, and her friend Jenny when she died – then joining the SOE and all that. But, after Hetty went, and her father dying last year – she started to break up. Then reading those reports on the camps, and the newsreels – that was the last straw.'

'Yes. She and Hetty were close, of course, over the years . . .' Dermot, as usual, left the nature, the degree, of this intimacy undefined.

But Robert, thrilled by Léonie's return to him and so forsaking his usual reticence, was happy to talk to his oldest friend, about things he could not have begun to talk about with anyone else. 'More than close. It was Hetty who always stood between Léa and me. You remember . . .' He smiled a fraction.

'Yes –'

'As long as Hetty was there I was always to play second fiddle.'

'I see.' Dermot did see, but did not care to comment further.

'Oh yes. That was exactly the problem between us. No other. And I couldn't help Léa – then. Hetty was always an *idée fixe*, an obsession with her. So that, when Léa saw those press reports and finally had to accept that Hetty couldn't have survived the camps, that she was dead, she couldn't face it. Because she had to accept that she was responsible for her death in a way, by running out on her when they met that time in Paris.'

'Running out? I didn't know – just that they'd met there, before the Gestapo arrived.'

'Yes, Léa left her – she told me. She was frightened of staying with her . . .'

'Frightened?'

'Of their old feelings for each other.'

'I see.' Dermot remained brief.

'So you do see, don't you? – what a long way Léa has to go. The guilt . . .'

'It's hard, yes.'

'And now she sees her agony as some sort of punishment for her earlier life with Hetty, her feelings there.'

'And how do you see it?' Dermot asked, by way of changing this, to him, delicate topic – the tragedy, always implicit, as far as he was concerned in any aberrant nature.

Robert drained his cup. 'Well, I loved them both. Now there's only Léa. So it's easier.'

'No longer in the middle.'

'Yes . . .' Robert paused, made aware, once more, of all the pain there had been in this triangle. 'But at least I can help Léa again now, as I've always wanted to. Because now she'll *let* me help her. The quite appalling thing is that it's taken Hetty's death for me to do this, for us to come together again.'

The two men looked out over the ruined demesne, hearing the tall dry summer grass rustle over the buried pleasure garden.

'It's really quite terrible about Hetty . . . But Léa will surely recover at Summer Hill,' Dermot said at last, emerging from his guarded mood, renewing a theme which had always absorbed him about the great house. 'Because you know there's something about the place – felt it almost as soon as I got back a month ago – something hopeful in the air, even when everything has gone to seed again.' He leant forward, finding his stride with a quite unusual enthusiasm. 'I've always felt, even when things were at their very worst here, in the old days, with old Lady Cordiner and Frances fighting and then all the terrible rows between Frances and Hetty, and the fire and the Black and Tan horrors – always felt there was a future somehow brewing in the ruins of things, under the dust-sheets, a phoenix in the ashes! Felt that people here – I used to say this to Hetty – could and would one day be unimaginably happy at Summer Hill. I can't account for the feeling, because so much *has* gone awry, and so often things have turned out for the very worst. And with Hetty and Pierre gone like that – what could be worse? The last straw, you'd think. Yet now there's you and Léa and Olivia here again. So once more – out of the blue, or the dark – there's a future for the place. How can one account for it all?'

'I can't really. Except that the house always seems to be there for saving people.'

'Or destroying them – like Frances and her mother. And poor Bunty.'

'Yes. Well, then, it's always saving *itself*, for something or somebody, for the *right* something or somebody.'

'Some sort of strange musical chairs.'

'I don't know what it is exactly,' Robert now took over Dermot's earlier passion. 'But I've felt something as you have here – the feeling of dead lives – old Lady Cordiner, Frances, Hetty now, and dozens of other Cordiners in the past – all influencing us. People who loved Summer Hill, or hated it, or the people in it, who lived out their dramas here with such passion that their imprint is still on the house somehow. *They're* still here – pushing us, to keep the place going, or maybe to live their lives for them, make up for their failures, faults, stupidities here, set the record straight, once and for all. I don't know . . .'

Robert gazed around him, searching the empty porch, as if trying to identify a whole host of ghosts. 'Everyone's still very much still here, aren't they? – sitting on the porch with us – as in some stiff Victorian family photograph. All of them. And they're all *watching* us – criticising, encouraging. Above all expecting us to get on and *do* something. Very Victorian, that. That's the feeling I have.'

'Yes, exactly.' Dermot lit his pipe, a drift of tobacco passing on the summer air. 'So, we'll have to do that then – try and put the place to rights again.'

'What is the situation, with Hetty and Pierre – and Summer Hill? I only had the rough details from you on the 'phone.'

'Hetty left no will, as far as I can ascertain. And in any case, as you know, Summer Hill never actually belonged to her or Pierre. All left to her, for use during her lifetime, by an "admirer". And I've told you who I think that is, the present Duke of Windsor. But I spoke to Mulrooney, the solicitor in Dublin, as soon as I got over – the man who dealt with the whole business originally. His "client", he told me, is quite willing that I should continue to have the legal administration of the house and estate, pending Hetty's possible return. And that if, after a period of five years, she doesn't show up, then we will reconsider the matter. And at that point his "client", he says, will very likely accept my recommendation as to who the place should go to then. Well, of course, I have and I shall recommend that you and Léa – and Olivia – have it at that point. Meanwhile, as the administrator now, I hope you and Léa *will* live here – and won't mind my living here, too!'

'Nothing would please us more, as you well know. But how should we arrange things – financially? What's the situation there?'

'Hetty had no bank account herself – she remained an undischarged bankrupt technically. I've had all the administration of the funds, some of it my own and Mortimer's money and what remained of Mulrooney's "client's" money after he bought the place back from Kennedy. There's presently only some £3,000 remaining at the bank here – pays Jack and Elly and Bridget. And the rates. And not much else. So we'll have to think about that. The roof's all right, that's the great thing – no damp or rot to speak of. But there will be soon. It's my idea that you and I share expenses here fifty-fifty –'

'Certainly not! Your share shouldn't be more than 25% at the most.'

They discussed these business affairs for five minutes longer. But in their enthusiasm for what lay before them – the restoration, once more, of this house which they both loved – the matter was hardly important to either of them. They would have enough money, together, to effect some immediate repairs on the house, and to maintain it. And that was all that mattered. They could live here now – start to rescue something from Hetty's death, rescue other things from the wreck of the war: a marriage for Robert, a happy retirement after nearly fifty years in the Army for Dermot. What Robert and Dermot had always seen as a world elsewhere for them was theirs now, willy-nilly, in this cast of fate, the ill wind that had blown them great good. They had both been away, estranged in heart and by distance from Summer Hill. Now they had come home.

Cabbage whites and red admirals zigzagged over the tall ragwort and wild grass which had practically obliterated all the paths. Swallows, darting and swooping over the ivy-choked walls, fed on the listless air, where midges and thunder flies formed a continual feast. The high-summer afternoon was dead-still and hot as Robert and Léonie pushed their way through the heavy undergrowth in the vegetable garden, searching the paths out with their feet, explorers in this jungle.

'Look, those lovely tall yellow flowers,' Léonie remarked, 'in the *vegetable* garden?'

'Must have seeded themselves here – Evening Primrose. *Oenothera*,' Robert added, his old passion for natural history returning now, in the place where he had learned these things. Léonie fingered the floppy, tulip-shaped flowers. 'They smell – in the evening,' he told her, swatting at the midges swarming above him.

Coming to the old vine house in a corner of the garden they found it collapsed at one end, glass broken, tendrils of vine spreading out all over the top, falling down in an arbour over a broken water barrel.

'Wonder if there are still any peaches inside?'

They pushed open the arched, diamond-paned door. A blackbird, disturbed, flew upwards against the glass, battering itself for an instant, before retreating, hiding among a collection of old apple boxes.

'Endless things to be done,' Robert said encouragingly.

'Too much . . .' Léonie was tired suddenly in the heat under the glass.

'We can do it. By degrees. We'll get a gardener. And help from the village.'

'Never was much good at gardening.'

'Doesn't matter. I like it.'

They walked down the central aisle, among nettles, the decayed entrail-like remains of long-dead tomato plants. Then they found the peaches on the wall at the end, more than half a dozen of them and ripe enough. Robert picked her one. The juice spilled down her chin as she bit into it.

'See! The peaches are still okay. We used to steal in here, eat them –' He stopped, for it had been he and Hetty, not Léonie, who, as children, had come in here, early on summer mornings years before, to do just this.

But Léonie knew this, too. 'You needn't stop,' she said. 'It was you and Hetty – who stole in here and ate then.' Her eyes flickered a little as if she were trying to clear them of something. 'You mustn't think I – that I can't bear the thought, the mention of Hetty.' Then, as if suddenly deciding something, she reached up, stretching far up the wall, for another peach which she gave to Robert. 'I can bear the thought of her – with you. What I couldn't bear was neither of you, I suppose. And the way I behaved to you, before the war – well, there was no reason for you to be kind to me, as you have been, after it. I misjudged you.'

He bit into the peach. 'No, I don't think you misjudged me. Just, neither of us could deal with each other – while Hetty was alive. We both loved her. Now she's not here, we can. I hope.'

' "Deal with each other" – sounds like a business! I hope it needn't be like that with us, Robert . . .' Some irony, a touch of life, had returned to her voice at last.

They took the other peaches back to the house. Robert had counted them. 'Just one each for everyone – Olivia, Dermot, Aunt Emily, Jack, Elly and Bridget.'

They smiled at the idea of how exactly the peaches had divided themselves up. For both of them it seemed a happy portent, this rediscovered bounty in the ruined vine house. There was promise here in the late sunlight over the garden, the smell of peaches, in the hem of Léonie's dress which she held up now like a dancer, cradling them. They had rescued something wonderful in the dust.

Certainly things changed for Léonie in the vine house that afternoon. She began to rise a fraction from her dead level. She went out with the others on the river that evening, trailing her hand in the black water by the overhanging willows. And, gradually in the days that followed, she took to life again in the old house, unpacking, settling things, storing, exploring.

She never, though, found the courage to enter Hetty's primrose bedroom. Elly took on the job there, of sorting and putting away Hetty's things – her clothes, books, knick-knacks, papers – packing them before they were sent to join so much else of the same sort belonging to earlier Cordiners, up in the attics. Only one thing she kept aside, found in Hetty's bureau: the snow-dome with the ivory miniature of Summer Hill inside, the little paperweight which on Frances's instructions, nearly fifty years before, she had thieved from old Lady Cordiner. Gazing at it now, she decided to return it, in her own person, just as she had taken it all those years before – replacing it where it had always been in Lady Cordiner's time, in the centre of the drawing room mantelpiece.

One afternoon a few days later Léonie noticed it, recognising it at once – as Hetty's most special charm, always kept by her bedside in their Dublin days together, taken with her everywhere when they had toured Ireland with Fonsy O'Grady's troupe.

How had it got there? She dared not ask, thinking this might break the magic of its sudden appearance. Instead, tumbling the snow inside so that it frothed over the miniature chimneys, she watched the flakes circle round the aerial chamber, falling lightly then, soon smothering the roofs and gables. How often before had she seen Hetty do just this, in a despondent moment, as a balm, a cure.

And she could not restrain her tears then, alone in the drawing room, gripped once more by the guilt of a terrible emotion – for a life that could not be returned and set before her, like the snow-dome.

She buried her face in her arms, unseeing, leaning on the mantelpiece. Behind her, as the snow settled everywhere in the glass dome, another special toy of Hetty's had started to move. The zoetrope, the magic Wheel of Life, was very slowly circling – the cow, vivacious again, about to renew its endless hurdles over the moon.

Robert found her, face still buried in her arms, a few minutes later. He saw the snow-dome in front of her, recognising it, knowing its meaning, the emotions it contained – for both of them. Picking it up, he set the flurry going again, re-animating it, holding it up briefly in front of him. Léonie had turned to him by now, watching his attentions here, to this object held between them now, shared, understood.

'It's all right, Léa,' he said quietly. 'She's gone. But she's still here.' He put the dome back in the centre of the mantelpiece. 'And will be,' he added, a sudden bright timbre to his voice. 'Because *we're* here, you and I, together again.' He gazed at her in the hot afternoon silence. 'We can start again now. We really can.'

'Yes . . .' she said. '*Yes*,' she repeated with much more conviction as she walked towards him.

14

'THIS PLACE DOESN'T look to have been bombed at all.' Robert, after a first week on the road, touring Germany, spoke to the army press liaison officer beside him, driving into the outskirts of Dortmund in Westphalia.

'Oh, Dortmund was bombed all right!' The Captain was derisive. 'Wait till you see the centre.'

Ten minutes later, leaving the practically untouched suburbs of heavy Prussian villas, they arrived at the centre, in one of the main streets. And now the view had changed completely. From end to end of the long straight thoroughfare, and all about them, the scene was one of utter desolation. Almost every building had been razed to the ground, collapsed in huge mounds of uncleared, blackened rubble, with a few houses left standing – but with only a single wall and chimney, windows open to the sky, cardboard cut-outs, standing free against the grey clouds, clotted with smoke from small fires everywhere, watched over by tattered figures cooking on open braziers amidst the ruins.

A vision of the underworld, Robert thought. Nobody could surely live here. And yet it was crowded with people that afternoon. They were everywhere, as if this was an ordinary town, yet all engaged in the most unlikely metropolitan things. Old women brewed up kettles in front of sackcloth shacks set up in front of grandiose ruined steps and porticoes. Others, like worker bees, clambered up and down the huge mounds of rubble, unceasingly, carrying things, going to and from the wrecked houses. A majority, it seemed, pushed handcarts piled with broken furnishings up and down the narrow central aisle of the street. All of them, at a glance, seemed full of purposeful life.

Yet on closer inspection it was clear that they were doing very little. They went – but they always returned. They were driven, yet aimless. And, as soon as they saw the military car, their attention was immediately diverted – crushing up against the windows, asking for something. A lift? Food? Money? It was not clear. And they did not insist. This vast collection of humanity – waiting, going, trudging, imploring, pressing against the car windows – all were strangers to life, with the sunken, expressionless faces of the mad, completely, obsessively absorbed in their own aimless acts.

'What are they all doing? –'

'Watch out, Corporal!' The Captain leant forward to the driver. They had narrowly missed running down an old woman pushing a handcart from a side-street.

'What are they all doing?' The Captain sat back, lighting a cigarette casually.

'Yes. All this moving about. The bombing must have stopped months ago here.'

'Oh yes – that. These people, they stay in their houses 'till the bitter end, 'till the place literally falls down about their ears. Then they move to the cellar, before it finally collapses on them. They get these handcarts then and try and move in somewhere else nearby. Determined to stay close to home, you see. That's the whole point. Their only chance as they see it, if they're to be reunited with their families, is to stay close to home – hoping for a son back from the war – long dead of course on the Russian front. Or a daughter from Berlin, most likely raped and killed by the Russians during their last assault there. That's all these people have in mind now – to try to get the family together again.'

'My God . . .' Robert, thinking of his own family, of Summer Hill, thought the Captain brutally insensitive. No doubt he had seen it all before. It had hardened him. He was a realist. Yet for Robert in some ways Dortmund was as bad as Dachau. Here the people had survived, only to live in hopeless hope, a living death.

'Yes, that's Dortmund,' the Captain said dismissively as they left the ruined city. 'A lot of people pretending they still have their homes. The D.P.s are better off in a way – you'll see this evening. At least they know they've lost everything. Can only start from scratch – if they start back at all. Should get to their camp in an hour or so. Luckily it's just beyond our 21st Army Group H.Q. at Bad Oeynausen. So we can put up there for a night or two. Get a decent meal – a wash and brush-up. Could do with that.' He sighed, taking out a very clean handkerchief, dabbing his face and neck. 'My God, the dirt of these towns. And the *people*. Soot and smuts, gets everywhere.'

A few hours later, coming over a rise, they suddenly found themselves in a quite different world: a group of absurdly ornate, nineteenth-century gingerbread villas, set in a landscape of immaculately kept grass, between groves of exotic trees. They had arrived at Bad Oeynausen, a large health resort once, built in the times of the Kaisers, long emptied of all its patients, where every villa and *kursaal* had been taken over now by the British occupation forces, as their army headquarters in Westphalia, so that the only things which marred this idyllic vision were the military notices everywhere – ARE YOU ARMED? – and the endless coloured wires of the Signal Corps running from one building to another.

'Where's the Displaced Persons' camp?'

'Over there, beyond the church, down the hill. They've a hospital there as well, in the old gymnasium, I think.' He snorted. 'Hospital, food, every comfort – all laid on. These D.P.s are too damn lucky really, ending up here. And some of them are sure to have been collaborators. Hardly deserve it . . .' He straightened his cuffs, his tie.

'They're not Germans, though, these D.P.s,' Robert said rather sharply.

'No. Poles for the most part. A few Russians.'

'Allies of ours.'

'All the same . . .' The Captain grimaced, remaining disgruntled at this largesse extended by the British occupation authorities. 'You should see them . . . Quite beyond everything really. And still coming in by the truckload. *Filthy.*'

An hour later Robert, accompanied by the supercilious Captain, walked over to the D.P. camp behind the health resort. The grey clouds had gone and a faint, hazy sun had appeared. The afternoon was very still as they moved beneath the lemon-yellow trees. Passing by the little Gothic church Robert heard the organ music, the sound of voices. He was startled by the familiar tune, the words, the strong male voices drifting out from the open porch doors.

We plough the fields and scatter,
The good seed on the land . . .

He thought of autumns at Summer Hill with Hetty years before, this very hymn heard so often in the family church beyond Cloone. And suddenly he was struck by an emotion so strong, so eerie, that he shuddered, as if someone was walking over his grave.

'Yes,' the Captain told him, noticing his surprise. 'Harvest festival obviously. Army choir rehearsing. Next Sunday.'

'What harvest?' Robert asked, astonished.

The Captain was surprised now. 'Well, the usual harvest, of course. It's August, isn't it? Or next month?'

They passed on. This would make a paragraph in one of his articles, Robert thought. A harvest festival – in this ruined, famished land. How quite extraordinary the English were, he thought, his realistic colonial blood beginning to boil: celebrating harvest festivals here, as if nothing had happened, as if there'd been no war at all, no complete desecration – only an hour away, in cities like Dortmund, where they were starving. And he'd hope to get this arrogant, ignorant Army Captain into the same article.

Moving through the sentry gate at the barbed wire perimeter fence and going on down the hill along an avenue of acacia trees, they came to another barbed wire fence with sentry posts, and behind it the heavily ornate granite gymnasium which housed the D.P. hospital. A medical orderly met them in the vast marble hall with its dry fountain in the centre.

'Robert Grant, of the *Express*, to see Surgeon-Major Fields,' the Captain told the man brusquely, stamping his boots as they waited.

Major Fields appeared beyond the central fountain in a white coat – a tall man, hawk-nosed, with a neat moustache. He took Robert's hand warmly.

'Mr Grant – very good of you to come all this way to see us.' The words were expected, formal, precise. But there was warmth in his precision. 'Always appreciated your articles in the *Express*. Particularly your Western Desert reports,

Superb. Nothing so dramatic here, I'm afraid. Though there are one or two things may interest you . . .'

'I'm sure, Major. Though it's not really war – it's the people that interest me, us . . .' They understood each other at once.

Moving from the huge hall they found themselves in an even larger and more ornate space, with marble pillars and friezes decorated with hefty Teutonic nymphs and fauns bathing, disporting themselves among waterlilies and bullrushes. For this was not a gymnasium, as the Captain had said, but the largest of the old *kursaals*, a long, gently-sloping swimming pool, empty now, but filled instead with a score of hospital cots.

'Rather makeshift,' the Surgeon-Major told him. 'But we've just had a lot of new arrivals this morning, terrible condition many of them. We've had to put some of them in here temporarily.'

Stepping down into the shallow end of the pool Robert moved among the patients, wrapped in grey army blankets, two medical orderlies attending them; there was a smell of ether, of some strong disinfectant, in the air. He gazed at the wan faces – old peasant men, crones, some young children, all with the same quite vacant, uncomprehending faces – incarcerated, terrorised by the Germans for years and now once more imprisoned by the liberating forces. These people no longer had any idea of where they were or what was happening to them. They were worse off even than the citizens of Dortmund. These people no longer knew what life was about at all, had lost even the obsession of aimlessness.

'Where are they from?'

'Slovakia mostly. Had a rough time. First with the Germans, then the Russians. And then a long journey – taken them months to get here. But these are the few lucky ones . . .'

They moved down the gentle slope towards the deep end of the pool. Robert saw an old peasant woman, still wearing a spotted headscarf, out of her cot, kneeling, apparently praying over the cot next to her, where a huddled shape lay, the face invisible.

'Now here's an interesting case I'd like to show you – just came in this morning – give you an idea what these people have been through. A woman from one of the Nazi concentration camps. We'll get the interpreter. Corporal?' He turned to one of the orderlies. 'Where's that Slovak interpreter? Should be with us. Can you find him, please?'

'A concentration camp – that old woman kneeling?'

'No. The younger one beyond. That's her friend Anna with whom she came in. We don't know who she is – seems to have lost her memory. Doesn't speak any Slovak – doesn't really speak at all. Except a few words of English – that's the strange thing. Here, I'll show you – the tattooed number mark inside her arm, the first we've had here, certainly from one of the concentration camps.'

They moved over to the far cot. Robert saw the shape beneath the blanket, an arm lying over the top, but the face invisible, turned away to the side.

'No need to wake her,' he told the Surgeon-Major. But, as if at the sound of his voice, the woman turned her head slowly round, her greasy, matted hair twisting over the pillow, neck thin as a swan's, a death's head staring up at him.

It was Hetty.

Robert's head began to buzz, the swimming pool walls, at the deep end now, beginning to shift and tilt, as he heard the voices again, the brash soldiers' choir belting out, 'We plough the fields and scatter . . .' He started to sway, so that Major Fields had to steady him.

'All right?'

Robert, regaining control, at once knelt down by the cot. 'Hetty?'

Her big blue eyes were the only really recognisable thing left in the wreck of her face, which was scarred, pock-marked, grey, the skin drum-tight over the sharp bones. And she seemed to recognise him, but with a quite unexpected anger in her expression, a malignancy which astonished him.

'Hetty?' He repeated her name more urgently.

'Yes,' she said finally, faintly but with a bitterness that made him shudder.

'You see,' the Major said enthusiastically. 'I told you – she speaks some English. Extraordinary.'

15

'A SK HER HOW the other woman got to Slovakia.' Robert, sitting with the peasant woman, the Slovak interpreter and Surgeon-Major Fields in his office, waited while the man translated his question, listening to the woman's response, before the interpreter turned back to him.

'The woman here, Anna – she was a farmer's wife. They had a hill farm in northern Slovakia, east of Cadca, way up in the Beskid mountains – that's part of the Tatras. This other woman – she calls her Eva, the "French woman" – arrived one day at the farm last February, she thinks it was, dying – of cold, hunger. Said she'd escaped from a German camp at Oswieckiem, fifty miles north of the border, in Poland. Anna and her husband took her in and hid her in the hay store – hiding her from the German patrols and the Slovak quislings, the Hlinka Guards. She got better gradually, very slowly . . .'

'And then? What then?'

The interpreter resumed his work before returning to Robert. 'Then the Russians came into Slovakia – from the east and the north. Fighting, raping, pillaging. There was panic everywhere. The Russians went up into the hills, the Tatras, pursuing fleeing Germans, Slovak collaborators, the Hlinka Guards. A group of these Guards had forced themselves into Anna's farmhouse, taking refuge. A Russian patrol tracked them there. There was a fight, a lot of shooting. The Russian patrol overwhelmed the place in the end – and of course assumed this woman and her husband, along with Eva in the hay store, were Nazi collaborators as well. They took them all down to Cadca – beat them, imprisoned them, tortured them. All the men were finally killed or executed. But the two women, Anna and the "French woman", Eva, were spared. Just raped, very badly treated. Eventually they escaped, when the Russian troops moved on from Cadca. The two women, with a group of other Slovaks, moved west into Bohemia then, finally getting over the border into Germany, first to a D.P. camp in Swabia and then here.'

'And the French woman's husband? She had a husband – what happened to him?' Robert asked. 'Ask her.'

'He died, she told her, during their escape from Oswieckiem,' the interpreter said after a further few minutes. 'She told her they'd run into a German patrol, north of Zywiec. They were crossing the Sola river. The Germans fired at them as they dodged over the ice – they hit him, but missed her. She fell into the water and got across. That's what she told Anna here. They could only speak in bad German, both of them, so she's not certain if she's got it right.'

'Thank her, will you?' Robert said to the interpreter. 'Thank her very much for looking after my friend. And tell her I'll make arrangements – with the Major here – for her to be properly resettled, and have money, when I get back to London.'

'Oswieckiem,' Robert said to the Major after the interpreter and Anna had left the office. 'That's Auschwitz.'

'Auschwitz? I thought no one had got out of there alive, let alone escaped from it.'

'How ill is she, Major?'

'Not one thing, more like half a dozen. Malnutrition, exhaustion. Remains of frostbite on her toes and fingers. She's also suffering the after-effects of smallpox. You can see those pock marks. Not to mention the cuts and abrasions everywhere, barely healed. And then of course, what with being raped and all the other appalling treatment, there's the mental trauma. She can't really speak, as you saw. And she's lost her memory. It's lucky you found her here. And recognised her. I'd never have known who she was or what to do with her. She'd just have ended up in some German lunatic asylum, never to be heard of again. As it is, she's alive. And thanks to you, now that we know about her, she's curable – with proper attention.'

'London?'

'Obviously. But there's no chance of our getting her there –'

'I think I could get her flown out, with the RAF.'

'Perhaps, with your contacts – at the *Express*. What an extraordinary story you have there – if it's true. An Englishwoman, escaping from Auschwitz. What did you say her name was? I'd like it for my records.'

'Cordiner. Henrietta Cordiner. And Irish, not English. You might have known her better as "Laura Bowen". She was a big cinema star twenty years ago.'

The Major searched his mind. 'No, can't say I do. But then I'm no great cinema-goer.' He looked out of the window at the line of acacia trees bordering the long avenue, their branches stirring in a faint breeze, a few leaves dropping, swirling up again in the wake of a jeep tearing up the hill. 'More interested in facts – in my work.' He leaned back in his chair, thinking. 'And they're really more interesting – aren't they? – when you think of your friend's escape . . .'

Robert walked back up the avenue alone five minutes later, passing through the perimeter fence and sentry post back into the main army camp. He stopped at the little Gothic church, hesitating a moment before going inside.

The choir had gone. But the organist was still there up in the gallery, invisible, playing a Bach organ prelude, the sound gradually swelling up, before reaching dazzlingly repeated crescendoes, so that the windows shook and the church seemed about to burst apart.

He stood there, at the back beneath the gallery, the evening sunlight, low down now, flooding directly through the open porch door. He sat down and listened to the triumphant music.

He had not taken it all in yet – not at all. Ten days before he had confirmed everything, a fresh start with Léonie, just the two of them, a whole future for them both at Summer Hill. But now there were three of them again. Was he at the end of something? Or the beginning? Or was he – as so often before with these two women – at an end and a beginning, a fearful balance, inextricably held between them, all three once more forming a precarious cat's cradle?

Hetty stayed on at the D.P. hosital for another few weeks while Robert completed his work in north Germany. Then, returning to Bad Oeynausen very briefly, and finding how she had recovered a little of her memory and health, he arranged to have her flown to London with the RAF, before he hurried on to Berlin and then Munich for the final two weeks of his assignment. Meanwhile, unable to telephone Summer Hill, he had sent a cable, and then a letter, to Léonie and Dermot, telling them the astonishing news, without hearing anything back from them as he continued his travels.

So it was, returning to London and going straight to the Royal Free Hospital without calling at his flat down the road in John Street, that he found Léonie, alone with Hetty, in a private room there. He seemed to have interrupted some intimacy as he opened the door – Léonie sitting on Hetty's bed, leaning away from her quickly.

'Darling!' Léonie jumped up. 'Here at last – we've been so waiting for you.' She stood up, embracing him, while Hetty, propped up on her pillows, looked at him with perhaps not quite so joyful an expression. He had brought a spray of pink and mauve chrysanthemums for her at the corner of High Holborn. But he held them now, absentmindedly, at a loss. Quite expecting to see Hetty alone, he felt an intruder, at a disadvantage – Hetty already much-visited, obviously by Léonie, surrounded by little gifts, cards, books, even a half-bottle of champagne – whereas he was a late-comer at this celebration. He made the best of it, giving Hetty her flowers, kissing her forehead.

'So,' she said, echoing his thoughts, 'late for the pe-party! We were waiting. Now we can open the champagne.' He noticed at once the very slightly tense and petulant tone to her voice.

'I couldn't get back from Berlin any sooner –'

'Never mind – you're here! That's the great thing.' She looked up at him. There was a haughty self-sufficiency in her expression. She had recovered in an extraordinary way – mind quite restored but in a pert, sharp, dismissive manner.

'You certainly look better.'

And she did. And so did Léonie, even more so. She was alight, alive in a way Robert had not seen in her for years, all her long depressions lifted in this miraculous return of her friend. Hetty was still dreadfully thin, scarred, pock-marked. But there was a strange fire in her eyes – that bitter dominant look which he had first noticed in the hospital at Bad Oeynausen, increased in the interval. Yes, despite – or was it because of? – the appalling physical punishments she had undergone, there was about her now, in her set, harsh expression, something which he last remembered seeing in her years before, as a wilful child, a young woman, when she had been a great picture star, that time in Egypt.

All her old domineering arrogance had returned, Robert saw. At Bad Oeynausen he had put it down to that temporary feeling of elation, of *Schadenfreude*, which survivors of great tragedies often feel. But now he saw it was no temporary characteristic. Hetty, abandoning all her reforms, had changed once more. And so, too, as part of this change – and because Léonie owed her life to her – Hetty held her once again in thrall.

Robert sensed this clearly. It explained his sharp initial feeling when he had first arrived in the room, of being an intruder. It was all perfectly clear – these submerged longings between the two of them, lying on the air, an air of celebration, warmth, joyous renewal – where he was loved, but not essential, where Hetty, always the survivor, the joker come up once more untimely, had returned to trump his suit and regain Léonie. He might as well have walked out of their lives there and then, he thought. But he did not.

'Oh yes!' Hetty said a few weeks later, when all three of them, with Dermot, were back in Summer Hill sitting by the first of the autumn fires in the big drawing room. 'It was *Madame Butterfly* that saved me!' She looked over at Léonie. Then she turned to Robert, with that same bright dizzy look which he had noticed in London. But now it was more obvious. There was madness in her eyes. 'Wouldn't have survived otherwise, not a chance. It was that first week, after we arrived. The *blockowa* – our block chief, the bloody Polish bitch – said was there anyone among us new arrivals who sang or played music? I put my hand up. So did Rosa – she played the accordion. It was for the camp orchestra, can you imagine. So we were taken over to another block, warm, much more comfortable, where the *kapo*, the head of the women's orchestra, Alma Rose, auditioned us. I was shaking with fear, no idea what to do. Then it came to me: *Madame Butterly* – of course! Those duets, Léa, we used to do here – you remember? "*Te voglio bene . . .*"'

'How could I forget?' Léonie looked at her happily.

'Well, I did it – sang and played it, doing both voices. And they took me. And Rosa. And from then on it was much easier. We had fairly decent clothes and *shoes* – you've no idea how important a pair of even half-decent shoes were there. In the winter – you were dead in a week without them. Anyway, from then on we played every morning and evening, on a sort of bandstand by the main gates of Birkenau, while the labour details marched in and out. And then there were the formal concerts, every month, for the SS officers. Hoess, the head of the camp, usually came, and his deputy Aumenier and Dr Mengele and our *Lagerführerin*

Mandel – these *savages*: they had to have music, can you imagine? Classic and *schmaltz*, Beethoven and the Beer Barrel Polka. And it all had to be done *perfectly*. And they had to have new music, new songs at every concert. So the copying was a frantic business. Orchestrating it, getting all the parts out, absolutely endless business, sixteen, eighteen hours a day. Rosa did a lot of that . . .'

'And all this, while the others – were going up in smoke?' Robert asked quietly.

'Oh yes, we knew all about *that*,' Hetty said offhandedly. 'Almost from the word go. The chimneys, the absolutely foul smell when the wind changed. But no one talked about it. You didn't talk about that in Birkenau. If the *kapos* or the SS heard you mention it – you were off into the ovens yourself. So you just did everything, but everything and *anything*, to stay alive, to make sure you weren't in the next selection. Or that you didn't get a note wrong at the next concert. Because if you did, Alma Rose – well, you'd be sacked from the orchestra. And that meant back to the labour blocks. And people didn't survive there for more than a month or two. And then there was always the rumour that Hoess was going to close down the orchestra. And that would have been sure death for us, as well. So you forgot about the others,' she said casually. 'You just thought of your own survival, nothing else.'

Robert was surprised, even horrified, by Hetty's insensitivity over all this. So, he saw, was Dermot. He was not sure about Léonie. Hetty had certainly changed completely. Hers was not the natural elation of the survivor at all. This heartlessness was the reason for her survival. Hetty had survived Auschwitz because she had regained all that steel-hard domineering need to win, that riding rough-shod over people, which had often characterised her early life and made her a great picture star. It was obvious: a matter of sink or swim in Auschwitz, Hetty had rediscovered all those quite ruthless characteristics of hers, abandoned before in her various renunciations and reforms – had swum, while the others, in millions, had gone up in smoke.

She continued her story in the same almost lively vein until she came to the events leading up to her escape, when some of the fire went out of her voice and she paused. 'Perhaps we wouldn't have gone through with the escape, if we'd known how close the Russians were getting to the camp. But the orchestra was about to be disbanded, we'd heard. And Pierre was getting desperate. He'd survived well enough in the early months, as a doctor in the main camp, and he could move around fairly freely – he had a black triangle – so I saw him quite often. But then Mengele got on to him, forced him to work in his "surgery" . . .'

She paused, as if about to comment on this Mengele's operations. But she dismissed the idea, as not part of her story, continuing in her bright, increasingly exalted mode. 'Anyway, it was my idea, getting away, because I suddenly had the opportunity. One of the senior SS officers, Oberscharfuehrer Linz he was called – something different from the rest, educated, been at university in Bonn, though he was still a brute – he took a fancy to me. I got to know him – he had the overall responsibility for the concerts, had a house next the camp. He wanted to sleep with me, said his wife was going to be away. I agreed – on one condition, if he beat me in a fencing duel . . .'

'A duel? But why?'

'I'd seen the scars on his face – knew he'd gone in for that sort of thing as a student. It was our only chance. I'd spoken to Pierre about it. We needed his uniforms, you see. The vain brute – he had dozens of them, in the house. So when his wife went away and the servants were out for the evening – that's what happened. He agreed. Said he'd arrange the swords – the *Schläger* sword the students use there.

'The plan was simple enough. If I won I'd kill him – and take the uniforms. Get dressed in one and take another back for Pierre. And then we'd simply walk out of the main gate that same night. Pierre spoke German fluently. And I'd have little or nothing to say. After all, we'd be two senior SS officers leaving the camp – none of the guards would dare question us. And I'd fixed up all the make-up for myself, no problem playing the part. Then we'd have the civilian clothes which we'd got together – beneath the uniforms. If it worked it'd be because of the sheer simplicity of it all. Quite a few others tried to escape – and one or two succeeded. But they were always caught, either before they got out of the camp at all or a few days later. And usually because their plans were too difficult, complicated. They hid out after evening roll call, between the two perimeter fences, in a big wood pile several times. But the dogs got them. Nobody had ever even tried just walking out of the main gate – and one reason was that no prisoner could ever get hold of or hope to mock up a complete senior SS officer's uniform. But now I had the chance of doing just this – and I took it. Nothing to lose. We were both of us desperate. We knew we'd certainly be killed, one way or another, if we stayed in the camp. The orchestra was definitely going to be closed down. And they wouldn't have let Pierre survive, after what he'd seen of Mengele's work. They were gassing and burning more than ever that winter, furiously, knowing the Russians were closing in on them. And I'd recovered. I was quite fit. We got special food in the orchestra. And I'd been practising with a stick for several weeks beforehand. This was our only chance. And far better to die fighting than being pushed into the gas chamber.' Her eyes were alight with a manic energy, living again now all the risks she had lived through then.

'But the Colonel?' Robert asked. 'Had he no suspicions – when you suggested this duel?'

'No. I told him I'd done it in France, with foils, when I was young. He liked the idea, in his twisted mind – quite certain he'd win and then have all the more pleasure in taking me afterwards. He was thrilled by the idea really. And he should have won. I'd never fenced with these broad *Schläger* swords before, like a bayonet, with a great soup plate thing as a hand guard. You chopped with it, more than parried or lunged. But I *did* win – he was just fighting to sleep with me. I was fighting for my life – and Pierre's.'

'What – what happened?'

'We fought in the basement of his house, alone. He'd sent the servants out beforehand so as to have me at his leisure afterwards . . .' She paused, an ugly look in her eyes.

'So – tell them what happened, Hetty!' Léonie, who had heard all this before, was anxious that Hetty, her protégée now almost, should display the full extent of her prowess.

'He laughed – that's what happened, which infuriated me. And he took it all too easily. To begin with. He wasn't used to lunging – that's not the German way – just parried my blows and chopped back now and then, not very seriously, playing with me. I knew he wouldn't be prepared for the lunge himself, so I held it back, my strong card. And when it came – well, he'd left himself open, tip of the sword went straight through his shirt. Then he started to fight, furiously, and it was touch and go for a while. But the first wound, you see! He was bleeding badly. He was too late . . .'

Hetty paused on a note of triumph. 'It was all fairly plain sailing then. Absolutely no trouble getting out of the camp – they just saluted us sharply. And we got right down near to the Slovak border all right, in about a week, travelling only at night in the freezing cold, until we had to cross the Sola river – when we ran straight into a German patrol. They were in the bushes on our side, resting, smoking. We more or less crashed into them. They were so surprised we were able to get away across the river, over the ice on one side, until they shot Pierre. They were shooting all round us, but wildly in the dark. They missed me. I stayed with Pierre, tried to pull him with me into the water, hoping he was only slightly wounded. But he wasn't, just pretending to be – kept shouting at me to go on, pushing me into the water. I fell into it. The current took me away down-river. I got to the far bank somehow – about half a mile downstream. Got clean away then. The dogs couldn't track me in the water. It was terrible.' She ended her story suddenly, curtly, almost viciously, then completely dried up, staring round her in a vacant, chilling way.

16

I N THE AUTUMN days that followed at Summer Hill, as Hetty slowly recovered and now that she was safe at last in her old home, something snapped in her mentally. She was either quite silent or else her manic ramblings increased. Her mind began to wander – bitterly, horrifyingly – among vile things.

Now that she was no longer under the daily threat of extinction, a pus of anger broke from her, which she fingered through, haphazardly resurrecting all the repressed memories, the horrors she had undergone, and much more witnessed, in the camp.

Walking with Dermot slowly down the old monkey puzzle avenue, or with Robert and Léonie on the porch steps, or with Léonie alone, back in her primrose bedroom, she would suddenly come out with, and elaborate on, some spectacularly brutal detail, speaking of it not with sanity or sympathy but with cruel emphasis, as if she had taken on the role of one of the SS guards herself – the vivid, bloodied images intruding on the lovely autumn air around Summer Hill like visions from hell.

'. . . they brought back the two who'd escaped a few days later – the dogs got them of course. The SS had their drums out as usual, all of us paraded in front of Hoess and Auminer. Then they were strung up on the gallow, with only a six-inch drop. They struggled for minutes on end, gasping for breath. We had to stand there for a whole hour, watching them sway . . .

'He was called "Ivan the Terrible", a huge man, one of the Russian *kapos*. He and two other of his *kapo* friends used to have competitions to see which of them could kill someone with just *one* blow. They'd choose just anyone, any group they happened upon. Ivan always won . . .

'Down at the ramp once, with a transport just in – we had to play there that day for some reason: the SS guard took the baby from the woman's arms – the baby'd been crying – and just dashed it to the ground. The dogs started to eat at it.'

All these vignettes were made the worse by being offered so casually, coldly, objectively – or else in a voice of rising frenzy, eyes wide and staring, as she bunched her hands, and cracked her finger joints. And when Robert tried to soften her approach to these memories, to calm her tortured spirit, she laughed at him.

'You – you've no idea! You weren't there,' she spat at him. 'You can't understand. No one can, if they weren't there.'

'Yes. But now it's over, Hetty. You're back, safe –'

'It's *not* over!' She was angrier still. 'Never! It never will be.'

Robert spoke to Dermot one morning, as they walked along the river drive on a squally September day. 'I suppose it's obvious,' he said. 'All a reaction. Now that she's survived she feels desperately guilty – about all the others who didn't. Can't face her own survival. And it shows up in this mad way – almost relishing the horrors, trying to immerse herself in them now, punish herself – suffer now for all that she didn't suffer herself at the time. And then there's Pierre. You notice? – apart from that first time, she doesn't talk about him at all. Hasn't really begun to think about that, accept his loss.'

'She needs attention.' Dermot looked out at the stormy water.

'Yes. Just the sort she had from Pierre. And Pierre isn't here any more.'

'Someone then.'

'Yes. But who? Léa and I – we'll have to go back to London soon.'

'I'm not much good at that sort of thing. I'll try . . .'

Robert and Dermot understood the apparently hopeless situation. But Léonie, when Robert talked to her alone, was much more optimistic.

'So you do see, don't you?' Robert said. 'What's happened.' And he repeated his diagnosis of Hetty which he had given to Dermot.

'Yes, of course I see all that,' she replied sharply.

'You don't seem to have seen it. You seem to go along with her, when she talks in this mad cold way –'

'I *do* see!' she interrupted him vehemently. 'I know her better than anyone else. She's suffering all the horrors now that she didn't then, and all the guilt. Of course! But she doesn't need another doctor or psychiatrist. She needs *me!*'

She looked at Robert defiantly. And he thought, yes, he'd been right in his initial intuitions at the London hospital a few weeks before. Once more Hetty had come between him and Léonie. Once more Léonie was about to be dragged into the maelstrom of Hetty's life. But this time he mustn't let it happen. He had made things up so well with her – this time he wouldn't lose her. He would fight – for Léonie's life, for his. And Hetty, however much he understood and sympathised with her, would have to take second place.

They were picking their way through the overgrown rock garden, the paths wild with blackberry briars. Léonie stopped to pick the over-ripe fruit, suddenly unconcerned with Robert. He watched her – the slightly chunky figure in a patterned smock dress, still with that lovely toss of silk-fine hair, greying now: an air of abundance about her, fruit-filled, almost as he remembered her that time they had first met in Paris, in the hall of her father's house in Passy, when she had looked at him, with such candour, as if certain then of all the happiness that was to come to them – as it had, as it could have gone on coming, but for Hetty. Yes, he would fight for her.

He said to her in the heavy silence, with no fight in his attitude or voice, speaking evenly, calmly. 'Léa, if you go that way with Hetty again – you'll never escape, not this time. You know that . . .'

Léonie swallowed a blackberry, offered him one. 'Oh, Robert, what do you mean?' she said lightly, equally reasonably. 'She *needs* help. And how could I not, after what she did for me – taking my place with the Gestapo in Paris, and in that terrible camp. There's no question.'

'Let's not go through all that again. You know perfectly well what I mean. Helping her is one thing. But you want her again as well –'

'It's *you* starting all that again, not me. Starting the old jealousy thing.'

'No. It's not jealousy. Just I know you too well – when you get involved with Hetty it's all or nothing. Seen it before. The obsession. You lose touch with reality. You two together – you won't have time for anyone else.'

She turned and faced him, herself calm still, a touch of pity for him in her expression. 'Anyone else? You mean you, don't you? As if *you* couldn't be included. As if one can only love one person at a time. But don't you see – if not jealous – how small-minded that attitude is? Always told you that. It needn't be either/or. It can be *all* of us, here at Summer Hill. You and I. And Hetty. And Olivia and Dermot . . .'

'So you've always said – making a crowd of it. But it'd really only be you and Hetty in the end.'

'It's just your immaturity that stops it, Robert. I've always known that, too!'

They were arguing now – a deep anger, all sorts of bitter emotion, rising in them. They were back where they had left off, when they had parted nearly ten years before in Hampstead. But Robert regained his control.

'It's not immaturity, Léa. Temperament, yes, mine and yours. And they're different, that's all. Of course we should help her – and I don't object to your loving her. But I'm just not interested – never have been – in sharing you with her.'

'Ah!' Léonie could not restrain the sneer in her voice. 'Not *able*, you mean.'

He shook his head. 'You see, you're losing touch already. Because a person doesn't want something it doesn't automatically mean that they fear it, or aren't capable of it. It can just as well be because that "thing" runs quite against the grain of their nature. It doesn't run against your nature. But it does mine. It's not a question of weakness or strength, nor even morals. It's just a fact: your inclinations are not mine.'

She listened. Or rather she half-listened, half-agreeing, half-not. She was on a knife-edge of impending decisions, and she hardly knew this either. As regards Hetty, she had given herself over once more to what she simply felt.

'And can we ever really change our character?' Robert went on. 'I doubt it. Look at you. Look at Hetty – back in all her old domineering ways again. Oh, this time she has a real excuse for it. But that's really part of her true nature as well – the need to dominate, exploit, hurt, for all that happened long ago to her. And that's what's happening now. She's hooked you again, with this cast-iron excuse of her terrible suffering. And that I can't live with in you – your hidden, obsessive thing again for Hetty. I can't live with that. That's too much against the grain.'

Léonie, refusing to admit the truth of any of this, as she always had with Robert, made no answer. Instead she changed the topic to one in which she could be sure of her ground and could thus renew her attack. 'And you? What about you and Hetty? You see nothing hypocritical there? As if you don't . . . as if you hadn't loved her?'

'I did. And I do. But it's not that sort of love. I have that for you now. Why won't you see that, before it's too late, and come with me?'

They had pushed on through the jungle of the rock garden, pulling briars aside, but now they had come to an impasse in the wilderness. Léonie turned back, taking a thorn from her hand.

'You're making it either/or again.'

'Yes.'

'That's blackmail!'

'No – I've tried to explain. It's just fact.'

Returning to the high lawn, they stood beneath the cedar tree, looking over the valley in the late sunlight, the house beneath them, covered in Virginia creeper, golden-yellow above the porch: the house, full of warmth and promise, where everyone could be happy.

Robert picked at the bark of the cedar, taking a bit in his hand, putting it to his nose, smelling all his years at Summer Hill. He was not just losing Léonie then, he knew. He was losing this house, his home, as well. And it was this that finally made him angry – this impending loss of his birthright – when Léonie said to him, 'Fact or blackmail, it amounts to the same thing.'

'For you. Not for me. And that's really what it's all about, isn't it? Always was, when you and Hetty get together. Always is with lovers. They just can't get to see anyone else's point of view.'

He put the bit of cedar bark in his pocket and started to walk down the wild lawn, back to the house.

'You don't love me!' she shouted after him. 'If you did, you'd *see* my point of view – over Hetty.'

He turned to her briefly, bitterly. 'It's not a point of view, Léa – it's just a blind obsession.'

He walked on alone towards the house.

He had lost Léonie, he thought, as he sat in a window seat, taking the train back to Dublin next morning. He had tried to make a fight for her. But you could not regain someone in the grip of such a fierce emotion – the need to sacrifice, to love, the need to return to their real nature. He had lost her, Hetty, Summer Hill. Or as good as lost it all. No doubt he would visit from time to time. But he would be a supernumerary now in the house. Hetty had regained her home once more, and that was right. But *he* had lost his home – and his wife. And that seemed atrocious.

He had hinted at nothing of this to Hetty when he had spoken to her alone before leaving. 'It's simply . . . I have all this work to finish in London. These German articles. And I must see Olivia in Dublin, before she gets started at Trinity.'

'Yes, well, you might have stayed on here a bit. Still, I don't know what would have happened to me – if you hadn't found me at that D.P. camp. I'd lost my memory, everything. Never have got back here at all. Or my wits back. Thank you . . .'

He had found it difficult to look at Hetty then, appalled by the brazen expression on her face, which quite belied her last words. Yet he did not think she was taking any victory from his departure, any triumph in having regained Léonie once more. Her expression was entirely self-serving – a busy, frustrated look, with something malign about it. Her face had reminded him of her mother's then. Frances had had just the same sort of embittered, self-justificatory look in her eyes, so often towards Hetty herself, when they had been children together at Summer Hill. And now that same expression, years later, had come to be levelled at him.

He looked out of the train window, at the stooks of corn piled up in a field, carts taking it away to a threshing machine and a smoking traction engine in the distance, a plough pulled behind a tractor in another field, the earth turning black in long furrows. 'We plough the fields and scatter, the good seed on the land,' he said quietly, remembering the choir at Bad Oeynausen six weeks earlier. And now he knew why he had felt that appalling emotion, when he had first heard the hymn outside the church – the feeling of someone walking over his grave. The message there had not, indeed, been one of celebration for harvest home. It had been a foretaste of the bitter harvest he was to reap, in finding and rescuing Hetty half an hour later – which would lose him his home.

In Dublin he met Olivia, just about to start her first term at Trinity, his old College. As a treat he took her to Jammets, near the front gates of the College, a French restaurant, done out in the belle époque style, all gilt, velvet and mahogany, where they had a table under a great mural of Diana the huntress, flying across the blue empyrean, bow in hand, pursuing a golden hind. Olivia, in a new tweed skirt and fine cotton blouse which she had bought out of money her father had given her, at Brown Thomas's store up the road, was beside herself.

'Oh, Daddy! This is such fun. I've not seen a place like this – ever, I think. And certainly never eaten like this!' She scanned the menu dizzily, unable to take it all in.

'Yes. It's good. Used to eat here. Oh, just once or twice when I was up at Trinity myself and in the money.'

'Did modern history, didn't you?'

'Yes. But modern languages will do you even better. Especially since you already have such good French. I'm so glad you're here . . .' He smiled at her, but it was not as full a smile as he would have liked.

At first, putting a good face on things, he gave only the merest hint as to what had passed at Summer Hill. But Olivia, knowing all too well the problems between her parents, and older and wiser in years thereby, soon sensed what had happened – soon realised how broken her father was behind his welcoming façade. And, loving him, she was hurt by his hurt. Yet, sharing some of his restrained temperament, she hoped not to show too much of her feelings over this – or to show them, at least, but not in too obvious a way.

So she said, looking through the elaborate menu more carefully. 'Daddy, I've never seen anything like it! Oysters and duck *à l'orange*. Can it be real? – after years of spam and dried eggs?'

'It's real. Though I've forgotten it all myself.'

'Well, you must eat it, eat it *all* then!'

'Olivia –'

'No. I mean treat yourself as well as me. You like food, don't you? I remember –'

'Yes, but not to make a pig of myself.'

'Well, let's *nearly* make pigs of ourselves. You deserve it . . .' She looked at him tenderly.

Her ploy had the desired effect. Robert did like good food, had tasted nothing of it in nearly six years. He brightened under the idea of being a bit lavish – but more particularly under his daughter's warm yet concerned gaze.

They ordered Galway oysters, pâté de foie gras, the duck *à l'orange* and a bottle of vintage Moët to go with it all. He gave the menu back to the elderly waiter in a wing collar and rather threadbare dark jacket. The food, the mood, were both supremely French. But not the waiter or his accent. He spoke in the broadest, sprightly Dublin tones when he said, 'Ah, that'll be fine, Sir. I couldn't have chosen betther meself.' Robert smiled at Olivia after he had left.

'It's wonderful, isn't it?' she said. 'Dublin. And three years here. I couldn't be happier. But you must be, too, Daddy . . .' And, when the champagne came in its cooler and the bubbles frothed a little in their glasses, she lifted hers and said, 'It's all somehow . . . so jaunty here in Dublin, isn't it? Everyone, the people, the mood. Not like dreary England. Let's be jaunty from now on, Daddy.' And they were.

But later, before the coffee, she asked him – she could not restrain herself – for more details of what had happened at Summer Hill.

'It's Hetty, isn't it? That's the real reason for Mummy staying down there.'

'Well –'

'Of course it is. Mummy's like that, isn't she? It was just the same with her friend Jenny. I know it now. I didn't really understand it before.'

'Well, Hetty and your Mama were always very close – the closest friends, long before Jenny.'

'Yes, but you and Hetty were even *closer* friends, long before that – before Mummy ever came on the scene – on that island, as children, weren't you?'

'Oh yes.'

'So it's *cruel* of Hetty. Taking Mummy over like that again. Because that's what she's doing, isn't it?'

'In a way, yes.' He made a hopeless gesture. Then he reminded himself how they were to be jaunty. 'But you have to remember how much they owe each other. Mummy would almost certainly have been in that camp – and dead now – but for Hetty.'

'And Hetty? – what does she owe Mama?'

'Oh, everything – long before, when they were close. Everything. I don't think Hetty would ever have become the person she is but for Mama. Her support.'

'But Hetty's become *awful* – by all accounts!'

'So might you – if you'd been through Auschwitz. Anyway, there's nothing to be done about it.'

'Isn't there?'

'No. I've tried, often enough. And this time it was all the more difficult. Because now they've finally proved how right they are for each other, and how right they were all along. Fate. The other two have gone – Jenny and Pierre. So now it's obvious to them – they were made for each other.'

'But that's nonsense! This "fate" business – because what about you and me? And us? All three of us. Isn't all that more important to Mummy? We're not "fate". We're real. She's still married to you, still my Mama. What can she *think* she's doing – giving all that up?'

Olivia was angry now, startlingly angry. Robert tried to calm her. 'She doesn't think she's given it all up. She thinks I've done that. Running away. And I haven't. It's just I can't live with Mummy *and* Hetty at Summer Hill. So *I'm* the one to blame, in her eyes.'

'Well, that's worse nonsense on her part!'

'So it seems. To us. But we're not her. It's nonsense to us. These . . . obsessions . . . always seem so, to outsiders.'

'Obsessions? Sounds more like an illness to me.'

'Perhaps.' He shrugged. 'So perhaps they'll cure each other . . .'

Olivia slumped back on the velvet banquette, sighed, fiddled with her napkin. 'It's still nonsense. You're just being kind about it all, about Mummy.'

'What else can I be? I've been angry about it before. Oh yes. But that didn't help anybody. So that's all there is to be now – as kind as we can about it all.'

He did not say anything more for a moment. But then, seeing Olivia's wan face, he reached across and took her hand on the table cloth. 'Come on, don't be sad. You and I – remember? – we're going to be jaunty.'

She said nothing. But then suddenly, waking up and smiling a bit, gripping his fingers, she said, 'Yes, we will be. And if there isn't you and Mummy – there'll always be you and me.'

And with this Robert was bright at last. And they both had proper smiles for each other. And later, when the coffee came, he said, 'Would you like to try a special Irish whiskey? They used to do one here, thirty years old or some such . . .'

'Yes,' she said, leaning back on the red velvet again, this time holding her head high. 'But Irish whiskey – in such a French restaurant?'

'Oh, they have everything here, in Ireland.' For a moment, after he had said this, he felt a spasm of sadness again. For he was losing everything in Ireland. But no, that was not true. Olivia would be here. He would see her, now and in the future. He had lost his home, his wife. But he had truly gained his daughter.

Robert was right. In the ensuing months, and the years that followed, Hetty and Léonie cured each other – for all their losses. At first it was a slow process. Luckily Hetty was still too frenzied then, with her violent memories of Auschwitz, to take in how she had, once more, destroyed Robert and Léonie's marriage. While Léonie, just as Robert had said to Olivia, reassured herself on this score by thinking how it was Robert, not she, who had broken things up.

Could he not see, quite objectively, how she *must* stay and help Hetty? – how Hetty's punishing daytime visions of the camp, her wicked commentaries on it and the far worse nightmares she suffered then and for years afterwards – how all this was directly due to her having abandoned Hetty in the Paris apartment? Could he not see, too, how she owed Hetty her life? For she doubted, even with all her SOE training, if she would have survived the Gestapo interrogations or the camp. Hetty, in doing both these things, had, as always, found a stronger heart than hers – found reserves, an extraordinary resilience against the worst life had to offer. Could Robert see none of this? Was he so morally and emotionally blind – so selfish?

And then on another, deeper emotional level Léonie returned to her old opinions about Robert. Why could he not have accepted her affection, her love for Hetty – and the fact that she loved him as well? Why could he not share in this loving? Robert, just as he had before, had broken this happy combination, when all three of them could have lived on at Summer Hill contentedly, had destroyed this obvious future in a house they all loved.

And this was simply his immaturity. Or his ridiculous puritan notions. Or both. She had not misjudged him, as she had told him in the old vine house. Unfortunately not. She had been right about him all along. People, she had to admit now, did not really change. And certainly she could not change herself now. She had remained true to her nature, had been quite prepared to love them both. But if Robert refused this natural scheme of things – well, then, that was his look-out. She would love Hetty alone.

And she did. As the months passed, autumn turning to winter, Hetty found a cure in this loving, her fevers and nightmares gradually subsiding, her health improving, memory and balance returning. So that soon, when the topic came up, she was able to talk quite rationally, as she and Lèonie thought, of Robert's defection.

'I suppose it's just his ... childishness,' Hetty said one winter afternoon, echoing Léonie's thoughts. They were in the basement still-room, sorting through boxes of Cox's orange pippins, wrapping them in newspaper, before storing them away on racked trays, so that the air reeked of apples, a crisp autumnal fulfilment. 'You see,' Hetty went on, 'you have to remember, losing both his parents, he has this terrible need to possess things, undivided possession, of a house or a person. That's the feeling that secretly dominates in him: possession.'

'But why? When, really, he had both of us?' Léonie threw a bad apple away.

'Men find it difficult to share things,' Hetty said easily. 'Learnt that long ago, with Craig. And I lost that sharing feeling myself in the camp. We were like men there, most of us. Had to be. You took everything, anything *for yourself.* If you didn't you were dead. But with you . . .' She paused, an apple in her hands, smelling it. 'With you I'm getting back to the real me, getting back what I lost, in the camp, losing Pierre.' She wrapped the apple up and put it on the tray; the two of them like squirrels in the dark room preparing for a long hibernation. 'Sharing . . . whether we learn this, or just have the gift more naturally as women, I don't know. But we do. We have to share . . .'

'It's such a pity, though. About Robert.' A note of passion had come into Léonie's calm voice. 'Because we could both have shared things with him, too. Especially him,' she added bitterly.

Hetty looked at Léonie quizzically, noting this urgency in her voice, sensing how it reflected a real love she still had for Robert, when a stab of jealousy rose in her. But was she jealous of Léonie, whom she now possessed so completely once more? – or of Robert, recipient of this love, as she suddenly felt a pang of her own old love for him. And the thought, a possessive masculine thought, which remained, even now, part of her character . . . intruded on her next words.

'Yes, especially him. But, Léa, perhaps it's not so easy sharing, when it comes to it. Perhaps it's better when there are just two of us?' She gazed at Léonie anxiously, in that old way of years before, when she had wanted her exclusively, needed to dominate and possess her completely.

And Léonie saw this and, fearing loss, said at once, 'Yes, perhaps it's easier that way.'

They finished storing the apples and went upstairs, where the maid Bridget – now that Elly was getting slow on her feet – brought them tea by the big log fire in the drawing room. Aunt Emily mostly took tea in her room now, with her oatcakes, and Dermot was out for the day, shooting with some of the neighbours.

'Whatever about Robert,' Hetty said, leaning forward, settling a log, 'people's real feelings are so . . . difficult. And one just has to get on with things. We have to.' She looked up at her with such a vulnerable expression, that Léonie knew that everything she had done, everything she had decided, in losing Robert – all this had been worth it. She was right to be linked with this woman for as long as life was. 'We have a le-le-life together here, don't we?' Hetty went on. 'You and I. And Dermot and Aunt Emily. And Jack and Elly.' Léonie nodded.

And they did. What they had both shared in so passionately – in Dublin years before and with Fonsy O'Grady's troupe and momentarily in Egypt – was now returned to them as a permanence at Summer Hill: a life together – the two women regaining all that was lost between them – love, companionship, dependency, touch. So that sleeping or waking, with each other or apart, they wove as the years drew on those silken threads, the unique lines of the heart which can grow between people who are, indeed, made for each other.

Hetty no longer had to act parts to her old friend. She had lived all those parts now, and more. She no longer, in her old petulant ways and means, had to dominate her. She had done this already, with so many people, won out over so many things. She was a survivor. She had survived everything. And this was almost enough to satisfy her. But not quite.

As Robert had said – people never really change their deepest characteristics. And this was true of Hetty. There remained – indeed after her full recovery six months later it became a disruptive itch – some of her old arrogance, a frustrated ambition to create, to succeed, to dominate in one sphere or another. And this urge she could not repress indefinitely. It came to intrude now and then, upsetting the balance of their lives – in rows, misunderstandings. So that recognising this, and seeing how, just as before, it could come to erode and destroy her relationship with Léonie, Hetty knew she must find some other outlet for this vivid, dangerous spirit of hers.

And she did. Going through all her old books and papers in the attics the following spring, she came across the novel she had begun years before, *Aquamarine*, the story of her early life in Domenica and Summer Hill. She took up the book again and by the autumn had completed it. She sent it to a London publisher who at once accepted it.

'How marvellous!' Léonie said when Hetty showed her the letter, the two of them sitting out on the porch after breakfast in the golden weather. 'Now – now we have everything!'

And they did.

EPILOGUE

ROBERT, BEFORE THE servants Pietro and his wife Maria came, and with nothing much better to do on the morning of his sixty-fifth birthday, went to his study desk in the Villa Serena and opened his journal, in which he wrote sporadically, remembering events in a jaunty way and generally bringing himself up to date by naming things, so to encourage the sense of his own otherwise rather isolated existence. The villa, designed to hug the almost sheer cliff-face, was built on a haphazard succession of different levels and extensions – not broad or tall but long, rather in the Spanish style, with a colonnaded serpentine terrace all along the front, set high up on Monte Marcello, facing the Poet's Gulf just south of Lerici on the Ligurian Riviera. He had bought this lovely maritime folly over fifteen years before, as a holiday retreat, just after he had married Catherine. But now she was gone, just a year before, and retiring from London he lived here on his own. Opening the ruled pages of the Italian school exercise book, taking out his old fountain pen, he started to write.

'*Crostini di Mozzarella, fritelle di Bel Paese, crostini di Mare, pizzette,*' I muttered first thing when I woke this morning, invoking Lucullan spirits, a litany of hot and cold *antipasti* running through my mind. The hot ones first – little rounds of baked bread and fritters garnished with seafood – for, though I saw from my window it was going to be midwinter warm today, it might start to cool early and it would be as well if Pietro and Maria had lots of piping-hot tit-bits on hand, along with the cold side dishes, of course: '*Prosciutto di Parma, Prosciutto di San Daniele,*' I addressed the sunrise, '*Salame di Felino, Lingua con Salsa Verde . . .*'

Splendid. I'd consider the other birthday dishes later, turning on my pillow – and it was only then that I felt the sick headache and remembered the nightmare. God! And I'd hoped that everything was going to be cloudless today, especially today, especially with so few complaints recently.

I've been pretty well lately, body and soul. So the headache and the bad dream surprised me. Perhaps I've been more worried than I care to admit by Olivia's not being here yet. She was due out on the Genoa flight yesterday. But fog had closed Heathrow down and she'd called to say she and William and Lottie hoped to get away first thing this morning, taking a hire car straight down as soon as she arrived. With any luck she'll still make the lunch party. Still, I suppose I wanted to be certain of her being here well beforehand, a little familial support against the impending crowd. Not that I'm expecting many outsiders. I think only Matteson, the consul in Genoa, and his pretty wife – and some stringer with *The Times* who said he *had* to interview me. The cheek of it! A paper I never much cared for – now gone quite to seed.

The other guests will be old friends. Hugh Latimer, of course – my publisher, amongst them. He and Molly spent Christmas in Rome, before going on to see Vesuvius – for some unfathomable reason. They're coming up on the *rapido* from Rome this morning. Of the rest of the guests – well, a dozen or more, English and Italian, people Catherine and I have come to know in this Lerici area, a few others I've come to know myself in the last year, having more or less retired here full time. Not that I mind living alone . . .

All the same, I'd like to have been sure of Olivia. She's had a difficult time this last year – what with her divorce and having to cope with the two children on her own. Still, that'll be another treat – seeing them before they go back to school. And lucky, too, that my bank account is fairly healthy, what with the royalties on that last African book, so that I was able to send Olivia a good whack of money this Christmas – which will more than cover all their air fares and so on. And then again I'll have all three of them with me out here afterwards to myself for nearly a week. No, Olivia could hardly have accounted for the nightmare.

Perhaps I'd slept with a crick in my neck all night, unable to right myself in the bed, like a sheep stuck on its back? That's possible. There's a stiffness about the top of my shoulders this morning. I'm sixty-five. No avoiding the fact.

But I shall certainly avoid it – and think about the celebratory wines instead. There's some quite decent champagne, though I've never really fancied that drink. Makes me burp, like an infant. Much better is the Barolo Classico I've been keeping – a lovely deep red-brown now, a 1955, just right at nearly ten years old. As for the white wine I've tasted nothing better than Bertini's Frascati which I got half a dozen cases of before Christmas, a dozen bottles already chilling in the fridge. Pietro stacked them away there yesterday. At least I hope he did.

A sweet wine after the Zabaglione? Well, I've never much cared for the local Cinque Terre, the famous Sciacchetra – liqueur-sweet, almost oily. And, besides, Pietro has got me something wonderful from Sardinia: an old Vernaccia – pale, gold, soft, but nothing cloying. Superb. Elixir of youth . . .

Yes, I'm far from being on my last legs. Though I sometimes find it a task to climb back up all the steps from the little bathing cove at the bottom of the cliff here. But I can still easily manage the shorter flight leading to the road above. I can even walk to the town if I've a mind to – and back. No trouble. After all, I crossed Africa only a few years ago, coast to coast, and quite a bit of it on foot. (Well, no, I mustn't lie – probably less than fifty miles actually on foot . . .) So, yes, I'm fit enough and don't believe I slept with a crick in my neck all night.

So why the bad dreams? No, let's be exact again: why the grotesque, excruciating, grinding nightmare? I thought I'd done with that sort of mental agony years ago, that the spirit on this last run in was finally calmed. And, yes, it *has* been calmed. After Catherine died, a year ago, things were difficult certainly. The dying, of course, though it was quite quick and mostly painless – and the missing her, which I don't suppose I have, or ever will get over.

But latterly, and apart from this, there's been a lot of real peace for me out here this last year. Olivia divorced – painful no doubt, but seeing the better side of it now, because she really is better off without him; my 'memoirs' written – published in London today, in fact to coincide with my birthday. And then, of course, last but not least the knighthood! What a laugh! But a surprise, too. I had that OBE after the war – services rendered as a war correspondent and so on. And I'd thought that was it. So yes, I was surprised – and moved, I suppose. Not because I felt I deserved it (don't think I did), but because I wished Catherine had been here to share it with me. Though in fact, remembering her droll honesty in everything, she might well have dissuaded me from accepting it. ('Oh God, Robert! – not that. You know it's all nonsense: a tin medal and a doll's ribbon, all frou-frou and pink satiny in a box, a clout with a phoney sword, gracious murmurings with HRH in that *heavy* throne room, band of the Grenadier Guards crashing through "Tales from the Vienna Woods" in the background. Not you at all . . .') But I did accept it – and no doubt will have to go through exactly the sort of ceremony Catherine would have envisaged. Still, that will be one more nice way to remember her, a confirmation of her sudden nicely malicious wit – almost Irish in that way. Though no one could have been more English: the proverbial rose – small, compact, sweet, peach-cheeked, that unflawed, creamy skin, so reserved on the surface – which made her quick words and wit, her sensuousness, all the more unexpected. I miss her. Badly.

Still I have found peace out here at last. And perhaps I've finally managed to come to terms with all my earlier life, with Hetty and Léonie. Come to terms with Summer Hill – with all that was won and lost there. I used to think it was only these two people, this house, that could ever give me real happiness. I was wrong. I was lucky to find an even greater happiness with Catherine out here at the Villa Serena – quite forgetting all the disappointments, horrors, nightmares of the old days. Yes, because of Catherine – but also in myself, finding that jauntiness of spirit – the very word Olivia recommended to me that evening together in Dublin, just after everything had come apart for me at Summer Hill. Yes, all that old *sturm und drang* was finally settled out here in Italy, over the last fifteen years. So that I came to see all that past with the two women and Summer Hill as another man's life.

So why the horror again last night?

Have I, in my mind and scribbling my 'memoirs' out here on the terrace in the sun these last years, simply repressed all this painful past, conveniently forgotten about it? It's true that I've written almost nothing about Hetty and Léonie or the great house in these 'memoirs' which are intended as a professional, not a personal, account: my life as a reporter, war correspondent, columnist, travel writer, author of sorts, all over the place in the old days. Fine. But did I in fact keep out everything in this autobiography that *really* mattered? No, surely not. Autobiography must reflect one's *nature*. I'm simply not a heart-on-the-sleeve sort of person. Not at all.

Now, let me think again about the party arrangements: Pietro's *pièce de résistance* today – *Tartufi Bianchi*! That wonderfully pungent, penetrating flavour and scent of these rare white truffles he's managed to get hold of from Turin, big as tennis balls, which he'll cook as *Filetti di Tacchino Bolognese*, the truffles sliced very finely over Turkey breasts and ham, then cooked gently in butter and the best grated Parmesan. This really is something. Pietro did it for Catherine some years ago, as a special treat on *her* birthday . . .

But I must stop thinking about Catherine all the time. An indulgence. I could think of her most of the day without any trouble. Her and the happiness – and her not being here any more. Oh yes, I've faced the facts. The pain, the loss. It's simply that I won't beat my breast about it – not that I'm cold or that I've repressed things.

Anyway, when I finally got out of bed this mroning, I felt better. The view out of the window – sharp blue sky over the bay, the Gulf a darker azure beyond, sunlight glittering on the white horses riding further out to sea. A day with an intense winter sparkle to it, the sort of atmosphere, so keen and bright, that you felt you could reach out and *touch* it – though that's the sort of sensuous idea and expression which would come much more naturally to Hetty than to me . . .

Robert paused in his writing. Here he was thinking of Hetty again, out of the blue, for no good reason. He got up and went to the kitchen, making himself a pot of coffee. But Hetty remained on his mind. Was this what the nightmare had come to tell him? – how he had avoided all the real issues, both in his life and his memoirs? But surely, he sought to persuade himself again, he was doing himself an injustice? He had never been that kind of writer. He had always dealt in facts, where there was some literary skill in their presentation no doubt, but little or no invention – he hoped. Nothing to be ashamed of there, he thought.

Yes, indeed, why should he ever have embarked on the treacherous slopes of 'truth telling' – the usually quite imponderable motives of private lives: all that dizzy confusion of high emotion when people, losing their heads, came to deal out hate and love like cards in a wild gambling game. He'd never been interested in that game. He'd had to play it with Hetty and Léonie long enough – had suffered it, and that was surely sufficient. Taking his coffee with him he returned to the study and his journal.

'No,' he continued these thoughts in the school exercise book.

I never enjoyed these sharp contradictions of emotion, as the other two seemed to. I've always believed that life should be susceptible to reason. The other two ran freewheel. I tended to keep in gear. Chalk and cheese. Though this didn't stop us from getting on in the old days. I have to admit – from falling in love and goodness knows what else. Rather the reverse: attraction of opposites, no doubt.

Well, all the confusion, this hot emotion, was in my 'lived' life, with them, not my written one, my 'memoirs'. And that, surely, was more than enough. Writing for publication in any sort of personal, intimate vein simply wouldn't have been me.

And there is another point: Hetty has done a lot of this 'truth telling' already, in her own writing, in many of her novels. She's just the sort of writer I'm not. That's always been her gift as a fine, intuitive novelist: fiction, where I've always worked with the facts. Yes, she's written extensively about all three of us, here and there throughout her novels – lightly or heavily disguised. But it's perfectly clear, to me at least, that it's us. We're all there, in our messy acts and emotions – the way we lived together, then didn't live, and lived again, and finally parted from each other.

Oh yes, at a distance, for Hetty, and Léa too, I've always remained the necessary third in that triangle – I can see that – necessary to support the other two corners, so that they've both kept in touch with me over the years, Hetty with her novels suitably inscribed – books to show me where I went wrong with them no doubt, all that I missed out on by not being more emotionally co-operative with them both. Books in this way as a sort of literary revenge? It's very possible. Or am I just being cynical, still hurt by it all, in my heart of hearts?

Perhaps this is true, for some of the dedications are full of real emotion towards me. However, the novels themselves – and this is what I'm really getting at – are filled with barely-disguised incidents from my life with her, in Domenica, at Summer Hill, right up to my finding her in Germany after the war. And the same is true of the details of my life with Léonie, which Léa must have talked to her about in their years together. Hetty, though she has so much herself, always needed to feed on other people, for her insecurities, her imagined failures. She's a very autobiographical novelist.

So it's obvious – Hetty has written this personal part of my life for me in this way. And if anyone, some nosy biographer, ever thought it worth it, they could easily find me there, in her novels, along with Léonie, rising to the top in this manner, like cream in a diary pan. Or perhaps, more honestly, like the fat you take off a stew, which you discard. For I've sometimes wondered how much I ever really meant to either of them – in terms of anything reasoned or reasonable – so obsessed have they always been with each other.

Or, again, is it me who's being unreasonable? Cynical? Hurt? For I did love them both – at different times, together. Can't deny that. Yes, there was love, on all sides, in different ways, times, places. What a strange nonsense it now seems. The three of us made up a droll caravanserai of love, each laden down with precious bales, deviously sold or bartered or swapped en route. Or wantonly lost in the sands, sometimes miraculously discovered again on a later journey. For years we all traded in emotions, haggled over its weights and measures, ran the silk road of kisses . . . But in the end – what disasters! So that I've come to think that the real urge we feel in love – is to end love, to be released from it, which is what I did out here at the Villa Serena: released long ago from those two women who made my life so happy, yet finally agonising.

So why the nightmare? Why shouldn't I just be happy now, freed from both of them at last, free from all the terrors, hopes and despairs of that past, free to enjoy what I've rescued from it all, by myself and with Catherine. And I've rescued a lot: Catherine, and a daughter I love dearly coming today with my two grandchildren, along with my old friend Hugh, and Molly, and the others. A knighthood, undeserved (but why worry about that? – someone has to get them; a lunch party with *Tartufi Bianchi* and Bertini's Frascati. Sixty-five, fit enough and still with my marbles. What more could one ask for?

What luck – if I were to die tomorrow – to have had all this life here at the Villa Serena, living high up, like a bird perched on this steep, bare cliff – a cliff that fists out and then subsides, running into this Poet's Gulf where Shelley drowned but which cradles me. Yes – and today so particularly to be grateful for: a midwinter sun still promising me things as I start out on my own midwinter. What more could one ask for? A small future, with few painful memories, no nightmares. 'Old men forget.' So be it. So very much be it.

He sipped his coffee. It had gone cold. He made another pot in the kitchen and took it out on to the terrace, warming in the sun now, the wicker chairs and table sheltered behind a tall glass windbreak. He sat down, gazing out over the bay. Small boats were returning after their night's fishing, the acetylene lamps doused on their bowsprits. 'Home is the hunter, home from the hill – and the sailor home from the sea,' he said to himself pleasurably.

Yet still he felt unsettled, nervy. And he knew why. He had avoided the crucial issue in his journal this morning – cleverly worked round it in every possible way. He had quite failed to face, to define, the nightmare itself. Here at least he was certainly avoiding an issue. This ghost, returned untimely, would have to be laid. Unwillingly he returned to his study desk.

'The nightmare,' he wrote. Then he felt the pain of it all over again, so that he paused. Then he hardened himself for the task.

It was quite short, simple even. It was its grinding repetition that made it awful. Hetty's words – her much younger face and voice, fourteen or so, when she was hardly more than a child, leaning over me, the words stammered out again and again: 'You're n-not going to g-get out of it so easily! You're not going to g-get out of it!'

But out of what? – for I wasn't *in* anything at that point. Both of us were in some open, quite unrecognisable space, a surrealist landscape, absolutely flat desert, with a highly-coloured enamel-blue sky. Hetty was standing above me. I was flat out on the bare earth, being pressed into it by some flimsy transparent material, thin gauze paper, the sort used in old flower presses. And these sheets were falling on me, one after the other, like great snowflakes, so insubstantial that I felt I could easily throw them off. But of course I couldn't, I was helpless, being suffocated by them, the sheets (pages from an empty book?) gradually pressing me underground – with Hetty's face then, that lovely wide brow, big oval blue eyes, locks of jet-black hair, becoming less and less clear, as she disappeared then, up into a flaming sky, but with her repeated words loud as ever: '. . . not g-going to g-get out of it, g-get out of it, g-get out of it!'

Then she disappeared altogether in the flames and I was deep underground, forced down by these innumerable leaves of paper which, like papier-mâché, were now solidifying all round me and I was fighting not to be buried alive, the paper rapidly hardening like stone, so that I would soon be a fossil myself, dead and embedded in the earth forever.

Well, there's the nightmare. Seems pretty inconclusive, to say the least. Does it mean anything? Well, that Hetty always liked to tease and hurt me, at that age, when we were adolescent – there's that, obviously. But what was I not going to get out of? There's the question. Some responsibility to her? Or to Léa? Some sort of unfinished business there? That *I* have failed to finish – as the guilty party? Can't be. I did everything I could then, to keep Léonie, to hold her. I wanted her with me then. We'd just made things up. I loved her. It was she who insisted on going back to her old ways with Hetty.

Or is it some long-lost debt I owe *Hetty*, something unfilfilled there? – going right back to our childhood? Dreams, bad dreams especially, are often about this, aren't they? – traumas from childhood, unresolved. Well, the only thing unresolved between us then was my loving her. And I can't be blamed for that. The blame was hers, if anybody's, in that she didn't love me in return. Or, at least, she didn't then. That was much later, up in the children's garden, and by then it was *too* late. I was with Léonie.

And what of the fire? Why did Hetty disappear, like the Virgin in some cheap religious painting, clouds of fire, ascending heavenwards? What's one to make of that? Just a reflection of how much I idolised her, I suppose, the infatuation I had for her when we were young. So the whole dream is simply a reflection of how much she once meant to me, that's all – a reflection of all the pain that long infatuation brought to me. Yes, that's it. Just a confirmation of that. So obvious really. All over and done with now. I've faced it, written it down. Now I can sleep easy . . .

Pietro and Maria arrived ten minutes later, meeting Robert in the kitchen, profuse with birthday greetings and a bunch of red hothouse carnations. Some of the food for the birthday party was up in their car at the top of the steps. Robert, still in his dressing gown, helped them down with it. And soon, with this bustle about the Villa, he began to feel better – and better still when he had bathed and dressed.

Afterwards he looked at himself in the bedroom mirror: the old linen tropical suit, almost Edwardian in cut, a red carnation rampant, one of the last of his tailored, Egyptian blue cotton shirts, a nicely faded silk polka dot tie, the comfy brown brogues which Duckers in Oxford still made for him . . . Quite the English gentleman, he thought, adding simple gold cufflinks and a dash of Trumper's cologne about his temples. No one would know him now for the rough colonial boy, brought up and orphaned on a ruined citrus farm in the West Indies, a boy from nowhere, an island, a mere speck, lost in the middle of the wide Sargasso Sea . . . Quite the gentleman? Quite the Knight, he might rather say. Sir Robert Grant . . . it didn't really sound too bad. A lot of nonsense and vanity, of course. All the same, he felt very much better now, the headache dissolved, the bad dream quite forgotten. He moved out on to the terrace then, with the post which Pietro had brought up from his box in Lerici.

There were quite a few Christmas cards and letters from various people – all of it delayed in the terrible Italian posts. He glanced through the letters quickly, picking a few out for more careful consideration later – until suddenly he started. The envelope in front of him was from Hetty. He saw the Irish stamp, and the postmark dated well before Christmas, addressed in that hurried, assured yet somehow naive scrawl of hers – the hand of an Edwardian *grande dame* full of natural hauteur which, if you had not known the woman, would have suggested someone cold, arrogant, ruthless.

And how real these qualities were in her, he thought, as he fingered the envelope gingerly. And yet they were only facets, he well remembered, among so many other quite opposite qualities, her grace, beauty, that sweet wit sometimes, above all that stammering vulnerability which could so easily overwhelm her, so that one knew how wonderful a person she was at heart – if only she could find and inhabit that lovely realm of her spirit as a permanence.

Robert's hand shook slightly as he opened the envelope with his tortoiseshell paper-knife. My God, he thought, so long since he'd first met her, since it had all been over between them – yet still there was the vague excitement.

Henrietta had written at length, the difficult script pushing right up to the margins of the notepaper. He wished she had used a typewriter. But she rarely had, even though latterly, the effects of her syphilis bringing an early arthritis, this would have made writing so much easier for her.

But, no, she had once written to him about the thrill of ink running over fine paper, the joy of her old Mentmore fountain pen. Or writing in pencil – that was wonderful, too, she had said, for then there was the added pleasure in the dry-sappy pine smell when you sharpened them, especially in bed, where she usually wrote in the mornings, surrounded by half a dozen soft-leaded artist's 'Imperials', their wafer-thin shavings curled into little crowned trumpets all over the patchwork quilt.

That was how he had last seen her, indeed, sitting up in the four-poster – moved near the window so that she could look straight out over the demesne and the river valley – when he had gone to Summer Hill three years before for Dermot's funeral. Since then he had only had messages on Christmas cards. What could Hetty want to say now – in this obviously long letter? What explanation, demand, justification? What was to be invoked now of all that he had won and lost at Summer Hill? His hand still trembled slightly as he opened the sheets of paper.

18 December 1964

Dear Robert,

Out of the blue for you once more, like that first time all those years ago when I landed on your family hearth in Domenica, a screeching bundle from nowhere, as I imagine. And this may be just as unexpected and possibly disrupting an arrival, though I hope not.

I want to ask you if you would look after all my papers, manuscripts, letters and so on – be my literary executor when I'm gone. I really don't want them getting into the hands of the nosy literary folk who've been at me already about them – these new gossipy biographers, dull academics, booksellers, auctioneers, libraries in Texas. I've heard from them all, and worse, seen some of them at the door, too, and don't really want any of that. Yet I want to preserve them nonetheless from the ruin that Summer Hill is likely to become when I'm gone. So I've had most of these papers packed in boxes and had Ronnie Ryan, my solicitor here, take them to the bank vault in Kilkenny.

I've kept them for you – really no other reason. You were always to have had them, if you survived. And you have, and will I'm sure, longer than me. But somehow I could never bring myself to talk about this, or give you these papers, face to face – since I felt you would too easily refuse or talk your way out of it in your clever old logical ways.

So I write, where you can't overwhelm me with your voice – where I hope, please, at this distance, you will think about it all calmly and accept the commission. You, together with Hugh Latimer of course, who publishes us both. You are the two trustees and literary executors named in my will. Future income (if any) from all my books is to be divided between you and Olivia, after 10% of these royalties go to the Royal Literary Fund. It's all in the will – with Ronnie Ryan, if I keel over tomorrow!

Robert paused in his reading. There was something missing in Hetty's résumé of her will. Of course! The house and lands of Summer Hill – and Léonie. No mention had been made of either. He supposed that Léonie was to have the house and estate, if she survived her, but that Hetty had been embarrassed to say so in the letter, knowing how he would feel, seeing this as a further betrayal on her part. Well, it would be, he thought, resuming his reading in a colder mood.

So you will think nicely about this imposition, won't you? At this distance it should be easier for you to do so. In writing like this we can surely stand back from each other a little, can't we? (Before we recede from each other altogether!) In writing, too, perhaps

I can make up for some of the pain which I – and Léonie, too – have caused you over the years. This may be more difficult. Words, since they've been our profession as well as our expression, have always been a bit of a problem between us. We were often too good at them, so that feeling was lost – wordy battles that go back such a long way!

I was at church here the other day and remembered how it was when we were children there: the one place we couldn't argue the toss, as we so often did then. Yes, I was reminded of all that, sitting in the same pew where we sat together years ago, bored and fiddly children, through so many Sunday mornings of enforced speechlessness. For it was in this church, I'm sure – during one of Canon Bradshaw's gracious, soft-voiced, interminable sermons – that for want of anything better to do we first calmed down and thought of each other properly, saw ourselves as other than nursery rivals contending for a 'parent', realised that we were not forever to be fractious children, permanent 'orphans', but sensed that one day we might find safety together – love even – which we did, however briefly.

Yes, when you and I couldn't speak and weren't arguing, we had the gift, I felt, of *looking* at each other properly, and finding truths there which had been quite lost with words. So look at me now, in your mind, when you consider this request, and I feel you may agree with it then. You may agree, too, because so many of these papers reflect Summer Hill, in one way or another, a place I know you've loved. As I have.

Latterly, I'm sure, you've wondered why I've spent so much time and effort and money I didn't really have in keeping up the house. Well, apart from loving it, I've tried to look after it because the house and family here reflect qualities of independence and spirit now sadly lacking in this for-so-long tyrannised, frightened and conformist country: qualities of plain speaking, of concern, of national and neighbourly involvement, as well as all that old wit-and-elegance-of-the-Anglo-Irish bit.

I saw these things as my own Irish inheritance and have wanted to maintain them – so continuing to 'protest', to ask embarrassing questions, long after most of my Protestant co-religionists in the Republic have disowned that spirit and took to large helpings of humble pie. It's certainly made me unpopular with them, just as the same sort of questioning has with my Catholic and republican neighbours. Though I'm as Irish as they are . . .

Forgive these asides. It's simply my instinct that you'll accept this request. Or is it just that I still have a small residue of vanity – in thinking you may still be interested in me, in what will survive of me at least, in these papers? Possibly. Though you can't deny your qualities as a meorialist. I've often noticed this in your columns, your books. (Yes, I read them, each time they arrive, with your neat, non-committal inscriptions.)

People like you who remember things in such detail, who want to get that detail on paper at all costs, are essentially memorialists – spies on time, old money-lenders fingering the days. You may not like to think of yourself as such. But I know it – know what lies behind that often brisk and literal, here-and-now façade of yours, when you've made out your gifts were aimed at nothing more than a deadline in Fleet Street.

I suspect you see yourself as a less creative writer than me – just a journalist, travel writer or whatever. But with your knowledge (as opposed to my intuition) about what *really* matters you've been just as creative as I. People, places, events in your books – even the near trivia you've sometimes dealt with in your journalism – all this in your style, your heart, you've set against the clock of life, the larger fates. That's been your great distinction – the unpretentious way you've set the transient against a background of last things. There's always been that light yet grave tone in your work that I've longed for in mine – which has been too unrelievedly in the wild laughter and tears-before-bedtime mode: romantic where you are classic, if you like.

So I do hope you will look after these papers. And read through them, for there are letters, diaries and so on, things you've never seen – not, with your own so independent spirit, in search of, or in any need of, me after I'm gone, but as evidence of my mind, the way I've seen all three of us, our lives, problems. And the way I've seen just you and me, from the beginning in Domenica: the people we were together then, or the couple we might have been, for there are comments on this as well. The children's garden . . . You, with your logic, your energy, have always been one for completing things, I for leaving them undone. Perhaps these papers will make some amends for that.

Of course, this idea of your needing me in this mental way: you may well feel just the opposite – that it is I, in this rather enfeebled, reclusive life in Ireland, now and when I'm gone, who might need you. But I have you in thought – in faith, if you like. Just as you were always so much 'there' for me when we were children, so you are still, even though *you* may not feel this now. And indeed I often gave you good reason for feeling this . . . I'm sorry. Anyway, knowing your doubts, your unhappinesses about me in the past, these papers are for you – as an explanation I hope of the many things I didn't or refused or wasn't able to tell you in the past, about me, about Léonie – and about *us*, that uniquely 'you and I' part of both our lives.

You know that aside from a few trivial pieces I've never published any autobiography. But I've written one all the same – and you'll find it among the papers, too. It's for you. Perhaps in reading it you may find that it completes our life somehow, makes the relationship whole; that we live together, as we once wanted to, live now what was unlived then. An impossible idea? I don't think so – simply two people sharing their true, their full shape and potential, which can only surely happen in thought – in words, not action.

You may feel of course that a good deal of you and I – our trials, tribulations together – already exists in some of my novels, which you tell me – if you tell me no more! – that you've read. But we've both been necessarily filtered and changed through the fiction there: me especially, changed completely – re-inventing myself, becoming so many 'others' in each story I wrote.

Who was I? Of course for many years I didn't know who my real father was. But I think that my temperament was such that I was never likely to understand my own nature in any deep sense anyway – just acted boldly, usually rashly, in accordance with what I *thought* it to be. My acting first and my writing later always took me away from myself, which was exactly the point of both these exercises! – to escape what I didn't know about, what I feared in myself: the emptiness there. But perhaps, if when you read this 'memoir', you will be able to fill that void suitably and know who I really was – you if anybody.

The autobiography isn't fiction. It's as true, warts and all, as I could get. But I know it isn't any ultimate reality either, the absolute truth about myself, or about my feelings towards you. The words here must always be tentative, unfertilised, hooks without eyes, I'm afraid: one side of a written dialogue waiting to be voiced, where you alone can play the other role. For the truth about us both is only ever likely to exist in some mid-way meeting of our thoughts, in the air between us as it were, a co-operative verity, which we failed to produce in fact but which I hope may be established now, when you read the autobiography – so that when you do, thinking of me, I'll be thinking of you. Be sure of that. And that's really the whole point, isn't it? – in life or death: it's the thought that counts!

My love,

Hetty.

Robert put down the letter. His hands were still shaking. But it was more from anger then, not excitement: anger at the thought confirmed – how this ghost, which he thought so well laid, had now returned. And then there were some of the details, phrases, which annoyed him. This talk of their meeting in mid-air, a 'co-operative verity', their living in her memoir 'all that was unlived then'.

It annoyed him because he knew well how, if Hetty had only thought like this years before, they would never have had to meet in mid-air. They could have met, could have lived and loved together in fact, not fancy, for he would not have married Léonie then. Almost everything she had said in the letter was perforce – the results of her own whims, choices, her own wildly swinging and divided nature. He had never wanted it that way – any mid-way, mid-air thing between them. He had just wanted her, in reality. And he knew that again now, astonished at the wave of emotion that swept over him. He could have calmed those ills of hers, restored those losses, balanced her divisive nature, just as much as Léonie ever had – if he had ever been given the chance. But Hetty had never given him that chance at all, all those years ago. Had she done so – why, they could both have been living together for years now at Summer Hill, happy in their old age ...

My God, he thought – his earlier idea that morning that he had quite got over Hetty! Yet here he was trembling with rage and emotion: all the old poisonous frustrations and obsessions returned. And, worse still, here she was telling him how, with this autobiography, he was going to have to live all his experiences with her over again, all the pain, the loss.

He re-read bits of the letter, grudgingly acknowledging the praise she gave him, the affection she confirmed. Yet still, in his annoyance, he refused to see the essential message there – how she was apologising for all her behaviour towards him, her behaviour alone – and hers with Léonie. He failed to see, clearly intimated between the lines, how fond she still was of him, how she was asking his forgiveness. Instead what he did notice was the mood of doom in the letter, Hetty sensing her end. And this surprised him. It was Léonie, as he knew from Olivia who saw her fairly regularly, who had been ill earlier the previous year, with stomach cramps, pains in the abdomen. Hetty, when he had last seen her, had been arthritic, with sporadic aches, but otherwise well. And her few messages to him since had confirmed her health. So why the leitmotif of 'last things' in the letter? Well, he wasn't going to worry about it now. A whiff of some herb blew out on to the terrace – rosemary, he was sure. And the smell roused him. Hetty's letter could wait and so could the others. He would go into the kitchen and chat with Maria, get in her way for a minute or two. The kitchen – cure for all ills ...

When he got there Maria was taking a tray of little *pizzette* out of the oven.

'Rosemary?' he asked her.

'No. Oregano.' She was very busy.

'Oh, that's funny. I could have sworn it was rosemary – "Rosemary for remembrance".'

He returned to the salon where Pietro had just come up from the small cellar and was organising the drinks.

'Warm enough to have it all on the terrace, I think, Pietro.'

'*Si*, Signor.'

He helped Pietro move the bottles and glasses out into the sun, lining them up on a table. Then he started to polish the glasses – anything to forget Hetty and her letter.

'Ice?' he asked Pietro. 'For the gin and tonic, if they *have* to have it.'

'*Si*, Signor.'

'And you have the Frascati well chilled, in the fridge?'

'*Si*, Signor.'

Pietro was no conversationalist. His wife usually more than made up for him in that way. But Robert decided he could not bother her again so soon. Instead he went back into the salon, thinking to tidy the place, before he saw how tidy it was already. He fidgeted about a bit, moving furniture, then replacing it. He went to the mantelpiece. But that was all perfectly tidy as well. Except – what was it? Something was wrong. Of course – the two small Chinese famille rose vases, which were always kept at either end of the shelf, were right next to each other now.

Had he or Maria moved them recently? He thought not, but could not be sure. As he returned them to their proper places, a smell of violets flooded the air. It made him start. He raised the neck of one of the vases, putting it to his nose. There was no doubt – it reeked: a deep, oily essence of violets. Léonie's violets. Her smell.

These were two Daoguang vases, Cordiner family heirlooms, which Henrietta – on behalf of Léonie, too – had given him as a Christmas present, over there, ten years before. But they were strange vases, since one or other of them – and neither had ever held flowers or perfume at Summer Hill – would offer from time to time, but only to certain people, this intense odour of violets. Hetty could smell it – and Robert, too. But for almost everyone else there was absolutely nothing there – as indeed there had not been for Robert in years. But now this morning, with this unmistakable odour, Léonie had returned, was in the room with him, just as Hetty had been half an hour before in her letter. But the presence of this new *revenant* disturbed Robert even more deeply than the nightmare or Hetty's letter; this sweet smell of Léonie returned to him, essence of their bed together in many places, of a woman who, despite everything, he knew he had once loved just as much as Hetty.

His hand was shaking again. He decided he needed a drink, a mid-morning whizzer. Even better, he would get it from the kitchen drinks cupboard – which would give him the excuse to bother Maria again.

*

The *pizzette* were delicious – the *Tartufi Bianchi* superb. The guests drank well and had a merry time. Hugh Latimer proposed a birthday toast, adding a few gracious words, to which Robert responded with equal brevity, before offering a toast to Pietro and Maria for the splendid feast.

Molly Latimer talked to Robert later. 'It's all so *nice*,' she said, head to one side, smiling, quizzical. Robert was as fond of her as of Hugh. He raised his glass of Frascati to her.

'And *you* are so nice.'

'I'm only sorry about Olivia.'

'She called from Genoa, flight was delayed. But she'll be here before we finish – plenty of time yet. Here, do get rid of that gassy champagne and try some of this Frascati . . .'

The British Consul from Genoa bearded Robert then and he switched to a more formal mode. The man congratulated him on everything – for the second time, for he and his pretty wife had done all this on arrival. Hugh Latimer, the more adept diplomat, finally rescued him and they went out together on to the terrace.

'A splendid review in the *Telegraph* already. I've a copy for you – got it in Rome. And both the Sundays are giving it lead reviews – I called the office. And an excellent subscription. I couldn't be better pleased – with your "memoirs" . . .' His eyes twinkled.

'My apotheosis . . .'

'I hope not! You'll write something more, won't you?'

'About what, dear Hugh? Can't really slog around the wild places much any more. And I'm not one for the vine-and-olive-grove Tuscan book, old British gent in a ruined *podere* squelching grapes with his bare toes in a vat. Not really my style – least of all living on this bare rock.' They gazed out over the Poet's Gulf, sipped their drinks.

'What will you do then?' Hugh asked.

This gave Robert his cue. And he took it, rather unwillingly. 'I had a letter from Hetty this morning, delayed in the post.'

'Yes?'

'You must have had the same request. She wants both of us to be her literary executors.'

'Yes. I had a note from her about that.'

'Well, that might keep me occupied for a bit – if I don't go before her, which is quite possible. She was fit enough when I last saw her.'

'Yes, she is. Saw her last autumn. She came over for her new novel.'

'But what do you think – about her papers? Lot of work there, I imagine. She should leave them all to that manuscript library in Texas, get a handsome price for them there, too, I imagine.'

'She doesn't want that. She said in her letter to me – she wants you to have them, particularly.'

'Yes, I know.' Robert was downcast. 'And that's the problem. I don't want to have to – well, live my life with her all over again.'

'No.'

'And of course I would, because she's written a proper autobiography as well, warts and all. She told me.'

Hugh perked up at this. 'Oh, I didn't know. That must be absolutely fascinating. *Her* life – my God.'

'Yes. But she may not want it published. She didn't say. Just left it to us, I suppose.'

'To you, Robert. You'd be the person to decide. Chief executor as it were – which you surely are, in truth.'

'I don't know, Hugh . . . I'm not keen on the whole thing, honestly. I'd sooner not be involved – far too much water under that bridge. I'd really prefer if you handled it, when it comes to the point –'

Just as he said this a searing pain shot through his head, the early-morning headache, after the nightmare, returning suddenly with a vengeance – like a needle passing through his skull. A further message from Hetty – just as he had denied her? He had had these strange intimations all morning. Of course, he did not believe in it all, the psychic thing, messages through the ether. Nonetheless he was unnerved by it, thinking he might as well amend his last statement. 'Well anyway, Hugh, I suppose I can't actually turn her down. I'll do something. I'll write to her.' As he said this the pain quite disappeared. Then Pietro came out on to the terrace.

'Telephone, Signor.'

Robert had taken several congratulatory calls already that morning and was tired of them. 'Tell them to leave a message, Pietro.'

'It's a long-distance, from Ireland, Signor. The man said it was urgent.'

'The *man?*'

'*Si*, Signor.'

Robert looked over at Hugh. 'I don't think I know any man in Ireland these days – just women. Unless it's the *Irish Times*, looking for an interview.' He stood up, finishing his Frascati. 'A few words of wisdom from the old sage at the Villa Serena? Can't be. I haven't won the Nobel prize. And I'm not Irish either.'

He pondered these last words as he went to the telephone in his study. Of course he supposed he was Irish, if he was anything. It was there, in Ireland, at Summer Hill, that almost everything that had really mattered in his heart had happened. Hetty's letter, and all the other strange intimations of the morning, were more than enough to confirm that emotional nationality. He picked up the telephone.

'A *what?*' Robert asked again. The line was crackling badly. Then it cleared.

'A *fire*, Sir Robert – at Summer Hill,' the voice shouted.

'Who's calling?'

'Mr Ryan – Ronnie Ryan – Miss Cordiner's solicitor, from Kilkenny. The point is –'

'A fire? Where? When?' Robert was still confused.

'Last night, or the early morning. Some of the bedrooms in the south wing, the landing above the hall. Started in Miss Cordiner's bedroom apparently. Luckily,

Jack Welsh downstairs smelt something, got the brigade out, and they had it under control in an hour or so. But the point is, Mr Grant – Miss Cordiner is all right, a few bruises, superficial burns – but Miss Straus, I'm afraid she died in the blaze. They couldn't get her out of the bedroom and –'

The line, which had cleared for a minute, was now crackling again and Robert did not hear the end of the sentence.

'Léonie?' he shouted.

'– Cordiner, she asked me to call you, so –'

The static was bad now. 'Of course –'

'– the funeral – Friday – been snowing heavily – I'm making the arrangements. Miss Cordiner asked me –'

'Yes, yes. Tell Miss Cordiner I'll be over right away. I'll fly over as soon as I can.'

'Fine. I'll tell – arrangements for Friday, at the house, so –'

The static returned and Robert heard no more, finally putting the telephone down. How much clearer the earlier messages from Ireland that morning had been – the fiery nightmare, the searing headaches, the whiff of rosemary when it was oregano, the smell of violets. And now their meaning was at last quite clear to Robert. Above all the note of doom in Hetty's letter made some sense now. But what sense? What exactly had happened? He returned to the terrace, taking Hugh aside, telling him of the call.

'Oh, my God – how quite appalling. Of course I'll come over with you.'

'What puzzles me though is how the fire started, midwinter, with all that Irish damp and wet. And the solicitor said it had been snowing heavily over there.'

'These old houses, fires in the drawing room – a log, a spark – after they'd gone to bed.'

'It started up *in* one of the bedrooms, though.'

'Faulty wiring?'

'They only had the electricity put in ten years ago.'

'Dear me, so all Hetty's papers gone, too. She worked in her bedroom.'

'No. I didn't tell you. She had all her papers and manuscripts packed up and sent to the bank. She wrote to me . . .'

As he said this something struck Robert. The note of doom in the letter . . . And then he thought he saw it: had Hetty sent all her papers away, intentionally, in *advance* of the fire? Was there something prepared in it all? No, it couldn't be. That was nonsense.

'We've got seats on tomorrow afternoon's flight from Genoa. Come back with us on that.'

'Yes. But let me wait and see what Olivia says when she gets here.'

Olivia arrived, with the two children, ten minutes later, the hire car skidding to a halt at the top of the Villa steps where Robert, seeing some other guests off, was waiting. Lottie and William, cooped up in the tiny Fiat for hours, jumped out all agog. Olivia got out on the other side much more slowly, leaning on the roof, looking at her father a moment, sighing, cradling her head in her arms.

'Oh – oh oh!' she groaned in mock dramatics. 'This *awful* little car.' She thumped it on the roof. 'Stalled on the autostrada. And now I've missed everything! You drunken, foody lot, you!'

She hurried round the car, rushing into her father's arms, embracing him. Then, hands on her shoulders, he held her apart from him for an instant, gazing at her: the same silk-fine, dark hair riding the high brow, something of the chunky build, same blackberry eyes, the very slightly pouty, sensuous lower lip – so little of her father in her looks, he thought, so much of her mother. And then, for the first time that day, Robert felt real pain as he hugged her again.

Huge moist flakes of snow fluttered through the air, icing the stone pineapples on the gate pillars, drifting across the fretworked gable-ends and diamond-paned windows of the little Gothic lodge: a Christmas card scene as Ronnie Ryan drove Robert and Hugh and Molly through the main gate of Summer Hill, Olivia with the two children in another car behind them. The funeral was in an hour's time.

They drove up the avenue. In the white drifts nothing was visible beyond the line of tall beech trees. The demesne was foreshortened everywhere, without length or breadth, in which none of the informal eighteenth-century landscaping showed, curtained by the gentle spirals of snow which muffled every sound. The car ran noiselessly over the spongy flakes, so that they seemed to be moving through a huge crystal ball, a vast toy, a glass ornament shaken out of its liquid, translucent peace, the snowflakes dancing in the orb; soon the travellers would reach the centrepiece of this conceit, the pinnacles and domes of some fairy-tale castle . . .

But the house when it came in view at the top of the rise was a sad sight. The east façade which gave out over the valley was grimed and blackened. Tongues of soot rose up the walls from gaping windows, the glass and casements were shattered, all the way up to the roof. A debris of snow-covered brick and plaster lay on the lawn in front. There was an air of something freshly killed about the house – still bloodied and warm, a body whose intimacies had been laid bare.

Ronnie Ryan – benign and portly, balding, in a dark suit and Homburg hat – looked up at the house as they rounded the old pleasure gardens, the astrolabe still there, its ribs, skeleton-like, rimmed in snow. 'A bad business – very bad altogether.'

'Which room exactly did the fire start in?'

'The primrose room – Miss Cordiner's room. Between twelve and one in the morning, they think. Jack Welsh, at the back, was awake – smelt something. Luckily his daughter Mary and her husband Seamus were staying, over from Birmingham last week. Seamus got upstairs quickly. But the whole landing was engulfed, smoke and flames. He only just managed to drag Miss Cordiner out of her room. Of course . . .' Ronnie Ryan paused. 'He'd – he'd no idea that Miss Straus was in the same room.'

Robert said nothing. The car drew up some distance from the portico. It had to. Mounds of snowy debris lay between them and the hall door. They all got out, as Olivia and the children arrived in the car behind. Robert, moving slowly through the thin flakes towards the house with his daughter, started to pick and poke vaguely over the mounds of burnt rubbish. Bits of charred furniture stuck out from the snow, sodden books, ice-encrusted carpets. The remains of a leather chesterfield sofa crouched beneath the snow.

'Look,' he said. 'That's the canterbury Hetty kept her books in, next to her bed.' He examined the smashed and charred antique. 'And there – that pembroke table. We did lessons on that, as children.' Moving on he came to a pile of sodden books. Lifting up one, he dusted the snow off it. *'The Boy's Book of Railways* – that was mine.' Beneath were a red-bound copy of *Punch* for 1898 and an old Victorian manual on beekeeping.

'Come on, Daddy, let's go in.' Olivia took his arm and they walked up the steps. Elly and Jack Welsh, a very elderly couple now, were waiting for them. They all went into the hall. The debris here, which had fallen from the walls and down the stairwell from the first-floor landing, had been almost entirely cleared away. But Robert's shoe squeaked over something on the floor. Bending down he picked up part of a broken crystal pendant, holding it for a moment, so that it glittered faintly in the snowy light from the open hall door. Then he looked up. The great Waterford chandelier, which had always hung right down through the house from the top of the stairwell, had gone completely. He put the piece of glass into his pocket. He felt he had come into a time of last mementoes for Summer Hill.

Then, turning, he suddenly saw Léonie's coffin, on trestle stands to one side of the hall, by the long Flemish tapestry. It was surrounded by laurel, ferns, holly, garlands of simple winter greenery. He moved towards it, stood there an instant, but could think of nothing – except of how much colder she must be than he was.

'Come into the drawing room, Daddy. There's a fire . . .'

'And Hetty?' He turned to Olivia who had been talking to Elly.

'She's upstairs, in another bedroom. Elly says she doesn't want –'

'I should see her.' Robert, as if pursued by something, was anxious to see Hetty, attend the church – complete all his business in Summer Hill as soon as possible and get away.

'No. She's not coming to the funeral. She doesn't want to see anyone 'till after it.'

Robert reluctantly joined the others in the long drawing room where there were sandwiches and whiskey – and a fire, two small electric fires. Robert huddled close to one of them, barely nibbling at a sandwich, sipping his whiskey, still numbed. Outside the tall windows the snow drifted lightly down, a soft shroud over the world.

An hour later the first of the mourners arrived, cars gliding silently up the long avenue, being parked in the yard, the people walking round, beginning to congregate under cover on the porch steps in greatcoats and scarves, stamping the snow off their shoes.

And, half an hour after that, Robert with Olivia and the two children were in the first of the hired cars, following the hearse down the avenue, before they turned right outside the front gates and started slowly down the narrow twisting hill road into the village of Cloone.

The snow had thinned in the early afternoon and the hill had been specially gritted beforehand. But even so the chauffeur nearly ran them into the back of the hearse, giving its bumper a sharp clip as their car skidded on, before almost colliding with a group of villagers paying their respects, hats off, standing in front of one of the old terraced estate cottages on the steep corner.

'Just the thing – at an Irish funeral: mourners up on a manslaughter charge . . .' Robert hoped to lighten the mood, without success.

But the service in the little church across the river, with Cranmer's vivid words and the hymn 'To be a pilgrim' played by the organist and a small choir out from the cathedral in Kilkenny – all this was beautiful, appropriate, moving.

Yet Robert, at one end of the front pew where he and Hetty had fiddled with boredom nearly sixty years before, found himself quite without emotion. Though he wanted to feel for this woman, cold beside him now on trestles a few yards away, who had once meant so much, had been so warm and close to him.

Why could he not feel for her now? It was surely nothing to do with all that had happened between them years before, her staying on with Hetty finally. He had long got over that. Why was it then? Just his restrained temperament once more? Surely not. Surely, at least at such times like this, he was capable of having, even showing, some emotion.

Then the thought suddenly struck him – perhaps it was because Hetty was not here, ever that vital third in his relationship with Léonie. A crucial player in this mourning was missing. But then had he really needed Léonie because he had failed with Hetty? Had he taken Léa on because, as her greatest friend, that was as close as he could get to Hetty – taking revenge against Hetty at the same time, for her coldness to him, by stealing Léonie from her?

Could his feelings for these two women have been so twisted? It was possible. He prayed he had not been so perverse, so immature, so selfish with them. He literally prayed then, something he had not done since he and Hetty had been children together sitting in this same pew.

'I have lifted up mine eyes unto the Lord and seen my salvation! . . .' He listened to the anthem, with the choir. Had he, he wondered, ever seen anything of the sort? Had he denied his salvation somehow? – a man incapable of any simple natural emotion, with a heart as cold as the white weather outside. He prayed – for some ordinary human feeling for this woman, once so loved, lying dead almost next to him.

Then, kneeling a few minutes later, he glanced over at Lottie and William at the end of the pew, bent right down, hidden beneath the wood, heads together, up to some vital business. They were bored – fiddling, whispering, disputing a hassock, pulling it one way, then another – lost in a secret world, see-saws of argument, affection, spite and making up. Children.

And at that moment the emotion he had hoped for suddenly swept over him, for the two children in their own right, and because they were him and Hetty years before in just the same place, and for Léonie finally, because she, whatever else, had become that vital third in their world, all those years ago at Summer Hill – a world she was leaving forever now. So that now he could feel for her completely.

And he saw then, with awful clarity, how there had been, and must still be, essentially three of them in the equation of their lives, that cat's cradle difficult – for him impossible in the end – to maintain, but which nonetheless contained the truth of all their lives: for him an unattainable truth.

And he could mourn that too, now – how for his own good or bad reasons he had refused to be part of that equation in the end, had abandoned the two women, had destroyed what might have been meant for them all – a life together, for the last twenty years, at Summer Hill.

Now he felt too much – a sense of guilt as well as love towards Léonie, a longing to make things up to her for betraying her in this way. So that he found the short journey through the snow, walking behind the undertakers carrying her coffin to the Cordiner family vault, almost unbearable.

'In sure and certain resurrection . . .' the rector intoned. But Robert could not look into the vault, bright from the reflected snow, as they put her among all the Cordiner ancestors, returning her here as well to what was her true home, from which, once more, he was excluded. When the vault door finally clanged shut he longed to be out of the whole place, back to the hotel in Dublin, a flight to the Villa Serena.

Afterwards, when most of the mourners had struggled purposefully back to Summer Hill in the snow, there was a reception, a funeral 'tea' – largely composed of strong drink – in the drawing room and hall.

After half an hour Robert could stand it no more. He would simply have to force himself on Hetty upstairs, offer condolences – then leave. He strode into the hall. Luckily Ronnie Ryan, just coming downstairs, met him there. 'Miss Cordiner – she wonders if you would like to go and see her now.'

Robert went upstairs with Ryan, along the corridor of the west wing, not touched in the fire. The solicitor stopped at one of the bedroom doors. With a moment's trepidation now, fearing the worst, emotionally and visually, Robert went inside.

He was astonished by what confronted him.

It was a large room – it had once been the best of the visitors' bedrooms. But now nothing of its old furnishings remained. It had been done up recently, completely and expensively redecorated, transformed, with two new large divan beds, loose-weave white wool counterpanes, white cane furniture, pretty wallpaper – a bathroom, he saw, built en suite into the next room: a bedroom with every modern comfort, warm and bright, the flowery curtains still open, giving out on to the snowy gardens.

Hetty sat on a high cane chair, next to a glass-topped table, covered in books, new novels, magazines, papers, with all her pens and pencils at the ready – a handsome new electric fire aglow at one side. But what astonished Robert most was her demeanour. Dressed in a smartly-cut tweed skirt, fluffy white cotton blouse and an embroidered sleeveless Russian waistcoat that he remembered her in years before, Hetty – apart from a slightly black eye and a light bandage round her forearm – looked formidably handsome, composed, a woman quite in charge of things. Robert had fully expected someone in bed – enfeebled, distraught, unhappy. Hetty in one of her most collapsed modes. Instead, here was a woman dressed, and against a background, straight out of an advertisement from *House and Garden*.

'Hetty . . .' He could not hide his surprise.

'Robert! – at last. How le-lovely.' She spoke casually, smiling faintly, rubbing her nose with one of her artist's 'Imperial' pencils.

'I – I thought you'd be in bed. Or something.'

'Yes, they all think that. That's the general idea. Just I can't be-bear funerals. Almost as be-bad as seeing people off at railway stations.' She looked at him in her old quizzical, haughty manner. 'You're surprised? Shouldn't be. Why should I have to face up to all that dreary chilling business in the church, coffins and things? Or that nonsense downstairs now. Nothing to do with Léa. All that I feel for her is up here.' She touched her head. 'Or down there.' She dropped her hand to a typescript on the glass-topped table. 'I won't be made to mourn people their way. Only mine. And mine's be-*better*,' she added tartly.

'Yes.' But Robert remained perplexed. He took the other white cane chair near her at the table. 'It's just – I hadn't expected you here.' He looked about the smart room.

'Oh, I had this done up all frou-frou and silk satiny for my American publisher and his wife when they come to visit. Harry Jacobson and Mary-Ann: they couldn't bear the cold in the other rooms. Overheard them talking one me-morning a few years ago. "Harry," she said, "I didn't just lightly fr-freeze in bed last night. I was *solid*." So I thought if he was going to go on publishing me I'd better do something about it.'

There was silence after this. Robert did not know quite what to say, so he said 'yes' rather inconclusively. Then, by way of changing the topic, he said, 'I got your letter, just a few days ago. Delayed in the Italian posts.'

'Good. I'm glad. I wondered – not hearing from you. I hope you weren't too pe-pe-put off by it?'

Now, for the first time there was a note of doubt in her voice, a feel of genuine, not breezy emotion. And Robert, unable to take much more of the latter, took his cue from this changed approach.

'Hetty, what really happened?' he asked. 'With you and Léa – and the fire. I've only heard the vaguest details from Ronnie Ryan.'

She looked away, raised her head, as if seeking inspiration from the pretty wallpaper. Then she looked back at him. And now there was a real emotion in her face. 'I thought you might guess it all from my letter.'

'Guess what? Apart from rather a note of doom in it all –'

'Exactly.'

'But why? You're looking so well – you weren't going to die.'

'No. But Léa was. We both were,' she added decisively. 'That was the whole point.'

'What point?' he asked, fearing his worst suspicions were going to be confirmed.'

'Léa hadn't been that well this last year –'

'I knew that, stomach pains, but nothing serious, you all said.'

'That's what we all thought. And the doctors. Nothing really wrong at all. But then a few months ago – it was all very quick. She had cancer, of the womb. And it was too late. They couldn't operate, they said. It had spread all over. She was in pain, and it got worse, even with the drugs – unbearable. Now do you see the pe-point, of the fire?'

'No –'

'And why Léa was in my bedroom when the fire started.'

And Robert was forced to see it all then. 'No, Hetty . . .' He paused. 'You, too.'

'Yes. I started it. Just bad luck – that Jack Welsh smelt the burning. And that Seamus was staying here. Dragged me out of the room. But didn't see Léa – didn't know she was in the room at all.' She picked up one of the new novels on the table. 'Review copies, what a chore. I was hoping not to have to do any more of them.' Then she looked at Robert quickly, just as he was about to speak. 'You don't have to ask me why.'

'No.'

'Twenty years with her here. And all that went before. I wanted no more of it, alone. We'd agreed a month ago – said when the pain got too bad. After Christmas, we thought.'

'Yes.'

'She'd seen Olivia in October when she was still okay. They all had a lovely long weekend here together, Olivia and the children. So we'd said our goodbyes, all my pe-papers in the vault, the letter I wrote you and Hugh. And then there was Christmas – which we managed. It was all as neat as it could be. Then last week, last Sunday, she could stand no more. It would have been the happier solution. For both of us.'

Hetty had regained some of her composure as she spoke, in all but her eyes which were frightened.

'I am sorry,' was all Robert could say.

She picked up the old snow-dome, using it now as a paperweight on the table, with its miniature of Summer Hill inside – starting to turn it slowly, so that the flakes began to drift over the tiny chimneys and gable-ends. 'Now, I'm back where I started,' she said. 'Wherever that is.' She gazed vacantly into the crystal.

Robert who, until that moment, with the others waiting for him downstairs, had been anxious to leave, suddenly found himself staring at the dome, transfixed, seeing the house complete inside it – inviolate, perfect, a glittering ageless emblem. And it struck at his heart then – feelings of all sorts of desertion. But he must leave. He had to.

'You're not rushing away at once, Robert?' She had read his thoughts.

'We have to, Hetty – the bad roads – before the light goes.' He glanced at the window. The light had not yet gone at all. Indeed it was rather brighter than it had been, the snow clouds lightening, the weather passing on, leaving a soft white glitter over the gardens.

'Oh, do stay the night. You're all expected. Biddy has made beds up all along this landing, there's food. Go tomorrow.' She glanced at him, still fingering the crystal dome. 'Or why go at all?' she added in just the same casual tone. 'Why not stay here, Robert?' She looked into the orb. 'Always your home – just as much as mine.'

She set the dome back on the table. The flakes started to settle gently over the house. She glanced up at him in the silence. 'Why don't you stay, Robert?'

The funeral party finished early, most of the guests equally anxious to get away in the bad weather. Olivia was with Molly Latimer in the drawing room. They had just finished helping Biddy, and two other local women in for the day, to clear away the tea things.

'Papa's so keen to get off,' Olivia said. 'We really should stay the night. Leaving Hetty on her own, just with Jack and Elly . . .'

'Yes.'

'I suppose she'll be all right. Such a strange house.' Olivia looked around the room, where the lights had not yet been switched on. 'That it doesn't give you the creeps at a time like this – half-burnt, fires, deaths, funerals. Yet there's still an air of – what is it? – safety, welcome?'

'Yes,' Molly said. 'It's always had that, whenever I've come over with Hugh. But then Irish houses nearly always do, don't they? That feeling of warmth – even when it's *freezing*.' Molly shivered.

They left the room and went into the hall. 'Better get our hats and coats together. It'll certainly be freezing in the car. And where on earth have the children got to?'

Lottie and William were at the top of the house, on the old nursery landing – which had been strictly forbidden them on earlier visits, as the boards were thought to be unsafe. It was gloomy since they dared not put on the lights, tip-toeing along, the floorboards creaking, exploring. A door was ajar. They pushed it open – then nearly jumped out of their skins.

A great crocodile stared up at them, its mouth a snarl of vicious teeth. Recovering from her fright, Lottie ventured into the room. William hung back. 'Come on, you coward! It's nothing. Just stuffed.' They moved further in. The room was filled with rubbish. But when they came to inspect it all more closely they were fascinated.

'Look! Bits of an old gun!' William said in wonder. 'A *real* gun, a rifle!'

'And all those other strange animals next door, do you see?'

They had come to the threshold of the adjoining room, gazing at the strange animals in the glass cases – the lemurs, the porcupine – ghostly beasts in the white gloom.

'What a place!' William said. But he was still a bit frightened. 'If we're caught we'll be for it, though.'

'You're just a coward,' Lottie said. 'I *like* it here.'

'So do I, but –'

'Look!' Lottie had found the long skeleton of a snake in an old tea-chest. Pulling it out, she shook the stringed vertebrae suddenly, rattling the evil thing in his face.

'Don't!' he yelled.

'Shush! – they'll hear us, cowardy.'

'I'm *not!*'

Returning the skeleton to its chest, she relented. 'Nice if we could play here.'

'Yes. But we can't. The floorboards aren't safe. And we're all going back to Dublin now – Mummy said, to the hotel.'

'Yes. Pity . . .'

'Come on then, or we'll miss the car.' He fingered the remains of the old Winchester rifle lovingly an instant before they left the playroom.

Hugh Latimer was in the library with Ronnie Ryan. They had been talking of the future. 'So what will happen now, do you think – the house, Miss Cordiner?'

'She shouldn't stay here on her own – that's certain. Take a service flat in Dublin.'

'Exactly. But do you think she'll *want* to stay on here?'

'Yes, I'm sure she will. That's the whole problem. Always seen it in her. Absolutely attached to the place. It'd be the devil's own job getting her out of here. No question. Won't be told – you know Miss Cordiner . . .'

'Yes, I know. Could she get any sort of a companion?'

Ronnie Ryan shrugged. 'Unlikely. Stuck way up here on the hill in this great place. And who could possibly make up for the last one, Mr Latimer?'

'No . . . I don't want to pry, but has she the money to keep the place up here?'

'Probably. Just about. But that's not the real problem – just keeping it up. The fact is that she could never live here on her own. Always a great one for *company*, Mr Latimer. And then, as far as money goes, there *is* the problem now. If anyone's to live here there'd have to be substantial repairs to the east wing, the landing, the hall. I don't suppose she'd see much change out of fifty or sixty thousand these days for that. No, my advice would be for her to get out of the place, before the roof comes off, get herself a nice warm service flat in Dublin. This place . . .' He sighed. 'It's beautiful. But it's done its turn, Mr Latimer. Gardens all gone to rack and ruin, the house itself half gutted in the fire. And the roof will be next – always is in Ireland. To keep it going now, well, it'd be flogging a dead horse.'

'Yes, I suppose so. A pity . . .' Hugh gazed around at the books, the old leather-bound volumes, ancient folios, set everywhere around two walls, as many modern books against the other two. 'I suppose we'd better be thinking of going – weather may turn bad again. And I should see Miss Cordiner before I leave.' Hugh looked out of the window. The snow had stopped, the cloud quite passed on, so that now, in mid-afternoon, there was still no need of the lights, a bright white glitter reflecting off the snow, shining into the library.

They stood up, moving to the door. But Hugh stopped suddenly, seeing a pile of artist sketch-books on the floor next to it, used as a door-stopper, it seemed.

He picked one up, opening it. It was dated '1902', the numerals set in a wonderfully elaborate mock-Gothic scroll. Turning the pages he saw the pen and ink and water-colour drawings – the perfect draughtsmanship, vivid, beautiful, witty, all quite original, with an accompanying text on each opposite page: an illustrated journal of life at Summer Hill, its routines and eccentricities, landscape, flora, fauna, its even more abundant and bizarre human life. The other sketch-books, he saw, were just the same. It was a startling collection.

'Oh, yes – Miss Emily's drawings,' Ronnie Ryan told him. 'A remarkable woman, sister of old Sir Desmond –'

'Yes. I met her briefly, years ago, just before she died. But I'd no idea – of all this!'

'Ah yes, just a few old scrapbooks, drawings and things. Kept her out of mischief, they said. She was, well – ninepence in the shilling.'

Hugh flicked through the pages again, his publisher's eye alert now. 'Worth a lot more than that, Mr Ryan, I'm certain. The whole story of a great house, over several generations, in words and pictures. Absolutely marvellous. Never seen anything like it.'

'You mean, there's money in it?'

'I should say so, yes. Thousands . . .'

They went back to the hall, meeting Olivia and Molly, getting their things together. 'Where *are* those children? We really should see Hetty – and leave before it gets dark.' Olivia was worried. 'What *is* Daddy doing up there?'

The group looked up the great staircase, waiting for him, wanting to go.

The daylight went quickly then. The snow lay thick and still about the house in the sudden dark. But the two hire cars, which had been engaged that morning at Dublin airport, stayed where they were on the gravel surround. Then one by one the lights came on in rooms about the house: in the drawing room, the library, the dining room – where Bridget started to lay places for eight on the long table – then in three of the other bedrooms in the west wing, the house gradually coming alive again in the strange airless calm of the night. The snow dazzled now, a myriad of tiny pinpoints reflecting the light from a half-moon over the silent valley.

Robert, having taken his overnight things upstairs to a bedroom next to Olivia's, spoke to her alone as he unpacked his few clothes.

'What happened? You'd been so mad to get off back to Dublin!'

'Yes.' He took his reading spectacles out of his pocket and put them with a book on the bedside table. 'I'd absolutely no intention of staying.'

'What changed your mind?'

He told her of his earlier conversation with Hetty, how she had asked them all to stay the night, at least – and then how, as an afterthought as it seemed, had said to him how Summer Hill was as much his home as hers.

'And?'

'Well, she'd been so casual about everything, the invitation, about telling me the place was mine as much as hers – no dramatics. So I thought I'd just tell her we'd stay overnight, the bad weather and so on. But I didn't say this. Because it was obvious what she really meant – which was that I, you, all of us, should live in the place with her, as a permanency. Obviously. You know that little snow-dome of the house, used to be kept on the drawing mantelpiece? – she was fingering it, gazing into it. It was quite clear what she meant.'

'And?' Olivia was on tenterhooks.

Robert took his dressing gown from the bag. 'So I said, I told her – the words just came out as if someone else was speaking – that we, I at least, would stay on for a bit. Nothing permanent, I thought. Just a week or two. Help her get things settled, see what she wanted to do, a flat in Dublin or something. Anyway, at that point, after I'd said I'd stay, her calm casual air quite vanished. She broke down, started to sob . . .'

Robert searched his coat pockets now for something. 'Everything she'd been repressing, about Mama, about me, I suppose, the future of the house – it all came out in a fearful rush.' He found some pipe-cleaners at last, putting them with the book and spectacles on the bedside table. 'So I will stay. More permanently, and of course I told her that then, seeing how she was, weeping over that frightful glass-topped table she got in to please her American publishers. Told her I'd stay – and help her put the place back in order a bit. What do you think?' He looked up at Olivia doubtfully.

'I think that's fine!' She smiled, came over and kissed him on the forehead. 'But I'm astonished . . .'

'Yes. But what else? Hetty's right. It was my home. Though I certainly shan't stay here in the winter,' he added quickly, shivering. 'Winter at the Villa Serena. But we could spend the summers here . . .'

'"We"?'

'Why not? The children at least. And whenever you can get away from London.'

'Why not indeed!' Olivia was excited at the prospect. 'The children love it here. And I've always loved the place. Except, well, I've never been entirely easy here, just visiting Mama, with Hetty – knowing how you've felt about them both. Now it'd be different.'

'Yes, it would.'

That third in the triangle had gone, he thought. Things therefore could not but be easier for him in one way, if sadder in another. There was a strange justice in it all. He was back where he had started with Hetty, more than fifty years before – where he had always wanted to be, alone again with her at Summer Hill. He had lost everything. Now, at the very last moment, he had regained it all.

They went down to supper half an hour later. Hetty joined them – Robert, Olivia, the two children, Hugh and Molly, Ronnie Ryan. Hetty, despite the fire, insisted on bringing out the two candelabra, lighting them. The occasion was not breezy or convivial. It was calm and sober, but filled with all sorts of secret or unspoken thoughts.

'We'll be able to play upstairs now as much as we want,' Lottie whispered to William over the chicken broth. Their mother had told them how they would be here much more often now.

'Those sketch-books of your great aunt Emily's – I've been looking at them in the library,' Hugh said half-way through the meal. 'They're absolutely wonderful. Do you think we might publish them – the best of them? They'd make a wonderful book. A series of books.'

'Yes. If you think so. But would anybody be-buy them?'

'I'm sure they would – great nostalgia for all that now, Edwardian country life and lives.'

'You mean – they'd really pay *money*?' Hetty asked, a little jealous now to hear of this other hidden literary bounty in the house.

'Yes, I'm sure –'

'And what of my "memoirs", Hugh? Will you pe-publish them? You've just done Robert's.'

'Yes, Robert told me – I'd no idea you'd written anything like that. Your life, Hetty . . . That would be a *real* bestseller . . .'

'Enough, with Aunt Emily's sketch-books, to repair the east wing?'

'More than enough, I should say – and put the rest of the place in order, too.'

Hetty smiled, lifting her glass. 'Well, to all of us, then – a future.' She looked round the table. 'And to absent fr-fr-friends . . .' She raised her glass to the portraits of all the Cordiner ancestors, who once more seemed to come alive in the flickering candlelight – and kept it raised a moment for the others in her mind then, for all the Cordiners in the family vault across the river, with Léonie.

The snow had quite moved away by morning, bringing a day of brilliant blue sky and sun, almost hot, which soaked down on the landscape – an enchantment of pearly folds and meringue twists, a crisp glitter on the garden terraces, creamy glaciers running down the lawn to the river gorge where the trees were canopied in powdery foam. It was a day so unexpected in an Irish winter – buoyant, tingling, fine, where land and sky made one vast empty canvas and there seemed no end of things in the air.

Robert, taking Hetty's arm, went for a short walk with her, down the porch steps and out over the gravel surround. Their boots crackled, pushing through the crisp surface, leaving deep footprints in the virgin snow as they moved between the white hillocks of debris from the fire. He came to the pile where he had found the old books the previous afternoon, digging about in it again now, rescuing the bound volume of *Punch* for 1898, then the Victorian manual on beekeeping. He rubbed the snow off it.

'Now there's a thing,' he said enthusiastically. 'Beekeeping. I've often thought of it: we should really keep some bees here, Hetty – at Summer Hill.'

Inside the great hall, with their mother beyond the green baize door in the back regions, talking to Jack and Elly, and the Latimers still upstairs, the two children wondered what to do, how to make best use of their sudden freedom.

Lottie gazed at the long Flemish tapestry. Then anchoring her arm about one of the hall pillars, she let her body swirl slowly round it, so that, as she turned, the stories in the weave came alive, a panorama of fearless hunters and their prey, of wonderful mediaeval courts, of invulnerable Kings and Queens.

'"The King was in the counting house counting out his money – the Queen was in the parlour eating bread and honey" . . .' she chanted to herself. She wondered where a house like this could ever end, there was so much of it – rooms and corridors, nooks and crannies – all unexplored, all waiting.

'Here, come and look at this!' William said, kneeling on the window box over on the far side of the hall. He was gazing at a small pane of stained glass set at the bottom corner of the tall window. It showed a yellow-eyed eagle, perched on an old helmet – with some writing beneath, the morning sun streaming through it all – illuminating the colours vividly. 'There's something written there,' he said when Lottie arrived. '"Audaces Fortuna Juvat" . . .' He made a rough stab at the Latin. 'What does it mean?'

'Oh, nothing – I don't know,' Lottie was forced to admit after a minute's inspection. 'Come on – there's much better things to do than look at that! Let's do something *really* brave and risky.'

'What?'

'There's another room upstairs in the attics, beyond the one with the croc. It's *locked* . . .'

'I don't think –'

'Come *on*!'

They tiptoed away, starting properly to explore the big house.